MARY STEWART'S MERLIN TRILOGY

By the same author

THE LAST ENCHANTMENT

TOUCH NOT THE CAT

THE HOLLOW HILLS

THE CRYSTAL CAVE

THE GABRIEL HOUNDS

AIRS ABOVE THE GROUND

THIS ROUGH MAGIC

THE MOON-SPINNERS

THE IVY TREE

MY BROTHER MICHAEL

NINE COACHES WAITING

THUNDER ON THE RIGHT

WILDFIRE AT MIDNIGHT

MADAM, WILL YOU TALK?

For children

A WALK IN WOLF WOOD

LUDO AND THE STAR HORSE

THE LITTLE BROOMSTICK

MARY STEWART'S MERLIN TRILOGY

THE CRYSTAL CAVE
THE HOLLOW HILLS
THE LAST ENCHANTMENT

WILLIAM MORROW AND COMPANY, INC.
New York *1980*

It is the policy of William Morrow and Company, Inc., and its imprints and affiliates, recognizing the importance of preserving what has been written, to print the books we publish on acid-free paper, and we exert our best efforts to that end.

Library of Congress Cataloging in Publication Data

Stewart, Mary, 1916–
Mary Stewart's Merlin trilogy.

CONTENTS: The crystal cave.—The hollow hills.—The last enchantment.
1. Merlin—Legends. I. Title. II. Title: Merlin trilogy.
PR6009.T46M4 1980 823'.914 80-21019
ISBN 0-688-00347-8

Printed in the United States of America

30 29 28 27 26 25 24

CONTENTS

MARY STEWART'S MERLIN TRILOGY

THE CRYSTAL CAVE

To the Memory of

MOLLIE CRAIG

with my love

CONTENTS

MERLIN

O Merlin in your crystal cave
Deep in the diamond of the day,
Will there ever be a singer
Whose music will smooth away
The furrow drawn by Adam's finger
Across the meadow and the wave?
Or a runner who'll outrun
Man's long shadow driving on,
Burst through the gates of history,
And hang the apple on the tree?
Will your sorcery ever show
The sleeping bride shut in her bower,
The day wreathed in its mound of snow,
And Time locked in his tower?

Edwin Muir

PROLOGUE

THE PRINCE OF DARKNESS

I am an old man now, but then I was already past my prime when Arthur was crowned King. The years since then seem to me now more dim and faded than the earlier years, as if my life were a growing tree which burst to flower and leaf with him, and now has nothing more to do than yellow to the grave.

This is true of all old men, that the recent past is misted, while distant scenes of memory are clear and brightly coloured. Even the scenes of my far childhood come back to me now sharp and high-coloured and edged with brightness, like the pattern of a fruit tree against a white wall, or banners in sunlight against a sky of storm.

The colours are brighter than they were, of that I am sure. The memories that come back to me here in the dark are seen with the new young eyes of childhood; they are so far gone from me, with their pain no longer present, that they unroll like pictures of something that happened, not to me, not to the bubble of bone that this memory used to inhabit, but to another Merlin as young and light and free of the air and spring winds as the bird she named me for.

With the later memories it is different; they come back, some of them, hot and shadowed, things seen in the fire. For this is where I gather them. This is one of the few trivial tricks—I cannot call it power—left to me now that I am old and stripped at last down to man. I can see still . . . not clearly or with the call of trumpets as I once did, but in the child's way of dreams and pictures in the fire. I can still make the flames burn up or die; it is one of the simplest of magics, the most easily learned, the last forgotten. What I cannot recall in dream I see in the flames, the red heart of the fire or the countless mirrors of the crystal cave.

The first memory of all is dark and fireshot. It is not my own memory, but later you will understand how I know these things. You would call it not memory so much as a dream of the past, something in the blood, something recalled from him, it may be, while he still bore me in his body. I believe that such things can be. So it seems to me right that I should start with him who was before me, and who will be again when I am gone.

This is what happened that night. I saw it, and it is a true tale.

It was dark, and the place was cold, but he had lit a small fire of wood, which smoked sullenly but gave a little warmth. It had been raining all day, and from the branches near the mouth of the cave water still dripped, and a steady trickle overflowed the lip of the well, soaking the ground below. Several times, restless, he had left the cave, and now he walked out below the cliff to the grove where his horse stood tethered.

With the coming of dusk the rain had stopped, but a mist had risen, creeping knee-high through the trees so that they stood like ghosts, and the grazing horse floated like a swan. It was a grey, and more than ever ghostly because it grazed so quietly; he had torn up a scarf and wound fragments of cloth round the bit so that no jingle should betray him. The bit was gilded, and the torn strips were of silk, for he was a king's son. If they had caught him, they would have killed him. He was just eighteen.

He heard the hoofbeats coming softly up the valley. His head moved, and his breathing quickened. His sword flicked with light as he lifted it. The grey horse paused in its grazing and lifted its head clear of the mist. Its nostrils flickered, but no sound came. The man smiled. The hoofbeats came closer, and then, shoulder-deep in mist, a brown pony trotted out of the dusk. Its rider, small and slight, was wrapped in a dark cloak, muffled from the night air. The pony pulled to a halt, threw up its head, and gave a long, pealing whinny. The rider, with an exclamation of dismay, slipped from its back and grabbed for the bridle to muffle the sound against her cloak. She was a girl, very young, who looked round her anxiously until she saw the young man, sword in hand, at the edge of the trees.

"You sound like a troop of cavalry," he said.

"I was here before I knew it. Everything looks strange in the mist."

"No one saw you? You came safely?"

"Safely enough. It's been impossible the last two days. They were on the roads night and day."

"I guessed it." He smiled. "Well, now you are here. Give me the bridle." He led the pony in under the trees, and tied it up. Then he kissed her.

After a while she pushed him away. "I ought not to stay. I brought the things, so even if I can't come tomorrow—" She stopped. She had seen the saddle on his horse, the muffled bit, the packed saddle-bag. Her hands moved sharply against his chest, and his own covered them and held her fast. "Ah," she said, "I knew. I knew even in my sleep last night. You're going."

"I must. Tonight."

She was silent for a minute. Then all she said was: "How long?"

He did not pretend to misunderstand her. "We have an hour, two, no more."

She said flatly: "You will come back." Then as he started to speak: "No. Not now, not any more. We have said it all, and now there is no more time. I only meant that you will be safe, and you will come back safely. I tell you, I know these things. I have the Sight. You will come back."

"It hardly needs the Sight to tell me that. I must come back. And then perhaps you will listen to me—"

"No." She stopped him again, almost angrily. "It doesn't matter. What does it matter? We have only an hour, and we are wasting it. Let us go in."

He was already pulling out the jewelled pin that held her cloak together, as he put an arm round her and led her towards the cave.

"Yes, let us go in."

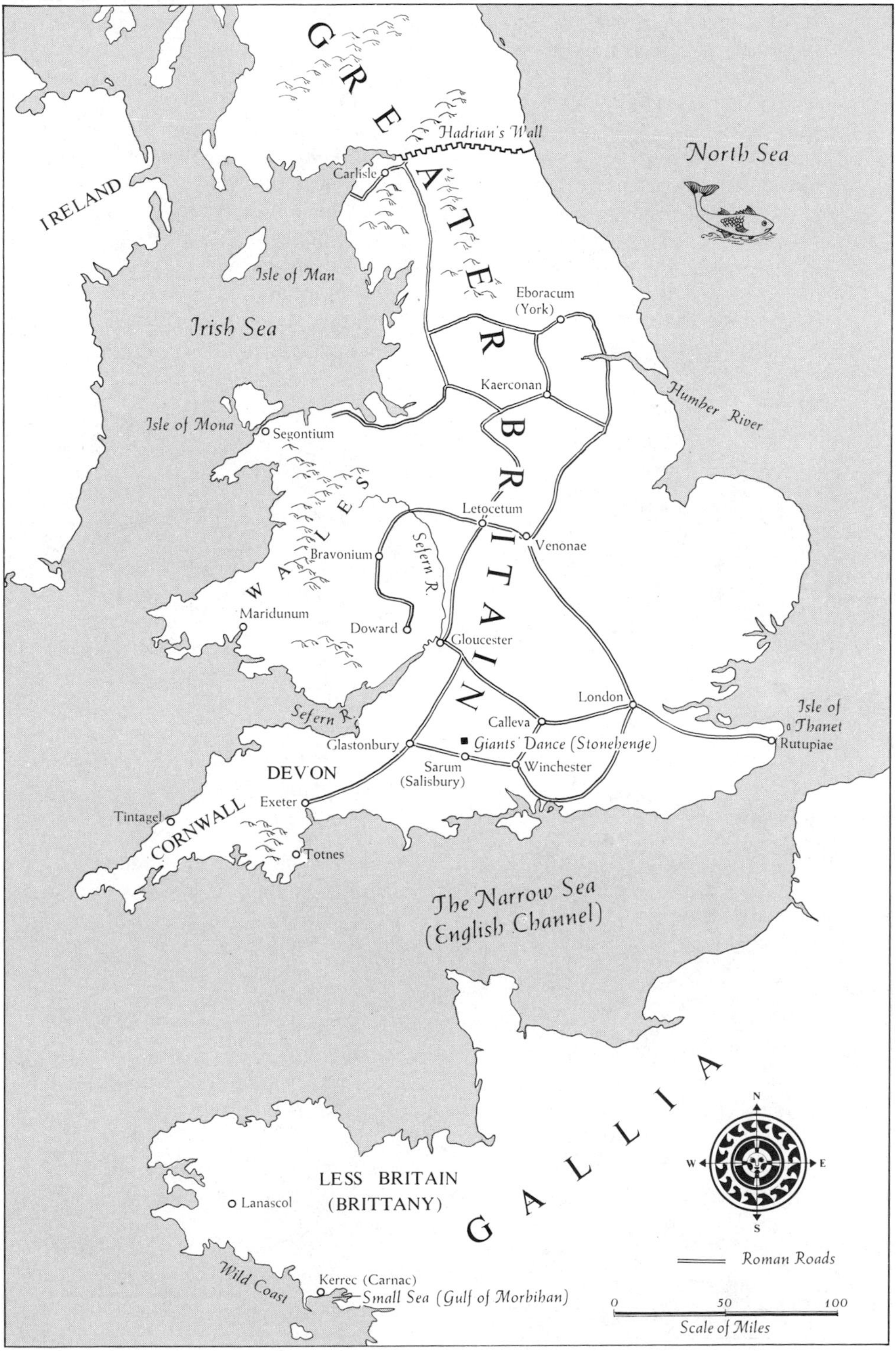
GREATER BRITAIN
Hadrian's Wall
North Sea
IRELAND
Carlisle
Isle of Man
Irish Sea
Eboracum
(York)
Kaerconan
Humber River
Isle of Mona
Segontium
WALES
Letocetum
Venonae
Bravonium
Sefern R.
Maridunum
Doward
Gloucester
London
Sefern R.
Calleva
Isle of
Thanet
Rutupiae
Glastonbury
Giants' Dance (Stonehenge)
Sarum
(Salisbury)
Winchester
DEVON
Exeter
Tintagel
CORNWALL
Totnes
The Narrow Sea
(English Channel)
GALLIA
LESS BRITAIN
(BRITTANY)
Lanascol
Wild Coast
Kerrec (Carnac)
Small Sea (Gulf of Morbihan)
N
W
E
S
Roman Roads
0
50
100
Scale of Miles

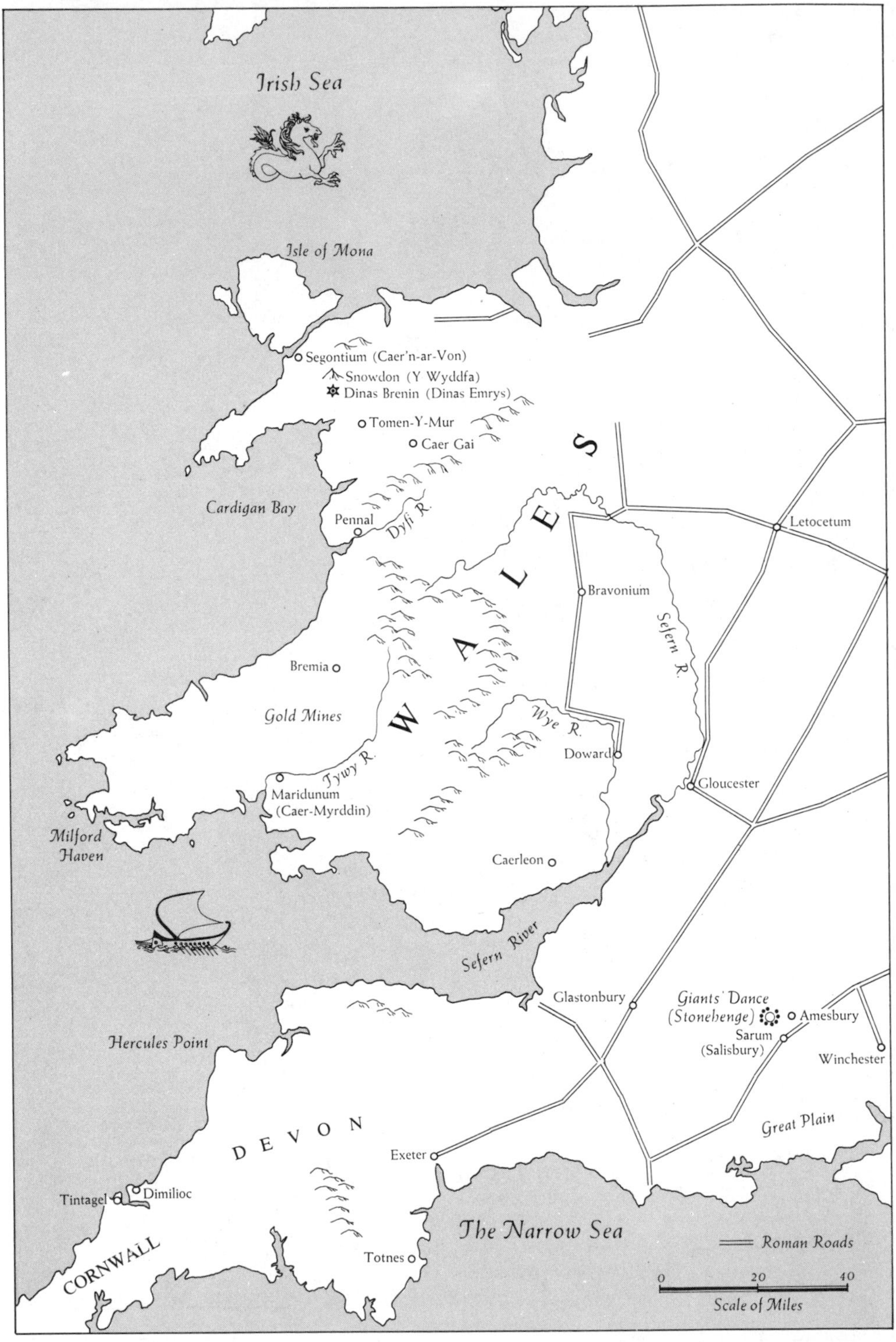

Irish Sea
Isle of Mona
Segontium (Caer'n-ar-Von)
Snowdon (Y Wyddfa)
Dinas Brenin (Dinas Emrys)
Tomen-Y-Mur
Caer Gai
Cardigan Bay
Pennal
Dyfi R.
W A L E S
Letocetum
Bravonium
Sefern R.
Bremia
Gold Mines
Wye R.
Doward
Tywy R.
Gloucester
Maridunum
(Caer-Myrddin)
Milford
Haven
Caerleon
Sefern River
Glastonbury
Giants' Dance
(Stonehenge)
Amesbury
Sarum
(Salisbury)
Winchester
Hercules Point
D E V O N
Great Plain
Exeter
Tintagel
Dimilioc
The Narrow Sea
Roman Roads
CORNWALL
Totnes
0
20
40
Scale of Miles

BOOK I

THE DOVE

1

The day my uncle Camlach came home, I was just six years old.

I remember him well as I first saw him, a tall young man, fiery like my grandfather, with the blue eyes and reddish hair that I thought so beautiful in my mother. He came to Maridunum near sunset of a September evening, with a small troop of men. Being only small, I was with the women in the long, old-fashioned room where they did the weaving. My mother was sitting at the loom; I remember the cloth; it was of scarlet, with a narrow pattern of green at the edge. I sat near her on the floor, playing knuckle-bones, right hand against left. The sun slanted through the windows, making oblong pools of bright gold on the cracked mosaics of the floor; bees droned in the herbs outside, and even the click and rattle of the loom sounded sleepy. The women were talking among themselves over their spindles, but softly, heads together, and Moravik, my nurse, was frankly asleep on her stool in one of the pools of sunlight.

When the clatter, and then the shouts, came from the courtyard, the loom stopped abruptly, and with it the soft chatter from the women. Moravik came awake with a snort and a stare. My mother was sitting very straight, head lifted, listening. She had dropped her shuttle. I saw her eyes meet Moravik's.

I was halfway to the window when Moravik called to me sharply, and there was something in her voice that made me stop and go back to her without protest. She began to fuss with my clothing, pulling my tunic straight and smoothing my hair, so that I understood the visitor to be someone of importance. I felt excitement, and also surprise that apparently I was to be presented to him; I was used to being kept out of the way in those days. I stood patiently while Moravik dragged the comb through my hair, and over my head she and my mother exchanged some quick, breathless talk which, hardly heeding, I did not understand. I was listening to the tramp of horses in the yard and the shouting of men, words here and there coming clearly in a language neither Welsh nor Latin, but Celtic with some accent like the one of Less Britain, which I understood because my nurse, Moravik, was a Breton, and her language came to me as readily as my own.

I heard my grandfather's great laugh, and another voice replying. Then he must have swept the newcomer indoors with him, for the voices receded, leaving only the jingle and stamp of the horses being led to the stables.

I broke from Moravik and ran to my mother.

"Who is it?"

"My brother Camlach, the King's son." She did not look at me, but pointed to the fallen shuttle. I picked it up and handed it to her. Slowly, and rather mechanically, she set the loom moving again.

"Is the war over, then?"

"The war has been over a long time. Your uncle has been with the High King in the south."

"And now he has to come home because my uncle Dyved died?" Dyved had been the heir, the King's eldest son. He had died suddenly, and in great pain, of cramps in the stomach, and Elen his widow, who was childless, had gone back to her father. Naturally there had been the usual talk of poison, but nobody took it seriously; Dyved had been well liked, a tough fighter and a careful man, but generous where it suited. "They say he'll have to marry. Will he, Mother?" I was excited, important at knowing so much, thinking of the wedding feast. "Will he marry Keridwen, now that my uncle Dyved—"

"What?" The shuttle stopped, and she swung round, startled. But what she saw in my face appeased her, for the anger went out of her voice, though she still frowned, and I heard Moravik clucking and fussing behind me. "Where in the world did you get that? You hear too much, whether you understand it or not. Forget such matters, and hold your tongue." The shuttle moved again, slowly. "Listen to me, Merlin. When they come to see you, you will do well to keep quiet. Do you understand me?"

"Yes, Mother." I understood very well. I was well accustomed to keeping out of the King's way. "But will they come to see me? Why me?"

She said, with a thin bitterness that made her look all at once older, almost as old as Moravik: "Why do you think?"

The loom clacked again, fiercely. She was feeding in the green thread, and I could see that she was making a mistake, but it looked pretty, so I said nothing, watching her and staying close, till at length the curtain at the doorway was pushed aside, and the two men came in.

They seemed to fill the room, the red head and the grey within a foot of the beams. My grandfather wore blue, periwinkle colour with a gold border. Camlach was in black. Later I was to discover that he always wore black; he had jewels on his hands and at his shoulder, and beside his father he looked lightly built and young, but as sharp and whippy as a fox.

My mother stood up. She was wearing a house-robe of dark brown, the colour of peat, and against it her hair shone like corn-silk. But neither of the two men glanced at her. You would have thought there was no one in the room but I, small as I was, by the loom.

My grandfather jerked his head and said one word: "Out," and the women hurried in a rustling, silent group from the chamber. Moravik stook her ground, puffed up with bravery like a partridge, but the fierce blue eyes flicked to her for a second, and she went. A sniff as she passed them was all that she dared. The eyes came back to me.

"Your sister's bastard," said the King. "There he is. Six years old this month, grown like a weed, and no more like any of us than a damned devil's whelp would be. Look at him! Black hair, black eyes, and as scared of cold iron as a changeling from the hollow hills. You tell me the devil himself got that one, and I'll believe you!"

My uncle said only one word, straight to her: "Whose?"

"You think we didn't ask, you fool?" said my grandfather. "She was whipped till the women said she'd miscarry, but never a word from her. Better if she had, perhaps—some nonsense they were talking, old wives' tales of devils coming in the dark to lie with young maids—and from the look of him they could be right."

Camlach, six foot and golden, looked down at me. His eyes were blue, clear as my mother's, and his colour was high. The mud had dried yellow on his soft doeskin boots, and a smell of sweat and horses came from him. He had come to look at me before even taking the dirt of travel off. I remember how he stared down at me, while my mother stood silent, and my grandfather glowered under his brows, his breath coming harsh and rapid, as it always did when he had put himself in a passion.

"Come here," said my uncle.

I took half a dozen steps forward. I did not dare go nearer. I stopped. From three paces away he seemed taller than ever. He towered over me to the ceiling beams.

"What's your name?"

"Myrddin Emrys."

"Emrys? Child of light, belonging to the gods . . . ? That hardly seems the name for a demon's whelp."

The mildness of his tone encouraged me. "They call me Merlinus," I ventured. "It's a Roman name for a falcon, the *corwalch.*"

My grandfather barked, "Falcon!" and made a sound of contempt, shooting his arm-rings till they jingled.

"A small one," I said defensively, then fell silent under my uncle's thoughtful look.

He stroked his chin, then looked at my mother with his brows up. "Strange choices, all of them, for a Christian household. A Roman demon, perhaps, Niniane?"

She put up her chin. "Perhaps. How do I know? It was dark."

I thought a flash of amusement came and went in his face, but the King swept a hand down in a violent gesture. "You see? That's all you get—lies, tales of sorcery, insolence! Get back to your work, girl, and keep your bastard out of my sight! Now that your brother's home, we'll find a man who'll take the pair of you from under my feet and his! Camlach, I hope you see the sense of getting yourself a wife now, and a son or two, since this is all I'm left with!"

"Oh, I'm for it," said Camlach easily. Their attention had lifted from me. They were going, and neither had touched me. I unclenched my hands and moved back softly, half a pace; another. "But you've got yourself a new queen meantime, sir, and they tell me she's pregnant?"

"No matter of that, you should be wed, and soon. I'm an old man, and these are troubled times. As for this boy"—I froze again—"forget him. Whoever sired him, if he hasn't come forward in six years, he'll not do so now. And if it had been Vortigern himself, the High King, he'd have made nothing of him. A sullen brat who skulks alone in corners. Doesn't even play with the other boys—afraid to, likely. Afraid of his own shadow."

He turned away. Camlach's eyes met my mother's, over my head. Some message passed. Then he looked down at me again, and smiled.

I still remember how the room seemed to light up, though the sun had gone now, and its warmth with it. Soon they would be bringing the rushlights.

"Well," said Camlach, "it's but a fledgling falcon after all. Don't be too hard on him, sir; you've frightened better men than he is, in your time."

"Yourself, you mean? Hah!"

"I assure you."

The King, in the doorway, glared briefly at me under his jutting brows, then with a puff of impatient breath settled his mantle over his arm. "Well, well, let be. God's sweet death, but I'm hungry. It's well past supper-time—but I suppose you'll want to go and soak yourself first, in your damned Roman fashion? I warn you, we've never had the furnaces on since you left . . ."

He turned with a swirl of the blue cloak and went out, still talking. Behind me I heard my mother's breath go out, and the rustle of her gown as she sat. My uncle put out a hand to me.

"Come, Merlinus, and talk to me while I bathe in your cold Welsh water. We princes must get to know one another."

I stood rooted. I was conscious of my mother's silence, and how still she sat.

"Come," said my uncle, gently, and smiled at me again.

I ran to him.

I went through the hypocaust that night.

This was my own private way, my secret hiding-place where I could escape from the bigger boys and play my own solitary games. My grandfather had been right when he said I "skulked alone in corners," but this was not from fear, though the sons of his nobles followed his lead—as children do—and made me their butt in their rough war-games whenever they could catch me.

At the beginning, it is true, the tunnels of the disused heating-system were a refuge, a secret place where I could hide and be alone; but I soon found a curiously strong pleasure in exploring the great system of dark, earth-smelling chambers under the palace floors.

My grandfather's palace had been, in times past, a vast country-house belonging to some Roman notable who had owned and farmed the land for several miles each way along the river valley. The main part of the house still stood, though badly scarred by time and war, and by at least one disastrous fire, which had destroyed one end of the main block and part of a wing. The old slaves' quarters were still intact round the courtyard where the cooks and house-servants worked, and the bath-house remained, though patched and plastered, and with the roof rough-thatched over the worst bits. I never remember the furnace working; water was heated over the courtyard fires.

The entrance to my secret labyrinth was the stoke-hole in the boiler-house; this was a trap in the wall under the cracked and rusting boiler, barely the height of a grown man's knee, and hidden by docks and nettles and a huge curved metal shard fallen from the boiler itself. Once inside, you could get under the rooms of the bath-house, but this had been out of use for so long that the space under the floors was too cluttered and foul even for me. I went the other way, under the main block of the palace. Here the old hot-air system had been so well built and maintained that even now the knee-high space under the floors was dry and airy, and plaster still clung to the brick pillars that held up the floors. In places, of course, a pillar had collapsed, or debris had fallen, but the traps which led from one room to another were solidly arched and safe, and I was free to crawl, unseen and unheard, even as far as the King's own chamber.

If they had ever discovered me I think I might have received a worse punishment than whipping: I must have listened, innocently enough, to dozens of secret councils, and certainly to some very private goings-on, but that side of it never occurred to me. And it was natural enough that nobody should give a thought to the dangers of eavesdropping; in the old days the flues had been cleaned by boy-slaves, and nobody much beyond the age of ten could ever have got through some of the workings; there were one or two places where even I was hard put to it to wriggle through. I was only once in danger of discovery: one afternoon when Moravik supposed I was playing with the boys and they in turn thought I was safe under her skirts, the red-haired Dinias, my chief tormentor, gave a younger boy such a shove from the roof-tree where they were playing that the latter fell and broke a leg, and set up such a howling that Moravik, running to the scene, discovered me absent and set the palace by the ears. I heard the noise, and emerged breathless and dirty from under the boiler, just as she started a hunt through the bath-house wing. I lied my way out of it, and got off with boxed ears and a scolding, but it was a warning; I never went into the hypocaust again by daylight, only at night before Moravik came to bed, or once or twice when I was wakeful and she was already abed and snoring. Most of the palace would be abed, too, but when there was a feast, or when my grandfather had guests, I would listen to the noise of voices and the singing; and sometimes I would creep as far as my mother's chamber, to hear the sound of her voice as she talked with her women. But one night I heard her praying, aloud, as one does sometimes when alone, and in the prayer was my name, "Emrys," and then her tears. After that I went another way, past the Queen's rooms, where almost every evening Olwen, the young Queen, sang to her harp among her ladies, until the King's tread came heavily down the corridor, and the music stopped.

But it was for none of these things that I went. What mattered to me—I see it clearly now—was to be alone in the secret dark, where a man is his own master, except for death.

Mostly I went to what I called my "cave." This had been part of some main chimney-shaft, and the top of it had crumbled, so that one could see the sky. It had held magic for me since the day I had looked up at midday and had seen, faint but unmistakable, a star. Now when I went in at night I would curl up on my bed of stolen stable-straw and watch the stars wheeling slowly across, and make my own bet with heaven, which was, if the moon should show over the shaft while I was there, the next day would bring me my heart's desire.

The moon was there that night. Full and shining, she stood clear in the center of the shaft, her light pouring down on my upturned face so white and pure that it seemed I drank it in like water. I did not move till she had gone, and the little star that dogs her.

On the way back I passed under a room that had been empty before, but which now held voices.

Camlach's room, of course. He and another man whose name I did not know, but who, from his accent, was one of those who had ridden in that day; I had found that they came from Cornwall. He had one of those thick, rumbling voices of which I caught only a word here and there as I crawled quickly through, worming my way between the pillars, concerned only not to be heard.

I was right at the end wall, and feeling along it for the arched gap to the next chamber, when my shoulder struck a broken section of flue pipe, and a loose piece of fireclay fell with a rattle.

The Cornishman's voice stopped abruptly. "What's that?"

Then my uncle's voice, so clear down the broken flue that you would have thought he spoke in my ear.

"Nothing. A rat. It came from under the floor. I tell you, the place is falling to pieces." There was the sound of a chair scraping back, and footsteps going across the room, away from me. His voice receded. I thought I heard the chink and gurgle of a drink being poured. I began slowly, slowly, to edge along the wall towards the trap.

He was coming back.

. . . "And even if she does refuse him, it will hardly matter. She won't stay here—at any rate, no longer than my father can fight the bishop off and keep her by him. I tell you, with her mind set on what she calls a higher court, I've nothing to fear, even if he came himself."

"As long as you believe her."

"Oh, I believe her. I've been asking here and there, and everyone says the same." He laughed. "Who knows, we may be thankful yet to have a voice at that heavenly court of hers before this game's played out. And she's devout enough to save the lot of us, they tell me, if she'll only put her mind to it."

"You may need it yet," said the Cornishman.

"I may."

"And the boy?"

"The boy?" repeated my uncle. He paused, then the soft footsteps resumed their pacing. I strained to hear. I had to hear. Why it should have mattered I hardly knew. It did not worry me overmuch to be called bastard, or coward, or devil's whelp. But tonight there had been that full moon.

He had turned. His voice carried clearly, careless, indulgent even.

"Ah, yes, the boy. A clever child, at a guess, with more there than they give him credit for . . . and nice enough, if one speaks him fair. I shall keep him close to me. Remember that, Alun; I like the boy . . ."

He called a servant in then to replenish the wine-jug, and under cover of this, I crept away.

That was the beginning of it. For days I followed him everywhere, and he tolerated, even encouraged me, and it never occurred to me that a man of twenty-one would not always welcome a puppy of six for ever trotting at his heels. Moravik scolded, when she could get hold of me, but my mother seemed pleased and relieved, and bade her let me be.

2

It had been a hot summer, and there was peace that year, so for the first few days of his homecoming Camlach idled, resting or riding out with his father or the men through the harvest fields and the valleys where the apples already dropped ripe from the trees.

South Wales is a lovely country, with green hills and deep valleys, flat water-meadows yellow with flowers where cattle grow sleek, oak forests full of deer, and the high blue uplands where the cuckoo shouts in springtime, but where, come winter, the wolves run, and I have seen lightning even with the snow.

Maridunum lies where the estuary opens to the sea, on the river which is marked Tobius on the military maps, but which the Welsh call Tywy. Here the valley is flat and wide, and the Tywy runs in a deep and placid meander through bog and water-meadow between the gentle hills. The town stands on the rising ground of the north bank, where the land is drained and dry; it is served inland by the military road from Caerleon, and from the south by a good stone bridge with three spans, from which a paved street leads straight uphill past the King's house, and into the square. Apart from my grandfather's house, and the barrack buildings of the Roman-built fortress where he quartered his soldiers and which he kept in good repair, the best building in Maridunum was the Christian nunnery near the palace on the river's bank. A few holy women lived there, calling themselves the Community of St. Peter, though most of the townspeople called the place Tyr Myrddin, from the old shrine of the god which had stood time out of mind under an oak not far from St. Peter's gate. Even when I was a child, I heard the town itself called Caer-Myrddin * : it is not true (as they say now) that men call it after me. The fact is that I, like the town and the hill behind it with the sacred spring, was called after the god who is worshipped in high places. Since the events which I shall tell of, the name of the town has been publicly changed in my honour, but the god was there first, and if I have his hill now, it is because he shares it with me.

My grandfather's house was set among its orchards right beside the river. If you climbed—by way of a leaning apple-tree—to the top of the wall, you could sit high over the towpath and watch the river-bridge for people riding in from the south, or for the ships that came up with the tide.

Though I was not allowed to climb the trees for apples—being forced to content myself with the windfalls—Moravik never stopped me from climbing to the top of the wall. To have me posted there as sentry meant that she got wind of new arrivals sooner than anyone else in the palace. There was a little raised

* *dd* is pronounced *th* as in *thus. Myrddin* is, roughly, *Murthin.* Caer-Myrddin is the modern Carmarthen.

terrace at the orchard's end, with a curved brick wall at the back and a stone seat protected from the wind, and she would sit there by the hour, dozing over her spindle, while the sun beat into the corner so hotly that lizards would steal out to lie on the stones, and I called out my reports from the wall.

One hot afternoon, about eight days after Camlach's coming to Maridunum, I was at my post as usual. There was no coming and going on the bridge or the road up the valley, only a local grain-barge loading at the wharf, watched by a scatter of idlers, and an old man in a hooded cloak who loitered, picking up windfalls along under the wall.

I looked over my shoulder towards Moravik's corner. She was asleep, her spindle drooping on her knee, looking, with the white fluffy wool, like a burst bulrush. I threw down the bitten windfall I had been eating, and tilted my head to study the forbidden tree-top boughs where yellow globes hung clustered against the sky. There was one I thought I could reach. The fruit was round and glossy, ripening almost visibly in the hot sun. My mouth watered. I reached for a foothold and began to climb.

I was two branches away from the fruit when a shout from the direction of the bridge, followed by the quick tramp of hoofs and the jingle of metal, brought me up short. Clinging like a monkey, I made sure of my feet, then reached with one hand to push the leaves aside, peering down towards the bridge. A troop of men was riding over it, towards the town. One man rode alone in front, bareheaded, on a big brown horse.

Not Camlach, or my grandfather; and not one of the nobles, for the men wore colours I did not know. Then as they reached the nearer end of the bridge I saw that the leader was a stranger, black-haired and black-bearded, with a foreign-looking set to his clothes, and a flash of gold on his breast. His wristguards were golden, too, and a span deep. His troop, as I judged, was about fifty strong.

King Gorlan of Lanascol. Where the name sprang from, clear beyond mistake, I had no idea. Something heard from my labyrinth, perhaps? A word spoken carelessly in a child's hearing? A dream, even? The shields and speartips, catching the sun, flashed into my eyes. Gorlan of Lanascol. A king. Come to marry my mother and take me with him overseas. She would be a queen. And I . . .

He was already setting his horse at the hill. I began to half-slither, half-scramble, down the tree.

And if she refuses him? I recognized that voice; it was the Cornishman's. And after him my uncle's: *Even if she does, it will hardly matter . . . I've nothing to fear, so even if he came himself . . .*

The troop was riding at ease across the bridge. The jingle of arms and the hammering of hoofs rang in the still sunlight.

He had come himself. He was here.

A foot above the wall-top I missed my footing and almost fell. Luckily my grip held, and I slithered safely to the coping in a shower of leaves and lichen just as my nurse's voice called shrilly:

"Merlin? Merlin? Save us, where's the boy?"

"Here—here, Moravik—just coming down."

I landed in the long grass. She had left her spindle and, kilting up her skirts, came running.

"What's the to-do on the river road? I heard horses, a whole troop by the noise— Saints alive, child, look at your clothes! If I didn't mend that tunic only this week, and now look at it! A tear you could put a fist through, and dirt from head to foot like a beggar's brat!"

I dodged as she reached for me. "I fell. I'm sorry. I was climbing down to tell you. It's a troop of horse—foreigners! Moravik, it's King Gorlan from Lanascol! He has a red cloak and a black beard!"

"Gorlan of Lanascol? Why, that's barely twenty miles from where I was born! What's he here for, I wonder?"

I stared. "Didn't you know? He's come to marry my mother."

"Nonsense."

"It's true!"

"Of course it's not true! Do you think I wouldn't know? You must not say these things, Merlin, it could mean trouble. Where did you get it?"

"I don't remember. Someone told me. My mother, I think."

"That's not true and you know it."

"Then I must have heard something."

"Heard something, heard something. Young pigs have long ears, they say. Yours must be for ever to the ground, you hear so much! What are you smiling at?"

"Nothing."

She set her hands on her hips. "You've been listening to things you shouldn't. I've told you about this before. No wonder people say what they say."

I usually gave up and edged away from dangerous ground when I had given too much away, but excitement had made me reckless. "It's true, you'll find it's true! Does it matter where I heard it? I really can't remember now, but I know it's true! Moravik—"

"What?"

"King Gorlan's my father, my real one."

"What?" This time the syllable was edged like the tooth of a saw.

"Didn't you know? Not even you?"

"No, I did not. And no more do you. And if you so much as breathe this to anyone— How do you know the name, even?" She took me by the shoulders and gave me a sharp little shake. "How do you even know this is King Gorlan? There's been nothing said of his coming, even to me."

"I told you. I don't remember what I heard, or where. I just heard his name somewhere, that's all, and I know he's coming to see the King about my mother. We'll go to Less Britain, Moravik, and you can come with us. You'll like that, won't you? It's your home. Perhaps we'll be near—"

Her grip tightened, and I stopped. With relief I saw one of the King's body-servants hurrying towards us through the apple-trees. He came up panting.

"He's to go before the King. The boy. In the great hall. And hurry."

"Who is it?" demanded Moravik.

"The King said to hurry. I've been looking everywhere for the boy—"

"Who is it?"

"King Gorlan from Brittany."

She gave a little hiss, like a startled goose, and dropped her hands. "What's his business with the boy?"

"How do I know?" The man was breathless—it was a hot day and he was stout—and curt with Moravik, whose status as my nurse was only a little higher with the servants than my own. "All I know is, the Lady Niniane is sent for, and the boy, and there'll be a beating for someone, by my reckoning, if he's not there by the time the King's looking round for him. He's been in a rare taking since the outriders came in, that I can tell you."

"All right, all right. Get back and say we'll be there in a few minutes."

The man hurried off. She whirled on me and grabbed at my arm. "All the sweet saints in heaven!" Moravik had the biggest collection of charms and talismans of anyone in Maridunum, and I had never known her pass a wayside shrine without paying her respects to whatever image inhabited it, but officially she was a Christian and, when in trouble, a devout one. "Sweet cherubim! And the child has to choose this afternoon to be in rags! Hurry, now, or there'll be trouble for both of us." She hustled me up the path towards the house, busily calling on her saints and exhorting me to hurry, determinedly refusing even to comment on the fact that I had been right about the newcomer. "Dear, dear St. Peter, why did I eat those eels for dinner and then sleep so sound? Today of all days! Here"—she pushed me in front of her into my room—"get out of those rags and into your good tunic, and we'll know soon enough what the Lord has sent for you. Hurry, child!"

The room I shared with Moravik was a small one, dark, and next to the servants' quarters. It always smelt of cooking smells from the kitchen, but I liked this, as I liked the old lichened pear tree that hung close outside the window, where the birds swung singing in the summer mornings. My bed stood right under this window. The bed was nothing but plain planks set across wooden blocks, no carving, not even a head or foot board. I had heard Moravik grumble to the other servants when she thought I wasn't listening, that it was hardly a fit place to house a king's grandson, but to me she said merely that it was convenient for her to be near the other servants; and indeed I was comfortable enough, for she saw to it that I had a clean straw mattress, and a coverlet of wool every bit as good as those on my mother's bed in the big room next to my grandfather. Moravik herself had a pallet on the floor near the door, and this was sometimes shared by the big wolfhound who fidgeted and scratched for fleas beside her feet, and sometimes by Cerdic, one of the grooms, a Saxon who had been taken in a raid long since, and had settled down to marry one of the local girls. She had died in childbed a year later, and the child with her, but he stayed on, apparently quite content. I once asked Moravik why she allowed the dog to sleep in the room, when she grumbled so much about the smell and the fleas; I forget what she answered, but I knew without being told that he was there to give warning if anyone came into the room during the night. Cerdic, of course, was the exception; the dog accepted him with no more fuss than the beating of his tail upon the floor, and vacated the bed for him. In a way, I suppose, Cerdic fulfilled the same function as the watchdog, and others besides. Moravik never mentioned him, and neither did I. A small child is supposed to sleep very soundly, but even then, young as I was, I would wake sometimes in the middle of the night, and lie quite still, watching the stars through the window beside me, caught like sparkling silver fish in the net of the pear tree's boughs. What passed between Cerdic and Moravik meant no more to me than that he helped to guard my nights, as she my days.

My clothes were kept in a wooden chest which stood against the wall. This was very old, with panels painted with scenes of gods and goddesses, and I think originally it had come from Rome itself. Now the paint was dirty and rubbed and flaking, but still on the lid you could see, like shadows, a scene taking place in what looked like a cave; there was a bull, and a man with a knife, and someone holding a sheaf of corn, and over in the corner some figure, rubbed almost away, with rays round his head like the sun, and a stick in his hand. The chest was lined with cedarwood, and Moravik washed my clothes herself, and laid them away with sweet herbs from the garden.

She threw the lid up now, so roughly that it banged against the wall, and pulled out the better of my two good tunics, the green one with the scarlet border. She shouted for water, and one of the maids brought it, running, and was scolded for spilling it on the floor.

The fat servant came panting again to tell us that we should hurry, and got snapped at for his pains, but in a very short time I was hustled once more along the colonnade, and through the big arched doorway into the main part of the house.

The hall where the King received visitors was a long, high room with a floor of black and white stone framing a mosaic of a god with a leopard. This had been badly scarred and broken by the dragging of heavy furniture and the constant passing of booted feet. One side of the room was open to the colonnade, and here in winter a fire was kindled on the bare floor, within a loose frame of stones. The floor and pillars near it were blackened with the smoke. At the far end of the room stood the dais with my grandfather's big chair, and beside it the smaller one for his Queen.

He was sitting there now, with Camlach standing on his right, and his wife, Olwen, seated at his left. She was his third wife, and younger than my mother, a dark, silent, rather stupid girl with a skin like new milk and braids down to her knees, who could sing like a bird, and do fine needlework, but very little else. My mother, I think, both liked and despised her. At any rate, against all expectation, they got along tolerably well together, and I had heard Moravik say that life for my mother had been a great deal easier since the King's second wife, Gwynneth, had died a year ago, and within the month Olwen had taken her place in the King's bed. Even if Olwen had cuffed me and sneered at me as Gwynneth did I should have liked her for her music, but she was always kind to me in her vague, placid way, and when the King was out of the way had taught me my notes, and even let me use her harp till I could play after a fashion. I had a feeling for it, she said, but we both knew what the King would say to such folly, so her kindness was secret, even from my mother.

She did not notice me now. Nobody did, except my cousin Dinias, who stood by Olwen's chair on the dais. Dinias was a bastard of my grandfather's by a slave-woman. He was a big boy of seven, with his father's red hair and high temper; he was strong for his age and quite fearless, and had enjoyed the King's favour since the day he had, at the age of five, stolen a ride on one of his father's horses, a wild brown colt that had bolted with him through the town and only got rid of him when he rode it straight at a breast-high bank. His father had thrashed him with his own hands, and afterwards given him a dagger with a gilded hilt. Dinias claimed the title of Prince—at any rate among the rest of the children—from then on, and treated his fellow-bastard, myself, with the utmost contempt. He stared at me now as expressionless as a stone, but his left hand—the one away from his father—made a rude sign, and then chopped silently, expressively, downwards.

I had paused in the doorway, and behind me my nurse's hand twitched my tunic into place and then gave me a push between the shoulder-blades. "Go on now. Straighten your back. He won't eat you." As if to give the lie to this, I heard the click of charms and the start of a muttered prayer.

The room was full of people. Many of them I knew, but there were strangers there who must be the party I had seen ride in. Their leader sat near the King's right, surrounded by his own men. He was the big dark man I had seen on the bridge, full-bearded, with a fierce beak of a nose and thick limbs shrouded in a scarlet cloak. On the King's other side, but standing below the dais, was my mother, with two of her women. I loved to see her as she was now, dressed like a princess, her long robe of creamy wool hanging straight to the floor as if carved of new wood. Her hair was unbraided, and fell down her back like rain. She had a blue mantle with a copper clasp. Her face was colourless, and very still.

I was so busy with my own fears—the gesture from Dinias, the averted face and downcast eyes of my mother, the silence of the people, and the empty middle of the floor over which I must walk—that I had not even looked at my grandfather. I had taken a step forward, still unnoticed, when suddenly, with a crash like a horse kicking, he slammed both hands down on the wooden arms of his chair, and thrust himself to his feet so violently that the heavy chair went back a pace, its feet scoring the oak planks of the platform.

"By the light!" His face was mottled scarlet, and the reddish brows jutted in knots of flesh above his furious little blue eyes. He glared down at my mother, and drew a breath to speak that could be heard clear to the door where I had paused, afraid. Then the bearded man, who had risen with him, said something in some accent I didn't catch, and at the same moment Camlach touched his arm, whispering. The King paused, then said thickly, "As you will. Later. Get them out of here." Then clearly, to my mother: "This is not the end of it, Niniane, I promise you. Six years. It is enough, by God! Come, my lord."

He swept his cloak up over one arm, jerked his head to his son, and, stepping down from the dais, took the bearded man by the arm, and strode with him towards the door. After him, meek as milk, trailed his wife Olwen with her women, and after her Dinias, smiling. My mother never moved. The King went by her without a word or a look, and the crowd parted between him and the door like a stubble-field under the share.

It left me standing alone, rooted and staring, three paces in from the door. As the King bore down on me I came to myself and turned to escape into the anteroom, but not quickly enough.

He stopped abruptly, releasing Gorlan's arm, and swung round on me. The blue cloak swirled, and a corner of the cloth caught my eye and brought the tears to it. I blinked up at him. Gorlan had paused beside him. He was younger than my uncle Dyved had been. He was angry, too, but hiding it, and the anger was not for me. He looked surprised when the King stopped, and said: "Who's this?"

"Her son, that your grace would have given a name to," said my grandfather, and the gold flashed on his armlet as he swung his big hand up and knocked me flat to the floor as easily as a boy would flatten a fly. Then the blue cloak swept by me, and the King's booted feet, and Gorlan's after him with barely a pause. Olwen said something in her pretty voice and stooped over me, but the King called to her, angrily, and her hand withdrew and she hurried after him with the rest.

I picked myself up from the floor and looked round for Moravik, but she was not there. She had gone straight to my mother, and had not even seen. I began to push my way towards them through the hubbub of the hall, but before I could reach my mother the women, in a tight and silent group round her, left the hall by the other door. None of them looked back.

Someone spoke to me, but I did not answer. I ran out through the colonnade, across the main court, and out again into the quiet sunlight of the orchard.

My uncle found me on Moravik's terrace.

I was lying on my belly on the hot flagstones, watching a lizard. Of all that day, this is my most vivid recollection; the lizard, flat on the hot stone within a foot of my face, its body still as green bronze but for the pulsing throat. It had small dark eyes, no brighter than slate, and the inside of its mouth was the colour of melons. It had a long, sharp tongue, which flicked out quick as a whip, and its feet made a tiny rustling noise on the stones as it ran across my finger and vanished down a crack in the flags.

I turned my head. My uncle Camlach was coming down through the orchard.

He mounted the three shallow steps to the terrace, soft-footed in his elegant laced sandals, and stood looking down. I looked away. The moss between the stones had tiny white flowers no bigger than the lizard's eyes, each one perfect as a carved cup. To this day I remember the design on them as well as if I had carved it myself.

"Let me see," he said.

I didn't move. He crossed to the stone bench and sat down facing me, knees apart, clasped hands between them.

"Look at me, Merlin."

I obeyed him. He studied me in silence for a while.

"I'm always being told that you will not play rough games, that you run away from Dinias, that you will never make a soldier or even a man. Yet when the King strikes you down with a blow which would have sent one of his deerhounds yelping to kennel, you make no sound and shed no tear."

I said nothing.

"I think perhaps you are not quite what they deem you, Merlin."

Still nothing.

"Do you know why Gorlan came today?"

I thought it better to lie. "No."

"He came to ask for your mother's hand. If she had consented you would have gone with him to Brittany."

I touched one of the moss-cups with a forefinger. It crumbled like a puff-ball and vanished. Experimentally, I touched another. Camlach said, more sharply than he usually spoke to me: "Are you listening?"

"Yes. But if she's refused him it will hardly matter." I looked up. "Will it?"

"You mean you don't want to go? I would have thought . . ." He knitted the fair brows so like my grandfather's. "You would be treated honourably, and be a prince."

"I am a prince now. As much a prince as I can ever be."

"What do you mean by that?"

"If she has refused him," I said, "he cannot be my father. I thought he was. I thought that was why he had come."

"What made you think so?"

"I don't know. It seemed—" I stopped. I could not explain to Camlach about the flash of light in which Gorlan's name had come to me. "I just thought he must be."

"Only because you have been waiting for him all this time." His voice was calm. "Such waiting is foolish, Merlin. It's time you faced the truth. Your father is dead."

I put my hand down on the tuft of moss, crushing it. I watched the flesh of the fingers whiten with the pressure. "She told you that?"

"No." He lifted his shoulders. "But had he been still alive he would have been here long since. You must know that."

I was silent.

"And if he is not dead," pursued my uncle, watching me, "and still has never come, it can surely not be a matter for great grief on anyone's part?"

"No, except that however base he may be, it might have saved my mother something. And me." As I moved my hand, the moss slowly unfurled again, as if growing. But the tiny flowers had gone.

My uncle nodded. "She would have been wiser, perhaps, to have accepted Gorlan, or some other prince."

"What will happen to us?" I asked.

"Your mother wants to go into St. Peter's. And you—you are quick and clever, and I am told you can read a little. You could be a priest."

"No!"

His brows came down again over the thin-bridged nose. "It's a good enough life. You're not warrior stock, that's certain. Why not take a life that will suit you, and where you'd be safe?"

"I don't need to be a warrior to want to stay free! To be shut up in a place like St. Peter's—that's not the way—" I broke off. I had spoken hotly, but found the words failing me. I could not explain something I did not know myself. I looked up eagerly: "I'll stay with you. If you cannot use me I—I'll run away to serve some other prince. But I would rather stay with you."

"Well, it's early yet to speak of things like that. You're very young." He got to his feet. "Does your face hurt you?"

"No."

"You should have it seen to. Come with me now."

He put out a hand, and I went with him. He led me up through the orchard, then in through the arch that led to my grandfather's private garden.

I hung back against his hand. "I'm not allowed in there."

"Surely, with me? Your grandfather's with his guests, he'll not see you. Come along. I've got something better for you than your windfall apples. They've been gathering the apricots, and I saved the best aside out of the baskets as I came down."

He trod forward, with that graceful cat's stride of his, through the bergamot and lavender, to where the apricot and peach trees stood crucified against the high wall in the sun. The place smelt drowsy with herbs and fruit, and the doves were crooning from the dove-house. At my feet a ripe apricot lay, velvet in the sun. I pushed it with my toe until it rolled over, and there in the back of it was the great rotten hole, with wasps crawling. A shadow fell over it. My uncle stood above me, with an apricot in each hand.

"I told you I'd got something better than windfalls. Here." He handed me one. "And if they beat you for stealing, they'll have to beat me as well." He grinned, and bit into the fruit he held.

I stood still, with the big bright apricot cupped in the palm of my hand. The garden was very hot, and very still, and quiet except for the humming of insects. The fruit glowed like gold, and smelt of sunshine and sweet juice. Its skin felt like the fur of a golden bee. I could feel my mouth watering.

"What is it?" asked my uncle. He sounded edgy and impatient. The juice of his apricot was running down his chin. "Don't stand there staring at it, boy! Eat it! There's nothing wrong with it, is there?"

I looked up. The blue eyes, fierce as a fox, stared down into mine. I held it out to him. "I don't want it. It's black inside. Look, you can see right through."

He took his breath in sharply, as if to speak. Then voices came from the other side of the wall; the gardeners, probably, bringing the empty fruit-baskets down ready for morning. My uncle, stooping, snatched the fruit from my hand and threw it from him, hard against the wall. It burst in a golden splash of flesh against the brick, and the juice ran down. A wasp, disturbed from the tree, droned past between us. Camlach flapped at it with a queer, abrupt gesture, and said to me in a voice that was suddenly all venom:

"Keep away from me after this, you devil's brat. Do you hear me? Just keep away."

He dashed the back of his hand across his mouth, and went from me in long strides towards the house.

I stood where I was, watching the juice of the apricot trickle down the hot wall. A wasp alighted on it, crawled stickily, then suddenly fell, buzzing on its back to the ground. Its body jack-knifed, the buzz rose to a whine as it struggled, then it lay still.

I hardly saw it, because something had swelled in my throat till I thought I would choke, and the golden evening swam, brilliant, into tears. This was the first time in my life that I remember weeping.

The gardeners were coming down past the roses, with baskets on their heads. I turned and ran out of the garden.

3

My room was empty even of the wolfhound. I climbed on my bed and leaned my elbows on the windowsill, and stayed there a long while alone, while outside in the pear tree's boughs the thrush sang, and from the courtyard beyond the shut door came the monotonous clink of the smith's hammer and the creak of the windlass as the mule plodded round the well.

Memory fails me here. I cannot remember how long it was before the clatter and the buzz of voices told me that the evening meal was being prepared. Nor can I remember how badly I was hurt, but when Cerdic, the groom, pushed the door open and I turned my head, he stopped dead and said: "Lord have mercy upon us. What have you been doing? Playing in the bull-shed?"

"I fell down."

"Oh, aye, you fell down. I wonder why the floor's always twice as hard for you as for anyone else? Who was it? That little sucking-boar Dinias?"

When I did not answer he came across to the bed. He was a small man, with bowed legs and a seamed brown face and a thatch of light-coloured hair. Standing on my bed as I was, my eyes were almost on a level with his.

"Tell you what," he said. "When you're a mite larger I'll teach you a thing or two. You don't have to be big to win a fight. I've a trick or two worth knowing, I can tell you. Got to have, when you're wren-size. I tell you, I can tumble a fellow twice my weight—and a woman too, come to that." He laughed, turned his head to spit, remembered where he was, and cleared his throat instead. "Not that you'll need my tricks once you're grown, a tall lad like you, nor with the girls neither. But you'd best look to that face of yours if you're not to scare them silly. Looks as if it might make a scar." He jerked his head at Moravik's empty pallet. "Where is she?"

"She went with my mother."

"Then you'd best come with me. I'll fix it up."

So it was that the cut on my cheek-bone was dressed with horse-liniment, and I shared Cerdic's supper in the stables, sitting on straw, while a brown mare nosed round me for fodder, and my own fat slug of a pony, at the full end of his rope, watched every mouthful we ate. Cerdic must have had methods of his own in the kitchens, too; the barm-cakes were fresh, there was half a chicken-leg each as well as the salt bacon, and the beer was full-flavoured and cool.

When he came back with the food I knew from his look that he had heard it all. The whole palace must be buzzing. But he said nothing, just handing me the food and sitting down beside me on the straw.

"They told you?" I asked.

He nodded, chewing, then added through a mouthful of bread and meat: "He has a heavy hand."

"He was angry because she refused to wed Gorlan. He wants her wed because of me, but till now she has refused to wed any man. And now, since my uncle Dyved is dead, and Camlach is the only one left, they asked Gorlan from Less Britain. I think my uncle Camlach persuaded my grandfather to ask him, because he is afraid that if she marries a prince in Wales—"

He interrupted at that, looking both startled and scared. "Whist ye now, child! How do you know all this? I'll be bound your elders don't tattle of these high matters in front of you? If it's Moravik who talks when she shouldn't—"

"No. Not Moravik. But I know it's true."

"How in the Thunderer's name do you know any such thing? Slaves' gossip?"

I fed the last bite of my bread to the mare. "If you swear by heathen gods, Cerdic, it's you who'll be in trouble, with Moravik."

"Oh, aye. That kind of trouble's easy enough to come by. Come on, who's been talking to you?"

"Nobody. I know, that's all. I—I can't explain how . . . And when she refused Gorlan my uncle Camlach was as angry as my grandfather. He's afraid my father will come back and marry her, and drive him out. He doesn't admit this to my grandfather, of course."

"Of course." He was staring, even forgetting to chew, so that saliva dribbled from the corner of his open mouth. He swallowed hastily. "The gods know—God knows where you got all this, but it could be true. Well, go on."

The brown mare was pushing at me, snuffing sweet breath at my neck. I handed her away. "That's all. Gorlan is angry, but they'll give him something. And my mother will go in the end to St. Peter's. You'll see."

There was a short silence. Cerdic swallowed his meat and threw the bone out of the door, where a couple of the stableyard curs pounced on it and raced off in a snarling wrangle.

"Merlin—"

"Yes?"

"You'd be wise if you said no more of this to anyone. Not to anyone. Do you understand?"

I said nothing.

"These are matters that a child doesn't understand. High matters. Oh, some of it's common talk, I grant you, but this about Prince Camlach—" He dropped a hand to my knee, and gripped and shook it. "I tell you, he's dangerous, that one. Leave it be, and stay out of sight. I'll tell no one, trust me for that. But you, you must say no more. Bad enough if you were rightwise a prince born, or even in the King's favour like that red whelp Dinias, but for you . . ." He shook the knee again. "Do you heed me, Merlin? For your skin's sake, keep silent and stay out of their way. And tell me who told you all this."

I thought of the dark cave in the hypocaust, and the sky remote at the top of the shaft. "No one told me. I swear it." When he made a sound of impatience and worry I looked straight at him and told him as much of the truth as I dared. "I have heard things, I admit it. And sometimes people talk over your head, not noticing you're there, or not thinking you understand. But at other times"—I paused—"it's as if something spoke to me, as if I saw things . . . And sometimes the stars tell me . . . and there is music, and voices in the dark. Like dreams."

His hand went up in a gesture of protection. I thought he was crossing himself, then saw the sign against the evil eye. He looked shamefaced at that, and dropped the hand. "Dreams, that's what it is; you're right. You've been asleep in some corner, likely, and they've talked across you when they shouldn't, and you've heard things you shouldn't. I was forgetting you're nothing but a child. When you look with those eyes—" He broke off, and shrugged. "But you'll promise me you'll say no more of what you've heard?"

"All right, Cerdic. I promise you. If you'll promise to tell me something in return."

"What's that?"

"Who my father was."

He choked over his beer, then with deliberation wiped the foam away, set down the horn, and regarded me with exasperation. "Now how in middle-earth do you think I know that?"

"I thought Moravik might have told you."

"Does she know?" He sounded so surprised that I knew he was telling the truth.

"When I asked her she just said there were some things it was better not to talk about."

"She's right at that. But if you ask me, that's her way of saying she's no wiser than the next one. And if you do ask me, young Merlin, though you don't, that's another thing you'd best keep clear of. If your lady mother wanted you to know, she'd tell you. You'll find out soon enough, I doubt."

I saw that he was making the sign again, though this time he hid the hand. I opened my mouth to ask if he believed the stories, but he picked up the drinking horn, and got to his feet.

"I've had your promise. Remember?"

"Yes."

"I've watched you. You go your own way, and sometimes I think you're nearer to the wild things than to men. You know she called you for the falcon?"

I nodded.

"Well, here's something for you to think about. You'd best be forgetting falcons for the time being. There's plenty of them around, too many, if truth be told. Have you watched the ring-doves, Merlin?"

"The ones that drink from the fountain with the white doves, then fly away free? Of course I have. I feed them in winter, along with the doves."

"They used to say in my country, the ring-dove has many enemies, because her flesh is sweet and her eggs are good to eat. But she lives and she prospers, because she runs away. The Lady Niniane may have called you her little falcon, but you're not a falcon yet, young Merlin. You're only a dove. Remember that. Live by keeping quiet, and by running away. Mark my words." He nodded at me, and put a hand down to pull me to my feet. "Does the cut still hurt?"

"It stings."

"Then it's on the mend. The bruise is nought to worry you, it'll go soon enough."

It did, indeed, heal cleanly, and left no mark. But I remember how it stung that night, and kept me awake, so that Cerdic and Moravik kept silent in the other corner of the room, for fear, I suppose, that it had been from some of their mutterings that I had pieced together my information.

After they slept I crept out, stepped past the grinning wolfhound, and ran along the hypocaust.

But tonight I heard nothing to remember, except Olwen's voice, mellow as an ousel's, singing some song I had not heard before, about a wild goose, and a hunter with a golden net.

4

After this, life settled back into its peaceful rut, and I think that my grandfather must eventually have accepted my mother's refusal to marry. Things were strained between them for a week or so, but with Camlach home, and settling down as if he had never left the place—and with a good hunting season coming up—the King forgot his rancour, and things went back to normal.

Except possibly for me. After the incident in the orchard, Camlach no longer went out of his way to favour me, nor I to follow him. But he was not unkind to me, and once or twice defended me in some petty rough-and-tumble with the other boys, even taking my part against Dinias, who had supplanted me in his favour.

But I no longer needed that kind of protection. That September day had taught me other lessons besides Cerdic's of the ring-dove. I dealt with Dinias myself. One night, creeping beneath his bedchamber on the way to my "cave," I chanced to hear him and his pack-follower Brys laughing over a foray of that afternoon when the pair of them had followed Camlach's friend Alun to his tryst with one of the servant-girls, and had stayed hidden, watching and listening, to the sweet end. When Dinias waylaid me next morning I stood my ground and—quoting a sentence or so—asked if he had seen Alun yet that day. He stared, went red and then white (for Alun had a hard hand and a temper to match it) and then sidled away, making the sign behind his back. If he liked to think it was magic rather than simple blackmail, I let him. After that, if the High King himself had ridden in claiming parentage for me, none of the children would have believed him. They left me alone.

Which was just as well, for during that winter part of the floor of the bath-house fell in, my grandfather judged the whole thing dangerous, and had it filled in and poison laid for the rats. So like a cub smoked from its earth, I had to fend for myself above ground.

About six months after Gorlan's visit, as we were coming through a cold February into the first budding days of March, Camlach began to insist, first to my mother and then to my grandfather, that I should be taught to read and write. My mother, I think, was grateful for this evidence of his interest in me; I myself was pleased and took good care to show it, though after the incident in the orchard I could have no illusions about his motives. But it did no harm to let Camlach think that my feelings about the priesthood had undergone a change. My mother's declaration that she would never marry, coupled with her increased withdrawal among her women and her frequent visits to St. Peter's to talk with the Abbess and such priests as visited the community, removed his worst fears—either that she would marry a Welsh prince who could hope to take over the kingdom in her right, or that my unknown father would come to claim her and legitimate me, and prove to be a man of rank and power who might supplant him forcibly. It did not matter to Camlach that in either event I was not much of a danger to him, and less than ever now, for he had taken a wife before Christmas, and already at the beginning of March it seemed that she was pregnant. Even Olwen's increasingly obvious pregnancy was no threat to him, for Camlach stood high in his father's favour, and it was not likely that a brother so much younger would ever present a serious danger. There could be no question; Camlach had a good fighting record, knew how to make men like him, and had ruthlessness and common sense. The ruthlessness showed in what he had tried to do to me in the orchard; the common sense showed in his indifferent kindness once my mother's decision removed the threat to him. But I have noticed this about ambitious men, or men in power—they fear even the slightest and least likely threat to it. He would never rest until he saw me priested and safely out of the palace.

Whatever his motives, I was pleased when my tutor came; he was a Greek who had been a scribe in Massilia until he drank himself into debt and ensuing slavery; now he was assigned to me, and because he was grateful for the change in status and the relief from manual work, taught me well and without the religious bias which had constricted the teaching I had picked up from my mother's priests. Demetrius was a pleasant, ineffectually clever man who had a genius for languages, and whose only recreations were dice and (when he won) drink. Occasionally, when he had won enough, I would find him happily and incapably asleep over his books. I never told anyone of these occasions, and indeed was glad of the chance to go about my own affairs; he was grateful for my silence, and in his turn, when I once or twice played truant, held his tongue and made no attempt to find out where I had been. I was quick to catch up with my studies and showed more than enough progress to satisfy my mother and Camlach, so Demetrius and I respected one another's secrets and got along tolerably well.

One day in August, almost a year after the coming of Gorlan to my grandfather's court, I left Demetrius placidly sleeping it off, and rode up alone into the hills behind the town.

I had been this way several times before. It was quicker to go up past the barrack walls and then out by the military road which led eastwards through the hills to Caerleon, but this meant riding through the town, and possibly being seen, and questions being asked. The way I took was along the river-bank. There was a gateway, not much used, leading straight out from our stableyard to the broad flat path where the horses went that towed the barges, and the path followed the river for quite a long way, past St. Peter's and then along the placid curves of the Tywy to the mill, which was as far as the barges went. I had never been beyond this point, but there was a pathway leading up past the mill-house and over the road, and then by the valley of the tributary stream that helped to serve the mill.

It was a hot, drowsy day, full of the smell of bracken. Blue dragonflies darted and glimmered over the river, and the meadowsweet was thick as curds under the humming clouds of flies.

My pony's neat hoofs tapped along the baked clay of the towpath. We met a big dapple grey bringing an empty barge down from the mill with the tide, taking it easy. The boy perched on its withers called a greeting, and the bargeman lifted a hand.

When I reached the mill there was no one in sight. Grain sacks, newly unloaded, were piled on the narrow wharf. By them the miller's dog lay sprawled in the hot sun, hardly troubling to open an eye as I drew rein in the shade of the buildings. Above me, the long straight stretch of the military road was empty. The stream tumbled through a culvert beneath it, and I saw a trout leap and flash in the foam.

It would be hours before I could be missed. I put the pony at the bank up to the road, won the brief battle when he tried to turn for home, then kicked him to a canter along the path which led upstream into the hills.

The path twisted and turned at first, climbing the steep stream-side, then led out of the thorns and thin oaks that filled the gully, and went north in a smooth level curve along the open slope.

Here the townsfolk graze their sheep and cattle, so the grass is smooth and shorn. I passed one shepherd boy, drowsy under a hawthorn bush, with his sheep at hand; he was simple, and only stared vacantly at me as I trotted past, fingering the pile of stones with which he herded his sheep. As we passed him he picked up one of them, a smooth green pebble, and I wondered if he was going to throw it at me, but he lobbed it instead to turn some fat grazing lambs which were straying too far, then went back to his slumbers. There were black cattle further afield, down nearer the river where the grass was longer, but I could not see the herdsman. Away at the foot of the hill, tiny beside a tiny hut, I saw a girl with a flock of geese.

Presently the path began to climb again, and my pony slowed to a walk, picking his way through scattered trees. Hazel-nuts were thick in the coppices, mountain ash and brier grew from tumbles of mossed rock, and the bracken was breast-high. Rabbits ran everywhere, scuttering through the fern, and a pair of jays scolded a fox from the safety of a swinging hornbeam. The ground was too hard, I supposed, to bear tracks well, but I could see no sign, either of crushed bracken or broken twigs, that any other horseman had recently been this way.

The sun was high. A little breeze swept through the hawthorns, rattling the green, hard fruit. I urged the pony on. Now among the oaks and hollies were pine trees, their stems reddish in the sunlight. The ground grew rougher as the path climbed, with bare grey stone outcropping through the thin turf, and a honeycombing of rabbit burrows. I did not know where the path led, I knew nothing but that I was alone, and free. There was nothing to tell me what sort of day this was, or what way-star was leading me up into the hill. This was in the days before the future became clear to me.

The pony hesitated, and I came to myself. There was a fork in the track, with nothing to indicate which would be the best way to go. To left, to right, it led away round the two sides of a thicket.

The pony turned decisively to the left, this being downhill. I would have let him go, but that at that moment a bird flew low across the path in front of me, left to right, and vanished beyond the trees. Sharp wings, a flash of rust and slate-blue, the fierce dark eye and curved beak of a merlin. For no reason, except that this was better than no reason, I turned the pony's head after it, and dug my heels in.

The path climbed in a shallow curve, leaving the wood on the left. This was a stand mainly of pines, thickly clustered and dark, and so heavily grown that you could only have hacked your way in through the dead stuff with an axe. I heard the clap of wings as a ring-dove fled from shelter, dropping invisibly out of the far side of the trees. It had gone to the left. This time I followed the falcon.

We were now well out of sight of the river valley and the town. The pony picked his way along one side of a shallow valley, at the foot of which ran a narrow, tumbling stream. On the far side of the stream the long slopes of turf went bare up to the scree, and above this were the rocks, blue and grey in the sunlight. The slope where I rode was scattered with hawthorn brakes throwing pools of slanted shadow, and above them again, scree, and a cliff hung with ivy where choughs wheeled and called in the bright air. Apart from their busy sound, the valley held the most complete and echo-less stillness.

The pony's hoofs sounded loud on the baked earth. It was hot, and I was thirsty. Now the track ran along under a low cliff, perhaps twenty feet high, and at its foot a grove of hawthorns cast a pool of shade across the path. Somewhere, close above me, I could hear the trickle of water.

I stopped the pony and slid off. I led him into the shade of the grove and made him fast, then looked about me for the source of the water.

The rock by the path was dry, and below the path was no sign of any water running down to swell the stream at the foot of the valley. But the sound of running water was steady and unmistakable. I left the path and scrambled up the grass at the side of the rock, to find myself on a small flat patch of turf, a little dry lawn scattered with rabbits' droppings, and at the back of it another face of cliff.

In the face of the rock was a cave. The rounded opening was smallish and very regular, almost like a made arch. To one side of this, the right as I stood looking, was a slope of grass-grown stones long ago fallen from above, and overgrown with oak and rowan, whose branches overhung the cave with shadow. To the other side, and only a few feet from the archway, was the spring.

I approached it. It was very small, a little shining movement of water oozing out of a crack in the face of the rock, and falling with a steady trickle into a round basin of stone. There was no outflow. Presumably the water sprang from the rock, gathered in the basin, and drained away through another crack, eventually to join the stream below. Through the clear water I could see every pebble, every grain of sand at the bottom of the basin. Hart's-tongue fern grew above it, and there was moss at the lip, and below it green, moist grass.

I knelt on the grass, and had put my mouth to the water, when I saw there was a cup. This stood in a tiny niche among the ferns. It was a handspan high, and made of brown horn. As I lifted it down I saw above it, half-hidden by the ferns, the small, carved figure of a wooden god. I recognized him. I had seen him under the oak at Tyr Myrddin. Here he was in his own hill-top place, under the open sky.

I filled the cup and drank, pouring a few drops on the ground for the god.

Then I went into the cave.

5

This was bigger than had appeared from outside. Only a couple of paces inside the archway—and my paces were very short—the cave opened out into a seemingly vast chamber whose top was lost in shadow. It was dark, but—though at first I neither noticed this nor looked for its cause—with some source of extra light that gave a vague illumination, showing the floor smooth and clear of obstacles. I made my way slowly forward, straining my eyes, with deep inside me the beginning of that surge of excitement that caves have always started in me. Some men experience this with water; some, I know, on high places; some create fire for the same pleasure: with me it has always been the depths of the forest, or the depths of the earth. Now, I know why; but then, I only knew that I was a boy who had found somewhere new, something he could perhaps make his own in a world where he owned nothing.

Next moment I stopped short, brought up by a shock which spilled the excitement through my bowels like water. Something had moved in the murk, just to my right.

I froze still, straining my eyes to see. There was no movement. I held my breath, listening. There was no sound. I flared my nostrils, testing the air cautiously round me. There was no smell, animal or human; the cave smelt, I thought, of smoke and damp rock and the earth itself, and of a queer musty scent I couldn't identify. I knew, without putting it into words, that had there been any other creature near me the air would have felt different, less empty. There was no one there.

I tried a word, softly, in Welsh. "Greetings." The whisper came straight back at me in an echo so quick that I knew I was very near the wall of the cave, then it lost itself, hissing, in the roof.

There was movement there—at first, I thought, only an intensifying of the echoed whisper, then the rustling grew and grew like the rustling of a woman's dress, or a curtain stirring in the draught. Something went past my cheek, with a shrill, bloodless cry just on the edge of sound. Another followed, and after them flake after flake of shrill shadow, pouring down from the roof like leaves down a stream of wind, or fish down a fall. It was the bats, disturbed from their lodging in the top of the cave, streaming out now into the daylight valley. They would be pouring out of the low archway like a plume of smoke.

I stood quite still, wondering if it was these that had made the curious musty smell. I thought I could smell them as they passed, but it wasn't the same. I had no fear that they would touch me; in darkness or light, whatever their speed, bats will touch nothing. They are so much creatures of the air, I believe, that as the air parts in front of an obstacle the bat is swept aside with it, like a petal carried downstream. They poured past, a shrill tide of them between me and the wall. Childlike, to see what the stream would do—how it would divert itself—I took a step nearer to the wall. Nothing touched me. The stream divided and poured on, the shrill air brushing both my cheeks. It was as if I did not exist. But at the same moment when I moved, the creature that I had seen moved, too. Then my outstretched hand met, not rock, but metal, and I knew what the creature was. It was my own reflection.

Hanging against the wall was a sheet of metal, burnished to a dull sheen. This, then, was the source of the diffused light within the cave; the mirror's silky surface caught, obliquely, the light from the cave's mouth, and sent it on into the darkness. I could see myself moving in it like a ghost, as I recoiled and let fall the hand which had leapt to the knife at my hip.

Behind me the flow of bats had ceased, and the cave was still. Reassured, I stayed where I was, studying myself with interest in the mirror. My mother had had one once, an antique from Egypt, but then, deeming such things to be vanity, she had locked it away. Of course I had often seen my face reflected in water, but never my body mirrored, till now. I saw a dark boy, wary, all eyes with curiosity, nerves, and excitement. In that light my eyes looked quite black; my hair was black, too, thick and clean, but worse cut and groomed than my pony's; my tunic and sandals were a disgrace. I grinned, and the mirror flashed a sudden smile that changed the picture completely and at once, from a sullen young animal poised to run or fight, to something quick and gentle and approachable; something, I knew even then, that few people had ever seen.

Then it vanished, and the wary animal was back, as I leaned forward to run a hand over the metal. It was cold and smooth and freshly burnished. Whoever had hung it—and he must be the same person who used the cup of horn outside—had either been here very recently, or he still lived here, and might come back at any moment to find me.

I was not particularly frightened. I had pricked to caution when I saw the cup, but one learns very young to take care of oneself, and the times I had been brought up in were peaceful enough, at any rate in our valley; but there are always wild men and rough men and the lawless and vagabonds to be reckoned with, and any boy who likes his own company, as I did, must be prepared to defend his skin. I was wiry, and strong for my age, and I had my dagger. That I was barely seven years old never entered my head; I was Merlin, and, bastard or not, the King's grandson. I went on exploring.

The next thing I found, a pace along the wall, was a box, and on top of it shapes which my hands identified immediately as flint and iron and tinderbox, and a big, roughly made candle of what smelled like sheep's tallow. Beside these objects lay a shape which—incredulously and inch by inch—I identified as the skull of a horned sheep. There were nails driven into the top of the box here and there, apparently holding down fragments of leather. But when I felt these, carefully, I found in the withered leather frameworks of delicate bone; they were dead bats, stretched and nailed on the wood.

This was a treasure cave indeed. No find of gold or weapons could have excited me more. Full of curiosity, I reached for the tinderbox.

Then I heard him coming back.

My first thought was that he must have seen my pony, then I realized he was coming from further up the hill. I could hear the rattling and scaling of small stones as he came down the scree above the cave. One of them splashed into the spring outside, and then it was too late. I heard him jump down on to the flat grass beside the water.

It was time for the ring-dove again; the falcon was forgotten. I ran deeper into the cave. As he swept aside the boughs that darkened the entrance, the light grew momentarily, enough to show me my way. At the back of the cave was a slope and jut of rock, and, at twice my height, a widish ledge. A quick flash of sunlight from the mirror caught a wedge of shadow in the rock above the ledge, big enough to hide me. Soundless in my scuffed sandals, I swarmed on to the ledge, and crammed my body into that wedge of shadow, to find it was in fact a gap in the rock, giving apparently on to another, smaller cave. I slithered in through the gap like an otter into the river-bank.

It seemed that he had heard nothing. The light was cut off again as the boughs sprang back into place behind him, and he came into the cave. It was a man's tread, measured and slow.

If I had thought about it at all, I suppose I would have assumed that the cave would be uninhabited at least until sunset, that whoever owned the place would be away hunting, or about his other business, and would return only at nightfall. There was no point in wasting candles when the sun was blazing outside. Perhaps he was here now only to bring home his kill, and he would go again and leave me the chance to get out. I hoped he would not see my pony tethered in the hawthorn brake.

Then I heard him moving, with the sure tread of someone who knows his way blindfold, towards the candle and the tinderbox.

Even now I had no room for apprehension, no room, indeed, for any but the one thought or sensation—the extreme discomfort of the cave into which I had crawled. It was apparently small, not much bigger than the large round vats they use for dyeing, and much the same shape. Floor, wall and ceiling hugged me round in a continuous curve. It was like being inside a large globe; moreover, a globe studded with nails, or with its inner surface stuck all over with small pieces of jagged stone. There seemed no inch of surface not bristling like a bed of strewn flints, and it was only my light weight, I think, that saved me from being cut, as I quested about blindly to find some clear space to lie on. I found a place smoother than the rest and curled there, as small as I could, watching the faintly defined opening, and inching my dagger silently from its sheath into my hand.

I heard the quick hiss and chime of flint and iron, and then the flare of light, intense in the darkness, as the tinder caught hold. Then the steady, waxing glow as he lit the candle.

Or rather, it should have been the slow-growing beam of a candle flame that I saw, but instead there was a flash, a sparkle, a conflagration as if a whole pitch-soaked beacon was roaring up in flames. Light poured and flashed, crimson, golden, white, red, intolerable into my cave. I winced back from it, frightened now, heedless of pain and cut flesh as I shrank against the sharp walls. The whole globe where I lay seemed to be full of flame.

It was indeed a globe, a round chamber floored, roofed, lined with crystals. They were fine as glass, and smooth as glass, but clearer than any glass I had ever seen, brilliant as diamonds. This, in fact, to my childish mind, was what they first seemed to be. I was in a globe lined with diamonds, a million burning diamonds, each face of each gem wincing with the light, shooting it to and fro, diamond to diamond and back again, with rainbows and rivers and bursting stars and a shape like a crimson dragon clawing up the wall, while below it a girl's face swam faintly with closed eyes, and the light drove right into my body as if it would break me open.

I shut my eyes. When I opened them again I saw that the golden light had shrunk and was concentrated on one part of the wall no bigger than my head, and from this, empty of visions, rayed the broken, brilliant beams.

There was silence from the cave below. He had not stirred. I had not even heard the rustle of his clothes.

Then the light moved. The flashing disc began to slide, slowly, across the crystal wall. I was shaking. I huddled closer to the sharp stones, trying to escape it. There was nowhere to go. It advanced slowly round the curve. It touched my shoulder, my head, and I ducked, cringing. The shadow of my movement rushed across the globe, like a wind-eddy over a pool.

The light stopped, retreated, fixed glittering in its place. Then it went out. But the glow of the candle, strangely, remained; an ordinary steady yellow glow beyond the gap in the wall of my refuge.

"Come out." The man's voice, not loud, not raised with shouted orders like my grandfather's, was clear and brief with all the mystery of command. It never occurred to me to disobey. I crept forward over the sharp crystals, and through the gap. Then I slowly pulled myself upright on the ledge, my back against the wall of the outer cave, the dagger ready in my right hand, and looked down.

6

He stood between me and the candle, a hugely tall figure (or so it seemed to me) in a long robe of some brown homespun stuff. The candle made a nimbus of his hair, which seemed to be grey, and he was bearded. I could not see his expression, and his right hand was hidden in the folds of his robe.

I waited, poised warily.

He spoke again, in the same tone. "Put up your dagger and come down."

"When I see your right hand," I said.

He showed it, palm up. It was empty. He said gravely: "I am unarmed."

"Then stand out of my way," I said, and jumped. The cave was wide, and he was standing to one side of it. My leap carried me three or four paces down the cave, and I was past him and near the entrance before he could have moved more than a step. But in fact he never moved at all. As I reached the mouth of the cave and swept aside the hanging branches I heard him laughing.

The sound brought me up short. I turned.

From here, in the light which now filled the cave, I saw him clearly. He was old, with grey hair thinning on top and hanging lank over his ears, and a straight growth of grey beard, roughly trimmed. His hands were calloused and grained with dirt, but had been fine, with long fingers. Now the old man's veins crawled and knotted on them, distended like worms. But it was his face which held me; it was thin, cavernous almost as a skull, with a high domed forehead and bushy grey brows which came down jutting over eyes where I could see no trace of age at all. These were closely set, large, and of a curiously clear and swimming grey. His nose was a thin beak; his mouth, lipless now, stretched wide with his laughter over astonishingly good teeth.

"Come back. There's no need to be afraid."

"I'm not afraid." I dropped the boughs back into place, and not without bravado walked towards him. I stopped a few paces away. "Why should I be afraid of you? Do you know who I am?"

He regarded me for a moment, seeming to muse. "Let me see you. Dark hair, dark eyes, the body of a dancer and the manners of a young wolf . . . or should I say a young falcon?"

My dagger sank to my side. "Then you do know me?"

"Shall I say I knew you would come some day, and today I knew there was someone here. What do you think brought me back so early?"

"How did you know there was someone here? Oh, of course, you saw the bats."

"Perhaps."

"Do they always go up like that?"

"Only for strangers. Your dagger, sir."

I put it back in my belt. "Nobody calls me sir. I'm a bastard. That means I belong to myself, no one else. My name's Merlin, but you knew that."

"And mine is Galapas. Are you hungry?"

"Yes." But I said it dubiously, thinking of the skull and the dead bats.

Disconcertingly, he understood. The grey eyes twinkled. "Fruit and honey cakes? And sweet water from the spring? What better fare would you get, even in the King's house?"

"I wouldn't get that in the King's house at this hour of the day," I said frankly. "Thank you, sir, I'll be glad to eat with you."

He smiled. "Nobody calls me sir. And I belong to no man, either. Go out and sit down in the sun, and I'll bring the food."

The fruit was apples, which looked and tasted exactly like the ones from my grandfather's orchard, so that I stole a sideways glance at my host, scanning him by daylight, wondering if I had ever seen him on the river-bank, or anywhere in the town.

"Do you have a wife?" I asked. "Who makes the honey cakes? They're very good."

"No wife. I told you I belonged to no man, and to no woman either. You will see, Merlin, how all your life men, and women too, will try to put bars round you, but you will escape those bars, or bend them, or melt them at your will, until, of your will, you take them round you, and sleep behind them in their shadow. . . . I get the honey cakes from the shepherd's wife, she makes enough for three, and is good enough to spare some for charity."

"Are you a hermit, then? A holy man?"

"Do I look like a holy man?"

"No." This was true. The only people I remember being afraid of at that time were the solitary holy men who sometimes wandered, preaching and begging, into the town; queer, arrogant, noisy men, with a mad look in their eyes, and a smell about them which I associated with the heaps of offal outside the slaughter-pens. It was sometimes hard to know which god they professed to serve. Some of them, it was whispered, were druids, who were still officially outside the law, though in Wales in the country places they still practiced without much interference. Many were followers of the old gods—the local deities—and since these varied in popularity according to season, their priests tended to switch allegiance from time to time where the pickings were richest. Even the Christian ones did this sometimes, but you could usually tell the real Christians, because they were the dirtiest. The Roman gods and their priests stayed solidly enshrined in their crumbling temples, but did very well on offerings likewise. The Church frowned on the lot, but could not do much about it. "There was a god at the spring outside," I ventured.

"Yes. Myrddin. He lends me his spring, and his hollow hill, and his heaven of woven light, and in return I give him his due. It does not do to neglect the gods of a place, whoever they may be. In the end, they are all one."

"If you're not a hermit, then, what are you?"

"At the moment, a teacher."

"I have a tutor. He comes from Massilia, but he's actually been to Rome. Who do you teach?"

"Until now, nobody. I'm old and tired, and I came to live here alone and study."

"Why do you have the dead bats in there, on the box?"

"I was studying them."

I stared at him. "Studying bats? How can you study bats?"

"I study the way they are made, and the way they fly, and mate, and feed. The way they live. Not only bats, but beasts and fish and plants and birds, as many as I see."

"But that's not studying!" I regarded him with wonder. "Demetrius—that's my tutor—tells me that watching lizards and birds is dreaming, and a waste of time. Though Cerdic—that's a friend—told me to study the ring-doves."

"Why?"

"Because they're quick, and quiet, and keep out of the way. Because they only lay two eggs, but still though everybody hunts them, men and beasts and hawks, there are still more ring-doves than anything else."

"And they don't put them in cages." He drank some water, regarding me. "So you have a tutor. Then you can read?"

"Of course."

"Can you read Greek?"

"A little."

"Then come with me."

He got up and went into the cave. I followed him. He lit the candle once more—he had put it out to save tallow—and by its light lifted the lid of the box. In it I saw the rolled shapes of books, more books together than I had ever imagined there were in the world. I watched as he selected one, closed the lid carefully, and unrolled the book.

"There."

With delight, I saw what it was. A drawing, spidery but definite, of the skeleton of a bat. And alongside it, in neat, crabbed Greek letters, phrases which I immediately, forgetting even Galapas' presence, began to spell out to myself.

In a minute or two his hand came over my shoulder. "Bring it outside." He pulled out the nails holding one of the dried leathery bodies to the box-lid, and lifted it carefully in his palm. "Blow out the candle. We'll look at this together."

And so, with no more question, and no more ceremony, began my first lesson with Galapas.

It was only when the sun, low over one wing of the valley, sent a long shadow creeping up the slope, that I remembered the other life that waited for me, and how far I had to go. I jumped to my feet.

"I'll have to go! Demetrius won't say anything, but if I'm late for supper they'll ask why."

"And you don't intend to tell them?"

"No, or they'd stop me coming again."

He smiled, making no comment. I doubt if I noticed then the calm assumptions on which the interview had been based; he had neither asked how I had come, nor why. And because I was only a child I took it for granted, too, though for politeness' sake I asked him:

"I may come again, mayn't I?"

"Of course."

"I—it's hard to say when. I never know when I'll get away—I mean, when I'll be free."

"Don't worry. I shall know when you are coming. And I shall be here."

"How can you know?"

He was rolling up the book with those long, neat fingers. "The same way I knew today."

"Oh! I was forgetting. You mean I go into the cave and send the bats out?"

"If you like."

I laughed with pleasure. "I've never met anyone like you! To make smoke signals with bats! If I told them they'd never believe me, even Cerdic."

"You won't tell even Cerdic."

I nodded. "That's right. Nobody at all. Now I must go. Goodbye, Galapas."

"Goodbye."

And so it was in the days, and in the months, that followed. Whenever I could, once and sometimes twice in the week, I rode up the valley to the cave. He certainly seemed to know when I was coming, for as often as not he was there waiting for me, with the books laid out; but when there was no sign of him I did as we had arranged and sent out the bats as a smoke signal to bring him in. As the weeks went by they got used to me, and it took two or three well-aimed stones sent up into the roof to get them out; but after a while this grew unnecessary; people at the palace grew accustomed to my absences, and ceased to question them, and it became possible to make arrangements with Galapas for meeting from day to day.

Moravik had let me go more and more my own way since Olwen's baby had been born at the end of May, and when Camlach's son arrived in September she established herself firmly in the royal nursery as its official ruler, abandoning me as suddenly as a bird deserting the nest. I saw less and less of my mother, who seemed content to spend her time with her women, so I was left pretty much to Demetrius and Cerdic between them. Demetrius had his own reasons for welcoming a day off now and again, and Cerdic was my friend. He would unsaddle the muddy and sweating pony without question, or with a wink and a lewd remark about where I had been that was meant as a joke, and was taken as such. I had my room to myself now, except for the wolfhound; he spent the nights with me for old times' sake, but whether he was any safeguard I have no idea. I suspect no; I was safe enough. The country was at peace, except for the perennial rumours of invasion from Less Britain; Camlach and his father were in accord; I was to all appearances heading willingly and at high speed for the prison of the priesthood, and so, when my lessons with Demetrius were officially done, was free to go where I wished.

I never saw anyone else in the valley. The shepherd only lived there in summer, in a poor hut below the wood. There were no other dwellings there, and beyond Galapas' cave the track was used only by sheep and deer. It led nowhere.

He was a good teacher, and I was quick, but in fact I hardly thought of my time with him as lessons. We left languages and geometry to Demetrius, and religion to my mother's priests; with Galapas to begin with it was only like listening to a story-teller. He had travelled when young to the other side of the earth, Aethiopia and Greece and Germany and all around the Middle Sea, and seen and learned strange things. He taught me practical things, too; how to gather herbs and dry them to keep, how to use them for medicines, and how to distil certain subtle drugs, even poisons. He made me study the beasts and birds, and—with the dead birds and sheep we found on the hills, and once with a dead deer—I learnt about the organs and bones of the body. He taught me how to stop bleeding, how to set a broken bone, how to cut bad flesh away and cleanse the place so that it heals cleanly; even—though this came later—how to draw flesh and sinews into place with thread while the beast is stunned with fumes. I remember that the first spell he taught me was the charming of warts; this is so easy that a woman can do it.

One day he took a book out of the box and unrolled it. "Do you know what this is?"

I was used to diagrams and drawings, but this was a drawing of nothing I could recognize. The writing was in Latin, and I saw the words *Aethiopia* and *Fortunate Islands,* and then right out in a corner, *Britannia.* The lines seemed to be scrawled everywhere, and all over the picture were trails of mounds drawn in, like a field where moles have been at work.

"Those, are they mountains?"

"Yes."

"Then it's a picture of the world?"

"A map."

I had never seen a map before. At first I could not see how it worked, but in a while, as he talked, I saw how the world lay there as a bird sees it, with roads and rivers like the radials of a spider's web, or the guidelines that lead the bee into the flower. As a man finds a stream he knows, and follows it through the wild moors, so, with a map, it is possible to ride from Rome to Massilia, or London to Caerleon, without once asking the way or looking for the milestones. This art was discovered by the Greek Anaximander, though some say the Egyptians knew it first. The map that Galapas showed me was a copy from a book by Ptolemy of Alexandria. After he had explained, and we had studied the map together, he bade me get out my tablet and make a map for myself, of my own country.

When I had done he looked at it. "This in the center, what is it?"

"Maridunum," I said in surprise. "See, there is the bridge, and the river, and this is the road through the market place, and the barrack gates are here."

"I see that. I did not say your town, Merlin, I said your country."

"The whole of Wales? How do I know what lies north of the hills? I've never been further than this."

"I will show you."

He put aside the tablet, and taking a sharp stick, began to draw in the dust, explaining as he did so. What he drew for me was a map shaped like a big triangle, not Wales only, but the whole of Britain, even the wild land beyond the Wall where the savages live. He showed me the mountains and rivers and roads and towns, London and Calleva and the places that cluster thick in the south, to the towns and fortresses at the ends of the web of roads, Segontium and Caerleon and Eboracum and the towns along the Wall itself. He spoke as if it were all one country, though I could have told him the names of the kings of a dozen places that he mentioned. I only remember this because of what came after.

Soon after this, when winter came and the stars were out early, he taught me their names and their powers, and how a man could map them as one would map the roads and townships. They made music, he said, as they moved. He himself did not know music, but when he found that Olwen had taught me, he helped me to make myself a harp. This was a rude enough affair, I suppose, and small, made of hornbeam, with the curve and fore-pillar of red sallow from the

Tywy, and strung with hair from my pony's tail, where the harp of a prince (said Galapas) should have been strung with gold and silver wire. But I made the string-shoes out of pierced copper coins, the key and tuning-pins of polished bone, then carved a merlin on the sounding-board, and thought it a finer instrument than Olwen's. Indeed it was as true as hers, having a kind of sweet whispering note which seemed to pluck songs from the air itself. I kept it in the cave: though Dinias left me alone these days, being a warrior while I was only a sucking clerk, I would not have kept anything I treasured in the palace, unless I could lock it in my clothes-chest, and the harp was too big for that. At home for music I had the birds in the pear tree, and Olwen still sang sometimes. And when the birds were silent, and the night sky was frosted with light, I listened for the music of the stars. But I never heard it.

Then one day, when I was twelve years old, Galapas spoke of the crystal cave.

7

It is common knowledge that, with children, those things which are most important often go unmentioned. It is as if the child recognizes, by instinct, things which are too big for him, and keeps them in his mind, feeding them with his imagination till they assume proportions distended or grotesque which can become equally the stuff of magic or of nightmare.

So it was with the crystal cave.

I had never mentioned to Galapas my first experience there. Even to myself I had hardly admitted what came sometimes with light and fire; dreams, I had told myself, memories from below memory, figments of the brain only, like the voice which had told me of Gorlan, or the sight of the poison in the apricot. And when I found that Galapas never mentioned the inner cave, and that the mirror was kept covered whenever I was there, I said nothing.

I rode up to see him one day in winter when frost made the ground glitter and ring, and my pony puffed out steam like a dragon. He went fast, tossing his head and dragging at the bit, and breaking into a canter as soon as I turned him away from the wood and along the high valley. I had at length grown out of the gentle, cream-coloured pony of my childhood, but was proud of my little Welsh grey, which I called Aster. There is a breed of Welsh mountain pony, hardy, swift, and very beautiful, with a fine narrow head and small ears, and a strong arch to the neck. They run wild in the hills, and in past times interbred with horses the Romans brought from the East. Aster had been caught and broken for my cousin Dinias, who had overridden him for a couple of years and then discarded him for a real war-horse. I found him hard to manage, with rough manners and a ruined mouth, but his paces were silken after the jogging I was used to, and once he got over his fear of me he was affectionate.

I had long since contrived a shelter for my pony when I came here in winter. The hawthorn brake grew right up against the cliff below the cave, and deep in the thickest part of it Galapas and I had carried stones to make a pen of which the back wall was the cliff itself. When we had laid dead boughs against the walls and across the top, and had carried a few armfuls of bracken, the pen was not only a warm, solid shelter, but invisible to the casual eye. This need for secrecy was another of the things that had never been openly discussed; I understood without being told that Galapas in some way was helping me to run counter to Camlach's plans for me, so—even though as time went on I was left more completely to my own devices—I took every precaution to avoid discovery, finding half a dozen different ways to approach the valley, and a score of stories to account for the time I spent there.

I led Aster into the pen, took off his saddle and bridle and hung them up, then threw down fodder from a saddle-bag, barred the entrance with a stout branch, and walked briskly up to the cave.

Galapas was not there, but that he had gone only recently was attested by the fact that the brazier which stood inside the cave mouth had been banked down to a glow. I stirred it till the flames leapt, then settled near it with a book. I had not come today by arrangement, but had plenty of time, so left the bats alone, and read peacefully for a while.

I don't know what made me, that day out of all the days I had been there alone, suddenly put the book aside, and walk back past the veiled mirror to look up at the cleft through which I had fled five years ago. I told myself that I was only curious to see if it was as I had remembered it, or if the crystals, like the visions, were figments of my imagination; whatever the reason, I climbed quickly to the ledge, and dropping on my hands and knees by the gap, peered in.

The inner cave was dead and dark, no glimmer reaching it from the fire. I crawled forward cautiously, till my hands met the sharp crystals. They were all too real. Even now not admitting to myself why I hurried, with one eye on the mouth of the main cave and an ear open for Galapas' return, I slithered down from the ledge, snatched up the leather riding jerkin which I had discarded and, hurrying back, thrust it in front of me through the gap. Then I crawled after.

With the leather jerkin spread on the floor, the globe was comparatively comfortable. I lay still. The silence was complete. As my eyes grew accustomed to the darkness, I could see the faintest grey glimmer from the crystals, but of the magic that the light had brought there was no sign.

There must have been some crack open to the air, for even in that dark confine there was a slight current, a cold thread of a draught. And with it came the sound I was listening for, the footsteps of someone approaching over the frosty rock . . .

When Galapas came into the cave a few minutes later I was sitting by the fire, my jerkin rolled up beside me, poring over the book.

Half an hour before dusk we put our books aside. But still I made no move to go. The fire was blazing now, filling the cave with warmth and flickering light. We sat for a while in silence.

"Galapas, there's something I want to ask you."

"Yes?"

"Do you remember the first day I came here?"

"Very clearly."

"You knew I was coming. You were expecting me."

"Did I say so?"

"You know you did. How did you know I would be here?"

"I saw you in the crystal cave."

"Oh, that, yes. You moved the mirror so that the candlelight caught me, and you saw my shadow. But that's not what I was asking you. I meant, how did you know I was going to come up the valley that day?"

"That was the question I answered, Merlin. I knew you were coming up the valley that day, because, before you came, I saw you in the cave."

We looked at one another in silence. The flames glowed and muttered between us, flattened by the little draught that carried the smoke out of the cave. I don't think I answered him at first, I just nodded. It was something I had known. After a while I said, merely: "Will you show me?"

He regarded me for a moment more, then got to his feet. "It is time. Light the candle."

I obeyed him. The little light grew golden, reaching among the shadows cast by the flickering of the fire.

"Take the rug off the mirror."

I pulled at it and it fell off into my arms in a huddle of wool. I dropped it on his bed beside the wall.

"Now go up on the ledge, and lie down."

"On the ledge?"

"Yes. Lie on your belly, with your head towards the cleft, so that you can see in."

"Don't you want me to go right in?"

"And take your jerkin to lie on?"

I was halfway up to the ledge. I whipped round, to see him smiling.

"It's no use, Galapas, you know everything."

"Some day you will go where even with the Sight I cannot follow you. Now lie still, and watch."

I lay down on the ledge. It was wide and flat and held me comfortably enough, prone, with my head pillowed on my bent arms, and turned towards the cleft.

Below me, Galapas said softly: "Think of nothing. I have the reins in my hand; it is not for you yet. Watch only."

I heard him move back across the cave towards the mirror.

The cave was bigger than I had imagined. It stretched upwards further than I could see, and the floor was worn smooth. I had even been wrong about the crystals; the glimmer that reflected the torchlight came only from puddles on the floor, and a place on one wall where a thin slither of moisture betrayed a spring somewhere above.

The torches, jammed into cracks in the cave wall, were cheap ones, of rag stuffed into cracked horns—the rejects from the workshops. They burned sullenly in the bad air. Though the place was cold, the men worked naked save for loincloths, and sweat ran over their backs as they hacked at the rock-face, steady ceaseless tapping blows that made no noise, but you could see the muscles clench and jar under the torchlit sweat. Beneath a knee-high overhang at the base of the wall, flat on their backs in a pool of seepage, two men hammered upwards with shortened, painful blows at rock within inches of their faces. On the wrist of one of them I saw the shiny pucker of an old brand.

One of the hewers at the face doubled up, coughing, then with a glance over his shoulder stifled the cough and got back to work. Light was growing in the cave, coming from a square opening like a doorway, which gave on a curved tunnel down which a fresh torch—a good one—came.

Four boys appeared, filthy with dust and naked like the others, carrying deep baskets, and behind them came a man dressed in a brown tunic smudged with damp. He had the torch in one hand and in the other a tablet which he stood studying with frowning brows while the boys ran with their baskets to the rock-face and began to shovel the fallen rock into them. After a while the foreman went forward to the face and studied it, holding his torch high. The men drew back, thankful it seemed for the respite, and one of them spoke to the foreman, pointing first at the workings, then at the seeping damp at the far side of the cave.

The boys had shovelled and scrabbled their baskets full, and dragged them back from the face. The foreman, with a shrug and a grin, took a silver coin from his pouch and, with the gambler's practiced flick, tossed it. The workmen craned to see. Then the man who had spoken turned back to the face and drove the pick in.

The crack widened, and dust rushed down, blotting out the light. Then in the wake of the dust came the water.

"Drink this," said Galapas.

"What is it?"

"One of my brews, not yours; it's quite safe. Drink it."

"Thanks. Galapas, the cave *is* crystal still. I—dreamed it differently."

"Never mind that now. How do you feel?"

"Odd . . . I can't explain. I feel all right, only a headache, but—empty, like a shell with the snail out of it. No, like a reed with the pith pulled out."

"A whistle for the winds. Yes. Come down to the brazier."

When I sat in my old place, with a cup of mulled wine in my hands, he asked: "Where were you?"

I told him what I had seen, but when I began to ask what it meant, and what he knew, he shook his head. "I think this has already gone past me. I do not know. All I know is that you must finish that wine quickly and go home. Do you realize how long you lay there dreaming? The moon is up."

I started to my feet. "Already? It must be well past suppertime. If they're looking for me—"

"They will not be looking for you. Other things are happening. Go and find out for yourself—and make sure you are part of them."

"What do you mean?"

"Only what I say. Whatever means you have to use, go with the King. Here, don't forget this." He thrust my jerkin into my arms.

I took it blindly, staring. "He's leaving Maridunum?"

"Yes. Only for a while. I don't know how long."

"He'll never take me."

"That's for you to say. The gods only go with you, Myrddin Emrys, if you put yourself in their path. And that takes courage. Put your jerkin on before you go out, it's cold."

I shoved a hand into the sleeve, glowering. "You've seen all this, something that's really happening, and I—I was looking into the crystals with the fire, and here I've got a hellish headache, and all for nothing . . . Some silly dream of slaves in an old mine. Galapas, when will you teach me to see as you do?"

"For a start, I can see the wolves eating you and Aster, if you don't hurry home."

He was laughing to himself as if he had made a great jest, as I ran out of the cave and down to saddle the pony.

8

It was a quarter moon, which gave just enough light to show the way. The pony danced to warm his blood, and pulled harder than ever, his ears pricked towards home, scenting his supper. I had to fight to hold him in, because the way was icy, and I was afraid of a fall, but I confess that—with Galapas' last remark echoing uncomfortably in my head—I let him go downhill through trees a good deal too fast for safety, until we reached the mill and the level of the towpath.

There it was possible to see clearly. I dug my heels in and galloped him the rest of the way.

As soon as we came in sight of town I could see that something was up. The towpath was deserted—the town gates would have been locked long since—but the town was full of lights. Inside the walls torches seemed to be flaring everywhere, and there was shouting and the tramp of feet. I slipped from the saddle at the stableyard gate, fully prepared to find myself locked out, but even as I reached to try it the gate opened, and Cerdic, with a shaded lantern in his hand, beckoned me in.

"I heard you coming. Been listening all evening. Where've you been, loverboy? She must have been good tonight."

"Oh, she was. Have they been asking for me? Have they missed me?"

"Not that I know of. They've got more to think about tonight than you. Give me the bridle, we'll put him in the barn for now. There's too much coming and going in the big yard."

"Why, what's going on? I heard the noise a mile off. Is it a war?"

"No, more's the pity, though it may end up that way. There's a message come this afternoon, the High King's coming to Segontium, and he'll lie there for a week or two. Your grandfather's riding up tomorrow, so everything's to be got ready mighty sharp."

"I see." I followed him into the barn, and stood watching him unsaddle, while half-absently I pulled straw from the pile and twisted a wisp for him. I handed this across the pony's withers. "King Vortigern at Segontium? Why?"

"Counting heads, they say." He gave a snort of laughter as he began to work the pony over.

"Calling in his allies, do you mean? Then there is talk of war?"

"There'll always be talk of war, so long as yon Ambrosius sits there in Less Britain with King Budec at his back, and men remember things that's better not spoken of."

I nodded. I could not remember precisely when I had been told, since nobody said it aloud, but everyone knew the story of how the High King had claimed the throne. He had been regent for the young King Constantius who had died suddenly, and the King's younger brothers had not waited to prove whether the rumours of murder were true or false; they had fled to their cousin Budec in Less Britain, leaving the kingdom to the Wolf and his sons. Every year or so the rumours sprang up again; that King Budec was arming the two young princes; that Ambrosius had gone to Rome; that Uther was a mercenary in the service of the Emperor of the East, or that he had married the King of Persia's daughter; that the two brothers had an army four hundred thousand strong and were going to invade and burn Greater Britain from end to end; or that they would come in peace, like archangels, and drive the Saxons out of the eastern shores without a blow. But more than twenty years had gone by, and the thing had not happened. The coming of Ambrosius was spoken of now as if it were accomplished, and already a legend, as men spoke of the coming of Brut and the Trojans four generations after the fall of Troy, or Joseph's journey to Thorny Hill near Avalon. Or like the Second Coming of Christ—though when I had once repeated this to my mother she had been so angry that I had never tried the joke again.

"Oh, yes," I said, "Ambrosius coming again, is he? Seriously, Cerdic, why is the High King coming to North Wales?"

"I told you. Doing the rounds, drumming up a bit of support before spring, him and that Saxon Queen of his." And he spat on the floor.

"Why do you do that? You're a Saxon yourself."

"That's a long time ago. I live here now. Wasn't it that flaxen bitch that made Vortigern sell out in the first place? Or at any rate you know as well as I do that since she's been in the High King's bed the Northmen have been loose over the land like a heath fire, till he can neither fight them nor buy them off. And if she's what men say she is, you can be sure none of the King's true-born sons'll live to wear the crown." He had been speaking softly, but at this he looked over his shoulder and spat again, making the sign. "Well, you know all this—or you would, that is, if you listened to your betters more often, instead of spending your time with books and such like, or chasing round with the People from the hollow hills."

"Is that where you think I go?"

"It's what people say. I'm not asking questions. I don't want to know. Come up, you." This to the pony as he moved over and started work, hissing, on the other flank. "There's talk that the Saxons have landed again north of Rutupiæ, and they're asking too much this time even for Vortigern to stomach. He'll have to fight, come spring."

"And my grandfather with him?"

"That's what he's hoping, I'll be bound. Well, you'd best run along if you want your supper. No one'll notice you. There was all hell going on in the kitchens when I tried to get a bite an hour back."

"Where's my grandfather?"

"How do I know?" He cocked his head at me, over the pony's rump. "Now what's to do?"

"I want to go with them."

"Hah!" he said, and threw the chopped feed down for the pony. It was not an encouraging sound.

I said stubbornly: "I've a fancy to see Segontium."

"Who hasn't? I've a fancy to see it myself. But if you're thinking of asking the King . . ." He let it hang. "Not but what it's time you got out of the place and saw a thing or two, shake you a bit out of yourself, it's what you need, but I can't say I see it happening. You'll never go to the King?"

"Why not? All he can do is refuse."

"All he can do—? Jupiter's balls, listen to the boy. Take my advice and get your supper and go to bed. And don't try Camlach, neither. He's had a right stand-up fight with that wife of his and he's like a stoat with the toothache. —You can't be serious?"

"The gods only go with you, Cerdic, if you put yourself in their path."

"Well, all right, but some of them have got mighty big hoofs to walk over you with. Do you want Christian burial?"

"I don't really mind. I suppose I'll work my way up to Christian baptism fairly soon, if the bishop has his way, but till then I've not signed on officially for anyone."

He laughed. "I hope they'll give me the flames when my turn comes. It's a cleaner way to go. Well, if you won't listen, you won't listen, but don't face him on an empty belly, that's all."

"I'll promise you that," I said, and went to forage for supper. After I had eaten, and changed into a decent tunic, I went to look for my grandfather.

To my relief Camlach was not with him. The King was in his bedchamber, sprawled at ease in his big chair before a roaring log fire, with his two hounds asleep at his feet. At first I thought the woman in the high-backed chair on the other side of the hearth was Olwen, the Queen, but then I saw it was my mother. She had been sewing, but her hands had dropped idle in her lap, and the white stuff lay still over the brown robe. She turned and smiled at me, but with a look of surprise. One of the wolfhounds beat his tail on the floor, and the other opened an eye and rolled it round and closed it again. My grandfather glowered at me from under his brows, but said kindly enough: "Well, boy, don't stand there. Come in, come in, there's a cursed draught. Shut the door."

I obeyed, approaching the fire.

"May I see you, sir?"

"You're seeing me. What do you want? Get a stool and sit down."

There was one near my mother's chair. I pulled it away, to show I was not sitting in her shadow, and sat down between them.

"Well? Haven't seen you for some time, have I? Been at your books?"

"Yes, sir." On the principle that it is better to attack than to defend, I went straight to the point. "I . . . I had leave this afternoon, and I went out riding, so I—"

"Where to?"

"Along the river path. Nowhere special, only to improve my horsemanship, so—"

"It could do with it."

"Yes, sir. So I missed the messenger. They tell me you ride out tomorrow, sir."

"What's that to you?"

"Only that I would like to come with you."

"You would like? You would like? What's this, all of a sudden?"

A dozen answers all sounding equally well jostled in my head for expression. I thought I saw my mother watching me with pity, and I knew that my grandfather waited with indifference and impatience only faintly tempered with amusement. I told the simple truth. "Because I am more than twelve years old, and have never been out of Maridunum. Because I know that if my uncle has his way, I shall soon be shut up, in this valley or elsewhere, to study as a clerk, and before that happens—"

The terrifying brows came down. "Are you trying to tell me you don't want to study?"

"No. It's what I want more than anything in the world. But study means more if one has seen just a little of the world—indeed, sir, it does. If you would allow me to go with you—"

"I'm going to Segontium, did they tell you that? It's not a feast-day hunting-party, it's a long ride and a hard one, and no quarter given for poor riders."

It was like lifting a heavy weight, to keep my eyes level on that fierce blue glare. "I've been practicing, sir, and I've a good pony now."

"Ha, yes, Dinias' breakdown. Well, that's about your measure. No, Merlin, I don't take children."

"Then you're leaving Dinias behind?"

I heard my mother gasp, and my grandfather's head, already turned away, jerked back to me. I saw his fists clench on the chair arm, but he did not hit me. "Dinias is a man."

"Then do Mael and Duach go with you, sir?" They were his two pages, younger than myself, and went everywhere with him.

My mother began to speak, in a breathless rush, but my grandfather moved a hand to stop her. There was an arrested look in the fierce eyes under the scowling brows. "Mael and Duach are some use to me. What use are you?"

I looked at him calmly. "Till now, of very little. But have they not told you that I speak Saxon as well as Welsh, and can read Greek, and that my Latin is better than yours?"

"Merlin—" began my mother, but I ignored her.

"I would have added Breton and Cornish, but I doubt if you will have much use for these at Segontium."

"And can you give me one good reason," said my grandfather dryly, "why I should speak to King Vortigern in any other language but Welsh, seeing that he comes from Guent?"

I knew from his tone that I had won. Letting my gaze fall from his was like retreating with relief from the battlefield. I drew a breath, and said, very meekly: "No, sir."

He gave his great bark of laughter, and thrust out a foot to roll one of the dogs over. "Well, perhaps there's a bit of the family in you after all, in spite of your looks. At least you've got the guts to beard the old dog in his den when it suits you. All right, you can come. Who attends you?"

"Cerdic."

"The Saxon? Tell him to get your gear ready. We leave at first light. Well, what are you waiting for?"

"To say good night to my mother." I rose from my stool and went to kiss her. I did not often do this, and she looked surprised.

Behind me, my grandfather said abruptly: "You're not going to war. You'll be back inside three weeks. Get out."

"Yes, sir. Thank you. Good night."

Outside the door I stood still for a full half minute, leaning against the wall, while my blood-beat steadied slowly, and the sickness cleared from my throat. *The gods only go with you if you put yourself in their path. And that takes courage.*

I swallowed the sickness, wiped the sweat off my palms, and ran to find Cerdic.

9

So it was that I first left Maridunum. At that time it seemed like the greatest adventure in the world, to ride out in the chill of dawn, when stars were still in the sky, and make one of the jostling, companionable group of men who followed Camlach and the King. To begin with, most of the men were surly and half asleep, and we rode pretty well in silence, breath smoking in the icy air, and the horses' hoofs striking sparks from the slaty road. Even the jingle of harness sounded cold, and I was so numb that I could hardly feel the reins, and could think of nothing else but how to stay on the excited pony and not get myself sent home in disgrace before we had gone a mile.

Our excursion to Segontium lasted eighteen days. It was my first sight of King Vortigern, who had at this time been High King of Britain for more than twenty years. Be sure I had heard plenty about him, truth and tales alike. He was a hard man, as one must be who had taken his throne by murder and held it with blood; but he was a strong king in a time when there was need for strength, and it was not altogether his fault that his stratagem of calling in the Saxons as mercenaries to help him had twisted in his hand like an edged sword slipping, and cut it to the bone. He had paid, and paid again, and then had fought; and now he spent a great part of every year fighting like a wolf to keep the ranging hordes contained along the Saxon Shore. Men spoke of him—with respect—as a fierce and bloodthirsty tyrant, and of his Saxon Queen, Rowena, with hatred as a witch; but though I had been fed from childhood on the tales of the kitchen slaves, I was looking forward to seeing them with more curiosity than fear.

In any event, I need not have been afraid; I saw the High King only from a distance. My grandfather's leniency had extended only to letting me go in his train; once there, I was of no more account—in fact of much less—than his pages Mael and Duach. I was left to fend for myself among the anonymous rabble of boys and servants, and, because my ways had made me no friends among my contemporaries, was left to myself. I was later to be thankful for the fact that, on the few occasions when I was in the crowd surrounding the two Kings, Vortigern did not lay eyes on me, and neither my grandfather nor Camlach remembered my existence.

We lay a week at Segontium, which the Welsh call Caer'n-ar-Von, because it lies just across the strait from Mona, the druids' isle. The town is set, like Maridunum, on the banks of an estuary, where the Seint River meets the sea. It has a splendid harbour, and a fortress placed on the rising ground above this, perhaps half a mile away. The fortress was built by the Romans to protect the harbour and the town, but had lain derelict for over a hundred years until Vortigern put part of it into repair. A little lower down the hill stood another more recent strong-point, built, I believe, by Macsen, grandfather of the murdered Constantius, against the Irish raiders.

The country here was grander than in South Wales, but to my eyes forbidding rather than beautiful. Perhaps in summer the land may be green and gentle along the estuary, but when I saw it first, that winter, the hills rose behind the town like storm-clouds, their skirts grey with the bare and whistling forests, and their crests slate blue and hooded with snow. Behind and beyond them all towers the great cloudy top of Moel-y-Wyddfa, which now the Saxons call Snow Hill, or Snowdon. It is the highest mountain in all Britain, and is the home of gods.

Vortigern lay, ghosts or no ghosts, in Macsen's Tower. His army—he never moved in those days with less than a thousand fighting men—was quartered in the fort. Of my grandfather's party, the nobles were with the King in the tower, while his train, of which I was one, was housed well enough, if a trifle coldly, near the west gate of the fort. We were treated with honour; not only was Vortigern a distant kinsman of my grandfather's, but it seemed to be true that the High King was—in Cerdic's phrase—"drumming up support." He was a big dark man, with a broad fleshy face and black hair as thick and bristled as a boar's, growing grey. There were black hairs on the back of his hands, and sprouting from his nostrils. The Queen was not with him; Cerdic whispered to me that he had not dared bring her where Saxons were so little welcome. When I retorted that he was only welcome himself because he had forgotten his Saxon and turned into good Welsh, he laughed and cuffed my ear. I suppose it was not my fault that I was never very royal.

The pattern of our days was simple. Most of the day was spent hunting, till at dusk we would return to fires and drink and a full meal, and then the kings and their advisers turned to talk, and their trains to dicing, wenching, quarrelling, and whatever other sports they might choose.

I had not been hunting before; as a sport it was foreign to my nature, and here everyone rode out hurly-burly in a crowd, which was something I disliked. It was also dangerous: there was plenty of game in the foothills, and there were some wild rides with necks for sale; but I saw no other chance of seeing the country, and besides, I had to find out why Galapas had insisted on my coming to Segontium. So I went out every day. I had a few falls, but got nothing worse than bruises, and managed to attract no attention, good or bad, from anyone who mattered. Nor did I find what I was looking for; I saw nothing, and nothing happened except that my horsemanship improved, and Aster's manners along with it.

On the eighth day of our stay we set off for home, and the High King himself, with an escort a hundred strong, went with us to set us on our road.

The first part of the way lay along a wooded gorge where a river ran fast and deep, and where the horses had to go singly or two abreast between the cliffs and the water. There was no danger for so large a party, so we went at ease, the gorge ringing with the sound of hoofs and bridle-chains and men's voices, and the occasional croak overhead as the ravens sailed off the cliffs to watch us. These birds do not wait, as some say, for the noise of battle; I have seen them follow armed bands of men for miles, waiting for the clash and the kill.

But that day we went safely, and near midday we came to the place where the High King was to part from us and ride back. This was where the two rivers met, and the gorge opened out into a wider valley, with forbidding icebound crags of slate to either side, and the big river running south, brown and swollen with melting snow. There is a ford at the watersmeet, and leading south from this a good road which goes dry and straight over high ground towards Tomen-y-Mur.

We halted just north of the ford. Our leaders turned aside into a sheltered hollow which was cupped on three sides by thickly wooded slopes. Clumps of bare alder and thick reeds showed that in summer the hollow would be marshland; on that December day it was solidly frostbound, but protected from the wind, and the sun came warmly. Here the party stopped to eat and rest. The kings sat apart, talking, and near them the rest of the royal party. I noticed that it included Dinias. I, as usual, finding myself not of the royal group, nor with the men-at-arms, nor yet the servants, handed Aster to Cerdic, then went apart, climbing a short way among the trees to a wooded dell where I could sit alone and out of sight of the others. At my back was a rock thawed by the sun, and from the other side of this came, muffled, the jingle of bits as horses grazed, the men's voices talking, and an occasional guffaw, then the rhythmic silences and mutterings that told me the dice had come out to pass the time till the kings completed their farewell. A kite tilted and swung above me in the cold air, the sun striking bronze from its wings. I thought of Galapas, and the bronze mirror flashing, and wondered why I had come.

King Vortigern's voice said suddenly, just behind me: "This way. You can tell me what you think."

I had whipped round, startled, before I realized that he, and the man he was speaking to, were on the other side of the rock that sheltered me.

"Five miles, they tell me, in either direction . . ." The High King's voice dwindled as he turned away. I heard footsteps on the frosty ground, dead leaves crackling, and the jar of nailed boots on stone. They were moving off. I stood up, taking it carefully, and peered over the rock. Vortigern and my grandfather were walking up through the wood together, deep in talk.

I remember that I hesitated. What, after all, could they have to say that could not already have been said in the privacy of Macsen's Tower? I could not believe that Galapas had sent me merely as a spy on their conference. But why else? Perhaps the god in whose way I had put myself had sent me here alone, today, for this. Reluctantly, I turned to follow them.

As I took the first step after them a hand caught my arm, not gently. "And where do you think you're going?" demanded Cerdic under his breath.

I shook him off violently. "Damn you, Cerdic, you nearly made me jump out of my skin! What does it matter to you where I'm going?"

"I'm here to look after you, remember?"

"Only because I brought you. No one tells you to look after me, these days. Or do they?" I looked at him sharply. "Have you followed me before?"

He grinned. "To tell you the truth, I never troubled. Should I have?"

But I persisted. "Did anyone tell you to watch me today?"

"No. But didn't you see who went this way? It was Vortigern and your grandfather. If you'd any idea of wandering after them, I'd think again if I was you."

"I wasn't going 'after them,' " I lied. "I was merely taking a look round."

"Then I'd do it elsewhere. They said special that the escort had to wait down here. I came to make sure you knew it, that's all. Very special about it, they was."

I sat down again. "All right, you've made sure. Now leave me again, please. You can come and tell me when we're due to move off."

"And have you belting off the minute my back's turned?"

I felt the blood rise to my cheeks. "Cerdic, I told you to go."

He said doggedly: "Look, I know you, and I know when you look like that. I don't know what's in your mind, but when you get that look in your eye there's trouble for somebody, and it's usually for you. What's to do?"

I said furiously: "The trouble's for you this time, if you don't do as I say."

"Don't go all royal on me," he said. "I was only trying to save you a beating."

"I know that. Forgive me. I had—something on my mind."

"You can tell me, can't you? I knew there'd been something biting you this last few days. What is it?"

"Nothing that I know of," I said truthfully. "Nothing you can help with. Forget it. Look, did the kings say where they were going? They could have talked their fill at Segontium, surely, or on the ride here?"

"They've gone to the top of the crag. There's a place up there at the end of the ridge where you can look right up and down the valley, all ways. There used to be an old tower there, they say. They call it Dinas Brenin."

"King's Fort? How big's the tower?"

"There's nothing there now but a tumble of stones. Why?"

"I—nothing. When do we ride home, I wonder?"

"Another hour, they said. Look, why don't you come down, and I'll cut you in on a dice game."

I grinned. "Thanks for nothing. Have I kept you out of your game, too? I'm sorry."

"Don't mention it. I was losing anyway. All right, I'll leave you alone, but you wouldn't think of doing anything silly now, would you? No sense in sticking your neck out. Remember what I told you about the ring-dove."

And at that exact moment, a ring-dove went by like an arrow, with a clap and whistle of wings that sent up a flurry of frost like a wake. Close behind her, a little above, ready to strike, went a merlin.

The dove rose a fraction as she met the slope, skimming up as a gull skims a rising wave, hurtling towards a thicket near the lip of the dell. She was barely a foot from the ground, and for the falcon to strike her was dangerous, but he must have been starving, for, just as she reached the edge of the thicket, he struck.

A scream, a fierce *kwik-ik-ik* from the falcon, a flurry of crashing twigs, then nothing. A few feathers drifted lazily down, like snow.

I started forward, and ran up the bank. "He got her!" It was obvious what had happened; both birds, locked together, had hurtled on into the thicket and crashed to the ground. From the silence, it was probable that they both now lay there, stunned.

The thicket was a steep tangle almost covering one side of the dell. I thrust the boughs aside and pushed my way through. The trail of feathers showed me my way. Then I found them. The dove lay dead, breast downwards, wings still spread as she had struck the stones, and with blood smearing bright over the iris of her neck feathers. On her lay the merlin. The steel ripping-claws were buried deep in the dove's back, the cruel beak half driven in by the crash. He was still alive. As I bent over them his wings stirred, and the bluish eyelids dropped, disclosing the fierce dark eye.

Cerdic arrived, panting, at my shoulder. "Don't touch him. He'll tear your hands. Let me."

I straightened. "So much for your ring-dove, Cerdic. It's time we forgot her, isn't it? No, leave them. They'll be here when we come back."

"Come back? Where from?"

I pointed silently to what showed ahead, directly in the path the birds had been taking. A square black gap like a door in the steep ground behind the thicket; an entrance hidden from casual sight, only to be seen if, for some reason, one pushed one's way in among the tangled branches.

"What of it?" asked Cerdic. "That's an old mine adit, by the look of it."

"Yes. That's what I came to see. Strike a light, and come along."

He began to protest, but I cut him short. "You can come or not, as you please. But give me a light. And hurry, there isn't much time." As I began to push my way towards the adit I heard him, muttering still, dragging up handfuls of dry stuff to make a torch.

Just inside the adit there was a pile of debris and fallen stone where the timber props had rotted away, but beyond this the shaft was smooth enough, leading more or less levelly into the heart of the hill. I could walk pretty nearly upright, and Cerdic, who was small, had to stoop only slightly. The flare of the makeshift torch threw our shadows grotesquely in front of us. It showed the grooves in the floor where loads had been dragged to daylight, and on walls and roof the marks of the picks and chisels that had made the tunnel.

"Where the hell do you think you're going?" Cerdic's voice, behind me, was sharp with nerves. "Look, let's get back. These places aren't safe. That roof could come in."

"It won't. Keep that torch going," I said curtly, and went on.

The tunnel bent to the right, and began to curve gently downhill. Underground one loses all sense of direction; there is not even the drift of wind on one's cheek that gives direction even on the blackest night; but I guessed that we must be winding our way deep into the heart of the hill on which had stood the old king's tower. Now and again smaller tunnels led off to left and right, but there was no danger of losing our way; we were in the main gallery, and the rock seemed reasonably good. Here and there had been falls from roof or wall, and once I was brought to a halt by a fall of rubble which almost blocked the way, but I climbed through, and the tunnel was clear beyond.

Cerdic had stopped at the barrier of rubble. He advanced the torch and peered after me. "Hey, look, Merlin, come back, for pity's sake! This is beyond any kind of folly. I tell you, these places are dangerous, and we're getting down into the very guts of the rock. The gods alone know what lives down here. Come back, boy."

"Don't be a coward, Cerdic, there's plenty of room for you. Come on through. Quickly."

"That I won't. If you don't come out this minute, I swear I'll go back and tell the King."

"Look," I said, "this is important. Don't ask me why. But I swear to you there's no danger. If you're afraid, then give me that torch, and get back."

"You know I can't do that."

"Yes, I know. You wouldn't dare go back to tell him, would you? And if you did leave me, and anything happened, what do you suppose would happen to you?"

"They say right when they say you're a devil's spawn," said Cerdic.

I laughed. "You can say what you like to me when we're back in daylight, but hurry now, Cerdic, please. You're safe, I promise you. There's no harm in the air today, and you saw how the merlin showed us the door."

He came, of course. Poor Cerdic, he could afford to do nothing else. But as he stood beside me again, with the torch held up, I saw him looking at me sideways, and his left hand was making the sign against the evil eye.

"Don't be long," he said, "that's all."

Twenty paces further, round a curve, the tunnel led into the cavern.

I made a sign to him to lift the torch. I could not have spoken. This vast hollow, right in the hill's heart, this darkness hardly touched by the torch's flare, this dead stillness of air where I could hear and feel my own blood beating—this, of course, was the place. I recognized every mark of the workings, the face seamed and split by the axes, and smashed open by the water. There was the domed roof disappearing into darkness, there in a corner some rusty metal where the pump had stood. There the shining moisture on the wall, no longer a ribbon, but a curtain of gleaming damp. And there where the puddles had lain, and the seepage under the overhang, a wide, still pool. Fully a third of the floor was under water.

The air had a strange smell all its own, the breath of the water and the living rock. Somewhere above, water dripped, each tap clear like a small hammer on metal. I took the smouldering faggot from Cerdic's hand, and went to the water's edge. I held the light as high as I could, out over the water, and gazed down. There was nothing to see. The light glanced back from a surface as hard as metal. I waited. The light ran, and gleamed, and drowned in darkness. There was nothing there but my own reflection, like the ghost in Galapas' mirror.

I gave the torch back to Cerdic. He hadn't spoken. He was watching me all the time with that sidelong, white-eyed look.

I touched his arm. "We can go back now. This thing's nearly out anyway. Come on."

We didn't speak as we made our way back along the curving gallery, past the rubble, through the adit and out into the frosty afternoon. The sky was a pale, milky blue. The winter trees stood brittle and quiet against it, the birches white as bone. From below a horn called, urgent, in the still metallic air.

"They're going." Cerdic drove the torch down into the frozen ground to extinguish it. I scrambled down through the thicket. The dove still lay there, cold, and stiff already. The merlin was there too; it had withdrawn from the body of its kill, and sat near it on a stone, hunched and motionless, even when I approached. I picked up the ring-dove and threw it to Cerdic. "Shove it in your saddle-bag. I don't have to tell you to say nothing of this, do I?"

"You do not. What are you doing?"

"He's stunned. If we leave him here he'll freeze to death in an hour. I'm taking him."

"Take care! That's a grown falcon—"

"He'll not hurt me." I picked up the merlin; he had fluffed his feathers out against the cold, and felt soft as a young owl in my hands. I pulled my leather sleeve down over my left wrist, and he took hold of this, gripping fiercely. The eyelids were fully open now, and the wild dark eyes watched me. But he sat still, with shut wings. I heard Cerdic muttering to himself as he bent to retrieve my things from the place where I had taken my meal. Then he added something I had never heard from him before. "Come on then, young master."

The merlin stayed docile on my wrist as I fell in at the back of my grandfather's train for the ride home to Maridunum.

10

Nor did it attempt to leave me when we reached home. I found, on examining it, that some of its wing feathers had been damaged in that hurtling crash after the ring-dove, so I mended them as Galapas had taught me, and after that it sat in the pear tree outside my window, accepting the food I gave it, and making no attempt to fly away.

I took it with me when next I went to see Galapas.

This was on the first day of February, and the frost had broken the night before, in rain. It was a grey leaden day, with low cloud and a bitter little wind among the rain. Draughts whistled everywhere in the palace, and curtains were fast drawn across the doors, while people kept on their woollen cloaks and huddled over the braziers. It seemed to me that a grey and leaden silence hung also over the palace; I had hardly seen my grandfather since we had returned to Maridunum, but he and the nobles sat together in council for hours, and there were rumours of quarrelling and raised voices when he and Camlach were closeted together. Once when I went to my mother's room I was told she was at her prayers and could not see me. I caught a glimpse of her through the half-open door, and I could have sworn that as she knelt below the holy image she was weeping.

But in the high valley nothing had changed. Galapas took the merlin, commended my work on its wings, then set it on a sheltered ledge near the cave's entrance, and bade me come to the fire and get warm. He ladled some stew out of the simmering pot, and made me eat it before he would listen to my story. Then I told him everything, up to the quarrels in the palace and my mother's tears.

"It was the same cave, Galapas, that I'll swear! But why? There was nothing there. And nothing else happened, nothing at all. I've asked as best I could, and Cerdic has asked about among the slaves, but nobody knows what the kings discussed, or why my grandfather and Camlach have fallen out. But he did tell me one thing; I am being watched. By Camlach's people. I'd have come to see you sooner, except for that. They've gone out today, Camlach and Alun and the rest, so I said I was going to the water-meadow to train the merlin, and I came up here."

Then as he was still silent, I repeated, worried into urgency: "What's happening, Galapas? What does it all mean?"

"About your dream, and your finding of the cavern, I know nothing. About the trouble in the palace, I can guess. You knew that the High King had sons by his first wife, Vortimer and Katigern and young Pascentius?"

I nodded.

"Were none of them there at Segontium?"

"No."

"I am told that they have broken with their father," said Galapas, "and Vortimer is raising troops of his own. They say he would like to be High King, and that Vortigern looks like having a rebellion on his hands when he can least afford it. The Queen's much hated, you know that; Vortimer's mother was good British, and besides, the young men want a young king."

"Camlach is for Vortimer, then?" I asked quickly, and he smiled.

"It seems so."

I thought about it for a little. "Well, when wolves fall out, don't they say the ravens come into their own?" As I was born in September, under Mercury, the raven was mine.

"Perhaps," said Galapas. "You're more likely to be clapped in your cage sooner than you expected." But he said it absently, as if his mind were elsewhere, and I went back to what concerned me most.

"Galapas, you've said you know nothing about the dream or the cavern. But this—this must have been the hand of the god." I glanced up at the ledge where the merlin sat, broodingly patient, his eyes half shut, slits of firelight.

"It would seem so."

I hesitated. "Can't we find out what he—what it means?"

"Do you want to go into the crystal cave again?"

"N-no, I don't. But I think perhaps I should. Surely you can tell me that?"

He said heavily, after a few moments: "I think you must go in, yes. But first, I must teach you something more. You must make the fire for yourself this time. Not like that—" smiling, as I reached for a branch to stir the embers. "Put that down. You asked me before you went away to show you something real. This is all I have left to show you. I hadn't realized . . . Well, let that go. It's time. No, sit still, you have no more need of books, child. Watch now."

Of the next thing, I shall not write. It was all the art he taught me, apart from certain tricks of healing. But as I have said, it was the first magic to come to me, and will be the last to go. I found it easy, even to make the ice-cold fire and the wild fire, and the fire that goes like a whip through the dark; which was just as well, because I was young to be taught such things, and it is an art which, if you are unfit or unprepared, can strike you blind.

It was dark outside when we had done. He got to his feet.

"I shall come back in an hour and wake you."

He twitched his cloak down from where it hung shrouding the mirror, put it round him, and went out.

The flames sounded like a horse galloping. One long, bright tongue cracked like a whip. A log fell down with a hiss like a woman's sigh, and then a thousand twigs crackled like people talking, whispering, chattering of news . . .

It faded all into a great brilliant blaze of silence. The mirror flashed. I picked up my cloak, now comfortably dry, and climbed with it into the crystal cave. I folded it and lay down on it, with my eyes fixed on the wall of crystal arching over me. The flames came after me, rank on bright rank, filling the air, till I lay in a globe of light like the inside of a star, growing brighter and ever brighter till suddenly it broke and there was darkness . . .

The galloping hoofs sparked on the gravel of the Roman road. The rider's whip cracked and cracked again, but the horse was already going full tilt, its nostrils wide and scarlet, its breath like steam in the cold air. The rider was Camlach. Far behind him, almost half a mile behind now, were the rest of the young men of his party, and still further behind them, leading his lamed and dripping horse, came the messenger who had taken the news to the King's son.

The town was alive with torches, men running to meet the galloping horse, but Camlach paid no heed to them. He drove the spiked spurs into the horse's sides, and galloped straight through the town, down the steep street, and into the outer yard of the palace. There were torches there, too. They caught the quick glint of his red hair as he swung from the horse and flung the reins into the hands of a waiting slave. The soft riding boots made no sound as he ran up the steps and along the colonnade that led to his father's room. The swift black figure was lost for a moment in shadow under the arch, then he flung the door wide and went through.

The messenger had been right. It had been a quick death. The old man lay on the carved Roman bed, and over him someone had thrown a coverlet of purple silk. They had somehow managed to prop his jaw, for the fierce grey beard jutted ceilingwards, and a little head-rest of baked clay beneath his neck held his head straight, while the body slowly froze iron-hard. There was no sign, the way he lay, that the neck was broken. Already the old face had begun to fall away, to shrink, as death pared the flesh down from the jut of the nose till it would be left simply in planes of cold candlewax. The gold coins that lay on his mouth and shut eyelids glimmered in the light of the torches at the four corners of the bed.

At the foot of the bed, between the torches, stood Niniane. She stood very still and upright, dressed in white, her hands folded quietly in front of her with a crucifix between them, her head bent. When the door opened she did not look up, but kept her eyes fixed on the purple coverlet, not in grief, but almost as if she were too far away for thought.

To her side, swiftly, came her brother, slim in his black clothes, glinting with a kind of furious grace that seemed to shock the room.

He walked right up to the bed and stood over it, staring down at his father. Then he put down a hand and laid it over the dead hands clasped on the purple silk. His hand lingered there for a moment, then drew back. He looked at Niniane. Behind her, a few paces back in the shadows, the little crowd of men, women, servants, shuffled and whispered. Among them, silent and dry-eyed, Mael and Duach stared. Dinias, too, all his attention fixed on Camlach.

Camlach spoke very softly, straight to Niniane. "They told me it was an accident. Is this true?"

She neither moved nor spoke. He stared at her for a moment, then with a gesture of irritation, looked beyond her, and raised his voice.

"One of you, answer me. This was an accident?"

A man stepped forward, one of the King's servants, a man called Mabon. "It's true, my lord." He licked his lips, hesitating.

Camlach showed his teeth. "What in the name of the devils in hell's the matter with you all?" Then he saw where they were staring, and looked down at his right hip, where, sheathless, his short stabbing dagger had been thrust through his belt. It was blood to the hilt. He made a sound of impatience and disgust and, pulling it out, flung it from him, so that it skittered across the floor and came up against the wall with a small clang that sounded loud in the silence.

"Whose blood did you think?" he asked, still with that lifted lip. "Deer's blood, that's all. When the message came, we had just killed. I was twelve miles off, I and my men." He stared at them, as if daring them to comment. No one moved. "Go on, Mabon. He slipped and fell, the man told me. How did it happen?"

The man cleared his throat. "It was a stupid thing, sir, a pure accident. Why, no one was even near him. It was in the small courtyard, the way through to the servants' rooms, where the steps are worn. One of the men had been carrying oil around to fill the lamps. He'd spilt some on the steps, and before he got back to wipe it up the King came through, in a bit of a hurry. He—he hadn't been expected there at the time. Well, my lord, he treads in the oil, and goes straight down on his back, and hits his head on the stone. That's how it happened, my lord. It was seen. There's those that can vouch for it."

"And the man whose fault it was?"

"A slave, my lord."

"He's been dealt with?"

"My lord, he's dead."

While they had been talking, there had been a commotion in the colonnade, as the rest of Camlach's party arrived and came hurrying along to the King's room after him. They had pressed into the room while Mabon was speaking, and now Alun, approaching the prince quietly, touched his arm.

"The news is all round the town, Camlach. There's a crowd gathering outside. A million stories going round—there'll be trouble soon. You'll have to show yourself and talk to them."

Camlach flicked him a glance, and nodded. "Go and see to it, will you? Bran, go with him, and Ruan. Shut the gates. Tell the people I'm coming out soon. And now, the rest of you, out."

The room emptied. Dinias lingered in the doorway, got not even a glance, and followed the rest. The door shut.

"Well, Niniane?"

In all this time she had never looked at him. Now she raised her eyes. "What do you want of me? It's true as Mabon tells you. What he didn't say was that the King had been fooling with a servant-girl and was drunk. But it was an accident, and he's dead . . . and you with all your friends were a good twelve miles away. So you're King now, Camlach, and there is no man can point a finger at you and say, 'He wanted his father dead.' "

"No woman can say that to me either, Niniane."

"I have not said it. I'm just telling you that the quarrels here are over. The kingdom's yours—and now it's as Alun says, you had better go and speak to the people."

"To you first. Why do you stand like that, as if you didn't care either way? As if you were scarcely with us here?"

"Perhaps because it's true. What you are, brother, and what you want, does not concern me, except to ask you one thing."

"And that is?"

"That you let me go now. He never would, but I think you will."

"To St. Peter's?"

She bent her head. "I told you nothing here concerned me any more. It has not concerned me for some time, and less than ever now, with all this talk about invasion, and war in the spring, and the rumours about shifts of power and the death of kings. . . . Oh, don't look at me like that; I'm not a fool, and my father talked to me. But you need not be afraid of me; nothing I know or can do can ever harm your plans for yourself, brother. I tell you, there is nothing I want out of life now except to be allowed to go in peace, and live in peace, and my son too."

"You said 'one thing.' That makes two."

For the first time something came to life in her eyes; it might have been fear. She said swiftly: "It was always the plan for him, your plan, even before it was my father's. Surely, after the day Gorlan went, you knew that even if Merlin's father could come riding in, sword in hand and with three thousand men at his back, I would not go to him? Merlin can do you no harm, Camlach. He will never be anything but a nameless bastard, and you know he is no warrior. The gods know he can do you no harm at all."

"And even less shut up as a clerk?" Camlach's voice was silky.

"Even less, shut up as a clerk. Camlach, are you playing with me? What's in your mind?"

"This slave who spilt the oil," he said. "Who was he?"

That flicker in her eyes again. Then the lids dropped. "The Saxon. Cerdic."

He didn't move, but the emerald on his breast glittered suddenly against the black as if his heart had jumped.

She said fiercely: "Don't pretend you guessed this! How could you guess it?"

"Not a guess, no. When I rode in the place was humming with whispers like a smashed harp." He added, in sudden irritation: "You stand there like a ghost with your hands on your belly as if you still had a bastard there to protect."

Surprisingly, she smiled. "But I have." Then as the emerald leapt again: "No, don't be a fool. Where would I get another bastard now? I meant that I cannot go until I know he is safe from you. And that we are both safe from what you propose to do."

"From what I propose to do to *you?* I swear to you there is nothing—"

"I am talking about my father's kingdom. But let it go now. I told you, my only concern is that St. Peter's should be left in peace . . . And it will be."

"You saw this in the crystal?"

"It is unlawful for a Christian to dabble in soothsaying," said Niniane, but her voice was a little over-prim, and he looked sharply at her, then, suddenly restless, took a couple of strides away into the shadows at the side of the room, then back into the light.

"Tell me," he said abruptly. "What of Vortimer?"

"He will die," she said indifferently.

"We shall all die, some day. But you know I am committed to him now. Can you not tell me what will happen this coming spring?"

"I see nothing and I can tell you nothing. But whatever your plans for the kingdom, it will serve no purpose to let even the smallest whisper of murder start, and I can tell you this, you're a fool if you think that the King's death was anything but an accident. Two of the grooms saw it happen, and the girl he'd been with."

"Did the man say anything before they killed him?"

"Cerdic? No. Only that it was an accident. He seemed concerned more for my son than for himself. It was all he said."

"So I heard," said Camlach.

The silence came back. They stared at one another. She said: "You would not."

He didn't answer. They stood there, eyes locked, while a draught crept through the room, making the torches gutter.

Then he smiled, and went. As the door slammed shut behind him a gust of air blew through the room, and tore the flames along from the torches, till shadow and light went reeling.

The flames were dying, and the crystals dim. As I climbed out of the cave and pulled my cloak after me, it tore. The embers in the brazier showed a sullen red. Outside, now, it was quite dark. I stumbled down from the ledge and ran towards the doorway.

"Galapas!" I shouted. "Galapas!"

He was there. His tall, stooping figure detached itself from the darkness outside, and he came forward into the cave. His feet, half-bare in his old sandals, looked blue with cold.

I came to a halt a yard from him, but it was as if I had run straight into his arms, and been folded against his cloak.

"Galapas, they've killed Cerdic."

He said nothing, but his silence was like words or hands of comfort.

I swallowed to shift the ache in my throat. "If I hadn't come up here this afternoon . . . I gave him the slip, along with the others. But I could have trusted him, even about you. Galapas, if I'd stayed—if I'd been there—perhaps I could have done something."

"No. You counted for nothing. You know that."

"I'll count for less than nothing now." I put a hand to my head: it was aching fiercely, and my eyes swam, still half-blind. He took me gently by the arm and made me sit down near the fire.

"Why do you say that? A moment, Merlin, tell me what has happened."

"Don't you know?" I said, surprised. "He was filling the lamps in the colonnade, and some oil spilled on the steps, and the King slipped in it and fell and broke his neck. It wasn't Cerdic's fault, Galapas. He spilt the oil, that's all, and he was going back, he was actually going back to clean it up when it happened. So they took him and killed him."

"And now Camlach is King."

I think I stared at him for some time, unseeing with those dream-blinded eyes, my brain for the moment incapable of holding more than the single fact.

He persisted, gently: "And your mother? What of her?"

"What? What did you say?"

The warm shape of a goblet was put into my hand. I could smell the same drink that he had given me before when I dreamed in the cave. "Drink that. You should have slept till I wakened you, then it wouldn't have come like this. Drink it all."

As I drank, the sharp ache in my temples dulled to a throb, and the swimming shapes round me drew back into focus. And with them, thought.

"I'm sorry. It's all right now, I can think again, I've come back. . . . I'll tell you the rest. My mother's to go into St. Peter's. She tried to make Camlach promise to let me go too, but he wouldn't. I think . . ."

"Yes?"

I said slowly, thinking hard now: "I didn't understand it all. I was thinking about Cerdic. But I believe he's going to kill me. I believe he will use my grandfather's death for this; he'll say that my slave did it . . . Oh, nobody will believe that I could take anything from Camlach, but if he does shut me up in a religious house, and then I die quietly, a little time after, then by that time the whispers will have worked, and nobody will raise a voice about it. And by that time, if my mother is just one of the holy women at St. Peter's, and no longer the King's daughter, she won't have a voice to raise, either." I cupped my hands round the goblet, looking across at him. "Why should anyone fear me so, Galapas?"

He did not answer that, but nodded to the goblet in my hands. "Finish it. Then, my dear, you must go."

"Go? But if I go back, they'll kill me, or shut me up . . . Won't they?"

"If they find you, they will try."

I said eagerly: "If I stayed here with you—nobody knows I come here—even if they found out and came after me, you'd be in no danger! We'd see them coming up the valley for miles, or we'd know they were coming, you and I . . . They'd never find me; I could go in the crystal cave."

He shook his head. "The time for that isn't come. One day, but not now. You can no more be hidden now, than your merlin could go back into its egg."

I glanced back over my shoulder at the ledge where the merlin had sat brooding, still as Athene's owl. There was no bird there. I wiped the back of a hand across my eyes, and blinked, not believing. But it was true. The firelit shadows were empty.

"Galapas, it's gone!"

"Yes."

"Did you see it go?"

"It went by when you called me back into the cave."

"I—which way?"

"South."

I drank the rest of the potion, then turned the goblet up to spill the last drops for the god. Then I set it down and reached for my cloak.

"I'll see you again, won't I?"

"Yes. I promise you that."

"Then I shall come back?"

"I promised you that already. Some day, the cave will be yours, and all that is in it."

Past him, in from the night, came a cold stray breath of air that stirred my cloak and lifted the hairs on my nape. My flesh prickled. I got up and swung the cloak round me and fastened the pin.

"You're going, then?" He was smiling. "You trust me so much? Where do you plan to go?"

"I don't know. Home, I suppose, to start with. I'll have time to think on the way there, if I need to. But I'm still in the god's path. I can feel the wind blowing. Why are you smiling, Galapas?"

But he would not answer that. He stood up, then pulled me towards him and stooped and kissed me. His kiss was dry and light, an old man's kiss, like a dead leaf drifting down to brush the flesh. Then he pushed me towards the entrance. "Go. I saddled your pony ready for you."

It was raining still as I rode down the valley. The rain was cold and small, and soaking; it gathered on my cloak and dragged at my shoulders, and mixed with the tears that ran down my face.

This was the second time in my life that I wept.

11

The stableyard gate was locked. This was no more than I had expected. That day I had gone out openly enough through the main yard with the merlin, and any other night might have chanced riding back the same way, with some story of losing my falcon and riding about till dark to look for it. But not tonight.

And tonight there would be no one waiting and listening for me, to let me in.

Though the need for haste was breathing on the back of my neck, I kept the impatient pony to a walk, and rode quietly along under the palace wall in the direction of the bridge. This and the road leading to it were alive with people and torches and noise, and twice in the few minutes since I had come in sight of it a horseman went galloping headlong out over the bridge, going south.

Now the wet, bare trees of the orchard overhung the towpath. There was a ditch here below the high wall, and over it the boughs hung, dripping. I slid off the pony's back and led him in under my leaning apple-tree, and tethered him. Then I scrambled back into the saddle, got unsteadily to my feet, balanced for a moment, and jumped for the bough above me.

It was soaking, and one of my hands slipped, but the other held. I swung my legs up, cocked them over the bough, and after that it was only the work of moments to scramble over the wall, and down into the orchard grasses.

There to my left was the high wall which masked my grandfather's garden, to the right the dovecote and the raised terrace where Moravik used to sit with her spinning. Ahead of me was the low sprawl of the servants' quarters. To my relief hardly a light showed. All the light and uproar of the palace was concentrated beyond the wall to my left, in the main building. From even further beyond, and muted by the rain, came the tumult of the streets.

But no light showed in my window. I ran.

What I hadn't reckoned on was that they should have brought him here, to his old place. His pallet lay now, not across the door, but back in the corner, near my bed. There was no purple here, no torches; he lay just as they had flung him down. All I could see in the half-darkness was the ungainly sprawled body, with an arm flung wide and the hand splayed on the cold floor. It was too dark to see how he had died.

I stooped over him and took the hand. It was cold already, and the arm had begun to stiffen. I lifted it gently to the pallet beside his body, then ran to my bed and snatched up the fine woollen coverlet. I spread it over Cerdic, then jerked upright, listening, as a man's voice called something in the distance, and then there were footsteps at the end of the colonnade, and the answer, shouted:

"No. He's not come this way. I've been watching the door. Is the pony in yet?"

"No. No sign." And then, in reply to another shout: "Well, he can't have ridden far. He's often out till this time. What? Oh, very well . . ."

The footsteps went, rapidly. Silence.

There was a lamp in its stand somewhere along the colonnade. This dealt enough light through the half-open door for me to see what I was doing. I silently lifted the lid of my chest, pulled out the few clothes I had, with my best cloak, and a spare pair of sandals. I bundled these all together in a bag, together with my other possessions, my ivory comb, a couple of brooches, a cornelian clasp. These I could sell. I climbed on the bed and pitched the bag out of the window. Then I ran back to Cerdic, pulled aside the coverlet, and, kneeling, fumbled at his hip. They had left his dagger. I tugged at the clasp with fingers that were clumsier even than the darkness made them, and it came undone. I took it, belt and all, a man's dagger, twice as long as my own, and honed to a killing point. Mine I laid beside him on the pallet. He might need it where he had gone, but I doubted it; his hands had always been enough.

I was ready. I stood looking down at him for a moment longer, and saw instead, as in the flashing crystal, how they had laid my grandfather, with the torchlight and the watchers and the purple. Nothing here but darkness, a dog's death. A slave's death.

"Cerdic." I said it half aloud, in the darkness. I wasn't weeping now. That was over. "Cerdic, rest you now. I'll send you the way you wanted, like a king."

I ran to the door, listened for a moment, then slipped through into the deserted colonnade. I lifted the lamp from its bracket. It was heavy, and oil spilled. Of course; he had filled it just that evening.

Back in my own room I carried the lamp over to where he lay. Now—what I had not foreseen—I could see how he had died. They had cut his throat.

Even if I had not intended it, it would have happened. The lamp shook in my hand, and hot oil splashed on the coverlet. A burning fragment broke from the wick, fell, caught, hissed. Then I flung the lamp down on the body, and watched for five long seconds while the flame ran into the oil and burst like blazing spray.

"Go with your gods, Cerdic," I said, and jumped for the window.

I landed on the bundle and went sprawling in the wet grass, then snatched it up and ran for the river wall.

Not to frighten the pony, I made for a place some yards beyond the apple tree, and pitched the bag over the wall into the ditch. Then back to the tree, and up it, to the high coping.

Astride of this, I glanced back. The fire had caught. My window glowed now, red with pulsing light. No alarm had yet been given, but it could only be a matter of moments before the flames were seen, or someone smelled the smoke. I scrambled over, hung by my hands for a moment, then let myself drop. As I got to my feet a shadow, towering, jumped at me and struck.

I went down with a man's heavy body on top of me, pinning me to the muddy grass. A splayed hand came hard down on my face, choking my cry off short. Just near me was a quick footstep, the rasp of drawn metal, and a man's voice saying, urgently, in Breton: "Wait. Make him talk first."

I lay quite still. This was easy to do, for not only had the force of the first man's attack driven the breath right out of my body, but I could feel his knife at my throat. Then as the second man spoke, my captor, with a surprised grunt, shifted his weight from me, and the knife withdrew an inch or two.

He said, in a tone between surprise and disgust: "It's only a boy." Then to me, harshly, in Welsh: "Not a sound out of you, or I'll slit your throat here and now. Understood?"

I nodded. He took his hand from my mouth, and getting up, dragged me to my feet. He rammed me back against the wall, holding me there, the knife pricking my collarbone. "What's all this? What are you doing bolting out of the palace like a rat with the dogs after it? A thief? Come on, you little rat, before I choke you."

He shook me as if I were indeed a rat. I managed to gasp: "Nothing. I was doing no harm! Let me go!"

The other man said softly, out of the darkness: "Here's what he threw over the wall. A bag full of stuff."

"What's in it?" demanded my captor. And to me, "Keep quiet, you."

He had no need to warn me. I thought I could smell smoke now, and see the first flicker of light as my fire took hold of the roof beams. I flattened myself back even further into the black shadow under the wall.

The other man was examining my bundle. "Clothes . . . sandals . . . some jewelry by the feel of it . . ."

He had moved out on to the towpath, and, with my eyes now used to the darkness, I could make him out. A little weasel of a man, with bent shoulders, and a narrow, pointed face under a straggle of hair. No one I had ever seen.

I gave a gasp of relief. "You're not the King's men! Who are you, then? What do you want here?"

The weaselly man stopped rooting in my bag, and stared.

"That's no concern of yours," said the big man who held me. "We'll ask the questions. Why should you be so scared of the King's men? You know them all, eh?"

"Of course I do. I live in the palace. I'm—a slave there."

"Marric"—it was the Weasel, sharply—"look over there, there's a fire started. They're buzzing like a wasp's nest. No point in wasting time here over a runaway slave-brat. Slit his throat and let's run for it while we can."

"A moment," said the big man. "He may know something. Look now, you—"

"If you're going to slit my throat anyway," I said, "why should I tell you anything? *Who are you?*"

He ducked his head forward suddenly, peering at me. "Crowing mighty fine all of a sudden, aren't you? Never mind who *we* are. A slave, eh? Running away?"

"Yes."

"Been stealing?"

"No."

"No? The jewelry in the bundle? And this—this isn't a slave's cloak." He tightened his grip on the stuff at my throat till I squirmed. "And that pony? Come on, the truth."

"All right." I hoped I sounded sullen and cowed enough for a slave now. "I did take a few things. It's the prince's pony, Myrddin's . . . I—I found it straying. Truly, sir. He went out today and he's not back yet. He'll have been thrown, he's a rotten horseman. I—it was a bit of luck—they won't miss it till I'm well away." I plucked at his clothes beseechingly. "Please, sir, let me go. Please! What harm could I do—?"

"Marric, for pity's sake, there's no time." The flames had taken hold now, and were leaping. There was shouting from the palace, and the Weasel pulled at my captor's arm. "The tide's going out fast, and the gods only know if she's there at all, this weather. Listen to the noise—they'll be coming this way any minute."

"They won't," I said. "They'll be too busy putting the fire out to think of anything else. It was well away when I left it."

"When you left it?" Marric hadn't budged; he was staring down at me, and his grip was less fierce. "Did *you* start that fire?"

"Yes."

I had their full attention now, even Weasel's.

"Why?"

"I did it because I hate them. They killed my friend."

"Who did?"

"Camlach and his people. The new King."

There was a short silence. I could see Marric better now. He was a big, burly man, with a bush of black hair, and black eyes that glinted in the fire.

"And," I added, "if I'd stayed, they'd have killed me, too. So I burned the place and ran away. Please let me go now."

"Why should they want to kill you? They'll want to now, of course, with the place going up like a torch—but why, before that? What had you done?"

"Nothing. But I was the old King's slave, and . . . I suppose I heard things. Slaves hear everything. Camlach thinks I might be dangerous . . . He has plans . . . I knew about them. Believe me, sir," I said earnestly, "I'd have served him as well as I did the old King, but then he killed my friend."

"What friend? And why?"

"Another slave, a Saxon, his name was Cerdic. He spilled oil on the steps, and the old King fell. It was an accident, but they cut his throat."

Marric turned his head to the other. "Hear that, Hanno? That's true enough. I heard it in the town." Then back to me: "All right. Now you can tell us a bit more. You say you know Camlach's plans?"

But Hanno interrupted again, this time desperately. "Marric, for pity's sake! If you think he's got something to tell us, bring him along. He can talk in the boat, can't he? I tell you, if we wait much longer we'll lose the tide, and she'll be gone. There's dirty weather coming by the feel of it, and it's my guess that they won't wait." And then in Breton: "We can as easy ditch him later as now."

"Boat?" I said. "You're going on the river?"

"Where else? Do you think we can go by road? Look at the bridge." Marric jerked his head sideways. "All right, Hanno. Get in. We'll go."

He began to drag me across the towpath. I hung back. "Where are you taking me?"

"That's our affair. Can you swim?"

"No."

He laughed under his breath. It was not a reassuring sound. "Then it won't matter to you which way we go, will it? Come along." And he clapped his hand once more over my mouth, swung me up as if I had been no heavier than my own bundle, and strode across the path to the oily dark glimmer that was the river.

The boat was a coracle, half hidden under the hanging bank. Hanno was already casting off. Marric went down the bank with a bump and a slither, dumped me in the lurching vessel, and clambered after me. As the coracle rocked out from under the bank he let me feel the knife again against the back of my neck. "There. Feel it? Now hold your tongue till we're clear of the bridge."

Hanno thrust off, and guided us out with the paddle into the current. A few feet from the bank I felt the river take hold of the boat, and we gathered speed. Hanno bent to the paddle and held her straight for the southern arch of the bridge.

Held in Marric's grip, I sat facing astern. Just as the current took us to sweep us southwards I heard Aster's high, frightened whinny as he smelt the smoke, and in the light of the now roaring fire I saw him, trailing a broken rein, burst from the wall's shadow and scud like a ghost along the towpath. Fire or no fire, he would make for the gate and his stable, and they would find him. I wondered what they would think, where they would look for me. Cerdic would be gone now, and my room with the painted chest, and the coverlet fit for a prince. Would they think I had found Cerdic's body, and in my fear and shock had dropped the lamp? That my own body was there, charred to nothing, in the remains of the servants' wing? Well, whatever they thought, it didn't matter. Cerdic had gone to his gods, and I, it seemed, was going to mine.

12

12

The black arch of the bridge swooped across the boat, and was gone. We fled downstream. The tide was almost on the turn, but the last of the ebb took us fast. The air freshened, and the boat began to rock.

The knife withdrew from my flesh. Across me Marric said: "Well, so far so good. The brat did us a good turn with his fire. No one was watching the river to see a boat slip under the bridge. Now, boy, let's hear what you have to tell us. What's your name?"

"Myrddin Emrys."

"And you say you were—hey, wait a minute! Did you say Myrddin? Not the bastard?"

"Yes."

He let out a long whistling breath, and Hanno's paddle checked, to dip again hurriedly as the coracle swung and rocked across the current. "You heard that, Hanno? It's the bastard. Then why in the name of the spirits of lower earth did you tell us you were a slave?"

"I didn't know who you were. You hadn't recognized me, so I thought if you were thieves yourselves, or Vortigern's men, you'd let me go."

"Bag, pony, and all . . . So it was true you were running away? Well," he added thoughtfully, "if all tales be true, you're not much to be blamed for that. But why set the place on fire?"

"That was true, too. I told you. Camlach killed a friend of mine, Cerdic the Saxon, though he had done nothing to deserve it. I think they only killed him because he was mine and they meant to use his death against me. They put his body in my room for me to find. So I burnt the room. His people like to go to their gods like that."

"And the devil take anyone else in the palace?"

I said indifferently: "The servants' wing was empty. They were all at supper, or out looking for me, or serving Camlach. It's surprising—or perhaps it isn't—how quickly people can switch over. I expect they'll put the fire out before it reaches the King's apartments."

He regarded me in silence for a minute. We were still racing with the turning tide, well out in the estuary now. Hanno gave no sign of steering to the further bank. I pulled my cloak closer round me and shivered.

"Who were you running to?" asked Marric.

"Nobody."

"Look, boy, I want the truth, or bastard prince or not, you'll go over the side now. Hear me? You'd not last a week if you hadn't someone to go to, to take service with. Who did you have in mind? Vortigern?"

"It would be sensible, wouldn't it? Camlach's going with Vortimer."

"He's what?" His voice sharpened. "Are you sure?"

"Quite sure. He was playing with the idea before, and he quarrelled with the old King about it. He and his lot would have gone anyway, I think. Now, of course, he can take the whole kingdom with him, and shut it against Vortigern."

"And open it for who else?"

"I didn't hear that. Who is there? You can imagine, he wasn't being very open about it until tonight, when his father the King lay dead."

"Hm." He thought for a minute. "The old King leaves another son. If the nobles don't want this alliance—"

"A baby? Aren't you being a bit simple? Camlach's had a good example in front of him; Vortimer wouldn't be where he is if his father hadn't done just what Camlach will do."

"And that is?"

"You know as well as I do. Look, why should I say any more till I know who you are? Isn't it time you told me?"

He ignored that. He sounded thoughtful. "You seem to know a lot about it. How old are you?"

"Twelve. I'll be thirteen in September. But I don't need to be clever to know about Camlach and Vortimer. I heard him say so himself."

"Did you, by the Bull? And what else did you hear?"

"Quite a lot. I was always underfoot. Nobody took any notice of me. But my mother's going into retirement now at St. Peter's, and I wouldn't give you a fig for my chances, so I cleared out."

"To Vortigern?"

I said, honestly: "I've no idea. I—I have no plans. It might have to be Vortigern in the end. What choice is there but him, and the Saxon wolves hanging at our throats for all time till they've torn Britain piecemeal and swallowed her? Who else is there?"

"Well," said Marric, "Ambrosius."

I laughed. "Oh, yes, Ambrosius. I thought you were serious. I know you're from Less Britain, I can tell by your voices, but—"

"You asked who we were. We are Ambrosius' men."

There was a silence. I realized that the river-banks had disappeared. Far off in the darkness to the north a light showed; the lighthouse. Some time back the rain had slackened and stopped. Now it was cold, with the wind off shore, and the water was choppy. The boat pitched and swung, and I felt the first qualm of sickness. I clutched my hands hard against my belly, against the cold as much as the sickness, and said sharply: "Ambrosius' men? Then you're spies? His spies?"

"Call us loyal men."

"Then it's true? It's true he's waiting in Less Britain?"

"Aye, it's true."

I said, aghast: "Then that's where you're going? You can't imagine you can get there in this horrible boat?"

Marric laughed, and Hanno said sourly, "We might have to, at that, if the ship's not there."

"What ship would be there in winter?" I demanded. "It's not sailing weather."

"It's sailing weather if you pay enough," said Marric dryly. "Ambrosius pays. The ship will be there."

His big hand dropped on my shoulder, not ungently. "Never mind that, there's still things I want to know."

I curled up, hugging my belly, trying to take big breaths of the cold clear air. "Oh, yes, there's a lot I could tell you. But if you're going to drop me overboard anyway, I've nothing to lose, have I? I might as well keep the rest of my information to myself—or see if Ambrosius will pay for it. And there's your ship. Look; if you can't see it yet, you must be blind. Now don't talk to me any more, I feel sick."

I heard him laugh again under his breath. "You're a cool one, and no mistake. Aye, there's the ship, I can see her clearly enough now. Well, seeing who you are, we'll take you aboard. And I'll tell you the other reason; I liked what you said about your friend. That sounded true enough. So you can be loyal, eh? And you've no call to be loyal to Camlach, by all accounts, or to Vortigern. Could you be loyal to Ambrosius?"

"I'll know when I see him."

His fist sent me sprawling to the bottom of the boat. "Princeling or not, keep a civil tongue in your head when you speak of him. There's many a hundred men think of him as their King, rightwise born."

I picked myself up, retching. A low hail came from near at hand, and in a moment we were rocking in the deeper shadow of the ship.

"If he's a man, that'll be enough," I said.

The ship was small, compact and low in the water. She lay there, unlighted, a shadow on the dark sea. I could just see the rake of her mast swaying—sickeningly, it seemed to me—against the scudding cloud that was only a little lighter than the black sky above. She was rigged like the merchantmen who traded in and out of Maridunum in the sailing weather, but I thought she looked cleaner built, and faster.

Marric answered the hail, then a rope snaked down overside, and Hanno caught it and made it fast.

"Come on, you, get moving. You can climb, can't you?"

Somehow, I got to my feet in the swinging coracle. The rope was wet, and jerked in my hands. From above an urgent voice came: "Hurry, will you? We'll be lucky if we get back at all, with the weather that's coming up."

"Get aloft, blast you," said Marric, roughly, giving me a shove. It was all it needed. My hands slipped, nerveless, from the rope, and I fell back into the coracle, landing half across the side, where I hung, gasping and retching, and beyond caring what fate overtook me or even a dozen kingdoms. If I had been stabbed or thrown into the sea at that point I doubt if I would even have noticed, except to welcome death as a relief. I simply hung there over the boat's side like a lump of sodden rags, vomiting.

I have very little recollection of what happened then. There was a good deal of cursing, and I think I remember Hanno urgently recommending Marric to cut his losses and throw me overboard; but I was picked up bodily and, somehow, slung up and into the waiting hands above. Then someone half-carried, half-dragged me below, and dropped me on a pile of bedding with a bucket to hand and the air from an open port blowing on my sweating face.

I believe the journey took four days. Rough weather there certainly was, but at least it was behind us, and we made spanking speed. I stayed below the whole time, huddled thankfully in the blankets under the port-hole, hardly venturing to lift my head. The worst of the sickness abated after a time, but I doubt if I could have moved, and mercifully no one tried to make me.

Marric came down once. I remember it vaguely, as if it were a dream. He picked his way in over a pile of old anchor chain to where I lay, and stood, his big form stooping, peering down at me. Then he shook his head. "And to think I thought we'd done ourselves a good turn, picking you up. We should have thrown you over the side in the first place, and saved a lot of trouble. I reckon you haven't very much more to tell us, anyway?"

I made no reply.

He gave a queer little grunt that sounded like a laugh, and went out. I went to sleep, exhausted.

When I woke, I found that my wet cloak, sandals and tunic had been removed, and that, dry and naked, I was cocooned deep in blankets. Near my head was a water jar, its mouth stoppered with a twist of rag, and a hunk of barley bread.

I couldn't have touched either, but I got the message. I slept.

Then one day shortly before dusk, we came in sight of the Wild Coast, and dropped anchor in the calm waters of Morbihan that men call the Small Sea.

BOOK II

THE FALCON

1

The first I knew of our coming to shore was being roused, still heavy with that exhausted sleep, by voices talking over me.

"Well, all right, if you believe him, but do you really think even a bastard prince would be abroad in those clothes? Everything soaking, not even a gilt clasp to his belt, and look at his sandals. I grant you it's a good cloak, but it's torn. More likely the first story was true, and he's a slave running away with his master's things."

It was, of course, Hanno's voice, and he was talking in Breton. Luckily I had my back to them, curled up in the welter of blankets. It was easy to pretend to be asleep. I lay still, and tried to keep my breathing even.

"No, it's the bastard all right; I've seen him in the town. I'd have known him sooner if we'd been able to show a light." The deeper voice was Marric's. "In any case it would hardly matter who he was; slave or royal bastard, he's been privy to a lot in that palace that Ambrosius will want to listen to. And he's a bright lad; oh, yes, he's what he says he is. You don't learn those cool ways and that kind of talking in the kitchens."

"Well, but . . ." The change in Hanno's voice made my skin shift on my bones. I kept very still.

"Well but what?"

The Weasel dropped his voice still further. "Maybe if we made him talk to us first . . . I mean, look at it this way. All that stuff he told us, hearing what King Camlach meant to do and all that. . . . If we'd got that information for ourselves and got away to report it, there'd be a fat purse for us, wouldn't there?"

Marric grunted. "And then when he gets ashore and tells someone where he comes from? Ambrosius would hear. He hears everything."

"Are you trying to be simple?" The question was waspish.

It was all I could do to keep still. There was a space between my shoulder-blades where the skin tightened cold over the flesh as if it already felt the knife.

"Oh, I'm not as simple as that. I get you. But I don't see that it—"

"Nobody in Maridunum knows where he went." Hanno's whisper was hurried and eager. "As for the men who saw him come on board, they'll think we've taken him off with us now. In fact, that's what we'll do, take him with us now, and there are plenty of places between here and the town . . ." I heard him swallow. "I told you before we put out, it's senseless to have spent the money on his passage—"

"If we were going to get rid of him," said Marric bluntly, "we'd have done better not to have paid his passage at all. Have a bit of sense, we'll get the money back now in any case, and maybe a good bit over."

"How do you make that out?"

"Well, if the boy has got information, Ambrosius'll pay the passage, you can be sure of that. Then if it turns out he is the bastard—and I'm certain he is—there might be extra in it for us. Kings' sons—or grandsons—come in useful, as who should know better than Ambrosius?"

"Ambrosius must know the boy's useless as a hostage." Hanno sounded sullen.

"Who's to tell? And if he's no use either way to Ambrosius, then we keep the boy and sell him and split the proceeds. So leave it be, I tell you. Alive, he might be worth something; dead, he's worth nothing at all, and we might find ourselves out of pocket over his passage."

I felt Hanno's toe prodding me, not gently. "Doesn't look worth much either way at the moment. Ever know anyone so sick? He must have a stomach like a girl. Do you even suppose he can walk?"

"We can find out," said Marric, and shook me. "Here, boy, get up."

I groaned, rolled over slowly, and showed them what I hoped was a wretchedly pale face. "What is it? Are we there?" I asked it in Welsh.

"Yes, we're there. Come on now, get to your feet, we're going ashore."

I groaned again, more dismally than before, and clutched my belly. "Oh, God, no, leave me alone."

"A bucket of sea water," suggested Hanno.

Marric straightened. "There's hardly time." He spoke in Breton again. "He looks as if we'd have to carry him. No, we'll have to leave him; we've got to get straight to the Count. It's the night of the meeting, remember? He'll already know the ship's docked, and he'll be expecting to see us before he has to leave. We'd better get the report straight to him, or there'll be trouble. We'll leave the boy here for the time being. We can lock him up and tell the watch to keep an eye on him. We can be back well before midnight."

"You can, you mean," said Hanno sourly. "I've got something that won't wait."

"Ambrosius won't wait, either, so if you want the money for that, you'd better come. They've half finished unloading already. Who's on watch?"

Hanno said something, but the creak of the heavy door as they pulled it shut behind them, and then the thudding of the bars dropping into their sockets drowned the reply. I heard the wedges go in, then lost the sound of their voices and footsteps in the noises of the off-loading operation that was shaking the ship—the creak of winches, the shouts of men above me and a few yards away on shore, the hiss and squeak of running hawsers, and the thud of loads being lifted and swung overside on to the wharf.

I threw the blankets off and sat up. With the ceasing of the dreadful motion of the ship I felt steady again—even well, with a sort of light and purged emptiness that gave me a strange feeling of well-being, a floating, slightly unreal sensation, like the power one has in dreams. I knelt up on the bedding and looked about me.

They had lanterns on the wharf to work by, and light from these fell through the small square port-hole. It showed me the wide-mouthed jar, still in place, and a new hunk of barley bread. I unstoppered the jar and tasted the water cautiously. It was musty, tasting of the rag, but good enough, and it cleared the metallic sickness from my mouth. The bread was iron-hard, but I soused it in water until I could break off a piece to chew. Then I got up, and levered myself up to look out of the port-hole.

To do this I had to reach for the sill and pull myself up by my hands, finding a hold for my toes on one of the struts that lined the bulkhead. I had guessed by the shape of my prison that the hold was in the bows, and I now saw that this was correct. The ship lay alongside a stone-built wharf where a couple of lanterns hung on posts, and by their light some twenty men—soldiers—were working to bring the bales and loaded crates off the ship. To the back of the wharf was a row of solid-looking buildings, presumably for storage, but tonight it looked as if the merchandise were bound elsewhere. Carts waited beyond the lamp posts, the hitched mules patient. The men with the carts were in uniform, and armed, and there was an officer superintending the unloading.

The ship was moored close to the wharf amidships, where the gang-plank was. Her forward hawser ran from the rail above my head to the wharf, and this had allowed the bow to swing out from land, so that between me and the shore lay about fifteen feet of water. There were no lights at this end of the ship; the rope ran down into a comfortable pool of darkness, and beyond that was the deeper darkness of the buildings. But I would have to wait, I decided, till the unloading was finished, and the carts—presumably the soldiers with them—moved off. There would be time later to escape, with only the watch on board, and perhaps even the lanterns gone from the wharf.

For of course I must escape. If I stayed where I was, my only hope of safety lay in Marric's goodwill, and this in its turn depended on the outcome of his interview with Ambrosius. And if for some reason Marric could not come back, and Hanno came instead . . .

Besides, I was hungry. The water and the hideous snack of soaked bread had set the juices churning in a ferociously empty belly, and the prospect of waiting two or three hours before anyone came back for me was intolerable, even without the fear of what that return might bring. And even if the best should happen, and Ambrosius send for me, I could not be too sure of my fate at his hands once he had all the information I could give him. Despite the bluff which had saved my life from the spies, this information was scanty enough, and Hanno had been right in guessing—and Ambrosius would know it—that I was useless as a hostage. My semi-royal status might impress Marric and Hanno, but neither being grandson to Vortigern's ally, nor nephew to Vortimer's, would be much of a recommendation to Ambrosius' kindness. It looked as if, royal or not, my lot would with luck be slavery, and without it, an unsung death.

And this I had no intention of waiting for. Not while the port-hole stood open, and the hawser ran, sagging only slightly, from just above me to the bollard on the wharf. The two spies, I supposed, were so little accustomed to dealing with prisoners of my size that they had not even given a thought to the port-hole. No man, not even the weaselly Hanno, could have attempted escape that way, but a slim boy could. Even if they had thought of it, they knew I could not swim, and they had not reckoned with the rope. But, eyeing it carefully as I hung there in the port-hole, I thought I could manage it. If the rats could go along it—I could see one now, a huge fat fellow, sleek with scraps, creeping down towards the shore—then so could I.

But I would have to wait. Meanwhile, it was cold, and I was naked. I dropped lightly back into the hold, and turned to hunt for my clothes.

The light from the shore was dim but sufficient. It showed me the small cage of my prison with the blankets tumbled on the pile of old sacks that had been my bed; a warped and splitting sea-chest against a bulkhead; a pile of rusty chain too heavy for me to shift; the water jar, and in the far corner—"far" meaning two paces away—the vile bucket still half-full of vomit. It showed me nothing else. It may have been a kindly impulse which had made Marric strip me of my sodden clothes, but either he had forgotten to return them, or they had been kept back to prevent me from doing this very thing.

Five seconds showed me that the chest contained nothing but some writing tablets, a bronze cup, and some leather sandal-thongs. At least, I thought, letting the lid down gently on this unpromising collection, they had left me my sandals. Not that I wasn't used to going barefoot, but not in winter, not on the roads. . . . For, naked or not, I had still to escape. Marric's very precautions made me more than ever anxious to get away.

What I would do, where I would go, I had no idea, but the god had sent me safely out of Camlach's hands and across the Narrow Sea, and I trusted my fate. As far as I had a plan I intended to get near enough to Ambrosius to judge what kind of man this was, then, if I thought there was patronage there, or even only mercy, I could approach him and offer him my story and my services. It never entered my head that there might be anything absurd about asking a prince to employ a twelve-year-old. I suppose that to this extent at least, I was royal. Failing Ambrosius' service, I believe I had some hazy idea of making my way to the village north of Kerrec where Moravik came from, and asking for her people.

The sacks I had been lying on were oldish, and beginning to rot. It was easy enough to tear one of them open at the seams for my head and arms to go through. It made a dreadful garment, but it covered me after a fashion. I ripped a second one, and pulled that over my head as well, for warmth. A third would be too bulky. I fingered the blankets longingly, but they were good ones, too thick to tear, and would have been impossibly hampering on my climb out of the ship. Reluctantly, I let them lie. A couple of the leather thongs, knotted together, made a girdle. I stuffed the remaining lump of barley bread into the front of my sack, swilled my face, hands, and hair with the rest of the water, then went again to the port-hole and pulled myself up to look out.

While I was dressing I heard shouts and the tramp of feet, as if the men had been formed up ready to march. I now saw that this had indeed happened. Men and carts were moving off. The last of the carts, heavily loaded, was just creaking away past the buildings with the whip cracking over the straining mules. With them went the tramp of marching feet. I wondered what the cargo was; hardly grain at that time of year; more likely, I thought, metal or ore, to be unloaded by troops and sent to the town under guard. The sounds receded. I looked carefully round. The lanterns still hung from the posts, but as far as I could see the wharf was deserted. It was time to go, before the watch decided to come forward to check on the prisoner.

For an active boy, it was easy. I was soon sitting astride the sill of the port-hole, with my body outside and my legs gripping the bulkhead while I reached up for the rope. There was a bad moment when I found I could not reach it, and would have to stand, holding myself somehow against the hull of the ship, above the black depths between ship and wharf where the oily water lapped and sucked, rustling its drifts of refuse against the dripping walls. But I managed it, clawing up the ship's side as if I had been another of the shoregoing rats, till at last I could stretch upright and grasp the hawser. This was taut and dry, and went down at a gentle angle towards the bollard on the wharf. I gripped it with both hands, twisted to face outwards, then swung my legs free of the ship and up over the rope.

I had meant to let myself down gently, hand over hand, to land in the shadows, but what I hadn't reckoned on, being no seaman, was the waterborne lightness of a small ship. Even my slender weight, as I hitched myself down the rope, made her curtsy, sharply and disconcertingly, and then, tilting, swing her bow suddenly in towards the wharf. The hawser sagged, slackened, drooped under my weight as the strain was loosed, then went down into a loop. Where I swung, clinging like a monkey, it suddenly hung vertical. My feet lost their grip and slid away from me; my hands could not hold my weight. I went down the ship's side on that hawser like a bead on a string.

If the ship had swung more slowly, I would have been crushed as she ground against the wharf-side, or drowned as I reached the bottom of the loop, but she went like a horse shying. As she jarred the edge of the wharf I was just above it, and the jerk loosened what was left of my grip and flung me clear. I missed the bollard by inches, and landed sprawling on the frost-hard ground in the shadow of a wall.

2

There was no time to wonder whether I was hurt. I could hear the slap of bare feet on the deck above me as the watch raced along to see what had happened. I bunched, rolled, and was on my feet and running before his bobbing lantern reached the side. I heard him shout something, but I had already dodged round the corner of the buildings, and was sure he had not seen me. Even if he had, I thought I was safe enough. He would check my prison first, and even then I doubted if he would dare leave the ship. I leaned for a moment or two against the wall, hugging the rope burns on my hands, and trying to adjust my eyes to the night.

Since I had come from near-darkness in my prison, this took no more than a few seconds, and I looked quickly about me to get my bearings.

The shed that hid me was the end one of the row, and behind it—on the side away from the wharf—was the road, a straight ribbon of gravel, making for a cluster of lights some distance away. This no doubt was the town. Nearer, just where the road was swallowed by darkness, was a dim and shifting gleam, which must be the tail light of the last wagon. Nothing else moved.

It was a fairly safe guess that any wagons so guarded were bound for Ambrosius' headquarters. I had no idea whether I could get to him, or even into any town or village, but all I wanted at this stage was to find something to eat, and somewhere warm where I could hide and eat it, and wait for daylight. Once I got my bearings, no doubt the god would lead me still.

He would also have to feed me. I had originally meant to sell one of my brooches for food, but now, I thought, as I jogged in the wake of the wagons, I would have to steal something. At the very worst, I still had a hunk of barley bread. Then somewhere to hide until daylight. . . . If Ambrosius was at "a meeting," as Marric had said, it would be worse than useless to go to his headquarters and ask to see him now. Whatever my sense of my own importance, it did not stretch to privileged treatment by Ambrosius' soldiers if I turned up dressed like this in his absence. Come daylight, we should see.

It was cold. My breath puffed, grey on the black and icy air. There was no moon, but the stars were out like wolves' eyes, glaring. Frost glittered on the stones of the road, and rang under the hoofs and wheels ahead of me. Mercifully there was no wind, and my blood warmed with running, but I dared not catch up with the convoy, which went slowly, so that from time to time I had to check and hang back, while the freezing air bit through the ragged sacks and I flailed my arms against my body for warmth.

Fortunately there was plenty of cover; bushes, sometimes in crouching clusters, sometimes singly, hunched as they had frozen in the path of the prevailing wind, still reaching after it with stiff fingers. Among them great stones stood, rearing sharp against the stars. I took the first of these for a huge milestone, but then saw others, in ranks, thrusting from the turf like storm-blasted avenues of trees. Or like colonnades where gods walked—but not gods that I knew. The starlight struck the face of the stone where I had paused to wait, and something caught my eye, a shape rudely carved in the granite, and etched by the cold light like lampblack. An axe, two-headed. The standing stones stretched away from me into darkness like a march of giants. A dry thistle, broken down to the stalk, stabbed my bare leg. As I turned away I glanced at the axe again. It had vanished.

I ran back to the road, clamping my teeth against the shivering. It was the cold, of course, that made me shiver; what else? The wagons had drawn ahead again, and I ran after, keeping to the turf at the road's edge, though this in fact seemed as hard as the gravel. The frost broke and squeaked under my sandals. Behind me the silent army of stones marched dwindling into the dark, and before me now were the lights of a town and the warmth of its houses reaching out to meet me. I think it was the first time that I, Merlin, had run towards light and company, run from solitude as if it were a ring of wolves' eyes driving one nearer the fire.

It was a walled town. I should have guessed it, so near the sea. There was a high earthwork and above that a palisade, and the ditch outside the earthwork was wide and white with ice. They had smashed the ice at intervals, so that it would not bear; I could see the black stars and the crisscross map of cracks just skinning over with grey glass as the new ice formed. There was a wooden bridge across to the gate, and here the wagons halted, while the officer rode forward to speak to the guards, and the men stood like rocks while the mules stamped and blew and jingled their harness, eager for the warmth of the stable.

If I had had any idea of jumping on the back of a wagon and being carried in that way, I had had to abandon it. All the way to the town the soldiers had been strung out in a file to either side of the convoy, with the officer riding out to one side where he could scan the whole. Now, as he gave the order to advance and break step for the bridge, he wheeled his horse and rode back himself to the tail of the column, to see the last cart in. I caught a glimpse of his face, middle-aged, bad-tempered and catarrhal with cold. Not the man to listen patiently, or even to listen at all. I was safer outside with the stars and the marching giants.

The gate thudded shut behind the convoy, and I heard the locks drive home.

There was a path, faintly discernible, leading off eastward along the edge of the ditch. When I looked that way I saw that, some way off, so far that they must mark some kind of settlement or farm well beyond the limits of the town, more lights showed.

I turned along the path at a trot, chewing at my chunk of barley bread as I went.

The lights turned out to belong to a fair-sized house whose buildings enclosed a courtyard. The house itself, two storeys high, made one wall of the yard, which was bounded on the other three sides by single-storey buildings—baths, servants' quarters, stables, bakehouse—the whole enclosure high-walled and showing only a few slit windows well beyond my reach. There was an arched gateway, and beside this in an iron bracket set at the height of a man's reach, a torch spluttered, sulky with damp pitch. There were more lights inside the yard, but I could hear no movement or voices. The gate, of course, was shut fast.

Not that I would have dared go in that way, to meet some summary fate at the porter's hands. I skirted the wall, looking hopefully for a way to climb in. The third window was the bakehouse; the smells were hours old, and cold, but still would have sent me swarming up the wall, save that the window was a bare slit which would not have admitted even me.

The next was a stable, and the next also. . . . I could smell the horse-smells and beast-smells mingling, and the sweetness of dried grass. Then the house, with no windows at all facing outwards. The bathhouse, the same. And back to the gate.

A chain clanged suddenly, and within a few feet of me, just inside the gate, a big dog gave tongue like a bell. I believe I jumped back a full pace, then flattened myself against the wall as I heard a door open somewhere close. There was a pause, while the dog growled and someone listened, then a man's voice said something curt, and the door shut. The dog grumbled to itself for a bit, snuffling at the foot of the gate, then dragged its chain back to the kennel, and I heard it settling again into its straw.

There was obviously no way in to find shelter. I stood for a while, trying to think, with my back pressed to the cold wall that still seemed warmer than the icy air. I was shaking so violently now with the cold that I felt as if my very bones were chattering. I was sure I had been right to leave the ship, and not to trust myself to the troops' mercy, but now I began to wonder if I dared knock at the gate and beg for shelter. I would get rough shrift as a beggar, I knew, but if I stayed out here I might well die of cold before morning.

Then I saw, just beyond the torchlight's reach, the low black shape of a building that must be a cattle shed or shippon, some twenty paces away and at the corner of a field surrounded by low banks crowned with thorn bushes. I could hear cattle moving there. At least there would be their warmth to share, and if I could force my chattering teeth through it, I still had a heel of barley bread.

I had taken a pace away from the wall, moving, I could have sworn, without a sound, when the dog came out of his kennel with a rush and a rattle, and set up his infernal baying again. This time the house door opened immediately, and I heard a man's step in the yard. He was coming towards the gate. I heard the rasp of metal as he drew some weapon. I was just turning to run when I heard, clear and sharp on the frosty air, what the dog had heard. The sound of hoofs, full gallop, coming this way.

Quick as a shadow, I ran across the open ground towards the shed. Beside it a gap in the bank made a gateway, which had been blocked with a dead thorn-tree. I shoved through this, then crept—as quietly as I could, not to disturb the beasts—to crouch in the shed doorway, out of sight of the house gate.

The shed was only a small, roughly built shelter, with walls not much more than man-height, thatched over, and crowded with beasts. These seemed to be young bullocks for the most part, too thronged to lie down, but seemingly content enough with each other's warmth, and some dry fodder to chew over. A rough plank across the doorway made a barrier to keep them in. Outside, the field stretched empty in the starlight, grey with frost, and bounded with its low banks ridged with those hunched and crippled bushes. In the center of the field was one of the standing stones.

Inside the gateway, I heard the man speak to silence the dog. The sounds of hoofs swelled, hammering up the iron track, then suddenly the rider was on us, sweeping out of the dark and pulling his horse up with a scream of metal on stone and a flurry of gravel and frozen turf, and the thud of the beast's hoofs right up against the wood of the gate. The man inside shouted something, a question, and the rider answered him even in the act of flinging himself down from the saddle.

"Of course it is. Open up, will you?"

I heard the door gate as it was dragged open, then the two men talking, but apart from a word here and there, could not distinguish what they said. It seemed, from the movement of the light, that the porter (or whoever had come to the gate) had lifted the torch down from its socket. Moreover, the light was moving this way, and both men with it, leading the horse.

I heard the rider say, impatiently: "Oh, yes, it'll be well enough here. If it comes to that, it will suit me to have a quick getaway. There's fodder there?"

"Aye, sir. I put the young beasts out here to make room for the horses."

"There's a crowd, then?" The voice was young, clear, a little harsh, but that might only be cold and arrogance combined. A patrician voice, careless as the horsemanship that had all but brought the horse down on its haunches in front of the gate.

"A fair number," said the porter. "Mind now, sir, it's through this gap. If you'll let me go first with the light . . ."

"I can see," said the young man irritably, "if you don't shove the torch right in my face. Hold up, you." This to the horse as it pecked at a stone.

"You'd best let me go first, sir. There's a thorn bush across the gap to keep them in. If you'll stand clear a minute, I'll shift it."

I had already melted out of the shed doorway and round the corner, where the rough wall met the field embankment. There were turfs stacked here, and a pile of brushwood and dried bracken that I supposed were winter bedding. I crouched down behind the stack.

I heard the thorn-tree being lifted and flung aside. "There, sir, bring him through. There's not much room, but if you're sure you'd as soon leave him out here—"

"I said it would do. Shift the plank and get him in. Hurry, man, I'm late."

"If you leave him with me now, sir, I'll unsaddle for you."

"No need. He'll be well enough for an hour or two. Just loosen the girth. I suppose I'd better throw my cloak over him. Gods, it's cold . . . Get the bridle off, will you? I'm getting in out of this . . ."

I heard him stride away, spurs clinking. The plank went back into place, and then the thorn-tree. As the porter hurried after him I caught something that sounded like, "And let me in at the back, where the father won't see me."

The big gate shut behind them. The chain rattled, but the dog stayed silent. I heard the men's steps crossing the yard, then the house door shut on them.

3

Even if I had dared to risk the torchlight and the dog, to scramble over the bank behind me and run the twenty paces to the gate, there would have been no need. The god had done his part; he had sent me warmth and, I discovered, food.

No sooner had the gate shut than I was back inside the shippon, whispering reassurance to the horse as I reached to rob him of the cloak. He was not sweating much; he must have galloped only the mile or so from the town, and in that shed among the crowded beasts he could take no harm from cold; in any case, my need came before his, and I had to have that cloak. It was an officer's cloak, thick, soft, and good. As I laid hold of it I found, to my excitement, that my lord had left me not only his cloak, but a full saddle-bag as well. I stretched up, tiptoe, and felt inside.

A leather flask, which I shook. It was almost full. Wine, certainly; that young man would never carry water. A napkin with biscuits in it, and raisins, and some strips of dried meat.

The beasts jostled, dribbling, and puffed their warm breath at me. The long cloak had slipped to trail a corner in the dirt under their hoofs. I snatched it up, clutched the flask and food to me, and slipped out under the barrier. The pile of brushwood in the corner outside was clean, but I would hardly have cared if it had been a dung-heap. I burrowed into it, wrapped myself warmly in the soft woollen folds, and steadily ate and drank my way through everything the god had sent me.

Whatever happened, I must not sleep. Unfortunately it seemed that the young man would not be here for more than an hour or two; but this with the bonus of food should be time enough to warm me so that I might bed down in comfort till daylight. I would hear movement from the house in time to slip back to the shed and throw the cloak into place. My lord would hardly be likely to notice that his marching rations had gone from his saddle-bag.

I drank some more wine. It was amazing how even the stale ends of the barley bread tasted the better for it. It was good stuff, potent and sweet, and tasting of raisins. It ran warm into my body, till the rigid joints loosened and melted and stopped their shaking, and I could curl up warm and relaxed in my dark nest, with the bracken pulled right up over me to shut out the cold.

I must have slept a little. What woke me I have no idea; there was no sound. Even the beasts in the shed were still.

It seemed darker, so that I wondered if it were almost dawn, when the stars fade. But when I parted the bracken and peered out I saw they were still there, burning white in the black sky.

The strange thing was, it was warmer. Some wind had risen, and had brought cloud with it, scudding drifts that raced high overhead, then scattered and wisped away so that shadow and starlight broke one after the other like waves across the frost-grey fields and still landscape, where the thistles and stiff winter grasses seemed to flow like water, or like a cornfield under the wind. There was no sound of the wind blowing.

Above the flying veils of cloud the stars were brilliant, studding a black dome. The warmth and my curled posture in the dark must (I thought) have made me dream of security, of Galapas and the crystal globe where I had lain curled, and watched the light. Now the brilliant arch of stars above me was like the curved roof of the cave with the light flashing off the crystals, and the passing shadows flying, chased by the fire. You could see points of red and sapphire, and one star steady, beaming gold. Then the silent wind blew another shadow across the sky with light behind it, and the thorn-trees shivered, and the shadow of the standing stone.

I must be buried too deep and snug in my bed to hear the rustle of the wind through grass and thorn. Nor did I hear the young man pushing his way through the barrier that the porter had replaced across the gap in the bank. For, suddenly, with no warning, he was there, a tall figure striding across the field, as shadowy and quiet as the wind.

I shrank, like a snail into its shell. Too late now to run and replace the cloak. All I could hope was that he would assume the thief had fled, and not search too near. But he did not approach the shed. He was making straight across the field, away from me. Then I saw, half in, half out of the shadow of the standing stone, the white animal grazing. His horse must have broken loose. The gods alone knew what it found to eat in that winter field, but I could see it, ghostly in the distance, the white beast grazing beside the standing stone. And it must have rubbed the girth till it snapped; its saddle, too, was gone.

At least in the time he would take to catch it, I should be able to get away . . . or better still, drop the cloak near the shed, where he would think it had slid from the horse's back, and then get back to my warm nest till he had gone. He could only blame the porter for the animal's escape; and justly; I had not touched the bar across the doorway. I raised myself cautiously, watching my chance.

The grazing animal had lifted its head to watch the man's approach. A cloud swept across the stars, blackening the field. Light ran after the shadow across the frost. It struck the standing stone. I saw that I had been wrong; it was not the horse. Nor—my next thought—could it be one of the young beasts from the shed. This was a bull, a massive white bull, full-grown, with a royal spread of horns and a neck like a thunder-cloud. It lowered its head till the dewlap brushed the ground, and pawed once, twice.

The young man paused. I saw him now, clearly, as the shadow lifted. He was tall and strongly built, and his hair looked bleached in the starlight. He wore some sort of foreign dress—trousers cross-bound with thongs below a tunic girded low on the hips, and a high loose cap. Under this the fair hair blew round his face like rays. There was a rope in his hand, held loosely, its coils brushing the frost. His cloak flew in the wind; a short cloak, of some dark colour I could not make out.

His cloak? Then it could not be my young lord. And after all, why should that arrogant young man come with a rope to catch a bull that had strayed in the night?

Without warning, and without a sound, the white bull charged. Shadow and light rushed with it, flickering, blurring the scene. The rope whirled, snaked into a loop, settled. The man leapt to one side as the great beast tore past him and came to a sliding stop with the rope snapping taut and the frost smoking up in clouds from the side-slipping hoofs.

The bull whirled, and charged again. The man waited without moving, his feet planted slightly apart, his posture casual, almost disdainful. As the bull reached him he seemed to sway aside, lightly, like a dancer. The bull went by him so close that I saw a horn shear the swirling cloak, and the beast's shoulder passed the man's thigh like a lover seeking a caress. The man's hands moved. The rope whipped up into a ring, and another loop settled round the royal horns. The man leaned against it, and as the beast came up short once more, turning sharp in its own smoke, the man jumped.

Not away. Towards the bull, clean on to the thick neck, with knees digging into the dewlap, and fierce hands using the rope like reins.

The bull stopped dead, his feet four-square, his head thrust downwards with his whole weight and strength against the rope. There was still no sound that I could hear, no sound of hoof or crack of rope or bellow of breath. I was half out of the brushwood now, rigid and staring, heedless of anything save the fight between man and bull.

A cloud stamped the field again with darkness. I got to my feet. I believe I meant to seize the plank from the shed and rush with it across the field to give what futile help I could. But before I could move the cloud had fled, to show me the bull standing as before, the man still on its neck. But now the beast's head was coming up. The man had dropped the rope, and his two hands were on the bull's horns, dragging them back . . . back . . . up. . . . Slowly, almost as if in a ritual of surrender, the bull's head lifted, the powerful neck stretched up, exposed.

There was a gleam in the man's right hand. He leaned forward, then drove the knife down and across.

Still in silence, slowly, the bull sank to its knees. Black flowed over the white hide, the white ground, the white base of the stone.

I broke from my hiding place and ran, shouting something—I have no idea what—across the field towards them.

I don't know what I meant to do. The man saw me coming, and turned his head, and I saw that nothing was needed. He was smiling, but his face in the starlight seemed curiously smooth and unhuman in its lack of expression. I could see no sign of stress or effort. His eyes were expressionless too, cold and dark, with no smile there.

I stumbled, tried to stop, caught my feet in the trailing cloak, and fell, rolling in a ridiculous and helpless bundle towards him, just as the white bull, slowly heeling over, collapsed. Something struck me on the side of the head. I heard a sharp childish sound which was myself crying out, then it was dark.

4

Someone kicked me again, hard, in the ribs. I grunted and rolled, trying to get out of range, but the cloak hampered me. A torch, stinking with black smoke, was thrust down, almost into my face. The familiar young voice said, angrily: "My cloak, by God! Grab hold of him, you, quick. I'm damned if I touch him, he's filthy."

They were all round me, feet scuffling the frost, torches flaring, men's voices curious, or angry, or indifferently amused. Some were mounted, and their horses skirmished on the edge of the group, stamping and fidgeting with cold.

I crouched, blinking upwards. My head ached, and the flickering scene above me swam unreal, in snatches, as if reality and dream were breaking and dovetailing one across the other to split the senses. Fire, voices, the rocking of a ship, the white bull falling . . .

A hand tore the cloak off me. Some of the rotten sacking went with it, leaving me with a shoulder and side bare to the waist. Someone grabbed my wrist and yanked me to my feet and held me. His other hand took me roughly by the hair, and pulled my head up to face the man who stood over me. He was tall, young, with light brown hair showing reddish in the torchlight, and an elegant beard fringing his chin. His eyes were blue, and looked angry. He was cloakless in the cold. He had a whip in his left hand.

He eyed me, making a sound of disgust. "A beggar's brat, and stinking, at that. I'll have to burn the thing, I suppose. I'll have your hide for this, you bloody little vermin. I suppose you were going to steal my horse as well?"

"No, sir. I swear it was only the cloak. I would have put it back, I promise you."

"And the brooch as well?"

"Brooch?"

The man holding me said: "Your brooch is still in the cloak, my lord."

I said quickly: "I only borrowed it, for warmth—it was so cold, so I—"

"So you just stripped my horse and left him to catch cold? Is that it?"

"I didn't think it would harm him, sir. It was warm in the shed. I would have put it back, really I would."

"For me to wear after you, you stinking little rat? I ought to slit your throat for this."

Someone—one of the mounted men—said: "Oh, leave it. There's no harm done except that your cloak will have to go to the fuller tomorrow. The wretched boy's half naked, and it's cold enough to freeze a salamander. Let him go."

"At least," said the young officer between his teeth, "it will warm me up to thrash him. Ah, no, you don't—hold him fast, Cadal."

The whip whistled back. The man who held me tightened his grip as I fought to tear free, but before the whip could fall a shadow moved in front of the torchlight and a hand came lightly down, no more than a touch, on the young man's wrist.

Someone said: "What's this?"

The men fell silent, as if at an order. The young man dropped the whip to his side, and turned.

My captor's grip had slackened as the newcomer spoke, and I twisted free. I might possibly have doubled away between the men and horses and run for it, though I suppose a mounted man could have run me down in seconds. But I made no attempt to get away. I was staring.

The newcomer was tall, taller than my cloakless young officer by half a head. He was between me and the torches, and I could not see him well against the flame. The flares swam still, blurred and dazzling; my head hurt, and the cold had sprung back at me like a toothed beast. All I saw was the tall shadowy figure watching me, dark eyes in an expressionless face.

I took a breath like a gasp. "It was you! You saw me, didn't you? I was coming to help you, only I tripped and fell. I wasn't running away—tell him that, please, my lord. I did mean to put the cloak back before he came for it. Please tell him what happened!"

"What are you talking about? Tell him what?"

I blinked against the glare of the torches. "About what happened just now. It was—it was you who killed the bull?"

"Who *what?*"

It had been quiet before, but now there was silence, complete except for the men's breathing as they crowded round, and the fidgeting of the horses.

The young officer said sharply: "What bull?"

"The white bull," I said. "He cut its throat, and the blood splashed out like a spring. That was how I got your cloak dirty. I was trying—"

"How the hell did you know about the bull? Where were you? Who's been talking?"

"Nobody," I said, surprised. "I saw it all. Is it so secret? I thought I must be dreaming at first, I was sleepy after the bread and wine—"

"By the Light!" It was the young officer still, but now the others were exclaiming with him, their anger breaking round me. "Kill him, and have done" . . . "He's lying" . . . "Lying to save his wretched skin" . . . "He must have been spying" . . .

The tall man had not spoken. Nor had he taken his eyes off me. From somewhere, anger poured into me, and I said hotly, straight to him: "I'm not a spy, or a thief! I'm tired of this! What was I to do, freeze to death to save the life of a horse?" The man behind me laid a hand on my arm, but I shook him off with a gesture that my grandfather himself might have used. "Nor am I a beggar, my lord. I'm a free man come to take service with Ambrosius, if he'll have me. That's what I came here for, from my own country, and it was . . . it was an accident that I lost my clothes. I—I may be young, but I have certain knowledge that is valuable, and I speak five languages . . ." My voice faltered. Someone had made a stifled sound like a laugh. I set my chattering teeth and added, royally: "I beg you merely to give me shelter now, my lord, and tell me where I may seek him out in the morning."

This time the silence was so thick you could have cut it. I heard the young officer take breath to speak, but the other put out a hand. He must, by the way they waited for him, be their commander. "Wait. He's not being insolent. Look at him. Hold the torch higher, Lucius. Now, what's your name?"

"Myrddin, sir."

"Well, Myrddin, I'll listen to you, but make it plain and make it quick. I want to hear this about the bull. Start at the beginning. You saw my brother stable his horse in the shed yonder, and you took the cloak off its back for warmth. Go on from there."

"Yes, my lord," I said. "I took the food from the saddle-bag, too, and the wine—"

"You were talking about *my* bread and wine?" demanded the young officer.

"Yes, sir. I'm sorry, but I'd hardly eaten for four days—"

"Never mind that," said the commander curtly. "Go on."

"I hid in the brushwood stack at the corner of the shed, and I think I went to sleep. When I woke I saw the bull, over by the standing stone. He was grazing there, quite quiet. Then you came, with the rope. The bull charged, and you roped it, and then jumped on its back and pulled its head up and killed it with a knife. There was blood everywhere. I was running to help. I don't know what I could have done, but I ran, all the same. Then I tripped over the cloak, and fell. That's all."

I stopped. A horse stamped, and a man cleared his throat. Nobody spoke. I thought that Cadal, the servant who had held me, moved a little further away.

The commander said, very quietly: "Beside the standing stone?"

"Yes, sir."

He turned his head. The group of men and horses was very near the stone. I could see it behind the horsemen's shoulders, thrusting up torchlit against the night sky.

"Stand aside and let him see," said the tall man, and some of them moved.

The stone was about thirty feet away. Near its base the frosty grass showed scuffled by boots and hoofprints, but no more. Where I had seen the white bull fall, with the black blood gushing from its throat, there was nothing but the scuffled frost, and the shadow of the stone.

The torch-bearer had shifted the torch to throw light towards the stone. Light fell now straight on my questioner, and for the first time I saw him plainly. He was not as young as I had thought; there were lines in his face, and his brows were down, frowning. His eyes were dark, not blue like his brother's, and he was more heavily built than I had supposed. There was a flash of gold at his wrists and collar, and a heavy cloak dropped in a long line from shoulder to heel.

I said, stammering: "It wasn't you. I'm sorry, it—I see now, I must have dreamed it. No one would come with a rope, and a short knife, alone against a bull . . . and no man could drag a bull's head up and slit its throat . . . it was one of my—it was a dream. And it wasn't you, I can see that now. I—I thought you were the man in the cap. I'm sorry."

The men were muttering now, but no longer with threats. The young officer said, in quite a different tone from any he had used before: "What was he like, this 'man in the cap'?"

His brother said quickly: "Never mind. Not now." He put out a hand, took me by the chin, and lifted my face. "You say your name is Myrddin. Where are you from?"

"From Wales, sir."

"Ah. So you're the boy they brought from Maridunum?"

"Yes. You knew about me? Oh!" Made stupid by the cold and by bewilderment, I made the discovery I should have made long ago. My flesh shivered like a nervous pony's with cold, and a curious sensation, part excitement, part fear. "You must be the Count. You must be Ambrosius himself."

He did not trouble to answer. "How old are you?"

"Twelve, sir."

"And who are you, Myrddin, to talk of offering me service? What can you offer me, that I should not cut you down here and now, and let these gentlemen get in out of the cold?"

"Who I am makes no difference, sir. I am the grandson of the King of South Wales, but he is dead. My uncle Camlach is King now, but that's no help to me either; he wants me dead. So I'd not serve your turn even as a hostage. It's not who I am, but what I am that matters. I have something to offer you, my lord. You will see, if you let me live till morning."

"Ah, yes, valuable information, and five languages. And dreams, too, it seems." The words were mocking, but he was not smiling. "The old King's grandson, you say? And Camlach not your father? Nor Dyved, either, surely? I never knew the old man had a grandson, barring Camlach's baby. From what my spies told me I took you to be his bastard."

"He used sometimes to pass me off as his own bastard—to save my mother's shame, he said, but she never saw it as shame, and she should know. My mother was Niniane, the old King's daughter."

"Ah." A pause. "Was?"

I said: "She's still alive, but by now she's in St. Peter's nunnery. You might say she joined them years ago, but she's only been allowed to leave the palace since the old King died."

"And your father?"

"She never spoke of him, to me or any man. They say he was the Prince of Darkness."

I expected the usual reaction to that, the crossed fingers or the quick look over the shoulder. He did neither. He laughed.

"Then no wonder you talk of helping kings to their kingdoms, and dream of gods under the stars." He turned aside then, with a swirl of the big cloak. "Bring him along, one of you. Uther, you may as well give him your cloak again before he dies in front of our eyes."

"Do you think I'd touch it after him, even if he were the Prince of Darkness in person?" asked Uther.

Ambrosius laughed. "If you ride that poor beast of yours in your usual fashion you'll be warm enough without. And if your cloak is dabbled with the blood of the Bull, then it's not for you, tonight, is it?"

"Are you blaspheming?"

"I?" said Ambrosius, with a sort of cold blankness.

His brother opened his mouth, thought better of it, shrugged, and vaulted into his grey's saddle. Someone flung the cloak to me, and—as I struggled with shaking hands to wrap it round me again—seized me, bundled me up in it anyhow, and threw me up like a parcel to some rider on a wheeling horse. Ambrosius swung to the saddle of a big black.

"Come, gentlemen."

The black stallion jumped forward, and Ambrosius' cloak flew out. The grey pounded after him. The rest of the cavalcade strung out at a hand-gallop along the track back to the town.

5

Ambrosius' headquarters was in the town. I learned later that the town had, in fact, grown up round the camp where Ambrosius and his brother had, during the last couple of years, begun to gather and train the army that had for so long been a mythical threat to Vortigern, and now, with the help of King Budec, and troops from half the countries of Gaul, was growing into a fact. Budec was King of Less Britain, and cousin of Ambrosius and Uther. He it was who had taken the brothers in twenty years ago when they—Ambrosius then ten years old, and Uther still at his nurse's breast—were carried overseas into safety after Vortigern had murdered their elder brother the King. Budec's own castle was barely a stone's throw from the camp that Ambrosius had built, and round the two strongpoints the town had grown up, a mixed collection of houses, shops and huts, with the wall and ditch thrown round for protection. Budec was an old man now, and had made Ambrosius his heir, as well as Comes or Count of his forces. It had been supposed in the past that the brothers would be content to stay in Less Britain and rule it after Budec's death; but now that Vortigern's grip on Greater Britain was slackening, the money and the men were pouring in, and it was an open secret that Ambrosius had his eye on South and West Britain for himself, while Uther—even at twenty a brilliant soldier—would, it was hoped, hold Less Britain, and so for another generation at least provide between the two kingdoms a Romano-Celtic rampart against the barbarians from the north.

I soon found that in one respect Ambrosius was pure Roman. The first thing that happened to me after I was dumped, cloak and all, between the door-posts of his outer hall, was that I was seized, unwrapped, and—exhausted by now beyond protest or question—deposited in a bath. The heating system certainly worked here; the water was steaming hot, and thawed my frozen body in three painful and ecstatic minutes. The man who had carried me home—it was Cadal, who turned out to be one of the Count's personal servants—bathed me himself. Under Ambrosius' own orders, he told me curtly, as he scrubbed and oiled and dried me, and then stood over me as I put on a clean tunic of white wool only two sizes too big.

"Just to make sure you don't bolt again. He wants to talk to you, don't ask me why. You can't wear those sandals in this house, Dia knows where you've been with them. Leastways, it's obvious where you've been with them; cows, was it? You can go barefoot, the floors are warm. Well, at least you're clean now. Hungry?"

"Are you joking?"

"Come along, then. Kitchen's this way. Unless, being a king's grand-bastard, or whatever it was you told him, you're too proud to eat in the kitchen?"

"Just this once," I said, "I'll put up with it."

He shot me a look, scowled, and then grinned. "You've got guts, I'll give you that. You stood up to them a fair treat. Beats me how you thought of all that stuff quick enough. Rocked 'em proper. I wouldn't have given two pins for your chances once Uther laid hands on you. You got yourself a hearing, anyway."

"It was true."

"Oh, sure, sure. Well, you can tell him all over again in a minute, and see you make it good, because he don't like them that wastes his time, see?"

"Tonight?"

"Certainly. You'll find that out if you live till morning; he doesn't waste much time sleeping. Nor does Prince Uther, come to that, but then he's not working, exactly. Not at his papers, that is, though they reckon he puts in a bit of uncommon hard labour in other directions. Come along."

Yards before we reached the kitchen door the smell of hot food came out to meet me, and with it the sound of frying.

The kitchen was a big room, and seemed, to my eye, about as grand as the dining-room at home. The floor was of smooth red tiles, there was a raised hearth at each end of the room, and along the walls the chopping-slabs with store-jars of oil and wine below them and shelves of dishes above. At one of the hearths a sleepy-eyed boy was heating the oil in a skillet; he had kindled fresh charcoal in the burners, and on one of these a pot of soup simmered, while sausages spat and crackled over a grill, and I could smell chicken frying. I noticed that—in spite of Cadal's implied disbelief in my story—I was given a platter of Samian ware so fine that it must be the same used at the Count's own table, and the wine came in a glass goblet and was poured from a glazed red jar with a carved seal and the label "Reserve." There was even a fine white napkin.

The cook-boy—he must have been roused from his bed to make the meal for me—hardly bothered to look who he was working for; after he had dished up the meal he scraped the burners hurriedly clean for morning, did an even sketchier job of scouring his pans, then with a glance at Cadal for permission, went yawning back to bed. Cadal served me himself, and even fetched fresh bread hot from the bakehouse, where the first batch had just come out for morning. The soup was some savoury concoction of shellfish, which they eat almost daily in Less Britain. It was smoking hot and delicious, and I thought I had never eaten anything so good, until I tried the chicken, crisp-fried in oil, and the grilled sausages, brown and bursting with spiced meat and onions. I mopped the platter dry with the new bread, and shook my head when Cadal handed a dish of dried dates and cheese and honey cakes.

"No, thank you."

"Enough?"

"Oh, yes." I pushed the platter away. "That was the best meal I ever ate in my life. Thank you."

"Well," he said, "hunger's the best sauce, they say. Though I'll allow the food's good here." He brought fresh water and a towel and waited while I rinsed my hands and dried them. "Well, I might even credit the rest of your story now."

I looked up. "What d'you mean?"

"You didn't learn your manners in a kitchen, that's for sure. Ready? Come along then; he said to interrupt him even if he was working."

Ambrosius, however, was not working when we got to his room. His table—a vast affair of marble from Italy—was indeed littered with rolls and maps and writing materials, and the Count was in his big chair behind it, but he sat half sideways, chin on fist, staring into the brazier which filled the room with warmth and the faint scent of apple-wood.

He did not look up as Cadal spoke to the sentry, and with a clash of arms the latter let me by.

"The boy, sir." This was not the voice Cadal had used to me.

"Thank you. You can go to bed, Cadal."

"Sir."

He went. The leather curtains fell to behind him. Ambrosius turned his head then. He looked me up and down for some minutes in silence. Then he nodded towards a stool.

"Sit down."

I obeyed him.

"I see they found something for you to wear. Have you been fed?"

"Yes, thank you, sir."

"And you're warm enough now? Pull the stool nearer the fire if you want to."

He turned straight in the chair, and leaned back, his hands resting on the carved lions' heads of the arms. There was a lamp on the table between us, and in its bright steady light any resemblance between the Count Ambrosius and the strange man of my dream had vanished completely.

It is difficult now, looking back from this distance in time, to remember my first real impression of Ambrosius. He would be at that time not much more than thirty years old, but I was only twelve, and to me, of course, he already seemed venerable. But I think that in fact he did seem older than his years; this was a natural result of the life he had led, and the heavy responsibility he had borne since he was a little younger than myself. There were lines round his eyes, and two heavy furrows between his brows which spoke of decision and perhaps temper, and his mouth was hard and straight, and usually unsmiling. His brows were dark like his hair, and could bar his eyes formidably with shadow. There was the faint white line of a scar running from his left ear half over his cheekbone. His nose looked Roman, high-bridged and prominent, but his skin was tanned rather than olive, and there was something about his eyes which spoke of black Celt rather than Roman. It was a bleak face, a face (as I would find) that could cloud with frustration or anger, or even with the hard control that he exerted over these, but it was a face to trust. He was not a man one could love easily, certainly not a man to like, but a man either to hate or to worship. You either fought him, or followed him. But it had to be one or the other; once you came within reach of him, you had no peace.

All of this I had to learn. I remember little now of what I thought of him, except for the deep eyes watching me past the lamp, and his hands clasped on the lions' heads. But I remember every word that was said.

He looked me up and down. "Myrddin, son of Niniane, daughter of the King of South Wales . . . and privy, they tell me, to the secrets of the palace at Maridunum?"

"I—did I say that? I told them I lived there, and heard things sometimes."

"My men brought you across the Narrow Sea because you said you had secrets which would be useful to me. Was that not true?"

"Sir," I said a little desperately, "I don't know what might be useful to you.

To them I spoke the language I thought they would understand. I thought they were going to kill me. I was saving my life."

"I see. Well, now you are here, and safely. Why did you leave your home?"

"Because once my grandfather had died, it was not safe for me there. My mother was going into a nunnery, and Camlach my uncle had already tried to kill me, and his servants killed my friend."

"Your friend?"

"My servant. His name was Cerdic. He was a slave."

"Ah, yes. They told me about that. They said you set fire to the palace. You were perhaps a little—drastic?"

"I suppose so. But someone had to do him honour. He was mine."

His brows went up. "Do you give that as a reason, or as an obligation?"

"Sir?" I puzzled it out, then said, slowly: "Both, I think."

He looked down at his hands. He had moved them from the chair arms, and they were clasped on the table in front of him. "Your mother, the princess." He said it as if the thought sprang straight from what we had been saying. "Did they harm her, too?"

"Of course not!"

He looked up at my tone. I explained quickly. "I'm sorry, my lord, I only meant, if they'd been going to harm her, how could I have left? No, Camlach would never harm her. I told you, she'd spoken for years of wanting to go into St. Peter's nunnery. I can't even remember a time when she didn't receive any Christian priest who visited Maridunum, and the Bishop himself, when he came from Caerleon, used to lodge in the palace. But my grandfather would never let her go. He and the Bishop used to quarrel over her—and over me. . . . The Bishop wanted me baptized, you see, and my grandfather wouldn't hear of it. I—I think perhaps he kept it as a bribe to my mother, if she'd tell him who my father was, or perhaps if she'd consent to marry where he chose for her, but she never consented, or told him anything." I paused, wondering if I was saying too much, but he was watching me steadily, and it seemed attentively. "My grandfather swore she should never go into the Church," I added, "but as soon as he died she asked Camlach, and he allowed it. He would have shut me up, too, so I ran away."

He nodded. "Where did you intend to go?"

"I didn't know. It was true, what Marric said to me in the boat, that I'd have to go to someone. I'm only twelve, and because I can't be my own master, I must find a master. I didn't want Vortigern, or Vortimer, and I didn't know where else to go."

"So you persuaded Marric and Hanno to keep you alive and bring you to me?"

"Not really," I said honestly. "I didn't know at first where they were going, I just said anything I could think of to save myself. I had put myself into the god's hands, and he had sent me into their path, and then the ship was there. So I made them bring me across."

"To me?"

I nodded. The brazier flickered, and the shadows danced. A shadow moved on his cheek, as if he was smiling. "Then why not wait till they did so? Why jump ship and risk freezing to death in an icy field?"

"Because I was afraid they didn't mean to bring me to you after all. I thought that they might have realized how—how little use I would be to you."

"So you came ashore on your own in the middle of a winter's night, and in a strange country, and the god threw you straight at my feet. You and your god between you, Myrddin, make a pretty powerful combination. I can see I have no choice."

"My lord?"

"Perhaps you are right, and there are ways in which you can serve me." He looked down at the table again, picked up a pen, and turned it over in his hand, as if he examined it. "But tell me first, why are you called Myrddin? You say your mother never told you who your father was? Never even hinted? Might she have called you after him?"

"Not by calling me Myrddin, sir. That's one of the old gods—there's a shrine just near St. Peter's gate. He was the god of the hill nearby, and some say of other parts beyond South Wales. But I have another name." I hesitated. "I've never told anyone this before, but I'm certain it was my father's name."

"And that is?"

"Emrys. I heard her talking to him once, at night, years ago when I was very small. I never forgot. There was something about her voice. You can tell."

The pen became still. He looked at me under his brows. "Talking to him? Then it was someone in the palace?"

"Oh, no, not like that. It wasn't real."

"You mean it was a dream? A vision? Like this tonight of the bull?"

"No, sir. And I wouldn't have called that a dream, either—it was real, too, in a different way. I have those sometimes. But the time I heard my mother. . . . There was an old hypocaust in the palace that had been out of use for years; they filled it in later, but when I was young—when I was little—I used to crawl in there to get away from people. I kept things there . . . the sort of things you keep when you're small, and if they find them, they throw them away."

"I know. Go on."

"Do you? I—well, I used to crawl through the hypocaust, and one night I was under her chamber, and heard her talking to herself, out loud, as you do when you pray sometimes. I heard her say 'Emrys,' but I don't remember what else." I looked at him. "You know how one catches one's own name, even if one can't hear much else? I thought she must be praying for me, but when I was older and remembered it, it came to me that the 'Emrys' must be my father. There was something about her voice . . . and anyway, she never called me that; she called me Merlin."

"Why?"

"After a falcon. It's a name for the *corwalch.*"

"Then I shall call you Merlin, too. You have courage, and it seems as if you have eyes that can see a long way. I might need your eyes, some day. But tonight you can start with simpler things. You shall tell me about your home. Well, what is it?"

"If I'm to serve you . . . of course I will tell you anything I can. . . . But—" I hesitated, and he took the words from me:

"But you must have my promise that when I invade Britain no harm will come to your mother? You have it. She shall be safe, and so shall any other man or woman you may ask me to spare for their kindness to you."

I must have been staring. "You are—very generous."

"If I take Britain, I can afford to be. I should perhaps have made some reservations." He smiled. "It might be difficult if you wanted an amnesty for your uncle Camlach?"

"It won't arise," I said. "When you take Britain, he'll be dead."

A silence. His lips parted to say something, but I think he changed his mind. "I said I might use those eyes of yours some day. Now, you have my promise, so let us talk. Never mind if things don't seem important enough to tell. Let me be the judge of that."

So I talked to him. It did not strike me as strange then that he should talk to me as if I were his equal, nor that he should spend half the night with me asking questions which in part his spies could have answered. I believe that twice, while we talked, a slave came in silently and replenished the brazier, and once I heard the clash and command of the guard changing outside the door. Ambrosius questioned, prompted, listened, sometimes wrting on a tablet in front of him, sometimes staring, chin on fist, at the table-top, but more usually watching me with that steady, shadowed stare. When I hesitated, or strayed into some irrelevancy, or faltered through sheer fatigue, he would prod me back with his questions towards some unseen goal, as a muleteer goads his mule.

"This fortress on the River Seint, where your grandfather met Vortigern. How far north of Caerleon? By which road? Tell me about the road. . . . How is the fortress reached from the sea?"

And: "The tower where the High King lodged, Maximus' Tower—Macsen's, you call it. . . . Tell me about this. How many men were housed there. What road there is to the harbour . . ."

Or: "You say the King's party halted in a valley pass, south of the Snow Hill, and the kings went aside together. Your man Cerdic said they were looking at an old stronghold on the crag. Describe the place . . . the height of the crag. How far one should see from the top, to the north . . . the south . . . the east."

Or: "Now think of your grandfather's nobles. How many will be loyal to Camlach? Their names? How many men? And of his allies, who? Their numbers . . . their fighting power . . . ?"

And then, suddenly: "Now tell me this. How did you know Camlach was going to Vortimer?"

"He said so to my mother," I told him, "by my grandfather's bier. I heard him. There had been rumours that this would happen, and I knew he had quarrelled with my grandfather, but nobody knew anything for certain. Even my mother only suspected what he meant to do. But as soon as the King was dead, he told her."

"He announced this straight away? Then how was it that Marric and Hanno heard nothing, apart from the rumours of the quarrel?"

Fatigue, and the long relentless questioning had made me incautious. I said, before I thought: "He didn't announce it. He told only her. He was alone with her."

"Except for you?" His voice changed, so that I jumped on my stool. He watched me under his brows. "I thought you told me the hypocaust had been filled in?"

I merely sat and looked at him. I could think of nothing to say.

"It seems strange, does it not," he said levelly, "that he should tell your mother in front of you, when he must have known you were his enemy? When his men had just killed your servant? And then, after he had told you of his secret plans, how did you get out of the palace and into the hands of my men, to 'make' them bring you with them to me?"

"I—" I stammered. "My lord, you cannot think that I—my lord, I told you I was no spy. I—all I have told you is true. He did say it, I swear it."

"Be careful. It matters whether this is true. Your mother told you?"

"No."

"Slaves' talk, then? That's all?"

I said desperately: "I heard him myself."

"Then where were you?"

I met his eyes. Without quite realizing why, I told the simple truth. "My lord, I was asleep in the hills, six miles off."

There was a silence, the longest yet. I could hear the embers settling in the brazier, and some distance off, outside, a dog barking. I sat waiting for his anger.

"Merlin."

I looked up.

"Where do you get the Sight from? Your mother?"

Against all expectation, he believed me. I said eagerly: "Yes, but it is different. She saw only women's things, to do with love. Then she began to fear the power, and let it be."

"Do you fear it?"

"I shall be a man."

"And a man takes power where it is offered. Yes. Did you understand what you saw tonight?"

"The bull? No, my lord, only that it was something secret."

"Well, you will know some day, but not now. Listen."

Somewhere, outside, a cock crowed, shrill and silver like a trumpet. He said: "That, at any rate, puts paid to your phantoms. It's high time you were asleep. You look half dead for lack of it." He got to his feet. I slid softly from the stool and he stood for a moment looking down at me. "I was ten when I sailed for Less Britain, and I was sick all the way."

"So was I," I said.

He laughed. "Then you will be as exhausted as I was. When you have slept, we'll decide what to do with you." He touched a bell, and a slave opened the door and stood aside, waiting. "You'll sleep in my room tonight. This way."

The bedchamber was Roman, too. I was to find that by comparison with, say, Uther's, it was austere enough, but to the eyes of a boy used to the provincial and often makeshift standards of a small outlying country, it seemed luxurious, with the big bed spread with scarlet wool blankets and a fur rug, the sheepskins on the floor, and the bronze tripod as high as a man, where the triple lamps, shaped like small dragons, mouthed tongues of flame. Thick brown curtains kept out the icy night, and it was very quiet.

As I followed Ambrosius and the slave past the guards—there were two on the door, rigid and unmoving except for their eyes which slid, carefully empty of speculation, from Ambrosius to me—it occurred to me for the first time to wonder whether he might be, perhaps, Roman in other ways.

But he only pointed to an archway where another of the brown curtains half hid a recess with a bed in it. I suppose a slave slept there sometimes, within call.

The servant pulled the curtain aside and showed me the blankets folded across the mattress, and the good pillows stuffed with fleece, then left me and went to attend Ambrosius.

I took off my borrowed tunic and folded it carefully. The blankets were thick, new wool, and smelt of cedarwood. Ambrosius and the slave were talking, but softly, and their voices came like echoes from the far end of a deep, quiet cave. It was bliss only to be in a real bed again, to lie, warm and fed, in a place that was beyond even the sound of the sea. And safe.

I think he said "Good night," but I was already submerged in sleep, and could not drag myself to the surface to answer. The last thing I remember is the slave moving softly to put out the lamps.

6

When I awoke next morning it was late. The curtains had been drawn back, letting in a grey and wintry day, and Ambrosius' bed was empty. Outside the windows I could see a small courtyard where a colonnade framed a square of garden, at the center of which a fountain played—in silence, I thought, till I saw that the cascade was solid ice.

The tiles of the floor were warm to my bare feet. I reached for the white tunic which I had left folded on a stool by the bed, but instead I saw that someone had put there a new one of dark green, the colour of yew trees, which fitted. There was a good leather belt to go with it, and a pair of new sandals replacing my old ones. There was even a cloak, this time of a light beech-green, with a copper brooch to fasten it. There was something embossed on the brooch; a dragon, enamelled in scarlet, the same device I had seen last night on the seal-ring he wore.

It was the first time that I remember feeling as if I looked like a prince, and I found it strange that this should happen at the moment when you would have thought I had reached the bottom of my fortunes. Here in Less Britain I had nothing, not even a bastard name to protect myself with, no kin, not even a rag of property. I had hardly spoken with any man except Ambrosius, and to him I was a servant, a dependant, something to be used, and only alive by his sufferance.

Cadal brought me my breakfast, brown bread and honeycomb and dried figs. I asked where Ambrosius was.

"Out with the men, drilling. Or rather, watching the exercises. He's there every day."

"What do you suppose he wants me to do?"

"All he said was, you could stay around here till you were rested, and to make yourself at home. I've to send someone to the ship, so if you'll tell me what your traps were that you lost, I'll have them brought."

"There was nothing much, I didn't have time. A couple of tunics and a pair of sandals wrapped in a blue cloak, and some little things—a brooch, and a clasp my mother gave me, things like that." I touched the expensive folds of the tunic I wore. "Nothing as good as this. Cadal, I hope I can serve him. Did he say what he wanted of me?"

"Not a word. You don't think he tells me his secret thoughts, do you? Now you just do as he says, make yourself at home, keep your mouth shut, and see you don't get into trouble. I don't suppose you'll be seeing much of him."

"I didn't suppose I would," I said. "Where am I to live?"

"Here."

"In this room?"

"Not likely. I meant, in the house."

I pushed my plate aside. "Cadal, does my lord Uther have a house of his own?"

Cadal's eyes twinkled. He was a short stocky man, with a square, reddish face, a black shag of hair, and small black eyes no bigger than olives. The gleam in them now showed me that he knew exactly what I was thinking, and moreover that everyone in the house must know exactly what had passed between me and the prince last night.

"No, he hasn't. He lives here, too. Cheek by jowl, you might say."

"Oh."

"Don't worry; you won't be seeing much of him, either. He's going north in a week or two. Should cool him off quickly, this weather . . . He's probably forgotten all about you by now, anyway." He grinned and went out.

He was right; during the next couple of weeks I saw very little of Uther, then he left with troops for the north, on some expedition designed half as an exercise for his company, half as a foray in search of supplies. Cadal had guessed right about the relief this would bring me; I was not sorry to be out of Uther's range. I had the idea that he had not welcomed my presence in his brother's house, and indeed that Ambrosius' continued kindness had annoyed him quite a lot.

I had expected to see very little of the Count after that first night when I had told him all I knew, but thereafter he sent for me on most evenings when he was free, sometimes to question me and to listen to what I could tell him of home, sometimes—when he was tired—to have me play to him, or, on several occasions, to take a hand at chess. Here, to my surprise, we were about even, and I do not think he let me beat him. He was out of practice, he told me; the usual game was dice, and he was not risking that against an infant soothsayer. Chess, being a matter of mathematics rather than magic, was less susceptible to the black arts.

He kept his promise, and told me what I had seen that first night by the standing stone. I believe, had he told me to, I would even have dismissed it as a dream. As time went on, the memory had grown blurred and fainter, until I had begun to think it might have been a dream fostered by cold and hunger and some dim recollection of the faded picture on the Roman chest in my room at Maridunum, the kneeling bull and the man with a knife under an arch studded with stars. But when Ambrosius talked about it, I knew I had seen more than was in the painting. I had seen the soldiers' god, the Word, the Light, the Good Shepherd, the mediator between the one God and man. I had seen Mithras, who had come out of Asia a thousand years ago. He had been born, Ambrosius told me, in a cave at mid-winter, while shepherds watched and a star shone; he was born of earth and light, and sprang from the rock with a torch in his left hand and a knife in his right. He killed the bull to bring life and fertility to the earth with its shed blood, and then, after his last meal of bread and wine, he was called up to heaven. He was the god of strength and gentleness, of courage and self-restraint. "The soldiers' god," said Ambrosius again, "and that is why we have re-established his worship here—to make, as the Roman armies did, some common meeting-ground for the chiefs and petty kings of all tongues and persuasions who fight with us. About his worship I can't tell you, because it is forbidden, but you will have gathered that on that first night I and my officers had met for a ceremony of worship, and your talk about bread and wine and bull-slaying sounded very much as if you had seen more of our ceremony than we are even allowed to speak about. You will know it all one day, perhaps. Till then, be warned, and if you are asked about your vision, remember that it was only a dream. You understand?"

I nodded, but with my mind filled, suddenly, with only one thing he had said. I thought of my mother and the Christian priests, of Galapas and the well of Myrddin, of things seen in the water and heard in the wind. "You want me to be an initiate of Mithras?"

"A man takes power where it is offered," he said again. "You have told me you don't know what god has his hand over you; perhaps Mithras was the god in whose path you put yourself, and who brought you to me. We shall see. Meanwhile, he is still the god of armies, and we shall need his help. . . . Now bring the harp, if you will, and sing to me."

So he dealt with me, treating me more as a prince than I had ever been treated in my grandfather's house, where at least I had had some sort of claim to it.

Cadal was assigned to me as my own servant. I thought at first he might resent this, as a poor substitute for serving Ambrosius, but he did not seem to mind, in fact I got the impression that he was pleased. He was soon on easy terms with me, and, since there were no other boys of my age about the place, he was my constant companion. I was also given a horse. At first they gave me one of Ambrosius' own, but after a day on that I asked shamefacedly if I might have something more my size, and was given a small stolid grey which—in my only moment of nostalgia—I called Aster.

So the first days passed. I rode out with Cadal at my side to see the country; this was still in the grip of frost, and soon the frost turned to rain so that the fields were churned mud and the ways were slippery and foul, and a cold wind whistled day and night across the flats, whipping the Small Sea to white on iron-grey, and blackening the northern sides of the standing stones with wet. I looked one day for the stone with the mark of the axe, and failed to find it. But there was another where in a certain light you could see a dagger carved, and a thick stone, standing a little apart, where under the lichen and the bird droppings stared the shape of an open eye. By daylight the stones did not breathe so cold on one's nape, but there was still something there, watching, and it was not a way my pony cared to go.

Of course I explored the town. King Budec's castle was in the center, on a rocky outcrop which had been crowned with a high wall. A stone ramp led up to the gate, which was shut and guarded. I often saw Ambrosius, or his officers, riding up this ramp, but never went myself any nearer than the guard post at the foot of it. But I saw King Budec several times, riding out with his men. His hair and his long beard were almost white, but he sat his big brown gelding like a man thirty years younger, and I heard countless stories of his prowess at arms and how he had sworn to be avenged on Vortigern for the killing of his cousin Constantius, even though it would take a lifetime. This, in fact, it threatened to do, for it seemed an almost impossible task for so poor a country to raise the kind of army that might defeat Vortigern and the Saxons, and gain a footing in Greater Britain. But soon now, men said, soon . . .

Every day, whatever the weather, men drilled on the flat fields outside the town walls. Ambrosius had now, I learned, a standing army of about four thousand men. As far as Budec was concerned they earned their keep a dozen times over, since not much more than thirty miles away his borders ran with those of a young king whose eye was weather-lifted for plunder, and who was held back only by rumours of Ambrosius' growing power and the formidable reputation of his men. Budec and Ambrosius fostered the idea that the army was mainly defensive, and saw to it that Vortigern learned nothing for certain: news of preparations for invasion reached him as before only in the form of rumours, and Ambrosius' spies made sure that these sounded like rumours. What Vortigern actually believed was what Budec was at pains that he should believe, that Ambrosius and Uther had accepted their fate as exiles, had settled in Less Britain as Budec's heirs, and were concerned with keeping the borders that would one day be their own.

This impression was fostered by the fact that the army was used as a foraging party for the town. Nothing was too simple or too rough for Ambrosius' men to undertake. Work which even my grandfather's rough-trained troops would have despised, these seasoned soldiers did as a matter of course. They brought in and stored wood in the town's yards. They dug and stored peat, and burned charcoal. They built and worked the smithies, making not only weapons of war, but tools for tilling and harvesting and building—spades, plough-shares, axes, scythes. They could break horses, and herd and drive cattle as well as butcher them; they built carts; they could pitch and mount guard over a camp in two hours flat, and strike it in one hour less. There was a corps of engineers who had half a square mile of workshops, and could supply anything from a padlock to a troop-ship. They were fitting themselves, in short, for the task of landing blindfold in a strange country and maybe living off it and moving fast across it in all weathers. "For," said Ambrosius once to his officers in front of me, "it is only to fair-weather soldiers that war is a fair-weather game. I shall fight to win, and after I have won, to hold. And Britain is a big country; compared with her, this corner of Gaul is no more than a meadow. So, gentlemen, we fight through spring and summer, but we do not retire at the first October frost to rest and sharpen our swords again for spring. We fight on—in snow, if we have to, in storm and frost and the wet mud of winter. And in all that weather and through all that time, we must eat, and fifteen thousand men must eat—well."

Shortly after this, about a month after my arrival in Less Britain, my days of freedom ended. Ambrosius found me a tutor.

Belasius was very different from Galapas and from the gentle drunkard Demetrius, who had been my official tutor at home. He was a man in his prime who was one of the Count's "men of business' and seemed to be concerned with the estimating and accounting side of Ambrosius' affairs; he was by training a mathematician and astronomer. He was half Gallo-Roman, half Sicilian, a tallish olive-faced man with long-lidded black eyes, a melancholy expression and a cruel mouth. He had an acid tongue and a sudden, vicious temper, but he was never capricious. I soon learned that the way to dodge his sarcasms and his heavy hand was to do my work quickly and well, and since this came easily to me and I enjoyed it, we soon understood one another, and got along tolerably well.

One afternoon towards the end of March we were working in my room in Ambrosius' house. Belasius had lodgings in the town, which he had been careful never to speak of, so I assumed he lived with some drab and was ashamed to risk my seeing her; he worked mainly in headquarters, but the offices near the treasury were always crowded with clerks and paymasters, so we held our daily tutorials in my room. This was not a large chamber, but to my eyes very well appointed, with a floor of red tiles locally made, carved fruitwood furniture, a bronze mirror, and a brazier and lamp that had come from Rome.

Today, the lamp was lit even in the afternoon, for the day was dark and overcast. Belasius was pleased with me; we were doing mathematics, and it had been one of the days when I could forget nothing, but walked through the problems he set me as if the field of knowledge were an open meadow with a pathway leading plain across it for all to see.

He drew the flat of his hand across the wax to erase my drawing, pushed the tablet aside, and stood up.

"You've done well today, which is just as well, because I have to leave early."

He reached out and struck the bell. The door opened so quickly that I knew his servant must have been waiting just outside. The boy came in with his master's cloak over his arm, and shook it out quickly to hold it for him. He did not even glance my way for permission, but watched Belasius, and I could see he was afraid of him. He was about my age, or younger, with brown hair cut close to his head in a curled cap, and grey eyes too big for his face.

Belasius neither spoke nor glanced at him, but turned his shoulders to the cloak, and the boy reached up to fasten the clasp. Across his head Belasius said to me: "I shall tell the Count of your progress. He will be pleased."

The expression on his face was as near a smile as he ever showed. Made bold by this, I turned on my stool. "Belasius—"

He stopped halfway to the door. "Well?"

"You must surely know . . . Please tell me. What are his plans for me?"

"That you should work at your mathematics and your astronomy, and remember your languages."

His tone was smooth and mechanical, but there was amusement in his eyes, so I persisted. "To become what?"

"What do you wish to become?"

I did not answer. He nodded, just as if I had spoken. "If he wanted you to carry a sword for him, you would be out in the square now."

"But—to live here as I do, with you to teach me, and Cadal as my servant . . . I don't understand it. I should be serving him somehow, not just learning . . . and living like this, like a prince. I know very well that I am only alive by his grace."

He regarded me for a moment under those long lids. Then he smiled. "It's something to remember. I believe you told him once that it was what you were, not who you were, that would matter. Believe me, he will use you, as he uses everyone. So stop wondering about it, and let it be. Now I must go."

The boy opened the door for him to show Cadal just pausing outside, with a hand raised to knock.

"Oh, excuse me, sir. I came to see when you'd be done for the day. I've got the horses ready, Master Merlin."

"We've finished already," said Belasius. He paused in the doorway and looked back at me. "Where were you planning to go?"

"North, I think, the road through the forest. The causeway's still good and the road will be dry."

He hesitated, then said, to Cadal rather than to me: "Then keep to the road, and be home before dark." He nodded, and went out, with the boy at his heels.

"Before dark?" said Cadal. "It's been dark all day, and it's raining now, besides. Look, Merlin"—when we were alone we were less formal—"why don't we just take a look along to the engineers' workshops? You always enjoy that, and Tremorinus ought to have got that ram working by now. What do you say we stay in town?"

I shook my head. "I'm sorry, Cadal, but I must go, rain or no rain. I've got the fidgets, or something, and I must get out."

"Well, then, a mile or two down to the port should do you. Come on, here's your cloak. It'll be pitch black in the forest; have a bit of sense."

"The forest," I said obstinately, turning my head while he fastened the pin. "And don't argue with me, Cadal. If you ask me, Belasius has the right ideas. *His* servant doesn't even dare to speak, let alone argue. I ought to treat you the same way—in fact I'll start straight away. . . . What are you grinning at?"

"Nothing. All right, I know when to give in. The forest it is, and if we lose ourselves and never get back alive, at least I'll have died with you, and won't have to face the Count."

"I really can't see that he'd care overmuch."

"Oh, he wouldn't," said Cadal, holding the door for me to go through. "It was only a manner of speaking. I doubt if he'd even notice, myself."

7

Once outside, it was not as dark as it had seemed, and it was warm, one of those heavy, dull days fraught with mists, and a small rain that lay on the heavy wool of our cloaks like frost.

About a mile to the north of the town the flattish salt-bitten turf began to give way to woodland, thin at first, with trees sticking up here and there solitary, with veils of white mist haunting their lower boughs or lying over the turf like pools, which now and then broke and swirled as a deer fled through.

The road north was an old one, paved, and the men who had built it had cleared the trees and scrub back on either side for a hundred paces, but with time and neglect the open verge had grown thick with whin and heather and young trees, so that now the forest seemed to crowd round you as you rode, and the way was dark.

Near the town we had seen one or two peasants carrying home fuel on their donkeys, and once one of Ambrosius' messengers spurred past us, with a stare, and what looked like a half-salute to me. But in the forest we met no one. It was the silent time between the thin birdsong of a March day and the hunting of the owls.

When we got among the big trees the rain had stopped, and the mist was thinning. Presently we came to a crossroads where a track—unpaved this time—crossed our own at right angles. The track was one used for hauling timber out of the forest, and also by the carts of charcoal burners, and, though rough and deeply rutted, it was clear and straight, and if you kept your horse to the edge, there was a gallop.

"Let's turn down here, Cadal."

"You know he said keep to the road."

"Yes, I know he did, but I don't see why. The forest's perfectly safe."

This was true. It was another thing Ambrosius had done; men were no longer afraid to ride abroad in Less Britain, within striking distance of the town. The country was constantly patrolled by his companies, alert and spoiling for something to do. Indeed, the main danger was (as I had once heard him admit) that his troops would over-train and grow stale, and look rather too hard for trouble. Meanwhile, the outlaws and disaffected men stayed away, and ordinary folk went about their business in peace. Even women could travel without much of an escort.

"Besides," I added, "does it matter what he said? He's not my master. He's only in charge of teaching me, nothing else. We can't possibly lose our way if we keep to the tracks, and if we don't get a canter now, it'll be too dark to press the horses when we get back to the fields. You're always complaining that I don't ride well enough. How can I, when we're always trotting along the road? Please, Cadal."

"Look, I'm not your master either. All right, then, but not far. And watch your pony; it'll be darker under the trees. Best let me go first."

I put a hand on his rein. "No. I'd like to ride ahead, and would you hold back a little, please? The thing is, I—I have so little solitude, and it's been something I'm used to. This was one of the reasons I had to come out this way." I added carefully: "It's not that I haven't been glad of your company, but one sometimes wants time to—well, to think things out. If you'll just give me fifty paces?"

He reined back immediately. Then he cleared his throat. "I told you I'm not your master. Go ahead. But go careful."

I turned Aster into the ride, and kicked him to a canter. He had not been out of his stable for three days, and in spite of the distance behind us he was eager. He laid his ears back, and picked up speed down the grass verge of the ride. Luckily the mist had almost gone, but here and there it smoked across the track saddle-high, and the horses plunged through it, fording it like water.

Cadal was holding well back; I could hear the thud of the mare's hoofs like a heavy echo of my pony's canter. The small rain had stopped, and the air was fresh and cool and resinous with the scent of pines. A woodcock flighted overhead with a sweet whispering call, and a soft tassel of spruce flicked a fistful of drops across my mouth and down inside the neck of my tunic. I shook my head and laughed, and the pony quickened his pace, scattering a pool of mist like spray. I crouched over his neck as the track narrowed, and branches whipped at us in earnest. It was darker; the sky thickened to nightfall between the boughs, and the forest rolled by in a dark cloud, wild with scent and silent but for Aster's scudding gallop and the easy pacing of the mare.

Cadal called me to stop. As I made no immediate response, the thudding of the mare's hoofs quickened, and drew closer. Aster's ears flicked, then flattened again, and he began to race. I drew him in. It was easy, as the going was heavy, and he was sweating. He slowed and then stood and waited quietly for Cadal to come up. The brown mare stopped. The only sound in the forest now was the breathing of the horses.

"Well," he said at length, "did you get what you wanted?"

"Yes, only you called too soon."

"We'll have to turn back if we're to be in time for supper. Goes well, that pony. You want to ride ahead on the way back?"

"If I may."

"I told you there's no question, you do as you like. I know you don't get out on your own, but you're young yet, and it's up to me to see you don't come to harm, that's all."

"What harm could I come to? I used to go everywhere alone at home."

"This isn't home. You don't know the country yet. You could lose yourself, or fall off your pony and lie in the forest with a broken leg—"

"It's not very likely, is it? You were told to watch me, why don't you admit it?"

"To look after you."

"It could come to the same thing. I've heard what they call you. 'The watchdog.' "

He grunted. "You don't need to dress it up. 'Merlin's black dog,' that's the way I heard it. Don't think I mind. I do as he says and no questions asked, but I'm sorry if it frets you."

"It doesn't—oh, it doesn't. I didn't mean it like that. . . . It's all right, it's only . . . Cadal—"

"Yes?"

"Am I a hostage, after all?"

"That I couldn't say," said Cadal woodenly. "Come along, then, can you get by?"

Where our horses stood the way was narrow, the center of the ride having sunk into deep mud where water faintly reflected the night sky. Cadal reined his mare back into the thicket that edged the ride, while I forced Aster—who would not wet his feet unless compelled—past the mare. As the brown's big quarters pressed back into the tangle of oak and chestnut there was suddenly a crash just behind her, and a breaking of twigs, and some animal burst from the undergrowth almost under the mare's belly, and hurtled across the ride in front of my pony's nose.

Both animals reacted violently. The mare, with a snort of fear, plunged forward hard against the rein. At the same moment Aster shied wildly, throwing me half out of the saddle. Then the plunging mare crashed into his shoulder, and the pony staggered, whirled, lashed out, and threw me.

I missed the water by inches, landing heavily on the soft stuff at the edge of the ride, right up against a broken stump of pine which could have hurt me badly if I had been thrown on it. As it was I escaped with scratches and a minor bruise or two, and a wrenched ankle that, when I rolled over and tried to put it to the ground, stabbed me with pain momentarily so acute as to make the black woods swim.

Even before the mare had stopped circling Cadal was off her back, had flung the reins over a bough, and was stooping over me.

"Merlin—Master Merlin—are you hurt?"

I unclamped my teeth from my lip, and started gingerly with both hands to straighten my leg. "No, only my ankle, a bit."

"Let me see . . . No, hold still. By the dog, Ambrosius will have my skin for this."

"What was it?"

"A boar, I think. Too small for a deer, too big for a fox."

"I thought it was a boar, I smelled it. My pony?"

"Halfway home by now, I expect. Of course you had to let the rein go, didn't you?"

"I'm sorry. Is it broken?"

His hands had been moving over my ankle, prodding, feeling. "I don't think so . . . No, I'm sure it's not. You're all right otherwise? Here, come on, try if you can stand on it. The mare'll take us both, and I want to get back, if I can, before that pony of yours goes in with an empty saddle. I'll be for the lampreys, for sure, if Ambrosius sees him."

"It wasn't your fault. Is he so unjust?"

"He'll reckon it was, and he wouldn't be far wrong. Come on now, try it."

"No, give me a moment. And don't worry about Ambrosius, the pony hasn't gone home, he's stopped a little way up the ride. You'd better go and get him."

He was kneeling over me, and I could see him faintly against the sky. He turned his head to peer along the ride. Beside us the mare stood quietly, except for her restless ears and the white edge to her eye. There was silence except for an owl starting up, and far away on the edge of sound another, like its echo.

"It's pitch dark twenty feet away," said Cadal. "I can't see a thing. Did you hear him stop?"

"Yes." It was a lie, but this was neither the time nor the place for the truth. "Go and get him, quickly. On foot. He hasn't gone far."

I saw him stare down at me for a moment, then he got to his feet without a word and started off up the ride. As well as if it had been daylight, I could see his puzzled look. I was reminded, sharply, of Cerdic that day at King's Fort. I leaned back against the stump. I could feel my bruises, and my ankle ached, but for all that there came flooding through me, like a drink of warm wine, the feeling of excitement and release that came with the power. I knew now that I had had to come this way; that this was to be another of the hours when not darkness, nor distance, nor time meant anything. The owl floated silently above me, across the ride. The mare cocked her ears at it, watching without fear. There was the thin sound of bats somewhere above. I thought of the crystal cave, and Galapas' eyes when I told him of my vision. He had not been puzzled, not even surprised. It came to me to wonder, suddenly, how Belasius would look. And I knew he would not be surprised, either.

Hoofs sounded softly in the deep turf. I saw Aster first, approaching ghostly grey, then Cadal like a shadow at his head.

"He was there all right," he said, "and for a good reason. He's dead lame. Must have strained something."

"Well, at least he won't get home before we do."

"There'll be trouble over this night's work, that's for sure, whatever time we get home. Come on, then, I'll put you up on Rufa."

With a hand from him I got cautiously to my feet. When I tried to put weight on the left foot, it still hurt me quite a lot, but I knew from the feel of it that it was nothing but a wrench and would soon be better. Cadal threw me up on the mare's back, unhooked the reins from the bough, and gave them into my hand. Then he clicked his tongue to Aster, and led him slowly ahead.

"What are you doing?" I asked. "Surely she can carry us both?"

"There's no point. You can see how lame he is. He'll have to be led. If I take him in front he can make the pace. The mare'll stay behind him. —You all right up there?"

"Perfectly, thanks."

The grey pony was indeed dead lame. He walked slowly beside Cadal with drooping head, moving in front of me like a smoke-beacon in the dusk. The mare followed quietly. It would take, I reckoned, a couple of hours to get home, even without what lay ahead.

Here again was a kind of solitude, no sounds but the soft plodding of the horses' hoofs, the creak of leather, the occasional small noises of the forest round us. Cadal was invisible, nothing but a shadow beside the moving wraith of mist that was Aster. Perched on the big mare at a comfortable walk, I was alone with the darkness and the trees.

We had gone perhaps half a mile when, burning through the boughs of a huge oak to my right, I saw a white star, steady.

"Cadal, isn't there a shorter way back? I remember a track off to the south just near that oak tree. The mist's cleared right away, and the stars are out. Look, there's the Bear."

His voice came back from the darkness. "We'd best head for the road." But in a pace or two he stopped the pony at the mouth of the southgoing track, and waited for the mare to come up.

"It looks good enough, doesn't it?" I asked. "It's straight, and a lot drier than this track we're on. All we have to do is keep the Bear at our backs, and in a mile or two we should be able to smell the sea. Don't you know your way about the forest?"

"Well enough. It's true this would be shorter, if we can see our way. Well . . ." I heard him loosen his short stabbing sword in its sheath. "Not that there's likely to be trouble, but best be prepared, so keep your voice down, will you, and have your knife ready. And let me tell you one thing, young Merlin, if anything should happen, then you'll ride for home and leave me to it. Got that?"

"Ambrosius' orders again?"

"You could say so."

"All right, if it makes you feel better, I promise I'll desert you at full speed. But there'll be no trouble."

He grunted. "Anyone would think you knew."

I laughed. "Oh, I do."

The starlight caught, momentarily, the whites of his eyes, and the quick gesture of his hand. Then he turned without speaking and led Aster into the track going south.

8

Though the path was wide enough to take two riders abreast, we went in single file, the brown mare adapting her long, comfortable stride to the pony's shorter and very lame step.

It was colder now; I pulled the folds of my cloak round me for warmth. The mist had vanished completely with the drop in temperature, the sky was clear, with some stars, and it was easier to see the way. Here the trees were huge; oaks mainly, the big ones massive and widely spaced, while between them saplings grew thickly and unchecked, and ivy twined with the bare strings of honeysuckle and thickets of thorn. Here and there pines showed fiercely black against the sky. I could hear the occasional patter as damp gathered and dripped from the leaves, and once the scream of some small creature dying under the claws of an owl. The air was full of the smell of damp and fungus and dead leaves and rich, rotting things.

Cadal trudged on in silence, his eyes on the path, which in places was tricky with fallen or rotting branches. Behind him, balancing on the big mare's saddle, I was still possessed by the same light, excited power. There was something ahead of us, to which I was being led, I knew, as surely as the merlin had led me to the cavern at King's Fort.

Rufa's ears pricked, and I heard her soft nostrils flicker. Her head went up. Cadal had not heard, and the grey pony, preoccupied with his lameness, gave no sign that he could smell the other horses. But even before Rufa, I had known they were there.

The path twisted and began to go gently downhill. To either side of us the trees had retreated a little, so that their branches no longer met overhead, and it was lighter. Now to each side of the path were banks, with outcrops of rock and broken ground where in summer there would be foxgloves and bracken, but where now only the dead and wiry brambles ran riot. Our horses' hoofs scraped and rang as they picked their way down the slope.

Suddenly Rufa, without checking her stride, threw up her head and let out a long whinny. Cadal, with an exclamation, stopped dead, and the mare pushed up beside him, head high, ears pricked towards the forest on our right. Cadal snatched at her bridle, pulled her head down, and shrouded her nostrils in the crook of his arm. Aster had lifted his head, too, but he made no sound.

"Horses," I said softly. "Can't you smell them?"

I heard Cadal mutter something that sounded like, "Smell anything, it seems you can, you must have a nose like a bitch fox," then, hurriedly starting to drag the mare off the track: "It's too late to go back, they'll have heard this bloody mare. We'd best pull off into the forest."

I stopped him. "There's no need. There's no trouble there, I'm certain of it. Let's go on."

"You talk fine and sure, but how can you know—?"

"I do know. In any case, if they meant us harm, we'd have known of it by now. They've heard us coming long since, and they must know it's only two horses and one of them lame."

But he still hesitated, fingering his short sword. The prickles of excitement fretted my skin like burrs. I had seen where the mare's ears were pointing—at a big grove of pines, fifty paces ahead, and set back above the right of the path. They were black even against the blackness of the forest. Suddenly I could wait no longer. I said impatiently: "I'm going, anyway. You can follow or not, as you choose." I jerked Rufa's head up and away from him, and kicked her with my good foot, so that she plunged forward past the grey pony. I headed her straight up the bank and into the grove.

The horses were there. Through a gap in the thick roof of pines a cluster of stars burned, showing them clearly. There were only two, standing motionless, with their heads held low and their nostrils muffled against the breast of a slight figure heavily cloaked and hooded against the cold. The hood fell back as he turned to stare; the oval of his face showed pale in the gloom. There was no one else there.

For one startled moment I thought that the black horse nearest me was Ambrosius' big stallion, then as it pulled its head free of the cloak I saw the white blaze on its forehead, and knew in a flash like a falling star why I had been led here.

Behind me, with a scramble and a startled curse, Cadal pulled Aster into the grove. I saw the grey gleam of his sword as he lifted it. "Who's that?"

I said quietly, without turning: "Put it up. It's Belasius . . . At least that's his horse. Another with it, and the boy. That's all."

He advanced. His sword was already sliding back into its housing. "By the dog, you're right, I'd know that white flash anywhere. Hey, Ulfin, well met. Where's your master?"

Even at six paces I heard the boy gasp with relief. "Oh, it's you, Cadal . . . My lord Merlin . . . I heard your horse whinny—I wondered— Nobody comes this way."

I moved the mare forward, and looked down. His face was a pale blur upturned, the eyes enormous. He was still afraid.

"It seems Belasius does," I said. "Why?"

"He—he tells me nothing, my lord."

Cadal said roundly: "Don't give us that. There's not much you don't know about him, you're never more than arm's length from him, day or night, everybody knows that. Come on, out with it. Where's your master?"

"I—he won't be long."

"We can't wait for him," said Cadal. "We want a horse. Go and tell him we're here, and my lord Merlin's hurt, and the pony's lame, and we've got to get home quickly . . . Well? Why don't you go? For pity's sake, what's the matter with you?"

"I can't. He said I must not. He forbade me to move from here."

"As he forbade us to leave the road, in case we came this way?" I said. "Yes. Now, your name's Ulfin, is it? Well, Ulfin, never mind the horse. I want to know where Belasius is."

"I—I don't know."

"You must at least have seen which way he went?"

"N-no, my lord."

"By the dog," exclaimed Cadal, "who cares where he is, as long as we get the horse? Look, boy, have some sense, we can't wait half the night for your master, we've got to get home. If you tell him the horse was for my lord Merlin, he won't eat you alive this time, will he?" Then, as the boy stammered something: "Well, all right, do you want us to go and find him ourselves, and get his leave?"

The boy moved then, jamming a fist to his mouth, like an idiot. "No . . . You must not . . . You must not . . . !"

"By Mithras," I said—it was an oath I cultivated at the time, having heard Ambrosius use it—"what's he doing? Murder?"

On the word, the shriek came.

Not a shriek of pain, but worse, the sound of a man in mortal fear. I thought the cry contained a word, as if the terror was shaped, but it was no word that I knew. The scream rose unbearably, as if it would burst him, then was chopped off sharply as if by a blow on the throat. In the dreadful silence that followed a faint echo came, in a breath from the boy Ulfin.

Cadal stood frozen as he had turned, one hand holding his sword, the other grasping Aster's bridle. I wrenched the mare's head round and lashed the reins down on her neck. She bounded forward, almost unseating me. She plunged under the pines towards the track. I lay flat on her neck as the boughs swept past us, hooked a hand in her neck-strap, and hung on like a tick. Neither Cadal nor the boy had moved or made a sound.

The mare went down the bank with a scramble and a slither, and as we reached the path I saw, so inevitably that I felt no surprise—nor indeed any thought at all—another path, narrow and overgrown, leading out of the track to the other side, just opposite the grove of pines.

I hauled on the mare's mouth, and when she jibbed, trying to head down the broader track for home, I lashed her again. She laid her ears flat and went into the path at a gallop.

The path twisted and turned, so that almost straight away our pace slackened, slowed, became a heavy canter. This was the direction from which that dreadful sound had come. It was apparent even in the starlight that someone had recently been this way. The path was so little used that winter grass and heather had almost choked it, but someone—something—had been thrusting a way through. The going was so soft that even a cantering horse made very little noise.

I strained my ears for the sound of Cadal coming after me, but could not hear him. It occurred to me only then that both he and the boy must have thought that, terrified by the shriek, I had run, as Cadal had bidden me, for home.

I pulled Rufa to a walk. She slowed willingly, her head up, her ears pricked forward. She was quivering; she, too, had heard the shriek. A gap in the forest showed three hundred paces ahead, so light that I thought it must mark the end of the trees. I watched carefully as we approached it, but nothing moved against the sky beyond.

Then, so softly that I had to strain my ears to make sure it was neither wind nor sea, I heard chanting.

My skin prickled. I knew now where Belasius was, and why Ulfin had been so afraid. And I knew why Belasius had said: "Keep to the road, and be home before dark."

I sat up straight. The heat ran over my skin in little waves, like catspaws of wind over water. My breathing came shallow and fast. For a moment I wondered if this was fear, then I knew it was still excitement. I halted the mare and slid silently from the saddle. I led her three paces into the forest, knotted the rein over a bough and left her there. My foot hurt when I put it to the ground, but the twinges were bearable, and I soon forgot them as I limped quickly towards the singing and the lighter sky.

9

I had been right in thinking that the sea was near. The forest ended in it, a stretch of sea so enclosed that at first I thought it was a big lake, until I smelled the salt and saw, on the narrow shingle, the dark slime of seaweeds. The forest finished abruptly, with a high bank where exposed roots showed through the clay which the tides had gnawed away year after year at the land's edge. The narrow strand was mainly of pebbles, but here and there bars of pale sand showed, and greyish, glimmering fans spreading fernlike between them, where shallow water ran seawards. The bay was very quiet, almost as if the frost of the past weeks had held it icebound, then, a pale line under the darkness, you could see the gap between the far headlands where the wide sea whitened. To the right—the south—the black forest climbed to a ridge, while to the north, where the land was gentler, the big trees gave shelter. A perfect harbour, you would have thought, till you saw how shallow it was, how at low tide the shapes of rock and boulder stuck black out of the water, shiny in the starlight with weed.

In the middle of the bay, so centered that at first I thought it must be man-made, was an island—what must, rather, be an island at high tide, but was now a peninsula, an oval of land joined to the shore by a rough causeway of stones, certainly man-made, which ran out like a navel cord to join it to the shingle. In the nearer of the shallow harbours made by the causeway and the shore a few small boats—coracles, I thought—lay beached like seals.

Here, low beside the bay, there was mist again, hanging here and there among the boughs like fishing nets hung out to dry. On the water's surface it floated in patches, spreading slowly till it curdled and thinned and then wisped away to nothing, only to thicken again elsewhere, and smoke slowly across the water. It lay round the base of the island so densely that this seemed to float on cloud, and the stars that hung above reflected a grey light from the mist that showed me the island clearly.

This was egg-shaped rather than oval, narrow at the causeway end, and widening towards the far end where a small hill, as regular in shape as a beehive, stood up out of the flat ground. Round the base of this hillock stood a circle of the standing stones, a circle broken only at the point facing me, where a wide gap made a gateway from which an avenue of the stones marched double, like a colonnade, straight down to the causeway.

There was neither sound nor movement. If it had not been for the dim shapes of the beached boats I would have thought that the shriek, the chanting, were figments of a dream. I stood just inside the edge of the forest, with my left arm round a young ash tree and the weight on my right foot, watching with eyes so completely adjusted to the dark of the forest that the mist-illumined island seemed as light as day.

At the foot of the hill, directly at the end of the central avenue, a torch flared suddenly. It lit, momentarily, an opening low in the face of the hill, and clearly in front of this the torch-bearer, a figure in a white robe. I saw, then, that what I had taken to be banks of mist in the shadow of the cromlechs were groups of motionless figures also robed in white. As the torch lifted I heard the chanting begin again, very softly, and with a loose and wandering rhythm that was strange to me. Then the torch and its bearer slowly sank earthwards, and I realized that the doorway was a sunken one, and he was descending a flight of steps into the heart of the hill. The others crowded after him, groups clotting, coalescing round the doorway, then vanishing like smoke being sucked into an oven door.

The chanting still went on, but so faint and muffled that it sounded no more than the humming of bees in a winter hive. No tune came through, only the rhythm which sank to a mere throb in the air, a pulse of sound felt rather than heard, which little by little tightened and quickened till it beat fast and hard, and my blood with it . . .

Suddenly, it stopped. There was a pause of dead stillness, but a stillness so charged that I felt my throat knot and swell with tension. I found I had left the trees and stood clear on the turf above the bank, my injury forgotten, my feet planted apart, flat and squarely on the ground, as if my body were rooted through them and straining to pull life from the earth as a tree pulls sap. And like the shoot of a tree growing and thrusting, the excitement in me grew and swelled, beating through somehow from the depths of the island and along the navel cord of the causeway, bursting up through flesh and spirit so that when the cry came at length it was as if it had burst from my own body.

A different cry this time, thin and edged, which might have meant anything, triumph or surrender or pain. A death cry, this time not from the victim, but from the killer.

And after it, silence. The night was fixed and still. The island was a closed hive sealed over whatever crawled and hummed within.

Then the leader—I assumed it was he, though this time the torch was out—appeared suddenly like a ghost in the doorway and mounted the steps. The rest came behind, moving not as people move in a procession, but slowly and smoothly, in groups breaking and forming, contained in pattern like a dance, till once more they stood parted into two ranks beside the cromlechs.

Again complete stillness. Then the leader raised his arms. As if at a signal, white and shining like a knife-blade, the edge of the moon showed over the hill.

The leader cried out, and this, the third cry, was unmistakably a call of triumphant greeting, and he stretched his arms high above his head as if offering up what he held between his hands.

The crowd answered him, chant and counterchant. Then as the moon lifted clear of the hill, the priest lowered his arms and turned. What he had offered to the goddess, he now offered to the worshippers. The crowd closed in.

I had been so intent on the ceremony at the center of the island that I had not watched the shore, or realized that the mist, creeping higher, was now blurring the avenue itself. My eyes, straining through the dark, saw the white shapes of the people as part of the mist that clotted, strayed, and eddied here and there in knots of white.

Presently I became aware that this, in fact, was what was happening. The crowd was breaking apart, and the people, in twos and threes, were passing silently down the avenue, in and out of the barred shadows which the rising moon painted between the stones. They were making for the boats.

I have no idea how long it had all taken, but as I came to myself I found that I was stiff, and where I had allowed my cloak to fall away I was soaked with the mist. I shook myself like a dog, backing again into the shelter of the trees. Excitement had spilled out of me, spirit as well as body, in a warm gush down my thighs, and I felt empty and ashamed. Dimly I knew that this was something different; this had not been the force I had learnt to receive and foster, nor was this spilled-out sensation the aftermath of power. That had left me light and free and keen as a cutting blade; now I felt empty as a licked pot still sticky and smelling with what it had held.

I bent, stiff-sinewed, to pull a swatch of wet and pallid grass, and cleaned myself, scrubbing my hands, and scooping mist drops off the turf to wash my face. The water smelt of leaves, and of the wet air itself, and made me think of Galapas and the holy well and the long cup of horn. I dried my hands on the inside of my cloak, drew it about me, and went back to my station by the ash tree.

The bay was dotted with the retreating coracles. The island had emptied, all but one tall white figure who came, now, straight down the center of the avenue. The mist cloaked, revealed, and cloaked him again. He was not making for a boat; he seemed to be heading straight for the causeway, but as he reached the end of the avenue he paused in the shadow of the final stone, and vanished.

I waited, feeling little except weariness and a longing for a drink of clear water and the familiarity of my warm and quiet room. There was no magic in the air; the night was as flat as old sour wine. In a moment, sure enough, I saw him emerge into the moonlight of the causeway. He was clad now in a dark robe. All he had done was drop his white robe off. He carried it over his arm.

The last of the boats was a speck dwindling in the darkness. The solitary man came quickly across the causeway. I stepped out from under the trees and down on to the shingle to meet him.

10

Belasius saw me even before I was clear of the trees' shadow. He made no sign except to turn aside as he stepped off the causeway. He came up, unhurried, and stood over me, looking down.

"Ah." It was the only greeting, said without surprise. "I might have known. How long have you been here?"

"I hardly know. Time passed so quickly. I was interested."

He was silent. The moonlight, bright now, fell slanting on his right cheek. I could not see the eyes veiled under the long dark lids, but there was something quiet, almost sleepy about his voice and bearing. I had felt the same after that releasing cry, there in the forest. The bolt had struck, and now the bow was unstrung.

He took no notice of my provocation, asking merely: "What brought you here?"

"I rode down when I heard the scream."

"Ah," he said again, then: "Down from where?"

"From the pine grove where you left your horse."

"Why did you come this way? I told you to keep to the road."

"I know, but I wanted to gallop, so we turned off into the main logging track, and I had an accident with Aster; he's wrenched a foreleg, so we had to lead him back. It was slow, and we were late, so we took a short cut."

"I see. And where is Cadal?"

"I think he thought I'd run for home, and he must have gone after me. At any rate he didn't follow me down here."

"That was sensible of him," said Belasius. His voice was still quiet, sleepy almost, but cat-sleepy, velvet sheathing a bright dagger-point. "But in spite of—what you heard—it did not in fact occur to you to run for home?"

"Of course not."

I saw his eyes glint for a moment under the long lids. " 'Of course not'?"

"I had to know what was going on."

"Ah. Did you know I would be here?"

"Not before I saw Ulfin and the horses, no. And not because you told me to keep to the road, either. But I—shall we say I knew something was abroad in the forest tonight, and that I had to find it?"

He regarded me for a moment longer. I had been right in thinking he would not look surprised. Then he jerked his head. "Come, it's cold, and I want my cloak." As I followed him up the grating shingle he added, over his shoulder: "I take it that Ulfin is still there?"

"I should think so. You have him pretty efficiently frightened."

"He has no need to be afraid, as long as he keeps away and sees nothing."

"Then it's true he doesn't know?"

"Whatever he knows or doesn't know," he said indifferently, "he has the sense to keep silent. I have promised him that if he obeys me in these things without question, then I shall free him in time to escape."

"Escape? From what?"

"Death when I die. It is normal to send the priests' servants with them."

We were walking side by side up the path. I glanced at him. He was wearing a dark robe, more elegant than anything I had seen at home, even the clothes Camlach wore; his belt was of beautifully worked leather, probably Italian, and there was a big round brooch at his shoulder where the moonlight caught a design of circles and knotted snakes in gold. He looked—even under the film which tonight's proceedings had drawn over him—Romanized, urbane, intelligent. I said: "Forgive me, Belasius, but didn't that kind of thing go out with the Egyptians? Even in Wales we would think it old-fashioned."

"Perhaps. But then you might say the Goddess herself is old-fashioned, and likes to be worshipped in the ways she knows. And our way is almost as old as she is, older than men can remember, even in songs or stones. Long before the bulls were killed in Persia, long before they came to Crete, long before even the sky-gods came out of Africa and these stones were raised to them, the Goddess was here in the sacred grove. Now the forest is closed to us, and we worship where we can, but wherever the Goddess is, be it stone or tree or cave, there is the grove called Nemet, and there we make the offering.—I see you understand me."

"Very well. I was taught these things in Wales. But it's a few hundred years since they made the kind of offering you made tonight."

His voice was smooth as oil. "He was killed for sacrilege. Did they not teach you—?" He stopped dead, and his hand dropped to his hip. His tone changed. "That's Cadal's horse." His head went round like a hunting dog's.

"I brought it," I said. "I told you my pony went lame. Cadal will have gone home. I suppose he took one of yours."

I unhitched the mare and brought her out into the moonlight of the open path. He was settling the dagger back in its sheath. We walked on, the mare following, her nose at my shoulder. My foot had almost ceased to hurt.

I said: "So, death for Cadal, too? This isn't just a question of sacrilege, then? Your ceremonies are so very secret? Is this a matter of a mystery, Belasius, or is what you do illegal?"

"It is both secret and illegal. We meet where we can. Tonight we had to use the island; it's safe enough—normally there's not a soul would come near it on the night of the equinox. But if word came to Budec there would be trouble. The man we killed tonight was a King's man; he's been held here for eight days now, and Budec's scouts have been searching for him. But he had to die."

"Will they find him now?"

"Oh, yes, a long way from here, in the forest. They will think a wild boar ripped him." Again that slanting glance. "You could say he died easily, in the end. In the old days he would have had his navel cut out, and would have been whipped round and round the sacred tree until his guts were wrapped round it like wool on a spindle."

"And does Ambrosius know?"

"Ambrosius is a King's man, too."

We walked for a few paces in silence. "Well, and what comes to me, Belasius?"

"Nothing."

"Isn't it sacrilege to spy on your secrets?"

"You're safe enough," he said dryly. "Ambrosius has a long arm. Why do you look like that?"

I shook my head. I could not have put it into words, even to myself. It was like suddenly having a shield put into your hand when you are naked in battle.

He said: "You weren't afraid?"

"No."

"By the Goddess, I think that's true. Ambrosius was right, you have courage."

"If I have, it's hardly the kind that you need admire. I thought once that I was better than other boys because there were so many of their fears I couldn't share or understand. I had others of my own, of course, but I learned to keep them to myself. I suppose that was a kind of pride. But now I am beginning to understand why, even when danger and death lie openly waiting in the path, I can walk straight by them."

He stopped. We were nearly at the grove. "Tell me why."

"Because they are not for me. I have feared for other men, but never in that way for myself. Not yet. I think what men fear is the unknown. They fear pain and death, because these may be waiting round any corner. But there are times when I know what is hidden, and waiting, or when—I told you—I see it lying straight in the pathway. And I know where pain and danger lie for me, and I know that death is not yet to come; so I am not afraid. This isn't courage."

He said slowly: "Yes. I knew you had the Sight."

"It comes only sometimes, and at the god's will, not mine." I had said too much already; he was not a man to share one's gods with. I said quickly, to turn the subject: "Belasius, you must listen to me. None of this is Ulfin's fault. He refused to tell us anything, and would have stopped me if he could."

"You mean that if there is any paying to be done, you're offering to do it?"

"Well, it seems only fair, and after all, I can afford to." I laughed at him, secure behind my invisible shield. "What's it to be? An old-fashioned religion like yours must have a few minor penalties held in reserve? Shall I die of the cramps in my sleep tonight, or get ripped by a boar next time I ride in the forest without my black dog?"

He smiled for the first time. "You needn't think you'll escape quite freely. I've a use for you and this Sight of yours, be sure of that. Ambrosius is not the only one who uses men for what they are worth, and I intend to use you. You have told me you were led here tonight; it was the Goddess herself who led you, and to the Goddess you must go." He dropped an arm round my shoulders. "You are going to pay for this night's work, Merlin Emrys, in coin that will content her. The Goddess is going to hunt you down, as she does all men who spy on her mystery—but not to destroy you. Oh, no; not Actaeon, my apt little scholar, but Endymion. She will take you into her embrace. In other words, you are going to study until I can take you with me to the sanctuary, and present you there."

I would have liked to say, "Not if you wrapped my guts round every tree in the forest," but I held my tongue. Take power where it is offered, he had said, and—remembering my vigil by the ash tree—there had been power there, of a kind. We should see. I moved—but courteously—from under the arm round my shoulders, and led the way up into the grove.

If Ulfin had been frightened before, he was almost speechless with terror when he saw me with his master, and realized where I had been.

"My lord . . . I thought he had gone home . . . Indeed, my lord, Cadal said—"

"Hand me my cloak," said Belasius, "and put this thing in the saddle-bag."

He threw down the white robe which he had been carrying. It fell loosely, unfolding, near the tree Aster was tied to, and as it dropped near him, the pony shied and snorted. At first I thought this was just at the ghostly fall of white near his feet, but then I saw, black on the white, dimmed even as it was by the darkness of the grove, the stains and splashing, and I smelled, even from where I stood, the smoke and the fresh blood.

Ulfin held the cloak up mechanically. "My lord"—he was breathless with fear and the effort of holding the restive horse at the same time—"Cadal took the pack horse. We thought my lord Merlin had gone back to the town. Indeed, sir, I was sure myself that he had gone that way. I told him nothing. I swear—"

"There's a saddle-bag on Cadal's mare. Put it there." Belasius pulled his cloak on and fastened it, then reached for the reins. "Hand me up."

The boy obeyed, trying, I could see, not only to excuse himself, but to gauge the strength of Belasius' anger. "My lord, please believe me, I said nothing. I'll swear it by any gods there are."

Belasius ignored him. He could be cruel, I knew; in fact, in all the time I knew him he never once spared a thought for another's anxiety or pain: more exactly, it never occurred to him that feeling could exist, even in a free man. Ulfin must have seemed at that moment less real to him than the horse he was controlling. He swung easily to the saddle, saying curtly, "Stand back." Then to me, "Can you manage the mare if we gallop? I want to get back before Cadal finds you're not home, and sets the place by the ears."

"I can try. What about Ulfin?"

"What about him? He'll walk your pony home, of course."

He swung his horse round, and rode out between the pine boughs. Ulfin had already run to bundle up the bloodstained robe and stuff it in the brown mare's saddle-bag. He hurried now to give me his shoulder, and somehow between us I scrambled into the saddle and settled myself. The boy stood back, silent, but I had felt how he was shaking. I suppose that for a slave it was normal to be so afraid. It came to me that he was even afraid to lead my pony home alone through the forest.

I hung on the rein for a moment and leaned down. "Ulfin, he's not angry with you; nothing will happen. I swear it. So don't be afraid."

"Did you . . . see anything, my lord?"

"Nothing at all." In the way that mattered this was the truth. I looked down at him soberly. "A blaze of darkness," I said, "and an innocent moon. But whatever I might have seen, Ulfin, it would not have mattered. I am to be initiated. So you see why he is not angry? That is all. Here, take this."

I slid my dagger from its sheath and flicked it to quiver point down in the pine needles.

"If it makes you easier," I said, "but you won't need it. You will be quite safe. Take it from me. I know. Lead my pony gently, won't you?"

I kicked the mare in the ribs and headed her after Belasius.

He was waiting for me—that is to say he was going at an easy canter, which quickened to a hand-gallop as I caught him up. The brown mare pounded behind him. I gripped the neck-strap and clung like a burr.

The track was open enough for us to see our way clearly in the moonlight. It sliced its way uphill through the forest to a crest from which, momentarily, one could see the glimmer of the town's lights. Then it plunged downhill again, and after a while we rode out of the forest on to the salt plains that fringed the sea.

Belasius neither slackened speed nor spoke. I hung on to the mare, watched the track over her shoulder, and wondered whether we would meet Cadal coming back for me with an escort, or if he would come alone.

We splashed through a stream, fetlock-deep, and then the track, beaten flat along the level turf, turned right in the direction of the main road. I knew where we were now; on our ride out I had noticed this track branching off just short of the bridge at the forest's edge. In a few minutes we would reach the bridge and the made road.

Belasius slackened his horse's pace and glanced over his shoulder. The mare thudded alongside, then he put up a hand and drew rein. The horses slowed to a walk.

"Listen."

Horses. A great many horses, coming at a fast trot along the paved road. They were making for the town.

A man's voice was briefly raised. Over the bridge came a flurry of tossing torches, and we saw them, a troop riding close. The standard in the torchlight showed a scarlet dragon.

Belasius' hand came hard down on my reins, and our horses stopped.

"Ambrosius' men," he said, at least that is what he began to say when, clear as cock-crow, my mare whinnied, and a horse from the troop answered her.

Someone barked an order. The troop checked. Another order, and horses headed our way at the gallop. I heard Belasius curse under his breath as he let go my rein.

"This is where you leave me. Hang on now, and see you guard your tongue. Even Ambrosius' arm cannot protect you from a curse." He lashed my mare across the quarters, and she jumped forward, nearly unseating me. I was too busy to watch him go, but behind me there was a splash and a scramble as the black horse jumped the stream and was swallowed by the forest seconds before the soldiers met me and wheeled to either side to escort me back to their officer.

The grey stallion was fidgeting in the blaze of torches under the standard. One of my escorts had hold of the mare's bit, and led me forward.

He saluted. "Only the one, sir. He's not armed."

The officer pushed up his visor. Blue eyes widened, and Uther's too-well-remembered voice said: "It had to be you, of course. Well, Merlin the bastard, what are you doing here alone, and where have you been?"

11

I didn't answer straight away. I was wondering how much to say. To any other officer I might have told a quick and easy half-truth, but Uther was likely to ride me hard, and for anyone who had been at a meeting both "secret and illegal," Uther was not just an officer, he was dangerous. Not that there was any reason for me to protect Belasius, but I did not owe information—or explanation—to anyone but Ambrosius. In any case, to steer aside from Uther's anger came naturally.

So I met his eyes with what I hoped was an expression of frankness. "My pony went lame, sir, so I left my servant to walk him home, and took my servant's horse to ride back myself." As he opened his mouth to speak, I hoisted the invisible shield that Belasius had put into my hand. "Usually your brother sends for me after supper, and I didn't wish to keep him waiting."

His brows snapped down at my mention of Ambrosius, but all he said was: "Why that way, at this hour? Why not by the road?"

"We'd gone some way into the forest when Aster hurt himself. We had turned east at the crossways into the logging track, and there was a path branching south from that which looked like a quicker way home, so we took it. The moonlight made it quite easy to see."

"Which path was this?"

"I don't know the forest, sir. I climbed the ridge and then down to a ford about a mile downstream."

He considered me for a moment, frowning. "Where did you leave your servant?"

"A little way along the second path. We wanted to be quite sure that it was the right way before he let me come on alone. He'll be about climbing the ridge now, I should think." I was praying, confusedly but sincerely, to whatever god might be listening, that Cadal was not at the moment riding back from town to find me.

Uther regarded me, sitting his fidgeting horse as if it did not exist. It was the first time I had realized how like his brother he was. And for the first time, too, I recognized something like power in him, and understood, young as I was, what Ambrosius had told me about his brilliance as a captain. He could judge me to a hairsbreadth. I knew he was looking straight through me, scenting a lie, not knowing where, or why, but wondering. And determined to find out . . .

For once he spoke quite pleasantly, without heat, even gently. "You're lying, aren't you? Why?"

"It's quite true, my lord. If you look at my pony when he comes in—"

"Oh, yes, that was true. I've no doubt I'll find he's lame. And if I send men back up the path they'll find Cadal leading him home. But what I want to know—"

I said quickly: "Not Cadal, my lord; Ulfin. Cadal had other duties, and Belasius sent Ulfin with me."

"Two of a kind?" The words were contemptuous.

"My lord?"

His voice cracked suddenly with temper. "Don't bandy words with me, you little catamite. You're lying about something, and I want to know what. I can smell a lie a mile off." Then he looked past me, and his voice changed. "What's that in your saddle-bag?" A jerk of his head at one of the soldiers flanking me. A corner of Belasius' robe was showing. The man thrust his hand into the bag and pulled it out. On the soiled and crumpled white the stains showed dark and unmistakable. I could smell the blood even through the bubbling resin of the torches.

Behind Uther the horses snorted and tossed their heads, scenting it, and the men looked at one another. I saw the torch-bearers eyeing me askance, and the guard beside me muttered something under his breath.

Uther said, violently: "By all the gods below, so that was it! One of them, by Mithras! I should have known, I can smell the holy smoke on you from here! All right, bastard, you that's so mighty free with my brother's name, and so high in his favour, we'll see what he has to say to this. What have you to say for yourself now? There's not much point in denying it, is there?"

I lifted my head. Sitting the big mare, I could meet him almost eye to eye. "Deny? I'm denying that I've broken a law, or done anything the Count wouldn't like—and those are the only two things that matter, my lord Uther. I'll explain to him."

"By God you will! So Ulfin took you there?"

I said sharply: "Ulfin had nothing to do with it. I had already left him. In any case, he is a slave, and does as I bid him."

He spurred his horse suddenly, right up to the mare. He leaned forward, gripping the folds of my cloak at the neck, and tightening the grip till he half-lifted me from the saddle. His face was thrust close to mine, his armed knee hurting my leg as the horses stamped and sidled together. He spoke through his teeth. "And you do as I bid you, hear that. Whatever you may be to my brother, you obey me, too." He tightened the grip still further, shaking me. "Understand, Merlin Emrys?"

I nodded. He swore as my brooch-pin scratched him, and let me go. There was a streak of blood on his hand. I saw his eyes on the brooch. He flicked his fingers to the torch-bearer, and the man pushed nearer, holding the flame high. "He gave you that to wear? The red dragon?" Then he stopped short as his eyes came up to my face and fixed there, stared, widened. The intense blue seemed to blaze. The grey stallion sidled and he curbed it sharply, so that the foam sprang.

"Merlin Emrys . . ." He said it again, this time to himself, so softly that I hardly caught it. Then suddenly he let out a laugh, amused and gay and hard, not like anything I had heard from him before.

"Well, Merlin Emrys, you'll still have to answer to him for where you've been tonight!" He wheeled his horse, flinging over his shoulder to the men: "Bring him along, and see he dosen't fall off. It seems my brother treasures him."

The grey horse jumped under the spur, and the troop surged after him. My captors, still holding the brown mare's bridle, pounded after, with me between them.

The druid's robe lay trampled and filthy in the dirt, where the troop had ridden over it. I wondered if Belasius would see it and take warning.

Then I forgot him. I still had Ambrosius to face.

Cadal was in my room. I said with relief: "Well, thank the gods you didn't come back after me. I was picked up by Uther's lot, and he's blazing mad because he knows where I went."

"I know," said Cadal grimly, "I saw it."

"What do you mean?"

"I did ride back for you. I'd made sure you'd had the sense to run for home when you heard that . . . noise, so I went after you. When I saw no sign of you on the way I just thought you must have got a tidy turn of speed out of the mare—the ground was fair smoking under *me,* I can tell you! Then when—"

"You guessed what was happening? Where Belasius was?"

"Aye." He turned his head as if to spit on the floor, recollected himself, and made the sign against the evil eye. "Well, when I got back here, and no sign of you, I knew you must've gone straight down to see what was going on. High-handed little fool. Might have got yourself killed, meddling with that lot."

"So might you. But you went back."

"What else could I do? You should've heard what I was calling you, too. Proper little nuisance was the least of it. Well, I was about half a mile out of town when I saw them coming, and I pulled aside and waited for them to pass. You know that old posting station, the ruined one? I was there. I watched them go by, and you at the back under guard. So I guessed he knew. I followed them back to town as close as I dared, and cut home through the side streets. I've only just got in. He found out, then?"

I nodded, beginning to unfasten my cloak.

"Then there'll be the devil to pay, and no mistake," said Cadal. "How did he find out?"

"Belasius had put his robe in my saddle-bag, and they found it. They think it was mine." I grinned. "If they'd tried it for size they'd have had to think again. But that didn't occur to them. They just dropped it in the mud and rode over it."

"About right, too." He had gone down on one knee to unfasten my sandals. He paused, with one in his hand. "Are you telling me Belasius saw you? Had words with you?"

"Yes. I waited for him, and we walked back together to the horses. Ulfin's bringing Aster, by the way."

He ignored that. He was staring, and I thought he had lost colour.

"Uther didn't see Belasius," I said. "Belasius dodged in time. He knew they'd heard one horse, so he sent me forward to meet them, otherwise I suppose they'd have come after us both. He must have forgotten I had the robe, or else chanced their not finding it. Anybody but Uther wouldn't even have looked."

"You should never have gone near Belasius. It's worse than I thought. Here, let me do that. Your hands are cold." He pulled the dragon brooch off and took my cloak. "You want to watch it, you do. He's a nasty customer—they all are, come to that—and him most of all."

"Did you know about him?"

"Not to say know. I might have guessed. It's right up his street, if you ask me. But what I meant was, they're a nasty lot to tangle with."

"Well, he's the archdruid, or at least the head of this sect, so he'll carry some weight. Don't look so troubled, Cadal, I doubt if he'll harm me, or let anyone else harm me."

"Did he threaten you?"

I laughed. "Yes. With a curse."

"They say these things stick. They say the druids can send a knife after you that'll hunt you down for days, and all you know is the whistling noise in the air behind you just before it strikes."

"They say all sort of things. Cadal, have I another tunic that's decent? Did my best one come back from the fuller? And I want a bath before I go to the Count."

He eyed me sideways as he reached in the clothes-chest for another tunic. "Uther will have gone straight to him. You know that?"

I laughed. "Of course. I warn you, I shall tell Ambrosius the truth."

"All of it?"

"All of it."

"Well, I suppose that's best," he said. "If anyone can protect you from them—"

"It's not that. It's simply that he ought to know. He has the right. Besides, what have I to hide from him?"

He said uneasily: "I was thinking about the curse . . . Even Ambrosius might not be able to protect you from that."

"Oh, that to the curse." I made a gesture not commonly seen in noblemen's houses. "Forget it. Neither you nor I have done wrong, and I refuse to lie to Ambrosius."

"Some day I'll see you scared, Merlin."

"Probably."

"Weren't you even scared of Belasius?"

"Should I be?" I was interested. "He'll do me no harm." I unhooked the belt of my tunic, and threw it on the bed. I regarded Cadal. "Would you be afraid if you knew your own end, Cadal?"

"Yes, by the dog! Do you?"

"Sometimes, in snatches. Sometimes I see it. It fills me with fear."

He stood still, looking at me, and there was fear in his face. "What is it, then?"

"A cave. The crystal cave. Sometimes I think it is death, and at other times it is birth or a gate of vision, or a dark limbo of sleep . . . I cannot tell. But some day I shall know. Till then, I suppose I am not afraid of much else. I shall come to the cave in the end, as you—" I broke off.

"As I what?" he said quickly. "What'll I come to?"

I smiled. "I was going to say 'As you will come to old age.' "

"That's a lie," he said roughly. "I saw your eyes. When you're seeing things, your eyes go queer; I've noticed it before. The black spreads and goes kind of blurred, dreaming-like—but not soft; no, your whole look goes cold, like cold iron, as if you neither saw nor cared about what's going on round you. And you talk as if you were just a voice and not a person . . . Or as if you'd gone somewhere else and left your body for something else to speak through. Like a horn being blown through to make the sound carry. Oh, I know I've only seen it a couple of times, for a moment, but it's uncanny, and it frightens me."

"It frightens me, too, Cadal." I had let the green tunic slide from my body to the floor. He was holding out the grey wool robe I wore for a bedgown. I reached absently for it, and sat down on the bed's edge, with it trailing over my knees. I was talking to myself rather than Cadal. "It frightens me, too. You're right, that's how it feels, as if I were an empty shell with something working through me. I say things, see things, think things, till that moment I never knew of. But you're wrong in thinking I don't feel. It hurts me. I think this may be because I can't command whatever speaks through me . . . I mean, I can't command it yet. But I shall. I know this, too. Some day I shall command this part of me that knows and sees, this god, and that really will be power. I shall know when what I foretell is human instinct, and when it is God's shadow."

"And when you spoke of my end, what was that?"

I looked up. Oddly enough it was less easy to lie to Cadal than it had been to Uther. "But I haven't seen your death, Cadal, no one's but my own. I was being tactless. I was going to say 'As you will come to a foreign grave somewhere . . .' " I smiled. "I know this is worse than hell to a Breton. But I think it will happen to you . . . That is, if you stay as my servant."

His look lightened, and he grinned. This was power, I thought, when a word of mine could frighten men like this. He said: "Oh, I'll do that all right. Even if he hadn't asked me to, I'd stay. You've an easy way with you that makes it a pleasure to look after you."

"Have I? I thought you found me a high-handed little fool, and a nuisance besides?"

"There you are, you see. I'd never have dared say that to anyone else your class, and all you do is laugh, and you twice royal."

"*Twice* royal? You can hardly count my grandfather as well as my—" I stopped. What stopped me was his face. He had spoken without thought, then, on a quick gasp, had tried to catch the words back into his mouth and unspeak them.

He said nothing, just stood there with the soiled tunic in his hand. I stood up slowly, the forgotten bedgown falling to the floor. There was no need for him to speak. I knew. I could not imagine how I had not known before, the moment I stood before Ambrosius in the frosty field and he stared down in the torchlight. He had known. And a hundred others must have guessed. I remembered now the sidelong looks of the men, the mutterings of the officers, the deference of servants which I had taken for respect for Ambrosius' commands, but which I saw now was deference to Ambrosius' son.

The room was still as a cave. The brazier flickered and its light broke and scattered in the bronze mirror against the wall. I looked that way. In the firelit bronze my naked body showed slight and shadowy, an unreal thing of firelight and darkness shifting as the flames moved. But the face was lit, and in its heavily defined planes of fire and shadow I saw his face as I had seen it in his room, when he sat over the brazier waiting for me to be brought to him. Waiting for me to come so that he could ask me about Niniane.

And here again the Sight had not helped me. Men that have god's-sight, I have found, are often human-blind.

I said to Cadal: "Everybody knows?"

He nodded. He didn't ask what I meant. "It's rumoured. You're very like him sometimes."

"I think Uther may have guessed. He didn't know before?"

"No. He left before the talk started to go round. That wasn't why he took against you."

"I'm glad to hear it," I said. "What was it, then? Just because I got across him over that business of the standing stone?"

"Oh, that, and other things."

"Such as?"

Cadal said, bluntly: "He thought you were the Count's catamite. Ambrosius doesn't go for women much. He doesn't go for boys either, come to that, but one thing Uther can't understand is a man who isn't in and out of bed with someone seven nights a week. When his brother bothered such a lot with you, had you in his house and set me to look after you and all that, Uther thought that's what must be going on, and he didn't half like it."

"I see. He did say something like that tonight, but I thought it was only because he'd lost his temper."

"If he'd bothered to look at you, or listen to what folks were saying, he'd have known fast enough."

"He knows now." I spoke with sudden, complete certainty. "He saw it, back there on the road, when he saw the dragon brooch the Count gave me. I'd never thought about it, but of course he would realize the Count would hardly put the royal cipher on his catamite. He had the torch brought up, and took a good look at me. I think he saw it then." A thought struck me. "And I think Belasius knows."

"Oh, yes," said Cadal, "he knows. Why?"

"The way he talked . . . As if he knew he daren't touch me. That would be why he tried to scare me with the threat of a curse. He's a pretty cool hand, isn't he? He must have been thinking very hard on the way up to the grove. He daren't put me quietly out of the way for sacrilege, but he had to stop me talking somehow. Hence the curse. And also—" I stopped.

"And also what?"

"Don't sound so startled. It was only another guarantee I'd hold my tongue."

"For the gods' sake, what?"

I shrugged, realized I was still naked, and reached for the bedgown again. "He said he would take me with him to the sanctuary. I think he would like to make a druid of me."

"He said that?" I was getting familiar with Cadal's sign to avert the evil eye. "What will you do?"

"I'll go with him . . . once, at least. Don't look like that, Cadal. There isn't a cat's chance in a fire that I'll want to go more than once." I looked at him soberly. "But there's nothing in this world that I'm not ready to see and learn, and no god that I'm not ready to approach in his own fashion. I told you that truth was the shadow of God. If I am to use it, I must know who He is. Do you understand?"

"How could I? What god are you talking about?"

"I think there is only one. Oh, there are gods everywhere, in the hollow hills, in the wind and the sea, in the very grass we walk on and the air we breathe, and in the bloodstained shadows where men like Belasius wait for them. But I believe there must be one who is God Himself, like the great sea, and all the rest of us, small gods and men and all, like rivers, we all come to Him in the end. —Is the bath ready?"

Twenty minutes later, in a dark blue tunic clipped at the shoulder by the dragon brooch, I went to see my father.

12

The secretary was in the anteroom, rather elaborately doing nothing. Beyond the curtain I heard Ambrosius' voice speaking quietly. The two guards at the door looked wooden.

Then the curtain was pulled aside and Uther came out. When he saw me he checked, hung on his heel as if to speak, then seemed to catch the secretary's interested look, and went by with a swish of the red cloak and a smell of horses. You could always tell where Uther had been; he seemed to soak up scents like a wash-cloth. He must have gone straight to his brother before he had even cleaned up after the ride home.

The secretary, whose name was Sollius, said to me: "You may as well go straight in, sir. He'll be expecting you."

I hardly even noticed the "sir." It seemed to be something I was already accustomed to. I went in.

He was standing with his back to the door, over by the table. This was strewn with tablets, and a stilus lay across one of them as if he had been interrupted while writing. On the secretary's desk near the window a half-unrolled book lay where it had been dropped.

The door shut behind me. I stopped just inside it, and the leather curtain fell closed with a ruffle and a flap. He turned.

Our eyes met in silence, it seemed for interminable seconds, then he cleared his throat and said: "Ah, Merlin," and then, with a slight movement of the hand, "Sit down."

I obeyed him, crossing to my usual stool near the brazier. He was silent for a moment, looking down at the table. He picked up the stilus, looked absently down at the wax, and added a word. I waited. He scowled down at what he had done, scored it out again, then threw the stilus down and said abruptly: "Uther has been to see me."

"Yes, sir."

He looked up under frowning brows. "I understand he came on you riding alone beyond the town."

I said quickly: "I didn't go out alone. Cadal was with me."

"Cadal?"

"Yes, sir."

"That's not what you told Uther."

"No, sir."

His look was keen now, arrested. "Well, go on."

"Cadal always attends me, my lord. He's—more than faithful. We went north as far as the logging track in the forest, and a short way along that my pony went lame, so Cadal gave me his mare, and we started to walk home." I took a breath. "We took a short cut, and came on Belasius and his servant. Belasius rode part of the way home with me, but it—it didn't suit him to meet Prince Uther, so he left me."

"I see." His voice gave nothing away, but I had the feeling that he saw quite a lot. His next question confirmed it. "Did you go to the druids' island?"

"You know about it?" I said, surprised. Then as he did not answer, waiting in cold silence for me to speak, I went on: "I told you Cadal and I took a short cut through the forest. If you know the island, you'll know the track we followed. Just where the path goes down to the sea there's a pine grove. We found Ulfin—that's Belasius' servant—there with the two horses. Cadal wanted to take Ulfin's horse and get me home quickly, but while we were talking to Ulfin we heard a cry—a scream, rather, from somewhere east of the grove. I went to see. I swear I had no idea the island was there, or what happened there. Nor had Cadal, and if he'd been mounted, as I was, he'd have stopped me. But by the time he'd taken Ulfin's horse and set off after me I was out of sight, and he thought I'd taken fright and gone home—which is what he'd told me to do—and it wasn't until he got right back here that he found I hadn't come this way. He went back for me, but by that time I'd come up with the troop." I thrust my hands down between my knees, clutching them tightly together. "I don't know what made me ride down to the island. At least, I do; it was the cry, so I went to see . . . But it wasn't only because of the cry. I can't explain, not yet . . ." I took a breath. "My lord—"

"Well?"

"I ought to tell you. A man was killed there tonight, on the island. I don't know who he was, but I heard that he was a King's man who has been missing for some days. His body will be found somewhere in the forest, as if a wild beast had killed him." I paused. There was nothing to be seen in his face. "I thought I should tell you."

"You went over to the island?"

"Oh, no! I doubt if I'd be alive now if I had. I found out later about the man who was killed. It was sacrilege, they said. I didn't ask about it." I looked up at him. "I only went down as far as the shore. I waited there in the trees, and watched it—the dance and the offering. I could hear the singing. I didn't know then that it was illegal . . . It's forbidden at home, of course, but one knows it still goes on, and I thought it might be different here. But when my lord Uther knew where I'd been he was very angry. He seems to hate the druids."

"The druids?" His voice was absent now. He still figeted with the stilus on the table. "Ah, yes. Uther has no love for them. He is one of Mithras' fanatics, and light is the enemy of darkness, I suppose. Well, what is it?" This, sharply, to Sollius, who came in with an apology, and waited just inside the door.

"Forgive me, sir," said the secretary. "There's a messenger from King Budec. I told him you were engaged, but he said it was important. Shall I tell him to wait?"

"Bring him in," said Ambrosius. The man came in with a scroll. He handed it to Ambrosius, who sat down in his great chair and unrolled it. He read it, frowning. I watched him. The flickering flames from the brazier spread, lighting the planes of the face which already, it seemed, I knew as well as I knew my own. The heart of the brazier glowed, and the light spread and flashed. I felt it spreading across my eyes as they blurred and widened . . .

"Merlin Emrys? Merlin?"

The echo died to an ordinary voice. The vision fled. I was sitting on my stool in Ambrosius' room, looking down at my hands clasping my knees. Ambrosius had risen and was standing over me, between me and the fire. The secretary had gone, and we were alone.

At the repetition of my name I blinked and roused myself.

He was speaking. "What do you see, there in the fire?"

I answered without looking up. "A grove of whitethorn on a hillside and a girl on a brown pony, and a young man with a dragon brooch on his shoulder, and the mist knee-high."

I heard him draw a long breath, then his hand came down and took me by the chin and lifted my face. His eyes were intent and fierce.

"It's true, then, this Sight of yours. I have been so sure, and now—now, beyond all doubt, it is true. I thought it was, that first night by the standing stone, but that could have been anything—a dream, a boy's story, a lucky guess to win my interest. But this . . . I was right about you." He took his hand from my face, and straightened. "Did you see the girl's face?"

I nodded.

"And the man's?"

I met his eyes then. "Yes, sir."

He turned sharply away and stood with his back to me, head bent. Once more he picked up the stilus from the table, turning it over and over with his fingers. After a while he said: "How long have you known?"

"Only since I rode in tonight. It was something Cadal said, then I remembered things, and how your brother stared tonight when he saw me wearing this." I touched the dragon brooch at my neck.

He glanced, then nodded. "Is this the first time you have had this—vision?"

"Yes. I had no idea. Now, it seems strange to me that I never even suspected—but I swear I did not."

He stood silent, one hand spread on the table, leaning on it. I don't know what I had expected, but I had never thought to see the great Aurelius Ambrosius at a loss for words. He took a turn across the room to the window, and back again, and spoke. "This is a strange meeting, Merlin. So much to say, and yet so little. Do you see now why I asked so many questions? Why I tried so hard to find what had brought you here?"

"The gods at work, my lord, they brought me here," I said. "Why did you leave her?"

I had not meant the question to come out so abruptly, but I suppose it had been pressing on me so long that now it burst out with the force of an accusation. I began to stammer something, but he cut me short with a gesture, and answered quietly.

"I was eighteen, Merlin, with a price on my head if I set foot in my own kingdom. You know the story—how my cousin Budec took me in when my brother the King was murdered, and how he never ceased to plan for vengeance on Vortigern, though for many years it seemed impossible. But all the time he sent scouts, took in reports, went on planning. And then when I was eighteen he sent me over myself, secretly, to Gorlois of Cornwall, who was my father's friend, and who has never loved Vortigern. Gorlois sent me north with a couple of men he could trust, to watch and listen and learn the lie of the land. Some day I'll tell you where we went, and what happened, but not now. What concerns you now is this . . . We were riding south near the end of October, towards Cornwall to take ship for home, when we were set upon, and had to fight for it. They were Vortigern's men. I don't know yet whether they suspected us, or whether they were killing—as Saxons and foxes do—for wantonness and the sweet taste of blood. The latter, I think, or they would have made surer of killing me. They killed my two companions, but I was lucky; I got off with a flesh wound, and a knock on the head that struck me senseless, and they left me for dead. This was at dusk. When I moved and looked about me it was morning, and a brown pony was standing over me, with a girl on his back staring from me to the dead men and back again, with never a sound." The first glimmer of a smile, not at me, but at the memory. "I remember trying to speak, but I had lost a lot of blood, and the night in the open had brought on a fever. I was afraid she would take fright and gallop back to the town, and that would be the end of it. But she did not. She caught my horse and got my saddle-bag, and gave me a drink, then she cleaned the wound and tied it up and then—God knows how—got me across the horse and out of that valley. There was a place she knew of, she said, nearer the town, but remote and secret; no one ever went there. It was a cave, with a spring— What is it?"

"Nothing," I said. "I should have known. Go on. No one lived there then?"

"No one. By the time we got there I suppose I was delirious; I remember nothing. She hid me in the cave, and my horse too, out of sight. There had been food and wine in my saddle-bag, and I had my cloak and a blanket. It was late afternoon by then, and when she rode home she heard that the two dead men had already been found, with their horses straying nearby. The troop had been riding north; it wasn't likely that anyone in the town knew there should have been three corpses found. So I was safe. Next day she rode up to the cave again, with food and medicines . . . And the next day, too." He paused. "And you know the end of the story."

"When did you tell her who you were?"

"When she told me why she could not leave Maridunum and go with me. I thought till then that she was perhaps one of the Queen's ladies—from her ways and her talk I knew she had been bred in a king's house. Perhaps she saw the same in me. But it didn't matter. Nothing mattered, except that I was a man, and she a woman. From the first day, we both knew what would happen. You will understand how it was when you are older." Again the smile, this time touching mouth as well as eyes. "This is one kind of knowledge I think you will have to wait for, Merlin. The Sight won't help you much in matters of love."

"You asked her to go with you—to come back here?"

He nodded. "Even before I knew who she was. After I knew, I was afraid for her, and pressed her harder, but she would not come with me. From the way she had spoken I knew she hated and feared the Saxons, and feared what Vortigern was doing to the kingdoms, but still she would not come. It was one thing, she said, to do what she had done, but another to go across the seas with the man who, when he came back, must be her father's enemy. We must end it, she said, as the year was ending, and then forget."

He was silent for a minute, looking down at his hands.

I said: "And you never knew she had borne a child?"

"No. I wondered, of course. I sent a message the next spring, but got no answer. I left it then, knowing that if she wanted me, she knew—all the world knew—where to find me. Then I heard—it must have been nearly two years later—that she was betrothed. I know now that this was not true, but then it served to make me dismiss it from my mind." He looked at me. "Do you understand that?"

I nodded. "It may even have been true, though not in the way you'd understand it, my lord. She vowed herself to the Church when I should have no more need of her. The Christians call that a betrothal."

"So?" He considered for a moment. "Whatever it was, I sent no more messages. And when later on there was mention of a child, a bastard, it hardly crossed my mind that it could be mine. A fellow came here once, a travelling eye-doctor who had been through Wales, and I sent for him and questioned him, and he said yes, there was a bastard boy at the palace of such and such an age, red-haired, and the King's own."

"Dinias," I said. "He probably never saw me. I was kept out of the way . . . And my grandfather did sometimes explain me away to strangers as his own. He had a few scattered around, here and there."

"So I gathered. So the next rumour of a boy—possibly the King's bastard, possibly his daughter's—I hardly listened to. It was all long past, and there were things to do, and always there was the same thought—if she had borne a child to me, would she not have let me know? If she had wanted me, would she not have sent word?"

He fell silent then, back in his own thoughts. Whether I understood it all then, as he talked, I do not now recollect. But later, when the pieces shook together to make the mosaic, it was clear enough. The same pride which had forbidden her to go with her lover had forbidden her, once she discovered her pregnancy, to call him back. And it helped her through the months that followed. More than that; if—by flight or any other means—she had betrayed who her lover was, nothing would have stopped her brothers from travelling to Budec's court to kill him. There must—knowing my grandfather—have been angry oaths enough about what they would do to the man who had fathered her bastard. And then time moved on, and his coming grew remote, and then impossible, as if he were indeed a myth and a memory in the night. And then the other long love stepped in to supersede him, and the priests took over, and the winter tryst was forgotten. Except for the child, so like his father; but once her duty to him was done, she could go to the solitude and peace which—all those years ago—had sent her riding alone up the mountain valley, as later I was to ride out alone by the same path, and looking perhaps for the same things.

I jumped when he spoke again. "How hard a time of it did you have, as a no-man's-child?"

"Hard enough."

"You believe me when I say I didn't know?"

"I believe anything you tell me, my lord."

"Do you hate me for this, very much, Merlin?"

I said slowly, looking down at my hands: "There is one thing about being a bastard and a no-man's-child. You are free to imagine your father. You can picture for yourself the worst and the best; you can make your father for yourself, in the image of the moment. From the time I was big enough to understand what I was, I saw my father in every soldier and every prince and every priest. And I saw him, too, in every handsome slave in the kingdom of South Wales."

He spoke very gently, above me. "And now you see him in truth, Merlin Emrys. I asked you, do you hate me for the kind of life I gave you?"

I didn't look up. I answered, with my eyes on the flames: "Since I was a child I have had the world to choose from for a father. Out of them all, Aurelius Ambrosius, I would have chosen you."

Silence. The flames leapt like a heartbeat.

I added, trying to make it light: "After all, what boy would not choose the King of all Britain for his father?"

His hand came hard under my chin again, turning my head aside from the brazier and my eyes from the flames. His voice was sharp. "What did you say?"

"What did I say?" I blinked up at him. "I said I would have chosen you."

His fingers dug into my flesh. "You called me King of all Britain."

"Did I?"

"But this is—" He stopped. His eyes seemed to be burning into me. Then he let his hand drop, and straightened. "Let it go. If it matters, the god will speak again." He smiled down at me. "What matters now is what you said yourself. It isn't given to every man to hear this from his grown son. Who knows, it may be better this way, to meet as men, when we each have something to give the other. To a man whose children have been underfoot since infancy, it is not given, suddenly, to see himself stamped on a boy's face as I am stamped on yours."

"Am I so like?"

"They say so. And I see enough of Uther in you to know why everyone said you were mine."

"Apparently he didn't see it," I said. "Is he very angry about it, or is he only relieved to find I'm not your catamite after all?"

"You knew about that?" He looked amused. "If he'd think with his brains instead of his body sometimes he'd be the better for it. As it is, we deal together very well. He does one kind of work, as I another, and if I can make the way straight, he'll make a king after me, if I have no—"

He bit off the word. In the queer little silence that followed I looked at the floor.

"Forgive me." He spoke quietly, equal to equal. "I spoke without thought. For so long a time I have been used to the idea that I had no son."

I looked up. "It's still the truth, in the sense you mean. And it's certainly the truth as Uther will see it."

"Then if you see it the same way, my path is the smoother."

I laughed. "I don't see myself as a king. Half a king, perhaps, or more likely a quarter—the little bit that sees and thinks, but can't do. Perhaps Uther and I between us might make one, if you go? He's larger than life already, wouldn't you say?"

But he didn't smile. His eyes had narrowed, with an arrested look. "This is how I have been thinking, or something like it. Did you guess?"

"No sir, how could I?" I sat up straight as it broke on me: "Is this how you thought you might use me? Of course I realize now why you kept me here, in your house, and treated me so royally, but I've wanted to believe you had plans for me—that I could be of use to you. Belasius told me you used every man according to his capacity, and that even if I were no use as a soldier, you would still use me somehow. This is true?"

"Quite true. I knew it straight away, before I even thought you might be my son, when I saw how you faced Uther that night in the field, with the vision still in your eyes, and the power all over you like a shining skin. No, Merlin, you will never make a king, or even a prince as the world sees it, but when you are grown I believe you will be such a man that, if a king had you beside him, he could rule the world. Now do you begin to understand why I sent you to Belasius?"

"He is a very learned man," I said cautiously.

"He is a corrupt man and a dangerous," said Ambrosius directly. "But he is a sophisticated and clever man who has travelled a good deal and who has skills you will not have had the chance to master in Wales. Learn from him. I don't say follow him, because there are places where you must not follow him, but learn all you can."

I looked up, then nodded. "You know about him." It was a conclusion, not a question.

"I know he is a priest of the old religion. Yes."

"You don't mind this?"

"I cannot yet afford to throw aside valuable tools because I don't like their design," he said. "He is useful, so I use him. You will do the same, if you are wise."

"He wants to take me to the next meeting."

He raised his brows but said nothing.

"Will you forbid this?" I asked.

"No. Will you go?"

"Yes." I said slowly, and very seriously, searching for the words: "My lord, when you are looking for . . . what I am looking for, you have to look in strange places. Men can never look at the sun, except downwards, at his reflection in things of earth. If he is reflected in a dirty puddle, he is still the sun. There is nowhere I will not look, to find him."

He was smiling. "You see? You need no guarding, except what Cadal can do." He leaned back against the edge of the table, half sitting, relaxed now and easy. "Emrys, she called you. Child of the light. Of the immortals. Divine. You knew that's what it meant?"

"Yes."

"Didn't you know it was the same as mine?"

"My name?" I asked, stupidly.

He nodded. "Emrys . . . Ambrosius; it's the same word. Merlinus Ambrosius—she called you after me."

I stared at him. "I—yes, of course. It never occurred to me." I laughed.

"Why do you laugh?"

"Because of our names. Ambrosius, prince of light . . . She told everyone that my father was the prince of darkness. I've even heard a song about it. We make songs of everything, in Wales."

"Some day you must sing it to me." Then he sobered suddenly. His voice deepened. "Merlinus Ambrosius, child of the light, look at the fire now, and tell me what you see." Then, as I looked up at him, startled, he said urgently: "Now, tonight, before the fire dies, while you are weary and there is sleep in your face. Look at the brazier, and talk to me. What will come to Britain? What will come to me, and to Uther? Look now, work for me, my son, and tell me."

It was no use; I was awake, and the flames were dying in the brazier; the power had gone, leaving only a room with rapidly cooling shadows, and a man and a boy talking. But because I loved him, I turned my eyes to the embers. There was utter silence, except for the hiss of ash settling, and the tick of the cooling metal.

I said: "I see nothing but the fire dying down in the brazier, and a burning cave of coal."

"Go on looking."

I could feel the sweat starting on my body, the drops trickling down beside my nose, under my arms, into my groin till my thighs stuck together. My hands worked on one another, tight between my knees till the bones hurt. My temples ached. I shook my head sharply to clear it, and looked up. "My lord, it's no use. I'm sorry, but it's no use. I don't command the god, he commands me. Some day it may be I shall see at will, or when you command me, but now it comes itself, or not at all." I spread my hands, trying to explain. "It's like waiting below a cover of cloud, then suddenly a wind shifts it and it breaks, and the light stabs down and catches me, sometimes full, sometimes only the flying edge of the pillars of sunlight. One day I shall be free of the whole temple. But not yet. I can see nothing." Exhaustion dragged at me. I could hear it in my voice. "I'm sorry, my lord. I'm no use to you. You haven't got your prophet yet."

"No," said Ambrosius. He put a hand down, and as I stood, drew me to him and kissed me. "Only a son, who has had no supper and who is tired out. Go to bed, Merlin, and sleep the rest of the night without dreaming. There is plenty of time for visions. Good night."

I had no more visions that night, but I did have a dream. I never told Ambrosius. I saw again the cave on the hillside, and the girl Niniane coming through the mist, and the man who waited for her beside the cave. But the face of Niniane was not the face of my mother, and the man by the cave was not the young Ambrosius. He was an old man, and his face was mine.

BOOK III

THE WOLF

1

I was five years with Ambrosius in Brittany. Looking back now, I see that much of what happened has been changed in my memory, like a smashed mosaic which is mended in later years by a man who has almost forgotten the first picture. Certain things come back to me plain, in all their colours and details; others—perhaps more important—come hazy, as if the picture had been dusted over by what has happened since, death, sorrow, changes of the heart. Places I always remember well, some of them so clearly that I feel even now as if I could walk into them, and that if I had the strength to concentrate, and the power that once fitted me like my robe, I might even now rebuild them here in the dark as I rebuilt the Giants' Dance for Ambrosius, all those years ago.

Places are clear, and ideas, which came to me so new and shining then, but not always the people: sometimes now as I search my memory I wonder if here and there I have confused them one with another, Belasius with Galapas, Cadal with Cerdic, the Breton officer whose name I forget now with my grandfather's captain in Maridunum who once tried to make me into the kind of swordsman that he thought even a bastard prince should want to be.

But as I write of Ambrosius, it is as if he were here with me now, lit against this darkness as the man with the cap was lit on that first frost-enchanted night in Brittany. Even without my robe of power I can conjure up against the darkness his eyes, steady under frowning brows, the heavy lines of his body, the face (which seems so young to me now) engraved into hardness by the devouring, goading will that had kept his eyes turned westward to his closed kingdom for the twenty-odd years it took him to grow from child to Comes and build, against all the odds of poverty and weakness, the striking force that grew with him, waiting for the time.

It is harder to write of Uther. Or rather it is hard to write of Uther as if he were in the past, part of a story that has been over these many years. Even more vividly than Ambrosius he is here with me; not here in the darkness—it is the part of me that was Myrddin that is here in the darkness. The part that was Uther is out there in the sunlight, keeping the coasts of Britain whole, following the design I made for him, the design that Galapas showed to me on a summer's day in Wales.

But there, of course, it is no longer Uther of whom I write. It is the man who was the sum of us, who was all of us—Ambrosius, who made me; Uther, who worked with me; myself, who used him, as I used every man who came to my hand, to make Arthur for Britain.

From time to time news came from Britain, and occasionally with it—through Gorlois of Cornwall—news of my home.

It seemed that after my grandfather's death, Camlach had not immediately deserted the old alliance with his kinsman Vortigern. He had to feel himself more secure before he would dare break away to support the "young men's party," as Vortimer's faction was called. Indeed, Vortimer himself had stopped short of open rebellion, but it seemed clear that this must come eventually. King Vortigern was back between the landslide and the flood; if he was to stay King of the British he must call on his Saxon wife's countrymen for help, and the Saxon mercenaries year by year increased their demands till the country was split and bleeding under what men openly called the Saxon Terror, and—in the West especially, where men were still free—rebellion only waited for a leader of leaders. And so desperate was Vortigern's situation becoming that he was forced against his better judgement to entrust the armed forces in the West more and more to Vortimer and his brothers, whose blood at least carried none of the Saxon taint.

Of my mother there was no news, except that she was safe in St. Peter's. Ambrosius sent her no message. If it came to her ears that a certain Merlinus Ambrosius was with the Count of Brittany, she would know what to think, but a letter or message direct from the King's enemy would endanger her unnecessarily. She would know, said Ambrosius, soon enough.

In fact it was five years before the break came, but the time went by like a tide-race. With the possibility of an opening developing in Wales and Cornwall, Ambrosius' preparations accelerated. If the men of the West wanted a leader he had every intention that it should be, not Vortimer, but himself. He would bide his time and let Vortimer be the wedge, but he and Uther would be the hammer that drove after it into the crack. Meanwhile hope in Less Britain ran high; offers of troops and alliances poured in, the countryside shook to the tramp of horses and marching feet, and the streets of the engineers and armourers rang far into the night as men redoubled their efforts to make two weapons in the time that before it had taken to make one. Now at last the break was coming, and when it came Ambrosius must be ready, and with no chance of failure. One does not wait half a lifetime gathering the material to make a killing spear, and then loose it at random in the dark. Not only men and materials, but time and spirit and the very wind of heaven must be right for him, and the gods themselves must open the gate. And for this, he said, they had sent me to him. It was my coming just at such a time with words of victory, and full of the vision of the unconquered god, which persuaded him (and even more important, the soldiers with him) that the time was at last approaching when he could strike with the certainty of victory. So—I found to my fear—he rated me.

Be sure I had never asked him again how he intended to use me. He made it clear enough, and between pride and fear and longing I fought to learn all that I could be taught, and to open myself for the power which was all I could give him. If he had wanted a prophet ready to hand he must have been disappointed; I saw nothing of importance during this time. Knowledge, I suppose, blocked the gates of vision. But this was the time for knowledge; I studied with Belasius till I outran him, learning, as he had never done, how to apply the calculations which to him were as much an art as songs were to me; even songs, indeed, I was to use. I spent long hours in the street of the engineers, and had frequently to be dragged by a grumbling Cadal from some oily piece of practical work which unfitted me, as he said, for any company but a bath-slave's. I wrote down, too, all I could remember of Galapas' medical teaching, and added practical experience by helping the army doctors whenever I could. I had the freedom of the camp and the town, and with Ambrosius' name to back me I took to this freedom like a hungry young wolf to his first full meal. I learned all the time, from every man or woman I met. I looked, as I had promised, in the light and the dark, at the sunshine and at the stale pool. I went with Ambrosius to the shrine of Mithras below the farmstead, and with Belasius to the gatherings in the forest. I was even allowed to sit silently at meetings between the Count and his captains, though nobody pretended that I would ever be much use in the field, "unless," said Uther once, half amused, half malicious, "he is to stand above us like Joshua holding the sun back, to give us more time to do the real work. Though joking apart, he might do worse . . . the men seem to think of him as something halfway between a Courier of Mithras and a splinter of the True Cross—saving your presence, brother—and I'm damned certain he'd be more use stuck up on a hill like a lucky charm where they can see him, than down in the field where he wouldn't last five minutes." He had even more to say when, at the age of sixteen, I gave up the daily sword practice which gave a man the minimum training in self-defense; but my father merely laughed and said nothing. I think he knew, though as yet I did not, that I had my own kind of protection.

So I learned from everyone; the old women who gathered plants and cobwebs and sea-weeds for healing; the travelling peddlers and quack healers; the horse doctors, the soothsayers, the priests. I listened to the soldiers' talk outside the taverns, and the officers' talk in my father's house, and the boys' talk in the streets. But there was one thing about which I learned nothing: by the time I left Brittany at seventeen, I was still ignorant of women. When I thought about them—which happened often enough—I told myself that I had no time, that there was a lifetime still ahead of me for such things, and that now I had work to do which mattered more. But I suppose the plain truth is that I was afraid of them. So I lost my desires in work, and indeed, I believe now that the fear came from the god.

So I waited, and minded my own business, which—as I saw it then—was to fit myself to serve my father.

One day I was in Tremorinus' workshop. Tremorinus, the master engineer, was a pleasant man who allowed me to learn all I could from him, gave me space in the workshops, and material to experiment with. This particular day I remember how when he came into the workshop and saw me busy over a model at my corner bench, he came over to have a look at it. When he saw what I was doing he laughed.

"I'd have thought there were plenty of those around without troubling to put up any more."

"I was interested in how they got them there." I tilted the scale model of the standing stone back into place.

He looked surprised. I knew why. He had lived in Less Britain all his life, and the landscape there is so seamed with the stones that men do not see them any more. One walks daily through a forest of stone, and to most men it seems dead stone . . . But not to me. To me they still said something, and I had to find out what; but I did not tell Tremorinus this. I added, merely: "I was trying to work it out to scale."

"I can tell you something straight away: that's been tried, and it doesn't work." He was looking at the pulley I had rigged to lift the model. "That might do for the uprights, but only the lighter ones, and it doesn't work at all for the cap-stones."

"No. I'd found that out. But I'd had an idea . . . I was going to tackle it another way."

"You're wasting your time. Let's see you getting down to something practical, something we need and can use. Now, that idea of yours for a light mobile crane might be worth developing . . ."

A few minutes later he was called away. I dismantled the model, and sat down to my new calculations. I had not told Tremorinus about them; he had more important things to think about, and in any case he would have laughed if I had told him I had learned from a poet how to lift the standing stones.

It had happened this way.

One day about a week before this, as I walked by the water that guarded the town walls, I heard a man singing. The voice was old and wavering, and hoarse with over-use—the voice of a professional singer who has strained it above the noise of the crowd, and through singing with the winter cold in his throat. What caught my attention was neither the voice nor the tune, which could hardly be picked out, but the sound of my own name.

Merlin, Merlin, where art thou going?

He was sitting by the bridge, with a bowl for begging. I saw that he was blind, but the remnant of his voice was true, and he made no gesture with his bowl as he heard me stop near him, but sat as one sits at a harp, head bent, listening to what the strings say, with fingers stirring as if they felt the notes. He had sung, I would judge, in kings' halls.

Merlin, Merlin, where art thou going
So early in the day with thy black dog?

I have been searching for the egg,
The red egg of the sea-serpent,
Which lies by the shore in the hollow stone.
And I go to gather cresses in the meadow,
The green cress and the golden grasses,
The golden moss that gives sleep,
And the mistletoe high on the oak, the druids' bough
That grows deep in the woods by the running water.

Merlin, Merlin, come back from the wood and the fountain!
Leave the oak and the golden grasses
Leave the cress in the water-meadow,
And the red egg of the sea-serpent
In the foam by the hollow stone!

Merlin, Merlin, leave thy seeking!
There is no diviner but God.

Nowadays this song is as well known as the one of Mary the Maiden, or the King and the Grey Seal, but it was the first time I had heard it. When he knew who it was who had stopped to listen, he seemed pleased that I should sit beside him on the bank, and ask questions. I remember that on that first morning we talked mostly of the song, then of himself; I found he had been as a young man on Mona, the druids' isle, and knew Caer'n-ar-Von and had walked on Snowdon. It was in the druids' isle that he had lost his sight; he never told me how, but when I told him that the sea-weeds and cresses that I hunted along the shore were only plants for healing, not for magic, he smiled and sang a verse I had heard my mother sing, which, he said, would be a shield. Against what, he did not say, nor did I ask him. I put money into his bowl, which he accepted with dignity, but when I promised to find a harp for him he went silent, staring with those empty eye-sockets, and I could see he did not believe me. I brought the harp next day; my father was generous, and I had no need even to tell him what the money was for. When I put the harp into the old singer's hands he wept, then took my hands and kissed them.

After that, right up to the time I left Less Britain, I often sought him out. He had travelled widely, in lands as far apart as Ireland and Africa. He taught me songs from every country, Italy and Gaul and the white North, and older songs from the East—strange wandering tunes which had come westward, he said, from the islands of the East with the men of old who had raised the standing stones, and they spoke of lores long forgotten except in song. I do not think he himself thought of them as anything but songs of old magic, poets' tales; but the more I thought about them, the more clearly they spoke to me of men who had really lived, and work they had really done, when they raised the great stones to mark the sun and moon and build for their gods and the giant kings of old.

I said something once about this to Tremorinus, who was kindly as well as clever, and who usually managed to find time for me; but he laughed and put it aside, and I said no more. Ambrosius' technicians had more than enough to think about in those days, without helping a boy to work out a set of calculations of no practical use in the coming invasion. So I let it be.

It was in the spring of my eighteenth year that the news came finally from Britain. Through January and February, winter had closed the seaways, and it was not till early March, taking advantage of the cold still weather before the gales began, that a small trading boat put into port, and Ambrosius got news.

Stirring news it was—literally so, for within a few hours of its coming, the Count's messengers were riding north and east, to gather in his allies at last, and quickly, for the news was late.

It appeared that Vortimer had finally, some time before, broken with his father and the Saxon Queen. Tired of petitioning the High King to break with his Saxon allies and protect his own people from them, several of the British leaders—among them the men of the West—had persuaded Vortimer to take matters into his own hands at last, and had risen with him. They had declared him King, and rallied to his banner against the Saxons, whom they had succeeded in driving back south and eastwards, till they took refuge with their longships in the Isle of Thanet. Even there Vortimer pursued them, and through the last days of autumn and the beginning of winter had beleaguered them there until they pleaded only to be allowed to depart in peace, packed up their goods, and went back to Germany, leaving their women and children behind them.

But Vortimer's victorious kingship did not last long. It was not clear exactly what had happened, but the rumour was that he had died of poison treacherously administered by a familiar of the Queen. Whatever the truth of the matter, he was dead, and Vortigern his father was once more in command. Almost his first act had been (and again the blame was imputed to his wife) to send yet again for Hengist and his Saxons to return to Britain. "With a small force," he had said, "nothing but a mobile peace-keeping force to help him impose order and pull together his divided kingdom." In fact, the Saxons had promised three hundred thousand men. So rumour said, and though it was to be supposed that rumour lied, it was certain at any rate that Hengist planned to come with a considerable force.

There was also a fragment of news from Maridunum. The messenger was no spy of Ambrosius; the news we got was, as it were, only the larger rumours. These were bad enough. It seemed that my uncle Camlach, together with all his nobles—my grandfather's men, the men that I knew—had risen with Vortimer and fought beside him in the four pitched battles against the Saxons. In the second, at Episford, Camlach had been killed, along with Vortimer's brother Katigern. What concerned me more was that after Vortimer's death reprisals had been levelled at the men who had fought with him. Vortigern had annexed Camlach's kingdom to join his own lands of Guent, and, wanting hostages, had repeated his action of twenty-five years earlier; he had taken Camlach's children, one of them still an infant, and lodged them in the care of Queen Rowena. We had no means of knowing if they were still alive. Nor did we know if Olwen's son, who had met the same fate, had survived. It seemed unlikely. Of my mother there was no news.

Two days after the news came, the spring gales began, and once more the seas were locked against us and against news. But this hardly mattered; indeed, it worked both ways. If we could get no news from Britain, they could have none of us, and of the final accelerated preparations for the invasion of Western Britain. For it was certain that the time had now come. It was not only a case of marching to the relief of Wales and Cornwall, but if there were to be any men left to rally to the Red Dragon, the Red Dragon would have to fight for his crown this coming year.

"You'll go back with the first boat," said Ambrosius to me, but without looking up from the map which was spread on the table in front of him.

I was standing over by the window. Even with the shutters closed and curtains drawn I could hear the wind, and beside me the curtains stirred in the draught. I said: "Yes, sir," and crossed to the table. Then I saw his finger was pointing on the map. "I'm to go to Maridunum?"

He nodded. "You'll take the first westbound boat, and make your way home from wherever it docks. You are to go straight up to Galapas and get what news there is from him. I doubt if you would be recognized in the town, but take no risks. Galapas is safe. You can make him your base."

"There was no word from Cornwall, then?"

"Nothing, except a rumour that Gorlois was with Vortigern."

"With Vortigern?" I digested this for a moment. "Then he didn't rise with Vortimer?"

"As far as my information goes, no."

"He's trimming, then?"

"Perhaps. I find it hard to believe. It may mean nothing. I understand he has married a young wife, and it may only be that he kept within walls all winter to keep her warm. Or that he foresaw what would happen to Vortimer, and preferred to serve my cause by staying safe and apparently loyal to the High King. But until I know, I cannot send to him directly. He may be watched. So you are to go to Galapas, for the news from Wales. I'm told Vortigern's holed up there somewhere, while the length of Eastern Britain lies open to Hengist. I'll have to smoke the old wolf out first, then weld the West against the Saxons. But it will have to be fast. And I want Caerleon." He looked up then. "I'm sending your old friend with you—Marric. You can send word back by him. Let's hope you find all well. You'll want news yourself, I dare say."

"It can wait," I said.

He said nothing to that, but raised his brows at me, and then turned back to the map. "Well, sit down and I'll brief you myself. Let's hope you can get away soon."

I indicated the swaying curtains. "I shall be sick all the way."

He looked up from the map, and laughed. "By Mithras, I hadn't thought of that. Do you suppose I shall be, too? A damned undignified way to go back to one's home."

"To one's kingdom," I said.

2

I crossed in early April, and on the same ship as before. But the crossing could not have been more different. This was not Myrddin, the runaway, but Merlinus, a well-dressed young Roman with money in his pocket, and servants in attendance. Where Myrddin had been locked naked in the hold, Merlinus had a comfortable cabin, and marked deference paid him by the captain. Cadal, of course, was one of my servants, and the other, to my own amusement though not his, was Marric. (Hanno was dead, having overreached himself, I gathered, in a little matter of blackmail.) Naturally I carried no outward sign of my connection with Ambrosius, but nothing would part me from the brooch he had given me; I wore this clipped inside the shoulder of my tunic. It was doubtful whether anyone would have recognized in me the runaway of five years ago, and certainly the captain gave no sign, but I held myself aloof, and was careful to speak nothing but Breton.

As luck would have it, the boat was going straight to the mouth of the Tywy and would anchor at Maridunum, but it had been arranged that Cadal and I were to be put off by boat as soon as the trader arrived in the estuary.

It was, in fact, my previous journey in reverse, but in the most important respect there was no difference. I was sick all the way. The fact that this time I had a comfortable bunk and Cadal to look after me, instead of sacks and a bucket in the hold, made not the slightest difference to me. As soon as the ship nosed out of the Small Sea, and met the windy April weather of the Bay, I left my brave stance in the bows and went below and lay down.

We had what they tell me was a fair wind, and we crept into the estuary and dropped anchor just before dawn, ten days before the Ides of April.

It was a still dawn, misty and cold. It was very quiet. The tide was just on the turn, beginning its flow up the estuary, and as our boat left the ship's side the only sound was the hiss and chuckle of water along her sides, and the soft splash of the paddles. Far away, faint and metallic, I could hear cocks crowing. Somewhere beyond the mist lambs were crying, answered by the deeper bleating of sheep. The air smelled soft, clear and salty, and in some curious way, of home.

We kept well out to the center of the stream, and the mist hid us from the banks. If we spoke at all, it was in whispers; once when a dog barked from the bank we heard a man speak to it almost as clearly as if he had been in the boat with us; this was sufficient warning, and we kept our voices down.

It was a strong spring tide, and took us fast. This was as well, for we had made anchor later than we should, and the light was growing. I saw the sailors who rowed us glance anxiously upwards and then lengthen their stroke. I leaned forward, straining my eyes for a glimpse of the bank I could recognize. Cadal said in my ear: "Glad to be back?"

"That depends on what we find. Mithras, but I'm hungry."

"That's not surprising," he said, with a sour chuckle. "What are you looking for?"

"There should be a bay—white sand with a stream coming down through trees—and a ridge behind it with a crest of pines. We'll put in there."

He nodded. The plan was that Cadal and I should be landed on the side of the estuary away from Maridunum, at a point I knew from which we could make our way unseen to join the road from the south. We would be travellers from Cornwall; I would do the talking, but Cadal's accent would pass with any but a native Cornishman. I had with me some pots of salve and a small chest of medicines, and if challenged could pass as a travelling doctor, a disguise that would serve as a pass to more or less anywhere I wanted to go.

Marric was still on board. He would go in with the trader, and disembark as usual at the wharf. He would try to find his old contacts in the town, and pick up what news he could. Cadal would go with me to the cave of Galapas, and act as connecting link with Marric to pass over what information I got. The ship was to lie for three days in the Tywy; when she sailed Marric would take the news back with her. Whether I and Cadal would be with him would depend on what we found; neither my father nor I forgot that after Camlach's part in the rebellion Vortigern must have been through Maridunum like a fox through a hen-run, and maybe his Saxons with him. My first duty was to get news of Vortigern, and send it back; my second to find my mother and see that she was safe.

It was good to be on land again; not dry land, for the grass at the head of the ridge was long and soaking, but I felt light and excited as the boat vanished under the mist and Cadal and I left the shore and made our way inland towards the road. I don't know what I expected to find in Maridunum; I don't even know that I cared overmuch; it was not the homecoming that made my spirits lift, but the fact that at last I had a job to do for Ambrosius. If I could not yet do a prophet's work for him, at least I could do a man's work, and then a son's. I believe that all the time I was half hoping that I would be asked to die for him. I was very young.

We reached the bridge without incident. Luck was with us there, for we fell in with a horse-trader who had a couple of nags in hand which he hoped to sell in the town. I bought one of them from him, haggling just enough to prevent suspicion; he was pleased enough with the price to throw in a rather worn saddle. By the time the transaction was finished it was full light and there were one or two people about, but no one gave us more than a cursory glance, except for one fellow who, apparently recognizing the horse, grinned, and said—to Cadal rather than to me—"Were you planning to go far, mate?"

I pretended not to hear, but from the corner of my eye saw Cadal spread his hands, shrug, and turn his eyes up in my direction. The look said, all too plainly, "I only follow where he goes, and he's crazy anyway."

Presently the towpath was empty. Cadal came alongside, and hooked a hand through the neck-strap. "He's right, you know. This old screw won't get you far. How far is it, anyway?"

"Probably not nearly as far as I remember. Six miles at the outside."

"Uphill most of the way, you said?"

"I can always walk." I smoothed a hand along the skinny neck. "He's not as much of a wreck as he looks, you know. There's not much wrong that a few good feeds won't put right."

"Then at least you won't have wasted your money. What are you looking at over that wall?"

"That's where I used to live."

We were passing my grandfather's house. It looked very little changed. From the cob's back I could just see over the wall to the terrace where the quince tree grew, its brilliant flame-coloured blossoms opening to the morning sun. And there was the garden where Camlach had given me the poisoned apricot. And there the gate where I had run in tears.

The cob plodded on. Here was the orchard, the apple trees already swelling with buds, the grass springing rough and green round the little terrace where Moravik would sit and spin, while I played at her feet. And here, now, was the place I had jumped over the wall the night I ran away; here was the leaning apple tree where I had left Aster tethered. The wall was broken, and I could see in across the rough grass where I had run that night, from my room where Cerdic's body lay on its funeral pyre. I pulled the cob to a halt and craned to see further. I must have made a clean sweep that night: the buildings were all gone, my room, and along with it two sides of the outer court. The stables, I saw, were still the same; the fire had not reached them, then. The two sides of the colonnade that had been destroyed had been rebuilt in a modern style that seemed to bear no relation to the rest, big rough stones and crude building, square pillars holding up a timber roof, and square, deep windows. It was ugly, and looked comfortless; its only virtue would be that it was weatherproof. You might as well, I thought, settling back in the saddle and putting the cob in motion, live in a cave . . .

"What are you grinning at?" asked Cadal.

"Only at how Roman I've become. It's funny, my home isn't here any more. And to be honest I don't think it's in Less Britain either."

"Where, then?"

"I don't know. Where the Count is, that's for sure. That will be this sort of place, I suppose, for some time to come." I nodded towards the walls of the old Roman barracks behind the palace. They were in ruins, and the place was deserted. So much the better, I thought; at least it didn't look as if Ambrosius would have to fight for it. Give Uther twenty-four hours, and the place would be as good as new. And here was St. Peter's, apparently untouched, showing no sign either of fire or spear. "You know something?" I said to Cadal, as we left the shadow of the nunnery wall and headed along the path towards the mill. "I suppose if I have anywhere I can call a home, it's the cave of Galapas."

"Doesn't sound all that Roman to me," said Cadal. "Give me a good tavern any day and a decent bed and some mutton to eat, and you can keep all the caves there are."

Even with this sorry horse, the way seemed shorter than I remembered it. Soon we had reached the mill, and turned up across the road and into the valley. Time fell away. It seemed only yesterday that I had come up this same valley in the sunshine, with the wind stirring Aster's grey mane. Not even Aster's—for there under the same thorn-tree was surely the same half-wit boy watching the same sheep as on my very first ride. As we reached the fork in the path, I found myself watching for the ring-dove. But the hillside was still, except for the rabbits scuttering among the young bracken.

Whether the cob sensed the end of his journey, or whether he merely liked the feel of grass under his feet and a light weight on his back, he seemed to quicken his step. Ahead of me now I could see the shoulder of the hill beyond which lay the cave.

I drew rein by the hawthorn grove.

"Here we are. It's up there, above the cliff." I slipped out of the saddle and handed the reins to Cadal. "Stay here and wait for me. You can come up in an hour." I added, on an afterthought: "And don't be alarmed if you see what you think is smoke. It's the bats coming out of the cave."

I had almost forgotten Cadal's sign against the evil eye. He made it now, and I laughed and left him.

3

Before I had climbed round the little crag to the lawn in front of the cave, I knew.

Call it foresight; there was no sign. Silence, of course, but then there usually had been silence as I approached the cave. This silence was different. It was only after some moments that I realized what it was. I could no longer hear the trickle of the spring.

I mounted to the top of the path, came out on the sward, and saw. There was no need to go into the cave to know that he was not there, and never would be again.

On the flat grass in front of the cave-mouth was a scatter of debris. I went closer to look.

It had been done not so very long ago. There had been a fire here, a fire quenched by rain before everything could properly be destroyed. There was a pile of sodden rubbish—half-charred wood, rags, parchment gone again to pulp but with the blackened edges still showing. I turned the nearest piece of scorched wood over with my foot; from the carving on it I knew what it was; the chest that had held his books. And the parchment was all that remained of the books themselves.

I suppose there was other stuff of his among the wreck of rubbish. I didn't look further. If the books had gone, I knew everything else would have gone too. And Galapas with them.

I went slowly towards the mouth of the cave. I paused by the spring. I could see why there had been no sound; someone had filled in the basin with stones and earth and more wreckage thrown out of the cave. Through it all the water welled still, sluggishly, oozing in silence over the stone lip and down to make a muddy morass of the turf. I thought I could see the skeleton of a bat, picked clean by the water.

Strangely enough, the torch was still on the ledge high beside the mouth of the cave, and it was dry. There was no flint or iron, but I made fire and, holding the torch before me, went slowly inside.

I think my flesh was shivering, as if a cold wind blew out of the cave and went by me. I knew already what I should find.

The place was stripped. Everything had been thrown out to burn. Everything, that is, except the bronze mirror. This, of course, would not burn, and I suppose it had been too heavy to be looted. It had been wrenched from the wall and stood propped against the side of the cave, tilted at a drunken angle. Nothing else. Not even a stir and whisper from the bats in the roof. The place echoed with emptiness.

I lifted the torch high and looked up towards the crystal cave. It was not there.

I believe that for a couple of pulses of the torchlight I thought he had managed to conceal the inner cave, and was in hiding. Then I saw.

The gap into the crystal cave was still there, but chance, call it what you will, had rendered it invisible except to those who knew. The bronze mirror had fallen so that, instead of directing light towards the gap, it directed darkness. Its light was beamed and concentrated on a projection of rock which cast, clear across the mouth of the crystal cave, a black wedge of shadow. To anyone intent only on the pillage and destruction in the cave below, the gap would be hardly visible at all.

"Galapas?" I said, trying it out on the emptiness. "Galapas?"

There was the faintest of whispers from the crystal cave, a ghostly sweet humming like the music I had once listened for in the night. Nothing human; I had not expected it. But still I climbed up to the ledge, knelt down and peered in.

The torchlight caught the crystals, and threw the shadow of my harp, trembling, clear round the lighted globe. The harp stood, undamaged, in the center of the cave. Nothing else, except the whisper dying round the glittering walls. There must be visions there, in the flash and counterflash of light, but I knew I would not be open to them. I put a hand down to the rock and vaulted, torch streaming, back to the floor of the cave. As I passed the tilted mirror I caught a glimpse of a tall youth running in a swirl of flame and smoke. His face looked pale, the eyes black and enormous. I ran out on to the grass. I had forgotten the torch, which flamed and streamed behind me. I ran to the edge of the cliff, and cupped a hand to my mouth to call Cadal, but then a sound from behind me made me whip round and look upwards.

It was a very normal sound. A pair of ravens and a carrion crow had risen from the hill, and were scolding at me.

Slowly this time, I climbed the path that led up past the spring and out on the hillside above the cave. The ravens went higher, barking. Two more crows made off low across the young bracken. There was a couple still busy on something lying among the flowering blackthorn.

I whirled the torch and flung it streaming to scatter them. Then I ran forward.

There was no telling how long he had been dead. The bones were picked almost clean. But I knew him by the discoloured brown rags that flapped under the skeleton, and the one old broken sandal which lay flung nearby among the April daisies. One of the hands had fallen from the wrist, and the clean, brittle bones lay near my foot. I could see where the little finger had been broken, and had set again, crookedly. Already through the bare rib-cage the April grass was springing. The air blew clean and sunlit, smelling of flowering gorse.

The torch had been stubbed out in the fresh grass. I stooped and picked it up. I should not have thrown it at them, I thought. His birds had given him a seemly waygoing.

A step behind me brought me round, but it was only Cadal.

"I saw the birds go up," he said. He was looking down at the thing under the blackthorn bushes. "Galapas?"

I nodded.

"I saw the mess down by the cave. I guessed."

"I hadn't realized I had been here so long."

"Leave this to me." He was stooping already. "I'll get him buried. Go you and wait down where we left the horse. I can maybe find some sort of tool down yonder, or I could come back—"

"No. Let him lie in peace under the thorn. We'll build the hill over him and let it take him in. We do this together, Cadal."

There were stones in plenty to pile over him for a barrow, and we cut sods with our daggers to turf it over. By the end of summer the bracken and foxgloves and young grasses would have grown right over and shrouded him. So we left him.

As we went downhill again past the cave I thought of the last time I had gone this way. I had been weeping then, I remembered, for Cerdic's death, for my mother's loss and Galapas', for who knew what foreknowledge of the future? *You will see me again,* he had said, *I promise you that.* Well, I had seen him. And some day, no doubt, his other promise would come true in its own fashion.

I shivered, caught Cadal's quick look, and spoke curtly. "I hope you had the sense to bring a flask with you. I need a drink."

4

Cadal had brought more than a flask with him, he had brought food—salt mutton and bread, and last season's olives in a bottle with their own oil. We sat in the lee of the wood and ate, while the cob grazed near us, and below in the distance the placid curves of the river glimmered through the April green of the fields and the young wooded hills. The mist had cleared, and it was a beautiful day.

"Well," said Cadal at length, "what's to do?"

"We go to see my mother. If she's still there, of course." Then, with a savagery that broke through me so suddenly that I had hardly known it was there: "By Mithras, I'd give a lot to know who did that up yonder!"

"Why, who could it be except Vortigern?"

"Vortimer, Pascentius, anyone. When a man's wise and gentle and good," I added bitterly, "it seems to me that any man's, every man's hand is against him. Galapas could have been murdered by an outlaw for food, or a herdsman for shelter, or a passing soldier for a drink of water."

"That was no murder."

"What, then?"

"I meant, that was done by more than one. Men in a pack are worse than lone ones. At a guess, it was Vortigern's men, on their way up from the town."

"You're probably right. I shall find out."

"You think you'll get to see your mother?"

"I can try."

"Did he—have you any messages for her?" It was, I suppose, the measure of my relationship with Cadal that he dared to ask the question.

I answered him quite simply. "If you mean did Ambrosius ask me to tell her anything, no. He left it to me. What I do tell her depends entirely on what's happened since I left. I'll talk to her first, and judge how much to tell her after that. Don't forget, I haven't seen her for a long time, and people change. I mean, their loyalties change. Look at mine. When I last saw her I was only a child, and I have only a child's memories—for all I know I misunderstood her utterly, the way she thought and the things she wanted. Her loyalties may lie elsewhere—not just the Church, but the way she feels about Ambrosius. The gods know there'd be no blame to her if she had changed. She owed Ambrosius nothing. She took good care of that."

He said thoughtfully, his eyes on the green distance threaded by the glinting river: "The nunnery hadn't been touched."

"Exactly. Whatever had happened to the rest of the town, Vortigern had let St. Peter's be. So you see I've to find out who is in which camp before I give any messages. What she hasn't known about for all these years, it won't hurt her to go on not knowing for as many more days. Whatever happens, with Ambrosius coming soon, I mustn't take the risk of telling her too much."

He began to pack away the remains of the meal while I sat, chin on hand, thinking, my eyes on the bright distance.

I added, slowly: "It's simple enough to find out where Vortigern is now, and if Hengist's landed already, and with how many men. Marric will probably find out without too much trouble. But there were other soundings the Count wanted me to take—things they'll hardly know about in the nunnery—so now that Galapas is dead, I'll have to try elsewhere. We'll wait here till dusk, then go down to St. Peter's. My mother will be able to tell me who I can still go to in safety." I looked at him. "Whatever king she favours, she's not likely to give me away."

"That's true enough. Well, let's hope they'll let her see you."

"If she knows who's asking for her, I imagine it will take more than a word from the Abbess to stop her from seeing me. Don't forget she's still a king's daughter." I lay back on the warm grass, my hands behind my head. "Even if I'm not yet a king's son . . ."

But, king's son or no, there was no getting into the nunnery.

I had been right in thinking there had been no damage done here. The high walls loomed unbroken and unscarred, and the gates were new and solid, of oak hinged and bolted with iron. They were fast shut. Nor—mercifully—did any welcoming torch burn outside. The narrow street was empty and unlit in the early dusk. At our urgent summons a small square window in the gate opened, and an eye was applied to the grille.

"Travellers from Cornwall," I said softly. "I must have word with the Lady Niniane."

"The Lady who?" It was the flat, toneless voice of the deaf. Wondering irritably why a deaf portress should be put at the gate, I raised my voice a little, going closer to the grille.

"The Lady Niniane. I don't know what she calls herself now, but she was sister of the late King. Is she with you still?"

"Aye, but she'll see nobody. Is it a letter you have? She can read."

"No, I must have speech with her. Go and take word to her; tell her it's—one of her family."

"Her family?" I thought I saw a flicker of interest in the eyes. "They're most of them dead and gone. Do you not get news in Cornwall? Her brother the King died in battle last year, and the children have gone to Vortigern. Her own son's been dead these five years."

"I knew that. I'm not her brother's family. And I'm as loyal as she is to the High King. Go and tell her that. And look—take this for your . . . devotions."

A pouch passed through the grille and was grabbed in a quick monkey-snatch. "I'll take a message for you. Give me your name. I don't say she'll see you, mind, but I'll take her your name."

"My name's Emrys." I hesitated. "She knew me once. Tell her that. And hurry. We'll wait here."

It was barely ten minutes before I heard the steps coming back. For a moment I thought it might be my mother, but it was the same old eyes that peered at me through the grille, the same clawed hand laying hold of the bars. "She'll see you. Oh no, not now, young master. You can't come in. Nor she can't come out yet, not till prayers is over. Then she'll meet you on the river walk, she says; there's another gate in the wall there. But not to let anyone see you."

"Very well. We'll be careful."

I could see the whites of the eyes turning, as she tried to see me in the shadows. "Knew you, she did, straight away. Emrys, eh? Well, don't worry that I'll say aught. These be troubled times, and the least said the better, no matter what about."

"What time?"

"An hour after moonrise. You'll hear the bell."

"I'll be there," I said, but the grille was already shut.

There was a mist rising again from the river. This would help, I thought. We went quietly down the lane which skirted the nunnery walls. It led away from the streets, down towards the towpath.

"What now?" asked Cadal. "It's two hours yet till moonrise, and by the look of the night we'll be lucky if we ever see a moon at all. You'll not risk going into the town?"

"No. But there's no sense in waiting about in this drizzle. We'll find a place out of the wet where we can hear the bell. This way."

The stableyard gate was locked. I wasted no time on it, but led the way to the orchard wall. No lights showed in the palace. We scrambled over where the wall was broken, and walked up through the damp grass of the orchard and into my grandfather's garden. The air was heavy with the smell of damp earth and growing things, mint and sweetbriar and moss and young leaves heavy with wet. Last year's ungathered fruit squelched under our feet. Behind us the gate creaked, emptily.

The colonnades were empty, the doors shut, the shutters fastened close over the windows. The place was all darkness and echoes and the scuttle of rats. But there was no damage that I could see. I suppose that, when Vortigern took the town, he had meant to keep the house for himself, and had somehow persuaded or forced his Saxons to bypass it in their looting as—from fear of the bishops—he had forced them to bypass St. Peter's. So much the better for us. We should at least have a dry and comfortable wait. My time with Tremorinus had been wasted indeed if I could not have picked every lock in the place.

I was just saying as much to Cadal when suddenly, round the corner of the house, treading softly as a cat on the mossy flagstones, came a young man walking fast. He stopped dead at the sight of us, and I saw his hand flash down to his hip. But even while Cadal's weapon hissed free of its sheath in reply the young man peered, stared, and then exclaimed: "Myrddin, by the holy oak!"

For a moment I genuinely didn't recognize him, which was understandable, since he was not much older than myself, and had changed as much in five years. Then, unmistakably, I saw who it was; broad shoulders, thrusting jaw, hair that even in the twilight showed red. Dinias, who had been prince and king's son when I was a nameless bastard; Dinias, my "cousin," who would not even recognize that much of a tie with me, but who had claimed the title of Prince for himself, and been allowed to get away with it.

He would hardly now be taken for a prince. Even in that fading light I could see that he was dressed, not poorly, but in clothes that a merchant might have worn, and he had only one jewel, an arm-ring of copper. His belt was of plain leather, his sword-hilt plain also, and his cloak, though of good stuff, was stained and frayed at the edge. About his whole person was that indefinable air of seediness which comes from relentless calculation from day to day or perhaps even from meal to meal.

Since in spite of the considerable changes he was still indisputably my cousin Dinias, it was to be supposed that once he had recognized me, there was little point in pretending he was wrong. I smiled and held out my hand. "Welcome, Dinias. Yours is the first known face I've seen today."

"What in the name of the gods are you doing here? Everyone said you were dead, but I didn't believe it."

His big head thrust out, peering close as the quick eyes looked me up and down. "Wherever you were, you've done all right, seemingly. How long have you been back?"

"We came today."

"Then you've heard the news?"

"I knew Camlach was dead. I'm sorry about that . . . if you were. As you'll know, he was no friend of mine, but that was hardly political . . ." I paused, waiting. Let him make the moves. I saw from the corner of an eye that Cadal was tensed and watchful, a hand still to his hip. I moved my own hand, palm downwards in a slight flattening movement, and saw him relax.

Dinias lifted a shoulder. "Camlach? He was a fool. I told him which way the wolf would jump." But as he spoke I saw his eyes slide sideways towards the shadows. It seemed that men watched their tongues these days in Maridunum. His eyes came back to me, suspicious, wary. "What's your business here, anyway? Why did you come back?"

"To see my mother. I've been in Cornwall, and all we got there was rumours of fighting, and when I heard Camlach was dead, and Vortimer, I wondered what had happened at home."

"Well, she's alive, you'll have found that out? The High King"—rather loudly—"respects the Church. I doubt if you'll get to see her though."

"You're probably right. I went up to the nunnery, and they wouldn't let me in. But I'll be here for a few days. I'll send a message in, and if she wants to see me, I imagine she'll find a way of doing so. But at least I know she's safe. It's a real stroke of luck, running into you like this. You'll be able to give me the rest of the news. I had no idea what I might find here, so as you see, I came in this morning quietly, alone with my servant."

"Quietly is right. I thought you were thieves. You're lucky I didn't cut you down and ask questions afterwards."

It was the old Dinias, the bullying note there again, an immediate response to my mild, excusing tone.

"Well, I wasn't taking any risks till I knew how the family stood. I went off to St. Peter's—I waited till dusk to do that—then I came to take a look around here. Is the place empty then?"

"I'm still living here. Where else?"

The arrogance rang as hollow as the empty colonnade, and for a moment I felt tempted to ask him for hospitality and see what he would say. As if the thought had struck him at the same moment he said quickly: "Cornwall, eh? What's the news from there? They say Ambrosius' messengers are scuttling across the Narrow Sea like waterflies."

I laughed. "I wouldn't know. I've been leading a sheltered life."

"You picked the right place." The contempt that I remembered so well was back in his voice. "They say old Gorlois spent the winter snugged down in bed with a girl barely turned twenty, and left the rest of the kings to play their own games out in the snow. They say she'd make Helen of Troy look like a market-woman. What's she like?"

"I never saw her. He's a jealous husband."

"Jealous of you?" He laughed, and followed it with a comment that made Cadal, behind me, suck in his breath. But the jibe had put my cousin back in humour, and off his guard. I was still the little bastard cousin, and of no account. He added: "Well, it would suit you. You had a peaceful winter, you with your goatish old Duke, while the rest of us tramped the country after the Saxons."

So he had fought with Camlach and Vortimer. It was what I had wanted to know. I said mildly: "I was hardly responsible for the Duke's policy. Nor am I now."

"Ha! It's as well for you. You knew he was in the north with Vortigern?"

"I knew he had left to join him—at Caer'n-ar-Von, was it? Are you going up there yourself?" I put the gentlest of queries into my voice, adding meekly: "I wasn't really in a position to hear much news that mattered."

A chill current of air eddied, loaded with damp, between the pillars. From some broken gutter above us water suddenly spilled over, to splash between us on the flagstones. I saw him gather his cloak round him. "Why are we standing here?" He spoke with a brusque heartiness that ran as false as the arrogance. "Come and exchange news over a flask of wine, eh?"

I hesitated, but only for a moment. It seemed obvious that Dinias had his own reasons for keeping out of the High King's eye; for one thing, if he had managed to live down his association with Camlach, he would surely be with Vortigern's army, not skulking here in this threadbare fashion in an empty palace. For another, now that he knew I was in Maridunum, I preferred to keep him under my eye than leave him now to go and talk to whom he would.

So I accepted with every appearance of flattered pleasure, only insisting that he must join me for supper, if he could tell me where a good meal was to be found, and a warm seat out of the wet . . . ?

Almost before the words were out he had me by the arm and was hurrying me across the atrium and out through the street door.

"Fine, fine. There's a place over on the west side, beyond the bridge. The food's good, and they get the kind of clients that mind their own business." He winked. "Not that you'll be wanting to bother with a girl, eh? Though you don't look as if they'd made a clerk of you after all . . . ? Well, no more for now, it doesn't do to look as though you've too much to talk about these days . . . You either fall foul of the Welsh or you fall foul of Vortigern—and the place is crawling with his spies just now. I don't know who it is they're looking for, but there's a story going about— No, take your trash away." This to a beggar who thrust a tray of rough-cut stones and leather laces in front of us. The man moved back without a word. I saw that he was blind in one eye from a cut; a hideous scar ran right up one cheek, and had flattened the bridge of the nose. It looked as if it had been a sword cut.

I dropped a coin on the tray as we passed, and Dinias shot me a look that was far from friendly. "Times have changed, eh? You must have struck it rich in Cornwall. Tell me, what happened that night? Did you mean to set the whole damned place on fire?"

"I'll tell you all about it over supper," I said, and would say no more till we reached the shelter of the tavern, and got a bench in the corner with our backs to the wall.

5

I had been right about Dinias' poverty. Even in the smoky murk of the tavern's crowded room I could see the threadbare state of his clothes, and sense the air half of resentment, half of eagerness, with which he watched while I ordered food and a jug of their best wine. While it was coming I excused myself and had a quick word aside with Cadal.

"I may get some of the facts we want from him. In any case I thought it better to stick to him—I'd rather he came under my eye for the moment. The odds are he'll be drunk enough by moonrise to be harmless, and I'll either get him bedded down safe with a girl, or if he's past it I'll see him home on my way to the nunnery. If I don't look like getting out of here by moonrise, get over yourself to the gate on the towpath to meet my mother. You know our story. Tell her I'm coming, but I fell in with my cousin Dinias and have to get rid of him first. She'll understand. Now get yourself some food."

"Watch your step, I would, Merlin. Your cousin, did you say? Proper daisy he is, and no mistake. He doesn't like you."

I laughed. "You think that's news? It's mutual."

"Oh. Well, as long as you watch it."

"I'll do that."

Dinias' manners were still good enough to make him wait till I had dismissed Cadal and sat down to pour the wine. He had been right about the food; the pie they brought us was stuffed full of beef and oysters in a thick, steaming gravy, and though the bread was made from barley meal it was fresh. The cheese was not, and was excellent. The tavern's other wares seemed to match the food; from time to time one got a glimpse of them as a girl peered giggling in through a curtained door, and some man put his cup down and hurried after her. From the way Dinias' eyes lingered on the curtain even while he ate, I thought I might have little difficulty in getting rid of him safely once I had the information I wanted.

I waited until he was halfway through his pie before I started asking questions. I hardly liked to wait longer for, from the way he reached for the wine-jug almost—in spite of his hunger—between every mouthful, I was afraid that if I left it too long he would not be clear-headed enough to tell me what I wanted.

Until I was quite sure how the land lay I was not prepared to venture on ground that might be tricky, but, my family being what it was, I could glean a good deal of the information Ambrosius wanted from simply asking questions about my relatives. These he answered readily enough.

To begin with, I had been presumed dead ever since the night of the fire. Cerdic's body had been destroyed, and the whole of that side of the courtyard along with it, and when my pony had found its way home and there was no sign of me, it could only be presumed that I had perished along with Cerdic and vanished the same way. My mother and Camlach had sent men out to search the countryside, but of course found no trace of me. It appeared there had been no suggestion of my having left by sea. The trading ship had not put in to Maridunum, and no one had seen the coracle.

My disappearance—not remarkably—had made very little stir. What my mother had thought about it no one knew, but she had apparently retired into the seclusion of St. Peter's very soon afterwards. Camlach had lost no time in declaring himself King, and for form's sake offered Olwen his protection, but since his own wife had one son and was heavy with another, it was an open secret that Queen Olwen would soon be married off to some harmless and preferably distant chieftain . . . And so on, and so on.

So much for news of the past, which was none of it news to me or news for Ambrosius. As Dinias finished his meal and leaned back against the wall loosening his belt, relaxed by the food and wine and warmth, I thought it time to steer near more immediate questions of the present. The tavern had filled up now, and there was plenty of noise to cover what we were saying. One or two of the girls had come out from the inner rooms, and there was a good deal of laughter and some horseplay. It was quite dark now outside, and apparently wetter than ever; men came in shaking themselves like dogs and shouting for mulled drinks. The atmosphere was heavy with peat smoke and charcoal from the grills and the smells of hot food and the reek of cheap oil-lamps. I had no fear of recognition: anyone would have had to lean right over our table and peer into my face to see me properly at all.

"Shall I send for more meat?" I asked.

Dinias shook his head, belched, and grinned. "No thanks. That was good. I'm in your debt. Now for your news. You've heard mine. Where have you been these past years?" He reached again for the jug of wine and up-ended it over his empty cup. "Damned thing's empty. Send for more?"

I hesitated. It appeared he had a poor head for wine, and I didn't want him drunk too soon.

He mistook my hesitation. "Come on, come on, you surely don't grudge me another jug of wine, eh? It isn't every day a rich young relative comes back from Cornwall. What took you there, eh? And what have you been doing all this time? Come on, young Myrddin, let's hear about it, shall we? But first, the wine."

"Well, of course," I said, and gave the order to the pot-boy. "But don't use my name here, if you don't mind. I'm calling myself Emrys now till I see which way the wind blows."

He accepted this so readily that I realized things were even trickier in Maridunum than I had thought. It seemed it was dangerous to declare oneself at all. Most of the men in the tavern looked Welsh; there were none I recognized, which was hardly surprising, considering the company I had kept five years ago. But there was a group near the door who, from their fair hair and beards, might have been Saxon. I supposed they were Vortigern's men. We said nothing until the pot-boy had dumped a fresh flask on the table in front of us. My cousin poured it, pushed his plate aside, leaned back and looked at me enquiringly.

"Well, come on, tell me about yourself. What happened that night you left? Who did you go with? You couldn't have been more than twelve or thirteen when you went, surely?"

"I fell in with a pair of traders going south," I told him. "I paid my way with one of the brooches that my gr—that the old King gave me. They took me with them as far as Glastonbury. Then I had a bit of luck—fell in with a merchant who was travelling west into Cornwall with glass goods from the Island, and he took me along." I looked down as if avoiding his eye, and twisted the cup between my fingers. "He wanted to set up as a gentleman, and thought it would do him credit to have a boy along who could sing and play the harp, and read and write as well."

"Hm. Very likely." I had known what he would think of my story, and indeed, his tone held satisfaction, as if his contempt of me had been justified. So much the better. It didn't matter to me what he thought. "Then?" he asked.

"Oh, I stayed with him for a few months, and he was pretty generous, he and his friends. I even made a fair amount on the side."

"Harping?" he asked, with a lift of the lip.

"Harping," I said blandly. "Also reading and writing—I did the man's accounts for him. When he came back north he wanted me to stay with him, but I didn't want to come back. Didn't dare," I added, disarmingly frank. "It wasn't hard to find a place in a religious house. Oh, no, I was too young to be anything but a layman. To tell you the truth, I quite enjoyed it; it's a very peaceful life. I've been busy helping them to write out copies of a history of the fall of Troy." His expression made me want to laugh, and I looked down at my cup again. It was good ware, Samian, with a high gloss, and the potter's mark was clear. A.M. *Ambrosius made me,* I thought suddenly, and smoothed the letters gently with my thumb as I finished for Dinias the account of the five harmless years spent by his bastard cousin. "I worked there until the rumours started coming in from home. I didn't pay much heed to them at first—rumours were always flying. But when we knew that it was true about Camlach's death, and then Vortimer's, I began to wonder what might have happened in Maridunum. I knew I had to see my mother again."

"You're going to stay here?"

"I doubt it. I like Cornwall, and I have a home there of a sort."

"Then you'll become a priest?"

I shrugged. "I hardly know yet. It's what they always meant me for, after all. Whatever the future is there, my place here is gone—if I ever had one. And I'm certainly no warrior."

He grinned at that. "Well, you never were, exactly, were you? And the war here isn't over; it's hardly begun, let me tell you." He leaned across the table confidentially, but the movement knocked his cup so that it rocked, and the wine washed up to the rim. He grabbed and steadied it. "Nearly spilled that, and the wine's nearly out again. Not bad stuff, eh? What about another?"

"If you like. But you were saying—?"

"Cornwall, now. I've always thought I'd like to go there. What are they saying there about Ambrosius?"

The wine was already talking. He had forgotten to be confidential; his voice was loud, and I saw one or two heads turn in our direction.

He took no notice. "Yes, I imagine you'd hear down there, if there was any news to hear. They say that's where he'll land, eh?"

"Oh," I said easily, "there's talk all the time. There has been for years, you know how it is. He hasn't come yet, so your guess is as good as mine."

"Like a bet on it?" I saw he had reached into the pouch at his waist and brought out a pair of dice, which he tossed idly from hand to hand. "Come on, give you a game?"

"No, thanks. At any rate, not here. Look, Dinias, I'll tell you what, we'll get another flask, or two if you like, and go home and drink them there?"

"Home?" He sneered, loose-lipped. "Where's that? An empty palace?"

He was still talking loudly, and from across the room I noticed someone watching us. Nobody I knew. Two men in dark clothes, one with fringe of black beard, the other thin-faced and red-headed, with a long nose like a fox. Welshmen, by the look of them. They had a flask on a stool in front of them, and cups in their hands, but the flask had been at the same level now for a good half hour. I glanced at Dinias. I judged he had reached the stage now of being disposed either to friendly confidences or a loud quarrel. To insist on leaving now might be to provoke that quarrel, and if we were being watched, and if the crowd near the door were indeed Vortigern's men, it would be better to stay here and talk quietly than to take my cousin out into the street, and perhaps be followed. What, after all, did a mention of Ambrosius' name matter? It would be on every man's lips, and if, as seemed likely, rumours had been flying more thickly than usual of late, everyone, Vortigern's friends and enemies alike, would be discussing them.

Dinias had dropped the dice on the table, and was pushing them here and there with a reasonably steady forefinger. At least they would give us an excuse for a heads-together session in our corner. And dice might take his attention off the wine flask.

I brought out a handful of small coins. "Look, if you really want a game. What can you put on the table?"

As we played I was conscious that Blackbeard and the foxy man were listening. The Saxons near the door seemed harmless enough; most of them were three parts drunk already, and talking too loudly among themselves to pay attention to anyone else. But Blackbeard seemed to be interested.

I threw the dice. Five and four. Too good; I wanted Dinias to win something. I could hardly offer him money to get him behind the curtain with a girl. Meanwhile, to put Blackbeard off the scent . . .

I said, not loudly, but very clearly: "Ambrosius, is it? Well, you know the rumours. I've heard nothing definite about him, only the usual stories that have been going the rounds these ten years. Oh, yes, men say he'll come to Cornwall, or Maridunum, or London, or Avon-mouth—you can take your pick . . . Your throw." Blackbeard's attention had shifted. I leaned closer to watch Dinias' throw, and lowered my voice. "And if he did come now, what would happen? You'll know this better than I. Would what's left of the West rise for him, or stand loyal to Vortigern?"

"The West would go up in flames. It's done that already, God knows. Double or quits? Flames like the night you left. God, how I laughed! Little bastard sets the place on fire and goes. Why did you? That's mine, double five. Throw you again."

"Right. Why did I go, you mean? I told you, I was afraid of Camlach."

"I didn't mean that. I mean why did you set the place on fire? Don't tell me it was an accident, because I don't believe you."

"It was a funeral pyre. I lit it because they killed my servant."

He stared, the dice for a moment still in his hands. "You fired the King's palace for a *slave?*"

"Why not? I happened to like my servant better than I liked Camlach."

He gave me a slightly fuddled look, and threw. A two and a four. I scooped back a couple of coins.

"Damn you," said Dinias, "you've no right to win, you've enough already. All right, again. Your servant, indeed! You've a mighty high tone for a bastard playing at being a scribe in a priest's cell."

I grinned. "You're a bastard, too, remember, dear cousin."

"Maybe, but at least I know who my father was."

"Keep your voice down, people are listening. All right, throw you again."

A pause while the dice rattled. I watched them rather anxiously. So far, they had tended to fall my way. How useful it would be, I thought, if power could be brought to bear on such small things; it would take no effort, and make the way smoother. But I had begun to learn that in fact power made nothing smoother; when it came it was like having a wolf by the throat. Sometimes I had felt like that boy in the old myth who harnessed the horses of the sun and rode the world like a god until the power burned him to death. I wondered if I would ever feel the flames again.

The dice fell from my very human fingers. A two and a one. No need to have the power if you could have the luck. Dinias gave a grunt of satisfaction and gathered them up, while I slid some coins towards him. The game went on. I lost the next three throws, and the heap beside him grew respectably. He was relaxing. No one was paying us any attention; that had been imagination. It was time, perhaps, for a few more facts.

"Where's the King now?" I asked.

"Eh? Oh, aye, the King. He's been gone from here nearly a month. Moved north as soon as the weather slackened and the roads were open."

"To Caer'n-ar-Von, you said—Segontium?"

"Did I? Oh, well, I suppose he calls that his base, but who'd want to be caught in that corner between Y Wyddfa and the sea? No, he's building himself a new stronghold, they say. Did you say you'd get another flask?"

"Here it comes. Help yourself, I've had enough. A stronghold, you said? Where?"

"What? Oh, yes. Good wine, this. I don't rightly know where he's building, somewhere in Snowdon. Told you. Dinas Brenin, they call it . . . Or would, if he could get it built."

"What's stopping him? Is there still trouble up there? Vortimer's faction still, or something new? They're saying in Cornwall that he's got thirty thousand Saxons at his back."

"At his back, on both sides—Saxons everywhere, our King has. But not with him. With Hengist—and Hengist and the King aren't seeing eye to eye. Oh, he's beset, is Vortigern, I can tell you!" Fortunately he was speaking quietly, his words lost in the rattle of dice and the uproar around us. I think he had half forgotten me. He scowled down at the table as he threw. "Look at that. The bloody things are ill-wished. Like King's Fort."

Somewhere the words touched a string of memory to a faint humming, as elusive and untraceable as a bee in the lime trees. I said casually, making my throw: "Ill-wished? How?"

"Hah, that's better. Should be able to beat that. Oh, well, you know these Northmen—if the wind blows colder one morning they say it's a dead spirit passing by. They don't use surveyors in that army, the soothsayers do it all. I heard he'd got the walls built four times to man height, and each time by next morning they'd cracked clear across. . . . How's that?"

"Not bad. I couldn't beat it, I'm afraid. Did he put guards on?"

"Of course. They saw nothing."

"Well, why should they?" It seemed that the luck was against us both; the dice were as ill-wished for Dinias as the walls for Vortigern. In spite of myself I threw a pair of doubles. Scowling, Dinias pushed half his pile towards me. I said: "It only sounds as if he picked a soft place. Why not move?"

"He picked the top of a crag, as pretty a place to defend as you'll find in all Wales. It guards the valley north and south, and stands over the road just where the cliffs narrow both sides, and the road is squeezed right up under the crag. And damn it, there's been a tower there before. The locals have called it King's Fort time out of mind."

King's Fort . . . Dinas Brenin . . . The humming swelled clear into a memory. Birches bone-white against a milk-blue sky. The scream of a falcon. Two kings walking together, and Cerdic's voice saying, *Come down, and I'll cut you in on a dice game."*

Before I even knew, I had done it, as neatly as Cerdic himself. I flicked the still turning dice with a quick finger. Dinias, up-ending the empty flask over his cup, never noticed. The dice settled. A two and a one. I said ruefully: "You won't have much trouble beating that."

He did beat it, but only just. He pulled the coins towards him with a grunt of triumph, then sprawled half across the table, his elbow in a pool of spilled wine. Even if I did manage, I thought, to let this drunken idiot win enough money off me, I would be lucky if I could get him even as far as the curtain leading to the brothel rooms. My throw again. As I shook the box I saw Cadal in the doorway, waiting to catch my eye. It was time to be gone. I nodded, and he withdrew. As Dinias glanced to see whom I had signalled to I threw again, and flicked a settling six over with my sleeve. One and three. Dinias made a sound of satisfaction and reached for the box.

"Tell you what," I said, "one more throw and we'll go. Win or lose, I'll buy another flask and we'll take it with us and drink it in my lodgings. We'll be more comfortable than here." Once I got him outside, I reckoned, Cadal and I could deal with him.

"Lodgings? I could have given you lodgings. Plenty of room there, you needn't have sent your man to look for lodgings. Got to be careful these days, you know. There. A pair of fives. Beat that if you can, Merlin the bastard!" He tipped the last of the wine down his throat, swallowed, and leaned back, grinning.

"I'll give you the game." I pushed the coins over to him, and made to stand up. As I looked round for the pot-boy to order the promised flask, Dinias slammed his hand down on the table with a crash. The dice jumped and rattled, and a cup went over, rolled, and smashed on the floor. Men stopped talking, staring.

"Oh, no, you don't! We'll play it out! Walk out just as the luck's turning again, would you? I'll not take that from you, or anyone else! Sit down and play, my bastard cousin—"

"Oh, for God's sake, Dinias—"

"All right, so I'm a bastard, too! All I can say is, better be the bastard of a king than a no-man's-child who never had a father at all!"

He finished with a hiccup, and someone laughed. I laughed too, and reached for the dice. "All right, we'll take them with us. I told you, win or lose, we'd take a flask home. We can finish the game there. It's time we drank one another into bed."

A hand fell on my shoulder, heavily. As I twisted to see who it was, someone came on my other side and gripped my arm. I saw Dinias stare upwards, gaping. Around us the drinkers were suddenly silent.

Blackbeard tightened his grip. "Quietly, young sir. We don't want a brawl, do we? Could we have a word with you outside?"

6

I got to my feet. There was no clue in the staring faces round me. Nobody spoke.

"What's all this about?"

"Outside, if you please," repeated Blackbeard. "We don't want a—"

"I don't in the least mind having a brawl," I said crisply. "You'll tell me who you are before I'll go a step with you. And to start with, take your hands off me. Landlord, who are these men?"

"King's men, sir. You'd best do as they say. If you've got nothing to hide—"

"'You've got nothing to fear'?" I said. "I know that one, and it's never true." I shoved Blackbeard's hand off my shoulder and turned to face him. I saw Dinias staring with his mouth slack. This, I supposed, was not the meek-voiced cousin he knew. Well, the time for that was past. "I don't mind these men hearing what you have to say. Tell me here. Why do you want to talk to me?"

"We were interested in what your friend here was saying."

"Then why not talk to him?"

Blackbeard said stolidly: "All in good time. If you'd tell me who you are, and where you come from—?"

"My name is Emrys, and I was born here in Maridunum. I went to Cornwall some years ago, when I was a child, and now had a fancy to come home and hear the news. That's all."

"And this young man? He called you 'cousin'."

"That was a form of speech. We are related, but not nearly. You probably also heard him call me 'bastard'."

"Wait a minute." The new voice came from behind me, among the crowd. An elderly man with thin grey hair, nobody I recognized, pushed his way to the front. "I know him. He's telling the truth. Why, that's Myrddin Emrys, sure enough, that was the old King's grandson." Then to me, "You won't remember me, sir. I was your grandfather's steward, one of them. I tell you this"—he stretched his neck, like a hen, peering up at Blackbeard—"King's men or no King's men, you've no business to lay a hand on this young gentleman. He's told you the truth. He left Maridunum five years ago—that's right, five, it was the night the old King died—and nobody heard tell where he'd gone. But I'll take any oath you like he would never raise a hand against King Vortigern. Why, he was training to be a priest, and never took arms in his life. And if he wants a quiet drink with Prince Dinias, why, they're related, as he told you, and who else would he drink with, to get the news of home?" He nodded at me, kindly. "Yes, indeed, that's Myrddin Emrys, that's a grown man now instead of a little boy, but I'd know him anywhere. And let me tell you, sir, I'm mightily glad to see you safe. It was feared you'd died in the fire."

Blackbeard hadn't even glanced at him. He was directly between me and the door. He never took his eyes off me. "Myrddin Emrys. The old King's grandson." He said it slowly. "And a bastard? Whose son, then?"

There was no point in denying it. I had recognized the steward now. He was nodding at me, pleased with himself. I said: "My mother was the King's daughter, Niniane."

The black eyes narrowed. "Is this true?"

"Quite true, quite true." It was the steward, his goodwill to me patent in his pale stupid eyes.

Blackbeard turned to me again. I saw the next question forming on his lips. My heart was thumping, and I could feel the blood stealing up into my face. I tried to will it down.

"And your father?"

"I do not know." Perhaps he would only think that the blood in my face was shame.

"Speak carefully, now," said Blackbeard. "You must know. Who got you?"

"I do not know."

He regarded me. "Your mother, the King's daughter. You remember her?"

"I remember her well."

"And she never told you? You expect us to believe this?"

I said irritably: "I don't care what you believe or what you don't believe. I'm tired of this. All my life people have asked me this question, and all my life people have disbelieved me. It's true, she never told me. I doubt if she told anyone. As far as I know, she may have been telling the truth when she said I was begotten of a devil." I made a gesture of impatience. "Why do you ask?"

"We heard what the other young gentleman said." His tone and look were stolid. " 'Better to be a bastard and have a king for a father, than a no-man's-child who never had a father at all!' "

"If I take no offense why should you? You can see he's in his cups."

"We wanted to make sure, that's all. And now we've made sure. The King wants you."

"The King?" I must have sounded blank.

He nodded. "Vortigern. We've been looking for you for three weeks past. You're to go to him."

"I don't understand." I must have looked bewildered rather than frightened. I could see my mission falling round me in ruins, but with this was a mixture of confusion and relief. If they had been looking for me for three weeks, this surely could have nothing to do with Ambrosius.

Dinias had been sitting quietly enough in his corner. I thought that most of what was said had not gone through to him, but now he leaned forward, his hands flat on the wine-splashed table. "What does he want him for? Tell me that."

"You've no call to worry." Blackbeard threw it at him almost disdainfully. "It's not you he wants. But I'll tell you what, since it was you led us to him, it's you who should get the reward."

"Reward?" I asked. "What talk is this?"

Dinias was suddenly stone sober. "I said nothing. What do you mean?"

Blackbeard nodded. "It was what you said that led us to him."

"He was only asking questions about the family—he's been away," said my cousin. "You were listening. Anybody could have listened, we weren't keeping our voices down. By the gods, if we wanted to talk treason would we have talked it here?"

"Nobody mentioned treason. I'm just doing my duty. The King wants to see him, and he's to come with me."

The old steward said, looking troubled now: "You can't harm him. He's who he says he is, Niniane's son. You can ask her yourself."

That brought Blackbeard round to face him quickly. "She's still alive?"

"Oh, yes, she's that all right. She's barely a stone's throw off, at the nunnery of St. Peter's, beyond the old oak at the crossways."

"Leave her alone," I said, really frightened now. I wondered what she might tell them. "Don't forget who she is. Even Vortigern won't dare to touch her. Besides, you've no authority. Either over me or her."

"You think not?"

"Well, what authority have you?"

"This." The short sword flashed in his hand. It was sharpened to a dazzle.

I said: "Vortigern's law, is it? Well, it's not a bad argument. I'll go with you, but it won't do you much good with my mother. Leave her alone, I tell you. She won't tell you any more than I."

"But at least we don't have to believe her when she says she doesn't know."

"But it's true." It was the steward, still chattering. "I tell you, I served in the palace all my life, and I remember it all. It used to be said she'd borne a child to the devil, to the prince of darkness."

Hands fluttered as people made the sign. The old man said, peering up at me: "Go with them, son, they'll not hurt Niniane's child, or her either. There'll come a time when the King will need the people of the West, as who should know better than he?"

"It seems I'll have to go with them, with the King's warrant so sharp at my throat," I said. "It's all right, Dinias, it wasn't your fault. Tell my servant where I am. Very well, you, take me to Vortigern, but keep your hands off me."

I went between them to the door, the drinkers making way for us. I saw Dinias stumble to his feet and come after. As we reached the street Blackbeard turned. "I was forgetting. Here, it's yours."

The purse of money jingled as it hit the ground at my cousin's feet.

I didn't turn. But as I went I saw, even without looking, the expression on my cousin's face as, with a quick glance to right and left, he stooped for the purse and tucked it into his waistband.

7

Vortigern had changed. My impression that he had grown smaller, less impressive, was not only because I myself, instead of being a child, was now a tall youth. He had grown, as it were, into himself. It did not need the makeshift hall, the court which was less a court than a gathering of fighting chiefs and such women as they kept by them, to indicate that this was a man on the run. Or rather, a man in a corner. But a cornered wolf is more dangerous than a free one, and Vortigern was still a wolf.

And he had certainly chosen his corner well. King's Fort was as I remembered it, a crag commanding the river valley, its crest only approachable along a narrow saddleback like a bridge. This promontory jutted out from a circle of rocky hills which provided in their shelter a natural corrie where horses could graze and where beasts could be driven in and guarded. All round the valley itself the mountains towered, grey with scree and still not green with spring. All the April rain had done was to bring a long cascade spilling a thousand feet from the summit to the valley's foot. A wild, dark, impressive place. If once the wolf dug himself in at the top of that crag, even Ambrosius would be hard put to it to get him out.

The journey took six days. We started at first light, by the road which leads due north out of Maridunum, a worse road than the eastbound way but quicker, even slowed down as we were by bad weather and the pace set by the women's litters. The bridge was broken at Pennal and more or less washed away, and nearly half a day was spent fording the Afon Dyfi, before the party could struggle on to Tomen-y-mur, where the road was good. On the afternoon of the sixth day we turned up the riverside track for Dinas Brenin, where the King lay.

Blackbeard had had no difficulty at all in persuading St. Peter's to let my mother go with him to the King. If he had used the same tactics as with me, this was understandable enough, but I had no opportunity to ask her, or even to find out if she knew any more than I did why Vortigern wanted us. A closed litter had been provided for her, and two women from the religious house travelled with her. Since they were beside her day and night it was impossible for me to approach her for private speech, and in fact she showed no sign of wanting to see me alone. Sometimes I caught her watching me with an anxious, even perhaps a puzzled look, but when she spoke she was calm and withdrawn, with never so much as a hint that she knew anything that Vortigern himself might not overhear. Since I was not allowed to see her alone, I had judged it better to tell her the same story I had told Blackbeard; even the same (since for all I knew he had been questioned) that I had told Dinias. She would have to think what she could about it, and about my reasons for not getting in touch with her sooner. It was, of course, impossible to mention Brittany, or even friends from Brittany, without risking her guess about Ambrosius, and this I dared not do.

I found her much changed. She was pale and quiet, and had put on weight, and with it a kind of heaviness of the spirit that she had not had before. It was only after a day or two, jogging north with the escort through the hills, that it suddenly came to me what this was; she had lost what she had had of power. Whether time had taken this, or illness, or whether she had abnegated it for the power of the Christian symbol that she wore on her breast, I had no means of guessing. But it had gone.

On one score my mind was set at rest straight away. My mother was treated with courtesy, even with distinction as befitted a king's daughter. I received no such distinction, but I was given a good horse, housed well at night, and my escort were civil enough when I tried to talk to them. Beyond that, they made very little effort with me; they would give no answer to any of my questions, though it seemed to me they knew perfectly well why the King wanted me. I caught curious and furtive glances thrown at me, and once or twice a look of pity.

We were taken straight to the King. He had set up his headquarters on the flat land between the crag and the river, from where he had hoped to oversee the building of his stronghold. It was a very different camp even from the makeshift ones of Uther and Ambrosius. Most of the men were in tents and, except for high earthworks and a palisade on the side towards the road, they apparently trusted to the natural defenses of the place—the river and crag on one side, the rock of Dinas Brenin on the other, and the impenetrable and empty mountains behind them.

Vortigern himself was housed royally enough. He received us in a hall whose wooden pillars were hung with curtains of bright embroidery, and whose floor of the local greenish slate was thickly strewn with fresh rushes. The high chair on the dais was regally carved and gilded. Beside him, on a chair equally ornate and only slightly smaller, sat Rowena, his Saxon Queen. The place was crowded. A few men in courtiers' dress stood near, but most of those present were armed. There was a fair sprinkling of Saxons. Behind Vortigern's chair on the dais stood a group of priests and holy men.

As we were brought in, a hush fell. All eyes turned our way. Then the King rose and, stepping down from the dais, came to meet my mother, smiling, and with both hands outstretched.

"I bid you welcome, Princess," he said, and turned to present her with ceremonial courtesy to the Queen.

The hiss of whispers ran round the hall, and glances were exchanged. The King had made it clear by his greeting that he did not hold my mother accountable for Camlach's part in the recent rebellion. He glanced at me, briefly but I thought with keen interest, gave me a nod of greeting, then took my mother's hand on his arm and led her up on to the dais. At a nod of his head, someone hurried to set a chair for her on the step below him. He bade her be seated, and he and the Queen took their places once more. Walking forward with my guards at my back, I stood below the dais in front of the King.

Vortigern spread his hands on the arms of his chair and sat upright, smiling from my mother to me with an air of welcome and even satisfaction. The buzz of whispers had died down. There was a hush. People were staring, expectant.

But all the King said was, to my mother: "I ask your pardon, Madam, for forcing this journey on you at such a time of year. I trust you were made comfortable enough?" He followed this up with smooth trivial courtesies while the people stared and waited, and my mother bent her head and murmured her polite replies, as upright and unconcerned as he. The two nuns who had accompanied her stood behind her, like waiting-women. She held one hand at her breast, fingering the little cross which she wore there as a talisman; the other lay among the brown folds on her lap. Even in her plain brown habit she looked royal.

Vortigern said, smiling: "And now will you present your son?"

"My son's name is Merlin. He left Maridunum five years ago after the death of my father, your kinsman. Since then he has been in Cornwall, in a house of religion. I commend him to you."

The King turned to me. "Five years? You would be little more than a child then, Merlin. How old are you now?"

"I am seventeen, sir." I met his gaze squarely. "Why have you sent for my mother and myself? I had hardly set foot in Maridunum again, when your men took me, by force."

"For that I am sorry. You must forgive their zeal. They only knew that the matter was urgent, and they took the quickest means to do what I wished." He turned back to my mother. "Do I have to assure you, Lady Niniane, that no harm will come to you? I swear it. I know that you have been in the House of St. Peter now for five years, and that your brother's alliance with my sons was no concern of yours."

"Nor of my son's, my lord," she said calmly. "Merlin left Maridunum on the night of my father's death, and from that day until now I have heard nothing from him. But one thing is certain, he had no part in the rebellion; why, he was only a child when he left his home—and indeed, now that I know he fled south that night, to Cornwall, I can only assume he went from very fear of my brother Camlach, who was no friend to him. I assure you, my lord King, that whatever I myself may have guessed of my brother's intentions towards you, my son knew nothing of them. I am at a loss to know why you should want him here."

To my surprise Vortigern did not even seem interested in my sojourn in Cornwall, nor did he look at me again. He rested his chin on his fist and watched my mother from under his brows. His voice and look were alike grave and courteous, but there was something in the air that I did not like. Suddenly I realized what it was. Even while my mother and the King talked, watching one another, the priests behind the King's chair watched me. And when I stole a glance out of the corners of my eyes at the people in the hall I found that here, too, there were eyes on me. There was a stillness in the room now, and I thought, suddenly: *Now he will come to it.*

He said quietly, almost reflectively: "You never married."

"No." Her lids drooped, and I knew she had become suddenly wary.

"Your son's father, then, died before you could be wed? Killed in battle, perhaps?"

"No, my lord." Her voice was quiet, but perfectly clear. I saw her hands move and tighten a little.

"Then he still lives?"

She said nothing, but bowed her head, so that her hood fell forward and hid her face from the other people in the hall. But those on the dais could still see her. I saw the Queen staring with curiosity and contempt. She had light blue eyes, and big breasts which bulged milk-white above a tight blue bodice. Her mouth was small. Her hands were as white as her breasts, but the fingers thick and ugly, like a servant's. They were covered with rings of gold and enamel and copper.

The King's brows drew together at my mother's silence, but his voice was still pleasant. "Tell me one thing, Lady Niniane. Did you ever tell your son the name of his father?"

"No." The tone of her voice, full and definite, contrasted oddly with the posture of bowed head and veiled face. It was the pose of a woman who is ashamed, and I wondered if she meant to look like this to excuse her silence. I could not see her face myself, but I saw the hand that held the fold of her long skirt. I was sharply reminded of the Niniane who had defied her father and refused Gorlan, King of Lanascol. Across that memory came another, the memory of my father's face, looking at me across the table in the lamplight. I banished it. He was so vividly in front of me that it seemed to me a wonder that the whole hall full of men could not see him. Then it came to me, sharply and with terror, that Vortigern had seen him. Vortigern knew. This was why we were here. He had heard some rumour of my coming, and was making sure. It remained to be seen whether I would be treated as a spy, or as a hostage.

I must have made some movement in spite of myself. My mother looked up, and I saw her eyes under the hood. She no longer looked like a princess; she looked like a woman who is afraid. I smiled at her, and something came back into her face, and I saw then that her fear was only for me.

I held myself still, and waited. Let him make the moves. Time enough to counter them when he had shown me the ground to fight from.

He twisted the big ring on his finger. "This is what your son told my messengers. And I have heard it said that no one else in the kingdom ever knew the name of his father. From what men tell me, Lady Niniane, and from what I know of you, your child would never be fathered by anyone base. Why not, then, tell him? It is a thing a man should know."

I said angrily, forgetting my caution: "What is it to you?"

My mother flashed me a look that silenced me. Then to Vortigern, "Why do you ask me these questions?"

"Lady," said the King, "I sent for you today, and for your son, to ask you one thing only. The name of his father."

"I repeat, why do you ask?"

He smiled. It was a mere baring of the teeth. I took a step. "Mother, he has no right to ask you this. He will not dare—"

"Silence him," said Vortigern.

The man beside me slapped a hand across my mouth, and held me fast. There was the hiss of metal as the other drew his sword and pressed it against my side. I stood still.

My mother cried out: "Let him go! If you hurt him, Vortigern, king or no king, I will never tell you, even if you kill me. Do you think I held the truth from my own father and my brother and even from my son for all these years, just to tell you for the asking?"

"You will tell me for your son's sake," said Vortigern. At his nod the fellow took his hand from my mouth, and stood back. But his hand was still on my arm, and I could feel the other's sword sharp through my tunic.

My mother had thrown back her hood now, and was sitting upright in her chair, her hands gripping the arms. Pale and shaken as she was, and dressed in the humble brown robe, she made the Queen look like a servant. The silence in the hall now was deathly. Behind the King's chair the priests stood staring. I held tightly to my thoughts. If these men were priests and magicians, then no thought of Ambrosius, not even his name, must come into my mind. I felt the sweat start on my body, and my thoughts tried to reach my mother and hold her, without forming an image which these men could see. But the power had gone, and there was no help here from the god; I did not even know if I was man enough for what might happen after she told them. I dared not speak again; I was afraid that if they used force against me she would speak to save me. And once they knew, once they started to question me . . .

Something must have reached her, because she turned and looked at me again, moving her shoulders under the rough robe as if she felt a hand touch her. As her eyes met mine I knew that this was nothing to do with power. She was trying, as women will, to tell me something with her eyes. It was a message of love and reassurance, but on a human level, and I could not understand it.

She turned back to Vortigern. "You choose a strange place for your questions, King. Do you really expect me to speak of these things here, in your open hall, and in the hearing of all comers?"

He brooded for a moment, his brows down over his eyes. There was sweat on his face, and I saw his hands twitch on the arms of the chair. The man was humming like a harp-string. The tension ran right through the hall, almost visibly. I felt my skin prickle, and a cold wolfspaw of fear walked up my spine. Behind the King one of the priests leaned forward and whispered. Then the King nodded. "The people shall leave us. But the priests and the magicians must remain."

Reluctantly, and with a buzz of chatter, people began to leave the hall. The priests stayed, a dozen or so men in long robes standing behind the chairs of the King and Queen. One of them, the one who had spoken to the King, a tall man who stood stroking his grey beard with a dirty ringed hand, was smiling. From his dress he was the head of them. I searched his face for signs of power, but, though the men were dressed in priests' robes, I could see nothing there but death. It was in all their eyes. More than that I could not see. The wolfspaw of cold touched my bones again. I stood in the soldier's grip without resistance.

"Loose him," said Vortigern. "I have no wish to harm the Lady Niniane's son. But you, Merlin, if you move or speak again before I give you leave, you will be taken from the hall."

The sword withdrew from my side, but the man still held it ready. The guards stood back half a pace from me. I neither moved nor spoke. I had never since I was a child felt so helpless, so naked of either knowledge or power, so stripped of God. I knew, with bitter failure, that if I were in the crystal cave with fires blazing and my master's eyes on me, I should see nothing. I remembered, suddenly, that Galapas was dead. Perhaps, I thought, the power had only come from him, and perhaps it had gone with him.

The King had turned his sunken eyes back to my mother. He leaned forward, his look suddenly fierce and intent.

"And now, Madam, will you answer my question?"

"Willingly," she said. "Why not?"

8

She had spoken so calmly that I saw the King's look of surprise. She put up a hand to push the hood back from her face, and met his eyes levelly.

"Why not? I see no harm in it. I might have told you sooner, my lord, if you had asked me differently, and in a different place. There is no harm now in men knowing. I am no longer in the world, and do not have to meet the eyes of the world, or hear their tongues. And since I know now that my son, too, has retired from the world, then I know how little he will care what the world says about him. So I will tell you what you want to know. And when I tell you, you will see why I have never spoken of this before, not even to my own father or to my son himself."

There was no sign of fear now. She was even smiling. She had not looked at me again. I tried to keep from staring at her, to school my face into blankness. I had no idea what she planned to say, but I knew that here would be no betrayal. She was playing some game of her own, and was secure in her own mind that this would avert whatever danger threatened me. I knew, for certain, that she would say nothing of Ambrosius. But still, everywhere in the hall, was death. Outside it had begun to rain, and the afternoon was wearing on towards twilight. A servant came in at the door bearing torches, but Vortigern waved him back. To do him justice, I believe he was thinking of my mother's shame, but I thought to myself: *There can be no help even there, no light, no fire* . . .

"Speak, then," said Vortigern. "Who fathered your son?"

"I never saw him." She spoke quite simply. "It was no man that I ever knew." She paused, then said, without looking at me, her eyes still level on the King: "My son will forgive me for what he is soon to hear, but you have forced me, and this he will understand."

Vortigern flashed me a look. I met it stonily. I was certain of her now.

She went on: "When I was only young, about sixteen, and thinking, as girls do, of love, it happened one Martinmas Eve, after I and my women had gone to bed. The girl who slept in my room was asleep, and the others were in the outer chamber, but I could not sleep. After a while I rose from my bed and went to the window. It was a clear night, with a moon. When I turned back to my bed-place I saw what I took to be a young man standing there, full in the middle of my bed-chamber. He was handsome, and young, dressed in a tunic and long mantle, with a short sword at his side. He wore rich jewels. My first thought was that he had broken in through the outer chamber while my women slept; my second was that I was in my shift, and barefoot, with my hair loose. I thought he meant mischief, and was opening my mouth to call out and wake the women, when the youth smiled at me, with a gesture as if to tell me to be quiet, he meant me no harm. Then he stepped aside into the shadow, and when I stole after, to look, there was no one there."

She paused. No one spoke. I remembered how she would tell me stories when I was a child. The hall was quite still, but I felt the man beside me quiver, as if he would have liked to move away. The Queen's red mouth hung open, half in wonder, half (I thought) in envy.

My mother looked at the wall above the King's head. "I thought it had been a dream, or a girl's fancy bred of moonlight. I went to bed and told no one. But he came again. Not always at night; not always when I was alone. So I realized it was no dream, but a familiar spirit who desired something from me. I prayed, but still he came. While I was sitting with my girls, spinning, or when I walked on dry days in my father's orchard, I would feel his touch on my arm, and his voice in my ear. But at these times I did not see him, and nobody heard him but I."

She groped for the cross on her breast and held it. The gesture looked so unforced and natural that I was surprised, until I saw that it was indeed natural, that she did not hold the cross for protection, but for forgiveness. I thought to myself, it is not the Christian God she should fear when she lies; she should be afraid of lying like this about the things of power. The King's eyes, bent on her, were fierce and, I thought, exultant. The priests were watching her as if they would eat her spirit alive.

"So all through that winter he came to me. And he came at night. I was never alone in my chamber, but he came through doors and windows and walls, and lay with me. I never saw him again, but heard his voice and felt his body. Then, in the summer, when I was heavy with child, he left me." She paused. "They will tell you how my father beat me and shut me up, and how when the child was born he would not give him a name fit for a Christian prince, but because he was born in September, named him for the sky-god, the wanderer, who has no house but the woven air. But I called him Merlin always, because on the day of his birth a wild falcon flew in through the window and perched above the bed, and looked at me with my lover's eyes."

Her glance crossed mine then, a brief flash. This, then, was true. And the Emrys, too, she had given me that in spite of them; she had kept that much of him for me after all.

She had looked away. "I think, my lord King, that what I have told you will not altogether surprise you. You must have heard the rumours that my son was not as ordinary boys—it is not possible always to be silent, and I know there have been whispers, but now I have told you the truth, openly; and so I pray you, my lord Vortigern, to let my son and me go back in peace to our respective houses of religion."

When she had finished there was silence. She bowed her head and pulled up her hood again to hide her face. I watched the King and the men behind him. I thought to see him angry, frowning with impatience, but to my surprise his brows smoothed out, and he smiled. He opened his mouth to answer my mother, but the Queen forestalled him. She leaned forward, licking her red lips, and spoke for the first time, to the priests.

"Maugan, is this possible?"

It was the tall man, the bearded high priest, who answered her. He spoke without hesitation, bland and surprisingly emphatic. "Madam, it is possible. Who has not heard of these creatures of air and darkness, who batten on mortal men and women? In my studies, and in many of the books I have read, I have found stories of children being born into the world in this fashion." He eyed me, fondling his beard, then turned to the King. "Indeed, my lord, we have the authority of the ancients themselves. They knew well that certain spirits, haunting the air at night between the moon and the earth, cohabit at their will with mortal women, in the shape of men. It is certainly possible that this royal lady—this virtuous royal lady—was the victim of such a creature. We know—and she has said herself—that this was rumoured for many years. I myself spoke with one of her waiting-women who said that the child could surely be begotten of none but the devil, and that no man had been near her. And of the son himself, when he was a child, I heard many strange things. Indeed, King Vortigern, this lady's story is true."

No one looked any longer at Niniane. Every eye in the place was on me. I could see in the King's face nothing that was not at once ferocious and innocent, a kind of eager satisfaction like a child's, or a wild beast's when it sees its prey loitering nearer. Puzzled, I held my tongue and waited. If the priests believed my mother, and Vortigern believed the priests, then I could not see where danger could come from. No faintest hint had turned men's thoughts towards Ambrosius. Maugan and the King seemed to hurry with eager satisfaction down the path that my mother had opened for them.

The King glanced at my guards. They had moved back from me, no doubt afraid to stand so near a demon's child. At his sign they closed in again. The man on my right still held his sword drawn, but down by his side and out of my mother's view. It was not quite steady. The man on my left surreptitiously loosened his own blade in its sheath. Both men were breathing heavily, and I could smell fear on them.

The priests were nodding sagely, and some of them, I noticed, held their hands in front of them in the sign to ward off enchantment. It seemed that they believed Maugan, they believed my mother, they saw me as the devil's child. All that had happened was that her story had confirmed their own belief, the old rumours. This, in fact, was what she had been brought here for. And now they watched me with satisfaction, but also with a kind of wary fear.

My own fear was leaving me. I thought I began to see what they wanted. Vortigern's superstition was legendary. I remembered what Dinias had told me about the stronghold that kept falling down, and the reports of the King's soothsayers that it was bewitched. It seemed possible that, because of the rumours of my birth, and possibly because of the childish powers I had shown before I left home, to which Maugan had referred, they thought I could advise or help them. If this was so, and they had brought me here because of my reputed powers, there might be some way in which I could help Ambrosius right from the enemy's camp. Perhaps after all the god had brought me here for this, perhaps he was still driving me. *Put yourself in his path* . . . Well, one could only use what was to hand. If I had no power to use, I had knowledge.

I cast my mind back to the day at King's Fort, and to the flooded mine in the core of the crag, to which the dream had led me. I would certainly be able to tell them why their foundations would not stand. It was an engineer's answer, not a magician's. But, I thought, meeting the oyster eyes of Maugan as he dry-washed those long dirty hands before him, if it was a magician's answer they wanted, they should have it. And Vortigern with them.

I lifted my head. I believe I was smiling. "King Vortigern!"

It was like dropping a stone into a pool, the room was so still, so centered on me. I said strongly: "My mother has told you what you asked her. No doubt you will tell me now in what way I can serve you, but first I must ask you to keep your royal promise and let her go."

"The Lady Niniane is our honoured guest." The King's reply seemed automatic. He glanced at the open arcade that faced the river, where the white lances of the rain hissed down across a dark grey sky. "You are both free to go whenever you choose, but this is no time to begin the long journey back to Maridunum. You will surely wish to lie the night here, Madam, and hope for a dry day tomorrow?" He rose, and the Queen with him. "Rooms have been prepared, and now the Queen will take you there to rest and make ready to sup with us. Our court here, and our rooms, are a poor makeshift, but such as they are, they are at your service. Tomorrow you will be escorted home."

My mother had stood when they did. "And my son? You still have not told us why you brought us here for this?"

"Your son can serve me. He has powers which I can use. Now, Madam, if you will go with the Queen, I will talk to your son and tell him what I want of him. Believe me, he is as free as you are. I constrained him only until you told me the truth I wished to hear. I must thank you now for confirming what I had guessed." He put out a hand. "I swear to you, Lady Niniane, by any god you like, that I do not hold his birth against him, now or ever."

She regarded him for a moment, then bowed her head and, ignoring his gesture, came down to me, holding out both her hands. I crossed to her and took them in my own. They felt small and cold. I was taller than she was. She looked up at me with the eyes that I remembered; there was anxiety in them, and the dregs of anger, and some message urgently spoken in silence.

"Merlin, I would not have had you know it this way. I would have spared you this." But this was not what her eyes were saying.

I smiled down at her, and said carefully: "Mother, you told me nothing today that shocked me. Indeed, there's nothing you could tell me about my birth that I do not already know. Set yourself at rest."

She caught her breath and her eyes widened, searching my face. I went on, slowly: "Whoever my father was, it will not be held against me. You heard what the King promised. That is all we need to know."

Whether she got this part of the message I could not guess. She was still taking in what I had said first. "You knew? You knew?"

"I knew. You surely don't imagine that in all the years I've been away from you, and with the kind of studies I've undertaken, I never found out what parentage I had? It's some years now since my father made himself known to me. I assure you, I've spoken with him, not once but many times. I find nothing in my birth of which I need to be ashamed."

For a moment longer she looked at me, then she nodded, and the lids drooped over her eyes. A faint colour had come up into her face. She had understood me.

She turned away, pulling her hood up again to hide her face, and put her hand on the King's arm. She went from the room, walking between him and the Queen, and her two women followed them. The priests remained, clucking and whispering and staring. I took no notice of them, but watched my mother go.

The King paused in the doorway, and I heard his voice bidding my mother goodbye. There was a crowd waiting in the outer porch. They made way for

Rowena and my mother, and the half-dozen women who were there followed them. I heard the swish of their dresses and the light voices of the women fade into the sound of the rain. Vortigern stood still in the doorway, watching them go. Outside the rain fell with a noise like a running river. It was darkening fast.

The King swung round on his heel and came back into the hall, with his fighting men behind him.

9

They crowded round me, muttering noisily, but holding back in a circle, like hounds before they close in for the kill. Death was back in the hall; I could feel it, but could not believe or understand it. I made a movement as if to follow my mother, and the swords of my guards lifted and quivered. I stood still.

I said sharply, to the King: "What's this? You gave your word. Are you so quickly forsworn?"

"Not forsworn. I gave my word that you should serve me, that I would never hold your birth against you. This is true. It is because of what I know about you, because you are the child of no man, that I have had you brought to me today. You will serve, Merlin, because of your birth."

"Well?"

He mounted the steps to the throne and sat down again. His movements were slow and deliberate. All the men of the court had crowded in with him, and with them the torch-bearers. The hall filled with smoky light and the rustle and creak of leather and the clank of mail. Outside the rain hissed down.

Vortigern leaned forward, chin on fist. "Merlin, we have learned today what in part we already suspected, that you are the child of no man, but of a devil. As such, you require mercy from no man. But because your mother is a king's daughter, and therefore something is due to you, I shall tell you why I brought you here. You know perhaps that I am building a stronghold here on the rock they call the Fortress?"

"Everyone knows it," I said, "and everyone knows that it will not stand, but falls down whenever it reaches man height."

He nodded. "And my magicians and wise men here, my advisers, have told me why. The foundations have not been properly laid."

"Well," I said, "that sounds remarkably like sense to me."

There was a tall old man to the King's right, beside the priests. His eyes were a bright angry blue under jutting white brows. He was watching me fixedly, and I thought I saw pity in his look. As I spoke, he put a hand up to his beard as if to hide a smile.

The King seemed not to have heard me. "They tell me," he said, "that a king's stronghold should be built on blood."

"They are talking, of course, in metaphors?" I said politely.

Maugan suddenly struck his staff on the floor of the dais. "They are talking literally!" he shouted. "The mortar should be slaked with blood! Blood should be sprinkled on the foundations. In ancient times no king built a fortress without observing this rite. The blood of a strong man, a warrior, kept the walls standing."

There was a sharp pause. My heart had begun to beat in slow, hard strokes that made the blood tingle in my limbs. I said, coldly: "And what has this to do with me? I am no warrior."

"You are no man, either," said the King harshly. "This is the magic, Merlin, that they have revealed to me, that I should seek out a lad who never had a father, and slake the foundations with his blood."

I stared at him, then looked round the ring of faces. There was shifting and muttering, and few eyes met mine, but I could see it in all their faces, the death I had smelled ever since I entered the hall. I turned back to the King.

"What rubbish is this? When I left Wales, it was a country for civilized men and for poets, for artists and for scholars, for warriors and kings who killed for their country, cleanly and in daylight. Now you talk of blood and human sacrifice. Do you think to throw modern Wales back to the rites of ancient Babylon and Crete?"

"I do not speak of 'human' sacrifice," said Vortigern. "You are the son of no man. Remember this."

In the stillness the rain lashed into the bubbling puddles on the ground outside. Someone cleared his throat. I caught the fierce blue glance of the old warrior. I had been right; there was pity there. But even those who pitied me were not going to raise a hand against this stupidity.

It had all come clear at last, like lightning breaking. This had been nothing to do with Ambrosius, or with my mother. She was safe enough, having merely confirmed what they wanted confirmed. She would even be honoured, since she had provided what they desired. And Ambrosius had never even entered their thoughts. I was not here as his son, his spy, his messenger; all they wanted was the "devil's child" to kill for their crude and dirty magic.

And, ironically enough, what they had got was no devil's child, not even the boy who once had thought to have power in his hands. All they had got was a human youth with no power beyond his human wits. But by the god, I thought, those might yet be enough . . . I had learned enough, power or no power, to fight them with their own weapons.

I managed to smile, looking beyond Maugan at the other priests. They were still making the sign against me, and even Maugan hugged his staff against his breast as if it had the power to protect him. "And what makes you so sure that my father the devil will not come to my aid?"

"Those are only words, King. There's no time to listen." Maugan spoke quickly and loudly, and the other priests pressed forward with him round the King's chair. They all spoke at once. "Yes, kill him now. There's no time to waste. Take him up to the crag and kill him now. You shall see that the gods will be appeased and the walls stand steady. His mother will not know, and even if she does, what can she do?"

There was a general movement, like hounds closing in. I tried to think, but I was empty even of coherent thought. The air stank and darkened. I could smell blood already, and the sword blades, held openly now against me, flashed in the torchlight. I fixed my eyes on the fireshot metal, and tried to empty my mind, but all I could see was the picked skeleton of Galapas, high on the hill in the sunlight, with the wings of the birds over him . . .

I said, to the swords: "Tell me one thing. Who killed Galapas?"

"What did he say? What did the devil's son say?" The question buzzed through the hall. A harsh voice said, loudly: "Let him speak." It was the old grey-bearded warrior.

"Who killed Galapas, the magician who lived on Bryn Myrddin above Maridunum?"

I had almost shouted it. My voice sounded strange, even to me. They fell silent, eyeing one another sideways, not understanding. Vortigern said: "The old man? They said he was a spy."

"He was a magician, and my master," I said. "And he taught me, Vortigern."

"What did he teach you?"

I smiled. "Enough. Enough to know that these men are fools and charlatans. Very well, Vortigern. Take me up to the crag and bring your knives with you, you and your soothsayers. Show me this fortress, these cracking walls, and see if I cannot tell you, better than they, why your fort will not stand. 'No man's child'!" I said it with contempt. "These are the things they conjure up, these foolish old men, when they can think of nothing else. Does it not occur to you, King, that the son of a spirit of darkness might have a magic that outstrips the spells of these old fools? If what they say is true, and if my blood will make these stones stand, then why did they watch them fall not once, not twice, but four times, before they could tell you what to do? Let me but see the place once, and I will tell you. By the God of gods, Vortigern, if my dead blood could make your fortress stand, how much better could my living body serve you?"

"Sorcery! Sorcery! Don't listen to him! What does a lad like him know of such matters?" Maugan began to shout, and the priests to cluck and chatter. But the old warrior said gruffly and sharply: "Let him try. There's no harm in that. Help you must have, Vortigern, be it from god or devil. Let him try, I say." And round the hall I heard the echoes from the fighting men, who would have no cause to love the priests: "Let him try."

Vortigern frowned in indecision, glancing from Maugan to the warriors, then at the grey arches where the rain fell. "Now?"

"Better now," they said. "There is not much time."

"No," I said clearly, "there is not much time." Silence again, all eyes on me. "The rain is heavy, Vortigern. What kind of king is it whose fortress is knocked down by a shower of rain? You will find your walls fallen yet again. This comes of building in the dark, with blind men for counsellors. Now take me to the top of your crag, and I will tell you why your walls have fallen. And if you listen to me instead of to these priests of darkness, I will tell you how to rebuild your stronghold in the light."

As I spoke, like the turning off of a tap, the downpour stopped. In the sudden quiet, men's mouths gaped. Even Maugan was dumb. Then like the pulling aside of a dark curtain, the sun came out.

I laughed. "You see? Come, King, take me to the top of the crag, and I will show you in sunlight why your walls fell down. But tell them to bring the torches. We shall need them."

10

Before we had fairly reached the foot of the crag I was proved right. The workmen could be seen crowded to the edge of the rock above, waiting for the King, and some of them had come down to meet him. Their foreman came panting up, a big man with rough sacking held gripped round his shoulders like a cloak, still sluicing with wet. He seemed hardly to have realized that the rain had stopped. He was pale, his eyes red-rimmed as if he had lacked sleep for nights. He stopped three paces away, eyeing the King nervously, and dashing the wet back of a hand across his face.

"Again?" said Vortigern briefly.

"Aye, my lord, and there's no one can say that it's a fault of ours, that I'll swear, any more than last time, or the times before. You saw yesterday how we were laying it this time. You saw how we cleared the whole site, to start again, and got right down to solid rock. And it is solid rock, my lord, I'll swear it. But still the wall cracks." He licked his lips, and his glance met mine and slid away from it, so that I knew he was aware of what the King and his soothsayers planned. "You're going up now, my lord?"

"Yes. Clear the men off the site."

The man swallowed, turned and ran up the twisting track. I heard him shouting. A mule was brought and the King mounted. My wrist was tied roughly to the harness. Magician or no, the sacrifice was to be given no chance of escape until he had proved himself. My guards kept close to my side. The King's officers and courtiers crowded round us, talking in low voices among themselves, but the priests held back, aloof and wary. I could see that they were not much afraid of the outcome; they knew as well as I did how much their magic was the power of their gods and how much illusion working on faith. They were confident that I could do no more than they; that even if I were one of their own kind they could find a way to defeat me. All I had to put against their smooth-worn rites was, they thought, the kind of bluff they were familiar with, and the luck that had stopped the rain and brought the sun out when I spoke.

The sun gleamed on the soaked grasses of the crag's crest. Here we were high above the valley where the river wound like a bright snake between its green verges. Steam rose from the roofs of the King's camp. Round the wooden hall and buildings the small skin tents clustered like toadstools, and men were no bigger than wood-lice crawling between them. It was a magnificent place, a true eagle's eyrie. The King halted his mule in a grove of wind-bitten oaks and pointed forward under the bare boughs.

"Yesterday you could have seen the western wall from here."

Beyond the grove was a narrow ridge, a natural hogsback or causeway, along which the workmen and their beasts had beaten a wide track. King's Fort was a craggy tower of rock, approached on one side by the causeway, and with its other three sides falling steeply away in dizzy slopes and cliffs. Its top was a plateau perhaps a hundred by a hundred paces, and would once have been rough grass with outcropping rock and a few stunted trees and bushes. Now it was a morass of churned mud round the wreck of the ill-wished tower. On three sides the walls of this had risen almost to shoulder height; on the fourth side the wall, newly split, sagged out in a chaos of piled stones, some fallen and half buried in mud, others still precariously mortared to outcrops of the living rock. Heavy poles of pine wood had been driven in here and there and canvas laid across to shelter the work from the rain. Some of the poles had fallen flat, some were obviously newly splintered by the recent crack. On those which were whole the canvas hung flapping, or had stretched and split with the wet. Everything was sodden, and pools stood everywhere.

The workmen had left the site and were crowded to one side of the plateau, near the causeway. They were silent, with fear in their faces. I could see that the fear was not of the King's anger at what had happened to the work, but of the force which they believed in and did not understand. There were guards at the entrance to the causeway. I knew that without them not one workman would have been left on the site.

The guards had crossed their spears, but when they recognized the King they drew them back. I looked up. "Vortigern, I cannot escape from you here unless I leap off the crag, and that would sprinkle my blood just where Maugan wants it. But neither can I see what is wrong with your foundations unless you loose me."

He jerked his head, and one of my guards freed me. I walked forward. The mule followed, stepping delicately through the thick mud. The others came after. Maugan had pressed forward and was speaking urgently to the King. I caught words here and there: "Trickery . . . escape . . . now or never . . . blood . . ."

The King halted, and the crowd with him. Someone said, "Here, boy," and I looked round to see the greybeard holding out a staff. I shook my head, then turned my back on them and walked forward alone.

Water stood everywhere, glinting in soggy pools between the tussocks, or on the curled fingers of young bracken thrusting through the pallid grass of winter. The grey rock glittered with it. As I walked slowly forward I had to narrow my eyes against the wet dazzle to see at all.

It was the western wall that had fallen. This had been built very near the edge of the crag, and though most of the collapse had been inwards, there was a pile of fallen stuff lying right out to the cliff's edge, where a new landslip showed raw and slimy with clay. There was a space in the north wall where an entrance was to be built; I picked my way through this between the piles of rubble and workmen's gear, and into the center of the tower.

Here the floor was a thick mess of churned mud, with standing puddles struck to blinding copper by the sun. This was setting now, in the last blaze of light before dusk, and glared full in my eyes as I examined the collapsed wall, the cracks, the angle of fall, the tell-tale lie of the outcrops.

All the time I was conscious of the stir and mutter of the crowd. From time to time the sun flashed on bared weapons. Maugan's voice, high and harsh, battered at the King's silence. Soon, if I did nothing and said nothing, the crowd would listen to him.

From where he sat his mule the King could see me through the gap of the north entrance, but most of the crowd could not. I climbed—or rather, mounted, such was my dignity—the fallen blocks of the west wall, till I stood clear of the building that remained, and they could all see me. This was not only to impress the King. I had to see, from this vantage point, the wooded slopes below through which we had just climbed, trying, now that I was clear of the crowd and the jostling, to recognize the way I had taken up to the adit, all those years ago.

The voices of the crowd, growing impatient, broke in on me, and I slowly lifted both arms towards the sun in a kind of ritual gesture, such as I had seen priests use in summoning spirits. If I at least made some show as a magician it might keep them at bay, the priests in doubt and the King in hope, till I had had time to remember. I could not afford to cast falteringly through the wood like a questing dog; I had to lead them straight and fast, as the merlin had once led me.

And my luck held. As I raised my arms the sun went in and stayed in, and the dusk began to thicken.

Moreover, with the dazzle out of my eyes, I could see. I looked back along the side of the causeway to the curve of the hill where I had climbed, all those years ago, to get away from the crowd round the two kings. The slopes were thickly wooded, more thickly than I remembered. Already, in the shelter of the corrie, some early leaves were out, and the woods were dark with thorn and holly. I could not recognize the way I had gone through the winter woods. I stared into the thickening dusk, casting back in memory to the child who had gone scrambling there . . .

We had ridden in from the open valley, along that stream, under the thick trees, over that low ridge and into the corrie. The kings, with Camlach and Dinias and the rest, had sat on that southern slope, below the knot of oaks. The cooking fires had been there, the horses there. It had been noon, and as I walked away—that way—I had trodden on my shadow. I had sat down to eat in the shelter of a rock . . .

I had it now. A grey rock, cleft by a young oak. And on the other side of the rock the kings had gone by, walking up towards King's Fort. A grey rock, cleft by a young oak beside the path. And straight from it, up through the steep wood, the flight-path of the merlin.

I lowered my arms, and turned. Twilight had fallen quickly in the wake of the grey clouds. Below me the wooded slopes swam thick with dusk. Behind Vortigern the mass of cloud was edged sharply with yellow, and a single shaft of misty light fell steeply on the distant black hills. The men were in dark silhouette, their cloaks whipping in the wet breeze. The torches streamed.

Slowly I descended from my viewpoint. When I reached the center of the tower floor I paused, full in the King's view, and stretched my hands out, palms down, as if I were feeling like a diviner for what lay below the earth. I heard the mutter go round, and the harsh sound of contempt from Maugan. Then I dropped my hands and approached them.

"Well?" The King's voice was hard and dry with challenge. He fidgeted in the saddle.

I ignored him, walking on past the mule and heading straight for the thickest part of the crowd as if it was not there. I kept my hands still by my sides, and my eyes on the ground; I saw their feet hesitate, shuffle, move aside as the crowd parted to let me through. I walked back across the causeway, trying to move smoothly and with dignity over the broken and sodden ground. The guards made no attempt to stop me. When I passed one of the torch-bearers I lifted a hand, and he fell in beside me without a word.

The track that the workmen and their beasts had beaten out of the hillside was a new one, but, as I had hoped, it followed the old deer-trod which the kings had taken. Halfway down, unmistakable, I found the rock. Young ferns were springing in the crevice among the roots of the oak, and the tree showed buds already breaking among last year's oak-galls. Without a moment's hesitation I turned off the track, and headed into the steep tangle of the woods.

It was far more thickly overgrown than I remembered, and certainly nobody had been this way in a long time, probably not since Cerdic and I had pushed our way through. But I remembered the way as clearly as if it had still been noon of that winter's day. I went fast, and even where the bushes grew more than shoulder height I tried to go smoothly, unregarding, wading through them as if they were a sea. Next day I paid for my wizard's dignity with cuts and scratches and ruined clothes, but I have no doubt that at the time it was impressive. I remember when my cloak caught and dragged on something how the torch-bearer jumped forward like a slave to loosen and hold it for me.

Here was the thicket, right up against the side of the dell. More rock had fallen from the slope above, piling between the stems of the thorn-trees like froth among the reeds of a backwater. Over it the bushes crowded, bare elderberry, honeysuckle like trails of hair, brambles sharp and whippy, ivy glinting in the torchlight. I stopped.

The mule slipped and clattered to a halt at my shoulder. The King's voice said: "What's this? What's this? Where are you taking us? I tell you, Merlin, your time is running out. If you have nothing to show us—"

"I have plenty to show you." I raised my voice so that all of them, pushing behind him, could hear me. "I will show you, King Vortigern, or any man who has courage enough to follow me, the magic beast that lies beneath your stronghold and eats at your foundations. Give me the torch."

The man handed it to me. Without even turning my head to see who followed, I plunged into the darkness of the thicket and pulled the bushes aside from the mouth of the adit.

It was still open, safely shored and square, with the dry shaft leading level into the heart of the hill.

I had to bend my head now to get in under the lintel. I stooped and entered, with the torch held out in front of me.

I had remembered the cave as being huge, and had been prepared to find that this, like other childhood memories, was false. But it was bigger even than I remembered. Its dark emptiness was doubled in the great mirror of water that had spread till it covered all the floor save for a dry crescent of rock six paces deep, just inside the mouth of the adit. Into this great, still lake the jutting ribs of the cave walls ran like buttresses to meet the angle of their own reflections, then on down again into darkness. Somewhere deeper in the hill was the sound of water falling, but here nothing stirred the burnished surface. Where, before, trickles had run and dripped like leaking faucets, now every wall was curtained with a thin shining veil of damp which slid down imperceptibly to swell the pool.

I advanced to the edge, holding the torch high. The small light of the flame pushed the darkness back, a palpable darkness, deeper even than those dark nights where the black is thick as a wild beast's pelt, and presses on you like a stifling blanket. A thousand facets of light glittered and flashed as the flames caught the sliding water. The air was still and cold and echoing with sounds like birdsong in a deep wood.

I could hear them scrambling along the adit after me. I thought quickly.

I could tell them the truth, coldly. I could take the torch and clamber up into the dark workings and point out faults which were giving way under the weight of the building work above. But I doubted if they would listen. Besides, as they kept saying, there was no time. The enemy was at the gates, and what Vortigern needed now was not logic and an engineer; he wanted magic, and something—anything—that promised quick safety, and kept his followers loyal. He himself might believe the voice of reason, but he could not afford to listen to it. My guess was that he would kill me first, and attempt to shore up the workings afterwards, probably with me in them. He would lose his workmen else.

The men came pouring in at the dark mouth of the adit like bees through a hive door. More torches blazed, and the dark slunk back. The floor filled with coloured cloaks and the glint of weapons and the flash of jewels. Eyes showed liquid as they looked around them in awe. Their breath steamed on the cold air. There was a rustle and mutter as of folk in a holy place, but no one spoke aloud.

I lifted a hand to beckon the King, and he came forward and stood with me at the edge of the pool. I pointed downwards. Below the surface something—a rock, perhaps—glimmered faintly, shaped like a dragon. I began to speak slowly, as it were testing the air between us. My words fell clear and leaden, like drops of water on rock.

"This is the magic, King Vortigern, that lies beneath your tower. This is why your walls cracked as fast as they could build them. Which of your soothsayers could have showed you what I show you now?"

His two torch-bearers had moved forward with him; the others still hung back. Light grew, wavering from the walls, as they advanced. The streams of sliding water caught the light and flowed down to meet their reflections, so that fire seemed to rise through the pool like bubbles in sparkling wine to burst at the surface. Everywhere, as the torches moved, water glittered and sparked, jets and splashes of light breaking and leaping and coalescing across the still surface till the lake was liquid fire, and down the walls the lightfalls ran and glittered like crystals; like the crystal cave come alive and moving and turning round me; like the starred globe of midnight whirling and flashing.

I took my breath in painfully, and spoke again. "If you could drain this pool, King Vortigern, to find what lay beneath it—"

I stopped. The light had changed. Nobody had moved, and the air was still, but the torchlight wavered as men's hands shook. I could no longer see the King: the flames ran between us. Shadows fled across the streams and staircases of fire, and the cave was full of eyes and wings and hammering hoofs and the scarlet rush of a great dragon stooping on his prey . . .

A voice was shouting, high and monotonous, gasping. I could not get my breath. Pain broke through me, spreading from groin and belly like blood bursting from a wound. I could see nothing. I felt my hands knotting and stretching. My head hurt, and the rock was hard and streaming wet under my cheek-bone. I had fainted, and they had seized me as I lay and were killing me: this was my blood seeping from me to spread into the pool and shore up the foundations of their rotten tower. I choked on breath like bile. My hands tore in pain at the rock, and my eyes were open, but all I could see was the whirl of banners and wings and wolves' eyes and sick mouths gaping, and the tail of a comet like a brand, and stars shooting through a rain of blood.

Pain went through me again, a hot knife into the bowels. I screamed, and suddenly my hands were free. I threw them up between me and the flashing visions and I heard my own voice calling, but could not tell what I called. In front of me the visions whirled, fractured, broke open in intolerable light, then shut again into darkness and silence.

11

I woke in a room splendidly lined with embroidered hangings, where sunlight spilled through the window to lay bright oblongs on a boarded floor.

I moved cautiously, testing my limbs. I had not been hurt. There was not even a trace of headache. I was naked, softly and warmly bedded in furs, and my limbs moved without a hint of stiffness. I blinked wonderingly at the window, then turned my head to see Cadal standing beside the bed, relief spreading over his face like light after cloud.

"And about time," he said.

"Cadal! Mithras, but it's good to see you! What's happened? Where is this?"

"Vortigern's best guest chamber, that's where it is. You fixed him, young Merlin, you fixed him proper."

"Did I? I don't remember. I got the impression that they were fixing me. Do you mean they're not still planning to kill me?"

"Kill you? Stick you in a sacred cave, more like, and sacrifice virgins to you. Pity it'd be such a waste. I could use a bit of that myself."

"I'll hand them over to you. Oh, Cadal, but it is good to see you! How did you get here?"

"I'd just got back to the nunnery gate when they came for your mother. I heard them asking for her, and saying they'd got you, and were taking the pair of you off to Vortigern at cocklight next day. I spent half the night finding Marric, and the other half trying to get a decent horse—and I might as well have saved myself the pains, I had to settle for that screw you bought. Even the pace you went, I was near a day behind you by the time you'd got to Pennal. Not that I wanted to catch up till I saw which way the land lay . . . Well, never mind, I got here in the end—at dusk yesterday—and found the place buzzing like a hive that's been trodden on." He gave a short bark of a laugh. "It was 'Merlin this', and 'Merlin that' . . . they call you 'the King's prophet' already! When I said I was your servant, they couldn't shove me in here fast enough. Seems there isn't exactly a rush to look after sorcerers of your class. Can you eat something?"

"No—yes. Yes, I can. I'm hungry." I pushed myself up against the pillows. "Wait a minute, you say you got here *yesterday?* How long have I slept?"

"The night and the day. It's wearing on for sunset."

"The night and the day? Then it's—Cadal, what's happened to my mother? Do you know?"

"She's gone, safe away home. Don't fret yourself about her. Get your food now, while I tell you. Here."

He brought a tray on which was a bowl of steaming broth, and a dish of meat with bread and cheese and dried apricots. I could not touch the meat, but ate the rest while he talked.

"She doesn't know a thing about what they tried to do, or what happened.

When she asked about you last night they told her you were here, 'royally housed, and high in the King's favour.' They told her you'd spat in the priests' eyes, in a manner of speaking, and prophesied fit to beat Solomon, and were sleeping it off, comfortable. She came to take a look at you this morning to make sure, and saw you sleeping like a baby, then she went off. I didn't get a chance to speak to her, but I saw her go. She was royally escorted, I can tell you; she'd half a troop of horse with her, and her women had litters nearly as grand as herself."

"You say I 'prophesied'? 'Spat in the priests' eyes'?" I put a hand to my head. "I wish I could remember . . . We were in the cave under King's Fort—they've told you about that, I suppose?" I stared at him. "What happened, Cadal?"

"You mean to tell me you don't remember?"

I shook my head. "All I know is, they were going to kill me to stop their rotten tower from falling down, and I put up a bluff. I thought if I could discredit their priests I might save my own skin, but all I ever hoped to do was to make a bit of time so that maybe I could get away."

"Aye, I heard what they were going to do. Some people are dead ignorant, you'd wonder at it." But he was watching me with the look that I remembered. "It was a funny kind of bluff, wasn't it? How did you know where to find the tunnel?"

"Oh, that. That was easy. I've been in these parts before, as a boy. I came to this very place once, years ago, with Cerdic who was my servant then, and I was following a falcon through the wood when I found that old tunnel."

"I see. Some people might call that luck—if they didn't know you, that is. I suppose you'd been right in?"

"Yes. When I first heard about the west wall cracking above, I thought it must be something to do with the old mine workings." I told him then, quickly, all that I could remember of what had happened in the cave. "The lights," I said, "the water glittering . . . the shouting . . . It wasn't like the 'seeings' I've had before—the white bull and the other things that I've sometimes seen. This was different. For one thing, it hurt far more. That must be what death is like. I suppose I did faint in the end. I don't remember being brought here at all."

"I don't know about that. When I got in to see you, you was just asleep, very deep, but quite ordinary, it seemed to me. I make no bones about it, I took a good look at you, to see if they'd hurt you, but I couldn't find any sign of it, bar a lot of scratches and grazes they said you'd got in the woods. Your clothes looked like it, too, I can tell you . . . But from the way you were housed here, and the way they spoke of you, I didn't think they'd dare raise a finger to you—not now. Whatever it was, a faint, or a fit or a trance, more like, you've put the wind up them proper, that you have."

"Yes, but how, exactly? Did they tell you?"

"Oh aye, they told me, the ones that could speak of it. Berric—he's the one that gave you the torch—he told me. He told me they'd all been set to cut your throat, those dirty old priests, and it seems if the King hadn't been at his wits' end, and impressed by your mother and the way the pair of you didn't seem frightened of them, he never would have waited. Oh, I heard all about it, don't worry. Berric said he'd not have given two pennies for your life back there in the hall when your mother told her story." He shot me a look. "All that rigmarole about the devil in the dark. Letting you in for this. What possessed her?"

"She thought it would help. I suppose she thought that the King had found out who my father was, and had had us dragged here to see if we had news of his plans. That's what I thought myself." I spoke thoughtfully. "And there was something else . . . When a place is full of superstition and fear, you get to feel it. I tell you, it was breathing goose-pimples all over me. She must have felt it, too. You might almost say she took the same line as I did, trying to face magic with magic. So she told the old tale about my being got by an incubus, with a few extra flourishes to carry it across." I grinned at him. "She did it well. I could have believed it myself if I hadn't known otherwise. But never mind, go on. I want to know what happened in the cavern. Do you mean I talked some kind of sense?"

"Well now, I didn't mean that, exactly. Couldn't make head or tail of what Berric told me. He swore he had it nearly word for word—it seems he has ambitions to be a singer or something . . . Well, what he said, you just stood there staring at the water running down the walls and then you started to talk, quite ordinary to start with, to the King, as if you was explaining how the shaft had been driven into the hill and the veins mined, but then the old priest—Maugan, isn't it?—started to shout 'This is fools' talk,' or something, when suddenly you lets out a yell that fair froze the balls on them—Berric's expression, not mine, he's not used to gentlemen's service—and your eyes turned up white and you put your hands up as if you was pulling the stars out of their sockets—Berric again, he ought to be a poet—and started to prophesy."

"Yes?"

"That's what they all say. All wrapped up, it was, with eagles and wolves and lions and boars and as many other beasts as they've ever had in the arena and a few more besides, dragons and such—and going hundreds of years forward, which is safe enough, Dia knows, but Berric said it sounded, the lot of it, as true as a trumpet, and as if you'd have given odds on it with your last penny."

"I may have to," I said dryly, "if I said anything about Vortigern or my father."

"Which you did," said Cadal.

"Well, I'd better know; I'm going to have to stick by it."

"It was all dressed up, like poets' stuff, red dragons and white dragons fighting and laying the place waste, showers of blood, all that kind of thing. But it seems you gave them chapter and verse for everything that's going to happen; the white dragon of the Saxons and the red dragon of Ambrosius fighting it out, the red dragon looking not so clever to begin with, but winning in the end. Yes. Then a bear coming out of Cornwall to sweep the field clear."

"A bear? You mean the Boar, surely; that's Cornwall's badge. Hm. Then he may be still for my father after all . . ."

"Berric said a bear. *Artos* was the word . . . he took notice, because he wondered about it himself. But you were clear about it, he says. Artos, you called him, Arthur . . . some name like that. You mean to tell me you don't remember a word of it?"

"Not a word."

"Well look, now, I can't remember any more, but if they start coming at you about it, you could find some way of getting them to tell you everything you said. It's quite the thing, isn't it, for prophets not to know what they were talking about? Oracles and that?"

"I believe so."

"All I mean is, if you've finished eating, and if you really feel all right, perhaps you'd better get up and dress. They're waiting for you out there."

"What for? For the god's sake, they don't want more advice? Are they moving the site of the tower?"

"No. They're doing what you told them to do."

"What's that?"

"Draining the pool by a conduit. They've been working all night and day getting pumps rigged up to get the water out through the adit."

"But why? That won't make the tower any safer. In fact it might bring the whole top of the crag in. Yes, I'm finished, take it away." I pushed the tray into his hands, and threw back the bed-covers. "Cadal, are you trying to tell me I said this in my—delirium?"

"Aye. You told them to drain the pool, and at the bottom they'd find the beasts that were bringing the King's fort down. Dragons, you said, red and white."

I sat on the edge of the bed, my head in my hands. "I remember something now . . . something I saw. Yes, that must be it . . . I did see something under the water, probably just a rock, dragon-shaped . . . And I remember starting to say something to the King about draining the pool . . . But I didn't tell them to drain it, I was saying 'Even if you drained the pool, it wouldn't help you.' At least, that's what I started to say." I dropped my hands and looked up. "You mean they're actually draining the place, thinking some water-beast is there underneath, rocking the foundations?"

"That's what you told them, Berric says."

"Berric's a poet, he's dressing it up."

"Maybe. But they're out there at it now, and the pumps have been working full blast for hours. The King's there, waiting for you."

I sat silent. He threw me a doubtful look, then took the tray out, and came back with towels and a silver basin of steaming water. While I washed he busied himself over a chest at the far side of the room, lifting clothes from it and shaking out the folds, while he talked over his shoulder. "You don't look worried. If they do drain that pool to the bottom, and there's nothing there—"

"There will be something there. Don't ask me what, I don't know, but if I said so . . . It's true, you know. The things I see this way are true. I have the Sight."

His brows shot up. "You think you're telling me news? Haven't you scared the toe-nails off me a score of times with what you say and the things you see that no one else can see?"

"You used to be scared of me, didn't you, Cadal?"

"In a way. But I'm not scared now, and I've no intention of being scared. Someone's got to look after the devil himself, as long as he wears clothes and needs food and drink. Now if you're done, young master, we'll see if these things fit you that the King sent for you."

"The King sent them?"

"Aye. Looks like the sort of stuff they think a magician ought to wear."

I went over to look. "*Not* long white robes with stars and moons on them, and a staff with curled snakes? Oh, really, Cadal—"

"Well, your own stuff's ruined, you've got to wear something. Come on, you'll look kind of fancy in these, and it seems to me you ought to try and impress them, the spot you're in."

I laughed. "You may be right. Let me see them. Hm, no, not the white, I'm not competing with Maugan's coven. Something dark, I think, and the black cloak. Yes, that'll do. And I'll wear the dragon brooch."

"I hope you do right to be so sure of yourself." Then he hesitated. "Look, I know it's all wine and worship now, but maybe we ought to make a break for it straight away, not wait to see which way the dice fall? I could steal a couple of horses—"

" 'Make a break for it'? Am I still a prisoner, then?"

"There's guards all round. Looking after you this time, not holding on to you, but by the dog, it comes to the same thing." He glanced at the window. "It'll be dusk before long. Look, I could spin some tale out there to keep them quiet, and maybe you could pretend to go to sleep again till dark—"

"No. I must stay. If I can get Vortigern to listen to me . . . Let me think, Cadal. You saw Marric the night we were taken. That means the news is on its way to my father, and if I'm any judge, he will move straight away. So far, lucky; the sooner the better; if he can catch Vortigern here in the West before he gets a chance to join again with Hengist . . ." I thought for a moment. "Now, the ship was due to sail three—no, four days ago—"

"It sailed before you left Maridunum," he said briefly.

"What?"

He smiled at my expression. "Well, what did you expect? The Count's own son and his lady hauled off like that—nobody knew for sure why, but there were stories going about, and even Marric saw the sense in getting straight back to Ambrosius with *that* tale. The ship sailed with the tide the same dawn; she'd be out of the estuary before you'd hardly ridden out of town."

I stood very still. I remember that he busied himself around me, draping the black cloak, surreptitiously pulling a fold to cover the dragon brooch that pinned it.

Then I drew a long breath. "That's all I needed to know. Now I know what to do. 'The King's prophet,' did you say? They speak truer than they know. What the King's prophet must do now is to take the heart out of these Saxon-loving vermin, and drive Vortigern out of this tight corner of Wales into some place where Ambrosius can smoke him out quickly and destroy him."

"You think you can do this?"

"I know I can."

"Then I hope you know how to get us both out of here before they find out whose side you're on!"

"Why not? As soon as I know where Vortigern is bound for, we'll take the news to my father ourselves." I settled the cloak to my shoulders, and grinned at him. "So steal those horses, Cadal, and have them waiting down by the stream. There's a fallen tree across the water; you can't miss the place; wait there where there's cover. I'll come. But first I must go and help Vortigern uncover the dragons."

I made for the door, but he got there ahead of me, and paused with his hand on the latch. His eyes were scared. "You really mean leave you on your own in the middle of that wolf-pack?"

"I'm not on my own. Remember that; and if you can't trust me, trust what is in me. I have learned to. I've learned that the god comes when he will, and how he will, rending your flesh to get into you, and when he has done, tearing himself free as violently as he came. Afterwards—now—one feels light and hollow and like an angel flying . . . No, they can do nothing to me, Cadal. Don't be afraid. I have the power."

"They killed Galapas."

"Some day they may kill me," I said. "But not today. Open the door."

12

They were all gathered at the foot of the crag where the workmen's track met the marshy level of the corrie. I was still guarded, but this time—at least in appearance—it was a guard of honour. Four uniformed men, with their swords safely sheathed, escorted me to the King.

They had laid duckboards down on the marshy ground to make a platform, and set a chair for the King. Someone had rigged a windbreak of woven saplings and brushwood on three sides, roofed it, and draped the lot with worked rugs and dyed skins. Vortigern sat there, chin on fist, silent. There was no sign of his Queen, or indeed of any of the women. The priests stood near him, but they kept back and did not speak. His captains flanked his chair.

The sun was setting behind the improvised pavilion in a splash of scarlet. It must have rained again that day; the grass was sodden, every blade heavy with drops. The familiar slate-grey clouds furled and unfurled slowly across the sunset. As I was led forward, they were lighting the torches. These looked small and dull against the sunset, more smoke than flame, dragged and flattened by the gusty breeze.

I waited at the foot of the platform. The King's eyes looked me up and down, but he said nothing. He was still reserving judgement. And why not, I thought. The kind of thing I seemed to have produced must be fairly familiar to him. Now he waited for proof of at least some part of my prophecy. If it was not forthcoming, this was still the time and the place to spill my blood. I wondered how the wind blew from Less Britain. The stream was a full three hundred paces off, dark under its oaks and willows.

Vortigern signed to me to take my place on the platform beside him, and I mounted it to stand at his right, on the opposite side from the priests. One or two of the officers moved aside from me; their faces were wooden, and they did not look at me, but I saw the crossed fingers, and thought: Dragon or no dragon, I can manage these. Then I felt eyes on me, and looked round. It was the greybeard. He was gazing fixedly at the brooch on my shoulder where my cloak had blown back from it. As I turned, his eyes lifted to mine. I saw his widen, then his hand crept to his side, not to make the sign, but to loosen his sword in its scabbard. I looked away. No one spoke.

It was an uncomfortable vigil. As the sun sank lower the chilly spring wind freshened, fretting at the hangings. Where puddles lay in the reedy ground the water rippled and splashed under the wind. Cold draughts knifed up between the duckboards. I could hear a curlew whistling somewhere up in the darkening sky, then it slanted down, bubbling like a waterfall, into silence. Above us the King's banner fluttered and snapped in the wind. The shadow of the pavilion lengthened on the soaked field.

From where we waited, the only sign of activity was some coming and going in the trees. The last rays of the sun, level and red, shone full on the west face of King's Fort, lighting up the head of the crag crowned with the wrecked wall. No workmen were visible there; they must all be in the cave and the adit. Relays of boys ran across and back with reports of progress. The pumps were working well and gaining on the water; the level had sunk two spans in the last half hour . . . If my lord King would have patience, the pumps had jammed, but the engineers were working on them and meanwhile the men had rigged a windlass and were passing buckets . . . All was well again, the pumps were going now and the level was dropping sharply . . . You could see the bottom, they thought . . .

It was two full hours of chill, numb waiting, and it was almost dark, before lights came down the track and with them the crowd of workmen. They came fast but deliberately, not like frightened men, and even before they came close enough to be clearly seen, I knew what they had found. Their leaders halted a yard from the platform, and as the others came crowding up I felt my guards move closer.

There were soldiers with the workmen. Their captain stepped forward, saluting.

"The pool is empty?" asked Vortigern.

"Yes, sir."

"And what lies beneath?"

The officer paused. He should have been a bard. He need not have paused to gather eyes: they were all on him already.

A gust of wind, sudden and stronger than before, tore his cloak to one side with a crack like a whip, and rocked the frame of the pavilion. A bird fled overhead, tumbling along the wind. Not a merlin: not tonight. Only a rook, scudding late home.

"There is nothing beneath the pool, sir." His voice was neutral, carefully official, but I heard a mutter go through the crowd like another surge of wind. Maugan was craning forward, his eyes bright as a vulture's, but I could see he did not dare to speak until he saw which way the King's mind was bending. Vortigern leaned forward.

"You are certain of this? You drained it to the bottom?"

"Indeed, sir." He signed to the men beside him, and three or four of them stepped forward to tip a clutter of objects in front of the platform. A broken mattock, eaten with rust, some flint axe-heads older than any Roman working, a belt buckle, a knife with its blade eaten to nothing, a short length of chain, a metal whip-stock, some other objects impossible to identify, and a few shards of cooking pots.

The officer showed a hand, palm up. "When I said 'nothing,' sir, I meant only what you might expect. These. And we got as near to the bottom as made no difference; you could see down to the rock and the mud, but we dredged the last bucket up, for good measure. The foreman will bear me out."

The foreman stepped forward then, and I saw he had a full bucket in his hand, the water slopping over the brim.

"Sir, it's true, there's naught there. You could see for yourself if you came up, sir, right to the bottom. But better not try it, the tunnel's awash with mud now, and not fit. But I brought the last pailful out, for you to see yourself."

With the word, he tipped the full bucket out, deluging the already sodden ground, and the water sloshed down to fill the puddle round the base of the royal standard. With the mud that had lain in the bottom came a few broken fragments of stone, and a silver coin.

The King turned then to look at me. It must be a measure of what had happened in the cavern yesterday that the priests still kept silent, and the King was clearly waiting, not for an excuse, but an explanation.

God knows I had had plenty of time to think, all through that long, cold silent vigil, but I knew that thinking would not help me. If he was with me, he would come now. I looked down at the puddles where the last red light of sunset lay like blood. I looked up across the crag where stars could be seen already stabbing bright in the clear east. Another gust of wind was coming; I could hear it tearing the tops of the oaks where Cadal would be waiting.

"Well?" said Vortigern.

I took a step forward to the edge of the platform. I felt empty still, but somehow I would have to speak. As I moved, the gust struck the pavilion, sharp as a blow. There came a crack, a flurry of sound like hounds worrying a deer, and a cry from someone, bitten short. Above our heads the King's banner whipped streaming out, then, caught in its ropes, bellied like a sail holding the full weight of the wind. The shaft, jerked sharply to and fro in soft ground loosened further by the thrown bucketful of water, tore suddenly free of the grabbing hands, to whirl over and down. It slapped flat on the sodden field at the King's feet.

The wind fled past, and in its wake was a lull. The banner lay flat, held heavy with water. The white dragon on a green field. As we watched, it sagged slowly into a pool, and the water washed over it. Some last faint ray from the sunset bloodied the water. Someone said fearfully, "An omen," and another voice, loudly, "Great Thor, the Dragon is down!" Others began to shout. The standard-bearer, his face ashen, was already stooping, but I jumped off the platform in front of them all and threw up my arms.

"Can any doubt the god has spoken? Look up from the ground, and see where he speaks again!"

Across the dark east, burning white hot with a trail like a young comet, went a shooting star, the star men call the firedrake or dragon of fire.

"There it runs!" I shouted. "There it runs! The Red Dragon of the West! I tell you, King Vortigern, waste no more time here with these ignorant fools who babble of blood sacrifice and build a wall of stone for you, a foot a day! What wall will keep out the Dragon? I, Merlin, tell you, send these priests away and gather your captains round you, and get you away from the hills of Wales to your own country. King's Fort is not for you. You have seen the Red Dragon come tonight, and the White Dragon lie beneath him. And by God, you have seen the truth! Take warning! Strike your tents now, and go to your own country, and watch your borders lest the Dragon follow you and burn you out! You brought me here to speak, and I have spoken. I tell you, the Dragon is here!"

The King was on his feet, and men were shouting. I pulled the black cloak round me, and without hurrying turned away through the crowd of workmen and soldiers that milled round the foot of the platform. They did not try to stop me. They would as soon, I suppose, have touched a poisonous snake. Behind me, through the hubbub, I heard Maugan's voice and thought for a moment they were coming after me, but then men crowded off the platform, and began thrusting their way through the mob of workmen, on their way back to the encampment. Torches tossed. Someone dragged the sodden standard up and I saw it rocking and dripping where presumably his captains were clearing a path for the King. I drew the black cloak closer and slipped into the shadows at the edge of the crowd. Presently, unseen, I was able to step round behind the pavilion.

The oaks were three hundred paces away across the dark field. Under them the stream ran loud over smooth stones.

Cadal's voice said, low and urgent: "This way." A hoof sparked on stone. "I got you a quiet one," he said, and put a hand under my foot to throw me into the saddle.

I laughed a little. "I could ride the firedrake itself tonight. You saw it?"

"Aye, my lord. And I saw you, and heard you, too."

"Cadal, you swore you'd never be afraid of me. It was only a shooting star."

"But it came when it came."

"Yes. And now we'd better go while we can go. Timing is all that matters, Cadal."

"You shouldn't laugh at it, master Merlin."

"By the god," I said, "I'm not laughing."

The horses pushed out from under the dripping trees and went at a swift canter across the ridge. To our right a wooded hill blocked out the west. Ahead was the narrow neck of valley between hill and river.

"Will they come after you?"

"I doubt it."

But as we kicked the beasts to a gallop between ridge and river a horseman loomed, and our horses swerved and shied.

Cadal's beast jumped forward under the spur. Iron rasped. A voice, vaguely familiar, said clearly: "Put up. Friend."

The horses stamped and blew. I saw Cadal's hand on the other's rein. He sat quietly.

"Whose friend?"

"Ambrosius'."

I said: "Wait, Cadal, it's the greybeard. Your name, sir? And your business with me?"

He cleared his throat harshly. "Gorlois is my name, of Cornwall."

I saw Cadal's movement of surprise, and heard the bits jingle. He still had hold of the other's rein, and the drawn dagger gleamed. The old warrior sat unmoving. There was no sound of following hoofs.

I said slowly: "Then, sir, I should rather ask you what your business is with Vortigern?"

"The same as yours, Merlin Ambrosius." I saw his teeth gleam in his beard. "I came north to see for myself, and to send word back to him. The West has waited long enough, and the time will be ripe, come spring. But you came early. I could have saved myself the pains, it seems."

"You came alone?"

He gave a short, hard laugh, like a dog barking. "To Vortigern? Hardly. My men will follow. But I had to catch you. I want news." Then, harshly: "God's grief, man, do you doubt me? I came alone to you."

"No, sir. Let him go, Cadal. My lord, if you want to talk to me, you'll have to do it on the move. We should go, and quickly."

"Willingly." We set the horses in motion. As they struck into a gallop I said over my shoulder: "You guessed when you saw the brooch?"

"Before that. You have a look of him, Merlin Ambrosius." I heard him laugh again, deep in his throat. "And by God, there are times when you have a look of your devil-sire as well! Steady now, we're nearly at the ford. It'll be deep. They say wizards can't cross water?"

I laughed. "I'm always sick at sea, but I can manage this." The horses plunged across the ford unhindered, and took the next slope at a gallop. Then we were on the paved road, plain to see in the flying starlight, which leads straight across the high ground to the south.

We rode all night, with no pursuit. Three days later, in the early morning, Ambrosius came to land.

BOOK IV

THE RED DRAGON

1

The way the chronicles tell it, you would think it took Ambrosius two months to get himself crowned King and pacify Britain. In fact, it took more than two years.

The first part was quick enough. It was not for nothing that he had spent all those years in Less Britain, he and Uther, developing an expert striking force the like of which had not been seen in any part of Europe since the disbanding nearly a hundred years ago of the force commended by the Count of the Saxon Shore. Ambrosius had, in fact, modelled his own army on the force of the Saxon Shore, a marvellously mobile fighting instrument which could live off the country and do everything at twice the speed of the normal force. Caesar-speed, they still called it when I was young.

He landed at Totnes in Devon, with a fair wind and a quiet sea, and he had hardly set up the Red Dragon when the whole West rose for him. He was King of Cornwall and Devon before he even left the shore, and everywhere, as he moved northwards, the chiefs and kings crowded to swell his army. Eldol of Gloucester, a ferocious old man who had fought with Constantine against Vortigern, with Vortigern against Hengist, with Vortimer against both, and would fight anywhere for the sheer hell of it, met him at Glastonbury and swore faith. With him came a host of lesser leaders, not least his own brother Eldad, a bishop whose devout Christianity made the pagan wolves look like lambs by comparison, and set me wondering where he spent the dark nights of the winter solstice. But he was powerful; I had heard my mother speak of him with reverence; and once he had declared for Ambrosius, all Christian Britain came with him, urgent to drive back the pagan hordes moving steadily inland from their landing-places in the south and east. Last came Gorlois of Tintagel in Cornwall, straight from Vortigern's side with news of Vortigern's hasty move out of the Welsh mountains, and ready to ratify the oath of loyalty which, should Ambrosius be successful, would add the whole kingdom of Cornwall for the first time to the High Kingdom of Britain.

Ambrosius' main trouble, indeed, was not lack of support but the nature of it. The native Britons, tired of Vortigern, were fighting-mad to clear the Saxons out of their country and get their homes and their own ways back, but a great majority of them knew only guerrilla warfare, or the kind of hit-and-ride-away tactics that do well enough to harass the enemy, but will not hold him back for long if he means business. Moreover, each troop came with its own leader, and it was as much as any commander's authority was worth to suggest that they might regroup and train under strangers. Since the last trained legion had withdrawn from Britain almost a century before, we had fought (as we had done before the Romans ever came) in tribes. And it was no use suggesting that, for instance, the men of Devet might fight beside the men of North Wales even with their own leaders; throats would have been cut on both sides before the first trumpet ever sounded.

Ambrosius here, as everywhere, showed himself master. As ever he used each man for what that man's strength was worth. He sowed his own officers broadcast among the British—for co-ordination, he said, no more—and through them quietly adapted the tactics of each force to suit his central plan, with his own body of picked troops taking the main brunt of attack.

All this I heard later, or could have guessed from what I knew of him. I could have guessed, also, what would happen the moment his forces assembled and declared him King. His British allies clamoured for him to go straight after Hengist and drive the Saxons back to their own country. They were not unduly concerned with Vortigern. Indeed, such power as Vortigern had had was largely gone already, and it would have been simple enough for Ambrosius to ignore him and concentrate on the Saxons.

But he refused to give way to pressure. The old wolf must be smoked out first, he said, and the field cleared for the main work of battle. Besides, he pointed out, Hengist and his Saxons were Northmen, and particularly amenable to rumours and fear; let Ambrosius once unite the British to destroy Vortigern, and the Saxons would begin to fear him as a force really to be reckoned with. It was his guess that, given the time, they would bring together one large force to face him, which might then be broken at one blow.

They had a council about it, at the fort near Gloucester where the first bridge crosses the Sefern river. I could picture it, Ambrosius listening and weighing and judging, and answering with that grave easy way of his, allowing each man his say for pride; then taking at the end the decision he had meant to take from the beginning, but giving way here and there on the small things, so that each man thought he had made a bargain and got, if not what he wanted, then something near it, in return for a concession by his commander.

The upshot was that they marched northwards within the week, and came on Vortigern at Doward.

Doward is in the valley of the Guoy, which the Saxons pronounce Way or Wye. This is a big river, which runs deep and placid-seeming through a gorge whose high slopes are hung with forests. Here and there the valley widens to green pastures, but the tide runs many miles up river, and these low meadows are often, in winter, awash under a roaring yellow flood, for the great Wye is not so placid as it seems, and even in summer there are deep pools where big fish lie and the currents are strong enough to overturn a coracle and drown a man.

Well north of the limit of the tidal floods, in a wide curve of the valley, stand the two hills called Doward. The one to the north is the greater, thick with forest and mined with caves inhabited, men say, by wild beasts and outlawed men. The hill called Lesser Doward is also forested, but more thinly, since it is rocky, and its steep summit, rising above the trees, makes a natural citadel so secure that it has been fortified time out of mind. Long before even the Romans came, some British king built himself a fortress on the summit which, with its commanding view, and the natural defenses of crag and river, made a formidable stronghold. The hill is wide-topped, and its sides steep and rough, and though siege engines could at one point be dragged up in dead ground, this ended in crags where the engines were useless. Everywhere except at this point there was a double rampart and ditch to get through before the outer wall of the fortress could be reached. The Romans themselves had marched against it once, and only managed to reduce it through treachery. This was in the time of Caratacus. Doward was the kind of place that, like Troy, must be taken from within.

This time also, it was taken from within. But not by treachery; by fire.

Everyone knows what happened there.

Vortigern's men were hardly settled after their headlong flight from Snowdon, when Ambrosius' army came up the valley of the Wye, and encamped due west of Doward Hill, at a place called Ganarew. I never heard what store of provisions Vortigern had; but the place had been kept prepared, and it was well known that there were two good springs within the fortress which had not yet been known to fail; so it might well have taken Ambrosius some time to reduce it by siege. But a siege was just what he could not afford, with Hengist gathering his forces, and the April seas opening between Britain and the Saxon shores. Besides, his British allies were restless, and would never have settled down for a prolonged siege. It had to be quick.

It was both quick and brutal. I have heard it said since that Ambrosius acted out of vengeance for his long-dead brother. I do not believe this to be true. Such long-standing bitterness was not in his nature, and besides, he was a general and a good fighting commander before he was even a man. He was driven only by necessity, and in the end, by Vortigern's own brutality.

Ambrosius besieged the place in the conventional way for about three days. Where he could, he drew up siege engines and tried to break the defenses. He did indeed breach the outer rampart in two places above what was still called Romans' Way, but when he found himself stopped by the inner rampart and his troops exposed to the defenders, he withdrew. When he saw how long the siege would take, and how, even in the three days, some of his British troops quietly left him and went off on their own, like hounds after the rumour of Saxon hares, he decided to make an end quickly. He sent a man to Vortigern with conditions for surrender. Vortigern, who must have seen the defection of some of the British troops, and who well understood Ambrosius' position, laughed, and sent back the messenger without a message, but with the man's own two hands severed, and bound in a bloody cloth to the belt at his waist.

He stumbled into Ambrosius' tent just after sundown of the third day, and managed to stay on his feet long enough to give the only message he was charged with.

"They say that you may stay here, my lord, until your army melts away, and you are left handless as I. They have food in plenty, sir, I saw it, and water—"

Ambrosius only said: "He ordered this himself?"

"The Queen," said the man. "It was the Queen." He pitched forward on the word at Ambrosius' feet, and from the dripping cloth at his belt the hands fell, sprawling.

"Then we will burn out the wasps' nest, queen and all," said Ambrosius. "See to him."

That night, to the apparent pleasure of the garrison, the siege engines were withdrawn from Romans' Way and the breached places in the outer rampart. Instead, great piles of brushwood and hewn branches were stacked in the gaps, and the army tightened its ring round the crest of the hill, with a circle of archers waiting, and men ready to cut down any who should escape. In the quiet hour before daylight the order was given. From every quarter the arrows, pointed with flaming, oil-soaked rags, showered into the fortress. It did not take long. The place was largely built of wood, and crowded with the wagons, provisions, beasts and their fodder. It burned fiercely. And when it was alight the brushwood outside the walls was fired, so that anyone leaping from the walls met another wall of fire outside. And outside that, the iron ring of the army.

They say that throughout, Ambrosius sat his big white horse, watching, till the flames made the horse as red as the Red Dragon above his head. And high on the fortress tower the White Dragon, showing against a plume of smoke, turned blood red as the flames themselves, then blackened and fell.

2

While Ambrosius was attacking Doward I was still at Maridunum, having parted from Gorlois on the ride south, and seen him on his way to meet my father.

It happened this way. All through that first night we rode hard, but there was no sign of pursuit, so at sunup we drew off the road and rested, waiting for Gorlois' men to come up with us. This they did during the morning, having been able, in the near-panic at Dinas Brenin, to slip away unobserved. They confirmed what Gorlois had already suggested to me, that Vortigern would head, not for his own fortress of Caer-Guent, but for Doward. And he was moving, they said, by the east-bound road through Caer Gai towards Bravonium. Once past Tomen-y-mur, there was no danger that we would be overtaken.

So we rode on, a troop now about twenty strong, but going easily. My mother, with her escort of fighting men, was less than a day ahead of us, and her party, with the litters, would be much slower than we were. We had no wish to catch up with them and perhaps force a fight which might endanger the women; it was certain, said Gorlois to me, that the latter would be delivered safely to Maridunum, "but," he added in his sharp, gruff way, "we shall meet the escort on their way back. For come back they will; they cannot know the King is moving east. And every man less for Vortigern is another for your father. We'll get news at Bremia, and camp beyond it to wait for them."

Bremia was nothing but a cluster of stone huts smelling of peat smoke and dung, black doorways curtained from wind and rain with hides or sacking, round which peered scared eyes of women and children. No men appeared, even when we drew rein in the midst of the place, and curs ran yapping round the horses' heels. This puzzled us, till (knowing the dialect) I called out to the eyes behind the nearest curtain, to reassure the people and ask for news.

They came out then, women, children, and one or two old men, crowding eagerly round us and ready to talk.

The first piece of news was that my mother's party had been there the previous day and night, leaving only that morning, at the Princess's insistence. She had been taken ill, they told me, and had stayed for half the day and the night in the head-man's house, where she was cared for. Her women had tried to persuade her to turn aside for a monastic settlement in the hills nearby, where she might rest, but she had refused, and had seemed better in the morning, so the party had ridden. It had been a chill, said the head-man's wife; the lady had been feverish, and coughing a little, but she had seemed so much better next morning, and Maridunum was not more than a day's ride; they had thought it better to let her do as she desired . . .

I eyed the squalid huts, thinking that, indeed, the danger of a few more hours in the litter might well be less than such miserable shelter in Bremia, so thanked the woman for her kindness, and asked where her man had gone. As to that, she told me, all the men had gone to join Ambrosius . . .

She mistook my look of surprise. "Did you not know? There was a prophet at Dinas Brenin, who said the Red Dragon would come. The Princess told me herself, and you could see the soldiers were afraid. And now he has landed. He is here."

"How can you know?" I asked her. "We met no messenger."

She looked at me as if I were crazed, or stupid. Had I not seen the firedrake? The whole village knew this for the portent, after the prophet had spoken so. The men had armed themselves, and had gone that very day. If the soldiers came back, the women and children would take to the hills, but everyone knew that Ambrosius could move more swiftly than the wind, and they were not afraid . . .

I let her run on while I translated for Gorlois. Our eyes met with the same thought. We thanked the woman again, gave her what was due for her care of my mother, and rode after the men of Bremia.

South of the village the road divides, the main way turning south-east past the gold mine and then through the hills and deep valleys to the broad valley of the Wye whence it is easy riding to the Sefern crossing and the south-west. The other, minor, road goes straight south, a day's ride to Maridunum. I had decided that in any case I would follow my mother south and talk to her before I rejoined Ambrosius; now the news of her illness made this imperative. Gorlois would ride straight to meet Ambrosius and give him the news of Vortigern's movements.

At the fork where our ways parted we came on the villagers. They had heard us coming and taken cover—the place was all rocks and bushes—but not soon enough; the gusty wind must have hidden our approach from them till we were almost on them. The men were out of sight, but one of their miserable pack-donkeys was not, and stones were still rolling on the scree.

It was Bremia over again. We halted, and I called out into the windy silence. This time I told them who I was, and in a moment, it seemed, the roadside was bristling with men. They came crowding round our horses, showing their teeth and brandishing a peculiar assortment of weapons ranging from a bent Roman sword to a stone spearhead bound on a hay-rake. They told the same story as their women; they had heard the prophecy, and they had seen the portent; they were marching south to join Ambrosius, and every man in the West would soon be with them. Their spirit was high, and their condition pitiful; it was lucky we had a chance to help them.

"Speak to them," said Gorlois to me. "Tell them that if they wait another day here with us, they shall have weapons and horses. They have picked the right place for an ambush, as who should know better than they?"

So I told them that this was the Duke of Cornwall, and a great leader, and that if they would wait a day for us, we would see they got weapons and horses. "For Vortigern's men will come back this way," I told them. "They are not to know that the High King is already fleeing eastwards: they will come back by this road, so we will wait for them here, and you will be wise to wait with us."

So we waited. The escort must have stayed rather longer than need be in Maridunum, and after that cold camp ride who could blame them? But towards dusk of the second day they came back, riding at ease, thinking maybe of a night's shelter at Bremia.

We took them nicely by surprise, and fought a bloody and very unpleasant little action. One roadside skirmish is very like another. This one differed only from the usual in being better generalled and more eccentrically equipped, but we had the advantages both of numbers and of surprise, and did what we had set out to do, robbed Vortigern of twenty men for the loss of only three of our own and a few cuts. I came out of it more creditably than I would have believed possible, killing the man I had picked out before the fighting swept over and past me and another knocked me off my horse and would possibly have killed me if Cadal had not parried the stroke and killed the fellow himself. It was quickly over. We buried our own dead and left the rest for the kites, after we had stripped them of their arms. We had taken care not to harm the horses, and when next morning Gorlois said farewell and led his new troops south-east, every man had a horse, and a good weapon of some kind. Cadal and I turned south for Maridunum, and reached it by early evening.

The first person I saw as we rode down the streets towards St. Peter's was my cousin Dinias. We came on him suddenly at a corner, and he jumped a foot and went white. I suppose rumours had been running like wildfire through the town ever since the escort had brought my mother back without me.

"Merlin. I thought—I thought—"

"Well met, cousin, I was coming to look for you."

He said quickly: "Look, I swear I had no idea who those men were—"

"I know that. What happened wasn't your fault. That isn't why I was looking for you."

"—and I was drunk, you know that. But even if I had guessed who they were, how was I to know they'd take you up on a thing like that? I'd heard rumours of what they were looking for, I admit, but I swear it never entered my head—"

"I said it wasn't your fault. And I'm back here again safely, aren't I? All's well that ends well. Leave it, Dinias. That wasn't what I wanted to talk to you about."

But he persisted. "I took the money, didn't I? You saw."

"And if you did? You didn't give information for money, you took it afterwards. It's different, to my mind. If Vortigern likes to throw his money away, then by all means rob him of it. Forget it, I tell you. Have you news of my mother?"

"I've just come from there. She's ill, did you know?"

"I got news on my way south," I said. "What's the matter with her? How bad?"

"A chill, they told me, but they say she's on the mend. I thought myself she still looked poor enough, but she was fatigued with the journey, and anxious about you. What did Vortigern want you for, in the end?"

"To kill me," I said briefly.

He stared, then began to stutter. "I—in God's name, Merlin, I know you and I have never been . . . that is, there've been times—" He stopped, and I heard him swallow. "I don't sell my kinsmen, you know."

"I told you I believed you. Forget it. It was nothing to do with you, some nonsense of his soothsayers'. But as I said, here I am safe and sound."

"Your mother said nothing about it."

"She didn't know. Do you think she'd have let him send her tamely home if she had known what he meant to do? The men who brought her home, they knew, you can be sure of that. So they didn't let it out to her?"

"It seems not," said Dinias. "But—"

"I'm glad of that. I'm hoping to get to see her soon, this time in daylight."

"Then you're in no danger now from Vortigern?"

"I would be, I suppose," I said, "if the place was still full of his men, but I was told at the gate that they've cleared out to join him?"

"That's so. Some rode north, and some east to Caer-Guent. You've heard the news, then?"

"What news?"

Though there was nobody else in the street, he looked over his shoulder in the old, furtive way. I slid down out of the saddle, and threw the reins to Cadal. "What news?" I repeated.

"Ambrosius," he said softly. "He's landed in the south-west, they say, and marching north. A ship brought the story yesterday, and Vortigern's men started moving out straight away. But—if you've just ridden in from the north, surely you'd meet them?"

"Two companies, this morning. But we saw them in good time, and got off the road. We met my mother's escort the day before, at the crossways."

" 'Met'?" He looked startled. "But if they knew Vortigern wanted you dead—"

"They'd have known I had no business riding south, and cut me down? Exactly. So we cut them down instead. Oh, don't look at me like that—it wasn't magician's work, only soldiers'. We fell in with some Welsh who were on their way to join Ambrosius, and we ambushed Vortigern's troop and cut them up."

"The Welsh knew already? The prophecy, was it?" I saw the whites of his eyes in the dusk. "I'd heard about that . . . the place is buzzing with it. The troops told us. They said you'd showed them some kind of great lake under the crag—it was that place we stopped at years ago, and I'll swear there was no sign of any lake then—but there was this lake of water with dragons lying in it under the foundations of the tower. Is it true?"

"That I showed them a lake, yes."

"But the dragons. What were they?"

I said, slowly: "Dragons. Something conjured out of nothing for them to see, since without seeing they would not listen, let alone believe."

There was a little silence. Then he said, with fear in his voice: "And was it magic that showed you Ambrosius was coming?"

"Yes and no." I smiled. "I knew he was coming, but not when. It was the magic that told me he was actually on his way."

He was staring again. "You knew he was coming? Then you did have tidings in Cornwall? You might have told me."

"Why?"

"I'd have joined him."

I looked at him for a moment, measuring. "You can still join him. You and your other friends who fought with Vortimer. What about Vortimer's brother, Pascentius? Do you know where he is? Is he still hot against Vortigern?"

"Yes, but they say he's gone to make his peace with Hengist. He'll never join Ambrosius, he wants Britain for himself."

"And you?" I asked. "What do you want?"

He answered quite simply, for once without any bluster or bravado. "Only a place I can call my own. This, if I can. It's mine now, after all. He killed the children, did you know?"

"I didn't, but you hardly surprise me. It's a habit of his, after all." I paused.

"Look, Dinias, there's a lot to say, and I've a lot to tell you. But first I've a favour to ask of you."

"What's that?"

"Hospitality. There's nowhere else I know of that I care to go until I've got my own place ready, and I've a fancy to stay in my grandfather's house again."

He said, without pretense or evasion: "It's not what it was."

I laughed. "Is anything? As long as there's a roof against this hellish rain, and a fire to dry our clothes, and something to eat, no matter what. What do you say we send Cadal for provisions, and eat at home? I'll tell you the whole thing over a pie and a flask of wine. But I warn you, if you so much as show me a pair of dice I'll yell for Vortigern's men myself."

He grinned, relaxing suddenly. "No fear of that. Come along, then. There's a couple of rooms still habitable, and we'll find you a bed."

I was given Camlach's room. It was draughty, and full of dust, and Cadal refused to let me use the bedding until it had lain in front of a roaring fire for a full hour. Dinias had no servant, except one slut of a girl who looked after him apparently in return for the privilege of sharing his bed. Cadal set her to carrying fuel and heating water while he took a message to the nunnery for my mother, and then went to the tavern for wine and provisions.

We ate before the fire, with Cadal serving us. We talked late, but here it is sufficient to record that I told Dinias my story—or such parts of it as he would understand. There might have been some personal satisfaction in telling him the facts of my parentage, but until I was sure of him, and the countryside was known to be clear of Vortigern's men, I thought it better to say nothing. So I told him merely how I had gone to Brittany, and that I had become Ambrosius' man. Dinias had heard enough already of my "prophecy" in the cavern at King's Fort to believe implicitly in Ambrosius' coming victory, so our talk ended with his promise to ride westwards in the morning with the news, and summon what support he could for Ambrosius from the fringes of Wales. He would, I knew, have been afraid in any case to do other than keep that promise; whatever the soldiers had said about the occasion there in King's Fort, it was enough to strike my simple cousin Dinias with the most profound awe of my powers. But even without that, I knew I could trust him in this. We talked till almost dawn, then I gave him money and said good night.

(He was gone before I woke next morning. He kept his word, and joined Ambrosius later, at York, with a few hundred men. He was honourably received and acquitted himself well, but soon afterwards, in some minor engagement, received wounds of which he later died. As for me, I never saw him again.)

Cadal shut the door behind him. "At least there's a good lock and a stout bar."

"Are you afraid of Dinias?" I asked.

"I'm afraid of everybody in this cursed town. I'll not be happy till we're quit of it and back with Ambrosius."

"I doubt if you need worry now. Vortigern's men have gone. You heard what Dinias said."

"Aye, and I heard what you said, too." He had stopped to pick up the blankets from beside the fire, and paused with his arms full of bedding, looking at me. "What did you mean, you're getting your own place here ready? You're never thinking of setting up house here?"

"Not a house, no."

"That cave?"

I smiled at his expression. "When Ambrosius has done with me, and the country is quiet, that is where I shall go. I told you, didn't I, that if you stayed with me you'd live far from home?"

"We were talking about dying, as far as I remember. You mean, live there?"

"I don't know," I said. "Perhaps not. But I think I shall need a place where I can be alone, away, aside from things happening. Thinking and planning is one side of life; doing is another. A man cannot be doing all the time."

"Tell that to Uther."

"I am not Uther."

"Well, it takes both sorts, as they say." He dumped the blankets on the bed. "What are you smiling at?"

"Was I? Never mind. Let's get to bed, we'll have to be early at the nunnery. Did you have to bribe the old woman again?"

"Old woman nothing." He straightened. "It was a girl this time. A looker, too, what I could see of her with that sack of a gown and a hood over her head. Whoever puts a girl like that in a nunnery deserves—" He began to explain what they deserved, but I cut him short.

"Did you find out how my mother was?"

"They said she was better. The fever's gone, but she'll not rest quiet till she's seen you. You'll tell her everything now?"

"Yes."

"And then?"

"We join Ambrosius."

"Ah," he said, and when he had dragged his mattress to lie across the door, he blew out the lamp and lay down without another word to sleep.

My bed was comfortable enough, and the room, derelict or no, was luxury itself after the journey. But I slept badly. In imagination I was out on the road with Ambrosius, heading for Doward. From what I had heard of Doward, reducing it would not be an easy job. I began to wonder if after all I had done my father a disservice in driving the High King out of his Snowdon fastness. I should have left him there, I thought, with his rotten tower, and Ambrosius would have driven him back to the sea.

It was with an effort almost of surprise that I recalled my own prophecy. What I had done at Dinas Brenin, I had not done of myself. It was not I who had decided to send Vortigern fleeing out of Wales. Out of the dark, out of the wild and whirling stars, I had been told. The Red Dragon would triumph, the White would fall. The voice that had said so, that said so now in the musty dark of Camlach's room, was not my own; it was the god's. One did not lie awake looking for reasons; one obeyed, and then slept.

3

It was the girl Cadal had spoken of who opened the nunnery gate to us. She must have been waiting to receive us, for almost as soon as Cadal's hand was lifted to the bell-pull the gate opened and she motioned us to come in. I got a swift impression of wide eyes under the brown hood, and a supple young body shrouded in the rough gown, as she latched the heavy gate and, drawing her hood closer over her face and hair, led us quickly across the courtyard. Her feet, bare in canvas sandals, looked cold, and were splashed with mud from the puddled yard, but they were slim and well-shaped, and her hands were pretty. She did not speak, but led us across the yard and through a narrow passage between two buildings, into a larger square beyond. Here against the walls stood fruit trees, and a few flowers grew, but these were mostly weeds and wild-flowers, and the doors of the cells that opened off the courtyard were unpainted and, where they stood open, gave on bare little rooms where simplicity had become ugliness and, too often, squalor.

Not so in my mother's cell. She was housed with adequate—if not royal—comfort. They had let her bring her own furniture, the room was limewashed and spotlessly clean, and with the change in the April weather the sun had come out and was shining straight in through the narrow window and across her bed. I remembered the furniture; it was her own bed from home, and the curtain at the window was one she had woven herself, the red cloth with the green pattern that she had been making the day my uncle Camlach came home. I remembered, too, the wolfskin on the floor; my grandfather had killed the beast with his bare hands and the haft of his broken dagger; its beady eyes and snarl had terrified me when I was small. The cross that hung on the bare wall at the foot of her bed was of dull silver, with a lovely pattern of locked but flowing lines, and studs of amethyst that caught the light.

The girl showed me the door in silence, and withdrew. Cadal sat down on a bench outside to wait.

My mother lay propped on pillows, in the shaft of sunshine. She looked pale and tired, and spoke not much above a whisper, but was, she told me, on the mend. When I questioned her about the illness, and laid a hand on her temples, she put me aside, smiling and saying she was well enough looked after. I did not insist: half of healing is in the patient's trust, and no woman ever thinks her own son is much more than a child. Besides, I could see that the fever had gone, and now that she was no longer anxious over me, she would sleep.

So I merely pulled up the room's single chair, sat down and began to tell her all she wanted to know, without waiting for her questions: about my escape from Maridunum and the flight like the arrow from the god's bow straight from Britain to Ambrosius' feet, and all that had happened since. She lay back against her pillows and watched me with astonishment and some slowly growing emotion which I identified as the emotion a cage-bird might feel if you set it to hatch a merlin's egg.

When I had finished she was tired, and grey stood under her eyes so sharply drawn that I got up to go. But she looked contented, and said, as if it was the sum and finish of the story, as I suppose it was, for her:

"He has acknowledged you."

"Yes. They call me Merlin Ambrosius."

She was silent a little, smiling to herself. I crossed to the window and leaned my elbows on the sill, looking out. The sun was warm. Cadal nodded on his bench, half asleep. From across the yard a movement caught my eye; in a shadowed doorway the girl was standing, watching my mother's door as if waiting for me to come out. She had put back her hood, and even in the shadows I could see the gold of her hair and a young face lovely as a flower. Then she saw me watching her. For perhaps two seconds our eyes met and held. I knew then why the ancients armed the cruellest god with arrows; I felt the shock of it right through my body. Then she had gone, shrinking close-hooded back into the shadow, and behind me my mother was saying:

"And now? What now?"

I turned my back on the sunlight. "I go to join him. But not until you are better. When I go I want to take news of you."

She looked anxious. "You must not stay here. Maridunum is not safe for you."

"I think it is. Since the news came in of the landing, the place has emptied itself of Vortigern's men. We had to take to the hill-tracks on our way south; the road was alive with men riding to join him."

"That's true, but—"

"And I shan't go about, I promise you. I was lucky last night, I ran into Dinias as soon as I set foot in town. He gave me a room at home."

"Dinias?"

I laughed at her astonishment. "Dinias feels he owes me something, never mind what, but we agreed well enough last night." I told her what mission I had sent him on, and she nodded.

"He"—and I knew she did not mean Dinias—"will need every man who can hold a sword." She knitted her brows. "They say Hengist has three hundred thousand men. Will he"—and again she was not referring to Hengist—"be able to withstand Vortigern, and after him Hengist and the Saxons?"

I suppose I was still thinking of last night's vigil. I said, without pausing to consider how it would sound: "I have said so, so it must be true."

A movement from the bed brought my eyes down to her. She was crossing herself, her eyes at once startled and severe, and through it all afraid. "Merlin—" but on the word a cough shook her, so that when she managed to speak again it was only a harsh whisper: "Beware of arrogance. Even if God has given you power—"

I laid a hand on her wrist, stopping her. "You mistake me, madam. I put it badly. I only meant that the god had said it through me, and because he had said it, it must be true. Ambrosius must win, it is in the stars."

She nodded, and I saw the relief wash through her and slacken her, body and mind, like an exhausted child.

I said gently: "Don't be afraid for me, Mother. Whatever god uses me, I am content to be his voice and instrument. I go where he sends me. And when he has finished with me, he will take me back."

"There is only one God," she whispered.

I smiled at her. "That is what I am beginning to think. Now, go to sleep. I will come back in the morning."

I went to see my mother again next morning. This time I went alone. I had sent Cadal to find provisions in the market, Dinias' slut having vanished when he did, leaving us to fend for ourselves in the deserted palace. I was rewarded, for the girl was again on duty at the gate, and again led me to my mother's room. But when I said something to her she merely pulled the hood closer without speaking, so that again I saw no more of her than the slender hands and feet. The cobbles were dry today, and the puddles gone. She had washed her feet, and in the grip of the coarse sandals they looked as fragile as blue-veined flowers in a peasant's basket. Or so I told myself, my mind working like a singer's, where it had no right to be working at all. The arrow still thrummed where it had struck me, and my whole body seemed to thrill and tighten at the sight of her.

She showed me the door again, as if I could have forgotten it, and withdrew to wait.

My mother seemed a little better, and had rested well, she told me. We talked for a while; she had questions about the details of my story, and I filled them in for her. When I got up to go I asked, as casually as I could:

"The girl who opened the gate; she is young, surely, to be here? Who is she?"

"Her mother worked in the palace. Keridwen. Do you remember her?"

I shook my head. "Should I?"

"No." But when I asked her why she smiled, she would say nothing, and in face of her amusement I dared not ask any more.

On the third day it was the old deaf portress; and I spent the whole interview with my mother wondering if she had (as women will) seen straight through my carefully casual air to what lay beneath, and passed the word that the girl must be kept out of my way. But on the fourth day she was there, and this time I knew before I got three steps inside the gate that she had been hearing the stories about Dinas Brenin. She was so eager to catch a glimpse of the magician that she let the hood fall back a little, and in my turn I saw the wide eyes, grey-blue, full of a sort of awed curiosity and wonder. When I smiled at her and said something in greeting she ducked back inside the hood again, but this time she answered. Her voice was light and small, a child's voice, and she called me "my lord" as if she meant it.

"What's your name?" I asked her.

"Keri, my lord."

I hung back, to detain her. "How is my mother today, Keri?"

But she would not answer, just took me straight to the inner court, and left me there.

That night I lay awake again, but no god spoke to me, not even to tell me she was not for me. The gods do not visit you to remind you what you know already.

By the last day of April my mother was so much better that when I went again to see her she was in the chair by the window, wearing a woollen robe over her shift, and sitting full in the sun. A quince tree, pinioned to the wall outside, was heavy with rosy cups where bees droned, and just beside her on the sill a pair of white doves strutted and crooned.

"You have news?" she asked, as soon as she saw my face.

"A messenger came in today. Vortigern is dead and the Queen with him. They say that Hengist is coming south with a vast force, including Vortimer's brother Pascentius and the remnant of his army. Ambrosius is already on his way to meet them."

She sat very straight, looking past me at the wall. There was a woman with her today, sitting on a stool on the other side of the bed; it was one of the nuns who had attended her at Dinas Brenin. I saw her make the sign of the cross on her breast, but Niniane sat still and straight looking past me at something, thinking.

"Tell me, then."

I told her all I had heard about the affair at Doward. The woman crossed herself again, but my mother never moved. When I had finished, her eyes came back to me.

"And you will go now?"

"Yes. Will you give me a message for him?"

"When I see him again," she said, "it will be time enough."

When I took leave of her she was still sitting staring past the winking amethysts on the wall to something distant in place and time.

Keri was not waiting, and I lingered for a while before I crossed the outer yard, slowly, towards the gate. Then I saw her waiting in the deep shadow of the gateway's arch, and quickened my step. I was turning over a host of things to say, all equally useless to prolong what could not be prolonged, but there was no need. She put out one of those pretty hands and touched my sleeve, beseechingly. "My lord—"

Her hood was half back, and I saw tears in her eyes. I said sharply: "What's the matter?" I believe that for a wild moment I thought she wept because I was going. "Keri, what is it?"

"I have the toothache."

I gaped at her. I must have looked as silly as if I had just been slapped across the face.

"Here," she said, and put a hand to her cheek. The hood fell right back. "It's been aching for days. Please, my lord—"

I said hoarsely: "I'm not a toothdrawer."

"But if you would just touch it—"

"Or a magician," I started to say, but she came close to me, and my voice strangled in my throat. She smelled of honeysuckle. Her hair was barley-gold and her eyes grey like bluebells before they open. Before I knew it she had taken my hand between both her own and raised it to her cheek.

I stiffened fractionally, as if to snatch it back, then controlled myself, and opened the palm gently along her cheek. The wide greybell eyes were as innocent as the sky. As she leaned towards me the neck of her gown hung forward slackly and I could see her breasts. Her skin was smooth as water, and her breath sweet against my cheek.

I withdrew the hand gently enough, and stood back. "I can do nothing about it." I suppose my voice was rough. She lowered her eyelids and stood humbly with folded hands. Her lashes were short and thick and golden as her hair. There was a tiny mole at the corner of her mouth.

I said: "If it's no better by morning, have it drawn."

"It's better already, my lord. It stopped aching as soon as you touched it."

Her voice was full of wonder, and her hand crept up to the cheek where mine had lain. The movement was like a caress, and I felt my blood jerk with a beat like pain. With a sudden movement she reached for my hand again and quickly, shyly, stooped forward and pressed her mouth to it.

Then the door swung open beside me and I was out in the empty street.

4

It seemed, from what the messenger had told me, that Ambrosius had been right in his decision to make an end of Vortigern before turning on the Saxons. His reduction of Doward, and the savagery with which he did it, had their effect. Those of the invading Saxons who had ventured furthest inland began to withdraw northwards towards the wild debatable lands which had always provided a beachhead for invasion. They halted north of the Humber to fortify themselves where they could, and wait for him. At first Hengist believed that Ambrosius had at his command little more than the Breton invading army—and he was ignorant of the nature of that deadly weapon of war. He thought (it was reported) that very few of the island British had joined Ambrosius; in any case the Saxons had defeated the British, in their small tribal forces, so often that they despised them as easy meat. But now as reports reached the Saxon leader of the thousands who had flocked to the Red Dragon, and of the success at Doward, he decided to remain no longer fortified north of the Humber, but to march swiftly south again to meet the British at a place of his own choosing, where he might surprise Ambrosius and destroy his army.

Once again, Ambrosius moved with Caesar-speed. This was necessary, because where the Saxons had withdrawn, they had laid the country waste.

The end came in the second week of May, a week hot with sunshine that seemed to come from June, and interrupted by showers left over from April—a borrowed week, and, for the Saxons, a debt called in by fate. Hengist, with his preparations half complete, was caught by Ambrosius at Maesbeli, near Conan's Fort, or Kaerconan, that men sometimes call Conisburgh. This is a hilly place, with the fort on a crag, and a deep ravine running by. Here the Saxons had tried to prepare an ambush for Ambrosius' force, but Ambrosius' scouts got news of it from a Briton they came across lurking in a hilltop cave, where he had fled to keep his woman and two small children from the axes of the Northmen. So Ambrosius, forewarned, increased the speed of his march and caught up with Hengist before the ambush could be fully laid, thus forcing him into open battle.

Hengist's attempt to lay an ambush had turned the luck against him; Ambrosius, where he halted and deployed his army, had the advantage of the land. His main force, Bretons, Gauls, and the island British from the south and southwest, waited on a gentle hill, with a level field ahead over which they could attack unimpeded. Among these troops, medleywise, were other native British who had joined him, with their leaders. Behind this main army the ground rose gently, broken only by brakes of thorn and yellow gorse, to a long ridge which curved to the west in a series of low rocky hills, and on the east was thickly forested with oak. The men from Wales—mountainy men—were stationed mainly on the wings, the North Welsh in the oak forest and, separated from them by the full body of Ambrosius' army, the South Welsh on the hills to the west. These forces, lightly armed, highly mobile and with scores to settle, were to hold themselves in readiness as reinforcements, the swift hammer-blows which could be directed during battle at the weakest points of the enemy's defense. They could also be relied upon to catch and cut down any of Hengist's Saxons who broke and fled the field.

The Saxons, caught, in their own trap, with this immense winged force in front of them, and behind them the rock of Kaerconan and the narrow defile where the ambush had been planned, fought like demons. But they were at a disadvantage: they started afraid—afraid of Ambrosius' reputation, of his recent ferocious victory at Doward, and more than both—so men told me—of my prophecy to Vortigern which had spread from mouth to mouth as quickly as the fires in Doward tower. And of course the omens worked the other way for Ambrosius. Battle was joined shortly before noon, and by sunset it was all over.

I saw it all. It was my first great battlefield, and I am not ashamed that it was almost my last. My battles were not fought with sword and spear. If it comes to that, I had already had a hand in the winning of Kaerconan before I ever reached it; and when I did reach it, was to find myself playing the very part that Uther had once, in jest, assigned to me.

I had ridden with Cadal as far as Caerleon, where we found a small body of Ambrosius' troops in possession of the fortress, and another on its way to invest and repair the fort at Maridunum. Also, their officer told me confidentially, to make sure that the Christian community—"all the community," he added gravely, with the ghost of a wink at me, "such is the commander's piety"—remained safe. He had been detailed, moreover, to send some of his men back with me, to escort me to Ambrosius. My father had even thought to send some of my clothes. So I sent Cadal back, to his disgust, to do what he could about Galapas' cave, and await me there, then myself rode north-east with the escort.

We came up with the army just outside Kaerconan. The troops were already deployed for battle and there was no question of seeing the commander, so we withdrew, as instructed, to the western hill where the men of the South Welsh tribes eyed one another distrustfully over swords held ready for the Saxons below. The men of my escort troop eyed me in something the same manner: they had not intruded on my silence on the ride, and it was plain they held me in some awe, not only as Ambrosius' acknowledged son, but as "Vortigern's prophet"—a title which had already stuck to me and which it took me some years to shed. When I reported with them to the officer in charge, and asked him to assign me a place in his troop, he was horrified, and begged me quite seriously to stay out of the fight, but to find some place where the men could see me, and know, as he put it, "that the prophet was here with them." In the end I did as he wished, and withdrew to the top of a small rocky crag hard by where, wrapping my cloak about me, I prepared to watch the battlefield spread out below like a moving map.

Ambrosius himself was in the center; I could see the white stallion with the Red Dragon glimmering above it. Out to the right Uther's blue cloak glinted as his horse cantered along the lines. The leader of the left wing I did not immediately recognize; a grey horse, a big, heavy-built figure striding it, a standard bearing some device in white which I could not at first distinguish. Then I saw what it was. A boar. The Boar of Cornwall. Ambrosius' commander of the left was none other than the greybeard Gorlois, lord of Tintagel.

Nothing could be read of the order in which the Saxons had assembled. All my life I had heard of the ferocity of these great blond giants, and all British children were brought up from babyhood on stories of their terror. They went mad in war, men said, and could fight bleeding from a dozen wounds, with no apparent lessening of strength or ferocity. And what they had in strength and cruelty they lacked in discipline. This seemed, indeed, to be so. There was no order that I could see in the vast surge of glinting metal and tossing horsehair which was perpetually on the move, like a flood waiting for the dam to break.

Even from that distance I could pick out Hengist and his brother, giants with long moustaches sweeping to their chests, and long hair flying as they spurred their shaggy, tough little horses up and down the ranks. They were shouting, and echoes of the shouts came clearly; prayers to the gods, vows, exhortations, commands, which rose towards a ferocious crescendo, till on the last wild shout of "Kill, kill, kill!" the axeheads swung up, glinting in the May sunlight, and the pack surged forward towards the ordered lines of Ambrosius' army.

The two hosts met with a shock that sent the jackdaws squalling up from Kaerconan, and seemed to splinter the very air. It was impossible, even from my point of vantage, to see which way the fight—or rather, the several different movements of the fight—was going. At one moment it seemed as if the Saxons with their axes and winged helms were boring a way into the British host; at the next, you would see a knot of Saxons cut off in a sea of British, and then, apparently engulfed, vanish. Ambrosius' center block met the main shock of the charge, then Uther's cavalry, with a swift flanking movement, came in from the east. The men of Cornwall under Gorlois held back at first, but as soon as the Saxons' front line began to waver, they came in like a hammer-blow from the left and smashed it apart. After that the field broke up into chaos. Everywhere men were fighting in small groups, or even singly and hand to hand. The noise, the clash and shouting, even the smell of sweat and blood mingled, seemed to come up to this high perch where I sat with my cloak about me, watching. Immediately below me I was conscious of the stirring and muttering of the Welshmen, then the sudden cheer as a troop of Saxons broke and galloped in our direction. In a moment the hilltop was empty save for me, only that the clamour seemed to have washed nearer, round the foot of the hill like the tide coming in fast. A robin lighted on a blackthorn at my elbow, and began to sing. The sound came high and sweet and uncaring through all the noise of battle. To this day, whenever I think of the battle for Kaerconan, it brings to mind a robin's song, mingled with the croaking of the ravens. For they were already circling, high overhead: men say they can hear the clash of swords ten miles off.

It was finished by sunset. Eldol, Duke of Gloucester, dragged Hengist from his horse under the very walls of Kaerconan to which he had turned to flee, and the rest of the Saxons broke and fled, some to escape, but many to be cut down in the hills, or the narrow defile at the foot of Kaerconan. At first dusk, torches were lit at the gate of the fortress, the gates were thrown open, and Ambrosius' white stallion paced across the bridge and into the stronghold, leaving the field to the ravens, the priests, and the burial parties.

I did not seek him out straight away. Let him bury his dead and clear the fortress. There was work for me down there among the wounded, and besides, there was no hurry now to give him my mother's message. While I had sat there in the May sunlight between the robin's song and the crash of battle, I knew that she had sickened again, and was already dead.

5

I made my way downhill between the clumps of gorse and the thorn-trees. The Welsh troops had vanished, long since, to a man, and isolated shouts and battle cries showed where small parties were still hunting down the fugitives in forest and hill.

Below, on the plain, the fighting was over. They were carrying the wounded into Kaerconan. Torches weaved everywhere, till the plain was all light and smoke. Men shouted to one another, and the cries and groans of the wounded came up clearly, with the occasional scream of a horse, the sharp commands from the officers, and the tramp of the stretcher-bearers' feet. Here and there, in the dark corners away from the torchlight, men scurried singly or in pairs among the heaped bodies. One saw them stoop, straighten, and scurry off. Sometimes where they paused there was a cry, a sudden moan, sometimes the brief flash of metal or the quick downstroke of a shortened blow. Looters, rummaging among the dead and dying, keeping a few steps ahead of the official salvage parties. The ravens were coming down; I saw the tilt and slide of their black wings hovering above the torches, and a pair perched, waiting, on a rock not far from me. With nightfall the rats would be there, too, running up from the damp roots of the castle walls to attack the dead bodies.

The work of salvaging the living was being done as fast and efficiently as everything else the Count's army undertook. Once they were all within, the gates would be shut. I would seek him out, I decided, after the first tasks were done. He would already have been told that I was safely here, and he would guess I had gone to work with the doctors. There would be time, later, to eat, and then it would be time enough to talk to him.

On the field, as I made my way across, the stretcher parties still strove to separate friend from foe. The Saxon dead had been flung into a heap in the center of the field; I guessed they would be burned according to custom. Beside the growing hill of bodies a platoon stood guard over the glittering pile of arms and ornaments taken from the dead men. The British dead were being laid nearer the wall, in rows for identification. There were small parties of men, each with an officer, bending over them one by one. As I picked my way through trampled mud oily and stinking with blood and slime I passed, among the armed and staring dead, the bodies of half a dozen ragged men—peasants or outlaws by the look of them. These would be looters, cut down or speared by the soldiers. One of them still twitched like a pinned moth, hastily speared to the ground by a broken Saxon weapon which had been left in his body. I hesitated, then went and bent over him. He watched me—he was beyond speech—and I could see he still hoped. If he had been cleanly speared, I would have drawn the blade out and let him go with the blood, but as it was, there was a quicker way for him. I drew my dagger, pulled my cloak aside out of the way, and carefully, so that I would be out of the jet of blood, stuck my dagger in at the side of his throat. I wiped it on the dead man's rags, and straightened to find a cold pair of eyes watching me above a levelled short sword three paces away.

Mercifully, it was a man I knew. I saw him recognize me, then he laughed and lowered his sword.

"You're lucky. I nearly gave it to you in the back."

"I didn't think of that." I slid the dagger back into its sheath. "It would have been a pity to die for stealing from that. What did you think he had worth taking?"

"You'd be surprised what you catch them taking. Anything from a corn plaster to a broken sandal strap." He jerked his head towards the high walls of the fortress. "He's been asking where you were."

"I'm on my way."

"They say you foretold this, Merlin? And Doward, too?"

"I said the Red Dragon would overcome the White," I said. "But I think this is not the end yet. What happened to Hengist?"

"Yonder." He nodded again towards the citadel. "He made for the fort when the Saxon line broke, and was captured just by the gate."

"I saw that. He's inside, then? Still alive?"

"Yes."

"And Octa? His son?"

"Got away. He and the cousin—Eosa, isn't it?—galloped north."

"So it isn't the end. Has he sent after them?"

"Not yet. He says there's time enough." He eyed me. "Is there?"

"How would I know?" I was unhelpful. "How long does he plan to stay here? A few days?"

"Three, he says. Time to bury the dead."

"What will he do with Hengist?"

"What do you think?" He made a little chopping movement downwards with the edge of his hand. "And long overdue, if you ask me. They're talking about it in there, but you could hardly call it a trial. The Count's said nothing as yet, but Uther's roaring to have him killed, and the priests want a bit of cold blood to round the day off with. Well, I'll have to get back to work, see if I can catch more civilians looting." He added as he turned away: "We saw you up there on the hill during the fighting. People were saying it was an omen."

He went. A raven flapped down from behind me with a croak, and settled on the breast of the man I had killed. I called to a torch-bearer to light me the rest of the way, and made for the main gate of the fortress.

While I was still some way short of the bridge a blaze of tossing torches came out, and in the middle of them, bound and held, the big blond giant that I knew must be Hengist himself. Ambrosius' troops formed a hollow square, and into this space his captors dragged the Saxon leader, and there must have forced him to his knees, for the flaxen head vanished behind the close ranks of the British. I saw Ambrosius himself then, coming out over the bridge, followed closely on his left by Uther, and on his other side by a man I did not know, in the robe of a Christian bishop, still splashed with mud and blood. Others crowded behind them. The bishop was talking earnestly in Ambrosius' ear. Ambrosius' face was a mask, the cold, expressionless mask I knew so well. I heard him say what sounded like, "You will see, they will be satisfied," and then, shortly, something else that caused the bishop at last to fall silent.

Ambrosius took his place. I saw him nod to an officer. There was a word of command, followed by the whistle and thud of a blow. A sound--it could hardly be called a growl—of satisfaction from the watching men. The bishop's voice, hoarse with triumph: "So perish all pagan enemies of the one true God! Let his body be thrown now to the wolves and kites!" And then Ambrosius' voice, cold and quiet: "He will go to his own gods with his army round him, in the manner of his people." Then to the officer: "Send me word when all is ready, and I will come."

The bishop started to shout again, but Ambrosius turned away unheeding and, with Uther and the other captains, strode back across the bridge and into the fortress. I followed. Spears flashed down to bar my way, then—the place was garrisoned by Ambrosius' Bretons—I was recognized, and the spears withdrawn.

Inside the fortress was a wide square courtyard, now full of a bustling, trampling confusion of men and horses. At the far side a shallow flight of steps led to the door of the main hall and tower. Ambrosius' party was mounting the steps, but I turned aside. There was no need to ask where the wounded had been taken. On the east side of the square a long double-storeyed building had been organized as a dressing station; the sounds coming from this guided me. I was hailed thankfully by the doctor in charge, a man called Gandar, who had taught me in Brittany, and who avowedly had no use for either priests or magicians, but who very much needed another pair of trained hands. He assigned me a couple of orderlies, found me some instruments and a box of salves and medicines, and thrust me—literally—into a long room that was little better than a roofed shed, but which now held some fifty wounded men. I stripped to the waist and started work.

Somewhere around midnight the worst was done and things were quieter. I was at the far end of my section when a slight stir near the entrance made me look round to see Ambrosius, with Gandar and two officers, come quietly in and walk down the row of wounded, stopping by each man to talk or, with those worst wounded, to question the doctor in an undertone.

I was stitching a thigh wound—it was clean, and would heal, but it was deep and jagged, and to everyone's relief the man had fainted—when the group reached me. I did not look up, and Ambrosius waited in silence until I had done and, reaching for the dressings the orderly had prepared, bandaged the wound. I finished, and got to my feet as the orderly came back with a bowl of water. I plunged my hands into this, and looked up to see Ambrosius smiling. He was still in his hacked and spattered armour, but he looked fresh and alert, and ready if necessary to start another battle. I could see the wounded men watching him as if they would draw strength just from the sight.

"My lord," I said.

He stooped over the unconscious man. "How is he?"

"A flesh wound. He'll recover, and live to be thankful it wasn't a few inches to the left."

"You've done a good job, I see." Then as I finished drying my hands and dismissed the orderly with a word of thanks, Ambrosius put out his own hand. "And now, welcome. I believe we owe you quite a lot, Merlin. I don't mean for this; I mean for Doward, and for today as well. At any rate the men think so, and if soldiers decide something is lucky, then it is lucky. Well, I'm glad to see you safe. You have news for me, I believe."

"Yes." I said it without expression, because of the men with us, but I saw the smile fade from his eyes. He hesitated, then said quietly: "Gentlemen, give us leave." They went. He and I faced one another across the body of the unconscious man. Nearby a soldier tossed and moaned, and another cried out and bit the sound back. The place smelled vile, of blood and drying sweat and sickness.

"What is this news?"

"It concerns my mother."

I think he already knew what I was going to tell him. He spoke slowly, measuring the words, as if each one carried with it some weight that he ought to feel. "The men who rode here with you . . . they brought me news of her. She had been ill, but was recovered, they said, and safely back in Maridunum. Was this not true?"

"It was true when I left Maridunum. If I had known the illness was mortal, I would not have left her."

" 'Was' mortal?"

"Yes, my lord."

He was silent, looking down, but without seeing him, at the wounded man. The latter was beginning to stir; soon he would be back with the pain and the stench and the fear of mortality. I said: "Shall we go out into the air? I've finished here. I'll send someone back to this man."

"Yes. And you must get your clothes. It's a cool night." Then, still without moving: "When did she die?"

"At sunset today."

He looked up quickly at that, his eyes narrow and intent, then he nodded, accepting it. He turned to go out, gesturing me to walk with him. As we went he asked me: "Do you suppose she knew?"

"I think so, yes."

"She sent no message?"

"Not directly. She said, 'When we meet again, it will be soon enough.' She is a Christian, remember. They believe—"

"I know what they believe."

Some commotion outside made itself heard, a voice barking a couple of commands, feet tramping. Ambrosius paused, listening. Someone was coming our way, quickly.

"We'll talk later, Merlin. You have a lot to tell me. But first we must send Hengist's spirit to join his fathers. Come."

They had heaped the Saxon dead high on a great stack of wood, and poured oil and pitch over them. At the top of the pyramid, on a platform roughly nailed together of planks, lay Hengist. How Ambrosius had stopped them robbing him I shall never know, but he had not been robbed. His shield lay on his breast, and a sword by his right hand. They had hidden the severed neck with a broad leather collar of the kind some soldiers use for throat guards. It was studded with gold. A cloak covered his body from throat to feet, and its scarlet folds flowed down over the rough wood.

As soon as the torches were thrust in below, the flames caught greedily. It was a still night, and the smoke poured upwards in a thick black column laced with fire. The edges of Hengist's cloak caught, blackened, curled, and then he was lost to sight in the gush of smoke and flames. The fire cracked like whips, and as the logs burned and broke, men ran, sweating and blackened, to throw more in. Even from where we stood, well back, the heat was intense, and the smell of burnt pitch and roasting meat came in sickening gusts on the damp night air. Beyond the lighted ring of watching men torches moved still on the battlefield, and one could hear the steady thud of spades striking into the earth for the British dead. Beyond the brilliant pyre, beyond the dark slopes of the far hills, the May moon hung, faint through the smoke.

"What do you see?"

Ambrosius' voice made me start. I looked at him, surprised. "See?"

"In the fire, Merlin the prophet."

"Nothing but dead men roasting."

"Then look and see something for me, Merlin. Where has Octa gone?"

I laughed. "How should I know? I told you all I could see."

But he did not smile. "Look harder. Tell me where Octa has gone. And Eosa. Where they will dig themselves in to wait for me. And how soon."

"I told you. I don't look for things. If it is the god's will that they should come to me, they come out of the flames, or out of the black night, and they come silently like an arrow out of ambush. I do not go to find the bowman; all I can do is stand with my breast bare and wait for the arrow to hit me."

"Then do it now." He spoke strongly, stubbornly. I saw he was quite serious. "You saw for Vortigern."

"You call it 'for' him? To prophesy his death? When I did that, my lord, I did not even know what I was saying. I suppose Gorlois told you what happened—even now, I couldn't tell you myself. I neither know when it will come, nor when it will leave me."

"Only today you knew about Niniane, and without either fire or darkness."

"That's true. But I can't tell you how, any more than how I knew what I told Vortigern."

"The men call you 'Vortigern's prophet.' You prophesied victory for us, and we had it, here and at Doward. The men believe you and have faith in you. So have I. Is it not a better title now to be 'Ambrosius' prophet'?"

"My lord, you know I would take any title from you that you cared to bestow. But this comes from somewhere else. I cannot call it, but I know that if it matters it will come. And when it comes, be sure I will tell you. You know I am at your service. Now, about Octa and Eosa I know nothing. I can only guess—and guess as a man. They fight still under the White Dragon, do they?"

His eyes narrowed. "Yes."

"Then what Vortigern's prophet said must still hold good."

"I can tell the men this?"

"If they need it. When do you plan to march?"

"In three days."

"Aiming for where?"

"York."

I turned up a hand. "Then your guess as a commander is probably as good as my guess as a magician. Will you take me?"

He smiled. "Will you be any use to me?"

"Probably not as a prophet. But do you need an engineer? Or an apprentice doctor? Or even a singer?"

He laughed. "A host in yourself, I know. As long as you don't turn priest on me, Merlin. I have enough of them."

"You needn't be afraid of that."

The flames were dying down. The officer in charge of the proceedings approached, saluted, and asked if the men might be dismissed. Ambrosius gave him leave, then looked at me. "Come with me to York, then. I shall have work for you there. Real work. They tell me the place is half ruined, and I'll need someone to help direct the engineers. Tremorinus is at Caerleon. Now, find Caius Valerius and tell him to look after you, and bring you to me in an hour's time." He added over his shoulder as he turned away: "And in the meantime if anything should come to you out of the dark like an arrow, you'll let me know?"

"Unless it really is an arrow."

He laughed, and went.

Uther was beside me suddenly. "Well, Merlin the bastard? They're saying you won the battle for us from the hilltop?" I noticed, with surprise, that there was no malice in his tone. His manner was relaxed, easy, almost gay, like that of a prisoner let loose. I supposed this was indeed how he felt after the long frustrations of the years in Brittany. Left to himself Uther would have charged across the Narrow Sea before he was fairly into manhood, and been valiantly smashed in pieces for his pains. Now, like a hawk being flown for the first time at the quarry, he was feeling his power. I could feel it, too: it clothed him like folded wings. I said something in greeting, but he interrupted me. "Did you see anything in the flames just now?"

"Oh, not you, too," I said warmly. "The Count seems to think all I have to do is to look at a torch and tell the future. I've been trying to explain it doesn't work like that."

"You disappoint me. I was going to ask you to tell my fortune."

"Oh, Eros, that's easy enough. In about an hour's time, as soon as you've settled your men, you'll be bedded down with a girl."

"It's not as much of a certainty as all that. How the devil did you know I'd managed to find one? They're not very thick on the ground just here—there's only about one man in fifty managed to get one. I was lucky."

"That's what I mean," I said. "Given fifty men and only one woman amongst them, then Uther has the woman. That's what I call one of the certainties of life. Where will I find Caius Valerius?"

"I'll send someone to show you. I'd come myself, only I'm keeping out of his way."

"Why?"

"When we tossed for the girl, he lost," said Uther cheerfully. "He'll have plenty of time to look after you. In fact, all night. Come along."

6

We went into York three days before the end of May.

Ambrosius' scouts had confirmed his guess about York; there was a good road north from Kaerconan, and Octa had fled up this with Eosa his kinsman, and had taken refuge in the fortified city which the Romans called Eboracum, and the Saxons Eoforwick, or York. But the fortifications at York were in poor repair, and the inhabitants, when they heard of Ambrosius' resounding victory at Kaerconan, offered the fleeing Saxons cold comfort. For all Octa's speed, Ambrosius was barely two days behind him, and at the sight of our vast army, rested, and reinforced by fresh British allies encouraged by the Red Dragon's victories, the Saxons, doubting whether they could hold the city against him, decided to beg for mercy.

I saw it myself, being right up in the van with the siege engines, under the walls. In its way it was more unpleasant even than a battle. The Saxon leader was a big man, blond like his father, and young. He appeared before Ambrosius stripped to his trews, which were of coarse stuff bound with thongs. His wrists likewise were bound, this time with a chain, and his head and body were smeared with dust, a token of humiliation he hardly needed. His eyes were angry, and I could see he had been forced into this by the cowardice—or wisdom, as you care to call it—of the group of Saxon and British notables who crowded behind him out of the city gate, begging Ambrosius for mercy on themselves and their families.

This time he gave it. He demanded only that the remnants of the Saxon army should withdraw to the north, beyond the old Wall of Hadrian, which (he said) he would count the border of his realm. The lands beyond this, so men say, are wild and sullen, and scarcely habitable, but Octa took his liberty gladly enough, and after him, eager for the same mercy, came his cousin Eosa throwing himself on Ambrosius' bounty. He received it, and the city of York opened its gates to its new king.

Ambrosius' first occupation of a town was always to follow the same pattern. First of all the establishment of order: he would never allow the British auxiliaries into the town; his own troops from Less Britain, with no local loyalties, were the ones that established and held order. The streets were cleaned, the fortifications temporarily repaired, and plans drawn up for the future work and put into the hands of a small group of skilled engineers who were to call on local labour. Then a meeting of the city's leaders, a discussion on future policy, an oath of loyalty to Ambrosius, and arrangements made for the garrisoning of the city when the army departed. Finally a religious ceremony of thanksgiving with a feast and a public holiday.

In York, the first great city invested by Ambrosius, the ceremony was held in the church, on a blazing day near the end of June, and in the presence of the whole army, and a vast crowd of people.

I had already attended a private ceremony elsewhere.

It was not to be expected that there was still a temple of Mithras in York. The worship was forbidden, and in any case would have vanished when the last legion left the Saxon Shore almost a century ago, but in the day of the legions the temple at York had been one of the finest in the country. Since there was no natural cave nearby, it had originally been built below the house of the Roman commander, in a large cellar, and because of this the Christians had not been able to desecrate and destroy it, as was their wont with the sacred places of other men. But time and damp had done their work, and the sanctuary had crumbled into disrepair. Once, under a Christian governor, there had been an attempt to turn the place into a chapel-crypt, but the next governor had been outspokenly, not to say violently, opposed to this. He was a Christian himself, but he saw no reason why the perfectly good cellar under his house should not be used for what (to him) was the real purpose of a cellar, namely, to store wine. And a wine store it had remained, till the day Uther sent a working party down to clean and repair it for the meeting, which was to be held on the god's own feast day, the sixteenth day of June. This time the meeting was secret, not from fear, but from policy, since the official thanksgiving would be Christian, and Ambrosius would be there to offer thanks in the presence of the bishops and all the people. I myself had not seen the sanctuary, having been employed during my first days in York on the restoring of the Christian church in time for the public ceremony. But on the feast of Mithras I was to present myself at the underground temple with others of my own grade. Most of these were men I did not know, or could not identify by the voice behind the mask; but Uther was always recognizable, and my father would of course be there, in his office as Courier of the Sun.

The door of the temple was closed. We of the lowest grade waited our turn in the antechamber.

This was a smallish, square room, lit only by the two torches held in the hands of the statues one to either side of the temple door. Above the doorway was the old stone mask of a lion, worn and fretted, part of the wall. To either side, as worn and chipped, and with noses and members broken and hacked away, the two stone torch-bearers still looked ancient and dignified. The anteroom was chill, in spite of the torches, and smelled of smoke. I felt the cold at work on my body; it struck up from the stone floor into my bare feet, and under the long robe of white wool I was naked. But just as the first shiver ran up my skin, the temple door opened, and in an instant all was light and colour and fire.

Even now, after all these years, and knowing all that I have learned in a lifetime, I cannot find it in me to break the vow I made of silence and secrecy. Nor, so far as I know, has any man done so. Men say that what you are taught when young can never be fully expunged from your mind, and I know that I, myself, have never escaped the spell of the secret god who led me to Brittany and threw me at my father's feet. Indeed, whether because of the curb on the spirit of which I have already written, or whether by intervention of the god himself, I find that my memory of his worship has gone into a blur, as if it was a dream. And a dream it may be, not of this time alone, but made up of all the other times, from the first vision of the midnight field, to this night's ceremony, which was the last.

A few things I remember. More torch-bearers of stone. The long benches to either side of the center aisle where men reclined in their bright robes, the masks turned to us, eyes watchful. The steps at the far end, and the great apse with the arch like a cave-mouth opening on the cave within, where, under the star-studded roof, was the old relief in stone of Mithras at the bull-slaying. It must have been somehow protected from the hammers of the god-breakers, for it was still strongly carved and dramatic. There he was, in the light of the torches, the young man of the standing stone, the fellow in the cap, kneeling on the fallen bull and, with his head turned away in sorrow, striking the sword into its throat. At the foot of the steps stood the fire-altars, one to each side. Beside one of them a man robed and masked as a Lion, with a rod in his hand. Beside the other the Heliodromos, the Courier of the Sun. And at the head of the steps, in the center of the apse, the Father waiting to receive us.

My Raven mask had poor eyeholes, and I could only see straight forward. It would not have been seemly to look from side to side with that pointed bird-mask, so I stood listening to the voices, and wondering how many friends were here, how many men I knew. The only one I could be sure of was the Courier, tall and quiet there by the altar fire, and one of the Lions, either him by the archway, or one of the grade who watched from somewhere along the makeshift benches.

This was the frame of the ceremony, and all that I can remember, except the end. The officiating Lion was not Uther, after all. He was a shorter man, of thick build, and seemingly older than Uther, and the blow he struck me was no more than the ritual tap, without the sting that Uther usually managed to put into it. Nor was Ambrosius the Courier. As the latter handed me the token meal of bread and wine, I saw the ring on the little finger of his left hand, made of gold, enclosing a stone of red jasper with a dragon crest carved small. But when he lifted the cup to my mouth, and the scarlet robe slipped back from his arm, I saw a familiar scar white on the brown flesh, and looked up to meet the blue eyes behind the mask, alight with a spark of amusement that quickened to laughter as I started, and spilled the wine. Uther had stepped up two grades, it seemed, in the time since I had last attended the mysteries. And since there was no other Courier present, there was only one place for Ambrosius . . .

I turned from the Courier to kneel at the Father's feet. But the hands which took my own between them for the vow were the hands of an old man, and when I looked up, the eyes behind the mask were the eyes of a stranger.

Eight days later was the official ceremony of thanksgiving. Ambrosius was there, with all his officers, even Uther, "for," said my father to me afterwards when we were alone, "as you will find, all gods who are born of the light are brothers, and in this land, if Mithras who gives us victory is to bear the face of Christ, why, then, we worship Christ."

We never spoke of it again.

The capitulation of York marked the end of the first stage of Ambrosius' campaign. After York we went to London in easy stages, and with no more fighting, unless you count a few skirmishes by the way. What the King had to undertake now was the enormous work of reconstruction and the consolidation of his kingdom. In every town and strongpoint he left garrisons of tried men under trusted officers, and appointed his own engineers to help organize the work of rebuilding and repairing towns, roads and fortresses. Everywhere the picture was the same; once-fine buildings ruined or damaged almost beyond repair; roads half obliterated through neglect; villages destroyed and people hiding fearfully in caves and forests; places of worship pulled down or polluted. It was as if the stupidity and lawless greed of the Saxon hordes had cast a blight over the whole land. Everything that had given light—art, song, learning, worship, the ceremonial meetings of the people, the feasts at Easter or Hallowmass or midwinter, even the arts of husbandry, all these had vanished under the dark clouds on which rode the northern gods of war and thunder. And they had been invited here by Vortigern, a British king. This, now, was all that people remembered. They forgot that Vortigern had reigned well enough for ten years, and adequately for a few more, before he found that the war-spirit he had unleashed on his country had outgrown his control. They remembered only that he had gained his throne by bloodshed and treachery and the murder of a kinsman—and that the kinsman had been the true king. So they came flocking now to Ambrosius, calling on him the blessings of their different gods, hailing him with joy as King, the first "King of all Britain," the first shining chance for the country to be one.

Other men have told the story of Ambrosius' crowning and his first work as King of Britain; it has even been written down, so here I will only say that I was with him for the first two years as I have told, but then, in the spring of my twentieth year, I left him. I had had enough of councils and marching, and long legal discussions where Ambrosius tried to reimpose the laws that had fallen into disuse, and the everlasting meetings with elders and bishops droning like bees, days and weeks for every drop of honey. I was even tired of building and designing; this was the only work I had done for him in all the long months I served with the army. I knew at last that I must leave him, get out of the press of affairs that surrounded him; the god does not speak to those who have no time to listen. The mind must seek out what it needs to feed on, and it came to me at last that what work I had to do, I must do among the quiet of my own hills. So in spring, when we came to Winchester, I sent a message to Cadal, then sought Ambrosius out to tell him I must go.

He listened half absently; cares pressed heavily on him these days, and the years which had sat lightly on him before now seemed to weigh him down. I have noticed that this is often the way with men who set their lives towards the distant glow of one high beacon; when the hilltop is reached and there is nowhere further to climb, and all that is left is to pile more on the flame and keep the beacon burning, why, then, they sit down beside it and grow old. Where their leaping blood warmed them before, now the beacon fire must do it from without. So it was with Ambrosius. The King who sat in his great chair at Winchester and listened to me was not the young commander whom I had faced across the map-strewn table in Less Britain, or even the Courier of Mithras who had ridden to me across the frostbound field.

"I cannot hold you," he said. "You are not an officer of mine, you are only my son. You will go where you wish."

"I serve you. You know that. But I know now how best I can serve you. You spoke the other day of sending a troop towards Caerleon. Who's going?"

He looked down at a paper. A year ago he would have known without looking. "Priscus, Valens. Probably Sidonius. They go in two days' time."

"Then I'll go with them."

He looked at me. Suddenly it was the old Ambrosius back again. "An arrow out of the dark?"

"You might say so. I know I must go."

"Then go safely. And some day, come back to me."

Someone interrupted us then. When I left him he was already going, word by word, through some laborious draft of the new statutes for the city.

7

The road from Winchester to Caerleon is a good one, and the weather was fine and dry, so we did not halt in Sarum, but held on northwards while the light lasted, straight across the Great Plain.

A short way beyond Sarum lies the place where Ambrosius was born. I cannot even call to mind now what name it had gone by in the past, but already it was being called by his name, Amberesburg, or Amesbury. I had never been that way and had a mind to see it, so we pressed on, and arrived just before sunset. I, together with the officers, was given comfortable lodging with the head man of the town—it was little more than a village, but very conscious now of its standing as the King's birthplace. Not far away was the spot where, many years ago, some hundred or more British nobles had been treacherously massacred by the Saxons and buried in a common grave. This place lay some way west of Amesbury, beyond the stone circle that men call the Giants' Dance, or the Dance of the Hanging Stones.

I had long heard about the Dance and had been curious to see it, so when the troop reached Amesbury, and were preparing to settle in for the night, I made my excuses to my host, and rode out westwards alone over the open plain. Here, for mile on mile, the long plain stretches without hill or valley, unbroken save for clumps of thorn-trees and gorse, and here and there a solitary oak stripped by the winds. The sun sets late, and this evening as I rode my tired horse slowly westwards the sky ahead of me was still tinged with the last rays, while behind me in the east the clouds of evening piled slate-blue, and one early star came out.

I think I had been expecting the Dance to be much less impressive than the ranked armies of stones I had grown accustomed to in Brittany, something, perhaps, on the scale of the circle on the druids' island. But these stones were enormous, bigger than any I had ever seen; and their very isolation, standing as they did in the center of that vast and empty plain, struck the heart with awe.

I rode some of the way round, slowly, staring, then dismounted and, leaving my horse to graze, walked forward between two standing stones of the outer circle. My shadow, thrown ahead of me between their shadows, was tiny, a pygmy thing. I paused involuntarily, as if the giants had linked hands to stop me.

Ambrosius had asked me if this had been "an arrow out of the dark." I had told him yes, and this was true, but I had yet to find out why I had been brought here. All I knew was that, now I was here, I wished myself away. I had felt something of the same thing in Brittany as I first passed among the avenues of stone; a breathing on the back of the neck as if something older than time were looking over one's shoulder; but this was not quite the same. It was as if the ground, the stones that I touched, though still warm from the spring sunlight, were breathing cold from somewhere deep below.

Half reluctantly, I walked forward. The light was going rapidly, and to pick one's way into the center needed care. Time and storm—and perhaps the gods of war—had done their work, and many of the stones were cast down to lie haphazard, but the pattern could still be discerned. It was a circle, but like nothing I had seen in Brittany, like nothing I had even imagined. There had been, originally, an outer circle of the huge stones, and where a crescent of these still stood I saw that the uprights were crowned with a continuous lintel of stones as vast as themselves, a great linked curve of stone, standing like a giants' fence across the sky. Here and there others of the outer circle were still standing, but most had fallen, or were leaning at drunken angles, with the lintel stones beside them on the ground. Within the bigger circle was a smaller one of uprights, and some of the outer giants had fallen against these and brought them flat. Within these again, marking the center, was a horse-shoe of enormous stones, crowned in pairs. Three of these trilithons stood intact; the fourth had fallen, and brought its neighbour down with it. Echoing this once again was an inner horse-shoe of smaller stones, nearly all standing. The center was empty, and crossed with shadows.

The sun had gone, and with its going the western sky drained of colour, leaving one bright star in a swimming sea of green. I stood still. It was very quiet, so quiet that I could hear the sound of my horse cropping the turf, and the thin jingle of his bit as he moved. The only other sound was the whispering chatter of nesting starlings among the great trilithons overhead. The starling is a bird sacred to druids, and I had heard that in past time the Dance had been used for worship by the druid priests. There are many stories about the Dance, how the stones were brought from Africa, and put up by giants of old, or how they were the giants themselves, caught and turned to stone by a curse as they danced in a ring. But it was not giants or curses that were breathing the cold now from the ground and from the stones; these stones had been put here by men, and their raising had been sung by poets, like the old blind man of Brittany. A lingering shred of light caught the stone near me; the huge knob of stone on one sandstone surface echoed the hole in the fallen lintel alongside it. These tenons and sockets had been fashioned by men, craftsmen such as I had watched almost daily for the last few years, in Less Britain, then in York, London, Winchester. And massive as they were, giants' building as they seemed to be, they had been raised by the hands of workmen, to the commands of engineers, and to the sound of music such as I had heard from the blind singer of Kerrec.

I walked slowly forward across the circle's center. The faint light in the western sky threw my shadow slanting ahead of me, and etched, momentarily in fleeting light, the shape of an axe, two-headed, on one of the stones. I hesitated, then turned to look. My shadow wavered and dipped. I trod in a shallow pit and fell, measuring my length.

It was only a depression in the ground, the kind that might have been made, years past, by the falling of one of the great stones. Or by a grave . . .

There was no stone nearby of such a size, no sign of digging, no one buried here. The turf was smooth, and grazed by sheep and cattle, and under my hands as I picked myself up slowly, were the scented, frilled stars of daisies. But as I lay I had felt the cold strike up from below, in a pang as sudden as an arrow striking, and I knew that this was why I had been brought here.

I caught my horse, mounted and rode the two miles back to my father's birthplace.

We reached Caerleon four days later to find the place completely changed. Ambrosius intended to use it as one of his three main stations along with London and York, and Tremorinus himself had been working there. The walls had been rebuilt, the bridge repaired, the river dredged and its banks strengthened, and the whole of the east barrack block rebuilt. In earlier times the military settlement at Caerleon, circled by low hills and guarded by a curve of the river, had been a vast place; there was no need for even half of it now, so Tremorinus had pulled down what remained of the western barrack blocks and used the material on the spot to build the new quarters, the baths, and some brand-new kitchens. The old ones had been in even worse condition than the bathhouse at Maridunum, and now, "You'll have every man in Britain asking to be posted here," I told Tremorinus, and he looked pleased.

"We'll not be ready a moment too soon," he said. "The rumour's going round of fresh trouble coming. Have you heard anything?"

"Nothing. But if it's recent news I wouldn't have had it. We've been on the move for nearly a week. What kind of trouble? Not Octa again, surely?"

"No, Pascentius." This was Vortimer's brother who had fought with him in the rebellion, and fled north after Vortimer's death. "You knew he took ship to Germany? They say he'll come back."

"Give him time," I said, "you may be sure he will. Well, you'll send me any news that comes?"

"Send you? You're not staying here?"

"No. I'm going on to Maridunum. It's my home, you know."

"I had forgotten. Well, perhaps we'll see something of you; I'll be here myself a bit longer—we've started work on the church now." He grinned. "The bishop's been at me like a gadfly: it seems I should have been thinking of that before I spent so much time on the things of this earth. And there's talk, too, of putting up some kind of monument to the King's victories. A triumphal arch, some say, the old Roman style of thing. Of course they're saying here in Caerleon that we should build the church for that—the glory of God with Ambrosius thrown in. Though myself I think if any bishop should get the credit of God's glory and the King's combined it should be Gloucester—old Eldad laid about him with the best of them. Did you see him?"

"I heard him."

He laughed. "Well, in any case you'll stay tonight, I hope? Have supper with me."

"Thanks. I'd like to."

We talked late into the night, and he showed me some of his plans and designs, and seemed flatteringly anxious that I should come back from Maridunum to see the various stages of the building. I promised, and next day left Caerleon alone, parrying an equally flattering and urgent request from the camp commandant to let him give me an escort. But I refused, and in the late afternoon came, alone, at last in sight of my own hills. There were rain clouds massing in the west, but in front of them, like a bright curtain, the slanting sunlight. One could see on a day like this why the green hills of Wales had been called the Black Mountains, and the valleys running through them the Valleys of Gold.

Bars of sunlight lay along the trees of the golden valleys, and the hills stood slate-blue or black behind them, with their tops supporting the sky.

I took two days for the journey, going easily, and noticing by the way, how the land seemed already to have got back its bloom of peace. A farmer building a wall barely looked my way as I rode by, and a young girl minding a flock of sheep smiled at me. And when I got to the mill on the Tywy, it seemed to be working normally; there were grain sacks piled in the yard, and I could hear the clack-clack-clack of the turning wheel.

I passed the bottom of the path which led up to the cave, and held on straight for the town. I believe I told myself that my first duty and concern was to visit St. Peter's to ask about my mother's death, and to see where she was buried. But when I got from my horse at the nunnery gate and lifted a hand to the bell, I knew from the knocking of my heart that I had told myself a lie.

I could have spared myself the deception; it was the old portress who let me in, and who led me straight, without being asked, through the inner court and down to the green slope near the river where my mother was buried. It was a lovely place, a green plot near a wall where pear trees had been brought early into blossom by the warmth, and where, above their snow, the white doves she had loved were rounding their breasts to the sun. I could hear the ripple of the river beyond the wall, and down through the rustling trees the note of the chapel bell.

The Abbess received me kindly, but had nothing to add to the account which I had received soon after my mother's death, and had passed on to my father. I left money for prayers, and for a carved stone to be made, and when I left, it was with her silver and amethyst cross tucked into my saddle-bag. One question I dared not ask, even when a girl who was not Keri brought wine for my refreshment. And finally, with my question unasked, I was ushered to the gate and out into the street. Here I thought for a moment that my luck had changed, for as I was untying my horse's bridle from the ring beside the gate I saw the old portress peering at me through the grille—remembering, no doubt, the gold I had given her on my first visit. But when I produced money and beckoned her close to shout my question in her ear, and even, after three repetitions, got through to her, the only answer was a shrug and the one word, "Gone," which—even if she had understood me—was hardly helpful. In the end I gave it up. In any case, I told myself, this was something that had to be forgotten. So I rode out of town and back over the miles to my valley with the memory of her face burned into everything I saw, and the gold of her hair lying in every shaft of the slanting sunlight.

Cadal had rebuilt the pen which Galapas and I had made in the hawthorn brake. It had a good roof and a stout door, and could easily house a couple of big horses. One—Cadal's own, I supposed—was already there.

Cadal himself must have heard me riding up the valley, because, almost before I had dismounted, he came running down the path by the cliff, had the bridle out of my hand, and, lifting both my hands in his, kissed them.

"Why, what's this?" I asked, surprised. He need have had no fears for my safety; the messages I had sent him had been regular and reassuring. "Didn't you get the message I was coming?"

"Yes, I got it. It's been a long time. You're looking well."

"And you. Is all well here?"

"You'll find it so. If you must live in a place like this, there's ways and ways of making it fit. Now get away up, your supper's ready." He bent to unbuckle the horse's girths, leaving me to go up to the cave alone.

He had had a long time in which to do it, but even so it came with a shock like a miracle. It was as it had always been, a place of green grass and sunlight. Daisies and heartsease starred the turf between the green curls of young bracken, and young rabbits whisked out of sight under the flowering blackthorn. The spring ran crystal clear, and crystal clear through the water of the well could be seen the silver gravel at the bottom. Above it, in its ferny niche, stood the carved figure of the god; Cadal must have found it when he cleared the rubbish from the well. He had even found the cup of horn. It stood where it had always stood. I drank from it, sprinkled the drops for the god, and went into the cave.

My books had come from Less Britain; the great chest was backed against the wall of the cave, where Galapas' box had been. Where his table had stood there was another, which I recognized from my grandfather's house. The bronze mirror was back in place. The cave was clean, sweet-smelling and dry. Cadal had built a hearth of stone, and logs were laid ready across it to light. I half expected to see Galapas sitting beside the hearth, and, on the ledge near the entrance, the falcon which had perched there on the night a small boy left the cave in tears. Deep among the shadows above the ledge at the rear was the gash of deeper shadow which hid the crystal cave.

That night, lying on the bed of bracken with the rugs pulled round me, I lay listening, after the dying of the fire, to the rustle of leaves outside the cave, and, beyond that, the trickle of the spring. They were the only sounds in the world. I closed my eyes and slept as I had not slept since I was a child.

8

Like a drunkard who, as long as there is no wine to be had, thinks himself cured of his craving, I had thought myself cured of the thirst for silence and solitude. But from the first morning of waking on Bryn Myrddin, I knew that this was not merely a refuge, it was my place. April lengthened into May, and the cuckoos shouted from hill to hill, the bluebells unfurled in the young bracken, and evenings were full of the sound of lambs crying, and still I had never once gone nearer the town than the crest of a hill two miles north where I gathered leaves and cresses. Cadal went down daily for supplies and for what news was current, and twice a messenger rode up the valley, once with a bundle of sketches from Tremorinus, once with news from Winchester and money from my father—no letter, but confirmation that Pascentius was indeed massing troops in Germany, and war must surely come before the end of summer.

For the rest I read, and walked on the hills, and gathered plants and made medicines. I also made music, and sang a number of songs which made Cadal look sideways at me over his tasks and shake his head. Some of them are still sung, but most are best forgotten. One of the latter was this, which I sang one night when May was in town with all her wild clouds of blossom, and greybell turned to bluebell along the brakes.

The land is grey and bare, the trees naked as bone,
Their summer stripped from them; the willow's hair,
The beauty of blue water, the golden grasses,
Even the bird's whistle has been stolen,
Stolen by a girl, robbed by a girl lithe as willow.

Blithe she is as the bird on the May bough,
Sweet she is as the bell in the tower,
She dances over the bending rushes
And her steps shine on the grey grass.

I would take a gift to her, queen of maidens,
But what is left to offer from my bare valley?
Voices of wind in the reeds, and jewel of rain,
And fur of moss on the cold stone.
What is there left to offer but moss on the stone?
She closes her eyes and turns from me in sleep.

The next day I was walking in a wooded valley a mile from home looking for wild mint and bitterweed, when, as if I had called her, she came up the path through the bluebells and bracken. For all I know, I may have called her. An arrow is an arrow, whichever god looses it.

I stood still by a clump of birches, staring as if she would vanish; as if I had indeed conjured her up that moment from dream and desire, a ghost in sunlight. I could not move, though my whole body and spirit seemed to leap at once to meet her. She saw me, and laughter broke in her face, and she came to me, walking lightly. In the chequer of dancing light and shadow as the birch boughs moved she still seemed insubstantial, as if her step would hardly stir the grasses, but then she came closer and it was no vision, but Keri as I remembered her, in brown homespun and smelling of honeysuckle. But now she wore no hood; her hair was loose over her shoulders, and her feet were bare. The sun glanced through the moving leaves, making her hair sparkle like light on water. She had her hands full of bluebells.

"My lord!" The small, breathless voice was full of pleasure.

I stood still with all my dignity round me like a robe, and under it my body fretting like a horse that feels curb and spur at the same time. I wondered if she were going to kiss my hand again, and if so, what I would do. "Keri! What are you doing here?"

"Why, gathering bluebells." The wide innocence of her look robbed the words of pertness. She held them up, laughing at me across them. God knows what she could see in my face. No, she was not going to kiss my hand. "Didn't you know I'd left St. Peter's?"

"Yes, they told me. I thought you must have gone to some other nunnery."

"No, never that. I hated it. It was like being in a cage. Some of them liked it, it made them feel safe, but not me. I wasn't made for such a life."

"They tried to do the same thing to me, once," I said.

"Did you run away, too?"

"Oh, yes. But I ran before they shut me up. Where are you living now, Keri?"

She did not seem to have heard the question. "You weren't meant for it, either? Being in chains, I mean?"

"Not those chains."

I could see her puzzling over this, but I was not sure what I had meant myself, so held my tongue, watching her without thought, feeling only the strong happiness of the moment.

"I was sorry about your mother," she said.

"Thank you, Keri."

"She died just after you'd left. I suppose they told you all about it?"

"Yes. I went to the nunnery as soon as I came back to Maridunum."

She was silent for a moment, looking down. She pointed a bare toe in the grass, a little shy dancing movement which set the golden apples at her girdle jingling. "I knew you had come back. Everyone's talking about it."

"Are they?"

She nodded. "They told me in the town that you were a prince as well as a great magician . . ." She looked up then, her voice fading to doubt, as she eyed me. I was wearing my oldest clothes, a tunic with grass stains that not even Cadal could remove, and my mantle was burred and pulled by thorns and brambles. My sandals were of canvas like a slave's; it was useless to wear leather through the long wet grass. Compared even with the plainly dressed young man she had seen before, I must look like a beggar. She asked, with the directness of innocence: "Are you still a prince, now that your mother is gone?"

"Yes. My father is the High King."

Her lips parted. "Your father? The King? I didn't know. Nobody said that."

"Not many people know. But now that my mother is dead, it doesn't matter. Yes, I am his son."

"The son of the High King . . ." She breathed it, with awe. "And a magician, too. I know that's true."

"Yes. That is true."

"You once told me you weren't."

I smiled. "I told you I couldn't cure your toothache."

"But you did cure it."

"So you said. I didn't believe you."

"Your touch would cure anything," she said, and came close to me.

The neck of her gown hung slack. Her throat was pale as honeysuckle. I could smell her scent and the scent of the bluebells, and the bittersweet juice of the flowers crushed between us. I put out a hand and pulled at the neck of the gown, and the drawstring snapped. Her breasts were round and full and softer than anything I had imagined. They rounded into my hands like the breasts of my mother's doves. I believe I had expected her to cry out and pull away from me, but she nestled towards me warmly, and laughed, and put her hands up behind my head and dug her fingers into my hair and bit me on the mouth. Then suddenly she let her whole weight hang against me so that, reaching to hold her, plunging clumsily into the kiss, I stumbled forward and fell to the ground with her under me and the flowers scattering round us as we fell.

It took me a long time to understand. At first it was laughter and snatched breathing and all that burns down into the imagination in the night, but still held down hard and steady because of her smallness and the soft sounds she made when I hurt her. She was slim as a reed and soft with it, and you would have thought it would make me feel like a duke of the world, but then suddenly she made a sound deep in her throat as if she was strangling, and twisted in my arms as I have seen a dying man twist in pain, and her mouth came up like something striking, and fastened on mine.

Suddenly it was I who was strangling; her arms dragged at me, her mouth sucked me down, her body drew me into that tight and final darkness, no air, no light, no breath, no whisper of waking spirit. A grave inside a grave. Fear burned down into my brain like a white hot blade laid across the eyes. I opened them and could see nothing but the spinning light and the shadow of a tree laid across me whose thorns tore like spikes. Some shape of terror clawed my face. The thorn-tree's shadow swelled and shook, the cave-mouth gaped and the walls breathed, crushing me. I struggled back, out, tore myself away and rolled over apart from her, sweating with fear and shame.

"What's the matter?" Even her voice sounded blind. Her hands still moved over the space of air where I had been.

"I'm sorry, Keri. I'm sorry."

"What do you mean? What's happened?" She turned her head in its fallen flurry of gold. Her eyes were narrow and cloudy. She reached for me. "Oh, if that's all, come here. It's all right, I'll show you, just come here."

"No." I tried to put her aside gently, but I was shaking. "No, Keri. Leave me. No."

"What's the matter?" Her eyes opened suddenly wide. She pushed herself up on her elbow. "Why, I do believe you've never done it before. Have you? Have you?"

I didn't speak.

She gave a laugh that seemed meant to sound gay, but came shrilly. She rolled over again and stretched out her hands. "Well, never mind, you can learn, can't you? You're a man, after all. At least, I thought you were . . ." Then, suddenly in a fury of impatience: "Oh, for God's sake. Hurry, can't you? I tell you, it'll be all right."

I caught her wrists and held them. "Keri, I'm sorry. I can't explain, but this is . . . I must not, that's all I know. No, listen, give me a minute."

"Let me go!"

I loosed her and she pulled away and sat up. Her eyes were angry. There were flowers caught in her hair.

I said: "This isn't because of you, Keri, don't think that. It has nothing to do with you—"

"Not good enough for you, is that it? Because my mother was a whore?"

"Was she? I didn't even know." I felt suddenly immensely tired. I said carefully: "I told you this was nothing to do with you. You are very beautiful, Keri, and the first moment I saw you I felt—you must know what I felt. But this is nothing to do with feeling. It is between me and—it is something to do with my—" I stopped. It was no use. Her eyes watched me, bright and blank, then she turned aside with a little flouncing movement and began to tidy her dress. Instead of "power," I finished: "—something to do with my magic."

"Magic." Her lip was thrust out like a hurt child's. She knotted her girdle tight with a sharp little tug, and began to gather up the fallen bluebells, repeating spitefully: "Magic. Do you think I believe in your silly magic? Did you really think I even had the toothache, that time?"

"I don't know," I said wearily. I got to my feet.

"Well, maybe you don't have to be a man to be a magician. You ought to have gone into that monastery after all."

"Perhaps." A flower was tangled in her hair and she put a hand up to pull it out. The fine floss glinted in the sun like gossamer. My eye caught the blue mark of a bruise on her wrist. "Are you all right? Did I hurt you?"

She neither answered nor looked up, and I turned away. "Well, goodbye, Keri."

I had gone perhaps six steps when her voice stopped me. "Prince—"

I turned.

"So you do answer to it?" she said. "I'm surprised. Son of the High King, you say you are, and you don't even leave me a piece of silver to pay for my gown?"

I must have stood staring like a sleepwalker. She tossed the gold hair back over her shoulder and laughed up at me. Like a blind man fumbling, I felt in the purse at my belt and came out with a coin. It was gold. I took a step back towards her to give it to her. She leaned forward, still laughing, her hands out, cupped like a beggar's. The torn gown hung loose from the lovely throat. I flung the coin down and ran away from her, up through the wood.

Her laughter followed me till I was over the ridge and down in the next valley and had flung myself on my belly beside the stream and drowned the feel and the scent of her in the rush of the mountain water that smelled of snow.

9

In June Ambrosius came to Caerleon, and sent for me. I rode up alone, arriving one evening well past supper-time, when the lamps had been lit and the camp was quiet. The King was still working; I saw the spill of light from headquarters, and the glimmer on the dragon standard outside. While I was still some way off I heard the clash of a salute, and a tall figure came out whom I recognized as Uther.

He crossed the way to a door opposite the King's, but with his foot on the bottom step saw me, stopped, and came back. "Merlin. So you got here. You took your time, didn't you?"

"The summons was hasty. If I am to go abroad, there are things I have to do."

He stood still. "Who said you were to go abroad?"

"People talk of nothing else. It's Ireland, isn't it? They say Pascentius has made some dangerous allies over there, and that Ambrosius wants them destroyed quickly. But why me?"

"Because it's their central stronghold he wants destroyed. Have you ever heard of Killare?"

"Who hasn't? They say it's a fortress that's never been taken."

"Then they say the truth. There's a mountain in the center of all Ireland, and they say that from the summit of it you can see every coast. And on top of that hill there's a fortress, not of earth and palisades, but of strong stones. That, my dear Merlin, is why you."

"I see. You need engines."

"We need engines. We have to attack Killare. If we can take it, you can reckon that there'll be no trouble there for a few years to come. So I take Tremorinus, and Tremorinus insists on taking you."

"I gather the King isn't going?"

"No. Now I'll say good night; I have business to attend to, or I would ask you in to wait. He's got the camp commandant with him, but I don't imagine they'll be long."

On this, he said a pleasant enough good night, and ran up the steps into his quarters, shouting for his servant before he was well through the door.

Almost immediately, from the King's doorway, came the clash of another salute, and the camp commandant came out. Not seeing me, he paused to speak to one of the sentries, and I stood waiting until he had done.

A movement caught my eye, a furtive stir of shadow where someone came softly down a narrow passage between the buildings opposite, where Uther was housed. The sentries, busy with the commandant, had seen nothing. I drew back out of the torchlight, watching. A slight figure, cloaked and hooded. A girl. She reached the lighted corner and paused there, looking about her. Then, with a gesture that was secret rather than afraid, she pulled the hood closer about her face. It was a gesture I recognized, as I recognized the drift of scent on the air, like honeysuckle, and from under the hood the lock of hair curling, gold in the torchlight.

I stood still. I wondered why she had followed me here, and what she hoped to gain. I do not think it was shame I felt, not now, but there was pain, and I believe there was still desire. I hesitated, then took a step forward and spoke.

"Keri?"

But she paid no attention. She slid out from the shadows and, quickly and lightly, ran up the steps to Uther's door. I heard the sentry challenge, then a murmur, and a soft laugh from the man.

When I drew level with Uther's doorway it was shut. In the light of the torch I saw the smile still on the sentry's face.

Ambrosius was still sitting at his table, his servant hovering behind him in the shadows.

He pushed his papers aside and greeted me. The servant brought wine and poured it, then withdrew and left us alone.

We talked for a while. He told me what news there was since I had left Winchester; the building that had gone forward, and his plans for the future. Then we spoke of Tremorinus' work at Caerleon, and so came to the talk of war. I asked him for the latest about Pascentius, "for," I said, "we have been waiting weekly to hear that he had landed in the north and was harrying the countryside."

"Not yet. In fact, if my plans come to anything, we may hear nothing more of Pascentius until the spring, and then we shall be more than prepared. If we allow him to come now, he may well prove more dangerous than any enemy I have yet fought."

"I've heard something about this. You mean the Irish news?"

"Yes. The news is bad from Ireland. You know they have a young king there, Gilloman? A young firedrake, they tell me, and eager for war. Well, you may have heard it, the news is that Pascentius is contracted to Gilloman's sister. You see what this could mean? Such an alliance as that might put the north and west of Britain both at risk together."

"Is Pascentius in Ireland? We heard he was in Germany, gathering support."

"That is so," he said. "I can't get accurate information about his numbers, but I'd say about twenty thousand men. Nor have I yet heard what he and Gilloman plan to do." He lifted an eyebrow at me, amused. "Relax, boy, I haven't called you here to ask for a prediction. You made yourself quite clear at Kaerconan; I'm content to wait, like you, on your god."

I laughed. "I know. You want me for what you call 'real work'."

"Indeed. This is it. I am not content to wait here in Britain while Ireland and Germany gather their forces and then come together on both our coasts like a summer storm, and meet in Britain to overwhelm the north. Britain lies between them now, and she can divide them before ever they combine to attack."

"And you'll take Ireland first?"

"Gilloman," he said, nodding. "He's young and inexperienced—and he is also nearer. Uther will sail for Ireland before the month's end." There was a map in front of him. He half turned it so that I could see. "Here. This is Gilloman's stronghold; you'll have heard of it, I don't doubt. It is a mountain fortress called Killare. I have not found a man who has seen it, but I am told it is strongly fortified, and can be defended against any assault. I am told, indeed, that it has never fallen. Now, we can't afford to have Uther sit down in front of it for months, while Pascentius comes in at the back door. Killare must be taken quickly, and it cannot—they tell me—be taken by fire."

"Yes?" I had already noticed that there were drawings of mine on the table among the maps and plans.

He said, as if at a tangent: "Tremorinus speaks very highly of you."

"That's good of him." Then, at my own tangent: "I met Uther outside. He told me what you wanted."

"Then will you go with him?"

"I'm at your service, of course. But sir"—I indicated the drawings—"I have made no new designs. Everything I have designed has already been built here. And if there is so much hurry—"

"Not that, no. I'm asking for nothing new. The machines we have are good—and must serve. What we have built is ready now for shipping. I want you for more than this." He paused. "Killare, Merlin, is more than a stronghold, it is a holy place, the holy place of the Kings of Ireland. They tell me the crest of the hill holds a Dance of stone, a circle such as you knew in Brittany. And on Killare, men say, is the heart of Ireland and the holy place of Gilloman's kingdom. I want you, Merlin, to throw down the holy place, and take the heart out of Ireland."

I was silent.

"I spoke of this to Tremorinus," he said, "and he told me I must send for you. Will you go?"

"I have said I will. Of course."

He smiled, and thanked me, not as if he were High King and I a subject obeying his wish, but as if I were an equal giving him a favour. He talked then for a little longer about Killare, what he had heard of it, and what preparations he thought we should make, and finally leaned back, saying with a smile: "One thing I regret. I'm going to Maridunum, and I should have liked your company, but now there is no time for that. You may charge me with any messages you care to."

"Thank you, but I have none. Even if I had been there, I would hardly have dared to offer you the hospitality of a cave."

"I should like to see it."

"Anyone will tell you the way. But it's hardly fit to receive a King."

I stopped. His face was lit with a laughter that all at once made him look twenty again. I set down my cup. "I am a fool. I had forgotten."

"That you were begotten there? I thought you had. I can find my way to it, never fear."

He spoke then about his own plans. He himself would stay in Caerleon, "for if Pascentius attacks," he told me, "my guess is that he will come down this way"—his finger traced a line on the map—"and I can catch him south of Carlisle. Which brings me to the next thing. There was something else I wanted to discuss with you. When you last came through Caerleon on your way to Maridunum in April, I believe you had a talk with Tremorinus?"

I waited.

"About this." He lifted a sheaf of drawings—not mine—and handed them across. They were not of the camp, or indeed of any buildings I had seen. There was a church, a great hall, a tower. I studied them for a few minutes in silence. For some reason I felt tired, as if my heart were too heavy for me. The lamp smoked and dimmed and sent shadows dancing over the papers. I pulled myself together, and looked up at my father. "I see. You must be talking about the memorial building?"

He smiled. "I'm Roman enough to want a visible monument."

I tapped the drawings. "And British enough to want it British? Yes, I heard that, too."

"What did Tremorinus tell you?"

"That it was thought some kind of monument to your victories should be erected, and to commemorate your kingship of a united kingdom. I agreed with Tremorinus that to build a triumphal arch here in Britain would be absurd. He did say that some churchmen wanted a big church built—the bishop of Caerleon, for instance, wanted one here. But surely, sir, this would hardly do? If you build at Caerleon you'll have London and Winchester, not to mention York, thinking it should have been there. Of them all, I suppose, Winchester would be the best. It is your capital."

"No. I've had a thought about this myself. When I travelled up from Winchester, I came through Amesbury . . ." He leaned forward suddenly. "What's the matter, Merlin? Are you ill?"

"No. It's a hot night, that's all. A storm coming, I think. Go on. You came through Amesbury."

"You knew it was my birthplace? Well, it seemed to me that to put my monument in such a place could give no cause for complaint—and there is another reason why it's a good choice." He knitted his brows. "You're like a sheet, boy. Are you sure you're all right?"

"Perfectly. Perhaps a little tired."

"Have you supped? It was thoughtless of me not to ask."

"I ate on the way, thank you. I have had all I needed. Perhaps—some more wine—"

I half rose, but before I could get to my feet he was on his, and came round the table with the jug and served me himself. While I drank he stayed where he was, near me, sitting back against the table's edge. I was reminded sharply of how he had stood this way that night in Brittany when I discovered him. I remember that I held it in my mind, and in a short while was able to smile at him.

"I am quite well, sir, indeed I am. Please go on. You were giving me the second reason for putting your monument at Amesbury."

"You probably know that it is not far from there that the British dead lie buried, who were slain by Hengist's treachery. I think it fitting—and I think there is no man who will argue with this—that the monument to my victory, to the making of one kingdom under one King, should also be a memorial for these warriors." He paused. "And you might say there is yet a third reason, more powerful than the other two."

I said, not looking at him, but down into the cup of wine, and speaking quietly: "That Amesbury is already the site of the greatest monument in Britain? Possibly the greatest in the whole West?"

"Ah." It was a syllable of deep satisfaction. "So your mind moves this way, too? You have seen the Giants' Dance?"

"I rode out to it from Amesbury, when I was on my way home from Winchester."

He stood up at that and walked back round the table to his chair. He sat, then leaned forward, resting his hands on the table. "Then you know how I am thinking. You saw enough when you lived in Brittany to know what the Dance was once. And you have seen what it is now—a chaos of giant stones in a lonely place where the sun and the winds strike." He added more slowly, watching me: "I have talked of this to Tremorinus. He says that no power of man could raise those stones."

I smiled. "So you sent for me to raise them for you?"

"You know they say it was not men who raised them, but magic."

"Then," I said, "no doubt they will say the same again."

His eyes narrowed. "You are telling me you can do it?"

"Why not?"

He was silent, merely waiting. It was a measure of his faith in me that he did not smile.

I said: "Oh, I've heard all the tales they tell, the same tales they told in Less Britain of the standing stones. But the stones were put there by men, sir. And what men put there once, men can put there again."

"Then if I don't possess a magician, at least I possess a competent engineer?"

"That's it."

"How will you do it?"

"As yet, I know less than half of it. But it can be done."

"Then will you do this for me, Merlin?"

"Of course. Have I not said I am here only to serve you as best I can? I will rebuild the Giants' Dance for you, Ambrosius."

"A strong symbol for Britain." He spoke broodingly now, frowning down at his hands. "I shall be buried there, Merlin, when my time comes. What Vortigern wanted to do for his stronghold in darkness, I shall do for mine in the light; I shall have the body of her King buried under the stones, the warrior under the threshold of all Britain."

Someone must have drawn the curtains back from the door. The sentries were out of sight, the camp silent. The stone doorposts and the heavy lintel lying across them framed a blue night burning with stars. All round us the vast shadows reared, giant stones linked like pleached trees where some hands long since bone had cut the signs of the gods of air and earth and water. Someone was speaking quietly; a king's voice; Ambrosius' voice. It had been speaking for some time; vaguely, like echoes in the dark, I heard it.

". . . and while the King lies there under the stone the Kingdom shall not fall. For as long and longer than it has stood before, the Dance shall stand again, with the light striking it from the living heaven. And I shall bring back the great stone to lay upon the grave-place, and this shall be the heart of Britain, and from this time on all the kings shall be one King and all the gods one God. And you shall live again in Britain, and for ever, for we will make between us a King whose name will stand as long as the Dance stands, and who will be more than a symbol; he will be a shield and a living sword."

It was not the King's voice; it was my own. The King was still sitting on the other side of the map-strewn table, his hands still and flat on the papers, his eyes dark under the straight brows. Between us the lamp dimmed, flickering in a draught from under the shut door.

I stared at him, while my sight slowly cleared. "What did I say?"

He shook his head, smiling, and reached for the wine jug.

I said irritably: "It comes on me like a fainting fit on a pregnant girl. I'm sorry. Tell me what I said?"

"You gave me a kingdom. And you gave me immortality. What more is there? Drink now, Ambrosius' prophet."

"Not wine. Is there water?"

"Here." He got to his feet. "And now you must go and sleep, and so must I. I leave early for Maridunum. You are sure you have no messages?"

"Tell Cadal he is to give you the silver cross with the amethysts."

We faced one another in a small silence. I was almost as tall as he. He said, gently: "So now it is goodbye."

"How does one say goodbye to a King who has been given immortality?"

He gave me a strange look. "Shall we meet again, then?"

"We shall meet again, Ambrosius."

It was then I knew that what I had prophesied for him was his death.

10

Killare, I had been told, is a mountain in the very center of Ireland. There are in other parts of this island mountains which, if not as great as those of our own country, could still merit the name. But the hill of Killare is no mountain. It is a gentle conical hill whose summit is, I suppose, no more than nine hundred feet high. It is not even forested, but clothed over with rough grass, with here and there a copse of thorn-trees, or a few single oaks.

Even so, standing where it does, it looms like a mountain to those approaching it, for it stands alone, the only hill at the center of a vast plain. On every hand, with barely the least undulation, the country stretches flat and green; north, south, east, west, it is the same. But it is not true that you can see the coasts from that summit; there is only the interminable view on every hand of that green gentle country, with above it a soft and cloudy sky.

Even the air is mild there. We had fair winds, and landed on a long, grey strand on a soft summer morning, with a breeze off the land smelling of bog myrtle and gorse and salt-soaked turf. The wild swans sailed the loughs with the half-grown cygnets, and the peewits screamed and tumbled over the meadows where their young nestled down between the reeds.

It was not a time, or a country, you would have thought, for war. And indeed, the war was soon over. Gilloman, the king, was young—they said not more than eighteen—and he would not listen to his advisers and wait for a good moment to meet our attack. So high was his heart that, at the first news of foreign troops landing on the sacred soil of Ireland, the young king gathered his fighting men together, and threw them against Uther's seasoned troops. They met us on a flat plain, with a hill at our backs and a river at theirs. Uther's troops stood the first wild, brave attack without giving ground even a couple of paces, then advanced steadily in their turn, and drove the Irish into the water. Luckily for them, this was a wide stream, and shallow, and, though it ran red that evening, many hundreds of Irishmen escaped. Gilloman the king was one of them, and when we got the news that he had fled west with a handful of trusted followers, Uther, guessing he would be making for Killare, sent a thousand mounted troops after him, with instructions to catch him before he reached the gates. This they just managed to do, coming up with him barely half a mile short of the fortress, at the very foot of the hill and within sight of the walls. The second battle was short, and bloodier than the first. But it took place in the night, and in the confusion of the mêlée Gilloman himself escaped once more, and galloped away with a handful of men, this time nobody knew where. But the thing was done; by the time we, the main body of the army, came to the foot of Mount Killare, the British troops were already in possession, and the gates were open.

A lot of nonsense has been talked about what happened next. I myself have heard some of the songs, and even read one account which was set down in a book. Ambrosius had been misinformed. Killare was not strong-built of great stones; that is to say, the outer fortifications were as usual of earthworks and palisades behind a great ditch, and inside that was a second ditch, deep, and with spikes set. The central fortress itself was certainly stone-walled, and the stones were big ones, but nothing that a normal team, with the proper tackle, could not handle easily. Inside this fortress wall were houses, of the most part built of wood, but also some strong places underground, as we have in Britain. Higher yet stood the innermost ring, a wall round the crest of the hill like a crown round the brow of a king. And inside this, at the very center and apex of the hill, was the holy place. Here stood the Dance, the circle of stones that was said to contain the heart of Ireland. It could not compare with the Great Dance of Amesbury, being only a single circle of unlinked stones, but it was impressive enough, and still stood firm with much of the circle intact, and two capped uprights near the center where other stones lay, seemingly without pattern, in the long grass.

I walked up alone that same evening. The hillside was alive with the bustle and roar, familiar to me from Kaerconan, of the aftermath of battle. But when I passed the wall that hedged the holy place, and came out towards the crest of the hill, it was like leaving a bustling hall for the quiet of some tower room upstairs. Sounds fell away below the walls, and as I walked up through the long summer grass, there was almost silence, and I was alone.

A round moon stood low in the sky, pale still, and smudged with shadow, and thin at one edge like a worn coin. There was a scatter of small stars, with here and there the shepherd stars herding them, and across from the moon one great star alone, burning white. The shadows were long and soft on the seeding grasses.

A tall stone stood alone, leaning a little towards the east. A little further was a pit, and beyond that again a round boulder that looked black in the moonlight. There was something here. I paused. Nothing I could put a name to, but the old, black stone itself might have been some dark creature hunched there over the pit's edge. I felt the shiver run over my skin, and turned away. This, I would not disturb.

The moon climbed with me, and as I entered the circle she lifted her white disc over the cap-stones and shone clear into the center of the ring. My footsteps crunched, dry and brittle, over a patch of ground where fires had recently been lit. I saw the white shapes of bones, and a flat stone shaped like an altar. The moonlight showed carving on one side, crude shapes twisted, of ropes or serpents. I stooped to run a finger over them. Nearby a mouse rustled and squeaked in the grass. No other sound. The thing was clean, dead, godless. I left it, moving on slowly through the moon-thrown shadows. There was another stone, domed like a beehive, or a navel-stone. And here an upright fallen, with the long grass almost hiding it. As I passed it, searching still, a ripple of breeze ran through the grasses, blurring the shadows and dimming the light like mist. I caught my foot on something, staggered, and came down to my knees at the end of a long flat stone which lay almost hidden in the grass. My hands moved over it. It was massive, oblong, uncarved, simply a great natural stone on to which now the moonlight poured. It hardly needed the cold at my hands, the hiss of the bleached grasses under the sudden run of wind, the scent of daisies, to tell me that this was the stone. All round me, like dancers drawing back from a center, the silent stones stood black. On one side the white moon, on the other the king-star, burning white. I got slowly to my feet and stood there at the foot of the long stone, as one might stand at the foot of a bed, waiting for the man in it to die.

It was warmth that woke me, warmth and the voices of men near me. I lifted my head. I was half-kneeling, half-lying with my arms and the upper part of my body laid along the stone. The morning sun was high, and pouring straight down into the center of the Dance. Mist smoked up from the damp grass, and its white wreaths hid the lower slopes of the hill. A group of men had come in through the stones of the Dance, and were standing there muttering among themselves, watching me. As I blinked, moving my stiff limbs, the group parted and Uther came through, followed by half a dozen of his officers, among whom was Tremorinus. Two soldiers pushed between them what was obviously an Irish prisoner; his hands were tied and there was a cut on one cheek where blood had dried, but he held himself well and I thought the men who guarded him looked more afraid than he.

Uther checked when he saw me, then came across as I got stiffly to my feet. The night must have shown still in my face, for in the group of officers behind him I saw the look I had grown used to, of men both wary and amazed, and even Uther spoke a fraction too loudly.

"So your magic is as strong as theirs."

The light was too strong for my eyes. He looked vivid and unreal, like an image seen in moving water. I tried to speak, cleared my throat, and tried again. "I'm still alive, if that's what you mean."

Tremorinus said gruffly: "There's not another man in the army would have spent the night here."

"Afraid of the black stone?"

I saw Uther's hand move in an involuntary gesture as if it sprang of itself to make the sign. He saw I had noticed, and looked angry. "Who told you about the black stone?"

Before I could answer, the Irishman said suddenly: "You saw it? Who are you?"

"My name is Merlin."

He nodded slowly. He still showed no sign of fear or awe. He read my thought, and smiled, as if to say, "You and I, we can look after ourselves."

"Why do they bring you here like this?" I asked him.

"To tell them which is the king-stone."

Uther said: "He has told us. It's the carved altar over there."

"Let him go," I said. "You have no need of him. And leave the altar alone. This is the stone."

There was a pause. Then the Irishman laughed. "Faith, if you bring the King's enchanter himself, what hope has a poor poet? It was written in the stars that you would take it, and indeed, it is nothing but justice. It's not the heart of Ireland that that stone has been but the curse of it, and maybe Ireland will be all the better to see it go."

"How so?" I asked him. Then, to Uther: "Tell them to loose him."

Uther nodded, and the men loosed the prisoner's hands. He rubbed his wrists, smiling at me. You would have thought we two were alone in the Dance. "They say that in times past that stone came out of Britain, out of the mountains of the west, in sight of the Irish Sea, and that the great King of all Ireland, Fionn

Mac Cumhaill was his name, carried it in his arms one night and walked through the sea with it to Ireland, and set it here."

"And now," I said, "we carry it a little more painfully back to Britain."

He laughed. "I would have thought the great magician that's yourself would have picked it up in one hand."

"I'm no Fionn," I said. "And now if you are wise, poet, you will go back to your home and your harp, and make no more wars, but make a song about the stone, and how Merlin the enchanter took the stone from the Dance of Killare and carried it lightly to the Dance of the Hanging Stones at Amesbury."

He saluted me, laughing still, and went. And indeed he did walk safely down through the camp and away, for in later years I heard the song he made.

But now his going was hardly noticed. There was a pause while Uther frowned down at the great stone, seeming to weigh it in his mind. "You told the King that you could do this thing. Is that true?"

"I said to the King that what men had brought here, men could take away."

He looked at me frowningly, uncertainly, still a little angry. "He told me what you said. I agree. It doesn't need magic and fine words, only a team of competent men with the right engines. Tremorinus!"

"Sir?"

"If we take this one, the king-stone, there will be no need to trouble overmuch with the rest. Throw them down where you can and leave them."

"Yes, sir. If I could have Merlin—"

"Merlin's team will be working on the fortifications. Merlin, get started, will you? I give you twenty-four hours."

This was something the men were practiced at; they threw down the walls and filled in the ditches with them. The palisades and houses, quite simply, we put to the flame. The men worked well, and were in good heart. Uther was always generous to his troops, and there had been goods in plenty to be looted, arm-rings of copper and bronze and gold, brooches, and weapons well made and inlaid with copper and enamel, in a way the Irish have. The work was finished by dusk, and we withdrew from the hill to the temporary camp which had been thrown up on the plain at the foot of the slope.

It was after supper when Tremorinus came to me. I could see the torches and the fires still lit at the top of the hill, throwing what was left of the Dance into relief. His face was grimy, and he looked tired.

"All day," he said bitterly, "and we've raised it a couple of feet, and half an hour ago the props cracked, and it's gone back again into its bed. Why the hell did you have to suggest that stone? The Irishman's altar would have been easier."

"The Irishman's altar would not have done."

"Well, by the gods, it looks as if you aren't going to get this one either! Look, Merlin, I don't care what he says, I'm in charge of this job, and I'm asking you to come and take a look. Will you?"

The rest is what the legends have been made of. It would be tedious now to relate how we did it, but it was easy enough; I had had all day to think about it, having seen the stone and the hillside, and I had had the engines in my mind since Brittany. Wherever we could we took it by water—downriver from Killare to the sea, and thence to Wales and still as far as possible by river, using the two great Avons, with little more than a score of dry miles to cross between them. I was not Fionn of the Strong Arm, but I was Merlin, and the great stone travelled home as smoothly as a barge on an untroubled water, with me beside it all the way. I suppose I must have slept on that journey, but I cannot remember doing so. I went wakeful, as one is at a death-bed, and on that one voyage of all those in my life, I never felt the movement of the sea, but sat (they tell me) calm and silent, as if in my chair at home. Uther came once to speak to me—angry, I suppose, that I had done so easily what his own engineers could not do—but he went away after a moment, and did not approach me again. I remember nothing about it. I suppose I was not there. I was watching still between day and night in the great bedchamber at Winchester.

The news met us at Caerleon. Pascentius had attacked out of the north with his force of German and Saxon allies, and the King had marched to Carlisle and defeated him there. But afterwards, safely back at Winchester, he had fallen ill. About this, rumours were rife. Some said that one of Pascentius' men had come in disguise to Winchester where Ambrosius lay abed of a chill, and had given him poison to drink. Some said the man had come from Eosa. But the truth was the same; the King was very sick at Winchester.

The king-star rose again that night, looking, men said, like a fiery dragon, and trailing a cloud of lesser stars like smoke. But it did not need the omen to tell me what I had known since that night on the crest of Killare, when I had vowed to carry the great stone from Ireland, and lay it upon his grave.

So it was that we brought the stone again to Amesbury, and I raised the fallen circles of the Giants' Dance into their places for his monument. And at the next Easter-time, in the city of London, Uther Pendragon was crowned King.

BOOK V

THE COMING OF THE BEAR

1

Men said afterwards that the great dragon star which blazed at Ambrosius' death, and from which Uther took the royal name of Pendragon, was a baleful herald for the new reign. And indeed, at the start, everything seemed to be against Uther. It was as if the falling of Ambrosius' star was the signal for his old enemies to rise again and crowd in from the darkened edges of the land to destroy his successor. Octa, Hengist's son, and Eosa his kinsman, counting themselves freed by Ambrosius' death from their promise to stay north of his borders, called together what force they could still muster for attack, and as soon as the call went out, every disaffected element rose to it. Warriors greedy for land and plunder crowded over afresh from Germany, the remnants of Pascentius' Saxons joined with Gilloman's fleeing Irish, and with whatever British thought themselves passed over by the new King. Within a few weeks of Ambrosius' death Octa, with a large army, was scouring the north like a wolf, and before the new King could come up with him had destroyed cities and fortresses clear down from the Wall of Hadrian to York. At York, Ambrosius' strong city, he found the walls in good repair, the gates shut, and men ready to defend themselves. He dragged up what siege engines he had, and settled down to wait.

He must have known that Uther would catch up with him there, but his numbers were such that he showed no fear of the British. Afterwards they reckoned he had thirty thousand men. Be that as it may, when Uther came up to raise the siege with every man he could muster, the Saxons outnumbered the British by more than two to one. It was a bloody engagement, and a disastrous one. I think myself that Ambrosius' death had shaken the kingdom; for all Uther's brilliant reputation as a soldier, he was untried as supreme commander, and it was already known that he had not his brother's calmness and judgement in the face of odds. What he lacked in wisdom, he made up in bravery, but even that would not defeat the odds that came against him that day at York. The British broke and ran, and were saved only by the coming of dusk, which at that time of year fell early. Uther—with Gorlois of Cornwall, his second in command—managed to rally his remaining force near the top of the small hill called Damen. This was steep, and offered cover of a kind, cliffs and caves and thick hazel-woods, but this could only be a temporary refuge from the Saxon host which triumphantly circled the base of the hill, waiting for morning. It was a desperate position for the British, and called for desperate measures. Uther, grimly encamped in a cave, called his weary captains together while the men snatched what rest they could, and with them thrashed out a plan for outwitting the huge host waiting for them at the foot of the hill. At first nobody had much idea beyond the need to escape, but someone—I heard later that it was Gorlois—pointed out that to retreat further was merely to postpone defeat and the destruction of the new kingdom: if escape was possible, then so was attack, and this seemed feasible if the British did not wait until daylight, but used what element of surprise there was in attacking downhill out of the dark and long before the enemy expected it. Simple tactics, indeed, that the Saxons might have expected from men so desperately trapped, but Saxons are stupid fighters, and as I have said before, lacking in discipline. It was almost certain that they would expect no move till dawn, and that they slept soundly where they had lain down that night, confident of victory, and with any luck three parts drunken on the stores they had taken.

To do the Saxons justice, Octa had posted scouts, and these were wide enough awake. But Gorlois' plan worked, helped by a little mist which crept before dawn up from the low ground and surrounded the base of the hill like a veil. Through this, twice as large as life, and in numbers altogether deceiving, the British came in a silent, stabbing rush at the first moment when there was light enough to see one's way across the rocks. Those Saxon outposts who were not cut down in silence, gave the alarm, but too late. Warriors rolled over, cursing, snatching their weapons up from where they lay beside them, but the British, silent no longer, swept yelling across the half-sleeping host, and cut it to pieces. It was finished before noon, and Octa and Eosa taken prisoner. Before winter, with the north swept clear of Saxons, and the burned longboats smoking quietly on the northern beaches, Uther was back in London with his prisoners behind bars, making ready for his coronation the following spring.

His battle with the Saxons, his near defeat and subsequent sharp, brilliant victory, was all that the reign needed. Men forgot the bale of Ambrosius' death, and talked of the new King like a sun rising. His name was on everyone's lips, from the nobles and warriors who crowded round him for gifts and honours, to the workmen building his palaces, and the ladies of his court flaunting new dresses like a field of poppies in a colour called Pendragon Red.

I saw him only once during these first weeks. I was at Amesbury still, superintending the work of raising the Giants' Dance. Tremorinus was in the north, but I had a good team, and after their experience with the king-stone at Killare, the men were eager to tackle the massive stones of the Dance. For the raising of the uprights, once we had aligned the stones, dug the pits and sunk the guides, there was nothing that could not be done with rope and shear-legs and plumb-line. It was with the great lintels that the difficulty lay, but the miracle of the building of the Dance had been done countless years before, by the old craftsmen who had shaped those gigantic stones to fit as surely one into the other as wood dovetailed by a master carpenter. We had only to find means to lift them. It was this which had exercised me all those years, since I first saw the capped stones in Less Britain, and began my calculations. Nor had I forgotten what I had learned from the songs. In the end I had designed a wooden crib of a kind which a modern engineer might have dismissed as primitive, but which—as the singer had been my witness—had done the task before, and would again. It was a slow business, but it worked. And I suppose it was a marvellous enough sight to see those vast blocks rising, stage by stage, and settling finally into their beds as smoothly as if they had been made of tallow. It took two hundred men to each stone as it was moved, drilled teams who worked by numbers and who kept up their rhythms, as rowers do, by music. The rhythms of the movement were of course laid down by the work, and the tunes were old tunes that I remembered from my childhood; my nurse had sung them to me, but she never sang the words that the men sometimes set to them. These tended to be lively, indecent, and intensely personal, and mostly concerning those in high places. Neither Uther nor I was spared, though the songs were never sung deliberately in my hearing. Moreover, when outsiders were present, the words were either correct or indistinguishable. I heard it said, long afterwards, that I moved the stones of the Dance with magic and with music. I suppose you might say that both are true. I have thought, since, that this must have been how the story started that Phoebus Apollo built with music the walls of Troy. But the magic and the music that moved the Giants' Dance, I shared with the blind singer of Kerrec.

Towards the middle of November the frosts were sharp, and the work was finished. The last camp fire was put out, and the last wagon-train of men and materials rolled away south back to Sarum. Cadal had gone ahead of me into Amesbury. I lingered, holding my fidgeting horse, until the wagons had rolled out of sight over the edge of the plain and I was alone.

The sky hung over the silent plain like a pewter bowl. It was still early in the day, and the grass was white with frost. The thin winter sun painted long shadows from the linked stones. I remembered the standing stone, and the white frost, the bull and the blood and the smiling young god with the fair hair. I looked down at the stone. They had buried him, I knew, with his sword in his hand. I said to him: "We shall come back, both of us, at the winter solstice." Then I left him and mounted my horse, and rode toward Amesbury.

2

News came of Uther in December; he had left London and ridden to Winchester for Christmas. I sent a message, got no reply, and rode out once more with Cadal to where the Giants' Dance stood frostbound and lonely in the center of the plain. It was the twentieth of December.

In a fold of the ground just beyond the Dance we tethered our horses and lit a fire. I had been afraid that the night might be cloudy, but it was crisp and clear, with the stars out in their swarms, like motes in moonlight.

"Get some sleep, if you can in this cold," said Cadal. "I'll wake you before dawn. What makes you think he'll come?" Then, when I made no reply: "Well, you're the magician, you should know. Here, just in case your magic won't put you to sleep, you'd better put the extra cloak on. I'll wake you in time, so don't fret yourself."

I obeyed him, rolling myself in the double thickness of wool, and lying near the fire with my head on my saddle. I dozed rather than slept, conscious of the small noises of the night surrounded by the immense stillness of that plain; the rustle and crack of the fire, the sound of Cadal putting new wood on it, the steady tearing sound of the horses grazing at hand, the cry of a hunting owl in the air. And then, not long before dawn, the sound I had been expecting; the steady beat of the earth beneath my head which meant the approach of horses.

I sat up. Cadal, blear-eyed, spoke morosely. "You've an hour yet, I reckon."

"Never mind. I've slept. Put your ear to the ground, and tell me what you hear."

He leaned down, listened for perhaps five heartbeats, then was on his feet and making for our horses. Men reacted quickly in those days to the sound of horsemen in the night.

I checked him. "It's all right. Uther. How many horses do you reckon?"

"Twenty, perhaps thirty. Are you sure?"

"Quite sure. Now get the horses saddled and stay with them. I'm going in."

It was the hour between night and morning when the air is still. They were coming at a gallop. It seemed that the whole of the frozen plain beat with the sound. The moon had gone. I waited beside the stone.

He left the troop some little way off, and rode forward with only one companion. I did not think they had yet seen me, though they must have seen the flicker of Cadal's dying fire in the hollow. The night had been bright enough with starlight, so they had been riding without torches, and their night sight was good; the two of them came on at a fast canter straight for the outer circle of the Dance, and at first I thought they would ride straight in. But the horses pulled up short with a crunch and slither of frost, and the King swung from the saddle. I heard the jingle as he threw the reins to his companion. "Keep him moving," I heard him say, and then he approached, a swift striding shadow through the enormous shadows of the Dance.

"Merlin?"

"My lord?"

"You choose your times strangely. Did it have to be the middle of the night?" He sounded wide awake and no more gracious than usual. But he had come.

I said: "You wanted to see what I have done here, and tonight is the night when I can show you. I am grateful that you came."

"Show me what? A vision? Is this another of your dreams? I warn you—"

"No. There's nothing of that here, not now. But there is something I wanted you to see which can only be seen tonight. For that, I'm afraid we shall have to wait a little while."

"Long? It's cold."

"Not so long, my lord. Till dawn."

He was standing the other side of the king-stone from me, and in the faint starlight I saw him looking down at it, with his head bent and a hand stroking his chin. "The first time you stood beside this stone in the night, men say you saw visions. Now they tell me in Winchester that as he lay dying he spoke to you as if you were there in his bedchamber, standing at the foot of the bed. Is this true?"

"Yes."

His head came up sharply. "You say you knew on Killare that my brother was dying, yet you said nothing to me?"

"It would have served no purpose. You could not have returned any sooner for knowing that he lay sick. As it was, you journeyed with a quiet mind, and at Caerleon, when he died, I told you."

"By the gods, Merlin, it was not for you to judge whether to speak or not! You are not King. You should have told me."

"You were not King either, Uther Pendragon. I did as he bade me."

I saw him make a quick movement, then he stilled himself. "That is easy to say." But from his voice I knew that he believed me, and was in awe of me and of the place. "And now that we are here, and waiting for the dawn, and whatever it is you have to show me, I think one or two things must be made clear between us. You cannot serve me as you served my brother. You must know that. I want none of your prophecies. My brother was wrong when he said that we would work together for Britain. Our stars will not conjoin. I admit I judged you too harshly, there in Brittany and at Killare; for that I am sorry, but now it is too late. We walk different ways."

"Yes. I know."

I said it without any particular expression, simply agreeing, and was surprised when he laughed, softly, to himself. A hand, not unfriendly, dropped on my shoulder. "Then we understand one another. I had not thought it would be so easy. If you knew how refreshing that is after the weeks I've had of men suing for help, men crawling for mercy, men begging for favours . . . And now the only man in the kingdom with any real claim on me will go his own way, and let me go mine?"

"Of course. Our paths will still cross, but not yet. And then we will deal together, whether we will or no."

"We shall see. You have power, I admit it, but what use is that to me? I don't need priests." His voice was brisk and friendly, as if he were willing away the strangeness of the night. He was rooted to earth, was Uther. Ambrosius would have understood what I was saying, but Uther was back on the human trail like a dog after blood. "It seems you have served me well enough already, at Killare, and here with the Hanging Stones. You deserve something of me, if only for this."

"Where I can be, I shall be at your service. If you want me, you know where to find me."

"Not at my court?"

"No, at Maridunum. It's my home."

"Ah, yes, the famous cave. You deserve a little more of me than that, I think."

"There is nothing that I want," I said.

There was a little more light now. I saw him slant a look at me. "I have spoken to you tonight as I have spoken to no man before. Do you hold the past against me, Merlin the bastard?"

"I hold nothing against you, my lord."

"Nothing?"

"A girl in Caerleon. You could call her nothing."

I saw him stare, then smile. "Which time?"

"It doesn't matter. You'll have forgotten, anyway."

"By the dog, I misjudged you." He spoke with the nearest to warmth I had yet heard from him. If he knew, I thought, he would have laughed.

I said: "I tell you, it doesn't matter. It didn't then, and less than that now."

"You still haven't told me why you dragged me here at this time. Look at the sky; it's getting on for dawn—and not a moment too soon, the horses will be getting cold." He raised his head towards the east. "It should be a fine day. It will be interesting to see what sort of job you've made of this. I can tell you now, Tremorinus was insisting, right up to the time I got your message, that it couldn't be done. Prophet or no prophet, you have your uses, Merlin."

The light was growing, the dark slackening to let it through. I could see him more clearly now, standing with head up, his hand once more stroking his chin. I said: "It's as well you came by night, so that I knew your voice. I shouldn't have known you in daylight. You've grown a full beard."

"More kingly, eh? There was no time to do anything else on campaign. By the time we got to the Humber . . ." He started to tell me about it, talking, for the first time since I had known him, quite easily and naturally. It may have been that now I was, of all his subjects, the only one kin to him, and blood speaks to blood, they say. He talked about the campaign in the north, the fighting, the smoking destruction the Saxons had left behind them. "And now we spend Christmas at Winchester. I shall be crowned in London in the spring, and already—"

"Wait." I had not meant to interrupt him quite so peremptorily, but things were pressing on me, the weight of the sky, the shooting light. There was no time to search for the words that one could use to a king. I said quickly: "It's coming now. Stand with me at the foot of the stone."

I moved a pace from him and stood at the foot of the long king-stone, facing the bursting east. I had no eyes for Uther. I heard him draw breath as if in anger, then he checked himself and turned with a glitter of jewels and flash of mail to stand beside me. At our feet stretched the stone.

In the east night slackened, drew back like a veil, and the sun came up. Straight as a thrown torch, or an arrow of fire, light pierced through the grey air and laid a line clear from the horizon to the king-stone at our feet. For perhaps twenty heartbeats the huge sentinel trilithon before us stood black and stark, framing the winter blaze. Then the sun lifted over the horizon so quickly that you could see the shadow of the linked circle move into its long ellipse, to blur and fade almost immediately into the wide light of a winter's dawn.

I glanced at the King. His eyes, wide and blank, were on the stone at his feet. I could not read his thoughts. Then he lifted his head and looked away from me at the outer circle where the great stones stood locked across the light. He took a slow pace away from me and turned on his heel, taking in the full circle of the Hanging Stones. I saw that the new beard was reddish and curled; he wore his hair longer, and a gold circle flashed on his helm. His eyes were blue as woodsmoke in the fresh light.

They met mine at last. "No wonder you smile. It's very impressive."

"That's with relief," I said. "The mathematics of this have kept me awake for weeks."

"Tremorinus told me." He gave me a slow, measuring look. "He also told me what you had said."

"What I had said?"

"Yes. 'I will deck his grave with nothing less than the light itself.' "

I said nothing.

He said slowly: "I told you I knew nothing of prophets or priests. I am only a soldier, and I think like a soldier. But this—what you have done here—this is something I understand. Perhaps there is room for us both, after all. I told you I spend Christmas at Winchester. Will you ride back with me?"

He had asked me, not commanded me. We were speaking across the stone. It was the beginning of something, but something I had not yet been shown. I shook my head. "In the spring, perhaps. I should like to see the crowning. Be sure that when you need me I shall be there. But now I must go home."

"To your hole in the ground? Well, if it's what you want . . . Your wants are few enough, God knows. Is there nothing you would ask of me?" He gestured with his hand to the silent circle. "Men will speak poorly of a King who does not reward you for this."

"I have been rewarded."

"At Maridunum, now. Your grandfather's house would be more suitable for you. Will you take it?"

I shook my head. "I don't want a house. But I would take the hill."

"Then take it. They tell me men call it Merlin's Hill already. And now it's full daylight, and the horses will be cold. If you had ever been a soldier, Merlin, you would know that there is one thing more important even than the graves of kings: not to keep the horses standing."

He clapped me on the shoulder again, turned with a swirl of the scarlet cloak, and strode to his waiting horse. I went to find Cadal.

3

When Easter came I still had no mind to leave Bryn Myrddin (Uther, true to his word, had given me the hill where the cave stood, and people already associated its name with me, rather than with the god, calling it Merlin's Hill) but a message came from the King, bidding me to London. This time it was a command, not a request, and so urgent that the King had sent an escort, to avoid any delay I might have incurred in waiting for company.

It was still not safe in those days to ride abroad in parties smaller than a dozen or more, and one rode armed and warily. Men who could not afford their own escort waited until a party was gathered, and merchants even joined together to pay guards to ride with them. The wilder parts of the land were still full of refugees from Octa's army, with Irishmen who had been unable to get a passage home, and a few stray Saxons trying miserably to disguise their fair skins, and unmercifully hunted down when they failed. These haunted the edges of the farms, skulking in the hills and moors and wild places, making sudden savage forays in search of food, and watching the roads for any solitary or ill-armed traveller, however shabby. Anyone with cloak or sandals was a rich man and worth despoiling.

None of this would have deterred me from riding alone with Cadal from Maridunum to London. No outlaw or thief would have faced a look from me, let alone risked a curse. Since events at Dinas Brenin, Killare, and Amesbury my fame had spread, growing in song and story until I hardly recognized my own deeds. Dinas Brenin had also been renamed; it had become Dinas Emrys, in compliment to me as much as to commemorate Ambrosius' landing, and the strong-point he had successfully built there. I lived, too, as well as I ever had in my grandfather's palace or in Ambrosius' house. Offerings of food and wine were left daily below the cave, and the poor who had nothing else to bring me in return for the medicines I gave them, brought fuel, or straw for the horses' bedding, or their labour for building jobs or making simple furniture. So winter had passed in comfort and peace, until on a sharp day in early March Uther's messenger, having left the escort in the town, came riding up the valley.

It was the first dry day after more than two weeks of rain and sleety wind, and I had gone up over the hill above the cave to look for the first growing plants and simples. I paused at the edge of a clump of pines to watch the solitary horseman cantering up the hill. Cadal must have heard the hoofbeats; I saw him, small below me, come out of the cave and greet the man, then I saw his pointing arm indicating which way I had gone. The messenger hardly paused. He turned his beast uphill, struck his spurs in, and came after me.

He pulled up a few paces away, swung stiffly out of the saddle, made the sign, and approached me.

He was a brown-haired young man of about my own age, whose face was vaguely familiar. I thought I must have seen him around Uther's train somewhere. He was splashed with mud to the eyebrows, and where he was not muddy his face was white with fatigue. He must have got a new horse in Maridunum for the last stage, for the animal was fresh, and restive with it, and I saw the young man wince as it threw its head up and dragged at the reins.

"My lord Merlin. I bring you greetings from the King, in London."

"I am honoured," I said formally.

"He requests your presence at the feast of his coronation. He has sent you an escort, my lord. They are in the town, resting their horses."

"Did you say 'requests'?"

"I should have said 'commands', my lord. He told me I must bring you back immediately."

"This was all the message?"

"He told me nothing more, my lord. Only that you must attend him immediately in London."

"Then of course I shall come. Tomorrow morning, when you have rested the horses?"

"Today, my lord. Now."

It was a pity that Uther's arrogant command was delivered in a slightly apologetic way. I regarded him. "You have come straight to me?"

"Yes, my lord."

"Without resting?"

"Yes."

"How long has it taken you?"

"Four days, my lord. This is a fresh horse. I am ready to go back today." Here the animal jerked its head again, and I saw him wince.

"Are you hurt?"

"Nothing to speak of. I took a fall yesterday and hurt my wrist. It's my right wrist, not my bridle hand."

"No, only your dagger hand. Go down to the cave and tell my servant what you have told me, and say he is to give you food and drink. When I come down I shall see to your wrist."

He hesitated. "My lord, the King was urgent. This is more than an invitation to watch the crowning."

"You will have to wait while my servant packs my things and saddles our horses. Also while I myself eat and drink. I can bind up your wrist in a few minutes. And while I am doing it you can give me the news from London, and tell me why the King commands me so urgently to the feast. Go down now; I shall come in a short while."

"But, sir—"

I said: "By the time Cadal has prepared food for the three of us I shall be with you. You cannot hurry me more than that. Now go."

He threw me a doubtful look, then went, slithering on foot down the wet hill-side and dragging the jibbing horse after him. I gathered my cloak round me against the wind, and walked past the end of the pine wood and out of sight of the cave.

I stood at the end of a rocky spur where the winds came freely down the valley and tore at my cloak. Behind me the pines roared, and under the noise the bare blackthorns by Galapas' grave rattled in the wind. An early plover screamed in the grey air. I lifted my face to the sky and thought of Uther and London, and the command that had just come. But nothing was there except the sky and the pines and the wind in the blackthorns. I looked the other way, down towards Maridunum.

From this height I could see the whole town, tiny as a toy in the distance. The valley was sullen green in the March wind. The river curled, grey under the grey sky. A wagon was crossing the bridge. There was a point of colour where a standard flew over the fortress. A boat scudded down-river, its brown sails full of the wind. The hills, still in their winter purple, held the valley cupped as one might hold in one's palms a globe of glass . . .

The wind whipped water to my eyes, and the scene blurred. The crystal globe was cold in my hands. I gazed down into it. Small and perfect in the heart of the crystal lay the town with its bridge and moving river and the tiny, scudding ship. Round it the fields curved up and over, distorting in the curved crystal till fields, sky, river, clouds held the town with its scurrying people as leaves and sepals hold a bud before it breaks to flower. It seemed that the whole countryside, the whole of Wales, the whole of Britain could be held small and shining and safe between my hands, like something set in amber. I stared down at the land globed in crystal, and knew that this was what I had been born for. The time was here, and I must take it on trust.

The crystal globe melted out of my cupped hands, and was only a fistful of plants I had gathered, cold with rain. I let them fall, and put up the back of a hand to wipe the water from my eyes. The scene below me had changed; the wagon and the boat had gone; the town was still.

I went down to the cave to find Cadal busy with his cooking pots, and the young man already struggling with the saddles of our horses.

"Let that alone," I told him. "Cadal, is there hot water?"

"Plenty. Here's a start and a half, orders from the King. London, is it?" Cadal sounded pleased, and I didn't blame him. "We were due for a change, if you ask me. What is it, do you suppose? He"—jerking his head at the young man—"doesn't seem to know, or else he's not telling. Trouble, by the sound of it."

"Maybe. We'll soon find out. Here, you'd better dry this." I gave him my cloak, sat down by the fire, and called the young man to me. "Let me see that arm of yours now."

His wrist was blue with bruising, and swollen, and obviously hurt to the touch, but the bones were whole. While he washed I made a compress, then bound it on. He watched me half apprehensively, and tended to shy from my touch, and not only, I thought, with pain. Now that the mud was washed off and I could see him better, the feeling of familiarity persisted even more strongly. I eyed him over the bandages. "I know you, don't I?"

"You wouldn't remember me, my lord. But I remember you. You were kind to me once."

I laughed. "Was it such a rare occasion? What's your name?"

"Ulfin."

"Ulfin? It has a familiar sound . . . Wait a moment. Yes, I have it. Belasius' boy?"

"Yes. You do remember me?"

"Perfectly. That night in the forest, when my pony went lame, and you had to lead him home. I suppose you were around underfoot most of the time, but you were about as conspicuous as a field mouse. That's the only time I remember. Is Belasius over here for the coronation?"

"He's dead."

Something in his tone made me cock an eye at him over the bandaged wrist. "You hated him as much as that? No, don't answer, I guessed as much back there, young as I was. Well, I shan't ask why. The gods know I didn't love him myself, and I wasn't his slave. What happened to him?"

"He died of a fever, my lord."

"And you managed to survive him? I seem to remember something about an old and barbarous custom—"

"Prince Uther took me into his service. I am with him now—the King."

He spoke quickly, looking away. I knew it was all I would ever learn. "And are you still so afraid of the world, Ulfin?"

But he would not answer that. I finished tying the wrist. "Well, it's a wild and violent place, and the times are cruel. But they will get better, and I think you will help to make them so. There, that's done. Now get yourself something to eat. Cadal, do you remember Ulfin? The boy who brought Aster home the night we ran into Uther's troops by Nemet?"

"By the dog, so it is." Cadal looked him upon and down. "You look a sight better than you did then. What happened to the druid? Died of a curse? Come along then, and get something to eat. Yours is here, Merlin, and see you eat enough for a human being for a change, and not just what might keep one of your precious birds alive."

"I'll try," I said meekly, and then laughed at the expression on Ulfin's face as he looked from me to my servant and back again.

We lay that night at an inn near the crossroads where the way leads off north for the Five Hills and the gold mine. I ate alone in my room, served by Cadal. No sooner had the door shut behind the servant who carried the dishes than Cadal turned to me, obviously bursting with news.

"Well, there's a pretty carry-on in London, by all accounts."

"One might expect it," I said mildly. "I heard someone say Budec was there, together with most of the kings from across the Narrow Sea, and that most of them, and half the King's own nobles, have brought their daughters along with an eye to the empty side of the throne." I laughed. "That should suit Uther."

"They say he's been through half the girls in London already," said Cadal, setting a dish down in front of me. It was Welsh mutton, with a good sauce made of onions, hot and savoury.

"They'd say anything of him." I began to help myself. "It could even be true."

"Yes, but seriously, there's trouble afoot, they say. Woman trouble."

"Oh, God, Cadal, spare me. Uther was born to woman trouble."

"No, but I mean it. Some of the escort were talking, and it's no wonder Ulfin wouldn't. This is real trouble. Gorlois' wife."

I looked up, startled. "The Duchess of Cornwall? This can't be true."

"It's not true yet. But they say it's not for want of trying."

I drank wine. "You can be sure it's only rumour. She's more than half as young again as her husband, and I've heard she's fair. I suppose Uther pays her some attention, the Duke being his second in command, and men make all they can of it, Uther being who he is. And what he is."

Cadal leaned his fists on the table and looked down at me. He was uncommonly solemn. "Attention, is it? They say he's never out of her lap. Sends her the best dishes at table each day, sees she's served first, even before he is, pledges her in front of everybody in the hall every time he raises his goblet. Nobody's talking of anything else from London to Winchester. I'm told they're laying bets in the kitchen."

"I've no doubt. And does Gorlois have anything to say?"

"Tried to pass it over at first, they say, but it got so that he couldn't go on pretending he hadn't noticed. He tried to look as if he thought Uther was just doing the pair of them honour, but when it came to sitting the Lady Ygraine—that's her name—on Uther's right, and the old man six down on the other side—" He paused.

I said, uneasily: "He must be crazed. He can't afford trouble yet—trouble of any kind, let alone this, and with Gorlois of all people. By all the gods, Cadal, it was Cornwall that helped Ambrosius into the country at all, and Cornwall who put Uther where he is now. Who won the battle of Damen Hill for him?"

"Men are saying that, too."

"Are they indeed?" I thought for a moment, frowning. "And the woman? What—apart from the usual dunghill stuff—do they say about her?"

"That she says little, and says less each day. I've no doubt Gorlois has plenty to say to her at night when they're alone together. Anyway, I'm told she hardly lifts her eyes in public now, in case she meets the King staring at her over his cup, or leaning across at table to look down her dress."

"That is what I call dunghill stuff, Cadal. I meant, what is she like?"

"Well, that's just what they don't say, except that she's silent, and as beautiful as this, that and the other thing." He straightened. "Oh, no one says she gives him any help. And God knows there's no need for Uther to act like a starving man in sight of a dish of food; he could have his platter piled high any night he liked. There's hardly a girl in London who isn't trying to catch that eye of his."

"I believe you. Has he quarrelled with Gorlois? Openly, I mean?"

"Not so that I heard. In fact, he's been over-cordial there, and he got away with it for the first week or so; the old man was flattered. But Merlin, it does sound like trouble; she's less than half Gorlois' age and spends her life mewed up in one of those cold Cornish castles with nothing to do but weave his war-cloaks and dream over them, and you may be sure it's not of an old man with a grey beard."

I pushed the platter aside. I remember I still felt wholly unconcerned about what Uther was doing. But Cadal's last remark came a little too near home for comfort. There had been another girl, once, who had had nothing to do but sit at home and weave a dream . . .

I said abruptly: "All right, Cadal. I'm glad to know. I just hope we can keep clear of it ourselves. I've seen Uther mad for a woman before, but they've always been women he could get. This is suicide."

"Crazed, you said. That's what men are saying, too," said Cadal slowly. "Bewitched, they call it." He looked down at me half-sideways. "Maybe that's why he sent young Ulfin in such a sweat to make sure you'd come to London. Maybe he wants you there, to break the spell?"

"I don't break," I said shortly. "I make."

He stared for a moment, shutting his mouth on what, apparently, he had been about to say. Then he turned away to lift the jug of wine. As he poured it for me, in silence, I saw that his left hand was making the sign. We spoke no more that night.

4

As soon as I came in front of Uther I saw that Cadal had been right. Here was real trouble.

We reached London on the very eve of the crowning. It was late, and the city gates were shut, but it seemed there had been orders about us, for we were hustled through without question, and taken straight up to the castle where the King lay. I was scarcely given time to get out of my mud-stained garments before I was led along to his bedchamber and ushered in. The servants withdrew immediately and left us alone.

Uther was ready for the night, in a long bedgown of dark brown velvet edged with fur. His high chair was drawn to a leaping fire of logs, and on a stool beside the chair stood a pair of goblets and a lidded silver flagon with steam curling gently from the spout. I could smell the spiced wine as soon as I entered the room, and my dry throat contracted longingly, but the King made no move to offer it to me. He was not sitting by the fire. He was prowling restlessly up and down the room like a caged beast, and after him, pace for pace, his wolf-hound followed him.

As the door shut behind the servants he said abruptly, as he had said once before:

"You took your time."

"Four days? You should have sent better horses."

That stopped him in his tracks. He had not expected to be answered. But he said, mildly enough: "They were the best in my stables."

"Then you should get winged ones if you want better speed than we made, my lord. And tougher men. We left two of them by the way."

But he was no longer listening. Back in his thoughts, he resumed his restless pacing, and I watched him. He had lost weight, and moved quickly and lightly, like a starving wolf. His eyes were sunken with lack of sleep, and he had mannerisms I had not seen in him before; he could not keep his hands still. He wrung them together behind him, cracking the finger-joints, or fidgeted with the edges of his robe, or with his beard.

He flung at me over his shoulder: "I want your help."

"So I understand."

He turned at that. "You know about it?"

I lifted my shoulders. "Nobody talks of anything else but the King's desire for Gorlois' wife. I understand you have made no attempt to hide it. But it is more than a week now since you sent Ulfin to fetch me. In that time, what has happened? Are Gorlois and his wife still here?"

"Of course they are still here. They cannot go without my leave."

"I see. Has anything yet been said between you and Gorlois?"

"No."

"But he must know."

"It is the same with him as with me. If once this thing comes to words, nothing can stop it. And it is the crowning tomorrow. I cannot speak with him."

"Or with her?"

"No. No. Ah, God, Merlin, I cannot come near her. She is guarded like Danaë."

I frowned. "He has her guarded, then? Surely that's unusual enough to be a public admission that there's something wrong?"

"I only mean that his servants are all round her, and his men. Not only his bodyguard—many of his fighting troops are still here, that were with us in the north. I can only come near her in public, Merlin. They will have told you this."

"Yes. Have you managed to get any message to her privately?"

"No. She guards herself. All day she is with her women, and her servants keep the doors. And he—" He paused. There was sweat on his face. "He is with her every night."

He flung away again with a swish of the velvet robe, and paced, soft-footed, the length of the room, into the shadows beyond the firelight. Then he turned. He threw out his hands and spoke simply, like a boy.

"Merlin, what shall I do?"

I crossed to the fire-place, picked up the jug and poured two goblets of the spiced wine. I held one out to him. "To begin with, come and sit down. I cannot talk to a whirlwind. Here."

He obeyed, sinking back in the big chair with the goblet between his hands. I drank my own, gratefully, and sat down on the other side of the hearth.

Uther did not drink. I think he hardly knew what he had between his hands. He stared at the fire through the thinning steam from the goblet. "As soon as he brought her in and presented her to me, I knew. God knows that at first I thought it was no more than another passing fever, the kind I've had a thousand times before, only this time a thousand times stronger—"

"And been cured of," I said, "in a night, a week of nights, a month. I don't know the longest time a woman has ever held you, Uther, but is a month, or even three, enough to wreck a kingdom for?"

The look he gave me, blue as a sword-flash, was a look from the old Uther I remembered. "By Hades, why do you think I sent for you? I could have wrecked my kingdom any time in these past weeks had I been so minded. Why do you think it has not yet gone beyond folly? Oh, yes, I admit there has been folly, but I tell you this is a fever, and not the kind I have had before, and slaked before. This burns me so that I cannot sleep. How can I rule and fight and deal with men if I cannot sleep?"

"Have you taken a girl to bed?"

He stared, then he drank. "Are you mad?"

"Forgive me, it was a stupid question. You don't sleep even then?"

"No." He set down the goblet beside him, and knitted his hands together. "It's no use. Nothing is any use. You must bring her to me, Merlin. You have the arts. This is why I sent for you. You are to bring her to me so that no one knows. Make her love me. Bring her here to me, while he is asleep. You can do it."

"Make her love you? By magic? No, Uther, this is something that magic cannot do. You must know that."

"It is something that every old wife swears she can do. And you—you have power beyond any man living. You lifted the Hanging Stones. You lifted the king-stone where Tremorinus could not."

"My mathematics are better, that is all. For God's sake, Uther, whatever men say of that, you know how it was done. That was no magic."

"You spoke with my brother as he died. Are you going to deny that now?"

"No."

"Or that you swore to serve me when I needed you?"

"No."

"I need you now. Your power, whatever it is. Dare you tell me that you are not a magician?"

"I am not the kind that can walk through walls," I said, "and bring bodies through locked doors." He made a sudden movement, and I saw the feverish brightness of his eyes, not this time with anger, but I thought with pain. I added: "But I have not refused to help you."

The eyes sparked. "You will help me?"

"Yes, I will help you. I told you when last we met that there would come a time when we must deal together. This is the time. I don't know yet what I must do, but this will be shown to me, and the outcome is with the god. But one thing I can do for you, tonight. I can make you sleep. No, be still and listen . . . If you are to be crowned tomorrow, and take Britain into your hands, tonight you will do as I say. I will make you a drink that will let you sleep, and you'll take a girl to your bed as usual. It may be better if there is someone besides your servant who will swear you were in your own chamber."

"Why? What are you going to do?" His voice was strained.

"I shall try to talk with Ygraine."

He sat forward, his hands tight on the arms of the chair. "Yes. Talk to her. Perhaps you can come to her where I cannot. Tell her—"

"A moment. A little while back you told me to 'make her love you.' You want me to invoke any power there is to bring her to you. If you have never spoken to her of your love, or seen her except in public, how do you know she would come to you, even if the way were free? Is her mind clear to you, my lord King?"

"No. She says nothing. She smiles, with her eyes on the ground, and says nothing. But I know. I know. It is as if all the other times I played at love were only single notes. Put together, they make the song. She is the song."

There was a silence. Behind him, on a dais in the corner of the room, was the bed, with the covers drawn back ready. Above it, leaping up the wall, was a great dragon fashioned of red gold. In the firelight it moved, stretching its claws.

He said suddenly: "When we last talked, there in the middle of the Hanging Stones, you said you wanted nothing from me. But by all the gods, Merlin, if you help me now, if I get her, and in safety, then you can ask what you will. I swear it."

I shook my head, and he said no more. I think he saw that I was no longer thinking of him; that other forces pressed me, crowding the firelit room. The dragon flamed and shimmered up the dark wall. In its shadow another moved, merging with it, flame into flame. Something struck at my eyes, pain like a claw. I shut them, and there was silence. When I opened them again the fire had died, and the wall was dark. I looked across at the King, motionless in his chair, watching me. I said, slowly: "I will ask you one thing, now."

"Yes?"

"That when I bring you to her in safety, you shall make a child."

Whatever he had expected, it was not this. He stared, then, suddenly, laughed. "That's with the gods, surely?"

"Yes, it is with God."

He stretched back in his chair, as if a weight had been lifted off his shoulders. "If I come to her, Merlin, I promise you that whatever I have power to do, I shall do. And anything else you bid me. I shall even sleep tonight."

I stood up. "Then I shall go and make the draught and send it to you."

"And you'll see her?"

"I shall see her. Good night."

Ulfin was half asleep on his feet outside the door. He blinked at me as I came out.

"I'm to go in now?"

"In a minute. Come to my chamber first and I'll give you a drink for him. See he takes it. It's to give him sleep. Tomorrow will be a long day."

There was a girl asleep in a corner, wrapped in a blue blanket on a huddle of pillows. As we passed I saw the curve of a bare shoulder and a tumble of straight brown hair. She looked very young.

I raised my brows at Ulfin, and he nodded, then jerked his head towards the shut door with a look of enquiry.

"Yes," I said, "but later. When you take him the drink. Leave her sleeping now. You look as if you could do with some sleep yourself, Ulfin."

"If he sleeps tonight I might get some." He gave a flicker of a grin at me. "Make it strong, won't you, my lord? And see it tastes good."

"Oh, he'll drink it, never fear."

"I wasn't thinking of him," said Ulfin. "I was thinking of me."

"Of you? Ah, I see, you mean you'll have to taste it first?"

He nodded.

"You have to try everything? His meals? Even love potions?"

"Love potions? For him?" He stared, open-mouthed. Then he laughed. "Oh, you're joking!"

I smiled. "I wanted to see if you could laugh. Here we are. Wait now, I won't be a minute."

Cadal was waiting for me by the fire in my chamber. This was a comfortable room in the curve of a tower wall, and Cadal had kept a bright fire burning and a big cauldron of water steaming on the iron dogs. He had got out a woollen bedgown for me and laid it ready across the bed.

Over a chest near the window lay a pile of clothes, a shimmer of gold cloth and scarlet and fur. "What's that?" I asked, as I sat down to let him draw off my shoes.

"The King sent a robe for tomorrow, my lord." Cadal, with an eye on the boy who was pouring the bath, was formal. I noticed the boy's hand shaking a little, and water splashed on the floor. As soon as he had finished, obedient to a jerk of Cadal's head, he scuttled out.

"What's the matter with that boy?"

"It isn't every night you prepare a bath for a wizard."

"For God's sake. What have you been telling him?"

"Only that you'd turn him into a bat if he didn't serve you well."

"Fool. No, a moment, Cadal. Bring me my box. Ulfin's waiting outside. I promised to make up a draught."

Cadal obeyed me. "What's the matter? His arm still bad?"

"It's not for him. For the King."

"Ah." He made no further comment, but when the thing was done and Ulfin had gone, and I was stripping for the bath, he asked: "It's as bad as they say?"

"Worse." I gave him a brief version of my conversation with the King.

He heard me out, frowning. "And what's to do now?"

"Find some way to see the lady. No, not the bedgown; not yet, alas. Get me a clean robe out—something dark."

"Surely you can't go to her tonight? It's well past midnight."

"I shall not go anywhere. Whoever is coming, will come to me."

"But Gorlois will be with her—"

"No more now, Cadal. I want to think. Leave me. Good night."

When the door had shut on him I went across to the chair beside the fire. It was not true that I wanted time to think. All I needed was silence, and the fire. Bit by bit, slowly, I emptied my mind, feeling thought spill out of me like sand from a glass, to leave me hollow and light. I waited, my hands slack on the grey robe, open, empty. It was very quiet. Somewhere, from a dark corner of the room, came the dry tick of old wood settling in the night. The fire flickered. I watched it, but absently, as any man might watch the flames for comfort on a cold night. I did not need to dream. I lay, light as a dead leaf, on the flood that ran that night to meet the sea.

Outside the door there were sounds suddenly, voices. A quick tap at the panel, and Cadal came in, shutting the door behind him. He looked guarded and a little apprehensive.

"Gorlois?" I asked.

He swallowed, then nodded.

"Well, show him in."

"He asked if you had been to see the King. I said you'd been here barely a couple of hours, and you had had time to see nobody. Was that right?"

I smiled. "You were guided. Let him come in now."

Gorlois came in quickly, and I rose to greet him. There was, I thought, as big a change in him as I had seen in Uther; his big frame was bent, and for the first time one saw straight away that he was old.

He brushed aside the ceremony of my greeting. "You're not abed yet? They told me you'd ridden in."

"Barely in time for the crowning, but I shall see it after all. Will you sit, my lord?"

"Thanks, but no. I came for your help, Merlin, for my wife." The quick eyes peered under the grey brows. "Aye, no one could ever tell what you were thinking, but you've heard, haven't you?"

"There was talk," I said carefully, "but then there always was talk about Uther. I have not heard anyone venture a word against your wife."

"By God, they'd better not! However, it's not that I've come about tonight. There's nothing you could do about that—though it's possible you're the only person who could talk some sense into the King. You'll not get near him now till after the crowning, but if you could get him to let us go back to Cornwall without waiting for the end of the feast . . . Would you do that for me?"

"If I can."

"I knew I could count on you. With things the way they are in the town just now, it's hard to know who's a friend. Uther's not an easy man to gainsay. But you could do it—and what's more, you'd dare. You're your father's son, and for my old friend's sake—"

"I said I'd do it."

"What's the matter? Are you ill?"

"It's nothing. I'm weary. We had a hard ride. I'll see the King in the morning early, before he leaves for the crowning."

He gave a brief nod of thanks. "That's not the only thing I came to ask you. Would you come and see my wife tonight?"

There was a pause of utter stillness, so prolonged that I thought he must notice. Then I said: "If you wish it, yes. But why?"

"She's sick, that's why, and I'd have you come and see her, if you will. When her women told her you were here in London, she begged me to send for you. I can tell you, I was thankful when I heard you'd come. There's not many men I'd trust just now, and that's God's truth. But I'd trust you."

Beside me a log crumbled and fell into the heart of the fire. The flames shot up, splashing his face with red, like blood.

"You'll come?" asked the old man.

"Of course." I looked away from him. "I'll come immediately."

5

Uther had not exaggerated when he said that the Lady Ygraine was well guarded. She and her lord were lodged in a court some way west of the King's quarters, and the court was crowded with Cornwall men-at-arms. There were armed men in the antechamber too, and in the bedchamber itself some half-dozen women. As we went in the oldest of these, a greyhaired woman with an anxious look, hurried forward with relief in her face.

"Prince Merlin." She bent her knees to me, eyeing me with awe, and led me towards the bed.

The room was warm and scented. The lamps burned sweet oil, and the fire was of applewood. The bed stood at the center of the wall opposite the fire. The pillows were of grey silk with gilt tassels, and the coverlet richly worked with flowers and strange beasts and winged creatures. The only other woman's room that I had seen was my mother's, with the plain wooden bed and the carved oak chest and the loom, and the cracked mosaics of the floor.

I walked forward and stood at the foot of the bed, looking down at Gorlois' wife.

If I had been asked then what she looked like I could not have said. Cadal had told me she was fair, and I had seen the hunger in the King's face, so I knew she was desirable; but as I stood in the airy scented room looking at the woman who lay with closed eyes against the grey silk pillows, it was no woman that I saw. Nor did I see the room or the people in it. I saw only the flashing and beating of the light as in a globed crystal.

I spoke without taking my eyes from the woman in the bed. "One of her women stay here. The rest go. You too, please, my lord." He went without demur, herding the women in front of him like a flock of sheep. The woman who had greeted me remained by her mistress's bed. As the door shut behind the last of them, the woman in the bed opened her eyes. For a few moments of silence we met each other eye to eye. Then I said: "What do you want of me, Ygraine?"

She answered crisply, with no pretense: "I have sent for you, Prince, because I want your help."

I nodded. "In the matter of the King."

She said straightly: "So you know already? When my husband brought you here, did you guess I was not ill?"

"I guessed."

"Then you can also guess what I want from you?"

"Not quite. Tell me, could you not somehow have spoken with the King himself before now? It might have saved him something. And your husband as well."

Her eyes widened. "How could I talk to the King? You came through the courtyard?"

"Yes."

"Then you saw my husband's troops and men at arms. What do you suppose would have happened had I talked to Uther? I could not answer him openly, and if I had met him in secret—even if I could—half London would have known it within the hour. Of course I could not speak to him or send him a message. The only protection was silence."

I said slowly: "If the message was simply that you were a true and faithful wife and that he must turn his eyes elsewhere, then the message could have been given to him at any time and by any messenger."

She smiled. Then she bent her head.

I took in my breath. "Ah. That's what I wished to know. You are honest, Ygraine."

"What use to lie to you? I have heard about you. Oh, I know better than to believe all they say in the songs and stories, but you are clever and cold and wise, and they say you love no woman and are committed to no man. So you can listen, and judge." She looked down at her hands, where they lay on the coverlet, then up at me again. "But I do believe that you can see the future. I want you to tell me what the future is."

"I don't tell fortunes like an old woman. Is this why you sent for me?"

"You know why I sent for you. You are the one man with whom I can seek private speech without arousing my husband's anger and suspicion—and you have the King's ear." Though she was but a woman, and young, lying in her bed with me standing over it, it was as if she were a queen giving audience. She looked at me very straight. "Has the King spoken to you yet?"

"He has no need to speak to me. Everyone knows what ails him."

"And will you tell him what you have just learned from me?"

"That will depend."

"On what?" she demanded.

I said slowly: "On you yourself. So far you have been wise. Had you been less guarded in your ways and your speech there would have been trouble, there might even have been war. I understand that you have never allowed one moment of your time here to be solitary or unguarded; you have taken care always to be where you could be seen."

She looked at me for a moment in silence, her brows raised. "Of course."

"Many women—especially desiring what you desire—would not have been able to do this, Lady Ygraine."

"I am not 'many women'." The words were like a flash. She sat up suddenly, tossing back the dark hair, and threw back the covers. The old woman snatched up a long blue robe and hurried forward. Ygraine threw it round her, over her white nightrobe, and sprang from the bed, walking restlessly over towards the window.

Standing, she was tall for a woman, with a form that might have moved a sterner man than Uther. Her neck was long and slender, the head poised gracefully. The dark hair streamed unbound down her back. Her eyes were blue, not the fierce blue of Uther's, but the deep, dark blue of the Celt. Her mouth was proud. She was very lovely, and no man's toy. If Uther wanted her, I thought, he would have to make her Queen.

She had stopped just short of the window. If she had gone to it, she might have been seen from the courtyard. No, not a lady to lose her head.

She turned. "I am the daughter of a king, and I come from a line of kings. Cannot you see how I must have been driven, even to think the way I am thinking now?" She repeated it passionately. "Can you not see? I was married at sixteen to the Lord of Cornwall; he is a good man; I honour and respect him. Until I came to London I was half content to starve and die there in Cornwall, but he brought me here, and now it has happened. Now I know what I must have, but it is beyond me to have it, beyond the wife of Gorlois of Cornwall. So what else would you have me do? There is nothing to do but wait here and be silent, because on my silence hangs not only the honour of myself and my husband and my house, but the safety of the kingdom that Ambrosius died for, and that Uther himself has just sealed with blood and fire."

She swung away to take two quick paces and back again. "I am no trashy Helen for men to fight over, die over, burn down kingdoms for. I don't wait on the walls as a prize for some brawny victor. I cannot so dishonour both Gorlois and the King in the eyes of men. And I cannot go to him secretly and dishonour myself in my own eyes. I am a lovesick woman, yes. But I am also Ygraine of Cornwall."

I said coldly: "So you intend to wait until you can go to him in honour, as his Queen?"

"What else can I do?"

"Was this the message I had to give him?"

She was silent.

I said: "Or did you get me here to read you the future? To tell you the length of your husband's life?"

Still she said nothing.

"Ygraine," I said, "the two are the same. If I give Uther the message that you love and desire him, but that you will not come to him while your husband is alive, what length of life would you prophesy for Gorlois?"

Still she did not speak. The gift of silence, too, I thought. I was standing between her and the fire. I watched the light beating round her, flowing up the white robe and the blue robe, light and shadow rippling upwards in waves like moving water or the wind over grass. A flame leapt, and my shadow sprang over her and grew, climbing with the beating light to meet her own climbing shadow and join with it, so that there across the wall behind her reared—no dragon of gold or scarlet, no firedrake with burning tail, but a great cloudy shape of air and darkness, thrown there by the flame, and sinking as the flame sank, to shrink and steady until it was only her shadow, the shadow of a woman, slender and straight, like a sword. And where I stood, there was nothing.

She moved, and the lamplight built the room again round us, warm and real and smelling of applewood. She was watching me with something in her face that had not been there before. At last she said, in a still voice: "I told you there was nothing hidden from you. You do well to put it into words. I had thought all this. But I hoped that by sending for you I could absolve myself, and the King."

"Once a dark thought is dragged into words it is in the light. You could have had your desire long since on the terms of 'any woman', as the King could on the terms of any man." I paused. The room was steady now. The words came clearly to me, from nowhere, without thought. "I will tell you, if you like, how you may meet the King's love on your terms and on his, with no dishonour to yourself or him, or to your husband. If I could tell you this, would you go to him?"

Her eyes had widened, with a flash behind them, as I spoke. But even so she took time to think. "Yes." Her voice told me nothing.

"If you will obey me, I can do this for you," I said.

"Tell me what I must do."

"Have I your promise, then?"

"You go too fast," she said dryly. "Do you yourself seal bargains before you see what you are committed to?"

I smiled. "No. Very well then, listen to me. When you feigned illness to have me brought to you, what did you tell your husband and your women?"

"Only that I felt faint and sick, and was no more inclined for company. That if I was to appear beside my husband at the crowning, I must see a physician tonight, and take a healing draught." She smiled a little wryly. "I was preparing the way, too, not to sit beside the King at the feast."

"So far, good. You will tell Gorlois that you are pregnant."

"That I am pregnant?" For the first time she sounded shaken. She stared.

"This is possible? He is an old man, but I would have thought—"

"It is possible. But I—" She bit her lip. After a while she said calmly: "Go on. I asked for your counsel, so I must let you give it."

I had never before met a woman with whom I did not have to choose my words, to whom I could speak as I would speak to another man. I said: "Your husband can have no reason to suspect you are pregnant by any man but himself. So you will tell him this, and tell him also that you fear for the child's health if you stay longer in London, under the strain of the gossip and the King's attentions. Tell him that you wish to leave as soon as the crowning is over. That you do not wish to go to the feast, to be distinguished by the King, and to be the center of all the eyes and the gossip. You will go with Gorlois and the Cornish troops tomorrow, before the gates shut at sunset. The news will not come to Uther until the feast."

"But"—she stared again—"this is folly. We could have gone any time this past three weeks if we had chosen to risk the King's anger. We are bound to stay until he gives us leave to go. If we go in that manner, for whatever reason—"

I stopped her. "Uther can do nothing on the day of the crowning. He must stay here for the days of feasting. Do you think he can give offense to Budec and Merrovius and the other kings gathered here? You will be in Cornwall before he can even move."

"And then he will move." She made an impatient gesture. "And there will be war, when he should be making and mending, not breaking and burning. And he cannot win: if he is the victor in the field, he loses the loyalty of the West. Win or lose, Britain is divided, and goes back into the dark."

Yes, she would be a queen. She was on fire for Uther as much as he for her, but she could still think. She was cleverer than Uther, clear-headed, and, I thought, stronger too.

"Oh, yes, he will move." I lifted a hand. "But listen to me. I will talk to the King before the crowning. He will know that the story you told Gorlois was a lie. He will know that I have told you to go to Cornwall. He will feign rage, and he will swear in public to be revenged for the insult put on him by Gorlois at the crowning . . . And he will make ready to follow you to Cornwall as soon as the feast is over—"

"But meanwhile our troops will be safely out of London without trouble. Yes, I see. I did not understand you. Go on." She drove her hands inside the sleeves of the blue robe, and clasped her elbows, cradling her breasts. She was not so ice-calm as she looked, the Lady Ygraine. "And then?"

"And you will be safely at home," I said, "with your honour and Cornwall's unbroken."

"Safely, yes. I shall be in Tintagel, and even Uther cannot come at me there. Have you seen the stronghold, Merlin? The cliffs of that coast are high and cruel, and from them runs a thin bridge of rock, the only way to the island where the castle stands. This bridge is so narrow that men can only go one at a time, not even a horse. Even the landward end of the bridge is guarded by a fortress on the main cliff, and within the castle there is water, and food for a year. It is the strongest place in Cornwall. It cannot be taken from the land, and it cannot be approached by sea. If you wish to shut me away for ever from Uther, this is the place to send me."

"So I have heard. This will be, then, where Gorlois will send you. If Uther follows, lady, would Gorlois be content to wait inside the stronghold with you for a year like a beast in a trap? And could his troops be taken in with him?"

She shook her head. "If it cannot be taken, neither can it be used as a base. All one can do is sit out the siege."

"Then you must persuade him that unless he is content to wait inside while the King's troops ravage Cornwall, he himself must be outside, where he can fight."

She struck her hands together. "He will do that. He could not wait and hide and let Cornwall suffer. Nor can I understand your plan, Merlin. If you are trying to save your King and your kingdom from me, then say so. I can feign sickness here, until Uther finds he has to let me go home. We could go home without insult, and without bloodshed."

I said sharply: "You said you would listen. Time runs short."

She was still again. "I am listening."

"Gorlois will lock you in Tintagel. Where will he go himself to face Uther?"

"To Dimilioc. It is a few miles from Tintagel, up the coast. It is a good fortress, and good country to fight from. But then what? Do you think Gorlois will not fight?" She moved across to the fireside and sat down, and I saw her steady her hands deliberately, spreading the fingers on her knee. "And do you think the King can come to me in Tintagel, whether Gorlois is there or no?"

"If you do as I have bid you, you and the King may have speech and comfort one of the other. And you will do this in peace. No"—as her head came up sharply—"this part of it you leave with me. This is where we come to magic. Trust me for the rest. Get yourself only to Tintagel, and wait. I shall bring Uther to you there. And I promise you now, for the King, that he shall not give battle to Gorlois, and that after he and you have met in love, Cornwall shall have peace. As to how this will be, it is with God. I can only tell you what I know. What power is in me now, is from him, and we are in his hands to make or to destroy. But I can tell you this also, Ygraine, that I have seen a bright fire burning, and in it a crown, and a sword standing in an altar like a cross."

She got to her feet quickly, and for the first time there was a kind of fear in her eyes. She opened her mouth as if to speak, then closed her lips again and turned back towards the window. Again she stopped short of it, but I saw her lift her head as if longing for the air. She should have been winged. If she had spent her youth walled in Tintagel it was no wonder she wanted to fly.

She raised her hands and pushed back the hair from her brows. She spoke to the window, not looking at me. "I will do this. If I tell him I am with child, he will take me to Tintagel. It is the place where all the dukes of Cornwall are born. And after that I have to trust you." She turned then and looked at me, dropping her hands. "If once I can have speech with him . . . even just that . . . But if you have brought bloodshed to Cornwall through me, or death to my husband, then I shall spend the rest of my life praying to any gods there are that you, too, Merlin, shall die betrayed by a woman."

"I am content to face your prayers. And now I must go. Is there someone you can send with me? I'll make a draught for you and send it back. It will only be poppy; you can take it and not fear."

"Ralf can go, my page. You'll find him outside the door. He is Marcia's grandson, and can be trusted as I trust her." She nodded to the old woman, who moved to open the door for me.

"Then any message I may have to send you," I said, "I shall send through him by my man Cadal. And now good night."

When I left her she was standing quite still in the center of the room, with the firelight leaping round her.

6

We had a wild ride to Cornwall.

Easter that year had fallen as early as it ever falls, so we were barely out of winter and into spring when, on a black wild night, we halted our horses on the clifftop near Tintagel, and peered down into the teeth of the wind. There were only the four of us, Uther, myself, Ulfin, and Cadal. Everything, so far, had gone smoothly and according to plan. It was getting on towards midnight on the twenty-fourth of March.

Ygraine had obeyed me to the letter. I had not dared, that night in London, to go straight from her quarters to Uther's chamber, in case this should be reported to Gorlois; but in any case Uther would be asleep. I had visited him early next morning, while he was being bathed and made ready for the crowning. He sent the servants away, except for Ulfin, and I was able to tell him exactly what he must do. He looked the better for his drugged sleep, greeted me briskly enough, and listened with eagerness in the bright, hollow eyes.

"And she will do as you say?"

"Yes. I have her word. Will you?"

"You know that I will." He regarded me straightly. "And now will you not tell me about the outcome?"

"I told you. A child."

"Oh, that." He hunched an impatient shoulder. "You are like my brother; he thought of nothing else . . . Still working for him, are you?"

"You might say so."

"Well, I must get one sooner or later, I suppose. No, I meant Gorlois. What will come to him? There's a risk, surely?"

"Nothing is done without risk. You must do the same as I, you must take the time on trust. But I can tell you that your name, and your kingdom, will survive the night's work."

A short silence. He measured me with his eyes. "From you, I suppose that is enough. I am content."

"You do well to be. You will outlive him, Uther."

He laughed suddenly. "God's grief, man, I could have prophesied that myself! I can give him thirty years, and he's no stay-at-home when it comes to war. Which is one good reason why I refuse to have his blood on my hands. So, on that same account . . ."

He turned then to Ulfin and began to give his orders. It was the old Uther back again, brisk, concise, clear. A messenger was to go immediately to Caerleon, and troops to be despatched from there to North Cornwall. Uther himself would travel there straight from London as soon as he was able, riding fast with a small bodyguard to where his troops would be encamped. In this way the King could be hard on Gorlois' heels, even though Gorlois would leave today, and the

King must stay feasting his peers for four more long days. Another man was to ride out immediately along our proposed route to Cornwall, and see that good horses were ready at short stages all the way.

So it came about as I had planned. I saw Ygraine at the crowning, still, composed, erect, and with downcast eyes, and so pale that if I had not seen her the night before, I myself would have believed her story true. I shall never cease to wonder at women. Even with power, it is not possible to read their minds. Duchess and slut alike, they need not even study to deceive. I suppose it is the same with slaves, who live with fear, and with those animals who disguise themselves by instinct to save their lives. She sat through the long, brilliant ceremony, like wax which at any moment may melt to collapse; then afterwards I caught a glimpse of her, supported by her women, leaving the throng as the bright pomp moved slowly to the hall of feasting. About halfway through the feast, when the wine had gone round well, I saw Gorlois, unremarked, leave the hall with one or two other men who were answering the call of nature. He did not come back.

Uther, to one who knew the truth, may not have been quite so convincing as Ygraine, but between exhaustion and wine and his ferocious exultation at what was to come, he was convincing enough. Men talked among themselves in hushed voices about his rage when he discovered Gorlois' absence, and his angry vows to take vengeance as soon as his royal guests had gone. If that anger were a little overloud and his threats too fierce against a Duke whose only fault was the protection of his own wife, the King had been intemperate enough before for men to see this as part of the same picture. And so bright now was Uther's star, so dazzling the luster of the crowned Pendragon, that London would have forgiven him a public rape. They could less easily forgive Ygraine for having refused him.

So we came to Cornwall. The messenger had done his work well, and our ride, in hard short stages of no more than twenty miles apiece, took us two days and a night. We found our troops waiting encamped at the place selected—a few miles in from Hercules Point and just outside the Cornish border—with the news that, however she had managed it, Ygraine was fast in Tintagel with a small body of picked men, while her husband with the rest of his force had descended on Dimilioc, and sent a call round for the men of Cornwall to gather to defend their Duke. He must know of the presence of the King's troops so near his border, but no doubt he would expect them to wait for the King's coming, and could have as yet no idea that the King was already there.

We rode secretly into our camp at dusk, and went, not to the King's quarters, but to those of a captain he could trust. Cadal was there already, having gone ahead to prepare the disguises which I meant us to wear, and to await Ralf's message from Tintagel when the time was ripe.

My plan was simple enough, with the kind of simplicity that often succeeds, and it was helped by Gorlois' habit, since his marriage, of riding back nightly where he could—from Dimilioc or his other fortresses—to visit his wife. I suppose there had been too many jests about the old man's fondness, and he had formed the habit (Ralf had told me) of riding back secretly, using the private gate, a hidden postern to which access wae difficult unless one knew the way. My plan was simply to disguise Uther, Ulfin, and myself to pass, if we were seen, as Gorlois and his companion and servant, and ride to Tintagel by night. Ralf would arrange to be on duty himself at the postern, and would meet us and lead us up the secret path. Ygraine had by some means persuaded Gorlois—this had been the greatest danger—not to visit her himself that night, and would dismiss all her women but Marcia. Ralf and Cadal had arranged between them what clothes we should wear: the Cornwall party had ridden from London in such a hurry on the night of the coronation feast that some of their baggage had been left behind, and it had been simple to find saddle-cloths with the blazon of Cornwall, and even one of Gorlois' familiar war-cloaks with the double border of silver.

Ralf's latest message had been reassuring; the time was ripe, the night black enough to hide us and wild enough to keep most men within doors. We set off after it was full dark, and the four of us slipped out of camp unobserved. Once clear of our own lines we went at a gallop for Tintagel, and it would have been only the keen eye of suspicion which could have told that this was not the Duke of Cornwall with three companions, riding quickly home to his wife. Uther's beard had been greyed, and a bandage came down one side of his face to cover the corner of his mouth, and give some reason—should he be forced to talk—for any strangeness in his speech. The hood of his cloak, pulled down low as was natural on such a fierce night, shadowed his features. He was straighter and more powerful than Gorlois, but this was easy enough to disguise, and he wore gauntlets to hide his hands, which were not those of an old man. Ulfin passed well enough as one Jordan, a servant of Gorlois whom we had chosen as being the nearest to Ulfin's build and colouring. I myself wore the clothes of Brithael, Gorlois' friend and captain: he was an older man than I, but his voice was not unlike mine, and I could speak good Cornish. I have always been good at voices. I was to do what talking proved necessary. Cadal came with us undisguised; he was to wait with the horses outside and be our messenger if we should need one.

I rode up close to the King and set my mouth to his ear. "The castle's barely a mile from here. We ride down to the shore now. Ralf will be there to show us in. I'll lead on?"

He nodded. Even in the ragged, flying dark I thought I saw the gleam of his eyes. I added: "And don't look like that, or they'll never think you're Gorlois, with years of married life behind you."

I heard him laugh, and then I wheeled my horse and led the way carefully down the rabbit-ridden slope of scrub and scree into the head of the narrow valley which leads down towards the shore.

This valley is little more than a gully carrying a small stream to the sea. At its widest the stream is not more than three paces broad, and so shallow that a horse can ford it anywhere. At the foot of the valley the water drops over a low cliff straight to a beach of slaty shingle. We rode in single file down the track, with the stream running deep down on the left, and to our right a high bank covered with bushes. Since the wind was from the south-west and the valley was deep and running almost north, we were sheltered from the gale, but at the top of the bank the bushes were screaming in the wind, and twigs and even small boughs hurtled through the air and across our path. Even without this and the steepness of the stony path and the darkness, it was not easy riding; the horses, what with the storm and some tension which must have been generated by the three of us—Cadal was as solid as a rock, but then he was not going into the castle—were wild and white-eyed with nerves. When, a quarter of a mile from the sea, we turned down to the stream and set the beasts to cross it, mine, in the lead, flattened its ears and balked, and when I had lashed it across and into a plunging canter up the narrow track, and a man's figure detached itself from the shadows ahead beside the path, the horse stopped dead and climbed straight up into the air till I felt sure it would go crashing over backwards, and me with it.

The shadow darted forward and seized the bridle, dragging the horse down. The beast stood, sweating and shaking.

"Brithael," I said. "Is all well?"

I heard him exclaim, and he took a pace, pressing closer to the horse's shoulder, peering upwards in the dark. Behind me Uther's grey hoisted itself up the track and thudded to a halt. The man at my horse's shoulder said, uncertainly: "My lord Gorlois . . . ? We did not look for you tonight. Is there news, then?"

It was Ralf's voice. I said in my own: "So we'll pass, at least in the dark?"

I heard his breath go in. "Yes, my lord . . . For the moment I thought it was indeed Brithael. And then the grey horse . . . Is that the King?"

"For tonight," I said, "it is the Duke of Cornwall. Is all well?"

"Yes, sir."

"Then lead the way. There is not much time."

He gripped my horse's bridle above the bit and led him on, for which I was grateful, as the path wae dangerous, narrow and slippery and twisting along the steep bank between the rustling bushes; not a path I would have wished to ride even in daylight on a strange and frightened horse. The others followed, Cadal's mount and Ulfin's plodding stolidly along, and close behind me the grey stallion snorting at every bush and trying to break his rider's grip, but Uther could have ridden Pegasus himself and foundered him before his own wrists even ached.

Here my horse shied at something I could not see, stumbled, and would have pitched me down the bank but for Ralf at its head. I swore at it, then asked Ralf: "How far now?"

"About two hundred paces to the shore, sir, and we leave the horses there. We climb the promontory on foot."

"By all the gods of storm, I'll be glad to get under cover. Did you have any trouble?"

"None, sir." He had to raise his voice to make me hear, but in that turmoil there was no fear of being heard more than three paces off. "My lady told Felix himself—that's the porter—that she had asked the Duke to ride back as soon as his troops were disposed at Dimilioc. Of course the word's gone round that she's pregnant, so it's natural enough she'd want him back, even with the King's armies so close. She told Felix the Duke would come by the secret gate in case the King had spies posted already. He wasn't to tell the garrison, she said, because they might be alarmed at his leaving Dimilioc and the troops there, but the King couldn't possibly be in Cornwall for another day at soonest . . . Felix doesn't suspect a thing. Why should he?"

"The porter is alone at the gate?"

"Yes, but there are two guards in the guard-room."

He had told us already what lay inside the postern. This was a small gate set low in the outer castle wall, and just inside it a long flight of steps ran up to the right, hugging the wall. Halfway up was a wide landing, with a guard-room to the side. Beyond that the stairs went up again, and at the top was the private door leading through into the apartments.

"Do the guards know?" I asked.

He shook his head. "My lord, we didn't dare. All the men left with the Lady Ygraine were hand-picked by the Duke."

"Are the stairs well lighted?"

"A torch. I saw to it that it will be mostly smoke."

I looked over my shoulder to where the grey horse came ghostly behind me through the dark. Ralf had had to raise his voice to make me hear above the wind which screamed across the top of the valley, and I would have thought that the King would be waiting to know what passed between us. But he was silent, as he had been since the beginning of the ride. It seemed he was indeed content to trust the time. Or to trust me.

I turned back to Ralf, leaning down over my horse's shoulder. "Is there a password?"

"Yes, my lord. It is *pilgrim.* And the lady has sent a ring for the King to wear. It is one the Duke wears sometimes. Here's the end of the path, can you see? It's quite a drop to the beach." He checked, steadying my horse, then the beast plunged down and its hoofs grated on shingle. "We leave the horses here, my lord."

I dismounted thankfully. As far as I could see, we were in a small cove sheltered from the wind by a mighty headland close to our left, but the seas, tearing past the end of this headland and curving round to break among the offshore rocks, were huge, and came lashing down on the shingle in torrents of white with a noise like armies clashing together in anger. Away to the right I saw another high headland, and between the two this roaring stretch of white water broken by the teeth of black rocks. The stream behind us fell seawards over its low cliff in two long cascades which blew in the wind like ropes of hair. Beyond these swinging waterfalls, and in below the overhanging wall of the main cliff, there was shelter for the horses.

Ralf was pointing to the great headland on our left. "The path is up there. Tell the King to come behind me and to follow closely. One foot wrong tonight, and before you could cry help you'd be out with the tide as far as the western stars."

The grey thudded down beside us and the King swung himself out of the saddle. I heard him laugh, that same sharp, exultant sound. Even had there been no prize at the end of the night's trail, he would have been the same. Danger was drink and dreams alike to Uther.

The other two came up with us and dismounted, and Cadal took the reins. Uther came to my shoulder, looking at the cruel race of water. "Do we swim for it now?"

"It may come to that, God knows. It looks to me as if the waves are up to the castle wall."

He stood quite still, oblivious of the buffeting of wind and rain, with his head lifted, staring up at the headland. High against the stormy dark, a light burned.

I touched his arm. "Listen. The situation is what we expected. There is a porter, Felix, and two men-at-arms in the guard-room. There should be very little light. You know the way in. It will be enough, as we go in, if you grunt your thanks to Felix and go quickly up the stair. Marcia, the old woman, will meet you at the door of Ygraine's apartments and lead you in. You can leave the rest to us. If there is any trouble, then there are three of us to three of them, and on a night like this there'll be no sound heard. I shall come an hour before dawn and send Marcia in for you. Now we shall not be able to speak again. Follow Ralf closely, the path is very dangerous. He has a ring for you and the password. Go now."

He turned without a word and trod across the streaming shingle to where the boy waited. I found Cadal beside me, with the reins of the four horses gathered in his fist. His face, like my own, was streaming with wet, his cloak billowing round him like a storm cloud.

I said: "You heard me. An hour before dawn."

He, too, was looking up at the crag where high above us the castle towered. In a moment of flying light through the torn cloud I saw the castle walls, growing out of the rock. Below them fell the cliff, almost vertical, to the roaring waves. Between the promontory and the mainland, joining the castle to the mainland cliff, ran a natural ridge of rock, its sheer side polished flat as a sword-blade by the sea. From the beach where we stood, there seemed to be no way out but the valley; not mainland fortress, nor causeway, nor castle rock, could be climbed. It was no wonder they left no sentries here. And the path to the secret gate could be held by one man against an army.

Cadal was saying: "I'll get the horses in there, under the overhang, in what shelter there is. And for my sake, if not for yon lovesick gentleman's, be on time. If they as much as suspicion up yonder that there's something amiss, it's rats in a trap for the lot of us. They can shut that bloody little valley as sharp as they can block the causeway, you know that? And I wouldn't just fancy swimming out the other way, myself."

"Nor I. Content yourself, Cadal, I know what I'm about."

"I believe you. There's something about you tonight . . . The way you spoke just now to the King, not thinking, shorter than you'd speak to a servant. And he said never a word, but did as he was bid. Yes, I'd say you know what you're about. Which is just as well, master Merlin, because otherwise, you realize, you're risking the life of the King of Britain for a night's lust?"

I did something which I had never done before; which I do not commonly do. I put a hand out and laid it over Cadal's where it held the reins. The horses were quiet now, wet and unhappy, huddling with their rumps to the wind and their heads drooping.

I said: "If Uther gets into the place tonight and lies with her, then before God, Cadal, it will not matter as much as the worth of a drop of that sea-foam there if he is murdered in the bed. I tell you, a King will come out of this night's work whose name will be a shield and buckler to men until this fair land, from sea to sea, is smashed down into the sea that holds it, and men leave earth to live among the stars. Do you think Uther is a King, Cadal? He's but a regent for him who went before and for him who comes after, the past and future King. And tonight he is even less than that: he is a tool, and she a vessel, and I . . . I am a spirit, a word, a thing of air and darkness, and I can no more help what I am doing than a reed can help the wind of God blowing through it. You and I, Cadal, are as helpless as dead leaves in the waters of that bay." I dropped my hand from his. "An hour before dawn."

"Till then, my lord."

I left him then, and, with Ulfin following, went after Ralf and the King across the shingle to the foot of the black cliff.

7

I do not think that now, even in daylight, I could find the path again without a guide, let alone climb it. Ralf went first, with the King's hand on his shoulder, and in my turn I held a fold of Uther's mantle, and Ulfin of mine. Mercifully, close in as we were to the face of the castle rock, we were protected from the wind: exposed, the climb would have been impossible; we would have been plucked off the cliff like feathers. But we were not protected from the sea. The waves must have been rushing up forty feet, and the master waves, the great sevenths, came roaring up like towers and drenched us with salt fully sixty feet above the beach.

One good thing the savage boiling of the sea did for us, its whiteness cast upwards again what light came from the sky. At last we saw, above our heads, the roots of the castle walls where they sprang from the rock. Even in dry weather the walls would have been unscalable, and tonight they were streaming with wet. I could see no door, nothing breaking the smooth streaming walls of slate. Ralf did not pause, but led us on under them towards a seaward corner of the cliff. There he halted for a moment, and I saw him move his arm in a gesture that meant 'Beware'. He went carefully round the corner and out of sight. I felt Uther stagger as he reached the corner himself and met the force of the wind. He checked for a moment and then went on, clamped tight to the cliff's face. Ulfin and I followed. For a few more hideous yards we fought our way along, faces in to the soaking, slimy cliff, then a jutting buttress gave us shelter, and we were stumbling suddenly on a treacherous slope cushiony with sea-pink, and there ahead of us, recessed deep in the rock below the castle wall, and hidden from the ramparts above by the sharp overhang, was Tintagel's emergency door.

I saw Ralf give a long look upwards before he led us in under the rock. There were no sentries above. What need to post men on the seaward ramparts? He drew his dagger and rapped sharply on the door, a pattern of knocks which we, standing as we were at his shoulder, scarcely heard in the gale.

The porter must have been waiting just inside. The door opened immediately. It swung silently open for about three inches, then stuck, and I heard the rattle of a chain bolt. In the gap a hand showed, gripping a torch. Uther, beside me, dragged his hood closer, and I stepped past him to Ralf's elbow, holding my mantle tightly to my mouth and hunching my shoulders against the volleying gusts of wind and rain.

The porter's face, half of it, showed below the torch. An eye peered. Ralf, well forward into the light, said urgently: "Quick, man. A pilgrim. It's me back, with the Duke."

The torch moved fractionally higher. I saw the big emerald on Uther's finger catch the light, and said curtly, in Brithael's voice: "Open up, Felix, and let us get in out of this, for pity's sake. The Duke had a fall from his horse this morning, and his bandage is soaking. There are just the four of us here. Make haste."

The chain bolt came off and the door swung wide. Ralf put a hand to it so that, ostensibly holding it for his master, he could step into the passage between Felix and Uther as the King entered.

Uther strode in past the bowing man, shaking the wet off himself like a dog, and returning some half-heard sound in answer to the porter's greeting. Then with a brief lift of the hand which set the emerald flashing again, he turned straight for the steps which led upwards on our right, and began quickly to mount them.

Ralf grabbed the torch from the porter's hand as Ulfin and I pressed in after Uther. "I'll light them up with this. Get the door shut and barred again. I'll come down later and give you the news, Felix, but we're all drenched as drowned dogs, and want to get to a fire. There's one in the guard-room, I suppose?"

"Aye." The porter had already turned away to bar the door. Ralf was holding the torch so that Ulfin and I could go past in shadow.

I started quickly up the steps in Uther's wake, with Ulfin on my heels. The stairs were lit only by a smoking cresset which burned in a bracket on the wall of the wide landing above us. It had been easy.

Too easy. Suddenly, above us on the landing, the sullen light was augmented by that from a blazing torch, and a couple of men-at-arms stepped from a doorway, swords at the ready.

Uther, six steps above me, paused fractionally and then went on. I saw his hand, under the cloak, drop to his sword. Under my own I had my weapon loose in its sheath.

Ralf's light tread came running up the steps behind us.

"My lord Duke!"

Uther, I could guess how thankfully, stopped and turned to wait for him, his back to the guards.

"My lord Duke, let me light you—ah, they've a torch up there." He seemed only then to notice the guards above us, with the blazing light. He ran on and up past Uther, calling lightly: "Holà, Marcus, Sellic, give me that torch to light my lord up to the Duchess. This wretched thing's nothing but smoke."

The man with the torch had it held high, and the pair of them were peering down the stairs at us. The boy never hesitated. He ran up, straight between the swords, and took the torch from the man's hand. Before they could reach for it, he turned swiftly to douse the first torch in the tub of sand which stood near the guard-room door. It went out into sullen smoke. The new torch blazed cleanly, but swung and wavered as he moved so that the shadows of the guards, flung gigantic and grotesque down the steps, helped to hide us. Uther, taking advantage of the swaying shadows, started again swiftly up the flight. The hand with Gorlois' ring was half up before him to return the men's salutes. The guards moved aside. But they moved one to each side of the head of the steps, and their swords were still in their hands.

Behind me, I heard the faint whisper as Ulfin's blade loosened in its sheath. Under my cloak, mine was half-drawn. There was no hope of getting past them. We would have to kill them, and pray it made no noise. I heard Ulfin's step lagging, and knew he was thinking of the porter. He might have to go back to him while we dealt with the guards.

But there was no need. Suddenly, at the head of the second flight of steps, a door opened wide, and there, full in the blaze of light, stood Ygraine. She was in white, as I had seen her before; but not this time in a night-robe. The long gown shimmered like lake water. Over one arm and shoulder, Roman fashion, she wore a mantle of soft dark blue. Her hair was dressed with jewels. She stretched out both her hands, and the blue robe and the white fell away from wrists where red gold glimmered.

"Welcome, my lord!" Her voice, high and clear, brought both guards round to face her. Uther took the last half-dozen steps to the landing in two leaps, then was past them, his cloak brushing the sword-blades, past Ralf's blazing torch, and starting quickly up the second flight of steps.

The guards snapped back to attention, one each side of the stair-head, their backs to the wall. Behind me I heard Ulfin gasp, but he followed me quietly enough as, calmly and without hurry, I mounted the last steps to the landing. It is something, I suppose, to have been born a prince, even a bastard one; I knew that the sentries' eyes were nailed to the wall in front of them by the Duchess's presence as surely as if they were blind. I went between the swords, and Ulfin after me.

Uther had reached the head of the stairway. He took her hands, and there in front of the lighted door, with his enemies' swords catching the torchlight below him, the King bent his head and kissed Ygraine. The scarlet cloak swung round both of them, engulfing the white. Beyond them I saw the shadow of the old woman, Marcia, holding the door.

Then the King said: "Come," and with the great cloak still covering them both, he led her into the firelight, and the door shut behind them.

So we took Tintagel.

8

We were well served that night, Ulfin and I. The chamber door had hardly shut, leaving us islanded halfway up the flight between the door and the guards below, when I heard Ralf's voice again, easy and quick above the slither of swords being sheathed:

"Gods and angels, what a night's work! And I still have to guide him back when it's done! You've a fire in the room yonder? Good. We'll have a chance to dry off while we're waiting. You can get yourselves off now and leave this trick to us. Go on, what are you waiting for? You've had your orders—and no word of this, mark you, to anyone that comes."

One of the guards, settling his sword home, turned straight back into the guard-room, but the other hesitated, glancing up towards me. "My lord Brithael, is that right? We go off watch?"

I started slowly down the stairs. "Quite right. You can go. We'll send the porter for you when we want to leave. And above all, not a word of the Duke's presence. See to it." I turned to Ulfin, big-eyed on the stairs behind me. "Jordan, you go up to the chamber door yonder and stand guard. No, give me your cloak. I'll take it to the fire."

As he went thankfully, his sword at last ready in his hand, I heard Ralf crossing the guard-room below, underlining my orders with what threats I could only guess at. I went down the steps, not hurrying, to give him time to get rid of the men.

I heard the inner door shut, and went in. The guard-room, brightly lit by the torch and the blazing fire, was empty save for ourselves.

Ralf gave me a smile, gay and threadbare with nerves. "Not again, even to please my lady, for all the gold in Cornwall!"

"There will be no need again. You have done more than well, Ralf. The King will not forget."

He reached up to put the torch in a socket, saw my face, and said anxiously: "What is it, sir? Are you ill?"

"No. Does that door lock?" I nodded at the shut door through which the guards had gone.

"I have locked it. If they had had any suspicion, they would not have given me the key. But they had none, how could they? I could have sworn myself just now that it was Brithael speaking there, from the stairs. It was—like magic." The last word held a question, and he eyed me with a look I knew, but when I said nothing, he asked merely: "What now, sir?"

"Get you down to the porter now, and keep him away from here." I smiled. "You'll get your turn at the fire, Ralf, when we have gone."

He went off, light-footed as ever, down the steps. I heard him call something, and a laugh from Felix. I stripped off my drenched cloak and spread it, with Ulfin's, to the blaze. Below the cloak my clothes were dry enough. I sat for a while, holding my hands before me to the fire. It was very still in the firelit chamber, but outside the air was full of the surging din of the waters and the storm tearing at the castle walls.

My thoughts stung like sparks. I could not sit still. I stood and walked about the little chamber, restlessly. I listened to the storm outside and, going to the door, heard the murmur of voices and the click of dice as Ralf and Felix passed the time down by the gate. I looked the other way. No sound from the head of the stairs, where I could just see Ulfin, or perhaps his shadow, motionless by the chamber door . . .

Someone was coming softly down the stairs; a woman, shrouded in a mantle, carrying something. She came without a sound, and there had been neither sound nor movement from Ulfin. I stepped out on to the landing, and the light from the guard-room came after me, firelight and shadow.

It was Marcia. I saw the tears glisten on her cheeks as she bent her head over what lay in her arms. A child, wrapped warm against the winter night. She saw me and held her burden out to me. "Take care of him," she said, and through the shine of the tears I saw the treads of the stairway outline themselves again behind her. "Take care of him . . ."

The whisper faded into the flutter of the torch and the sound of the storm outside. I was alone on the stairway, and above me a shut door. Ulfin had not moved.

I lowered my empty arms and went back to the fire. This was dying down, and I made it burn up again, but with small comfort to myself, for again the light stung me. Though I had seen what I wanted to see, there was death somewhere before the end, and I was afraid. My body ached, and the room was stifling. I picked up my cloak, which was almost dry, slung it round me, and crossed the landing to where in the outer wall was a small door under which the wind drove like a knife. I thrust the door open against the blast, and went outside.

At first, after the blaze of the guard-room, I could see nothing. I shut the door behind me and leaned back against the damp wall, while the night poured over me like a river. Then things took shape around me. In front and a few paces away was a battlemented wall, waist high, the outer wall of the castle. Between this wall and where I stood was a level platform, and above me a wall rising again to a battlement, and beyond this the soaring cliff and the walls climbing it, and the shape of the fortress rising above me step by step to the peak of the promontory. At the very head of the rise, where we had seen the lighted window, the tower now showed black and lightless against the sky.

I went forward to the battlement and leaned over. Below was an apron of cliff, which would in daylight be a grassy slope covered with sea-pink and white campion and the nests of sea-birds. Beyond it and below, the white rage of the bay. I looked down to the right, the way we had come. Except for the driving arcs of white foam, the bay where Cadal waited was invisible under darkness.

It had stopped raining now, and the clouds were running higher and thinner. The wind had veered a little, slackening. It would drop towards dawn. Here and there, high and black beyond the racing clouds, the spaces of the night were filled with stars.

Then suddenly, directly overhead, the clouds parted, and there, sailing through them like a ship through running waves, the star.

It hung there among the dazzle of smaller stars, flickering at first, then pulsing, growing, bursting with light and all the colours that you see in dancing water. I watched it wax and flame and break open in light, then a racing wind would fling a web of cloud across it till it lay grey and dull and distant, lost to the eye among the other, minor stars. Then, as the swarm began their dance again it came again, gathering and swelling and dilating with light till it stood among the other stars like a torch throwing a whirl of sparks. So on through the night, as I stood alone on the ramparts and watched it; vivid and bright, then grey and sleeping, but each time waking to burn more gently, till it breathed light rather than beat, and towards morning hung glowing and quiet, with the light growing round it as the new day promised to come in clear and still.

I drew breath, and wiped the sweat from my face. I straightened up from where I had leaned against the ramparts. My body was stiff, but the ache had gone. I looked up at Ygraine's darkened window where, now, they slept.

9

I walked slowly back across the platform towards the door. As I opened it I heard from below, clear and sharp, a knocking on the postern gate.

I took a stride through to the landing, pulling the door quietly shut behind me, just as Felix came out of the lodge below, and made for the postern. As his hand went out to the chain-bolt, Ralf whipped out behind him, his arm raised high. I caught the glint in his fist of a dagger, reversed. He jumped, cat-footed, and struck with the hilt. Felix dropped where he stood. There must have been some slight sound audible to the man outside, above the roaring of the sea, for his voice came sharply: "What is it? Felix?" And the knocking came again, harder than before.

I was already halfway down the flight. Ralf had stooped to the porter's body, but turned as he saw me coming, and interpreted my gesture correctly, for he straightened, calling out clearly:

"Who's there?"

"A pilgrim."

It was a man's voice, urgent and breathless. I ran lightly down the rest of the flight. As I ran I was stripping my cloak off and winding it round my left arm. Ralf threw me a look from which all the gaiety and daring had gone. He had no need even to ask the next question; we both knew the answer.

"Who makes the pilgrimage?" The boy's voice was hoarse.

"Brithael. Now open up, quickly."

"My lord Brithael! My lord—I cannot—I have no orders to admit anyone this way . . ." He was watching me as I stooped, took Felix under the armpits, and dragged him with as little noise as I could, back into the lodge and out of sight. I saw Ralf lick his lips. "Can you not ride to the main gate, my lord? The Duchess will be asleep, and I have no orders—"

"Who's that?" demanded Brithael. "Ralf, by your voice. Where's Felix?"

"Gone up to the guard-room, sir."

"Then get the key from him, or send him down." The man's voice roughened, and a fist thudded against the gate. "Do as I say, boy, or by God I'll have the skin off your back. I have a message for the Duchess, and she won't thank you for holding me here. Come now, hurry up!"

"The—the key's here, my lord. A moment." He threw a desperate look over his shoulder as he made a business of fumbling with the lock. I left the unconscious man bundled out of sight, and was back at Ralf's shoulder, breathing into his ear:

"See if he's alone first. Then let him in."

He nodded, and the door opened on its chain-bolt. Under cover of the noise it made I had my sword out, and melted into the shadow behind the boy, where the opening door would screen me from Brithael. I stood back against the wall. Ralf put his eye to the gap, then drew back, with a nod at me, and began to slide the chain out of its socket. "Excuse me, my lord Brithael." He sounded abject and confused. "I had to make sure . . . Is there trouble?"

"What else?" Brithael thrust the door open so sharply that it would have thudded into me if Ralf had not checked it. "Never mind, you did well enough." He strode in and stopped, towering over the boy. "Has anyone else been to this gate tonight?"

"Why, no, sir." Ralf sounded scared—as well he might—and therefore convincing. "Not while I've been here, and Felix said nothing . . . Why, what's happened?"

Brithael gave a grunt, and his accoutrements jingled as he shrugged. "There was a fellow down yonder, a horseman. He attacked us. I left Jordan to deal with him. There's been nothing here, then? No trouble at all?"

"None, my lord."

"Then lock the gate again and let none in but Jordan. And now I must see the Duchess. I bring grave news, Ralf. The Duke is dead."

"The Duke?" The boy began to stammer. He made no attempt to shut the gate, but left it swinging free. It hid Brithael from me still, but Ralf was just beside me, and in the dim light I saw his face go pinched and blank with shock. "The Duke—d-dead, my lord? Murdered?"

Brithael, already moving, checked and turned. In another pace he would be clear of the door which hid me from him. I must not let him reach the steps and get above me.

"Murdered? Why, in God's name? Who would do that? That's not Uther's way. No, the Duke took the chance before the King got here, and we attacked the King's camp tonight out of Dimilioc. But they were ready. Gorlois was killed in the first sally. I rode with Jordan to bring the news. We came straight from the field. Now lock that gate and do as I say."

He turned away and made for the steps. There was room, now, to use a sword. I stepped out from the shadow behind the door.

"Brithael."

The man whirled. His reactions were so quick that they cancelled out my advantage of surprise. I suppose I need not have spoken at all, but again there are certain things a prince must do. It cost me dear enough, and could have cost me my life. I should have remembered that tonight I was no prince; I was fate's creature, like Gorlois whom I had betrayed, and Brithael whom I now must kill. And I was the future's hostage. But the burden weighed heavy on me, and his sword was out almost before mine was raised, and then we stood measuring one another, eye to eye.

He recognized me then, as our eyes met. I saw the shock in his, and a quick flash of fear which vanished in a moment, the moment when my stance and my drawn sword told him that this would be his kind of fight, not mine. He may have seen in my face that I had already fought harder than he, that night.

"I should have known you were here. Jordan said it was your man down there, you damned enchanter. Ralf! Felix! Guard—ho there, guard!"

I saw he had not grasped straight away that I had been inside the gate all along. Then the silence on the stairway, and Ralf's quick move away from me to shut the gate told its own story. Fast as a wolf, too quickly for me to do anything, Brithael swept his left arm with its clenched mailed fist smashing into the side of the boy's head. Ralf dropped without a sound, his body wedging the gate wide open.

Brithael leapt back into the gateway. "Jordan! Jordan! To me! Treachery!"

Then I was on him, blundering somehow through his guard, breast to breast, and our swords bit and slithered together with whining metal and the clash of sparks.

Rapid steps down the stairs. Ulfin's voice: "My lord—Ralf—"

I said, in gasps: "Ulfin . . . Tell the King . . . Gorlois is dead. We must get back . . . Hurry . . ."

I heard him go, fast up the stairs at a stumbling run. Brithael said through his teeth: "The King? Now I see, you pandering whoremaster."

He was a big man, a fighter in his prime, and justly angry. I was without experience, and hating what I must do, but I must do it. I was no longer a prince, or even a man fighting by the rules of men. I was a wild animal fighting to kill because it must.

With my free hand I struck him hard in the mouth and saw the surprise in his eyes as he jumped back to disengage his sword. Then he came in fast, the sword a flashing ring of iron round him. Somehow I ducked under the whistling blade, parried a blow and held it, and lashed a kick that took him full on the knee. The sword whipped down past my cheek with a hiss like a burn. I felt the hot sting of pain, and the blood running. Then as his weight went on the bruised knee, he trod crookedly, slipped on the soaked turf and fell heavily, his elbow striking a stone, and the sword flying from his hand.

Any other man would have stepped back to let him pick it up. I went down on him with all the weight I had, and my own sword shortened, stabbing for his throat.

It was light now, and growing lighter. I saw the contempt and fury in his eyes as he rolled away from the stabbing blade. It missed him, and drove deep into a spongy tuft of sea-pink. In the unguarded second as I fought to free it, his tactics shifted to match mine, and with that iron fist he struck me hard behind the ear, then, wrenching himself aside, was on his feet and plunging down the dreadful slope to where his own sword lay shining in the grass two paces from the cliff's edge.

If he reached it, he would kill me in seconds. I rolled, bunching to get my feet, flinging myself anyhow down the slimy slope towards the sword. He caught me half on to my knees. His booted foot drove into my side, then into my back. The pain broke in me like a bubble of blood and my bones melted, throwing me flat again, but I felt my flailing foot catch the metal, and the sword jerked from its hold in the turf to skid, with how gentle a shimmer, over the edge. Seconds later, it seemed, we could hear, thin and sweet through the thunder of the waves, the whine of metal as it struck the rocks below.

But before even the sound reached us he was on me again. I had a knee under me and was dragging myself up painfully. Through the blood in my eyes I saw the blow coming, and tried to dodge, but his fist struck me in the throat, knocking me sideways with a savagery that spreadeagled me again on the wet turf with the breath gone from my body and the sight from my eyes. I felt myself roll and slip and, remembering what lay below, blindly drove my left hand into the turf to stop myself falling. My sword was still in my right hand. He jumped for me again, and with all the weight of his big body brought both feet down on my hand where it grasped the sword. The hand broke across the metal guard. I heard it go. The sword snapped upwards like a trap springing and caught him across his outstretched hand. He cursed in a gasp, without words, and recoiled momentarily. Somehow, I had the sword in my left hand. He came in again as quickly as before, and even as I tried to drag myself away, he made a quick stride forward and stamped again on my broken hand. Somebody screamed. I felt myself thrash over, mindless with pain, blind. With the last strength I had I jabbed the sword, hopelessly shortened, up at his straddled body, felt it torn from my hand, and then lay waiting, without resistance, for the last kick in my side that would send me over the cliff.

I lay there breathless, retching, choking on bile, my face to the ground and my left hand driven into the soft tufts of sea-pink, as if it clung to life for me. The beat and crash of the sea shook the cliff, and even this slight tremor seemed to grind pain through my body. It hurt at every point. My side pained as though the ribs were stove in, and the skin had been stripped from the cheek that lay pressed hard into the turf. There was blood in my mouth, and my right hand was a jelly of pain. I could hear someone, some other man a long way off, making small abject sounds of pain.

The blood in my mouth bubbled and oozed down my chin into the ground, and I knew it was I who was groaning. Merlin the son of Ambrosius, the prince, the great enchanter. I shut my mouth on the blood and began to push and claw my way to my feet.

The pain in my hand was cruel, the worst of all; I heard rather than felt the small bones grind where their ends were broken. I felt myself lurching as I got to my knees, and dared not try to stand upright so near the cliff's edge. Below me a master wave struck, thundered, fountained up into the greying light, then fell back to crash into the next rising wave. The cliff trembled. A sea-bird, the first of the day, sailed overhead, crying.

I crawled away from the edge and then stood up.

Brithael was lying near the postern gate, on his belly, as if he had been trying to crawl there. Behind him on the turf was a wake of blood, glossy on the grass like the track of a snail. He was dead. That last desperate stroke had caught the big vein in the groin, and the life had pumped out of him as he tried to crawl for help. Some of the blood that soaked me must be his.

I went on my knees beside him and made sure. Then I rolled him over and over till the slope took him, and he went after his sword into the sea. The blood would have to take care of itself. It was raining again, and with luck the blood would be gone before anyone saw it.

The postern gate stood open still. I reached it somehow and stood, supporting myself with a shoulder against the jamb. There was blood in my eyes, too. I wiped it away with a wet sleeve.

Ralf had gone. The porter also. The torch had burnt low in its socket and the smoky light showed the lodge and stairway empty. The castle was quiet. At the top of the stairway the door stood partly open, and I saw light there and heard voices. Quiet voices, urgent but unalarmed. Uther's party must still be in control; there had been no alarm given.

I shivered in the dawn chill. Somewhere, unheeded, the cloak had dropped from my arm. I didn't trouble to look for it. I let go of the gate and tried standing upright without support. I could do it. I started to make my way down the path towards the bay.

10

There was just light enough to see the way; light enough, too, to see the dreadful cliff and the roaring depths below. But I think I was so occupied with the weakness of my body, with the simple mechanics of keeping that body upright and my good hand working and the injured hand out of trouble, that I never once thought of the sea below or the perilous narrowness of the strip of safe rock. I got past the first stretch quickly, and then clawed my way, half crawling, down the next steep slide across the tufted grasses and the rattling steps of scree. As the path took me lower, the seas came roaring up closer beside me, till I felt the spray of the big waves salt with the salt blood on my face. The tide was full in with morning, the waves still high with the night's wind, shooting icy tongues up the licked rock and bursting beside me with a hollow crash that shook the very bones in my body, and drenched the path down which I crawled and stumbled.

I found him halfway up from the beach, lying face downwards within an inch of the edge. One arm hung over the brink, and at the end of it the limp hand swung to the shocks of air disturbed by the waves. The other hand seemed to have stiffened, hooked to a piece of rock. The fingers were black with dried blood.

The path was just wide enough. Somehow I turned him over, pulling and shifting him as best I could till he was lying close against the cliff. I knelt between him and the sea.

"Cadal. Cadal."

His flesh was cold. In the near-darkness I could see that there was blood on his face, and what looked like thick ooze from some wound up near the hair. I put my hand to it; it was a cut, but not enough to kill. I tried to feel the heartbeat in his wrist, but my numbed hand kept slipping on the wet flesh and I could feel nothing. I pulled at his soaked tunic and could not get it open, then a clasp gave way and it tore apart, laying the chest bare.

When I saw what the cloth had hidden I knew there was no need to feel for his heart. I pulled the sodden cloth back over him, as if it could warm him, and sat back on my heels, only then attending to the fact that men were coming down the path from the castle.

Uther came round the cliff as easily as if he were walking across his palace floor. His sword was ready in his hand, the long cloak gathered over his left arm. Ulfin, looking like a ghost, came after him.

The King stood over me, and for some moments he did not speak. Then all he said was:

"Dead?"

"Yes."

"And Jordan?"

"Dead too, I imagine, or Cadal would not have got this far to warn us."

"And Brithael?"

"Dead."

"Did you know all this before we came tonight?"

"No," I said.

"Nor of Gorlois' death?"

"No."

"If you were a prophet as you claim to be, you would have known." His voice was thin and bitter. I looked up. His face was calm, the fever gone, but his eyes, slaty in the grey light, were bleak and weary.

I said briefly: "I told you. I had to take the time on trust. This was the time. We succeeded."

"And if we had waited until tomorrow, these men, aye, and your servant here as well, would still be living, and Gorlois dead and his lady a widow . . . And mine to claim without these deaths and whisperings."

"But tomorrow you would have begotten a different child."

"A legitimate child," he said swiftly. "Not a bastard such as we have made between us tonight. By the head of Mithras, do you truly think my name and hers can withstand this night's work? Even if we marry within the week, you know what men will say. That I am Gorlois' murderer. And there are men who will go on believing that she was in truth pregnant by him as she told them, and that the child is his."

"They will not say this. There is not a man who will doubt that he is yours, Uther, and rightwise King born of all Britain."

He made a short sound, not a laugh, but it held both amusement and contempt. "Do you think I shall ever listen to you again? I see now what your magic is, this 'power' you talk of . . . It is nothing but human trickery, an attempt at statecraft which my brother taught you to like and to play for and to believe was your mystery. It is trickery to promise men what they desire, to let them think you have the power to give it, but to keep the price secret, and then leave them to pay."

"It is God who keeps the price secret, Uther, not I."

"God? God? What god? I have heard you speak of so many gods. If you mean Mithras—"

"Mithras, Apollo, Arthur, Christ—call him what you will," I said. "What does it matter what men call the light? It is the same light, and men must live by it or die. I only know that God is the source of all the light which has lit the world, and that his purpose runs through the world and past each one of us like a great river, and we cannot check or turn it, but can only drink from it while living, and commit our bodies to it when we die."

The blood was running from my mouth again. I put up my sleeve to wipe it away. He saw, but his face never changed. I doubt if he had even listened to what I said, or if he could have heard me for the thunder of the sea. He said merely, with that same indifference that stood like a wall between us:

"These are only words. You use even God to gain your ends. 'It is God who tells me to do these things, it is God who exacts the price, it is God who sees that others should pay . . .' For what, Merlin? For your ambition? For the great prophet and magician of whom men speak with bated breath and give more worship than they would a king or his high priest? And who is it pays this debt to

God for carrying out your plans? Not you. The men who play your game for you, and pay the price. Ambrosius. Vortigern. Gorlois. These other men here tonight. But you pay nothing. Never you."

A wave crashed beside us and the spume showered the ledge, raining down on Cadal's upturned face. I leaned over and wiped it away, with some of the blood. "No," I said.

Uther said, above me: "I tell you, Merlin, you shall not use me. I'll no longer be a puppet for you to pull the strings. So keep away from me. And I'll tell you this also. I'll not acknowledge the bastard I begot tonight."

It was a king speaking, unanswerable. A still, cold figure, with behind his shoulder the star hanging clear in the grey. I said nothing.

"You hear me?"

"Yes."

He shifted the cloak from his arm, and flung it to Ulfin, who held it for him to put on. He settled it to his shoulders, then looked down at me again. "For what service you have rendered, you shall keep the land I gave you. Get back, then, to your Welsh mountains, and trouble me no more."

I said wearily: "I shall not trouble you again, Uther. You will not need me again."

He was silent for a moment. Then he said abruptly: "Ulfin will help you carry the body down."

I turned away. "There is no need. Leave me now."

A pause, filled with the thunder of the sea. I had not meant to speak so, but I was past caring, or even knowing, what I said. I only wanted him gone. His sword-point was level with my eyes. I saw it shift and shimmer, and thought for a moment that he was angry enough to use it. Then it flashed up and was rammed home in its housing. He swung round and went on his way down the path. Ulfin edged quietly past without a word, and followed his master. Before they had reached the next corner the sea had obliterated the sound of their footsteps.

I turned to find Cadal watching me.

"Cadal!"

"That's a king for you." His voice was faint, but it was his own, rough and amused. "Give him something he swears he's dying for, and then, 'Do you think I can withstand this night's work?' says he. A fine old night's work he's put in, for sure, and looks it."

"Cadal—"

"You, too. You're hurt . . . your hand? Blood on your face?"

"It's nothing. Nothing that won't mend. Never mind that. But you—oh, Cadal—"

He moved his head slightly. "It's no use. Let be. I'm comfortable enough."

"No pain now?"

"No. It's cold, though."

I moved closer to him, trying to shield his body with my own from the bursting spray as the waves struck the rock. I took his hand in my own good one. I could not chafe it, but pulled my tunic open and held it there against my breast. "I'm afraid I lost my cloak," I said. "Jordan's dead, then?"

"Yes." He waited for a moment. "What—happened up yonder?"

"It all went as we had planned. But Gorlois attacked out of Dimilioc and got himself killed. That's why Brithael and Jordan rode this way, to tell the Duchess."

"I heard them coming. I knew they'd be bound to see me and the horses. I had to stop them giving the alarm while the King was still . . ." He paused for breath.

"Don't trouble," I said. "It's done with, and all's well."

He took no notice. His voice was the merest whisper now, but clear and thin, and I heard every word through the raging of the sea.

"So I mounted and rode up a bit of the way to meet them . . . the other side of the water . . . then when they came level I jumped the stream and tried to stop them." He waited for a moment. "But Brithael . . . that's a fighter, now. Quick as a snake. Never hesitated. Sword straight into me and then rode over me. Left me for Jordan to finish."

"His mistake."

His cheek-muscles moved slightly. It was a smile. After a while he asked: "Did he see the horses after all?"

"No. Ralf was at the gate when he came, and Brithael just asked if anyone had been up to the castle, because he'd met a horseman below. When Ralf said no he accepted it. We let him in, and then killed him."

"Uther." It was an assumption, not a question. His eyes were closed.

"No. Uther was still with the Duchess. I couldn't risk Brithael taking him unarmed. He would have killed her, too."

The eyes flared open, momentarily clear and startled. *"You?"*

"Come, Cadal, you hardly flatter me." I gave him a grin. "Though I'd have done you no credit, I'm afraid. It was a very dirty fight. The King wouldn't even know the rules. I invented them as I went along."

This time it really was a smile. "Merlin . . . little Merlin, that couldn't even sit a horse . . . You kill me."

The tide must be on the turn. The next wave that thundered up sent only the finest spray which fell on my shoulders like mist. I said: "I have killed you, Cadal."

"The gods . . ." he said, and drew a great, sighing breath. I knew what that meant. He was running out of time. As the light grew I could see how much of his blood had soaked into the soaking path. "I heard what the King said. Could it not have happened without . . . all this?"

"No, Cadal."

His eyes shut for a moment, then opened again. "Well," was all he said, but in the syllable was all the acquiescent faith of the past eight years. His eyes were showing white now below the pupil, and his jaw was slack. I put my good arm under him and raised him a little. I spoke quickly and clearly:

"It will happen, Cadal, as my father wished and as God willed through me. You heard what Uther said about the child. That alters nothing. Because of this night's work Ygraine will bear the child, and because of this night's work she will send him away as soon as he is born, out of the King's sight. She will send him to me, and I shall take him out of the King's reach, and keep him and teach him all that Galapas taught me, and Ambrosius, and you, even Belasius. He will be the sum of all our lives, and when he is grown he will come back and be crowned King at Winchester."

"You know this? You promise me that you know this?" The words were scarcely recognizable. The breath was coming now in bubbling gasps. His eyes were small and white and blind.

I lifted him and held him strongly against me. I said, gently and very clearly: "I know this. I, Merlin, prince and prophet, promise you this, Cadal."

His head fell sideways against me, too heavy for him now as the muscles went out of control. His eyes had gone. He made some small muttering sound and then, suddenly and clearly, he said, "Make the sign for me," and died.

I gave him to the sea, with Brithael who had killed him. The tide would take him, Ralf had said, and carry him away as far as the western stars.

Apart from the slow clop of hoofs, and the jingle of metal, there was no sound in the valley. The storm had died. There was no wind, and when I had ridden beyond the first bend of the stream, I lost even the sound of the sea. Down beside me, along the stream, mist hung still, like a veil. Above, the sky was clear, growing pale towards sunrise. Still in the sky, high now and steady, hung the star.

But while I watched it the pale sky grew brighter round it, flooding it with gold and soft fire, and then with a bursting wave of brilliant light, as up over the land where the herald star had hung, rose the young sun.

THE LEGEND OF MERLIN

Vortigern, King of Britain, wishing to build a fortress in Snowdon, called together masons from many countries, bidding them build a strong tower. But what the stonemasons built each day collapsed each night and was swallowed up by the soil. So Vortigern held council with his wizards, who told him that he must search for a lad who never had a father, and when he had found him should slay him and sprinkle his blood over the foundations, to make the tower hold firm. Vortigern sent messengers into all the provinces to look for such a lad, and eventually they came to the city that was afterwards called Carmarthen. There they saw some lads playing before the gate, and being tired, sat down to watch the game. At last, towards evening, a sudden quarrel sprang up between a couple of youths whose names were Merlin and Dinabutius. During the quarrel Dinabutius was heard to say to Merlin: "What a fool must thou be to think thou art a match for me! Here am I, born of the blood royal, but no one knows what thou art, for never a father hadst thou!" When the messengers heard this they asked the bystanders who Merlin might be, and were told that none knew his father, but that his mother was daughter of the King of South Wales, and that she lived along with the nuns in St. Peter's Church in that same city.

The messengers took Merlin and his mother to King Vortigern. The King received the mother with all the attention due to her birth, and asked her who was the father of the lad. She replied that she did not know. "Once," she said, "when I and my damsels were in our chambers, one appeared to me in the shape of a handsome youth who, embracing me and kissing me, stayed with me some time, but afterwards did as suddenly vanish away. He returned many times to speak to me when I was sitting alone, but never again did I catch sight of him. After he had haunted me in this way for a long time, he lay with me for some while in the shape of a man, and left me heavy with child." The King, amazed at her words, asked Maugantius the soothsayer whether such a thing might be. Maugantius assured him that such things were well known, and that Merlin must have been begotten by one of the "spirits there be betwixt the moon and the earth, which we do call incubus daemons."

Merlin, who had listened to all this, then demanded that he should be allowed to confront the wizards. "Bid the wizards come before me, and I will convict them of having devised a lie." The King, struck by the youth's boldness and apparent lack of fear, did as he asked and sent for the wizards. To whom Merlin spoke as follows: "Since ye know not what it is that doth hinder the foundation being laid of this tower, ye have given counsel that the mortar thereof should be slaked with my blood, so that the tower should stand forthwith. Now tell me, what is it that lieth hid beneath the foundation, for somewhat is there that doth not allow it to stand?" But the wizards, afraid of showing ignorance, held their peace. Then said Merlin (whose other name is Ambrosius): "My lord the

King, call thy workmen and bid them dig below the tower, and a pool shalt thou find beneath it that doth forbid the walls to stand." This was done, and the pool uncovered. Merlin then commanded that the pool should be drained by conduits; two stones, he said, would be found at the bottom, where two dragons, red and white, were lying asleep. When the pool was duly drained, and the stones uncovered, the dragons woke and began to fight ferociously, until the red had defeated and killed the white. The King, amazed, asked Merlin the meaning of the sight, and Merlin, raising his eyes to heaven, prophesied the coming of Ambrosius and the death of Vortigern. Next morning, early, Aurelius Ambrosius landed at Totnes in Devon.

After Ambrosius had conquered Vortigern and the Saxons and had been crowned King he brought together master craftsmen from every quarter and asked them to contrive some new kind of building that should stand for ever as a memorial. None of them were able to help him, until Tremorinus, Archbishop of Caerleon, suggested that the King should send for Merlin, Vortigern's prophet, the cleverest man in the kingdom, "whether in foretelling that which shall be, or in devising engines of artifice." Ambrosius forthwith sent out messengers, who found Merlin in the country of Gwent, at the fountain of Galapas where he customarily dwelt. The King received him with honour, and first asked him to foretell the future, but Merlin replied: "Mysteries of such kind be in no wise to be revealed save only in sore need. For if I were to utter them lightly or to make laughter, the spirit that teaches me would be dumb and would forsake me in the hour of need." The King then asked him about the monument, but when Merlin advised him to send for the "Dance of the Giants that is in Killare, a mountain in Ireland," Ambrosius laughed, saying it was impossible to move stones that everyone knew had been set there by giants. Eventually, however, the King was persuaded to send his brother Uther, with fifteen thousand men, to conquer Gilloman, King of Ireland, and bring back the Dance. Uther's army won the day, but when they tried to dismantle the giant circle of Killare and bring down the stones, they could not shift them. When at length they confessed defeat, Merlin put together his own engines, and by means of these laid the stones down easily, and carried them to the ships, and presently brought them to the site near Amesbury where they were to be set up. There Merlin again assembled his engines, and set up the Dance of Killare at Stonehenge exactly as it had stood in Ireland. Shortly after this a great star appeared in the likeness of a dragon, and Merlin, knowing that it betokened Ambrosius' death, wept bitterly, and prophesied that Uther would be King under the sign of the Dragon, and that a son would be born to him "of surpassing mighty dominion, whose power shall extend over all the realms that lie beneath the ray (of the star)."

The following Easter, at the coronation feast, King Uther fell in love with Ygraine, wife of Gorlois, Duke of Cornwall. He lavished attention on her, to the scandal of the court; she made no response, but her husband, in fury, retired from the court without leave, taking his wife and men-at-arms back to Cornwall. Uther, in anger, commanded him to return, but Gorlois refused to obey. Then the King, enraged beyond measure, gathered an army and marched into Cornwall, burning the cities and castles. Gorlois had not enough troops to withstand him, so he placed his wife in the castle of Tintagel, the safest refuge, and himself prepared to defend the castle of Dimilioc. Uther immediately laid siege to Dimilioc, holding Gorlois and his troops trapped there, while he cast about for some way of breaking into the castle of Tintagel to ravish Ygraine. After some days he asked advice from one of his familiars called Ulfin. "Do thou therefore give me counsel in what wise I may fulfill my desire," said the King, "for, and I do not, of mine inward sorrow shall I die." Ulfin, telling him what he knew already—that Tintagel was impregnable—suggested that he send for Merlin. Merlin, moved by the King's apparent suffering, promised to help. By his magic arts he changed Uther into the likeness of Gorlois, Ulfin into Jordan, Gorlois' friend, and himself into Brithael, one of Gorlois' captains. The three of them rode to Tintagel, and were admitted by the porter. Ygraine taking Uther to be her husband the Duke, welcomed him, and took him to her bed. So Uther lay with Ygraine that night, "and she had no thought to deny him in aught he might desire." That night, Arthur was conceived.

But in the meantime fighting had broken out at Dimilioc, and Gorlois, venturing out to give battle, was killed. Messengers came to Tintagel to tell Ygraine of her husband's death. When they found "Gorlois," apparently still alive, closeted with Ygraine, they were speechless, but the King then confessed the deception, and a few days later married Ygraine.

Uther Pendragon was to reign fifteen more years. During those years he saw nothing of his son Arthur, who on the night of his birth was carried down to the postern gate of Tintagel and delivered into the hands of Merlin, who cared for the child in secret until the time came for Arthur to inherit the throne of Britain.

Throughout Arthur's long reign Merlin advised and helped him. When Merlin was an old man he fell dotingly in love with a young girl, Vivian, who persuaded him, as the price of her love, to teach her all his magic arts. When he had done so she cast a spell on him which left him bound and sleeping; some say in a cave near a grove of whitethorn trees, some say in a tower of crystal, some say hidden only by the glory of the air around him. He will wake when King Arthur wakes, and come back in the hour of his country's need.

AUTHOR'S NOTE

No novelist dealing with Dark Age Britain dares venture into the light without some pen-service to the Place-Name Problem. It is customary to explain one's usage, and I am at once less and more guilty of inconsistency than most. In a period of history when Celt, Saxon, Roman, Gaul and who knows who else shuttled to and fro across a turbulent and divided Britain, every place must have had at least three names, and anybody's guess is good as to what was common usage at any given time. Indeed, the "given time" of King Arthur's birth is somewhere around 470 A.D., and the end of the fifth century is as dark a period of Britain's history as we have. To add to the confusion, I have taken as the source of my story a semi-mythological, romantic account written in Oxford by a twelfth-century Welshman,* who gives the names of places and people what one might call a post-Norman slant with an overtone of clerical Latin. Hence in my narrative the reader will find Winchester as well as Rutupiæ and Dinas Emrys, and the men of Cornwall, South Wales, and Brittany instead of Dumnonii, Demetae, and Armoricans.

My first principle in usage has been, simply, to make the story clear. I wanted if possible to avoid the irritating expedient of the glossary, where the reader has to interrupt himself to look up the place-names, or decide to read straight on and lose himself mentally. And non-British readers suffer further; they look up Calleva in the glossary, find it is Silchester, and are none the wiser until they consult a map. Either way the story suffers. So wherever there was a choice of names I have tried to use the one that will most immediately put the reader in the picture: for this I have sometimes employed the device of having the narrator give the current crop of names, even slipping in the modern one where it does not sound too out of place. For example: "Maesbeli, near Conan's Fort, or Kaerconan, that men sometimes call Conisburgh." Elsewhere I have been more arbitrary. Clearly, in a narrative whose English must be supposed in the reader's imagination to be Latin or the Celtic of South Wales, it would be pedantic to write of Londinium when it is so obviously London; I have also used the modern names of places like Glastonbury and Winchester and Tintagel, because these names, though mediaeval in origin, are so hallowed by association that they fit contexts where it would obviously be impossible to intrude the modern images of (say) Manchester or Newcastle. These "rules" are not, of course, intended as a criticism of any other writer's practice; one employs the form the work demands; and since this is an imaginative exercise which nobody will treat as authentic history, I have allowed myself to be governed by the rules of poetry: what communicates simply and vividly, and sounds best, is best.

The same rule of ear applies to the language used throughout. The narrator,

* Or (possibly) Breton.

telling his story in fifth-century Welsh, would use in his tale as many easy colloquialisms as I have used in mine; the servants Cerdic and Cadal would talk some kind of dialect, while, for instance, some sort of "high language" might well be expected from kings, or from prophets in moments of prophecy. Some anachronisms I have deliberately allowed where they were the most descriptive words, and some mild slang for the sake of liveliness. In short, I have played it everywhere by ear, on the principle that what sounds right is acceptable in the context of a work of pure imagination.

For that is all *The Crystal Cave* claims to be. It is not a work of scholarship, and can obviously make no claim to be serious history. Serious historians will not, I imagine, have got this far anyway, since they will have discovered that the main source of my story-line is Geoffrey of Monmouth's *History of the Kings of Britain.*

Geoffrey's name is, to serious historians, mud. From his Oxford study in the twelfth century he produced a long, racy hotch-potch of "history" from the Trojan War (where Brutus "the King of the Britons" fought) to the seventh century A.D., arranging his facts to suit his story, and when he got short on facts (which was on every page), inventing them out of the whole cloth. Historically speaking, the *Historia Regum Brittaniae* is appalling, but as a story it is tremendous stuff, and has been a source and inspiration for the great cycle of tales called the Matter of Britain, from Malory's *Morte d'Arthur* to Tennyson's *Idylls of the King,* from *Parsifal* to *Camelot.*

The central character of the *Historia* is Arthur, King of the first united Britain. Geoffrey's Arthur is the hero of legend, but it is certain that Arthur was a real person, and I believe the same applies to Merlin, though the "Merlin" that we know is a composite of at least four people—prince, prophet, poet and engineer. He appears first in legend as a youth. My imaginary account of his childhood is coloured by a phrase in Malory: "the well of Galapas,* where he wont to haunt," and by a reference to "my master Blaise"—who becomes in my story Belasius. The Merlin legend is as strong in Brittany as in Britain.

One or two brief notes to finish with.

I gave Merlin's mother the name Niniane because this is the name of the girl (Vivian/Niniane/Nimue) who according to legend seduced the enchanter in his dotage and so robbed him of his powers, leaving him shut in his cave to sleep till the end of time. No other women are associated with him. There is so strong a connection in legend (and indeed in history) between celibacy, or virginity, and power, that I have thought it reasonable to insist on Merlin's virginity.

Mithraism had been (literally) underground for years. I have postulated a local revival for the purpose of my story, and the reasons given by Ambrosius seem likely. From what we know of the real Ambrosius, he was Roman enough to follow the "soldiers' god." †

About the ancient druids so little is known that (according to the eminent scholar I consulted) they can be considered "fair game." The same applies to the megaliths of Carnac (Kerrec) in Brittany, and to the Giants' Dance of Stonehenge near Amesbury. Stonehenge was erected around 1500 B.C., so I only

* So *fontes galabes* is sometimes translated.

† Bede, the 7th C. historian, calls him "Ambrosius, a Roman." *(Ecclesiastical History of the English Nation.)*

allowed Merlin to bring one stone from Killare. At Stonehenge it is true that one stone—the largest—is different from the rest. It comes originally, according to the geologists, from near Milford Haven, in Wales. It is also true that a grave lies within the circle; it is off center, so I have used the midwinter sunrise rather than the midsummer one towards which the Dance is oriented.

All the places I describe are authentic, with no significant exception but the cave of Galapas—and if Merlin is indeed sleeping there "with all his fires and travelling glories around him," one would expect it to be invisible. But the well is there on Bryn Myrddin, and there is a burial mound on the crest of the hill.

It would seem that the name "merlin" was not recorded for the falcon *columbarius* until mediaeval times, and the word is possibly French; but its derivation is uncertain, and this was sufficient excuse for a writer whose imagination had already woven a series of images from the name before the book was even begun.

Where Merlin refers to the potter's mark A.M., the *A* would be the potter's initial or trade mark; the *M* stands for *Manu,* literally "by the hand of."

The relationship between Merlin and Ambrosius has (I believe) no basis in legend. A ninth-century historian, Nennius, from whom Geoffrey took some of his material, called his prophet "Ambrosius." Nennius told the story of the dragons in the pool, and the young seer's first recorded prophecy. Geoffrey, borrowing the story, calmly equates the two prophets: "Then saith Merlin, that is also called Ambrosius. . . ." This throwaway piece of "nerve," as Professor Gwyn Jones calls it,* gave me the idea of identifying the "prince of darkness" who fathered Merlin—gave me, indeed, the main plot of *The Crystal Cave.*

My greatest debt is obviously to Geoffrey of Monmouth, master of romance. Among other creditors too numerous to name and impossible to repay, I should like especially to thank Mr. Francis Jones, County Archivist, Carmarthen; Mr. and Mrs. Morris of Bryn Myrddin, Carmarthen; Mr. G.B. Lancashire of The Chase Hotel, Ross-on-Wye; Brigadier R. Waller, of Wyaston Leys, Monmouthshire, on whose land lie Lesser Doward and the Romans' Way; Professor Hermann Brück, Astronomer Royal for Scotland, and Mrs. Brück; Professor Stuart Piggott of the Department of Archaeology at Edinburgh University; Miss Elizabeth Manners, Headmistress of Felixstowe College; and Mr. Robin Denniston, of Hodder & Stoughton Ltd., London.

February 1968—February 1970. M.S.

* Introduction to the Everyman ed. of *History of the Kings of Britain.*

ACKNOWLEDGEMENTS

Edwin Muir's poem "Merlin" is reprinted by permission of Faber and Faber Ltd. from the *Collected Poems, 1921–58.*

The poem on page 152 is a free translation of verses appearing in *Barzaz Breiz; Chants Populaires de la Bretagne,* by the Vicomte de la Villemarqué (Paris, 1867).

The Legend of Merlin is based on the translation of Geoffrey of Monmouth's *History of the Kings of Britain* which was first published in the Everyman's Library, Vol. 577, by J. & M. Dent in 1912.

THE HOLLOW HILLS

To the memory of

my father

CONTENTS

There was a boy born,
A winter king.
Before the black month
He was born,
And fled in the dark month
To find shelter
With the poor.

He shall come
With the spring
In the green month
And the golden month
And bright
Shall be the burning
Of his star.

M.S.

Routes taken by Merlin
0 20 40
Miles
Dunpelydyr
Caer Eidyn
MANAU
GUOTODIN
Alaunus R.
Bremenium
STRATHCLYDE
Hadrian's Wall
Segedunum
German Sea
Luguvallium
Ituna Estuary
RHEGED
Galava
Mediobogdum
Glannaventa
Alauna
IRELAND
Isle of Man
Eboracum
(York)
NORTHERN
ANGLES
Abus R.
Irish Sea
Isle of Mona
Segontium
GWYNEDD
Deva
Viroconium
POWYS
EAST
ANGLES
EAST
SAXONS
Severn R.
DYFED
Glevum
Maridunum
Tywy R.
Nidum
Caerleon
Severn R.
London
Vagniacae
Calleva
Thames R.
Rutupiae
Uxella R.
Wall of Ambrosius
Medway R.
Winchester
SAXON SHORE
Hercules Point
DUMNONIA
Vindocladia
Dimilioc
Isca
Potters' Bay
Tintagel
Camelford
The Narrow Sea
Cassiterides
GALLIA

BOOK I

THE WAITING

1

There was a lark singing somewhere high above. Light fell dazzling against my closed eyelids, and with it the song, like a distant dance of water. I opened my eyes. Above me arched the sky, with its invisible singer lost somewhere in the light and floating blue of a spring day. Everywhere was a sweet, nutty smell which made me think of gold, and candle flames, and young lovers. Something, smelling not so sweet, stirred beside me, and a rough young voice said: "Sir?"

I turned my head. I was lying on turf, in a hollow among furze bushes. These were full of blossom, golden, sweet-smelling flames called out by the spring sun. Beside me a boy knelt. He was perhaps twelve years old, dirty, with a matted shag of hair, and clad in some coarse brown cloth; his cloak, made of skins roughly stitched together, showed rents in a dozen places. He had a stick in one hand. Even without the way he smelled I could have guessed his calling, for all around us his herd of goats grazed among the furze bushes, cropping the young green prickles.

At my movement he got quickly to his feet and backed off a little, peering, half wary and half hopeful, through the filthy tangle of hair. So he had not robbed me yet. I eyed the heavy stick in his hand, vaguely wondering through the mists of pain whether I could help myself even against this youngster. But it seemed that his hopes were only for a reward. He was pointing at something out of sight beyond the bushes. "I caught your horse for you. He's tied over there. I thought you were dead."

I raised myself to an elbow. Round me the day seemed to swing and dazzle. The furze blossom smoked like incense in the sun. Pain seeped back slowly, and with it, on the same tide, memory.

"Are you hurt bad?"

"Nothing to matter, except my hand. Give me time, I'll be all right. You caught my horse, you say? Did you see me fall?"

"Aye, I was over yonder." He pointed again. Beyond the mounds of yellow blossom the land rose, smooth and bare, to a rounded upland broken by grey rock seamed with winter thorn. Behind the shoulder of the land the sky had that look of limitless and empty distance which spoke of the sea. "I saw you come riding up the valley from the shore, going slow. I could see you was ill, or maybe sleeping on the horse. Then he put his foot wrong—a hole, likely—and you came off. You've not been lying long. I'd just got down to you."

He stopped, his mouth dropping open. I saw shock in his face. As he spoke I had been pushing myself up till I was able to sit, propped by my left arm, and carefully lift my injured right hand into my lap. It was a swollen, crusted mass of dried blood, through which fresh red was running. I had, I guessed, fallen on it when my horse had stumbled. The faint had been merciful enough. The pain was growing now, wave on wave grinding, with the steady beat and drag of the tide over shingle, but the faintness had gone, and my head, though still aching from the blow, was clear.

"Mother of mercy!" The boy was looking sick. "You never did that falling from your horse?"

"No. It was a fight."

"You've no sword."

"I lost it. No matter. I have my dagger, and a hand for it. No, don't be afraid. The fighting's done. No one will hurt you. Now, if you'll help me onto my horse, I'll be on my way."

He gave me an arm as I got to my feet. We were standing at the edge of a high green upland studded with furze, with here and there stark, solitary trees thrust into strange shapes by the steady salt wind. Beyond the thicket where I had lain the ground fell away in a sharp slope scored by the tracks of sheep and goats. It made one side of a narrow, winding valley, at the foot of which a stream raced, tumbling, down its rocky bed. I could not see what lay at the foot of the valley, but about a mile away, beyond the horizon of winter grass, was the sea. From the height of the land where I stood one could guess at the great cliffs which fell away to the shore, and beyond the land's farthest edge, small in the distance, I could see the jut of towers.

The castle of Tintagel, stronghold of the Dukes of Cornwall. The impregnable fortress rock, which could only be taken by guile, or by treachery from within. Last night, I had used both.

I felt a shiver run over my flesh. Last night, in the wild dark of the storm, this had been a place of gods and destiny, of power driving towards some distant end of which I had been given, from time to time, a glimpse. And I, Merlin, son of Ambrosius, whom men feared as a prophet and visionary, had been in that night's work no more than the god's instrument.

It was for this that I had been given the gift of Sight, and the power that men saw as magic. From this remote and sea-locked fortress would come the King who alone could clear Britain of her enemies, and give her time to find herself; who alone, in the wake of Ambrosius, the last of the Romans, would hold back the fresh tides of the Saxon Terror, and, for a breathing space at least, keep Britain whole. This I had seen in the stars, and heard in the wind: it was I, my gods had told me, who would bring this to pass; this I had been born for. Now, if I could still trust my gods, the promised child was begotten; but because of him—because of me—four men had died. In that night lashed by storm and brooded over by the dragon-star, death had seemed commonplace, and gods waiting, visible, at every corner. But now, in the still morning after the storm, what was there to see? A young man with an injured hand, a King with his lust satisfied, and a woman with her penance beginning. And for all of us, time to remember the dead.

The boy brought my horse up to me. He was watching me curiously, the wariness back in his face.

"How long have you been here with your goats?" I asked him.

"A sunrise and a sunrise."

"Did you see or hear anything last night?"

Wariness became, suddenly, fear. His eyelids dropped and he stared at the ground. His face was closed, blank, stupid. "I have forgotten, lord."

I leaned against my horse's shoulder, regarding him. Times without number

I had met this stupidity, this flat, expressionless mumble; it is the only armour available to the poor. I said gently: "Whatever happened last night, it is something I want you to remember, not to forget. No one will harm you. Tell me what you saw."

He looked at me for perhaps ten more seconds of silence. I could not guess what he was thinking. What he was seeing can hardly have been reassuring; a tall young man with a smashed and bloody hand, cloakless, his clothes stained and torn, his face (I have no doubt) grey with fatigue and pain and the bitter dregs of last night's triumph. All the same the boy nodded suddenly, and began to speak.

"Last night in the black dark I heard horses go by me. Four, I think. But I saw no one. Then, in the early dawn, two more following them, spurring hard. I thought they were all making for the castle, but from where I was, up there by the rocks, I never saw torches at the guard-house on the cliff top, or on the bridge going across to the main gate. They must have gone down the valley there. After it was light I saw two horsemen coming back that way, from the shore below the castle rock." He hesitated. "And then you, my lord."

I said slowly, holding him with my eyes: "Listen now, and I will tell you who the horsemen were. Last night, in the dark, King Uther Pendragon rode this way, with myself and two others. He rode to Tintagel, but he did not go by the gate-house and the bridge. He rode down the valley, to the shore, and then climbed the secret path up the rock and entered the castle by the postern gate. Why do you shake your head? Don't you believe me?"

"Lord, everyone knows the King had quarrelled with the Duke. No one could get in, least of all the King. Even if he did find the postern door, there's none would dare open it to him."

"They opened last night. It was the Duchess Ygraine herself who received the King into Tintagel."

"But—"

"Wait," I said. "I will tell you how it happened. The King had been changed by magic arts into a likeness of the Duke, and his companions into likenesses of the Duke's friends. The people who let them into the castle thought they were admitting Duke Gorlois himself, with Brithael and Jordan."

Under its dirt the boy's face was pale. I knew that for him, as for most of the people of this wild and haunted country, my talk of magic and enchantment would come as easily as stories of the loves of kings and violence in high places. He said, stammering: "The King—the King was in the castle last night with the Duchess?"

"Yes. And the child that will be born will be the King's child."

A long pause. He licked his lips. "But—but—when the Duke finds out . . ."

"He won't find out," I said. "He's dead."

One filthy hand went to his mouth, the fist rammed against his teeth. Above it his eyes, showing white, went from my injured hand to the bloodstains on my clothing, then to my empty scabbard. He looked as if he would have liked to run away, but did not dare even do that. He said breathlessly: "You killed him? You killed our Duke?"

"Indeed no. Neither I nor the King wished him dead. He was killed in battle. Last night, not knowing that the King had already ridden secretly for Tintagel, your Duke sallied out from his fortress of Dimilioc to attack the King's army, and was killed."

He hardly seemed to be listening. He was stammering: "But the two I saw this morning . . . It was the Duke himself, riding up from Tintagel. I saw him. Do you think I don't know him? It was the Duke himself, with Jordan, his man."

"No. It was the King with his servant Ulfin. I told you the King took the Duke's likeness. The magic deceived you, too."

He began to back away from me. "How do you know these things? You—you said you were with them. This magic—who are you?"

"I am Merlin, the King's nephew. They call me Merlin the enchanter."

Still backing, he had come up against a wall of furze. As he looked this way and that, trying which way to run, I put out a hand.

"Don't be afraid. I'll not hurt you. Here, take this. Come, take it, no sensible man should fear gold. Call it a reward for catching my horse. Now, if you'll help me onto his back, I'll be on my way."

He made a half movement forward, ready to snatch and run, but then he checked, and his head went round, quick as a wild thing's. I saw the goats had already stopped grazing and were looking eastwards, ears pricked. Then I heard the sound of horses.

I gathered my own beast's reins in my good hand, then looked round for the boy to help me. But he was already running, whacking the bushes to chase the goats in front of him. I called to him and, as he glanced over his shoulder, flung the gold. He snatched it up and then was gone, racing up the slope with his goats scampering round him.

Pain struck at me again, grinding the bones of my hand together. The cracked ribs stabbed and burned my side. I felt the sweat start on my body, and round me the spring day wavered and broke again in mist. The noise of approaching hoofs seemed to hammer with the pain along my bones. I leaned against my horse's saddle, and waited.

It was the King riding again for Tintagel, this time for the main gate, and by daylight, with a company of his men. They came at a fast canter along the grassy track from Dimilioc, four abreast, riding at ease. Above Uther's head the Dragon standard showed red on gold in the sunlight. The King was himself again; the grey of his disguise had been washed from his hair and beard, and the royal circlet glinted on his helmet. His cloak of kingly scarlet was spread behind him over his bay's glossy flanks. His face looked still, calm and set; a bleak enough look, and weary, but with over all a kind of contentment. He was riding to Tintagel, and Tintagel was his at last, with all that lay within the walls. For him, it was an end.

I leaned against my horse's shoulder and watched them come level with me.

It was impossible for Uther not to see me, but he never glanced my way. I saw, from the troop behind him, the curious glances as I was recognized. No man was there but must have some inkling now of what had happened last night in Tintagel, and of the part I had played in bringing the King to his heart's desire. It was possible that the simpler souls among the King's companions might have expected the King to be grateful; to reward me; at the very least to recognize and acknowledge me. But I, who had dealt all my life with kings, knew that where there is blame as well as gratitude, blame must be allotted first, lest it should cling to the King himself. King Uther could only see that, by what he called the failure of my foreknowledge, the Duke of Cornwall had died even while he, the King, was lying with the Duchess. He did not see the Duke's death for what it was, the grim irony behind the smiling mask that gods show when they want men to do their will. Uther, who had small truck with gods, saw only that by waiting even one day he might have had his way with honour and in the sight of men. His anger with me was genuine enough, but even if it were not, I knew that he must find someone to blame: whatever he felt about the Duke's death—and he could hardly fail to see it as a miraculously open gate to his marriage with Ygraine—he must in public be seen to show remorse. And I was the public sacrifice to that remorse.

One of the officers—it was Caius Valerius, who rode at the King's shoulder—leaned forward and said something, but Uther might never have heard. I saw Valerius look doubtfully back at me, then with a half-shrug, and a half-salute to me, he rode on. Unsurprised, I watched them go.

The sound of hoofs dwindled sharply down the track towards the sea. Above my head, between one wing-beat and the next, the lark's song shut off, and he dropped from the bright silence to his rest in the grass.

Not far from me a boulder jutted from the turf. I led the horse that way and somehow, from the boulder's top, scrambled into the saddle. I turned the beast's head east by north for Dimilioc, where the King's army lay.

2

Gaps in memory can be merciful. I have no recollection of reaching the camp, but when, hours later, I swam up out of the mists of fatigue and pain I was within doors, and in bed.

I awoke to dusk, and some faint and swimming light that may have been firelight and candle flame; it was a light hazed with colour and drowned with shadows, threaded by the scent of wood-smoke and, it seemed distantly, the trickle and splash of water. But even this warm and gentle consciousness was too much for my struggling senses, and soon I shut my eyes and let myself drown again. I believe that for a while I thought I was back in the edges of the Otherworld, where vision stirs and voices speak out of the dark, and truth comes with the light and the fire. But then the aching of my bruised muscles and the fierce pain in my hand told me that the daylight world still held me, and the voices that murmured across me in the dusk were as human as I.

"Well, that's that, for the moment. The ribs are the worst of it, apart from the hand, and they'll mend soon enough; they're only cracked."

I had a vague feeling that I knew the voice. At any rate I knew what he was: the touch on the fresh bandages was deft and firm, the touch of a professional. I tried to open my eyes again, but the lids were leaden, gummed together and sticky with sweat and dried blood. Warmth came over me in drowsy waves, weighting my limbs. There was a sweet, heavy smell; they must have given me poppy, I thought, or stunned me with smoke before they dressed the hand. I gave up, and let myself drift back from the shore. Over the dark water the voices echoed, softly.

"Stop staring at him and bring the bowl nearer. He's safe enough in this state, never fear." It was the doctor again.

"Well, but one's heard such stories." They were speaking Latin, but the accents were different. The second voice was foreign; not Germanic, nor yet from anywhere on the Middle Sea. I have always been quick at languages, and even as a child spoke several dialects of Celtic, along with Saxon and a working knowledge of Greek. But this accent I could not place. Asia Minor, perhaps? Arabia?

Those deft fingers gently turned my head on the pillow, and parted my hair to sponge the bruises. "Have you never seen him before?"

"Never. I hadn't imagined him so young."

"Not so young. He must be two and twenty."

"But to have done so much. They say his father the High King Ambrosius never took a step, in the last year or two, without talking it over with him. They say he sees the future in a candle flame and can win a battle from a hilltop a mile away."

"They would say anything, of him." The doctor's voice was prosaic and calm. Brittany, I thought, I must have known him in Brittany. The smooth Latin had some overtone I remembered, without knowing how. "But certainly Ambrosius valued his advice."

"Is it true he rebuilt the Giants' Dance near Amesbury, that they call the Hanging Stones?"

"That's true enough. When he was a lad with his father's army in Brittany he studied to be an engineer. I remember him talking to Tremorinus—that was the army's chief engineer—about lifting the Hanging Stones. But that wasn't all he studied. Even as a youth he knew more about medicine than most men I've met who practise it for a livelihood. I can't think of any man I'd rather have by me in a field hospital. God knows why he chooses to shut himself away in that godforsaken corner of Wales now—at least, one can guess why. He and King Uther never got on. They say Uther was jealous of the attention his brother the King paid Merlin. At any rate, after Ambrosius' death, Merlin went nowhere and saw no one, till this business of Uther and Gorlois' Duchess. And it seems as if that's brought him trouble enough. . . . Bring the bowl nearer, while I clean his face. No, here. That's right."

"That's a sword cut, by the look of it."

"A glancing scratch from the point, I'd say. It looks worse than it is, with all the blood. He was lucky there. Another inch and it would have caught his eye. There. It's clean enough; it won't leave a scar."

"He looks like death, Gandar. Will he recover?"

"Of course. How not?" Even through the lulling of the nepenthe, I recognized the quick professional reassurance as genuine. "Apart from the ribs and the hand, it's only cuts and bruising, and I would guess a sharp reaction from whatever has been driving him the last few days. All he needs is sleep. Hand me that ointment there, please. In the green jar."

The salve was cool on my cut cheek. It smelled of valerian. Nard, in the green jar . . . I made it at home. Valerian, balm, oil of spikenard . . . The smell of it took me dreaming out among the mosses at the river's edge, where water ran sparkling, and I gathered the cool cress and the balsam and the golden moss . . .

No, it was water pouring at the other side of the room. He had finished, and had gone to wash his hands. The voices came from farther off.

"Ambrosius' bastard, eh?" The foreigner was still curious. "Who was his mother, then?"

"She was a king's daughter, Southern Welsh, from Maridunum in Dyfed. They say he got the Sight from her. But not his looks; he's a mirror of the late King, more than Uther ever was. Same colouring, black eyes, and that black hair. I remember the first time I saw him, back in Brittany when he was a boy; he looked like something from the hollow hills. Talked like it, too, sometimes; that is, when he talked at all. Don't let his quiet ways fool you; it's more than just book-learning and luck and a knack of timing; there's power there, and it's real."

"So the stories are true?"

"The stories are true," said Gandar flatly. "There. He'll do now. No need to stay with him. Get some sleep. I'll do the rounds myself, and come and take a look at him again before I go to bed. Good night."

The voices faded. Others came and went in the darkness, but these were voices without blood, belonging to the air. Perhaps I should have waited and waked to listen, but I lacked the courage. I reached for sleep and drew it round me like a blanket, muffling pain and thought together in the merciful dark.

When I opened my eyes again it was to darkness lit by calm candle-light. I was in a small chamber with a barrel roof of stone and rough-hewn walls where the once bright paint had darkened and flaked away with damp and neglect. But the room was clean. The floor of Cornish slate had been well scrubbed, and the blankets that covered me were fresh-smelling and thick, and richly worked in bright patterns.

The door opened quietly, and a man came in. At first, against the stronger light beyond the doorway, I could only see him as a man of middle height, broad shouldered and thickly built, dressed in a long plain robe, with a round cap on his head. Then he came forward into the candle-light, and I saw that it was Gandar, the chief physician who travelled with the King's armies. He stood over me, smiling.

"And about time."

"Gandar! It's good to see you. How long have I slept?"

"Since dusk yesterday, and now it's past midnight. It was what you needed. You looked like death when they brought you in. But I must say it made my job a lot easier to have you unconscious."

I glanced down at the hand which lay, neatly bandaged, on the coverlet in front of me. My body was stiff and sore inside its strapping, but the fierce pain had died to a dull aching. My mouth was swollen, and tasted still of blood mingled with the sick-sweet remnants of the drug, but my headache had gone, and the cut on my face had stopped hurting.

"I'm thankful you were here to do it," I said. I shifted the hand a little to ease it, but it was no use. "Will it mend?"

"With the help of youth and good flesh, yes. There were three bones broken, but I think it's clean." He looked at me curiously. "How did you come by it? It looked as if a horse had trodden on you and then kicked your ribs in. But the cut on your face, that was a sword, surely?"

"Yes. I was in a fight."

His brows went up. "If that was a fight, then it wasn't fought by any rules I ever heard of. Tell me—wait, though, not yet. I'm on fire to know what happened—we all are—but you must eat first." He went to the door and called, and presently a servant came in with a bowl of broth and some bread. I could not manage the bread at first, but then sopped a little of it in the broth, and ate that. Gandar pulled a stool up beside the bed, and waited in silence till I had finished. At length I pushed the bowl aside, and he took it from me and set it on the floor.

"Now do you feel well enought to talk? The rumours are flying about like stinging gnats. You knew that Gorlois was dead?"

"Yes." I looked about me. "I'm in Dimilioc itself, I take it? The fortress surrendered, then, after the Duke was killed?"

"They opened the gates as soon as the King got back from Tintagel. He'd already had the news of the skirmish, and the Duke's death. It seems that the Duke's men, Brithael and Jordan, rode to Tintagel as soon as the Duke fell, to take the Duchess the news. But you'd know that; you were there." He stopped short, as he saw the implications. "So that was it! Brithael and Jordan—they ran into you and Uther?"

"Not into Uther, no. They never saw him; he was still with the Duchess. I was outside with my servant Cadal—you remember Cadal?—guarding the doors. Cadal killed Jordan, and I killed Brithael." I smiled, wryly, with my stiff mouth. "Yes, you may well stare. He was well beyond my weight, as you can see. Do you wonder I fought foul?"

"And Cadal?"

"Dead. Do you think otherwise that Brithael would have got to me?"

"I see." His gaze told again, briefly, the tally of my hurts. When he spoke, his voice was dry. "Four men. With you, five. It's to be hoped the King counts it worth the price."

"He does," I said. "Or he will soon."

"Oh, aye, everyone knows that. Give him time only to tell the world that he is guiltless of Gorlois' death, and to get him buried with honour, so that he can marry the Duchess. He's gone back to Tintagel already, did you know? He must have passed you on the road."

"He did," I said dryly. "Within a yard or two."

"But didn't he see you? Or surely—he must have known you were hurt?" Then my tone got through to him. "You mean he saw you, like that, and left you to ride here alone?" I could see that he was shocked, rather than surprised. Gandar and I were old acquaintances, and I had no need to tell him what my relationship had been with Uther, even though he was my father's brother. From the very beginning, Uther had resented his brother's love for his bastard son, and had half feared, half despised my powers of vision and prophecy. He said hotly: "But when it was done in his service—"

"Not his, no. What I did, I did because of a promise I made to Ambrosius. It was a trust he left with me, for his kingdom." I left it at that. One did not speak to Gandar of gods and visions. He dealt, like Uther, with things of the flesh. "Tell me," I said, "those rumours you were talking of. What are they? What do people think happened at Tintagel?"

He gave a half-glance over his shoulder. The door was shut, but he lowered his voice. "The story goes that Uther had already been in Tintagel, with the Duchess Ygraine, and that it was you who took him there and put him in the way of entering. They say you changed the King by enchantment into a likeness of the Duke, and got him past the guards and into the Duchess's bedchamber. They say more than that; they say she took him to her bed, poor lady, thinking he was her husband. And that when Brithael and Jordan took her the news of Gorlois' death, there was 'Gorlois' sitting large as life beside her at breakfast. By the Snake, Merlin, why do you laugh?"

"Two days and nights," I said, "and the story has grown already. Well, I suppose that is what men will believe, and go on believing. And perhaps it is better than the truth."

"What is the truth, then?"

"That there was no enchantment about our entry into Tintagel, only disguise, and human treachery."

I told him the story then, exactly as it had happened, with the tale I had given the goat-herd. "So you see, Gandar, I sowed that seed myself. The nobles and the King's advisers must know the truth, but the common folk will find the tale of magic, and a blameless Duchess, better to believe—and, God knows, easier—than the truth."

He was silent for a while. "So the Duchess knew."

"Or we would not have got in," I said. "It shall not be said, Gandar, that this was a rape. No, the Duchess knew."

He was silent again, for rather longer. Then he said, heavily: "Treachery is a hard word."

"It is a true one. The Duke was my father's friend, and he trusted me. It would never have occurred to him that I would help Uther against him. He knew how little I cared for Uther's lusts. He could not guess that my gods demanded that I should help him satisfy this one. Even though I could not help myself, it was still treachery, and we shall suffer for it, all of us."

"Not the King." He said it positively. "I know him. I doubt if the King will feel more than a passing guilt. You are the one who is suffering for it, Merlin, just as you are the one who calls it by its name."

"To you," I said. "To other men this will remain a story of enchantment, like the dragons which fought at my bidding under Dinas Emrys, and the Giants' Dance which floated on air and water to Amesbury. But you have seen how Merlin the King's enchanter fared that night." I paused, and shifted my hand on the coverlet, but shook my head at the question in his face. "No, no, let be. It's better already. Gandar, one other truth about that night must be known. There will be a child. Take it as hope, or take it as prophecy, you will see that, come Christmas, a boy will be born. Has he said when he will marry her?"

"As soon as it's decent. Decent!" He repeated the word on a short bark of laughter, then cleared his throat. "The Duke's body is here, but in a day or two they'll carry him to Tintagel to bury him. Then, after the eight days' mourning, Uther is to marry the Duchess."

I thought for a moment. "Gorlois had a son by his first wife. Cador, he was called. He must be about fifteen. Have you heard what is to become of him?"

"He's here. He was in the fight, beside his father. No one knows what has passed between him and the King, but the King gave an amnesty to all the troops that fought against him in the action at Dimilioc, and he has said, besides, that Cador will be confirmed Duke of Cornwall."

"Yes," I said. "And Ygraine's son and Uther's will be King."

"With Cornwall his bitter enemy?"

"If he is," I said wearily, "who is to blame him? The payment may well be too long and too heavy, even for treachery."

"Well," said Gandar, suddenly brisk, gathering his robe about him, "that's with time. And now, young man, you'd better get some more rest. Would you like a draught?"

"Thank you, no."

"How does the hand feel?"

"Better. There's no poison there; I know the feel of it. I'll give you no more trouble, Gandar, so stop treating me like a sick man. I'm well enough, now that I've slept. Get yourself to bed, and forget about me. Good night."

When he had gone I lay listening to the sounds of the sea, and trying to gather, from the god-filled dark, the courage I would need for my visit to the dead.

Courage or no, another day passed before I found the strength to leave my chamber. Then I went at dusk to the great hall where they had put the old Duke's body. Tomorrow he would be taken to Tintagel for burial among his fathers. Now he lay alone, save for the guards, in the echoing hall where he had feasted his peers and given orders for his last battle.

The place was cold, silent but for the sounds of wind and sea. The wind changed and now blew from the northwest, bringing with it the chill and promise of rain. There was neither glazing nor horn in the windows, and the draught stirred the torches in their iron brackets, sending them sideways, dim and smoking, to blacken the walls. It was a stark, comfortless place, bare of paint, or tiling, or carved wood; one remembered that Dimilioc was simply the fortress of a fighting man; it was doubtful if Ygraine had ever been here. The ashes in the hearth were days old, the half-burned logs dewed with damp.

The Duke's body lay on a high bier in the center of the hall, covered with his war cloak. The scarlet with the double border of silver and the white badge of the Boar was as I had seen it at my father's side in battle. I had seen it, too, on Uther as I led him disguised into Gorlois' castle and his bed. Now the heavy folds hung to the ground, and beneath them the body had shrunk and flattened, no more than a husk of the tall old man I remembered. They had left his face uncovered. The flesh had sunk, grey as twice-used tallow, till the face was a moulded skull, showing only the ghost of a likeness to the Gorlois I had known. The coins on his eyes had already sunk into the flesh. His hair was hidden by his war helm, but the familiar grey beard jutted over the badge of the Boar on his chest.

I wondered, as I went forward soft-footed over the stone floor, by which god Gorlois had lived, and to which god he had gone in dying. There was nothing here to show. Christians, like other men, put coins on the eyes. I remembered other death-beds, and the press of spirits waiting round them; there was nothing here. But he had been dead three days, and perhaps his spirit had already gone through that bare and windy gap in the wall. Perhaps it had already gone too far for me to reach it and make my peace.

I stood at the foot of his bier, the man I had betrayed, the friend of my father Ambrosius the High King. I remembered the night he had come to ask me for my help for his young wife, and how he had said to me: "There are not many men I'd trust just now, but I trust you. You're your father's son." And how I had said nothing, but watched the firelight stain his face red like blood, and waited my chance to lead the King to his wife's bed.

It is one thing to have the gift of seeing the spirits and hearing the gods who move about us as we come and go; but it is a gift of darkness as well as light. The shapes of death come as clear as those of life. One cannot be visited by the future without being haunted by the past; one cannot taste comfort and glory without the bitter sting and fury of one's own past deeds. Whatever I had thought to encounter near the dead body of the Duke of Cornwall, it would hold no comfort and no peace for me. A man like Uther Pendragon, who killed in open battle and open air, would think no more of this than a dead man dead. But I, who in obeying the gods had trusted them even as the Duke had trusted me, had known that I would have to pay, and in full. So I had come, but without hope.

There was light here from the torches, light and fire. I was Merlin; I should be able to reach him; I had talked with the dead before. I stood still, watching the flaring torches, and waited.

Slowly, all through the fortress, I could hear the sounds dwindling and sinking to silence as men finally went to rest. The sea soughed and beat below the window, the wind plucked at the wall, and ferns growing there in the crevices rustled and tapped. A rat scuttled and squeaked somewhere. The resin bubbled in the torches. Sweet and foul, through the sharp smoke, I smelled the smell of death. The torchlight winked blank and flat from the coins on the dead eyes.

The time crawled by. My eyes ached with the flame, and the pain from my hand, like a biting fetter, kept me penned in my body. My spirit was pared down to nothing, blind as the dead. Whispers I caught, fragments of thought from the still and sleepy guards, meaningless as the sound of their breathing, and the creak of leather or chime of metal as they stirred involuntarily from time to time. But beyond these, nothing. What power I had been given on that night at Tintagel had drained from me with the strength that had killed Brithael. It had gone from me and was working, I thought, in a woman's body; in Ygraine, lying even now beside the King in that grim and battered near-isle of Tintagel, ten miles to the south. I could do nothing here. The air, solid as stone, would not let me through.

One of the guards, the one nearest me, moved restlessly, and the butt of his grounded spear scraped on the stone. The sound jarred the silence. I glanced his way involuntarily, and saw him watching me.

He was young, rigid as his own spear, his fists white on the shaft. The fierce blue eyes watched me unwinkingly under thick brows. With a shock that went through me like the spear striking I recognized them. Gorlois' eyes. It was Gorlois' son, Cador of Cornwall, who stood between me and the dead, watching me steadily, with hatred.

In the morning they took Gorlois' body south. As soon as he was buried, Gandar had told me, Uther planned to ride back to Dimilioc to rejoin his troops until such time as he could marry the Duchess. I had no intention of waiting for his return. I called for provisions and my horse and, in spite of Gandar's protestations that I was not yet fit for the journey, set out alone for my valley above Maridunum and the cave in the hill which the King had promised should remain, in spite of everything, my own.

3

No one had been inside the cave during my absence. This was hardly to be wondered at, since the people held me in much awe as an enchanter, and moreover it was commonly known that the King himself had granted me the hill Bryn Myrddin. Once I left the main road at the water-mill, and rode up the steep tributary valley to the cave which had become my home, I saw no one, not even the shepherd who commonly watched his flocks grazing the stony slopes.

In the lower reaches of the valley the woods were thick; oaks still rustled their withered leaves, chestnut and sycamore crowded close, fighting for the light, and hollies showed black and glinting between the beeches. Then the trees thinned, and the path climbed along the side of the valley, with the stream running deep down on the left, and to the right slopes of grass, broken by scree, rising sharply to the crags that crowned the hill. The grass was still bleached with winter, but among the rusty drifts of last year's bracken the bluebell leaves showed glossy green, and blackthorn was budding. Somewhere, lambs were crying. That, and the mewing of a buzzard high over the crags, and the rustle of the dead bracken where my tired horse trod, were all the sounds in the valley. I was home, to the solace of simplicity and quiet.

The people had not forgotten me, and word must have gone round that I was expected. When I dismounted in the thorn grove below the cliff and stabled my horse in the shed there I found that bracken had been freshly strewn for bedding, and a netful of fodder hung from a hook beside the door; and when I climbed to the little apron of lawn which lay in front of my cave I found cheese and new bread wrapped in a clean cloth, and a goatskin full of local thin, sour wine, which had been left for me beside the spring.

This was a small spring, a trickle of pure water welling out of a ferny crack in the rock to one side of the entrance to the cave. The water ran down, sometimes in a steady flow, sometimes no more than a sliding glimmer over the mosses, to drip into a rounded basin of stone. Above the spring the little statue of the god Myrddin, he of the winged spaces of the air, stared from between the ferns. Beneath his cracked wooden feet the water bubbled and dripped into the stone basin, lipping over into the grass below. Deep in the clear water metal glinted; I knew that the wine and bread, like the thrown coins, had been left as much as an offering to the god as to me; in the minds of the simple folk I had already become part of the legend of the hill, their god made flesh who came and went as quietly as the air, and brought with him the gifts of healing.

I lifted down the cup of horn which stood above the spring, filled it from the goatskin, then poured wine for the god, and drank the rest myself. The god would know whether there was more in the gesture than ritual homage. I myself was tired beyond thought, and had no prayer to offer; the drink was for courage, nothing more.

To the other side of the cave entrance, opposite the spring, was a tumble of grass-grown stones, where saplings of oak and mountain ash had seeded themselves, and grew in a thick tangle against the rocky face. In summer their boughs cast a wide pool of shade, but now, though overhanging it, they did nothing to conceal the entrance to the cave. This was a smallish arch, regular and rounded, as if made by hand. I pushed the hanging boughs aside and went in.

Just inside the entrance the remnants of a fire still lay in white ash on the hearth, and twigs and damp leaves had drifted over it. The place smelled already of disuse. It seemed strange that it was barely a month since I had ridden out at the King's urgent summons to help him in the matter of Ygraine of Cornwall. Beside the cold hearth stood the unwashed dishes from the last, hasty meal my servant had prepared before we set out.

Well, I would have to be my own servant now. I put the goatskin of wine and the bundle of bread and cheese on the table, then turned to re-make the fire. Flint and tinder lay to hand where they had always lain, but I knelt down by the cold faggots and stretched out my hands for the magic. This was the first magic I had been taught, and the simplest, the bringing of fire out of the air. It had been taught me in this very cave, where as a child I had learned all I knew of natural lore from Galapas, the old hermit of the hill. Here, too, in the cave of crystal which lay deeper in the hill, I had seen my first visions, and found myself as a seer. "Some day," Galapas had said, "you will go where even with the Sight I cannot follow you." It had been true. I had left him, and gone where my god had driven me; where none but I, Merlin, could have gone. But now the god's will was done, and he had forsaken me. Back there in Dimilioc, beside Gorlois' bier, I had found myself to be an empty husk; blind and deaf as men are blind and deaf; the great power gone. Now, weary though I was, I knew I would not rest until I saw if, here in my magic's birthplace, the first and smallest of my powers was left to me.

I was soon answered, but it was an answer I would not accept. The westering sun was dropping red past the boughs at the cave mouth, and the logs were still unkindled, when finally I gave up, with the sweat running scalding on my body under my gown, and my hands, outstretched for the magic, trembling like those of an old man. I sat by the cold hearth and ate my supper of bread and cheese and watered wine in the chill of the spring dusk, before I could gather even strength enough to reach for the flint and tinder and try with them.

Even this, a task that every wife does daily and without thought, took me an age, and set my maimed hand bleeding. But in the end fire came. A tiny spark flew in among the tinder and started a slow, creeping flame. I lit the torch from it, and then, carrying the flame high, went to the back of the cave. There was something I still must do.

The main cavern, high-roofed, went a long way back. I stood with the torch held high, looking up. At the back of the cave was a slope of rock leading up to a wide ledge, which in its turn climbed into the dark, high shadows. Invisible among these shadows was the hidden cleft beyond which lay the inner cave, the globed cavity lined with crystals where, with light and fire, I had seen my first visions. If the lost power lay anywhere, it lay there. Slowly, stiff with fatigue, I climbed the ledge, then knelt to peer through the low entrance to the inner cave. The flames from my torch caught the crystals, and light ran round the globe. My harp still stood where I had left it, in the center of the crystal-studded floor. Its shadow shot towering up the shimmering walls, and flame sparked from the copper of the string-shoes, but no stir of the air set it whispering, and its own arching shadows quenched the light. I knelt there for a long time, eyes wide and staring, while round me light and shadow shivered and beat. But my eyes ached, empty of vision, and the harp stayed silent.

At length I withdrew, and made my way down into the main cave. I remember that I picked my way slowly, carefully, like a man who has never been that way before. I thrust the torch under the dry wood I had piled for a fire, till the logs caught, crackling; then went out and found my saddle-bags, and lugged them back into the human comfort of the firelight, and began to unpack them.

My hand took a long time to heal. For the first few days it pained me constantly, throbbing so that I was afraid it was infected. During the day this did not matter so much, for there were tasks to do; all that my servant had done for me for so long that I hardly knew how to set about it; cleaning, preparing food, tending my horse. Spring came slowly to South Wales that year, and there was no grazing yet on the hill, so I had to cut and carry fodder for him, and walk farther than I cared to in search of the healing plants I needed. Luckily food for myself was always forthcoming; gifts were left almost daily at the foot of the small cliff below the lawn. It may have been that the country folk had not yet heard that I was out of favour with the King, or it may simply have been that what I had done for them in the way of healing outweighed Uther's displeasure. I was Merlin, son of Ambrosius; or, as the Welsh say it, Myrddin Emrys, the enchanter of Myrddin's Hill; and in another way, I suppose, the priest of the old god of the hollow hill, Myrddin himself. What gifts they would have brought for him they brought now for me, and in his name I accepted them.

But if the days were full enough, the nights were bad. I seemed always wakeful, less perhaps from the pain of my hand than from the pain of my memories: where Gorlois' death chamber had been empty, my own cave was full of ghosts. Not the spirits of the loved dead whom I would have welcomed; but the spirits of those I had killed went past me in the dark with thin sounds like the cry of bats. At least, this is what I told myself. I believe now that I was often touched with fever: the cave still housed the bats that Galapas and I had studied, and it must have been these I heard, passing to and from the cave mouth during the night. But in my memory of this time they are the voices of dead men, restless in the dark.

April went by, wet and chill, with the winds that searched you to the bone. This was the bad time, empty except for pain, and idle except for the barest efforts to live. I believe I ate very little; water and fruit and black bread was my staple diet. My clothes, never sumptuous, became threadbare with no one to care for them, and then ragged. A stranger seeing me walking the hill paths would have taken me for a beggar. Days passed when I did little but huddle over the smoking fire. My chest of books was unopened, my harp was left where it stood. Even had my hand been whole, I could have made no music. As for magic, I dared not put myself to the test again.

But gradually, like Ygraine waiting in her cold castle to the south, I slid into a sort of calm acceptance. As the weeks went by my hand healed, cleanly enough. I was left with two stiff fingers, and a scar along the outer edge of the palm, but the stiffness passed with time, and the scar never troubled me. And as time passed the other wounds healed, too. I grew used to loneliness, as I had been accustomed to solitude, and the nightmares ceased. Then as May drew on the winds changed, grew warm, and grass and flowers came springing. The grey clouds packed away, and the valley was full of sunlight. I sat for hours in the sun at the mouth of the cave, reading, or preparing the plants I had gathered, or from time to time watching—but no more than idly—for the approach of a rider which would mean a message. (Even so, I thought, must my old teacher Galapas have sat here many a time in the sunlight, looking down the valley where, one day, a small boy would come riding.) And I built up again my stock of plants and herbs, wandering farther and farther from the cave as my strength came back to me. I never went into the town, but now and again when poor folk came for medicines or for healing, they brought snatches of news. The King had married Ygraine with as much pomp and ceremony as such a hasty union would permit, and he had seemed merry enough since the wedding, though quicker to anger than he used to be, and would have sudden morose fits when folk learned to avoid him. As for the Queen, she was silent, acceding in everything to the King's wishes, but rumour had it that her looks were heavy, as if she mourned in secret. . . .

Here my informant shot a quick sidelong look at me, and I saw his fingers move to make the sign against enchantment. I let him go on, asking no more questions. The news would come to me in its own time.

It came almost three months after my return to Bryn Myrddin.

One day in June, when a hot morning sun was just lifting the mist from the grass, I went up the hill to find my horse, which I had tethered out to graze on the grassland above the cave. The air was still, and the sky was full of singing larks. Over the green mound where Galapas lay buried the blackthorns showed green leaves budding through fading snowbanks of flowers, and bluebells were thick among the fern.

I doubt if I actually needed to tether my horse. I usually carried with me the remnants of the bread my benefactors left for me, so when he saw me coming he would advance to the end of his tether and stand waiting, expectant.

But not today. He was standing at the far stretch of his rope, on the edge of the hill, head up and ears pricked, apparently watching something away down the valley. I walked over to him and, while he nuzzled in my hand for the bread, looked where he had been looking.

From this height I could see the town of Maridunum, small in the distance, clinging to the north bank of the placid Tywy as it wound its way down its wide green valley towards the sea. The town, with its arched stone bridge and its harbour, lies just where the river widens towards the estuary. There was the usual huddle of masts beyond the bridge, and nearer, on the towpath that threaded its way along the silver curves of the river, a slow grey horse towed a grain barge up to the mill. The mill itself, lying where the stream from my own valley met the river, was hidden in woodland; out of these trees ran the old military road which my father had repaired, straight as a die through five open miles, to the barracks near Maridunum's eastern gate.

On this road, perhaps a mile and a half beyond the water-mill, there was a cloud of dust where horsemen skirmished. They were fighting; I saw the flash of metal. Then the group resolved itself, clearer through the dust. There were four mounted men, and they were fighting three to one. The lone man seemed to be trying to escape, the others to surround him and cut him down. At length he burst free in what looked like a desperate bid for escape. His horse, pulled round hard, struck one of the others on the shoulder, and its rider fell, dislodged by a heavy blow. Then the single man, crouched and spurring hard, turned his horse off the road and across the grass, making desperately for the cover afforded by the edge of the woodland. But he did not reach it. The other two spurred after him; there was a short, wild gallop, then they had caught him up, one on each side, and as I watched he was dragged from his horse and beaten to his knees. He tried to crawl away, but he had no chance. The two horsemen circled, their weapons flashing, and the third man, apparently uninjured, had remounted and was galloping to join them. Then suddenly he checked his horse, so sharply that it reared. I saw him fling up an arm. He must have shouted a warning, for the other two, abruptly abandoning their victim, wheeled their beasts, and the three of them galloped off, full stretch, with the loose horse pelting behind them, to be lost to sight eastwards beyond the trees.

Next moment I saw what had startled them. Another group of horsemen was approaching from the direction of the town. They must have seen the retreating trio, but it soon appeared that they had seen nothing of the attack, for they came on at a canter, riding at ease. I watched them as they drew level with the place where the fallen man—injured or dead—must be lying. They passed it without slackening pace. Then they, too, were lost to sight below the woodland.

My horse, finding no more bread, nipped me, then jerked his head away sharply, ears flattened. I caught him by the halter, pulled up the tether, peg and all, and turned his head downhill.

"I stood on this spot once before," I told him, "while a King's messenger came riding to see me and bid me go and help the King to his desire. I had power that day; I dreamed I held the whole world cupped in my hands, shining and small. Well, maybe I've nothing today but the hill I stand on, but that might be a Queen's messenger lying down yonder, with a message still in his pouch. Message or not, he'll need help if he's still alive. And you and I, my friend, have had our fill of idleness. It's time to be doing again."

In a little less than twice the time it would have taken my servant to do the job, I had the horse bridled, and was on my way down the valley. Reaching the mill road, I turned my horse's head to the right, and drove my heels in.

The place where I had seen the horseman fall was near the edge of the woods, where the bushes were thick, a place of bracken and undergrowth and scattered trees. The smell of horses still hung in the air, with the tang of trampled bracken and sweet briar and, foul through it all, the smell of vomit. I dismounted and tethered my horse, then pushed my way forward through the thick growth.

He lay on his face, half hunched as he had crawled and collapsed, one hand still trapped under his body, the other outflung and gripping a tuft of bracken. A youth, lightly built but well grown, fifteen, perhaps, or a little more. His clothes, torn and grimed and bloodstained by the fight and his crawl through the thorns, had been good, and there was a glint of silver on one wrist, and a silver brooch at his shoulder. So they had not managed to rob him, if robbery had been the motive for the attack. His pouch was still at his belt, and fastened.

He made no move as I approached him, so I thought him insensible, or dead. But when I knelt beside him I saw the slight movement as his hand clenched more tightly on the stems of bracken, and I realized that he was exhausted or hurt beyond all caring. If I were one of his murderers come to finish him off, he would lie there and let me.

I spoke gently. "Be easy, I shan't hurt you. Lie still a moment. Don't try to move."

There was no response. I laid careful hands on him, feeling for wounds and broken bones. He flinched from my touch, but made no sound. I satisfied myself soon that no bones were broken. There was a bloodied swelling near the back of his head, and one shoulder was already blackened with bruising, but the worst that I could see was a patch of crushed and bleeding flesh on the hip, which looked—and indeed later proved—to be where a horse's hoof had struck him.

"Come," I said at length, "turn over, and drink this."

He moved then, though wincing from the touch of my arm round his shoulder, and turned slowly round. I wiped the dirt and sickness from his mouth and held my flask to his lips; he gulped greedily, coughed, and then, losing strength again, leaned heavily against me, his head drooping against my chest. When I put the flask back to his mouth he turned his head away. I could feel him using all his strength not to cry out against the pain. I stoppered the flask and put it away.

"I have a horse here. You must try and sit him somehow, and I'll get you home, where I can see to your hurts." Then, when he made no response: "Come now. Let's get you out of this before they decide to come back and finish what they started."

He moved then, abruptly, as if these were the first words that had got through to him. I saw his hand grope down to the pouch at his belt, discover it was still there, and then fall limply away. The weight against my chest sagged suddenly. He had fainted.

So much the better, I thought, as I laid him down gently and went to bring up my horse. He would be spared the painful jolting of the ride, and by the gods' mercy I might have him in bed with his hurts bandaged before he woke. Then in the very act of stooping to lift him again I paused. His face was dirty, grime mingled with bloodstains from scratches and a cut above the ear. Under the mask of dirt and blood the skin was drained and grey. Brown hair, shut eyes, a slack mouth. But I recognized him. It was Ralf, Ygraine's page, who had let us into Tintagel that night, and who with Ulfin and myself had guarded the Duchess's chamber until the King had had his desire.

I stooped and lifted the Queen's messenger, and heaved his unconscious body across my waiting horse.

4

Ralf did not regain his senses during the journey up to the cave, and only after I had washed and bound his wounds and put him into bed did he open his eyes. He stared at me for a few moments, but without recognition.

"Don't you know me?" I said. "Merlinus Ambrosius. You brought your message safely enough. See." I held up the wallet, still sealed. But his eyes, cloudy and unfocused, slid past it, and he turned his head against the pillow, wincing as he felt the pain from the bruising on the back of his neck. "Very well," I told him, "sleep now. You're in safe hands."

I waited beside him till he drifted back into sleep, then took the wallet and its contents out to my seat in the sunlight. The seal was, as I had expected, the Queen's, and the superscription was mine. I broke the seal and read the letter.

It was not from the Queen herself, but from Marcia, Ralf's grandmother and the Queen's closest confidante. The letter was brief enough, but held all I wanted to know. The Queen was indeed pregnant, and the child would be born in December. The Queen herself—said Marcia—seemed happy to be bearing the King's child, but, where she spoke of me at all, spoke with bitterness, throwing on me the responsibility for her husband Gorlois' death. "She says little, but it is my belief that she mourns in secret, and that even in her great love for the King there will always be the shadow of guilt. Pray God her feeling for the child may not be tainted with it. As for the King, it is seen that he is angry, though he is as ever kind and loving to my lady, and there is no man who doubts but that the child is his. Alas, I could find it in me to fear for the child at the King's hands, if it were not unthinkable that he should so grieve the Queen. Wherefore, Prince Merlin, I beg by this letter to commend to you as your servant my grandson Ralf. For him, too, I fear at the King's hands; and I believe that, if you will take him, service abroad with a true prince is better than here with a King who counts his service as betrayal. There is no safety for him in Cornwall. So pray you, lord, let Ralf serve you now, and after you, the child. For I think I understand what you were speaking of when you said to my lady, 'I have seen a bright fire burning, and in it a crown, and a sword standing in an altar like a cross.' "

Ralf slept until dusk. I had lit the fire and made broth, and when I took it to the back of the cave where he lay I saw his eyes open, watching me. There was recognition in them now, and a wariness that I could not quite understand.

"How do you feel now?"

"Well enough, my lord. I—this is your cave? How did I come here? How did you find me?"

"I had gone up to the hill above here, and from there I saw you being attacked. The men were frightened off, and ran away, leaving you. I went down to get you, and carried you up here on my horse. So you recognize me now, do you?"

"You've let your beard grow, but I'd have known you, my lord. Did I speak to you before? I don't remember anything. I think they hit me on the head."

"They did. How is it now?"

"A headache. But not bad. It's my side"—wincing—"that hurts most."

"One of the horses struck you. But there's no real damage done; you'll be well enough in a few days. Do you know who they were?"

"No." He knitted his brows, thinking, but I could see the effort hurt him, so I stopped him.

"Well, we can talk later. Eat now."

"My lord, the message—"

"I have it safely. Later."

When I went back to him he had finished the broth and bread, and looked more like himself. He would not take more food, but I made him drink a little wine, and watched the colour come back into his face. Then I drew up a chair, and sat down beside the bed.

"Better?"

"Yes." He spoke without looking at me. He looked down at his hands, nervously plucking at the covers in front of him. He swallowed. "I—I haven't thanked you yet, my lord."

"For what? Picking you up and bringing you here? It was the only way to get your news."

He glanced up at that, and for a startled second I realized that he thought it was no more than the truth. I saw then what there was in that look he had given me; he was afraid of me. I thought back to that night in Tintagel, the gay youth who had dealt so bravely for the King, and so truly with me. But for the moment I let it go. I said:

"You brought me the news I wanted. I've read your grandmother's letter. You know what she tells me in it about the Queen?"

"Yes."

"And about yourself?"

"Yes." He shut his mouth on the syllable, and looked away, sullen, like someone unfairly trapped and held for questioning, who is determined not to answer. It seemed that, whatever Marcia's motives for sending him to me, he himself was far from willing to offer me service. From which I guessed that she had told him nothing about her hopes for the future.

"All right, we'll leave that for the moment. But it seems that somebody wants to harm you, whoever it may be. If those men this morning weren't just roadside cutthroats, it would help to know who they were, and who paid them. Have you no idea who they might have been?"

"No," still mumbling.

"It's of some interest to me," I said mildly. "They might conceivably want to kill me, too."

That startled him out of his resentment. "Why?"

"If you were attacked out of revenge for the part you played at Tintagel, then presumably they will attack me as well. If you were attacked for the message you carried to me, I want to know why. If they were plain thieves, which seems the most likely, then they may still be hereabouts, and I must get a message to the troopers down at the barracks."

"Oh. Yes, I see." He looked disconcerted and slightly ashamed. "But it's true, my lord; I don't know who they were. I—it was of interest to me, too. I've been trying to think, all this time, but I've no idea. There's no clue that I can remember. They didn't wear badges; at least I don't think so . . ." His brows drew together, painfully. "I'd have noticed badges, surely, if they'd had them?"

"How were they dressed?"

"I—I hardly noticed. Leather tunics, I think, and chainmail caps. No shields, but swords and daggers."

"And they were well mounted. I saw that. Did you hear their speech?"

"Not that I remember. They hardly spoke, a shout or two, that was all. British speech, but I couldn't tell where from. I'm not good at accents."

"There was nothing you can think of that might have marked them for King's men?"

This was probing too near the wound. He went scarlet, but said levelly enough: "Nothing. But is it likely?"

"I wouldn't have thought so," I said. "But kings are queer cattle, and queerest of all when they have bad consciences. Well, then, Cornishmen?"

The flush had ebbed, leaving him if possible more sickly pale than before. His eyes were sullen and unhappy. This was the wound itself; this was a thought he had lived with. "Duke's men, you mean?"

"They told me before I left Dimilioc that the King was to confirm young Cador as Duke of Cornwall. That's one man, Ralf, who will have no love for you. He won't stop to consider that you were the Duchess's man, and were serving her as you were bidden. He is full of hatred, and it might extend to vengeance. One could hardly blame him if it did."

He looked faintly surprised, then in some odd way set at ease by this dispassionate handling. After a bit he said, with an attempt at the same tone: "They might have been Cador's men, I suppose. There was nothing to show it, one way or the other. Maybe I'll remember something." He paused. "But surely, if Cador intended to kill me, he could have cut me down in Cornwall. Why come all the way here? To follow me to you? He must hate you as much."

"More," I said. "But if he had intended to kill me, he knew where to find me; the whole world knows that. And he'd have come before this."

He eyed me doubtfully. Then he appeared to find an explanation for my apparent lack of fear. "I suppose no one would dare come after you here, for fear of your magic?"

"It would be nice to think so," I agreed. There was no point in telling him how thin my defenses were. "Now, that's enough for the moment. Rest again, and you'll find you feel better tomorrow. Will you sleep, do you think? Are you in pain?"

"No," he said, not truthfully. Pain was a weakness he would not admit to me. I stooped and felt for the heartbeat in his wrist. It was strong and even. I let the wrist drop, and nodded at him. "You'll live. Call me in the night if you want me. Good night."

Ralf did not in fact remember anything more next morning that would give a clue to the identity of his attackers, and I forbore for a few days from questioning him further about the contents of Marcia's letter. Then one evening, when I judged he was better, I called him to me. It had been a damp day, and the evening had brought a chill with it, so I had lit a fire, and sat with my supper beside it.

"Ralf, bring your bowl and eat beside me where it's warm. I want to talk to you."

He came obediently. He had somehow managed to mend and tidy his clothes, and now, with the cuts and bruises fading, and with colour back in his face, he was almost himself again, except for a limp where the wound on his hip had not yet mended; and except, still, for his silence, and the sullen shadow of wariness in his face. He limped across and sat where I pointed.

"You said you knew what else was in your grandmother's letter to me besides news of the Queen?" I asked him.

"Yes."

"Then you know she sent you to take service with me, because she feared the King's displeasure. Did the King himself give you any reason to fear him?"

A slight shake of the head. He would not meet my eyes. "Not to fear him, no. But when the alarm came of a Saxon landing on the south coast, and I asked to ride with his men, he would not take me." His voice was sullen and furious. "Even though he took every other Cornishman who had fought against him at Dimilioc. But myself, who had helped him, he dismissed."

I looked thoughtfully at the bent head, the hot averted cheek. This, of course, was the reason for his attitude to me, the wary resentment and anger. He could only see, understandably enough, that through his service to me and the King he had lost his place near the Queen; worse, he had incurred his Duke's anger, had been disgraced as a Cornish subject and banished from his home to a kind of service he disdained.

I said: "Your grandmother tells me little except that she feels you had better seek a career for yourself outside Cornwall. Leave that for a moment; you can't seek anything much until your leg is healed. But tell me, did the King ever say anything to you directly about the night of Gorlois' death?"

A pause, so long that I thought he would not answer. Then he said: "Yes. He told me that I had served him well, and he—he thanked me. He asked me if I wanted a reward. I said no, the service was reward enough. He didn't like that. I think he wanted to give me money, and requite me, and forget it. He said then that I could no longer serve him or the Queen. That in serving him I had betrayed my master the Duke, and that a man who had betrayed one master could betray another."

"Well?" I said. "Is that all?"

"All?" His head jerked up at that. He looked startled and contemptuous. *"All?* An insult like that? And it was a lie, you know it was! I was my lady's man, not Duke Gorlois'! I did not betray the Duke!"

"Oh, yes, it was an insult. You can't expect the King to be level-headed yet, when he himself feels as guilty as Judas. He's got to put the betrayal on someone's shoulders, so it's yours and mine. But I doubt if you're in actual danger from him. Even a doting grandmother could hardly call that a threat."

"Who was talking about threats?" said Ralf hotly. "I didn't come away because I was afraid! Someone had to bring the message, and you saw how safe that was!"

It was hardly the tone a servant uses. I hid my amusement and said mildly: "Don't ruffle your feathers at me, young cockerel. No one doubts your courage. I'm sure the King does not. Now, tell me about this Saxon landing. Where? What happened? I've had no news from the south for over a month now."

In a little while he answered me civilly enough. "It was in May. They landed south of Vindocladia. There's a deep bay there, they call it Potters' Bay. I forget its real name. Well, it's outside federated territory, in Dumnonia, and that was against all the agreements the Federates made. You would know that."

I nodded. It is hard to remember now, looking back down the years to the time I write of, Uther's time, that today men hardly remember even the name of Federate. The first of the Federated Saxons were the followers of Hengist and Horsa, who had been called in by King Vortigern as mercenary help to establish him on his stolen throne. When the fighting was done, and the rightful princes Ambrosius and Uther had fled to Brittany, the usurper Vortigern would have dismissed his Saxon mercenaries; but they refused to withdraw, demanding territory where they could settle, and promising, as federated settlers, to fight as Vortigern's allies. So, partly because he dared not refuse them, partly because he foresaw that he might need them again, Vortigern gave them the coastal stretches in the south, from Rutupiae to Vindocladia—the stretch that was called the Saxon Shore. In the days of the Romans it had been so called because the main Saxon landings had been there; by Uther's time the name had taken on a direr and truer significance. On a clear day you could see the Saxon smoke from London Wall.

It had been from this secured base, and from similar enclaves in the north-east, that the new attacks had come when my father was King. He had killed Hengist and his brother, and had driven the invaders back, some northwards into the wild lands beyond Hadrian's Wall, and others behind their old boundaries, where once again—but this time forcibly—they had been bound by treaty. But a treaty with a Saxon is like writing in water: Ambrosius, not trusting to the prescribed boundaries, had thrown up a wall to protect the rich lands which marched with the Saxon Shore. Until his death the treaty—or the Wall—had held them, nor had they openly joined in the attacks led by Hengist's son Octa and Eosa his kinsman in the early days of Uther's reign; but they were uneasy neighbours: they provided a beach-head for any wandering longships, and the Saxon Shore grew crowded and still more crowded, till even Ambrosius' Wall looked frail protection. And everywhere along the eastern shores raiders came in from the German Sea, some to burn and rape and sail again, others to burn and rape and stay, buying or extorting new territory from the local kings.

Such an attack, now, Ralf was describing to me.

"Well, of course the Federates broke the agreement. A new war-band—thirty ships it was—landed in Potters' Bay, well west of the boundary, and the Federates welcomed them and came out in force to help them. They established a beach-head near the river's mouth and started to push up towards Vindocladia. I think if they had once got to Badon Hill—what is it?"

He broke off, staring at me. There was amazement in his face, and a touch of fear.

"Nothing," I said. "I thought I heard something outside, but it's only the wind."

He said slowly: "You looked for a moment the way you did that night at Tintagel, when you said the air was full of magic. Your eyes went strange, all black and blurred, as if you were seeing something, out there beyond the fire." He hesitated. "Was it prophecy?"

"No. I saw nothing. All I heard was a sound like horses galloping. It was only the wild geese going over in the wind. If it was prophecy, it will come again. Go on. You were speaking of Badon Hill."

"Well, the Saxons can't have known that King Uther was in Cornwall, with all the force he'd brought down to fight Duke Gorlois. He gathered his army and called on the Dumnonians to help him, and marched to drive the

Saxons back." He paused, compressing his lips, then finished briefly: "Cador went with him."

"Did he indeed?" I was thoughtful. "You didn't happen to hear what had passed between them?"

"Only that Cador had been heard to say that since he couldn't defend his part of Dumnonia alone he didn't mind fighting alongside the Devil himself, as long as the Saxons could be cleared from the coast."

"He sounds a sensible young man."

Ralf, hot on his grievance, was not listening. "You see, he didn't exactly make peace with Uther—"

"Yes. One gathers that."

"—but he did march with him! And I could not! I went to him, and to my lady, and begged to go, but he wouldn't take me!"

"Well," I said, reasonably, "how could he?"

That stopped him. He stared at me, ready to be angry again. "What do you mean? If *you* think me a traitor—"

"You're the same age as Cador, aren't you? Then try to show as much common sense. Think. If Cador was to go into battle beside the King, then the King, for your sake, could hardly take you. Uther may suffer a few pangs of conscience when he lays eyes on you, but Cador must see you as one of the causes of his father's death. Do you think he would bear you near him, however much he may need the King and his legions? Now do you see why you were left at home, and then sent north to me?"

He was silent. I said, gently: "What's done is done, Ralf. Only a child expects life to be just; it's a man's part to stand by the consequence of his deeds. As we both shall, believe me. So put all this behind you, and take what the gods send. Your life is not over because you have had to leave the court, or even because you have had to leave Cornwall."

There was a longer silence. Then he picked up his empty bowl and mine and got to his feet. "Yes, I see. Well, since for the moment I can't do much else, I'll stay and serve you. But not because I'm afraid of the King, or because my grandmother wants to get me out of Duke Cador's way. It's because I choose. And indeed"—he swallowed—"I reckon I owe it to you." His tone was neither grateful nor conciliatory. He stood there like a soldier, stiffly, the bowls clutched to his ribs.

"Then start paying your debt and wash the supper dishes," I said equably, and picked up a book.

He hung on his heel a moment, but I neither spoke nor looked up. He went then, without another word, to draw water from the spring outside.

5

Bruises on the young heal quickly, and Ralf was soon active again, and insistent that he no longer needed doctoring. The wound on his hip, however, gave some trouble, and left him limping for a week or two.

In "choosing" to stay with me, he had made the best of a bad job, since for the time being he was tied to the cave by his injury and by the loss of his horse, but he served me well, mastering what resentment he might yet feel towards me and his new position. He was silent still, but this suited me, and I went quietly about my affairs, while Ralf gradually fell into my ways, and we got along tolerably well together. Whatever he thought of my quarters in the cave, and the menial tasks which between us we had to do, he made it clear that he was a page serving a prince. Somehow, through the days that followed, I found myself relieved, bit by bit, of burdensome work which I had begun to take for granted; I had leisure again to study, to replenish my store of medicines, even to make music. It was strange at first, and then in some way comforting, to lie wakeful in the night and hear the boy's untroubled breathing from the other side of the cave. After a while, I found I was sleeping better; as the nightmares receded, strength and calmness came back; and if power still withheld itself, I no longer despaired of its return.

As for Ralf, though I could see that he still fretted against his exile—to which, of course, he could see no clear end—he was never less than courteous, and as time went on seemed to accept his banishment with a better grace, and either lost or hid his unhappiness in a kind of contentment.

So the weeks went by, and the valley fields yellowed towards harvest, and the message came at last from Tintagel. One evening in August, towards dusk, a messenger came spurring up the valley. Ralf was not with me. I had sent him that afternoon across the hill to the hut where the shepherd, Abba, lived all summer. I had been treating Abba's son Ban, who was simple, for a poisoned foot; this was almost healed, but still needed salves.

I went out to meet the messenger. He had dismounted below the cliff, and now clambered up to the flat alp in front of the cave. He was a young man, spruce and lively, and his horse was fresh. I guessed from this that his message was not urgent; he had taken his time, and come at his ease. I saw him take in my ragged robe and threadbare mantle in one swift, summing glance, but he doffed his cap and went on one knee. I wondered if the salute was for the enchanter, or for the King's son.

"My lord Merlin."

"You are welcome," I said. "From Tintagel?"

"Yes, sir. From the Queen." A quick upward glance. "I came privily, without the King's knowledge."

"So I had imagined, or you would have borne her badge. Get up, man. The grass is damp. Have you had supper?"

He looked surprised. It was not thus, I reckoned, that most princes received their messengers. "Why, no, sir, but I bespoke it at the inn."

"Then I won't keep you from it. I've no doubt it will be better than you'd get here. Well then, your business? You've brought a letter from the Queen?"

"No letter, sir, just the message that the Queen desires to see you."

"Now?" I asked sharply. "Is there anything wrong with her, or with the child she bears?"

"Nothing. The doctors and the women say that all is well. But"—he dropped his eyes—"it seems she has that on her mind which makes her want to talk with you. As soon as possible, she said."

"I see." Then, with my voice as carefully neutral as his: "Where is the King?"

"The King plans to leave Tintagel in the second week of September."

"Ah. So any time after that it will be 'possible' for me to see the Queen."

This was rather more frank than he cared for. He flashed me a glance, then looked at the ground again. "The Queen will be pleased to receive you then. She has bidden me make arrangements for you. You will understand that it will not do for you to be received openly in the castle of Tintagel." Then, in a burst of candour: "You must know, my lord, there is no man's hand in Cornwall but will be against you. It would be better if you came disguised."

"As for that," I said, fingering my beard, "you will see that I'm half disguised already. Don't worry, man, I understand; I'll be discreet. But you'll have to tell me more. She gave no reason for this summons?"

"None, my lord."

"And you heard nothing—no gossip from among the women, things like that?"

He shook his head, then, at the look in my face, added quickly: "My lord, she was urgent. She did not say so, but it must concern the child, what else?"

"Then I will come." I thought he looked shocked. As he lowered his eyes, I said, sharply: "Well, what did you expect? I am not the Queen's man. No, nor the King's either, so there's no need to look scared."

"Whose, then?"

"My own, and God's. But you can go back to the Queen and tell her I will come. What arrangements have you made for me?"

He hurried, relieved, on to his own ground. "There is a small inn at a ford of the river Camel, in the valley about five miles from Tintagel. It is kept by a man called Caw. He is a Cornishman, but his wife Maeve was one of the Queen's women, and he will keep his counsel. You can stay there without fear; they will expect you. You may send messages to Tintagel, if you will, by one of Maeve's sons—it would not be wise to go near the castle until the Queen sends for you. Now for the journey. The weather should still be fine in mid-September, and the seas are usually calm enough, so—"

"If you are about to advise me that it is easier to go by sea, you're wasting your breath," I said. "Has no one ever told you that enchanters can't cross water? At least, not with any comfort. I should be seasick did I so much as cross the Severn River in the ferry. No, I go by road."

"But the main road takes you past the barracks at Caerleon. You might be recognized. And then the bridge at Glevum is guarded by King's troops."

"Very well. I'll take the river crossing, but make it a short one." I knew that he was right. To go by the main road through Caerleon and then by the Glevum Bridge would, even without the prospect of discovery by Uther's troops, put several days on my journey. "I'll avoid the military road. There's a good track along the coast through Nidum; I'll go that way, if you can bespeak me a boat at the mouth of the Ely River?"

"Very well, my lord." And so it was arranged. I would cross from the Ely to the mouth of the Uxella in the country of the Dumnonii, and from there I would find my way south-west by the tracks, avoiding the roads where I might fall in with Uther's troops or Cador's men.

"Do you know the way?" he asked me. "For the last part, of course, Ralf can guide you."

"Ralf will not be with me. But I can find it. I've been through that country before, and I have a tongue in my head."

"I can arrange for horses—"

"Better not," I said. "We agreed, did we not, that I would be better disguised? I'll use a disguise that has served me before. I'll be a travelling eye doctor, and a humble fellow like that doesn't expect to post with fresh horses all the way. Have no fear, I shall be safe, and, when the Queen wants me, I shall be there."

He was satisfied, and stayed for a while longer answering my questions and giving me what news there was. The King's brief punitive expedition against the coastal raiders had been successful, and the newcomers had been pushed back behind the agreed boundaries of the Federated West Saxons. For the moment things were quiet in the south. From the north had come rumours of tougher fighting where Anglian raiders, from Germany, had crossed the coast near the Alaunus River in the country of the Votadini. This is the country that we of Dyfed call Manau Guotodin, and it is from here that the great King Cunedda came, invited a century ago by the Emperor Maximus, to drive the Irish from Northern Wales and settle there as allies to the Imperial Eagles. These were, I suppose, the first of the Federates; they drove the Irish out, and afterwards remained in Northern Wales, which they called Gwynedd. A descendant of Cunedda held it still; Maelgon, a stark king and a good warrior, as a man would have to be to keep that country in the wake of the great Magnus Maximus.

Another descendant of Cunedda still held the Votadini country: a young king, Lot, as fierce and as good a fighter as Maelgon; his fortress lay near the coast south of Caer Eidyn, in the center of his kingdom of Lothian. It was he who had faced and beaten off the latest attack of the Angles. He had been given his command by Ambrosius, in the hope that with him the kings of the north—Gwalawg of Elmet, Urien of Gore, the chiefs of Strathclyde, King Coel of Rheged—would form a strong wall in the north and east. But Lot, it was said, was ambitious and quarrelsome; and Strathclyde had sired nine sons already and (while they fought like young bull seals each for his square of territory) was cheerfully siring more. Urien of Gore had married Lot's sister and would stand firm, but was, it was said, too close in Lot's shadow. The strongest of them was still (as in my father's time) Coel of Rheged, who held with a light hand all the smaller chiefs and earls of his kingdom, and brought them together faithfully against the smallest threat to the sovereignty of the High Kingdom.

Now, the Queen's messenger told me, the King of Rheged, with Ector of Galava and Ban of Benoic, had joined with Lot and Urien to clear the north of trouble, and for the time being they had succeeded. On the whole the news was cheering. The harvest had been good everywhere, so hunger would not drive any more Saxons across before winter closed the seaways. We should have peace for a time; enough time for Uther to settle any unrest caused by the quarrel with Cornwall and his new marriage, to ratify such alliances as Ambrosius had made, and to strengthen and extend his system of defenses.

At length the messenger took his leave. I wrote no letters, but sent news of Ralf to his grandmother, and a message of compliance to the Queen, with thanks for the gift of money she had sent me by the messenger's hand to provide for my journey. Then the young man rode off cheerfully down the valley towards the good company and the better supper that awaited him at the inn. It remained now for me to tell Ralf.

This was more difficult even than I had expected. His face lit when I told him about the messenger, and he looked eagerly about for the man, seeming very disappointed when he found that he had already gone. Messages from his grandmother he received almost impatiently, but plied me with questions about the fighting south of Vindocladia, listening with such eagerness to all I could tell him of that and the larger news that it was obvious that his forced inaction in Maridunum fretted him far more than he had shown. When I came to the Queen's summons he showed more animation than I had seen in him since he had come to me.

"How long before we set out?"

"I did not say 'we' would set out. I shall go alone."

"Alone?" You would have thought I had struck him. The blood sprang under the thin skin and he stood staring with his mouth open. Eventually he said, sounding stifled: "You can't mean that. You can't."

"I'm not being arbitrary, believe me. I'd like to take you, but you must see it isn't possible."

"Why not? You know everything here will be perfectly safe; in any case, you've left it before. And you can't travel alone. How would you go on?"

"My dear Ralf. I've done it before."

"Maybe you have, but you can't deny I've served you well since I've been here, so why not take me? You can't just go to Tintagel—back to where things are happening—and leave me here! I warn you"—he took a breath, eyes blazing, all his careful courtesy collapsing in ruins—"I warn you, my lord, if you go without me, I shan't be here when you come back!"

I waited till his gaze fell, then said mildly: "Have some sense, boy. Surely you see why I can't take you? The situation hasn't changed so much since you had to leave Cornwall. You know what would happen if any of Cador's men recognized you, and everyone knows you round about Tintagel. You'd be seen, and the word would go round."

"I know that. Do you still think I'm afraid of Cador? Or of the King?"

"No. But it's foolish to run into danger when one doesn't need to. And the messenger certainly seemed to think there was still danger."

"Then what about you? Won't you be in danger, too?"

"Possibly. I shall have to go disguised, as it is. Why do you think I've been letting my beard grow all this while?"

"I didn't know. I never thought about it. Do you mean you've been expecting the Queen to send for you?"

"I didn't expect this summons, I admit," I said. "But I know that, come Christmas, when the child is born, I must be there."

He stared. "Why?"

I regarded him for a moment. He was standing near the mouth of the cave, against the sunset, just as he had come in from his trip across the hill to the shepherd's hut. He was still clutching the osier basket which had held the salves. It held a small bundle now, wrapped in a clean linen cloth. The shepherd's wife, who lived across in the next valley, sent bread up weekly to her man; some of this Abba regularly sent on to me. I could see the boy's fists clenched bone-white on the handle of the basket. He was tense, as angry and fretting as a fighting dog held back in the slips. There was something more here, I was sure, than home-sickness, or disappointment at missing an adventure.

"Put that basket down, for goodness' sake," I said, "and come in. That's better. Now, sit down. It's time that you and I talked. When I accepted your service, I did not do so because I wanted someone to scour the cooking pots and carry gifts from Abba's wife on baking day. Even if I am content with my life here on Bryn Myrddin, I'm not such a fool as to think it contents you—or would do so for long. We are waiting, Ralf, no more. We have fled from danger, both of us, and healed our hurts, and now there is nothing to do but wait."

"For the Queen's childbed? Why?"

"Because as soon as he is born, the Queen's son will be given to me to care for."

He was silent for a full minute before he said, sounding puzzled: "Does my grandmother know this?"

"I think she suspects that the child's future lies with me. When I last spoke with the King, on that night at Tintagel, he told me he would not acknowledge the child who would be born. I think this is why the Queen has sent for me."

"But . . . not to acknowledge his eldest son? You mean he will send him away? Will the Queen agree? A baby—surely they would never send it to *you*? How could you keep it? And how can you even know it will be a boy?"

"Because I had a vision, Ralf, that night in Tintagel. After you had let us in through the postern gate, while the King was with Ygraine, and Ulfin kept guard outside the chamber, you diced with the porter in the lodge by the postern. Do you remember?"

"How could I ever forget? I thought that night would never end."

I did not tell him that it had not ended yet. I smiled. "I think I felt the same, while I waited alone in the guard-room. It was then that I saw—was shown—for certain why God had required me to do as I had done, shown for sure that my prophecies had been true. I heard a sound on the stairs, and went out of the guard-room onto the landing. I saw Marcia, your grandmother, coming down the steps towards me from the Queen's room, carrying a child. And though it was only March, I felt the chill of midwinter, and then I saw the stairs and the shadows clear through her body, and knew it was a vision. She put the child into my arms and said, 'Take care of him.' She was weeping. Then she vanished, and the child too, and the winter's chill went with her. But this was a true picture, Ralf. At Christmas I shall be there, waiting, and Marcia will hand the Queen's son into my care."

He was silent for a long time. He seemed awed by the vision. But then he said, practically: "And I? Where do I come into this? Is this why my grand-mother told me to stay with you and serve you?"

"Yes. She saw no future for you near the King. So she made sure you would be near his son."

"A baby?" His voice was blank. He sounded horrified, and far from flattered. "You mean that if the King won't acknowledge the child, you'll have to keep it? I don't understand. Oh, I can see why my grandmother concerns herself, and even why you do, but not why she dragged me into it! What sort of future does she think there is in looking after a king's bastard that won't be acknowledged?"

"Not a king's bastard," I said. "A king."

There was silence but for the fluttering of the fire. I had not spoken with power, but with the full certainty of knowledge. He stared, open-mouthed, and shaken.

"Ralf," I said, "you came to me in anger, and you stayed from duty, and you have served me as well and as faithfully as you knew how. You were no part of my vision, and I don't know if your coming here, or the wounds that held you here with me, were part of God's plan; I have had no message from my gods since Gorlois died. But I do know now, after these last weeks, that there is no one I would sooner choose to help me. Not with the kind of service you have given till now: when this winter comes it isn't a servant I shall need; I shall need a fighting man who is loyal, not to me or to the Queen, but to the next High King."

He was pale, and stammering. "I had no idea. I thought . . . I thought . . ."

"That you were suffering a kind of exile? In a way, we both were. I told you it was a waiting time." I looked down at my hands. It was dark now outside the cave; the sun had gone, and dusk drew in. "Nor do I know clearly what lies ahead, except danger and loss and treachery, and in the end some glory."

He sat quiet, without moving, till I roused myself from my thoughts and smiled at him. "So now, perhaps, you will accept that I don't doubt your courage?"

"Yes. I'm sorry I spoke as I did. I didn't understand." He hesitated, chewing his lip, then sat forward, hands on knees. "My lord, you really don't know why the Queen has sent for you now?"

"No."

"But because you know that your vision of the birth was a true one, you know that you will go safely this time to Cornwall, and return?"

"You could say so."

"Then if your magic is always true, might it not be because I go with you to protect you that you make the journey safely?"

I laughed. "I suppose it's a good quality in a fighting man, never to admit defeat. But can't you see, taking you would only be taking two risks instead of one. Because my bones tell me I shall be safe, it doesn't mean that you will."

"If you can be disguised, so can I. If you even say that we must go as beggars and sleep in the ditches . . . whatever the danger . . ." He swallowed, sounding all at once very young. "What is it to you if I run a risk? *You* are to be safe, you told me so. So taking me can't endanger you, and that's all that matters. Won't you let me take my own risks? Please?"

His voice trailed away. Silence again, and the fire flickering. Time was, I thought, not without bitterness, when I would only have had to watch the flames to find the answer there. Would he be safe? Or would I carry the burden of yet another death? But all that the firelight showed me was a youth who needed to find manhood. Uther had denied it to him; I could not let my conscience do the same.

At length I said heavily: "I told you once that men must stand by their own deeds. I suppose that means I have no right to stop you taking your own risks. Very well, you may come. . . . No, don't thank me. You'll dislike me thoroughly enough before we're done. It will be a damned uncomfortable journey, and before we set out, you'll have work to do that won't suit you."

"I'm used to that," he said, and straightened, laughing. He was shining, excited, the gaiety that I remembered back in his face. "But you don't mean you're going to teach me magic?"

"I do not. But I shall have to teach you a little medicine, whether you like it or not. I shall be a travelling eye doctor; it's a good passport anywhere, and one can pay one's way easily without spending the Queen's gold abroad where questions might be asked. So you will have to be my assistant, and that means learning to mix the salves properly."

"Well, if I must, but God help the patients! You know I can't tell one herb from the other."

"Never fear, I wouldn't let you touch them. You can leave me to select the plants. You'll just prepare them."

"And if any of Cador's men show signs of recognizing us, just try some of my salves on them," he said buoyantly. "Talk about magic, it'll be easy. The eye doctor's skilled assistant will simply strike them blind."

6

We came to the inn at Camelford two days before the middle of September.

The Camel valley is winding, with steep sides clothed with trees. For the last part of the way we followed the track along the waterside. The trees were closely crowded, and the path where we rode was so thickly padded with moss and small, dark-green ferns that our horses' hoofs made no sound. Beside us the river wrangled its way down through granite boulders that glittered in the sun. Around and above us the dense hangers of oak and beech were turning yellow, and acorns crunched among the dead leaves where the horses trod. Nuts ripened in the thickets; the willows trailed amber leaves in the tugging shallows; and wherever the bright sun splashed through the boughs it shimmered on the spiders' webs of autumn furred and glittering, sagging deep with dew.

Our journey had been uneventful. Once south of the Severn and beyond hourly danger of recognition, we had ridden at ease, and in pleasant stages. The weather, as so often in September, was warm and bright, but with a crisp feel to the air that made riding a pleasure. Ralf had been in high spirits all the way, in spite of poor clothes, an undistinguished horse (bought with some of the Queen's gold) and the work he had had to do for me making the washes and ointments with which I largely paid our way. We were only questioned once, by a troop of King's men who came on us just short of Hercules Point. Uther kept the old Roman camp there garrisoned as a strongpoint, and by the purest mischance we fell foul of a scouting party which was making its way home by the moorland track we followed. We were taken to the camp and questioned, though it seemed this was merely a matter of form as, after a cursory look at our baggage, my story was accepted. We were sent on our way with our flasks refilled with the ration wine, the richer for a copper coin given me by a man off duty who followed us out of the camp and begged a pot of salve from me.

I found the men's vigilance interesting, and would have liked to know more of the state of affairs in the north, but that would have to wait. To have asked questions here would have attracted attention I did not want. No doubt I would find out what I wished to know from the Queen herself.

"Did you see anyone you knew?" I asked Ralf, as we headed over the moors at a brisk canter away from the gate of the camp.

"None. Did you?"

"I'd met the officer before, a few years ago. His name is Priscus. But he gave no sign of recognizing me."

"I wouldn't have known you myself," said Ralf. "And it isn't just the beard. It's the way you walk, your voice, everything. It's like that night at Tintagel, when you were disguised as the Duke's captain. I'd known him all my life, and I'd have sworn you were he. It's no wonder folks are talking about magic. I thought it was magic myself."

"This is easier," I said. "If you carry a trade or a skill with you men think about that, instead of looking at you too closely."

Indeed, I had troubled very little with disguise. I had bought a new riding cloak, brown, with a hood which could be pulled about my face, and I spoke Celtic with the accent of Brittany. This is a tongue close to the Cornish one, and would be understood where we were going. This, with the beard, and my humble tradesman's bearing, should keep any but my intimates from knowing me. Nothing would part me from the brooch my father had given me, with its royal cipher of the Red Dragon on gold, but I wore it clipped inside the breast of my tunic, and had threatened Ralf with every fate in the Nine Books of Magic if he call me "my lord" even in private.

We reached Camelford towards evening. The inn was a small squat building of daubed stone built where the coast road ran down into the ford. It was at the top of the bank, just clear of flood level. Ralf and I, approaching by the country track along the river, came on it from the rear. It seemed a pleasant place, and clean. Someone had given the stones a wash of red ochre, the colour of the rich earth thereabouts, and fat poultry picked about among the ricks at the edge of a swept yard. A chained dog dozed in the shade of a mulberry tree heavy with fruit. There was a tidy stack of firewood against the byre, and the midden was fully twenty feet from the back door.

As luck would have it, the innkeeper's wife was out at the back with a maidservant, taking in bedding which had been spread over the bushes in the sun. As we approached the dog flew out, barking, at the length of his chain. The woman straightened, shading her eyes against the light, and staring.

She was a young woman, broadly built and lively looking, with a fresh, high colour and prominent light-blue eyes. Her bad teeth and plump figure gave away a rash passion for sweetmeats, and the lively blue eyes spoke even more clearly of other pleasures. They ran now over Ralf, who rode ahead of me, appraised him as likely, but young for it; then, more hopefully, over me, to dismiss me finally as less likely, and probably too poor to pay my shot anyway. Then, as her gaze returned to Ralf, I saw her recognize him. She stiffened, looking quickly back at me. Her mouth fell open, and I thought for an anxious moment that she was going to curtsy, but then she had command of herself. A word sent the maid packing indoors with an armful of bedding, a shrill bidding to the dog drove him back, ears down and growling, into the mulberry shade, then she was greeting us, smiling widely, eyes curious and excited.

"You'll be the eye doctor, likely?"

We drew our horses to a halt in the dust of the yard. "Indeed, mistress. My name is Emrys, and this is my servant Ban."

"We've been expecting you. Your beds is bespoke." Then under her breath as she came close to my horse's shoulder: "You be very welcome, my lord, and Ralf, too. I declare he do look a handspan taller than when I seen him last. Will you be pleased to come in?"

I dismounted and handed the reins to Ralf. "Thank you. It's good to be here; we're both weary. Ralf will look after the horses himself. Now before we go in, Maeve, give me the news from Tintagel. Is all well with the Queen?"

"Yes, indeed, sir, praise be to all the saints and fairies. You need have no worries there, surely."

"And the King? He's still at Tintagel?"

"Aye, my lord, but the word goes that he'll ride out any day now. You'll not have long to bide. You're as safe here as anywhere in Cornwall. We'll have good enough warning of troops moving, and you can hear them on this road a mile off. And never worry about Caw—that's my husband; he's a Duke's man, sure enough, but he'll do nothing to harm my lady, and besides, he always does as I tell him. Leastways, not always. There's some things he don't do near often enough for my liking." This with a burst of cheery laughter. I saw Ralf grinning as he led the horses away, then Maeve, talking loudly about beds and supper-time, and the sore eyes of her youngest which could do with looking at, led me through the back door of the inn.

When I saw her husband later that evening I knew that I need have no fears for his discretion. He was a dry stick of a man, and silent as an oyster. He came in as we were sitting down to supper, stared at Ralf, nodded at me, then went about his business of serving wine without a word spoken. His wife treated him—and all comers—with the same rough, frank kindliness, and saw to it without fuss that we were well served and comfortably housed. It was as good a house of its kind as I have ever been in, and the food was excellent.

Understandably, the inn was always busy, but there was little danger of our being recognized. My character as a travelling healer was not only my pass to people's incurious acceptance; it gave Ralf and me the excuse to go abroad in the countryside. Each day early we would take food and wine with us, and make our way up by one of the deep, densely wooded glens that fed the Camel valley, to the windy upland that lay between Camelford and the sea. Ralf knew all the ways. We would separate, more often than not, and each choose some hidden point of vantage from which he could watch the two roads which Uther and his men might take out of Tintagel. He might turn north-east along the coast for Dimilioc and the camp near Hercules Point, or—if he was making straight for Winchester or the trouble centers along the Saxon Shore—he would follow the valley tracks through Camelford and from there climb south-east to the military road which ran along the spine of Dumnonia. Here on the wind-swept heights the forest thins, and there are great tracts of broken moorland treacherous with bog and watched over by strange stony hills. The old Roman road, crumbling fast in that wild country, but still serviceable, runs straight through Isca, into the kinder lands behind Ambrosius' Wall. It was my guess that this latter was the way that Uther would take, and I wanted to see who rode with him. Ralf and I gave it out that I was searching for plants for my medicines, and indeed I came back each evening to my meeting-place with him with a pouch full of roots and berries which did not grow at home, and which I was glad to have. Luckily the weather continued fine, and no one wondered to see us ride abroad. They were too glad to have a doctor staying there who, each evening, would treat any who came to him, and ask no more than they could afford to pay.

So the days went by, serene and still, while we waited for the King to move, and the Queen to send word.

It was a week before he rode out. He went the way I had expected, and I was there watching.

There is a place where the track from Tintagel to Camelford runs straight for some quarter of a mile along the foot of a steeply wooded bank. For the most part the wood is too steep and thickly grown to penetrate, but there were places at the wood's edge open to the sun, stony banks deep in ferns and drifting thistledown, where brambles and bracken grew in thickets over the rocks.

The blackthorn bushes were high, and glinting with fruit. Some of the little sloe-plums were still greenish, but most were ready; black bloomed over pale blue with ripeness. There is an extract one can make of the fruit which is sovereign for a flux of the bowels: one of Maeve's children had been suffering in this way, and I had promised a draught that night. It would need no more than a handful, but the fruit was ripe to perfection, and so tempting that I went on gathering. If the berries are crushed and added in a certain way to juniper-wine they make a good drink, rich, astringent and powerful. I had told Maeve of it, and she wanted to try it.

My bag was almost full when I heard, like a soft thunder in the distance, horses coming steadily along the track below me. I withdrew quickly into the edge of the wood, and watched from hiding. Soon the head of the column came in sight; then the long train of dust, filled with the beat of trotting hoofs, the clash of mail, the coloured glint of pennants, rolled past along the foot of the slope. A thousand, perhaps more. I stood stone-still in the shadow of the trees, and watched them go by.

A horse's length to the front the King rode, and behind him, on his left hand, his standard-bearer carried the Red Dragon. Other colours showed through the dust, but there was no wind to move the banners, and though I strained my eyes the length of the column, I could not swear to most that I saw. Nor did I glimpse the one I was watching for, though it might well have been there. I waited till the last horseman disappeared at a smart trot round a bend in the road, then I made my way to the place where I had arranged to meet Ralf.

He met me halfway, panting. "Did you see them?"

"Yes. Where were you? I sent you to watch the other road."

"I was watching. There was nothing stirring there, nothing at all. I was on my way back here when I heard them, so I ran. I almost missed them—only saw the tail end. It was the King, wasn't it?"

"It was. Ralf, could you pick out the devices? Did you see any that you knew?"

"I saw Brychan, and Cynfelin, but no others from Dyfnaint that I recognized. The men from Garlot were there, and Cernyw, too, I think, and others I thought I knew, but there was too much dust to make sure. They were round that bend before I could get a good sight of them."

"Was Cador there?"

"My lord, I'm sorry, I didn't see."

"No matter. If the others were there from Cornwall, you may be sure he would be. No doubt they'll know at the inn. And had you forgotten that you were not to call me 'my lord,' even when we were alone?"

"I'm sorry . . . Emrys." It was a measure of our new, easier relationship that he should add, with a suspicious meekness: "And had you forgotten that my name is Ban?" Then, laughing as he dodged my cuff at his head: "Do you have to call me after the half-wit?"

"It's the first name that came into my head. It's a king's name too, the King of Benoic, so you can take your choice which was your sponsor."

"Benoic? Where's that?"

"In the north. Come now, we'll get back to the inn. I doubt if the Queen will send before tomorrow, but I've a draught to make tonight, and it's a decoction that takes time. Here, carry these."

I was right; the messenger came next morning. Ralf had gone out down the road to watch for him, and the two of them came back together, with the news that I was to ride to Tintagel immediately for my audience with the Queen.

I had not confessed it to Ralf, nor even hardly admitted it to myself, but I was apprehensive about the coming interview with Ygraine. On that night at Tintagel when the child was conceived I had been certain, in every way a seer can be certain, that the boy who was to be born would be given to me to foster, and that I should be the guardian of a great King. Uther himself, in his bitterness and anger over Gorlois' death, had sworn to reject the "bastard" he had begotten, and from Marcia's letter I knew he was still of the same mind. But in the six long months since that March night I had had no direct message from Ygraine, and no means of knowing whether she would obey her husband, or whether as the time drew near she would find it impossible to face separation from her child. I had gone over in my mind a hundred times all the arguments I might bring to bear, remembering half incredulously the sureness with which I had spoken to her before, and to the King. Indeed my god had been with me then. And in truth, and how bitterly, was he gone from me now. There were even times when, lying wakeful in the night, I saw my sure visions in the past as chances, illusions, dreams fed by desire. I remembered the King's bitter words to me. *"I see now what your magic is, this 'power' you talk of. It is nothing but human trickery, an attempt at statecraft which my brother taught you to like and to play for, and to believe was your mystery. You use even God to gain your ends. 'It is God who tells me to do these things, it is God who exacts the price, it is God who sees that others should pay . . .' For what, Merlin? For your ambition? And who is it pays this debt to God for carrying out your plans? Not you. The men who play your game for you, and pay the price. But you pay nothing."* When I listened to such words as these, heard clearly in the nights when nothing else spoke to me, I wondered if I had read my vision of the future aright, or if everything I had done and dreamed of had been a mockery. Then, thinking of those who had paid with death for my dream, I would wonder if that death had not been kinder than this desert of self-doubt where I lay fixed, waiting in vain for even the smallest of my gods to speak to me. Oh, yes, I paid. Every night of those nine long months I paid.

But now it was day, and I would soon find out what the Queen wanted with me. I remember how restlessly I fidgeted around while Ralf saddled my horse and made ready. Maeve was with the maids in the kitchen, washing the sloes for the wine-making. A pan of them was on the stove, coming to the simmer. It seemed a strange memory to take with me on my visit to the Queen, the smell of sloe wine. Suddenly I found the pungent sweetness intolerable, and made, choking, for the air outside. But then one of the girls came running to ask something about the mixing, and in answering her I forgot my sickness, and then all at once Ralf was at my elbow to summon me, and the three of us—Ralf, the messenger and I—were heading for Tintagel at a hand-gallop through the soft, blowing September noon.

7

It was only a few months since I had last seen Ygraine, but she seemed very much changed. At first I thought this was only the pregnancy; her once-slim body was greatly swollen and, though her face was full of the bloom of health, she had that pinched and shadowy look that women get around the eyes and mouth. But the change was deeper than this; it was in the expression of her eyes, in her gestures, the way she sat. Where before she had seemed young and burning, a wild bird beating her wings against the wires of the cage, now she seemed to brood, wings clipped, gravid, a creature of the ground.

She received me in her own chamber, a long room above the curtain wall, with a deep circular recess where the turret stood at the north-west corner. There were windows in the long wall facing south-west, and through these the sunlight fell freely, but the Queen was sitting by one of the narrow turret windows, through which came the breeze of the soft September afternoon, and the eternal noise of the sea on the rocks below. So much was still here, then, of the Ygraine I remembered. It was like her, I thought, to choose the wind and the sea sounds, rather than the sunlight. But even here, in spite of the light and air, one got the feeling of a cage: this was the room in which the young wife of Gorlois the old Duke had passed those pent years before the fateful trip to London where she had met the King. Now, after that brief flight, she was penned again, by her love for the King, and by the weight of his child. I never loved a woman, except one, but I have pitied them. Now, looking at the Queen, young, beautiful, and with her heart's desire, I pitied her even as I feared her for what she might say to me.

She was alone. I had been led by a chamberlain through the outer room where the women span and weaved and gossiped. Bright eyes looked at me in momentary curiosity, and the chattering was stilled, only to begin again as soon as I had passed. There was no recognition in their faces, only perhaps here and there some disappointment at the sight of so ordinary and humble a fellow. No diversion here. To them I was a messenger, to be received by the Queen in the King's absence; that was all.

The chamberlain rapped on the door of the inner chamber and then withdrew. Marcia, Ralf's grandmother, opened the door. She was a grey-haired woman with Ralf's eyes in a lined and anxious face, but in spite of her age she bore herself as straight as a girl. Though she was expecting me, I saw her eyes rest on me for a moment without recognition, then with a flicker of surprise. Even Ygraine looked startled for a moment, then she smiled and held out her hand.

"Prince Merlin. Welcome." Marcia curtsied to the air somewhere between me and the Queen, and withdrew. I went forward to kneel and kiss the Queen's hand.

"Madam."

She raised me kindly. "It was good of you to come so quickly for such a strange summons. I hope the journey was easy?"

"Very easy. We are well lodged with Maeve and Caw, and so far no one has recognized me, or even Ralf. Your secret is safe."

"I must thank you for taking so much care of it. I promise you I'd not have known you until you spoke."

I fingered my chin, smiling. "As you see, I've been preparing for some time."

"No magic this time?"

"As much as there was before," I said.

She looked at me straightly then, the beautiful dark-blue eyes meeting mine in the way I remembered, and I saw that this was still the old Ygraine, direct as a man, and with the same high pride. The heavy stillness was just an overlay, the milky calm that seems to come on women in pregnancy. Beneath the stillness, the placidity, was the old fire. She spread her hands out. "Looking at me now, do you still tell me that when you spoke to me that night in London, and promised me the King's love, there was no magic there?"

"Not in the ruse that brought the King to you, madam. In what happened after, perhaps."

" 'Perhaps'?" There was a quick lift to her voice that warned me. Ygraine might be a Queen, with mettle as high as a man's, but she was a woman nearing her seventh month. My fears were my own, and must stay my own. I hesitated, searching for words, but she went on quickly, burningly, as if to convince herself across my silence: "When you first spoke with me and told me you could bring the King to me, there was magic there, I know there was. I felt it, and I saw it in your face. You told me that your power came from God, and that in obeying you I was God's creature, even as you were. You said that because of the magic that would bring Uther to me, the kingdom should have peace. You spoke of crowns and altars. . . . And now, see, I am Queen, with God's blessing, and I am heavy with the King's child. Dare you tell me now that you deceived me?"

"I did not deceive you, madam. That was a time full of visions, and a passion of dreams and desires. We are quit of those now, and we are sober, and it is daylight. But magic is here, growing in you, and this time it is fact, not vision. He will be born at Christmas, they tell me."

" 'He? You sound very sure."

"I am sure."

I saw her press her lips together as if at a sudden spasm of pain, then she looked away from me, down at her hands which lay folded across her belly. When she spoke, she spoke calmly, straight to her hands, or to what they covered. "Marcia told me of the messages she sent to you in the summer. But you must have known, without her telling you, the way my lord the King thinks of this matter."

I waited, but she seemed to expect an answer. "He told me himself," I said. "If he's still of the same mind now as he was then, he won't acknowledge the child as his heir."

"He is still of the same mind." Her eyes came swiftly up to mine again. "Don't misunderstand me, he has not the faintest doubt of me, nor ever had. He knows that I was his from the first moment I saw him, and that from that moment, on one excuse or another, I never lay with the Duke. No, he does not doubt me; he knows the child is his. And for all his high speech"—there was the glimmer of a smile, and suddenly her voice was indulgent, the voice of a woman speaking of her child or of a loved husband—"and for all his rough denials, he knows your power and fears it. You told him a child would come out of that night, and he would trust your word, even if he could not trust mine. But none of this alters the way he feels about it. He blames himself—and you, and even the child—for the Duke's death."

"I know."

"If he had waited, he says, Gorlois would still have died that night, and I would have been Queen, and the child conceived in wedlock, so that no one could question his parentage or call him bastard."

"And you, Ygraine?"

She was silent for a long time. She turned that lovely head of hers and gazed out of the window, where the sea birds swung and tilted, crying, on the wind. I saw, I am not sure how, that her calm was that of a soldier who has won one battle, and rests before the next. I felt my nerves tighten. I did not hold Ygraine lightly, should the battle be with me.

She said, very quietly: "What the King says may well be true. I don't know. But what's done is done, and it is the child who must concern me now. This is why I sent for you." A pause. I waited. She faced me again. "Prince Merlin, I fear for the child."

"At the King's hands?" I asked.

This was too straight, even for Ygraine. Her eyes were cold, and her voice. "This is insolence, and folly, too. You forget yourself, my lord."

"I?" I spoke as coldly. "It is you who forget, madam. If my mother had been wed to Ambrosius when he begot me, Uther would not now be King, nor would I have helped him to your bed to beget the child you carry. There should be no talk of insolence or folly from you to me. I know, who better, what chance there is in Britain for a prince conceived out of wedlock and unacknowledged by his sire."

She had flushed as red as she was pale before. Her eyes dropped from mine, their anger dying. She spoke simply, like a girl. "You are right, I had forgotten. I ask your pardon. I'd forgotten, too, what it was like to talk freely. There is no one here besides Marcia and my lord, and I cannot talk to Uther about the child."

I had been standing all this while; now I turned aside to bring up a chair and set it near her in the turret embrasure. I sat down. Things had changed between us, suddenly, as when a wind changes. I knew then that the battle was not with me, but with herself, her own woman's weakness. She was watching me now as a woman in pain watches her doctor. I said gently: "Well, I am here. And I am listening. What did you send for me to tell me?"

She drew in her breath. When she spoke her voice was calm, but no more than a whisper. "That if this child is a boy, the King will not allow me to rear him. If it's a girl I may keep her, but a boy so begotten cannot be acknowledged as a prince and legitimate heir, so he must not remain here, even as a bastard." Visibly, she steadied herself. "I told you, Uther does not doubt me. But because of what happened that night, my husband's death, and all the talk of magic, he swears that men may still believe that the Duke and not himself begot this child. There will be other sons, he says, whose begetting no man will question, and among them he will find the heir to the High Kingdom."

"Ygraine," I said, "I know what a heavy thing it is—however it happens—for a woman to lose her child. Perhaps there is no heavier grief. But I think the King is right. The boy should not remain here to be reared as a bastard in times so wild and uncertain. If there should be other heirs, declared and acknowledged by the King, they might count him a danger to themselves, and certainly they would be a danger for him. I know what I'm talking about; this is what happened in my own childhood. And I, as a royal bastard, found fortune as this prince may never find it; I had my father's protection."

A pause. She nodded without speaking, her eyes once again on the hands that lay in her lap.

"And if the child is to be sent away," I said, "it's better that he should be taken straight from the birth chamber, before you have had time even to hold him. Believe me"—I spoke quickly, though she had not moved—"this is true. I'm speaking now as a doctor."

She moistened her lips. "Marcia says the same."

I waited a moment, but she said no more. I started to speak, found my voice come hoarsely, and cleared my throat. In spite of myself, my hands tightened on the arms of my chair. But my voice was calm and steady as I came to the core of the interview. "Has the King told you where the child is to be fostered?"

"No. I told you it wasn't easy to talk to him about it. But when he last spoke of it he said he would take counsel; and he spoke of Brittany."

"Brittany?" For all my care, the word came out with a cutting edge. I fought to recover my calm. My hands had clenched on the chair, and I relaxed them and held them still. So, my doubts were real. Oddly enough, the knowledge hardened me. If I must fight the King as well as Ygraine—yes, and my Delphic gods as well—then I would do so. As long as I could see the ground to fight from . . . "So Uther will send him to King Budec?"

"It seems so." She seemed to have noticed nothing strange in my manner. "He sent a messenger a month ago. That was just before I sent to ask you to come. Budec is the obvious choice, after all."

This was true. King Budec of Less Britain was a cousin of the King's. It was he who, some thirty years ago, had taken my father and the young Uther under his protection when the usurper Vortigern murdered their elder brother King Constans, and in his capital of Kerrec they had assembled and trained the army which had won the High Kingdom back from Vortigern. But I shook my head. "Too obvious. If anyone should look for the boy to harm him, they'll guess where to go. Budec can't protect him all the time. Besides—"

"Budec cannot care for my child as he should be cared for!" The words came forcibly, stopping me short, but the interruption was not uncivil. It came almost like a cry. It was plain that she had not heard a word I had said. She was fighting herself, choosing words. "He is old, and besides, Brittany is a long way off, and less secure even than this Saxon-ridden land. Prince Merlin, I—Marcia and I—we think that you—" The hands suddenly twisted together in her lap. Her voice changed. "There is no one else we can trust. And Uther—whatever Uther says, he knows that his kingdom, or any part of it, would be safe in your hands. You are Ambrosius' son, and the child's closest kinsman. Everyone knows your power, and fears it—the child would be safe with you to protect him. It's you who must take him, Merlin!" She was begging me now. "Take him safe, somewhere away from this cruel coast, and rear him for me. Teach him as you were taught, and rear him as a King's son should be reared, and then when he is grown, bring him back and let him take his place as you did, at the next King's side."

She faltered. I must have been staring at her like a fool. She fell quiet, twisting her hands. There was a long silence, filled with the scent of the salt wind and the crying of the gulls. I had not been aware of rising, but I found myself standing at the window with my back to the Queen, staring out at the sky. Below the turret wall the gulls wheeled and mewed in the wind, and far below, at the foot of the black cliff, the sea dashed and whitened. But I saw and heard nothing. My hands were pressed down hard on the stone of the sill, and when at length I lifted them and straightened they showed a mottled bar of bloodless flesh where the stone had bitten in. I began to chafe them, only now feeling the small hurt as I turned back to meet the Queen's eyes. She too had hold of herself again, but I saw strain in her face, and a hand plucked at her gown.

I said flatly: "Do you think you can persuade the King to give him to me?"

"No. I don't think so. I don't know." She swallowed. "Of course I can talk to him, but—"

"Then why send for me to ask me this, if you have no power to sway the King?"

She was white, and her lips worked together, but she kept her head up and faced me. "I thought that if you agreed, my lord, you could—you would—"

"I can do nothing with Uther now. You should know that." Then, in sudden, bitter comprehension. "Or did you send for me as you did last time, hoping for magic to order, as if I were an old spell-wife, or a country druid? I would have thought, madam—" I stopped. I had seen the flinching in her eyes, and the drawn pallor round her mouth, and I remembered what she carried in her. My anger died. I turned up a hand, speaking gently: "Very well. If it can be done, Ygraine, I will do it, even if I have to talk to Uther myself to remind him of his promise."

"His promise? What did he promise you, and when?"

"When he first sent for me, and told me of his love for you, he swore to obey me in anything, if only he could have his way." I smiled at her. "It was meant as a bribe rather than a promise, but no matter, we'll hold it to him as a royal oath."

She began to thank me, but I stopped her. "No, no, keep your thanks. I may not succeed with the King; you know how little he loves me. You were wise to send secretly, and you'll be wiser not to let him know we talked of this together."

"He shan't know from me."

I nodded. "Now, for the child's sake and your own, you must put your fears aside. Leave this to me. Even if we can't move the King, I promise you that wherever the child is fostered, I shall make it my business to watch over him. He will be kept safely, and reared as a King's son should be reared. Will that content you?"

"If it has to, yes."

She drew a long breath then and moved at last, rising from her chair and, still gracefully in spite of her bulk, pacing down the long room to one of the far windows. I made no move to follow her. She stood there for a while with her back to me, in silence. When at length she turned, she was smiling. She lifted a hand to beckon me and I went to her.

"Will you tell me one thing, Merlin?"

"If I can."

"That night when we spoke in London, before you brought the King to me here. You talked of a crown, and a sword standing in an altar like a cross. I have wondered so much about it, thinking . . . Tell me now, truly. Was it my crown you saw? Or did you mean that this child—this boy who has cost so much—that he will be King?"

I should have said to her: "Ygraine, I do not know. If my vision was true; if I was a true prophet, then he will be King. But the Sight has left me, and nothing speaks to me in the night or in the fire, and I am barren. I can only do as you do, and take the time on trust. But there is no going back. God will not waste all the deaths."

But she was watching me with the eyes of a woman in pain, so I said to her: "He will be King."

She bent her head and stood silent for a few moments, watching the sunlight on the floor, not as if thinking, but as if listening to what stirred within her. Then she looked up at me again.

"And the sword in the altar?"

I shook my head. "Madam, I don't know. It has not come yet. If I am to know, I will be shown."

She put out a hand. "One more thing . . ." From something in her voice, I knew that this mattered most to her. Not knowing what was coming, I braced myself to lie. She said: "If I must lose this child . . . Shall I have others, Merlin?"

"That is three things you have asked me, Ygraine."

"You won't answer?"

I had spoken only to gain time, but at the flash of fear and doubt in her eyes I was glad to tell her the truth. "I would answer you, madam, but I do not know."

"How is that?" she asked sharply.

I lifted my shoulders. "That again I cannot answer. Further than this boy you carry, I have not seen. But it seems probable, since he is to be King, that you will have no other sons. Girls, maybe, to bring you comfort."

"I shall pray for it," she said simply, and led the way back to the embrasure. She gestured me to sit. "Will you not take a cup of wine with me now, before you leave? I've received you poorly, I'm afraid, after asking such a journey of you, but I was in torment until I had talked with you. Won't you sit down with me now for a little while, and tell me what the news is with you?"

So I stayed a short while longer and, after I had given her my meager news, I asked where Uther was bound with his troops. She told me that he was heading, not for his capital at Winchester as I had supposed, but northwards to Viroconium, where he had called a council of leaders and petty kings from the north and north-east. Viroconium is the old Roman town which lies on the border of Wales, with the mountains of Gwynedd between it and the threat of the Irish Shore. It was still at this time a market center, and the roads were well maintained. Once out of the Dumnonian Peninsula, Uther could make good speed north by the Glevum Bridge. He might even, if the weather stayed fair and the country quiet, be back for the Queen's lying-in. For the moment, Ygraine told me, the Saxon Shore was quiet; after Uther's victory at Vindocladia the invaders had retired on the hospitality of the federated tribes. There was no clear news from the north, but the King (she told me) feared some kind of concerted action there in the spring between the Picts of Strathclyde and the invading Angles: the meeting of the Kings at Viroconium had been called in an attempt to thrash out some kind of united plan of defense.

"And Duke Cador?" I asked her. "Does he stay here in Cornwall, or go on to Vindocladia to watch the Saxon Shore?"

Her answer surprised me. "He is going north with the King, to the council."

"Is he indeed? Then I'd better guard myself." At her quick look I nodded. "Yes, I shall go straight to the King. Time grows short, and it's luck for me that he's travelling north. He's bound to take his troops by the Glevum Bridge, so Ralf and I can cross by the ferry and get there before him. If I intercept him north of the Severn, there's nothing to show him that I ever left Wales."

Soon after that I took my leave. When I left her she was standing by the window again. Her head was held high, and the breeze was ruffling her dark hair. I knew then that when the time came the child would not be taken from a weeping and regretful woman, but from a Queen, who was content to let him go to his destiny.

Not so with Marcia. She was waiting for me in the anteroom, bursting with questions, regrets, and anger against the King which she barely smothered into discretion. I reassured her as best I could, swore several times on every god in every shrine and hollow hill in Britain that I would do my utmost to get possession of the child and keep him safe, but when she started to ask me for spells for protection in childbed, and to talk of wet-nurses, I left her talking, and made for the door.

Forgetting herself in her agitation, she followed me and grabbed my sleeve. "And did I tell you? The King says she must have his own physician, a man he can trust to put the right stories about afterwards, and say nothing about where the poor mite goes for fostering. As if it wasn't more important that my lady should be properly looked after! Give any doctor enough gold, and he'd swear his own mother's life away, everybody knows that."

"Certainly," I said gravely. "But I know Gandar well, and there's no one better. The Queen will be in good hands."

"But an army doctor! What can he know about childbirth?"

I laughed. "He served with my father's army in Brittany for a long time. Where there are fighting men, there are also their women. My father had a standing army in Brittany of fifteen thousand men, encamped. Believe me, Gandar has had plenty of experience."

With that she had to be content. She was talking again about wet-nurses when I left her.

She came to the inn that night, cloaked and hooded, and riding straight as a man. Maeve led her to the room her family shared, drove out everyone—including Caw—who was still awake, then took Ralf to talk to his grandmother. I was in bed before she left.

Next morning Ralf and I set out for Bryn Myrddin, with a flask or two of sloe wine to cheer us on our way. To my surprise, Ralf seemed every bit as cheerful as he had been on the way south. I wondered if, after the brief spell back in the scene of his childhood, service with me had begun to look like freedom. He had heard all the news from his grandmother; he told it me as we rode; most of it was what I had learned already from the Queen, with some court gossip added which was entertaining but hardly informative, except for the talk which was inevitably going round about Uther's rejection of the child.

Ralf, to my secret amusement, seemed as anxious now as Marcia for me to get custody of the baby.

"If the King refuses, what will you do?"

"Go to Brittany to talk to King Budec."

"Do you think he'll let you stay with the prince?"

"Budec is my kinsman too, remember."

"Well, but would he risk offending King Uther? Would he keep it secret from him?"

"That I can't tell you," I said. "If it had been Hoel, now—Budec's son—that would be different. He and Uther always fought like dogs after the same bitch."

I did not add that the description was in fact more accurate than was decent. Ralf merely nodded, chewing (we had stopped on a sunny hillside to eat), and reached for a flask. "Have some of this?" He was offering me the sloe wine.

"God of green grapes, boy, no! It won't be ready to drink for a year. Wait till next harvest's ripe, and open it then."

But he insisted, and unstoppered the flask. It certainly smelled odd and, he admitted, tasted worse. When I suggested, not unkindly, that Maeve had probably made a mistake and given him the medicine for the flux, he spat the mouthful out on the grass, then asked me a little stiffly what I was laughing at.

"Not at you. Here, let me taste the stuff. . . . Well, there's nothing in it that there shouldn't be; but I must have been thinking of something else when they asked me about the mixing. No, I was laughing at myself. All these months—these years, even—hammering at heaven's doors to get what? A baby and a wet-nurse. If you insist on staying with me, Ralf, the next few years will certainly bring new experiences for both of us."

He merely nodded; he was busy pursuing present anxieties.

"If we have to go to Brittany, you mean we might have to stay disguised like this? For *years?*" He flicked with a contemptuous finger at the coarse stuff of his cloak.

"That will depend. Not quite like this, I hope. Hold step till you reach your bridges, Ralf."

His face showed me that this was not how enchanters were expected to talk. They built their own bridges, or flew across without them. "Depend on the King, you mean? Must you seek him out? My grandmother says, if it's put about that the baby's stillborn, it could be handed to you secretly, and the King never know."

"You forget. Men must know if a prince is born. How else, when Uther dies, can they be brought to accept him?"

"Then what are you going to do, my lord?"

I shook my head, not answering. He took my silence for refusal to tell him, and accepted it with no more questions. For my part, I had perforce to take my own advice about crossing bridges; I was waiting to see a way over. With the Queen won, the harder half of the game was played; now I must plan how best to deal with the King—whether to seek his consent openly, or go first to Budec. But as we sat finishing our meal I was not thinking overmuch about Brittany, or the King, or even the child; I was content to rest in the sun and let the time go over. What had just happened at Tintagel had happened without my contriving. Something was moving; there was a kind of breathing brightness in the air, the wind of God brushing by, invisible in sunlight. Even for men who cannot see or hear them, the gods are still there, and I was not less than a man. I had not the arrogance—or the hardihood—to test my power again, but I put on hope, as a naked man welcomes rags in a winter storm.

8

The weather held, so we went easily, taking care not to tread too closely on the heels of Uther's force; if we were caught west of the Uxella marshes—or indeed south of the Severn at all—it would be only too obvious where we had been. Uther usually moved fast, and there was nothing to delay him here in settled country, so we followed cautiously, waiting until his army should be clear of the southern end of the Severn ferry. If we were lucky with the ferry and, once we were across the Severn, made good speed northwards, we should be able (having apparently just come innocently for the purpose from Maridunum) to fall in with the troops on their way up the Welsh border, and try to have speech with the King.

On the way south we had avoided the main road, but had used the pack tracks which run near the coast, winding in and out of the valleys. Now, since we dared not fall too far behind Uther, we kept as closely as we dared to the straight route along the ridges, but avoiding the paved road where the posting stations might be left guarded in the army's wake.

We were even more careful than we had been formerly. After we had left the shelter of Maeve's roof we sought out no more inns. Indeed, the ways we went boasted of no inns even had we looked for them; we lodged where we could—in wood-cutters' cabins, sheep shelters, even once or twice in the lee of a stack of bracken cut for bedding—and blessed the mild weather. It was wild country through which we went. There are high ridged stretches of moorland, where heather grows among the granite tors, and the land is good to feed nothing except the sheep and the wild deer; but just below the rocky spine of the land the forest begins. On the uplands the trees grow sparsely, raked by the wind, already in early autumn half scoured of leaves. But lower, in every dip and valley, the forest is dense, of trees crowded and hugely grown, impassable with undergrowth as toughly woven as a fisherman's net. Here and there, unnoticed until you stumble across them, are crags and bouldered screes of rock thickly clothed with thorn and creeper, invisible and deadly as a wolf trap. Even more dangerous are the stretches of bog, some black and slimy, some innocent and green as a meadow, where a man on horseback can sink from sight as easily and almost as quickly as a spoon sinking into a bowl of gruel. There are secret ways through these places, known to the beasts and the forest dwellers, but mostly men shun them. At night the soft ground flickers with marshlights and strange dancing flames which, men say, are the souls of the wandering dead.

Ralf had known the ways in his own country, but once we struck the low-lying marshy forests through which the Uxella and its tributaries flow towards the Severn we had to go more cautiously, relying on information from the people of the forest, charcoal-burners and woodmen, and once or twice a solitary hermit or holy man who offered us a night's shelter in some cave or woodland shrine.

Ralf seemed to enjoy the rough travel and rougher lodging, and even the danger that seemed to lie about us in forest and track, and the threat of the army so few miles ahead. Both of us grew daily more unkempt and more like the roles we had assumed. It might be said that our disguise was more necessary here even than in Tintagel; woe betide the King's messenger or merchant who rides off the guarded road in these parts, but the poor are received kindly, vagrants or holy men with nothing to steal, and Ralf and I, as poor travelling healers, met welcome everywhere. There was nowhere we could not buy food and shelter with a copper penny and a pot of medicine. The marsh folk always need medicine, living as they do at the edge of the fetid bogland, with agues and swollen joints and the fear of fever. They build their huts right at the borders of the scummed pools, just clear of the deep black mud at the edge, or even set them on stilts right over the stagnant water. The huts crack and rot and fall to pieces every year, and have to be patched each spring, but in spring and autumn the flocks of travelling birds fly down to drink, in summer the waters are full of fish and the forest of game, and in winter the folk break the ice and lie in wait for the deer to come and drink. And always the place is loud with frogs; I have eaten these many times in Brittany, and it is true that they make a good meal. So the folk of the marshes cling to their stinking cabins, and eat well and drink the standing water, and die of the fever and the flux; nor do they fear the walking fires which haunt the marsh at night, for these are the souls of men they knew.

We were still twelve miles short of the ferry, and it was growing dusk, when the first hint of trouble came. The oak forests had given way to a lighter woodland of birch and alder, the trees crowding so closely to the sides of the track that we had to lie low on the horses' necks to avoid the whipping branches. Though there had been no rain the ground was very soft, and now and again our horses' hoofs splashed deep in the black mire. Soon, somewhere near us, I smelled the marsh, and before long through the thinning trees we could see the dull glimmer of the bog pools reflecting the last light from the sky. My horse stumbled, floundering, and Ralf, who was riding ahead of me, checked and put a quick hand to my rein. Then he pointed ahead.

Ahead of us, a different light pricked the dusk: the steady, dull yellow of candle or rushlight. The hut of a marsh dweller. We rode towards it.

The dwelling was not set over the water, but the ground was very wet, and was no doubt flooded in bad weather, for the hut was raised on piles, and approached by a narrow causeway of logs sawn short and jammed together across a ten-foot moat of mud.

A dog barked. I could see a man, a shadow against the dully lit interior of the hut, peering out at us. I hailed him. The marsh dwellers speak a tongue of their own, but they understand the Celtic of the Dumnonii.

"My name is Emrys. I'm a travelling doctor, and this is my servant. We're making for the ferry at Uxella. We came by the forest because the King's army is on the road. We're looking for shelter, and can pay for it."

If there was one thing the poor folk of these parts understood, it was the need for a man to keep out of the way of troops on the march. In a few moments a bargain was struck, the dog was hauled back into the hut and tied up, and I was picking my way gingerly across the slippery logs, leaving Ralf to tend the horses and tether them on the driest piece of ground he could find.

Our host's name was Nidd; he was a short, agile-looking fellow with black hair and a black bristle of beard. His shoulders and arms looked immensely strong, but he limped badly from a leg which had been broken, then set by guesswork and left to knit crooked. His wife, who was probably little more than thirty, was white-haired and bent double on herself with rheumatism; she looked and moved like an old woman, and her face was drawn into tight lines round a toothless mouth. The hut was cramped and foul-smelling, and I would rather have slept in the open, but the evening had turned chilly, and neither Ralf nor I wished to spend a night out in the sodden forest. So when we had had our fill of black bread and broth we accepted the space of floor offered us, and prepared to lie down wrapped in our cloaks, and take what rest we could. I had mixed a potion for the woman, and she was already asleep, huddled against the other wall under a pile of skins, but Nidd made no move to join her. He went instead to the doorway, peering again into the night, as if expecting someone. Ralf's eyes met mine, and his brows lifted; his hand moved towards his dagger. I shook my head. I had heard the light, quick footsteps on the causeway. The dog made no sound, but his tail beat the floor. The curtain of rough-tanned deerhide was pushed aside from the doorway, and a boy came running in, his mouth one huge grin in a filthy face. He stopped short when he saw Ralf and me, but his father said something in patois and the boy, still eyeing us curiously, dumped the bundle of faggots he carried on the table and undid the thong that held it together. Then, with a swift wary look at me, he pulled from the middle of the faggots a dead fowl, a few strips of salted pork, a bundle which he shook out to reveal a pair of good leather trews, and a well-sharpened knife of the kind issued to the soldiers of the King's armies.

I approached the table, holding out my hand. The man stood watchful, but made no move, and after a moment the boy dropped the knife into my palm. I weighed it in my hand, considering. Then I laughed and dropped it point down, to the table. It stuck there beside the fowl, quivering.

"You've had good hunting tonight, haven't you? That's easier than waiting for the wild duck to flight in at dawn. So, the King's army lies nearby? How near?"

The boy merely stared, too shy to answer, but with the help of his father I got the information bit by bit.

It was not reassuring. The army had made camp barely five miles away. The boy had lurked in a tree at the forest's edge, watching his chance to steal food, and had overheard scraps of talk among the men who had gone in among the trees to relieve themselves. It seemed, if the boy had rightly understood what he had heard, that though the main body of the army would no doubt head on its way in the morning, a troop was to be detached and sent directly to Caerleon, with a message for the commander there. They would obviously go by the quickest way, the river crossing. They would certainly commandeer whatever boats were available.

I looked at Ralf. He was already fastening his cloak. I nodded, and turned to Nidd.

"We must go, I'm afraid. We must get to the ferry before the King's troops, and no doubt they'll ride at first light. We'll have to leave now. Can the boy guide us?"

The boy would do anything, it seemed, for the copper penny I gave him, and he knew all the ways through the marsh. We thanked our host, left the fee and medicines we had promised, and were soon on our way, with the boy—whose name was Ger—at my horse's head.

There were stars, and a quarter moon, but hazed over with fitful cloud. I could barely see the path, but the boy never hesitated. He seemed able to see even in the dark under the trees. The beasts trod softly enough on the forest floor, but the boy made no sound at all.

It was difficult to tell, what with the dark, the bad going and the winding track, what kind of distance we were covering. It seemed a long time before the trees dwindled and thinned, and the way stretched clearer ahead of us. As the moon grew stronger, the clouds diffusing her pale light, I could see more clearly. We were still in the marsh; water gleamed on either hand, islanded with blackness. Underfoot mud pulled and sucked at the horses' hoofs. Rushes swished and rustled shoulder high. There was a noise of frogs everywhere, and now and again a splash as something took to the water. Once, with a clap and a call and a flash of white, a feeding bird shot off not a yard in front of my horse's hoofs, and, had it not been for the boy's hand on the reins, I must have been unseated and thrown into the water. After that my horse picked his way nervously, starting even at the faint sucking sounds from the pools where the marshlights flickered and bubbles popped under the wisps of vapour which hung and floated over the water. Here and there, sticking up black out of the bog, was the stripped skeleton of a tree.

It was a strange, dead-looking landscape, and smelling of death. From Ralf's silence, I knew that he was afraid. But our guide, at my horse's head, plodded on through the wandering mists and the wisps of fire that were the souls of his fathers. The only sign he gave was when, at a fork in the track, we passed a hollow tree, a thick trunk twice the height of a man, with a gaping hole in the bark, and inside this a greenish glow that, with the help of the moonlight, faintly lit a crouching shape of eyes, mouth, and crudely carved breasts. The old goddess of the crossways, the Nameless One, who sits staring from her hollowed log like the owl who is her creature; and in front of her, decaying with the greenish glow that folk call enchanter's light, an offering of fish, laid in an oyster shell. I heard Ralf's breath go in, and his hand flickered in a defensive gesture. The boy Ger, without even looking aside, muttered the word under his breath, and held straight on.

Half an hour later, from the head of a rise of solid ground, we saw the wide, moonlit stretch of the estuary, and smelled salt on the clean and moving air.

Down by the shore where the ferry plied there was a red glimmer of light, the flame of the cresset on the wharf. The road to it, clear in the moonlight, crossed the ridge not far from us and ran straight downhill to the shore. We drew rein, but when I turned to thank the boy I found that he had already vanished, melting back into the darkness as silently as one of the wandering marshlights fading. We headed our weary horses down towards the distant glimmer.

When we reached the ferry we found that our luck had deserted us as swiftly and as decisively as our guide. The cresset burned on its post at the strip of shingle where the ferry beached, but the ferry was not there. Straining my ears, I thought I heard, above the ripple of water, the splashing of oars some way out on the estuary. I gave a hail, but got no reply.

"It looks as if he expects to come back to this side soon," said Ralf, who had been exploring. "There's a fire in the hut, and he's left the door open."

"Then we'll wait inside," I said. "It's not likely the King's troops will set out before cock-crow. I can't imagine his message to Caerleon is as urgent as that, or he'd have sent a rider posting last night. See to the horses, then come in and get some rest."

The ferryman's hut was empty, but the remains of a fire still glowed in the ring of stones that served for a hearth. There was a pile of dry kindling beside it, and before long a comforting tongue of flame licked up through the wood and set the turf glowing. Ralf was soon dozing in the warmth, while I sat watching the flames and listening for the return of the ferry.

But the sound that roused me was not the sound of a keel grating on shingle; it was the soft and distant thudding of a troop of horse coming at the canter.

Before my hand could reach Ralf's shoulder to shake him awake, he was on his feet.

"Quick, my lord, if we ride fast along the shingle—the tide's not full yet—"

"No. They'd hear us, and in any case the horses are too tired. How far away would you say they were?"

He was at the door in two strides, his head slanted, listening. "Half a mile. Less. They'll be here in a few minutes. What are you going to do? We can't hide. They'll see the horses, and the country's open as a map in the sand."

This was true. The road down which the horsemen were coming ran straight up from the shore to the head of the ridge. To right and left of it lay the marshlands, glinting with water, and white with mist. Behind us the estuary stretched glimmering, throwing back the moonlight.

"What you can't run from, you must face," I said. "No, not like that"—as the boy's hand went to his sword—"not against King's men, and we wouldn't stand a chance anyway. There's a better way. Get the bags, will you?"

I was already stripping off my stained and ragged tunic. He threw me a doubtful look, but ran to obey. "You won't get away with that doctor disguise again."

"I don't intend to try. When fate forces your hand, Ralf, go with it. It looks as if I may get to see the King sooner than I'd hoped to."

"Here? But you—he—the Queen—"

"The Queen's secret will be safe. I've been thinking how to deal with this if it happened. We'll let them think we've just come south from Maridunum, hoping to see the King."

"But the ferryman? If they check with him?"

"It could be awkward, but we'll have to chance it. Why should they, after all? Even if they do, I can deal with it. Men will believe anything of the King's enchanter, Ralf, even that he could cross the estuary on a cloud, or ford it knee high at flood-tide."

While we were talking he had unstrapped one of the saddle-bags and pulled out of it the decent dark robe and stitched doeskin boots I had worn for my interview with the Queen, while I bent over the bucket of water by the door and swilled the weariness of the journey and the stench of the marshlander's hut off my face and hands. *When fate forces you,* I had said to Ralf. I felt my blood running fast and light with the hope that this stroke—ill luck we had thought it—might be the first cold, dangerous touch of the god's hand.

When the troop rode up, halting with a clatter and slither of shingle in front of the ferryman's hut, I was standing waiting for them in the open doorway, with the firelight behind me, and the bright moonlight catching the royal Dragon at my shoulder.

Behind me in the shadows I heard Ralf mutter thankfully: "Not Cornwall's men. They won't know me."

"But they'll know me," I said. "That's Ynyr's badge. They're Welshmen from Guent."

The officer was a tall man, with a thin hawk face and a white scar twisting the corner of his mouth. I did not remember him, but he stared, saluted, and said: "By the Raven himself! How came you here, sir?"

"I must have words with the King. How far away is his camp?"

As I spoke, a kind of ripple of movement went among the troop, horses fidgeting and one suddenly rearing as if curbed too nervously. The officer snapped something over his shoulder, then turned back to me. I heard him swallow before he answered me.

"Some eight miles off, sir."

There was something more here, I thought, than surprise at finding me in this deserted place, and the awe that I was accustomed to meeting among common men. I felt Ralf move up close behind me to my shoulder. A half-glance showed me the sparkle in his eyes; show Ralf danger, and he came alive.

The officer said abruptly: "Well, my lord, this has saved us something. We were on the way to Caerleon. We had the King's orders to find you and bring you to him."

I caught the sharp intake of Ralf's breath. I thought fast, through a sudden quickening of the heart. This explained the soldiers' reaction; they thought the King's enchanter must have had magical foreknowledge of the King's will. On a plainer level, it settled the matter of the ferryman; if this troop was an escort for me, they would not now need to cross the ferry. Ralf could buy the man's silence when I had gone with the troops. I would not risk taking the boy back within reach of Uther's displeasure.

There was no harm in driving the point home. I said pleasantly: "So I have saved you the trip to Bryn Myrddin. I'm glad. Where did the King plan to receive me? At Viroconium? I didn't think he meant to lie at Caerleon."

"Nor does he," said the man. I could hear the effort of control, but his voice was hoarse, and he cleared his throat. "You—you knew the King was travelling north to Viroconium?"

"How not?" I asked him. From the edge of my eye I saw the nods and head-turning among the men that also asked *How not?* "But I had a mind to talk to him sooner than that. Did he charge you with a letter for me?"

"No, sir. Instructions to take you to him, that was all." He leaned forward in the saddle. "I think it was on account of the message he got last evening from Cornwall. Ill news, I think, though he told no one what it was. He seemed angry. Then he gave the order to fetch you."

He waited, looking down at me as if I would be sure to know the contents of the message.

I was only too afraid that I did. Someone had recognized us, or made a guess, and sent to tell the King. The messenger could easily have passed us on the road. So, whatever was to happen between Uther and myself, I had to get Ralf out of danger first. And although I was not afraid for the Queen at Uther's hands, there were others—Maeve, Caw, Marcia, the child himself. . . . The skin on my nape stung and roused like a dog's that smells danger. I took a long, steadying breath and looked about me. "You have a spare horse? My beast is weary and must be led. My servant will rest here, and go back at first light with the ferry, to make ready for me at home. The King will no doubt see me escorted there when my business with him is done."

The officer's voice, apologetic but definite, cut across Ralf's furious whisper of dissent. "If it please you, sir, you will both come. Those were my orders. We have horses. Shall we ride?"

At the lift of his hand the men were already moving forward to close us round. There was nothing to be done. He had his orders, and I would risk more by arguing than by obeying. Besides, every minute's delay might bring the ferry back. I had heard nothing, but the fellow must have seen the soldiers' torches, and might even now be heading back for custom.

A trooper came up with the spare horses and took our own beasts in hand. We mounted. The officer barked an order, and the troop wheeled and fell in behind us.

We were barely two hundred paces from the shore when I heard, clear behind me, the sound of a boat's bottom grating on shingle. No one else paid any attention. The officer was busy telling me about the council to be held in the north, and behind me I could hear Ralf's voice, gay and amused, promising the troopers "a skin of sloe wine, the best stuff you ever tasted. A recipe of my master's. It's what they give you with the rations now in Caerleon, so you'll see what you've missed. That's what comes of sending messages for a wizard, who knows everything that's happened before it's even happened at all. . . ."

The King was abed when we arrived at the camp, and we were lodged—and guarded—in a tent not far from his. We said nothing to each other that could not be overheard. And, danger or no danger, it was the most comfortable lodging we had had since we left the inn at Camelford. Ralf was soon asleep, but I lay wakeful, watching the empty dark, listening to the little wind which had sprung up throwing handfuls of rain against the walls of the tent, and telling myself: "It must happen. It must happen. The god sent me the vision. The child was given to me." But the dark stayed empty, and the wind swept the tent walls and withdrew into silence, and nothing came.

I turned my head on its uneasy pillow, and saw dimly the shine of Ralf's eyes, watching me. But he turned over without speaking, and soon his breathing slackened again into sleep.

9

The King received me alone, soon after dawn.

He was armed and ready for the road, but bareheaded. His helmet with its gold circlet lay on a stool beside his chair, and his sword and shield stood propped against the box which held the travelling altar of Mithras that he always carried with him. The tent was hung with skins and worked curtains, but it was chilly, and draughts crept everywhere. Outside were the sounds of the army breaking camp. I could hear the snap and flutter of the Dragon standard by the entrance.

He greeted me briefly. His face still wore the bleak expression I remembered, empty of friendliness, but I could see neither anger nor enmity there. His look was cool and summing, his voice brisk.

"You and your Sight have saved me a little trouble, Merlin."

I bent my head. If he asked no questions I need answer none. I came to the point. "What do you want with me?"

"Last time we spoke together I was harsh with you. I have since thought that this was perhaps unworthy of a king to whom you had just done a service."

"You were bitter at the Duke's death."

"As to that, he fought against his King. Whatever the circumstances, he raised a sword to me, and he died. It's done, and it is past. We, you and I, are left with the future. This is what concerns me now."

"The child," I said, assenting.

The blue eyes narrowed. "Who sent you the news? Or is this still the Sight?"

"Ralf brought the news. When he left your court, he came to me. He serves me now."

He considered that for a moment, his brows drawing together, then smoothing as he found no harm in it. I watched him. He was a tall man, with reddish hair and beard, and a fair, high-coloured skin that made him look younger than his years. It was just over a year, I thought, since my father had died and Uther had lifted the Pendragon standard. Kingship had steadied him; I could see discipline in his face as well as the lines drawn there by passion and temper, and kingship along with his victories clothed him like a cloak.

He moved a hand, dismissively, and I knew that Ralf need fear him no longer. "I said the past was past, but there is one thing I must ask you. On that night in Tintagel when this child was begotten, I bade you keep away from me and trouble me no more. Do you remember?"

"I remember."

"And you replied that you would not trouble me again, that I should not need your service again. Was this foresight, or only anger?"

I said quietly: "When I spoke, I spoke the words that came to me. I thought they were foresight. All the words I spoke and the things I did throughout that night I took as if they came straight from the gods. Why do you ask? Have you sent for me now to command service of me?"

"To ask it, rather."

"As a prophet?"

"No. As a kinsman."

"Then I'll tell you, as a kinsman, that it was not prophecy that night, nor was it anger, sir, but only grief. I was grieving for my servant's death, and for the deaths of Gorlois and his companions. But now, as you say, the past is past. If I can serve you, you have only to command me."

But, I thought, as I waited for him to speak, if it was no prophecy, then none of that night was God's and He never spoke to me. No, I had told the truth when I said that Uther would have no need for my service; it had not been Uther whom I served that night; it was not Uther I would serve now. I remembered the words of the other King, my father: *"You and I between us, Merlin, we will make such a king as the world has never known."* It was the dead King, and the one still unborn, who commanded me.

If there had been any hesitation in my manner, Uther had not noticed it. He nodded, then set his elbow on his knee and his chin on his fist and thought for a while, frowning.

"There is one other thing I said that night. I told you that I would not acknowledge the child begotten then. I spoke in anger, but now I speak coldly, after taking thought and counsel, and I tell you, Merlin, that I'm still of the same mind."

He seemed to expect an answer, but I was silent. He went on, half irritably: "Don't misunderstand me, I don't doubt the Queen. I believe her when she tells me that she never lay with Gorlois after he brought her to London. The child is mine, yes, but he cannot be my heir, nor can he be reared in my house. If the child is a girl, then none of this matters, but if it is a boy it would be folly to rear him as heir to the High Kingdom, when men will only have to count on their fingers to say that Gorlois begot him of his wife Ygraine, half a month before the High King married her." He looked at me. "You must know this as well as I do, Merlin. You have lived in kings' houses. There will always be those who doubt his birth, so there will always be those who would try to pull him off the throne in favour of men with a 'better claim,' and God knows there will always be claims in plenty. And the best claims will be those of my other sons. So, even brought up as my bastard at my court, the child is dangerous. He may try to come at the kingship by the deaths of my other children. By the Light, this is not unknown. I will not have my house a battleground. I must beget myself another son, an undoubted heir, conceived in wedlock to the satisfaction of all men, and reared at my side when the kingdom is settled and the Saxon wars are over. Do you accept this?"

"You are the King, Uther, and the child's father."

It was hardly an answer, but he nodded as if I had agreed. "There is more. This child is not only dangerous, he'll be a victim of danger. If men can say that he was not mine, that he must have been begotten by Gorlois on Ygraine his wife, then it follows that he is the true son of the Duke of Cornwall, with a claim on the younger son's portion of the lands which Cador holds, now that I've confirmed him as Duke in his father's place. You see? King's son or Duke's, Cador is bound to be the child's enemy, and there are some who'd follow him quickly enough."

"Is Cador loyal to you?"

"I trust him." He gave a short laugh. "So far. He's young, but hard-headed. He wants Cornwall, and he won't risk anything that could lose it—yet. But later, who knows? And when I am gone . . ." He let it hang. "No, Cador is not my enemy, but there are others who are."

"Who?"

"God knows, but what king was ever without them? Even Ambrosius . . . they're still saying he died of poison. I know you told me this was not true, but even so I have Ulfin taste my food. Ever since I took Octa and Eosa prisoner, they've been the storm center for every disaffected leader who thinks he can see his way to a crown like Vortigern's—backed with Saxon forces, and paid for with British lives and lands. But what else can I do? Let them go, to raise the Federates against me? Or kill them, and give their sons in Germany a grievance to be wiped out in blood? No, Octa and his cousin are my hostages. Without them, Colgrim and Badulf would have been here long since, and the Saxon Shore would have burst its bounds and be lapping at Ambrosius' Wall. As it is, I'm buying time. You can't tell me anything, Merlin? Have you heard anything, or seen?"

He was not asking for prophecy; Uther looked askance and white-eyed at things of the Otherworld, like a dog that sees the wind. I shook my head.

"Of your enemies? Nothing, except that when Ralf came to me after leaving your court, he was set upon, and nearly killed. The men had no badge. They may have thought he was your messenger, or perhaps the Queen's. Troops from the barracks hunted the woods, but found no trace of them. More than that, I've heard nothing. But be sure that if I ever learn anything I will tell you."

He gave a brief nod, then went on, slowly, choosing his words. His manner was abrupt, almost reluctant. For myself, my mind was spinning, and I had to fight to hold myself calm and steady. We were coming now onto the battleground, but it must be a very different battle from the one I had planned for. "You and I," he had said. He would hardly have sent for me unless I was to have some concern in the child's future.

He was going over the same ground that Ygraine and I had covered. ". . . so you see why, if the child is a boy, he cannot stay with me, yet if I send him away, he is beyond my power to protect. But protection he must have. Bastard or no, he is my child and the Queen's, and if we have no other sons he must one day be declared my heir to the High Kingdom." He turned up a hand. "You see where this leaves me. I must consign him to a guardian who will keep him in safety for the first few years of his life . . . at least until this torn kingdom is settled and safe, and in the hands of strong and loyal allies, and my own declared heirs."

He waited again for my agreement. I nodded, then said, carefully neutral: "Have you chosen this guardian?"

"Yes. Budec."

So the Queen had been right, and the decision was made. But still he had sent for me. I held myself still and said, so flatly that it sounded indifferent: "It was the obvious choice."

He shifted in his chair and cleared his throat. I saw with some surprise that he was uneasy, nervous even. He even looked half pleased at my commendation of his choice. The knowledge steadied me. I realized that I had been so single-minded—so wrapped in what I had believed was my and the child's driving fate—that I had seen Uther falsely as the enemy. He was not so concerned: the plain fact was that Uther was a war-leader harassed perpetually by the strife in and around his borders, working desperately against time to patch a dam here, a sea-wall there, against the piling floodwater; and to him this affair of the child, though it might prove one day vitally important, was now little but a rub in the way of major issues, something he wanted out of the way and delegated. He had spoken without emotion, and indeed had set the thing out fairly enough. It was possible that he had sent for me, genuinely, to ask my advice, as his brother had been used to do. In which case . . . I wetted dry lips, and schooled myself to listen quietly, an adviser with a man beset by trouble.

He was speaking again, something about a letter. The message which had come yesterday. He pointed to the stool beside him where the parchment lay, crumpled as if he had thrown it down in anger. "Did you know about this?"

I picked the letter up and smoothed it out. It was brief, a message from Brittany, that had been sent to the King at Tintagel and brought here after him. King Budec had fallen sick of a fever, it said, during the summer. He had seemed on the way to recovery, then, towards the end of August, he had quite suddenly died. The letter finished with protestations of formal friendship from the new king, Hoel, Uther's "devoted cousin and ally . . ."

I looked up. Uther had sat back in his chair, shifting a fold of the scarlet mantle over his arm. Everything seemed quite still. Outside, the wind had dropped. The sounds of the camp came from far away, faintly. Uther's chin was sunk on his chest, and he was watching me with a mixture of worry and impatience.

I was noncommittal. "This is heavy news. Budec was a good man and a good friend."

"Heavy enough, even if it had not destroyed my plans. I was preparing to send messages even when this letter came. Now I can't see my way clear. Have they told you that I go to a council of kings at Viroconium?"

"Audagus told me." Audagus was the officer who had escorted us from the ferry.

He threw out a hand. "Then you see how much I want to turn aside to deal with this. But it must be dealt with now. This is why I sent for you."

I flicked the seal with a forefinger. "You won't send the child to Hoel, then? He swears himself your devoted cousin and ally."

"He may be my devoted cousin and ally, but he's also a—" Uther used a phrase that became a soldier rather than a king in council. "I never liked him, nor he me. Oh, Mithras knows he would never mean harm to a son of mine, but he's not the man his father was, and he might not be able to protect the boy from his ill-wishers. No, I'll not send him to Hoel. But what other court can I send him to? Reckon it for yourself." He told over a few names, all powerful men, all of them kings whose lands lay in the southern part of the country, behind the Wall of Ambrosius. "Well? Do you see my problem? If he goes to one of the nobles or petty kings here in safe country he could still be in danger from an ambitious man; or worse, become a tool of treachery and rebellion."

"So?"

"So I come to you. You are the only man who can steer me between these clashing rocks. On the one hand, the child must be sworn and acknowledged my own, in case there is no other heir. On the other, he must be taken away out of danger for himself and the kingdom, and brought up in ignorance of his birth until the time comes when I send for him." He turned over a hand on his knee and asked me as simply as he had asked me once before: "Can you help me?"

I answered him as simply. The bewilderment, the confused whirl of thought, settled suddenly into a pattern, like coloured leaves blown down into a tapestry on the grass when the spinning wind drops still. "Of course. You need wreck no part of your kingdom on either of these rocks. Listen, and I will tell you how. You told me you had 'taken counsel.' Other men, then, know of your plans to send the boy to Budec?"

"Yes."

"Have you spoken to anyone of this letter, and your doubts of Hoel?"

"No."

"Good. You will give it out that your plan stays as formerly, and that the boy will go to Hoel's court at Kerrec. You will write to Hoel requesting this. Have someone make all arrangements to send the boy with his nurse and attendants as soon as the weather allows. See that it is given out that I will accompany him there myself."

He was frowning, intent, and I could see protest in his face, but he made none. He said merely: "And?"

"Next," I said, "I must be at Tintagel for the birth. Who is her physician?"

"Gandar." He seemed about to say something more, then changed his mind and waited.

"Good. I'm not suggesting I should attend her." I smiled. "In view of what I shall suggest, that might lead to some rather dangerous rumours. Now, will you be there yourself for the laying-in?"

"I shall try, but it's doubtful."

"Then I shall be there to attest the child's birth, as well as Gandar and the Queen's women, and whoever you can appoint. If it is a boy, the news will be sent to you by beacon, and you will declare him your son by the Queen, and, in default of a son begotten in wedlock, your heir until another prince shall be born."

He took some time over that, frowning, and obviously reluctant to commit himself. But it was only the conclusion of what he had himself said to me. Finally he nodded and spoke a little heavily: "Very well. It is true. Bastard or not, he is my heir until I get another. Go on."

"Meantime the Queen will keep her chamber, and once he has been seen and sworn to, the child will be taken back to the Queen's apartments and kept there, seen only by Gandar and the women. Gandar can arrange this. I myself will leave openly, by the main gate and the bridge. Then after dark I shall go down secretly to the postern gate on the cliff, to receive the child."

"And take him where?"

"To Brittany. No, wait. Not to Hoel, nor by the ship which everyone will be watching. Leave that part of it to me. I shall take him to someone I know in Brittany, on the edge of Hoel's kingdom. He will be safe, and well cared for. You have my word for it, Uther."

He brushed that aside as if there had been no need for me to say it. He was already looking lighter, glad to be relieved of a care that must, among the weighty cares of the kingdom, seem trivial, and—with the child still only a weight in a woman's womb—unreal. "I'll have to know where you take him."

"To my own nurse, who reared me and the other royal children, bastard and true alike, in the nurseries at Maridunum. Her name is Moravik, and she's a Breton. After the sack by Vortigern she went home to her people. She has married since. While the child is sucking, I can think of no better place. He won't be looked for in such a humble home. He will be guarded, but better than that, he will be hidden and unknown."

"And Hoel?"

"He will know. He must. Leave Hoel to me."

Outside a trumpet sounded. The sun was growing stronger, and the tent was warm. He stirred, and flexed his shoulders, as a man does when he lays off his armour. "And when men find that the child is not on the royal ship, but has vanished? What do we tell them?"

"That for fear of the Saxons in the Narrow Sea the prince was sent, not by the royal ship, but privily, with Merlin, to Brittany."

"And when it is found he is not at Hoel's court?"

"Gandar and Marcia will swear to it that I took the child safely. What will be said I can't tell you, but there's no one who will doubt me, or that the child is safe as long as he's under my protection. And what my protection means you know. I imagine that men will talk of enchantments and vanishings, and wait for the child to reappear when my spells are lifted."

He said prosaically: "They're more like to say the ship foundered and the child is dead."

"I shall be there to deny it."

"You mean you won't stay with the boy?"

"I must not, not yet. I'm known."

"Then who will be with him? You said he would be guarded."

For the first time I hesitated fractionally. Then I met his eyes. "Ralf."

He looked startled, then angry, then I saw him thinking back past his anger. He said slowly: "Yes. I was wrong there, too. He will be true."

"There is no one truer."

"Very well, I am content. Make what arrangements you please. It's in your hands. You of all men in Britain will know how to protect him." His hands came down hard on the arms of his chair. "So, that is settled. Before we march today I shall send a message to the Queen telling her what I have decided."

I thought it wise to ask: "Will she accept it? It's no easy thing for a woman to bear, even a queen."

"She knows my decision, and she will do as I say. There's one thing, though, where she'll have her way; she wants the child baptized a Christian."

I glanced at the Mithras altar against the tent wall. "And you?"

He lifted his shoulders. "What does it matter? He will never be King. And if he were, then he would pay service where he had to, in the sight of the people." A hard, straight look. "As my brother did."

If it was a challenge I declined it, saying merely: "And the name?"

"Arthur."

The name was strange to me, but it came like an echo of something I had heard long before. Perhaps there had been Roman blood in Ygraine's family . . . The Artorii; that would be it. But that was not where I had heard the name. . . .

"I'll see to it," I said. "And now, with your permission, I'll send the Queen a letter, too. She'll lie the easier for being assured of my loyalty."

He nodded, then stood up and reached for his helmet. He was smiling, a cold ghost of the old malicious smile with which he had baited me when I was a child. "It's strange, isn't it, Merlin the bastard, that I should talk so easily of trusting the body of my own ill-begotten son to the one man in the kingdom whose claim to the throne is better than his? Are you not flattered?"

"Not in the least. You'd be a fool if you didn't know by now that I have no ambitions towards your crown."

"Then don't teach my bastard any, will you?" He turned his head, shouting for a servant, then back to me. "And none of your damned magic, either."

"If he's your son," I said dryly, "he won't take very kindly to magic. I shall teach him nothing except what he has the need and the right to know. You have my word on it."

On that we parted. Uther would never like me, nor I him, but there was a kind of cold mutual respect between us, born of our shared blood and the different love and service we had given to Ambrosius. I should have known that he and I were linked in this as closely as the two sides of the same counter, and that we would move together whether we willed it or not. The gods sit over the board, but it is men who move under their hands for the mating and the kill.

I should have known; but I had been so used to God's voice in the fire and stars that I had forgotten to listen for it in the counsels of men.

Ralf was waiting, alone in the guarded tent. When I told him the result of my talk with the King, he was silent a long time. Then he said: "So it will all happen, just as you said it would. Did you expect it to come like this? When they brought us here last night, I thought you were afraid."

"I was, but not in the way you mean."

I expected him to ask how, but oddly, he seemed to understand. His cheek flushed and he busied himself over some detail of packing. "My lord, I have to tell you . . ." His voice was stifled. "I have been very wrong about you. At first I—because you are not a man of war, I thought—"

"You thought I was a coward? I know."

He looked up sharply. "You knew? You didn't mind?" This, obviously, was almost as bad as cowardice.

I smiled. "When I was a child among budding warriors, I grew used to it. Besides, I have never been sure myself how much courage I have."

He stared at that, then burst out: "But you are afraid of nothing! All the things that have happened—this journey—you'd have thought we were riding out on a summer morning, instead of going by paths filled with wild beasts and outlaws. And when the King's men took us—even if he is your uncle, that's not to say you'd never be in danger from him. Everyone knows the King's unchancy to cross. But you just looked cold as ice, as if you expected him to do what you wanted, just as everyone does! You, afraid? You're not afraid of anything that's real."

"That's what I mean," I said. "I'm not sure how much courage is needed to face human enemies—what you'd call 'real'—knowing they won't kill you. But foreknowledge has its own terrors, Ralf. Death may not lie just at the next corner, but when one knows exactly when it will come, and how . . . It's not a comfortable thought."

"You mean you do know?"

"Yes. At least, I think it's my death that I see. At any rate it is darkness, and a shut tomb."

He shivered. "Yes, I see. I'd rather fight in daylight, even thinking I might die perhaps tomorrow. At least it's always 'perhaps tomorrow,' never 'now.' Will you wear the doeskin boots for riding, my lord, or change them now?"

"Change them. Thank you." I sat down on a stool and stretched out a foot for him. He knelt to pull off my boots. "Ralf, there is something else I must tell you. I told the King you were with me, and that you would go to Brittany to guard the child."

He looked up at that, struck still. "You told him *that?* What did he say?"

"That you were a true man. He agreed, and approved you."

He sat back on his heels, my boots in his bands, gaping at me.

"He has had time to think, Ralf, as a king should think. He has also had time—as kings do—to still his conscience. He sees Gorlois now as a rebel, and the past as done with. If you wish to go back into his service he will receive you kindly, and give you a place among his fighting men."

He did not answer, but stooped forward again and busied himself fastening my boots. Then he got to his feet and pulled back the flap of the tent, calling to a man to bring up the horses. "And hurry. My lord and I ride now for the ferry."

"You see?" I said. "Your own decision this time, freely given. And yet who can say it is not as much a part of the pattern as the 'chance' of Budec's death?" I got to my feet, stretching, and laughed. "By all the living gods, I'm glad that things are moving now. And gladder for the moment of one thing more than any other."

"That you're to get the child so easily?"

"Oh, that, of course. No, I really meant that now at last I can shave off this damnable beard."

10

By the time Ralf and I reached Maridunum my plans, so far as could be at this stage, were made. I sent him by the next ship to Brittany, with letters of condolence to Hoel, and with messages to supplement the King's. One letter, which Ralf carried openly, merely repeated the King's request that Hoel should give shelter to the baby during his infancy; the other, which Ralf was to deliver secretly, assured Hoel that he would not be burdened with the charge of the child, nor would we come by the royal ship or at the time ostensibly fixed. I begged his assistance for Ralf in all the arrangements for the secret journey at Christmas that I planned. Hoel, easy-going and lazy by nature, and less than fond of his cousin Uther, would be so relieved, I knew, that he would help Ralf and myself in every way known to him.

With Ralf gone, I myself set out for the north. It was obvious that I would not be able to leave the baby too long in Brittany; the refuge with Moravik would serve for a while, till men's interest died down, but after that it might be dangerous. Brittany was the place (as I had said to the Queen) where Uther's enemies would look for the child; the fact that the child was not—had never been—at his publicly declared refuge at Hoel's court might make them believe that the talk of Brittany had been nothing but a false trail. I would make certain that no real trail would lead them to Moravik's obscure village. But this was only safe as long as the boy was an infant. As soon as he grew and began to go about, some query or rumour might start. I knew how easily this could happen, and for the child of a poor house to be so cared for and guarded as must happen here, it would be very easy for some question to start a rumour, and a rumour to grow too quickly into a guess at the truth.

More than this, once the child was weaned from women and the nursery, he would have to be trained, if not as a young prince, than as a young noble and a warrior. It was obvious that Bryn Myrddin, on no count, could be his home: he must have the comfort and safety of a noble house around him. In the end I had thought of a man who had been a friend of my father's, and whom I had known well. His name was Ector, styled Count of Galava, one of the nobles who fought under King Coel of Rheged, Uther's most considerable ally in the north.

Rheged is a big kingdom, stretching from the mountainous spine of Britain right to the western coast, and from the Wall of Hadrian in the north clear down to the plain of Deva. Galava, which Ector held under Coel, lies about thirty miles in from the sea, in the north-west corner of the kingdom. Here there is a wild and mountainous tract of country, all hills and water and wild forest; in fact, one of the names it goes by is the Wild Forest. Ector's castle lies on the flat land at the end of one of the long lakes that fill these valleys. There was in past time a Roman fortress there, one of a chain on the military road running from Glannaventa on the coast to join the main way from Luguvallium to York. Between

Galava and the port of Glannaventa lie steep hills and wild passes, easily defended, and inland is the well-guarded country of Rheged itself.

When Uther had talked of fostering the child in some safe castle he had thought only of the rich, long-settled lands inside Ambrosius' Wall, but even without his fears of the nobles' loyalty, I would have counted that country dangerous; these were the very lands that the Saxons, immured along the Shore, coveted most dearly. It was these lands which, I guessed, they would fight for first and most bitterly. In the north, in the heart of Rheged, where no one would look for him and where the Wild Forest itself would guard him, the boy could grow up as safely as God would allow, and as freely as a deer.

Ector had married a few years back. His wife was called Drusilla, of a Romano-British family from York. Her father, Faustus, had been one of the city magistrates who had defended the city against Hengist's son Octa, and had been one of those urgent to advise the Saxon leader to yield himself to Ambrosius. Ector himself was fighting at the time in my father's army. It was in York that he had met Drusilla, and had married her. They were both Christians, and this was possibly why their paths and Uther's had not often crossed. But I, along with my father, had been to Faustus' house in York, and Ambrosius had there taken part in many long discussions about the settlement of the northern provinces.

The castle at Galava was well protected, being built on the site of the old Roman fort, with the lake before it, and a deep river on the one hand, and the wild mountains near. It could be approached only from the open water, or by one of the easily watched and defended valley passes. But it did not have the air of a fortress. Trees grew near it, now rich with autumn, and there were boats out and men fishing where the river flowed deep and still through its sedgy flatlands. The green meadows at the waters' head were full of cattle, and there was a village crowded under the castle walls as there had been in the Roman Peace. Two full miles beyond the castle walls lay a monastery, and so secluded were the valleys that right up on the heights above the tree-line, where the land stretched bare of all but short grass and stones, one saw the strange little blue-fleeced sheep that breed in Rheged, with some shepherd boy cheerfully braving the wolves and fierce hill foxes with the protection of a stick and a single dog.

I travelled alone, and quietly. Though the hated beard had gone, and with it the heavy disguise, I managed the journey unnoticed and unrecognized, and came to Galava towards late afternoon on a bright, crisp October day.

The great gates were wide open, giving on a paved yard where men and boys were unloading a wagon of straw. The oxen stood patiently, chewing their cud; near them a lad was watering a pair of sweating horses. Dogs barked and skirmished, and hens pecked busily among the fallen straw. There were trees in the yard, and to either side of the steps up to the main door someone had planted beds of marigolds, which blazed orange and yellow in the late sunshine. It looked like a prosperous farm rather than a fortress, but through an open door I could see the rows of freshly burnished weapons, and from behind one of the high walls came shouted orders and the clash of men drilling.

I had barely paused between the posts of the archway when the porter was barring my way and asking my business. I handed him my Dragon brooch, wrapped in a small pouch, and bade him take it to his master. He came hurrying back to the gate within minutes, and the chamberlain, puffing in his wake, showed me straight in to Count Ector.

Ector was not much changed. He was a man of medium height, growing now into middle age; if my father had lived they would have been of an age now, I reckoned, which made him something over forty. He had a brown beard going grey, and brown skin with the blood springing healthily beneath it. His wife was more than ten years younger; she was tall, a statuesque woman still in her twenties, reserved and a little shy, but with smoky-blue eyes that belied her cool manner and distant speech. Ector had the air of a contented man.

He received me alone, in a small chamber where spears and bows stood stacked against the walls, and the hearth was four deep in deer-hounds. The fire was heaped as high as a funeral pyre with pine logs blazing, and small wonder, for the narrow windows were unglazed and open to the brisk October air, and the wind whined like another hound in the bowstrings that were stacked there.

He gripped my arms with a bearlike welcome, beaming. "Merlinus Ambrosius! Here's a pleasure indeed! What is it, two years? Three? There's been water under the bridge, aye, and stars fallen, since we last met, eh? Well, you're welcome, welcome. I can't think of any man I'd rather see under my roof! You've been making a name for yourself, haven't you? The tales I've heard tell . . . Well, well, but you can tell me the truth of it yourself. God's sweet death, boy, you get more like him by the day! Thinner, though, thinner. You look as if you've seen no red meat for a year. Come, sit down by the fire now, and let me send for supper before we talk."

The supper was enormous and excellent, and would have served me ten times over. Ector ate enough for three, and pressed me to finish the rest. While we ate we exchanged news. He had heard of the Queen's pregnancy, and spoke of it, but for the moment I let it go, and asked him instead what had happened at Viroconium. Ector had attended the King's council there, and was but newly returned home.

"Success?" he asked, in reply to my question. "It's hard to say. It was well attended. Coel of Rheged, of course, and all from these lands"—he named half a dozen neighbours—"except Riocatus of Verterae, who sent to say he was sick."

"I gather you didn't believe it?"

"When I believe anything that jackal says," said Ector forcibly, "I'm a spit-licker too. But the wolves were there, all of them, so the scavengers hardly matter."

"Strathclyde?"

"Oh, aye, Caw was there. You know the Picts in the western half of his land have been giving trouble—when haven't they given trouble, come to that? But for all Caw's Pictish himself, he'll co-operate with any plan that'll help him keep control of that wild territory of his, so he was well disposed to the idea of the council. He'll help, I'm sure of it. Whether he can control that pack of sons he's sired is another matter. Did you know that one of them, Heuil, a wild young blackguard scarcely old enough (you'd have thought) to lift a spear, took one of Morien's girls by force last spring when she was on her way to the monastery her father had promised her to since birth? He lifted his spear to *her* easily enough; by the time her father got the news she was over the border with him, and in no condition for any monastery, however broad-minded." He chuckled. "Morien cried rape, of course, but everyone was laughing, so he made the best of it. Strathclyde had to pay, naturally, and he and Morien sat on opposite benches at Viroconium, and Heuil wasn't there at all. Ah, well, but they agreed to sink their differences. King Uther managed it well enough, so what between Rheged and Strathclyde, there's half the northern frontier solid for the King."

"And the other half?" I asked. "What about Lot?"

"Lot?" Ector snorted. "That braggart! He'd swear allegiance to the Devil and Hecate combined if it would get him a few more acres for himself. He cares no more for Britain than that hound by the hearthstone. Less. He and his wild brood of brothers sitting on that cold rock of theirs. They'll fight when it pays them, and that's all." He fell silent, scowling at the fire, poking with a foot at the hound nearest him; it yawned with pleasure, and flattened its ears. "But he talks well, and maybe I'm blackguarding him. Times are changing, and even barbarians like Lot ought to be able to see that unless we band together with a strong oath, and keep it, it'll be the Flood Year all over again."

He was not referring to an actual flood, but to the year of the great invasion a century ago, when the Picts and Saxons, joined with the Scots from Ireland, poured across Hadrian's Wall with axe and fire. Maximus commanded then, in Segontium. He drove them back and broke them, and won for Britain a time of peace, and for himself an empire and a legend.

I said: "Lothian is a key to the defense that Uther's planning, even more than Rheged or Strathclyde. I'd heard tell—I don't know if it's true?—that there are Angles settled on the Alaunus, and that the strength of the Anglian Federates south of York along the Abus has doubled since my father's death?"

"It's true." He spoke heavily. "And south of Lothian there's only Urien on the coast, and he's another carrion crow, picking at Lot's leavings. Nay, that may be another one I'm doing an injustice to. He's married to Lot's sister, when all's done, so he'd be bound to cry the same way. Talking of which—"

"Talking of what?" I asked, as he paused.

"Marriage." He scowled, then began to grin. "If it wasn't so plaguy dangerous, it would be funny. You knew Uther had a bastard girl, I forget her name, she must be seven or eight years old?"

"Morgause. Yes, I remember her. She was born in Brittany."

Morgause was a sideslip of Uther's by a girl in Brittany who had followed him to Britain hoping, I suppose, for marriage, since she was of good family, and the only woman, so far as anyone knew then for certain, who had borne him a child. (It had always been a matter of amazement, and a good deal of private and public conjecture among Uther's troops, how he managed to avoid leaving a train of bastards in his wake like seedlings following the sower down a furrow. But this girl was, to public knowledge, the only one. And I believe to Uther's knowledge, too. He was a fair man and a generous one, and no girl had suffered any loss worse than maidenhead through him.) He had acknowledged the child, kept both child and mother at one of his houses, and after the mother's marriage to a lord of his household, had taken the girl into his own. I had seen her once or twice in Brittany, a thin pale-haired girl with big eyes and a mouth folded small.

"What about Morgause?" I asked.

"Uther was casting out feelers for marrying her to Lot, come the time she'll be ready for bedding."

I cocked an eyebrow at him. "And what did Lot think about that?"

"Eh, you'd have laughed to watch him. Black as a wolverine at the suggestion that Uther's byblow was good enough, but careful to keep his talk sweet in case there's no other daughter born in the right bed now the King's wedded.

Bastards—and their mates—have inherited kingdoms before now. Saving your presence, of course."

"Of course. Lot casts his eyes as high as that, then?"

He gave a short nod. "High as the High Kingdom itself, you can take my word for it."

I digested that, frowning. I had never met Lot; he was at this time scarcely older than myself—somewhere in his early twenties—and though he had fought under my father, his path and mine had not crossed. "So Uther wants to tie Lothian to him, and Lot wants to be tied? Whether it's for his own ambition or not, it means surely that Lot will fight for the High King when the time comes? And Lothian is our main bulwark against the Angles and the other invaders from the north."

"Oh, aye, he'll fight," said Ector. "Unless the Angles offer him a better bribe than Uther does."

"Do you mean that?" I was alarmed. Ector, for all his bluff ways, was a shrewd observer, and few men knew more about the changing shifts of power along our shores.

"Maybe I was putting it a trifle high. But for my money Lot's unscrupled and ambitious, and that's a combination that spells danger to any overlord who can't placate him."

"How is he with Rheged?" I was thinking of the child to be lodged here perhaps at Galava, with Lot east by north across the Pennines.

"Oh, friends, friends. As good friends as two big hounds each with his own full platter of meat. No, it's not yet a matter for concern, and may never be. So forget it, and drink up." He drank deeply himself, set down his cup and wiped his mouth. Then he fixed me with a sharp and curious eye. "Well? You'd better get to it, boy. You didn't come all this way for a good supper and a brattle with an old farmer. Tell me how I can serve Ambrosius' son?"

"It is Ambrosius' nephew you will be serving," I said, and told him the rest. He heard me out in silence. For all his warmth and heartiness, there was nothing impulsive or overquick about Ector. He had been a cold-brained and calculating officer; a valuable man in any circumstance, from a pitched fight to a long and careful siege. After a sharp glance of surprise and a lift of the brows when I spoke of the King's decision and my guardianship of the child, he listened without moving and without taking his eyes off me.

When I had finished, he stirred. "Well . . . I'll say one thing to start with, Merlin; I'm glad and proud you should have come to me. You know how I felt about your father. And to tell you the truth, boy"—he cleared his throat, hesitated, then looked away into the fire as he spoke—"it always sorrowed my heart that you yourself were a bastard. And that's between these four walls, I don't have to tell you. Not that Uther's made a bad shot at being High King—"

"A far better shot than I'd ever have made," I said, smiling. "My father used to say that Uther and I, between us, shared out some of the qualities of a good king. It was a dear dream of his that some day, between us, we might fashion one. And this is the one." Then, as his head went up, "Oh, I know, a baby not yet born. But all the first part has happened as I knew it must happen: a child begotten by Uther and given to me to raise. I know this is the one. I believe he will be such a king as this poor country has never had before, and may never see again."

"Your stars tell you this?"

"It has been written there, certainly, and who writes among the stars but God?"

"Well, God grant it is so. There's coming a time, Merlin, maybe not next year, or for five years, or even for ten, but it is coming—when the Flood Year will come again, and pray God that this time there's a king here to raise the sword of Maximus against it." He turned his head sharply. "What's that? That sound?"

"Only the wind in the bowstrings."

"I thought it was a harp sounding. Strange. What is it, boy? Why do you look so?"

"Nothing."

He looked at me doubtfully for a moment longer, then grunted and fell silent, and behind us the long humming stretched out, a cold music, something from the air itself. I remembered how, as a child, I had lain watching the stars and listening for the music which (I had been told) they made as they moved. This must, I thought, be how it sounded.

A servant came in then with logs to replenish the fire, and the sound died. When he had gone, and the door had shut behind him, Ector spoke again in quite a different tone. "Well, I'll do it, of course, and proud to. You're right; in the next few years I can't see that Uther will have much time for him, and for that matter he'd be hard put to it to keep the child safe. Tintagel might have done, but as you say, there's Cador there . . . Does the King know that you've come to me?"

"No. Nor will I tell him, yet."

"Indeed?" He thought it over for a moment, frowning a little. "Do you think he'll be content with that?"

"Possibly. I don't know. He didn't press me too hard about Brittany. I think that just now he wants as little to do with it as need be. The other thing is"—I smiled a little wryly—"the King and I have a truce declared, but I wouldn't bank on its staying that way; and out of sight, out of mind. If I'm to have anything to do with the child's teaching, then it had better be at a fair distance from the High King."

"Aye, I've heard that, too. It's never a wise thing to help kings to their heart's desire. Will the boy be a Christian?"

"The Queen wants it, so he'll be baptized in Brittany if I can arrange it. He's to be called Arthur."

"You'll stand for him?"

I laughed. "I believe the fact that I was never baptized myself puts me out of the running."

His teeth showed. "I forgot you were a pagan. Well, I'm glad to hear about the boy. There'd have been a peck of trouble else."

"Your wife, you mean? She's so devout?"

"Poor lass," he said, "she has nothing else since our second died. There'll be no more, they say. In fact it will be God's mercy if we take this boy into our house; my son Cei's a headstrong little ruffian for all he's only three, and the women spoil him. It will be good to have the second child. What did you say his name was to be? Arthur? You'll leave this with me to talk over with Drusilla? Though there's no question, she'll be as glad as I am to have him. And I can tell you that she's close-mouthed enough, for all she's a woman. He'll be safe with us."

"I was sure of it. It doesn't need the stars to tell me that." But when I began to thank him, he cut me short.

"Well, then, that's settled. We can talk over the details later. I'll speak with Drusilla tonight. You'll stay a while of course?"

"Thank you, but I can't—no longer than it takes to rest myself and my horse. I have to be at Tintagel again in December, and before that I must be home when Ralf gets back from Brittany. There's a lot to be arranged."

"A pity. But you'll be back. I'll look forward to it." He grinned, stirring the hounds again. "I'll enjoy seeing you installed as tutor to the household, or whatever you think will give you some claim on the boy. And I own I should like to see Cei licked into shape. Maybe he'll mind his manners with you, if he thinks he can be turned into a toad for disobeying you."

"Bats are my speciality," I said, smiling. "You are very good, and I'll never be out of your debt. But I'll find a place of my own."

"Look, boy, Ambrosius' son doesn't wander the countryside looking for a home while I have four walls and a fireplace to offer him. Why not here?"

"Because I might be recognized, and where Merlin is for the next few years, men will look for Arthur near him. No, I must stay unknown. A household as big as this is too risky, and, with all my thanks to you, four walls are not always the best shelter for such as me."

"Ah, yes. A cave, isn't it? Well, there are a few hereabouts, they tell me, if you turn the wolves out first. Well, you know your own business. But tell me, what of the Queen? You didn't say where she stood in this? What woman would let her first child be taken from the bed where she bore him, and never try to see him again or make herself known to him?"

"The Queen herself sent for me secretly, and asked me to take him. She has suffered, I know, but it's the King's will, and she knows that it's more than a whim born of anger; she sees the dangers as well as he. And she is a queen before she is a woman." I added, carefully: "I think that the Queen is not a woman for a family, any more than Uther is a family man. They are man and woman for each other, and outside their bed they are King and Queen. It may be that in the future Ygraine will wonder, and ask questions; but that is with the future. For the moment she is content to let him go."

After this we talked on, late into the night, arranging as far as we could the details of the time ahead. Arthur would be left in Brittany until he was three or four years old, then at a safe time of year Ralf would bring him across from Brittany to Ector's home.

"And you?" asked Ector. "Where will you be?"

"Not in Brittany, for the same reason that I can't live here. I shall vanish, Ector, It's a talent that magicians have. And when I do appear again, it will be somewhere that draws men's eyes away from Brittany and Galava." When he questioned me further, I laughed, and refused to enlighten him.

"Truth to tell, my plans are not yet fixed. Now, I've kept you out of your bed for long enough. Your wife will be wondering what sort of mystery man you have been closeted with all these hours. I'll make my apologies when you present me in the morning."

"And I'll make my own now," he said, getting to his feet. "But that's one apology I enjoy making. You miss a lot, you know, Merlin—but then you can't know."

"I know," I said.

"You do? Then you must think it's worth it, life without women?"

"For me, yes."

"Well, then, come this way to your cold bed," he said, and held the door for me.

11

The boy was born on the eve of Christmas, an hour before midnight.

Just before the birth I and the two nobles appointed as witnesses were called into the Queen's chamber, where Gandar attended with Marcia and other women of the Queen's household. One of these was a girl called Branwen who had lately been brought to bed of a dead child; she was to be the child's wet-nurse. When all was done, the baby washed and swaddled, and the Queen sleeping, I took my leave and rode out of the castle and along the track towards Dimilioc. As soon as the lights of the gate-house were out of view I turned my horse aside down the steep path into the valley which runs from the high fields above the headland down to the shore.

The castle at Tintagel is built on a promontory of rock, or near-island, a crag jutting up out of the fearsome seas, which is joined to the cliffs of the mainland only by a narrow causeway. To either side of this causeway the cliffs drop away sheer to small bays of rock and shingle tucked in under the cliff. From one of these a path, narrow and precarious, and passable only on a receding tide, leads up the face of the cliff to a small gate let into the roots of the castle wall. This is the postern, the secret entrance to the castle. Inside is a narrow stairway of stone leading up to the private door of the royal apartments.

Halfway up the steep stairway was a broad landing, and a guard-room. Here I was to wait, until the child was judged fit to be taken abroad into the winter's cold. There were no guards: months past, the King had had the postern sealed, and the guard-room's other door, giving on the main part of the castle, had been built up. For tonight the postern gate had been opened, but no porter manned it; only Ulfin the King's man, and Valerius, his friend and trusted officer, waited there to let me in. Valerius took me up to the guard-room, while Ulfin went out down the path into the bay to take my horse. Ralf was not with me. He had gone to ensure that the Breton ship was waiting as it had promised, and he was also to bring horses and to keep watch each night in the bay below the secret path.

I waited for two days and nights. There was a pallet in the guard-room, and Ulfin himself had kindled a fire to banish the disused chill of the place, and from time to time brought food and fuel, and the news from above stairs. He would have waited on me if I had let him; he was grateful still for some kindness I had shown to him in the past, and I think the King's disfavour had distressed him. But I sent him back to his post at the Queen's door, and spent the waiting time alone.

At the other side of the landing, in the outer wall of the castle and opposite the guard-room door, was another door leading out onto a narrow, level platform skirted waist-high by a battlement. It was not overlooked by any of the castle windows, and below it, between the castle wall and the sea, was an apron of grass sloping down to the edge of the sheer cliffs. In summer the place was alive with nesting sea birds, but now, in midwinter, it was barren and crisp with frost. From below, incessantly, came the suck and hush and thud of the winter sea.

Each day, at dawn and sunset, I walked out to this platform to see if the weather had changed. But for three days there was no change. The air was cold, and below me the grass, grey with rime, was barely distinguishable in the thick mist that held the whole place shrouded, from the invisible sea below the invisible cliffs to the pale blur where the winter sun fought to clear the sky. Below the blanket of mist the sea was quiet, as quiet as it ever is on that raging coast. And every midnight, before I slept, I went out into the icy dark and looked upwards for the stars. But there was only the blank pall of the mist.

Then on the third night, the wind came. A small wind from the west, that crept across the battlements and in under the doors and set the flames fluttering blue round the birch logs. I stood up, listening. I had a hand to the latch of the door when I heard a sound, in the quiet, from the head of the stairway. The door to the Queen's apartments had opened and shut again, gently. I opened the door and looked upwards.

Someone was coming softly down the stairs; a woman, shrouded in a mantle, carrying something. I stepped out onto the landing, and the light from the guard-room door came after me, firelight and shadow.

It was Marcia. I saw the tears glisten on her cheeks as she bent her head over what lay in her arms. A child, wrapped warm against the winter night. She saw me and held her burden out to me. "Take care of him," she said. "Take care of him, as God loves him and you."

I took the child from her. Inside the woollen wrappings I caught the glint of cloth of gold. "And the token?" I asked. She handed me a ring. It was one I had often seen on Uther's hand, made of gold, enclosing a stone of red jasper with a dragon crest carved small. I slipped it on my own finger, and saw her instinctive movement of protest, stilled as she remembered who I was.

I smiled. "For safekeeping only. I shall put it away for him."

"My lord prince . . ." She bent her head. Then she threw a quick glance over her shoulder to where the girl Branwen, hooded and cloaked, was coming down the stairway, with Ulfin behind her carrying a pack with her effects. Marcia turned back to me swiftly and laid a hand on my arm. "You will tell me where you are taking him?" It was a plea, whispered.

I shook my head. "I'm sorry. It's better that no one should know."

She was silent, her lips working. Then she straightened herself. "Very well. But you promise me that he will be safe? I'm not asking you as a man, or even as a prince. I'm asking you from your power. He will be safe?"

So Ygraine had said nothing, even to Marcia. Marcia's guess at the future was still only a guess. But in the days to come both these women would feel the bitter need for each other's confidence. It would be cruel to leave the Queen isolated with her knowledge and her hopes. It is not true that women cannot keep secrets. Where they love, they can be trusted to death and beyond, against all sense and reason. It is their weakness, and their great strength.

I met Marcia's eyes full for a moment. "He will be King," I said. "The Queen knows it. But for the child's sake, you will tell no one else."

She bent her head again, without replying. Ulfin and Branwen were beside us. Marcia leaned forward gently and drew back a fold of the shawl from the child's face. The baby was sleeping. The eyelids, curiously full, lay over the shut eyes like pale shells. There was a thick down of dark hair on his head. Marcia stooped and kissed him lightly on the head. He slept on, undisturbed. She pulled the fold of wool back to shelter him, then with gentle expert hands settled the bundle closer into my arms. "So. Hold his head so. You will be careful going down the path?"

"I will be careful."

She opened her mouth to speak again, then shook her head quickly, and I saw a tear slide from her cheek to fall on the child's shawl. Then she turned abruptly away, and started back up the stairs.

I carried the baby down the secret path. Valerius went ahead, with his sword drawn and ready, and behind me, with Ulfin's arm to help her, came Branwen. As we reached the bottom and stepped on the grating pebbles, Ralf's shadow detached itself from the immense darkness of the cliffs, and we heard his quick, relieved greeting, and the tread of hoofs on the shingle.

He had brought a mule for the girl, tough and sure-footed. He settled her in the saddle, then I handed the baby up to her, and she folded him close in the warmth of her cloak. Ralf vaulted to the back of his own horse and took the mule's rein in hand. I was to lead the pack-mule. This time I planned to travel as an itinerant singer—a harper is free of kings' courts where a drug-peddler is not—and my harp was strapped to the mule's saddle. Ulfin gave me the lead-rein, then held my gelding for me; it was fresh, and anxious to be moving and warm itself. I said my thanks and farewells, then he and Valerius started back up the cliff path. They would seal the postern again behind them.

I turned my horse's head into the wind. Ralf and the girl had already put their mounts to the bank. I saw the dim shapes pause above me, waiting, and the pale oval of Ralf's face as he turned back to watch me. Then his arm went out, pointing.

"Look!"

I turned.

The mist was lifting, drawing back from a sparkling sky. Faintly, high over the castle promontory, grew a hazy moon of light. Then the last cloud blew clear, billowing before the west wind like a sail blowing towards Brittany, and in its wake, blazing through the sparkle of the lesser stars, grew the great star that had lit the night of Ambrosius' death, and now burned steady in the east for the birth of the Christmas King.

We set spurs to our horses and rode for the ship.

12

The wind stayed fair for Brittany, and we came in sight of the Wild Coast at dawn on the fifth day. Here the sea is never quiet; the cliffs, high and dangerous, towered black with the early light behind them and the teeth of the sea gnawing white at the base; but once round Vindanis Point the seas flattened and ran calmer, and I was even able to leave my cabin in time to watch our arrival at the wharf south of Kerrec which my father and King Budec had built years back when the invasion force was being assembled here.

The morning was still, with a touch of frost and a thin mist pearling the fields. The country hereabouts is flat, field and moorland stretching inland where the wind scours the grass with salt, and for miles nothing grows but pine and wind-bitten thorn. Thin streams wind between steep mudbanks down to the bays and inlets that bite everywhere into the coast, and at low tide the flats teem with shellfish and are loud with the cries of wading birds. For all its dour seeming it is a rich country, and had provided a haven not only for Ambrosius and Uther when Vortigern murdered their brother the King, but for hundreds of other exiles who fled from Vortigern and the threat of the Saxon Terror. Even then, they found parts of the country already peopled by the Celts of Britain. When the Emperor Maximus, a century before, had marched on Rome, those British troops who survived his defeat had straggled back to the refuge of this friendly land. Some had gone home, but a great many had remained to marry and settle; my kinsman, King Hoel, came of one such family. The British had indeed settled in such numbers that men called the peninsula Britain also, dubbing it Less Britain, as their homeland was known as Greater Britain. The language spoken here was still recognizably the same as that of home, and men worshipped the same gods, but the memories of older gods still visibly held the land, and the place was strange. I saw Branwen gazing out over the ship's rail with wide eyes and wondering face, and even Ralf, who had travelled here before as my messenger, had a look of awe as we drew nearer the wharf and saw, beyond the huts and the piles of casks and bales, the first ranks of the standing stones.

These line the fields of Less Britain, rank on rank, like old grey warriors waiting, or armies of the dead. They have stood there, men say, since time began. No one knows why, or how they came there. But I had long known that they were raised, not by giants or gods or even enchanters, but by human engineers whose skill lives on only in song. These skills I learned, when as a boy I lived in Brittany, and men called it magic. For all I know they may be right. One thing is certain, though men's hands lifted the stones, and are long since dust under their roots, the gods they served still walk there. When I have gone between the stones at night, I felt eyes on my back.

But now the sun was up, gilding the granite surfaces, and throwing the shadows of the stones slanting blue across the frost. The wharf-side was already busy; carts stood ready for loading, and men and boys ran about the business of tying up and unloading the ship. We were the only passengers, but no one cast more than a glance at the travellers in their decent, sober clothes; the musician with the harp in his baggage and his wife and baby beside him, with his servant in attendance. Ralf had lifted the baby from Branwen's arms, and supported her as she trod gingerly down the gangplank. She was silent and pale, and leaned heavily on him. I saw, as he bent over her, how—suddenly, it seemed—he had grown from boy to man. He would be turned sixteen now, and though Branwen was perhaps a year older than he, Ralf might well be taken for her husband, rather than I. He looked brisk and bright, sleek as a springtime cockerel in his neat new clothes. He was the only one of our party, I thought sourly, feeling the wharf tilt and sway under me as if it had still been the heaving deck, who had weathered the passage well.

The escort he had arranged was waiting for us. Not the escort of troops which King Hoel had wanted to provide, but simply a mule litter for Branwen and the child, with a muleteer and one other man, who had brought horses for Ralf and myself. This man came forward now to greet me. From his bearing I judged him to be an officer, but he was not in uniform, and there was nothing to show that the escort came from the King. Nor apparently had the officer been told anything about us, beyond the fact that we were to be led into town and housed there until the King should send for us.

He greeted me civilly, but without the courtesies of rank. "You are welcome, sir. The King sends his greetings, and I am here to escort you into town. I trust you had a good voyage?"

"They tell me so," I said, "but neither I nor the lady are inclined to believe them."

He grinned. "I thought she looked a little green. I know how she feels. I'm not a great one for the sea, myself. And you, sir? Can you ride as far as the town? It's little more than a mile."

"I can try," I said. We exchanged courtesies while Ralf helped Branwen into the litter and drew the curtains against the morning chill. As she settled herself into the warmth the baby woke and began to cry. He had very good lungs, had Arthur. I suppose I must have winced. I saw a gleam of amusement in the officer's face, and said dryly:

"Are you married?"

"Yes, indeed."

"I used to think sometimes what I might be missing. Now I begin to know."

He laughed at that. "One can always escape. It's the best reason I know for being a soldier. Will you mount, sir?"

He and I rode side by side on the way into the town. Kerrec was a sizeable settlement, half civil, half military, walled and moated, clustered round a central hill where the King's stronghold lay. Near the ramp which led up to the castle gate was the house where my father had lived during his years of exile, while he and King Budec assembled and trained the army which had invaded Britain to claim it back for him, her rightful King.

And now, perhaps, her next and greater King was here at my side, still yelling lustily, muffled in a litter, and being carried over the wooden bridge that spanned the moat, and in through the gate of the town.

My companion was silent beside me. Behind us the others rode at ease; they chatted among themselves, the sound of their voices and the sharp clop of the horses' hoofs on the cobbles and the jingling of bits sounding loud in the still and misty daybreak. The town was just waking. Cocks crowed from yards and middens; here and there doors were opened and women, shawled against the cold, could be seen moving with pails or armfuls of kindling to start the day's work.

I was glad of my companion's silence as I looked about me. Even in the five years since I had left it the place seemed to have changed completely. I suppose one cannot pull a standing army out of a town where it has been built and trained for years, and not leave an echoing shell. The army, indeed, had been mainly quartered outside the walls, and the camps had long since been dismantled and gone back to grassland. But in the town, though King Budec's own troops remained, the orderly bustle and the air of purpose and expectancy which had characterized the place in my father's time had gone. In the street of the engineers, where I had served my apprenticeship with Tremorinus, there were a few workshops open and already clanging in the early dawn, but the air of high purpose had gone with the crowd and the clamour, and something almost like desolation had taken its place. I was glad that the way to our lodging did not pass my father's house.

We were lodged with a decent couple, who made us welcome; Branwen and the baby were carried straight off to some women's fastness, while I was shown to a good room where a fire blazed and breakfast was spread waiting beside it. A servant carried the baggage in, and would have stayed to wait on me, but Ralf dismissed him and served the meal himself. I bade him eat with me, and he did so, cheerful and brisk as if the last week or so had been spent holidaying, and when we had done asked if I wanted to go out to explore the town. I gave him leave, but said that I would stay within doors. I am a strong man, and do not readily tire, but it takes more than a mile on dry land and a good breakfast to dispel the grinding sickness and exhaustion of a winter voyage. So I bade Ralf merely see to it that Branwen and the child were comfortable, and, after he had gone, composed myself to rest and wait for the King's summons.

It came at lamplighting, and Ralf with it, wide-eyed, with a robe over his arm of soft combed wool dyed a rich dark blue, with a border worked in gold and silver thread.

"The King sent this for you. Will you wear it?"

"Certainly. It would be an insult to do anything else."

"But it's a prince's robe. People will wonder who you are."

"Not a prince's, no. A singer's robe of honour. This is a civilized country, Ralf, like my own. It's not only princes and soldiers who are held in high esteem. When will King Hoel receive me?"

"In an hour's time, he says. He will receive you alone, before you sing in the hall. What are you laughing at?"

"King Hoel being cunning from necessity. There's only one catch about going as a singer to Hoel's court; he happens to be tone deaf. But even a tone deaf king will receive a travelling singer, to get his news. So he receives me alone. Then if the barons in his hall want to hear me, he doesn't have to sit through it."

"He sent that harp along, though." Ralf nodded to the instrument which stood shrouded near the lamp.

"He sent it, yes, but it was never his; it's my own." He looked at me in surprise. I had spoken more curtly than I had meant to. All day the silent harp had stood there, untouched, but speaking to me of memories, of most, indeed, that I had ever had of happiness. As a boy here in Kerrec, in my father's house, I had played it almost nightly. I added: "It was one I used here, years ago. Hoel's father must have kept it for me. I don't suppose it's been touched since I last played it. I'd better try it before I go. Uncover it, will you?"

A scratch at the door then heralded a slave with a ewer of steaming water. While I washed, and combed my hair, then let the slave help me into the sumptuous blue robe, Ralf uncovered the harp and set it ready.

It was bigger than the one I had brought with me. That was a knee harp, easy to transport; this was a standing harp, with a greater range and a tone which would reach the corners of a King's hall. I tuned it carefully, then ran my fingers over the strings.

To remember love after long sleep; to turn again to poetry after a year in the market place, or to youth after resignation to drowsy and stiffening age; to remember what once you thought life could hold, after telling over with muddied and calculating fingers what it has offered; this is music, made after long silence. The soul flexes its wings, and, clumsy as any fledgling, tries the air again. I felt my way, groping back through the chords, for the passion that slept there in the harp, exploring, testing as a man tests in the dark ground which once he knew in daylight. Whispers, small jags of sound, bunches of notes dragged sharply. The wires thrilled, catching the firelight, and the long running chords lapsed into the song.

There was a hunter at the moon's dark
Who sought to lay a net of gold in the marshes.
A net of gold, a net heavy as gold.
And the tide came in and drowned the net,
Held it invisible, deep, and the hunter waited,
Crouching by the water in the moon's dark.

They came, the birds flighting the dark,
Hundred on hundred, a king's army.
They landed on the water, a fleet of ships,
Of king's ships, proud with silver, silver masted,
Swift ships, fierce in battle,
Crowding the water in the moon's dark.

The net was heavy beneath them, hidden,
waiting to catch them.
But he lay still, the young hunter, with idle hands.

Hunter, draw in your net. Your children
will eat tonight,
And your wife will praise you, the cunning hunter.

He drew in his net, the young hunter,
drew it tight and fast.
It was heavy, and he drew it to shore, among the reeds.
It was heavy as gold, but nothing was there but water.
There was nothing in it but water, heavy as gold,
And one grey feather,
From the wing of a wild goose.

They had gone, the ships, the armies,
into the moon's dark.

And the hunter's children were hungry,
and his wife lamented.
But he slept dreaming, holding the wild goose feather.

King Hoel was a big, thick-bodied man in his middle thirties. During the time I had spent in Kerrec—from my twelfth to my seventeenth year—I had seen very little of him. He had been a lusty and dedicated fighting man, while I was only a youth, and busy with my studies in hospital and workshop. But later he had fought with my father's troops in Greater Britain, and there we had come to know and to like one another. He was a man of big appetites and, as such men often are, good natured and tending to laziness. Since I had last seen him he had put on flesh, and his face had the flush of good living, but I had no doubt he would be as stalwart as ever in the field.

I started by speaking of his father King Budec and the changes that had come, and we talked for a while of past times.

"Ah, yes, those were good years." He stared, chin on fist, into the fire. He had received me in his private chamber, and after we had been served with wine, had dismissed the servants. His two deer-hounds lay stretched on the skins at his feet, dreaming still of the chase they had had that day. His hunting spears, freshly cleaned, stood against the wall behind his chair, their blades catching the firelight. The King stretched his massive shoulders, and spoke wistfully. "I wonder, when will such years come again?"

"You are talking of the fighting years?"

"I am talking of Ambrosius' years, Merlin."

"They will come again, with your help now." He looked puzzled, then startled, and uneasy. I had spoken prosaically enough, but he had caught the implications. Like Uther, he was a man who liked everything normal, open and ordinary. "You mean the child? The bastard? After all we've heard about it, he'll be the one to succeed Uther?"

"Yes. I promise you."

He fidgeted with his cup, and his eyes slid away from mine. "Ah, yes. Well, we shall keep him safely. But tell me, why the secrecy? I had a letter from Uther asking me openly enough to care for the boy. Ralf couldn't tell me much more than was in the letters he brought. I'll help, of course, every way I can, but I don't want a quarrel with Uther. His letter to me made it pretty clear that this boy's only his heir in default of a better claim."

"That's true. Don't be afraid, I don't want a quarrel, either, between you and Uther. One doesn't throw a precious morsel down between two fighting-dogs and expect it to survive. Until there is a boy with what Uther calls a better claim, he's as anxious as I am to keep this one safe. He knows what I'm doing, up to a point."

"Ah." He cocked an eye at me, intrigued. I had been right about him. He might be well disposed towards Britain, but he was not above doing a quietly back-handed turn to Britain's King. "Up to what point?"

"The time when the baby is weaned, and grown enough to need men's company and to be taught men's arts. Four years, perhaps, or less. After that I shall take him back from you, and he must go home to Britain. If Uther asks where he is, he will have to be told, but until he does—well, there's no need to seek him out, is there? Myself, I doubt if Uther will question you at all. I think he would forget this child if he could. In any case, if there is blame, it is mine. He put the boy in my charge, to rear as I thought fit."

"But will it be safe to take him back? If Uther's sending him here now because of enemies at home, are you sure it will be better then?"

"It's a risk that will have to be taken. I want to be near the child as he grows. It should be in Britain, and therefore it must be in secret. There are bad times coming, Hoel, for us all. I cannot yet see what will happen, beyond these facts; that this boy—this bastard if you like—will have enemies, even more than Uther has. You call him bastard; so will other men with ambition. His secret enemies will be more deadly even than the Saxons. So he must be hidden until the time comes for him to take the crown, and then he must take it with no cast of doubt, and be raised King in the sight of all Britain."

" 'He must be'? You have seen things, then?" But before I could answer he shied quickly away from the strange ground, and cleared his throat. "Well, I'll keep him safe for you, as well as I may. Just tell me what you want. You know your own business, always did. I'll trust you to keep me right with Uther." He gave his great laugh. "I remember how Ambrosius used to say that your judgment in matters of policy, even when you were a youngling, was worth ten of any bedroom emperor's." My father, naturally, had said no such thing, and in any case would hardly have said it to Hoel, who had a fair reputation himself as a lover, but I took it as it was intended, and thanked him. He went on: "Well, tell me what you want. I confess I'm puzzled. . . . These enemies you talk of, won't they guess he's in Brittany? You say Uther made no secret of his plans, and when the time comes for the royal ship to sail and it's seen that you and the child aren't on it, won't they simply think he was sent over earlier, and search first for him here in Brittany?"

"Probably. But by that time he'll be disposed of in the place I've arranged for him, and that's not the kind of place where Uther's nobles would think of looking. And I myself will be gone."

"What place is that? Am I to know?"

"Of course. It's a small village near your boundary, north, towards Lanascol."

"What?" He was startled, and showed it. One of the hounds stirred and opened an eye. "North? At the edge of Gorlan's land? Gorlan is no friend to the Dragon."

"Nor to me," I said. "He's a proud man, and there is an old score between his house and my mother's. But he has no quarrel with you?"

"No, indeed," said Hoel fervently, with the respect of one fighting man for another.

"So I believed. So Gorlan isn't likely to make forays into the edge of your territory. What's more, who would dream that I would hide the child so near him? That with all Brittany to choose from, I'd leave him within bowshot of Uther's enemy? No, he'll be safe. When I leave him, I'll do so with a quiet mind. But that's not to say I'm not deeply in your debt." I smiled at him. "Even the stars need help at times."

"I'm glad to hear it," said Hoel gruffly. "We mere kings like to think we have our parts to play. But you and your stars might make it a bit easier for us, perhaps? Surely, in all that great forest north of here, there must be safer places than the very edge of my lands?"

"Possibly, but it happens that I have a safe house there. The one person in both the Britains who'll know exactly what to do with the child for the next four years, and will care for him as she would for her own."

"She?"

"Yes. My own nurse, Moravik. She's a Breton born, and after Maridunum was sacked in Camlach's war she left South Wales and went home. Her father owned a tavern north of here at a place called Coll. Since he'd grown too old for work, a fellow called Brand kept it for him. Brand's wife was dead, and soon after Moravik returned home she and Brand married, just to keep things right in the sight of God . . . and, knowing Moravik, I'm not just talking about the inn's title deeds. . . . They keep the place still. You must have passed it, though I doubt if you'd ever stop there—it stands where two streams join and a bridge crosses them. Brand's a retired soldier of your own, and a good man—and in any case will do as Moravik bids him." I smiled. "I never knew a man who didn't, except perhaps my grandfather."

"Ye—es." He still sounded doubtful. "I know the village, a handful of huts by the bridge, that's all. . . . As you say, hardly a likely place to hunt a High King's heir. But an inn? Isn't that in itself a risk? With men—Gorlan's, too, since it's a time of truce—coming and going from the road?"

"So, no one will question your messengers or mine. My man Ralf will stay there to guard the boy, and he'll need to stay abreast of news, and get messages to you from time to time, and to me."

"Yes. Yes, I see. And when you take the child there, what's your story?"

"No one will think twice about a travelling harper plying his trade on a journey. And Moravik has put a story round that will explain the sudden appearance of Ralf and the baby and his nurse. The story, if anyone questions it, will be that the girl, Branwen, is Moravik's niece, who bore a child to her master over in Britain. Her mistress cast her from the house, and she had no other place to go, but the man gave her money for the passage to her aunt's house in Brittany, and paid the travelling singer and his man to escort her. And the singer's man, meanwhile, will decide to leave his master and stay with the girl."

"And the singer himself? How long will you stay there?"

"Only as long as a travelling singer might, then I'll move on and be forgotten. By the time anyone even thinks to look farther for Uther's child, how can they find him? No one knows the girl, and the baby is only a baby. Every house in the country has one or more to show."

He nodded, chewing it over this way and that, and asked a few more questions. Finally he admitted: "It will serve, I suppose. What do you want me to do?"

"You have watchers in the kingdoms that march with yours?"

He laughed shortly. "Spies? Who hasn't?"

"Then you'll hear quickly enough if there's any hint of trouble from Gorlan or anyone else. And if you can arrange for some quick and secret contact with Ralf, should it be necessary—?"

"Easy. Trust me. Anything I can do, short of war with Gorlan . . ." He gave his deep chuckle again. "Eh, Merlin, it's good to see you. How long can you stay?"

"I'll take the boy north tomorrow, and with your permission will go unescorted. I'll come back as soon as I see all is safe. But I'll not come here again. You might be expected to receive a travelling singer once, but not actually to encourage him."

"No, by God!"

I grinned. "If this weather holds, Hoel, could the ship stay for me for a few days?"

"For as long as you like. Where do you plan to go?"

"Massilia first, then overland to Rome. After that, eastwards."

He looked surprised. "You? Well, here's a start! I'd always thought of you being as fixed as your own misty hills. What put that into your head?"

"I don't know. Where do ideas come from? I have to lose myself for a few years, till the child needs me, and this seemed to be the way. Besides, there was something I heard." I did not tell him that it had only been the wind in the bowstrings. "I've had a mind lately to see some of the lands I learned about as a boy."

We talked on then for a while. I promised to send letters back with news from the eastern capitals, and, as far as I could, I gave him points of call to which he would send his own tidings and Ralf's about Arthur.

The fire died down and he roared for a servant. When the man had been and gone—

"You'll have to go and sing in the hall soon," said Hoel. "So if we've got all clear, we'll leave it at that, shall we?" He leaned back in his chair. One of the hounds got to its feet and pushed against his knee, asking for a caress. Over the sleek head the King's eyes gleamed with amusement. "Well now, you've still to give me the news from Britain. And the first thing you can do is to tell me the inside story of what happened nine months ago."

"If you in your turn will tell me what the public story is."

He laughed. "Oh, the usual stories that follow you as closely as your cloak flapping in the wind. Enchantments, flying dragons, men carried through the air and through walls, invisibly. I'm surprised, Merlin, that you take the trouble to come by ship like an ordinary man, when your stomach serves you so ill. Come now, the story."

It was very late when I got back to our lodging. Ralf was waiting, half asleep in the chair by the fire in my room. He jumped up when he saw me, and took the harp from me.

"Is all well?"

"Yes. We go north in the morning. No, thank you, no wine. I drank with the King, and they made me drink again in the hall."

"Let me take your cloak. You look tired. Did you have to sing to them?"

"Certainly." I held out a handful of silver and gold pieces, and a jewelled pin. "It's nice to think, isn't it, that one can earn one's keep so handsomely? The jewel was from the King, a bribe to stop me singing, otherwise they'd have had me there yet. I told you this was a cultured country. Yes, cover the big harp. I'll take the other with me tomorrow." Then as he obeyed me: "What of Branwen and the baby?"

"Went to bed three hours since. She's lying with the women. They seem very pleased to have a baby to look after." He finished on a note of surprise which made me laugh.

"Did he stop crying?"

"Not for an hour or two. They didn't seem to mind that, either."

"Well, no doubt he'll start again at cock-crow, when we rouse them. Now go to bed and sleep while you can. We start at first light."

13

There is a road leading almost due north out of the town of Kerrec, the old Roman road which runs straight as a spear-cast across the bare, salty grassland. A mile out of town, beyond the ruined posting station, you can see the forest ahead of you like a slow tidal wave approaching to swallow the salt flats. This is a vast stretch of woodland, deep and wild. The road spears straight into it, aiming for the big river that cuts the country from east to west. When the Romans held Gallia there was a fort and settlement beyond the river, and the road was built to serve it; but now the river marks the boundary of Hoel's kingdom, and the fort is one of Gorlan's strongholds. The writ of neither king runs far into the forest, which stretches for countless hilly miles, covering the rugged center of the Breton peninsula. What traffic there is keeps to the road; the wild land is served only by the tracks of charcoal-burners and wood-cutters and men who move secretly outside the law. At the time of which I write the place was called the Perilous Forest, and was reputed to be magic-bound and haunted. Once leave the road and plunge into the tracks that twist through the tangled trees, and you could travel for days and hardly see the sun.

When my father had held command in Brittany under King Budec, his troops had kept order even in the forest, as far as the river where King Budec's land ended and King Gorlan's began. They had cut the trees well back to either side of the road, and opened up some of the subsidiary tracks, but this had been neglected, and now the saplings and the bushes had crowded in. The paved surface of the road had long since been broken by winter, and here and there it crumbled off into patches of iron-hard mud that in soft weather would be a morass.

We set out on a grey, cold day, with the wind tasting faintly of salt. But though the wind blew damp from the sea it brought no rain with it, and the going was fair enough. The huge trees stood on either hand like pillars of metal, holding a weight of low, grey sky. We rode in silence, and after a few miles the thickly encroaching growth of the underwood forced us, even on this road, to ride in single file. I was in the lead, with Branwen behind me, and Ralf in the rear leading the pack-mule. I had been conscious for the first hour or so of Ralf's tension, the way his head turned from side to side as he watched and listened; but we saw and heard nothing except the quiet winter life of the forest; a fox, a pair of roe deer, and once a shadowy shape that might have been a wolf slipping away among the trees. Nothing else; no sound of horses, no sign of men.

Branwen showed no hint of fear. When I glanced back I saw her always serene, sitting the neat-footed mule stolidly, with an unmoved calm that held no trace of uneasiness. I have said little about Branwen, because I have to confess that I remember very little about her. Thinking back now over the span of years, I see only a brown head bent over the baby she carried, a rounded cheek and downcast eyes and a shy voice. She was a quiet girl who—though she talked easily enough to Ralf—rarely addressed me of her own will, being painfully in awe of me both as prince and enchanter. She seemed to have no inkling of any risk or danger in our journey, nor did she seem stirred—as most girls would have been—by the excitement of travelling abroad to a new country. Her imperturbable calm was not due to confidence in myself or Ralf; I came to see that she was meek and biddable to the point of stupidity, and her devotion to the baby was such as to blind her to all else. She was the kind of woman whose only life is in the bearing and rearing of children, and without Arthur she would, I am sure, have suffered bitterly over the loss of her own baby. As it was, she seemed to have forgotten this, and spent the hours in a kind of dreamy contentment that was exactly what Arthur needed to make the discomforts of the journey tolerable.

Towards noon we were deep in the forest. The branches laced thick overhead, and in summer would have shut out the sky like a pitched shield, but above the bare boughs of winter we could see a pale and shrouded point of light where the sun struggled to be through. I watched for a sheltered place where we could leave the road without showing too many traces, and presently, just as the baby woke and began to fret, saw a break in the undergrowth and turned my horse aside.

There was a path, narrow and winding, but in the sparse growth of winter it was passable. It led into the forest for a hundred paces or so before it divided, one path leading on deeper among the trees, the other—no more than a deer-trod—winding steeply up to skirt the base of a rocky spur. We followed the deer-trod. This picked its way through fallen boulders tufted with dead and rusty fern, then led upwards round a stand of pines, and faded into the bleached grass of a tiny clearing above the rock. Here, in a hollow, the sun came with a faint warmth. We dismounted, and I spread a saddle-cloth in the most sheltered spot for the girl, while Ralf tethered the horses below the pines and threw down feed from the hay nets. Then we sat ourselves down to eat. I sat at the lip of the hollow, with my back against a tree, a post from which I could see the main path running below the rock. Ralf stayed with Branwen. It had been a long time since we had broken our fast, and we were all hungry. The baby, indeed, had begun to yell lustily as the mule scrambled up the steep path. Now he found his cries stifled against the girl's nipple, and fell silent, sucking busily.

The forest was very quiet. Most wild creatures lie still at noon. The only thing moving was a carrion crow, which flapped heavily down onto a pine above us, and began to caw. The horses finished their feed and dozed, hip-shotten, heads low. The baby still fed, but more slowly, drowsing into milky sleep. I leaned back against the stem of the tree. I could hear Branwen murmuring to Ralf. He said something, and I heard her laugh, then through the murmur of the two young voices I caught another, distant, sound. Horses, at the trot.

At my word the boy and girl fell abruptly silent. Ralf was on his feet in the blink of an eye, and kneeling beside me to watch the path below. I signed Branwen to stay where she was. I need not have troubled; she had turned a wondering look on us, then the baby hiccupped, and she held him to her shoulder, patting him, all her attention on him again. Ralf and I knelt at the edge of the clearing, watching the path below.

The horses—there were two of them by the sound of it—could not be woodcutters' beasts nor the slow train of the charcoal-burners. Trotting horses, in the

Perilous Forest, meant only one thing, trouble. And travellers who carried, as we did, gold for the baby's keep were quarry for any outlaws and disaffected men. Hampered as we were by Branwen and Arthur, both fighting and flight were impossible. Nor was it easy, with the baby, to keep silent and let danger pass by so closely. I had made it clear to Ralf that whatever happened he was to stay with the girl and, at the least hint of danger, leave it to me to devise some way of drawing the danger away. Ralf had protested, mutinied, then finally seen the sense of it and sworn to obey.

So now when I whispered, "Only two, I think. If they don't come up this way, they'll not see us. Get to the horses. And for God's sake tell the girl to keep the baby quiet," he merely nodded, melting back from my side. He stooped to whisper to Branwen, and I saw her nod placidly, shifting the child to her other breast. Ralf slipped like a shadow among the pines where the horses stood. I waited, watching the path.

The riders were approaching. There was no other sound except the crow, still cawing high in the pine tree. Then I saw them. Two horses, trotting single file; poor beasts, heavy bred and none too well fed by the look of them, careless how they put their feet, and having to be hauled up by their cursing riders at every hole or root across the path. It was a fair enough guess that the men were outlaws. They were as unkempt as their beasts, and looked half savage, and dangerous. They were dressed in what looked like old uniforms, and on the arm of one of them was a dirty badge, half torn away. It looked like Gorlan's. The fellow in the rear rode carelessly, lolling in the saddle as if half drunken, but the man in front pricked at the alert, as such men learn to do, his head moving from side to side like that of a questing dog. He held a bow at the ready. Through the rotten leather of the sheath at his thigh I saw the long knife, burnished to a killing point.

They were almost below me. They were passing. There had been no sound from the baby, nor from our horses, hidden among the pines. Only the carrion crow, balancing high in the sunshine, scolded noisily.

I saw the fellow with the bow lift his head. He said something over his shoulder, in a thick accent I could not catch. He grinned, showing a row of rotten teeth, then lifted his bow, notched it, and sent an arrow whizzing into the pine. It hit. The crow shot upwards off the bough with a yell, then fell, transfixed. It landed within two paces of Branwen and the child, flapped for a second or two, then lay still.

As I dodged back and ran for the pines I heard both men laughing. Now the marksman would come to retrieve his arrow. Already I could hear him forcing his beast through the underbrush. I picked up the arrow, crow and all, and flung it out over the edge of the hollow. It landed down among the boulders. From the path the man could not have seen where the bird fell; it was a chance that he might believe it had fluttered there, and would ride no farther. I saw Branwen's eyes, startled and wondering, as I ran past her. But she did not stir, and the baby slept at her breast. I gave her a sign which was meant to convey reassurance, approval, and warning all in one, and ran for my horse.

Ralf was holding the beasts quiet, heads together, muffling eyes and nostrils with his cloak. I paused beside him, listening. The outlaws were coming on. They must not have seen the crow; they came on without pausing, making for the pines.

I seized my sorrel's bridle from Ralf, and turned it to mount. The horse circled, treading the dry stalks and snapping twigs. I heard the sudden clatter and tramp as the outlaws dragged their beasts to a standstill. One of them said, "Listen!" in Breton, and there was the rasp of metal as weapons came hissing out. I was in the saddle. My own sword was out. I pulled the sorrel's head round, and had opened my mouth to shout when I heard another cry from the path, then the same voice yelling "Look! Look there!" and my horse reared sharply back on its haunches as something broke out of the bushes beside me and went by so close that it almost brushed my leg.

It was a hind, white against the winter forest. She scudded through the pines like a ghost, bounded along the top of the hollow where we had lain, stood poised for a moment in view at the edge, then vanished down the steep, boulder-strewn slope, straight into the path of the two outlaws. I heard shouts of triumph from below, the crack of a whip, the sudden thud and flurry of hoofs as the men wrenched their horses back to the path and lashed them to a gallop. They were giving hunting calls. I jumped from the saddle, threw the sorrel's reins to Ralf, and ran back to my place above the rock. I reached it in time to see the two of them going back full tilt the way they had come. Ahead of them, dimly seen for a moment, like a scud of mist through the bare trees, fled the white hind. Then the laughter, the hunting cries, the hammer of hard-driven horses, echoed plunging back through the forest, and was gone.

14

The river which marks the boundary of Hoel's kingdom flows right through the heart of the forest. In places it cuts a deep gorge between overhanging banks of trees, and everywhere in the central part of the forest the land is seamed by small, wild valleys where tributary streams wind or tumble into the main. But there is a place, almost in the center of the forest, where the river valley is wider and more gentle, forming a green basin where men have tilled the fields, and over the years have cut back the forest to make grazing land round the small settlement called Coll, which in Breton means the Hidden Place. Here there had been, in past times, a Roman transit camp on the road from Kerrec to Lanascol. All that remained of this now was the squared outline where the original ditch had been dug beside the tributary. Here lay the village. On two sides of it the stream made a natural defense or moat; for the rest, the Roman ditch had been cleared and widened, and filled with water. Inside this were steep defensive earthworks, crowned with palisades. The bridge had been a stone one in Roman times; the piles still stood and were spanned now with planking. Though the village lay near Gorlan's border, it was accessible from it only through the narrow pass cut by the river, and there the road had crumbled almost back to the original rocky path that wolves and wild men had used before the Romans ever came. Coll was well named.

Brand's tavern lay just inside the gate. The main street of the village was little more than a dirty alley floored unevenly with cobbles. The inn stood a little way back from this, on the right. It was a low building, roughly built of stone, with mortar slapped haphazardly into the gaps. The outbuildings round the yard were no more than wattle huts, daubed with mud. The roof was newly thatched, with good close work of reeds held down by a net of rope weighted with heavy stones. The door was open, as the door of an inn should be, with a heavy curtain of skins hung across the opening to keep the weather out. Through the chimney hole at one end rose a sluggish column of smoke that smelled of peat.

We arrived at dusk when the gates were closing. Everywhere mingled with the peat smoke came the smells of supper cooking. There were few people about; the children had been called in long since, and the men were home at their supper. Only a few hungry-looking dogs skulked here and there; an old woman hurried past with a shawl held over her face and a fowl squawking under her other arm; a man led a yoke of weary oxen along the street. I could hear the clink of a smith's anvil not far away, and smell the sharp fume of burned hoofs.

Ralf eyed the inn dubiously. "It looked better in October, on a sunny day. It's not much of a place, is it?"

"All the better," I said. "No one will come looking in a place like this for the son of the King of Britain. Go in now and play your part, while I hold the horses."

He pushed aside the curtain and went in. I helped Branwen dismount, and settled her on one of the benches beside the door. The baby woke, and began to whimper, but almost immediately Ralf came out again, followed by a big, burly man and a boy. The man must be Brand himself; he had been a fighting man and still bore himself like one, and I saw the puckered seam of an old wound across the back of one hand.

He hesitated, uncertain how to greet me. I said quickly: "You'll be the innkeeper? I'm Emrys the singer, who was to bring your wife's niece along with us, with the baby. You're expecting us, I believe?"

He cleared his throat. "Indeed, indeed. You're most welcome. My wife's been looking for you this week past." He saw the boy staring, and added sharply: "What are you waiting for? Take the horses round the back."

The boy darted to obey. Brand, ducking his head at me and indicating the door of the inn with a gesture that was half invitation, half salute, said: "Come in, come in. Supper's cooking." Then, doubtfully, "It's mighty rough company we get here, but maybe—"

"I'm used to rough company," I said tranquilly, and preceded him through the door.

This was not a time of year for much coming and going on the roads, so the place was not crowded. There were some half-dozen men, dimly seen in a room lit only by one tallow candle and the light from the peat fire. The talk hushed as we went in, and I saw the looks at the harp I carried, and the whisper that went round. Nobody spared a glance for the girl carrying the baby. Brand said, a shade too quickly: "On through there. That far door, behind the fire." Then the door shut behind us, and there in the back room stood Moravik, fists on her hips, waiting to greet us.

Like everyone else whom one has not seen since childhood, she had shrunk. When I had last seen her I had been a boy of twelve, and tall for my age. Even then she had seemed much bigger than I was, a creature of bulk and commanding voice, surrounded by the aura of authority and infallible decisions left over from the nursery. Now she came no higher than my collar-bone, but she still had the bulk and the voice, and—I was to find—the authority. Though I had turned out to be the favoured son of the High King of all Britain, I was still, obviously, the wayward small boy from her first nursery.

Her first words were characteristic. "And a fine time of night to come, with the gates just shutting! You could have been out in that forest all night, and a precious lot there'd have been left of you by morning, what with the wolves, and worse, that lives out there. And damp, too, I shouldn't wonder—sweet saints and stars preserve us, look at your cloak? Get it off this minute, and come to the fire. There's a good supper cooking, special for you. I remember all the things you like, and I never thought to see you sitting at my table again, young Merlin, not after that night when the place burned down round you, and there was nothing to be found of you in the morning but a few burned bones in your room." Then suddenly she came forward with a rush and had hold of me. There were tears on her face. "Eh, Merlin, little Merlin, but it's good to see you again."

"And you, Moravik." I embraced her. "I swear you must have got younger every year since you left Maridunum. And now you're putting me in your debt again, you and your good man here. I'll not forget it, and neither will the King. Now, this is Ralf, my companion, and this"—drawing the girl forward—"is Branwen, with the child."

"Eh, the baby! The good Goddess save us all! What with seeing you,

Merlin, I'd forgotten all about him! Come near the fire, girl, don't stand there in the draught. Come to the fire, and let me see him . . . Eh, the lamb, the bonny lamb. . . ."

Brand touched my arm, grinning. "And now, what with seeing *him,* she'll forget everything else, my lord. It's lucky she got the supper ready for you before she got a sight of the baby. Sit you down here. I'll serve you myself."

Moravik had made a rich mutton stew, satisfying and very hot. The mutton of the Breton salt flats is as good even as anything we get in Wales. There were dumplings with the stew, and good new bread hot from the oven. Brand brought a jug of red wine, very much better than anything we can make at home. He waited on us while Moravik busied herself with Branwen and the baby, whose whimpering had broken now into lusty crying, only to be stilled by Branwen's breast. The fire blazed and crackled, the room was warm and smelled of good food and wine, the firelight traced the shape of the girl's cheek, and the baby's head. I became conscious of someone watching me, and turned my head to see Ralf's eyes on my face. He opened his mouth as if to speak, but at that moment some clamour from the outer room made Brand set the wine-jug down on the table, excuse himself quickly to me, and hurry out. He left the door slightly ajar. Beyond it I could hear voices raised in what sounded like persuasion or argument. Brand answered, quietly, but the clamour persisted.

He came back into the room, looking worried, and shut the door behind him. "My lord, there's those outside who saw you come in, and saw you'd a harp with you. Now, well, it's only natural, my lord, they want a song. I tried to argue them out of it, said you were tired, and had come a long way, but they insisted. Said they'd pay for your supper, between them, if the song was a good one."

"Well," I said, "why not let them?"

His mouth dropped open. "But—sing to them? You?"

"Don't you hear anything in Brittany?" I asked him. "I really am a singer. And it wouldn't be the first time I've earned my fee."

From her place near Branwen beside the fire, Moravik looked up quickly. "Here's a new start! Potions and such I knew about, learned from that old hermit above the mill, and even magic—" crossing herself. "But music? Who taught you?"

"Queen Olwen taught me the notes," I said, adding, to Brand, "That was my grandfather's wife, a Welsh girl who sang like a laverock. Then later when I was here in Brittany with Ambrosius I learned from a master. You may have heard him, perhaps? An old blind singer, who had travelled and made music in every country in the world."

Brand nodded as if he knew the man I spoke of, but Moravik looked doubtfully at me, tut-tutting, and shaking her head. I suppose no one who has reared a boy from babyhood, and not seen him since his twelfth year, ever thinks he can be a master at anything. I grinned at them. "Why, I played in front of King Hoel, back there in Kerrec. Not that he's anything of a judge, but Ralf has heard me, too. Ask him, if you think I can't earn my supper."

Brand said doubtfully: "But you'll not want to be singing to the likes of them, my lord?"

"Why not? A travelling minstrel sings where he's hired to sing. And that's what I am, while I'm in Less Britain." I got to my feet. "Ralf, bring me the harp. Finish the wine yourself, and then get to bed. Don't wait for me."

I went out into the tavern's public room. This had filled up now; there were about twenty men there, crowded in the smoky warmth. When I went in there were shouts of "The singer, the singer!" and "A tale, a tale!"

"Make room for me then, good people," I said. A stool was vacated for me near the fire, and someone poured me a cup of wine. I sat down and began to tune the harp. They fell still, watching me.

They were simple folk, and such folk like tales of marvels. When I asked them what they would have, they asked for this tale and that of gods and battles and enchantments, so in the end—my mind, I think, on the child sleeping in the next room—I gave them the story of Macsen's Dream. This is as much a tale of magic as any of the rest, though its hero is the Roman commander Magnus Maximus, who was real enough. The Celts call him Macsen Wledig, and the legend of Macsen's Dream was born in the singing valleys of Dyfed and Powys, where every man claims Prince Macsen as his own, and the stories have gone from mouth to mouth until, if Maximus himself appeared to tell them the truth, no one would believe him. It's a long story, the Dream, and every singer has his own version of it. This is the one I sang that night:

Macsen, Emperor of Rome, went hunting, and being tired in the heat of the day lay down to sleep on the banks of the great river that flows towards Rome, and he dreamed a dream.

He dreamed that he journeyed along the river towards its source, and came to the highest mountain in the world; and from there followed another fair flowing river through the rich fields and broad woodlands till he reached the mouth of the river, and there at its mouth was a city of turrets and castles crowded round a fair harbour. And in that harbour lay a ship of gold and silver with no man on board, but with all sails set and shivering to the wind out of the east. He crossed a gangplank made of the white bone of a whale, and the ship sailed.

And soon, after a sunset and a sunset, he came to the fairest island of all the world, and leaving the ship, he traversed the island from sea to sea. And there on the western shore he saw an island at hand across a narrow strait. And on the near shore where he stood was a fair castle, with an open gate. Then Macsen entered the castle and found himself in a great hall with golden pillars, and walls dazzling with gold and silver and precious stones. In that hall two youths sat playing chess on a silver board, and near them an old man in an ivory chair carved chessmen for them out of crystal. But Macsen had no eyes for all this splendour. More beautiful than silver and ivory and precious stones was a maiden, who sat still as a queen in her golden chair. The moment the Emperor saw her he loved her, and, raising her, he embraced her and begged her to be his wife. But in the very moment of the embrace he woke, and found himself in the valley outside Rome, with his companions watching him.

Then Macsen leaped to his feet and told his dream; and messengers were sent the length and breadth of the world, to find the land he had traversed, and the castle with the beautiful maiden. And after many months, and a score of false journeys, one man found them, and came home to tell his master. The island, most beautiful in all the world, was Britain, and the castle by the western sea was Caer Seint, by Segontium, and the island across the shining strait was Mona, isle of druids. So Macsen journeyed to Britain, and found everything just as he had dreamed it, and requested the hand of the maiden from her father and her brothers, and made her his Empress. Her name was Elen, and she bore Macsen two sons and a daughter, and in her honour he built three castles, in Segontium,

Caerleon and Maridunum, which was called Caer Myrddin in honour of the god of high places.

Then, because Macsen stayed in Britain and forgot Rome, they made a new emperor in Rome, who set his standard on the walls and defied Macsen. So Macsen raised an army of the Britons, and, with Elen and her brothers at his side, set out for Rome; and he conquered Rome. Thereafter he stayed in Rome, and Britain saw him no more, but Elen's two brothers took the British forces back to their homes, and to this day the seed of Macsen Wledig reigns in Britain.

When I had done, and the last note had hummed away to nothing in the smoky stillness, there was a roar of applause, cups thumping on the tables, and rough voices calling for more music, and more wine. Another cupful was pressed on me, and while I drank and rested before singing again, the men went back to talking among themselves, but softly, lest they disturb the singer's thoughts.

It was as well they could not guess at them; I was wondering what they would do if they knew that the last and latest scion of Maximus lay sleeping on the other side of the wall. For this part of the legend, at least, was true, that my father's family was descended straight from Maximus' marriage with the Welsh princess Elen. The rest of the legend, like all such tales, was a kind of dreaming distortion of the truth, as if an artist, reassembling a broken mosaic from a few worn and random fragments, rebuilt the picture in his own shimmering new colours, with here and there the pieces of the old, true picture showing plain.

The facts were these. Maximus, a Spaniard by birth, had commanded the armies in Britain under his general Theodosius at a time when Saxons and Picts were raiding the coasts constantly, and the Roman province of Britain looked like crumbling to its fall. Between them the commanders repaired the Wall of Hadrian, and held it, and Maximus himself rebuilt and garrisoned the great fortress at Segontium in Wales, and made it his headquarters. This is the place that is called Caer Seint by the British; it is the "fair castle" of the Dream, and here it must have been that Maximus met his Welsh Elen, and married her.

Then in the year that Ector had called the Flood Year it was Maximus (though his enemies denied him the credit) who after months of bitter fighting drove the Saxons back and constructed the provinces of Strathclyde and Manau Guotodin, buffer states, in whose shelter the people of Britain—his people—might live in peace. Already "Prince Macsen" to the folk of Wales, he was declared Emperor by his troops, and so might have remained, but for the events everyone knows of which took him abroad to avenge his old general's murder, and thereafter to march on Rome itself.

He never came back; here again the Dream is true; but not because he conquered Rome and stayed to rule it. He was defeated there, and later executed, and though some of the British forces who had gone with him came home and pledged themselves to his widow and his sons, the brief peace was over. With Maximus dead the Flood came again, and this time there was no sword to stop it.

Small wonder, in the dark years that followed, that the short stretch of Maximus' victorious peace should appear to men like a lost age as golden as any the poets sing. Small wonder that the legend of "Macsen the Protector" had grown and grown until his power compassed the earth, and in their dark times men spoke of him as of a god-sent saviour. . . .

My thoughts went back to the baby sleeping in the straw. I lifted the harp again, and when they hushed for me, sang them another song:

There was a boy born,
A winter king.
Before the black month
He was born,
And fled in the dark month
To find shelter
With the poor.

He shall come
With the spring
In the green month
And the golden month
And bright
Shall be the burning
Of his star.

"And did you earn your supper?" asked Moravik.

"Plenty to drink, and three copper coins." I laid them on the table and put the leather bag containing the King's gold beside them. "That's for your care of the child. I'll send more when it's needed. You'll not regret this, you and Brand. You've nursed kings before, Moravik, but never such a king as this one will be."

"What do I care for kings? That's nought but a bonny bairn, that should never have been set to such a journey in this weather. He should be home in his own nursery, and you can tell your King Uther that from me! Gold, indeed!" But the leather bag had vanished into some fastness of her skirt, and the coins with it.

"He's come to no harm on the journey?" I asked quickly.

"None that I can see. That's a good, strong boy, and like to flourish as well as any of my children. He's abed now, and those two young things with him, poor children, so keep your voice down and let them sleep."

Branwen and the child lay on a pallet in the far corner of the room, away from the fire. Their bed was underneath the flight of rough wooden steps which led up to a platform, like a small loft such as they use for hay in kings' stables. Indeed there was hay stacked there, and our beasts had been led in from the yard at the back, and were tethered now under the loft. A donkey, which I suppose was Brand's own, stood near them in the straw.

"Brand brought yours in," said Moravik. "There isn't much room, but he daren't leave them outside in the byre. That sorrel of yours with the white blaze, someone might know it for King Hoel's own, and there'd be questions asked that weren't too easy to answer. I've put you up above, and the boy. It's maybe not what you're used to, but it's soft, and it's clean."

"It'll be fine. But don't send me to bed yet, please, Moravik. May I stay up and talk to you?"

"Hm. Send you to bed, indeed! Aye, you always did look meek and talk soft, and you doing exactly as you wanted all the time. . . ." She sat down by the fire, spreading her skirts, and nodded to a stool. "Well, now, sit down and let me look at you. Mercy me, and here's a change! Who'd ever have thought it, back there in Maridunum, with hardly a decent rag to your name, that you'd turn out a son of the High King himself, and a doctor and a singer . . . and the sweet saints only know what else besides!"

"A magician, you mean?"

"Well, that never surprised me, the way I heard you'd been running off to the old man at Bryn Myrddin." She crossed herself, and her hand closed on an amulet at her neck. I had seen it glinting in the firelight; it was hardly a Christian symbol. So Moravik still hedged herself around with every talisman she could find. In this she was like most of the folk bred in the Perilous Forest, with its tales of old hauntings, and things seen in the twilight and heard in the wind. She nodded at me. "Aye, you always were a queer lad, with your solitary ways, and the things you'd say. Always knew too much, you did. I thought it was with listening at doors, but it seems I was wrong. 'The King's prophet,' they tell me you're called now. And the doings I've heard about, if the half of them's to be believed, which I doubt they're not . . . Well, now, tell me. Tell me everything."

The fire had burned low, almost to ash. There was silence from the next room now; the drinkers had either gone home, or settled to sleep. Brand had climbed the ladder an hour since, and snored softly beside Ralf. In the corner beside the dozing beasts, Branwen and the child slept, unmoving.

"And now here's this new start," said Moravik softly. "This baby here, you tell me he's the son of the High King, Uther himself, that won't own to him. Why do you have to take it on yourself to look after him? I'd have thought there's others he might ask, that could do it easier."

"I can't answer for King Uther," I said, "but for myself, you might say the child was a trust left to me by my father, and by the gods."

"The gods?" she asked sharply. "What talk is this for a good Christian man?"

"You forget, I was never baptized."

"Not even yet? Aye, I remember the old King would have none of it. Well, that's no concern of mine now, only of your own. But this child here, is he christened?"

"No. There's been no time. If you want to, then have him christened."

" 'If you want to'? What way is that to talk? What 'gods' were you talking of just now?"

"I hardly know. They—he—will make himself known in his own good time. Meanwhile have the boy christened, Moravik. When he leaves Brittany he's to be reared in a Christian household."

She was satisfied. "As soon as may be. I'll see him right with the dear Lord and his saints, trust me for that. And I've hung the vervain charm over his crib, and seen the nine prayers said. The girl says his name's Arthur. What sort of a name is that?"

"You would say Artos," I told her. This is a name meaning "Bear" in Celtic. "But don't call him by that name here. Give him some other name that you can use, and forget the other."

"Emrys, then? Ah, I thought that would make you smile. I'd always hoped that one day there'd be a child I could call after you."

"No, after my father Ambrosius, as I was called." I tried the names over to myself, in Latin and then in the Celtic tongue. *"Artorius Ambrosius, last of the Romans . . . Artos Emrys, first of the British . . ."* Then aloud to Moravik, smiling:

"Yes, call him so. Once, long ago, I foretold it, the coming of the Bear, a king called Arthur, who would knit past and future. I had forgotten, till now, where I had heard the name before. Christen him so."

She was silent for a few minutes. I saw her quick eyes searching my face. "In trust to you, you said. A king such as there hasn't been before. He will be King, then? You swear he will be King?" Then suddenly: "Why do you look like that, Merlin? I saw you look the same way a while back when the girl put the child to her breast. What is it?"

"I don't know . . ." I spoke slowly, my eyes on the last glimmer of fire where the burned logs hollowed round a red cave. "Moravik, I have done what I have done because God—whichever god he is—drove me to do it. Out of the dark he told me that the child which Uther begot of Ygraine that night at Tintagel would be King of all Britain, would be great, would drive the Saxons out of our shores and knit our poor country into a strong whole. I did nothing of my own will, but just for this, that Britain might not go down into the dark. It came to me whole, out of the silence and the fire, and as a certainty. Then for a time I saw nothing and heard nothing, and wondered if, in my love for my father and my father's land, I had been led astray, and had seen vision where there was nothing but hope and desire. But now, see, there it lies, just as the god told me." I looked at her. "I don't know if I can make you understand, Moravik. Visions and prophecies, gods and stars and voices speaking in the night . . . things seen cloudy in the flames and in the stars, but real as pain in the blood, and piercing the brain like ice. But now . . ." I paused again. ". . . now it is no longer a god's voice or a vision, it is a small human child with lusty lungs, a baby like any other baby, who cries, and sucks milk, and soaks his swaddling clothes. One's visions do not take account of this."

"It's men who have visions," said Moravik. "It's women who bear the children to fulfill them. That's the difference. And as for that one there"—she nodded towards the corner—"we shall see what we shall see. If he lives—and why should he not live, he's strong enough?—if he lives he has a good chance to be King. All we can do now is see that he makes a man. I'll do my part as you've done yours. The rest is with the good God."

I smiled at her. Her sturdy common sense seemed to have lifted a great weight from me. "You're right. I was a fool ever to doubt. What will come, will come."

"Then sleep on that."

"Yes. I'll go to bed now. You have a good man there, Moravik. I'm glad of it."

"Between us, boy, we'll keep your little King safely."

"I'm sure of that," I said, and after we had talked a little longer I climbed the ladder to bed.

That night I dreamed. I was standing in a field I knew near Hoel's town of Kerrec. It was a place of ancient holiness, where once a god had walked and I had seen him. In my dream I knew that I had come in the hope of seeing him again.

But the night was empty. All that moved was the wind. The sky arched high, bright with indifferent stars. Across its black dome, soft through the glitter of the fiercer stars, lay the long track of light they call the Galaxy. There was no cloud. About me stretched the field, just as I remembered it, bitten by the wind and sown by the sea's salt, with bare thorn trees hunched along the banks, and, solitary in the center, a single giant stone. I walked towards it. In the scattered light of the stars I cast no shadow, nor was there a shadow by the stone. Only the grey wind blurring the grass, and behind the stone the faint drifting of the stars that is not movement, but the heavens breathing.

Still the night was empty. My thoughts arrowed up into the shell of silence, and fell back spent. I was trying, with every grain of skill and power which I had fought and suffered for, to recall the god whose hand had been over me then, and whose light had led me. I prayed aloud, but heard no sound. I called on my magic, my gift of eyes and mind that men called the Sight, but nothing came. The night was empty, and I was failing. Even my human vision was failing, night and starlight melting into a blur, like something seen through running water. . . .

The sky itself was moving. The earth held still, but heaven itself was moving. The Galaxy gathered and narrowed into a shaft of light, then froze still as a stream in the bite of winter. A shaft of ice—no, a blade, it lay across the sky like a king's sword, with the great jewels blazing in the hilt. Emerald I saw, topaz, sapphires, which in the tongue of swords mean power and joy and justice and clean death.

For a long time the sword lay there, still, like a weapon newly burnished, waiting for the hand which will lift and wield it. Then, of itself, it moved. Not as a weapon is lifted in battle, or in ceremony, or sport. But as a blade slides home to its housing it slid, how gently, down towards the standing stone, dropping into it as a sword slips resting into its scabbard.

Then there was nothing but the empty field and the whistling wind, and a grey stone standing.

I woke to the darkness of the inn room, and a single star, small and bright, showing through a gap above the rafters. Below me the beasts breathed sweet breath, while all around were the snores and stirrings of the sleepers. The place smelled warmly of horses and peat smoke and hay and mutton stew.

I lay unmoving, flat on my back, watching the little star. I hardly thought about the dream. Vaguely, I remembered that there had been talk of a sword, and now this dream . . . But I let it pass me. It would come. I would be shown. God was back with me; time had not lied. And in an hour or two it would be morning.

BOOK II

THE SEARCH

1

The gods, all of them, must be accustomed to blasphemy. It is a blasphemy even to question their purposes, and to wonder, as I had done, who they were or if they even existed is blasphemy itself. Now I knew my god was back with me, that his purpose was working, and though I still saw nothing clearly, I knew that his hand would be over me when the time was right, and I would be guided, driven, shown—it did not matter which, nor in what form he came. He would show me that, too. But not yet. Today was my own. The dreams of the night had vanished with the stars that made them. This morning the wind was only the wind, and the sunlight nothing but light.

I do not think I even looked back. I had no fear for Ralf or the child. The Sight may be an uncomfortable thing to possess, but foreknowledge of catastrophe relieves the possessor of the small frets of day to day. A man who has seen his own old age and bitter end does not fear what may come to him at twenty-two. I had no doubts about my own safety, or the boy's whose sword I had seen—twice now—drawn and shining. So I was free to dread nothing worse than the next sea voyage, which took me, suffering but alive, to the port of Massilia on the Inland Sea, and landed me there on a bright February day which, in Britain, we would have called summer.

Once there, it did not matter who saw me and reported meeting me. If it should be noised abroad that Prince Merlin had been seen in Southern Gaul, or Italy, then perhaps Uther's enemies would watch me for a while, hoping for a lead to the vanished prince. Eventually they would give up and search elsewhere, but by that time the trail would be cold. In Kerrec the visit of the inconspicuous singer would be forgotten, and Ralf, quietly anonymous in the forest tavern, would be able to come and go without fear between Coll and the castle at Kerrec, with news of the child's progress for Hoel to transmit to me. So, once landed in Massilia, and recovered from my voyage, I set about making open preparations for my journey eastwards.

With no need this time for disguise, I travelled in comfort, if not in princely style. Appearances had never troubled me; a man makes his own; but I had friends to visit, and if I could not do them honour, at least I must not shame them. So I hired a body-servant and bought horses and baggage mules and a slave to look after them, and set off for my first destination, which was Rome.

The road out of Massilia is a straight, sun-beaten ribbon of white dust running along the shore where the villages built by Caesar's veterans crouch among their carefully tended olive groves and vines. We set out at sunrise with our horses' shadows long behind us. The road was still dewed, and the air smelled of dung and peppery cypress and the smoke of the early fires. Cockerels crowed and curs ran out yapping at our horses' heels. Behind me the two servants talked, low voiced, not to intrude on me. They seemed decent men; the

freeman, Gaius, had seen service before, and came to me well recommended. The other, Stilicho, was the son of a Sicilian horse-dealer who had cheated himself into debt and sold his son to pay it. Stilicho was a thin, lively youth with a cheerful eye and unquenchable spirits. Gaius was solemn and efficient, and more conscious of my dignity than I had ever been myself. When he discovered my royal status he took on an aura of pomp which amused me, and impressed Stilicho into silence for almost twenty minutes. I believe that thereafter it was continually used as a threat or a bribe for service. Certainly, whatever means the two of them employed, I was to find my journey almost a miracle of smoothness and comfort.

Now, as my horse pricked his ears at the morning sun, I felt my mood lift to meet the growing brilliance. It was as if the griefs and doubts of the last year streamed back from me like my horse's shadow. As I set off eastwards with my little train I was for the first time in my life free; free of the world in front of me, and free of the obligations at my back. Until this moment I had lived always towards some goal; I had sought for and then served my father, and after his death had waited in grief until, with Arthur, my servitude might start again. Now the first part of my work was done; the boy was safe and, as my gods and my stars could be trusted, he would remain so. I was still young, and facing the sun, and, call it solitude or call it freedom, I had a new world in front of me and a span of time ahead when at last I could travel the lands of which as a boy I had been taught so much, and which I had longed to see.

So in time I came to Rome, and walked on the green hills between the cypresses, and talked with a man who had known my father when he was the age I was now. I lodged in his house, and wondered how I had ever thought my father's house in Kerrec a palace, or seen London as a great city, or even a city at all. Then from Rome to Corinth, and overland through the valleys of the Argolid where goats grazed the baked summer hills, and people lived, wilder than they, among the ruins of cities built by giants. Here at last I saw stones greater even than those in the Giants' Dance, lifted and set just as the songs had told me, and as I travelled farther east I saw lands yet emptier with giant stones standing in desert sunlight, and men who lived as simply as roving wolf-packs, but who made songs as easily as the birds, and as marvellously as the stars moving in their courses. Indeed, they know more about the movements of the stars than any other men; I suppose their world is made up of the empty spaces of the desert and the sky. I spent eight months with a man near Sardis, in Maeonia, who could calculate to a hair's breadth, and with whose help I could have lifted the Giants' Dance in half the time had it been twice as great. Another six months I spent on the coast of Mysia, near Pergamum, in a great hospital where sick men flock for treatment, rich and poor alike. I found much that was new to me there in the art of healing; in Pergamum they use music with the drugs to heal a man's mind through dreams, and his body after it. Truly the god must have guided me when he sent me to learn music as a child. And all the time, on all my journeys, I learned smatterings of strange tongues, and heard new songs and new music, and saw strange gods worshipped, some in holy places, and some in manners we would call unclean. It is never wise to turn aside from knowing, however the knowing comes.

Through all this time I rested, steady and secure, in the knowledge that, back there in the Perilous Forest in Brittany, the child grew and thrived in safety.

Messages from Ralf came occasionally, sent by King Hoel to await me at

certain prearranged ports of call. This way I learned that, as soon as might be, Ygraine was pregnant again. She was delivered in due time of a daughter, who was called Morgian. By the time I read them, the letters were of course long out of date, but as far as the boy Arthur was concerned I had my own more immediate source of reassurance. I watched, in the way I have, in the fire.

It was in a brazier lit against the chill of a Roman evening that I first watched Ralf make the journey through the forest to Hoel's court. He travelled alone and unremarked, and when he set out again in the misty dark to make for home he was not followed. In the depths of the forest I lost him, but later the smoke blew aside to show me his horse safely stabled, and Branwen smiling in the sunlit yard with the baby in her arms. Several times after that I watched Ralf's journey, but always smoke or darkness seemed to gather and lie like mist along the river, so that I could not see the tavern, or follow him through the door. It was as if, even from me, the place was guarded. I had heard it said that the Perilous Forest of Brittany was spellbound land; I can affirm that this is true. I doubt if any magic less potent than mine could have spied through the wall of mist that hid the inn. Glimpses I had, no more than that, from time to time. Once, fleetingly, I saw the baby playing among a litter of puppies in the yard while the bitch licked his face and Brand looked on, grinning, till Moravik burst scolding out of her kitchen to snatch the child up, wipe his face with her apron, and vanish with him indoors. Another time I saw him perched aloft on Ralf's horse while it was drinking at the trough, and yet again astride the saddle in front of Ralf, hanging on to the mane with both hands while the beast trotted down to the river's edge. I never saw him closely, or even clearly, but I saw enough to know that he thrived and grew strong.

Then, when he was four years old, the time came when Ralf was to take him from the Forest's protection and seek Count Ector's.

The night his ship set sail from the Small Sea of Morbihan I was lying under a black Syrian sky where the stars seem to burn twice as big and ardent as the stars at home. The fire I watched was a shepherd's, lit against the wolves and mountain lions, and he had given me its hospitality when my servants and I were benighted crossing the heights above Berytus. The fire was stacked high with wind-dried wood, and blazed fiercely against the night. Somewhere beyond it I could hear Stilicho talking, then the rough mutter of the shepherd, and laughter shushed by Gaius' grave tones, till the roar and crackling of the fire drowned them. Then the pictures came, fragmentary at first, but as clear and vivid as the visions I had had as a boy in the crystal cave. I watched the whole journey, scene by scene, in one night's vision, as you can dream a lifetime between night and morning. . . .

This was my first clear sight of Ralf since I had parted from him in Brittany. I hardly knew him. He was a tall young man now, with the look of a fighter, and an air of decision and responsibility that gave him weight and sat well on him. I had left it to Hoel's and his discretion whether or not an armed escort would be needed to convoy his "wife and child" to the ship: in the event they played safe, though it was obvious that the secret was still our own. Hoel had contrived that a wagon-load of goods should be dispatched through the forest under the escort of half a dozen troopers; when it set off back towards Kerrec and the wharf where the ship lay, what more natural than that the young man and his family should travel back to Kerrec with the return load—I never saw what was in those corded bales—using its protection for themselves? Branwen rode in the wagon, and so, in the end, did Arthur. It looked to me as if he had already outgrown women's care; he would have spent all his time with the troopers, and it took Ralf's authority to make him ride concealed in the wagon with Branwen, rather than on the saddle-bow at the head of the troop. After the little party had reached the ship and embarked safely, four of the troop took ship along with Ralf, apparently convoying those precious bales to their destination. So the ship set sail. Light glittered on the firelit sea, and the little ship had red sails which spread against a breezy sky of sunset, till they dwindled and vanished small in the blowing fire.

It was in a blaze of sunrise, perhaps lit only by the Syrian flames, that the ship docked at Glannaventa. I saw the ropes made fast and the party cross the gangplank to be met by Ector himself, brown and smiling, with a full-armed body of men. They bore no badge. They had brought a wagon for the cargo, but as soon as they were clear of the town the wagon was left to follow, while out of it came a litter for Branwen and Arthur, and then the party rode as fast as might be for Galava, up the military road through the mountains which lie between Ector's castle and the sea. The road climbs through two steep passes with between them a low-lying valley sodden with marsh, which is flooded right through till late spring. The road is bad, broken by storm and torrents and winter frosts, and in places where the hillsides had slipped in flood time the road has vanished, and all that remains of it are the ghosts of the old tracks that were there before the Romans came. Wild country and a wild road, but straight going on a May day for a body of well armed men. I watched them trotting along, the litter swinging between its sturdy mules, through flame-lit dawn and firelit day, till suddenly with evening the mist rolled down dark from the head of the pass, and I saw in it the glitter of swords that spelled danger.

Ector's party was clattering downhill from the second summit, slowing to a walk at a steep place where crags crowded the edge of the road. From here it was only a short descent to the broad river valley and the good flat road to the waterhead where the castle stands. In the distance, still lit by evening, were the big trees and the blossoming orchards and the gentle green of the farmlands. But up in the pass among the grey crags and the rolling mist it was dark, and the horses slipped and stumbled on a steep scree where a torrent drove across the way and the road had collapsed into the water's bed. The rush of water must have blanketed all other sound from them. No one saw, dim behind the mist, the other men waiting, mounted and armed.

Count Ector was at the head of the troop, and in the middle of it, surrounded, the litter lurched and swung between its mules with Ralf riding close beside it. They were approaching the ambush; were beside it. I saw Ector's head turn sharply, then he checked his horse so suddenly that it tried to rear and instead plunged, slipping on the scree as Ector's sword flashed out and his arm went up. The troopers, surrounding the litter as best they might on the rushing slope, stood to fight. At the moment of clashing, shouting attack I saw what none of the troop appeared yet to have seen, other shadows riding down out of the mist beyond the crags.

I believe I shouted. I made no sound, but I saw Ralf's head go up like a hound's at his master's whistle. He yelled, wheeling his horse. Men wheeled with him, and met the new attack with a crash and flurry that sent sparks up from the swords like a smith's hammer from the anvil.

I strained my eyes through the visionary firelight to see who the attackers were. But I could not see. The wrestling, clashing darkness, the sparkling swords, the shouting, the wheeling horses—then the attackers vanished into the mist as suddenly as they had come, leaving one of their number dead on the scree, and carrying another bleeding across a saddle.

There was nothing to be gained by pursuing them across mountains thick with the misty twilight. One of the troopers picked up the fallen man and flung him across a horse. I saw Ector point, and the trooper searched the body looking, apparently, for identification, but finding none. Then the guard formed again round the litter, and rode on. I saw Ralf, surreptitious, winding a rag round his left arm where a blade had hacked in past the shield. A moment later I saw him, laughing, stoop in the saddle to say through the curtains of the litter: "Well, but you're not grown yet. Give it a year or two, and I promise you we'll find you a sword to suit your size." Then he reached to pull the leather curtains of the litter close. When I strained my sight to see Arthur, smoke blew grey across the scene and the shepherd called something to his dog, and I was back on the scented hillside with the moon coming out above the ruins of the temple where nothing remains now of the Goddess but her nightowls brooding.

So the years passed, and I used my freedom in travels which I have told of in other places; there is no room for them here. For me they were rich years, and lightly borne, and the god's hand lay gently on me, so that I saw all I asked to see; but in all the time there was no message, no moving star, nothing to call me home.

Then one day, when Arthur was six years old, the message came to me near Pergamum, where I was teaching and working in the hospital.

It was early spring, and all day rain had been falling like whips on the streaming rock, darkening the white limestone and tearing ruts in the pathway which leads down to the hospital cells by the sea. I had no fire to bring me the vision, but in that place the gods stand waiting by every pillar, and the air is heavy with dreams. This was only a dream, the same as other men's, and came in a moment of exhausted sleep.

A man had been carried in late in the night, with a leg badly gashed and the life starting to pump out of the great vein. I and the other doctor on duty had worked over him for more than three hours, and afterwards I had gone out into the sea to wash off the blood which had gushed thick and then hardened on me. It was possible that the patient would live; he was young, and slept now with the blood staunched and the wound safely stitched. I stripped off my soaked loincloth—that climate allows one to work near naked on the bloodier jobs—swam till I was clean, then stretched on the still warm sand to rest. The rain had stopped with evening, and the night was calm and warm and full of stars.

It was no vision I had, but a kind of dream of wakefulness. I lay (as I thought) open-eyed, watching, and watched by, the bright swarm. Among that fierce host of stars was one distant one, cloudy, its light faint among the others like a lamp in a swirl of snow. Then it swam closer, closer still, till its clouded air blotted out the brighter stars, and I saw mountains and shore, and rivers running like the veins of a leaf through the valleys of my own country. Now the snow swirled thicker, hiding the valleys, and behind the snow was the growl of thunder, and the shouting of armies, and the sea rose till the shore dissolved, and salt ran up the rivers and the green fields bleached to grey, and blackened to desert with their veins showing like dead men's bones.

I woke knowing that I must go back. It was not yet, the flood, but it was coming. By the next snow-time, or the next, we would hear the thunder, and I must be there, between the King and his son.

2

I had planned to go home by Constantinopolis, and letters had already gone ahead of me. Now I would have preferred to take a quicker way, but the only ship I could get was one plying north close inshore towards Chalcedon, which lies just across the strait from Constantinopolis. Arrived here, delayed by freakish winds and uncertain weather, luck still seemed against me; I had just missed a westbound ship, they told me, and there was no other due to leave for a week or more. From Chalcedon the trade is mostly small coastbound craft; the bigger shipping uses the great harbour of Constantinopolis. So I took the ferry over, not averse, in spite of the need I felt for haste, to seeing the city of which I had heard so much.

I had expected the New Rome to surpass the old Rome in magnificence, but found Constantine's city a place of sharper contrasts, with squalor crowding close behind the splendour, and that air of excitement and risk which is breathed in a young city looking forward to prosperity, still building, spreading, assimilating, and avid to grow rich.

Not that the foundation was new; it had been capital of Byzantium since Byzas had settled his folk there a thousand years before; but it was almost a century and a half now since the Emperor Constantine had moved the heart of the empire eastwards, and started to build and fortify the old Byzantium and call it after himself.

Constantinopolis is a city marvellously situated on a tongue of land which holds a natural harbour they call the Golden Horn, and rightly; I had never imagined such a traffic of richly laden ships as I saw in the brief crossing from Chalcedon. There are palaces and rich houses, and government buildings with corridors like a maze and the countless officials employed by the government coming and going like bees in a hive. Everywhere there are gardens, with pavilions and pools, and fountains constantly gushing; the city has an abundance of sweet water. To the landward side Constantine's Wall defends the city, and from its Golden Gate the great thoroughfare of the Mese runs, magnificently arcaded through most of its length, through three fora decorated with columns, to end at the great triumphal arch of Constantine. The Emperor's immense church dedicated to the Holy Wisdom sits high over the walls that edge the sea. It was a magnificent city, and a splendid capital, but it had not the air of Rome as my father had spoken of it, or as we had thought of it in Britain; this was still the East, and the city looked to the East. Even the dress, though men wore the Roman tunic and mantle, had the look of Asia, and, though Latin was spoken everywhere, I heard Greek and Syrian and Armenian in the markets, and once beyond the arcades of the Mese you might have supposed yourself in Antioch.

It is a place not easy to picture, if one has never been beyond Britain's shores. Above everything it was exciting, with an air full of promise. It was a city looking forward, where Rome and Athens and even Antioch had seemed to be looking back; and London, with its crumbling temples and patched-up towers and men always watching with their hands to their swords, seemed as remote and near as savage as the ice-lands of the northmen.

My host in Constantinopolis was a connection of my father's, distant, but not too distant to let him greet me as cousin. He was descended from one Adean, brother-in-law of Maximus, who had been one of Maximus' officers and had followed him on the final expedition to Rome. Adean had been wounded outside Rome and left for dead, but rescued and nursed back to health by a Christian family. Later he had married the daughter of the house, turned Christian, and though he never took service with the Eastern Emperor (being content with the pardon granted him through his father-in-law's intercession) his son entered the service of Theodosius II, made a fortune at it, and was rewarded with a royally connected wife and a splendid house near the Golden Horn.

His great-grandson bore the same name, but pronounced it with the accent of Byzantium: Ahdjan. He was still discernibly of Celtic descent, but looked, you might say, like a Welshman gone bloodless by being drawn too high towards the sun. He was tall and thin, with the oval face and pale skin, and the black eyes set straight, that you see in all their portraits. His mouth was thin-lipped, bloodless too; the court servant's mouth, close-lipped with keeping secrets. But he was not without humour, and could talk wisely and entertainingly, a rarity in a country where men—and women—argue perpetually about matters of the spirit in terms of the more than stupid flesh. I had not been in Constantinopolis half a day before I found myself remembering something I had read in a book of Galapas': "If you ask someone how many obols a certain thing costs, he replies by dogmatizing on the born and unborn. If you ask the price of bread, they answer you, the Father is greater than the Son, and the Son is subordinate to Him. If you ask is my bath ready, they answer you, the Son has been made out of nothing."

Ahdjan received me very kindly, in a splendid room with mosaics on the walls and a floor of golden marble. In Britain, where it is cold, we put the pictures on the floor and hang thick coverings over walls and doors; but they do things differently in the East. This room glittered with colour; they use a lot of gold in their mosaics, and with the faintly uneven surface of the tesserae this has the effect of glimmering movement, as if the wall-pictures were tapestries of silk. The figures are alive, and full of colour, some of them very beautiful. I remembered the cracked mosaic at home in Maridunum, which as a child I had thought the most wonderful picture in the world; it had been of Dionysos, with grapes and dolphins, but none of the pictures was whole, and the god's eyes had been badly mended, and showed a cast. To this day I see Dionysos with a squint. One side of Ahdjan's room opened to a terrace where a fountain played in a wide marble pool, and cypress and laurel grew in pots along the balustrade. Below this the garden lay, scented in the sun, with rose and iris and jasmine (though it was hardly into April) competing with the scent of a hundred shrubs, and everywhere the dark fingers of cypress, gilded with tiny cones, pointing straight at the brilliant sky. Below the terraces sparkled the waters of the Horn, as thickly populated with ships as a farm pond at home is with water-beetles.

There was a letter waiting for me, from Ector. After Ahdjan and I had exchanged greetings, I asked his leave, then unrolled and read it.

Ector's scribe wrote well, though in long periods which I knew were a gloss on what that forthright gentleman had actually said. But the news, sorted out from the poetry and the perorations, bore out what I already knew or suspected. In more than guarded phrases he conveyed to me that Arthur (for the scribe's sake he wrote of "the family, Drusilla and both the boys") was safe. But for how long "the place" might be safe, said Ector, he could not guess, and went on to give me the news as his informers reported it.

The danger of invasion, always there but for the last few years sporadic, had begun to grow into something more formidable. Octa and Eosa, the Saxon leaders defeated by Uther in the first year of his reign, and kept prisoner since then in London, were still safely held; but lately pressure had been brought to bear—not only by the Federates, but by some British leaders who were afraid of the growing discontent along the Saxon Shore—on King Uther to free the Saxon princes on terms of treaty. Since he had refused this, there had been two armed attempts to release them from prison. These had been punished with brutal severity, and now other factions were pressing Uther to kill the Saxon leaders out of hand, a course he was apparently afraid to take for fear of the Federates. These, firmly ensconced along the Shore, and crowding too close for comfort even to London, were again showing threatening signs of inviting reinforcements from abroad, and pressing up into the rich country near Ambrosius' Wall. Meanwhile there were worse rumours: a messenger had been caught, and under torture had confessed, that he carried tokens of friendship from the Angles on the Abus in the east, to the Pictish kings of the wild land west of Strathclyde. But nothing more, added Ector, than tokens; and he personally did not think that trouble could yet come from the north. Between Strathclyde and the Abus, the kingdoms of Rheged and Lothian still stood firm.

I skimmed through the rest, then rolled up the letter. "I must go straight home," I told Ahdjan.

"So soon? I was afraid of it." He signed to a servant, who lifted a silver flagon from a bowl of snow, and poured the wine into glass goblets. Where the snow had come from I did not know; they have it carried by night from the hilltops, and stored underground in straw. "I'm sorry to lose you, but when I saw the letter, I was afraid it might be bad news."

"Not bad yet, but there will be bad to come." I told him what I could of the situation, and he listened gravely. They understand these things in Constantinopolis. Since Alaric the Goth took Rome, men's ears are tuned to listen for the thunder in the north. I went on: "Uther is a strong king and a good general, but even he cannot be everywhere, and this division of power makes men uncertain and afraid. It's time the succession was made sure." I tapped the letter. "Ector tells me the Queen is with child again."

"So I had heard. If this is a boy he'll be declared the heir, won't he? Hardly a time for a baby to inherit a kingdom, unless he had a Stilicho to look after his interests." He was referring to the general who had protected the empire of the young Emperor Honorius. "Has Uther anyone among his generals who could be left as regent if he were killed?"

"For all I know they'd be as likely to kill as to protect."

"Well, Uther had better live, then, or allow the son he's already got to be his legitimate heir. He must be—what? Seven? Eight? Why cannot Uther do the sensible thing and declare him again, with you to become regent if the King should be killed during the boy's minority?" He looked at me sideways over his glass. "Come, Merlin, don't raise your brows at me like that. The whole world knows you took the child from Tintagel and have him hidden somewhere."

"Does the world say where?"

"Oh, yes. The world spawns solutions the way that pool yonder spawns frogs. The general opinion is that the child is safe in the island of Hy-Brasil, nursed by the white paps of nine queens, no less. It's no wonder he flourishes. Or else that he is with you, but invisible. Disguised perhaps as a pack-mule?"

I laughed. "How would I dare? What would that make Uther?"

"You'd dare anything, I think. I was hoping you'd dare tell me where the boy is, and all about him . . . No?"

I shook my head, smiling. "Forgive me, but not yet."

He moved a hand gracefully. They understand secrets, too, in Constantinopolis. "Well, at least you can tell me if he's safe and well?"

"I assure you of it."

"And will succeed, with you as regent?"

I laughed, shook my head, and drained my wine. He signalled to the slave, who was standing out of hearing, and the man hurried to refill my glass. Ahdjan waved him away. "I've had a letter, too, from Hoel. He tells me that King Uther has sent men in search of you, and that he doesn't speak of you with kindness, though everyone knows how much he owes you. There are rumours, too, that even the King himself does not know where his son is hidden, and has spies out searching. Some say the boy is dead. There are also those who say that you keep the young prince close for your own ambitious ends."

"Yes," I agreed equably, "there would be some who say that."

"You see?" He threw out a hand. "I try to goad you into speaking, and you are not even angry. Where another man would protest, would even fear to go back, you say nothing, and—I'm afraid—decide to take ship straight for home."

"I know the future, Ahdjan, that's the difference."

"Well, I don't know the future, and it's obvious you won't tell me, but I can make my own guess at the truth. What men are saying is just that truth twisted: you keep the boy close because you know he must one day be King. You can tell me this, though. What will you do when you get back? Bring him out of hiding?"

"By the time I get back the Queen's child should be born," I said. "What I do must depend on that. I shall see Uther, of course, and talk to him. But the main thing, as I see it, is to let the people of Britain know—friend and enemy alike— that Prince Arthur is alive and thriving, and will be ready to show himself beside his father when the time comes."

"And that's not yet?"

"I think not. When I reach home I hope I shall see more clearly. With your leave, Ahdjan, I'll take the first ship."

"As you will, of course. I shall be sorry to lose your company."

"I regret it, too. It's been a happy chance that brought me after all to Constantinopolis. I might have missed seeing you, but I was delayed by bad weather and lost the ship I should have got at Chalcedon."

He said something civil, then looked startled as he saw the implications. "Delayed? You mean you were on your way home already? Before you saw the letter? You knew?"

"No details. Only that it was time I was home."

"By the Three!" For a moment I had seen the Celt looking out of his eyes, though it was the Christian god that he swore by; they only have one other oath in Constantinopolis, and that is "By the One," and they fight to the death over them. Then he laughed. "By the Three! I wish I'd had you beside me last week in the Hippodrome! I lost a cool thousand on the Greens—a sure thing, you'd have sworn, and they ran like three-legged cows. Well, it seems that whatever prince has you to guide him, he's lucky. If *he* had had you, I might have had an empire today, instead of a respectable government post—and lucky to get that without being a eunuch besides."

He nodded as he spoke at the great mosaic on the main wall of the room behind us. I had noticed it already, and wondered vaguely at the Byzantine strain of melancholy which decorates a room with such scenes instead of the livelier designs one sees in Greece and Italy. I had already observed, in the entrance hall, a crucifix done life-size with mourning figures and Christian devices all round it. This, too, was an execution, but a noble one, on the battlefield. The sky was dark, done with chips of slate and lapis hammered into clouds like iron, with among them the staring heads of gods. The horizon showed a line of towers and temples with a crimson sun setting behind. It seemed meant to be Rome. The wide plain in front of the walls was the scene of the battle's end: to the left the defeated host, men and horses dead or dying on a field scattered with broken weapons; to the right the victors, clustered behind the crowned leader, and bathed in a shaft of light descending from a Christ poised in blessing above the other gods. At the victor's feet the other leader knelt, his neck bared to the executioner's blade. He was lifting both arms towards his conqueror, not for mercy, but in formal surrender of the sword which lay across his hands. Below him, in the corner of the picture, was written *Max.* On the right, below the victor, were stamped the words *Theod. Imp.*

"By the One!" I said, and saw Ahdjan smile; but he could not have known what had brought me so quickly to my feet. He rose gracefully and followed me to the wall, obviously pleased at my interest.

"Yes, Maximus' defeat by the Emperor. Good, isn't it?" He smoothed a hand over the silken tesserae. "The man who did it can't have known much of the ironies of war. In spite of all this, you might say it came out even enough in the end. That hang-dog fellow on the left behind Maximus is Hoel's ancestor, the one who took the remnants of the British contingent home. This holy-looking gentleman shedding blood all over the Emperor's feet is my great-great-grandfather, to whose conscience and good business sense I owe both my fortune and the saving of my soul."

I hardly listened. I was staring at the sword in Maximus' hand. I had seen it before. Glowing on the wall behind Ygraine. Flashing home to its scabbard in Brittany. Now here, the third time, imaged in Maximus' hand outside the walls of Rome.

Ahdjan was watching me curiously. "What is it?"

"The sword. So it was his sword."

"What was? Have you seen it, then?"

"No. Only in a dream. Twice, I've seen it in dreams. Now here for the third time, in a picture . . ." I spoke half to myself, musing. Sunlight, striking up off the pool on the terrace, sent light rippling across the wall, so that the sword shimmered in Macsen's hands; and the jewels in its hilt showed green and yellow and vivid blue. I said, softly: "So that is why I missed the ship at Chalcedon."

"What do you mean?"

"Forgive me, I hardly know. I was thinking of a dream. Tell me, Ahdjan, this picture . . . Are those the walls of Rome? Maximus wasn't murdered at Rome, surely?"

"Murdered?" Ahdjan, speaking primly, looked amused. "The word on our side of the family is 'executed.' No, it wasn't at Rome. I think the artist was being symbolic. It happened at Aquileia. You may not know it; it's a small place near the mouth of the Turrus River, at the northern end of the Adriatic."

"Do ships call there?"

His eyes widened. "You mean to go?"

"I would like to see the place where Macsen died. I would like to know what became of his sword."

"You won't find that at Aquileia," he said. "Kynan took it."

"Who?"

He nodded at the picture. "The man on the left. Hoel's ancestor, who took the British back home to Brittany. Hoel could have told you." He laughed at my expression. "Did you come all this way for that piece of information?"

"It seems so," I said. "Though until this moment I didn't know it. Are you telling me that Hoel has that sword? It's in Brittany?"

"No. It was lost long since. Some of the men who went home to Greater Britain took his things with them; I suppose they would have taken his sword to give his son."

"And?"

"That's all I know. It's a long time ago and all it is now is a family tale, and the half of it's probably not true. Does it matter so much?"

"Matter?" I said. "I hardly know. But I've learned to look close at most things that come my way."

He was watching me with a puzzled look, and I thought he would question me further, but after a short hesitation he said merely: "I suppose so. Will you walk out now into the garden? It's cooler. You looked as if your head hurt you."

"That? It was nothing. Someone playing a lyre on the terrace down there. It isn't in tune."

"My daughter. Shall we go down and stop her?"

On the way down he told me of a ship due to leave the Horn in two days' time. He knew the master, and could bespeak me a passage. It was a fast ship, and would dock at Ostia, whence I would certainly find a vessel plying westwards.

"What about your servants?"

"Gaius is a good man. You could do worse than employ him yourself. I freed Stilicho. He's yours if he'll stay, and he's a wizard with horses. It would be cruelty for me to take him to Britain; his blood's as thin as an Arabian gazelle's."

But when the morning came Stilicho was there at the quayside, stubborn as the mules he had handled with such skill, his belongings in a stitched sack, and a cloak of sheepskin sweltering round him in the Byzantine sun. I argued with him, traducing even the British climate, and my simple way of living which he might find tolerable in a country where the sun shines, but would be hardship itself in that land of icy winds and wet. But, seeing finally that he would have his way even if he paid his own passage with the money I had given him as a parting gift, I gave way.

To tell the truth I was touched, and glad to have his company on the long voyage home. Though he had had none of Gaius' training as a body-servant, he was quick and intelligent, and had already shown skill in helping me with plants and medicines. He would be useful, and besides, after all these years away life at Bryn Myrddin looked a little lonelier than it had used to, and I knew well that Ralf would never come back to me.

3

It was late summer when I reached Britain. Fresh news met me on the quay, in the person of one of the King's chamberlains, who greeted me with passionate relief, and such a total absence of surprise that I told him: "You should be in my business."

He laughed. He was Lucan, whom I had known well when my father was King, and he and I were on terms. "Soothsaying? Hardly. This is the fifth ship I've met. I own I expected you, but I never thought to see you so soon. We heard you went east a long while back, and we sent messengers, hoping to reach you. Did they find you?"

"No. But I was already on my way."

He nodded, as if I had confirmed his thoughts. He had been too close to my father, Ambrosius, to question the power that guided me. "You knew the King was sick, then?"

"Not that, no. Only that the times were dangerous, and I should get home. Uther ill? That's grave news. What's the sickness?"

"A wound gone bad. You knew he's been seeing to the rebuilding of the Saxon Shore defenses, and training the troops there himself? Well, an alarm was raised about longships up the Thames—they'd been seen level with Vagniacae—too near London for comfort. A small foray, nothing serious, but he was first into it as usual, and got a cut, and the wound didn't heal. This was two months since, and he's still in pain, and losing flesh."

"Two months? Hasn't his own physician been attending him?"

"Indeed yes. Gandar's been there from the beginning."

"And he could do nothing?"

"Well," said Lucan, "according to him the King was mending, and he says—along with the other doctors who've been consulted—that there's nothing to fear. But I've watched them conferring in corners, and Gandar looks worried." He glanced at me sideways. "There's a kind of uneasiness—you might even call it apprehension—infecting the whole court, and it's going to be hard to keep it contained there. I don't have to tell you, it's a bad time for the country to doubt if their leader's going to be fit to lead them. In fact, rumours have started already. You know the King can't have the bellyache without a scare of poison; and now they whisper about spells and hauntings. And not without reason; the King looks, sometimes, like a man who walks with ghosts. It was time you came home."

We were already moving along the road from the port. The horses had been there ready saddled at the quayside, and an escort waiting; this more for ceremony than for safety; the road to London is well-travelled and guarded. It occurred to me that perhaps the armed men who rode with us were there, not to see that I came to the King unharmed, but that I came there at all.

I said as much dryly, to Lucan. "It seems the King wants to make sure of me."

He looked amused, but only said with his courtier's smoothness: "Perhaps he was afraid that you might not care to attend him. Shall we say that a physician who fails to cure a king does not always add to his reputation."

"Does not always survive, you mean. I trust poor Gandar's still alive?"

"So far." He paused, then said neutrally: "Not that I'm much of a judge, but I'd have said it's not the King's body that lacks a cure, but his mind."

"So it's my magic that's wanted?" He was silent. I added: "Or his son?"

His eyelids drooped. "There are rumours about him, too."

"I'm sure there are." My voice was as bland as his. "One piece of news I did hear on my travels, that the Queen was pregnant again. I reckon she should have been brought to bed a month ago. What is the child?"

"It was a son, stillborn. They say that it was this sent the King out of his mind, and fevered his wound again. And now there are rumours that the eldest son is dead, too. In fact some say he died in infancy, that there is no son." He paused. His gaze fixed on his horse's ears, but there was the faintest of queries in his voice.

"Not true, Lucan," I said. "He's alive, a fine boy, and growing fast. Don't be afraid, he'll be there when he's needed."

"Ah." It was a long exhalation of relief. "Then it's true he's with you! This is the news that will heal the kingdom, if not the King. You'll bring the boy to London now?"

"First I must see the King. After that, who knows?"

A courtier knows when a subject has been turned, and Lucan asked no more questions, but began to talk of more general news. He told me in more detail what I had already learned from Ector's letters; Ector had certainly not exaggerated the situation. I took care not to ask too many questions about the possible danger in the north, but Lucan spoke of it himself, of the manning of strongpoints north of Rheged along the old line of Hadrian's Wall, and then of Lot's contribution to the defense of the north-east. "He's making hard going of it. Not because the raids are bad—the place has been quiet lately—but perhaps because of that very fact. The small kings don't trust Lot; they say he's a hard man and niggardly with spoils, and cares little for any interests except his own. When they see there's no fighting to be done yet, and nothing to win, they desert him wholesale and take their men home to till the fields." He made a sound of contempt, as near to a snort as a courtier ever gets. "Fools, not to see that whether they like their commander or not, they'll have no fields to till, nor families to till them for, unless they fight."

"But Lot's whole interest lies in his alliances, especially to the southward. I suppose that that with Rheged is safe enough? Why do his allies distrust him? Do they suspect him of lining his own nest at their expense? Or perhaps of something worse?"

"That I can't tell you." His voice was wooden.

"Is there no one else Uther can appoint as commander in the north?"

"Not unless he goes himself. He can't demote Lot. His daughter is promised to him."

I said, startled: "His daughter? Do you mean that Lot accepted Morgause after all?"

"Not Morgause, no," said Lucan. "I doubt that marriage wasn't tempting enough for Lothian, for all the girl's turned out such a beauty. Lot's an ambitious man, he'd not dangle after a bastard when there was a true-born princess to be had. I meant the Queen's daughter; Morgian."

"Morgian? But she can hardly be five years old!"

"Nevertheless, she's promised, and you know that's binding between kings."

"If I don't, who should?" I said dryly, and Lucan knew what I was thinking of: my own mother who had borne me to Ambrosius with no bond but a promise made in secret; and my father who had let the promise bind him as securely as a ceremonial oath.

We came in sight of London Wall then, and the traffic of the morning market thronged about us. Lucan had given me plenty to think about, and I was glad when the escort closed up, and he was silent, and left me to my thoughts.

I had expected to find Uther attended, and about some at least of his affairs, but he was still keeping his own chamber, and alone.

As I was led through the antechambers towards his room I saw nobles, officers and servants all waiting, and there was an apprehensive quiet about the crowded rooms which told its own tale. Men conferred in small groups, low-voiced and worried, the servants looked nervous and edgy, and in the outer corridors, where merchants and petitioners waited, there was the patient despondency of men who have already passed the point of hope.

Heads turned as I went through, and I heard the whisper run ahead of me like wind through a waste land, and a Christian bishop, forgetting himself, said audibly: "God be praised! Now we'll see the spell lifted." One or two men whom I knew started forward with warm greetings, and a spate of questions ready, but I smiled and shook my head and went through with no more than a quick word. And since with kings one can never quite rule out the thought of malice or murder, I checked the faces that I knew: somewhere in this crowd of armed and jewelled lords there might be one who would not welcome my return to the King's side; someone who watched for Uther to fail before his son was grown; someone who was Arthur's enemy, and therefore mine.

Some of them I knew well, but even these, as I greeted them, I studied. The leaders from Wales, Ynyr of Guent, Mador and Gwilim from my own country of Dyfed. Not Maelgon himself from Gwynedd, but one of his sons, Cunedda. Beside them, with a handful of their countrymen, Brychan and Cynfelin from Dyfnaint, and Nentres of Garlot, whom I had watched ride out with Uther from Tintagel. Then the men from the north; Ban of Benoic, a big, handsome man so dark that he might have been, like Ambrosius and myself, a descendant of the Spaniard Maximus. Beside Ban stood his cousin from Brittany, whose name I could not recall. Then Cadwy and Bors, two of the petty kings from Rheged, neighbours of Ector's; and another neighbour, Arrak, one of the numerous sons of Caw of Strathclyde. These I marked carefully, recalling what I knew of them. Nothing of importance yet, but I would remember, and watch. Rheged himself I did not see, nor Lot; it was to be assumed that their affairs in the north were more pressing even than the King's illness. But Urien, Lot's brother-in-law, was here, a thin, red-haired man with the light-blue eyes and high colour of temper; and Tudwal of Dinpelydr, who ran with him; and his blood-brother Aguisel, of whose private doings in his cold fortress near Bremenium I had heard strange tales.

There were others I did not know, and these I scanned briefly as I passed them. I could find out later who they were, from Lucan, or from Caius Valerius, who stood over near the King's door. Beside Valerius was a young man I thought I should recognize; a strongly built, sunburned man of twenty or so, with a face that I found faintly familiar. I could not place him. He watched me from his stance near Uther's doorway, but he neither spoke nor made any sign of greeting. I said under my breath to Lucan: "The man near the door, by Valerius. Who is he?"

"Cador of Cornwall."

I knew it now, the face I had last seen watching by Gorlois' body in the midnight hall of Dimilioc. And with the same look; the chill blue eyes, the frowning bar of brows, the warrior's face grown with the years more than ever like his father's and every whit as formidable.

Perhaps I need look no further. Of all those present he had most reason to hate me. And he was here, though Lucan had told me he was commander of the Irish Shore. In Rheged's absence, and Lot's, I supposed that he was the nearest there to Uther, except only myself.

I had to pass within a yard of him to get to the door of the King's room. I held his eyes deliberately, and he returned my look, but neither saluted nor bent his head. The blue eyes were cold and impassive. Well, I thought, as I greeted Valerius beside him, we should see. No doubt I could find out from Uther why he was here. And how much, if the King failed to recover, the young Duke stood to gain.

Lucan had gone in to tell the King of my arrival. Now he came out again and beckoned me forward. On his heels came Gandar. I would have paused to speak with him, but he shook his head quickly.

"No. He wants you to go straight in. By the Snake, Merlin, I'm glad to see you! But have a care . . . There, he's calling. A word with you later?"

"Of course. I'll be grateful."

There was another, peremptory call from inside the room. Gandar's eyes, heavy with worry, met mine again briefly as he stood aside to let me pass. The servant shut the door behind us and left me with the King.

4

He was up, and dressed in a house robe open at the front, with beneath it a tunic girded by a jewelled belt with a long dagger thrust through. His sword, the King's sword Falar, lay across its hangers below the gilded dragon that climbed the wall behind the bed. Though it was still summer there had been through the night a chill breeze from the north, and I was glad—my blood thin, I suppose, from my travels—to see a brazier glowing red on the empty hearth, with chairs set near.

He came quickly across the room to greet me, and I saw that he limped. As I answered his greeting I studied his face for signs of the sickness or distraction that I had been led to expect. He was thinner than before, with new lines to his face which made him look nearer fifty than forty (which was his age), and I saw that drawn look under the eyes which is one of the signs of long-gnawing pain or sleeplessness. But apart from the slight limp he moved easily enough, and with all the restless energy I remembered. And his voice was the same as ever, strong and quick with arrogant decision.

"There's wine there. We will serve ourselves. I want to talk to you alone. Sit down."

I obeyed him, pouring the wine and handing him a goblet. He took it, but set it down without drinking, and seated himself across from me, pulling the robe about his knees with an abrupt, almost angry gesture. I noticed that he did not look at me, but at the brazier, at the floor, at the goblet, anywhere not to meet my eyes. He spoke with the same abruptness, wasting no time on civilities about my journey. "They will have told you that I have been ill."

"I understood you still were," I said. "I'm glad to see you on your feet and so active. Lucan told me about the skirmish at Vagniacae; I understand it's about two months now since you were wounded?"

"Yes. It was nothing much, a spear glancing, not deep. But it festered, and took a long time to heal."

"It's healed now?"

"Yes."

"Does it still pain you?"

"No."

He almost snapped the word, pushing himself suddenly back in his chair to sit upright with his hands clenched on the arms, and his eyes on mine at last. It was the hard blue gaze I remembered, showing nothing but anger and dislike. But now I recognized both look and manner for what they were, those of a man driven against his will to ask help where he had sworn never again to ask it. I waited.

"How is the boy?"

If the sudden question surprised me, I concealed it. Though I had told Hoel and Ector that the King need only be told of the child's whereabouts if he demanded to know, it had seemed wise to send reports from time to time—couched in phrases that no one but the King would understand—of the boy's health and progress. Since Arthur had been at Galava the reports had gone to Hoel, and thence to Uther; nothing was to pass directly between Galava and the King. Hoel had written to me that, in all the years, Uther had made no direct enquiry about the boy. It was to be inferred that now he had no idea of his son's whereabouts.

I said: "You should have had a report since the last one I saw. Has it not come?"

"Not yet. I wrote myself a month ago to ask Hoel where the boy was. He has not replied."

"Perhaps his answer went to Tintagel, or to Winchester."

"Perhaps. Or perhaps he is not prepared to answer my question?"

I raised my brows. "Why not? It was always understood, surely, that the secrecy should not extend to you. Has he refused to answer you before?"

He said coldly, disconcerted and covering it: "I did not ask. There has been no need before."

This told me something beyond what I already knew. The King had only felt the need to locate Arthur since the Queen's last miscarriage. I had been right in thinking that, if she had given him other sons, he would have preferred to forget the "bastard" in Brittany. It also told me something I did not like: if he felt a need for Arthur now, this summons might be to tell me that my guardianship was ended before it had really begun.

To give myself time, I ignored what he had just said. "Then depend upon it, Hoel's answer is on its way. In any case it doesn't matter, since I am here to answer you instead."

His look was still stony, allowing no guesses. "They tell me you have been abroad all these years. Did you take him with you?"

"No. I thought it better to keep away from him till the time came when I could be of use to him. I made sure of his safety, then after I had left Brittany I kept close touch." I smiled slightly. "Oh, nothing that your spies could have seen . . . or any other man's. You know I have ways of my own. I took no risks. If you yourself have no inkling now of his whereabouts, you may be sure that no one else has."

I saw from the brief flicker in his eyes before the lids veiled them that I had guessed rightly: messages and constant reports of my movements had been sent back to him. No doubt, wherever he could, he had had me watched. It was no more than I expected. Kings live by information. Uther's enemies had probably watched me, too, and perhaps the King's own informants might have picked up some kind of lead to them. But when I asked him about this, he shook his head. He was silent for a while, following some private track of his own. He had not looked at me again. He reached for the goblet at his elbow, but not to drink; he fidgeted with it, turning it round and round where it stood. "He'll be seven years old now."

"Eight this coming Christmas, and strong for his age and well doing. You need have no fears for him, Uther."

"You think not?" Another flash, of bitterness stronger than any anger. In spite of my outward calmness I felt a violent moment of apprehension: if, contrary to appearances, the King's sickness was in fact mortal, what chance would the boy have at the head of this kingdom now, with half the petty kings (I saw Cador's face again) at his throat? And how was even I to know, through the light and the smoke, what the god's smile portended?

"You think not?" said the King again. I saw his fingerbones whiten where he held the goblet, and wondered that the thin silver did not crush. "When we last spoke together, Merlin, I asked a service of you, and I have no doubt it has been faithfully performed. I believe that service has almost reached its end. No, listen to me!" This though I had not spoken, nor even taken breath to speak. He talked like a man in a corner, attacking before he is even in danger. "I don't have to remind you what I said to you before, nor do I have to ask if you obeyed me. Wherever you have kept the boy, however you have trained him, I take it he is ignorant of his birth and standing, but that he is fit to come to me and stand before all men as a prince and my heir."

The blood ran hot under my skin in a flush I could feel. "Are you trying to tell me that you think the time has come?"

I had forgotten to school my voice. The silver goblet went back on the table with a rap. The angry blue eyes came back to me. "A king does not 'try to tell' his servants what they must do, Merlin."

I dropped my eyes with an effort and slowly, deliberately unclenched the apprehension that gripped me, the way one levers open the jaws of a fighting dog. I felt his angry stare on me, and heard the breath whistle through his pinched nostrils. Make Uther really angry, and it might take me years to fight my way back to the boy's side. I was aware in the silence that he shifted in his chair as if in sudden discomfort. In a breath or two I was able to look up and say: "Then supposing you tell me, King, whether you sent for me to discuss your health, or your son. Either way, I am still your servant."

He stared at me in rigid silence, then his brow slowly cleared, and his mouth relaxed into something like amusement. "Whatever you are, Merlin, you are hardly that. And you were right; I am trying to tell you something, something which concerns both my health and my son. By the Scorpion, why can I not find the words? I have sent for you not to demand my son of you, but to tell you that, if your healing skill fails me now, he must needs be King."

"You told me just now that you were healed."

"I said the wound was healed. The poison has gone, and the pain, but it has left a sickness behind it of a kind that Gandar cannot cure. He told me to look to you."

I remembered what Lucan had told me about the King who walked with ghosts, and I thought of some of the things I had seen at Pergamum. "You don't look to me like a man who is mortally ill, Uther. Are you speaking of a sickness of the mind?"

He didn't answer that, but when he spoke, it was not in the voice of a man changing the subject. "Since you were abroad, I have had two more children by the Queen. Did you know that?"

"I heard about the girl Morgian, but I didn't know about this last stillbirth until today. I'm sorry."

"And did this famous Sight of yours tell you that there would be no more?" Suddenly, he slammed the goblet down again on the table beside his chair. I saw that the silver had indeed dented under his fingers' pressure. He got to his feet with the violence of a thrown spear. I could see then that what I had taken for energy was a kind of drawn and dangerous tightness, nerves and sinews twanging like bowstrings. The hollows under his cheekbones showed sharp as if something had eaten him empty from within. "How can anyone be a King who is less than a man?" He flung this question at me, and then strode across the room to the window, where he leaned his head against the stone, looking out at the morning.

Now at last I understood what he had been trying to tell me. He had sent for me once before, to this very room, to tell me how his love for Ygraine, Gorlois' wife, was eating him alive. Then, as now, he had resented having to call upon my skill; then, as now, he had shown this same feverish and tightly drawn force, like a bowstring ready to snap. And the cause had been the same. Ambrosius had once said to me, "If he would think with his brains instead of his body sometimes he'd be the better for it." Until this matter of Ygraine, Uther's violent sexual needs had served his ends—not only of pleasure and bodily ease, but because his men, soldiers like himself, admired the prowess which, if not boasted of, was at any rate unconcealed. To them it was a matter for envy, amusement and admiration. And to Uther himself it was more than bodily satisfaction; it was an affirmation of self, a pride which was part of his own picture of himself as a leader.

He still neither moved nor spoke. I said: "If you find it hard to talk to me, would you rather I consulted with your other doctors first?"

"They don't know. Only Gandar."

"Then with Gandar?"

But in the end he told me himself, pacing up and down the room with that quick, limping stride. I had risen when he did, but he motioned me back impatiently, so I stayed where I was, turned away from him, leaning back in my chair beside the brazier, knowing that he walked up and down the room only because he would not face me as he talked. He told me about the raid at Vagniacae and the defending party he had led, and the sharp bitter skirmish on the shingle. The spear thrust had taken him in the groin, not a deep wound but a jagged one, and the blade had not been clean. He had had the cut bound up, and because it did not trouble him overmuch, had disregarded it; on a new alarm about a Saxon landing in the Medway, he had followed this up immediately, taking no rest until the menace was over. Riding had been uncomfortable, but not very painful, and there had been no warning until it was too late that the wound had begun to fester. In the end even Uther had to admit that he could no longer sit his horse, and he had been carried in a litter back to London. Gandar, who had not been with the troops, had been sent for, and under his care, slowly, the poison had dried up, and the festering scars healed. The King still limped slightly where the muscles had knitted awry, but there was no pain, and everything had seemed to be set for full recovery. The Queen had been all this time at Tintagel for her lying-in, and as soon as he was better himself, Uther made ready to go to her. Apparently quite recovered, he had ridden to Winchester, where he had halted his party to hold a council. Then, that night, there had been a girl—

Uther stopped talking abruptly, and took another turn of the room, which sent him back to the window. I wondered if he imagined I had thought him faithful to the Queen, but it had never occurred to me. Where Uther was, there had always been a girl.

"Yes?" I said.

And then at last the truth came out. There had been a girl and Uther had taken her to bed, as he had taken so many others in passing but urgent lust. And he found himself impotent.

"Oh, yes"—as I began to speak—"it has happened before, even to me. It happens to us all at times, but this should not have been one of the times. I wanted her, and she was skillful, but I tell you there was nothing—nothing. . . . I thought that perhaps I was weary from the journey, or that the discomfort of the saddle—it was no more than discomfort—had fretted me overmuch, so I waited there in Winchester to rest. I lay with the girl again, with her and with others. But it was no use, not with any of them." He swung away from the window then and came back to where I sat. "And then a messenger came from Tintagel to say that the Queen had been brought to bed early, of a stillborn prince." He was looking down at me, almost with hatred. "That bastard you hold for me. You've always been sure, haven't you, that he would be King after me? It seems you were right, you and your damned Sight. I'll get no other children now."

There was no point in commiseration, and he would not have wanted it from me. I said merely: "Gandar's skill in surgery is as great as mine. You can have no reason to doubt it. I will look at you if you wish, but I should like to talk to Gandar first."

"He has not your way with drugs. There is no man living who knows more about medicine. I want you to make me some drug that will bring life back to my loins. You can do this, surely? Every old woman swears she can concoct love potions—"

"You've tried them?"

"How could I try them without telling every man in my army—yes, and every woman in London—that their King is impotent? And can you hear the songs and stories if they knew this about me?"

"You are a good king, Uther. People don't mock that. And soldiers don't mock the men who lead them to victory."

"How long can I do that, the way I am? I tell you I am sick in more than body. This thing eats at me . . . I cannot live as half a man. And as for my soldiers—how would you like to ride a gelding into battle?"

"They'd follow you even if you rode in a litter, like a woman. If you were yourself, you would know that. Tell me, does the Queen know?"

"I went on from Winchester to Tintagel. I thought that, with her . . . but . . ."

"I see." I was matter of fact. The King had told me enough, and he was suffering. "Well, if there is a drug that will help you, be sure I shall find it. I learned more of these things in the East. It may be that this is only a matter of time and treatment. We have seen this happen too often to think of it as the end. You may yet get another son to supplant the 'bastard' I hold for you."

He said harshly: "You don't believe that."

"No. I believe what the stars tell me, if I have read them rightly. But you can trust me to help you as best I can: whatever happens, it's with the gods. Sometimes their ways seem cruel; who knows this better than you and I? But there is something else I have seen in the stars, Uther; whoever succeeds you, it will not be yet. You'll fight and win your own battles for a few years to come."

From his face, I knew then that he had feared worse things than his impotence. I saw, from the lightening of his look, that the cure of mind and body might well have begun. He came back to his chair, sat, and picking up the goblet, drained it, and set it down.

"Well," he said, and smiled for the first time, "now I shall be the first to believe the people who say that the King's prophet never lies. I shall be glad to take your word on this. . . . Come, fill the cups again, Merlin, and we'll talk. You have a lot to tell me; I can listen now."

So we talked for a while longer. When I began to tell him what I knew of Arthur, he listened calmly and with deep attention; I realized from the way he spoke that for some time now he must, whether consciously or not, have been pinning his hopes on his eldest born. I told him where the boy was now, and to my relief he raised no objections; indeed, after a few questions and a pause for thought he nodded approvingly.

"Ector is a good man. I might have thought of him myself, but as you know I was telling over the kings' courts, and never spared a thought for such as he. Yes, it will do . . . Galava is a good place, and safe. . . . And by the Light Himself, if the treaties I have made in the north hold good, I shall see that it remains so. And what you tell me about the boy's status there, and training . . . It will do well. If blood and training tell, he'll be a good fighter and a man whom men can trust and follow. We must see that Ector gets the best master-at-arms in the country."

I must have made a slight movement of protest, because he smiled again. "Oh, never fear, I can be secret too. After all, if he is to have the most illustrious teacher in the land, then the King must try to match him. How do you propose to get yourself up there to Galava, Merlin, without having half Britain follow you looking for magic and medicines?"

I answered with something vague. My public coming to London had served its purpose; already the buzz would have gone out that Prince Arthur was alive and thriving. As to my next disappearance, I did not yet know how or when it must be done; I could hardly think beyond the fact that the King had accepted all my plans, and that there was no question of Arthur's being removed from my care. I suspected that, as before, it was a decision taken with relief; once I had gone to my secret post at Galava, the King would forget me more readily than ever would the good folk at Maridunum.

He was speaking of it now. Unless the need came sooner, he said, he would send for the boy when he was grown—fourteen or so, and ready to lead a troop—and present him publicly, ratifying the young prince as his heir.

"Providing still that I have no other," he added, with a flash of the old hard look, and dismissed me to go and talk with Gandar.

5

Gandar was waiting for me in the room which had been allotted to me. While I had been talking with the King my baggage had been brought from the ship, and unpacked by my servant Stilicho. I showed Gandar the drugs I had brought with me, and after we had talked the King's case over, suggested that he send an assistant to study their use and preparation with me over the next few days, before I left London. If he had no one whom he could sufficiently trust to tend the King and be silent about it, I would lend him Stilicho.

At his look of surprise, I explained. As I have said, Stilicho had discovered a fair talent for preparing the dried plants and roots I had brought with me from Pergamum. He could not read, of course, but I put signs on the jars and boxes, and to begin with allowed him to handle only the harmless ones. But he proved reliable, and oddly painstaking for so lively a boy. I have learned since that men of his race have this facility with plants and drugs, and that the little kings of that country dare not eat even an unblemished apple without a taster. I was pleased to have found a servant who could be of use to me in this way, and had taught him a good deal. I would have been sorry to leave him behind in London, so was relieved when Gandar replied that he had an assistant he could trust, who should be sent to me as soon as I was ready.

I started work immediately. At my request Stilicho had been given a small chamber to himself, with a charcoal stove, and a table, and the various bowls and implements he needed. The room adjoined my own, with no door between, but I had had a double thickness of curtain hung across the doorway. Stilicho had by no means come to terms with the British summer, and kept his room at eruption point with heat.

It was about three days before I found a formula which promised some help for the King, and sent a message to Gandar. He, gasping before he had fairly got through the curtains, came himself, but instead of the assistant I expected he brought a girl with him, a young maiden whom I recognized after a moment as Morgause, the King's bastard daughter. She could be no more than thirteen or fourteen, but she was tall for her age, and it was true that she was beautiful. At that age many girls only show promise of beauty; Morgause had the thing itself, and even I, who am no judge of women, could see that this might be a beauty to send men mad. Her body was slight with a child's slenderness, but her breasts were full and pointed and her throat round as a lily stem. Her hair was rosy gold, streaming long and unbound over the golden-green robe. The large eyes that I remembered were gold-green too, liquid and clear as a stream running over mosses, and the small mouth lifted into a smile over kitten's teeth as she dropped a deep reverence to me.

"Prince Merlin." It was a demure child's voice, little more than a whisper. I saw Stilicho glance round from his work, then stand staring.

I gave her my hand. "They told me you had grown into a beauty, Morgause. Some man will be fortunate. You're not contracted yet? Then all the men in London have been slow."

The smile deepened, folding itself into dimples at the corner of her mouth. She did not speak. Stilicho, catching my glance, bent over his work again, but not, I thought, with quite the concentration it required.

"Phew," said Gandar, fanning himself. I could see the sweat already beading his broad face. "Do you have to work in a tepidarium?"

"My servant comes from a more blessed corner of the earth than this. They breed salamanders in Sicily."

"More blessed, you call it? I'd die in an hour."

"I'll have him bring the things out into my chamber," I offered.

"No need, for me. I'll not stay. I only came to present you my assistant, who will care for the King. Aye, you may well look surprised. You'll hardly believe me, but this child here is skilled already with drugs. Seems she had a nurse in Brittany, one of their wise women, who taught her the gathering and drying and preparing, and since she came over here she's been eager to learn more. But an army medical unit didn't seem quite the place for her."

"You surprise me," I said dryly. The girl Morgause had moved near the table where Stilicho was working, and bent her graceful little head towards him. A tress of the rose-gold hair brushed his hand. He labelled two jars at random, both wrongly, before he recovered himself and reached for a knife to melt the seals again.

"So," said Gandar, "when she heard the King needed drugs, she asked to look after them. She's practised enough, no fear of that, and the King has consented. For all she's young, she knows how to keep her counsel, and who better to care for him and keep his secrets than his own daughter?"

It was a good idea, and I said so. Gandar himself, though nominally the King's chief physician, had charge of the army medical teams. Until this recent wounding the King had hardly needed his personal care, and in any action or threat of it Gandar's place would be with the army. In Uther's present predicament his own daughter, so fortunately skilled, would answer very well.

"She's more than welcome to learn all she can here." I turned to the girl. "Morgause, I've distilled a drug which I think will help the King. I've copied out the formula for you here—can you make it out? Good. Stilicho has the ingredients, if he'll take time to label them correctly . . . Now, I'll leave him to show you how to compound the medicine. If you give him half an hour to get his apparatus out of this steam bath—"

"No need, for me," she said in a demure echo of Gandar. "I like the heat."

"Then I'll leave you," said Gandar with relief. "Merlin, will you come and sup with me tonight, or are you with the King?"

I followed him out into the cool airiness of my own room. From beyond the curtain came the murmur, hesitant with shyness, of the servant's voice, and an occasional soft question from the girl.

"It'll be all right, you'll see," said Gandar. "No need to look so doubtful."

"Was I? Not about the medicine, at any rate, and I'll take your word for the girl's skill."

"In any case, you'll surely stay a little while, and see how she does?"

"Certainly. I don't want to be too long in London, but I can give it a few days. You'll be here yourself?"

"Yes. But there's been such a marked change in him even in these last three days since you came, that I can't see he'll need me in attendance much longer."

"Let's hope it continues," I said. "To tell you the truth, I'm not much troubled . . . Certainly not for his general health. And for the impotence—if he gets ease and sleep, his mind may stop tormenting his body, and the condition may right itself. This seems to be happening already. You know how these things go."

"Oh, aye, he'll mend"—he glanced towards the curtained door and dropped his voice—"as far as need be. As to whether we can get the stallion back to the stand again, I can't see that it matters, now that we know there's a prince safe, and growing, and likely for the crown. We'll get him out of his distemper, and if by God's grace and the drugs you brought he lives to fight . . . and stays king of the pack—"

"He'll do that."

"Well . . ." he said, and let it go. I may say here that the King did in fact mend rapidly. The limp disappeared, he slept well and put on flesh, and I learned some time later from one of his chamberers that, although the King was never again the Bull of Mithras that his soldiers had laughed over and admired, and though he fathered no more children, he took certain satisfactions in his bed, and the unpredictable violences of his temper declined. As a soldier he was soon, again, the single-minded warrior who had inspired his troops and led them to victory.

When Gandar had gone, I went back into the boy's room to find Morgause slowly conning over the paper I had given her, while Stilicho showed her, one by one, the simples for distillation, the powders for sleeping draughts, the oils for massage of the pulled muscles. Neither of them saw me come in, so I watched for a few minutes in silence. I could see that Morgause missed nothing, and that, though the boy still watched her sideways and tended to shy from her beauty like a colt from fire, she seemed as oblivious of his sex as a princess should be of a slave.

The heat of the room was making my head ache. I crossed quickly to the table. Stilicho's monologue stopped short, and the girl looked up and smiled.

I said: "You understand it all? Good. I'll leave you now with Stilicho. If there's anything you want to know that he can't tell you, send for me."

I turned then to give instructions to the boy, but to my surprise Morgause made a quick movement towards me, laying a hand on my sleeve.

"Prince—"

"Morgause?"

"Must you really go? I—I thought you would teach me, you yourself. I want so much to learn from you."

"Stilicho can teach you all you need to know about the drugs the King will want. If you wish, I will show you how to help him over the pain of the tightened muscles, but I should have thought his bath-slave would do that better."

"Oh, yes. I know. I wasn't thinking of things like that: it's easy enough to learn what is needed for the King's care. It was—I had hoped for more. When I asked Gandar to bring me to you, I had thought—I had hoped—"

The sentence died and she drooped her head. The rose-gold hair fell in a gleaming curtain to hide her face. Through it, as through rain, I saw her eyes watching me, thoughtful, meek, childlike.

"You had hoped—?"

I doubt if even Stilicho, four paces away, heard the whisper. "—that you might teach me a little of your art, my lord Prince." Her eyes appealed to me, half hopeful and half afraid, like a bitch expecting to be whipped.

I smiled at her, but I knew my manner was stiff and my voice over-formal. I can face an armed enemy more easily than a young girl pleading like this, with a pretty hand on my sleeve, and her scent sweet on the hot air like fruit in a sunny orchard. Strawberries, was it, or apricots. . . ? I said quickly: "Morgause, I've no art to teach you that you cannot learn as easily from books. You read, don't you? Yes, of course you do, you read the formula. Then learn from Hippocrates and Galen. Let them be your masters; they were mine."

"Prince Merlin, in the arts I speak of you have no master."

The heat of the room was overpowering. My head hurt me. I must have been frowning, because she came close with a gentle dipping movement, like a bird nestling, and said rapidly, pleadingly: "Don't be angry with me. I've waited so long, and I was so sure that the chance had come. My lord, all my life I have heard people speak of you. My nurse in Brittany—she told me how she used to see you walking through the woods and by the seashore, gathering the cresses and roots and the white berries of the thunder-bough, and how sometimes you went with no more sound than a ghost, and no shadow even on a sunny day."

"She was telling stories to frighten you. I am a man like other men."

"Do other men talk to the stars as if they were friends in a familiar room? Or move the standing stones? Or follow the druids into Nemet and not die under the knife?"

"I did not die under the druids' knife because the archdruid was afraid of my father," I said bluntly. "And when I was in Brittany I was hardly a man, and certainly not a magician. I was a boy then, learning my trades as you are learning yours. I was barely seventeen when I left there."

She seemed hardly to have heard. I noticed how still she was, the long eyes shadowed under the curtaining hair, the narrow white hands folded below her breast against the green gown. She said: "But you are a man now, my lord, and can you deny that you have worked magic here in Britain? Since I have been here with my father the King, I have heard you spoken of as the greatest enchanter in the world. I have seen the Hanging Stones, which you lifted and set in their place, and I have heard how you foretold Pendragon's victories and brought the star to Tintagel, and made the King's son vanish away to the isle of Hy-Brasil—"

"So you heard that here, too, did you?" I tried for a lighter tone. "You'd better stop, Morgause, you're scaring my servant, and I don't want him running off, he's too useful."

"Don't laugh at me, my lord. Do you deny that you have the arts?"

"No, I don't deny it. But I couldn't teach you the things you want to know. Certain kinds of magic you can learn from any adept, but the arts which are mine are not mine to give away. I could not teach them to you, even if you were old enough to understand them."

"I could understand them now. I already have magic—such magic as young maids can learn, no more. I want to follow you and learn from you. My lord Merlin, teach me how to find power like yours."

"I've told you it isn't possible. You will have to take my word for that. You are too young. I'm sorry, child. I think that for power like mine you will always be too young. I doubt if any woman could go where I go and see what I see. It is not an easy art. The god I serve is a hard master."

"What god? I only know men."

"Then learn from men. What I have of power I cannot teach you. I have told you it is not my gift."

She watched me without comprehension. She was too young to understand. The light from the stove glimmered on the lovely hair, the wide, clever brows, the full breasts, the small, childish hands. I remembered that Uther had offered her to Lot, and that Lot had rejected her in favour of the young half-sister. I wondered if Morgause knew; and, compassionately, what would become of her.

I said gently: "It's true, Morgause. He only lends his power for his own ends. When they are achieved, who knows? If he wants you, he will take you, but don't walk into the flames, child. Content yourself with such magic as young maids can use."

She began to speak, but we were interrupted. Stilicho had been heating something in a bowl over the burner, and was no doubt so busy straining to hear what was being said that he let the bowl tilt, and some of the liquid spilled onto the flames. There was a hiss and a spitting, and a cloud of herb-smelling steam billowed thick between me and the girl, obscuring her. Through it I saw her hands, those still hands, moving quickly to fan the pungent mist away from her eyes. My own were watering. Vision blurred and glittered. The pain in my head blinded me. The movement of the small white hands through the steam was weaving a pattern like a spell. The bats went past me in a cloud. Somewhere near me the strings of my harp whimpered. The room shrank round me, chilled to a globe of crystal, a tomb . . .

"I'm sorry, master. Master, are you ill? Master?"

I shook myself awake. My vision cleared. The steam had thinned, and the last of it was wisping away through the window. The girl's hands were still again, folded as before; she had shaken her hair back, and was watching me curiously. Stilicho had lifted the bowl from the burner, and peered at me across it, anxious and scared.

"Master, it's one you mix yourself. You said there was no harm in it . . ."

"No harm at all. But another time, watch what you're doing." I looked down at the girl. "I'm sorry, did I frighten you? It's nothing, a headache, I get them sometimes. Sudden, and soon gone. Now I must go. I leave London at the end of the week. If you need my help before then, send to me and I shall be glad to come." I smiled, and reached out a hand to touch her hair. "No, don't look so downcast, child. It's a hard gift to have, and not for young maids."

She curtsied to me again as I went out, the small lovely face hidden once more behind the curtaining hair.

6

I think this was the only time in my life that I saw Bryn Myrddin not as the home I was eager to reach, but as a mere halting place on a journey. And once I had arrived in Maridunum, instead of welcoming the familiar quiet of the valley, the company of my books, the time to think and to work with my music and my medicines, I found myself fretting to be away, all my being straining northwards to where the boy lived who was to be my life from this time on.

All I knew of him, apart from the cryptic reassurances which had come to me through Hoel and Ector, was that he was healthy and strong, though smaller for his age than Cei, Ector's own son, had been. Cei was eleven years old now, to Arthur's eight, and as familiar to my visions as the young prince. I had watched Arthur scuffling with the older boy, riding a horse that to my coward's eye looked far too big for him, playing at swordsmanship with staves, and then with swords: I suppose these must have been blunted, but all I saw was the dangerous flash of the metal, and here, though Cei had the strength and the longer reach, I could see that Arthur was quick as a sword himself. I watched the pair of them fishing, climbing, racing through the edge of the Wild Forest in a vain bid to escape Ralf who (with the help of Ector's two most trusted men) rode guard on Arthur at all times, day or night. All this I watched in the fire, in the smoke or the stars, and once where there were none of these and the message was straining to be through, in the side of a precious crystal goblet which Ahdjan was displaying to me in his palace by the Golden Horn. He must have wondered at my sudden inattention, but probably put it down to indigestion after one of his lavish meals, which to an Eastern host is rather a compliment than otherwise.

I could not even be sure that I should recognize Arthur when I saw him, nor could I tell what kind of boy he had grown to be. Daring I could see, and gaiety, and stubborn strength, but of his real nature I could be no judge; visions may fill the mind's eye, but it takes blood to engage the heart. I had not even heard him speak. Nor had I as yet any clear idea how to enter his life when I did reach the north country, but every night of my journey from London to Bryn Myrddin I walked outside under the stars, searching for what they had to tell me, and always the Bear hung there straight ahead of me, glittering, speaking of the dark north and cool skies and the smell of pines and mountain water.

Stilicho's reaction when he saw the cave where I lived was not what I expected. When I had left home to go on my travels, since I was to be away for so long, I had hired help to look after the place for me. I had left money with the miller on the Tywy, asking him to send one of his servants up from time to time; it was apparent that this had been done, for the place was clean, dry and well provisioned. There was even fresh bedding for the horses, and we had barely dismounted before the girl from the mill came panting after us up the track with goats' milk and fresh bread and five or six newly caught trout. I thanked her, and then, because I would not let Stilicho clean the fish at the holy well, asked her to show him where the runaway water trickled down below the cliff. While I checked over my sealed jars and bottles, making sure that the lock on my chest was untouched and that the books and instruments within were undamaged, I could hear the two young voices outside still clacking busily as the mill wheel, with a good deal of laughter as each tried to make the other understand the foreign tongue.

When at length the girl went and the boy came in with the fish neatly gutted and split ready for roasting, he seemed happily prepared to find the place as convenient and comfortable as any of the houses we had stayed in on my travels. At first I put this down in some amusement to the compensation he had just discovered, but I found later that he had in fact been born and reared in just such a cave in his own country, where people of the lower sort are so poor that the owners of a well-placed and dry cavern count themselves lucky, and often have to fight like foxes to keep their den to themselves. Stilicho's father, who had sold him with rather less thought than one would give to an unwanted puppy, had been well able to spare him out of a family of thirteen; his room in the cave had been more valuable than his presence. As a slave, his quarters had been in the stables, or more usually out in the yard, and even since he had been in my service I was aware that I had lodged in places where the grooms were worse housed than the horses. The chamber he had occupied in London was the first he had ever had to himself. To him my cave on Bryn Myrddin was spacious and even luxurious, and now it promised further pleasures which did not often come the way of a young slave in the sharp competition of the servant's quarters.

So he settled in cheerfully, and word soon got round that the enchanter was back in his hill, and the folk came for drugs, and paid as they had always done with food and comforts. The miller's girl, whose name was Mai, seized every opportunity to come up the valley with food from the mill, and sometimes with the people's offerings which she brought for them. Stilicho, in his turn, made a practice of calling at the mill every time he went down to the town for me. And before very long it appeared that Mai had made him welcome in every way known to her. One night when I could not sleep I went out onto the lawn beside the holy well to look at the stars, and heard, in the night's quiet, the horses moving and stamping restlessly in their shed below the cliff. It was a night bright with stars and a white scythe of a moon, so I did not need a torch, but called softly to Stilicho to follow me and trod quickly down to the thorn grove to find out what was disturbing the beasts. It was only when I saw, through the half-opened door, the two young bodies coupling in the straw, that I realized Stilicho was there before me. I withdrew without being seen, and went back to my own bed to think.

A few days later when I talked to the boy, and told him that I planned to go north soon, but wanted no one to know of it, so would leave him behind to cover my retreat, he was enthusiastic, and fervent in protestations of faithfulness and secrecy. I was sure I could trust him; another gift he had besides his facility with drugs, he was a marvellous liar. I am told that this, too, is a gift of his people. My only fear was that he might lie too well, like his horse-trading father, and cheat himself and me into trouble. But it was a risk I had to take, and I judged him too loyal to me, and too happy in his life at Bryn Myrddin, to put it at risk. When he asked (trying not to sound too eager) when I would be gone, I could only tell him that I was waiting for a time, and a sign. As always, he accepted what I said, simply and without question. He would as soon have questioned a priestess mouthing in her shrine—they hold the Old Religion in Sicily—or Hephaistos himself when he breathed flame from the mountains. I had found that he believed every tale the people told of me, and would have shown no surprise if I had vanished in a puff of smoke or conjured gold from thin air. I suspected that, like Gaius, he made the most of his status as my servant; certainly Mai was terrified of me, and could not be persuaded to set foot beyond the thorn grove. Which was just as well for the plans I had in mind.

It was no magic sign that I was waiting for. If I had been certain it was safe, I would have set off for the north soon after I had reached home from London. But I knew that I would be watched. Uther would almost certainly continue to have me spied upon. There was no danger in this—not, that is, from the King; but if one man can buy a spy's loyalty, so can another, and there must be many others who, even only for curiosity, would be watching me. So I curbed my impatience, stayed where I was, and went about my business, waiting for the watchers to show themselves.

One day I sent Stilicho down with the horses to the forge at the edge of the town. Both animals had been shod for the journey from London, and though normally the shoes would have been removed before winter, I wanted my own mare left shod in preparation for my journey. Her girth buckles, too, were in need of repair, so Stilicho had ridden down, and was to do some errands in the town while the smith looked after the animals.

It was a day of frost, dry and still, but with the kind of thick sky that cuts the rays from the sun and lets it hang red and cold and low. I went over the hilltop to the hut of Abba the shepherd. His son Ban, the simpleton, had cut his hand a few days ago on a stake, and the wound had festered. I had cut the swelling and bound it with salve, but I knew that Ban could be trusted no more than a bandaged dog, and would worry the thing off if it hurt him.

I need not have troubled; the bandage was still in place, and the wound healing fast and neatly. Ban—I have noticed this with simple folk—mended like a child or a wild animal. Which was just as well, since he was one of those men who can hardly pass a week without injuring themselves in some way. After I had tended the hand I stayed. The hut was in a sheltered part of the valley, and Abba's sheep were all in fold. As sometimes happens, there were early lambs due, though it was only December. I stayed to help Abba with a hard lambing where the simpleton's hand would not have served him. By the time the twin lambs were curled, dry and sleeping, on Ban's knee near the fire, with the ewe watching nearby, the short winter's day had drawn to a red dusk. I took my leave, and walked home over the hilltop. The way took me across my own valley higher up, and it was dark when I reached the pine wood above the cave. The sky had cleared, the night was still and brightly starred, with a blurred moon throwing blue shadows on the frost. And shadows I saw, moving. I stopped dead, and stood to watch.

Four men, on the flat lawn outside my cave. From the thorn thicket below the cliff came the movement and clink of their tethered horses. I could hear the mutter of the men's voices as they huddled together, conferring. Two of them had swords in their hands.

Every moment the moonlight strengthened and fresh stars showered out into the frosty sky. Far away at the foot of the valley I heard the bark of a dog. Then, faintly, the clip of hoofs coming at a gentle pace. The intruders below me heard it, too. One of them gave a low command, and the group turned and made at speed for the path which would take them down to the grove.

They had barely reached the head of the path when I spoke from directly above them. "Gentlemen?"

You would have thought I had fallen straight from heaven in a chariot of flame. I suppose it was alarming enough, to be addressed out of the dark by a man they thought they had just heard riding up the valley some half-mile away. Besides, any man who sets out to spy on a magician starts more than half terrified, and ready to believe any marvel. One of them cried out in fear, and I heard a stifled oath from the leader. In the starlight their faces, upturned, looked grey as the frost.

I said: "I am Merlin. What do you want with me?"

There was a silence, in which the hoof-beats came nearer, quickening as the horses scented home and supper. I caught a movement below me as if they were half minded to turn and run. Then the leader cleared his throat. "We come from the King."

"Then put up your foolish swords. I will come down."

When I reached them I saw they had obeyed me, but their hands hovered not far from their weapons, and they huddled close together.

"Which of you is the leader?"

The biggest of them stepped forward. He was civil, but with truculence behind it. He had not relished that moment of fear. "We were waiting for you, Prince. We bring messages from the King."

"With swords drawn? Well, you are only four to one, after all."

"Against enchantment," said the man, nettled.

I smiled. "You should have known that my enchantment would never work against King's men. You could have been sure of your welcome." I paused. Their feet shuffled in the frost. One of them muttered something, half curse, half invocation, in his own dialect. I said: "Well, this is hardly the place to talk. My home is open to all comers, as you see. Why did you not kindle the fire and light the lamps and wait for me in comfort?"

More shuffling. They exchanged glances. No one answered. Clearly where we stood the scuffled frost showed their tracks up to the cave mouth. So, they had been inside. "Well," I said, "be welcome now."

I crossed to the holy well where the wooden image of the god stood, barely visible in its dark niche. I lifted down the cup, poured for him and drank. I invited the leader with a gesture. He hesitated, then shook his head. "I am a Christian. What god is that?"

"Myrddin," I said, "the god of high places. This was his hill before it was mine. He lends it to me, but he watches it still."

I saw the movement I had been waiting for among the men. Hands were behind backs as they made the sign against enchantment. One of them, then another, came forward to take the cup, drink, and spill for the god. I nodded at them. "It does not do to forget that the old gods still watch from the air and wait in the hollow hills. How else did I know you were here?"

"You knew?"

"How not? Come in." I turned in the cave mouth, holding back the boughs that half screened the entrance. None of them moved, except the leader, and he took one step only, then hesitated. "What's the matter?" I asked him. "The cave is empty, isn't it? Or isn't it? Did you find something amiss when you went in, that you are afraid to tell me?"

"There was nothing amiss," said the leader. "We didn't go in—that is—" He cleared his throat, and tried again. "Yes, we went inside, only a pace over the threshold, but—" He stopped. There was muttering, and more glances, and I heard, "Go on, tell him, Crinas."

Crinas started again. "The truth is, sir—"

His story was a long time coming, with many hesitations and promptings, but I got it in the end, still waiting in the cave mouth with the troopers standing round in a half circle, like wary cattle.

It seemed they had come to Maridunum a day or so before, waiting their chance to ride up to the cave unobserved. They had had orders not to approach me openly, for fear that other watchers (whose presence the King suspected) might waylay them and take from them any message I might put into their hands.

"Yes?"

The man cleared his throat. This morning, he said, they had seen my mare tethered outside the smithy, saddled and shod. When they asked the smith where I was he told them nothing, leaving them to assume that I was somewhere in the town, with business to pursue that would keep me until the mare was ready. They had imagined that whoever else was watching me would be staying near me in the town, so had seized the chance and ridden up to the cave.

Another pause. They could see nothing in that darkness, but I could feel they were straining to guess my reactions to their story. I said nothing, and the man swallowed, and ploughed on.

The next part of the story had, at least, the ring of truth. During their wait in Maridunum they had asked, among other idle-sounding questions, the way to the cave. Be sure they had been told, with nothing spared about the holiness of the place, and the power and awesomeness of its owner. The people of the valley were very proud of their enchanter, and my deeds would lose nothing in the telling. So the men had ridden up the valley half afraid already.

They had found, as they expected, a deserted cave. The frost outside held the lawn blank and printless. All that had met them was the silence of the winter hills, broken only by the trickle of the spring. They had lit a torch and peered in through the entrance; the cave was orderly but empty, and the ashes were cold. . . .

"Well?" I asked, as Crinas stopped.

"We knew you were not there, sir, but there was a feeling about the place . . . When we called out there was no reply, but then we heard something rustling in the dark. It seemed to come from the inner cave, where the bed is with the lamp beside it—"

"Did you go in?"

"No, sir."

"Or touch anything?"

"No, sir," he said quickly. "We—we did not dare."

"It's just as well," I said. "And then?"

"We looked all about us, but there was no one. But all the time that sound. We began to be afraid. There had been stories . . . One of the men said you might be there watching, invisible. I told him not to be a fool, but indeed there was a feeling . . ."

"Of eyes in one's back? Of course there was. Go on."

He swallowed. "We shouted again. And then—they came down out of the roof. The bats, like a cloud."

We were interrupted then. Stilicho had reached the grove and seen the troopers' horses tied there. I heard the shed door slam shut on our horses, then the boy came racing up the twisting pathway and across the flat grass, dagger in hand.

He was shouting something. Moonlight caught the blade of the long knife, held low and level, ready to stab. Metal rasped as the men whirled to defend themselves. I took two swift strides forward, pushing them aside, and bore down hard on the boy's knife hand, bringing him up short.

"No need. They're King's men. Put up." Then, as the others put their weapons back: "Were you followed, Stilicho?"

He shook his head. He was trembling. A slave is not trained to arms like a free man's son. Indeed, it was only since we had come to Bryn Myrddin that I had let him carry a knife at all. I let him go, and turned back to Crinas. "You were telling me about the bats. It sounds to me as if you had let the stories trouble you overmuch, Crinas. If you disturbed the bats, they might certainly alarm you for a moment, but they are only bats."

"But that was not all, my lord. The bats came down, yes, out of the roof, somewhere in the dark, and went past us into the air. It was like a plume of smoke, and the air stank. But after they had gone by us we heard another sound. It was music."

Stilicho, standing close to me, stared from them to me, wide-eyed in the dusk. I saw they were making the sign again.

"Music all around us," said the man. "Soft, like whispering, running round and round the wall of the cave in an echo. I'm not ashamed, my lord, we came out of that cave, and we did not dare go in again. We waited for you outside."

"With swords drawn against enchantment. I see. Well, there is no need to wait longer in the cold. Will you not come in now? I assure you that you will not be harmed, so long as you do not raise a hand against me or my servant. Stilicho, go in and kindle the fire. Now, gentlemen? No, don't try to go. Remember you have not yet given me the King's message."

Finally, between threats and reassurance, they came in, treading very softly indeed, and not speaking above a whisper. The leader consented to sit with me, but none of the others would come in as far, preferring to sit between the fire and the mouth of the cave. Stilicho hurried to warm wine and spices, and hand it round.

Now that they were in the light I could see that they were not dressed in the uniform of the King's regular troops; there was neither badge nor blazon to be seen; they might be taken for the armed troops of any petty leader. They certainly carried themselves like soldiers, and though they paid Crinas no obvious deference, it was apparent that there was some difference of rank between them.

I surveyed them. The leader sat stolidly, but the others fidgeted under my gaze, and I saw one of them, a thin, smallish man with black hair and a pale face, still surreptitiously making the sign.

At length I spoke: "You have come, you tell me, with messages from the King. Did he charge you with a letter?"

Crinas answered me. He was a big man, reddish fair, with light eyes. Some Saxon blood, perhaps; though there are red Celts as fair as this. "No, sir. Only to convey his greetings, and ask after his son's welfare."

"Why?"

He repeated my question in apparent surprise. "Why, my lord?"

"Yes, why? I have been gone from the court four months. In that time the

King has had reports. Why should he send you now, and to me? He knows the child is not here. It seems obvious"—I lingered on the word, looking from one to the other of the armed men—"that he could not be safe here. The King also knew that I would wait at Bryn Myrddin for a while before I left to join Prince Arthur. I expect to be spied on, but I find it hard to believe that he sent you with such a message."

The three beyond the fire looked at one another. A broad fellow with a red, pimpled face shifted his sword-belt forward nervously, his hand playing unthinkingly with the hilt. I saw Stilicho's eyes on him; then he moved round with the wine-jug to stand nearby.

Crinas held my eyes for a moment in silence, then nodded. "Well, sir, all right. You've smoked us out. I didn't hope to get away with a thin tale like that, not with you. It was all I could think of at a jump, when you surprised us like that."

"Very well. You are spies. I still want to know why?"

He lifted his broad shoulders. "You know, sir, who better, what kings are. It wasn't for us to question when we were told to come here and look the place over without letting you see us." Behind him the others nodded, agreeing anxiously. "And we did no harm, my lord. We never came into the cave. That much was true."

"No, and you told me why not."

He turned up a hand. "Well, sir, I don't say but you do right to be angry. I'm sorry. This isn't our normal business, as you'll guess, but orders are orders."

"What were you ordered to find out?"

"Nothing special, just ask around, and take a look at the place, and find out when you were going." A quick look sideways, to see how I was taking it. "It was my understanding that there was a lot you hadn't told the King, and he wanted to find out. Did you know he had you followed from the minute you left London?"

Another grain of truth. "I guessed it," I said.

"Well, there you are." He managed to say it as if it explained everything. "It's a way kings have, trusting nobody and wanting to know everything. It's my belief—if you'll excuse me for saying it, my lord—"

"Go on."

"I think the King didn't believe what you told him about where you were keeping the young prince. Maybe he thought you'd shift him, and keep him hidden, like before. So he sent us on the quiet, hoping we'd find some clue."

"Perhaps. Wanting knowledge is a disease of kings. And speaking of that, is there any worsening of the King's health which might have made him suddenly anxious for news?"

I saw, as clearly as if he had said it, that he wished he had thought of this himself. He hesitated, then decided that where it could be told, the truth was safer. "As to that, my lord, we've no information, and I've not seen him myself lately. But they say the sickness has passed, and he's back in the field."

This tallied with what I had been told. I said nothing for a while, but watched them thoughtfully. Crinas drank, with an assumption of ease, but his eyes on me were wary. At length I said: "Well, you have done as you were bidden, and found out what the King wanted. I am still here, and the child is not. The King must trust me for the rest. As for when I am going, I will tell him in my own good time."

Crinas cleared his throat. "That's an answer we'd sooner not take, sir." His voice came over-loud, like a braggart's, but he was not bluffing. The others shared his fear, but without his measure of courage; though this was no comfort to me; I knew that frightened men are dangerous. One of the troopers—the small fellow with black eyes shifting in a face pale with nerves—leaned forward and plucked at his leader's sleeve. I caught the mutter of, "Better go. Don't forget who he is . . . Quite enough now . . . Make him angry."

I said crisply: "I am not angry. You are doing your duty, and it is not your fault if the King trusts no one, but must have each story ratified twice over. You may tell him this"—I paused as if for thought, and saw them craning—"that his son is where I told him, safe and thriving, and that I am only waiting for good weather to make the voyage."

"Voyage?" Crinas asked sharply.

I lifted my brows. "Come now. I thought all the world knew where Arthur was. In any case, the King will understand."

One of the men said hoarsely: "Yes, we knew, but it was only a whisper. Then it's true about the island?"

"Quite true."

"Hy-Brasil?" asked Crinas. "That's a myth, my lord, saving your presence."

"Did I give it a name? I am not responsible for the whispers. The place has many names, and enough stories are told about it to fill the Nine Books of Magic . . . And every man who sees it sees something different. When I took Arthur there—"

I paused to drink, as a singer wets his throat before touching the chords. The three in front of me were all attention now. I did not look at Crinas, but spoke past him, giving my voice the tale-teller's extra pitch and resonance.

"You all know that the child was handed to me three nights after he was born. I took him to a safe place, then when the time was right and the world quiet, I carried him westwards, to a coast I know. There, below the cliffs, is a bay of sand where the rocks stand up like the fangs of wolves, and no boat or swimmer can live when the tide is breaking round them. To right and left of the bay the sea has driven arches through the cliff. The rocks are purple and rose-coloured and pale as turquoise in the sun, and on a summer's evening when the tide is low and the sun sinking, men see on the horizon land that comes and goes with the light. It is the Summer Isle, which (they say) floats and sinks at the will of heaven, the Island of Glass through which the clouds and stars can be seen, but which for those who dwell there is full of trees and grass and springs of sweet water . . ."

The pale-faced man was straining forward, open-mouthed, and I saw the shoulders of another shift under his woollen cloak as if with cold. Stilicho's eyes were like shield-bosses.

". . . It is the Isle of Maidens, where kings are carried at their endings. And there will come a day—"

"My lord! I have seen it myself!" That the pale man should interrupt a prophet apparently on the point of prophecy showed a nerve scraped raw. "I have seen it myself! When I was a boy I saw it! Clear, as clear as the Cassiterides on a fair day after rain. But it seemed an empty land."

"It is not empty. And it is not only there when men like you can see it. It can be found even in winter, for those who know how to find it. But there are not many who can travel to it and then return."

Crinas had listened without moving, his face expressionless. "Then he's on Cornish land?"

"You know it too?"

There was no hint of mockery in my voice, but he said with a snap: "I do not," and set down his empty cup and made ready to rise. I saw his hand go to his sword-belt. "Is this the message we have to take back to the King?"

At a movement of his head the others rose with him. Stilicho set the wine-jug down with a clatter, but I shook my head at him and laughed. "It would go hard with you, I think, if that were all. And hard with me, to have fresh spies set on me. For all our sakes, I'll set his mind at rest. Will you bear a letter back to London for me?"

Crinas stood still a moment, his eyes fast on mine. Then he relaxed, his thumb hooking harmlessly in his belt. When I heard his breath of relief I knew how near he had been to questioning me further in the only way he knew. "Willingly, sir."

"Then wait a while longer. Sit down again. Fill their cups, Stilicho."

The letter to Uther was brief. I began by asking after his health, then wrote that, according to my private sources of information, the prince was well. As soon as the spring came, I told him, I intended to travel and see the boy myself. Meantime I would watch him in my own way, and send the King all the news there was.

After I had sealed the message I took it back into the outer cave. The men had been talking quickly among themselves in undertones, while Stilicho hovered with the wine-jug. They broke off as I came in, and got to their feet. I handed the letter to Crinas.

"Anything else I have to say is in that letter. He will be satisfied." I added: "Even if your mission did not work out precisely to orders, you have nothing to fear from the King. Leave me now, and the god of going watch you on your way."

They went at last, perhaps not so grateful as they might have been for my parting invocation. As they hurried out across the frost I saw the quick sidelong glances into the shadows, and the hunching of cloaks close round their shoulders as if the night were breathing on their backs. As they passed the holy well every one of them made a sign, and I do not think that the last—Crinas'—was the sign of the Cross.

7

The sound of their horses' hoofs dwindled down the valley track. Stilicho came racing back from the cliff above the grove.

"They've all gone." His eyes were wide, dilated not only with the frosty dark. "My lord, I thought they were going to kill you."

"It was possible. They were brave men, and they were frightened. It's a risky combination, especially as one of them was a Christian."

He was on to that as quickly as a house dog on to a rat. "Meaning he didn't believe you?"

"Meaning just that. He was sure he didn't believe me, but he wouldn't have staked anything on its being a lie. Now find me some food, Stilicho, will you? It doesn't matter what, but hurry, and put together what you can for a journey. I'll see to my clothes myself. Is the mare ready?"

"Why, yes, lord, but—you're going tonight?"

"As soon as I can. This is the chance I have been waiting for. They've shown themselves, and by the time they find that the trail I gave them is false I shall be gone—vanished to the island beyond the west. . . . Now, you know what to do; we've talked of it many times."

This was true. We had planned that, when I went, Stilicho would remain at Bryn Myrddin, fetching and carrying supplies as usual, keeping up for as long as he could the illusion that I was still at home. I had built up a store of medicines, and for some time now had let him compound the simpler ones himself and dispense them to the poor folk who came up the valley, so they would not suffer by my absence, and it would be a little time before anyone would raise a question. We might not gain much time in this way, but I should gain enough. Once I was across the nearer hills and had reached the valley tracks in the forest, I would be hard indeed to follow.

So now Stilicho merely nodded, and ran to do as I bade him. In a very short time food was ready, and while I ate he packed together what I would need for the journey. I could see he was bursting with questions, so I let him talk. I could talk to him haltingly in his own tongue, but mainly he got along with his fluent but heavily accented Latin. Since we had left Constantinopolis most of his natural lively spirits had flowed in my direction; he had to talk to someone, and it would have been cruelty to insist on the silent respect which Gaius had tried to instill. Besides, this is not my way. So, as he hurried about his tasks, the questions came eagerly.

"My lord, if that man Crinas didn't really believe in the Isle of Glass, and he had to have the information about the prince, why did he go away?"

"To read my letter. He thinks the truth will be in that."

His eyes widened. "But he'll never dare open a letter to the King! Did you write the truth in it?"

I raised my brows at him. "The truth? Don't you believe in the Isle of Glass, either?"

"Oh, yes. Everyone knows about that." He was solemn. "Even in Sicily we knew of the invisible island beyond the west. But that's not where you're going now, *I'd* stake anything on that!"

"Why so sure?"

He gave me a limpid look. "You, lord? Across the Western Sea? In winter? I'll believe anything, but not that! If you could use magic instead of a ship, we'd have journeyed more easily in the Middle Sea. Do you remember the storm off Pylos?"

I laughed. "With no magic but mandragora . . . Too well, I remember it. No, Stilicho, I gave nothing away in the letter. That letter will never get to the King. They weren't King's men."

"Not King's men?" He paused, open-mouthed, to stare, then remembered himself and stooped again over the saddlebag he was packing. "How do you know? Did you know them?"

"No. But Uther doesn't use troops to spy; how could he hope to keep them secret? These are troops, sent—as Crinas told me—to ask questions in the market and the taverns in Maridunum, and then to search this place while we were out of it, and find, if not the prince, some clue to him. They weren't even spies. What spy would dare go back to his master and say he had been discovered, but had been given a letter to carry for his victim, with the information in it? I tried to make it easy for them, and it's possible they think they deceived me, but in any case they had to take the chance and get their hands on the letter. I give Crinas best, he's a quick thinker. When I caught them at it, he did well enough. It wasn't his fault that the other man gave him away."

"What do you mean, lord?"

"The small man with the pale face. I heard him say something in his own tongue. I doubt if Crinas heard it. He was speaking in Cornish. So later I spoke of the Isle of Glass, and described the bay, and he knew of that, too, and the Cassiterides. They are islands off the Cornish coast, ones in which even Crinas must believe."

"Cornish?" asked the boy, trying the word.

"From Cornwall, in the south-west."

"Queen's men, then?" Stilicho had not spent all his time in London in the stillroom with Morgause. He listened almost as much as he talked, and had regaled me continually since we left Uther's court with what "they" were saying about every subject under the sun. "They said she was still in the south-west after the last lying-in."

"That's true. And she might use Cornishmen for secret work, but I think not. Neither the King nor the Queen keep Cornish troops close to them these days."

"There are Cornish troops at Caerleon. I heard it in the town."

I looked up sharply. "Are there indeed? Under whom?"

"I didn't hear. I could find out." He was looking at me eagerly, but I shook my head.

"No. The less you know about it, the better. Leave it now. They'll stop watching me for the length of time it takes to read that letter, and by the time they find someone who can read Greek—"

"Greek?"

"The King has a Greek secretary," I said blandly. "I didn't see why I should make it easy. And I doubt if they know I suspect them. They'll be in no hurry. Besides, I put something in the letter to make them think I would stay here until spring."

"Will they come back?"

"I doubt it. What are they to do? Come back to tell me they read the King's letter, and are not King's men? As long as they think I'm here, they will be afraid to do that, in case I report to the King. They dare not kill me, and they dare not let me find out who they are. They will keep away. As it is, the next time you go into Maridunum, see that a message is sent to the garrison commander to watch for these Cornishmen, and tell him to report what has happened to the King. We may as well use his spies to guard us from the others. . . . There, I've finished. You've packed the food? Fill the flask now, will you? Meanwhile, if anyone does come up here, what is your story?"

"That you have been out daily on the hillside, and that you went last towards Abba's valley, and that I think you must be staying to help him with the sheep." He looked up doubtfully. "They won't believe me."

"Why not? You're an accomplished liar. Be careful, you're spilling that wine."

"A prince help with the sheep? It's not very likely."

"I've done stranger things," I said. "They'll believe you. In any case, it's true. Where do you think I got the bloodstains on my old cloak today?"

"Killing someone, I thought."

He was quite serious. I laughed. "That doesn't happen often, and usually by mistake."

He shook his head in unbelief, and stoppered the wine. "If those men had drawn swords on you, my lord, would you have stopped them with magic?"

"I hardly needed magic, with your dagger so ready. I haven't thanked you yet for your courage, Stilicho. It was well done."

He looked surprised. "You're my master."

"I bought you for money, and gave you back the freedom you were born with. What sort of a debt is that?"

He merely looked without understanding, and presently said: "There, all's ready, lord. You will want your thick boots, and the sheepskin cloak. Shall I get Strawberry ready while you dress?"

"In a moment," I said. "Come here. Look at me. I have promised you that you will be safe here. This is true; I have seen no danger coming, not for you. But once I am clear away, if you are afraid, go down to the mill and stay there."

"Yes, lord."

Don't you believe me?"

"Yes."

"Then why are you afraid?"

He hesitated, swallowing. Then he said: "The music they spoke of, lord. What was it? Was it really from the gods?"

"In a way. My harp speaks sometimes, of itself, when the air moves. I think that's what they heard and, because they were guilty, they were afraid."

He glanced over to the corner where the big harp stood. I had had it send across from Brittany, and since I had come home had used it constantly, restoring the other to its place. "That one? How could it, lord, muffled like that against the air?"

"No, not that one. That harp stays dumb until I touch it. I meant the little one I travelled with. I made it myself, here in this cave with Galapas the magician to help me."

He wetted his lips. You could see that this was hardly a reassurance. "I've not seen it since we got home. Where do you keep it?"

"I was going to show you anyway, before I left. Come, boy, there's no need for you to fear it. You've carried it yourself a thousand times. Now, get me a torch, and come and see."

I led him to the back of the main chamber. I had never shown him the crystal cave, and, because I kept my chest of books and my table across the rough rock-slope that led to the ledge, he had never climbed that way and found it. Now I motioned him to help me shift the table, and holding the torch high, mounted to the shadowy ledge where the crystal cave lay hidden. I knelt down at the entrance and beckoned him forward beside me.

The torch in my hand threw firelight, glimmering through moving smoke, round the globed walls of crystal. Here as a boy I had seen my first visions in the leap and flash of moving flame. Here I had seen myself begotten, the old King dead, the tower of Vortigern built on water, the dragon of Ambrosius leaping to victory. Now the globe was empty but for the harp which stood there, with its shadow thrown clear round the sparkling walls.

I glanced down at the boy's face. Awe was stirring in it, even at the empty globe and the empty shadows.

"Listen," I said. I said it loudly, and as my voice stirred the still air the harp whispered, and the music ran humming round and round the crystal walls.

"I was going to show you the cave," I said. "If ever you want to hide, hide here. I did myself, as a boy. Be sure the gods will watch over you, and you will be safe. Where safer, then right in God's hand, in his hollow hill? Now, go and see to Strawberry. I'll bring the harp down myself. It's time I was gone."

When morning came I was fifteen miles away, riding north through the oak forest which lies along the valley of the Cothi. There is no road there, only tracks, but I knew them well, and I knew the glass-blowers' hut deep in the wood. At this time of the year it would be empty.

I and my mare shared its shelter half that December day. I watered her at the stream, and threw fodder that I had brought into a corner of the hut. I myself was not hungry. There was something else for me to feed on; that deep excited feeling of lightness and power which I recognized. The time had been right, and something lay ahead of me. I was on my way.

I drank a mouthful of wine, wrapped myself warmly in Abba's sheepskins, and fell asleep as soundly and thoughtlessly as a child.

I dreamed again of the sword, and I knew, even through the dream, that this came straight from the god. Ordinary dreams are never so clear; they are jumbles of desires and fears, things seen and heard, and felt though unknown. This came clear, like a memory.

I saw the sword close for the first time, not vast and dazzling, like the sword of stars over Brittany, or dim and fiery as it had shimmered against the dark wall in Ygraine's chamber. It was just a sword, beautiful in the way of a weapon, with the jewels on the hilt set in gold scrollwork, and the blade glimmering and eager, as if it would fight of itself. Weapons are named for this; some are eager fighters, some dogged, some unwilling; but all are alive.

This sword was alive; it was drawn, gripped in the hand of an armed man. He was standing by a fire, a camp fire lit apparently in the middle of a darkened plain, and he was the only person to be seen in all that plain. A long way behind him I saw, dim against the dark, the outline of walls and a tower. I thought of the mosaic I had seen in Ahdjan's house, but it was not Rome this time. The outline of the tower was familiar, but I could not remember where I had seen it, nor even be sure that I had not seen it only in dreams.

He was a tall man, cloaked, and the dark cloak fell in a long heavy line from shoulder to heel. The helmet hid his face. His head was bent, and he held the sword naked across his hands. He was turning it over and over, as if weighing its balance, or studying the runes on the blade. The firelight flashed and darkened, flashed and darkened, as the blade turned. I caught one word, KING, and then again, KING, and saw the jewels sparking as the sword turned. I saw then that the man had a circle of red gold on his helmet, and that his cloak was purple. Then as he moved the firelight lit the ring on his finger. It was a gold ring carved with a dragon.

I said: "Father? Sir?" but, as sometimes happens in dreams, I could make no sound. But he looked up. There were no eyes under the peak of the helmet. Nothing. The hands that held the sword were the hands of a skeleton. The ring shone on bone.

He held the sword out to me, flat across the skeleton hands. A voice that was not my father's said: "Take it." It was not a ghost's voice, or the voice of bidding that comes with vision: I have heard these, and there is no blood in them; it is as if the wind breathed through an empty horn. This was a man's voice, deep and abrupt and accustomed to command, with a rough edge to it such as comes from anger, or sometimes from drunkenness; or sometimes, as now, from fatigue.

I tried to move, but I could not, any more than I could speak. I have never feared a spirit, but I feared this man. From the blank of shadow below the helmet came the voice again, grim, and with a faint amusement, that crept along my skin like the brush of a wolf's pelt felt in the dark. My breath stopped and my skin shivered. He said, and now I clearly heard the weariness in the voice: "You need not fear me. Nor should you fear the sword. I am not your father, but you are my seed. Take it, Merlinus Ambrosius. You will find no rest until you do."

I approached him. The fire had dwindled, and it was almost dark. I put my hands out for the sword, and he reached to lay it across them. I held still, though my flesh shrank from touching his bony fingers; but they were not there to touch. As the sword left his grip it fell, through his hands and through mine, and between us to the ground. I knelt, groping in the darkness, but my hand met nothing. I could feel his breath above me, warm as a living man's, and his cloak brushed my cheek. I heard him say: "Find it. There is no one else who can find it." Then my eyes were open and it was full noon, and the strawberry mare was nuzzling at me where I lay, with her mane brushing my face.

8

December is certainly no time for travelling, especially for one whose business does not allow him to use the roads. The winter woods are open and clear of undergrowth, but there are many places in the remoter valleys where there is no clear going save along the stream-side, and that is tortuous and rough, and the banks are apt to be dangerously broken—or even washed right away—with floods and bad weather. Snow, at least, I was spared, but on the second day out of Bryn Myrddin the weather worsened to a cold wind with flurries of sleet, and there was ice in all the ways.

Going was slow. On the third day, towards dusk, I heard wolves howling somewhere up near the snow-line. I had kept to the valleys, travelling in deep forest still, but now and again where the forest thinned I had caught glimpses of the hilltops, and they were white with fresh snow. And there was more to come; the air had the smell of snow, and the soft cold bite on one's cheek. The snow would drive the wolves down lower. Indeed, as dark drew in and the trees crowded closer I thought I saw a shadow slipping away between the trunks, and there were sounds in the underbrush which might have been made by harmless creatures such as deer or fox; but I noticed that Strawberry was uneasy; her ears flattened repeatedly, and the skin on her shoulders twitched as if flies were settling there.

I rode with my chin on my shoulder and my sword loose in its sheath. *"Mevysen"*—I spoke to my Welsh mare in her own language—"when we find this great sword that Macsen Wledig is keeping for me, you and I will no doubt be invincible. And find it we must, it seems. But just at the moment I'm as scared of those wolves as you are, so we'll go on till we find some place that's defensible with this poor weapon and my poorer skill, and we'll sit the night out together, you and I."

The defensible place was a ruinous shell of a building deep in the forest. Literally a shell; it was all that remained of a smallish erection the shape of a kiln, or a beehive. Half of it had fallen away, leaving the standing part like an egg broken endways, the curving half-dome backed against the wind and offering some sort of protection from the intermittent sleet. Most of the fallen masonry had been removed—probably stolen for building stone—but there was still a ragged rampart of broken stuff behind which it was possible to take shelter, and conceal myself and the mare.

I dismounted, and led her in. She picked her way between the mossed stones, shook her wet neck, and was soon settled quietly enough with her nosebag, under the dry curve of the dome. I set a heavy rock on the end of her rope, then pulled the dead fronds of some fern from a dry corner under the wall, dried her damp hide with it, and covered her. She seemed to have lost her fears, and munched steadily. I made myself as comfortable as I could with one saddle-bag for a dry seat, and what remained to me of food and wine. I would have dearly liked to light a fire, as much against the wolves as for comfort, but there might be other enemies than wolves looking for me by now, so, with my sword ready to hand, I huddled into my sheepskins and ate my cold rations and fell at last into a waking doze which was the nearest to sleep that danger and discomfort would allow.

And dreamed again. No dream, this time, of kings or swords or stars moving, but a dream half-waking, broken and uneasy, of the small gods of small places; gods of hills and woods and streams and crossways; the gods who still haunt their broken shrines, waiting in the dusk beyond the lights of the busy Christian churches, and the dogged rituals of the greater gods of Rome. In the cities and the crowded places men have forgotten them, but in the forests and the wild hill country the folk still leave offerings of food and drink, and pray to the local guardians of the place who have dwelled there time out of mind. The Romans gave them Roman names, and let them be; but the Christians refuse to believe in them, and their priests berate the poorer folk for clinging to the old ways—and no doubt for wasting offerings which would do better at some hermit's cell than at some ancient holy place in the forest. But still the simple folk creep out to leave their offerings, and when these vanish by morning, who is to say that a god has not taken them?

This, I thought, dreaming, must be such a place. I was in the same forest, and the apse of stone where I sat was the same, even to the rampart of mossed boulders in front of me. It was dark, and my ears were filled with the roaring of the upper boughs where the night wind poured across the forest. I heard nothing approaching, but beside me the mare stirred and breathed gustily into the fodder-bag, and lifted her head, and I looked up to see eyes watching me from the darkness beyond the rampart.

Held by sleep, I could not move. In equal silence, and very swiftly, others came. I could discern them only as shadows against the cold darkness; not wolves, but shadows like men; small figures appearing one by one, like ghosts, and with no more sound, until they ringed me in, eight of them, standing shoulder to shoulder across the entrance to my shelter. They stood there, not moving or speaking, eight small shadows, as much part of the forest and the night as the gloom cast by the trees. I could see nothing except—when high over the bare trees a cloud swept momentarily clear of the winter stars—the gleam of watching eyes.

No movement, no word. But suddenly, without any conscious change, I knew I was awake. And they were still there.

I did not reach for my sword. Eight to one is not a kind of odds that makes sense, and besides, there are other ways to try first. But even those I never got a chance to use. As I moved, taking breath to speak, one of them said something, a word that was blown away in the wind, and the next thing I knew I was being thrown back forcibly against the wall behind me, while rough hands forced a gag into my mouth, and my hands were pulled behind my back and the wrists bound tightly together. They half lifted, half dragged me out of the walled shelter, and flung me down outside with my back against the bruising stones that formed the rampart. One of them produced flint and iron, and after a long struggle managed to set light to the twist of rag stuck in a cracked ox horn which did duty as a torch; the thing burned sullenly with a feeble and stinking light, but with its help they set to work to hunt through the saddle-bags, and examine the mare herself with careful curiosity. Then they brought the torch to where I sat with two of them standing over me and, thrusting the reeking rag almost into my face, examined me much as they had done the mare.

It seemed clear from the fact that I was still alive that they were not simple robbers; indeed, they took nothing from the saddle-bags, and though they disarmed me of sword and dagger, they did not search me further. I began to fear, as they looked me over closely with nods and grunted comments of satisfaction, that they had actually been looking for me. But in that case, I thought, if they had wanted to know my destination, or had been paid to find it out, they would have done better to stay invisible, and follow me. No doubt I would have led them in the end to Count Ector's doorstep.

Their comments told me nothing about their business with me, but they did tell me something as important: these men spoke in a tongue I had never heard before, but all the same I knew it; the Old Tongue of the Britons, which my master Galapas had taught me.

The Old Tongue has still something the same form as our own British language, but the people who speak it have for so long lived away from other men that their speech has altered, adding its own words and changing its accent until now it takes study and a good ear to follow it at all. I could hear the familiar inflections, and here and there a word recognizable as the Welsh of Gwynedd, but the accent had changed, slurred and strange through five hundred years of isolation, with words surviving that had long fallen out of use in other dialects, and sounds added like the echoes of the hills themselves, and of the gods and wild creatures that dwell there.

It told me who these men must be. They were the descendants of those tribesmen who had, long since, fled to the remoter hills, leaving the cities and the cultivable lands to the Romans, and after them to Cunedda's federates from Guotodin, and had roosted, like homeless birds, in the high tracts of the forest where living was scarce and no better men would dispute it with them. Here and there they had fortified a hilltop and held it, but in most cases any hill that could be so fortified was desirable to conquerors, so was eventually stormed or starved out and taken. So, hilltop by hilltop, the remnants of the unconquered had retreated, till there was left to them only the crags and caves and the bare land which the snow locked in winter. There they lived, seen by none except by chance, or when they wished it. It was they, I guessed, who crept down by night to take the offerings from the country shrines. My waking dream had been true enough. These, perhaps, were all who could be seen by living eyes, of the dwellers in the hollow hills.

They were talking freely—as freely as such folk ever do—not knowing I could understand them. I kept my eyelids lowered, and listened.

"I tell you, it must be. Who else would be travelling in the forest on a night like this? And with a strawberry mare?"

"That's right. Alone, they said, with a red roan mare."

"Maybe he killed the other, and stole the mare. He's hiding, that's certain. Why else lie out here in winter without a fire, and the wolves coming down this low?"

"It's not the wolves he's afraid of. Depend on it, this is the man they were wanting."

"And paying for."

"They said he was dangerous. He didn't look it to me."

"He had a sword drawn ready."
"But he never picked it up."
"We were too quick for him."
"He had seen us. He had time. You shouldn't have taken him like that, Cwyll. They didn't say take him. They said find him and follow him."
"Well, it's too late now. We've taken him. What do we do? Kill him?"
"Llyd will know."
"Yes. Llyd will know."
They did not speak as I have reported it, but in snatches one across the other, brief phrases bandied to and fro in that strange, sparse language. Presently they left me where I lay between my two guards, and withdrew a short distance. To wait, I supposed, for Llyd.
Some twenty minutes later he came, with two companions; three more shadows suddenly no longer part of the forest's blackness. The others crowded round him, talking and pointing, and presently he seized the torch—which was now little more than a singed rag smelling of pitch—and strode towards me. The others crowded after.
They stood in a half circle round me as they had stood before. Llyd held the torch high, and it showed me my captors, not clearly, but enough to know them again. They were small men, dark-haired, with surly lined faces beaten by weather and hard living to a texture like gnarled wood. They were dressed in roughly tanned skins, and breeches of thick, coarse-woven cloth dyed the browns and greens and murreys that you can make with the mountain plants. They were variously armed, with clubs, knives, stone axes chipped to a sheen, and—the one who had given the orders until Llyd came—with my sword.
Llyd said: "They have gone north. There is no one in the forest to hear or see. Take the gag out."
"What's the use?" It was the fellow holding my sword who spoke. "He doesn't know the Old Tongue. Look at him. He does not understand. When we spoke just now of killing him he did not look afraid."
"What does that tell us except that he is brave, which we know already? A man attacked and tied as he is might well be expecting death, but there is no fear in his eyes. Do as I say. I know enough to ask him his name and where he is bound for. Take out the gag. And you, Pwul, and Areth, see if you can find dry stuff to burn. Let us have good light to see him by."
One of the two beside me reached for the knot, and got the gag loosened. It had cut my mouth at the corner, and was foul with blood and spittle, but he thrust it into his pouch. Theirs was a degree of poverty that wasted nothing. I wondered how much "they" had offered to pay for me. If Crinas and his followers had tracked me this far and set the hill-dwellers to watch me and discover where I was bound, Cwyll's hasty action had spoiled that plan. But it had also spoiled mine. Even if they decided now to let me go, so that they could follow me in secret, my journey was fruitless. Forewarned though I was, I could never elude these watchers. They see everything that moves in the forest, and they can send messages as quickly as the bees. I had known all along that the forest would be full of watchers, but normally they stay out of sight and mind their own concerns. Now I saw that my only hope of reaching Galava unbetrayed was to enlist them. I waited to hear what their leader had to say.
He spoke slowly, in bad Welsh. "Who are you?"
"A traveller. I go north to the house of an old friend."

"In winter?"

"It was necessary."

"Where . . ." He searched for the words. ". . . where do you come from?"

"Maridunum."

This, it appeared, tallied with what "they" had told them. He nodded. "Are you a messenger?"

"No. Your men have seen what I carry."

One of them said quickly, in the Old Tongue: "He carries gold. We saw it. Gold in his belt, and some stitched in the mare's girth."

The leader regarded me. I could not read his face; it was about as transparent as oak bark. He said over his shoulder, without taking his eyes off me: "Did you search him?" He was speaking his own language.

"No. We saw what was in his pouch when we took his weapons."

"Search him now."

They obeyed him, not gently. Then they stood back and showed him what they had found, crowding to look by the light of the meager torch. "The gold; look how much. A brooch with the Dragon of the King's house. Not a badge; feel the weight, it is gold. A brand with the Raven of Mithras. And he rides from Maridunum towards the north, and secretly." Cwyll pulled my cloak again across the exposed brand and stood up. "It must be the man the soldiers told us about. He is lying. He is the messenger. We should let him go and follow him."

But Llyd spoke slowly, staring down at me. "A messenger carrying a harp, and the sign of the Dragon, and the brand of the Raven? And he rides alone out of Maridunum? No. There is only one man it can be; the magician from Bryn Myrddin."

"Him?" This was the man who held my sword. It went slack, suddenly, in his grasp, and I saw him swallow and take a fresh grip. "Him, the magician? He is too young. Besides, I have heard of that magician. They say he is a giant, with eyes that freeze you to the marrow. Let him go, Llyd, and we will follow him, as the soldiers asked us."

Cwyll said, uncomfortably: "Yes, let him go. Kings are nothing to us, but a magician is unchancy to harm."

The others crowded close, curious and uneasy.

"A magician? They said nothing about that, or we would never have touched him."

"He's no magician, see how he's dressed. Besides, if he knew magic, he could have stopped us."

"He was asleep. Even enchanters have to sleep."

"He was awake. He saw us. He did nothing."

"We gagged him first."

"He is not gagged now, and see, he says nothing."

"Yes, let him go, Llyd, and we will get the money the soldiers offered. They said they would pay us well."

More mutters, and nods of assent. Then one man said, thoughtfully: "He has more on him than they offered us."

Llyd had not spoken for some time, but now he broke angrily across the talk. "Are we thieves? Or hirelings to give information for gold? I told you before, I will not blindly do as the soldiers asked us, for all their money. Who are they that we, the Old Ones, should do their work? We will do our own. There are things here that I should like to know. The soldiers told us nothing. Perhaps this man will. I think there are great matters afoot. Look at him; that is no man's messenger. That is a man who counts among men. We will untie him, and talk. Light the fire, Areth."

While he had been talking the two he had bidden had brought together a pile of boughs and fallen stuff, and built a pyre ready for lighting. But there could have been no dry twig in the forest that night. Though the sleet showers had stopped some while back, all was dripping wet, and the ground felt spongy as if it must be soaked right to the earth's center.

Llyd made a sign to the two who guarded me. "Untie his hands. And one of you, bring food and drink."

One of them hurried off, but the other hesitated, fingering his knife. Others crowded round, arguing. Llyd's authority, it seemed, was not that of a king, but of an accepted leader whose companions have the right to query and advise. I caught fragments of what they were saying, and then Llyd clearly: "There are things we must know. Knowledge is the only power we have. If he will not tell us of his own will, then we shall have to make him. . . ."

Areth had managed to set the damp stuff smouldering, but it gave neither heat nor light, only an intermittent gusting of smoke, acrid and dirty, which blew into all quarters as the wind wandered, making the eyes smart and choking the breath.

It was time, I thought, that I made an end. I had learned enough. I said, clearly, in the Old Tongue: "Stand back from the fire, Areth."

There was a sudden complete silence. I did not look at them. I fixed my eyes on the smoking logs. I blotted out the bite of my bound wrists, the pain of my bruises, the discomfort of my soaked clothes. And, as easily as a breath taken and then released on the night air, the power ran through me, cool and free. Something dropped through the dark, like a fire arrow, or a shooting star. With a flash, a shower of white sparks that looked like burning sleet, the logs caught, blazing. Fire poured down through the sleet, caught, gulped, billowed up again gold and red and gloriously hot. The sleet hissed in onto the fire, and, as if it had been oil, the fire fed on it, roaring. The noise of it filled the forest and echoed like horses galloping.

I took my eyes from it at last, and looked about me. There was no one there. They had vanished as if they had indeed been spirits of the hills. I was alone in the forest, lying against the tumbled rocks, with the steam rising already from my drying clothes, and the bonds biting painfully into my wrists.

Something touched me from behind. The blade of a stone knife. It slid between the flesh of my wrists and the ropes, sawing at my bonds. They gave way. Stiffly, I flexed my shoulders and began to chafe the bruised wrists. There was a thin cut, bleeding, where the knife had caught me. I neither spoke nor looked behind me, but sat still, chafing my wrists and hands.

From somewhere behind me a voice spoke. It was Llyd's. He spoke in the Old Tongue.

"You are Myrddin called Emrys or Ambrosius, son of Ambrosius the son of Constantius who sprang from the seed of Macsen Wledig?"

"I am Myrddin Emrys."

"My men took you in error. They did not know."

"They know now. What will you do with me?"

"Set you on your journey when you choose to go."

"And meanwhile question me, and force me to tell you of the grave matters that concern me?"

"You know we can force you to do nothing. Nor would we. You will tell us what you wish, and go when you wish. But we can watch for you while you sleep, and we have food and drink. You are welcome to what we have to offer."

"Then I accept it. Thank you. Now, you have my name. I have heard yours, but you must give it to me yourself."

"I am Llyd. My ancestor was Llyd of the forests. There is no man here who is not descended from a god."

"Then there is no man here who need fear a man descended from a king. I shall be glad to share your supper and talk with you. Come out now, and share the warmth of my fire."

The food was part of a cold roast hare, with a loaf of black bread. They had venison, fresh killed, the result of tonight's foray; this they kept for the tribe, but thrust the pluck into the fire to roast, and along with it the carcass of a black hen and some flat uncooked cakes that looked, and smelled, as if they had been mixed with blood. It was an easy guess where these and the hare had been picked up; one sees such things at every crossways stone in that part of the country. It is no blasphemy in these people to take the wayside sacrifices: as Llyd had said to me, they consider themselves descended from the gods and entitled to the offerings; and indeed, I see no harm in it. I accepted the bread, and a piece of venison heart, and a horn of the strong sweet drink they make themselves from herbs and wild honey.

The ten men sat round the fire, while Llyd and I, a little apart from them, talked.

"These soldiers," I said, "who wanted me followed. What sort of men were they?"

"Five men, soldiers fully armed, but with no blazon."

"Five? One of them red-haired, big, in a brown jerkin and a blue cloak? And another on a pied horse?" This was the only horse recognizable to Stilicho, who had glimpsed its white patches in the murk of the grove. They must have had a fifth man, left on watch at the foot of the valley. "What did they say to you?"

But Llyd was shaking his head. "There was no man such as you describe, nor any such horse. The leader was a fair man, thin as a hay-fork, with a beard. They asked us only to watch for a man on a strawberry roan mare, who rode alone, on business that they had no knowledge of. But they said their master would pay well to know where he went."

He threw the bone he had been gnawing over his shoulder, wiped his mouth, and met my eyes straightly. "I said I would not ask your business, but tell me this much, Myrddin Emrys. Why is the son of the High King Ambrosius and the kin of Uther Pendragon hiding alone in the forest while Urien's men hunt him, wishing him ill?"

"Urien's men?"

There was deep satisfaction in his voice. "Ah. Some things your magic will not tell you. But in these valleys, no one moves but we know of it. No one comes here but he is marked and followed until we know his business. We know Urien of Gore. These men were his, and spoke the tongue of his country."

"Then you can tell me about Urien," I said. "I know of him; a small king of a small country, brother by marriage to Lot of Lothian. There is no reason that I know why he should hunt me. I am on King's business, and Urien has no quarrel with me or with the King. He and his brother of Lothian are allies of Rheged and of the King. Has Urien, then, become the creature of some other man? Duke Cador?"

"No. Only of King Lot."

I was silent. The fire roared and above us the forest stirred and ruffled. The wind was dying. I was thinking savagely. That Crinas and his gang were Cador's I had no doubt; now it seemed that there had been other spies from the north, watching and waiting, and that somehow they had stumbled across my trail. Urien, Lot's jackal. And Cador. Two of Uther's most powerful allies, his right hand and his left; and the moment the King began to fail they had spies out looking for the prince. . . . The pattern broke and re-formed as a reflection in a pool re-forms after a rock has been thrown into it; but not the same pattern; the rock is there in the center, changing everything. King Lot, the betrothed of Morgian the High King's daughter. King Lot.

I said at length: "I heard you say these men had ridden on north. Were they going straight to report to Urien, or still trying to find and follow me?"

"To follow you. They said they would cast farther north to find some trace of you. If they find none they will seek us out at a place we arranged with them."

"And will you meet them there?"

He spat sideways, not troubling to answer.

I smiled. "I shall go on tomorrow. Will you guide me to a path that the troopers will not know?"

"Willingly, but to do that I must know where you are making for."

"I am following a dream I had," I told him. He nodded. These folk of the hills find this reasonable. They work by instinct like animals, and they read the skies and wait for portents. I thought for a minute, then asked him: "You spoke of Macsen Wledig. When he left these islands to go to Rome, did any of your people go with him?"

"Yes. My own great-grandfather led them under Macsen."

"And came back?"

"Indeed."

"I told you I had had a dream. I dreamed that a dead king spoke to me, and told me that before I could raise the living one I had a quest to fulfill. Did you ever hear what became of Macsen's sword?"

He threw up a hand in a sign I had never seen before. But I recognized what it was, a strong sign against strong magic. He muttered to himself, some rune in words I did not know, then, hoarsely, to me: "So. It has come. Arawn be praised, and Bilis, and Myrddin of the heights. I knew these were great matters. I felt it on my skin as a man feels the rain falling. So this is what you seek, Myrddin Emrys?"

"This is what I seek. I have been East, and was told there that the sword, with the best of the Emperor's treasure, came back to the West. I think I have been led here. Can you help me further?"

He shook his head slowly. "No. Of that matter I knew nothing. But there are those in the forest who can help you. The word was handed down. That is all I can tell you."

"Your great-grandfather said nothing?"

"I did not say that. I will tell you what he said." He dropped into the singsong voice that the tale-tellers use. I knew he would give me the exact words; these people hand words down from generation to generation, changeless and as precisely worked as the chasing on a cup. "The sword was laid down by a dead Emperor, and shall be lifted by a living one. It was brought home by water and by land, with blood and with fire, and by land and water shall it go home, and lie hidden in the floating stone until by fire it shall be raised again. It shall not be lifted except by a man rightwise born of the seed of Britain."

The chanting stopped. The others round the fire had stopped their talking to listen; I saw eyes glint white, and hands move in the ancient sign. Llyd cleared his throat, spat again, and said gruffly: "That's all. I told you it would be no help."

"If I am to find the sword," I said, "help will come, no fear of that. And now I know I am getting near to it. Where the song is, the sword cannot be far away. And after I have found it . . . I think you know where I am going."

"Where else should Myrddin Emrys be going, secretly and on a winter journey, except to the Prince's side?"

I nodded. "He is beyond your territory, Llyd, but not beyond the eyes of your people. Do you know where he is?"

"No. But we will."

"I'm content that you should. Watch me if you wish, and when you see where I am going, watch him for me. This is a king, Llyd, who will deal as justly with the Old Ones of the hills as ever he does with the kings and bishops who meet in Winchester."

"We will watch him for you."

"Then I shall go north, as I was going before, and wait for guidance. Now, with your permission, I should like to sleep."

"You will be safe," said Llyd. "At first light we will see you on your way."

9

The way they showed me was a path no better and no worse than I had followed hitherto, but it was easier to follow by the secret signs they told me of, and it was shorter even than keeping to the road. There were sudden twists and ascents to narrow passes which, without the signs, I would not have suspected of holding a way through. I would ride up some narrow, tree-filled gorge with an apparently solid wall of mountain straight ahead, and the sound of a torrent swelling and echoing between the rocks; but always, when I reached it, there was the pass, narrow and often dangerous, but clear, leading through some (till now) invisible cleft into the steep descent beyond. So for two days more I journeyed, seeing no one, resting little, and keeping myself and the mare alive on what the Old Ones had given me.

On the morning of the third day the mare cast a shoe. As luck would have it we were in easy ground, a ridge of smooth sheep-turf between valley and valley, deserted at this season, but smooth going. I dismounted, and led Strawberry along the ridge, scanning the valleys below me for signs of a road, or the smoke of a settlement. I knew roughly where I was now; though mist and snowstorms veiled the higher crests, I had seen, when they lifted, the white top of the great Snow Hill which holds up the winter sky. I had ridden this way before by the road, and recognized the shape of some of the nearer hills. I was sure that I had not far to travel to find a road, and a smith.

I had considered trying, myself, to remove Strawberry's other three shoes, but the going had been hard as iron, and if I had not kept her shod, she would have been lame long since. Besides, we were running out of food, and there was none to find in the winter ways. I must take the risk of being seen and recognized.

It was a still clear day of frost. At about noon I saw the smoke of a village, and a few minutes later the gleam of water in the valley below it. I turned the mare's head downhill. We went gently down under the shelter of sparsely set oaks, whose boughs still held a rustle of dead leaves. Soon I could see, below ahead of us through the bare trunks, the grey glitter of the river sliding between its banks.

Just above it I halted the mare at the edge of the oak wood. No movement, no sound, except the noisy river which drowned even the distant sound of barking dogs that marked the village.

I was certain that I was now not far from the course of the road. My best hope for a forge was where road and river met. Such places are generally near a ford or a bridge. Keeping just within the edge of the oak wood, I led Strawberry gently on towards the north.

So we journeyed for another hour or so, when suddenly the valley took a turn to the north-west, and there ahead of me, joining it from a neighbour valley, ran the open belt of green that spoke of a road. And I could hear, clear on the winter's stillness, the metallic clang of a hammer.

There was no sign of the settlement, but where the road met the river the woods were very thick, and I knew that any village in these parts would be built on some hillock or rising ground from which men might defend themselves. The smith, in his solitary forge down by the water, need have no such fears. Such men are too useful, and have nothing worth the taking, and besides, there is still about them some of the old awe that hangs over the places where roads and waters meet.

The smith himself might indeed have been another of the Old Ones. He was a small man, bent by his trade, but immensely broad of shoulder, with arms knotted with muscle and covered with a pelt as thick as a bear's. His hands, broad and cracked, were almost as black as his hair.

He looked up from his work as my shadow fell across the doorway. I greeted him, then tied the mare to a ring by the door and sat down to wait, glad of the heat of the fire which was being blown to a blaze by a boy in a leather apron. The smith answered my greeting, with a sharp stare from under his brows, then without pausing in the rhythm of his work, went back to his hammering. He was making a share. With a hiss of steam and the gradual dulling of the strokes, the share slowly greyed and cooled to its cutting edge. The smith muttered something to the boy at the bellows, who let the air run out, then, picking up the water bucket, left the forge. The smith, setting down his hammer, straightened and stretched. He hooked a wine skin down from the wall and drank, then wiped his mouth. The expert eyes ran over the mare. "Did you bring the shoe?" I had half expected him to speak the Old Tongue, but it was plain Welsh. "Otherwise it'll take more time than you like to spare, I dare say. Or will I just take the other three off?"

I grinned. "And pay me for them?"

"I'd do it for nothing," said the smith, showing a blacktoothed grin.

I handed him the cast shoe. "Put this back on and there's a penny in it for you."

He took the thing and examined it, turning it slowly in those horny hands. Then he nodded, and picked up the mare's foot.

"Going far?"

Part of a smith's payment was, of course, whatever news his customers could give him. I had expected this, and had a story ready. He rasped and listened, while the mare stood quietly between us, head down and ears slack. After a while the boy came back with a full bucket and tipped water into the tub. He had taken a long time, and he breathed as if he had been hurrying. If I thought about it at all, I imagined that he had seized, boy-like, the opportunity to spend as long over the errand as he could, and had had to hurry back. The smith made no comment, other than to grunt at him to get back to his bellows, and soon the fire roared up, and the shoe began to glow to red heat.

I suppose I should have been more alert, though to be here at all was a risk I had had to take. And there had been a chance that the troopers asking for the rider with the strawberry mare had not passed this way. But it seemed that they had.

What with the roar of the furnace and the clanging hammer I heard nothing of any approach, just saw, suddenly, the shadows between me and the doorway, then the four men standing there. They were all armed, and they all held their weapons ready, as if they were fully prepared to use them. Two of them held spears, none the less deadly for being home-made, one had a woodsman's hacking knife, its blade honed to a bright edge that would go through living oak, and the fourth held, with some expertness, a Roman short sword.

The last one was the spokesman. He greeted me civilly enough, while the smith held his hammering, and the boy stared.

"Who are you, and where are you bound for?"

I answered him in his own dialect, and without moving from where I sat. "My name is Emrys, and I am travelling north. I have had to come out of my way because, as you see, my mare has cast a shoe."

"Where are you from?"

"From the south, where we do not send armed men against a stranger who passes through our village. What are you afraid of, coming four to one?"

He growled something, and the two with the spears grounded them, shuffling their feet. But the swordsman stood firm.

"You speak our language too well to be a stranger. I think you are the man we have been told to look for. Who are you?"

"No stranger to you, Brychan," I said calmly. "Did you get that sword at Kaerconan, or did we take it when we cut Vortigern's troops to pieces at the crossroads by Bremia?"

"Kaerconan?" The sword-point wavered and fell. "You fought there, for Ambrosius?"

"I was there, yes."

"And at Bremia? With Duke Gorlois?" The point dropped completely. "Wait, you said your name was Emrys? Not Myrddin Emrys, the prophet that won the battle for us, and then doctored our hurts? Ambrosius' son?"

"The same."

The men of my race do not easily bend the knee, but as he slid his sword back into his belt and showed his blackened teeth in a wide grin of pleasure, the effect was the same. "By all the gods, so it is! I didn't know you, sir. Put your weapons up, you fools, can't you see he's a prince, and no meat of ours?"

"Small blame to them if they can't see any such thing," I said, laughing. "I'm neither prince nor prophet now, Brychan, *braud.* I'm travelling secretly, and I need help . . . and silence."

"You shall have anything we can give you, my lord." He had caught my involuntary glance towards the smith and the staring boy, and added quickly: "There's no man here will say a word, look you. No, nor boy neither."

The boy nodded, swallowing. The smith said gruffly: "If I'd known who you were—"

"You'd not have sent your boy scampering off to take the news to the village?" I said. "No matter. If you are a King's man as Brychan is, I can trust you."

"We are all King's men here," said Brychan harshly, "but if you were Uther's worst enemy, instead of his brother's son and the winner of his battles, I would help you, and so would my kinsmen and every man in these parts. Who was it saved this arm of mine after Kaerconan? It's thanks to you that I was able to carry this sword against you today." He clapped the hilt at his belt. I remembered the arm; one of the Saxon axes had driven deep into the flesh, hacking a collop of muscle and laying the bone bare. I had stitched the arm and treated it; whether it was the virtue of the medicine, or Brychan's faith in anything "the

King's prophet" might do, the arm had healed. A great part of its strength was gone for ever, but it served him. "And as for the rest of us," he finished, "we're all your men, my lord. You're safe here, and your secrets with you. We all know where the future of these lands lies, and that's in your hands. Myrddin Emrys. If we'd known you were the 'traveller' those soldiers were seeking, we'd have held them here till you came—aye, and killed them if you'd so much as nodded your head." He gave a fierce look round him, and the others nodded, muttering their agreement. Even the smith grunted some sort of assent, and brought his hammer clanging down as if it was an axe on an enemy's neck.

I said something to them, of thanks and acknowledgement. I was thinking that I had been out of the country too long; for too long had been talking with statesmen and lords and princes. I had begun to think as they were thinking. It was not only the nobles and the fighting kings who would help Arthur to the high throne and maintain him there; it was the folk of Britain, rooted in the land, feeding it and drawing life from it like its own trees, who would lift him there and fight for him. It was the faith of the people, from the high lands to the low, that would make him High King of all the realms and islands in a full sense which my father had dreamed of but had been unable to achieve in the short time allowed him. It had been the dream, too, of Maximus, the would-be emperor who had seen Britain as the foremost in a yoke of nations pulling the same way against the cold wind from the north. I looked at Brychan with his disabled arm, at his kinsmen, poor men of a poor village they would die to defend, at the smith and his ragged boy, and thought of the Old Ones keeping faith in their cold caves with the past and the future, and thought: this time it will be different. Macsen and Ambrosius tried it with force of arms, and laid the paving stones. Now, God and the people willing, Arthur will build the palace. And then, suddenly: that it was time I left courts and castles and went back into the hills. It was from the hills that help would come.

Brychan was speaking again. "Will you not come to the village with us now, my lord? Leave the smith here to finish your mare, and come yourself up to my house, and rest and eat and give us your news. We are sharp set, all of us, to know why troopers should come seeking you, with money in their hands, and as urgent about it as if there was a kingdom at stake."

"There is. But not for the High King."

"Ah," he said. "They would have had us believe they were King's troops, but I thought they were not. Whose, then?"

"They serve Urien of Gore."

The men exchanged glances. Brychan's look was bright with intelligence. "Urien, eh? And why should Urien pay for news of you? Or maybe it was news of Prince Arthur he'd be paying for?"

"The two are the same," I said, nodding. "Or soon will be. He wants to know where I am going."

"So he can follow you to the boy's hiding-place. Yes. But how would that profit Urien of Gore? He's a small man, and not likely to get bigger. Or—wait, I have it, of course. It would profit his kinsman, Lot of Lothian?"

"I think so. I've been told that Urien is Lot's creature. You may be sure he is working for him."

Brychan nodded, and said slowly: "And King Lot is promised to a lady that's like to be Queen if Arthur dies . . . So he's paying troops to find where the boy is kept? My lord, that adds up to something I don't like the smell of."

"Nor I. We may be wrong, Brychan, but my bones tell me we are right. And there may be others besides Lot and Urien. Were these men the only ones? You had no Cornishmen pass this way?"

"No, my lord. Rest easy, if any others come this way, they'll get no help." He gave a short bark of laughter. "I'd trust your bones sooner than most men's pledged word. We'll see no danger follows you to the little prince. . . . If any pursuit of you comes through Gwynedd we'll see that it bogs down as surely as a stag's scent fails when he takes to water. Trust us, my lord. We're your men, as we were your father's. We know nothing of this prince you hold in your hand for us, but if he's yours, and you tell us to follow him and serve him, then, Myrddin Emrys, we'll be his men as long as we can hold swords. That's a promise, and it's for you that we make it."

"Then I'll accept it for him, and give you my thanks." I got to my feet. "Brychan, it would be better if I did not come to the village with you, but there is something you could do for me now, if you will. I need food for the next few days, and wine for my flask, and fodder for the mare. I have money. Could you get these for me?"

"Nothing easier, and you can put away your money. Did you take money of me when you mended my arm? Give us an hour, and we'll get all you want, and no word said. The boy can come with us—folk are used to seeing him bring goods down to the forge. He'll bring what you need."

I thanked him again, and we talked for a little longer, while I gave him what news there was from the south; then they took their leave. It is a matter of fact that, then or at any time, none of them, down to the boy, said a word to any man about my visit.

The boy had not yet returned from the village when the smith finished his job. I paid him his fee and commended him on his work. He took this as no more than his due, and, though he must have heard all that had passed between Brychan and me, showed no awe of me. Indeed, I have never seen why any man skilled in his trade, and surrounded by the articles of his craft, should be in awe of princes. Their task differs, that is all.

"Which way do you ride?" he asked me. Then, as I hesitated: "I told you not to fear me. If that magpie Brychan and his brothers can be silent, then so can I. I serve the road and all men on it, and I'm no more a King's man than any smith who is bound to serve the road, but I spoke to Ambrosius once. And my grandfather's grandfather, why, he shod the horse of the Emperor Maximus himself." He mistook the reason for the look on my face. "Aye, you may well stare. That's a long time ago. But even then, my granda told me, this anvil had been worked by father and son and father and son further back than the oldest man in the village could remember. Why, it's said hereabouts that the first smith who set up his iron here had been taught his trade by Weland Smith himself. So who else would the Emperor come to? Look."

He pointed at the door, which was set wide open, back against the wall. It was made of oak, adzed smooth as beaten silver, and age and weather had so bleached and polished it that its surface was bone pale, meshed and rippled like grey water. From a hook nearby hung a bag of iron nails, and then a rack of branding irons. All over the silky wood of the door were the scars of brands where the generations of smiths had tried them as they were fashioned.

An *A* caught my eye, but the brand was new, still charred and black. Beneath it and overlaid by it was some sign that looked like a bird flying; then an arrow, and an eye, and one or two cruder signs scrawled in with red-hot metal by idle jesters waiting for the smith to finish a job. But to one side, clear of them all, faded so that they were only dark silver on light, were the letters *M.I.* Just below these was a deeper scar on the door, a half-moon indented, with the marks of nails. It was at this that the smith was pointing. "They say that's where the Emperor's stallion kicked out, but I don't believe it. When I and mine handle a horse, be he the wildest stallion straight off the hills, he doesn't kick. But that, there, above it, that's true enough. The brand was made there, for the horses Macsen Wledig took east with him, the time he killed the King of Rome."

"Smith," I said, "that is the only part of your legend that is false. The King of Rome killed Maximus, and took his sword. But the men of Wales brought it back here to Britain. Was the sword made here, too?"

He was a long time replying, and I felt my heart quicken as I waited. But at last he said, reluctantly: "If it was, I have never heard ot it." It was obvious that it had cost him a struggle not to add the sword to the forge's credit, but he had told me the truth.

"I was told," I said, "that somewhere in the forest is a man who knows where the Emperor's sword is hidden. Have you heard of this, or do you know where I can find it?"

"No, how should I? They say there is a holy man a long way north of here who knows everything. But he lives north of the Deva, in another country."

"That is the way I was riding," I said. "I shall seek him out."

"Then if you don't want to meet yon soldiers, don't go by the road. Six miles north of here there's a crossroads, where the road for Segontium heads west. Keep by the river from here, and it'll take you clear across the corner till the west-bound road crosses it."

"But I'm not going to Segontium. If I bear too far to the west—"

"You leave the river where it meets the road again. Straight across from the ford the track runs up into the forest, through a shaw of hollies, and after that it's plain enough to see. It'll carry you on northwards, and never a glimpse of a road you'll see till you reach the Deva. If you ask the ferryman there about the holy man in the Wild Forest, he'll tell you the way. You go by the river. It's a good track, and impossible to miss."

I have found that people never say this unless, in fact, the way is very easy to miss. However, I said nothing and, the boy arriving at that moment with the provisions, helped him stow them. As we did so he whispered: "I heard what he said, lord. Don't listen to him. It's a bad track to follow, and the river's high. Stay with the road."

I thanked him and gave him a coin for his pains. He went back to his bellows, and I turned to take my leave of the smith, who had vanished into some dark and cluttered recess at the back of the smithy. I could hear the clattering of metal, and his whistling between his broken teeth. I called out above it. "I'm on my way now. My thanks." Then my breath caught in my throat. Suddenly, back in the dark clutter behind the chimney, the newly leaping flame had lit the outline of a face.

A stone face; a familiar face once seen at every crossways. One of the first Old Ones, the god of going, the other Myrddin whose name was Mercury, or Hermes, lord of the high roads and bearer of the sacred snake. As one born in September, he was mine. He lay back now, the old Herm who had once stood out in the open watching the passers-by, head propped against the wall, the moss and lichen on him long since dried to powdered grey. Clearly under the blurred and fretted lines of carving I recognized the flat face rimmed with beard, the blank eyes as oval and bulging as grapes, the hands clasped across the belly, the once protruding genitals smashed and mutilated.

"If I had known you were there, Old One," I said, "I would have poured the wine for you."

The smith had reappeared at my elbow. "He gets his rations, never fear. There's none who serves the road would dare neglect him."

"Why did you bring him in?"

"He never stood here. He was at the ford I told you of, where the old track that they call Elen's Causeway crossed the river Seint. When the Romans built their new road to Segontium they put their post station right in front of him. So he was brought here, I never heard how."

I said slowly: "At the ford you told me of? Then I think I must go that way after all." I nodded to the smith, then raised a hand in salute to the god. "Go with me now," I said to him, "and help me find this way—which it is impossible to miss."

He went with me for the first part of the way; indeed, so long as the track clung to the river's bank it could hardly be missed. But towards late afternoon, when the dim winter sun hung low to its setting, a mist began to gather and hang near the water, thickening with dusk into a damp and blinding fog. It might have been possible to follow the sound of water, though under the mist this was misleading, sometimes loud and near at hand, at others muted and deceivingly distant; but where the river took a bend, the track cut straight across, and twice, following this, I found myself astray and picking a way through the deep forest with no sign or sound of the river. In the end, astray for the third time, I dropped the reins on Strawberry's neck, and let her pick her own way, reflecting that, ironically, had I risked the road I would have been safe enough. I would have heard the troopers approaching, and have been safe from their eyes had I withdrawn only a few yards into the fog-bound forest.

There must be a moon above the low-lying mist. This drifted like lighted cloud, not solid, but rivers of vapour with dark between, banks of pale stuff clinging round the trees like snow. Through it, hiding and showing, the gaunt trees laced their back boughs overhead. Underfoot the forest floor was thick as velvet and as quiet to walk on.

Strawberry plodded steadily on, without hesitation, following some path unseen to me, or some instinct of her own. Now and again she pricked her ears, but at something I could neither hear nor see, and once she checked and flung up her head sideways, coming as near as she ever did to shying, but before I could pick up the reins again, she slacked her ears, dropped her head, and quickened her pace along the invisible line of her choosing. I let her alone. Whatever was drifting past us in the misty silence, it would do us no harm. If this was the way—and I was sure now that it was—we were protected.

An hour after full dark, the mare carried me softly out of the trees, across a hundred paces or so of flat ground, and came to a halt in front of a looming square of blackness that could only be a building. There was a water trough outside. She lowered her head, blew, and began to drink.

I dismounted and pushed open the door of the building. It was the posting station the smith had told me of, empty now and half derelict, but apparently still in use by travellers such as myself. In one corner a pile of half-charred logs showed where a fire had been lit recently, and in another stood a bed made from some tolerably clean planks laid across stones to raise it from the draught. It was rough comfort, but better than some we had had. I fell asleep within the hour to the sound of Strawberry's munching, and slept deeply and dreamlessly till morning.

When I woke, it was in the dusk of dawn, the sun not yet up. The mare dozed in her corner, slack-hipped. I went out to the trough for water to wash with.

The mist had gone, and with it the milder air. The ground was grey with frost. I looked about me.

The posting station stood a few paces back from the road which ran straight as a spear from east to west through the forest. Along this line the woodland had been cleared when the Romans made the road, the trees felled and the undergrowth hacked down a hundred paces back to either side from the gravelled way. Now saplings had grown up again and the low growth was thick and tangled, but still, near where I stood, I thought I could see under it the line of the old track that had been there before the Romans came. The river, smooth here and quiet-running, slid over the ruins of the causeway that took the road through it, hock deep. Beyond this, at the farther edge of the cleared land, I could see, black against the grey winter oaks, the shaw of holly which marked my road to the north.

Satisfied, I cracked the wafer of ice on the water of the trough and washed. As I did so, behind me the sun came up between the trees in the red of a cold dawn. Shadows grew and sharpened, barring the stiff grass. The frost sparkled. Light grew, like the smith's furnace under the bellows. When I turned, the sun, low and dazzling, blazed into my eyes, blinding me. The winter trees stood black and unbodied against a sky like a forest fire. The river ran molten.

There was something between me and the river, a tall shape, massive and yet insubstantial against the blaze, standing knee deep in the underbrush at the edge of the road. Something familiar, but familiar in another setting, of darkness, and strange places, and outland gods. A standing stone.

For a sharp moment I wondered if I was still asleep, and this was my dream again. I put up an arm against the light and narrowed my eyes under it, peering.

The sun came clear of the tree-tops. The shadow of the forest moved back. The stone stood clear against the sparkling forest.

It was not after all a standing stone. Nothing strange at all, or out of place. It was an ordinary milestone, perhaps two cubits taller than was normal, but bearing only the usual inscription to an emperor, and below this the message: A. SEGONTIO. M . P . XXII.

When I approached it I saw the reason for its height; instead of being sunk in the turf it had been mounted on a squared plinth of stone. A different stone. The plinth where the Herm had stood? I stooped to push the frosted grass aside. The red sunlight struck the stone, showing a mark on the plinth that might have been an arrow. Then I saw what it was: the remains of some ancient writing, the ogam letters blurred and worn till they showed like the fletching on a shaft, and a barbed head pointing westwards.

Well, I thought, why not? The signs were simple, but messages do not always come from the gods beyond the stars. My god had spoken to me before in ways as small as this, and I had told myself only yesterday to look low as well as high for the things of power. And here they were—a cast horsehoe, a word from a wayside smith, and some scratches on a stone—conspiring to turn me aside from my northern journey and take me westwards to Segontium. I thought again, why not? Who knew but that the sword might really have been made down at the forge yonder, and chilled in the Seint River, and that after his death they had carried it home to his wife's country, where she lodged still with his infant son? Somewhere in Segontium, the Caer Seint of Macsen Wledig, the King's Sword of Britain might lie, waiting to be lifted in fire.

10

The inn I stayed at in Segontium was a comfortable one, at the edge of town, but now serving the main highway. A few travellers lodged there, but the place mostly served food and drink to the local men who attended the market, or who were on their way with goods down to the port.

The place had seen better days, having been built to serve the soldiers at the vast barracks above the town. It must have stood there, at the least, for a couple of hundred years; originally it had been well built of stone, with one handsome room, almost a hall, where a vast fireplace stood, and oaken beams as solid as iron held up the roof. The remains of the benches and the stout tables were still there, stained and burned, and here and there hacked where the daggers of drunken legionaires had carved their names, along with other things less respectable. It was a marvel that anything remained: some of the stone had been pillaged, and once at least the inn had been burned by raiders from Ireland, so that now the stone oblong of the hall was all that remained, and the blackened beams held up a roof of thatch instead of tiles. The kitchen was no more than a lean-to of daubed wattle behind the great fireplace.

But there was a big fire of logs blazing, and a smell of good ale, with bread baking in the oven outside; and a shed with decent bedding and fodder for the mare. I saw her warm and groomed and fed before I went into the inn myself to bespeak a bed-place and a meal.

At that time of year the port was all but closed to traffic; few travellers were on the roads, and men did not stay out late drinking, but got themselves home to their beds soon after dusk. No one looked curiously at me, or ventured a question. The inn was quiet early, and I went to bed and slept soundly.

In the morning it was fine, with one of those glittering sharp days that December sometimes throws down like bright gold among the lead of winter's coinage. I breakfasted early, looked in at the mare, then left her resting and went out on foot.

I turned east, away from the town and the port, along the river's bank where, on rising ground about half a mile above the town, stood the remains of Segontium Roman fortress. Macsen's Tower stands just outside it, a little way down the hill. Here the High King Vortigern had lodged his men when my grandfather the King of South Wales had ridden up from Maridunum with his train to talk with him. I, a boy of twelve, had been with them, and on that journey had discovered for the first time that the dreams of the crystal cave were true. Here, in this wild and quiet corner of the world, I had first felt power, and found myself as a seer.

That had been a winter journey, too. As I walked up the weedy road towards the gateway set between its crumbling towers, I tried to conjure again the colours of cloaks and banners and bright weapons where now, in the blue shadows of morning, lay only the unprinted frost.

The vast complex of buildings was deserted. Here and there on the naked and fallen masonry the black marks of fire told their story. Elsewhere you could see where men had taken the great stones, stripping the very paving from the streets and carrying it off for their own building. There were dry thistles in the window spaces, and young trees rooted on the walls. A well-shaft gaped, choked with rubble. The cisterns brimmed with rain water, which slopped out through the grooves on the edge where men had sharpened their swords. No, there was nothing to see. The place was empty, even of ghosts. The winter sun shone down on a wise and crumbling waste land. The silence was complete.

I remember that as I walked through the shells of the buildings I was thinking, not of the past, not even of my present quest, but practically, as Ambrosius' engineer, of the future. I was weighing up the place as Tremorinus the chief engineer and I had been used to do: shifting this, repairing that, making the towers good, abandoning the north-easterly blocks to make good the west and south . . . Yes, if Arthur should ever need Segontium . . .

I had come to the top of the rise, the center of the fort where the Commandant's house—Maximus' house—had stood. It was as derelict as the rest. The great door still hung on rotting hinges, but the lintel was broken and sagging, and the place was dangerous. I went cautiously inside. In the main chamber there was daylight spilling through gaps in the roof, and piles of rubble half hid the walls where paint still showed, flaked and dark with damp. In the dimness I could see the remains of a table—too massive to take away, and not worth chopping for kindling—and behind it the shredded remnants of leather hangings on the wall. A general had sat here once, planning to conquer Rome, as formerly Rome had conquered Britain. He had failed, and died, but in failing he had sown the seeds of an idea which after him another king had picked up. "It will be one country, a kingdom in its own right," my father had said, "not merely a province of Rome. Rome is going, but for a while at least, we can stand." And through this came the memory of another voice, the voice of the prophet who sometimes spoke through me: "And the kingdoms shall be one Kingdom, and the gods one God."

It would be time to listen to those ghostly voices when a general sat there once again. I turned back into the bright morning stillness. Where, in this waste land, was the end of my quest?

From here you could see the sea, with the small crowded houses of the port, and across from this the druids' isle that is called Mona, or Von, so that the people call the place Caer-y-n'ar Von. To the other side, behind me, reared the Snow Hill, Y Wyddfa, where if a man could climb and live among the snows, he would meet the gods walking. Against its distant whiteness showed, dark and ruined, the remains of Macsen's Tower. And suddenly, from this new angle, I saw it afresh. The tower of my dream; the tower in the picture on Ahdjan's wall . . . I left the Commandant's house and walked quickly out of the fortress gate towards it.

It stood in a wilderness of tumbled stones, but I knew that near it, dug into the side of the little valley beyond the gate, and running in almost beneath the tower itself, was the temple of Mithras; and on the thought I found that my feet had led me, with no will of my own, down the path which led to the Mithraeum door.

There were steps here, cracked and slippery. Halfway down the flight one tread thrust upwards vertically, half blocking the stairway, and at the foot was a pile of mud and shards, fouled by rats and prowling dogs. The place stank of damp and dirt and some ancient noisomeness that might have been spilled blood. On the ruined wall above the steps some roosting birds had whitened the stones; the dung was greening over now with slime. A jackdaw's perch, perhaps? A raven of Mithras? A merlin? I trod cautiously forward over the slimy flags, and paused in the temple doorway.

It was dark, but some sunlight had followed me in, and there was enough light from a hole broken in the roof somewhere, so that I could see dimly. The temple was as filthy and forlorn as the stairway that led to it. Only the strength of the vaulted roof had saved the place from falling in under the weight of the hillside above. The furnishings had gone long since, the braziers, benches, carvings; this, like the scoured ruin overhead, was a shell empty of its tenant. The four lesser altars had been broken and defaced, but the central altar stood there still, fixed and massive, with its carved dedication to the unconquered god, MITHRAE INVICTO, but above the altar, in the apse, axe and hammer and fire had obliterated the story of the bull and the conquering god. All that remained of the picture of the bull-slaying was an ear of wheat, down in one corner, its carving still sharp and new and miraculously unspoiled. The air, sour with the smell of some fungus, caught at the lungs.

It seemed fitting to say a prayer to the god departed. As I spoke aloud, something in the echo of my voice came, not like an echo, but an answer. I had been wrong. The place was not yet empty. It had been holy, and was stripped of its holiness; but something was still held down to that cold altar. The sour smell was not the smell of fungus. It was unlit incense, and cold ashes, and unsaid prayers.

I had been his servant once. There was no one here but I. Slowly, I walked forward into the center of the temple, and held out my open hands.

Light, and colour, and fire. White robes and chanting. Fires licking upwards like light blowing. The bellow of a dying bull and the smell of blood. Outside somewhere the sun blazing and a city rejoicing to welcome its new king, and the sound of laughter and marching feet. Round me incense pouring heavy and sweet, and a voice that said through it, calm and small: "Throw down my altar. It is time to throw it down."

I came to myself coughing, with the air round me swirling thick with dust, and the sound of a crash still echoing round and round the vaulted chamber. The air trembled and rang. At my feet lay the altar, hurled over on its back into the curve of the apse.

I stared, dazed still and with swimming sight, at the hole it had torn in the floor where it had stood. My head sang with the echo; the hands I held stiffly before me were filthy, and one of them showed a bleeding gash. The altar was heavy, of massive stone, and in my right mind I would never have laid hands to it; but here it lay at my feet, with the echo of its fall dying in the roof, followed by the whisper of settling masonry as the crumbled pavement began to slide down into the hole where the altar had stood.

Something showed in the depths of the hole: a hard straight edge and a corner too sharp for stone. A box. I knelt down and reached for it.

It was of metal, and very heavy, but the lid lifted easily. Whoever had buried it had trusted the god's protection rather than a lock. Inside, my hands met canvas cloth, long rotten, which tore; then inside that again, wrappings of oiled leather. Something long and slender and supple; here at last it was. Gently, I took the wrappings off the sword and held it naked across my hands.

A hundred years since they had put it here, those men who had made their way back from Rome. It shone in my hands, as bright and dangerous and beautiful as on the day it had been made. It was no wonder, I thought, that already in that hundred years it had become a thing of legend. It was easy to believe that the old smith, Weland himself, who was old before the Romans came, might have made this last artifact before he faded with the other small gods of wood and stream and river, into the misty hills, leaving the crowded valleys to the bright gods of the Middle Sea. I could feel the power from the sword running into my palms, as if I held them in water where lightning struck. *Whoso takes this sword from under this stone is rightwise King born of all Britain . . .* The words were clear as if spoken, bright as if carved on the metal. I, Merlin, only son of Ambrosius the King, had taken the sword from the stone. I, who had never given an order in battle, nor led so much as a troop; who could not handle a war stallion, but rode a gelding or a quiet mare. I, who had never even lain with a woman. I, who was no man, but only eyes and a voice. A spirit, I had said once, a word. No more.

The sword was not for me. It would wait.

I wrapped the beautiful thing up again in the filthy wrappings, and knelt to replace it. I saw that the box was deeper than I had thought; there were other objects there. The rotten canvas had fallen away to show the shape, gleaming in the dimness, of a wide-mouthed dish, a krater such as I had seen on my travels in countries east of Rome. It seemed to be of red gold, studded with emeralds. Beside it, still half muffled in wrappings, gleamed the bright edge of a lance-head. The rim of a platter showed, crusted with sapphire and amethyst.

I leaned forward to lay the sword back in its place. But before I could do it, without any warning, the heavy lid of the box fell shut with a crash. The noise set the echoes drumming again, and brought down with it a cascade of stone and plaster from the apse and the crumbling walls above. It happened so quickly that in the single moment of my own sharp recoil the box, hole and all had vanished from view under the rubble.

I was left kneeling there in the choking cloud of dust, with the shrouded sword held fast in my filthy and bleeding hands. From the apse, the last of the carving had vanished. It was only a curved wall, showing blank, like the wall of a cave.

11

The ferryman at the Deva knew the holy man of whom the smith had spoken. It seemed he lived in the hills above Ector's fortress, at the edge of the great tract of mountain land they call the Wild Forest. Though I no longer felt myself to need the hermit's guidance, it would do no harm to talk to him, and his cell—a chapel, the ferryman called it—lay on my way, and might give me lodging until I considered how best to present myself at Count Ector's gates.

Whether or not the possession of the sword had in fact carried power with it, I travelled fast and easily, and with no more alarms. A week after leaving Segontium we—the mare and I—cantered easily along the green margin of a wide, calm lake, making for a light which showed pale in the early dusk, high as a star among the trees on the other shore.

It was a long way round the lake, and it was full dark when at last I trotted the tired mare up the forest track into a clearing and saw, against the soft and living darkness of the forest, the solid wedge of the chapel roof.

It was a smallish oblong building set back against the trees at the far side of a large clearing. All round the open space the pines stood in a dark and towering wall, but above was a roof of stars, and beyond the pines, on every side, the glimmer of the snow-clad heights that cupped this corrie high in the hills. To one side of the clearing, in a basin of mossy rock, stood a still, dark pool; one of those springs that well up silently from below, for ever renewing itself without sound. The air was piercingly cold, and smelled of pines.

There were mossed and broken steps leading up to the chapel door. This was open, and inside the building the light burned steadily. I dismounted and led the mare forward. She pecked against a stone, her hoof rapping sharply. You would have thought that anyone living in this solitary place would have come out to investigate, but there was no sound, no movement. The forest hung still. Only, far overhead, the stars seemed to move and breathe as they do in the winter air. I slipped the mare's bridle off over her ears, and left her to drink at the well. Gathering my cloak round me, I trod up the mossy steps, and entered the chapel.

It was small, oblong in shape, with a highish barrel roof; a strange building to find in the wild heart of the forest, where at most one might have expected a rough-built hut, or at least a cave, or dwelling contrived among the stones. But this had been built as a shrine, a holy place for some god to dwell in. The floor was of stone flags, clean and unbroken. In the center, opposite the door, stood the altar, with a thick curtain of some worked stuff hung behind it. The altar itself was covered with a clean, coarse cloth, on which stood the lighted lamp, a simple, country-made thing which nevertheless gave a strong and steady light. It had recently been filled with oil, and the wick was trimmed and unsmoking. To one side of the altar, on the step, was a stone bowl of the kind I had seen used for sacrifice; it had been scoured white, and held sweet water. To the other side stood a lidded pot of some dark metal, pierced, such as the Christians use to burn incense. The air of the chapel still held, faintly, the sweet gummy smell. Three bronze lamps, triple-branched, stood unlit against a wall.

The rest of the chapel was bare. Whoever kept it, whoever had lighted the lamp and burned the incense, slept elsewhere.

I called aloud: "Is anyone there?" and waited for the echoes to run up into the roof and die. No answer.

My dagger was in my hand; it had sprung there without conscious thought on my part. I had met this kind of situation before, and it had only meant one thing; but that had been in Vortigern's time, the time of the Wolf. Such a man as this hermit, living alone in a solitary place, trusted to the place itself, its god and its holiness, to protect him. It should have been enough, and in my father's time had certainly been so. But things had changed, even in the few years since his death. Uther was no Vortigern, but it seemed sometimes that we were sliding back to the time of the Wolf. The times were wild and violent, and filled with alarms of war; but more than this, faiths and loyalties were changing faster than men's minds could grow to apprehend them. There were men about who would kill even at the altar's horns. But I had not thought there were any such in Rheged, when I chose it for Arthur's sanctuary.

Struck by an idea, I stepped carefully past the altar and drew back the edge of the curtain. My guess had been right; there was a space behind the curtain, a semicircular recess which was apparently used as storage room; dimly the lamplight showed a clutter of stools and oil jars and sacred vessels. At the back of the recess a narrow doorway had been cut in the wall.

I went through. It was here, obviously, that the keeper of the place lived. There was a small square chamber built on the end of the chapel, with a low window deeply recessed, and another door giving, presumably, straight on the forest. I felt my way across in the dimness and pushed the door open. Outside the starlight showed me the rampart of pine trees crowding close, and to one side a lean-to shed, with its overhanging roof sheltering a stack of fuel. Nothing else.

Leaving the door wide, I surveyed what I could see of the room. There was a wooden bed with skins and blankets piled on it, a stool, and a small table with a cup and platter where the remains of a meal lay half-eaten. I picked up the cup; it was half full of thin wine. On the table a candle had burned down into a mess of tallow. The smell of the dead candle still hung there, mixed with the smell of the wine and the dead embers on the hearth. I put a finger to the tallow; it was still soft.

I went back into the chapel. I stood by the altar, and shouted again. There were two windows, one to either side, high in the wall; they were unglazed, open on the forest. If he was not too far away, he would surely hear me. But again there was no reply.

Then, huge and silent as a ghost, a great white owl swept in through one window and sailed across the lamplit space. I caught a glimpse of the cruel beak, the soft wings, the great eyes, blind and wise, then it was gone with no more sound than a spirit makes. It was only the *dillyan wen,* the white owl which haunts every tower and ruin in the country, but my flesh crept on my bones. From outside came the long, sad, terrible cry of the owl, and after it, like an echo, the sound of a man moaning.

Without his moaning I would not have found him till daylight. He was robed and hooded in black, and he lay face down under the dark trees at the edge of the clearing, beyond the spring. A jug fallen from his hand showed what his errand had been. I stooped and gently turned him over.

He was an old man, thin and frail, with bones that felt as brittle as a bird's. When I had made sure that none was broken, I picked him up in my arms and carried him back indoors. His eyes were half open, but he was still unconscious; in the lamplight I could see how one side of his face was dragged down as if a statuary had run his hand down suddenly over the clay, blurring the outline. I put him into his bed, wrapped warm. There was kindling left by the hearth, and what looked like a winter-stone ready among the ashes. I brought more fuel, then made fire and, when the stone was warm, drew it out, wrapped it in cloth, and put it to the old man's feet. For the moment there was nothing more that could be done for him, so after I had seen to the mare I made a meal for myself, then settled by the dying fire to watch through the rest of the night.

For four days I tended him, while none came near except the forest creatures and the wild deer, and at night the white owl haunting the place as if it waited to convoy his spirit home.

I did not think he could recover; his face was fallen in and grey, and I had seen the same blue tinge round the mouths of dying men. From time to time he seemed to come half to the surface, to know I was beside him. At such times he was restless always, fretting, I understood, about the care of the shrine. When I tried to talk to him and reassure him, he seemed not to understand, so in the end I drew back the curtains that parted the room from the shrine, so that he might see the lamp still burning in its place on the altar.

It was a strange time for me, by day tending the chapel and its keeper, and by night snatching sleep while I watched the sick man and waited for his restless muttering to make sense. There was a small store of meal and wine in the place, and with the dried meat and raisins left in my pack, I had sufficient food. The old man could scarcely swallow; I kept him alive on warm wine mixed with water, and a cordial I made for him from the medicines I carried. Each morning I was amazed that he had lived through the night. So I stayed, tending the place by day, and by night spending long hours beside him watching, or else in the chapel where the smell of incense slowly faded and the sweet air of the pines floated in and set the flame of the lamp aslant in its well of oil.

Now when I look back on that time it is like an island in moving waters. Or like a dreaming night which gives rest and impetus between the hard days. I ought to have been impatient to get on with my journey, to meet Arthur and to talk with Ralf again and arrange with Count Ector how best, without betraying either of us, I might enter the fabric of Arthur's life. But I troubled myself with none of these things. The shrouding forest, the still and glowing shrine, the sword lying where I had hidden it under the thatch of the shed, these held me there, serene and waiting. One never knows when the gods will call or come, but there are times when their servants feel them near, and this was such a time.

On the fifth night, as I carried in wood to build the fire, the hermit spoke to me from the bed. He was watching me from his pillows, and though he had not the strength to lift his head, his eyes were level and clear.

"Who are you?"

I set down the wood and went over to the bedside. "My name is Emrys. I was passing through the forest, and came on the shrine. I found you by the well, and brought you back to your bed."

"I . . . remember. I went to get water . . ." I could see the effort that the memory cost him, but intelligence was back in his eyes, and his speech, though blurred, was clear enough.

"You were taken ill," I told him. "Don't trouble yourself now. I'll get you something to drink, then you must rest again. I have a brew here which will strengthen you. I am a doctor; don't be afraid of it."

He drank, and after a while his colour seemed better, and his breathing easier. When I asked him if he was in pain, his lips said, "No," without sound, and he lay quietly for a while, watching the lamp beyond the doorway. I made the fire up and propped him higher on his pillows to ease his breathing, then sat down and waited with him. The night was still; from close outside came the hooting of the white owl. I thought: *You will not have long to wait, my friend.*

Towards midnight the old man turned his head easily on the pillows and asked me suddenly: "Are you a Christian?"

"I serve God."

"Will you keep the shrine for me when I am gone?"

"The shrine shall be kept. Trust me for it."

He nodded, as if satisfied, and lay quiet for a time. But I thought something still troubled him; I could see it working behind his eyes. I heated more wine and mixed the cordial and held it to his lips. He thanked me with courtesy, but as if he was thinking of something else, and his eyes went back to the lighted doorway of the shrine.

I said: "If you wish, I will ride down and bring you a Christian priest. But you will have to tell me the way."

He shook his head, and closed his eyes again. After a while he said, thinly: "Can you hear them?"

"I can hear nothing but the owl."

"Not that, no. The others."

"What others?"

"They crowd at the doors. Sometimes on a night of midsummer you can hear them crying like young birds, or like flocks on the far hills." He moved his head on the pillow. "Did I do wrong, I wonder, to shut them out?"

I understood him then. I thought of the bowl of sacrifice, the well outside, the unlit lamps in the sacred nine of an older religion than any. And I think some part of my mind was with the white shadow that floated through the forest boughs outside. The place, if my blood told me aright, had been holy time out of mind. I asked him gently: "Whose was the shrine, father?"

"It was called the place of the trees. After that the place of the stone. Then for a while it had another name . . . but now down in the village they call it the chapel in the green."

"What was the other name?"

He hesitated, then said: "The place of the sword."

I felt the nape of my neck prickle, as if the sword itself had touched me. "Why, father? Do you know?"

He was silent for a moment, and his eyes watched me, considering. Then he gave the ghost of a nod, as if he had reached some conclusion that satisfied him. "Go into the shrine and draw the cloth from the altar."

I obeyed him, lifting the lamp down to the step in front of the altar, and taking off the cloth that had draped it to the ground. It had been possible to see even through the covering cloth that the altar was not a table such as the Christians commonly use, but as high as a man's waist, and of the Roman shape. Now I saw that this was indeed so. It was the twin of the one in Segontium, a Mithras altar with a squared front and the edge scrolled to frame the carving. And carving there had been, though it was there no longer. I could make out the words MITHRAE and INVICTO across the top, but on the panel below where other words had been, a sword had been cut clear through them, its hilt, like a cross, marking the center of the altar. The remains of the other letters had been gouged away, and the sword blade carved in high relief among them. It was rough carving, but clear, and as familiar to my eyes as that hilt was already familiar to my hand. I realized then, staring at it, that the sword in the stone was the only cross the chapel held. And above it, only the dedication to Mithras Unconquered remained. The rest of the altar was bare.

I went back to the old man's bedside. His eyes waited, with a question in them. I asked him: "What does Macsen's sword do here, carved like a cross in the altar?"

His eyes closed, then opened again, lightly. He fetched a long, light breath. "So. It is you. You have been sent. It was time. Sit down again, while I tell you." As I obeyed him, he said, strongly enough, but in a voice stretched thin as wire: "There is just time to tell you. Yes, it is Macsen's sword, him the Romans called Maximus, who was Emperor here in Britain before the Saxons ever came, and who married a British princess. The sword was forged south of here, they say, from iron found in Snow Hill within sight of the sea, and tempered with water that runs from that hill into the sea. It is a sword for the High King of Britain, and was made to defend Britain against her enemies."

"So when he took it to Rome, it availed him nothing?"

"It is a marvel it did not break in his hand. But after he was murdered they brought the sword home to Britain, and it is ready for the King's hand that can find it, and finding, raise."

"And you know where they hid it?"

"I never knew that, but when I was a boy and came here to serve the gods, the priest of the shrine told me that they had taken it back to the country where it was made, to Segontium. He told me the story, as it happened in this very place, years before his time. It was . . . it was after the Emperor Macsen had died at Aquileia by the Inland Sea, and those of the British who were left came home. They came through Brittany, and landed here on the west, and took the road home through the hills, and they came by here. Some of them were servants of Mithras, and when they saw this place was holy, they waited here for the summer midnight, and prayed. But most were Christians, and one was a priest, so when the others had done they asked him to say a mass. But there was neither cross nor cup, only the altar as you see it. So they talked together, and went to where their horses were standing, and took from the bundles tied there treasure beyond counting. And among the treasure was the sword, and a great krater, a grail of the Greek fashion, wide and deep. They stood the sword over against the altar for a cross, and they drank from the grail, and it was said afterwards that no man was there that day but found his spirit satisfied. They left gold for the shrine, but the sword and the grail they would not leave. One of them took a chisel and a hammer and made the altar as you see it. Then they rode away with the treasure, and did not come this way again."

"It's a strange story. I never heard it before."

"No man has heard it. The keeper of the shrine swore by the old gods and the new that he would say nothing save to the priest who came after. And I, in my turn, was told." He paused. "It is said that one day the sword itself will come back to the shrine, to stand here for a cross. So in my time I have struggled to keep the shrine clean of all but what you see. I took the lights away, and the offering bowls, and threw the crooked knife into the lake. The grass has grown now over the stone. I drove out the owl that nested in the roof, and I took the silver and copper coins from the well and gave them to the poor." Another long pause, so long that I thought he had gone. But then his eyes opened again. "Did I do right?"

"How can I tell? You did what you thought was right. No one can do more than that."

"What will you do?" he asked.

"The same."

"And you will tell no man what I have told you, save him who should know?"

"I promise."

He lay quietly, with trouble still in his face, and his eyes intent on something distant and long ago. Then, imperceptibly but as definitely as a man stepping into a cold stream to cross it, he made a decision. "Is the cloth still off the altar?"

"Yes."

"Then light the nine lamps and fill the bowl with wine and oil, and open the doors to the forest, and carry me where I can see the sword again."

I knew that if I lifted him, he would die in my hands. His breath laboured harshly in the thin chest, and the frail body shook with it. He turned his head on the pillows, feebly now.

"Make haste." When I hesitated, I saw fear touch his face. "I tell you I must see it. Do as I say."

I thought of the shrine scoured and swept of all its ancient sanctities; and then of the sword itself, hidden with the King's gold in the roof-beams of the stable outside. But it was too late even for that. "I cannot lift you, father," I said, "but lie still. I will bring the altar to you."

"How can you—?" he began, then stopped with wonder growing in his face, and whispered: "Then bring it quickly, and let me go."

I knelt beside the bed, facing away from him, looking at the red heart of the fire. The logs had fallen from their blaze into a glowing cave, crystals glimmering in a globe of fire. Beside me the difficult breathing came and went like the painful beat of my own blood. The beat surged in my temples, hurting me. Deep in my belly the pain grew and burned. The sweat ran scalding down my face, and my bones shook in their sheath of flesh as, grain by grain and inch by shining inch, I built that altar-stone for him against the dark, blank wall. It rose slowly, solid, and blotted out the fire. The surface of the stone was lucent against the dark, and ripples of light touched it and wavered acorss it, as if it floated on sunlit water. Then, lamp by lamp, I lit the nine flames so that they floated with the stone like riding-lights. The wine brimmed in the bowl, and the censer smoked. INVICTO, I wrote, and groped, sweating, for the name of the god. But all that came was the single word INVICTO, and then the sword stood forward out of the stone like a blade from a splitting sheath, and the blade was white iron with runes running down it in the wavering water-light, below the flashing hilt and the word in the stone, TO HIM UNCONQUERED . . .

It was morning, and the first birds were stirring. Inside, the place was very quiet. He was dead, gone as lightly as the vision I had made for him out of shadows. It was I who, stiff and aching, moved like a ghost to cover the altar and tend the lamp.

BOOK III

THE SWORD

1

When I had promised the dying man to see that the chapel was cared for, I had not thought of doing this myself. There was a monastery in one of the little valleys not far from Count Ector's castle, and it should not be hard to find someone from there who would live here and care for the place. This did not mean I must hand over the sword's secret to him; it was mine now, and the end of its story was in my hands.

But as the days passed, I thought better of my decision to approach the brothers. To begin with, I was forced to inaction, and given time to think.

I buried the old man's body, and just in time, as the next day the snow came, falling thick, soft and silent, to shroud the forest deep, and island the chapel and block the tracks. To tell the truth I was glad to stay; there was enough food and fuel, and both the mare and I needed the rest.

For two weeks or more the snow lay; I lost track of days, but Christmas came and went, and the start of the year. Arthur was nine years old.

So perforce I kept the shrine. I supposed that whoever came as keeper would, like the old man, fight to keep the place clear for his own God, but in the meantime I was content to let what god would take the place. I would open it again to any who would use it. So I put away the altar cloth, and cleaned the three bronze lamps and set them about the altar and lighted the nine flames. About the stone and the spring I could do nothing until the snow melted. Nor could I find the curving knife, and for this I was thankful; that Goddess is not one to whom I would willingly open a door. I kept the sweet holy-water in her bowl of sacrifice, and at morning and evening burned a pinch of incense. The white owl came and went at will. By night I shut the chapel door to keep out the cold and the wind, but it was never locked, and all day it stood open, with the lights shining out over the snow.

Some time after the turn of the year the snow melted, and the tracks through the forest showed black and deep in mire. Still I made no move. I had had time to think, and I saw that I must surely have been led up to the chapel by the same hand that had guided me to Segontium. Where better could I stay to be near Arthur without attracting attention? The chapel provided the perfect hiding-place. I knew well enough that the place would be held in awe, and its guardian with it. The "holy man of the forest" would be accepted without question. Word would go round that there was a new and younger holy man, but, country memories being long, folk would recall how each hermit as he died had been succeeded by his helper, and before long I would simply be "the hermit of the Wild Forest" in my turn and in my own right. And with the chapel as my home and my cure, I could visit the village for supplies, talk to the people, and in this way get news, at the same time ensuring that Count Ector would hear of my installation in the Wild Forest.

About a week after the thaw started, before I would risk taking Strawberry down through the knee-deep mud of the tracks, I had visitors. Two of the forest people; a small, thick-set dark man dressed in badly cured deerskins, which stank, and a girl, his daughter, wrapped in coarse woollen cloth. They had the same swarthy looks and black eyes as the hill men of Gwynedd, but under its weather-beaten brown the girl's face was pinched and grey. She was suffering, but dumbly like an animal; she neither moved nor made a sound when her father unwrapped the rags from her wrist and forearm swollen and black with poison.

"I have promised her that you will heal her," he said simply.

I made no comment then, but took her hand, speaking gently in the Old Tongue. She hung back, afraid, until I explained to the man—whose name was Mab—that I must heat water and cleanse my knife in the fire; then she let him lead her inside. I cut the swelling, and cleaned and bound the arm. It took a long time, and the girl made no sound throughout, but under the dirt her pallor grew, so when I had done and had wrapped clean bandages round the arm I heated wine for both of them, and brought out the last of my dried raisins, and meal cakes to go with them. These last I had made myself, trying my hand at them as I had so often watched my servant do at home. At first my cakes had been barely eatable, even when sopped in wine, but lately I had got the trick of it, and it gave me pleasure to see Mab and the girl eat eagerly, and then reach for more. So from magic and the voices of gods to the making of meal cakes: this, perhaps the lowest of my skills, was not the one in which I took least pride.

"Now," I said to Mab, "it seems that you knew I was here?"

"Word went through the forest. No, do not look like that, Myrddin Emrys. We tell no one. But we follow all who move in the forest, and we know all that passes."

"Yes. Your power. I was told so. I may need its help, while I stay here keeping the chapel."

"It's yours. You have lighted the lamps again."

"Then give me the news."

He drank, and wiped his mouth. "The winter has been quiet. The coasts are bound with storms. There was fighting in the south, but it is over and the borders are whole. Cissa has taken ship to Germany. Aelle stays, with his sons. In the north there is nothing. Gwarthegydd has quarrelled with his father Caw, but when did that breed ever rest quiet? He has fled to Ireland, but that is nothing. They say also that Riagath is with Niall in Ireland. Niall has feasted with Gilloman, and there is peace between them."

It was a bare recital of facts, told through with neither expression nor real understanding, as if learned by rote. But I could piece it together. The Saxons, Ireland, the Picts of the north; threats on all sides, but no more than threats: not yet.

"And the King?" I asked.

"Is himself, but not the man he was. Where he was brave, now he is angry. His followers fear him."

"And the King's son?" I waited for the answer. How much did these folk really see?

The black eyes were unreadable. "They say he is on the Isle of Glass, but then what do you do here in the Wild Forest, Myrddin Emrys?"

"I tend the shrine. You are welcome to it. All are welcome."

He was silent for a while. The girl crouched beside the fire, watching me, her fear apparently gone. She had finished eating, but I had seen her slip a couple of the meal cakes into the folds of her clothes, and smiled to myself.

I said to Mab: "If I should need to send a message, would your people take it?"

"Willingly."

"Even to the King?"

"We would contrive that it should reach him."

"As for the King's son," I said, "you say that you and your people see all that passes in the forest. If my magic should reach out to the King's son in his hiding-place, and call him to me through the forest, will he be safe?"

He made the strange sign that I had seen Llyd's men make, and nodded. "He will be safe. We will watch him for you. Did you not promise Llyd that he would be our King as well as the king of those in the cities of the south?"

"He is everyone's King," I said.

The girl's arm must have healed cleanly, for he did not bring her back. Two days later a freshly snared pheasant appeared at the back door, with a skin of the honey mead. In my turn I cleared the drifted snow from the stone, and put a cup in the place made for it above the spring. I never saw anyone near either, but there were signs I recognized, and when I left part of a new batch of meal cakes at the back door they would vanish overnight, and some offering appear in their place—a piece of venison, perhaps, or the leg of a hare.

As soon as the forest tracks were clear I saddled Strawberry and rode down towards Galava. The way led down the banks of the stream, and along the northern shore of a lake. This was a smaller lake than the great stretch of water at whose head Galava lay; it was little more than a mile long, and perhaps a third of a mile wide, with the forest crowding down on every hand right to the water. About midway along, but nearer the southern shore, was an island, not large, but thickly grown with trees, a piece of the surrounding forest broken off and thrown down into the quiet water. It was a rocky island, its trees crowding steeply up towards the high crags which reared at the center. These were of grey stone, outlined still with the last of the snow, and looking for all the world like the towers of a castle. On that day of leaden stillness there was about them a kind of burnished brightness. The island swam above its own reflection, the mirrored towers seeming to sink, fathoms deep, into the still center of the lake.

From the other end of this lake the stream flowed out again, this time as a young river, swollen with snow water, cutting its way deep and fast through beds of pallid rushes and black marshland seamed with willow and alder, towards Galava. In a mile or so the valley widened, and the marsh gave way to the cultivated land and the walls of small farms, and the cottages of the settlement crowding close under the protection of the castle walls. Beyond Ector's towers, jutting grey and uncompromising through the black winter trees, was the great lake which stretched as far as the eye could see, to merge with the sullen sky.

The first place I came to was a farm set a short way back from the riverside. It was not the kind of farm we have in the south and south-west, built on the Roman plan, but a place such as I had become used to seeing here in the north. There was a cluster of circular buildings, the farmhouse and the sheds for the beasts, all within a big irregular ring protected by a palisade of wood and stone. As I passed the gate a dog hurtled to the end of his chain, barking. A man, the owner by his dress, appeared in the doorway of a barn and stood staring. He had a billhook in his hand. I reined in and called a greeting. He came forward with a look of curiosity, but with the wariness that one saw everywhere in the country nowadays when a stranger approached.

"Where are you bound, stranger? For the Count's castle of Galava?"

"No. Only to the nearest place where I may buy food—meat and meal and perhaps some wine. I've come from the chapel up there in the forest. You know it?"

"Who doesn't? How does the old man up there, old Prosper? We've not seen him since before the snow."

"He died at Christmas."

He crossed himself. "You were with him?"

"Yes. I keep the chapel now." I gave no details. If he liked to assume I had been there for some time, helping the chapel's keeper, that was all to the good. "My name is Myrddin," I told him. I had decided to use my own name, rather than the "Emrys." Myrddin was a common enough name in the west, and would not necessarily be connected with the vanished Merlin; on the other hand, if Arthur was still known as "Emrys," it might provoke questions if a stranger of that name suddenly appeared in the district, and began to spend time in the boy's company.

"Myrddin, eh? Where are you from?"

"I kept a hill shrine for a time in Dyfed."

"I see." His eyes summed me, found me harmless, and he nodded. "Well, each to his task. No doubt your prayers serve us in their way as much as the Count's sword when it's needed. Does he know of the change up yonder?"

"I've seen no one since I came. The snow fell just after Prosper died. What sort of man is this Count Ector?"

"A good lord and a good man. And his lady as good as he. You'll not lack while they hold the forest."

"Has he sons?"

"Two, and likely boys both. You'll see them, I dare say, when the weather loosens. They ride in the forest most days. No doubt the Count will send for you when he comes home; he's away now, and the elder son with him. They expect him back at the turn of spring." He turned his head and called, and a woman appeared in the doorway of the house. "Catra, here's the new man from the chapel. Old Prosper died at midwinter: you were right he wouldn't last the new year in. Have you bread to spare from the baking, and a skin of wine? Good sir, you'll take a bite with us till the fresh batch comes from the oven?"

I accepted, and they made me welcome, and found me all I needed, bread and meal and a skin of wine, sheeps' tallow to make candles, oil for the lamps and chopped feed for the mare. I paid for them, and Fedor—he told me his name—helped me pack my saddle-bags. I asked no more questions, but listened to all he told me of local news, and then, well content, rode back to the shrine. The news would get to Ector, and the name; he would be the one person who would immediately connect the new hermit of the Wild Forest with the Myrddin who had vanished with the winter from his cold hilltop in Wales.

I rode down again at the beginning of February, this time to the village itself, where I found that the folk knew all about my coming and, as I had guessed, accepted me already as part of the place. Had I tried to find a niche in village or castle I would still, I knew, have been "the foreigner" and "the stranger" and a subject of ceaseless gossip, but holy men were a class apart, and often wanderers, and the good folk took them as they came. I had been relieved to find that they never came up to the chapel; there was too much of its ancient awesomeness still hanging about the place. They were most of them Christians, and turned for their comfort to the community of brothers nearby, but old beliefs die hard, and I was regarded with more respect, I believe, than the abbot himself.

The same image of ancient holiness clung, I had found, about the island in the lake. I had asked one of the hill men about it. It was known, he told me, as Caer Bannog, which means the Castle in the Mountains, and was said to be haunted by Bilis the dwarf king of the Otherworld. It was reputed to appear and disappear at will, sometimes floating invisible, as if made of glass. No one would go near it, and though people fished on the lake in summer and animals were grazed on the flat grassland at the western end where the river flowed into the valley, no one ventured near the island. Once a fisherman, caught in a sudden storm, had had his boat driven onto the island, and had passed a night there. When he came home next day he was mad, and talked of a year spent in a great castle made of gold and glass, where strange and terrible creatures guarded a hoard of treasure beyond man's counting. No one was tempted to go and look for the treasure, for the fisherman was dead, raving, within the week. So no man set foot now on the island, and though (they said) you could see the castle clearly sometimes of a fine sunset evening, when a boat rowed nearer it vanished clear away, and it was well known that if you set foot on the shore, the island would sink beneath you.

Such stories are not always to be dismissed as shepherds' tales. I had thought about it often, this other "isle of glass" that I found now almost on my doorstep, and wondered if its reputation would make it a safe hiding-place for Macsen's sword. It would be some years yet before the boy Arthur could take and lift the sword of Britain, and meanwhile it was neither safe nor fitting that it should be hidden in the roof of a beasts' shed out there in the forest. It was a marvel, I had sometimes thought, that it did not set light to the thatch. If it was indeed the King's sword of Britain, and Arthur was to be the King who would lift it, it must lie in a place as holy and as haunted as the shrine where I myself had found it. And when the day came the boy must be led to it himself, even as I had been led. I was the god's instrument, but I was not the god's hand.

So I had wondered about the island. And then, one day, I was sure.

I went down to the village again in March for my monthly supplies. When I rode back along the lake side the sun was setting, and a light mist wreathed along the water's surface. It made the island seem a long way off, and floating, so that one might well imagine it ghostly, and ready to sink under a random foot. The sun, sinking in splendour, caught the crags, and sent them flaming up from the dark hangers of trees behind. In this light the strange formations of the rock looked like high embattled towers, the crest of a sunlit castle standing above the trees. I looked, thinking of the legends, then looked again, and reined Strawberry in sharply and sat staring. There, across the flat sheen of the lake, above the floating mist, was the tower of my dream again, Macsen's Tower, whole once more and built out of the sunset. The tower of the sword.

I took the sword across next day. The mist was thicker than ever, and hid me from anyone who might have been there to see.

The island lay less than two hundred paces from the south shore of the lake. I would have swum the mare across, but found that she could go through breast high. The lake was still as glass, and as silent. We forged across with no more splashing than the wild deer make, and saw no living thing but a pair of diver ducks, and a heron beating slowly past in the mist.

I left the mare grazing, and carried the sword up through the trees till I reached the foot of the towered crags. I think I knew what I would find. Bushes and young trees grew thickly along the scree at the foot of the cliffs, but the boughs were barely budding, and through them I could see an opening, giving on a narrow passageway which led steeply downwards into the cliffs. I had brought a torch with me. I lit it, then went quickly down the steep passage, and found myself in a deep inner cavern where no light came.

In front of my feet lay a sheet of water, black and still, flooring half the cavern. Beyond the pool, against the back of the cavern, stood a low block of stone; I could not tell if it was a natural ledge, or if men's hands had squared it, but it stood there like an altar, and to one side of it a bowl had been hollowed in the stone. This was full of water, which in the smoky torchlight looked red as blood. Here and there from the roof water welled slowly, dripping down. Where it struck the surface of the pool the water broke with the sound of a plucked harp-string, its echo rippling away with the widening rings of torchlight. But where it dripped dull on stone it had not, as you might expect, worn the rock into hollows, but had built pillars, and above these from the dripping rocks hung solid stone icicles that had grown to meet the pillars below. The place was a temple, pillared in pale marble and floored with glass. Even I, who was here by right, and hedged with power, felt my scalp tingle.

By land and water shall it go home, and lie hidden in the floating stone until by fire it shall be raised again. So had the Old Ones said, and they would have recognized this place as I did; as the dead fisherman did who came back from the Otherworld raving of the halls of the dark King. Here, in Bilis' antechamber, the sword would be safe till the youth came who had the right to lift it.

I waded forward through the pool. The floor sloped and the water deepened. Now I could see how the dark passageway ran on, back and down behind the stone table, until the roof met the water's surface and the passage vanished below the level of the lake. Ripples ringed and lapsed against the rock, and the echoes ran round the walls and broke between the pillars. The water was ice-cold. I laid the sword, still wrapped as I had found it, on the stone table. I went back across the pool. The place sang with echoes. I stood still, while they sank to a humming murmur and then died. My very breathing sounded all at once too loud, an intrusion. I left the sword to its silent waiting, and went quickly back up towards daylight. The shadows parted and let me through.

2

April came, when Ector was expected home. For the first week of the month it rained and blew, weather like winter, so that the forest roared like the sea and the draughts through the shrine kept the nine lights plunging sidelong and smoking. The white owl watched from the place where she sat her eggs in the roof.

Then I woke in the night to silence. The wind had dropped, the pines were still. I rose and threw my cloak about me and went out. Outside the moon was high, and there in the north the Bear wheeled so low and brilliant that one felt one could reach up and touch it, were it not that its touch would burn. My blood ran light and free; my body felt rinsed and new clean as the forest. For the rest of the night I slept no more than a lover does, and at first light rose and broke my fast and went to saddle Strawberry.

The sun rose brilliant in a clear sky, and its early light poured into the glade. Yesterday's rain lay thick and glittering on the grasses and the new young curls of fern; it dripped and steamed from the pines so that their scent pierced the air. Beyond their bloomed crests the encircling hills smoked white towards the sky.

I let the mare out of the shed, and was carrying the saddle over to her when suddenly she lifted her head from her grazing, and put her ears up. Seconds later I heard what she had heard, the beat of hoofs, coming at a fast gallop, far too fast for safety on a twisting path seamed with roots and overhung by branches. I set the saddle down, and waited.

A neat black horse, galloped hard on a tight rein, burst out of the forest, came to a sliding stop three paces from me, and the boy who had been lying along his back like a leech slid, all in the same movement, to the ground. The horse was sweating hard, and the bit dripped foam. Red showed inside the blown nostrils. That neat-footed gallop and the collected stop had been a matter of hard control, then. Nine years old? At his age I had been riding a fat pony which had to be kicked to a trot.

He gathered the reins competently in one hand and held the horse still when it tried to thrust past him to the water. He did it absently; his attention was all on me.

"Are you the new holy man?"

"Yes."

"Prosper was a friend of mine."

"I'm sorry."

"You don't much look like a hermit. Are you really keeping the chapel now?"

"Yes."

He chewed his lip thoughtfully, regarding me. It was a look of appraisal, a weighing-up. Under it, as under no other I had encountered, I could feel my muscles clench themselves to hold nerves and heart-beats steady. I waited. I knew that, as ever, my face gave nothing away. What he must be seeing was merely a harmless-looking man, unarmed, saddling an undistinguished horse for his routine ride down the valley for supplies.

He came apparently to a decision. "You won't tell anyone you saw me?"

"Why, who's looking for you?"

His lips parted, surprised. I got the impression that I had been supposed to say: "Very well, sir." Then he turned his head sharply, and I heard it, too. Hoofs coming, soft on the mossy ground. Fast, but not so fast as the hard-ridden black.

"You haven't seen me, remember?" I saw his hand start towards his pouch, then stop halfway. He grinned, and the sudden flash startled me: till that moment he had been so like Uther, but that sudden lighting of the face was Ambrosius', and the dark eyes were Ambrosius', too. Or mine.

"I'm sorry." He said it politely, but very fast. "I do assure you I'm not doing anything wrong. At least, not very. I'll let him catch me soon. But he won't let me ride the way I like to." He grabbed the saddle, ready to mount.

"If you ride like that on these tracks," I said, "I don't blame him. Do you need to go? Get inside there while I throw him off the scent, and I'll put your horse somewhere to cool off."

"I knew you weren't a holy man," he said, in the tone of someone conveying a compliment, and throwing me the reins, he vanished through the back doorway.

I led the black horse across to the shed, and shut the door on him. I stood there for a moment or two, breathing deeply as a man does when he comes out of rough water, steadying myself. Ten years, waiting for this. I had broken Tintagel's defenses for Uther, and killed Brithael its captain, with a steadier pulse than I had now. Well, he was here, and we should see. I went to the edge of the clearing to meet Ralf.

He was alone, and furious. His big chestnut came up the track at a slamming canter, with Ralf crouched low on its neck. There was a thin scarlet mark on one cheek where a branch had whipped his face.

The sun was full on the clearing, and he must have been dazzled. I thought for a moment he was going to ride right over me. Then he saw me, and reined his horse hard to its haunches.

"Hey, you! Did a boy ride through here a few minutes ago?"

"Yes." I spoke softly, and put my hand up to the rein. "But hold a moment—"

"Out of the way, fool!" The chestnut, feeling the spurs go home, reared violently, tearing the rein from my hand. On the same breath Ralf said, thunderstruck: "My lord!" and hauled the horse sideways. The striking hoofs missed me by inches. Ralf came out of the saddle as lightly as the boy Arthur, and reached for my hand to kiss it.

I drew it back quickly. "No. And get off your knee, man. He's here, so watch what you do."

"Sweet Christ, my lord, I nearly ran you down! The sun in my eyes—I couldn't see who it was!"

"So I imagined. A rather rough welcome, though, for the new hermit, Ralf? Are those the usual manners of the north?"

"My lord—my lord, I'm sorry. I was angry . . ." Then, honestly: "Only because he fooled me. And even when I sighted the young devil I couldn't come up with him. So I . . ." Then what I had said got through to him. His voice trailed off, and he stood back, taking me in from head to foot as if he could hardly believe his eyes. "The new hermit *You?* You mean *you* are the 'Myrddin' of the shrine? . . . Of course! How stupid of me, I never connected him with you . . . And I'm sure no one else has—I haven't heard so much as a hint that it might be Merlin himself—"

"I hope you never will. All I am now is the keeper of the shrine, and so I shall remain, as long as it's necessary."

"Does Count Ector know?"

"Not yet. When is he due home?"

"Next week."

"Tell him then."

He nodded, and then laughed, the surprise giving way to excitement, and what looked like pleasure. "By the Rood, it's good to see you again, my lord! Are you well? How have you fared? How did you come here? And now—what will happen now?"

The questions came pouring out. I put up a hand, smiling. "Look," I said quickly, "we'll talk later. We'll arrange a time. But now, will you go and lose yourself for an hour or so, and let me make the boy's acquaintance on my own?"

"Of course. Will two hours do? You'll get a lot of credit for that—I'm not usually thrown off his track so easily." He glanced round the glade, but with his eyes only, not moving his head. The place was still in the morning sun, and silent but for the cock thrush singing. "Where is he? In the chapel? Then in case he's watching us, you'd better do some misdirecting."

"With pleasure." I turned and pointed up one of the tracks which led out of the glade. "Will that one do? I don't know where it goes, but it might suffice to lose you."

"If it doesn't kill me," he said resignedly. "Of course it had to be that one, didn't it? In the normal way I'd just call that a bad guess, but seeing it's you—"

"It was only a random choice, I assure you. I'm sorry. Is it so dangerous?"

"Well, if I'm supposed to be looking for Arthur there, it's guaranteed to keep me out of the way for quite some time." He gathered the reins, miming hasty agreement for the benefit of the unseen watcher. "No, seriously, my lord—"

" 'Myrddin.' No lord of yours now, nor of any man's."

"Myrddin, then. No, it's a rough track but it's rideable—just. What's more, it's just the way that devil's cub would have chosen to take . . . I told you, nothing you do can ever be quite random." He laughed. "Yes, it's good to have you back. I feel as if the world had been lifted off my shoulders. These last few years have been pretty full ones, believe me!"

"I believe you." He mounted, saluting, and I stepped back. He went across the glade at a canter, and then the sound of hoofs dwindled up the ferny track and was gone.

The boy was sitting on the table's edge, eating bread and honey. The honey was running off his chin. He slid to his feet when he saw me, wiped the honey off with the back of his hand, licked the hand and swallowed.

"Do you mind very much? There seemed to be plenty, and I was starving."

"Help yourself. There are dried figs in that bowl on the shelf."

"Not just now, thank you. I've had enough. I'd better water Star now, I think. I heard Ralf go."

As we led the horse across to the spring, he told me: "I call him Star for that white star on his forehead. Why did you smile then?"

"Only because when I was younger than you I had a pony called Aster; that means Star in Greek. And like you, I escaped from home one day and rode up into the hills and came across a hermit living alone—it was a cave he lived in, not a chapel, but it was just as lonely—and he gave me honey cakes and fruit."

"You mean you ran away?"

"Not really. Only for the day. I just wanted to get away alone. One has to, sometimes."

"Then you did understand? Is that why you sent Ralf away, and didn't tell him I was here? Most people would have told him straight away. They seem to think I need looking after," said Arthur in a tone of grievance. The horse lifted a streaming muzzle and blew the drops from its nostrils and turned from the water. We began to walk back across the clearing. He looked up. "I haven't thanked you yet. I'm much obliged to you. Ralf won't get into trouble, you know. I never tell when I give them the slip. My guardian would be angry, and it's not their fault. Ralf will come back this way, and I'll go with him then. And don't worry yourself, either; I won't let him harm you. It's always me he blames, anyway." That sudden grin again. "It's always my fault, as a matter fact. Cei is older than me, but I get all the ideas."

We had reached the shed. He made as if to hand me the reins, then, as he had done before, stopped in mid-gesture, led the horse in himself and tied him up. I watched from the doorway.

"What's your name?" I asked.

"Emrys. What's yours?"

"Myrddin. And, oddly enough, Emrys. But then that's a common name where I come from. Who is your guardian?"

"Count Ector. He's Lord of Galava." He turned from his task, his cheeks flushed. I could see he was waiting for the next question, the inevitable question, but I did not ask it. I had spent twelve years myself having to tell every man who spoke to me that I was the bastard of an unknown father: I did not intend to force this boy through the same confession. Though there were differences. If I was any judge, he had better defenses already than I had had at twice his age. And as the well-guarded foster son of the Count of Galava, he did not have to live, as I had, with bastard shame. But then, I thought again, watching him, the differences between this child and myself went deeper: I had been content with very little, not guessing my power; this boy would never be content with less than all.

"And how old are you?" I asked him. "Ten?"

He looked pleased. "As a matter of fact I've just had my ninth birthday."

"And can ride already better than I do now."

"Well, your'e only a—" He bit it off, and went scarlet.

"I only started work as a hermit at Christmas," I said mildly. "I've really ridden around the place quite a lot."

"What doing?"

"Travelling. Even fighting, when I had to."

"Fighting? Where?"

As we talked I had led him round to the front entrance of the chapel, and up the steps. These were mossed with age, and steep, and I was surprised at the child's lightness of foot as he trod up them beside me. He was a tall boy, sturdily built, with bones that gave promise of strength. There was another kind of promise, too. Uther's sort; he would be a handsome man. But the first impression one got of Arthur was of a controlled swiftness of movement almost like a dancer's or a skilled swordsman's. There was something in it of Uther's restlessness, but it was not the same; this sprang from some deep inner core of harmony. An athlete would have talked of co-ordination, an archer of a straight eye, a sculptor of a steady hand. Already in this boy, they came together in the impression of a blazing but controlled vitality.

"What battles were you in? You would be young, even when the Great Wars were being fought? My guardian says that I will have to wait until I am fourteen before I go to war. It's not fair, because Cei is three years older, and I can beat him three times out of four. Well, twice perhaps . . . Oh!"

As we went in through the chapel doorway the bright sunlight behind us had thrown our shadows forward, so that at first the altar had been hidden. Now, as we moved, the light reached it, the strong light of early morning, by some freak falling straight on the carved sword so that the blade seemed to lift clear and shining from its shadows on the stone.

Before I could say a word he had darted forward and reached for the hilt. I saw his hand meet the stone, and the shock of it go through his flesh. He stood like that for seconds, as if tranced, then dropped the hand to his side and stepped back, still facing the altar.

He spoke without looking at me. "That was the queerest thing. I thought it was real. I thought, 'There is the most beautiful and deadly sword in the world, and it is for me,' And all the time it wasn't real."

"Oh, it's real," I said. Through the dazzling swirl of sun-motes I saw the boy, hazed with brightness, turn to stare at me. Behind him the altar shimmered white with the ice-cold fire. "It's real enough. Some day it will lie on this very altar, in the sight of all men. And he who then dares to touch and lift it from where it lies shall . . ."

"Shall what? What shall he do, Myrddin?"

I blinked, shook the sun from my eyes, and steadied myself. It is one thing to watch what is happening elsewhere on middle-earth; it is quite another to see what has not yet come out of the heavens. This last, which men call prophecy, and which they honour me for, is like being struck through the entrails by that whip of God that we call lightning. But even as my flesh winced from it I welcomed it as a woman welcomes the final pang of childbirth. In this flash of vision I had seen it as it would happen in this very place; the sword, the fire, the young King. So my own quest through the Middle Sea, the painful journey to Segontium, the shouldering of Prosper's tasks, the hiding of the sword in Caer Bannog—now I knew for certain that I had read the god's will aright. From now, it was only waiting.

"What shall I do?" the voice demanded, insistent.

I do not think the boy was conscious of the change in the question. He was fixed, serious, burning. The end of the lash had caught him, too. But it was not yet time. Slowly, fighting the other words away, I gave him all he could understand.

I said: "A man hands on his sword to his son. You will have to find your own. But when the time comes, it will be there for you to take, in the sight of all men."

The Otherworld drew back then, and let me through, back into the clear April morning. I wiped the sweat from my face and took a breath of sweet air. It felt like a first breath. I pushed back the damp hair and gave my head a shake. "They crowd me," I said irritably.

"Who do?"

"Oh," I said, "those who keep wake here." His eyes watched me, at stretch, ready for wonders. He came slowly down the altar steps. The stone table behind him was only a table, with a sword rudely carved. I smiled at him. "I have a gift, Emrys, which can be useful and very powerful, but which is at times inconvenient, and always damnably uncomfortable."

"You mean you can see things that aren't there?"

"Sometimes."

"Then you're a magician? Or a prophet?"

"A little of both, shall we say. But that is my secret, Emrys. I kept yours."

"I shan't tell anyone." That was all, no promises, no oaths, but I knew he would keep to it. "You were telling the future then? What did it mean?"

"One cannot always be sure. Even I am not always sure. But one thing for certain, some day, when you are ready, you will find your own sword, and it will be the most beautiful and deadly sword in the world. But now, just for the moment, would you find me a drink of water? There's a cup beside the spring."

He brought it, running. I thanked him and drank, then handed it back. "Now, what about those dried figs? Are you still hungry?"

"I'm always hungry."

"Then next time you come, bring your rations with you. You might pick a bad day."

"I'll bring you food if you want it. Are you very poor? You don't look it." He considered me again, head aslant. "At least, perhaps you do, but you don't speak as if you were. If there's anything you'd like, I'll try and get it for you."

"Don't trouble yourself. I have all I need, now," I said.

3

Ralf came back duly, with questions in his eyes, but none on his lips except those he might ask a stranger.

He came too soon for me. There were nine years to get through, and judgments to make. And too soon, I could see, for the boy, though he received Ralf with courtesy, and then stood silent under the lash of that eloquent young man's tongue. I gathered from Arthur's expression that if it had not been for my presence he might have been thrashed by more than words. I understood that he lived under hard discipline: that kings must be brought up harder than other men he must have known, but not that the rule applied to him. I wondered what rule applied to Cei, and what Arthur thought the discrimination meant. He took it well, and when it was finished and I offered Ralf the appeasement of wine, went meekly enough to serve it.

When at length he was sent to lead the horses out, I said quickly to Ralf: "Tell Count Ector I would rather not come down to the castle. He'll understand that. The risks are too great. He'll know where we can meet in safety, so I'll leave it to him to suggest a place. Would he normally come up here, or might that make people wonder?"

"He never came before, when Prosper was here."

"Then I'll come down whenever he sends a message. Now, Ralf, there's not much time, but tell me this. You've no reason to suppose that anyone has suspected who the boy is? There's been no one watching about the place, nothing suspicious at all?"

"Nothing."

I said slowly: "Something I saw, when you first brought him over from Brittany. On the journey across by the pass, your party was attacked. Who were they? Did you see?"

He stared. "You mean up there by the rocks between here and Mediobogdum? I remember it well. But how did you know that?"

"I saw it in the fire. I watched constantly then. What is it, Ralf? Why do you look so?"

"It was a queer thing," he said slowly. "I've never forgotten it. That night, when they attacked us, I thought I heard you call my name. A warning, clear as a trumpet, or a dog barking. And now you say you were watching." He shifted his shoulders as if at a sudden draught, then grinned. "I'd forgotten about you, my lord. I'll have to get used to it again, I suppose. Do you still watch us? It could be an awkward thought, at times."

I laughed. "Not really. If there was danger it would come through to me, I think. Otherwise it seems I can leave it to you. But come, tell me, did you ever find out who it was attacked you that night?"

"No. They wore no blazon. We killed two of them, and there was nothing on them to show whose men they were. Count Ector thought they must be outlaws or robbers. I think so, too. At any rate there's been nothing since then, nothing at all."

"I thought not. And now there must be nothing to connect Myrddin the hermit with Merlin the enchanter. What has been said about the new holy man of the chapel in the green?"

"Only that Prosper had died and that God had sent a new man at the appointed time, as he has always done. That the new man is young, and quiet-seeming, but not as quiet as he seems."

"And just what do they mean by that?"

"Just what they say. You don't always bear yourself just like a humble hermit, sir."

"Don't I? I can't think why not; it's what I normally am. I must guard myself."

"I believe you mean that." He was smiling, as if amused. "I shouldn't worry, they just think you must be holier than most. It's always been a haunted place, this, and more so now, it seems. There are stories of a spirit in the shape of a huge white bird that flies in men's faces if they venture too far up the track, and—oh, all the usual tales you always get about hauntings, silly country stories, things one can't believe. But two weeks back—did you know that a troop of men was riding this way from somewhere near Alauna, and a tree fell across the way, with no wind blowing, and no warning?"

"I hadn't heard that. Was anyone hurt?"

"No. There's another path; they used that."

"I see."

He was watching me curiously. "Your gods, my lord?"

"You might call them that. I hadn't realized I was to be so closely guarded."

"So you knew something like this might happen?"

"Not until you told me. But I know who did it, and why."

He frowned, thinking. "But if it was done deliberately . . . If I am to bring Emrys this way again—"

"Emrys will be safe. And he is your safe conduct, too, Ralf. Don't fear them."

I saw his brows twitch at the word "fear," then he nodded. I thought he seemed anxious, even tense. He asked me: "How long do you suppose you will be here?"

"It's hard to judge. You must know it depends on the High King's health. If Uther recovers fully, it may be that the boy will stay here until he is fourteen, and ready to go to his father. Why, Ralf? Can you not resign yourself to obscurity for a few more years? Or do you find it too taxing riding guard on that young gentleman?'

"No—that is, yes. But—it isn't that . . ." He stammered, flushing.

I said, amused: "Who is she?"

I did not quite understand his scowling look until, after a pause, he asked: "How much else did you see, when you watched Arthur in the fire?"

"My dear Ralf!" It was not just the moment to tell him that the stars tend only to mirror the fate of kings and the will of gods. I said mildly: "The Sight doesn't as a rule take me beyond bedchamber doors. I guessed. Your face is about as concealing as a gauze curtain. And you must remember to call him Emrys even when you are angry."

I'm sorry. I didn't mean— Not that there was anything you couldn't have watched—I mean, I've never even been in her bedchamber . . . I mean, she's—oh hell and damnation, I should have known you'd know all about it. I didn't mean to be insolent. I'd forgotten you never take anything the way other men do. I never know where I am with you. You've been away too long. . . . There are the horses now. He seems to have saddled yours as well. I thought you said you weren't coming down today after all?"

"I hadn't intended to. It must be Emrys' idea."

It was. As soon as he saw us in the doorway, Arthur called out: "I brought your horse, too, sir. Will you not ride down part of the way with us?"

"If we go at my pace, not yours."

"We'll walk the whole way if you like."

"Oh, I won't subject you to that. But we'll let Ralf lead the way, shall we?"

The first part of the descent was steep. Ralf went in front and Arthur behind him, and the black horse must have been very sure-footed indeed, for Arthur rode with his chin on his shoulder the whole way, talking to me. To anyone who did not know, it might have seemed that it was the boy who had nine years to make up; I hardly had to question him; all the detail, small and great, of his life came tumbling out, till I knew as much about Count Ector's household and the boy's place in it as he knew himself—and more besides.

We came at length down from the edge of the pines into a wood of oak and chestnut where the going was easier, and after half a mile or so struck into the easy track along the lake. Caer Bannog floated, sunlit, above its secret. The valley widened ahead of us, and presently, cloudy along its green curve, showed the line of willows that marked the river.

Where the river left the lake I checked my horse. As I took my leave of them the boy asked quickly: "May I come back soon?"

"Come whenever you like—whenever you can. But you must promise me one thing."

He looked wary, which meant that what he promised, he would keep. "What's that?"

"Don't come without Ralf, or whoever escorts you. Don't break away next time. This is not called the Wild Forest for nothing."

"Oh, I know it's supposed to be haunted, but I'm not afraid of what lives in the hills, not now that I've seen—" He checked, and changed direction without a tremor "—not with you there. And if it's wolves, I have my dagger, and wolves don't attack by day. Besides, there are no wolves that could catch Star."

"I was thinking of a different kind of wild beast."

"Bears? Boars?"

"No, men."

"Oh." The syllable was a shrug. It was bravery, of course; there were outlaws here as well as anywhere, and he must have heard stories, but it was innocence as well. Such had been Count Ector's care of him. The most vulnerable and sought-for head in the kingdoms, and danger was still only a story to him.

"All right," he said, "I promise." I was satisfied. The guardians from the hollow hills might watch him for me, but guarding him was another thing. That took Ector's kind of power, and mine.

"My greetings to Count Ector," I told Ralf, and saw that he had understood my thoughts. We parted then. I stood watching them ride off along the turf by the river, the black horse fighting to be away and snatching at the bit, Ralf's big chestnut simmering alongside, while the boy talked excitedly, gesturing. At length he must have got his way, for suddenly Ralf's heels moved, and the chestnut leaped forward into a gallop. The black, set alight a fraction later, tore after it. As the two flying figures vanished round a shaw of birch trees, the smaller turned in the saddle, and waved. It had begun.

He was back next day, trotting decorously into the clearing with Ralf half a length in the rear. Arthur carried a gift of eggs and honey cakes and the information that Count Ector was still away, but the Countess seemed to think contact with the holy man might do good where it was most needed, and was glad to let him come meanwhile. The Count would arrange to see me as soon as he got back.

Arthur gave me the message, not Ralf, and obviously saw nothing in it but the strict precautions of a guardian who he must have long ago decided was over-zealous to an uncomfortable degree.

Four of the eggs were broken. "Only Emrys," said Ralf, "could possibly have imagined he could carry eggs on that wild colt of his."

"You must admit he did very well only to break four."

"Oh, aye, only Emrys could have done it. I've never had a quieter ride since I last escorted you."

He went off then on some excuse. Arthur washed the eggs out of his horse's mane and then settled down to help me eat the honey cakes, and ply me with questions about the world that lay outside the Wild Forest.

A few days later Ector returned to Galava, and arranged through Ralf to meet me.

Word would have gone round by now that the boy Emrys had ridden up two or three times to the chapel in the green, and people might well expect Count Ector or his lady to send for the new incumbent to look him over. It was arranged that Ector and I were to meet as if by chance at Fedor's farm. Fedor himself and his wife could be trusted, I was told, with anything; the other folk there would only see the hermit calling for supplies as usual, and the Count riding by and taking the opportunity to speak with him.

We were shown into a smallish, smoke-filled room, and our host brought wine and then left us.

Ector had hardly altered, save to add a little grey to his hair and beard. When, after the first greetings were over, I told him so, he laughed. "That's hardly surprising. You tip a gilded cuckoo's egg into my quiet nest and think to find me carefree? No, no, man, I was only jesting. Neither Drusilla nor I would have been without the boy. Whatever comes of it in the end, these have been good years, and if we've done a good job, we had the finest stuff in the world to work on."

He plunged then into an account of his stewardship. Five years is a long time, and there was a great deal to say. I spoke hardly at all, but listened readily. Some of what he told me I knew already, from the fire, or from the boy's own talk. But if I was familiar enough with the tenor of Arthur's life here in Galava, and could judge its results for myself, what came chiefly out of Ector's talk of him was the deep affection which he and his wife felt for their charge. Not only these two, but the rest of the household who had no idea who Arthur was held him, apparently, in the same affection. My impressions of him had been right; there was courage and quick wit and a burning desire to excel. Not enough cool sense and caution, perhaps—faults like his father's—"but who the devil wants a young boy to be cautious? That much he'll learn the first time he's hurt, or, worse, when he finds a man that can't be trusted," said Ector gruffly, obviously torn between pride in the boy and in his own successful guardianship.

When I began to talk of this, and to thank him for what he had done, he cut me off abruptly.

"Well, now, you've got yourself settled nicely in here, from all I hear about it. That was a fine chance, wasn't it, that led you up to the Green Chapel in time to take old Prosper's place?"

"Chance?" I said.

"Oh, aye, I'd forgotten who I was talking to. It's a long time since we had an enchanter in these parts. Well, to a jogging mortal like me it would have come as chance. Whatever it was, it's the best thing; you couldn't have taken a place in the castle, as it happens; we've got a man here who knows you well; Marcellus, him that married Valerius' sister. He's my master-at-arms. Maybe I shouldn't have taken him on, knowing you'd be likely to come back, but he's one of the best officers in the country, and God knows we're going to need all we have, here in the north. He's the best swordsman in the country, too. For the boy's sake, I couldn't miss the chance." He shot me a sharp look from under his brows. "What are you laughing at? Wasn't that chance, either?"

"No," I said, "it was Uther." I told him of the talk I had had with the King on the subject of Arthur's training. "How like Uther to send a man who knew me. But then he never did have room for more than one thought at a time. . . . Well, I'll keep away. Can you find a good reason for letting the boy ride up to see me?"

He nodded. "I've given it about that I know of you, and you're a learned man and have travelled widely, and there are things you can teach the boys that they'd not learn from Abbot Martin or the fathers. I'll let it be known that they may ride up your way whenever they wish."

" 'They'? Hasn't Cei outgrown a tutor, even an unorthodox one?"

"Oh, he wouldn't come for the learning." His father's voice held a kind of rueful pride. "He's like me, is Cei, not a thought in his head but what you might call the arts of the field. Not that even so he'll be the kind of swordsman Arthur's shaping for, but he's dogged and takes all the pains in the world. He'll not come twice if there's book learning to be discussed, but you know what boys are, what one has the other wants, and I couldn't keep him away if I tried, after all Arthur's been saying. He's talked of nothing else since I got home, even told Drusilla it was his holy duty to ride up there every day to see you got sufficient food. Yes, you may well laugh. Did you set a spell on him?"

"Not that I'm aware of. I'd like to see Cei again. He was a fine boy."

"It's not easy for him," said Ector, "knowing the younger one is near as good as he is already, for all the three years' difference, and is likely to surpass him when they both come to man. And when they were younger it was always 'Remember to let Emrys have as much as you—he's the foster-son, and a guest.' It might have been easier if there'd been others. Drusilla's had the hardest time of it, not liking to favour one or the other, but having to let Cei see all the way that he was the real son, without letting Arthur feel he was on the outside. Cei's done well enough by the other boy, even if he does tend to jealousy, but there'll be nothing to fear in the future, I assure you. Show him where he can be loyal, and no one will shift him. Like his father; a slow dog, but where he grips, he holds."

He talked on a little longer, and I listened, remembering my own very different upbringing as the bastard and outsider at another court. Where I had been quiet and showed no talents that could rouse jealousy in boy or man, Arthur by his very nature must shine out among the other boys in the castle like a young dragon hatching in a clutch of pond newts.

At last Ector sighed, drank, and set down his cup. "But there, those are nursery tales now, and long past. Cei stays by me now, among the men, and there's Bedwyr to keep Arthur company. When I said 'they' I wasn't thinking of Cei. We've another boy with us now. I brought him back with me from York. Bedwyr, his name is, son of Ban of Benoic. Know him?"

"I've met him."

"He asked me to take Bedwyr for a year or two. He'd heard Marcellus was here with me, and wanted Bedwyr to learn from him. He's about the same age as Arthur, so I wasn't sorry when Ban made the suggestion. You'll like Bedwyr. A quiet boy; not a great brain, so Abbot Martin tells me, but a good lad, and seems to like Emrys. Even Cei thinks twice before he tangles with the pair of them. Well, that's that, isn't it? It's just to be hoped Abbot Martin doesn't try to spoke the wheel."

"Is it likely?"

"Well, the boy was baptized a Christian. It's thought that Prosper served God in the later years, but it's well known that the Green Chapel has housed other gods than the true Christ in its time. What do you do now, up there in the forest?"

"I believe in giving due honour to whatever god confronts you," I said. "That's common sense in these days, as well as courtesy. Sometimes I think the gods themselves have not yet got it clear. The chapel is open to the air and the forest, and they come in who will."

"And Arthur?"

"In a Christian household, Arthur will owe duty to Christ's God. What he does on the field of battle may be another matter. I don't know yet which god will give the boy his sword—though I doubt if Christ was much of a swordsman. But we shall see. May I pour you more wine?"

"What? Oh, thank you." Ector blinked, wetted his lips, and changed the subject. "Ralf was saying you'd asked about that ambush at Mediobogdum five years back. They were robbers, no more. Why do you ask? Have you reason to think that someone's interested now?"

"I had some small trouble on the way north," I said. "Ralf tells me there has been nothing here."

"Nothing. I've been twice myself to Winchester and once to London, and there's never a soul so much as questioned me, which they'd have been quick to do if anyone had thought the boy might be anywhere in the north."

"Lot has never approached you or shown interest?"

Another quick look. "Him, eh? Well, nothing would surprise me there. Some of the trouble we've been having in these parts might easily have been avoided if that same gentleman had minded his kingdom's business instead of paying court to a throne."

"So they say that, do they? It's the King's place he's after, not just a place at the King's side?"

"Whatever he's after, they're handfast now, he and Morgian: they'll be married as soon as the girl is twelve years old. There's no way out of *that* union now, even if Uther wanted to end it."

"And you don't like it?"

"No one does, up in this part of the country. They say that Lot's stretching his borders all the time, and not always with the sword. There's talk of meetings. If he gets too much power by the time the High King fails, we might well find ourselves back in the time of the Wolf. The Saxons coming every spring and burning and raping as far as the Pennine Way, aye, and the Irish coming down to join them, and more of our men taking to the high hills and what cold comfort they can find there."

"How recently did you see the King?"

"Three weeks past. When he lay at York he sent for me, and asked privately about the boy."

"How did he look?"

"Well enough, but the cutting edge was gone. You understand me?"

"Very well. Was Cador of Cornwall with him?"

"No. He was still at Caerleon then. I have heard since—"

"At Caerleon?" I asked sharply. "Cador himself was there?"

"Yes," said Ector, surprised. "He'd be there just before you left home. Did you not know?"

"I should have known," I said. "He sent a party of armed men to search my home on Bryn Myrddin, and to watch my movements. I gave them the slip, I think, but what I didn't reckon on was being watched by two parties at the same time. Urien of Gore had men there in Maridunum, too, and they traced me north into Gwynedd." I told him about Crinas, and Urien's party, and he listened, frowning. I asked him: "You haven't heard reports of any such up here? They'd ask no questions openly, but wait and watch, and listen."

"No. If there were strangers, it would have been reported. You must have shaken them off. Be easy, Cador's men will never come this way. He's in Segontium now, did you know?"

"When I was there I heard he was expected. Do you know if he plans to make his headquarters at Segontium, now Uther's put him in charge of the Irish Shore defenses? Has there been talk of re-investing it?"

"There was talk, yes, but I doubt if it will ever come to anything. That's a task that'll take more time and money than Uther is likely to spare, or to have, just yet. If I can make a guess, Cador will garrison Segontium and the frontier fortresses, and base himself inland where he can keep his forces moving to the points of attack. Perhaps at Deva. Rheged himself is in Luguvallium. We do what we can."

"And Urien? I trust he's fixed on the east, where he belongs?"

"Well dug in on his rock," said Ector, with grim satisfaction. "And one thing's for sure. Until Lot marries Morgian with every bishop in the realm in attendance, and proof positive of consummation, he won't stir a hand to bring Uther down, or let Urien do so, either. Nor will he find Arthur. If they haven't had a sniff of the boy in nine years, they'll never pick the scent up now. So be easy. By the time Morgian is twelve, and ready for bedding, Arthur will be fourteen, and coming to the time when the King has promised to bring him before the kingdom. It will be time then to deal with Lot and Urien, and if the time comes before then, why, it is with God."

On that we parted, and I rode back alone to the shrine.

4

After this Arthur, sometimes with the other two boys, but usually just with Bedwyr, rode up to the chapel to see me two or three times a week. Cei was a big fair-haired boy, with a look of his father, and his manner to Arthur was a compound of patronage and hectoring affection which must have been galling at times to the younger boy. But Arthur seemed fond of his foster-brother, and eager to share with him the pleasure (for so he seemed to find it) of his visits to me. Cei enjoyed the tales I had to tell of foreign lands and the histories of fighting and conquests and battle, but he grew quickly tired of discussing the way people lived and governed their countries, and the talk of their legends and beliefs, which Arthur loved. As time went by Cei stayed more often at home, going (the other two told me) on sport or business with his father; hunting sometimes, or on patrol, or accompanying Count Ector on his occasional visits to his neighbours. After the first year, I rarely saw Cei at all.

Bedwyr was quite different, a quiet boy of Arthur's own age, gentle and dreamy as a poet, and a natural follower. He and Arthur were like two sides of the same apple. Bedwyr trailed, doglike in devotion, after the other boy; he made no attempt to hide his love for Arthur, but there was nothing soft about him, for all his gentle ways and poet's eyes. He was a plain boy, with his nose flattened in some fight, and badly set, and the scar of some nursery burn on his cheek. But he had character and kindness, and Arthur loved him. As the son of Ban, a petty king, Bedwyr was the superior even of Cei, and as far as any of the boys knew, right out of Arthur's star. But this never occurred to either Bedwyr or Arthur; the one offered devotion, the other accepted it.

One day I said to them: "Do you know the story of Bisclavaret, the man who became a wolf?" Bedwyr, without troubling to answer, brought the harp out from under its shroud, and put it gently by me. Arthur, prone on the bed with chin on fist and eyes brilliant in the firelight—it was a chill afternoon of late spring—said impatiently: "Oh, let be. Never mind the music. The story." Then Bedwyr curled beside him on the blankets, and I tuned the strings and started.

It is an eerie tale, and Arthur took it with sparkling face, but Bedwyr grew quieter than ever, all eyes. It was growing dark when they went home, with a husky servant that day for escort. Arthur, alone with me next day, told me how Bedwyr had woken in the night with the nightmare. "But do you know, Myrddin, when we were on the way home yesterday, when he must have been full of the story, we saw something slink off beyond the trees and we thought it was a wolf, and Bedwyr made me ride between him and Leo. I know he was frightened, but he said it was his right to protect me, and I suppose it was, since he is a king's son, and I—"

He stopped. It was as near as he had ever got to the boggy ground. I said nothing, but waited.

"—and I was his friend."

I talked to him then about the nature of courage, and the moment passed. I remember what he said afterwards of Bedwyr. I was to remember it many times in later years, when, on even less certain ground, the trust between him and Bedwyr held true.

He said now, seriously, as if at nine years old he knew: "He is the bravest companion, and the truest friend in all the world."

Ector and Drusilla had, of course, taken care to see that Arthur knew all that was good to know about his father and the Queen. He knew, too, as much as everyone in the country knew about the young heir who waited—in Brittany, in the Isle of Glass, in Merlin's tower?—to succeed to the kingdom. He told me once, himself, the story that was current about the "rape at Tintagel." The legend had lost nothing in the telling. By now, it seemed, men believed that Merlin had spirited the King's party, horses and all, invisibly within the walls of the stronghold, and out again in the broad light of next morning.

"And they say," finished Arthur, "that a dragon curled on the turrets all night, and in the morning Merlin flew off on him, in a trail of fire."

"Do they? It's the first I heard of that."

"Don't you know the story?" asked Bedwyr.

"I know a song," I said, "which is closer to the truth than anything you've heard up here. I got it from a man who'd once been in Cornwall."

Ralf was there that day, listening silently, amused. I raised my brows at him and he shook his head slightly. I had not thought he would have let Arthur know he came from Tintagel, and indeed I doubt if anyone now would have guessed. He spoke as nearly as might be with the accent of the north.

So I told the boys the story, the truth as I knew it—and who knew better?—without the extra trimmings of fantasy that time and ignorance had added to it. And God knows it was magical enough without; God's will and human love driving forward together in the black night under the light of the great star, and the seed sown which would make a king.

"So God had his way, and the King through him, and men—as men always do—made mistakes and died for them. And in the morning the enchanter rode away alone, to nurse his broken hand."

"No dragon?" This from Bedwyr.

"No dragon," I said.

"I prefer the dragon," said Bedwyr firmly. "I shall go on believing the dragon. Riding away alone, that's a let-down. A real enchanter wouldn't do that, would he, Ralf?"

"Of course not," said Ralf, getting to his feet. "But we must. Look, it's dusk already."

He was ignored. "I'll tell you what I don't understand," said Bedwyr, "and that's a King who would risk setting the whole kingdom at blaze for a woman. Keeping faith with your peers is surely more important than having any woman. I'd never risk losing anything that really mattered, just for that."

"Nor would I," said Arthur slowly. He had been thinking hard about it, I could see. "But I think I understand it, all the same. You have to reckon with love."

"But not to risk friendship for it," said Bedwyr quickly.

"Of course not," said Arthur. I could see that he was thinking in general terms, where Bedwyr meant one friendship, one love.

Ralf began to speak again, but at that moment something, a shadow, swept silently across the lamplight. The boys hardly glanced up; it was only the white owl, sailing silently in through the open window to its perch in the beams. But its shadow went across my skin like a hand of ice, and I shivered.

Arthur looked up quickly. "What is it, Myrddin? It's only the owl. You look as if you'd seen a ghost."

"It was nothing," I said. "I don't know."

I did not know, either, then, but I know now. We had been speaking Latin, as we usually did, but the word he had used for the shadow across the light was the Celtic one, *guenhwyvar.*

Be sure I told them, too, about their own country, and about the times recently past, of Ambrosius and the war he had fought against Vortigern, and how he had knit the kingdoms together into one, and made himself High King, and brought to the length and breadth of the land justice, with a sword at its back, so that for a short span of years men could go peacefully about their affairs anywhere in the country, and not be molested; or if they were, could seek, and get, the King's justice equally for high or low. Others had given them the stories as history; but I had been there, and closer to affairs than most, being at the High King's side and, in some cases, the architect of what had happened. This, of course, they could not be allowed to guess: I told them merely that I had been with Ambrosius in Brittany, and thereafter at the battle of Kaerconan, and through the next years of the rebuilding. They never asked how or why I was there, and I think this was out of delicacy, in case I should be forced to confess how I had served in some humble capacity as assistant to the engineers, or even as a scribe. But I still remember the questions Arthur poured out about the way the Count of Britain—as Ambrosius then styled himself—had assembled, trained and equipped his army, how he had shipped it across the Narrow Sea to the land of the Dumnonii where he had set up his standard as High King before he swept northwards to burn Vortigern out of Doward, and finally to smash the vast army of the Saxons at Kaerconan. Every detail of organization, training, and strategy I had to recall for him as best I could, and every skirmish of which I could tell them anything was fought over and over again by the two boys, poring over maps drawn in the dust.

"They say there will be war again soon," said Arthur, "and I am too young to go." He mourned over it, openly, like a dog which is bidden to stay at home on a hunting morning. It was three months before his tenth birthday.

It was not all talk of war and high matters, of course. There were days when the boys played like young puppies, running and wrestling, racing their horses along the riverside, swimming naked in the lake and scaring every fish within miles, or taking bows with Ralf up to the hills to look for hares or pigeons. Sometimes I went with them, but hunting was not a sport I cared for. It was different when it occurred to me to rummage out the old hermit's fishing rod and take it to try the waters of the lake. We would pass the time happily there, Arthur fishing with more fury than success, myself watching him, and talking. Bedwyr did not care for fishing, and on these occasions went with Ralf, but Arthur, even on the days when wind or weather made fishing useless, seemed to prefer to stay with me rather than go with Ralf or even Bedwyr to look for sport in the forest.

Looking back, I do not remember now that I ever paused to question this.

The boy was my whole life, my love for him so much a part of every day that I was content to take the time as it came, accepting straight from the gods the fact that the boy seemed to like above all else to be with me. I told myself merely that he needed to escape from the crowded household, from the patronage of an elder brother preparing now for a position which he himself could never hope for, and also a chance to be with Bedwyr in a world of imagination and brave deeds where he felt himself to belong. I would not allow myself to ascribe it to love, and if I had guessed the nature of the love, could have offered no comfort then.

Bedwyr stayed at Galava for more than a year, leaving for home in the autumn before Arthur's eleventh birthday. He was to return the following summer. After he had gone Arthur moped visibly for a week, was unwontedly quiet for another, then recovered his spirits with a bound, and rode up to see me, in defiance of the weather, rather more often than before.

I have no idea what reasons Ector gave for letting him come so often. Probably he needed no reason: as a rule the boy rode out daily except in the foulest weather, and if nothing was volunteered as to where he went, nothing would be asked. It became known, as it was bound to, that he came often to the Green Chapel where the wise man lived, but if people thought about it at all, they commended the boy's sense in seeking out a man known for his learning, and let it be.

I never attempted to teach Arthur in the way that Galapas, my master, had taught me. He was not interested in reading or figuring, and I made no attempt to press them on him; as King, he would employ other men in these arts. What formal learning he needed, he received from Abbot Martin or others of the community. I detected in him something of my own ear for languages, and found that, besides the Celtic of the district where he lived, he had retained a smattering of Breton from his babyhood, and Ector, mindful of the future, had been at pains to correct his northern accent into something which the British of all parts would understand. I decided to teach him the Old Tongue, but was amazed to find that he already knew enough of it to follow a sentence spoken slowly. When I asked where he had learned it he looked surprised and said: "From the hill people, of course. They are the only ones who speak it now."

"And you have spoken with them?"

"Oh, yes. When I was little once I was out with one of the soldiers and he was thrown and hurt himself, and two of the hill people came to help me. They seemed to know who I was."

"Did they indeed?"

"Yes. After that I saw them quite often, here and there, and I learned to speak with them a little. But I'd like to learn more."

Of my other skills, music and medicine, and all the knowledge I had so gladly amassed about the beasts and birds and wild things, I taught him nothing. He would have no need of them. He cared only about beasts to hunt them, and there, already, he knew almost as much as I about the ways of wild deer and wolf and boar. Nor did I share with him much of my knowledge about engines; here again it would be other men who would make and assemble them; he needed only to learn their uses, and most of this he was taught along with the arts of war he learned from Ector's soldiers. But as Galapas had done with me, I taught him how to make maps and read them, and I showed him the map of the sky.

One day he said to me: "Why do you look at me sometimes as if I reminded you of someone else?"

"Do I?"
"You know you do. Who is it?"
"Myself, a little."
His head came up from the map we were studying. "What do you mean?"
"I told you, when I was your age I used to ride up into the hills to see my friend Galapas. I was remembering the first time he taught me to read a map. He made me work a great deal harder than ever I make you."
"I see." He said no more, but I thought he was downcast. I wondered why he should imagine I could tell him anything about his parentage; then it occurred to me that he might expect me to "see" such things at will. But he never asked me.

5

There was no war that year, or the next. In the spring after Arthur's twelfth birthday Octa and Eosa at last broke from prison, and fled south to take refuge behind the boundaries of the Federated Saxons. The whisper went that they had been helped by lords who professed themselves loyal to Uther. Lot could not be blamed directly, nor Cador; no one knew who were the traitors, but rumours were rife, and helped to swell the feeling of unease throughout the country. It seemed as if Ambrosius' forceful uniting of the kingdoms were to go for nothing: each petty king, taking Lot's example, carved and kept his own boundaries. And Uther, no longer the flashing warrior men had admired and feared, depended too much on the strength of his allies, and turned a blind eye to the power they were amassing.

The rest of that year passed quietly enough, but for the usual tale of forays from north and south of the wild debatable land to either side of Hadrian's Wall, and summer landings on the east coast which were not (it was said) wholeheartedly repelled by the defenders there. Storms in the Irish Sea kept the west peaceful, and Cador, I was told, had made a beginning on the fortifications at Segontium. King Uther, heedless of the advisers who told him that when trouble came it would come first from the north, stayed between London and Winchester, throwing his energies into keeping the Saxon Shore patrolled and Ambrosius' Wall fortified, with his main force ready to move and strike wherever the invaders broke the boundaries. Indeed there seemed little to turn him yet towards the north: the talk of a great alliance of invaders was still only talk, and the small raids continued along the southern coast throughout the year, keeping the King down there to combat them. The Queen left Cornwall at this time, and moved to Winchester with all her train. Whenever the King could, he joined her there. It was observed, of course, that he no longer frequented other women as he had been used to do, but no rumour of impotence had gone around: it seemed as if the girls who had known of it had seen it simply as a passing phase of his illness, and said nothing. When it was seen now that he spent all his time with the Queen, the story went round that he had taken vows of fidelity. So, though the girls might mourn their lover, those citizens rejoiced who had been wont to lock their daughters away when word went round that the King was coming, and praised him for adding goodness to his powers as a fighting man.

These latter he certainly seemed to have recovered, though there were stories of the uncertain temper he showed, and of sudden ferocities in the treatment of defeated enemies. But on the whole this was welcomed as a sign of strength at a time when strength was needed.

I myself seemed to have managed to drop safely out of sight. If people wondered from time to time where I had gone, some said that I had crossed the Narrow Sea again and resumed my travels, others, that I had retired once more into a new solitude to continue my studies. I heard from Ralf and Ector—and sometimes, innocently, from Arthur—that there were rumours of me from all parts of the country. It was said that when the King first fell sick, Merlin had appeared immediately in a golden ship with a scarlet sail and ridden to the palace to heal him, and afterwards vanished into the air. He had been seen next at Bryn Myrddin, though none had seen him ride there. (This in spite of the fact that I had changed horses at the usual places, and stayed every night in a public tavern.) And since then, the talk went, Merlin the enchanter had been wont to appear and vanish here and there all over the country. He had healed a sick woman near Aquae Sulis, and a week later had been seen in the Caledonian Forest, four hundred miles away. The host of tales grew, coined by idle folk anxious for the importance that such "news" would give them. Sometimes, as had happened before, wandering healers or would-be prophets would style themselves "another Merlin," or even use my very name: this inspired trust in the healers, and if the patient recovered, did no harm. If the patient died, folk tended to say simply, "It cannot have been Merlin after all; *his* magic would have succeeded." And since the false Merlin would by that time have completely vanished, my reputation would survive the imposture. So I kept my secret, and lost nothing. Certainly no wandering suspicion lighted on the quiet keeper of the Green Chapel.

I had contrived from time to time to send messages of reassurance to the King. My chief fear was that he would grow impatient, and either send for the boy too soon, or by some hasty inadvertence betray Ector or myself to the people who watched him. But he remained silent. Ector, speaking of it to me, wondered if the King still thought the danger of treachery too great to have the boy by him in London, or if he still hoped against bitter hope that some day he would get another son.

Myself I think it was neither. He was beset, was Uther, with treachery and trouble and the lack of the fine health that he was used to; and besides, the Queen started to ail that winter. He had neither time nor mind to give to the young stranger who was waiting to take what he himself found it harder and harder to hold.

As for the Queen, there had been many times during the years when I had wondered at her silence. Ralf had, through means of his own, kept secretly in touch with his grandmother who served Ygraine, and through her had assured the Queen of her son's well-being. But from all accounts Ygraine, though she loved her daughter Morgian, and would have loved her son as dearly, was able to watch—indifferently enough, it seemed—her children used as tools of royal policy. Morgian and Arthur were, to her, pledges only of her love for the King, and having given them birth, she turned back to her husband's side. Arthur she had barely seen, and was content to know that one day he would emerge from his fastness safe and strong, in the King's time of need. Morgian, to whom she had given all the mother-love of which she was capable, was to be sent (without a backward glance, said Marcia in a letter to Ralf) to the marriage bed which would join the cold northern kingdom and its grim lord to Uther's side in the coming struggle. When I had tried to show Arthur something of the all-consuming sexual love which had obsessed Uther and Ygraine, I had spoken only half the truth. She was Uther's first, then she was Queen; and though she was the bearer of princes, she cared no more than the hawk does when its fledglings fly. As things stood, for her sake, it was better so; and, I thought, for Arthur too. All he needed now, he had from Ector and his gentle wife.

I kept no contact with Bryn Myrddin, but in some roundabout way Ector got news for me. Stilicho had married Mai, the miller's girl, and the child was a boy. I sent my felicitations and a gift of money, and a threat of various dire enchantments should he let either of his new family touch the books and the instruments that remained at the cave. Then I forgot about them.

Ralf married, too, during my second summer in the Wild Forest. His reason was not the same as Stilicho's; he had wooed the girl long enough, and only found his happiness in her bed after a Christian wedding. Even if I had not known the girl was virtuous, and that Ralf had been fretting after her like a curbed colt for a year or more, I could have guessed it from his relaxed and glowing strength as the weeks went by. She was a beautiful girl, gay and good, and with her maidenhead gave him all her worship. As for Ralf, he was a normal young man and had looked here and there, as young men will, but after his marriage I never knew him to look aside again, though he was handsome, and in later years was not unnaturally high in the King's favour and found many who tried to use him as a stepping stone to power as much as to pleasure. But he was never to be used.

I believe that there were those in Galava who wondered why such an able young gentleman was kept riding guard on Ector's foster-son when even young Cei joined his father and the troops whenever there was an alarm, but Ralf had a high temper, and a fine self-assurance these days, and had, besides, the Count's orders to quote. It might have been hard if his wife had taunted him, but she was soon with child, and too thankful to have him tied at home near her ever to question it. Ralf himself fretted a little, I know, but he confessed to me once when we were alone that if he could only see Arthur acknowledged and set in his rightful place beside the High King, he would count it a good life's work.

"You told me the gods were driving us that night at Tintagel," he said. "I am no familiar of the gods, as you are, but I can think of no youth I have known who is worthier to take up the High King's sword when he has to lay it down."

All reports bore this out. When I went down to the village for supplies, or to the tavern for gossip, I heard plenty about Ector's foster-son "Emrys." Even then his was a personality that gathers legend as a drip-stone gathers lime.

I heard a man say once, in the crowded tavern room: "I tell you this, if you told me he was one of the Dragon's breed, a bastard of the High King that's gone, I'd believe you."

There were nods, and someone said: "Well, why not? He could be a bastard of Uther's, couldn't he? It's always surprised me that there aren't more of those around. He was one for the women, sure enough, before his sickness put the fear of hell on him."

Someone else said: "If there were more, you can be sure he'd have acknowledged them."

"Aye, indeed," said the fellow who had spoken first. "That's true. He never showed any more shame than the farm bull, and why should he? They say that the girl he got in Brittany—Morgause, was it?—is high in his favour at court, and goes everywhere with him. Those are all we know of, the two girls, and the prince that's being reared at some foreign court."

Then the talk passed, as it often did these days, to the succession, and the young Prince Arthur growing up somewhere in the foreign kingdom to which Merlin the enchanter had secretly spirited him away.

Though how long he might be kept hidden I could not guess. Watching him come riding up the forest track, or diving and wrestling with Bedwyr in the summer waters of the lake, or drinking in the wonders I showed him as the earth absorbs rain, it was a marvel to me that everyone did not see, as I could, the kingship shining from him as it had shone in that moment's flashing vision from the sword in the altar-stone.

6

Then came the year that, even now, is called the Black Year. It was the year after Arthur's thirteenth birthday. The Saxon leader Octa died at Rutupiae, of some infection caught in the long imprisonment; but his cousin Eosa went to Germany, and there met Octa's son Colgrim, and it was not hard to guess at their counsels. The King of Ireland crossed the sea, but not to the Irish Shore, where Cador waited for him at Deva, and Maelgon of Gwynedd behind the scrambled-up fortifications of Segontium; but his sails were watched from Rheged's shore as he made landfall in Strathclyde and was received kindly by the Pictish kings there. These latter had had a treaty with Britain since Macsen's time, renewed with Ambrosius; but what answer they would make now to Ireland's proposals no man could guess.

Other troubles hit nearer home and more immediately. It was a year of starvation. The spring was long and cold and wet, the fields everywhere flooded, long past the time when corn should have been sown and growing. Cattle disease was everywhere in the south, and in Galava even the hardy blue-fleeced hill sheep died, their feet rotted away so that they could not move on the fells to feed themselves. Late frost blasted the fruit buds, and even as the green corn grew, it turned brown and rotted in the stagnant fields. Strange tales came north. A druid had run mad and attacked Uther for leading the country away from the Old Religion; and a Christian bishop stood up in church and railed against him for being a pagan. There was a story of an attempt on the King's life, and of the hideous way in which the King had punished the men responsible.

So spring and summer wore through, in disaster, and by the beginning of autumn the country lay like a waste land. People died of starvation. Folk talked of a curse laid on the country; but whether God was angry because the country shrines still claimed their sacrifices, or whether the old gods of hill and woodland exacted vengeance for neglect, no one was sure. All that was certain was that there was a blight on the land, and the King ailed. There was a meeting of nobles in London demanding that Uther should name his heir. But it seemed—Ector told me this—as if he still feared, not knowing friend from foe; all he would say was that his son lived and thrived, and would be presented to the nobles at the next Easter feast. Meanwhile his daughter Morgian passed her twelfth birthday, and would be taken north for her wedding at Christmas.

With the autumn the weather changed, and a mild, dry season set in. It was too late to help the crops or the dying cattle, but grateful to men starved of the sun, and the bright weather came in time to ripen some of the fruit that the spring storms and the summer rot had left on the trees. In the Wild Forest the mists curled through the pines in the early morning, and the September dews glittered everywhere on the cobwebs. Ector left Galava to meet with Rheged and his allies at Luguvallium. The King of Ireland had sailed for home and there was still peace in Strathclyde, but the defense line along the Ituna Estuary from Alauna to Luguvallium was to be manned, and there was talk of Ector as its commander. Cei went with his father. Arthur, scarce three months from his fourteenth birthday, tall enough for sixteen, and already (according to Ralf) a notable swordsman, fretted visibly, and grew daily more silent. He spent all his days now in the forest, often with me (though not so much as formerly), but most of the time, Ralf told me, hunting or taking breakneck rides through the rough country.

"If only the King would make some move," said Ralf to me. "The boy will kill himself else. It's as if he knew that there was something in the future for him, something unguessed at, but that gives him no peace. I'm afraid he'll break his neck before it happens. That new horse of his—Canrith he calls it—I wouldn't care to get astride it myself, and that's the truth. I can't think what possessed Ector to give it to him; a guilt gift perhaps."

I thought he was right. The white stallion had been left for Arthur when Ector took Cei up to Luguvallium with him. Bedwyr had gone, too, though he was no older than Arthur. Ector was hard put to it to explain to Arthur why he could not go. But until Uther spoke, we could do nothing.

The full moon came, the September moon that they call the harvester. It shone out in a dry mild night over the rotting fields, doing no good that anyone could see except light the outlaws who crept out of their fastnesses to pillage the outlying farms, or the troops who were constantly on the move these days to one or the other point of threat.

I could not sleep. My head ached, and phantoms crowded close, as they do when they bring vision; but nothing came forward into light or shape; nothing spoke. It was like suffering the threat of thunder, as close as the blankets that wrapped me, but without the lightning to break it, or the cleansing rain to bring a clear sky. When day broke at last, grey and misty, I rose, took bread, and a handful of olives from the crock, and went down through the forest to the lake, to wash the aching of the night away.

It was a quiet morning, so still that you could not tell where the mist ended and the surface of the lake began. The water met the flattened shingle of the beach without movement and without sound. Behind me the forest stood wrapped in the mist, its scents still sleeping. It seemed a kind of desecration to break the hush and plunge into that virgin water, but the fresh chill of it washed away the clinging strands of the night, and when I came out and was dry again and dressed, I ate my breakfast with pleasure, then settled down with my fishing rod to wait for the morning rise, and hope for a breeze at sun-up to ruffle the glassy water.

The sun came up at last, pale through the mist, but brought no breeze with it. The tops of the trees swam up out of the greyness, and at the far side of the lake the dark forest lifted, cloudy, towards the smoking hilltops. The water was bloomed with mist, like a pearl.

No ring or ripple broke the glassy water, no sign of a breeze to come. I had just decided that I might as well go, when I heard something coming fast through the forest at my back. Not a horseman; too light for that, and coming too fast through the brake.

I stayed as I was, half-turned, waiting. A prickling ran up the skin of my back, and I remembered the night's sleepless pain. The tingling ran into my fingers; I found I was clutching the rod until it hurt the flesh. All night, then, this had been coming. All night this had been waiting to happen. All night? If I was not mistaken, I had been waiting for this for fourteen years.

Fifty paces along the lake-side from where I sat, a stag broke cover. He saw me immediately, and stopped short, head high, poised to break the other way. He was white. In contrast the wide branches on his brow looked like polished bronze, and his eyes showed red as garnet. But he was real; there were stains of sweat on the white hide, and the thick hair of belly and neck was tagged with damp. A trail of yellow loosestrife had caught round his neck, and hung there like a collar. He looked back over his shoulder, then, stiff-legged, leaped from the bank into the water, and in two more bounds was shoulder-deep and swimming straight out into the lake.

The polished water broke and arrowed back. The splash was echoed by a crashing deep in the forest. Another beast coming, headlong.

I had been wrong in thinking that nothing could come through the forest as fast as a fleeing deer. Arthur's white hound, Cabal, broke from the trees exactly where the stag had broken, and hurled himself into the water. Seconds later Arthur himself, on the stallion Canrith, burst out after it.

He checked his horse on the shore, bringing it up rearing, fetlock deep. He had his bow strung ready in his hand. He pulled the stallion sideways and raised the bow, sighting from the back of the plunging horse. But deer swim low; only the stag's head showed above water, a wedge spearing away fast, its antlers flat behind it on the surface like boughs trailing. The hound, swimming strongly, was in line with it. Arthur lowered the bow, and turned the stallion back to breast the bank. In the moment before his spurs struck he saw me. He shouted something, and came cantering along the shingle.

His face was blazing with excitement. "Did you see him? Snow-white, and a head like an emperor! I never saw the like in my life! I'm going round. Cabal was closing, he'll hold him till I get there. Sorry I spoiled your fishing."

"Emrys—"

He checked impatiently. "What?"

"Look. He's making for the island."

He swung to look where I pointed. The stag had vanished into the mist, and the hound with him. There was no sign of them but the fading ripples flattening towards the shore.

"The island, is it? Are you sure?"

"Certain."

"All the devils of hell," he said angrily. "What a cursed piece of luck! I thought I had him when Cabal sprang him so close." He hung on the rein, hesitating, staring out over the clouded lake while the stallion fretted, sidling. I suppose he was as much in awe of the place as anyone brought up in that valley. Then he set his mouth, curbing Canrith sharply. "I'm going to the island. I can say goodbye to the stag, I suppose—that was too good to be true—but I'm damned if I lose Cabal. Bedwyr gave him to me, and I've no mind to lose him to Bilis or anyone else, either in this world or the other." He put two fingers to his mouth and whistled shrilly. "Cabal! Cabal! Here, sir, here!"

"It's no good, you'll hardly turn him now."

"No." He took a breath. "Well, there's nothing for it, it'll have to be the island. If your magic will reach that far, Myrddin, send it with me now."

"It's with you always, you know that. You're not going to swim him across, are you?"

"He'll go," said Arthur, a little breathlessly, as he forced the reluctant stallion towards the water. "It's too far to go round. If that beast takes to the crags, and Cabal follows it—"

"Why not take the boat? It's quicker, and that way you can bring Cabal back."

"Yes, but the wretched thing'll need bailing. It always does."

"I bailed it this morning. It's quite ready."

"Did you? That's the first bit of luck today! You were going out, then? Will you come with me?"

"No. I'll stay here. Come now, Emrys, go and find your hound."

For a moment boy and horse were quite still. Arthur stared down at me, something showing in his face that was half speculation, half awe, but which was quickly swallowed up in the larger impatience. He slid off the stallion's back and pushed the reins into my hand. Then he unstrung his bow and slung it across his shoulder and ran to the boat. This was a primitive flat-bottomed affair which usually lay beached in a reedy inlet a short way along the shore. He launched it with one flying shove, and jumped in. I stood on the shingle, holding the horse, watching him. He poled it out through the shallows, then had the oars out, and began to row.

I pulled the rolled cloth from behind the horse's saddle, slung it over the animal's steaming back, then tethered him where he could graze, and went back to my seat at the edge of the lake.

The sun was well up now, and gaining power. A kingfisher flashed by. Gauze-winged flies danced over the water. There was a smell of wild mint, and a dabchick crept out from a tangle of water forget-me-not. A dragonfly, tiny, with a scarlet body, clung pulsing to a reed. Under the sun the mist moved gently, smoking off the glassy water, shifting and restless like the phantoms of the night, like the smoke of the enchanted fire. . . .

The shore, the scarlet dragonfly, the white horse grazing, the cloudy forest at my back, faded, became phantoms themselves. I watched, my eyes wide and fixed on that silent and sightless cloud of pearl.

He was rowing hard, chin on shoulder as he neared the island. It loomed first as a swimming shape of shadow, growing to a shoreline hung over with the low boughs of trees. Behind the trees, misty and unreal, the shapes of rocks soared like a great castle brooding on its crag. Where the strand met the water lay a line of gleaming silver, drawn sharp between the island and its image. The cloudy trees and the high towers of the crags floated weightless on the water, phantoms themselves in the phantom mist.

The boat forged ahead. Arthur glanced over his shoulder, calling the hound's name.

"Cabal! Cabal!"

The call echoed loudly across the water, swam up the high crags, and died. There was no sign of either hound or stag. He bent to his oars again, sending the light boat leaping through the water.

Its bottom grated on shingle. He jumped out. He pulled it up and trod up through the narrow verge of grass. The light was stronger now as the sun rose higher, reflecting from white mist and white water. Over the shore the boughs of birch and rowan reached low, still heavy with moisture. The rowan berries were red as flame, and glossy. The turf was powdered with daisies and speedwell and small yellow pimpernel. Late foxgloves crowded down the banks, their spires thrusting through the trails of blackberry. Meadowsweet, rusting over with autumn, filled the air with its thick honey-scent.

The boy thrust the hanging boughs aside, plunged through the bramble trails, and stood squarely on the flowery turf, narrowing his eyes at the crags above him. He called again, and again the sound echoed away emptily, and died. The mist was lifting faster now, rolling upwards towards the tops, showing the lower reaches of rock bathed in a clear but swimming light. Suddenly he stiffened, gazing upwards. Midway up the crags, along what looked no more than a seam in the rock, the white stag cantered easily, light as a drift of the mist that wreathed away to air below it.

Arthur ran forward up the slope. His footsteps on the thick turf made no sound. He brushed waist-high through brakes of yellowing fern. sending the bright drops scattering, and came out at the foot of the cliff.

He paused again, looking about him. He seemed held by the same awe that had touched him earlier. He looked, not afraid, but as a man looks who knows that by a movement he may start something of which he cannot see the end. He craned his neck, searching the towering crags above him. There was no sign of the white stag, but the rocks looked more than ever like a castle crowned with the sun.

He took a breath, shaking his head as if he came out of water, then he spoke again, but quietly. "Cabal? Cabal?"

From somewhere very near him, bursting the awed silence, came the baying of the hound. There was something in it of excitement, something of fear. It came from the cliff. The boy looked round him, sharply. Then, behind the green curtain of the trees, he saw the cave. As he started forward Cabal bayed again, not in fear or pain, but like a beast questing.

With no more hesitation, Arthur plunged into the darkness of the cave.

He could never say afterwards how he found his way. I think he must have picked up the torch and flint I had left there, and lit it, but he remembers nothing of that. Perhaps what he does remember is the truth: there seemed, he said, to be everywhere some faintly diffused and swimming light, as if reflected from the burnished surface of the pool deep in the pillared cave.

There, beyond the shining pool, the sword lay on its table. From the rock above a trickle of water had run and dripped, the lime on it hardening through the years until the oiled leather of the wrappings, though proof enough to keep the metal bright, had hardened under the dripping till it felt like stone. In this the thing had rested, the crust of lime forming to hide all but its shape, the long slenderness of the weapon and the hilt formed like a cross.

It still looked like a sword, but a stone one, some random accident of dripping limestone. Perhaps he remembered the other hilt he had grasped in the Green Chapel, or perhaps for a moment he, too, saw the future break open in front of him. With an action too quick for thought, and too instinctive to prevent, he laid his hand to the hilt.

He spoke to me, as if I stood beside him. Indeed, I suppose I was as near to him, and as real, as the white hound that crouched, whining at the pool's edge.

"I pulled at it, and it came clear of the stone. It is the most beautiful sword in the world. I shall call it Caliburn."

The mist had gone from the forest now, sucked up by the sun. But it still lay over the island; this was invisible, floating on its sea of pearl.

I did not know how much time had passed. The sun was hot, beating down on the lake cupped in its hills. My eyes ached from the glare of water. I blinked them, moved, and stretched my stiff limbs.

There was a movement behind me; a sudden trampling, as if the white stallion had got loose. I turned quickly.

Thirty paces away, softly as a cloud, Cador of Cornwall rode out of the wood on a grey horse, with a troop at his back.

7

I believe that the thought uppermost in my mind was anger that I had not been warned. I was not only thinking of Arthur's guardians among the hill people; but even for me, Merlin, there had been no hint of danger in the sky, and the vision which had blanketed the troop's approach from my eyes and hearing had held nothing but light and promise leaping at last towards fulfillment. The only mitigation of my anger was that Arthur had not been found with me, and the only faint hope of safety lay in maintaining my character as hermit and trusting that Cador would not recognize me, and would ride on before the boy returned from the island.

All this went through my mind in the space it took Cador to raise a hand to halt the men behind him, and for me to pick up the discarded fishing rod and get to my feet. With some lie already forming on my lips I turned humbly to face Cador as he rode forward, to halt his grey ten paces off. Then all hope of remaining unrecognized vanished as behind him among the troop I saw Ralf with a gag in his mouth, and a trooper on either side of him.

I straightened. Cador bent his head, saluting me as low as he would have done the King. "Well met, Prince Merlin."

"Is it well met?" I was savagely angry. "Why have you taken my servant? He's none of yours now. Loose him."

He made a sign, and the troopers released Ralf's arms. He tore the gag from his mouth.

"Are you hurt?" I asked him.

"No." He was angry too, and bitter. "I'm sorry, sir. They fell on me as I was riding up through the forest. When they recognized me, they thought you might be near. They gagged me so that I could not give warning. They wanted to take you unawares."

"Don't blame yourself. It was no fault of yours." I had myself under control now, groping all the while for the shreds of the vision which had fled. Where was Arthur now? Still on the island, with Cabal and the wonderful sword? Or already on his way back through the mist? But I could see nothing except what was here, in plain daylight, and I knew that the spell was broken and I could not reach him.

I turned on Cador. "You go about your business strangely, Duke! Why did you lay hands on Ralf? You could have found me here any time you cared to ride this way. The forest is free to everyone, and the Green Chapel is open day and night. I would not have run from you."

"So you are the hermit of the chapel in the green?"

"I am he."

"And Ralf serves you?"

"He serves me."

He signed to his men to stay where they were, and himself rode forward, nearer where I stood. The white stallion screamed and plunged as the grey horse passed it. Cador drew to a halt beside me, and looked down, his brows raised. "And that horse? Is it yours? A strange choice for a hermit?"

I said acidly: "You know it is not mine. If you caught Ralf in the forest, then no doubt you saw one of Count Ector's sons as well. They were riding together. The boy came here to fish. I don't know how long he'll be; he often stays away half the day." I turned decisively away from the water. "Ralf, wait here for him. And you, my lord Duke, since you were so urgent to see me that you mishandled my servant, will you come with me now to the chapel, and say what you have to say in privacy? And you can tell me, too, what—besides this private hunt of yours—brings you and the men of Cornwall so far north?"

"War brings me; war, and the King's command. I doubt if even here you have been too isolated to know of Colgrim's threats? But you might say it was a happy chance that made me ride this way." He smiled, and added, pleasantly: "And this was hardly a private hunt. Did you not know, Prince Merlin, that men have been searching the length and breadth of the land to find you?"

"I was aware of it. I did not choose to be found. Now, Duke, will you come with me? Leave Ralf to wait here for the boy—"

"Count Ector's son, eh?" He had made no move to follow me away from the water's edge. He sat his big horse easily, still smiling. His manner was confident and assured. "And you really expect me to ride with you and leave Ralf to wait for this—son of Count Ector? No doubt to spirit him away for another span of years? Believe me, Prince—"

From the water, sharply, came Cabal's bark, the warning of a hound alert to danger. Then a word from Arthur, silencing the hound. The sound of oars as the boat jumped forward, suddenly driven hard through the water.

Cador swung his horse to face the sound, and in spite of myself I moved with him. My look must have been grim, for two of his officers spurred forward.

"Keep them back," I said sharply, and he flashed me a look and then lifted a hand. The men stopped short, a spear-cast off. I spoke quietly, for Cador alone:

"If you don't want Ector at your throat, with all Rheged behind him—yes, and Colgrim sweeping in to pick the fragments apart—let Ralf and the boy go now. Anything you have to say can be said to me. I shall not try to escape you. But for my life, Duke Cador, the King himself will answer."

He hesitated, glancing from the misty lake to where his troopers stood. They had pricked to the alert. I did not think they had recognized me, or realized what quarry their Duke was hunting today; but they had seen his interest in the sounds from behind the mist, and though they stayed where they were near the edge of the wood, the spears stirred and rattled like a reed-bed in the wind.

"As to that—" began Cador, but he was interrupted.

The boat ran out of the mist's edge and cut through the shallows. Seconds before it grounded Cabal, with a growl in his throat, flung himself over the thwart and made for the shore. One of the officers swung his horse round and drew his sword. Cador heard it, and shouted something. The man hesitated, and the hound, leaping up the bank, silent now, went in a rush for Cador himself. They grey horse reared back. The hound missed his grab, caught the edge of the saddle-cloth. It tore, and a piece came away in his jaws.

Behind me, Arthur yelled at the hound and ran the boat hard ashore. Ralf jumped forward, intending, I could see, to grab Cabal, but the troopers nearest him spurred forward and crossed their spears with a clash, holding him back. Cabal tossed the torn cloth over his shoulder and turned snarling to attack the men who held Ralf. One of them hefted his spear ready, and swords flashed out. Cador barked an order. The swords went up. The Duke lifted, not his sword, but his whip, and spurred the big grey round as the hound gathered himself to spring.

I took a stride forward under the whip, gripped the hound's collar, and threw my weight against his. I could scarcely hold him. Arthur's voice came fiercely, *"Cabal! Back!"* and even as the hound's pull slackened the boy jumped from the boat and in two strides was between me and Cador with the new sword naked and shining in his hand.

"You," he panted, "sir—whoever you are . . ." The sword's point slanted up at the Duke's breastbone. "Keep back! If you touch him, I swear I'll kill you, even if you had a thousand men at your back."

Cador slowly lowered the whip. I let Cabal go, and he sank to the ground behind Arthur, growling. Arthur stood squarely in front of me, angry and undoubtedly dangerous. But the Duke did not even seem to notice the sword or its threat. His eyes were on the boy's face. They flicked to mine, momentarily, then back to the boy.

All this had passed in a few breathless seconds. The Duke's men were still moving forward, the officers ranging to his side. As someone shouted an order, I shot a hand out and caught Arthur's arm and swung him round to face me, with his back to the Cornishmen.

"Emrys! What folly is this? There is no danger here, except from your hound. You should control him better. Take him now, and get yourself straight back to Galava with Ralf."

I had never spoken to him so in all the years he had known me. He stood still, his mouth slackening with surprise, like someone who has been struck for nothing. While he still stared dumbly I added, curtly: "This gentleman and I are acquainted. Why should you think he means me harm?"

"I—thought—" he stammered. "I thought—they had Ralf—and swords drawn on you—"

"You thought wrongly. I'm grateful to you, but as you see, I need no help. Put up your sword now, and go."

His eyes searched my face again, briefly, then he looked down at the sword he held. The sunlight blazed from it and the jewelled hilt sparkled. His hand looked young and tense on the hilt. I remembered the feel and fit of that hilt, and the life that ran back from the blade, clear into the sinews and the leaping blood. He had braved the very halls of the Otherworld for this, and had brought the bright thing back from darkness into the light that owned it, to find his first danger waiting, and himself—with the wonderful sword—its equal. And I had spoken to him like this.

I gave his arm a little shake, and released it. "Go. No one will stop you."

He rubbed it where I had gripped him, not stirring. His color was just beginning to come back, and with it a smoulder of anger. He looked so like Uther that I said, brutal with apprehension: "Go now and leave us, do you hear? I shall have time for you tomorrow."

"Emrys?" It was Cador, smoothly. Before I could stop him the boy had turned, and I saw that it was too late for pretense. Cador was looking from Arthur's face to mine, and there was excitement in his eyes.

"That is my name," said Arthur. He sounded sullen, narrowing his eyes up at the Duke against the sun. Then he seemed to notice the badge on the other's shoulder. "Cornwall? What are you doing so far north of your command, and with what authority do you lead your troops across our land?"

"Across your land? Count Ector's?"

"I'm his foster-son. But perhaps," said Arthur, silky with cold courtesy, "you have already passed Galava and spoken with his lady?"

He knew, of course, that Cador had not; he had not long ridden out of Galava himself. But Cador had given him the chance to recover the pride that I had damaged. He stood very straight, his back firmly turned to me, his eyes level on the Duke's.

Cador said: "So you are a ward of Count Ector's? Who is your father, then, Emrys?"

Arthur did not jib at this question now. He said coolly: "That, sir, I am not at liberty to tell you. But my breeding is not something of which I need to be ashamed."

This set Cador at pause. There was a curious expression on his face. He knew, of course. How could he not have known, the moment the boy flew out of the mist to my defense? From before that moment, it had been beyond repair. But there was still a chance that the others might not guess; Cador's big grey stood between Arthur and the troop, and even while the thought crossed my mind he turned and made a sign, and the officers and men moved back, once again beyond earshot.

I was calm now, knowing what I must do. The first thing was to salvage Arthur's pride, and whatever love I had not already destroyed by destroying this hour for him. I touched him gently on the shoulder. "Emrys, will you give us leave now? The Duke of Cornwall will not harm me, and he and I must talk together. Will you ride up to the chapel now with Ralf, and wait for me there?"

I expected Cador to intervene, but he sat without stirring. He was not watching the boy's face now, but the sword, still bare and flashing in Arthur's hand. Then he seemed to come to himself with a start. He signed to his men again, and Ralf, released, brought Canrith forward for Arthur, and mounted his own horse. He looked worried and questioning, wondering, probably, whether to take what I said at face value, or whether he must try to escape with Arthur into the forest.

I nodded to him. "Up to the shrine, Ralf. Wait for me there, if you will. Have no fear for me; I shall come later."

Arthur still hesitated, his hand on Canrith's bridle. Cador said: "It's true, Emrys, I mean him no harm. Don't be afraid to leave him. I know better than to tangle with enchanters. He'll come to you safely, never fear."

The boy threw me a strange look. He still looked doubtful, almost dazed. I said gently, not caring now who heard me: "Emrys—"

"Yes?"

"I have to thank you. It is true that I thought there was danger. I was afraid."

The sullen look lifted. He did not smile, but the anger died from his face, and life came back into it, as vividly as the bright sword leaping from its dull sheath. I knew then that nothing I had done had even smudged the edges of his love for me. He said, with little to be heard in his tone except exasperation: "How long will it be before you realize that I would give my life itself to keep you from hurt?"

He glanced down again at the sword in his hand, almost as if he wondered how it had got there. Then he looked up, straight at Cador.

"If you harm him in any way, the kingdoms will not be wide enough to hold us both. I swear it."

"Sir," said Cador, speaking, warrior to warrior, with grave courtesy, "that I well believe. I swear to you that I shall not harm him or anyone, save only the King's enemies."

The boy held his eyes for a moment longer, then nodded. He swallowed, and the tension went out of him. Then he leaped astride his horse, saluted Cador formally, and, without another word, rode off along the lake-side track. Cabal ran with him, and Ralf followed. I saw the boy glance back as he reached the bend in the track that would carry him out of my sight. Then they were gone, and I was alone with Cador and the men of Cornwall.

8

"Well, Duke?" I said.

He did not answer immediately, but sat biting his lip, staring down at the saddle-bow. Then, without turning, he signalled one of his officers who came forward and took his bridle as he dismounted. "Take the men down the shore a hundred paces. Water the horses, and wait for me there."

The man went, and the troop wheeled and clattered out of sight beyond a jut of woodland. Cador gathered his cloak over his arm and looked about him.

"Shall we talk here?"

We sat down where a flat rock overhung the water. He drew his dagger, for no worse purpose than to draw patterns in the wild thyme. When he had done a circle, and fitted a triangle inside it, he spoke to the ground. "He's a fine boy."

"He is."

"And like his sire."

I said nothing.

The dagger drove into the ground and stayed there. His head came up. "Merlin, why should you think I am his enemy?"

"Are you not his enemy?"

"No, by all the gods! I shall tell no one where he is unless you give me leave. There, you see? You look amazed. You thought of me as his enemy, and yours. Why?"

"If any man has reason for enmity, Cador, you have. It was through my action and Uther's that your father was killed."

"That is not quite true. You planned to betray my father's bed, but not my father himself. It was his own rashness, or bravery if you like, that caused his death. I believe that you did not foresee it. Besides, if I am to hate you because of that night, how much more should I hate Uther Pendragon?"

"And do you not?"

"God's death, man, have you not heard that I ride beside him and serve him as his chief captain?"

"I had heard it. And I wondered why. You must know how I have doubted you."

He laughed, a harsh laugh, like his father's rough bark. "You made it clear. I don't blame you. No, I don't hate Uther Pendragon; neither, I confess, do I love him. But when I was a boy I saw enough of divided kingdoms; Cornwall is mine, but she cannot stand alone. There is only one future for Cornwall now, and this is the same future as Britain's. I am linked to Uther, whether I like it or not. I will not bring division again, to see the people suffer. So I am Uther's man . . . or, which is nearer the truth, the High King's."

I watched the kingfisher, reassured now that the troop had gone, dive in a jewelled splash below us. He came up with a fish, shook his feathers, and flashed away. I said: "Did you send men to spy on me in Maridunum, years back, before I came north?"

His lips thinned. "Those. Yes, they were mine . . . and fine work they made of it! You guessed straight away, didn't you?"

"It was an obvious conclusion. They were Cornish, and your troops were at Caerleon. I learned later that you yourself had been there. Am I to be blamed if I thought you were trying to find Arthur?"

"Not at all. That is exactly what I was trying to do. But not to harm him." He frowned down again at the dagger. "Remember those years, Prince Merlin, and think how it was with me then. The King ailing, and for all one could see, pledging more and more power to Lot and his friends. He offered Morgause in marriage before ever Morgian was born, did you know that? And even now, I doubt if he really sees where Lot's ambition is leading him . . . I tried to tell him myself, but from me it came like an echo of the same ambition. I feared what would happen to the kingdoms should Uther die—or should Uther's son die. And though I didn't doubt your power to protect that son in your own way, there's a place for my way as well." The dagger thudded back into the turf. "So I wanted to find him, and watch him. As, for a different reason, I have been watching Lot."

"I see. You never thought of approaching me yourself and telling me this?"

He looked sideways at me, the corners of his mouth lifting. "If I had, would you have believed me?"

"It's probable. I am not easy to deceive."

"And told me where the boy was?"

I smiled. "That. No."

He hunched a shoulder. "Well, there's your answer. I sent my foolish spies, and found nothing. I even lost you. But I never meant you harm, I swear it. And though I may once have been your enemy, I was never Arthur's. Will you believe that now?"

I looked around me at the tranquil day, the sunlit trees, the light mist lifting from the lake. "I should have known it long ago. All day I have been wondering why I had had no warning of danger."

"If I were Arthur's enemy," he said, smiling, "I would know better than to try and snatch him from under Merlin's arm and eye. So if there had been danger in the air today, you would have known it?"

I drew a breath. I felt light again as the summer air around me. "I am sure of it. It worried me, that I had let you come so close today, and never felt the cold on my skin. Nor do I feel it now. Duke Cador, I should ask your forgiveness, if you will give it me."

"Willingly." He began to clean the tip of his dagger in the grass. "But if I am not his enemy, Merlin, there are those who are. I don't have to tell you about the dangers of this Christmas marriage; not only for Arthur's claim to the throne, but the dangers for the kingdom itself."

I nodded. "Division, strife, the dark end to a dark year. Yes. Is there anything more you can tell me about King Lot, that all men do not already know?"

"Nothing definite, not more than before. I am hardly in Lot's private councils. But I can tell you this; if Uther delays much longer over proclaiming his son, the nobles may decide to choose his successor among themselves. And the choice is there, ready, in Lot who is a tried and known warrior, who has fought at the King's hand, and is—will be soon—the King's son-in-law."

"Successor?" I said. "Or supplanter?"

"Not openly, no. Morgian would not see Lot stepping across her father's body to the kingdom. But once he is married to her, and is the King's apparent heir until Arthur is produced, then Arthur himself, when he does appear, will have to show both a stronger claim and a stronger backing."

"He has both."

"The claim, yes. But the backing? Lot has more men at his back than I." I said nothing, but after a bit he nodded. "Yes. I see. If he is backed by you, yourself in person . . . You can enforce his claim?"

"I can try. I shall have help. Yours, too, I hope?"

"You have it."

"You shame me, Cador."

"Hardly that," he said. "You were right. It was true that I hated you. I was young then, but I have come to see things differently; perhaps more clearly. For my own sake, if for nothing else, I cannot stand by and see Uther so bound to Lot, and Lot succeeding in his ambition. Arthur's is the one strong claim which can't be denied, and his is the one hand which can hold the kingdoms together—if any hand can do it now. Oh, yes, I would support him."

I was reflecting that even at fifteen Cador had been a realist; now, his tough-minded common sense was like a gust of cold air through a musty council-chamber. "Does Lot know this?" I asked him.

"I have made it clear, I think. Lot knows I would oppose him, and so would the northern lords of Rheged, and the kings of Wales. But there are others I am not sure of, and many who will be swayed either way if their lands are threatened. The times are dangerous, Merlin. You knew Eosa went to Germany, and was consorting with Colgrim and Badulf? Yes? Well, news came a short while ago that long-ships had been massing across the German Sea from Segedunum and that the Picts have opened their harbours to them."

"I had not heard that. Then there'll be fighting before winter?"

He nodded. "Before the month is out. That's why I am here. Maelgon stays on the Irish Shore, but the danger is not on the west; not yet. The attack will come from east and north."

"Ah." I smiled. "Then certain things will be made clear very soon, I think."

He had been watching me intently. Now his mouth relaxed, and he nodded again. "You see it? Of course you do. Yes, one good thing may come out of this clash—Lot must declare himself. If, as rumour has it, he has been making advances to the Saxons, then he will have to declare for Colgrim. If he wants Morgian, and the High Kingdom along with her, he'll have to fight for Uther." He laughed with genuine amusement. "It's Octa's death that has brought Colgrim raging straight across the German Sea, and forced Lot's hand. If he'd waited for the spring, Lot would have had Morgian, and could have received Colgrim too, and used the Saxons to set himself up as High King, like Vortigern before him. As it is, we shall see."

"Where is the King?" I asked.

"On his way north. He should be at Luguvallium within the week."

"He'll lead the field himself?"

"He intends to, though as you know he's a sick man. It seems that Colgrim may have forced Uther's hand, too. I think he will send for Arthur now. I think he will have to."

"Whether he sends or not," I said, "Arthur will be there." I saw the excitement spring to Cador's face again, and asked him: "Will you give him escort, Duke?"

"Willingly, by God! You'll come with him?"

I said: "After this, where he is, I am."

"And you'll be needed," he said meaningly. "Pray God Uther has not left it too late. Even with proof of Arthur's parentage, and the King's own sword fast in his hand, it won't be easy to persuade the nobles to declare for an untried boy . . . And Lot's faction will fight back every foot of the way. Better to take them by surprise, like this. The boy will need all you can throw into the scale for him."

I smiled. "He can throw in quite a lot himself. He's to be reckoned with, Cador, make no mistake. He's no kingmaker's toy."

He grinned. "You don't need to tell me that. Did you know he was more like you than ever like the King?"

I spoke with my eyes on the glittering surface of the lake. "I think it is my sword, not Uther's, which will carry him to the kingship."

He sat up sharply. "Yes. That sword. Where in middle-earth did he find that sword?"

"On Caer Bannog."

His eyes widened. "He went *there?* Then, by God, he's welcome to it and all it brings him! I'd not have dared! What took him there?"

"He went to save the hound. It had been given him by his friend. You might call it chance that took him there."

"Oh, aye. The same kind of chance that brought me along the lake-side today, to find a poor hermit, and a boy called Ambrosius, who holds a sword which might well befit a king?"

"Or an emperor," I said. "It's the sword of Macsen Wledig."

"So?" He drew in his breath. I saw the same look in his eyes as there had been in the Cornish troopers' when I spoke of the enchanted island. "This was the claim you were speaking of? You found that sword for him? You cast your net wide, Merlin."

"I cast no net. I go with the time."

"Yes. I see." He drew another long breath, and looked about him as if he saw the day for the first time, with all its sunlight and moving breezes and the island floating on the water. "And now for you, and for him and all of us, the time is come?"

"I think so. He found the sword where I had laid it, and you came, hard on its finding. All the year the King has been urged to make proclamation and he has done nothing. So instead, we will do it. You lie tonight at Galava?"

"Yes." He sat up, pushing the dagger home in its sheath with a rap. "You'll join us there? We ride at sun-up."

"I shall be there tonight," I said, "and Arthur with me. Today he stays with me in the forest. We have things to say to one another."

He looked at me curiously. "He knows nothing yet?"

"Nothing," I said. "I promised the King."

"Then until the King speaks publicly, I'll see he learns nothing. Some of my men may suspect, but they are all loyal. You needn't fear them."

I got to my feet, and he followed suit. He raised a hand to his watching officer in the distance. I heard the words of command, and the sounds of the troop mounting. They rode towards us along the lake-side.

"You have a horse?" asked Cador. "Or shall I leave one with you now?"

"Thank you, no. I have one. I'll walk back to the chapel when I'm ready. There's something I have to do first."

He looked again at the sunlit forest, the still lake, the dreaming hills, as if power or magic must be ready to fall on me from their light. "Something still to do? Here?"

"Indeed." I picked up the fishing rod. "I still have to catch my dinner, and for two now, instead of one. And see, this day of days has even produced a breeze for me. If Arthur can lift the sword of Maximus from the lake, surely I shall be granted at least two decent fish?"

9

Ralf met me at the edge of the clearing, but we could not have much talk, because Arthur was nearby, sitting in the sun on the chapel steps, with Cabal at his feet.

I told Ralf quickly what he must do. He was to ride down now to the castle and tell Drusilla what had happened, that Arthur was safe with me, and that we would join Duke Cador on the ride north tomorrow. A message was to go ahead to Count Ector, and one to the King. Meanwhile Ralf was to ask the Countess to arrange with Abbot Martin to have the shrine tended during my absence.

"And are you going to tell him now?" asked Ralf.

"No. It's for Uther to tell him."

"Don't you think he may guess already, after what happened down yonder? He's been silent ever since, but with a look to him as if he'd been given more than a sword. What is that sword, Merlin?"

"It's said that Weland Smith himself made it, long ago. What is sure is that the Emperor Maximus used it, and that his men brought it home for the King of Britain."

"That one? And he tells me he found it on Caer Bannog . . . I begin to see . . . And now you take him to the King. Are you trying to force Uther's hand? Do you think the King will accept him?"

"I am sure of it. Uther must claim him now. I think we may find that he has sent for him already. You'd better go, Ralf. There'll be time to talk later. You'll ride with us, of course."

"You think I'd let you leave me behind?" He spoke gaily, but I could see that he was torn between relief and regret; on the one hand the knowledge that the long watch was over, on the other, that Arthur would now be taken from his care and committed to mine and the King's. But there was happiness, too, that he would soon be back in the press of affairs in an open position of trust, and able to wield his sword against the kingdom's enemies. He saluted me, smiling, then turned and rode off down the tracks towards Galava.

The hoof-beats faded down through the forest. Sunlight poured into the clearing. The last of the water-drops had vanished from the pines, and the smell of resin filled the air. A thrush was singing somewhere. Late harebells were thick among the grass, and small blue butterflies moved over the white flowers of the blackberry. There was a hive of wild bees under the roof of the chapel; their humming filled the air, the sound of summer's end.

Through a man's life there are milestones, things he remembers even into the hour of his death. God knows that I have had more than a man's share of rich memories; the lives and deaths of kings, the coming and going of gods, the founding and destroying of kingdoms. But it is not always these great events that stick in the mind: here, now, in this final darkness, it is the small times that come back to me most vividly, the quiet human moments which I should like to live again, rather than the flaming times of power. I can still see, how clearly, the golden sunlight of that quiet afternoon. There is the sound of the spring, and the falling liquid of the thrush's song, the humming of the wild bees, the sudden flurry of the white hound scratching for fleas, and the sizzling sound of cooking where Arthur knelt over the wood fire, turning the trout on a spit of hazel, his face solemn, exalted, calm, lighted from within by whatever it is that sets such men alight. It was his beginning, and he knew it.

He did not ask me much, though a thousand questions must have been knocking at his lips. I think he knew, without knowing how, that we were on the threshold of events too great for talk. There are some things that one hesitates to bring down into words. Words change an idea by definitions too precise, meanings too hung about with the references of every day.

We ate in silence. I was wondering how to tell him, without breaking my promise to Uther, that I proposed to take him with me to the King. I thought that Ralf was wrong; the boy did not begin to guess the truth; but he must be wondering about the events of the day, not only the sword, but what there was between myself and Cador, and why Ralf had been so handled. But he said nothing, not even asking why Ralf had gone away and left him here alone with me. He seemed content with the moment. The angry little skirmish down by the lake might never have been.

We ate in the open air, and when we had finished, Arthur, without a word, removed the dishes and brought water in a bowl for me to wash with. Then he settled beside me on the chapel steps, lacing the fingers of his hands round one knee. The thrush still sang. Blue and shadowed, and misty with presence, the hills brooded, chin on knees, round the valley. I felt myself crowded already by the forces that waited there.

"The sword," he said. "You knew it was there, of course."

"Yes, I knew."

"He said . . . He called you an enchanter?" There was the faintest of queries in his voice. He wasn't looking at me. He sat on the step below me, head bent, looking down at the fingers laced round his knee.

"You knew that. You have seen me use magic."

"Yes. The first time I came here, when you showed me the sword in the stone altar, and I thought it was real . . ." He stopped abruptly, and his head came up. His voice was sharp with discovery. "It *was* real! This is the one, isn't it?" The one the stone sword was carved from? Isn't it? Isn't it?"

"Yes."

"What sword is it, Myrddin?"

"Do you remember my telling you—you and Bedwyr—the story of Macsen Wledig?"

"Yes, I remember it well. You said that was the sword carved in the altar here." Again that note of discovery. "This is the same? His very sword?"

"Yes."

"How did it come there, on the island?"

I said: "I put it there, years back. I brought it from the place where it had been hidden."

He turned fully then, and looked at me. A long look. "You mean you found it? It's your sword?"

"I didn't say that."

"You found it by magic? Where?"

"I can't tell you that, Emrys. Some day you may need to search for the place yourself."

"Why should I?"

"I don't know. But a man's first need is a sword, to use against life, and conquer it. Once it is conquered, and he is older, he needs other food, for the spirit . . ."

After a bit I heard him say, softly: "What are you seeing, Myrddin?"

"I was seeing a settled and shining land, with corn growing rich in the valleys, and farmers working their fields in peace as they did in the time of the Romans. I was seeing a sword growing idle and discontented, and the days of peace stretching into bickering and division, and the need of a quest for the idle swords and the unfed spirits. Perhaps it was for this that the god took the grail and the spear back from me and hid them in the ground, so that one day you might set out to find the rest of Macsen's treasure. No, not you, but Bedwyr . . . It is his spirit, not yours, which will hunger and thirst, and slake itself in the wrong fountains."

As if from far away, I heard my own voice die, and silence come back. The thrush had flown, the bees seemed quiet. The boy was on his feet now, and staring.

He said, with all the force of simplicity: "Who are you?"

"My name is Myrddin Emrys, but I am known as Merlin the enchanter."

"Merlin? But then—but that means you are—you were—" He stopped, and swallowed.

"Merlinus Ambrosius, son of Ambrosius the High King? Yes."

He stood silent for a long time. I could see him thinking back, remembering, assessing. Not guessing about himself—he had been too deeply rooted, and for too long, in the person of Ector's bastard foster-son. And, like everyone else in the kingdom, he assumed that the prince was being royally reared in some court beyond the sea.

He spoke at length quietly, but with such a kind of inward force and joy that one wondered how he could contain it. What he said surprised me. "Then the sword was yours. You found it, not I. I was only sent to bring it to you. It is yours. I will get it for you now."

"No, wait, Emrys—"

But he had already gone. He brought the sword, running, and held it out to me.

"Here. It's yours." He sounded breathless. "I ought to have guessed who you were . . . Not away in Brittany with the prince, as some people have it, but here, in your own country, waiting till the time came to help the High King. You are the seed of Ambrosius. Only you could have found it, and I found it only because you sent me there. It is for you. Take it."

"No. Not for me. Not for a bastard seed."

"Does that make a difference? Does it?"

"Yes," I said gently.

He was silent. The sword sank to his side and was quenched in his shadow. I mistook his silence, and I remember that at the time I was relieved merely that he said no more.

I got to my feet. "Bring it now into the chapel. We'll leave it there, where it belongs, on the god's altar. Whichever god is sovereign in this place will watch it for us. It must wait here till the time comes for it to be claimed in the sight of men, by the legitimate heir to the kingdom."

"So. That's why you sent me for it? To bring it for him?"

"Yes. In due time it will be his."

A little to my surprise he smiled, apparently satisfied. He nodded calmly. We took the sword together into the chapel. He laid it on the altar, above its carved replica. They were the same. His hand left the hilt, lingeringly, and he stepped back to my side.

"And now," I said, "I have something to tell you. The Duke of Cornwall brought news—"

I got no further. The sound of hoofs, approaching rapidly through the forest, brought Cabal up, roach-backed and growling. Arthur whipped round. His voice was sharp.

"Listen! Is that Cornwall's troop back again? Something must be wrong . . . Are you sure they mean you well?"

I put a hand to his arm and he stopped, then, at the look on my face, asked: "What is it, then? Were you expecting this?"

"No. Yes. I hardly know. Wait, Emrys. Yes, this had to come. I thought it must. The day is not over yet."

"What do you mean?"

I shook my head. "Come with me and meet them."

It was not Cornwall's troops that came clattering into the clearing. The Dragon glittered, red on gold. King's men. The officer halted his troop and rode forward. I saw his eye take in the wild clearing, the overgrown shrine, my own plain robes; it touched the boy at my side, no more than a touch, then came back to my face, and he saluted, bowing low.

The greeting was formal, in the King's name. It was followed by the news I had already had from Cador; that the King was marching north with his army, and would lie at Luguvallium, there to face the threat from Colgrim's forces. The man went on to tell me, looking troubled, that of late the King's sickness seemed to have taken hold of him again, and there were days when he had not the strength to ride, but proposed, if need be, to take the field in a litter. "And this is the message I was charged to give you, my lord. The High King, remembering the strength and help you gave to the army of his brother Aurelius Ambrosius, asks that you will come now out of your fastness, and go to him where he waits to meet his enemies." The message came, obviously, by rote. He finished: "My lord, I am to tell you that this is the summons you have been waiting for."

I bent my head. "I was expecting it. I had already sent to tell the King I was coming, and Emrys of Galava with me. You are to escort us? Then no doubt you will have the goodness to wait a while until we are ready. Emrys"—I turned to Arthur, standing in a white trance of excitement at my side—"come with me."

He followed me back into the chapel. As soon as we were out of sight of the troop he caught at my arm. "You're taking me? You're really taking me? And if it comes to a battle—"

"Then you shall fight in it."

"But my father, Count Ector . . . He may forbid it."

"You will not fight beside Count Ector. These are king's troops and you go with me. You will fight with the King."

He said joyously: "I knew this was a day of marvels! I thought at first that the white stag had led me to the sword, that it was for me. But now I see that it was just a sign that today I should ride to my first battle . . . What are you doing?"

"Watch now," I said. "I told you I would leave the sword in the god's protection. It has lain long enough in the darkness. Let us leave it now in the light."

I stretched out my hands. From the air the pale fire came, running down the blade, so that runes—quivering and illegible—shimmered there. Then the fire spread, engulfing it, till, like a brand too brightly flaring, the flames died, and when they had gone, there stood the altar, pale stone, with nothing against it but the stone sword.

Arthur had not seen me use this kind of power before, and he watched open-mouthed as the flames broke out of the air and caught at the stone. He drew back, awed and a little frightened, and the only colour in his face was the wanlight cast by the flames.

When it was done he stood very still, licking dry lips. I smiled at him.

"Come, be comfortable. You have seen me use magic before."

"Yes. But seeing this—this kind of thing . . . All this time, when Bedwyr and I were with you, you never let us know what sort of man you were . . . This power; I had no idea. You told us nothing of it."

"There was nothing to tell. There was no need for me to use it, and it wasn't something you could learn from me. You will have different skills, you and Bedwyr. You won't need this one. Besides, if you do, I shall be there to give it to you."

"Will you? Always? I wish I could believe that."

"It is true."

"How can you know?"

"I know," I said.

He stared at me for a moment longer, and in his face I could see a whole world of uncertainty and bewilderment and desire. It was a boy's look, immature and lost, and it was gone in a moment, replaced by his normal armour of bright courage. He smiled then, and the sparkle was back. "You may regret that, you know! Bedwyr's the only person who can stand me for long."

I laughed. "I'll do my best. Now, if you will, tell them to bring our horses out."

When I was ready I went out to join the waiting men. Arthur was not mounted and fretting to be off, as I had expected; he was holding my horse for me, like a groom. I saw his eyes widen a little when he saw me; I had put on my best clothes, and my black mantle was lined with scarlet and pinned on the shoulder by the Dragon brooch of the royal house. He saw that I was amused and had guessed his thought, and smiled a little in return as he swung himself up on his white stallion. I took care that he should not see what I was thinking then; that the youth with the plain mantle and the bright, proud look did not need a brooch to declare himself Pendragon, and royal. But he drew the stallion soberly in behind my mild roan mare, and the men were watching me.

So we left the chapel of the Wild Forest in the care of whichever god owned it, and rode down towards Galava.

BOOK IV

THE KING

1

The danger from the Saxons had been more immediate even than Cador had supposed. Colgrim had moved fast. By the time Arthur and I with our escort approached Luguvallium we found, just south-east of the town, the King's forces and Cador's moving into position with the men of Rheged, to face an enemy already massing in great numbers for the attack.

The British leaders were closeted with the King in his tent. This had been pitched on the summit of a small hill which lay behind the field of battle. There had in times past been some kind of a fortress there, and a few ruined walls still stood, with the remains of a tower, and lower down on the slopes were the tumbled stones and weedy garths of an abandoned village. The place was a riot of blackberry and nettle, with huge old apple trees still standing among the fallen stones, golden with ripening fruit. Here, below the hill, the baggage trains were rumbling into place; the trees and the half-ruined walls would provide shelter for the emergency dressing station. Soon the apparent chaos would resolve itself; the King's armies still fought with a pattern of the Roman discipline enforced by Ambrosius. Looking at the huge spreading host of the enemy, the field of spears and axes and the horse-hair tossing in the breeze like the foam of an advancing sea, I thought that we would need every last scruple of strength and courage that we could muster. And I wondered about the King.

Uther's tent had been pitched on a little level lawn, before the ruined tower. As our troop rode towards it through the noise and bustle of the battalions assembling into fighting order, I saw men turn to stare, and even above the shouts of command and the clash of arms could hear the word go round. "It's Merlin. Merlin. Merlin the prophet is here. Merlin is with us." Men turned, stared, shouted, and elation seemed to spread like a buzz through the field. A fellow with the device of Dyfed shouted as I passed, in my own tongue: "Are you with us then, Myrddin Emrys, *braud,* and have you seen the shooting star for us today?"

I called back, clearly, so that it could be heard: "Today it is a rising star. Watch for it, and the victory."

As I dismounted with Arthur and Ralf at the foot of the hill, and walked up to Uther's tent, I heard the word spread through the field with a rush like the wind racing over ripe corn.

It was a bright September day, full of sunlight. Outside the King's tent the Dragon blew, scarlet on yellow. I went straight in, with Arthur on my heels. The boy had armed himself at Galava, and looked at every point a young warrior. I had expected him to appear with Ector's blazon, but he carried no device, and his cloak and tunic were of plain white wool. "It's my colour," he had said, when he saw me looking. "The white horse, the white hound, and I shall carry a white shield. Since I have no name, I shall write on it myself. My device will be my own, when I get it." I had said nothing, but I thought now, as the boy trod forward beside me across the King's tent, that if he had deliberately courted all men's eyes on the field of battle, he could not have done better. The unmarked white, and his air of eager and shining youth, stood out among the tossing brilliance of colour on that bright morning, as surely as if the trumpets had already proclaimed him prince. And as Uther greeted us, I could see the same thought in the eager and hungry gaze he fixed on the boy's face.

Myself, I was shocked at Uther's appearance. It bore out the reports I had had of him, of a man visibly failing, "as if a canker gnawed at his guts, not with pain but with daily wasting." He was thin and his colour was bad, and I noticed that from time to time his hand went to his chest, as if he found it hard to draw breath. He was splendidly dressed, with gold and jewels glinting on his armour; the stuff of his great cloak was gold, too, with scarlet dragons entwined. He held himself upright, kingly in the great chair. There was grey now in the reddish hair and beard, but his eyes were vivid and alive as ever, burning in their deep sockets. The thinness of his face made it look more hawk-like, and if possible more kingly than before. The flashing gold and jewels and the great cloak hid the thinness of his body. Only the wrists and bony hands showed where the long wasting sickness had gnawed the flesh away.

Arthur waited behind me with Ralf as I went forward. Count Ector was there, near the King, along with Coel of Rheged, and Cador, and a dozen other of Uther's leaders whom I knew. I saw Ector eyeing Arthur with a kind of wonder. I did not see Lot anywhere.

Uther greeted me with a courtesy only thinly overlaying the eagerness below. It is possible that he had intended there and then to present his son to the commanders, but there was no time. Trumpets were sounding outside. Uther hesitated, looking indecisive, then he made a sign to Ector who stepped forward and formally presented Arthur to the King as his foster-son Emrys of Galava. Arthur, with this new quiet and self-contained maturity, knelt to kiss the King's hand. I saw Uther's hand close on his, and I thought he would speak then, but at that moment the trumpets shrilled again, nearer, and the door of the tent was pulled open. Arthur stood back. Uther—the effort was apparent—tore his eyes from the boy's face and gave the word. The commanders saluted hurriedly and dispersed to mount and gallop away to their stations. The ground shook to the trampling of horses, and the air to the shouting and the clash of metal. Four men ran in with poles, and I saw then that Uther's chair was a kind of litter, a big carrying-chair, in which he could be borne onto the battlefield. Someone ran to him with his sword and put it into his hand, whispering as he did so, and the four fellows bent to the poles, waiting for the King's word.

I stood back. If any memory came to me of the young, tough commander who had fought so ably at his brother's side through all the early years of war, it touched me now with no feeling of pity or regret, as the King turned his head and smiled, the same fierce, eager smile that I knew. The years had dropped away from him. If it had not been for the litter, I could have sworn that he was a whole man. There was even colour in his cheeks, and his whole person glittered.

"My servant here tells me you have foretold us victory already?" He laughed, a young man's laugh, full and ringing. "Then you have indeed brought us today all that we could desire. Boy!"

Arthur, at the tent door speaking to Ector, stopped and looked back. The King beckoned. "Here. Stay by me."

Arthur flashed an enquiring look at his foster-father, then at me. I nodded. As the boy moved to obey the King I saw Ector make a sign to Ralf, and the latter moved quietly with Arthur to the left of the King's litter. Ector hung on his heel a moment in the tent doorway, but Uther was saying something to his son, and Arthur was bent to listen. The Count hitched his cloak over his shoulder, nodded abruptly to me, and went out. The trumpets sounded again, and then the sunshine and the shouting were all about us as the King's chair was carried out towards the waiting troops.

I did not follow it down the hillside, but stayed where I was, on the high ground beside the tent, while below me on the wide field the armies formed. I saw the King's chair set down, and the King himself stand to speak to the men. From this distance I could hear nothing of what was said, but when he turned and pointed to where I stood high in the sight of the whole army, I heard the shout of "Merlin!" again, and the cheers. There was an answering shout from the enemy, a yell of derision and defiance, and then the clamour of trumpets and the thunder of the horses drowned everything, and shook the day.

Beside the tower wall stood an ancient apple tree, its bark now gnarled and thick with lichen like verdigris, but its boughs heavy with yellow fruit. In front of it was a tumble of stone with a plinth where perhaps there had once been an altar or a statue. I stepped up onto this, with my back to the laden apple tree, and watched the course of the fighting.

There was still no sign of Lot's banner. I beckoned a fellow running past—he was a medical orderly on his way to the dressing station lower down the hill—and asked him: "Lot of Lothian? Are his troops not come?"

"There's no sign of them yet, sir. I don't know why. Maybe they're to be held back as reserves on the right?"

I glanced where he was pointing. To the right of the field was the winding glimmer of a stream, flanked for some fifty paces to either hand by broken and sedgy ground. Beyond this the field rose through alder and willow and scrubby oak to thicker woodland. Between the trees the slope was rough and broken, but not too steep for horses, and the woods could well hide half an army. I thought I could see the glint of spear-heads through the thick of the trees. Lot, coming from the north-east, would have had early news of the Saxon advance, and would hardly have come late for the battle. He must be there, waiting and watching. But not, I was sure, by order as a reserve placed there by the King. The dilemma that Cador and I had spoken of might well be resolved today for Lot: if Uther looked like winning the victory, then Lot could throw his army in and share the time of triumph and its aftermath of reward and power; but if Colgrim should bear away the day, then Lot would have the chance of fixing his interest with the Saxon conquerors—in time, moreover, to deny his marriage with Morgian and take whatever power the new Saxon rule would offer him. I might well, I thought sourly, be doing the man an injustice, but my bones told me I was not. I wished there had been time to learn before the battle what Uther's dispositions had been. If Lot was anywhere at hand he would not miss this battle, of all battles, with the chances it held for him. I wondered how soon he would see me, or hear that I had come. And once he knew, he would have no doubt at all of the identity of the white-cloaked youth on the white horse, who fought so close on the King's left hand.

It was evident that the High King's presence, even in a litter, had cheered and fortified the British. Though, borne as he was in his chair, he could not lead the charge, he was there with the Dragon above him, right in the center of the field, and, though the press of his followers round him would hardly let an enemy get within striking distance, the fighting was fiercest round the Dragon, and from time to time I saw the flutter of the golden cloak and the flash of the King's own sword. Out on the right rode the King of Rheged, flanked by Caw and at least three of his sons. Ector too was on the right, fighting with dogged ferocity, while Cador on the left showed all the dash and dazzle of the Celt on his day of luck. Arthur I knew to be endowed by nature with the qualities of both, but today he would doubtless be more than content with his position guarding the King's left side. Ralf, in his turn, held himself back to guard Arthur's. I watched the chestnut horse swerve and turn and rear, never more than a pace away from the white stallion's flank.

This way and that the battle went. Here a banner would go down, swamped apparently under the savage tide of attack, then somehow there would be a recovery, and the British would press forward under the swinging axes, and push back the yelling waves of Saxons. From time to time a solitary horseman—a messenger, it could be assumed—spurred off eastwards across the boggy land by the stream, and up into the trees. And now it was certain that Lot's force was there, hidden and waiting in the wood. And, as surely as if I had read his mind, I knew that he was waiting there by no orders from the King. Whatever calls for help those messengers brought to him, he would delay his coming until he saw how the day went. So, for two fierce hours, lengthening through midday to three, the British forces fought, deprived of what should have been their fresh fighting right. The King of Rheged fell wounded, and was carried back: his forces held their position, but it could be seen that they were wavering. And still the men of Lothian held back. Soon, if they did not come in, it might be too late.

All at once, it seemed that it was. There was a shout from the center, a shout of anger and despair. There, in the thick of the press round the King's chair, I saw the Dragon standard waver, rock violently, then slope to its fall. Suddenly, for all the distance, it was as if I was there, close by the King's chair, seeing it all clearly. A body of Saxons, huge fair giants, some of them red with unfelt wounds, had rushed the group that surrounded the King, breaking it, it seemed, with sheer weight and ferocity. Some were cut down, some were forced back by desperate fighting, but two got through. They smashed their way forward, axes whirling, on the King's left. One axe struck the shaft of the standard, which splintered, rocked, and began to fall. The man who had carried it went down with the blood spouting from his severed wrist, and disappeared under the mashing hoofs. With scarcely a pause the axe wheeled through its bright arc towards the King. Uther was on his feet, his sword up to meet the axeman, but Ralf's sword whirled and bit, and the Saxon fell clear across the King's chair, his blood gushing out over the golden cloak. The King was pinned back under the fallen man's weight. The other Saxon rushed forward yelling. Ralf, cursing, fought to thrust his horse between the helpless King and the new attacker, but the Saxon, towering above the British, brushed their weapons aside as a mad bull brushes the long grass, and charged forward. It seemed nothing could stop him reaching the King. I saw Arthur drive his horse forward, just as the rocking standard fell, striking the white stallion across the chest. The stallion reared, screaming. Arthur, holding the horse with his knees, seized the falling standard, and shouting flung it clear across the King's chair into a soldier's ready grip, then swung the screaming, striking horse right into the path of the giant Saxon. The great axe whirled into its flashing circle, and came down. The stallion swerved and leaped, and the blow missed, but glancing spent from the boy's sword, knocked it spinning from his hand. The stallion climbed high again, striking out with those killing forefeet, and the axeman's face vanished in a pash of bright blood. The white horse plunged back to the side of the King's chair and Arthur's hand went down to his dagger. Then quiet, but clear as a shout, the King called, "Here!" and flung his own sword, hilt first, into the air. Arthur's hand shot out and caught it by the hilt. I saw it catch the light. The white horse reared again. The standard was up, and streaming in the wind, scarlet on gold. There was a great shout, spreading out from the center of the field where the white stallion, treading blood, leaped forward under the Dragon banner. Shouting, the men surged with him. I saw the standard-bearer hesitate fractionally, looking back at the King, but the King waved him forward, then lay back, smiling, in his chair.

And now, too late for whatever spectacular intervention Lot had intended, the Lothian troops swept down out of the woodland and swelled the ranks of the attacking British. But the day was already won. There was no man there on the field who had not seen what happened. There, white on a white horse, the King's fighting spirit had leaped, it seemed, out of his failing body, and run ahead, like the spark on the tip of a fighting spear, straight to the heart of the Saxon forces.

Soon, as the Saxons, breaking from stand to fighting stand, were pressed gradually backwards towards the marshes that fringed the field, and the British followed them with steadily growing ferocity and triumph, men started to run in behind the fighting troops to bring out the hurt and the dying. Uther's chair, which should have been borne back at the same time, was forging forward steadily in Arthur's wake. But the main press of the fighting was no longer round it; that was well forward of the field where, under the Dragon, everyone could see the white stallion and the white cloak and the flashing blade of the King's sword.

My post as a visible presence on the hill was no longer either heeded or necessary. I went down to where the emergency dressing station had been set up below the fallen tangles of the apple orchard. Already the tents were filling, and the orderlies were hard at work. I sent a boy running for my box of instruments and, taking off my cloak, slung it over the low boughs of an apple tree to make a shelter from the sun's rays; and as the next stretcher went by me I called to the bearers to set the wounded man down in the improvised shade.

One of the bearers was a lean and greying veteran whom I recognized. He had worked as orderly for me at Kaerconan. I said: "A moment, Paulus, don't hurry away. There are plenty to do the carrying; I'd rather have your help here."

He looked pleased that I had recognized him. "I thought you might need me, sir. I've got my kit with me." He knelt on the other side of the unconscious man, and together we began to slit the leather tunic away where it was torn open by a bloody gash.

"How is it with the King?" I asked him.

"Hard to say, sir. I thought he'd gone, and a lot else gone with him, but he's there now with Gandar, and sitting peaceful as a babe, and smiling. As well he might."

"Indeed . . . That's far enough, I think. Let me look . . ." It was an axe wound, and the leather and metal of the man's tunic had been driven deep into the hacked flesh and splintered bone. I said: "I doubt if there's much we can do here, but we'll try. God's on our side today, and he may well be on this poor fellow's, too. Hold this, will you? . . . As you were saying, well he might. The luck won't change now."

"Luck, is it? Luck on a white horse, you might say. A fair treat it was to see that youngster, the way he pushed through just at the right moment. It needed something like that, with the King falling back as if he was dead, and the Dragon going down. We were looking for King Lot then, but no sign of him. Believe me, sir, another half-minute and we'd have been going the other way. Battle's like that; it makes you wonder sometimes, to think what hangs on a few seconds and a bit of luck. A piece of nice timing like that, and the right person to do it—that's all it takes, and you've won or lost a kingdom."

We worked for a while in silence then, quickly, because the man was beginning to stir under my hands, and I had to finish before he woke to cruel life. When I had done all I could, and we were bandaging, Paulus said, ruminatively: "Funny thing."

"What?"

"Remember Kaerconan, sir?"

"Will I ever forget it?"

"Well, that youngster had a look of *him*—Ambrosius, I mean, that was Count of Britain then. White horse and all, and the Dragon flying over it. Men were saying so . . . And the name's the same, sir, isn't it? Emrys? Connection of yours, perhaps?"

"Perhaps."

"Ah, well," said Paulus, and asked no more questions. He did not need to say more; I knew already that rumours must have been flying round the camp from the moment that Arthur and I had ridden in with the escort. Let them run. Uther had shown his hand. And between the boy's bravery, and the luck of the battle and his own misjudgment, Lot would have a hard struggle of it now to change the King's mind, or to persuade the other nobles that Uther's son was no fit leader.

The man between us woke then and began to scream, and there was no more time for talking.

2

By nightfall the field was cleared of the fallen. The King had withdrawn when it was seen that the tide of victory was sure, and not to be stemmed by any late action of the Saxons. The battle over, the main forces of the British fell back on the township two miles to the north-west, leaving Cador, with Caw of Strathclyde, to hold the field. Lot had not stayed to test his position with the other leaders, but had withdrawn into the town as soon as the fighting was done, and had gone like Ajax to his quarters, since when no man had seen him. Already stories were going round about his fury at the King's action in favouring the strange youth on the battlefield, and his black silence when he heard that Emrys was bidden with me to the victory feast, where no doubt he would be further honoured. There were rumours, too, about the reason for the belated entrance into battle of Lot's troops. No one went so far as to speak of treachery, but it was said openly that, had he delayed much longer, and had not Arthur performed his small miracle, Lothian's inaction might have cost Uther the victory. Men wondered too, aloud, whether Lot would emerge from his sullen silence to share in the feast which was decreed for the following night. But I knew that he could not keep away. He dared not. Though he had said nothing, he must certainly know who "Emrys" was, and if he was ever to discredit him and seize the power he had schemed for, he would have to do it now.

After the emergency cases had been dealt with at the orchard dressing station, the medical units had also moved back to the town, where a hospital had been set up. I went with them, and dealt with a steady stream of cases all afternoon and evening. Our losses had not been heavy as such things commonly go, but still the burial parties would be hard at work all night, watched by the wolves and the gathering ravens. From the marshes came the distant flicker of flames, where the Saxon dead were burning.

I finished work in the hospital at about midnight, and was in an outer room, watching while Paulus packed my instruments away, when I heard someone coming quickly across the court outside, and was aware of a stir near the door behind me.

Call me an old fool if you like, remembering back through the years to what never happened, and you may be more than half right; but it was not only love which made me recognize his coming before I even turned my head. A current of fresh sweet air blew with him, cutting through the fumes of drugs and the stench of sickness and fear. The very lamps burned brighter.

"Merlin?" He spoke softly, as one does in a sickroom, but the excitement of the day was still in his voice. I looked at him smiling, then more sharply.

"Are you hurt? You young fool, why didn't you come to me sooner? Let me see."

He drew back the arm in its stiffened sleeve. "Can't you tell black Saxon blood when you see it? I never had a scratch. Oh, Merlin, what a day! And what a King! To go out in the field crippled and in a chair—that's real courage, far more than it takes to ride into a fight with a good horse and a good sword. I'll swear *I* never even had to think . . . it was so easy . . . Merlin, it was splendid! It's what I was born for—I know it now! And did you see what happened? What the King did? His sword? I'll swear it pulled me forward of its own will, not mine . . . And then the shouting and the way the soldiers moved forward, like the sea. I never even had to use a spur on Canrith . . . Everything moved so fast, and yet so slowly and clearly, every moment seemed to last for ever. I never knew one could be blazing hot and ice-cold all at the same moment, did you?"

He did not wait for answers, but talked on, fast and sparkling, his eyes alight still with the thrill of battle and the overwhelming experience of the day. I hardly listened, but I watched him, and watched the faces of the orderlies and servants, and of those men who were still awake and near enough to hear us. I saw it begin: even so, after battle, Ambrosius' very presence had given the wounded strength, and the dying comfort. Whatever it was he had had about him, Arthur had the same; I was to see it often in the future; it seemed that he shed brightness and strength round him where he went, and still had it ever renewed in himself. As he grew older, I knew it would be renewed more hardly and at a cost, but now he was very young, with the flower of manhood still to come. After this, I thought, who could maintain that youth itself made him unfit for kingship? Not Lot, stiffened in his ambition, grimly scheming for a dead king's throne. It was Arthur's very youth which had whistled up today the best that men had in them, as a huntsman calls up the following pack, or an enchanter whistles up the wind.

He recognized, in one of the beds a man who had fought near him, and went softly down the hospital room to speak to him, and then to others. Two of them, at least, I heard him call by name.

Give him the sword, my dream had said, *and his own nature will do the rest. Kings are not created out of dreams and prophecies: before ever you began to work for him, he was what you see now. All you have done is to guard him while he grew. You, Merlin, are a smith like Weland of the black forge; you made the sword and gave it a cutting edge, but it carves its own way.*

"I saw you up there beside the apple tree," said Arthur gaily. He had followed me out of the hospital room, and I had stopped in the anteroom to give instructions to a night orderly. "The men were saying it was an omen. That when you were there, above us on the hill, the fight was as good as won. And it's true, because through it all, even when I wasn't thinking, I could feel you watching me. Quite close beside me, too. It was like a shield at one's back. I even thought I heard—"

He stopped in mid-sentence. I saw his eyes widen and fix on something beyond me. I looked to see what had gagged him.

Morgause would be two and twenty now, and she was even lovelier than when I had last seen her. She wore grey, a long plain gown of dove-colour which should have made her look like a nun, but somehow did not. She wore no jewels, and needed none. Her skin was pale as marble, and the long eyes that I remembered were gold-green under the tawny lashes. Her hair, as befitted a woman still unwed, fell loose and shining over her shoulders, and was bound back from her brow with a broad band of white.

"Morgause!" I said, startled. "You should not be here!" Then I remembered her skills, and saw behind her two women and a page carrying boxes and linen cloths. She must have been working, as I had, among the wounded; or possibly she still attended the King, and had been with him. I added, quickly: "No, I see; forgive me, and forgive my lack of greeting. Your skill is welcome here. Tell me, how is the King?"

"He has recovered, my lord, and is resting. He seems well enough, and his spirits are good. It seems it was a notable fight. I wish I might have seen it." She glanced past me then at Arthur, an interested, summing look. It was obvious that she recognized him as the youth who had won everyone's praise that day, but it seemed that the King had not yet told her who he was. There was no hint of such a knowledge in her face or voice as she made him a reverence. "Sir."

The colour was up in Arthur's face, bright as a banner. He stammered some kind of greeting, suddenly sounding no more than an awkward boy; he whose boyhood had never been awkward.

She took it coolly, then turned her eyes back to me, dismissing him as a woman of twenty dismisses a child. I thought: No, she does not know yet.

She said, in that light, sweet voice: "My lord Merlin, I came with a message to you from the King. Later, when you have rested, he would like to speak with you."

I said doubtfully: "It's very late. Would he not be better to sleep?"

"I think he would sleep better if he spoke with you first. He was impatient to see you as soon as he came back from the field, but he needed to rest, so I gave him a draught, and he slept then. He's awake now. Can you come within the hour?"

"Very well."

She curtsied again with lowered eyes, and went, as quietly as she had come.

3

I supped alone with Arthur. I had been allotted a room whose window overlooked a strip of garden on the river bank; the garden was a terrace enclosed by gates and high walls. Arthur's room adjoined mine, and both were approached through an anteroom where guards stood armed. Uther was taking no chances.

My room was large and well appointed, and a servant waited there with food and wine. We spoke little while we ate. I was tired and hungry, and Arthur showed his usual appetite, but after his flow of exalted spirits he had fallen strangely quiet, probably, I thought, out of deference to me. For my part I could think of little else but the coming interview with Uther, and of what the morrow might bring; at that moment I could bring nothing to them myself but a sort of weariness of the spirit, which I told myself was no more than reaction from a long journey and a hard day. But I thought it was more than that, and felt like a man who comes out of a sunlit plain into boggy ground, where mist hangs heavy.

Ulfin, Uther's body-servant, came to take me to the King. From the way his look lingered on Arthur I could see he knew the truth, but he said nothing of it as he led me through the corridors to the King's chamber. Indeed he seemed to have little room in his mind for anything but anxiety about the King's health. When I was ushered into Uther's presence, I could see why. Even since the morning, the change was startling. He was in bed, propped in a furred bedgown against pillows, and, shorn of the kingly trappings of armour and scarlet and gold tissue, anyone could see how mortally wasted his body was. Now I could see his death clearly in his face. It would not be tonight, nor should it be tomorrow, but it must come soon; and this, I told myself, must be the cause of the formless dread that was weighing on me. But, though weak and weary, the King seemed pleased to see me, and eager to talk, so I pushed my foreboding aside. Even with tonight and tomorrow, Uther and I and whatever was working for us should have time to see our soaring star riding high and safe to his bright zenith.

He talked first of the battle, and of the day's events. It was evident that all his doubts were set aside, and that (though he would not admit it) he was regretting the lost years since Arthur had come near manhood. He plied me with questions, and, though afraid of taxing him too much, I could see that he would rest better when he knew all I had to tell him. So, as clearly and quickly as I could, I told him the story of the past years, all the details of the boy's life in the Wild Forest that could not be put into the reports I had sent him. I told him, too, what suspicions and certainties I had had about Arthur's enemies; when I spoke about Lot he made no sign, but he heard me out without interruption. Of the sword of Maximus I said nothing. The King had himself today publicly put his own sword into his son's hand; he could not have declared more openly that the boy was his favoured heir. Macsen's sword, when there was need for it, would be given by the god. Between the two gifts was still a dark gap of fate through which I could not see; there was no need to trouble the King with it.

When I had done he lay back on his pillows a while in silence, his eyes on a far corner of the room, deep in thought. Then he spoke.

"You were right, Merlin. Even where it was hard to understand, and where not understanding I condemned you, you were right. The god had us all in his hand. And doubtless it was the god himself who put it in my mind to deny my son and leave him in your care, to be brought in safety and secrecy to such manhood as this. At least it has been granted me to see what manner of man I begot on that wild night at Tintagel, and what kind of a king will come after me. I should have trusted you better, bastard, as my brother did. I don't need to tell you that I am dying, do I? Gandar hums and haws and begs the question, but you'll admit the truth, King's prophet?"

The question was peremptory, requiring an answer. When I said, "Yes," he smiled briefly, with a look almost of satisfaction. I found myself liking Uther better now than I ever had before, seeing him bring this kind of bleak courage to his coming death. This was what Arthur had recognized in him today, the kingly quality to which he had come late, but not too late. It could be that now, almost in the moment of fulfillment of the past years, he and I found ourselves united in the person of the boy.

He nodded. The strain of the day and night was beginning to show, but his look was friendly and his manner still crisp. "Well, we've cleared the past. The future is with him, and with you. But I'm not dead yet, and I'm still High King. The present is with me. I sent for you to tell you that I shall proclaim Arthur my heir tomorrow at the victory feast. There'll never be a better moment. After what happened today no one can argue his fitness; he has already proved himself in public, more, in the sight of the army. Even if I wished to, I doubt if I could keep his secret any longer; rumour has run through the camp like a fire through straw. He knows nothing yet?"

"It seems not. I would have thought he would begin to guess, but it seems not. You'll tell him yourself tomorrow?"

"Yes. I'll send for him in the morning. For the rest of the time, Merlin, stay by him and keep him close."

He spoke then about his plans for the morrow. He would talk with Arthur, and then in the evening, when everyone had recovered from the fighting, and erased the scars of battle, Arthur would be brought with glory and acclaim in front of the nobles at the victory feast. As for Lot—he came to it flatly and without excuse—there was doubt as to what Lot would do, but he had lost too much public credit over his delay in the battle, and even as the betrothed of the King's daughter he would hardly dare (Uther insisted) stand up in public against the High King's own choice. He said nothing about the darker possibility, that Lot might even have thrown his weight onto the Saxons' side of the balance; he saw the delay only as a bid for credit—that Lot's intervention should seem to carry the British to victory. I listened, and said nothing. Whatever the truth of that, the trouble would soon be other men's and not the King's.

He spoke then of Morgian, his daughter. The marriage, firmly contracted as it was, must go through; it could hardly be broken now without offering a mortal and dangerous insult to Lot and the northern kings who hunted with him. And as things had fallen out, it would be safer so; Lot would by the same token not dare to refuse the marriage, and by accepting it would bind himself publicly to Arthur; an Arthur already (months before the marriage) proclaimed, accepted, and established. Uther had almost said "and crowned," but let the sentence drift. He was looking tired now, and I made a move to leave him, but one of the thin hands lifted, and I waited. He did not speak for a few moments, but lay back with closed eyes. Somewhere a draught crept through the room, and the candles guttered. The shadows wavered, throwing dark across his face. Then the light steadied, and I could see his eyes, still bright in their deep sockets, watching me.

I heard his voice, thin with effort now, asking me something. Not asking, no. Uther the High King was begging me to stay beside Arthur, to finish the work I had begun, to watch him, advise him, guard him . . .

His voice faded, but the eyes watched me, intent, and I knew what they were saying. *"Tell me the future, Merlin, prophet of kings. Prophesy for me."*

"I shall be with him," I said, "and the rest of it I have said before. He will bear a king's sword, and with that sword he will do all and more than men hope for. Under him the countries will be one, and there shall be peace, and light before darkness. And when there is peace I myself will go back into my solitude, but I will be there, waiting, always, to be called up as quickly as a man might whistle for the wind."

I was not speaking with vision: this was something which has never come to me when asked for, and besides, visions did not live easily in the same room as Uther. But to comfort him I spoke from remembered prophecies, and from a knowledge of men and times, which sometimes comes to the same thing. It satisfied him, which was all that was needed.

"That is all I wanted to know," he said. "That you will stay near him, and serve him at all times . . . Perhaps, if I had listened to my brother, and kept you near me . . . You have promised, Merlin. There is no man who has more power, not even the High King."

He said it without rancour, in the tone of one making a plain statement. His voice was tired suddenly, the voice of a sick man.

I got to my feet. "I'll leave you now, Uther. You had better sleep. What is the draught Morgause gives you?"

"I don't know. Some poppy-smelling thing; she puts it in warm wine."

"Does she sleep here, near you?"

"No. Along the corridor, in the first of the women's rooms. But don't disturb her now. There's some of the drug still in that jar yonder."

I crossed the room, picked up the jar, and sniffed it. The potion, whatever it was, was already mixed in wine; the smell was sweet and heavy; poppy there was and other things I recognized, but it was not quite familiar. I dipped a finger in and put it to my lips. "Has anyone touched it since she mixed it?"

"Eh?" He had been drifting away, not in sleep, but as sick men do. "Touched it? No one that I have seen, but there's no one will try to poison me. It's well known that all my food is tasted. Call the boy in, if you wish."

"No need," I said. "Let him sleep." I poured some into a cup, but when I lifted it to my mouth he said with sudden vigour: "Don't be a fool! Let be!"

"I thought you said it would not be poisoned."

"No matter of that, we'll not take the chance."

"Do you not trust Morgause?"

"Morgause?" He knitted his brows, as if at an irrelevancy. "Of course, why not? When she has cared for me all these years, refusing to wed, even when . . .

But no matter of that. Her fate is 'in the smoke,' she says, and she is content to wait for it. She riddles like you, sometimes, and I've scant patience with riddles, as you may remember. No, how could I doubt my daughter? But tonight of all nights we must be wary, and of all men, except my son, I can least spare you." He smiled then, momentarily the Uther that I remembered, hard and gay, and slightly malicious. "At least, not until he is proclaimed, and then no doubt you and I will well spare one another."

I smiled. "Meantime I'll taste your wine. Calm yourself, I can smell nothing hurtful, and I assure you that my death is not yet."

I did not add, "So let me make sure that you live to proclaim your son tomorrow." This strange shadow that brooded still behind my shoulder, it could not be my own death, nor (I knew) was it Arthur's, but it might, against all probability, be the King's. I took a sip, letting the wine rest for a moment on my tongue, then swallowed. The King lay back on his pillows and watched me, tranquil once more. I sipped again, then crossed the room to sit down by the great bed, and, more idly now, we talked: of the past seamed with memories; of the future, shadows still across glory. We understood one another tolerably well at the last, Uther and I. When it was patent that the wine was harmless I poured a draught for him, watched him drink it, then called his servant Ulfin, and left him to sleep.

4

All was so far well. Even if Uther died tonight—and nothing in his look or in my bones told me that he would—all was surely still set fair. I, with Cador's backing and Ector's support, could proclaim Arthur to the nobles as well as the King could, and prestige with power behind it had every chance of forcing the thing through. The King's gesture in flinging his sword to the boy in battle would be, to many of the soldiers, proof enough of Arthur's right to succeed him, and the warriors who had followed him so gladly today would follow him still. It was surely only the dissidents of the north-east who would not rejoice to see the days of uncertainty finished, and the succession pass clear and undoubted into Arthur's hands.

Then why, I thought, as I trod quietly along the corridors towards my own chamber, was my heart so heavy in me; what was this foreboding black enough for a death? Why, if this was a heavy matter that my blood prophesied, could I not see it? What shadow hung, clawed and waiting, over the day's bright success?

A moment later, as I nodded to the guard outside my antechamber, and went quietly through into the room itself, I saw the edge of the shadow. Beyond the doorway connecting Arthur's room to my own I could see his bed. It was empty.

I went quickly back to the antechamber, and had stooped to shake the sleeping servant awake, when my nostrils caught a familiar smell, the drug that had been in the King's wine. I dropped the man's shoulder and left him snoring, and in three swift strides was back in the corridor. Before I had said a word, the guard flattened himself back against the wall, as if afraid of what he saw in my face.

But I spoke softly: "Where is he?"

"My lord, he's safe. There's no reason for alarm . . . We had our orders, there was no harm could come to him. The other guard saw him right to the door, and stayed there—"

"Where is he?"

"In the women's rooms, my lord. When the girl came to him—"

"Girl?" I asked sharply.

"Indeed, my lord. She came here. We stopped her, of course, wouldn't let her in, but then he came out to the door himself. . . ." Reassured now by my silence, the man was relaxing. "Indeed, my lord, all's well. It was one of the Lady Morgause's women, the black-haired one, you may have noticed her, plump as a robin, and the prettiest, as was proper for my young lord this night—"

I had noticed her; small and rounded, with a high colour and black eyes bright as a bird's. A pretty creature, very young, and healthy as a summer's day. But I bit my lip. "How long ago?"

"Two hours, as near as might be." A grin touched his mouth. "Time enough. My lord, where's the harm? Even if we'd tried, how could we have stopped him? We didn't let her in; we'd had our orders, and he knew it; but when he said he'd go with her, what could we do? After all, it's a fair end to a man's first battle day."

I said something to him, and went back into my room. The fellow was right enough, the guards had done their duty as they saw it, and this was one situation in which no guard would have interfered. And where indeed was the harm? The boy had seized one half of his manhood today out under the sun; it was inevitable that the rest should come to him tonight. As his sword had quenched its lust for blood, so the boy would burn alive till he quenched his own excitement in a girl's body. Anybody, I thought bitterly, but a god-bound prophet would have foreseen this. Any normal guardian would let this night take its normal course. But I was Merlin, and the room was full of shadows, and I was afraid.

I stood there alone, with the shadows pressing round me, controlling myself to coldness, facing the fear. The blackness came from my mind; very well, was it human merely, was it black jealousy, that Arthur at fourteen should take so easily a pleasure that at twenty I had burned for even as he, and had fumbled, failing? Or was it a fear worse than jealousy, the fear of losing or even sharing a love so dear and lately found; or was I fearful only for him, knowing what a girl could do to rob a man of power? And as this thought struck me I knew I was acquitted; the shadows were not from this. I had known, that day at twenty, when I fled from the girl's angry and derisive laughter, that for me there had been a cold choice between manhood and power, and I had chosen power. But Arthur's power would be different, that of full and fierce manhood, that of a king. He had shown me often enough that however much he might love and learn from me, he was Uther's son in the flesh; he wanted all that manhood could give. It was right that he should lie with his first girl tonight. I ought to smile, like the sentry, and go to bed myself and sleep, leaving him to his pleasure.

But the cold in my entrails and the sweat on my face were not there for nothing. I stood still, while the lamp flared and dimmed and flared again, and thought.

Morgause, I thought, one of Morgause's girls. And she'd drugged my servant, who might have come to tell me that Arthur had gone two hours since to her chamber. . . . And Morgause is Morgian's half-sister, and might be in Lot's pay, with the promise of some rich future should Lot become King. True, she had made no attempt on the King, but she knew he always used a taster, and it would have served no purpose to be rid of him until Lot was married to Morgian and able to declare himself legitimately heir to the High Kingdom. But now Uther was dying, and Arthur had appeared, with a claim which would eclipse Lot's. If Morgause was indeed an enemy, and wanted Arthur put out of the way before tomorrow's feast, then the boy might even now be drugged, captive in Lot's hands, or dying . . .

This was folly. It was not for death that the god had given him the sword and shown him to me as High King. There was no reason for Morgause to wish him ill. As his half-sister she might expect more from Arthur as King than from Lot, her sister's husband. Arthur's death, I thought coldly, would not profit her. But death was here, in a form and with a smell I did not know. A smell like treachery, something remembered dimly from my childhood, when my uncle planned to betray his father's kingdom, and to murder me. It was not a matter of reason, but of knowing. Danger was here, and I had to find it.

I could not walk through the house, asking where Arthur was. If he was happily bedded with a girl, this was something he would never forgive me. I would have to find him by other means, and since I was Merlin, the means were here. Standing rigid there in the dim chamber, with my hands held stiff-fisted at my sides, I stared at the lamp. . . .

I know that I never moved from the place or left my chamber, but in my memory now it seems as if I went out, silent and invisible as a ghost, across the antechamber, past the guard, and along the dim corridor towards Morgause's door. The other sentry was there; he was full awake, and watching, but he never saw me.

There was no sound from within. I went in.

In the outer room the air was heavy and warm, and smelled of scents and lotions such as women use. There were two beds there, and sleepers in them. On the threshold of the inner chamber Morgause's page was curled on the floor, sleeping.

Two beds, each with its sleeper. One was an old woman, grey-haired, mouth open, snoring slightly. The other slept silently, and over her pillow the long black hair lay heavy, braided for the night. The little dark girl slept alone.

I knew it now, the horror that oppressed me; the one thing that, looking for larger issues of death and treachery and loss, I had never thought of. I have said men with god's sight are often human-blind: when I exchanged my manhood for power it seemed I had made myself blind to the ways of women. If I had been simple man instead of wizard I would have seen the way eye answered eye back there at the hospital, have recognized Arthur's silence later, and known the woman's long assessing look for what it was.

Some magic she must have had, to blind me so. It may be that now, knowing I could do nothing, she let the magic lapse and thin; or let it waver as she sank towards sleep. Or it may be only that my power outstripped hers, and she had no shield against me. God knows I did not want to look, but I was nailed there by my own power, and because there is no power without knowledge, and no knowledge without suffering, the walls and door of Morgause's sleeping chamber dissolved in front of me, and I could see.

Time enough, the guard had said. They had indeed had time enough. The woman lay, naked and wide-legged, across the covers of the bed. The boy, brown against her whiteness, lay sprawled over her in the heavy abandonment of pleasure. His head was between her breasts, half turned from me; he was not asleep, but the next thing to it, his face close and quiet, his blind mouth searching her flesh as a puppy nuzzles for its mother's nipple. Her face I saw clearly. She held his head cradled, and about her body was the same heavy languor, but her face showed none of the tenderness that the gesture seemed to express. And none of the pleasure. It held a secret exultation as fierce as I have ever seen on a warrior's face in battle; the gilt-green eyes were wide and fixed on something invisible beyond the dark; and the small mouth smiled, a smile somewhere between triumph and contempt.

5

He came back to his room just before daylight. The first bird had whistled, and a few moments later the sudden jargoning of the early chorus almost drowned the clink of arms at the outer door, and his soft word to the guard. He came in, his eyes full of sleep, and stopped short just inside the door when he saw me sitting in the high-backed chair beside the window.

"Merlin! Up at this hour? Couldn't you sleep?"

"I haven't yet been to bed."

He came suddenly wide awake, sharpened and alert. "What is it? What's wrong? Is it the King?"

At least, I thought, he doesn't jump to the conclusion that I stayed awake to question his night's doings. And one thing he must never know; that I followed him through that door.

I said: "No, not the King. But you and I must talk before the day comes."

"Oh, the gods, not now, if you love me," he said, half laughing, and yawned. "Merlin, I've got to sleep. Did you guess where I'd gone, or did the guard tell you?"

As he came forward into the room I could smell her scent on him. I felt sickened, and I suppose I was shaken. I said curtly: "Yes, now. Wash yourself, and wake up. I have to talk to you."

I had put out all the lamps but one, and this was burning low, only half competing with the leaden light of dawn. I saw his face go rigid. "By what right—?" He checked himself, and I saw the quick control come down over his anger. "Very well. I suppose you do have the right to question me, but I don't like the time you choose."

It was something altogether different from the injured boyish anger he had shown before, how short a time ago, beside the lake. So far they had already taken him between them, the sword and the woman. I said: "I have no right to question you, and I've no intention of doing so. Calm yourself, and listen. It's true I want to talk to you—among other things—about what happened tonight, but not for the reasons you seem to impute to me. Who do you think I am, Abbot Martin? I don't dispute your right to take your pleasure as and where you wish." He was still hostile, between anger and pride. To relax him and pass the moment over, I added mildly: "Perhaps it wasn't wise to venture through this house at night where there are men who hate you for what you did yesterday. But how can I blame you for going? You showed yourself a man in battle, why not then in your bed?" I smiled. "Though I've never lain with a woman myself, I've known what it is to want one. For the pleasure you had, I'm glad."

I stopped. His face had been pale with anger; now even in that lack of light I could see the anger drain away, and with it the last vestiges of colour. It was as if blood and breath had stopped together. His eyes looked black. He narrowed them at me as if he could not see me properly, or as if he were seeing me for the first time, and could not get me in focus. It was a discomforting look, and I am not easily discomforted.

"You have never lain with a woman?"

Somehow, to the matters boiling in my mind, the question came as sheer irrelevancy. I said, surprised: "I said so. I believe it's a matter of common knowledge. I also believe it's a fact that some men hold in contempt. But those—"

"Are you a eunuch, then?"

The question was cruel; his manner, harsh and abrupt, made it seem meant so. I had to wait a moment before I answered.

"No. I was going to add, that those who hold chastity in contempt are not men whose contempt would disturb me. Have I yours, then?"

"What?" He had obviously not heard a word of what I had been saying. He jerked himself free of whatever strong emotion was riding him, and made for his room like a man who is choking, and in need of air. As he went he said, muffled: "I'll go and wash."

The door shut behind him. I stood up quickly and set my hands on the window sill, leaning out into the chill September dawn. A cock was crowing; from farther off others answered it. I found that I was shaking; I, Merlin, who had watched while kings and priests and princes plotted my death openly in front of my eyes; who had talked with the dead; who could make storm and fire and call the wind. Well, I had called this wind; I must face it. But I had counted on his love for me to get us both through what I had to tell him. I had not reckoned on losing his respect—and for such a reason—at this moment.

I told myself that he was young; that he was Uther's son, fresh from his first woman, and in the flush of his new sexual pride. I told myself that I had been a fool to see love given back where I gave it, when what the boy was rendering to me was no more than I had given my own tutor Galapas, affection tinged with awe. I told myself these and other things, and by the time he came back I was seated again, calm and waiting, with two goblets of wine poured ready on a table at my hand. He took one without a word, then sat across the room from me, on the edge of my bed. He had washed even his hair; it was still damp, and clung to his brow. He had changed his bedgown for day dress, and in the short tunic, without mantle or weapon, looked like a boy again, the Arthur of the summer and the Wild Forest.

I had been casting round carefully for what to say, but now could find nothing. It was Arthur who broke the silence, not looking at me, turning the goblet round and round in his hands, watching the swirl of wine as if his life depended on it.

He said, flatly, and as if it explained everything, as I suppose it did:

"I thought you were my father."

It was like facing an opponent's sword, only to find that the sword and the enemy are in fact illusions, but in the same moment to feel that the very ground on which one has made one's stand is a shaking bog. I fought to rearrange my thoughts.

Respect and love, yes, I had had these from him, but they could have been given to me for the man I was; in fact, only in such a way does a boy give them to his father. But other things became suddenly plain; above all the deference which he would have given to no other man but Ector, his obedience, his assumption of my ready welcome, and more than all—I saw it like the sudden rift of daffodil sky which opened in the grey beyond the window—the shining anticipation with which he had come with me to Luguvallium. I remembered my own ceaseless childhood search for my father, and how I had looked for and seen him everywhere, in every man who looked my mother's way. Arthur had had only his foster-parents' story of noble bastardy, and a vague promise of recognition "when you are grown enough to bear arms." As children do—as I had done—he had said little, but waited and wondered, ceaselessly. Then into this perpetual search and expectation I had come, with some mystery about me, and I suppose the air that Ralf had spoken of, of a man used to deference and moved by some strong purpose. The boy may have seen his own likeness to me; more likely others, Bedwyr even, had commented on it. So he had waited, reaching his own conclusions, prepared to give love, accept authority and trust me for the future. Then came the sword, a gift, it seemed, from me; father to son. And the discovery that had followed hard on it, that I was Ambrosius' son, and the Merlin of the thousand legends told at every fireside. Bastard or no, suddenly he had found himself, and he was royal.

So he had followed me to the King at Luguvallium, seeing himself as Ambrosius' grandson and great-nephew to Uther Pendragon. From this knowledge had come that flashing confidence in battle. He must have thought this was why Uther had flung him the sword, because in default of the absent prince, he, bastard or not, was the next in blood. So he had led the charge, and afterwards accepted the duties and the favours due to a prince.

It also explained why he had never seemed to suspect that he might be the "lost" prince. The stares and whispers and the deference he received he had put down to recognition as my son. He accepted, as most men did, the fact that the High King's heir was abroad at a foreign court, and thought nothing more about it. And once he imagined he had found his place, why should he think again? He was mine, and he was royal, and through me he had a place at the center of the kingdom. Now all at once, cruelly enough, as he must see it, he found himself not only deprived of ambition and the place he had dreamed of, but even of a place as a man's acknowledged son. I, who had lived my youth as a bastard and a no-man's-child, knew how that canker can eat: Ector had tried to spare Arthur this by telling him that he would one day be acknowledged nobly; it had never struck me that he would count in love and confidence on the acknowledgment coming from me.

"Even my name, you see." The dull apology of his tone was worse than the cruelty that shock had brought from him before.

At least, if I could heal nothing else, I could heal his pride. The cost would be counted presently, but he had to know now. I had many times thought how, if it were left to me, I would tell him. Now I spoke straight, the simple truth. "We bear the same name because we are in fact kin to one another. You are not my son, but we are cousins. You, like me, are a grandson of Constantius and a descendant of Maximus the Emperor. Your true name is Arthur, and you are the legitimate son of the High King and Ygraine his Queen."

I thought the silence this time would never break. At my first word his eyes had come up from watching the swirling wine, and fastened on me. His brows were knitted like those of a deaf man straining to hear. The red washed through his face like blood staining a white cloth, and his lips parted. Then he set the goblet down very carefully, and standing up, came to the window near me, and, just as I had done earlier, set his hands on the sill and leaned out into the air.

A bird flew into the bough beside him and began to sing. The sky faded to heron's-egg green, then slowly cooled to hyacinth where thin flakes of cloud floated. Still he stood there, and I waited, without movement or speech.

At length, without turning, he spoke to the bough with its singing bird. "Why this way? Fourteen years. Why not where I belonged?"

So at last I told him the whole story. I began with the vision Ambrosius had shared with me, of the kingdoms united under one king, Dumnonia to Lothian, Dyfed to Rutupiae; Romano-Briton and Celt and loyal *foederatus* fighting as one to keep Britain clear of the black flood that was drowning the rest of the Empire; a version, humbler and more workable, of Maximus' imperial dream, adapted and handed down by my grandfather to my father, and lodged in me by my master's teaching and by the god who had marked me for his service. I told him about Ambrosius' death without other issue, and the ravelled clue the god had thrust into my hand, bidding me follow it. About the sudden passion of the new King Uther for Ygraine, wife of Cornwall's Duke, and about my own connivance at their union, shown by the god that this was the union which would bring its next king to Britain. About Gorlois' death and Uther's remorse, mingled as it was with relief at a death he had more than half wished, but wanted publicly to disclaim and disown; then the consequent banishment of myself and Ralf, and Uther's own threats to disown the child so begotten. Then finally, how pride and common sense between them prevailed, and the child had been handed to me to look after through the dangerous first years of Uther's reign; and how since then the King's illness and the growing power of his enemies had forced him to leave his son in hiding. About some things I said nothing: I did not tell Arthur what I had seen waiting for him, of greatness or pain or glory; and I said no word about Uther's impotence. Nor did I speak of the King's desperate wish for another son to supplant the "bastard" of Tintagel; these were Uther's secrets, and he would not have long now to keep them.

Arthur listened in silence, without interruption. Indeed, at first without movement, so that one might have thought his whole attention was on the slowly brightening sky outside the window, and the song of the blackbird on the bough. But after a while he turned and—though I was not looking at him—I felt his eyes on me at last. When I came to the Coronation feast, and the King's demand for me to bring him to Ygraine's bed, he moved again, going softly across to his former place on the bed. My tale of that wild night when he was begotten was told plainly, exactly as it had happened. But he listened as if it had been the same half-enchanted tale I had told him in the Wild Forest with Bedwyr beside him, himself curled half-sitting, half-lying on my bed, chin on fist, his dark eyes, calm now and shining, on my face.

As I came towards an end it was to be seen that the tale fitted in with all that I had taught him in the past, so that now I was just handing him the last links in the golden lineage and saying, in effect: "All that I have ever taught or told you is summed up in you, yourself."

I stopped at length, and took a draught of wine. He uncurled swiftly from the bed and, bringing the jug, poured more into my goblet. When I thanked him, he stooped and kissed me.

"You," he said quietly, "you, from the very beginning. I wasn't so far wrong after all, was I? I'm as much yours as the King's—more; and Ector's too . . . Then Ralf, I'm glad to know about Ralf. I see . . . Oh, yes, now I begin to see a lot of things." He paced about the room, talking in snatches, half to himself, as restless as Uther. "So much—it's too much to take in, I'll have to have time . . . I'm glad it was you who told me. Did the King mean to tell me himself?"

"Yes. He would have talked to you earlier, if there had been time. I hope there will still be time."

"What do you mean?"

"He's dying, Arthur. Are you ready to be King?"

He stood there, the wine-jug still in his hand, hollow-eyed with lack of sleep, thoughts crowding in on him too fast for expression. *"Today?"*

"I think so. I don't know. Soon."

"Will you be with me?"

"Of course. I told you so."

It was only then, as he set down the jug, smiling, and turned to put out the lamp, that the other thing struck him. I saw the moment when his breath stopped, then was let out again cautiously, the way a man tries his breathing after a mortal stroke.

He had his back to me, reaching up to quench the lamp. I saw that his hand was quite steady. But the other hand, which he tried to hide from me, was making the sign against evil. Then, being Arthur, he did not stay turned away, but faced me.

"I have something to tell *you* now."

"Yes?"

The words came like something being dragged up from a depth. "The woman I was with tonight was Morgause." Then, as I did not speak, sharply: "You knew?"

"Only when it was too late to stop you. But I should have known. Before I ever went to see the King, I knew that something was wrong. Oh, no, nothing of what it was, only that the shadows pressed on me."

"If I had stayed in my room, as you told me . . ."

"Arthur. The thing has happened. It's no use saying 'if this' and 'if that'; can't you see that you're innocent? You obeyed your nature, it's something young men will do. But I, I am to blame. You could curse me, if you wished, for my promise to the King, and for all this secrecy. If I had told you sooner about your birth—"

"You told me to stay here. Even if you didn't know what ill was in the wind, you knew that if I obeyed you I would be safe. If I had obeyed you, I'd be more than safe, I would still be—" He bit off some word I did not quite hear, then finished, "—clean of this thing. Blame *you?* The blame is mine, and God knows it and will judge between us."

"God will judge us all."

He took three restless strides across the room and back again. "Of all women, my sister, my father's daughter . . ." The words came hard, like a morsel one gags on. I could see the horror clinging to him, like a slug to a green plant. His left hand still made the sign against evil: it is a pagan sign; the sin has been a heavy one before the gods since time began. He halted suddenly, squarely in front of me, even at this moment able to think beyond himself. "And Morgause herself? When she knows what you have just told me, what will she think, knowing the sin we've committed between us? What will she do? If she falls into despair—"

"She will not fall into despair."

"How can you know? You said you didn't know women. I believe that for women these matters are heavier." Horror struck at him again as he thought why. "Merlin, if there should be a child?"

I think there has been no moment in my life when I have had to exert more self-command. He was staring wildly at me; if I had let my thoughts show in my face, God only knows what he might have done. As he spoke the last sentence it was as if the formless shadows which had clawed and brooded over me all night suddenly took form and weight. They were there, clinging round my shoulders, vultures, heavy-feathered and stinking of carrion. I, who had schemed for Arthur's conception, had waited blind and idle while his death also was conceived.

"I shall have to tell her." His voice was edged, desperate. "Straight away. Even before the High King declares me. There may be those who guess, and she may hear . . ."

He talked on, a little wildly, but I was too busy with my own thoughts to listen. I thought: if I tell him that she knew already, that she is corrupt and that her power, such as it is, is corrupt; if I tell him that she used him deliberately to gather more power to herself; if I tell him these things now, while he is shaken out of his wits by all that has happened in this last day and night, he will take his sword and kill her. And when she dies the seed will die that is to grow corrupt as she is, and eat at his glory as this slug of horror eats at his youth. But if he kills them now he will never use a sword again in God's service, and their corruption will have claimed him before his work is even begun.

I said calmly: "Arthur. Be still now, and listen. I told you, what is done is done, and men must learn to stand by their deeds. Now hear me. One day soon you will be High King, and as you know, I am the King's Prophet. So listen to the first prophecy I shall make for you. What you did, you did in innocence. You alone of Uther's seed are clean. Has no one ever told you the gods are jealous? They insure against too much glory. Every man carries the seed of his own death, and you will not be more than a man. You will have everything; you cannot have more; and there must come a term to every life. All that has happened tonight is that you yourself have set that term. What more could a man want, that he determines his own death? Every life has a death, and every light a shadow. Be content to stand in the light, and let the shadow fall where it will."

He grew quieter as he listened, and at length asked me, calmly enough: "Merlin, what must I do?"

"Leave this to me. For yourself, put it behind you, forget about the night, and think of the morning. Listen, there are the trumpets. Go now, and get some sleep before the day begins."

So, imperceptibly, was the first link forged in the new chain that bound us. He slept, to be ready for the great doings of the morrow, and I sat watchful, thinking, while the light grew and the day came.

6

Ulfin, the King's chamberer, came at length to bid Arthur to the King's presence. I woke the boy, and later saw him go, silent and self-contained, showing a sort of impossible calm like smooth ice over a whirlpool. I think that, being young, he had already begun to put behind him the shadow of the night; the burden was mine now. This was a pattern which was common in the years to come.

As soon as he was gone, ushered out with a ceremony wherein I could see Ulfin remembering that night so long ago, of the boy's conception, and which Arthur himself accepted as if he had known it all his life, I called a servant and bade him bring the Lady Morgause to me.

The man looked surprised, then doubtful; it was to be surmised that the lady was used to do her own summoning. I had neither time nor patience this morning for such things. I said briefly: "Do as I say," and the fellow went, scuttling.

She kept me waiting, of course, but she came. This morning she wore red, the colour of cherries, and over the shoulders of the gown her hair looked rosy fair, larch buds in spring, the colour of apricots. Her scent was heavy and sweet, apricots and honeysuckle mixed, and I felt my stomach twist at the memory. But there was no other resemblance to the girl I had loved—had tried to love—so long ago: in Morgause's long-lidded green eyes there was not even the pretense of innocence. She came in smiling that close-lipped smile, with the prick of a charming dimple at the corner of her mouth, and, making me a reverence, crossed the room gracefully to seat herself in the high-backed chair. She disposed her robe prettily about her, dismissed her women with a nod, then lifted her chin and looked at me enquiringly. Her hands lay still and folded against the soft swell of her belly, and in her the gesture was not demure, but possessive.

Somewhere, coldly, a memory stirred. My mother, standing with her hands held so, facing a man who would have murdered me. "I have a bastard to protect." I believe that Morgause read my thoughts. The dimple deepened prettily, and the gold-fringed lids drooped.

I did not sit, but remained standing across the window from her. I said, more harshly than I had intended: "You must know why I sent for you."

"And you must know, Prince Merlin, that I am not used to being sent for."

"Let us not waste time. You came, and it's just as well. I wish to speak with you while Arthur is still with the King."

She opened her eyes wide at me. "Arthur?"

"Don't make those innocent eyes at me, girl. You knew his name when you took him to your bed last night."

"Can the poor boy not even keep his bed secrets from you?" The light pretty voice was contemptuous, meant to sting. "Did he come running to your whistle to tell you about it, along with everything else? I'm surprised you let him off the chain long enough to take his pleasure last night. I wish you joy of him, Merlin the kingmaker. What sort of king is a half-trained puppy going to make?"

"The sort who is not ruled from his bed," I said. "You have had your night, and that was too much. The reckoning comes now."

Her hands moved slightly in her lap. "You can do me no harm."

"No, I shall do you no harm." The flicker in her eyes showed that she had noticed the change of phrase. "But I am also here," I said, "to see that you do Arthur no harm. You will leave Luguvallium today, and you will not come back to the court."

"I leave court? What nonsense is this? You know that I look after the King; he depends on me for his medicines, I am his nurse. I and his chamberer look after him in all things. You cannot imagine that the King will ever agree to let me go."

"After today," I said, "the King will never want to see you again."

She stared. Her colour was high. This, I could see, mattered to her. "How can you say that? Even you, Merlin, cannot stop me from seeing my father, and I assure you he will not want to let me go. You surely don't mean to tell him what has happened? He's a sick man, a shock might kill him."

"I shall not tell him."

"Then what will you say to him? Why should he agree to having me sent away?"

"That is not what I said, Morgause."

"You said that after today the King would never want to see me again."

"I was not speaking of your father."

"I don't see—" She took a sharp breath, and the green-gilt eyes widened. "But you said . . . the King?" Her breath shortened. "You were speaking of that boy?"

"Of your brother, yes. Where is your skill? Uther is marked for death."

Her hands were working together in her lap. "I know. But . . . you say it comes today?"

I echoed my own question. "Where is your magic? It comes today. So you had better leave, had you not? Once Uther is gone, who will protect you here?"

She thought for a moment. The lovely green-gilt eyes were narrow and sly, not lovely at all. "Against what? Against Arthur? You're so sure you can make them accept him as King? Even if you do, are you trying to tell me that I will need protection against him?"

"You know as well as I do that he will be King. You have skill enough for that, and—in spite of what you said to anger me—skill enough to know what kind of a king. You may not need protection against him, Morgause, but it is certain that you will need it against me." Our eyes locked. I nodded. "Yes. Where he is, I am. Be warned, and go while you can. I can protect him from the kind of magic you wove last night."

She was calm again, seeming to draw into herself. The small mouth tightened in its secret smile. Yes, she had power of a kind. "Are you so sure you are proof against women's magic? It will snare you in the end, Prince Merlin."

"I know it," I said calmly. "Do not think I have not seen my end. And all our ends, Morgause. I have seen power for you, and for the thing you carry, but no joy. No joy, now or ever."

Outside the window, against the wall, was an apricot tree. The sun warmed the fruit, globe on golden globe, scented and heavy. Warmth reflected from the stone wall, and wasps hummed among the glossy leaves, sleepy with scent. So, once before, in a sweet-smelling orchard, I had met hatred and murder, eye to eye.

She sat very still, her hands locked against her belly. Her eyes held mine, seeming to drink at them. The scent of honeysuckle thickened, visibly, drifting in green-gold haze across the lighted window, mingling with the sunshine and the smell of apricots. . . .

"Stop it!" I said contemptuously. "Do you really think that your girl's magic can touch me? No more now than it could before. And what are you trying to do? This is hardly a matter of magic. Arthur knows now who he is, and he knows what he did last night with you. Do you think he will bear you near him? Do you think that he will watch daily, monthly, while a child grows in your belly? He is not a cold or a patient man. And he has a conscience. He believes that you sinned in innocence, as he did. If he thought otherwise, he might act."

"Kill me, you mean?"

"Do you not deserve killing?"

"He sinned, if you call it sin, as much as I."

"He did not know he was sinning, and you did. No, don't waste your breath on me. Why pretend? Even without your magic, you must know that half the court has whispered it since he and I rode in together yesterday. You knew he was Uther's son."

For the first time there was a shade of fear in her face. She said obstinately: "I did not know. You cannot prove I knew. Why should I do such a thing?"

I folded my arms and leaned a shoulder back against the wall. "I will tell you why. First, because you are Uther's daughter, and like him a seeker after casual lusts. Because you have the Pendragon blood in you that makes you desire power, so you take it as it mostly offers itself to women, in a man's bed. You knew your father the King was dying, and feared that there would be no place of power for you as half-sister of the young King whose Queen would later dispossess you. I think you would not have hesitated to kill Arthur, but that you would have less standing, even, at Lot's court, with your own sister as Queen. Whoever became High King would have no need of you, as Uther has. You would be married to some small king and taken to some corner of the land where you would pass your time bearing his children and weaving his war cloaks, with nothing in your hands but the petty power of a family, and what women's magic you have learned and can practise in your little kingdom. That is why you did what you did, Morgause. Because, no matter what it was, you wanted a claim on the young King, even if it was to be a claim of horror and of hatred. What you did last night you did coldly, in a bid for power."

"Who are you to talk to me so? You took power where you could find it."

"Not where I could find it; where it was given. What you have got you took, against all laws of God and men. If you had acted unknowingly, in simple lust, there would be no more to say. I told you, so far he thinks you have no blame. This morning, when he knew what he had done, his first thought was for your distress." I saw the flash of triumph in her eyes, and finished, gently: "But you are not dealing with him, you are dealing with me. And I say that you shall go."

She got swiftly to her feet. "Why did you not tell him then, and let him kill me? Would you not have wanted that?"

"To add another and worse sin? You talk like a fool."

"I shall go to the King!"

"To what purpose? He will spare no thought for you today."

"I am always by him. He will need his drugs."

"I am here now, and Gandar. He will not need you."

"He'll see me if I say I've come to say farewell! I tell you, I will go to him!"

"Then go," I said. "I'll not stop you. If you were thinking of telling him the truth, think again. If the shock kills him, Arthur will be High King all the sooner."

"He would not be accepted! They wouldn't accept him! Do you think Lot will stand by and listen to you? What if I tell *them* what Arthur did last night?"

"Then Lot would become High King," I said equably. "And how long would he let you live, bearing Arthur's child? Yes, you'd better think about it, hadn't you? Either way, there is nothing you can do, except go while you can. Once your sister is married at Christmas, get Lot to find you a husband. That way, you may be safe."

Suddenly, at this, she was angry, the anger of a spitting cat in a corner. "You condemn me, you! You were a bastard, too . . . All my life I have watched Morgian get everything. Morgian! That child to be a Queen, while I . . . Why, she even learns magic, but she has no more idea how to use it for her own ends than a kitten has! She'd do better in a nunnery than on a Queen's throne, and I—I . . ." She stopped on a little gasp, and caught her underlip in her teeth. I thought she changed what she had been about to say. ". . . I, who have something of the power which has made you great, Merlin my cousin, do you think I will be content to be nothing?" Her voice went flat, the voice of a wise-woman speaking a curse which will stick. "And that is what you will be, who are no man's friend, and no woman's lover. You are nothing, Merlin, you are nothing, and in the end you will only be a shadow and a name."

I smiled at her. "Do you think you can frighten me? I see further than you, I believe. I am nothing, yes; I am air and darkness, a word, a promise. I watch in the crystal and I wait in the hollow hills. But out there in the light I have a young king and a bright sword to do my work for me, and build what will stand when my name is only a word for forgotten songs and outworn wisdom, and when your name, Morgause, is only a hissing in the dark." I turned my head then, and called the servant. "Now enough of this, there is no more to say between us. Go and make yourself ready, and get you from court."

The man had come in, and was waiting inside the door glancing, I thought apprehensively, from one to the other of us. From his look, he was a black Celt from the mountains of the west; it is a race that still worships the old gods, so it is possible he could feel, if only partly, some of the stinging presences still haunting the room.

But for me, now, the girl was only a girl, tilting a pretty, troubled face to mine, so that the rose-gold hair streamed from her pale forehead down the cherry gown. To the servant waiting beside the door, it should have seemed an ordinary leave-taking, but for those stinging shadows. She never glanced his way, or guessed what he might see.

When she spoke her voice was composed, calm and low. "I shall go to my sister. She lies at York till the wedding."

"I shall see to it that an escort is ready. No doubt the wedding will still be at Christmas, according to plan. King Lot should join you soon, and give you a place at your sister's court."

There was a brief flash at that, discreetly veiled. I might have tried a guess at what she planned there—that she hoped, even at this late date, to take her sister's place at Lot's side—but I was weary of her. I said: "I'll bid you farewell, then, and a safe journey."

She made a reverence, saying, very low: "We shall meet again, cousin."

I said formally, "I shall look forward to it." She went then, slight, erect, hands folded close again, and the servant shut the door behind her.

I stood by the window, collecting my thoughts. I felt weary, and my eyes were gritty from lack of sleep, but my mind was clear and light, already free of the girl's presence. The fresh air of morning blew in to disperse the evil lingering in the room, till, with the last fading scent of honeysuckle, it was gone. When the servant came back I rinsed face and hands in cold water, then, bidding him follow me, went back to the hospital dormitory. The air was cleaner there, and the eyes of dying men easier to bear than the presence of the woman who was with child of Mordred, Arthur's nephew and bastard son.

7

King Lot, brooding on the edge of affairs, had not been idle. Certain busy gentlemen, friends of his, were seen to be hurrying here and there, protesting to anyone who would listen that it would be more appropriate for Uther to declare his heir from one of his great palaces in London or Winchester. This haste, they said, was unseemly: the thing should be done by custom, with due notice and ceremony, and backed by the blessing of the Church. But they whispered in vain. The ordinary people of Luguvallium, and the soldiers who at present outnumbered them, thought otherwise. It was obvious now that Uther was near his end, and it seemed not only necessary, but right, that he should declare his successor straight away, near the field where Arthur had in a fashion declared himself. And if there was no bishop present, what of it? This was a victory feast and was held, so to speak, still in the field.

The house where the King held court in Luguvallium was packed to the doors, and well beyond them. Outside, in the town and around it, where the troops held their own celebration, the air was blue with the smoke of fires, and thick with the smell of roasting meat. Officers on their way to the King's feast had to work quite hard to turn a blind eye to the drunkenness in camp and street, and a deaf ear to the squeals and giggles coming from quarters where women were not commonly allowed to be.

I hardly saw Arthur all day. He was closeted with the King until afternoon, and in the end only left to allow his father to rest before the feast. I spent most of the day in the hospital. It was peaceful there, compared with the crush near the royal apartments. All day, it seemed, the corridors outside my rooms and Arthur's were besieged; by men who wanted favours from the new prince, or just his notice; by men who wanted to talk with me, or to court my favour by gifts; or simply by the curious. I let it be known that Arthur was with the King, and would speak with no one before the time of the feast. To the guards I gave private orders that if Lot should seek me out, I was to be called. But he made no approach. Nor, according to the servants I questioned, was he to be seen in the town.

But I took no chances, and early that morning sent to Caius Valerius, a King's officer and an old acquaintance of mine, for extra guards for my rooms and Arthur's, to reinforce the duty sentries outside the main door, in the antechamber, and even at the windows. And before I went to the hospital I made my way to the King's rooms, to have a word with Ulfin.

It may perhaps seem strange that a prophet who had seen Arthur's crowning so plain and clear and ringed with light should take such pains to guard him from his enemies. But those who have had to do with the gods know that when those gods make promises they hide them in light, and a smile on a god's lips is not always a sign that you may take his favour for granted. Men have a duty to make sure. The gods like the taste of salt; the sweat of human effort is the savour of their sacrifices.

The guards on duty at the King's door lifted their spears without a challenge and let me straight through into the outer chamber. Here pages and servants waited, while in the second chamber sat the women who helped to nurse the King. Ulfin was, as ever, beside the door of the King's room. He rose when he saw me, and we talked for a little while, of the King's health, of Arthur, of the events of yesterday and the prospects for tonight; then—we were talking softly, apart from the women—I asked him:

"You knew Morgause had left the court?"

"I heard so, yes. Nobody knows why."

"Her sister Morgian is waiting in York for the wedding," I said, "and anxious for her company."

"Oh, yes, we heard that." It was to be inferred from the woodenness of his expression that nobody had believed it.

"Did she come to see the King?" I asked.

"Three times." Ulfin smiled. It was apparent that Morgause was no favourite of his. "And each time she was turned away because the prince was still with him."

A favoured daughter for twenty years, and forgotten in as many hours for a true-born son. *"You were a bastard, too,"* she had reminded me. Years ago, I remembered, I had wondered what would become of her. She had had position and authority of a sort here with Uther, and might well have been fond of him. She had (the King had hinted yesterday) refused marriage to stay near him. Perhaps I had been too harsh with her, driven by the horror of foreknowledge and my own single-minded love for the boy. I hesitated, then asked him: "Did she seem much distressed?"

"Distressed?" said Ulfin crisply. "No, she looked angry. She's bad to cross, is that lady. Always been so, from a child. One of her maids was crying, too; I think she'd been whipped." He nodded towards one of the pages, a fair boy, very young, kicking his heels at a window. "He was the one sent to turn her away the last time, and she laid his cheek open with her nails."

"Then tell him to take care it does not fester," I said, and such was my tone that Ulfin looked sharply at me, cocking a brow. I nodded. "Yes, it was I who sent her away. Nor did she go willingly. You'll know why, one day. Meanwhile, I take it that you look in now and again upon the King? The interview isn't tiring him overmuch?"

"On the contrary, he's better than I've seen him for some time. You'd think the boy was a well to drink at; the King never takes his eyes from him, and gains strength by the hour. They'll take their midday meal together."

"Ah. Then it will be tasted? That's what I came to ask."

"Of course. You can be easy, my lord. The prince will be safe."

"The King must take some rest before the feast."

He nodded. "I've persuaded him to sleep this afternoon after he has eaten."

"Then will you also—which will be more difficult—persuade the prince that he should do the same? Or, if not rest, then at least go straight to his rooms, and stay in them till the hour of feasting?"

Ulfin looked dubious. "Will he consent to that?"

"If you tell him that the order—but you'd better call it a request—came from me."

"I'll do that, my lord."

"I shall be in the hospital. You'll send for me, of course, if the King needs me. But in any case you must send to tell me the moment the prince leaves him."

It was about the middle of the afternoon when the fair-haired page brought the message. The King was resting, he told me, and the prince had gone to his rooms. When Ulfin had given the prince my message the latter had scowled, impatient, and had said sharply (this part of the message came demurely, verbatim) that he was damned if he'd skulk indoors for the rest of the day. But when Ulfin had said the message came from Prince Merlin the prince had stopped short, shrugged, and then gone to his rooms without further word.

"Then I shall go, too," I said. "But first, child, let me see that scratched cheek." When I had put salve on it, and sent him scampering back to Ulfin, I made my way through corridors more thronged than ever to my rooms.

Arthur was by the window. He turned when he heard me.

"Bedwyr is here, did you know? I saw him, but could not get near. I sent a message that we'd ride out this afternoon. Now you say I may not."

"I'm sorry. There will be other times to talk to Bedwyr, better than this."

"Heaven and earth, they couldn't be worse! This place stifles me. What do they want with me, that pack in the corridors outside?"

"What most men want of their prince and future King. You will have to get used to it."

"So it seems. There's even a guard here, outside the window."

"I know. I put him there." Then, answering his look: "You have enemies, Arthur. Have I not made it clear?"

"Shall I always have to be hemmed in like this, surrounded? One might as well be a prisoner."

"Once you are undoubted King you can make your own dispositions. But until then, you must be guarded. Remember that here we are only in an emergency camp: once in the King's capital, or in one of his strong castles, you'll have your own houshold, chosen by yourself. You'll be able to see all you want of Bedwyr, or Cei, or anyone else you may appoint. It will be freedom of a sort, as much as you can ever have now. Neither you nor I can go back to the Wild Forest again, Emrys. That's over."

"It was better there," he said, then gave me a gentle look, and smiled. "Merlin."

"What is it?"

He started to say something, changed his mind, shook his head instead and said abruptly: "At this feast tonight. You'll be near me?"

"Be sure of it."

"The King has told me how he will present me to the nobles. Do you know what will happen then? These enemies you speak of—"

"Will try to prevent the assembly from accepting you as Uther's heir."

He considered for a moment, briefly. "May they carry arms in the hall?"

"No. They'll try some other way."

"Do you know how?"

I said: "They can hardly deny your birth to the King's face, and with me there and Count Ector they can't quarrel with your identity. They can only try to discredit you; shake the faith of the waverers, and try to swing the army's vote. It's your enemies' misfortune that this has come on a battlefield where the army outnumbers the council of nobles three to one—and after yesterday the army will take some convincing that you are not fit to lead them. It's my guess that there will be something staged, something that will take men by surprise and shake their belief in you, even in Uther."

"And in you, Merlin?"

I smiled. "It's the same thing. I'm sorry, I can't see further yet than that. I can see death and darkness, but not for you."

"For the King?" he asked sharply.

I did not answer. He was silent for a moment, watching me, then, as if I had answered, he nodded, and asked:

"Who are these enemies?"

"They are led by the King of Lothian."

"Ah," he said, and I could see he had not let his senses be stifled through the brief hours of that crowded day. He had seen and heard, watched and listened. "And Urien who runs with him, and Tudwal of Dinpelydr, and—whose is the green badge with the wolverine?"

"Aguisel's. Did the King say anything to you about these men?"

He shook his head. "We talked mostly of the past. Of course he has heard all about me from you and Ector over these past years, and"—he laughed—"I doubt if any son ever knew more about his father and his father's father than I, with all you have told me; but telling is not the same. There was a lot of knowing to make up."

He talked on for a little about the interview with the King, speaking of the missed years without regret, and with the cool common sense that I had come to see was part of his character. That much, I thought, was not from Uther; I had seen it in Ambrosius, and in myself, in what men called coldness. Arthur had been able to stand back from the events of his youth; he had thought the thing through, and with the clear sight that would make him a king he had set feeling aside and come to the truth. Even when he went on to speak of his mother it was evident that he saw the matter much as Ygraine had done, and with the same hard expediency of outlook. "If I had known that my mother was still alive, and had been so willingly parted from me, it might have come hard to me, as a child. But you and Ector spared me that by telling me she was dead, and now I see it as you say she saw it; that to be a prince one must be ruled always by necessity. She did not give me up for nothing." He smiled, but his voice was still serious. "It was true as I told you. I was better in the Wild Forest thinking myself motherless, and your bastard, than waiting yearly in my father's castle for the Queen to bear another child to supplant me."

In all those years I had never seen it so. I had been blinded by my larger purposes, thinking all the time of his safety, of the kingdom's future, of the gods' will. Until the boy Emrys had burst into my life that morning in the Wild Forest, he had hardly been a person to me, only a symbol, another life (as it were) for my father, a tool for me. After I came to know and love him I had seen only the deprivations we had subjected him to, with his high temper and leaping ambition to be first and best, and his quick generosity and affection. It was no use telling myself that without me he might never have come near his heritage at all; I had lived with guilt for all that he had been robbed of.

No question but that he had felt the deprivation, the bite of dispossession. But even here, even now in the moment of finding himself, he could see clearly what that princely childhood would have meant. I knew he was right. Even apart from the daily dangers, he would have had a hard time of it beside Uther, and the high qualities, wasting with time and hope deferred, might have turned sour. But the admission, to absolve me, had to come from him. Now it lifted my guilt from me as cool air lifts a marsh mist.

He was still speaking of his father. "I like him," he said. "He has been a good king as far as it was in him. Standing apart from him as I have done, I have been able to listen to men talking, and to judge. But as a father—as to how we would have dealt together, that's another matter. There is time still to know my mother. She will need comfort soon, I think."

He referred only once, briefly, to Morgause.

"They say she has left the town?"

"She went this morning while you were with the King."

"You spoke with her? How did she take it?"

"Without distress," I said, with perfect truth. "You needn't fear for her."

"Did you send her away?"

"I advised her to go. As I advise you to put it out of your mind. For the moment, at any rate, there is nothing to be done. Except—I suggest—sleep . . . Today has been hard, and will be harder for both of us before it's done. So if you can forget the crowds outside and the guard beyond the window, I suggest we both sleep till sundown."

He yawned suddenly, widely, like a young cat, then laughed. "Have you put a spell on me to make sure of it? Suddenly I feel I could sleep for a week. . . . All right, I'll do as you say, but may I send a message to Bedwyr?"

He did not speak of Morgause again, and I think that soon, in the final preparations for the evening's feast, he forgot her. Certainly the haunted look of the morning had left him, and it seemed to me that no shadow touched him now; doubt and apprehension would have wisped off his charged and shining youth like water-drops from white-hot metal. Even if he had guessed, as I did, what the future held—that it was greater than he could have imagined, and in the end more terrible—I doubt if it would have dimmed his brightness. When one is fourteen, death at forty seems still to be several lifetimes away.

An hour after sundown, they came for us to lead us to the hall of feasting.

8

The hall was packed to the doors. If the place had seemed crowded before, by the time the trumpets sounded for the feast there was barely breathing-room in the corridors; it seemed as if even those sturdy Roman-built walls must bulge and crumble under the press of excited humanity. For rumour had run like a forest fire through the countryside that this was no ordinary victory feast, and even from parts of the province twenty or thirty miles off people were pouring into Luguvallium to be there for the great occasion.

It would have been impossible to sift and select the followers of those privileged nobles who were allowed into the main hall where the King would sit. At a feast of this kind men expected to leave their weapons outside, and this was enforced, till the antechamber, stacked as it was with thickets of spears and swords, looked like a grove of the Wild Forest. More than this the guards could not do, save run an eye over each man's person as he entered the hall, to see that he carried only the knife or dagger he needed for his food.

By the time the company was assembled the sky outside was paling to dusk, and torches were lit. Soon, with the smoky torchlight and the mild evening, the food and wine and talk and laughter, the place was uncomfortably warm, and I watched the King anxiously. He seemed in good enough spirits, but his colour was too high and his skin had a glazed, transparent look that I have seen before in men who are pushed to the limits of their strength. But he was perfectly in command of himself, talking cheerfully and courteously to Arthur on his right, and to the others about him, though at times he would fall into silence and seem to be drifting, forgetfully, into some place far away from which he would recall himself with a jerk. At one point he asked me—I was seated on his left—if I knew why Morgause had not come to see him that day. He asked without concern, without even much interest; it was obvious that he had not taken in the fact that she had left the court. I told him that she had wanted to go to her sister at York, and that since the King had been unable to see her I myself had given her permission, and sent her with an escort. I added quickly that the King need have no fears for his health, since I was here and would attend him personally. He nodded and thanked me, but as if my offer of help was something no longer needed: "I have had the best doctors I could have had this day; victory, and this boy beside me." He laid a hand on Arthur's arm, and laughed. "You heard what the Saxon dogs were calling me? The half-dead King. I heard them shouting it when I was carried forward in my chair . . . And so in truth I think I was, but now I have both victory and life."

He had spoken clearly, and men leaned forward to listen, and afterwards murmured approval, while the King went back to picking at his food. Ulfin and I had both warned him that he must eat and drink sparingly, but there had been no need for such advice; he had little appetite, and Ulfin saw to it that his wine was well watered. And Arthur's, too. He sat beside his father, his back straight as a spear, and the tension and excitement of the occasion had taken some of the colour from his cheeks. For once he hardly seemed to notice what he was eating. He spoke little, and then only when he was addressed, answering briefly and obviously only for courtesy. Most of the time he sat silent, his eyes on the throng in the hall below the royal dais. I, who knew him, could see what he was doing; he was telling over face by face, blazon by blazon, the toll of the men who were there, and noting where they sat. Noting also how they looked. This face was hostile, that friendly, this undecided and ready to be swayed by promises of power or gain, that foolish or merely curious. I could read them myself, as clearly as if they were red and white pieces ready on the board to play, but for a youth not yet turned fifteen, and on such a highly charged occasion, it was a marvel that he could collect himself to watch them so. Years afterwards he was still able to tally exactly the forces which assembled for and against him that first night of his power. Only twice did that cool look linger and soften; on Ector, not far from where we sat, solid, dependable Ector, beaming a little moist-eyed across his wine as he watched his foster-son jewelled and resplendent in white and silver at the High King's side. (I thought that Cei's glance beside him was less than enthusiastic, but Cei had, at best, low brows and a narrow face that gave even his enthusiasms a grudging look.) Down the hall, beside his father the King of Benoic, was Bedwyr, his plain face flushed and his soul, as they say, in his eyes. The two boys' eyes met and met again during the feasting. Here, already, the next strong thread was being woven of the new kingdom's pattern.

The feast wore on. I watched Uther carefully, wondering if he could last until the proclamation was made and the thing done, or if he would lack the strength to see it through. In which case I would have to choose the moment to intervene, or the work would have to be done with fighting. But his strength held. At last he looked round and raised a hand, and the trumpets rang out for silence. The clamour hushed, and all eyes turned to the high table. This had been deliberately raised, for it was beyond the King's strength to stand. Even so, upright in his great chair, with the blaze of lights and banners behind him, he looked alert and splendid, commanding silence.

He laid his hands along the carved arms of his chair, and began to speak. He was smiling.

"My lords, you all know why we are met here tonight. Colgrim has been put to flight, and his brother Badulf, and already reports have been coming back that the enemy is fled in disorder back towards the coast, beyond the wild lands to the north." He went on to speak of the previous day's victory, as decisive, he said, as his brother's victory at Kaerconan had been, and as potent an augury for the future. "The power of our enemies, which has been massing and threatening for so many years, is broken and driven back for a time. We have a breathing space. But more important than this, my lords, we have seen how this breathing space was won; we have seen what unity can do, and what we might suffer from the lack of it. Singly, what could we do, the kings of the north, the kings of the south and west? But together, held and fighting together, with one leader and one plan, we can thrust the sword of Macsen again into the heart of the enemy."

He had spoken, of course, figuratively, but I caught Arthur's half-start of recollection, and the flash of a glance across at me, before he went back to his steady scrutiny of the hall.

The King had paused. Ulfin, behind him, moved forward with a goblet of wine, but the King motioned it aside, and began to speak again. His voice was stronger, with the ring almost of his old vigour. "For this is a lesson which the last years have taught us. There must be one leader, one strong High King to whom all the kingdoms pay undoubted homage. Without this, we are back where we were before the Romans came. We are divided and lost as Gaul and Germany have been divided and lost; we splinter into small peoples, fighting each other as wolves do for food and space, and never turning against the common enemy; we become a submerged province of Rome, sliding with her to her downfall, instead of a new kingdom emerging as a unit with its own laws, its own people, its own gods. With the right king, faithfully followed, I believe that this will come. Who knows, the Dragon of Britain may be lifted, if not as high as the Eagles of Rome, then with a pride and a vision that will be even farther seen."

The silence was absolute. It could have been Ambrosius speaking. Or Maximus himself, I thought. So do the gods speak when they are waited for.

This time the pause was longer. The King had contrived that it should seem like an orator's, a pause to gather eyes, but I saw how his hands whitened on the chair-arms, how carefully he used the pause to gather strength. I thought I was the only one who noticed; hardly an eye was on Uther, they all watched the boy at his right. All, that is, except the King of Lothian; he was watching the High King, with a kind of eagerness in his face. Ulfin, as the King paused, was beside him again with the goblet; catching my eye, he touched it to his own lips, tasted, then gave it to the King, who drank. There was no way of disguising the tremor in the hand which raised the goblet to his mouth, but before he could betray his weakness further, Ulfin had gently taken the thing from his hand, and set it down. All this, I saw, Lot had followed, still with that same concentrated eagerness. He must recognize how sick Uther was, and minute by minute he must be hoping for the High King's strength to fail him. Either Morgause had told him, or he had guessed what I knew for certain, that Uther would not live long enough physically to establish Arthur on the throne, and that in the free-for-all which might develop round the person of so young a ruler, Arthur's enemies would find their chance.

When Uther began to speak again his voice had lost much of its vigour, but the silence was so complete that he hardly needed to raise it. Even those men who had drunk too much were solemnly intent as the King began to speak again about the battle, about those who had distinguished themselves, and the men who had fallen; finally, about the part Arthur had played in saving the day, and then about Arthur himself.

"You have all known, for these many years, that my son by Ygraine my Queen was being nurtured and trained for the kingship in lands away from these, and in hands stronger than, alas, my own have been since my malady overtook me. You have known that when the time came, and he was grown, he would be declared by name, Arthur, as my heir, and your new King. Now be it known to all men where their lawful prince has spent the years of his youth; first under the protection of my cousin Hoel of Brittany, then in the house of my faithful servant and fellow-soldier, Count Ector of Galava. And all the time he has been guarded and taught by my kinsman Merlin called Ambrosius, to whose hands he was committed at his birth, and whose fitness for the guardianship no man can question. Nor will you question the reasons which prompted me to send the prince away until such time as he might publicly be shown to you. It is a practice common enough among the great, to rear their children in other courts, where they may stay unspoiled by arrogance, uncorrupted by flattery, and safe from the contriving of treachery and ambition." He waited for a moment to regain his breath. He was looking down at the table as he spoke, and met no one's eyes, but here and there a man shifted in his seat or glanced at another; and Arthur's cool gaze took note of it.

The King went on: "And those of you who had wondered what sort of shifts might be used to train a prince, other than sending him as a boy into battle, and into council alongside his father, have seen yesterday how he received the King's sword easily from the King's hand, and led the troops to victory as surely as if he had been High King himself and a seasoned warrior."

Uther's breath was short now, and his colour bad. I saw Lot's eyes intent, and Ulfin's worried look. Cador was frowning. I thought briefly back, with thankfulness, to the talk I had had with him beside the lake. Cador and Lot: had Cador been less his father's son, how easy it would have been for the two of them to tear the land north and south, parcel it out between them like a pair of fighting dogs, while the landless pup whined starving.

"And so," said the High King, and in the silence his gasping breath was horribly apparent, "I present to you all my true born and only son, Arthur called Pendragon, who will be High King after my death, and who will carry my sword in battle from this time on."

He reached his hand to Arthur, and the boy stood up, straight and unsmiling, while the shouting and the cheering went roaring up into the smoky roof. The noise must have been heard clear through the town. When men paused to draw breath the echoes of the acclamation could be heard running out through the streets as a fire runs through stubble on a dry day. There was approval in the shouting, there was obvious relief that at last the issue was clear, and there was joy. I saw Arthur, cool as a cloud, assessing which lay where. But from where I sat I could also see the pulse leaping below the rigid jawline. He stood as a swordsman stands, at rest after one victory, but alert for the next challenge.

It came. Clear above the shouting and the thumping of drinking-vessels on the boards came Lot's voice, harsh and carrying.

"I challenge the choice, King Uther!"

It was like throwing a boulder down into the path of a fast-flowing stream. The noise checked; men stared, muttered, shifted and looked about them. Then all at once it could be seen that the stream divided. There was cheering still for Arthur and the King's choice, but here and there were shouts of "Lothian! Lothian!" and through it all Lot said strongly: "An untried boy? A boy who has seen one battle? I tell you, Colgrim will be back all too soon, and are we to have a boy to lead us? If you must hand on your sword, King Uther, hand it to a tried and seasoned leader, to be held in trust for this young boy when he is grown!" He finished the challenge with a crash of his fist on the table, and round him the clamour broke out again: "Lothian! Lothian!" and then farther off down the hall, confusedly, other challenges being shouted down by "Pendragon!" and "Cornwall!" and even "Arthur!" It was to be seen then, as the clamour mounted, that only the fact that men were unarmed prevented worse things than insults being hurled from side to side of the hall. The servants had backed to the walls, and chamberlains bustled here and there, white-faced and placatory. The King, ashen, threw up a hand, but the gesture went almost unnoticed. Arthur neither moved nor spoke, but he had gone rather pale.

"My lords! My lords!" Uther was shaking, but with rage; and rage, as I knew, was as dangerous to him as a spear thrust. I saw that Lot knew it, too. I laid a hand on Uther's arm. "All will be well," I told him softly. "Sit back now and let them shout it out. Look, Ector is speaking."

"My lord King!" Ector's voice was brisk, friendly, matter-of-fact, cooling the atmosphere in the hall. He spoke as if addressing the King alone. The effect was noticeable; the hall grew quiet as men strained to hear him. "My lord King, the King of Lothian has challenged your choice. He has a right to speak, as all your subjects have a right to speak before you, but not to challenge, not even to question, what you have said tonight." Raising his voice a little he turned to the listening hall. "My lords, this is not a matter of choice or election; a king's heir is begotten, not chosen by him, and where chance has provided such a begetting as this, what question is there? Look at him now, this prince who has been presented to you. He has been in my household for ten years, and I, my lords, knowing him as I do, tell you that here is a prince to be followed—not later, not 'when he is further grown,' but now. Even if I could not stand before you here to attest his birth, you have only to look at him and to think back to yesterday's field, to know that here, with all fortune and God's blessing, we have our true and rightful King. This is not open to challenge, even to question. Look at him, my lords, and remember yesterday! Who more fit to unite the kings from all the corners of Britain? Who more fit to wield his father's sword?"

There were shouts of "True! True!" and "What doubt can there be? He is Pendragon, and therefore our King!" and a hubbub of voices that was louder and more confused even than before. Briefly, I remembered my father's councils, their power and order; then I saw again how Uther shook, ashen in his great chair. The times were different; this was the way he had had to do it; he could not enforce it other than by public acclaim.

Before he could speak, Lot was smoothly on his feet again. He was no longer shouting; he spoke weightily, with an air of reason, and a courteous inclination towards Ector. "It was not the prince's begetting that I challenged, it was the fitness of a young and untried youth to lead us. We know that the battle yesterday was only the preliminary, the first move in a longer and more deadly fight even than Ambrosius faced, a struggle such as we have not seen since the days of Maximus. We need better leadership than is shown by a day's luck in a skirmish. We need, not a sick king's deputy, but a man vested with all the authority and God-given blessing of an anointed ruler. If this young prince is indeed fit to carry his father's sword, would his father be content to yield it to him now, before us all?"

Silence again, for three heart-beats. Every man there knew what it meant for the King formally to hand over the royal sword; it was abdication. Only I, of all the men in the hall except perhaps Ulfin, knew that it mattered nothing whether or not Uther abdicated now; Arthur would be King before night. But Uther did not know, and whether, even knowing his weakness, Uther was great enough to renounce publicly the power which had been the breath of life to him was not known even to me. He was sitting quite straight, apparently impassive, and only one as near to him as I could see how the palsy from time to time shook his body, so that light shivered in the circlet of red gold that bound his brow, and shook in the jewels on his fingers. I rose quietly from my chair and went to stand close beside him, at his left hand. Arthur, frowning, glanced questioningly at me. I shook my head at him.

The King licked his lips, hesitating. Lot's change of tone had puzzled him, as, it could be seen, it had puzzled others in the hall. But it had also relieved the waverers, those who were scared by the idea of rebellion, but found relief from their fear of the future in his air of reason and his deference to the High King. There were murmurs of approval and agreement. Lot spread his hands wide, as if including with him everyone in the body of the hall, and said, with that air of speaking reasonably for all of them: "My lords, if we could but see the King give his chosen heir the royal sword with his own hands, what could we do but acknowledge him? Afterwards, it will be time enough to discuss how best to face the coming wars."

Arthur's head turned slightly, like a hound's that catches an unfamiliar scent. Ector too looked round at the other men, surprised perhaps and distrustful of the apparent capitulation. Cador, silent at the other side of the room, stared at Lot as though he would drag his soul out from his eyes. Uther bent his head slightly, a gesture of abnegation which became him like nothing I had seen in him before.

"I am willing."

A chamberlain went running. Uther leaned back in the great chair, shaking his head as Ulfin proffered wine again. I dropped a hand unobtrusively to the wrist beside me; his pulse was all anyhow, a grasshopper pulse in a wrist gone suddenly frail and stringy, which before had been narrow with nerve and sinew. His lips were dry, and his tongue came out to moisten them. He said softly: "There's some trick here, but I can't see it. Can you?"

"Not yet."

"He has no real following. Not even among the army, after yesterday. But now . . . you may have to deal with it. They don't want facts, or even promises. You know them, what they want is a sign. Can you not give them one?"

"I don't know. Not yet. The gods come when they come."

Arthur had caught the whisper. He was as tight as a strung bow. Then he looked across the hall, and I saw his mouth relax slightly. I followed his look. It was Bedwyr, scarlet with fury, held down forcibly in his seat by his father's heavy hand. Otherwise I think that he would have been at Lot's throat with his bare hands.

The chamberlain came running, with Uther's battle sword laid, scabbarded, across his palms. The rubies in the hilt glinted balefully. The scabbard was of silver gilded, crusted with fine gold-work and gems. There was no man there but had seen the sword a hundred times at Uther's side. The man laid it flat on the table in front of the King. Uther's thin hand went out to the hilt, the fingers curving round it without thinking, fitting to the guard, a caress rather than a grip, the hold of the good fighting man. Arthur watched him, and I could see the flicker of puzzlement between his brows. He was thinking of the sword in the stone up there in the Wild Forest, wondering no doubt where that came into this formal scene of abdication.

But I, as the fire from the great rubies burned against my eyes, knew at last what the gods were doing. It was clear from the beginning, fire and dragon-star and the sword in the stone. And the message did not come through the smoke from the doubly-smiling god, it was clear as the flame in the ruby. Uther's sword would fail, as Uther himself had failed. But the other would not. It had come by water and by land and lay waiting now for this, to bring Arthur his kingdom, and keep and hold it, and afterwards go from men's sight for ever. . . .

The King laid firm hold of the hilt, and drew his sword. "I, Uther Pendragon, do by this token give to Arthur my son—"

There was a great gasp, then a hubbub of noise. Men cried out fearfully, "A sign! A sign!" and someone shouted, "Death! It means death!" and the whispers that had been stilled by victory, waking again: "What hope for us, a wasted land, and a maimed king, and a boy without a sword?"

As the sword came clear of the scabbard Uther lurched to his feet. He held it crookedly, half-lifted, staring down at it with ashen face and his mouth half open, struck still like a man out of his wits. The sword was broken. A handspan from the point the metal had snapped jaggedly, and the break shone raw and bright in the torchlight.

The King made some sound; it was as if he tried to speak, but the words choked in his throat. The sword sank with a clatter to the board. As his legs failed under him, Ulfin and I took him gently by the arms and eased him back into his chair. Arthur moved, fast as a mountain cat, to bend over him. "Sir? Sir?"

The he straightened slowly, his eyes on me. There was no need for me to tell him what every man in the hall could see. Uther was dead.

9

Uther dead did more than Uther dying could have done to control the panic that had swept the hall. Every man there was held, silent and still, on his feet, watching the High King as we lowered him gently against the back of the chair. In the stillness the flames in the torches rustled like silk, and the goblet Ulfin had dropped rolled ringing in a half circle and back again. I leaned forward over the dead King and closed his eyes.

Then Lot's voice, collected and forceful: "A sign indeed! A dead king and a broken sword! Do you still say, Ector, that God has appointed this boy to lead us against the Saxon invader? A maimed land indeed, with nothing between us and the Terror but a boy with a broken sword!"

Confusion again. Men shouting, turning to one another, staring about them in fear and amazement. Part of my mind noted, coldly, that Lot had not been surprised. Arthur, eyes blazing in a face paler than ever with shock, straightened from his father's body and whipped round to face the shouting in the hall, but I said swiftly, "No. Wait," and he obeyed me. But his hand had dropped to his dagger and gripped there, whitening. I doubt if he knew it, or, knowing, could have stopped himself. The turmoil of astonishment and fear jarred from wall to wall like waves in the wind.

Through the commotion came Ector's voice again, harsh and shaken, but sturdily matter-of-fact as before, brushing aside the strands of superstitious fear like a broom clearing cobwebs. "My lords! Is this seemly? Our High King is dead, here before our eyes. Dare we oppose his plain will when his eyes are hardly closed? We all saw what caused his death, the sight of the royal sword, which yesterday was whole, broken in its sheath. Are we to let this—accident"—he dropped the word heavily into the hush—"frighten us like children from doing what it is plain that we should do? If you look for a sign, there it is." He pointed at Arthur, standing straight as a pine beside the dead King's chair. "As one king falls, another is ready in his place. God sent him today for this. We must acknowledge him."

A pause, full of murmuring, while men looked at one another. There were nods, and shouts of agreement, but here and there still looks of doubt, and voices calling out, "But the sword? The broken sword?"

Ector said sturdily: "King Lot here called it a sign, this broken sword. A sign of what? I say, my lords, of treachery! This sword did not break in the High King's hand, nor in his son's."

"That's true," said another voice forcibly. Bedwyr's father, the King of Benoic, was on his feet. "We all saw it, whole in the battle. And by God, we saw it used!"

"But since then?" The questions came from every quarter of the hall. "Afterwards? Would the King have sent for it had he known it to be broken?" Then from some speaker at the end of the hall, invisible in the press: "But would the High King have consented to hand it to the boy, if it had still been whole?" And another voice, which I thought was Urien's: "He knew he was dying. He gave up the maimed land with the broken sword. It is for the strongest now to take up the kingship."

Ector, darkly flushed, broke in again: "I spoke the truth when I talked of treachery! In good time did the High King present his heir to us, or Britain would indeed be maimed, torn apart by disloyal dogs such as you, Urien of Gore!"

Urien shouted with anger, and his hand went to his dagger. Lot spoke to him, sharply, under cover of the tumult, and he subsided. Lot was smiling, his eyes narrow and watchful. His voice came smoothly: "We all know what interest Count Ector has in proclaiming his ward High King."

There was a sudden, still pause. I saw Ector glance round him, as if he would have conjured a weapon out of the air. Arthur's hand clenched tighter on his dagger's hilt. Then suddenly there was a stir from the right of the hall, where Cador stood forward among his men. The white Boar of Cornwall stretched and hunched itself on his sleeve as he moved. He looked round for quiet, and got it. Lot turned his head quickly; it was evident that he did not know what to expect. Ector controlled himself and subsided, rumbling. All around I saw the frightened men, the waverers, the time-servers, looking to Cador as men look for a lead in danger.

Cador's voice was clear and totally lacking in emotion. "What Ector says is true. I myself saw the High King's sword after the battle, when his son handed it back to him. It was whole and unmarked, save with the blood of the enemy."

"Then how is it broken? Is it treachery? Who broke it?"

"Who indeed?" said Cador. "Not the gods, for sure, whatever King Lot may think. The gods do not break the swords of the kings they favour with victory. They give them, and give them whole."

"Then if Arthur is our king," cried someone, "what sword have they given him?"

Cador looked up the hall: it was to be seen that he was expecting me to speak. But I said nothing. I had drawn back to stand behind Arthur in the shadow of the King's great chair. It was my place, and it was time they saw me take it. There was a kind of waiting pause, as heads turned to where I stood, a black shadow behind the boy's white and silver. Men shuffled and murmured. There were those here who had known my power, and there was no man present who doubted it. Not even Lot; the whites of his eyes showed as he looked askance. But when I still did not speak, there were smiles. I could see the tension in Arthur's shoulders and I spoke to him in silence with my will. *"Not yet, Arthur, not yet. Wait."*

He was silent. He had picked up the broken sword, and was gently fitting it back into its scabbard. As it went, it gave one sharp flash and then was quenched.

"You see?" said Cador to the hall. "Uther's sword is gone, and so is he. But Arthur has a sword, his own, and greater than this royal one that men have broken. The gods gave it to him. I saw it in his hand myself."

"When?" they asked. "Where? What gods? What sword was this?"

Cador waited, smiling, for the buzz of questions to die. He stood easily, a big man with that air of his of relaxed but ready power. Lot was biting his lip, and frowning. There was sweat thick on his forehead, and his eyes shifted round the hall, reckoning the tally of those who still supported him. From his look, he had still hoped that Cador might range himself against Arthur.

Cador had not looked at him. "I saw him once with Merlin," he told the company, "up in the Wild Forest, and he carried a sword more splendid than any I have seen before, jewelled like an Emperor's, and with a blade of light so bright that it turned the eyes."

Lot cleared his throat. "An illusion. It was done by magic. You said Merlin was there. We all know what that means. If Merlin is Arthur's master—"

A man interrupted, smallish, with black hair and a high colour. I recognized Gwyl from the western coast, on whose hills the druids meet still. "And if it was magic, what then? Look you, a king who has magic in his hand is a king to follow."

This brought a yell of approval. Fists hammered on the tables. Many of the men in the hall were mountain Celts, and this was talk they understood. "That is true, that is true! Strength is good, but of what use is it without luck? And our new King, though he is young, has both. It was true what Uther said, good training and good counsel. What better counsel could he have, than Merlin to stand beside him?"

"Good training indeed," shouted a boy's voice, "that doesn't hang back in battle till it's almost too late!" It was Bedwyr, forgetting himself. His father quenched him with a cuff to the side of the head, but the blow fell lightly, and the admonitory hand slid over to ruffle the boy's hair. There were smiles. The heat was cooling. The ferment brought about by the stroke of superstitious fear had passed, and men were calming, ready now to listen and to think. One or two who had seemed to favour Lot and his faction were seen to withdraw a little from him. Then someone called out: "Why doesn't Merlin speak? Merlin knows what we should do. Let him tell us!" Then the shouting began: "Merlin! Merlin! Let Merlin speak!"

I let them shout for a few minutes. Then when they were ready to tear the hall stone from stone to hear me, I spoke. I neither moved nor raised my voice, standing there between the dead King and the living one, but they hushed, listening.

"I have two things to tell you," I said. "First, that the King of Lothian was wrong. I am not Arthur's master. I am his servant. And the second is what the Duke of Cornwall has already told you; that between us and the Saxon Terror is a King, young and whole, with a sword given straight into his hand by God."

Lot could see the moment slipping from him. He looked around him, shouting: "A fine sword indeed, that appears in his hand as an illusion, and vanishes from it in battle!"

"Don't be a fool," said Ector gruffly. "That was one I lent him that was cut from him in the fight. My second best, too, so I'm not repining."

Someone laughed. There were smiles, and when Lot spoke again there was defeat under the sick rage in his voice. "Then where did he get this sword of marvels, and where is it now?"

I said: "He went alone to Caer Bannog and lifted it from its place below the lake."

Silence. There was no one here who did not know what that meant. I saw hands moving to make the sign against enchantment.

Cador stirred. "It is true. I myself saw Arthur come back from Caer Bannog with the thing in his hand, wrapped in an old scabbard as if it had lain in hiding for a hundred years."

"Which it had," I said into the silence. "Listen, my lords, and I will tell you what sword this is. It is the sword which Macsen Wledig took to Rome, and which was brought back to Britain by his people and hidden until it should please the gods to lead a King's son to find it. Must I remind you of the prophecy? It was not my prophecy, it was made before I was born; that the sword should come by water and by land, treasured in darkness and locked in stone, until he should come who is rightwise king born of all Britain, and lift it from its hiding-place. And there it has lain, my lords, safe in Caer Bannog, in Bilis' castle, until by magic signs sent from the gods did Arthur find it, and lifted it easily into his hand."

"Show us!" they cried. "Show us!"

"I shall show you. The sword lies now on the altar in the chapel of the Wild Forest where I laid it. It shall lie there till Arthur lifts it in the sight of you all."

Lot was beginning to be afraid; they were against him now, and by his actions he had confirmed himself as Arthur's enemy. But so far I had spoken quietly, without power, and he still saw a chance. The obstinacy which had driven him, and the stupidity of his own hope of power, sustained him now. "I have seen that sword, the sword in the altar of the Green Chapel. Many of you have seen it! It is Macsen's sword, yes, but it is made of stone!"

I moved then. I lifted my arms high. From somewhere, a breeze ran in through the open windows and stirred the coloured hangings so that behind Arthur the scarlet Dragon clawed up the golden banner, and sent my shadow towering like the Dragon's shadow, with arms raised like wings. The power was here. I heard it in my voice.

"And from the stone has he lifted it, and will lift it again, in the sight of you all. And from this day on, the chapel shall be called the Chapel Perilous, for if any man who is not the rightful King shall so much as touch the sword, it shall burn like levin in his hand."

Someone in the crowd said strongly: "If he has indeed got the sword of Macsen, he got it by God's gift, and if he has Merlin beside him, then by any god he follows, I follow him!"

"And I," said Cador.

"And I! And I!" came the shouts from the hall. "Let us all see this magic sword and this perilous altar!"

Every man was on his feet. The shouting rose and echoed in the roof. "Arthur! Arthur!"

I dropped my arms. *"Now, Arthur, it is now."*

He had not once looked at me, but he heard my thought, and I felt the power going out of me towards him. I could see it growing round him as he stood there, and every man in the hall could see it too. He raised a hand, and they waited for him. His voice came clear and firm: no boy's voice, but that of a man who has fought his first decisive battles, there in the field, and here in the hall.

"My lords. You saw how fate sent me to my father without a sword, as was fitting. Now treachery has broken the weapon he would have given me, and treachery has tried to take with it my birthright that is proven in front of you all, and was attested by my father the High King in open hall. But as Merlin has told you, God had already put another, greater weapon into my hand, and I shall indeed take it up in front of you all, as soon as I may come with all this company, to the Perilous Chapel."

He paused. It is not easy to speak after the gods have spoken. He finished simply, cool water after the flames. The torches had died to red and my shadow had dwindled from the wall. The Dragon banner hung still.

"My lords, we shall ride there in the morning. But now it is seemly that we should attend the High King, and see his body laid in kingly fashion, and guards set, before it can be taken to its resting-place. Then those who will may take up their swords and spears, and ride with me."

He finished. Cador came striding up the hall and with him Ector, and Gwyl, and Bedwyr's father King Ban, and a score of others. I stepped quietly back, leaving Arthur standing there alone, with the King's guard behind him. I made a sign, and servants stooped to lift and carry out the chair where, all this time, the dead King had sat stiffening, with no man looking his way save only Ulfin, who was weeping.

10

As soon as I left the hall I sent a servant running with a message that a swift horse was to be made ready for me. Another fetched my sword and cloak, and very soon, without attracting much notice, I was able to slip quietly through the thronged corridors and out to the courtyard.

The horse was there, ready. I thought I recognized it, then saw from its housings that it was Ralf's big chestnut. Ralf himself waited at its head, his face strained and anxious. Beyond the high walls of the courtyard the town hummed like a tumbled skep of bees, and lights were everywhere.

"What's this?" I asked him. "Didn't they get my message right? I go alone."

"So they said. The horse is for you. He's faster than your own, and sure on his feet, and he knows the forest tracks. And if you do meet trouble—" He left the sentence unfinished, but I understood him. The horse was trained to battle, and would fight for me like an extra arm.

"Thank you." I took the reins from him, and mounted. "They're expecting me at the gate?"

"Yes. Merlin"—he still kept a hand on the reins—"let me come with you. You shouldn't ride alone. You've a bad enemy there who'll stop at nothing."

"I know that. You'll serve me better by staying here and seeing that no one rides after me. Are the gates shut?"

"Yes, I saw to it. No rider but you leaves this place now until Arthur and the others ride out. But they tell me that there were two men slipped out before the company left the hall."

I frowned. "Lot's?"

"No one seems clear on that. They said they were messengers taking the news of the King's death south."

"No messenger was sent," I said curtly. I had ordered this myself. The news of the High King's death, with the fear and uncertainty it would engender, must not be carried beyond the walls until there could go with it news of a new King and a new crowning.

Ralf nodded. "I know. These two got through just before the order came. It could just be someone hoping for a purse—one of the chamberlains, perhaps, sending word south as soon as it happened. But it could just as soon be Lot's men, you know it could. What could he be planning? To break Macsen's sword, as he broke Uther's?"

"You think he could?"

"N—no. But if he can do nothing, then why are you riding up there now? Why not wait and ride up with the prince?"

"Because it's true that Lot will stop at nothing now to destroy Arthur's claim. He's worse than ambitious now, he's frightened. He'll do anything to discredit me, and shake men's faith in the sword as God's gift. So I must go. God does not defend himself. Why are we here, if not to fight for him?"

"You mean—? I see. They could desecrate the shrine, or destroy the altar . . . If they could even prevent your being there to receive the King . . . And they may kill the servant you left to tend the shrine. Is that it?"

"Yes."

He took the chestnut by the bit, so roughly that it jibbed, snorting. "Then do you think that Lot would hesitate to murder you?"

"No. But I don't think he'll succeed. Now let me go, Ralf. I shall be safe enough."

"Ah." There was relief in his voice. "You mean there are no more deaths in the stars tonight?"

"There is death for someone. It's not for me, but I'll take no one with me, to put more at risk. Which is why you are not coming, Ralf."

"Oh, God, if that's all—"

I laid the reins on the chestnut's neck and it gathered itself, sidling. "We had this fight once before, Ralf, and I gave way. But not tonight. I can't force you to obey me; you are not mine now. But you are Arthur's, and your duty is to stay with him and bring him safely to the chapel. Now let me go. Which gate?"

There was a stretched pause, then he stepped back. "The south. God go with you, my dear lord."

He turned his head and called an order to the guard. The courtyard gate swung open, and crashed shut again behind my galloping horse.

There was half a moon, shadow-edged, thin silver. It lit the familiar track along the valley. The willows along the river's edge stood humped above blue shadows. The river ran fast, full with rain. The sky sparkled with stars, and brighter than any of them burned the Bear. Then moon, stars and river were blotted from sight as the chestnut, feeling my heels, stretched his great stride and carried me at his sure gallop into the blackness of the Wild Forest.

For the first part of the way the track went straight and smooth, and here and there through breaks in the leafage the pale moon sifted down, throwing a faint grey light to the forest floor. Roots, ribbing the pathway, rapped under the horse's hoofs. I lay low on his neck to avoid the sweeping branches. Presently the track began to climb, gently at first, then steep and twisting as the forest ran up into the foothills. Here and there the way bent sharply to avoid crags which thrust up among the crowded trees. Somewhere deep down on the left was the noise of a mountain stream, fed like the river with the autumn rains. Save for the horse's thudding gallop there was no sound. The trees hung still. No breeze could penetrate so far into the thick darkness. Nothing else stirred. If deer, or wolf, or fox were abroad that night, I never saw them.

The way grew steeper. The chestnut, sure-footed, breasted the rough track with heaving ribs and stride at last slackening to a heavy canter. Not far now. A gap in the boughs above let starlight through, and I could see ahead where a twist of the path took it round like a tunnel into yet thicker blackness. An owl cried, away to the left. From the right, another answered. The sounds burst in my brain like a war cry as the chestnut took the bend, and I hauled at his mouth, throwing my whole weight back on the rein. A better horseman could have stopped him in time. But not I, and I had left it just too late.

He pulled to a plunging, trampling stop, but travelling as he was his hoofs ploughed up the muddy track, and he hurtled half-sideways towards the tree which lay fallen full across the way. A pine, dry and long-dead, with its branches thrusting out pointed and rigid as the spikes of a cavalry trap. Too high and too dense to jump, even had it lain in the open moonlight and not just at the darkest bend in the track. The place was well chosen. To one side of the track there was a steep and rocky drop forty feet to the rush of the stream; to the other a thicket of thorn and holly, too dense for a horseman to thrust through. There was no space even to swerve. Had we gone round the corner at a gallop, the horse would have been speared on the boughs, and I myself flung headlong against their crippling spikes.

If the enemy lay hidden, expecting me to gallop hard onto the spikes, there might be a few seconds in which we could get back from the ambush and off the track into deep forest. I turned the chestnut sharply and lashed the reins down. He came round fast, rearing, scoring his side along the wall of thorns and driving the sharp end of some branch deep into my thigh. Then suddenly, as if spurred, he snorted and hurled himself forward. Under us the path broke open with a crashing of boughs. A black pit gaped. The horse lurched, pitched half down, then went over in a thrashing of hoofs. I was flung clear over his shoulder into the space between the pit and the fallen tree. I lay for a moment half-stunned, while the horse, with a heave and a scramble, floundered out of the shallow pit and stood trembling, while two men, daggers in hand, broke out of the forest and came running.

I had been flung into the deepest of the dark shadow, and I suppose I was lying so still that for the moment I was invisible. The noise the stream made drowned most other sounds, and they may have thought I had been flung straight down into the gully. One of them ran to the edge, peering downwards, while the other pushed past the horse and came warily forward to the edge of the pit.

They had not had time to dig this deep enough, only deep enough to lame the horse and to throw me. Now in the black darkness it acted as a kind of protection, preventing them both from jumping me at once. The one near me called out to his fellow, but the rush of water below us drowned the words. Then he took a cautious step forward past the pit towards me. I saw the faint glimmer of the weapon in his hand.

I rolled, got him by the ankle, and heaved. He yelled, pitching forward half into the hole, then twisted free, slashed sideways with his dagger, and rolled away quickly to his feet. The other threw a knife. It struck the tree behind me and fell somewhere. One weapon the less. But now they knew where I was. They drew back beyond the pit, one to each side of the track. In the hand of one man I saw the glint of a sword, but could see nothing of the other. There was no sound but the rush of water.

At least the narrowness of the path, while it made for a good ambush, had effectively stopped them bringing up their own horses. Mine was dead lame. Their beasts must be tethered somewhere behind them in the trees. It was impossible to scramble through the fallen pine behind me; they would have caught and speared me there in seconds. Nor could I get through the wall of thorn. All that was left was the gully; if I could get down there unseen, somehow get past them and back into the open forest, perhaps even find their horses . . .

I moved cautiously sideways, towards the rim of the gully. I had my free hand out, feeling my way. There were bushes, and here and there saplings or young trees, rooted in the rocks. My hand met smooth bark, gripped it, tested it.

I moved warily crabwise, over the edge. My eyes were still on that glimmer of metal, the sword beyond the pit. The man was still there. My groping foot slid down a sharp and muddy step, the rim of the gully. A bramble snatched at it.

So did a man's hand. He had used my own trick. He had slid quietly down the bank, flattened himself there, and waited. Now he flung his whole weight, sharply, on my foot and, caught off balance, I fell. His knife just missed me, biting deep into the bank bare inches from my face as I pitched down past him.

He had meant to send me crashing down the rocky bank, to be broken and stunned on the rocks below, where they could follow and finish me together. If he had been content with this, he might have succeeded. But his lunge with the knife shook his own balance, and besides, as he grabbed at me, instead of resisting I went with him, stamping hard downwards at the grabbing hand. My boot went into something soft; he grunted with pain, then yelled something as my weight broke his grip, and, loosing whatever hold he had, he went hurtling with me down the steep side of the gully.

I had been falling the faster of the two, and I landed first, halfway down, hard up against the stem of a young pine. My attacker rolled after me in a crash of broken bushes and a shower of stones. As he hurtled against me in a flying tangle of limbs I braced myself to meet him. I flung myself over him, clamping my body hard over his, clasping his arms with both of mine and pinning him with my weight. I heard him cry out with pain. One leg was doubled under him. He lashed out with the other, and I felt a spur rake my leg through the soft leather of my boot. He fought furiously, thrashing and twisting under me like a landed fish. At any moment he would dislodge me from my purchase against the pine, and we would fall together to the gully. I struggled to hold him, and to get my dagger hand free.

The other murderer had heard us fall. He shouted something from the brink above, then I could hear him letting himself down the slope towards us. He came cautiously, but fast. Too fast. I shifted my grip on the man beneath me, forcing my full weight down to hold his arms pinned. I heard something crack; it sounded like a dead twig, but the fellow screamed. I managed to drag my right hand from under him. My fist was clamped round the dagger and the hilt had bitten into the flesh. I lifted it. Some stray glimmer of moonlight touched his eyes, a foot from mine; I could smell the fear and pain and hatred. He gave a wild heave that nearly unseated me, wrenching his head sideways from the coming blow. I reversed the dagger and struck with all the strength of the shortened blow at the exposed neck, just behind the ear.

The blow did not reach him. Something—a rock, a heavy billet of wood, hurled down from above—struck me hard on the point of the shoulder. My arm jerked out, useless, paralyzed. The dagger spun away into the blackness. The other murderer crashed down the last few feet through the bushes and rocks above me. I heard his drawn sword scrape on stone. The moon marked it as it whipped upwards to strike. I tried to wrench myself clear of my opponent, but he clung close, teeth and all, grappling like a hound, holding me there for that hacking sword to finish me.

It finished him. His companion jumped, and slashed downwards at the place where, a second before, my exposed back had been, plain in the moonlight. But I was already half free, and falling, my clothes tearing from my opponent's grasp, and my fist bloody from his teeth. It was his back that met the sword. It drove in.

I heard the metal grate on bone, then the screams covered the sound, and I was free of him and half-sliding, half-falling, towards the noise of the water.

A bush checked me, tore at me, let me through. A bough whipped me across the throat. A net of brambles ripped what was left of my clothing to ribbons. Then my hurtling body hit a boulder, checked, lay breathless and half-stunned against it for the two long moments it took to let me hear the second murderer coming after me. Then with no warning but a sudden gentle shift of earth the boulder went from under me and I fell down the last sheer drop straight to the slab of rock over which the icy water slid, racing, towards the edge of a deep pool.

If I had fallen into the pool itself I might not have been hurt. If I had struck one of the great boulders where the water dashed and wrangled, I would probably have been killed. But I fell into a shallow, long flat stretch of rock across which the water slid no more than a span deep, before plunging on and down into the next of the forest pools. I landed on my side, half-stunned and winded. The icy rush filled my mouth, nose, eyes, weighing down my heavy clothes, dragging at my bruised limbs. I was sliding with it along the greasy rock. My hands clawed for a hold, slipped, missed, scraped with bending nails.

Beside me with a thud and splash that shook the very rock, the second murderer landed, slipped, regained his foothold in the rushing water, and for the second time swung the sword high. It caught the moonlight. There were stars behind it. A sword lying clear acorss the night sky, in a blaze of stars. I took my hands from the rock, and the stream rolled me over to face the sword. The water blinded me. The noise of the cascade shook my bones apart. There was a flash like a shooting star, and the sword came down.

It was like a dream that repeated itself. Once before I had sat near a fire in the forest, with the small dark hill men waiting round me in a half circle, their eyes gleaming at the edge of the firelight like the eyes of forest creatures.

But this fire they had lit themselves. In front of it my torn clothes steamed, drying. Myself they had wrapped in their own cloaks, sheepskins, smelling too reminiscently of their first owners, but warm and dry. My bruises ached, and here and there a sharper pain told me where some stroke, unfelt in the scrimmage, had gone home. But my bones were whole.

I had not been unconscious long. Beyond the circle of firelight lay the two dead men, and near them a sharpened stake and a heavy club from which the blood had not yet been wiped. One of the men was still cleaning his long knife in the ground.

Mab brought me a bowl of hot wine, with something pungent overlying the taste of the grapes. I drank, sneezed, and pushed myself up straight.

"Did you find their horses?"

He nodded. "Over yonder. Your own is lame."

"Yes. Tend him for me, will you? When I get up to the shrine I'll send the servant down this way. He can lead the lame one home. Bring me one of the others now, and get me my clothes."

"They're still wet. It's barely ten minutes since we got you out of the pool."

"No matter," I said, "I must go. Mab, above here on the track there's a fallen tree, and a pit beside it. Will you ask your people to clear the path before morning?"

"They are there already. Listen."

I heard it then, beyond the rush of the stream and the crackling of the fire, Axe and mattock thudding, above us in the forest. Mab met my eyes. "Will the new King ride this way, then?"

"He may." I smiled. "How soon did you hear?"

"One of our people came from the town to tell us." He showed a gap of broken teeth. "Not by the gates you locked, master . . . But we knew before that. Did you not see the shooting star? It went across the heavens from end to end, crested like a dragon and riding a trail of smoke. So we knew you would come. But we were up beyond the Wolves' Road when the firedrake ran, and we were almost too late. I am sorry."

"You came in time," I said. "I'm in your debt for my life. I shan't forget it."

"I was in yours," he said. "Why did you ride alone? You should have known there was danger."

"I knew there was death, but I wanted no more deaths on my hands. Pain is another thing, and is soon over." I got to my feet, stiffly. "If I'm ever to move again, Mab, I must move now. My clothes?"

The clothes were wet still, a mass of mud and rents. But apart from the sheepskins there was nothing else; the hill people are small, and nothing of theirs would have fitted me. I shrugged myself into what was left of my court clothing, and took the bridle of a stolid brown horse from one of the men. The wound in my thigh was bleeding again, and from the feel of it there were splinters there. I got them to sling one of the sheepskins over the saddle, and climbed gingerly on.

"Shall we come with you?" they asked me.

I shook my head. "No. Stay and see the road cleared. In the morning, if you wish, come to the shrine. There will be a place there for you all."

The moonlit space at the forest's center was as still as a painted picture, and as unreal as a midnight dream. Moonlight edged the chapel roof and silvered the furred tops of the surrounding pines. The doorway showed an oblong of gold, where the nine lamps shone steadily round the altar.

As I rode softly round to the back the door opened there, and the servant peered fearfully out. All was well, he told me; no one had been by. But his eyes stretched wide when he saw the state I was in, and he was obviously glad when I handed the bridle to him and told him to leave me. Then I went in thankfully to the firelight to tend my hurts and change my clothing.

Slowly the silence seeped back. A brush of soft wind over the tree-tops swept the last sound of retreating hoofs away; it crept in through the chapel, thinning the lamp flames and drawing thin lines of smoke which smelled like sweet gums burning. Outside in the clearing the moon and stars poured their rare light down. The god was here. I knelt before the altar, emptying myself of mind and will, till through me I felt the full tide of God's will flowing, and bearing me with it.

The night lay silver and quiet, waiting for the torches and trumpets.

11

They came at last. Lights and clamour and the trampling of horses flowed nearer through the forest, till the clearing was filled with flaring torchlight and excited voices. I heard them through the waking sleep of vision, dim, echoing, remote, like bells heard from the bottom of the sea.

The leaders had come forward. They paused in the doorway. Voices hushed, feet shuffled. All they would see was the swept and empty chapel, deserted but for one man standing facing them across the stone altar. Round the altar the nine lamps still dealt their steady glow, showing the carved stone sword and the legend MITHRAE INVICTO, and lying across the top of the altar the sword itself, unsheathed, bare on the bare stone.

"Put out the torches," I told them. "There will be no need of them."

They obeyed me, then at my signal pressed forward into the chapel.

The place was small, the throng of men great. But the awe of the occasion prevailed; orders were given, but subdued; soft commands which might have come from priests in ritual rather than warriors recently in battle. There were no rites to follow, but somehow men kept their places; kings and nobles and kings' guards within the chapel, the press of lesser men outside in the silent clearing and overflowing into the gloom of the forest itself. There, they still had lights; the clearing was ringed with light and sound where the horses waited and men stood with torches ready; but forward under the open sky men came lightless and weaponless, as beseemed them in the presence of God and their King. And still, this one night of all the great nights, there was no priest present; the only intermediary was myself, who had been used by the driving god for thirty years, and brought at last to this place.

At length all were assembled, according to order and precedence. It was as if they had divided by arrangement, or more likely by instinct. Outside, crowding the steps, waited the little men from the hills; they do not willingly come under a roof. Inside the chapel, to my right, stood Lot, King of Lothian, with his group of friends and followers; to the left Cador, and those who went with him. There were a hundred others, perhaps more, crowded into that small and echoing space, but these two, the white Boar of Cornwall, and the red Leopard of Lothian, seemed to face one another balefully from either side of the altar, with Ector four-square and watchful at the door between them. Then Ector, with Cei behind him, brought Arthur forward, and after that I saw no one but the boy.

The chapel swam with colour and the glint of jewels and gold. The air smelled cold and fragrant, of pines and water and scented smoke. The rustle and murmuring of the throng filled the air and sounded like the rustle of flames licking through a pile of fuel, taking hold. . . .

Flames from the nine lamps, flaring and then dying; flames licking up the stone of the altar; flames running along the blade of the sword until it glowed white hot. I stretched my hands out over it, palms flat. The fire licked my robe, blazing white from sleeve and finger, but where it touched, it did not even singe. It was the ice-cold fire, the fire called by a word out of the dark, with the searing heat at its heart, where the sword lay. The sword lay in its flames as a jewel lies embedded in white wool. *Whoso taketh this sword* . . . The runes danced along the metal: the emeralds burned. The chapel was a dark globe with a center of fire. The blaze from the altar threw my shadow upwards, gigantic, into the vaulted roof. I heard my own voice, ringing hollow from the vault like a voice in a dream.

"Take up the sword, he who dares."

Movement, and men's voices, full of dread. Then Cador: "That is the sword. I would know it anywhere. I saw it in his hand, full of light. It is his, God witness it. I would not touch it if Merlin himself bade me."

There were cries of, "Nor I, nor I," and then, "Let the King take it up, let the High King show us Macsen's sword."

Then finally, alone, Lot's voice, gruffly: "Yes. Let him take it. I have seen, by God's death, I have seen. If it is his indeed, then God is with him, and it is not for me."

Arthur came slowly forward. Behind him the place was dim, the crowd shrunk back into darkness, the shuffle and murmur of their presence no more than the breeze in the forest trees outside. Here between us, the white light blazed and the blade shivered. The darkness flashed and sparkled, a crystal cave of vision, crowded and whirling with bright images. A white stag, collared with gold. A shooting star, dragon-shaped, and trailing fire. A king, restless and desirous, with a dragon of red gold shimmering on the wall behind him. A woman, white-robed and queenly, and behind her in the shadows a sword standing in an altar like a cross. A circle of vast linked stones standing on a windy plain with a king's grave at its center. A child, handed into my arms on a winter night. A grail, shrouded in mouldering cloth, hidden in a dark vault. A young king, crowned.

He looked at me through the pulse and flash of vision. For him, they were flames only, flames which might burn, or not; that was for me. He waited, not doubtful, nor blindly trusting; waiting only.

"Come," I said gently. "It is yours."

He put his hand through the white blaze of fire and the hilt slid cool into the grip for which, a hundred and a hundred years before, it had been made.

Lot was the first to kneel. I suppose he had most need. Arthur raised him, speaking without either rancour or cordiality; the words of a sovereign lord who is able to see past a present wrong to a coming good.

"I could not find it in me, Lot of Lothian, to quarrel with any man this day, least of all my sister's lord. You shall see that your doubts of me were groundless, and you and your sons after you will help me guard and hold Britain as she should be held."

To Cador he said simply: "Until I get myself another heir, Cador of Cornwall, you are he."

To Ector he spoke long and quietly, so that no man could hear save they two, and when he raised him, kissed him.

Thereafter for a long span of time he stood by the altar, as men knelt before him and swore loyalty on the hilt of the sword. To each one he spoke, directly as a boy, and grandly as a king. Between his hands, held like a cross, Caliburn shone with his own light only, but the altar with its nine dead lamps was dark.

As each man took his oath and pledged himself, he withdrew, and the chapel slowly emptied. As it grew quieter, the encircling forest filled with life and expectation and noise, where they crowded, clamorously excited now, waiting for their sworn King. They were bringing up the horses out of the wood, and the clearing filled with torchlight and trampling and the jingling of accoutrements.

Last of all Mab and the men of the hills withdrew, and save for the bodyguard ranged back against the shadowed wall, the King and I were alone.

Stiffly, for pain still locked my bones, I came round the altar till I stood before him. He was almost as tall as I. The eyes that looked back at me might have been my own.

I knelt in front of him and put out my hands for his. But he cried out at that, and pulled me to my feet, and kissed me.

"You do not kneel to me. Not you."

"You are High King, and I am your servant."

"What of it? The sword was yours, and we two know it. It doesn't matter what you call yourself, my servant, cousin, father, what you will—you are Merlin, and I'm nothing without you beside me." He laughed then, naturally, the grandeur of the occasion fitting him as easily as the hilt had fitted his hand. "What became of your state robe? Only you could have worn that dreadful old thing on such an occasion. I shall give you a robe of gold tissue, embroidered with stars, as befits your position. Will you wear it for me?"

"Not even for you."

He smiled. "Then come as you are. You'll ride down with me now, won't you?"

"Later. When you have time to look round for me, you will find that I am beside you. Listen, they are ready to take you to your place. It's time to go."

I went with him to the door. The torches still tossed flaring, though the moon had set long since and the last of the stars had died into a morning sky. Golden and tranquil, the light grew.

They had brought the white stallion up to the steps. When Arthur made to mount they would not let him, but Cador and Lot and half a dozen petty kings lifted him between them to the saddle, and at last men's hopes and joy rang up into the pines in a great shout. So they raised to be king Arthur the young.

I carried the nine lamps out of the chapel. Come daylight, I would take them where they now belonged, up to the caves of the hollow hills, where their gods had gone. Of the nine, all had been overturned, the oil spilled unburned along the floor. With them lay the stone bowl, shattered, and a pile of dust and crumbled fragments where the cold fire had struck. When I swept these away, with the oil that had soaked into them, it could be seen that the carving had gone from the front of the altar. These were the fragments that I held, caked with oil. All that was left of the carving on the altar's face was the hilt of the sword, and a word.

I swept and cleaned the place and made it fair again. I moved slowly, like an old man. I still remember how my body ached, and how at length, when I knelt again, my sight blurred and darkened as if still blind with vision, or with tears.

The tears showed me the altar now, bare of the nine-fold light that had pleasured the old, small gods; bare of the soldier's sword and the name of the soldiers' god. All it held now was the hilt of the carved sword standing in the stone like a cross, and the letters still deep and distinct about it: TO HIM UNCONQUERED.

THE LEGEND

When Aurelius Ambrosius was High King of Britain, Merlin, also called Ambrosius, brought the Giants' Dance out of Ireland and set it up near Amesbury, at Stonehenge. Shortly after this a great star appeared in the likeness of a dragon, and Merlin, knowing that it betokened Ambrosius' death, wept bitterly, and prophesied that Uther would be King under the sign of the Dragon, and that a son would be born to him "of surpassing mighty dominion, whose power shall extend over all the realms that lie beneath the ray (of the star)."

The following Easter, at the Coronation feast, King Uther fell in love with Ygraine, wife of Gorlois, Duke of Cornwall. He lavished attention on her, to the scandal of the court; she made no response, but her husband, in fury, retired from the court without leave, taking his wife and men-at-arms back to Cornwall. Uther, in anger, commanded him to return, but Gorlois refused to obey. Then the King, enraged beyond measure, gathered an army and marched into Cornwall, burning the cities and castles. Gorlois had not enough troops to withstand him, so he placed his wife in the castle of Tintagel, the safest refuge, and himself prepared to defend the castle of Dimilioc. Uther immediately laid siege to Dimilioc, holding Gorlois and his troops trapped there, while he cast about for some way of breaking into the castle of Tintagel to ravish Ygraine. After some days he asked advice from one of his familiars called Ulfin, who suggested that he send for Merlin. Merlin, moved by the King's apparent suffering, promised to help. By his magic arts he changed Uther into the likeness of Gorlois, Ulfin into Jordan, Gorlois' friend, and himself into Brithael, one of Gorlois' captains. The three of them rode to Tintagel, and were admitted by the porter. Ygraine, taking Uther to be her husband the Duke, welcomed him, and took him to her bed. So Uther lay with Ygraine that night, "and she had no thought to deny him in aught he might desire."

But in the meantime fighting had broken out at Dimilioc, and in the battle Ygraine's husband, the Duke, was killed. Messengers came to Tintagel to tell Ygraine of her husband's death. When they found "Gorlois," apparently still alive, closeted with Ygraine, they were speechless, but the King then confessed the deception, and a few days later married Ygraine. Some say that Ygraine's sister Morgause was married on the same day to Lot of Lothian, and the other sister Morgan le Fay was put to school in a nunnery, where she learned necromancy, and thereafter was wedded to King Urien of Gore. But others aver that Morgan was Arthur's own sister, born after him of the marriage of King Uther and Ygraine his Queen, and that Morgause was also his sister, but not by the same mother.

Uther Pendragon was to reign for fifteen more years, and during those years he saw nothing of his son Arthur. Before the child was born Merlin sought out the King and spoke with him. "Sir, ye must purvey you for the nourishing of your child." "As thou wilt," said the King, "be it." So on the night of his birth the child Arthur was carried down to the postern gate of Tintagel and delivered into the hands of Merlin, who took him to the castle of Sir Ector, a faithful knight. There Merlin had the child christened, and named him Arthur, and Sir Ector's wife took him as her foster son.

All through Uther's reign the country was sorely troubled by the Saxons and the Scots from Ireland. The two Saxon leaders whom the King had imprisoned managed to escape from London and fled thence to Germany, where they gathered a great army which struck terror throughout the kingdom. Uther himself was stricken with a grievous malady, and appointed Lot of Lothian, who was betrothed to his daughter Morgause, as his chief captain. But as often as Lot put the enemy to flight, they came back in even greater strength, and the country was laid waste. Finally Uther, though sorely ill, gathered his barons together and told them that he himself must lead the armies, so a litter was made for him, and he was carried in it at the head of his army against the enemy. When the Saxon leaders learned that the British King had taken the field against them in a litter, they disdained him, saying that he was half-dead already, and it would not become them to fight him. But Uther, with a return of his old strength, laughed and called out: "They call me the half-dead king, and so indeed I was. But I would rather conquer them in this wise, than be conquered by them and live in shame." So the army of the Britons defeated the Saxons. But the King's malady increased, and the woes of the kingdom. Finally, when the King lay close to death, Merlin appeared and approached him in the sight of all the lords and bade him acknowledge his son Arthur as the new King. Which he did, and afterwards died, and was buried by the side of his brother Aurelius Ambrosius within the Giants' Dance.

After his death the lords of Britain came together to find their new King. No one knew where Arthur was kept, or where Merlin was to be found, but they thought the King would be recognized by a sign. So Merlin had a great sword fashioned, and fixed it by his magic art into a great stone shaped like an altar, with an anvil of steel in it, and floated the stone on water to a great church in London, and set it up there in the churchyard. There were gold letters on the sword which said: "Whoso pulleth out this sword of this stone and anvil, is rightwise king born of all England." So a great feast was made, and at the feast all the lords came to try who could pull the sword from the stone. Among them came Sir Ector, and Kay his son, with Arthur, who had neither sword nor blazon, following as a squire. When they came to the jousting Sir Kay, who had forgotten his sword, sent Arthur back to look for it. But when Arthur returned to the house where they were lodging, everyone was gone and the doors were locked, so in impatience he rode to the churchyard, and drew the sword from the stone, and took it to Sir Kay. Then of course the sword was recognized, but even when Arthur showed that he alone of all men could pull it from the stone, there were those who cried out against him, saying it was great shame to them and to the realm to accept as king a boy of no high blood born, and that fresh trial must be made at Candlemas. So at Candlemas all the greatest in the land came together, and then again at Pentecost, but none of them could pull the sword from the stone, save only Arthur. But still some of the lords were angry and would not accept him, until in the end the common people cried out: "We will have Arthur unto our king, we will put him no more in delay, for we all see that it is God's will that he shall be our king, and who that holdeth against it, we will slay him." So Arthur was accepted by the people, high and low, and all men rich and poor kneeled to him and begged his mercy because they had delayed him so long, and he forgave them. Then Merlin told them all who Arthur was, and that he was no bastard, but begotten truly by King Uther upon Ygraine, three hours after the death of her husband the Duke. So they raised to be king Arthur the young.

AUTHOR'S NOTE

Like its predecessor, *The Crystal Cave,* this novel is a work of the imagination, though firmly based in both history and legend. Not perhaps equally in both: so little is known about Britain in the fifth century A.D. (the beginning of the "Dark Ages") that one is almost as dependent on tradition and conjecture as on fact. I for one like to think that where tradition is so persistent—and as immortal and self-perpetuating as the stories of the Arthurian Legend—there must be a grain of fact behind even the strangest of the tales which have gathered round the meager central facts of Arthur's existence. It is exciting to interpret these sometimes weird and often nonsensical legends into a story which has some sort of coherence as human experience and imaginative truth.

I have tried with *The Hollow Hills* to write a story which stands on its own, without reference to its forerunner, *The Crystal Cave,* or even to whatever explanatory notes follow here. Indeed, I only add these notes for the benefit of those readers whose interest may go beyond the novel itself, but who are not familiar enough with the ramifications of the Arthurian Legend to follow the thinking behind some parts of my story. It may give them pleasure to trace for themselves the seeds of certain ideas and the origins of certain references.

In *the Crystal Cave* I based my story mainly on the "history" related by Geoffrey of Monmouth,* which is the basis of the later and mainly mediaeval tales of "Arthur and his Court," but I set the action against the fifth-century Romano-British background, which is the real setting for all that we know of the Arthurian Fact.† We have no fixed dates, but I have followed some authorities who postulate 470 A.D. or thereabouts as the date of Arthur's birth. The story of *The Hollow Hills* covers the hidden years between that date and the raising of the young Arthur to be war-leader *(dux bellorum)* or, as legend has had it for more than a thousand years, King of Britain. What I would like to trace here are the threads I have woven to make this story of a period of Arthur's life which tradition barely touches, and history touches not at all.

That Arthur existed seems certain. We cannot say even that much for certain about Merlin. "Merlin the magician," as we know him, is a composite figure built almost entirely out of song and legend; but here again one feels that for such a legend to persist through the centuries, some man of power must have existed, with gifts that seemed miraculous to his own times. He first appears in legend as a youth, even then possessed of strange powers. On this story as related

---

* *History of the Kings of Britain,* translated by Sebastian Evans and revised by Charles W. Dunn (Everyman's Library, 1912).

† See *Roman Britain and the English Settlements,* R. G. Collingwood and J. N. L. Myres (Oxford, 1937); *Celtic Britain,* Nora K. Chadwick Vol. 34 in the series *Ancient Peoples and Places,* ed. Glyn Daniel (Thames and Hudson, 1963).

by Geoffrey of Monmouth I have built an imaginary character who seemed to me to grow out of and epitomize the time of confusion and seeking that we call the Dark Ages. Geoffrey Ashe, in his brilliant book *From Caesar to Arthur,** describes this "multiplicity of vision":

> When Christianity prevailed and Celtic paganism crumbled into mythology, a great deal of this sort of thing was carried over. Water and islands retained their magic. Lake-sprites flitted to and fro, heroes travelled in strange boats. The haunted hills became fairy-hills, belonging to vivid fairy folk hardly to be paralleled among other nations. Where barrows existed they often fitted this role. Unseen realms intersected the visible, and there were secret means of communication and access. The fairies and the heroes, the ex-gods and the demigods, jostled the spirits of the dead in kaleidoscopic confusion . . . Everything grew ambiguous. Thus, long after the triumph of Christianity, there continued to be fairy-hills; but even those which were not barrows might be regarded as havens for disembodied souls . . . There were saints of whom miracles were reported; but similar miracles, not long since, might have been the business of fully identifiable gods. There were glass castles where a hero might lie an age entranced; there were blissful fairylands to be reached by water or by cave-passageways . . . Journeys and enchantments, combats and imprisonments—theme by theme—the Celtic imagination articulated itself in story. Yet any given episode might be taken as fact or imagination or religious allegory or all three at once.

Merlin, the narrator of *The Hollow Hills,* the "enchanter" and healer gifted with the Sight, is able to move in and out of the different worlds at will. And as Merlin's legend is linked with the caves of glass, the invisible towers, the hollow hills where he now sleeps for all time, so I have seen him as the link between the worlds; the instrument by which, as he says, "all the kings become one King, and all the gods one God." For this he abnegates his own will and his desire for normal manhood. The hollow hills are the physical point of entry between this world and the Otherworld, and Merlin is their human counterpart, the meeting point for the interlocking worlds of men, gods, beasts and twilight spirits.

One meeting of the real and the fantasy worlds can be seen in the figure of Maximus. Magnus Maximus, the soldier with the dream of empire, was a fact; he commanded at Segontium until the time when he crossed to Gaul in his vain bid for power. "Macsen Wledig" is a legend, one of the Celtic "seeking" stories later to flower into the Quest of the Holy Grail. In this novel I have linked the facts of Arthur's great precursor and his imperial dream to the sword episodes of the Arthurian Legend, and lent them the shape of a Quest story.

The tale of the "Sword of Maximus" is my invention. It follows the archetypal "seeking and finding" pattern of which the Quest of the Grail, which later attached itself to the Arthurian Legend, is only one example. The stories of the Holy Grail, identifying it with the Cup from the Last Supper, are twelfth-century tales modelled in their main elements on some early Celtic "quest" stories; in fact they have elements even older. These Grail stories show certain

* Published by Collins, 1960. See also *The Quest for Arthur's Britain,* ed. Geoffrey Ashe (Pall Mall Press, 1968).

points in common, changing in detail, but fairly constant in form and idea. There is usually an unknown youth, the *bel inconnu,* who is brought up in the wilds, ignorant of his name or parentage. He leaves his home and rides out in search of his identity. He comes across a Waste Land, ruled by a maimed (impotent) king; there is a castle, usually on an island, on which the youth comes by chance. He reaches it in a boat belonging to a royal fisherman, the Fisher King of the Grail Legends. The Fisher King is sometimes identified with the impotent king of the Waste Land. The castle on the island is owned by a king of the Otherworld, and there the youth finds the object of his quest, sometimes a cup or a lance, sometimes a sword, broken or whole. At the quest's end he wakes by the side of the water with his horse tethered near him, and the island once again invisible. On his return from the Otherworld, fertility and peace are restored to the Waste Land. Some tales figure a white stag collared with gold, who leads the youth to his destination.

For further reference see *Arthurian Literature in the Middle Ages;* A Collaborative History edited by R. S. Loomis (Oxford University Press, 1959); and *The Evolution of the Grail Legend* by D. D. R. Owen (University of St. Andrews Publications, 1968).

SOME OTHER BRIEF NOTES

Segontium. Geoffrey of Monmouth in the *Vita Merlini* tells us of cups made by Weland the Smith in Caer Seint (Segontium), which were given to Merlin. There is also another story of a sword made by Weland which was given to Merlin by a Welsh king. There is a brief reference in *The Anglo-Saxon Chronicle* for the year 418 A.D. "In this year the Romans collected all the treasures which were in Britain and hid some in the earth so that no one afterwards could find them, and some they took with them into Gaul."

Galava. The main body of legend places King Arthur in the Celtic countries of the west, Cornwall, Wales, Brittany. In this I have followed the legends. But there is evidence which supports another strong tradition of Arthur in the north of England and in Scotland. So this story moves north. I have placed the traditional "Sir Ector of the Forest Sauvage" (who reared the young Arthur) at Galava, the modern Ambleside in the Lake District. I have often wondered if "the fountain of Galabes * where he (Merlin) wont to haunt" could be identified with the Roman Galava or Galaba. (In *The Crystal Cave* I gave it a different interpretation. The mediaeval romancers make "Galapas" a gaint—a version of the old guardian of the spring or waterway.) The fostering of Arthur on Ector, and the lodging at Galava of Bedwyr, are feasible; we find in Procopius that, as in later times, boys of good family were sent away to be educated. As for the "chapel in the green," once I had invented a shrine in the Wild Forest I could not resist calling it the Green Chapel, after the mediaeval Arthurian poem of *Sir Gawaine and the Green Knight,* which has its setting somewhere in the Lake District.

Ambrosius' Wall. This is the Wansdyke, or Woden's Dyke, so called by the Saxons, who saw it as the work of the gods. It ran from Newbury to the Severn,

* *Fontes galabes.*

and parts of it are still traceable. It was probably built some time between 450 and 475 A.D., so I have ascribed it to Ambrosius.

Caer Bannog. This name, old Celtic for "the castle of the peaks," is my own interpretation of the various names—Carbonek, Corbenic, Caer Benoic, etc.—given to the castle where the youth finds the Grail.

There is a Celtic legend in which Arthur carries off a cauldron (magic vessel or grail) and a wonderful sword from Nuadda or Llyd, King of the Otherworld.

Cei and Bedwyr. They are Arthur's companions in legend. Cei was Ector's son and became Arthur's seneschal. Bedwyr's name was later mediaevalized to Bedivere, but in his relationship with Arthur he seems to be the original of Lancelot. Hence the reference to the *guenhwyvar* (white shadow: Guinevere) which falls between the boys on page 520.

Cador of Cornwall. When Arthur died without issue, we are told that he left his kingdom to Cador's son.

Morgause. On the subject of Arthur's unwitting incest with his sister, there is a rich confusion of legend. The most usual story is that he lay with his half-sister Morgause, wife (or mistress) of Lot, and begot Mordred, who was eventually his downfall. His own sister Morgan, or Morgian, became "Morgan le Fay," the enchantress. Morgause is said to have borne four sons to Lot, who later were to become Arthur's devoted followers. This seemed unlikely if Arthur had lain with her when she was Lot's wife, so I have taken my own way through the confusion of the stories, with the suggestion that after leaving the court Morgause will lose no time in taking her sister's place as Lot's queen. I believe there was in the fifth century a nunnery near Caer Eidyn (Edinburgh) in Lothian to which Morgian could have retired. This could be the "house of witches" or "wise women" of legend, and it is tempting to suppose that Morgian and her nuns came from there to take Arthur away and nurse him after his last battle against Mordred at Camlann.

Coel, King of Rheged, is the original of the Old King Cole of the nursery rhymes. We are told that Hueil, one of the nineteen sons of Caw of Strathclyde, was much disliked by Arthur. Another of the sons, Gildas the monk, seems to have returned this dislike. It is he who, in 540 A.D., wrote *The Loss and Conquest of Britain,* without once mentioning Arthur by name, though he refers to the Battle of Badon Hill, the last of Arthur's twelve great battles, in which he broke the Saxon power. From the tone of Gildas' book it is to be inferred that, if Arthur was a Christian at all, his Christianity went no further than lip-service. At any rate he was no friend to the monks.

Caliburn is the most pronounceable of the names for Arthur's sword, which was later romanticized as Excalibur. White was Arthur's colour; his white hound, Cabal, has a place in legend. Canrith means "white phantom."

It will be seen from these necessarily sketchy notes that any given episode of my story may—to quote Geoffrey Ashe again—"be taken as fact or imagination or religious allegory or all three at once." In this, if in nothing else, it is wholly true to its time.

M.S.

November 1970–November 1972

THE LAST ENCHANT-MENT

To one who was dead
and is alive again,
who was lost,
and is found

CONTENTS

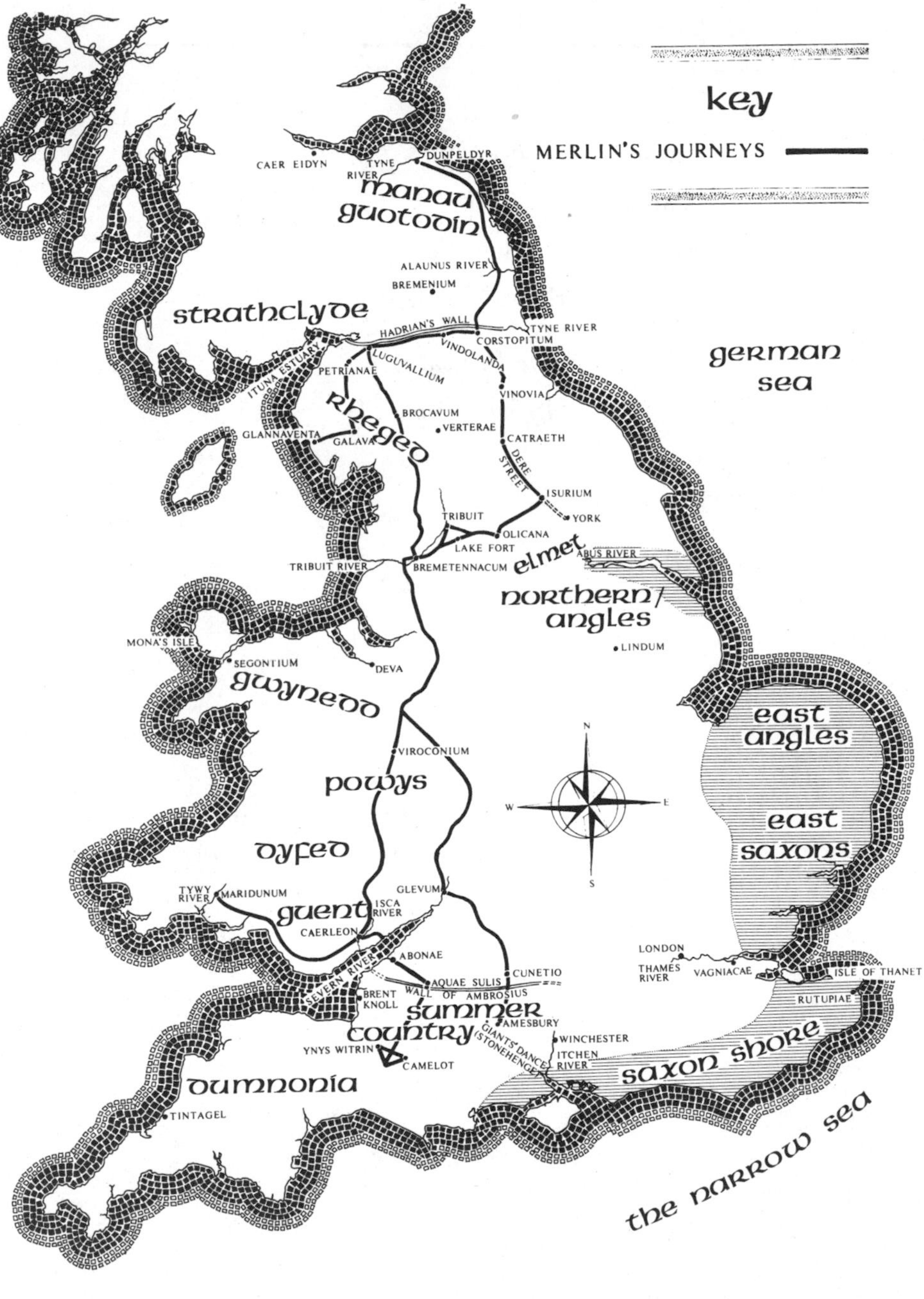

key
MERLIN'S JOURNEYS
CAER EIDYN
TYNE RIVER
DUNPELDYR
manau guotodin
ALAUNUS RIVER
BREMENIUM
strathclyde
HADRIAN'S WALL
TYNE RIVER
CORSTOPITUM
VINDOLANDA
ITUNA ESTUARY
PETRIANAE
LUGUVALLIUM
german sea
VINOVIA
BROCAVUM
VERTERAE
rheged
GLANNAVENTA
GALAVA
CATRAETH
DERE STREET
ISURIUM
YORK
TRIBUIT
OLICANA
LAKE FORT
TRIBUIT RIVER
BREMETENNACUM
elmet
ABUS RIVER
northern/angles
MONA'S ISLE
SEGONTIUM
LINDUM
DEVA
gwynedd
east angles
VIROCONIUM
powys
N
W
E
S
dyfed
east saxons
TYWY RIVER
MARIDUNUM
GLEVUM
guent
ISCA RIVER
CAERLEON
ABONAE
SEVERN RIVER
AQUAE SULIS
CUNETIO
LONDON
THAMES RIVER
VAGNIACAE
ISLE OF THANET
BRENT KNOLL
WALL OF AMBROSIUS
summer country
AMESBURY
RUTUPIAE
YNYS WITRIN
CAMELOT
GIANTS' DANCE (STONEHENGE)
WINCHESTER
ITCHEN RIVER
saxon shore
dumnonia
TINTAGEL
the narrow sea

BOOK I

DUNPELDYR

1

Not every king would care to start his reign with the wholesale massacre of children. This is what they whisper of Arthur, even though in other ways he is held up as the type itself of the noble ruler, the protector alike of high and lowly.

It is harder to kill a whisper than even a shouted calumny. Besides, in the minds of simple men, to whom the High King is the ruler of their lives, and the dispenser of all fates, Arthur would be held accountable for all that happened in his realm, evil and good alike, from a resounding victory in the battlefield to a bad rain-storm or a barren flock.

So, although a witch plotted the massacre, and another king gave the order for it, and though I myself tried to shoulder the blame, the murmur still persists: that in the first year of his reign Arthur the High King had his troops seek out and destroy some score of newly born babies in the hope of catching in that bloody net one single boy-child, his bastard by incest with his half-sister Morgause.

Calumny, I have called it, and it would be good to be able to declare openly that the story is a lie. But it is not quite that. It is a lie that he ordered the slaughter; but his sin was the first cause of it, and though it would never have occurred to him to murder innocent children, it is true that he wanted his own child killed. So it is just that some of the blame should rest on him; just, too, that some of it should cling to me. For I, Merlin, who am accounted a man of power and vision, had waited idly by while the dangerous child was engendered, and the tragic term set to the peace and freedom which Arthur could win for his people. I can bear the blame, for now I am beyond men's judgment, but Arthur is still young enough to feel the sting of the story, and be haunted by thoughts of atonement; and when it happened he was younger still, in all the first white-and-golden flush of victory and kingship, held up on the love of the people, the acclamation of the soldiers, and the blaze of mystery that surrounded the drawing of the sword from the stone.

It happened like this. King Uther Pendragon lay with his army at Luguvallium in the northern kindgom of Rheged, where he was to face a massive Saxon attack under the brothers Colgrim and Badulf, grandsons of Hengist. The young Arthur, still little more than a boy, was brought to this, his first field, by his foster-father Count Ector of Galava, who presented him to the King. Arthur had been kept in ignorance of his royal birth and parentage, and Uther, though he had kept himself informed of the boy's growth and progress, had never once seen him since he was born. This because, during the wild night of love when Uther had lain with Ygraine, then the wife of Gorlois, Duke of Cornwall and Uther's most faithful commander, the old duke himself had been killed. His death, though no fault of Uther's, weighed so heavily on the King that he swore never to claim for his own any child born of that night's guilty love. In due course Arthur had been handed to me to rear, and this I had done, at a far remove from both King and Queen. But there had been no other son born to them, and at last King Uther, who had ailed for some time, and who knew the danger of the Saxon threat he faced at Luguvallium, was forced to send for the boy, to acknowledge him publicly as his heir and present him to the assembled nobles and petty kings.

But before he could do so, the Saxons attacked. Uther, though too sick to ride at the head of the troops, took the field in a litter, with Cador, Duke of Cornwall, in command of the right, and on the left King Coel of Rheged, with Caw of Strathclyde and other leaders from the north. Only Lot, King of Lothian and Orkney, failed to take the field. King Lot, a powerful king but a doubtful ally, held his men in reserve, to throw them into the fight where and when they should be needed. It was said that he held back deliberately in the hope that Uther's army would be destroyed, and that in the event the kingdom might fall to him. If so, his hopes were defeated. When, in the fierce fighting around the King's litter in the center of the field, young Arthur's sword broke in his hand, King Uther threw to his hand his own royal sword, and with it (as men understood it) the leadership of the kingdom. After that he lay back in his litter and watched the boy, ablaze like some comet of victory, lead an attack that put the Saxons to rout.

Afterwards, at the victory feast, Lot headed a faction of rebel lords who opposed Uther's choice of heir. At the height of the brawling, contentious feast, King Uther died, leaving the boy, with myself beside him, to face and win them over.

What happened then has become the stuff of song and story. Enough here to say that by his own kingly bearing, and through the sign sent from the god, Arthur showed himself undoubted King.

But the evil seed had already been sown. On the previous day, while he was still ignorant of his true parentage, Arthur had met Morgause, Uther's bastard daughter, and his own half-sister. She was very lovely, and he was young, in all the flush of his first victory, so when she sent her maid for him that night he went eagerly, with no more thought of what the night's pleasure might bring but the cooling of his hot young blood and the loss of his maidenhood.

Hers, you may be sure, had been lost long ago. Nor was she innocent in other ways. She knew who Arthur was, and sinned with him knowingly, in a bid for power. Marriage, of course, she could not hope for, but a bastard born of incest might be a powerful weapon in her hand when the old King, her father, died, and the new young King took the throne.

When Arthur found what he had done, he might have added to his sin by killing her, but for my intervention. I banished her from court, bidding her take horse for York, where Uther's true-born daughter Morgan was lodged with her attendants, awaiting her marriage to the King of Lothian. Morgause, who like everyone else in those days was afraid of me, obeyed me and went, to practise her woman's spells and nourish her bastard in exile. Which she did, as you will hear, at her sister Morgan's expense.

But of that later. It would be better, now, to go back to the time when, in the breaking of a new and auspicious day, with Morgause out of mind and on her way to York, Arthur Pendragon sat in Luguvallium of Rheged, to receive homage, and the sun shone.

I was not there. I had already done homage, in the small hours between moonlight and sunrise, in the forest shrine where Arthur had lifted the sword of Maximus from the stone altar, and by that act declared himself the rightful King. Afterwards, when he, with the other prices and nobles, had gone in all the pomp and splendour of triumph, I had stayed alone in the shrine. I had a debt to pay to the gods of the place.

It was called a chapel now—the Perilous Chapel, Arthur had named it—but it had been a holy place long before men had laid stone on stone and raised the altar. It was sacred first to the gods of the land itself, the small spirits that haunt hill and stream and forest, together with the greater gods of air, whose power breathes through cloud and frost and speaking wind. No one knew for whom the chapel had first been built. Later, with the Romans, had come Mithras, the soldiers' god, and an altar was raised to him within it. But the place was still haunted with all its ancient holiness; the older gods received their sacrifices, and the ninefold lights still burned unquenched by the open doorway.

All through the years when Arthur had been hidden, for his own safety, with Count Ector in the Wild Forest, I had stayed near him, known only as the keeper of the shrine, the hermit of the Chapel in the Green. Here I had finally hidden the great sword of Maximus (whom the Welsh called Macsen) until the boy should come of an age to lift it, and with it drive the kingdom's enemies out and destroy them. The Emperor Maximus himself had done so, over a hundred years before, and men thought of the great sword now as a talisman, a godsent sword of magic, to be wielded only for victory, and only by the man who had the right. I, Merlinus Ambrosius, kin to Macsen, had lifted it from its long hiding-place in the earth, and had laid it aside for the one to come who would be greater than I. I hid it first in a flooded cave below the forest lake, then, finally, on the chapel altar, locked like carving in the stone, and shrouded from common sight and touch in the cold white fire called by my art from heaven.

From this unearthly blaze, to the wonder and terror of all present, Arthur had raised the sword. Afterwards, when the new King and his nobles and captains had gone from the chapel, it could be seen that the wildfire of the new god had scoured the place of all that had formerly been held sacred, leaving only the altar, to be freshly decked for him alone.

I had long known that this god brooked no companions. He was not mine, nor (I suspected) would he ever be Arthur's, but throughout the sweet three corners of Britain he was moving, emptying the ancient shrine, and changing the face of worship. I had seen with awe, and with grief, how his fires had swept away the signs of an older kind of holiness; but he had marked the Perilous Chapel—and perhaps the sword—as his own, beyond denying.

So all through that day I worked to make the shrine clean again and fit for its new tenant. It took a long time; I was stiff from recent hurts, and from a night of sleepless vigil; besides, there are things that must be performed decently and in order. But at length all was done, and when shortly before sunset, the servant of the shrine came back from the town, I took the horse he had brought, and rode down through the quiet woods.

It was late when I came to the gates, but these were open, and no one challenged me as I rode in. The place was still in a roar; the sky was alight with bonfires, the air throbbed with singing, and through the smoke one could smell roasting meats and the reek of wine. Even the presence of the dead King, lying there in the monastery church with his guards around him, could not put a bridle on men's tongues. The times were too full of happening, the town too small: only the very old and the very young found sleep that night.

I found none, certainly. It was well after night when my servant came in, and after him Ralf.

He ducked his head for the lintel—he was a tall young man—and waited till the door was shut, regarding me with a look as wary as any he had ever given me in the past when he had been my page and feared my powers.

"You're still up?"

"As you see." I was sitting in the high-backed chair beside the window. The servant had brought a brazier, kindled against the chill of the September night. I had bathed, and looked to my hurts again, and let the servant put me into a loose bedgown, before I sent him away and composed myself to rest. After the climax of fire and pain and glory that had brought Arthur to the kingship, I, who had lived my life only for that, felt the need for solitude and silence. Sleep would not come yet, but I sat, content and passive, with my eyes on the brazier's idle glow.

Ralf, still armed and jewelled as I had seen him that morning at Arthur's side in the chapel, looked tired and hollow-eyed himself, but he was young, and the night's climax was for him a new beginning, rather than an end. He said abruptly: "You should be resting. I gather that you were attacked last night on the way up to the chapel. How badly were you hurt?"

"Not mortally, though it feels bad enough! No, no, don't worry, it was bruises rather than wounds, and I've seen to them. But I'm afraid I lamed your horse for you. I'm sorry about that."

"I've seen him. There's no real damage. It will take a week, no more. But you—you look exhausted, Merlin. You should be given time to rest."

"And am I not to be?" As he hesitated, I lifted a brow at him. "Come, out with it. What don't you want to say to me?"

The wary look broke into something like a grin. But his voice, suddenly formal, was quite expressionless, the voice of the courtier who is not quite sure which way, as they say, the deer will run. "Prince Merlin, the King has desired me to bid you to his apartments. He wants to see you as soon as it is convenient for you." As he spoke his eye lingered on the door in the wall opposite the window. Until last night Arthur had slept in that annexe of my chamber, and had come and gone at my bidding. Ralf caught my eye, and the grin became real.

"In other words, straight away," he said. "I'm sorry, Merlin, but that's the message as it came to me through the chamberlain. They might have left it till morning. I was assuming you would be asleep."

"Sorry? For what? Kings have to start somewhere. Has he had any rest yet himself?"

"Not a hope. But he's got rid of the crowd at last, and they cleared the royal rooms while we were up at the shrine. He's there now."

"Attended?"

"Only Bedwyr."

That, I knew, meant, besides his friend Bedwyr, a small host of chamberers and servants, and possibly, even, a few people still waiting in the antechambers.

"Then ask him to excuse me for a few minutes. I'll be there as soon as I've dressed. Will you send Lleu to me, please?"

But this he would not have. The servant was sent with the message, and then, as naturally as he had done in the past when he was a boy, Ralf helped me himself. He took the bedgown from me and folded it, and gently, with care for my stiff limbs, eased me into a day-robe, then knelt to put my sandals on and fasten them.

"Did the day go well?" I asked him.

"Very well. No shadow on it."

"Lot of Lothian?"

He glanced up, grimly amused. "Kept his place. The affair of the chapel has left its brand on him . . . as it has on all of us." The last phrase was muttered, as if to himself, as he bent his head to buckle the second sandal.

"On me, too, Ralf," I said. "I am not immune from the god's fire, either. As you see. How is Arthur?"

"Still on his own high and burning cloud." This time the amusement held affection. He got to his feet. "All the same, I think he's already looking ahead for storms. Now, your girdle. It this the one?"

"It will do. Thank you. Storms? So soon? I suppose so." I took the girdle from him and knotted it. "Do you intend to stay with him, Ralf, and help him weather them, or do you count your duty done?" Ralf had spent the last nine years in Galava of Rheged, the remote corner of the country where Arthur had lived, unknown, as the ward of Count Ector. He had married a northern girl, and had a young family.

"To tell you the truth I've not thought about that yet," he said. "Too much has happened, all too quickly." He laughed. "One thing, if I stay with him, I can see that I'll look back with longing on the peaceful days when I had nothing to do but ride guard on those young dev—this is, on Bedwyr and the King! And you? You will hardly stay here as the hermit of the Green Chapel now? Will you come out of your fastness, and go with him?"

"I must. I have promised. Besides, it is my place. Not yours, though, unless you wish it. Between us, we made him King, and that is the end of the first part of the story. You have a choice now. But you'll have plenty of time to make it." He opened the door for me, and stood aside to let me pass him. I paused. "We whistled up a strong wind, Ralf. Let us see which way it will blow us."

"You'd let it?"

I laughed. "I have a speaking mind that tells me I may have to. Come, let us start by obeying this summons."

There were a few people still in the main antechamber to the King's apartments, but these were mostly servants, clearing and bearing away the remains of a meal that the King had apparently just finished. Guards stood woodenly at the door to the inner rooms. On a low bench near a window a young page lay fast asleep; I remembered seeing him when I had come this way three days ago to talk with the dying Uther. Ulfin, the King's body-servant and chief chamberlain, was absent. I could guess where he was. He would serve the new King with all the devotion he had given to Uther, but tonight he would be found with his old master in the monastery church. The man who waited by Arthur's door was a stranger to me, as were half the servants there; they were men and women who normally served Rheged's own king in his castle, and who were helping with the extra pressure of work brought by the occasion, and the High King's presence.

But they all knew me. As I entered the antechamber there was a sudden silence, and a complete cessation of movement, as if a spell had been cast. A servant carrying platters balanced along his arm froze like someone faced with the Gorgon's head, and the faces that turned to me were frozen similarly, pale and gape-mouthed, full of awe. I caught Ralf's eye on me, sardonic and affectionate. His brow quirked. "You see?" it said to me, and I understood more fully his own hesitation when he came to my room with the King's message. As my servant and companion he had been close to me in the past, and had many times, in prophecy, and in what men call magic, watched and felt my power at work; but the power that had blazed and blown through the Perilous Chapel last night had been something of quite a different order. I could only guess at the stories that must have run, swift and changing as the wildfire itself, through Luguvallium; it was certain that the humbler folk had talked of nothing else all day. And like all strange tales, it would grow with the telling.

So they stood staring. As for the awe that frosted the air, like the cold wind that comes before a ghost, I was used to that. I walked through the motionless crowd to the King's door, and the guard moved aside without a challenge, but before the chamberlain could lay a hand to the door it opened, and Bedwyr came out.

Bedwyr was a quiet, dark boy, a month or two younger than Arthur. His father was Ban, the King of Benoic, and a cousin of a king of Brittany. The two boys had been close friends since childhood, when Bedwyr had been sent to Galava to learn the arts of war from Ector's master-at-arms, and to share the lessons I gave Emrys (as Arthur was then called) at the shrine in the Wild Forest. He was already showing himself to be that strange contradiction, a born fighting man who is also a poet, at home equally with action and with the world of fancy and music. Pure Celt, you might say, where Arthur, like my father the High King Ambrosius, was Roman. I might have expected to see in Bedwyr's face the same awe left by the events of the miraculous night as in the faces of the humbler men present, but I could see only the aftermath of joy, a sort of uncomplicated happiness, and a sturdy trust in the future.

He stood aside for me, smiling. "He's alone now."

"Where will you sleep?"

"My father is lodging in the west tower."

"Good night, then, Bedwyr."

But as I moved to pass him he prevented me. He bent quickly and took my hand, then snatched it to him and kissed it. "I should have known you would see that it all came right. I was afraid, for a few minutes there in the hall, when Lot and his jackals started that treacherous fracas—"

"Hush," I said. He had spoken softly, but there were ears to hear. "That's over for the present. Leave it. And go straight to your father in the west tower. Do you understand?"

The dark eyes glimmered. "King Lot lodges, they tell me, in the eastern one?"

"Exactly."

"Don't worry. I've already had the same warning from Emrys. Good night, Merlin."

"Good night, and a peaceful sleep to us all. We need it."

He grinned, sketched a half-salute, and went. I nodded to the waiting servant and went in. The door shut behind me.

The royal rooms had been cleared of the apparatus of sickness, and the great bed stripped of its crimson covers. The floor tiles were freshly scoured and polished, and over the bed lay new unbleached sheets, and a rug of wolfskins.

The chair with the red cushion and the dragon worked on the back in gold stood there still, with its footstool and the tall tripod lamp beside it. The windows were open to the cool September night, and the air from them sent the lamp-flames sideways and made strange shadows on the painted walls.

Arthur was alone. He was over by a window, one knee on a stool that stood there, his elbows on the sill. The window gave, not on the town, but on the strip of garden that edged the river. He gazed out into the dark, and I thought I could see him drinking, as from another river, deep draughts of the fresh and moving air. His hair was damp, as if he had just washed, but he was still in the clothes he had worn for the day's ceremonies; white and silver, with a belt of Welsh gold set with turquoises and buckled with enamel-work. He had taken off his sword-belt, and the great sword Caliburn hung in its sheath on the wall beyond the bed. The lamplight smouldered in the jewels of the hilt; emerald, topaz, sapphire. It flashed, too, from the ring on the boy's hand; Uther's ring carved with the Dragon crest.

He heard me, and turned. He looked rarefied and light, as if the winds of the day had blown through him and left him weightless. His skin had the stretched pallor of exhaustion, but his eyes were brilliant and alive. About him, already there and unmistakable, was the mystery that falls like a mantle on a king. It was in his high look, and the turn of his head. Never again would "Emrys" be able to lurk in shadow. I wondered afresh how through all those hidden years we had kept him safe and secret among lesser men.

"You wanted me," I said.

"I've wanted you all day. You promised to be near me while I went through this business of hatching into a king. Where were you?"

"Within call, if not within reach. I was at the shrine—the chapel—till almost sunset. I thought you'd be busy."

He gave a little crack of laughter. "You call it that? It felt like being eaten alive. Or perhaps like being born . . . and a hard birth at that. I said 'hatching,' didn't I? Suddenly to find oneself a prince is hard enough, but even that is as different from being a king as the egg is from the day-old chick."

"At least make it an eaglet."

"In time, perhaps. That's been the trouble, of course. Time, there's been no time. One moment to be nobody—someone's unacknowledged bastard, and glad to be given the chance to get within shouting distance of a battle, with maybe a glimpse of the King himself in passing; the next—having drawn a couple of breaths as prince and royal heir—to be High King myself, and with such a flourish as no king can ever have had before. I still feel as if I'd been kicked up the steps of the throne from a kneeling position right down on the floor."

I smiled. "I know how you feel, more or less. I was never kicked half as high, but then I was a great deal lower down to start with. Now, can you slow down sufficiently to get some sleep? Tomorrow will be here soon enough. Do you want a sleeping potion?"

"No, no, when did I ever? I'll sleep as soon as you've gone. Merlin, I'm sorry to ask you to come here at this late hour, but I had to talk to you, and there's been no chance till now. Nor will there be tomorrow."

He came away from the window as he spoke, and crossed to a table where papers and tablets were lying. He picked up a stilus, and with the blunt end smoothed the wax. He did it absently, his head bent so that the dark hair swung forward, and the lamplight slid over the line of his cheek and touched the black lashes fringing the lowered lids. My eyes blurred. Time ran back. It was Ambrosius my father who stood there, fidgeting with the stilus and saying to me: "If a king had you beside him, he could rule the world. . . ."

Well, his dream had come true at last, and the time was now. I blinked memory away, and waited for the day-old King to speak.

"I've been thinking," he said abruptly. "The Saxon army was not utterly destroyed, and I have had no firm report yet about Colgrim himself, or Badulf. I think they both got safely away. We may hear within the next day or so that they have taken ship and gone, either home across the sea or back to the Saxon territories in the south. Or they may simply have taken refuge in the wild lands north of the Wall, and be hoping to regroup when they have gathered strength again." He looked up. "I have no need to pretend to you, Merlin. I am not a seasoned warrior, and I've no means of judging how decisive that defeat was, or what the possibilities are of a Saxon recovery. I've taken advice, of course. I called a quick council at sunset, when the other business was concluded. I sent for—that is, I would have liked you to be there, but you were still up at the chapel. Coel couldn't be there, either. . . . You'd know he was wounded, of course; you probably saw him yourself? What are his chances?"

"Slight. He's an old man, as you know, and he got a nasty slash. He bled too much before help got to him."

"I was afraid of it. I did go to see him, but was told he was unconscious, and they were afraid of inflammation of the lungs. . . . Well, Prince Urbgen, his heir, came in his stead, with Cador, and Caw of Strathclyde. Ector and Ban of Benoic were there, too. I talked it over with them, and they all say the same thing: someone will have to follow Colgrim up. Caw has to go north again as soon as may be; he has his own frontier to hold. Urbgen must stay here in Rheged, with his father the king at death's door. So the obvious choice would be Lot or Cador. Well, it cannot be Lot, I think you will agree there? For all his oath of fealty, there in the chapel, I won't trust him yet, and certainly not within reach of Colgrim."

"I agree. You'll send Cador, then? You can surely have no more doubts of him?"

Cador, Duke or Cornwall, was indeed the obvious choice. He was a man in the prime of his strength, a seasoned fighter, and loyal. I had once mistakenly thought him Arthur's enemy, and indeed he had had cause to be; but Cador was a man of sense, judicious and far-sighted, who could see beyond his hatred of Uther to the larger vision of a Britain united against the Saxon Terror. So he had supported Arthur. And Arthur, up there in the Perilous Chapel, had declared Cador and his sons the heirs to the kingdom.

So Arthur said merely: "How could I?" and scowled for a moment longer at the stilus. Then he dropped it on the table, and straightened. "The thing is, with my own leadership so new—" He looked up then, and saw me smiling. The frown vanished, to be replaced by a look I knew: eager, impetuous, the look of a boy, but behind it a man's will that would burn its way through any opposition. His eyes danced. "Yes, you're right, as usual. I'm going myself."

"And Cador with you?"

"No. I think I must go without him. After what happened, my father's death, and then the—" he hesitated—"then what happened up in the chapel yonder . . . if there is to be more fighting, I must be there myself, to lead the armies, and be seen to finish the work we started."

He paused, as if still expecting question or protest, but I made none.

"I thought you would try to prevent me."

"No. Why? I agree with you. You have to prove yourself to be above luck."

"That's it exactly." He thought for a moment. "It's hard to put it into words, but ever since you brought me to Luguvallium and presented me to the King, it has seemed—not like a dream exactly, but as if something were using me, using all of us. . . ."

"Yes. A strong wind blowing, and carrying us all with it."

"And now the wind has died down," he said, soberly, "and we are left to live life by our own strength only. As if—well, as if it had all been magic and miracles, and now they had gone. Have you noticed, Merlin, that no one man has spoken of what happened up yonder in the shrine? Already it's as if it had happened well in the past, in some song or story."

"One can see why. The magic was real, and too strong for many of those who witnessed it, but it has burned down into the memories of all who saw it, and into the memory of the folk who make the songs and legends. Well, that is for the future. But we are here now, and with the work still to do. And one thing is certain; only you can do it. So you must go ahead and do it in your own way."

The young face relaxed. His hands flattened on the table as he leaned his weight on them. For the first time it could be seen that he was very tired, and that it was a kind of relief to let the weariness sweep over him, and with it the need for sleep.

"I should have known you would understand. So you see why I must go myself, without Cador. He didn't like it, I confess, but he saw the point in the end. And to be honest, I would have liked him with me. . . . But this is something I must do alone. You might say it's as much for my own reassurance as for the people's. I can say that to you."

"Do you need reassurance?"

A hint of a smile. "Not really. In the morning I shall probably be able to believe everything that happened on the battlefield, and know it for real, but now it's still like being in the edges of a dream. Tell me, Merlin, can I ask Cador to go south to escort Queen Ygraine, my mother, from Cornwall?"

"There's no reason why not. He is Duke of Cornwall, so since Uther's death her home at Tintagel must fall under his protection. If Cador was able to sink his hatred of Uther into the common weal, he must long ago have been able to forgive Ygraine for her betrayal of his father. And now you have declared his sons your heirs to the High Kingdom, so all scores are paid. Yes, send Cador."

He looked relieved. "Then all's well. I've already sent a courier to her, of course, with the news. Cador should meet her on the road. They will be in Amesbury by the time my father's body arrives there for burial."

"Do I take it, then, that you want me to escort the body to Amesbury?"

"If you will. I cannot possibly go myself, as I should, and it must be royally escorted. Better you, perhaps, who knew him, than I, who am so recently royal. Besides, if he is to lie beside Ambrosius in the Dance of the Hanging Stones, you should be there to see the king-stone shifted and the grave made. You'll do that?"

"Certainly. It should take us, going in a seemly way, about nine days."

"By that time I should be there myself." A sudden flash. "With average luck, that is. I'm expecting word soon, about Colgrim. I'll be going after him in about four hours' time, as soon as it's full light. Bedwyr goes with me," he added, as if that should be a comfort and a reassurance.

"And what of King Lot, since I have gathered he does not go with you?"

At that I got a blank look, and a tone as smooth as any politician's. "He leaves, too, at first light. Not for his own land . . . not, that is, until I find which way Colgrim went. No, I urged King Lot to go straight to York. I believe Queen Ygraine will go there after the burial, and Lot can receive her. Then, once his marriage with my sister Morgan is celebrated, I suppose I can count him an ally, like it or not. And the rest of the fighting, whatever comes between now and Christmastime, I can do without him."

"So, I shall see you in Amesbury. And after that?"

"Caerleon," he said, without hesitation. "If the wars allow it, I shall go there. I've never seen it, and from what Cador tells me it must be my headquarters now."

"Until the Saxons break the treaty and move in from the south."

"As of course they will. Until then. God send there will be time to breathe first."

"And to build another stronghold."

He looked up quickly. "Yes. I was thinking of that. You'll be there to do it?" Then, with sudden urgency: "Merlin, you swear you will always be there?"

"As long as I am needed. Though it seems to me," I added lightly, "that the eaglet is fledging fast enough already." Then, because I knew what lay behind the sudden uncertainty: "I shall wait for you at Amesbury, and I shall be there to present you to your mother."

2

Amesbury is little more than a village, but since Ambrosius' day it has taken some kind of grandeur to itself, as befits his birthplace, and its nearness to the great monument of the Hanging Stones that stand on the windy Sarum plain. This is a linked circle of vast stone, a gigantic Dance, which was raised first in times beyond men's memory. I had (by what folk persisted in seeing as "magic art") rebuilt the Dance to be Britain's monument of glory, and the burial-place of her kings. Here Uther was to lie beside his brother Ambrosius.

We brought his body without incident to Amesbury and left it in the monastery there, wrapped in spices and coffined in hollowed oak, under its purple pall before the chapel altar. The King's guard (who had ridden south with his body) stood vigil, and the monks and nuns of Amesbury prayed beside the bier. Queen Ygraine being a Christian, the dead king was to be buried with all the rites and ceremonies of the Christian church, though in life he had barely troubled even to pay lip-service to the Christians' God. Even now he lay with gold coins glinting on the eyelids, to pay the fee of a ferryman who had exacted such toll for centuries longer than Saint Peter of the Gate. The chapel itself had apparently been erected on the site of a Roman shrine; it was little more than an oblong erection of daub and wattle, with wooden shafts holding up a roof of thatch, but it had a floor of fine mosaic work, scrubbed clean and hardly damaged. This, showing scrolls of vine and acanthus, would offend no Christian souls, and a woven rug lay centrally, probably to cover whatever pagan god or goddess floated naked among the grapes.

The monastery reflected something of Amesbury's new prosperity. It was a miscellaneous collection of buildings huddled anyhow around a cobbled yard, but these were in good repair, and the Abbot's house, which had been vacated for the Queen and her train, was well built of stone, with wooden flooring, and a big fireplace at one end with a chimney.

The headman of the village, too, had a good house, which he made haste to offer me for lodging, but explaining that the King would follow me soon, I left him in an uproar of extra preparation, and betook myself with my servants to the tavern. This was small, with little pretension to comfort, but it was clean, and fires were kept burning high against the autumn chills. The innkeeper remembered me from the time I had lodged there during the rebuilding of the Dance; he still showed the awe that the exploit had raised in him, and made haste to give me the best room, and to promise me fresh poultry and a mutton pie for supper. He showed relief when I told him that I had brought two servants with me, who would serve me in my own chamber, and banished his own staring pot-boys to their posts at the kitchen burners.

The servants I had brought were two of Arthur's. In recent years, living alone in the Wild Forest, I had cared for myself, and now had none of my own.

One was a small, lively man from the hills of Gwynedd; the other was Ulfin, who had been Uther's own servant. The late King had taken him from a rough servitude, and had shown him kindness, which Ulfin repaid with devotion. This would now belong to Arthur, but it would have been cruel to deny Ulfin the chance of following his master's body on its last journey, so I had asked for him by name. By my orders he had gone to the chapel with the bier, and I doubted if I would see him before the funeral was over. Meantime, the Welshman, Lleu, unpacked my boxes and bespoke hot water, and sent the more intelligent of the landlord's boys across to the monastery with a message from me to be delivered to the Queen on her arrival. In it I bade her welcome, and offered to wait on her as soon as she should be rested enough to send for me. News of the happenings in Luguvallium she had had already; now I added merely that Arthur was not yet in Amesbury, but was expected in time for the burial.

I was not in Amesbury when her party arrived. I rode out to the Giants' Dance to see that all was ready for the ceremony, to be told on my return that the Queen and her escort had arrived shortly after noon, and that Ygraine with her ladies was settled into the Abbot's house. Her summons to me came just as afternoon dimmed into evening.

The sun had gone down in a clouded sky, and when, refusing the offer of an escort, I walked the short distance to the monastery, it was already almost dark. The night was heavy as a pall, a mourning sky, where no stars shone. I remembered the great king-star that had blazed for Ambrosius' death, and my thoughts went again to the King who lay nearby in the chapel, with monks for mourners, and the guards like statues beside the bier. And Ulfin, who, alone of all those who saw him die, had wept for him.

A chamberlain met me at the monastery gate. Not the monks' porter; this was one of the queen's own servants, a royal chamberlain I recognized from Cornwall. He knew who I was, of course, and bowed very low, but I could see that he did not recall our last meeting. It was the same man, grown greyer and more bent, who had admitted me to the Queen's presence some three months before Arthur's birth, when she had promised to confide the child to my care. I had been disguised then, for fear of Uther's enmity, and it was plain that the chamberlain did not recognize, in the tall prince at the gate, the humbled bearded "doctor" who had called to consult with the Queen.

He led me across the weedy courtyard toward the big thatched building where the Queen was lodged. Cressets burned outside the door and here and there along the wall, so that the poverty of the place showed starkly. After the wet summer weeds had sprouted freely among the cobbles, and the corners of the yard were waist-high in nettles. Among these the wooden ploughs and mattocks of the working brothers stood, wrapped in sacking. Near one doorway was an anvil, and on a nail driven into the jamb hung a line of horse-shoes. A litter of thin black piglings tumbled, squealing, out of our way, and were called by a sow's anxious grunting through the broken planks of a half-door. The holy men and women of Amesbury were simple folk. I wondered how the queen was faring.

I need not have feared for her. Ygraine had always been a lady who knew her own mind, and since her marriage to Uther she had kept a most queenly state, urged to this, possibly, by the very irregularity of that marriage. I remembered the Abbot's house as a humble dwelling, clean and dry, but boasting no comfort. Now in a few short hours the Queen's people had seen to it that it was luxurious. The walls, of undressed stone, had been hidden by hangings of scarlet and green and peacock blue, and one beautiful Eastern carpet that I had brought for her from Byzantium. The wooden floor was scrubbed white, and the benches that stood along the walls were piled with furs and cushions. A great fire of logs burned on the hearth. To one side of this was set a tall chair of gilded wood, cushioned in embroidered wool, with a footstool fringed with gold. Across from this stood another chair with a high back, and arms carved with dragons' heads. The lamp was a five-headed dragon in bronze. The door to the Abbot's austere sleeping chamber stood open, and beyond it I caught a glimpse of a bed hung with blue, and the sheen of a silver fringe. Three or four women—two of them no more than girls—were busying themselves in the bedchamber and over the table, which, at the end of the room away from the fire, stood ready for supper. Pages dressed in blue ran with dishes and flagons. Three white greyhounds lay as near to the fire as they dared go.

As I entered, there was a pause in the bustle and chatter. All eyes turned to the doorway. A page bearing a wine-jar, caught within a yard of the door, checked, swerved, and stared, showing the whites of his eyes. Someone at the table dropped a wooden trencher, and the greyhounds pounced on the fallen cakes. The scrabbling of their claws and their munching were the only sounds in the room to be heard through the rustling of the fire.

"Good evening," I said pleasantly. I answered the women's reverences, watched gravely while a boy picked up the fallen trencher and kicked the dogs out of the way, then allowed myself to be ushered by the chamberlain toward the hearthplace.

"The Queen—" he was beginning, when the eyes turned from me to the inner door, and the greyhounds, arched and wagging, danced to meet the woman who came through it.

But for the hounds and the curtsying women, a stranger might have thought that here was the Abbess of the place come to greet me. The woman who entered was as much a contrast to the rich room as that room had been to the squalid courtyard. She was dressed from head to foot in black, with a white veil covering her hair, its ends thrown back over her shoulders, and its soft folds pinned to frame her face like a wimple. The sleeves of her gown were lined with some grey silken stuff, and there was a cross of sapphires on her breast, but to the somber black and white of her mourning there was no other relief.

It was a long time since I had seen Ygraine, and I expected to find her changed, but even so I was shocked at what I saw. Beauty was still there, in the lines of bone and the great dark-blue eyes and the queenly poise of her body; but grace had given way to dignity, and there was a thinness about the wrists and hands that I did not like, and shadows near her eyes almost as blue as the eyes themselves. This, not the ravages of time was what shocked me. There were signs everywhere that a doctor could read all too clearly.

But I was here as prince and emissary, not a physician. I returned her smile of greeting, bowed over her hand, and led her to the cushioned chair. At a sign from her the boys ran to collar the greyhounds and take them aside, and she settled herself, smoothing her skirt. One of the girls moved a footstool for her, and then, with lowered eyelids and folded hands, stayed beside her mistress's chair.

The Queen bade me be seated, and I obeyed her. Someone brought wine, and across the cups we exchanged the commonplaces of the meeting. I asked her how she did, but with purely formal courtesy, and I knew she could read nothing of my knowledge in my face.

"And the King?" she asked at length. The word came from her as if forced, with a kind of pain behind it.

"Arthur promised to be here. I expect him tomorrow. There has been no news from the north, so we have no means of knowing if there has been more fighting. The lack of news need not alarm you; it only means that he will be here as soon as any courier he might have sent."

She nodded, with no sign of anxiety. Either she could not think much beyond her own loss, or she took my tranquil tone as a prophet's reassurance. "Did he expect more fighting?"

"He stayed as a cautionary measure, no more. The defeat of Colgrim's men was decisive, but Colgrim himself escaped, as I wrote to you. We had no report on where he had gone. Arthur thought it better to make sure that the scattered Saxon forces could not re-form, at least while he came south for his father's burial."

"He is young," she said, "for such a charge."

I smiled. "But ready for it, and more than able. Believe me, it was like seeing a young falcon take to the air, or a swan to the water. When I took leave of him, he had not slept for the better part of two nights, and was in high heat and excellent health."

"I am glad of it."

She spoke formally, without expression, but I thought it better to qualify. "The death of his father came as a shock and a grief, but as you will understand, Ygraine, it could not come very near his heart, and there was much to be done that crowded out sorrow."

"I have not been so fortunate," she said, very low, and looked down at her hands.

I was silent, understanding. The passion that had driven Uther and this woman together, with a kingdom at stake for it, had not burned out with the years. Uther had been a man who needed women as most men need food and sleep, and when his kingly duties had taken him away from the Queen's bed, his own was rarely empty; but when they were together he had never looked aside, nor given her cause for grief. They had loved each other, King and Queen, in the old high way of love, which had outlasted youth and health and the shifts of compromise and expediency which are the price of kingship. I had come to believe that their son Arthur, deprived as he had been of royal status, and brought up in obscurity, had fared better in his foster-home at Galava than he would have done at his father's court, where with both King and Queen he would have come far behind the best.

She looked up at last, her face serene again. "I had your letter, and Arthur's, but there is so much more that I want to hear. Tell me what happened at Luguvallium. When he left to ride north against Colgrim, I knew he was not fit to do so. He swore he must take the field, even if he had to be carried in a litter. Which, I understand, is what happened?"

For Ygraine, the "he" of Luguvallium was certainly not her son. What she wanted was the story of Uther's last days, not the tale of Arthur's miraculous coming into his kingdom. I gave it to her.

"Yes. It was a great fight, and he fought it greatly. They carried him to the battlefield in a chair, and all through the fighting his servants kept him there, in the very thick of the battle. I had Arthur brought down from Galava at his orders, for him to be publicly acknowledged, but Colgrim attacked suddenly, and the King had to take the field without making the proclamation. He kept Arthur near him, and when he saw the boy's sword broken in the fight, threw him his own. I doubt if Arthur, in the heat of the battle, saw the gesture for what it was, but everyone else did who was near. It was a great gesture, made by a great man."

She did not speak, but her eyes rewarded me. Ygraine knew, none better, that Uther and I had never loved one another. Praise from me was something quite other than the flattery of the court.

"And afterwards the King sat back in his chair and watched his son carry the fight through to the enemy, and, untried as he was, bear his part in the rout of the Saxons. So later, when he presented the boy at last to the nobles and the captains, his work was half done. They had seen the sword of kingship handed over, and they had seen how worthily it had been used. But there was, in fact, some opposition. . . ."

I hesitated. It was that very opposition that had killed Uther; only a few hours before time, but as surely as the blow from an axe. And King Lot, who had led the opposing faction, was contracted to marry Ygraine's daughter Morgan.

Ygraine said calmly: "Ah, yes. The King of Lothian. I heard something of it. Tell me."

I should have known her. I gave her the whole story, omitting nothing. The roaring opposition, the treachery, the sudden, silencing death of the King. I told her of Arthur's eventual acclamation by the company, though dwelling lightly on my part in that. *("If he has indeed got the sword of Macsen, he got it by God's gift, and if he has Merlin beside him, then by any god he follows, I follow!")* Nor did I dwell on the scene in the chapel, but told her merely of the oath-taking, of Lot's submission, and Arthur's declaration of Gorlois' son Cador as his heir.

At this, for the first time, the beautiful eyes lightened, and she smiled. I could see that this was news to her, and must go some way to assuaging the guilt of her own part in Gorlois' death. Apparently Cador, either through delicacy, or because he and Ygraine still held aloof from one another, had not told her himself. She put out her hand for her wine, and sat sipping it while I finished the tale, the smile still on her mouth.

One other thing, one most important thing, would also have been news to her; but of this I said nothing. But the unspoken part of the tale was loud in my own mind so that when Ygraine spoke next, I must have jumped like a dog to the whip. "And Morgause?"

"Madam?"

"You have not spoken of her. She must have grieved for her father. It was a fortunate thing that she could be near him. He and I have both had cause to thank God for her skills."

I said, neutrally: "She nursed him with devotion. I am sure that she will miss him bitterly."

"Does she come south with Arthur?"

"No. She has gone to York, to be with her sister Morgan."

To my relief she asked no more questions about Morgause, but turned the subject, asking where I was lodged.

"In the tavern," I told her. "I know it from the old days, when I was working here. It's a simple kind of place, but they have taken pains to make me comfortable. I shan't be here for long." I glanced round me at the glowing room. "For yourself, do you plan a long stay, madam?"

"A few days only." If she had noticed my look at the luxury surrounding her, she gave no sign of it. I, who am not normally wise in the ways of women, realized suddenly that the richness and beauty of the place were not for Ygraine's own comfort, but had been deliberately contrived as a setting for her first meeting with her son. The scarlet and gold, the scents and waxlights, were this ageing woman's shield and enchanted sword.

"Tell me—" She spoke abruptly, straight out of the preoccupation that, through all else, bound her. "Does he blame me?"

It was the measure of my respect for Ygraine that I answered her directly, with no pretense that the subject was not uppermost in my mind as well. "I think you need have no fear of this meeting. When he first knew of his parentage, and of his inheritance, he wondered why you and the King had seen fit to deny him that birthright. He could not be blamed if, at first, he felt himself wronged. He had already begun to suspect that he was royal, but he assumed that—as in my case—the royalty came sideways. . . . When he knew the truth, with the elation came the wondering. But—and I swear that this is true—he gave no hint of bitterness or anger; he was anxious only to know why. When I had told him the story of his birth and fostering, he said—and I will give you his exact words—'I see it as you say she saw it; that to be a prince one must be ruled always by necessity. She did not give me up for nothing.' "

There was a little silence. Through it I heard echoing, unspoken save in my memory, the words with which he had finished: "I was better in the Wild Forest, thinking myself fatherless, and your bastard, Merlin, than waiting yearly in my father's castle for the Queen to bear another child to supplant me."

Her lips relaxed, and I saw her sigh. The soft underlids of her eyes had a faint tremor, which stilled as if a finger had been laid on a thrumming string. Colour came into her face, and she looked at me as she had looked all those years ago, when she had begged me to take the baby away and hide him from Uther's anger. "Tell me . . . what is he like?"

I smiled slightly. "Did they not tell you, when they brought you news of the battle?"

"Oh, yes, they told me. He is as tall as an oak tree and as strong as Fionn, and slew nine hundred men with his own hand alone. He is Ambrosius come again, or Maximus himself, with a sword like the lightning, and the witchlight round him in battle like the pictures of the gods at the fall of Troy. And he is Merlin's shadow and spirit, and a great hound follows him everywhere, to whom he speaks as to a familiar." Her eyes danced. "You may guess from all this that the messengers were black Cornishmen from Cador's troop. They would always rather sing a poem than state a fact. I want fact."

She always had. Like her, Arthur had dealt with facts, even as a child; he left the poetry to Bedwyr. I gave her what she wanted. "The last bit is almost true, but they got it the wrong way round. It is Merlin who is Arthur's shadow and spirit, like the great hound who is real enough; that's Cabal his dog that his friend Bedwyr gave him. For the rest, what shall I say? You'll see for yourself tomorrow. . . . He is tall and favours Uther rather than you, though he has my father's colouring; his eyes and hair are as dark as mine. He is strong, and full of courage and endurance—all the things your Cornishmen told you, brought down to life-size. He has the hot blood and high temper of youth, and he can be impulsive or arrogant, but under it all he has hard sense and a growing power of control, like any good man of his age. And he has what I consider a very great virtue. He is willing to listen to me."

This won another smile from her, with real warmth in it. "You mean to jest, but I am with you in counting that a virtue! He is lucky to have you. As a Christian, I am not allowed to believe in your magic—indeed, I do not believe in it as the common folk do; but whatever it is, and wherever it comes from, I have seen your power working, and I know that it is good, and that you are wise. I believe that whatever owns and moves you is what I call God. Stay with my son."

"I shall stay as long as he needs me."

Silence fell between us then, while we both looked at the fire. Ygraine's eyes dreamed under their long shadowed lids, and her face grew still once more, and tranquil; but I thought it was the waiting stillness of the forest depth, where overhead the boughs roar in the wind, and the trees feel the storms shaking them to the very root.

A boy came tiptoeing to kneel on the hearth and pile fresh logs on the fire. Flames crept, crackled, leaped into light. I watched them. For me, too, the pause was merely one of waiting; the flames were only flames.

The boy went away quietly. The girl took the goblet from the Queen's relaxed hand, and held her own out, a timid gesture, for my cup. She was a pretty creature, slim as a wand, with grey eyes and light-brown hair. She looked half-scared of me, and was careful, as I gave her the cup, not to touch my hand. She went quickly away with the empty vessels. I said softly: "Ygraine, is your physician here with you?"

Her eyelids fluttered. She did not look at me, but answered softly. "Yes. He travels with me always."

"Who is it?"

"His name is Melchior. He says he knows you."

"Melchior? A young man I met in Pergamum when I studied medicine there?"

"The same. Not so young now. He was with me when Morgan was born."

"He is a good man," I said, satisfied.

She glanced at me sideways. The girl was still out of hearing, with the rest of the women at the other side of the room. "I should have known I could hide nothing from you. You won't let my son know?"

I promised readily. That she was mortally ill I had known as soon as I saw her, but Arthur, not knowing her, and having no skill in medicine, might notice nothing. Time enough for that later. Now was for beginnings rather than endings.

The girl came and whispered to the Queen, who nodded and stood up. I rose with her. The chamberlain was advancing with some ceremony, lending the borrowed chamber yet another touch of royalty. The Queen half turned to me, her hand lifting to invite me with her to table, when suddenly the scene was interrupted. From somewhere outside came the distant call of a trumpet; then another, nearer, and then, all at once, the clash and excitement of arriving horsemen, somewhere beyond the monastery walls.

Ygraine's head went up, with something of the old lift of youth and courage. She stood very still. "The King?" Her voice was light and quick. Round the listening room, like an echo, went the rustle and murmur of the women. The girl beside the Queen was as taut as a bowstring, and I saw a vivid blush of excitement run up clear from neck to forehead.

"He is early," I said. My voice sounded flat and precise. I was subduing a pulse in my own wrist, which had quickened with the swelling hoof-beats. Fool, I told myself, fool. He is about his own business now. You loosed him, and lost him; that is one hawk who will never be hooded again. Stay back in the shadows, king's prophet; see your visions and dream your dreams. Leave life to him, and wait for his need.

A knock at the door, and a servant's quick voice. The chamberlain went bustling, but before him a boy came pelting with the message hurriedly relayed, and stripped of its courtly phrasing:

"With the Queen's leave . . . The King is here and wants Prince Merlin. Now, he says."

As I went I heard the silent room break into hubbub behind me, as the pages were sent scurrying to refurbish the tables, and bring fresh waxlights and scents and wine; and the women, clucking and crooning like a yardful of fowl, bustled after the Queen into the bedchamber.

3

"She's here, they tell me?" Arthur was hindering, rather than helping, a servant drag off his muddied boots. Ulfin had after all come back from the chapel; I could hear him in the adjoining room, directing the servants of the household in the unpacking and bestowing of Arthur's clothes and furnishings. Outside, the town seemed to have burst open with noise and torches and the stamping of horses and the shouting of orders. Now and again one could hear, distinct through the hubbub, the squealing giggle of a girl. Not everyone in Amesbury was in mourning.

The King himself gave little sign of it. He kicked free of his boots at last and shrugged the heavy cloak off his shoulders. His eyes came to me in an exact parody of Ygraine's sidelong look. "Have you spoken with her?"

"Yes. I've just left her. She was about to give me supper, but now I think she plans to feed you instead. She only got here today, and you'll find her tired, but she has had some rest, and she'll rest again all the better for having seen you. We hardly expected you before morning."

" 'Caesar-speed.' " He grinned, quoting one of my father's phrases; no doubt I, as his teacher, had over-used it rather. "Only myself and a handful, of course. We pushed ahead. The rest of them will come up later. I trust they will be here in time for the burial."

"Who is coming?"

"Maelgon of Gwynedd, and his son Maelgon. Urbgen's brother from Rheged—old Coel's third son, his name's Morien, isn't it? Caw couldn't come either, so he's sent Riderch—not Heuil, I'm glad to say, I never could stand that foul-mouthed braggart. Then, let me see, Ynyr and Gwilim, Bors . . . and I am told that Ceretic of Elmet is on his way from Loidis."

He went on to name a few others. It seemed that most of the northern kings had sent sons or substitutes; naturally with the remnant of the Saxon armies still haunting the north they would want to stay watching their own borders. So much, indeed, Arthur was saying through the splashing of the water his servant poured for him to wash himself in. "Bedwyr's father went home, too. He pleaded some urgency, but between ourselves I think he wanted to keep an eye for me on Lot's movements."

"And Lot?"

"Headed for York. I took the precaution of having him watched. Sure enough he's on his way. Is Morgan there still, or did she come south to meet the Queen?"

"She's still at York. There is one king you haven't mentioned yet."

The servant gave him a towel, and Arthur disappeared into it, scrubbing his wet hair dry. His voice came muffled. "Who?"

"Colgrim," I said mildly.

He emerged abruptly from the towel, skin glowing and eyes bright. He looked, I thought, about ten years old. "Need you ask?" The voice was not ten years old; it was a man's, full of mock arrogance, which under the mischief was real. Well, you gods, I thought, you put him there; you cannot count this as hubris. But I caught myself making the sign.

"No, but I am asking."

He was serious at once.

"It was tougher work than we'd expected. You might say that the second half of the battle was still to fight. We broke their strength at Luguvallium, and Badulf has died of wounds, but Colgrim was unhurt, and rallied what was left of his forces some way to the east. It wasn't just a case of hunting down fugitives; they had a formidable force there, and a desperate one. If we had gone in any less strength, they might even have turned the tables on us. I doubt if they would have attacked again—they were making for the east coast, and home, but we caught them halfway there, and they made a stand on the Glein River. Do you know that part of the country?"

"Not well."

"It's wild and hilly, deep in forest, with river glens winding south out of the uplands. Bad fighting country, but that was against them as well as us. Colgrim himself got away again, but thre's no chance now that he can pause and remuster any sort of force in the north. He rode east; that's one of the reasons that Ban stayed behind, though he was good enough to let Bedwyr come south with me again." He stood still, obedient now to his servant's hands as he was dressed, a fresh cloak flung over his shoulder and the pin made fast. "I'm glad," he finished, briefly.

"That Bedwyr's here? So I—"

"No. That Colgrim escaped again."

"Yes?"

"He's a brave man."

"Nevertheless, you will have to kill him."

"I know that. Now . . ." The servant stepped back, and the King stood ready. They had dressed him in dark grey, his cloak collared and lined with rich fur. Ulfin came from the bedchamber, holding a carved casket lined with embroidery, where Uther's royal circlet lay. The rubies caught the light, answering the flash from the jewels at Arthur's shoulder and breast. But when Ulfin proffered the box he shook his head. "Not now, I think."

Ulfin shut the box and went from the room, taking the other man with him. The door latched behind them. Arthur looked at me, in another echo of Ygraine's own hesitation. "Am I to understand that she expects me now?"

"Yes."

He fidgeted with the brooch at his shoulder, pricked his finger, and swore. Then, with a half-smile at me: "There's not much precedent for this sort of thing, is there? How does one meet the mother who gave one away at birth?"

"How did you greet your father?"

"That's different, you know it is."

"Yes. Do you want me to present you?"

"I was going to ask you to. . . . Well, we'd better get on with it. Some situations don't improve with keeping. . . . Look, you are sure about the supper? I've eaten nothing since dawn."

"Certain. They were running for fresh meats when I left."

He took a breath, like a swimmer before a deep dive. "Then shall we go?"

She was waiting beside her chair, standing in the light of the fire. Colour had run up into her cheeks, and the glow of the fire pulsed over her skin and made the white wimple rosy. She looked beautiful, with the shadows purged away, and youth lent back by the firelight and the brilliance of her eyes.

Arthur paused on the theshold. I saw the blue flash of Ygraine's sapphire cross as her breast rose and fell. Her lips parted, as if to speak, but she was silent. Arthur paced forward slowly, so dignified and stiff that he looked even younger than his years. I went with him, rehearsing in my mind the right words to say, but in the end there was no need to say anything. Ygraine the Queen, who had weathered worse moments in her time, took the occasion into her hands. She watched him for a moment, staring at him as if she would look right through his soul, then she curtsied to the ground, and said: "My lord."

He put a hand out quickly, then both hands, and raised her. He gave her the kiss of greeting, brief and formal, and held her hands for a little longer before he dropped them. He said: "Mother?" trying it out. It was what he had always called Drusilla, Count Ector's wife. Then, with relief: "Madam? I am sorry I could not be here in Amesbury to greet you, but there was still danger in the north. Merlin will have told you? But I came as quickly as I could."

"You made better speed than we could have hoped for. I trust you prospered? And that the danger from Colgrim's force is over?"

"For the moment. We have time, at least, to breathe . . . and to do what is to be done here in Amesbury. I am sorry for your grief and loss, madam. I—" He hesitated, then spoke with a simplicity that, I could see, comforted her and steadied him. "I can't pretend to you that I grieve as perhaps I should. I hardly knew him as a father, but all my life I have known him as a king, and a strong one. His people will mourn him, and I, too, mourn him as one of them."

"You have it in your hands to guard them as he tried to guard them." A pause, while they measured one another again. She was a fraction the taller of the two. Perhaps the same thought touched her; she motioned him toward the chair where I had been sitting, and herself sank back against the embroidered cushions. A page came running with wine, and there was a general breathing and rustle of movement. The Queen began to speak of tomorrow's ceremony; answering her, he relaxed, and soon they were talking more freely. But still behind the courtly exchanges could be felt all the turmoil of what lay between them unspoken, the air so charged, their minds so locked on one another, that they had forgotten my presence as completely as if I had been one of the servants waiting by the laden table. I glanced that way, then at the women and girls beside the Queen; all eyes were on Arthur, devouring him, the men with curiosity and some awe (the stories had reached them soon enough), the women with something added to the curiosity, and the two girls in a dazzled trance of excitement.

The chamberlain was hovering in a doorway. He caught my eye and looked a question. I nodded. He crossed to the Queen's side and murmured something. She assented with a kind of relief, and rose to her feet, the King with her. I noticed that the table was now laid for three, but when the chamberlain came to my elbow I shook my head. After supper their talk would be easier, and they could dismiss the servants. They would be better alone. So I took my leave, ignoring Arthur's glance almost of entreaty, and made my way back to the tavern to see if my fellow-guests there had left any of the supper for me.

Next day was bright and sunlit, with the clouds packed away low on the horizon, and a lark singing somewhere as if it were spring. Often a bright day at the end of September brings frost with it, and a searching wind—and nowhere can the winds search more keenly than on the stretches of the Great Plain. But the day of Uther's burial was a day borrowed from spring; a warm wind and a bright sky, and the sun golden on the Dance of the Hanging Stones.

The ceremonial by the grave was long, and the colossal shadows of the Dance moved round with the sun until the light blazed down full in the center, and it was easier to look at the ground, at the grave itself, at the shadows of clouds massing and moving like armies across the distances, than at the Dance's center where the priests stood in their robes, and the nobles in mourning white, with jewels flashing against the eyes. A pavilion had been erected for the Queen. She stood in its shade, composed and pale among her ladies, showing no sign of fatigue or illness. Arthur, with me beside him, stood at the foot of the grave.

At last it was done. The priests moved off, and after them the King and the royal party. As we crossed the grass toward the horses and litters, already behind us could be heard the soft thudding of earth on wood. Then from above came another sound to mask it. I looked up. High in the September sky could be seen a stream of birds, swift and black and small, gossiping and calling as they went southward. The last flock of swallows, taking the summer with them.

"Let us hope," said Arthur softly, at my elbow, "that the Saxons are taking the hint. I could do with the winter's length, both for the men and for myself, before the fighting starts again. Besides, there's Caerleon. I wish I could go today."

But of course he had to stay, as had we all, as long as the Queen remained in Amesbury. She went straight back to the monastery after the ceremony, and did not appear publicly again, but spent her time resting, or with her son. He was with her as much as his affairs allowed, while her people prepared to make the journey to York as soon as she should feel able to travel.

Arthur hid his impatience, and busied himself with the troops at exercise, or in long hours of talk with his friends and captains. Each day I could see him more and more absorbed in what he was doing, and what he faced. I myself saw little of him or of Ygraine; much of my time was spent out at the Giants' Dance, directing the sinking of the king-stone once more into its bed above the royal grave.

At last, eight days after Uther's burial, the Queen's party set off for the north. Arthur watched them decently out of sight along the road to Cunetio, then gave a great breath of relief, and pulled the fighting men out of Amesbury as neatly and quickly as pulling a stopper from a flask. It was the fifth day of October, and it was raining, and we were bound, as I knew to my cost, for the Severn estuary, and the ferry across to Caerleon, City of Legions.

4

Where the ferry crosses, the Severn estuary is wide, with big tides that come up fast over thick red mud. Boys watch the cattle night and day, for a whole herd can sink in the tidal mud and be lost. And when the spring and autumn tides meet the river's flow a wave builds up like the wave I once saw in Pergamum after the earthquake. On the south side the estuary is bounded by cliffs; the north shore is marshy, but a bowshot from the tide-mark there is well-drained gravel, lifting gently to open woodland of oak and sweet chestnut.

We pitched camp on the rising ground in the lee of the woods. While this was being done, Arthur, with Ynyr and Gwilim, the kings of Guent and Dyfed, went on a tour of exploration, then after supper he sat in his tent to receive the headmen from the settlements nearby. Numbers of the local folk crowded to see the new young King, even the fisherfolk who have no homes but the cliff caves and their frail-skinned coracles. He spoke with them all, accepting homage and complaint alike. After an hour or two of it, I asked leave with a look, got it, and went out into the air. It was a long time since I had smelled the hills of my own country, and besides, there was a place nearby that I had long wanted to visit.

This was the once-famous shrine of Nodens, who is Nuatha of the Silver Hand, known in my country as Llud, or Bilis, King of the Otherworld, whose gates are the hollow hills. He it was who had guarded the sword after I had raised it from its long grave below the floor of Mithras' temple at Segontium. I had left it in his keeping in the lake cave that was known to be sacred to him, before carrying it finally up to the Green Chapel. To Llud, also, I had a debt to pay.

His shrine by the Severn was far older than Mithras' temple, or the chapel in the forest. Its origins had long been lost, even in song or story. It had been a hill fortress first, with maybe a stone or a spring dedicated to the god who cared for the spirits of dead men. Then iron was found, and all through Roman times the place was mined, and mined richly. It may have been the Romans who first called the place the Hill of the Dwarfs, after the small dark men of the west who worked there. The mine had long since been closed, but the name persisted, and so did the stories, of the Old Ones who were seen lurking in the oak woods, or who came thronging out of the earth's depths on nights of storm and starlight to join the train of the dark king, as he rode from his hollow hill with his wild rout of ghosts and enchanted spirits.

I reached the top of the hill behind the camp, and walked down between the scattered oaks toward the stream at the valley's foot. There was a ripe autumn moon that showed me my way. The chestnut leaves, already loosened and drifting, fell here and there quietly to the grass, but the oaks still held their leaves, so that the air was full of rustling as the dry boughs stirred and whispered. The land after the rain smelled rich and soft, ploughing weather, nutting weather, the squirrel-time for winter's coming.

Below me on the shadowed slope something moved. There was a stirring of grasses, a pattering, then, like the sound of a hail-storm sweeping past, a herd of deer went by, as swiftly as swallows flying. They were very near. The moonlight struck the dappled coats and the ivory tips of the tines. So close they were that I even saw the liquid shine of their eyes. There were pied deer and white, ghosts of dapple and silver, scudding as lightly as their own shadows, and as swiftly as a sudden squall of wind. They fled by me, down to the valley foot, between the breasts of the rounded hills and up round a curve of oak trees, and were gone.

They say that a white deer is a magical creature. I believe that this is true. I had seen two such in my life, each one the herald of a marvel. These, too, seen in the moonlight, scudding like clouds into the trees' darkness, seemed things of magic. Perhaps, with the Old Ones, they haunted a hill that still held an open gate to the Otherworld.

I crossed the stream, climbed the next hill, and made my way up toward the ruinous walls that crowned it. I picked my way through the debris of what looked like ancient outworks, then climbed the last steep rise of the path. There was a gate set in a high, creeper-covered wall. It was open. I went in.

I found myself in the precinct, a wide courtyard stretching the full width of the flat hilltop. The moonlight, growing stronger every moment, showed a stretch of broken pavement furred with weeds. Two sides of the precinct were enclosed by high walls with broken tops; on the other two there had once been large buildings, of which some portions were still roofed. The place, in that light, was still impressive, roofs and pillars showing whole in the moonlight. Only an owl, flying silently from an upper window, showed that the place had long been deserted, and was crumbling back into the hill.

There was another building set almost in the middle of the court. The gable of its high roof stood up sharply against the moon, but moonlight fell through empty windows. This, I knew, must be the shrine. The buildings that edged the courtyard were what remained of the guest-houses and dormitories where pilgrims and suppliants had lodged; there were cells, walled in, windowless and private, such as I had known at Pergamum, where people slept, hoping for healing dreams, or visions of divination.

I went softly forward over the broken pavement. I knew what I would find; a shrine full of dust and cold air, like the abdicated temple of Mithras at Segontium. But it was possible, I told myself, as I trod up the steps and between the still-massive doorposts of the central *cella,* that the old gods who had sprung, like the oak trees and the grass and the rivers themselves—it was possible that these beings made of the air and earth and water of our sweet land, were harder to dislodge than the visiting gods of Rome. Such a one, I had long believed, was mine. He might still be here, where the night air blew through the empty shrine, filling it with the sound of the trees.

The moonlight, falling through the upper windows and the patches of broken roof, lit the place with a pure, fierce light. Some sapling, rooted high up in the masonry, swayed in the breeze, so that shadow and cold light moved and shifted over the dimness within. It was like being at the bottom of a wellshaft; the air, shadow and light, moved like water against the skin, as pure and as cold. The mosaic underfoot, rippled and uneven where the ground had shifted beneath it, glimmered like the floor of the sea, its strange sea-creatures swimming in the swaying light. From beyond the broken walls came the hiss, like foam breaking, of the rustling trees.

I stood there, quite still and silent, for a long time. Long enough for the owl to sail back on hushed wings, drifting to her perch above the dormitory. Long enough for the small wind to drop again, and the water-shadows to fall still. Long enough for the moon to move behind the gable, and the dolphins under my feet to vanish in darkness.

Nothing moved or spoke. No presence there. I told myself, with humility, that this meant nothing. I, once so powerful an enchanter and prophet, had been swept on a mighty tide to God's very gates, and now was dropping back on the ebb to a barren shore. If there were voices here I would not hear them. I was as mortal as the spectral deer.

I turned to leave the place. And smelled smoke.

Not the smoke of sacrifice; ordinary wood-smoke, and with it the faint smells of cooking. It came from somewhere beyond the ruined guest-house of the precinct's north side. I crossed the courtyard, went in through the remains of a massive archway, and, guided by the smell and then by faint firelight, found my way to a small chamber, where a dog, waking, began to bark, and the two who had been sleeping by the fire got abruptly to their feet.

It was a man and a boy, father and son by the look of them; poor people, to judge by their worn and shabby clothing, but with some look about them of men who are their own masters. In this I was wrong, as it happened.

They moved with the speed of fear. The dog—it was old and stiff, with a grey muzzle and a white eye—did not attack, but stood its ground, growling. The man was on his feet more quickly than the dog, with a long knife in his hand; it was honed and bright and looked like a sacrificial weapon. The boy, squaring up to the stranger with all the bravado of twelve or so, held a heavy billet of firewood.

"Peace to you," I said, then repeated it in their own tongue. "I came to say a prayer, but no one answered, so when I smelled the fire I came across to see if the god still kept servants here."

The knife-point sank, but he gripped it still, and the old dog growled. "Who are you?" demanded the man.

"Only a stranger who is passing this place. I had often heard of Nodens' famous shrine, and seized the time to visit it. Are you its guardian, sir?"

"I am. Are you looking for a night's lodging?"

"That was not my intention. Why? Do you still offer it?"

"Sometimes." He was wary. The boy, more trusting, or perhaps seeing that I was unarmed, turned away and placed the billet carefully on the fire. The dog, silent now, edged forward to touch my hand with its greyed muzzle. Its tail moved.

"He's a good dog, and very fierce," said the man, "but old, and deaf." His manner was no longer hostile. At the dog's action the knife had vanished.

"And wise," I said. I smoothed the upraised head. "He's one who can see the wind."

The boy turned, wide-eyed. "See the wind?" asked the man, staring.

"Have you not heard that of a dog with a white eye? And, old and slow as he is, he can see that I come with no intent to hurt you. My name is Myrddin Emrys, and I live west of here, near Maridunum, in Dyfed. I have been travelling, and am on my way home." I gave him my Welsh name; like everyone else, he would have heard of Merlin the enchanter, and awe is a bad hearth-friend. "May I come in and share your fire for a while, and will you tell me about the shrine you guard?"

They made way for me, and the boy pulled a stool out of a corner somewhere. Under my questions, at length, the man relaxed and began to talk. His name was Mog: it is not really a name, meaning, as it does, merely "a servant," but there was a king once who did not disdain to call himself Mog Nuatha, and the man's son was called, even more grandly, after an emperor. "Constant will be the servant after me," said Mog, and went on to talk with pride and longing of the great period of the shrine, when the pagon emperor rebuilt and re-equipped it only half a century before the last of the legions left Britain. From long before this time, he told me, a "Mog Nuatha" had served the shrine with all his family. But now there were only himself and his son; his wife was from home, having gone down that morning to market, and to spend the night with her ailing sister in the village.

"If there's room left, with all that's there now," the man grumbled. "You can see the river from the wall yonder, and when we saw the boats crossing I sent the boy to have a look. The army, he says it is, along with the young King—" He broke off, peering through the firelight at my plain robe and cloak. "You're no soldier, are you? Are you with them?"

"Yes to the last, and no to the first. As you can see, I am no soldier, but I am with the King."

"What are you, then? A secretary?"

"Of a sort."

He nodded. The boy, listening and absorbed, sat crosslegged beside the dog at my feet. His father asked: "What's he like, this youngster that they say King Uther handed the sword to?"

"He is young, but a man turned, and a good soldier. He can lead men, and he has enough sense to listen to his elders."

He nodded again. Not for these folk the tales and hopes of power and glory. They lived all their lives on this secluded hilltop, with this one direction to their days; what happened beyond the oak trees did not concern them. Since the start of time no one had stormed the holy place. He asked the only question that, to these two, mattered: "Is he a Christian, this young Arthur? Will he knock down the temple, in the name of this new-fangled god, or will he respect what's gone before?"

I answered him tranquilly, and as truly as I knew how: "He will be crowned by the Christian bishops, and bend his knees to his parents' God. But he is a man of this land, and he knows the gods of this land, and the people who still serve those gods on the hills and by the springs and fording-places." My eye had caught, on a broad shelf opposite the fire, a crowd of objects, carefully arranged. I had seen similar things in Pergamum and other places of divine healing; they were offerings to the gods; models of parts of the human body, or carved statues of animals or fish, that carried some message of supplication or gratitude. "You will find," I told Mog, "that his armies will pass by without harm, and that if he ever comes here himself he will say a prayer to the god and make an offering. As I did, and as I will."

"That's good talking," said the boy suddenly, and showed a white-toothed grin.

I smiled at him, and dropped two coins into the outstretched palm. "For the shrine, and for its servants."

Mog grunted something, and the boy Constant slid to his feet and went to a cupboard in the corner. He came back with a leather bottle and a chipped cup for me. Mog lifted his own cup up off the floor and the boy tipped the liquor in. "Your health," said Mog. I answered, and we drank. The stuff was mead, sweet and strong.

Mod drank again, and drew his sleeve across his mouth. "You've been asking about times long past, and we've told you as best we may. Now do you, sir, tell us what's been happening up there in the north. All we heard down here were stories of battles, and kings dying and being made. Is it true the Saxons have gone? Is it true that King Uther Pendragon kept this prince hidden all this time, and brought him out, sudden as a thunderclap, there in the battlefield, and he killed four hundred of the Saxon beasts with a magic sword that sang and drank blood?"

So once more I told the story, while the boy quietly fed the fire, and the flames spat and leaped and shone on the carefully polished offerings ranged on the shelf. The dog slept again, its head on my foot, the fire hot on its rough coat. As I talked the bottle passed and the mead went down in it, and at last the fire dwindled and the logs fell to ash, and I finished my tale with Uther's burial and Arthur's plans to hold Caerleon in readiness for the spring campaigning.

My host upended the bottle and shook it. "It's out. And a better night's work it never did. Thank you, sir, for your news. We live our own ways up here, but you'll know, being down in the press of affairs, that even things happening out yonder in Britain"—he spoke of it as if of a foreign land, a hundred miles from his quiet refuge—"can have their echoes, in pain and trouble sometimes, in the small and lonely places. We'll pray you're right about the new King. You can tell him, if ever you get near enough to have speech with him, that as long as he's loyal to the true land, he has two men here who are his servants, too."

"I shall tell him." I rose. "Thank you for the welcome, and the drink. I'm sorry I disturbed your sleep. I'll go and leave you to it now."

"Go now? Why, it's getting on for the dawning. They'll have locked you out of your lodging, that's for sure. Or were you in the camp down yonder? Then no sentry'll let you through, without you've got the King's own token. You'd best stay here. No," as I started some sort of protest, "there's a room still kept, just as it was in the old days, when they came here from far and wide to have the dreams. The bed's good, and the place is kept dry. You'd fare worse in many a tavern. Do us the favour and stay."

I hesitated. The boy nodded at me, eyes bright, and the dog, which had risen when I rose, wagged its tail and gave a wide, whining yawn, stretching the stiff forepaws.

"Yes. Stay," begged the boy.

I could see that it would mean something to them if I complied. To stay would be to bring back some of the ancient sanctity of the place; a guest in the guest-house, so carefully swept and aired and kept for the guests who no longer came.

"I shall be glad to," I said.

Constant, beaming, thrust a torch into the ashes and held it till it kindled. "Then come this way."

As I followed him his father, settling himself once more in his blankets by the hearth, said the time-honoured words of the healing-place.

"Sleep soundly, friend, and may the god send you a dream."

Whoever sent it, the dream came, and it was a true one.

I dreamed of Morgause, whom I had driven from Uther's court at Luguvallium, with an escort detailed to take her with safe ceremony across the high Pennines, and then southeast to York, where her half-sister Morgan lay.

The dream came fitfully, like those hilltop glimpses one gets through blowing cloud on a dark day. Which, in the dream, it was. I saw the party first on the evening of a wet and windy day, when fine rain blowing downwind turned the gravel of the road into a slippery track of mud. They had paused on the bank of a river swollen by rain. I did not recognize the place. The road led down into the river, in what should have been a shallow ford, but now showed as a racing tumble of white water which broke and foamed round an island that split the flood like a ship sailing. There was no house in sight, not even a cave. Beyond the ford the road twisted eastward among its sodden trees, and up through rolling foothills toward the high fells.

With dusk falling fast, it seemed that the party would have to spend the night here, and wait for the river to go down. The officer in command of the party seemed to be explaining as much to Morgause; I could not hear what was said, but he looked angry, and his horse, tired though it was, kept on the fret. I guessed that the choice of route had not been his: the normal way from Luguvallium is by the high moorland road that leaves the west highway at Brocavum and crosses the mountains by Verterae. This last, kept fortified and in fine repair, would have offered the party a staging post, and would have been the obvious choice for a soldier. Instead, they must have taken the old hill road which branches southeast from the five-way crossing near the camp on the River Lune. I had never been that way. It was not a road that had been kept in any kind of order. It led up the valley of the Dubglas and across the high moors, and thence through the mountains by the pass formed by the Tribuit and the Isara rivers. Men call this pass the Pennine Gap, and in past time the Romans kept it fortified and the roads open and patrolled. It is wild country—and still, among the remote summits and cliffs above the tree line, are caves where the Old Ones live. If this was indeed the road Morgause was taking, I could only wonder why.

Cloud and mist; rain in long grey showers; the swollen river piling its white bow-waves against the driftwood and bending willows of the river island. Then darkness and a gap of time hid the scene from me.

Next time I saw them they were halted, somewhere high in the pass, with tree-hung cliffs to the right of the road, and to the left a wide, falling prospect of forest, with a winding river at the foot of the valley, and hills beyond. They had halted by a milestone near the crest of the pass. Here a track branched off downhill to where, in a distant hollow of the valley, lights showed. Morgause was pointing toward these, and it seemed that there was an argument in progress.

Still I could hear nothing, but the cause of the dispute was obvious. The officer had thrust forward to Morgause's side and was leaning forward in his saddle, arguing fiercely, pointing first at the milestone and then at the road ahead. A late gleam from the west showed, etched by shadow on the stone, the name OLICANA. I could not see the mileage, but what the officer said was clear; that it would be folly to forgo the known comforts that awaited them in Olicana for the chance that the distant house (if such it was) could accommodate the party. His men, crowding near, were openly supporting him. Beside her, Morgause's women watched her anxiously, one might have said beseechingly.

After a while, with a resigned gesture, Morgause gave way. The escort re-formed. The women closed up beside her, smiling. But before the party had gone ten paces one of the women called out sharply, and then Morgause herself, loosing the reins on her horse's neck, put out a hand delicately into the air, as if groping for support, and swayed in her saddle. Someone cried out again. The women crowded to hold her. The officer, turning back, spurred his horse alongside hers and stretched an arm to support her drooping form. She collapsed against him, and lay inert.

There was nothing for it but to accept defeat. Within minutes the party was slithering and thudding down the track toward the distant light in the valley. Morgause, shrouded fast in her big cloak, lay motionless and fainting in the officer's arms.

But I knew, who am wary of witches, that within the shelter of the rich furred hood she was awake, and smiling her small triumphant smile, as Arthur's men carried her to the house to which, for her own reasons, she had led them, and where she planned to stay.

When the mists of vision parted next, I saw a bedchamber finely appointed, with a gilded bed and crimson covers, and a brazier burning red, throwing its light on the woman who lay there against the pillows. Morgause's women were there, the same who had attended her in Luguvallium, the young maid called Lind who had led Arthur to her mistress's bed, and the old woman who had slept the night through in a drugged slumber. The girl Lind looked pale and tired; I remembered that Morgause, in her rage with me, had had her whipped. She served her mistress warily, with shut lips and downcast eyes, while the old woman, stiff from the long, damp ride, went slowly about her tasks, grumbling as she went, but with side-long glances to make sure her mistress did not heed her. As for Morgause, she showed no sign of sickness or even fatigue. I had expected none. She lay back on the crimson pillows, the narrow green-gilt eyes staring out through the chamber walls at something far away and pleasurable, and smiling the same smile I had seen on her lips as Arthur lay beside her, sleeping.

I must have woken here, shaken out of the dream by hatred and distress, but the god's hand was still on me, because I went back into sleep and into the same room. It must have been later, after some span of time; days, even; however long it had taken Lot, King of Lothian, to wait through the ceremonies at Luguvallium, then gather his troops together and head south and eastward, by the same devious route, for York. No doubt his main force had gone directly, but he, with a small party of fast horsemen, had hastened to the meeting place with Morgause.

For that it had been prearranged was now clear. She must have got a message to him before she herself left the court, then she had forced her escort to ride slowly, taking time, and finally had contrived, by her feigned illness, to seek shelter in the privacy of a friend's house. I thought I saw her plan. Having failed in her bid for power through her seduction of Arthur, she had somehow persuaded Lot to this tryst, and now with her witch's wiles she would be set on winning his favour, to find a position of some sort at the court of her sister, Lot's future queen.

Next moment, as the dream changed, I saw the sort of wiles that she was using; witchcraft of a kind, I suppose, but the kind that any woman knows how to use. There was the bedchamber again, with the brazier dealing out a glow of warmth, and beside it, on a low table, food and wine in silver dishes. Morgause stood beside the brazier, the rosy glow playing on the white gown and creamy skin, and glimmering on the long shining hair that fell to her waist in rivulets of apricot light. Even I, who loathed her, had to admit that she was very lovely. The long green-gold eyes, thickly fringed by their golden lashes, watched the door. She was alone.

The door opened and Lot came in. The King of Lothian was a big dark man, with powerful shoulders and hot eyes. He favoured jewels, and glittered with arm rings and finger rings and a chain on his breast set with citrine and amethyst. At his shoulder, where the long black hair touched his cloak, was a magnificent pin of garnet and worked gold, in the Saxon style. Fine enough, I thought grimly, to have been a guest-gift from Colgrim himself. There was rain on his hair and cloak.

Morgause was speaking. I could hear nothing. It was a vision of movement and colour only. She made no move of welcome, nor did he seem to expect it. He showed no surprise at seeing her. He spoke once, briefly, then stooped to the table, and, picking up the silver jug, splashed wine from it into a cup with such haste and carelessness that the crimson stuff slopped over the table and onto the floor. Morgause laughed. There was no answering smile from Lot. He drank the wine down, deeply as if he needed it, then threw the cup to the floor, strode past the brazier and with his big hands, still marked and muddied from the ride, laid hold of the two sides of her gown at the neck, and ripped it apart, baring her body to the navel. Then he had hold of her, and his mouth was on hers, devouring her. He had not troubled to shut the door. I saw it shift wider, and the girl Lind, scared doubtless by the crash of the fallen cup, peer in, white-faced. Like Lot, she showed no surprise at what she saw, but, frightened perhaps by the man's violence, she hesitated, as if about to run to her mistress's aid. But then she saw, as I had seen the half-naked body melt, clinging, against the man's, and the woman's hands sliding up into the black wet hair. The torn gown slipped down to lie in a huddle on the floor. Morgause said something, and laughed. The man's grip on her shifted. Lind shrank back, and the door closed. Lot swung Morgause up and took four long strides to the bed.

Witch's wiles indeed, Even for a rape it would have been precipitate: for a seduction it was a record. Call me innocent, or stupid, or what you will, but at first I could only think, held there in the clouds of dreaming, that some spell had been at work. I believe I thought hazily of drugged wine, Circe's cup, and men turned into rutting swine. It was not until some time later, when the man reached a hand from the bed-covers and turned up the wick of the lamp, and the woman, dazed with sex and sleep, sat up smiling against the crimson pillows and drew the furs up to cover herself, that I began to suspect the truth. He padded across the floor, through the fallen wreck of his own clothes, poured another cupful of wine, drained it, then refilled it and took it back to Morgause. Then he heaved himself back into the bed beside her, sat back himself against the bed-head, and began to talk. She, half sitting, half lying against him, nodded and answered, seriously and at length. As they talked, his hand slid down to fondle her breasts; he did it half absently, as was natural enough in a man like Lot, who was used to women. But Morgause, the maiden with the unbound hair and demure little voice? Morgause noticed the gesture no more than the man. Only then, with a jar like an arrow thudding deep into a shield, did I see the truth.

They had been here before. They were familiar. Even before she had lain with Arthur, Lot had had her, and many times. They were so used to one another that they could lie twined naked on a bed and, busily and earnestly, talk. . . . About what?

Treachery. That was, naturally, my first thought. Treachery against the High King, whom both, for differing reasons, had cause to hate. Morgause, long jealous of the half-sister who must always take precedence of her, had laid siege to Lot and taken him to her bed. There had, it was to be supposed, been other lovers, too. Then came Lot's bid for power at Luguvallium. It failed, and Morgause, not guessing at the strength and clemency that would make Arthur accept him back among his allies, turned to Arthur himself in her own desperate play for power.

And now? She had magic of a kind. It was possible that she knew, as I knew, that in that night's incest with Arthur she had conceived. A husband she must have, and who better than Lot? If he could be persuaded that the child was his, she might cheat the hated young sister of marriage and kingdom, and build a nest where the cuckoo could hatch out in safety.

It looked as if she would succeed. When next I saw through the dream-smoke they were laughing together, and she had freed her body of the covers and was seated high on the furs against the crimson curtains of the bed-head, with the rose-gold hair streaming down behind her shoulders like a mantle of silk. The front of her body was bare, and on her head was Lot's royal circlet of white gold, glimmering with citrines and the milk-blue pearls of the northern rivers. Her eyes shone bright and narrow as a purring cat's, and the man was laughing with her as he lifted the cup and drank what looked like a toast to her. As he lifted it the cup rocked, and wine slopped over the brim to spill down her breasts like blood. She smiled, not stirring, and the king leaned forward, laughing, and sucked it off.

The smoke thickened. I could smell it, as if I was there in the room, close by the brazier. Then mercifully I was awake in the cool and tranquil night, but with the nightmare still crawling like sweat on the skin.

To anyone but me, knowing them as I knew them, the scene would have offered no offense. The girl was lovely, and the man fine enough, and if they were lovers, why, then, she had the right to look toward his crown. There should have been nothing to flinch at in the scene, any more than in a dozen such that one sees on any summer evening along the hedgerows, or in the midnight hall. But about a crown, even such a one as Lot's, there is something sacred: it is a symbol of that mystery, the link between god and king, king and people. So to see the crown on that wanton head, with the king's own head, bared of its royalty, bent below it like a beast's pasturing, was profanity, like spittle on an altar.

So I rose, and plunged my head in water, and washed the sight away.

5

When we reached Caerleon at noon next day, a bright October sun was drying the ground, and frost lay indigo-blue in the lee of walls and buildings. The alders along the river bank, their black boughs hung with yellow coins of leaves, looked bright and still, like stitchery against the background of pale sky. Dead leaves, still rimmed with frost, crunched and rustled under our horses' hoofs. The smells of new bread and roasting meat wound through the air from the camp kitchens, and brought sharply to mind my visit here with Tremorinus, the master engineer who had rebuilt the camp for Ambrosius, and included in his plans the finest kitchens in the country.

I said as much to my companion—it was Caius Valerius, my friend of old—and he grunted appreciatively.

"Let us hope the King takes due time for a meal before he starts his inspection."

"I think we can trust him for that."

"Oh, aye, he's a growing boy." It was said with a sort of indulgent pride, with no faintest hint of patronage. From Valerius it came well; he was a veteran who had fought with Ambrosius at Kaerconan and since then with Uther; he was also one of the captains who had been with Arthur at the battle on the River Glein. If men of this stamp could accept the youthful King with respect, and trust him for leadership, then my task was indeed done. The thought came unmixed with any sense of loss or declining, but with a calm relief that was new to me. I thought: I am growing old.

I became conscious that Valerius had asked me something. "I'm sorry. I was thinking. You said?"

"I asked if you were going to stay here till the crowning?"

"I think not. He may need me here for a while, if he's set on rebuilding. I'm hoping I shall have leave to go after Christmas, but I'll come back for the crowning."

"If the Saxons give us leave to hold it."

"As you say. To leave it till Pentecost would seem to be a little risky, but it's the bishops' choice, and the King would be wiser not to gainsay them."

Valerius grunted. "Maybe if they put their minds to it, and do some serious praying, God will hold the spring offensive back for them. Pentecost, eh? Do you suppose they're hoping for fire from heaven again . . . theirs, this time, perhaps?" He eyed me sideways. "What do you say?"

As it happened, I knew the legend to which he referred. Since the coming of the white fire into the Perilous Chapel, the Christians had been wont to refer to their own story, that once, at Pentecost, fire had fallen from heaven onto their god's chosen servants. I saw no reason to quarrel with such an interpretation of what had happened at the Chapel: it was necessary that the Christians, with their growing power, should accept Arthur as their God-appointed leader. Besides, for all I knew, they were right.

Valerius was still waiting for me to answer. I smiled. "Only that if they know from whose hand the fire falls, they know more than I do."

"Oh, aye, that's likely." His tone was faintly derisive. Valerius had been on garrison duty in Luguvallium on the night when Arthur lifted the sword from the fire in the Perilous Chapel, but, like everyone else, he had heard the tale. And, like everyone else, he shied away from what had happened there. "So you're leaving us after Christmas? Are we to know where for?"

"I'm going home to Maridunum. It's five—no, six years since I was there. Too long. I'd like to see that all is well."

"Then see that you do get back for the crowning. There will be great doings here at Pentecost. It would be a pity to miss them."

By then, I thought, she would be near her time. I said aloud: "Oh, yes. With or without the Saxons, we shall have great doings at Pentecost."

Then we spoke of other things until our quarters were reached, and we were bidden to join the King and his officers for meat.

Caerleon, the old Roman City of the Legions, had been rebuilt by Ambrosius, and since then kept garrisoned and in good repair. Arthur now set himself to enlarge it almost to its original capacity, and make it, besides, a king's stronghold and dwelling-place as well as a fortress. The old royal city of Winchester was reckoned now to be too near the borders of the Saxon federated territory, and too vulnerable, besides, to new invasion, situated as it is on the Itchen River, where longboats had landed before now. London was still safely held by the British, nor had any Saxons attempted to thrust up into the Thames valley, but in Uther's time the longboats had penetrated as far as Vagniacae, and Rutupiae and the Isle of Thanet had long been securely in Saxon hands. The threat was felt to be there, and growing yearly, and since Uther's accession London had begun—imperceptibly at first, and then with increasing speed—to show decay. Now it was a city fallen on evil days; many of its buildings had collapsed through age and neglect; poverty showed itself everywhere, as markets moved away, and those who could afford to do so left for safer places. It would never, men said, be a capital city again.

So until his new stronghold should be ready to counter any serious invasion from the Saxon Shore, Arthur planned to make Caerleon his headquarters. It was the obvious choice. Within eight miles of it was Ynyr's capital of Guent, and the fortress itself, lying in a loop of the river but beyond the danger of flood, had mountains at its back, and was additionally protected on the east by marshes at the watersmeet of the Isca and the little Afon Lwyd. Of course Caerleon's very strength restricted it; it could defend only a small portion of the territory under Arthur's shield. But for the present it could provide the headquarters for his policy of mobile defense.

I was with him all through that first winter. He did ask me once, with a smiling lift of the brows, if I was not going to leave him for my cave in the hills, but I said merely: "Later," and let it be.

I told him nothing about the dream I had had that night at Nodens' shrine. He had enough to think about, and I was only too thankful that he seemed to have forgotten the possible consequences of that night with Morgause. Time enough to talk to him when the news came from York about the wedding.

Which it did, in good time to stop the court's preparation to go north for the celebrations at Christmas. A long letter came first, from Queen Ygraine to the King; one came for me with the same courier, and was brought to me where I walked by the river. All morning I had been watching the laying of a conduit, but for the moment work had ceased, as the men went for their midday bread and wine. The troops drilling on the parade ground near the old amphitheatre had dispersed, and the winter day was still and bright, with a pearled mist.

I thinked the man, waiting, letter in hand, until he had gone. Then I broke the seal.

The dream had been a true one. Lot and Morgause were married. Before ever Queen Ygraine and her party reached York, the news had gone before them, that the lovers were handfast. Morgause—I was reading between the lines here—had ridden into the city with Lot, flushed with triumph and decked with his jewels, and the city, preparing for a royal wedding, with a sight of the High King himself, made the best of its disappointment, and, with northern thrift, held the wedding feast just the same. The King of Lothian, said Ygraine, had borne himself meekly to her, and had made gifts to the chief men of the city, so his welcome had been warm enough And Morgan—I could read the relief in the plain words—Morgan had showed neither anger nor humiliation; she had laughed aloud, and then wept with what appeared to be sheer relief. She had gone to the feasting in a gay red gown, and no girl had been merrier, even though (finished Ygraine with the touch of acid that I remembered) Morgause had worn her new crown from rising to bedtime. . . .

As for the Queen's own reaction, I thought that this, too, was one of relief. Morgause, understandably, had never been dear to her, whereas Morgan was the only child she had had by her to rear. It was clear that, while prepared to obey King Uther, both she and Morgan had disliked the marriage with the black northern wolf. I did, indeed, wonder if Morgan knew more about him than she had told her mother. It was even possible that Morgause, being what she was, had boasted that she and Lot had already lain together.

Ygraine herself showed no suspicion of this, nor of the bride's pregnancy as a possible reason for the hasty marriage. It was to be hoped that there was no hint, either, in the letter she had sent to Arthur. He had too much on his mind now; there would be time yet for the anger and the distress. He must be crowned first, and then be free to go about his formidable task of war without being shackled by what was women's business—and would, all too soon, be mine.

Arthur flung the letter down. He was angry, that was plain, but holding it on the rein.

"Well? I take it you know?"

"Yes."

"How long have you known?"

"The Queen your mother wrote to me. I have just read the letter. I imagine it carries the same news as yours."

"That is not what I asked you."

I said mildly: "If you are asking me, did I know this was going to happen, the answer is yes."

The angry dark gaze kindled. "*You did?* Why did you not tell me?"

"For two reasons. Because you were occupied with things that matter more, and because I was not quite sure."

"You? Not sure? Come, Merlin! This from you?"

"Arthur, all that I knew or suspected of this came to me in a dream, one night some weeks ago. It came not like a dream of power, or divination, but like a nightmare brought on by too much wine, or by too much thinking about that hellcat and her works and ways. King Lot had been in my mind, and so had she. I dreamed I saw them together, and she was trying on his crown. Was that enough, do you think, for me to make you a report that would have set the court by the ears, and you, maybe, racing up to York to quarrel with him?"

"It would have been enough, once." His mouth showed a stubborn and still angry line. I saw that the anger sprang from anxiety, striking at the wrong time about Lot's intentions.

"That," I said, "was when I was the King's prophet. No," at his quick movement, "I belong to no man else. I am yours, as always. But I am a prophet no longer, Arthur. I thought you understood."

"How could I? What do you mean?"

"I mean that the night at Luguvallium, when you drew the sword I had hidden for you in the fire, was the last time that the power visited me. You did not see the place afterwards, when the fire was gone and the chapel empty. It had broken the stone where the sword lay, and destroyed the sacred relics. Me, it did not destroy, but I think the power was burned out of me, perhaps for ever. Fires fade to ash, Arthur. I thought you must surely have guessed."

"How could I?" he said again, but his tone had changed. It was no longer angry and abrupt, but slow and thinking. As I, after Luguvallium, had felt myself ageing, then Arthur had, for good and all, left his boyhood. "You've seemed the same as always. Clear-headed, and so sure of yourself that it's like asking advice of an oracle."

I laughed. "They were not always so clear, by all accounts! Old women, or witless girls mumbling in the smoke. If I've been sure of myself during these past weeks, it's because the advice I have been asked for concerns my professional skills, no more."

" 'No more?' Enough, one would think, for any king to call on, if that were all he had known from you. . . . But yes, I think I see. It's the same for you as for me; the dreams and visions have gone, and now we have a life to live by the rules of men. I should have understood. You did, when I went myself after Colgrim." He walked over to the table where Ygraine's letter lay, and rested a fist on the marble. He leaned on it, frowning downward, but seeing nothing. Then he looked up. "And what of the years that are to come? The fighting will be bitter, and it will not be over this year, or the next. Are you telling me that I shall have nothing from you now? I'm not talking about your engines of war, or your knowledge of medicine; I'm asking you if I am not to have the 'magic' that the soldiers tell me about, the help that you gave to Ambrosius and to my father?"

I smiled. "That, surely." He was thinking, I knew, of the effect my prophecies, and sometimes my presence, had had on the fighting troops. "What the armies think of me now, they will go on thinking. And where is the need for further prophecies concerning the wars you are embarked on? Neither you nor your troops will need reminding at every turn. They know what I have said. Out there in the field, the length and width of Britain, there is glory for you, and for them. You will have success, and success again, and in the end—I do not know how far ahead—you will have victory. That is what I said to you, and it is still true. It is the work you were trained for: go and do it, and leave me to find a way to do mine."

"Which is, now that you've flown your eagle chick, and yourself stay earthborne? To wait for victory, then help me build again?"

"In time," I indicated the crumpled letter. "But more immediately, to deal with such things as this. After Pentecost, with your leave, I shall go north to Lothian."

A moment of stillness, while I saw the flush of relief colour his face. He did not ask what I meant to do there, but said merely: "I shall be glad. You know that. I doubt if we need to discuss why this happened?"

"No."

"You were right before, of course. As ever. What she wanted was power, and it did not matter to her how she took it. Or, indeed, where she looked for it. I can see that now. I can only be glad to feel myself absolved of any claim she might make on me." A small movement of his hand brushed Morgause and her plots aside. "But two things remain. The most important is that I still need Lot as an ally. You were right—again!—in not telling me of your dream. I would certainly have quarrelled with him. As it is—"

He paused, with a lift of the shoulders. I nodded.

"As it is you can accept Lot's marriage to your half-sister, and count it as sufficient alliance to hold him to your banner. Queen Ygraine, it seems, has acted wisely, and so has Morgan, your sister. This is, after all, the match that King Uther originally proposed. We may safely ignore the reasons for it now."

"All the more easily," he said, "because it seems that Morgan is not ill pleased. If she had shown herself slighted . . . That was the second problem I spoke of. But it seems to be no problem after all. Did the Queen tell you in her letter that Morgan showed nothing but relief?"

"Yes. And I have questioned the courier who brought the letters from York. He tells me that Urbgen of Rheged was at York for the wedding, and that Morgan hardly saw Lot for watching him."

Urbgen was now King in Rheged, old King Coel having died soon after the battle at Luguvallium. The new king was a man in his late forties, a notable warrior, and still a vigorous and handsome man. He had been widowed two or three years ago.

Arthur's look quickened with interest. "Urbgen of Rheged? Now that would be a match! It's the one I'd have preferred all along, but when the match was made with Lot, Urbegen's wife was still living. Urbgen, yes . . . Along with Maelgon of Gwynedd, he's the best fighting man in the north, and there has never been any doubt of his loyalty. Between those two, the north would be held firmly . . ."

I finished it for him. "And let Lot and his queen do what they will?"

"Exactly. Would Urbegen take her, do you think?"

"He will count himself lucky. And I believe she will fare better than she could ever have done with the other. Depend upon it, you'll be receiving another courier soon. And that is an informed guess, not a prophecy."

"Merlin, do you mind?"

It was the King who asked me, a man as old and wise as myself; a man who could see past his own crowding problems, and guess what it might mean to me, to walk in dead air where once the world had been a god-filled garden.

I thought for a little before I answered him. "I'm not sure. There have been times like this before, passive times, ebb after flood; but never when we were still on the threshold of great events. I am not used to feeling helpless, and I own that I cannot like it. But if I have learned one thing during the years when the god has been with me, it is to trust him. I am old enough now to walk tranquilly, and when I look at you I know that I have been fulfilled. Why should I grieve? I shall sit on the hilltops and watch you doing the work for me. That is the guerdon of age."

"Age? You talk as if you were a greybeard! What are you?"

"Old enough. I'm nearly forty."

"Well, then, for God's sake—?"

And so, in laughter, we passed the narrow corner. He drew me then to the window table where my scale models of the new Caerleon stood, and plunged into a discussion of them. He did not speak of Morgause again, and I thought: I spoke of trust, what sort of trust is this? If I fail him, then I shall indeed be only a shadow and a name, and my hand on the sword of Britain was a mockery.

When I asked leave to go to Maridunum after Twelfth Night, he gave it half absently, his mind already on the next task to hand for the morning.

The cave I had inherited from Galapas the hermit lay some six miles east of Maridunum, the town that guards the mouth of the River Tywy. My grandfather, the King of Dyfed, had lived there, and I, brought up as a neglected bastard in the royal household, had been allowed by a lazy tutor to run wild. I had made friends with the wise old recluse who lived in the cave on Bryn Myrddin, a hill sacred to the sky-god Myrddin, he of the light and the wild air. Galapas had died long ago, but in time I made the place my home, and the folk still came to visit Myrddin's healing spring, and to receive treatment and remedies from me. Soon my skill as a doctor surpassed even the old man's, and with it my reputation for the power that men call magic, so now the place was known familiarly as Merlin's Hill. I believe that the simpler folk even thought that I was Myrddin himself, the guardian of the spring.

There is a mill set on the Tywy, just where the track for Bryn Myrddin leaves the road. When I reached it I found that a barge had come up-river, and was moored there. Its great bay horse grazed where it could on the winter herbage, while a young man unloaded sacks onto the wharf. He worked singlehanded; the barge master must be withindoors slaking his thirst; but it was only one man's job to lift the half-score of grain sacks that had been sent up for grinding from some winter store. A child of perhaps five years old trotted to and fro, hindering the work, and talking ceaselessly in a weird mixture of Welsh and some other tongue familiar but so distorted—and lisping besides—that I could not catch it. Then the young man answered in the same tongue, and I recognized it, and him. I drew rein.

"Stilicho!" I called. As he set the sack down and turned, I added in his own tongue: "I should have let you know, but time was short, and I hardly expected to be here so soon. How are you?"

"My lord!" He stood amazed for a moment, then came running across the weedy yard to the road's edge, wiped his hands down his breeches, reached for my hand, and kissed it. I saw tears in his eyes, and was touched. He was a Sicilian who had been my slave on my travels abroad. In Constantinople I had freed him, but he had chosen to stay with me and return to Britain, and had been my servant while I had lived on Bryn Myrddin. When I went north he married the miller's daughter, Mai, and moved down the valley to live at the mill.

He was bidding me welcome, talking in the same excited, broken tongue as the child. What Welsh he had learned seemed to have deserted him for the moment. The child came up and stood, finger in mouth, staring.

"Yours?" I asked him. "He's a fine boy."

"My eldest," he said with pride. "They are all boys."

"All?" I asked, raising a brow at him.

"Only three," he said, with the limpid look I remembered, "and another soon."

I laughed and congratulated him, and hoped for another strong boy. These Sicilians breed like mice, and at least he would not, like his own father, be forced to sell children into slavery to buy food for the rest. Mai was the miller's only daughter, and would have a fat patrimony.

Had already, I found. The miller had died two years back; he had suffered from the stone, and would take neither care nor medicine. Now he was gone, and Stilicho was miller in his stead.

"But your home is cared for, my lord. Either I or the lad who works for me ride up every day to make sure all is well. There's no fear that anyone would dare go inside; you'll find your things just as you left them, and the place clean and aired . . . but of course there'll be no food there. So if you were wanting to go up there now . . ." He hesitated. I could see he was afraid of presuming. "Will you not honour us, lord, by sleeping here for tonight? It'll be cold up yonder, and damp with it, for all that we've had the brazier lit every week through the winter, like you told me, to keep the books sweet. Let you stay here, my lord, and the lad will ride up now to light the brazier, and in the morning Mai and I can go up—"

"It's good of you," I said, "but I shan't feel the cold, and perhaps I can get the fires going myself . . . more quickly, even, than your lad, perhaps?" I smiled at his expression; he had not forgotten some of the things he had seen when he served the enchanter. "So thank you, but I'll not trouble Mai, except perhaps for some food? If I might rest here for a while, and talk to you, and see your family, then ride up into the hill before dark? I can carry all I shall need until tomorrow."

"Of course, of course . . . I'll tell Mai. She'll be honoured . . . delighted. . . ." I had already caught a glimpse of a pale face and wide eyes at a window. She would be delighted, I knew, when the awesome Prince Merlin rode away again; but I was tired from the long ride, and had, besides, smelled the savoury stew cooking, which no doubt could easily be made to go one further. So much, indeed, Stilicho was naïvely explaining: "There's a fat fowl on the boil now, so all will be well. Come you in, and warm yourself, and rest till suppertime. Bran will see to your horse, while I get the last sacks off the barge, and it away back to town. So come your ways, lord, and welcome back to Bryn Myrddin."

Of all the many times I had ridden up the high valley-side toward my home on Bryn Myrddin, I do not quite know why I should remember this one so clearly. There was nothing special to mark it; it was a home-coming, no more.

But up to this moment, so much later, when I write of it, every detail of that ride remains vivid. The hollow sound of the horse's hoofs on the iron ground of winter; the crunch of leaves underfoot, and snap of brittle twigs; the flight of a woodcock and the clap of a startled pigeon. Then the sun, falling ripe and level as it does just before candle-time, lighting the fallen oak-leaves where they lay in shadow, edged with rime like powdered diamond; the holly boughs rattling and ringing with the birds I disturbed from feeding on the fruit; the smell of damp juniper as my horse pushed through; the sight of a single spray of whin flowers struck to gold by the sunlight, with the night's frost already crisping the ground and making the air pure and thin as chiming crystal.

I stabled my horse in the shed below the cliff, and climbed the path to the little alp of turf before the cave. And there was the cave itself, with its silence, and the familiar scents, and the still air stirring only to the faint movement of velvet on velvet, where the bats in the high lantern of the rock heard my familiar step, and stayed where they were, waiting for the dark.

Stilicho had told me the truth; the place was well cared for, dry and aired, and though it was colder by a cloak's thickness even than the frosty air outside, that would soon mend. The brazier stood ready for kindling, and fresh dry logs were set on the open hearth near the cave's entrance. There was tinder and flint on the usual shelf; in the past I had rarely troubled to use them, but this time I took them down, and soon had a flame going. It may be that, remembering a former, tragic home-coming, I was half-afraid to test (even in this tranquil after-time) the least of my powers; but I believe that the decision was made through caution rather than through fear. If I still had power to call on, I would save it for greater things than the making of a flame to warm me. It is easier to call the storm from the empty sky than to manipulate the heart of a man; and soon, if my bones did not lie to me, I should be needing all the power I could muster, to pit against a woman; and this is harder to do than anything concerning men, as air is harder to see than a mountain.

So I lit the brazier in my sleeping chamber, and kindled the logs at the doorway, then unpacked my saddlebags and went out with the pitcher to draw water from the spring. This trickled out of a ferny rock beside the cave mouth, and lisped through the hanging lace of rime, to drip into a round stone basin. Above it, among the mosses, and crowned with icy glitter, stood the image of the god Myrddin, who keeps the roads of the sky. I poured a libation to him, then went in to look to my books and medicines.

Nothing had taken harm. Even the jars of herbs, sealed and tied as I had taught Stilicho to do it, seemed fresh and good. I uncovered the great harp that stood at the back of the cave, and carried it near the fire to tune it. Then, having made my bed ready, I mulled some wine and drank it, sitting by the leaping fire of logs. Finally, I unwrapped the small knee-harp that had been with me on all my travels, and carried it back to its place in the crystal cave. This was a small inner cave, with its opening set high in the rear wall of the main cavern, and so placed behind a jut of rock that in the normal way the shadows hid it from sight. When I was a boy it had been my gate of vision. Here, in the inner silence of the hill, folded deep in darkness and in solitude, no sense could play except the eye of the mind, and no sound come.

Except, as now, the murmur of the harp as I set it down. It was the one I had made as a boy, so finely strung that the very air could set it whispering. The sounds were weird and sometimes beautiful, but somehow outside the run of music as we know it, as the song of the grey seal on the rocks is beautiful, but is the sound of the wind and the waves rather than of a beast. The harp sang to itself as I set it down, with a kind of slumbrous humming, like a cat purring to be back on its own hearthstone.

"Rest you there," I told it, and at the sound of my voice running round the crystal walls it hummed again.

I went back to the bright fire, and the stars gemming the black sky outside. I lifted the great harp to me and—hesitating at first, and then more easily—made music.

Rest you here, enchanter, while the light fades,
Vision narrows, and the far
Sky-edge is gone with the sun.
Be content with the small spark
Of the coal, the smell
Of food, and the breath
Of frost beyond the shut door.
Home is here, and familiar things;
A cup, a wooden bowl, a blanket,
Prayer, a gift for the god, and sleep.

(And music, says the harp,
And music.)

6

With the spring came, inevitably, trouble. Colgrim, sniffing his way cautiously back along the eastern coasts, landed within the old federated territories, and set about raising a new force to replace the one defeated at Luguvallium and the Glein.

I was back in Caerleon by that time, busy with Arthur's plans for the establishment there of his new mobile cavalry force.

The idea, though startling, was not altogether new. With Saxon Federates already settled, and by treaty, in the southeastern districts of the island, and with the whole eastern seaboard continually at risk, it was impossible to set up and effectively maintain a fixed line of defense. There were, of course, certain defensive ramparts already in existence, of which Ambrosius' Wall was the greatest. (I omit Hadrian's Great Wall here; it was never a purely defensive structure, and had been, even in the Emperor Macsen's time, impossible to keep. Now it was breached in a score of places; and besides, the enemy was no longer the Celt from the wild country to the north; he came from the sea. Or he was already, as I have explained, within the gates of southeast Britain.) The others Arthur set himself to extend and refurbish, notably the Black Dyke of Northumbria, which protects Rheged and Strathclyde, and the older Wall that the Romans originally built across the high chalk downlands south of the Sarum plain. The King planned to extend this wall northward. The roads through it were to be left open, but could be shut fast if any attempt was made by the enemy to move toward the Summer Country to the west. Other defensive works were planned, soon to be under way. Meanwhile, all the King could hope to do was fortify and man certain key positions, establish signal stations between these, and keep open the communicating roads. The kings and chiefs of the British would keep each his own territory, while the High King's work would be to maintain a fighting force that could be taken at need to help any of them, or be thrown into whatever breach was made in our defenses. It was the old plan with which Rome had successfully defended her province for some time before the withdrawal of the legions: the Count of the Saxon Shore had commanded just such a mobile force, and indeed Ambrosius, more recently, had done the same.

But Arthur planned to go further. "Caesar-speed," as he saw it, could be made ten times as speedy if the whole force were mounted. Nowadays, when one sees cavalry troops daily on the roads and in the parade grounds, this seems a normal enough thing; but then, when he first thought of it and put it to me, it came with all the force of the surprise attack he hoped to achieve with it. It would take time, of course; the beginnings, perforce, would be modest. Until enough of the troops were trained to fight from horseback, it would have to be a smallish, picked force drawn from among the officers and his own friends. This granted, the plan was feasible. But no such plan could be put into being without the right horses, and of these we could command relatively few. The cobby little native beasts, though hardy, were neither speedy enough nor big enough to carry an armed man into battle.

We talked it over for days and nights, going into every detail, before Arthur would put the idea before his commanders. There are those—the best, too, often among them—who are opposed to any kind of change; and unless every argument can be met, the waverers are drawn to cast with the noes. Between them Arthur and Cador, along with Gwilim of Dyfed and Ynyr from Caer Guent, hammered the thing out over the map tables. I could contribute little to the war-talk, but I did solve the problem of the horses.

There is a race of horses that are said to be the best in the world. Certainly they are the most beautiful. I had seen them in the East, where the men of the desert prize them more than their gold or their women; but they could be found, I knew, nearer than that. The Romans had brought some of these creatures back from North Africa into Iberia, where they had interbred with the thicker-bodied horses from Europe. The result was a splendid animal, fast and fiery, but strong with it, and supple, and biddable as a war-horse should be. If Arthur would send across to see what might be bought, then as soon as the weather would allow safe transportation, the makings of a mounted force could be his by the following summer.

So when I got back to Caerleon in the spring, it was to put in motion the building of big new stable-blocks, while Bedwyr was dispatched overseas to do the horse-trading.

Caerleon was already transformed. Work on the fortress itself had gone quickly and well, and now other buildings were springing up nearby, of sufficient comfort and grandeur to grace a temporary capital. Though Arthur would use the commandant's house inside the walls as battle headquarters, another house (which the folk called "the palace") was being built outside, in the lovely curve of the Isca River, by the Roman bridge. When finished this would be a large house, with several courtyards for guests and their servants. It was well built, of stone and brickwork, with painted plaster and carved pillars at the doors. Its roof was gilded, like that of the new Christian church, which was on the site of the old Mithras temple. Between these two buildings and the parade ground to the west of them, houses and shops were springing up, making a bustling township where before there had only been a small village settlement. The folk, proud of Arthur's choice of Caerleon, and willing to ignore the reasons for it, worked with a will to make the place worthy of a new reign, and a king who would bring peace.

He brought peace of a sort by Pentecost. Colgrim, with his new army, had broken bounds in the eastern regions. Arthur fought him twice, once not far south of the Humber, the second time nearer the Saxon boundary, in the reedy fields of Linnuis. In the second of these battles Colgrim was killed. Then, with the Saxon Shore uneasily recoiling into quiet once more, Arthur came back to us, in time to meet Bedwyr disembarking with the first contingent of the promised horses.

Valerius, who had been to help disembark them, was enthusiastic.

"High as your breast, and strong with it, and as gentle as maidens. Some maidens, that is. And fast, they say, as greyhounds, though they're still stiff from the voyage, and it'll take time before they get their land-legs again. And beautiful! There's many a maiden, gentle or otherwise, who'd sacrifice to Hecate for eyes as big and dark, or skins as silken . . ."

"How many did he bring? Mares as well? When I was in the East they parted only with the stallions."

"Mares as well. A hundred stallions in this first lot, and thirty mares. Better off than the army on campaign, but still fierce competition, eh?"

"You've been at war too long," I told him.

He grinned and went, and I called my assistants and went up through the new cavalry lines to make sure that all would be ready to receive the horses, and to check yet again the new, light field-harness that the saddler's workshops had made for them.

As I went, the bells began to ring from the gilded towers. The High King was home, and preparations for the crowning could begin.

Since I had watched Uther crowned I had travelled abroad, and seen splendours—in Rome, Antioch, Byzantium—beside which anything that Britain could do was like the mumming of gaudy tumblers; but there was about that ceremony at Caerleon a young and springtime glory that none of the riches of the East could have procured. The bishops and priests were splendid in scarlet and purple and white, set off the more brilliantly by the browns and sables of the holy men and women who attended them. The kings, each with his following of nobles and fighting men, glittered with jewels and gilded arms. The walls of the fortress, crested with the shifting and craning heads of the people, stirred with bright hangings, and rang with cheering. The ladies of the court were gay as kingfishers; even Queen Ygraine, in a glow of pride and happiness, had put aside her mourning robes, and shone like the rest. Morgan, beside her, had certainly none of the air of a rejected bride; she was only a little less richly dressed than her mother, and showed the same smiling, royal composure. It was difficult to remember how young she was. The two royal ladies kept their places among the women, not coming to Arthur's side. I heard, here and there, murmurs among the ladies, and perhaps even more among the matrons, who had their eyes on the empty side of the throne; but to me it was fitting that there should be no one yet to share his glory. He stood alone in the center of the church, with the light from the long windows kindling the rubies to a blaze, and laying panels of gold and sapphire along the white of his robe, and on the fur that trimmed the scarlet mantle.

I had wondered if Lot would come. Gossip had gathered, like a boil, to bursting-point before we knew; but come, in the end, he did. Perhaps he felt that he would lose more by staying away than by braving the King and Queen and his slighted princess, for, a few days before the ceremony, his spears were seen, along with those of Urien of Gore, and Aguisel of Bremenium, and Tydwal who kept Dunpeldyr for him, flouting the sky to the northeast. This train of northern lords stayed encamped together a little beyond the township, but they came crowding in to join the celebrations as if nothing untoward had ever happened at Luguvallium or York. Lot himself showed a confidence too easy to be called bravado; he was relying, perhaps, on the fact that he was now hand-kin to Arthur. Arthur said as much, privately, to me; in public he received Lot's ceremonious courtesies blandly. I wondered, with fear, if Lot yet suspected that he had the King's unborn child at his mercy.

At least Morgause had not come. Knowing the lady as I did, I thought she might have come and faced even me, for the pleasure of flaunting her crown in front of Ygraine, and her swollen belly in front of Arthur and myself. But whether for fear of me, or whether Lot's nerve had failed him and he had forbidden it, she stayed away, with her pregnancy as the plea. I was beside Arthur when Lot gave his queen's excuses; there was no hint of any extra knowledge in his face or voice, and if he saw Arthur's sudden glance at me, or the slight paling of his cheeks, he gave no sign. Then the King had himself in hand again, and the moment passed.

So the day wore through its brilliant, exhausting hours. The bishops spared no touch of holy ceremonial, and, for the pagans present, the omens were good. I had seen signs other than that of the Cross being made in the street as the procession passed, and at the street corners fortunes were told with bones and dice and gazing, while peddlers did a brisk trade with every kind of charm and luck-piece. Black cockerels had been killed at dawning, and offerings made at ford and crossroads, where the old Herm used to wait for traveller's gifts. Outside the city, in mountain and valley and forest, the small dark folk of the upper hills would be watching their own omens and petitioning their own gods. But in the city center, on church and palace and fortress alike, the Cross caught the sun. As for Arthur, he went through the long day with calm and pale-faced dignity, stiff with jewels and embroidery, and rigid with ceremony, a puppet for the priests to sanctify. If this was needed to declare his authority finally in the eyes of the people, then this was what he would do. But I, who knew him, and who stood at his side all through that endless day, could sense neither dedication nor prayer in that still composure. He was probably, I thought, planning the next fighting foray to the east. For him, as for all who had seen it, the kingdom had been taken into his hand when he lifted the great sword of Maximus from its long oblivion, and made his vow to the listening forests. The crown of Caerleon was only the public seal of what he had held in his hand then, and would hold until he died.

Then, after the ceremony, the feast. One feast is much like another, and this one was remarkable only for the fact that Arthur, who loved his food, ate very little, but glanced about him from time to time as if he could hardly wait for the feasting to stop, and the time of affairs to come back.

He had told me that he would want to talk with me that night, but he was kept till late, with the press of people around him, so I saw Ygraine first. She retired early from the feasting, and when her page came to me with a whispered message, I caught a nod from Arthur, and followed him.

Her rooms were in the King's house. Here the sounds of the revelry could be heard only faintly, against the more distant noise of the town's rejoicing. The door was opened to me by the same girl who had been with her at Amesbury; she was slender in green, with pearls in the light-brown hair, and eyes showing green as her gown: not the gleaming witch-colour of Morgause, but a clear grey-green, making one think of sunlight on a forest stream reflecting the young leaves of spring. Her skin was flushed with excitement and the feasting, and she smiled at me, showing a dimple and excellent teeth, as she curtsied me toward the Queen.

Ygraine gave me a hand. She looked tired, and the magnificent gown of purple, with its shimmer of pearls and silver, showed up her pallor, and the shadows at mouth and eyes. But her manner, composed and cool as always, betrayed no trace of fatigue.

She came straight to the point. "So, he got her pregnant."

Even as the knife-twist of fear went through me, I saw that she had no suspicion of the truth; she was referring to Lot, and to what she took to be the reason for his rejection of her daughter Morgan in favour of Morgause.

"It seems so." I was equally blunt. "At least it saves Morgan's face, which is all that need concern us."

"It's the best thing that could have happened," said Ygraine flatly. She smiled faintly at my look. "I never liked that marriage. I favoured Uther's first idea, when he offered Morgause to Lot years ago. That would have been enough for him, and honour for her. But Lot was ambitious, one way or another, even then, and nothing would please him but Morgan herself. So Uther agreed. At that time he would have agreed to anything that sealed the northern kingdoms against the Saxons; but while for policy's sake I saw that it had to be done, I am too fond of my daughter to want her shackled to that wayward and greedy traitor."

I put up my brows at her. "Strong words, madam."

"Do you deny the facts?"

"Far from it. I was there at Luguvallium."

"Then you will know how much, in loyalty, Lot's betrothal to Morgan bound him to Arthur, and how much marriage would have bound him, if profit pointed another way."

"Yes. I agree. I'm only glad that you yourself see it like that. I was afraid that the slight to Morgan would anger you and distress her."

"She was angry at first, rather than distressed. Lot is among the foremost of the petty kings, and, like him or not, she would have been queen of a wide realm, and her children would have had a great heritage. She could not like being displaced by a bastard, and one, besides, who has not shown her kindness."

"And when the bethrothal was first mooted, Urbgen of Rheged still had a wife."

The long lids lifted, and her eyes studied my impassive face. "Just so," was all she said, without surprise. It was said as if at the end of a discussion, rather than the beginning.

It was no surprise that Ygraine had been thinking along the same lines as Arthur and myself. Like his father Coel, Urbgen had shown himself staunch to the High King. "Rheged's" deeds in the past, and more recently at Luguvallium, were chronicled along with those of Ambrosius and Arthur, as the sky accepts the light of the setting and the rising sun.

Ygraine was saying, thoughtfully: "It might answer, at that. There's no need to ensure Urbgen's loyalty, of course, but for Morgan it would be power of the kind that I think she can manage, and for her sons. . . ." She paused. "Well, Urbgen has two already, both young men grown, and fighters like their sire. Who is to say that they will ever reach his crown? And the king of a realm as wide as Rheged cannot breed too many sons."

"He is past his best years, and she is still very young." I made it a statement, but she answered calmly:

"And so? I was not much older than Morgan when Gorlois of Cornwall married me."

For the moment, I believe, she had forgotten what that marriage had meant: the caging of a young creature avid to spread her wings and fly; the fatal passion of King Uther for Gorlois' lovely duchess; the death of the old duke, and then the new life, with all its love and pain.

"She will do her duty," said Ygraine, and now I saw that she had remembered, but her eyes did not falter. "If she was willing to accept Lot, whom she feared, she will take Urbgen willingly, should Arthur suggest it. It's a pity that Cador is too nearly related for her to have him. I would have liked to see her settled near to me in Cornwall."

"They are not blood kin." Cador was the son, by his first wife, of Ygraine's husband Gorlois.

"Too close," said Ygraine. "Men forget things too quickly, and there would be whispers of incest. It would not do, even to hint at a crime so shocking."

"No. I see that." My voice sounded level and cool.

"And besides, Cador is to wed, come summer, when he gets back to Cornwall. The King approves." She turned hand over in her lap, admiring, apparently, the glint of the rings on it. "So perhaps it would be as well to speak of Urbgen to the King, just as soon as some portion of his mind is free to think of his sister?"

"He has already thought of her. He discussed it with me. I believe he will send to Urbgen very soon."

"Ah! And then—" For the first time a purely human and female satisfaction warmed her voice with something uncommonly like spite. "And then we shall see Morgan take what is due to her in wealth and precedence over that redhaired witch, and may Lot of Lothian deserve the snares she set for him!"

"You think she trapped him deliberately?"

"How else? You know her. She wove her spells for this."

"A very common kind of spell," I said dryly.

"Oh, yes. But Lot has never lacked women, and no one can deny that Morgan is the better match, and as pretty a lass besides. And for all the arts Morgause boasts, Morgan is better able to be queen of a great kingdom. She was bred for it, as the bastard was not."

I watched her curiously. Beside her chair the brown-haired girl sat on her stool half asleep. Ygraine seemed careless of what she might overhear. "Ygraine, what harm did Morgause ever do to you that makes you so bitter against her?"

The red came up in her face like a flag, and for a moment I thought she would try to set me down, but we were neither of us young any more, or needing the armour of self-love. She spoke simply: "If you are thinking that I hated having a lovely young girl always near me, and near to Uther, with a right to him that went back beyond my own, it is true. But it was more than that. Even when she was a young girl—twelve, thirteen, no more—I thought of her as corrupt. That is one reason why I welcomed the match with Lot. I wanted her away from court."

This was straighter than I had expected. "Corrupt?" I asked.

The Queen's glance slid momentarily to the girl on the stool beside her. The brown head was nodding, the eyelids closed. Ygraine lowered her voice, but spoke clearly and carefully. "I am not suggesting that there was anything evil in her relationship with the King, though she never behaved to him like a daughter; nor was she fond of him as a daughter should be; she cajoled favours from him, no more than that. When I called her corrupt, I spoke of her practice of witchcraft. She was drawn to it always, and haunted the wise-women and the charlatans, and any talk of magic brought her staring awake like an owl at night-time. And she tried to teach Morgan, when the princess was only a child. That is what I cannot forgive. I have no time for such things, and in the hands of such as Morgause . . ."

She broke off. Vehemence had made her raise her voice, and I saw that the girl, like the owl, was also staring awake. Ygraine, recollecting herself, bent her head, a touch of colour in her face again.

"Prince Merlin, you must pardon me. I meant no disrespect."

I laughed. I saw, to my amusement, that the girl must have heard; she was laughing, too, but silently, dimpling at me from beyond her mistress's shoulder. I said: "I am too proud to think of myself in the same breath as girls dabbling with spells. I am sorry about Morgan. It is true that Morgause has power of a sort, and it is also true that such things can be dangerous. Any power is hard to hold, and power misused recoils on the user."

"Perhaps some day, if you get the chance, you will tell Morgan so." She smiled, trying for a lighter tone. "She will listen to you, where she would shrug her shoulders at me."

"Willingly." I tried to sound willing, like a grandfather called in to lecture the young.

"It may be that when she finds herself a queen with real power, she will cease to hanker for another sort." She turned the subject. "So now that Lot has a daughter of Uther's, even if only a bastard, will he consider himself bound to Arthur's banner?"

"That I cannot tell you. But unless the Saxons make heavy enough gains to make it worth Lot's while to try another betrayal, I think he will keep what power he has, and fight for his own land, if not for the High King's sake. I see no trouble there." I did not add: "Not of that kind." I finished merely: "When you go back to Cornwall, madam, I will send letters if you like."

"I should be grateful. Your letters were a great comfort to me before, when my son was at Galava."

We talked for a while longer, mainly of the day's events. When I would have asked after her health, she put the query aside with a smile that told me she knew as much as I, so I let it be, asking instead about Duke Cador's projected marriage. "Arthur has mentioned it. Who is it to be?"

"The daughter of Dinas. Did you know him? Her name is Mariona. The marriage was arranged, alas, when they were both children. Now Mariona is of age, so when the duke is home again they will be wed."

"I knew her father, yes. Why did you say 'alas'?"

Ygraine looked with a fond smile at the girl by her chair. "Because otherwise there would have been no difficulty in finding a match for my little Guenever."

"I am sure," I said, "that that will prove more than easy."

"But such a match," said the Queen, and the girl made a smiling mouth and lowered her lashes.

"If I dared use divination in your presence, madam," I said, smiling, "I would predict that one as splendid will present itself, and soon."

I spoke lightly, in formal courtesy, and was startled to hear in my voice an echo, though faint and soon lost, of the cadences of prophecy.

Neither of them heard it. The Queen was holding a hand to me, bidding me good night, and the girl Guenever held the door for me, sinking, as I passed, into a smiling curtsy of humility and grace.

7

"It's mine!" said Arthur, violently. "You only have to count! I heard the men talking about it in the guard-room. They didn't know I was near enough to hear them. They said she was big-bellied by Twelfth Night, and lucky to catch Lot so early, they could pass it off as a seven-month child. Merlin, you know as well as I do that he never came near her at Luguvallium! He wasn't there until the very night of the battle, and that night—that was the night—" He stopped, choking on it, and turned with a swirl of robes to pace the floor again.

It was well after midnight. The sounds of revelry from the town were fainter now, muted with the chill of the hour before dawn. In the King's room the candles had burned low into a welter of honeyed wax. Their scent mingled with the sharp smoke from a lamp that needed trimming.

Arthur turned sharply on his heel and came back to stand in front of me. He had taken off the crown and jewelled chain, and laid his sword aside, but he still wore the splendid coronation robe. The furred cloak lay across the table like a stream of blood in the lamplight. Through the open door of his bed-chamber I could see the covers turned back ready on the great bed, but, late though the hour was, Arthur showed no sign of fatigue. His every movement was infused with a kind of nervous fury.

He controlled it, speaking quietly. "Merlin, when we spoke that night of what had happened—" A breathing pause, then he changed course with ferocious directness: "When I lay incestuously with Morgause, I asked you what would happen if she should conceive. I remember what you said. I remember it well. Do you?"

"Yes," I said unwillingly, "I remember it."

"You said to me, 'The gods are jealous, and they insure against too much glory. Every man carries the seed of his own death, and there must come a term to every life. All that has happened tonight is that you yourself have set that term.' "

I said nothing. He faced me with the straight, uncompromising look that I was to come to know so well.

"When you spoke to me like that, were you telling me the truth? Was the prophecy a sure one, or were you finding words of comfort for me, so that I could face what was to come next day?"

"It was the truth."

"You meant that if she bore a child to me, you could foresee that he—she?—would be my death?"

"Arthur," I said, "prophecy does not work like that. I neither knew, in the way most men think of 'knowing,' that Morgause would conceive, nor that the child would be a mortal danger for you. I only knew, all the time you were with the woman, that the birds of death were on my shoulders, weighing me down and stinking of carrion. My heart was heavy with dread, and I could see death, as I thought, linking the two of you together. Death and treachery. But how, I did not know. By the time I understood it, the thing was done, and all that was left was to await what the gods chose to send."

He paced away from me again, over toward the bed-chamber door. He leaned there in silence, his shoulder to the jamb, his face away from me, then thrust himself off and turned. He crossed to the chair behind the big table, sat down, and regarded me, chin on fist. His movements were controlled and smooth, as always, but I, who knew him, could hear the curb-chain ring. He still spoke quietly. "And now we know the carrion-birds were right. She did conceive. You told me something else that night, when I admitted my fault. You said I had sinned unknowingly and was innocent. Is innocence, then, to be punished?"

"It's not uncommon."

" 'The sins of the fathers'?"

I recognized the phrase as a quotation from the Christian scriptures. "Uther's sin," I said, "visited on you."

"And mine, now, on the child?"

I said nothing. I did not like the way the interview was going. For the first time, talking with Arthur, I did not seem able to take control. I told myself I was weary, that I was still in the ebbtide of power, that my time would come again; but the truth is I was feeling a little like the fisherman in the Eastern tale who unstoppered a bottle and let out a genie many times more powerful than himself.

"Very well," said the King. "My sin and hers must be visited on the child. It must not be allowed to live. You will go north and tell Morgause so. Or if you prefer, I shall give you a letter telling her so myself."

I took breath, but he swept on without giving me time to speak.

"Quite apart from your forebodings—which God knows I would be a fool not to respect—can you not see how dangerous this thing could be now, if Lot should find out about it? It's plain enough what has happened. She feared she might be pregnant, and to save her shame she set herself to snare a husband. Who better than Lot? She had been offered to him before; for all we know she had wanted him, and now saw a chance to outshine her sister and give herself a place and a name, which she would lack after her father's death." His lips thinned. "And who knows better than I that if she set herself to get a man, any man, he would go to her for the whistle?"

"Arthur, you talk of her 'shame.' You don't think you were the first she took to her bed, do you?"

He said, a little too quickly: "I never did think so."

"Then how do you know she had not lain with Lot before you? That she was not already pregnant to him, and took *you* in the hope of snaring some kind of power and favour to herself? She knew Uther was dying; she feared that Lot, by his action at Luguvallium, had forfeited the King's favour. If she could father Lot's child on you . . ."

"This is guesswork. This is not what you said that night."

"No. But think back. It would fit the facts of my foreboding equally well."

"But not the force of them," he said sharply. "If the danger from this child is real, then what does it matter who fathered it? Guesswork won't help us."

"I'm not guessing when I tell you that she and Lot were lovers before ever you went to her bed. I told you I had had a dream that night at Nodens' shrine. I saw them meet at a house some way off an ill-frequented road. It must have been by prearrangement. They met like people who have been lovers for a long time. This child may in fact be Lot's, and not yours."

"And we've got it the wrong way round? I was the one she whistled up to save her shame?"

"It's possible. You had come from nowhere, eclipsing Lot as you would soon eclipse Uther. She made her bid to father Lot's child on you, but then had to abandon the attempt, for fear of me."

He was silent, thinking. "Well," he said at length, "time will tell us. But are we to wait for it? No matter whose child this is, it is a danger; and it doesn't take a prophet to see how that could be . . . or a god to act on it. If Lot ever knows—or believes—that his eldest child is fathered by me, how long do you think this chary loyalty of his will last? Lothian is a key point, you know that. I need that loyalty; I have to have it. Even if he had wedded my own sister Morgan, I could hardly have trusted him, whereas now . . ." He threw out a hand, palm up. "Merlin, it's done every day, in every village in the kingdom. Why not in a king's house? Go north for me, and talk to Morgause."

"You think she would listen? If she had not wanted the child, she would not have scrupled to get rid of it long since. She didn't take you for love, Arthur, and she bears you no friendship for letting her be driven from court. And to me"—I smiled sourly—"she bears a most emphatic and justified ill-will. She would laugh in my face. More than that: she would listen, and laugh at the power her action had given her over us, and then she would do whatever she thought would hurt us most."

"But—"

"You thought she might have persuaded Lot into marriage merely for her own sake, or to score from her sister. No. She took him because I foiled her plans to corrupt and own you, and because at heart, whatever the time may force him to do now, Lot is your enemy and mine, and through him she may one day do you harm."

A sharpening silence. "Do you believe this?"

"Yes."

He stirred. "Then I am still right. She must not bear the child."

"What are you going to do? Pay someone to bake her bread with ergot?"

"You will find some way. You will go—"

"I will do nothing in the matter."

He came to his feet, like a bow snapping upright when the string breaks. His eyes glittered in the candlelight. "You told me you were my servant. You made me King, you said by the god's wish. Now I am King, and you will obey me."

I was taller than he, by two fingers' breadth. I had outfaced kings before, and he was very young. I gave it just long enough, then said, gently:

"I am your servant, Arthur, but I serve the god first. Do not make me choose. I have to let him work the way he wills."

He held my eyes a moment longer, then drew a long breath, and released it as if it had been a weight he was holding. "To do this? To destroy, perhaps, the very kingdom you said he had sent me to build?"

"If he sent you to build it, then it will be built. Arthur, I don't pretend to understand this. I can only tell you to trust the time, as I do, and wait. Now, do as you did before, put it aside and try to forget it. Leave it with me."

"What will you do?"

"Go north."

A moment of quickening stillness, then he said: "To Lothian? But you said you would not go."

"No. I said I would do nothing about killing the child. But I can watch Morgause, and perhaps, in time, judge better what we must do. I will send to tell you what happens."

There was another silence. Then the tension went out of him, and he turned away, beginning to loosen the clasp of his belt. "Very well." He started to ask some question, then bit it back and smiled at me. Having shown the whip, he was now concerned, it seemed, to retreat on the old trust and affection. "But you will stay for the rest of the feasting? If the wars allow, I have to stay here myself for eight days before I can take horse again."

"No. I think I must be gone. Better perhaps while Lot is still here with you. That way I can melt into the countryside before ever he gets home, and watch and wait, and take what action I can. With your leave, I'll go tomorrow morning."

"Who goes with you?"

"Nobody. I can travel alone."

"You must take someone. It's not like riding home to Maridunum. Besides, you may need a messenger."

"I'll use your couriers."

"All the same . . ." He had got the belt undone. He threw it over a chair. "Ulfin!"

A sound from the next room, then discreet footsteps. Ulfin, carrying a long bedgown over one arm, came in from the bedchamber, stifling a yawn. "My lord?"

"Have you been in there all the while?" I asked sharply.

Ulfin, wooden-faced, reached to undo the clasps at the King's shoulder. He held the long outer robe as the King stepped out of it. "I was asleep, my lord."

Arthur sat down and thrust out a foot. Ulfin knelt to ease the shoe from it. "Ulfin, my cousin Prince Merlin goes north tomorrow, on what may prove a long and hard journey. I shall dislike losing you, but I want you to go with him."

Ulfin, shoe in hand, looked up at me and smiled. "Willingly."

"Should you not stay with the King?" I protested. "This week of all weeks—"

"I do as he tells me," said Ulfin simply, and stooped to the other foot.

As you do, in the end. Arthur did not say the words aloud, but they were there in the quick glance he gave me as he stood again for Ulfin to gird the bedgown round him.

I gave up. "Very well. I shall be glad to have you. We leave tomorrow, and I should warn you that we may be away for some considerable time." I gave him what instructions I could, then turned back to Arthur. "Now, I had better go. I doubt if I shall see you before I set off. I'll send you word as soon as I can. No doubt I shall know where you are."

"No doubt." He sounded all at once grim, very much the war-leader. "Can you spare a moment or two more? Thank you, Ulfin, leave us now. You'll have your own preparations to make. . . . Merlin, come and see my new toy."

"Another?"

"Another? Oh, you're thinking about the cavalry. Have you seen the horses Bedwyr brought?"

"Not yet. Valerius told me about them."

His eyes kindled. "They are splendid! Fast, fiery, and gentle. I am told they can live on hard rations if they have to, and that their hearts are so high that they will gallop all day, and then fight with you to the death. Bedwyr brought grooms with them. If everything they say is true, then surely we shall have a cavalry force to conquer the world! There are two trained stallions, white ones, that are real beauties, even finer than my Canrith. Bedwyr chose them especially for me. Over here . . ." As he spoke he led the way across the room toward a pillared archway closed by a curtain. "I haven't had time to try them yet, but surely I can throw off my chains for an hour or two tomorrow?"

His voice was that of a restive boy. I laughed. "I hope so. I am more fortunate than the King: I shall be on my way."

"On your old black gelding, no doubt."

"Not even that. A mule."

"A mule? Ah, of course. You go disguised?"

"I must. I can hardly ride into Lothian's stronghold as Prince Merlin."

"Well, take care. You're certain you don't want an escort, at least for the first part of the way?"

"Certain. I shall be safe. What's this you are going to show me?"

"Only a map. Here."

He pulled the curtain back. Beyond it was a kind of anteroom, little more than a broad portico giving on a small private courtyard. Torchlight winked on the spears of the guards on duty there, but otherwise the place was empty, bare even of furniture except for a huge table, rough-adzed out of oak. It was a map table, but instead of the usual sandtray it held, I saw, a map made of clay, with mountains and valleys, coasts and rivers, modelled by some clever sculptor, so that there, plain to see, lay the land of Britain as a highflying bird might view it from the heavens.

Arthur was plainly delighted at my praise. "I knew you would be interested! They only finished setting it up yesterday. Splendid, isn't it? Do you remember teaching me to make maps in the dust? This is better than scraping the sand into hills and valleys that change when you breathe on them. Of course, it can still be remodelled as we find out more. North of Strathclyde is anybody's guess . . . but then, by God's mercy, nothing north of Strathclyde need concern me. Not yet, anyway." He fingered a peg, carved and coloured like a red dragon, that stood over "Caerleon." "Now, which way do you plan to go tommorow?"

"I thought, by the west road through Deva and Bremet. I have a call to make at Vindolanda."

His finger followed the route northward till it reached Bremetannacum (which is commonly spoken of now as Bremet), and paused. "Will you do something for me?"

"Willingly."

"Go by the east. It's not so much farther, and the road is better for most of the way. Here, see? If you turn off at Bremet, you'll take this road through the mountain gap." His finger traced it out: east from Bremetennacum, up the old road following the Tribuit River, then over the pass and down through Olicana into the Vale of York. There Dere Street runs, a good, fast highway still, up through Corstopitum and the Wall and thence still north, right into Manau Guotodin, where lies Lot's capital of Dunpeldyr.

"You'll have to retrace your steps for Vindolanda," said Arthur, "but not far. You'll lose nothing in time, I believe. It's the road through the Pennine Gap that I want you to take. I've never been that way myself. I've had reports that it's quite feasible—you should have no difficulty, just the two of you—but it's too broken in places for a troop of cavalry. I shall be sending parties up to repair it. I shall have to fortify it, too . . . you agree? With parts of the eastern seaboard so open to the enemy, if they should get a grip on the easterly plains this will be their way into our British heartland in the west. There are two forts there already; I am told they could be made good. I want you to look at them for me. Don't take time over it; I can get detailed reports from the surveyors; but if you can go that way, I would like to have your thoughts about it."

"You shall have them."

As he straightened from the map, a cock crowed outside somewhere. The courtyard was grey. He said quietly: "For the other matter we spoke of, I am in your hands. God knows I should be thankful to be so." He smiled. "Now we had better get to our beds. You have a journey to face, and I another day of pleasure. I envy you! Good night, and God go with you."

8

Next day, furnished with food for two days' journey, and three good mules from one of the baggage trains, Ulfin and I set off on the journey northward.

I had made journeys before in circumstances as dangerous as this, when to be recognized would be to court disaster, or even death. I had, perforce, become adept at disguise; this had given rise to yet another legend about "the enchanter," that he could vanish at will into thin air to escape his enemies. I had certainly perfected the art of melting into a landscape: what I did in fact was assume the tools of some trade, and then frequent places where no one would expect a prince to be. Men's eyes are focused on what, not who, a traveller is, who goes labelled with his skill. I had travelled as a singer when I needed access to a prince's court as well as a humble tavern, but more often I went as a travelling physician or eye-doctor. This was the guise I liked best. It allowed me to practise my skill where it was most needed, among the poor, and it gave me access to any kind of house except the noblest.

This was the disguise I chose now. I took my small harp, but only for my private use: I dared not risk my skill as a singer earning me a summons to Lot's court. So the harp, muffled and wrapped into anonymity, hung on the baggage-mule's shabby saddle, while my boxes of unguents and roll of implements were carried plain to be seen.

The first part of our way I knew well, but after we reached Bremetennacum, and turned toward the Pennine Gap, the country was unfamiliar.

The Gap is formed by the valleys of three great rivers. Two of these, the Wharfe and the Isara, spring from the limestone on the Pennine tops and flow, meandering, eastward. The other, an important stream with countless smaller tributaries, lapses toward the west. It is called the Tribuit. Once through the Gap and into the valley of the Tribuit, an enemy's way would be clear to the west coast, and the last embattled corners of Britain.

Arthur had spoken of two forts lying within the Gap itself. I had gathered from seemingly idle questions put to local men in the tavern at Brementennacum that in times past there had been a third fort guarding the western mouth of the pass, where the Tribuit valley widens out toward the lowlands and the coast. It had been built by the Romans as a temporary marching camp, so much of the turf and timber structure would have decayed and vanished, but it occurred to me that the road serving it would stand a survey, and, if it were still in reasonable condition, could provide a quick corner-cut for cavalry coming down from Rheged to defend the Gap.

From Rheged to Olicana, and York. The road Morgause must have taken to meet Lot.

That settled it. I would take the same road, the road of my dream at Nodens' shrine. If the dream had been a true one—and I had no doubt of it—there were things I wished to learn.

We left the main road just beyond Bremetennacum, and headed up the Tribuit valley on the gravel of a neglected Roman road. A day's ride brought us to the marching camp.

As I had suspected, little was left of it but the banks and ditches, and some rotting timber where the gateways had once stood. But like all such camps it was cleverly placed, on a flank of moorland that looked in every direction over clear country. The hillside had a tributary stream at foot, and to the west the river flowed through flatlands toward the sea. Placed as the camp was, so far west, we might hope that it would not be needed for defense; but as a staging-camp for cavalry, or as a temporary base for a swift foray through the Gap, it was ideal.

I had been unable to find anyone who knew its name. When I wrote my report to Arthur that night, I called it merely "Tribuit."

Next day we struck out across country toward the first of the forts of which Arthur had spoken. This lay in the arm of a marshy stream, near the beginning of the pass. The stream spread out beside it into a lake, from which the place took its name. Though ruinous, it could, I judged, be speedily brought into repair. There was abundant timber in the valley, and plenty of stone and deep moorland turf available.

We reached it toward late afternoon, and, the air being balmy and dry, and the fortress walls promising sufficient shelter, we made camp there. Next morning we began the climb across the ridge toward Olicana.

Well before midday we had climbed clear of the forest and onto heathland. It was a fine day, with mist drawing back from the sparkling sedges, and the song of water bubbling from every crevice in the rock, where the rills tumbled down to fill the young river. Rippling, too, with sound was the morning sky, where curlews slanted down on ringing streams of song toward their nests in the grass. We saw a she-wolf, heavy with milk, slink across the road ahead, with a hare in her mouth. She gave us a brief, indifferent glance, then slipped into the shelter of the mist.

It was a wild way, a Wolf Road such as the Old Ones love. I kept my eye on the rocks that crowned the screes, but saw no sign that I could recognize of their remote and comfortless eyries. I had no doubt, though, that we were watched every step of the way. No doubt, either, that news had gone north on the winds that Merlin the enchanter was on the road, and secretly. It did not trouble me. It is not possible to keep secrets from the Old Ones; they know all that comes or goes in forest and hill. They and I had come to an understanding long since, and Arthur had their trust.

We halted on the summit of the moor. I looked around me. The mist had lifted now, dispersing under the steadily strengthening sun. All around us stretched the moor, broken with grey rock and bracken, with, in the distance, the still-misty heights of fell and mountain. To the left of the road the ground fell away into the wide Isara valley, where water glinted among crowding trees.

It could not have looked more unlike the rain-dimmed vision of Nodens' shrine, but there was the milestone with its legend, OLICANA; and there, to the left, the track plunging steeply down toward the valley trees. Among them, only just visible through the leafage, showed the walls of a considerable house.

Ulfin, ranging his mule alongside mine, was pointing.

"If only we had known, we might have found better lodging there."

I said slowly: "I doubt it. I think we were better under the sky."

He shot me a curious glance. "I thought you had never been this way, sir? Do you know the place?"

"Shall we say that I know of it? And would like to know more. Next time we pass a village, or if we see a shepherd on the hill, find out who owns that villa, will you?"

He threw me another look, but said no more, and we rode on.

Olicana, the second of Arthur's two forts, lay only ten miles or so to the east. To my surprise the road, heading steeply downward, then crossing a considerable stretch of boggy moorland, was in first-class condition. Ditches and embankments alike looked to have been recently repaired. There was a good timber bridge across the Isara itself, and the ford of the next tributary was cleared and paved. We made good speed in consequence, and came in the early evening into settled country. At Olicana there is a sizable township. We found lodgings in a tavern that stood near the fortress walls, to serve the men of the garrison.

From what I had seen of the road, and the orderly appointments of the town's streets and square, it came as no surprise that the walls of the fortress itself were in the same good order. Gates and bridges were sound and stout, and the ironwork looked fire-new. By carefully idle questions, and by listening to the talk in the tavern at supper-time, I was able to gather that a skeleton garrison had been placed here in Uther's time, to watch the road into the Gap and to keep an eye on the signal towers to the east. It had been an emergency measure, taken hastily during the worst years of the Saxon Terror, but the same men were still here, despairing of recall, bored to distraction, but kept to a tingling pitch of efficiency by a garrison commander who deserved something better (one gathered) than this dismal outpost of inaction.

The simplest way to gather the information I needed was to make myself known to this officer, who could then see that my report was sent straight back to the King. Accordingly, leaving Ulfin in the tavern, I presented myself at the guardroom with the pass Arthur had supplied.

From the speed with which I was passed through, and the lack of surprise at my shabby appearance, and refusal even to state my name or my business to anyone but the commander himself, it could be judged that messengers were frequent here. Secret messengers, at that. If this really was a forgotten outpost (and admittedly nor I nor the King's advisers had known of it) then the only messengers who would come and go so assiduously were spies. I began to look forward all the more to meeting the commander.

I was searched before being taken in, which was only to be expected. Then a couple of the guards escorted me through the fort to the headquarters building. I looked about me. The place was well lighted, and as far as I could see, roads, courtyards, well, exercise ground, workshops, barracks were in mint repair. We passed carpenters' shops, harness-makers, smithies. From the padlocks on the granary doors, I deduced that the barns were fully stocked. The place was not large but was still, I reckoned, undermanned. There could be accommodation for Arthur's cavalry almost before the force could be formed.

My pass was taken through, then I was shown into the commander's room, and the guards withdrew, with a neatness that told its own story. This was where the spies came; and usually, I supposed, as late as this.

The commander received me standing, a tribute not to me but to the King's seal. The first thing that struck me was his youth. He could not have been more than twenty-two. The second thing was that he was tired. Lines of strain were scored into his face: his youth, the solitary post up here, in charge of a bored and hardbitten contingent of men; the constant watchfulness as the tides of invasion flowed and ebbed along the eastern coasts; all this, winter and summer, without help and without backing. It seemed true that after Uther had sent him here four years ago—four years—he had forgotten all about him.

"You have news for me?" The flat tone disguised no eagerness; that had long since been dissipated by frustration.

"I can give you what news there is when my main business is done. I have been sent, rather, to get information from you, if you will be good enough to supply it. I have a report to send to the High King. I would be glad if a messenger could take it to him as soon as it is completed."

"That can be arranged. Now? A man can be ready within the half hour."

"No. It's not so urgent. If we might talk first, please?"

He sat down, motioning me to a chair. For the first time a spark of interest showed. "Do you mean that the report concerns Olicana? Am I to know why?"

"I shall tell you, of course. The King asked me to find out all I could about this place, and also about the ruined fortress in the pass, the one they call Lake Fort."

He nodded. "I know it. It's been a wreck for nearly two hundred years. It was destroyed in the Brigantian rebellion, and left to rot. This place suffered the same fate, but Ambrosius had it rebuilt. He had plans for Lake Fort, too, so I have been told. If I had had a mandate, I might have—" He checked himself. "Ah, well . . . You came from Bremet? Then you'll know that a couple of miles north of that road there is another fort—nothing there, only the site—but I would have thought it equally vital to any strategy involving the Gap. Ambrosius saw it so, they tell me. He saw that the Gap could be a key point of his strategy." There was no perceptible emphasis on the "he," but the inference was clear. Uther had not only forgotten the existence of Olicana and its garrison, he had either ignored or misunderstood the importance of the road through the Pennine Gap. As this young man, in his helpless isolation, had not.

I said quickly: "And now the new King sees it, too. He wants to refortify the Gap, not only with a view to closing and holding it against penetration from the east, if that becomes necessary, but also to using the pass as a quick line of attack. He has charged me to see what there is to be done. I think you can expect the surveyors up after my reports have been studied. This place is in a state of readiness that I know the King did not expect. He will be pleased."

I told him something then about Arthur's plans for the formation of the cavalry force. He listened eagerly, his weary boredom forgotten, and the questions he put showed that he knew a great deal about affairs on the eastern seaboard. He assumed, besides, a surprisingly intimate knowledge of Saxon movements and strategy.

I left that aside for the moment, and began to put my own questions about Olicana's accommodation and supplies. After little more than a minute of it he got to his feet, and, crossing to a chest locked with another of the great padlocks, opened it, and brought out tablets and rolls on which, it transpired, were lists, fully detailed, of all I wanted to know.

I studied these for a few minutes, then became conscious that he was waiting, watching me, with other lists in his hand.

"I think," he began, then hesitated. In a moment he made up his mind to continue. "I don't think that King Uther, in the last years, ever quite appreciated what the road through the Gap might mean in the coming struggle. When I was sent here—when I was young—I saw it as an outpost only, a place, you might say, to practise on. It was better than Lake Fort then but only just. . . . It took quite a time to get it into working shape. . . . Well, you know what happened, sir. The war moved north and south; King Uther was sick, and the country divided; we seemed to be forgotten. I sent couriers from time to time, with information, but got no acknowledgement. So for my own instruction and, I admit, entertainment, I began to send out men—not soldiers, but boys from the town mostly, with a taste for adventure—and gathered information. I am at fault, I know, but . . ." He stopped.

"You kept it to yourself?" I prompted him.

"With no wrong motive," he said hastily. "I did send one courier, with some information I judged to be of value, but heard no more of him or of the papers he carried. So I no longer wanted to commit anything to messengers who might not be received by the King."

"I can assure you that anything I send to the King has only to reach him safely to get his immediate attention."

While we had been talking he had been studying me covertly, comparing, I suppose, my shabby appearance with the manner I had made no attempt, with him, to disguise. He said slowly, glancing down at the lists he held: "I have the King's pass and seal, so I am to trust you. Am I to know your name?"

"If you wish. It is for you only. I have your promise?"

"Of course," he said, a shade impatiently.

"Then I am Myrddin Emrys, commonly known as Merlin. As you will gather, I am on a private journey, so I am known as Emrys, a travelling doctor."

"Sir—"

"No," I said quickly, "sit down again. I only told you so that you could be sure your information will reach the King's ear, and quickly. May I see it now?"

He laid the lists down in front of me. I studied them. More information: plans of fortified settlements, numbers of troops and armaments, troop movements carefully chronicled, supplies, ships . . .

I looked up, startled. "But these are plans of *Saxon* dispositions?"

He nodded. "Recent, too, sir. I had a stroke of fortune last summer. I was put in touch—it doesn't matter how—with a Saxon, a third-generation federate. Like a lot of the old federates, he wants to keep to the old order. These Saxons hold their pledged word sacred, and besides"—a glimmer of a smile on the grim young mouth—"they mistrust the incomers. Some of these new adventurers want to displace the wealthy federates just as much as they want to drive out the British."

"And this information comes from him. Can you trust it?"

"I think so. The parts I could check I have found to be true. I don't know how good or how recent the King's own information is, but I think you should draw his attention to the section—here—about Elesa, and Cerdic Elesing. That means—"

"Elesa's son. Yes. Elesa being our old friend Eosa?"

"That's right, Horsa's son. You would know that after he and his kinsman Octa escaped from Uther's prison, Octa died, at Rutupiae, but Eosa made for Germany and drummed up Octa's sons Colgrim and Badulf to make the attack in the north. . . . Well, what you may not have known was that before he died, Octa was claiming the title of 'king' here in Britain. It didn't amount to much more than the chieftainship he had had before, as Hengist's son; neither Colgrim nor Badulf seems to have set much store by it; but now they are dead, too, and, as you see . . ."

"Eosa makes the same claim. Yes. With any more success?"

"It seems so. King of the West Saxons, he calls himself, and his young son Cerdic is known as 'the Aetheling.' They claim descent from some far-back hero or demigod. That's usual, of course, but the point is that his people believe in it. You can see that this gives a new kind of colour to the Saxon invasions."

"It could alter what you were saying about the old-established federates."

"Indeed. Eosa and Cerdic have that sort of standing, you see. This talk of a 'kingdom' . . . He's promising stability—*and rights*—to the old federates, and a quick killing to the incomers. He's genuine, too. I mean, he's shown himself to be more than a clever adventurer; he's established the legend of a heroic kingship, he's accepted as a law-giver, and powerful enough to enforce new customs. Changed the grave-customs, even . . . they don't burn their dead now, I'm told, or even bury them with their arms and grave-goods in the old way. According to Cerdic the Aetheling, it's wasteful." That grim little smile again. "They get their priests to cleanse the dead man's weapons ritually, and then they re-use them. They now believe that a spear once used by a good fighter will make its next owner as good, or better . . . and a weapon taken from a defeated warrior will fight the harder for being given a second chance. I tell you, a dangerous man. The most dangerous, perhaps, since Hengist himself."

I was impresed, and said so. "The King shall see this as soon as I can get it to him. It will be brought to his attention straight away, I promise you that. You must know how valuable it is. How soon can you have copies made?"

"I already have copies. These can go straight away."

"Good. Now, if you'll allow me, I'll add a word to your report, and put my own report on Lake Fort in with them."

He brought writing materials and set them in front of me, then made for the door. "I'll arrange for a courier."

"Thank you. A moment, though—"

He paused. We had been speaking in Latin, but there was something about his use of it that told me he came from the West Country. I said: "They told me in the tavern that your name was Gerontius. Do I hazard a guess that it was once Gereint?"

He smiled. It took years off him. "It still is, sir."

"It's a name that Arthur will be glad to know," I said, and turned to my writing.

He stood still for a moment, then went to the door, opened it, and spoke with someone outside. He came back, and, crossing to a table in the corner, poured wine and set a goblet by me. I heard him draw breath once, as if to speak, but he was silent.

At last I was finished. He went to the door again, and came back, followed this time by a man, a wiry fellow, looking as if he had just wakened up, but dressed ready for the road. He carried a leather pouch with a strong lock. He was ready to go, he said, putting away the packages Gereint handed to him; he would eat on the way.

Gereint's terse instructions to him showed once more how good his information was. "You'll do best to go by Lindum. The King will have left Caerleon by now, and be heading back toward Linnuis. By the time you reach Lindum you'll get news of him."

The man nodded briefly, and went. So within a few hours of my reaching Olicana, my report, with how much more, was on its way back. Now I was free to turn my thoughts toward Dunpeldyr and what I would find there.

But first, to pay Gereint for his service. He poured more wine, and settled, with an eagerness that must have been foreign to him for a long time, to ply me with questions about Arthur's accession at Luguvallium, and the activities since then at Caerleon. He deserved good measure, and I gave it. Only when the midnight rounds were almost due did I get to my own questions.

"Soon after Luguvallium, did Lot of Lothian ride this way?"

"Yes, but not through Olicana itself. There's a road—it's little more than a track now—that cuts aside from the main road, and leads due east. It's a bad road, and skirts some dangerous bogland, so though it's the quickest way for anyone heading north, it is very little used."

"But Lot used it, even though he was heading south for York? To avoid being seen in Olicana, do you suppose?"

"That did not occur to me," said Gereint. "Not, that is, until later. . . . He has a house on that road. He would go there to lodge, rather than come into the town here."

"His own house? I see. Yes, I saw it from the pass. A snug place, but lonely."

"As to that," he said, "he uses it very little."

"But you knew he was there?"

"I know most things that go on hereabouts." A gesture at the padlocked chest. "Like an old wife at the cottage door, I have little else to do but observe my neighbours."

"I have reason to be grateful for it. Then you must know who met Lot at his house in the hills?"

His eyes held mine for a full ten seconds. Then he smiled. "A certain semi-royal lady. They arrived separately, and they left separately, but they reached York together." His brows lifted. "But how did *you* know this, sir?"

"I have my own ways of spying."

He said calmly: "So I believe. Well, now all is settled and correct in the sight of God and mankind. The King of Lothian has gone with Arthur from Caerleon into Linnuis, while his new queen waits at Dunpeldyr to bear the child. You knew, of course, about the child?"

"Yes."

"They have met here before," said Gereint, with a nod that added plainly, "and now we see the results of that meeting."

"Have they indeed? Often? And since when?"

"Since I came here, perhaps three or four times." His tone was not that of one passing on tavern gossip, but merely briskly informative. "Once they were here for as much as a month together, but they kept themselves close. It was a matter of report only; we saw nothing of them."

I thought of the bedchamber with its regal crimson and gold. I had been right. Long-time lovers, indeed. If only I could believe what I had suggested to Arthur, that the child could, in fact, be Lot's own. At least, from the neutral tone that Gereint had used, that was what most men assumed as yet.

"And now," he said, "love has had its way, in spite of policy. Is it presumptuous in me to ask if the High King is angry?"

He had earned an honest answer, so I gave him one.

"He was angry, naturally, at the way the marriage was made, but now he sees that it will serve as well as the other. Morgause is his half-sister, so the alliance with King Lot must still hold. And Morgan is free for whatever other marriage may suggest itself."

"Rheged," he said immediately.

"Possibly."

He smiled, and let the subject drop. We talked for a little longer, then I rose to go.

"Tell me something," I asked him. "Did your information run to a knowledge of Merlin's whereabouts?"

"No. Two travellers were reported, but there was no hint of who they might be."

"Or where they were bound?"

"No, sir."

I was satisfied. "Need I insist that no one is to know who I am? You will not include this interview in your report."

"That's understood. Sir—"

"What is it?"

"About this report of yours on Tribuit and Lake Fort. You said that surveyors would be coming up. It occurs to me that I could save them a good deal of time if I sent working parties over immediately. They could start on the preliminaries—clearing, gathering turf and timber, quarrying, digging the ditches. . . . If you would authorize the work?"

"I? I have no authority."

"No authority?" He repeated blankly, then began to laugh. "No, I see. I can hardly start quoting Merlin's authority, or people might ask how it came my way. And they might remember a certain humble traveller who peddled herbs and simples. . . . Well, since that same traveller brought me a letter from the High King, my own authority will doubtless suffice."

"It's had to do so for long enough," I agreed, and took my leave, well satisfied.

9

So we journeyed north. Once we had joined the main road north from York, the way they call Dere Street, going was easy, and we made fair speed. Sometimes we lodged in taverns, but, the weather being fine and hot, more often than not we would ride on as long as the light lasted, then make camp in some flowering brake near the road. Then after supper I would make music for myself, and Ulfin would listen, dreaming his own dreams while the fire died to white ash, and the stars came out.

He was a good companion. We had known one another since we were boys, I with Ambrosius in Brittany, where he gathered the army that was to conquer Vortigern and take Britain, Ulfin as servant—slave-boy—to my tutor Belasius. His life had been a hard one with that strange and cruel man, but after Belasius' death Uther had taken the boy into his service, and there Ulfin had soon risen to a place of trust. He was now about five-and-thirty years old, brown-haired and grey-eyed, very quiet, and self-contained in the way of men who know they must live their lives out alone, or as the companions of other men. The years as Belasius' catamite had left their mark.

One evening I made a song, and sang it to the low hills north of Vinovia, where the busy small rivers wind deep in their forested valleys, but the great road strikes across the higher land, through leagues of whin and bracken, and over the long heather moorlands where the only trees are pine and alder and groves of silver birch.

We were camped in one such coppice, where the ground was dry underfoot, and the slender birch boughs hung still in the warm evening, tenting us with silk.

This was the song. I called it a song of exile, and I have heard versions of it since, elaborated by some famous Saxon singer, but the first was my own:

He who is companionless
Seeks oftentimes the mercy
The grace
Of the creator, God.
Sad, sad the faithful man
Who outlives his lord.
He sees the world stand waste
As a wall blown on by the wind,
As an empty castle, where the snow
Sifts through the window-frames,
Drifts on the broken bed
And the black hearth-stone.

Alas, the bright cup!
Alas, the hall of feasting!
Alas the sword that kept
The sheep-fold and the apple-orchard
Safe from the claw of the wolf!
The wolf-slayer is dead.
The law-giver, the law-upholder is dead,
While the sad wolf's self, with the eagle, and the raven,
Come as kings, instead.

I was lost in the music, and when at length I laid the last note to rest and looked up, I was taken aback to see two things: one that Ulfin, sitting on the other side of the fire, was listening rapt, with tears on his face; the other, that we had company. Neither Ulfin nor I, enclosed in the music, had noticed the two travellers approaching us over the soft mosses of the moorland way.

Ulfin saw them in the same moment that I did, and was on his feet, knife ready. But it was obvious that there was no harm in them, and the knife was back in its sheath before I said, "Put up," or the foremost of the intruders smiled, and showed a placating hand.

"No harm, masters, no harm. I've always been fond of a bit of music, and you've got quite a talent there, you have indeed."

I thanked him, and, as if the words had been an invitation, he came nearer to the fire and sat, while the boy who was with him thankfully humped the packs off his shoulders and sank down likewise. He stayed in the background, away from the fire, though with the darkness of late evening a cool little breeze had sprung up, making the warmth of the burning logs welcome.

The newcomer was a smallish man, elderly, with a neat greying beard and unruly brows over myopic brown eyes. His dress was travel-worn but neat, the cloak of good cloth, the sandals and belt of soft-cured leather. Surprisingly, his belt buckle was of gold—or else thickly gilded—and worked in an elaborate pattern. His cloak was fastened with a heavy disk brooch, also gilded, with a design beautifully worked, a curling triskele set in filigree within a deeply fluted rim. The boy, whom at first I took to be his grandson, was similarly dressed, but his only jewel was something that looked like a charm worn on a thin chain at his neck. Then he reached forward to unroll the blankets for the night, and as his sleeve slid back I saw on his forearm the puckered scar of an old brand. A slave, then; and from the way he stayed back from the fire's warmth, and silently busied himself unpacking the bags, he was one still. The old man was a man of property.

"You don't mind?" The latter was addressing me. Our own simple clothes and simpler way of life—the bedding rolls under the birches, the plain plates and drinking horns, and the worn saddlebags we used for pillows—had told him that here were travellers no more than his equals, if that. "We got out of our way a few miles back, and were thankful to hear your singing and see the light of the fire. We guessed you might not be too far from the road, and now the boy tells me it lies just over yonder, thanks be to Vulcan's fires! The moorlands are all very well by daylight, but after dark treacherous for man or beast. . . ."

He talked on, while Ulfin, at a nod from me, rose to fetch the wine-flask and offer it to him. But the newcomer demurred, with a hint of complacency.

"No, no. Thank you, my good sir, but we have food. We need not trouble you—except, if you will allow it, to share your fire and company for the night? My name is Beltane, and my servant here is called Ninian."

"We are Emrys and Ulfin. Please be welcome. Will you not take wine? We carry enough."

"I also. In fact, I shall take it ill if you don't both join me in a drink of it. Remarkable stuff, I hope you'll agree. . . ." Then, over his shoulder: "Food, boy, quickly, and offer these gentlemen some of the wine that the commandant gave me."

"Have you come far?" I asked him. The etiquette of the road does not allow you to ask a man directly where he has come from or whither he is bound, but equally it is etiquette for him to tell you, even though his tale may be patently untrue.

Beltane answered without hesitation, through the chicken leg the boy had handed him.

"From York. Spent the winter there. Usually get out before this onto the road, but waited there . . . Town very full . . ." He chewed and swallowed, adding more clearly: "It was a propitious time. Business was good, so I stayed on."

"You came by Catraeth?" He had spoken in the Brtish tongue, so, following suit, I gave the place its old name. The Romans called it Cataracta.

"No. By the road east of the plain. I do not advise it, sir. We were glad to turn onto the moor tracks to strike across for Dere Street at Vinovia. But this fool"—a hitch of a shoulder at the slave—"missed the milestone. I have to depend on him; my sight is poor, except for things as near to me as this bit of fowl. Well, Ninian was counting the clouds, as usual, instead of watching the way, and by dusk-fall we had no idea where we were, or if we had passed the town already. Are we past it now? I fear we must be."

"I'm afraid so, yes. We passed through it late in the afternoon. I'm sorry. You had business there?"

"My business lies in every town."

He sounded remarkably unworried. I was glad of this, for the boy's sake. The latter was at my elbow with the wine-flask, pouring with grave concentration; Beltane, I judged, was all bark and bustle; Ninian showed no trace of fear. I thanked him, and he glanced up and smiled. I saw then that I had misjudged Beltane; his strictures, indeed, looked to be justified; it was obvious that the boy's thoughts, in spite of the seeming concentration on his tasks, were leagues away; the sweet, cloudy smile came from a dream that held him. His eyes, in the shadow-light of moon and fire, were grey, rimmed with darkness like smoke. Something about them, and about the absent grace of his movements, was surely familiar . . . I felt the night air breathing on my back, and the hairs on my nape lifted like the fur of a night-prowling cat.

Then he had turned away without speaking, and was stooping beside Ulfin with the flask.

"Try it, sir," Beltane urged me. "It's good stuff. I got it from one of the garrison officers at Ebor . . . God knows where *he* laid hands on it, but it's better not to ask, eh?" The ghost of a wink, as he chewed once more at his chicken.

The wine was certainly good, rich, smooth and dark, a rival to any I had tasted even in Gaul or Italy. I complimented Beltane on it, wondering as I spoke what service could have elicited payment like this.

"Aha!" he said, with that same complacency. "You're wondering what I could have done to chisel stuff like this out of him, eh?"

"Well, yes, I was," I admitted, smiling. "Are you a magician, that you can read thoughts?"

He chuckled. "Not that kind. But I know what you're thinking now, too."

"Yes?"

"You're busy wondering if I'm the King's enchanter in disguise. I'll warrant! You'd think it might take his kind of magic to charm a wine like that out of Vitruvius. . . . And Merlin travels the roads the same as I do; a simple tradesman you'd take him for, they say, with maybe one slave for company, maybe not even that. Am I right?"

"About the wine, yes, indeed. I take it, then, that you are more than just a 'simple tradesman'?"

"You could say so." Nodding, self-important. "But about Merlin, now. I hear he's left Caerleon. No one knew where he was bound, or on what errand, but that's always the way with him. They were saying in York that the High King would be back in Linnuis before the turn of the moon, but Merlin disappeared the day after the crowning." He looked from me to Ulfin. "Have you had any news of what's afoot?"

His curiosity was no more than the natural newsmongering of the travelling tradesman. Such folk are great bringers and exchangers of news; they are made welcome for it everywhere, and reckon on it as a valuable stock-in-trade.

Ulfin shook his head. His face was wooden. The boy Ninian was not even listening. His head was turned away toward the scented dark of the moorlands. I could hear the broken, bubbling call of some late bird stirring on its nest; joy came and went in the boy's face, a flying gleam as evanescent as starlight on the moving leaves above us. Ninian had his refuge, it seemed, from a garrulous master and the day's drudgery.

"We came from the west, yes, from Deva," I said, giving Beltane the information he angled for. "But what news I have is old. We travel slowly. I am a doctor, and can never move far without work."

"So? Ah, well," said Beltane, biting with relish into a barley bannock, "no doubt we will hear something when we get to the Cor Bridge. You're bound that way, too? Good, good. But you needn't fear to travel with me! I'm no enchanter, in disguise or otherwise, and even if Queen Morgause's men were to promise gold, or threaten death by fire, I could make shift to prove it!"

Ulfin looked up sharply, but I said merely: "How?"

"By my trade. I have my own brand of magic. And for all they say Merlin is master of so much, mine is one skill you can't pretend to if you haven't had the training. And that"—with the same cheerful complacency—"takes a lifetime."

"May we know what it is?" The question was mere courtesy. This patently was the moment of revelation he had been working for.

"I'll show you." He swallowed the last crumb of bannock, wiped his mouth delicately, and took another drink of wine. "Ninian! Ninian! You'll have time for your dreaming soon! Get the pack out, and feed the fire. We want light."

Ulfin reached behind him and threw a fresh faggot on. The flames leaped high. The boy fetched a bulky roll of soft leather, and knelt beside me. He undid the ties and unrolled the thing along the ground in the firelight.

It went with a flash and a shimmer. Gold caught the rich and dancing light, enamels in black and scarlet, pearly shell, garnet and blue glass—bedded or pinned along the kidskin were pieces of jewellery, beautifully made. I saw brooches, pins, necklaces, amulets, buckles for sandals or belts, and one little nest of enchanting silver acorns for a lady's girdle. The brooches were mostly of the round sort he was wearing, but one or two were of the old bow design, and I saw some animals, and one very elaborate curly dragonlike creature done with great skill in garnet set with cell-work and filigree.

I looked up to see Beltane watching me eagerly. I gave him what he wanted. "This is splendid work. Beautiful. It is as fine as any I have seen."

He glowed with simple pleasure. Now that I had placed him, I could let myself be easy. He was an artist, and artists live on praise as bees on nectar. Nor do they much concern themselves in anything beyond their own art; Beltane had been barely interested in my own calling. His questions were harmless enough, a travelling salesman probing for news; and with the events at Luguvallium still a story for every fireside, what finer morsel of news could there be than some hint of Merlin's whereabouts? It was certain that he had no idea who he was talking to. I asked a few questions about the work, these out of genuine interest; I have always learned where I could about any man's skills. His answers soon showed me that he had certainly made the jewels himself; so the service for which the wine had been a reward was also explained.

"Your eyesight," I said. "You spoiled it with this work?"

"No, no. My eyesight is poor, but it is good for close work. In fact, it has been my blessing as an artist. Even now, when I am no longer young, I can see details very finely, but your face, my good sir, is by no means clear; and as for these trees around us, for such I take them to be . . ." He smiled and shrugged. "Hence my keeping this idle dreamer of a boy. He is my eyes. Without him I could hardly travel as I do, and indeed, I am lucky to have got here safely, even with his eyes, the little fool. This is no country to leave the roads and venture across bogland."

His sharpness was a matter of routine. The boy Ninian ignored it; he had taken the chance of showing me the jewellery to stay near the fire.

"And now?" I asked the goldsmith. "You have shown me work fit for kings' courts. Too good, surely, for the marketplace? Where are you taking it?"

"Need you ask? To Dunpeldyr, in Lothian. With the king newly wed, and the queen as lovely as mayflowers and sorrelbuds, there will surely be trade for such as I."

I stretched my hand to the warmth of the blaze. "Ah, yes," I said. "He married Morgause in the end. Pledged to one princess and married to another. I heard something of that. You were there?"

"I was indeed. And small blame to King Lot, that's what everyone was saying. The Princess Morgan is fair enough, and right enough a king's daughter, but the other one—well, you know how the talk goes. No man, let alone a man like Lot of Lothian, could come within arm's length of that lady and not lust to bed her."

"Your eyesight was good enough for that?" I asked him. I saw Ulfin smile.

"I didn't need eyesight." He laughed robustly. "I have ears, and I hear the talk that goes around, and once I got near enough to smell the scent she uses, and catch the colour of her hair in the sunlight, and hear her pretty voice. So I got my boy to tell me what she looked like, and I made this chain for her. Do you think her lord will buy it of me?"

I fingered the lovely thing; it was of gold, each link as delicate as floss, holding flowers of pearl and citrine set in filigree. "He would be a fool if he did not. And if the lady sees it first, he certainly will."

"I reckon on that," he said, smiling. "By the time I get to Dunpeldyr, she should be well again, and thinking of finery. You knew, did you? She was brought to bed two full weeks ago, before her time."

Ulfin's sudden stillness made a pause of silence as loud as a shout. Ninian looked up. I felt my own nerves tighten. The goldsmith sensed the sharpening of the attention he was getting, and looked pleased. "Had you not heard?"

"No. Since we passed Isurium we have not lodged in towns. Two weeks ago? This is certain?"

"Certain, sir. Too certain, maybe, for some folks' comfort." He laughed. "Never have I seen so many folk counting on their fingers that never counted before! And count as they may, with the best will in the world, they make it September for the child's conceiving. That," said the little gossip, "would be at Luguvallium, when King Uther died."

"I suppose so," I said indifferently. "And King Lot? The last I heard, he was gone to Linnuis, to join Arthur there."

"He did, that's true. He'll hardly have got the news yet. We got it ourselves when we lay for a night at Elfete, on the east road. That was the way her courier took. He had some tale of avoiding trouble by going that way, but it's my belief he'd been told to take his time. By the time King Lot gets news of the birthing, it'll be a more decent interval since the wedding day."

"And the child?" I asked it idly. "A boy?"

"Aye, and from all accounts a sickly one, so with all his haste Lot still may not have got himself an heir."

"Ah, well," I said, "he has time." I turned the subject. "Are you not afraid to travel as you do, with so much valuable cargo?"

"I confess I have had fears about it," he admitted. "Yes, yes, indeed. You must understand that commonly, when I shut my workshop, and take to the roads for summer, I carry with me only such stuff as the folks like to buy in the markets, or, at best, gauds for merchants' wives. But luck was against me, and I could not get these jewels done in time to show them to Queen Morgause before she went north, so needs must I carry them after her. Now my luck is to fall in with an honest man like yourself; I don't need to be a Merlin to tell such things . . . I can see you're honest, and a gentleman like myself. Tell me, will my luck hold tomorrow? May we have your company, my good sir, as far as Cor Bridge?"

I had made up my mind already about that. "As far as Dunpeldyr if you will. I'm bound there. And if you stop by the way to sell your wares, that suits me, too. I recently had a piece of news that tells me there is no haste for me to be there."

He was delighted, and fortunately did not see Ulfin's look of surprise. I had already decided that the goldsmith might be useful to me. I judged that he would hardly have outstayed the spring weather in York, making up the rich jewels he had shown me, without some sort of assurance that Morgause would at least look at them. As he talked cheerfully on, needing very little encouragement to tell me more about the happenings in York, I found that I had been right. Somehow he had managed to engage the interest of Lind, Morgause's young handmaid, and had persuaded her, in return for a pretty trinket or two, to speak of his wares to the queen. Beltane himself had not been sent for, but Lind had taken one or two of his pieces to show her mistress, and had assured the goldsmith of Morgause's interest. He told me all about it at some length. For a while I let him talk on, then said causually: "You said something about Morgause and Merlin. Did I understand that she had soldiers out looking for him? Why?"

"No, you misunderstood me. I was speaking in jest. When I was in York, listening as I do to the talk of the place, I heard someone say that Merlin and she had quarrelled at Luguvallium, and that she spoke of him now with hatred, where before she had spoken with envy of his art. And lately, of course, everyone was wondering where he had gone. Queen or no, little harm could she do a man like that!"

And you, I thought, are luckily short of sight, otherwise I should have to be wary of a perceptive and garrulous little man. As it was, I was glad I had fallen in with him. I was still thinking about it, but idly, as finally even he decided it was time to sleep, and we let the fire go low and rolled ourselves in our blankets under the trees. His presence would give credence to my disguise, and he could be, if not my eyes, my ears and information at the court of Morgause. And Ninian, who acted as his eyes? The cold breeze stirred my nape again, and my idle calculations dislimned like a shadow when the sun goes in. What was this? Foreknowledge, the half-forgotten stirring of a kind of power? But even that speculation died as the night breeze hushed through the delicate birch boughs and the last faggot sank to ash. The dreamless night closed in. About the sickly child at Dunpeldyr I would not think at all, except to hope that it would not thrive, and so leave me no problem.

But I knew that the hope was vain.

10

It is barely thirty miles from Vinovia to the town at the Cor Bridge, but it took us six days' journeying. We did not keep to the road, but travelled by circuitous and sometimes rough ways, visiting every village and farmstead, however humble, that lay between us and the bridge.

With no reason for haste, the journey passed pleasantly. Beltane obviously took great pleasure in our company, and Ninian's lot was made easier by the use of mules to carry his awkward packs. The goldsmith was as garrulous as ever, but he was a good-hearted man, and moreover a meticulous and honest craftsman, which is something to respect. Our wandering progress was made slower than ever by the time he took over his work—repair-work, mostly, in the poorer places; in the bigger villages, or at taverns, he was of course occupied all the time.

So was the boy, but on the journeys between settlements, and in the evenings by the camp fire, we struck up a strange kind of friendship. He was always quiet, but after he found that I knew the ways of birds and beasts, that a detailed knowledge of plants went with my physician's skill, and that I could, at night, even read the map of the stars, he kept near me whenever he could, and even brought himself to question me. Music he loved, and his ear was true, so I began to teach him how to tune my harp. He could neither read nor write, but showed, once his interest was engaged, a ready intelligence that, given time and the right teacher, could be made to blossom. By the time we reached Cor Bridge I was beginning to wonder if I could be that teacher, and if Ninian could be brought—his master permitting—to serve me. With this in mind, I kept my eyes open whenever we passed some quarry or farmstead, in case there might be some likely slave I could buy to serve Beltane, and persuade him to release the boy.

From time to time the small cloud oppressed me still, the hovering chill of some vague foreboding that made me restless and apprehensive; trouble was there at my whistle, looking for somewhere to strike. After a while I gave up trying to see where that stroke might fall. I was certain that it could not concern Arthur, and if it was to concern Morgause, then there would be time enough to let it worry me. Even in Dunpeldyr I thought I should be safe enough: Morgause would have other things on her mind, not least the return of her lord, who could count on his fingers as well as any man.

And the trouble might be no deep matter, but the trivial annoyance of a day, soon forgotten. It is hard to tell, when the gods trail the shadows of foreknowledge across the light, whether the cloud is one that will blot out a king's realm, or make a child cry in its sleep.

At length we came to Cor Bridge, in the rolling country just south of the Great Wall. In Roman times the place was called Corstopitum. There was a strong fort there, well placed where Dere Street, from the south, crossed the great east-west road of Agricola. In time a civilian settlement sprang up in this favoured spot, and soon became a thriving township, accepting all the traffic, civil and military, from the four quarters of Britain. Nowadays the fort is a tumbledown affair, much of its stone having been pillaged for new buildings, but west of it, on a curve of rising ground edged by the Cor Burn, the new town still grows and prospers, with houses, inns, and shops, and a thriving market which is the liveliest relic of its prosperity in Roman times.

The fine Roman bridge, which gives the place its modern name, still stands, spanning the Tyne at the point where the Cor Burn runs into it from the north. There is a mill there, and the bridge's timbers groan all day under the loads of grain. Below the mill is a wharf where shallow-draught barges can tie up. The Cor is little more than a stream, relying on its steep tumble of water to drive the mill wheel, but the great River Tyne is wide and fast, flowing here over bright shingle between its gracious banks of trees. Its valley is broad and fertile, full of fruit trees standing deep in growing corn. From this flowery and winding tract of green the land rises toward the north to rolling moorland, where, under the windy stretches of sky, sudden blue lakes wink in the sun. In winter it is a bleak country, where wolves and wild men roam the heights, and come sometimes over-close to the houses; but in summer it is a lovely land, with forests full of deer, and fleets of swans sailing the waters. The air over the moors sparkles with bird-song, and the valleys are alive with skimming swallows and the bright flash of kingfishers. And along the edge of the whinstone runs the Great Wall of the Emperor Hadrian, rising and dipping as the rock rises and dips. It commands the country from its long cliff-top, so that from any point of it fold upon fold of blue distance fades away east or westward, till the eye loses the land in the misty edge of the sky.

It was not country I had known before. I had come this way, as I had told Arthur, because I had a call to make. One of my father's secretaries, whom I had known first in Brittany and thereafter in Winchester and Caerleon, had come north after Ambrosius' death, to retirement of a sort here in Northumbria. The pension he received from my father had let him buy a holding near Vindolanda, in a sheltered spot beside the Agricolan Road, with a couple of strong slaves to work it. There he had settled, growing rare plants in his favoured garden, and writing, so I had been told, a history of the times he had lived through. His name was Blaise.

We lodged in the old part of the town, at a tavern within the purlieus of the original fortress. Beltane, with sudden, immovable obstinacy, had refused to pay the toll exacted at the bridge, so we crossed at the ford some half-mile downstream, then turned along the river past the forge, coming into the town by its old east gate.

Night was falling when we got there, so we put up at the first tavern we found. This was a respectable place not far from the main market square. Late though the hour was, there was still plenty of coming and going. Servants were gossiping at the cistern while they filled their water jars; through the laughter and talk came the cool splash of a fountain; in some house nearby a woman was singing a weaving-song. Beltane was in high glee at the prospects for trading on the morrow, and in fact started business that same night, when the tavern filled up after supper-time. I did not stay to see how he did. Ulfin reported a bath house still in commission near the old west wall, so I spent the evening there and then retired, refreshed, to bed.

Next morning Ulfin and I breakfasted together in the shade of the huge plane tree which grew beside the inn. It promised to be a hot day.

Early as we were, Beltane and the boy were before us. The goldsmith had already set up his stall in a strategic place near the cistern; which meant merely that he, or rather Ninian, had spread some rush matting on the ground, and on that had laid out such gauds as might appeal to the eyes and purses of ordinary folk. The fine work was carefully hidden away in the lining of the bags.

Beltane was in his element, talking incessantly to any passerby who paused even for a moment to look at the goods; a complete lesson in jewelcraft was given away, so to speak, with every piece. The boy, as usual, was silent. He patiently rearranged the items that had been handled and carelessly dropped back on the matting, and he took the money, or sometimes exchange-goods such as food or cloth. Between-times he sat cross-legged, stitching at the frayed straps of his sandals, which had given a lot of trouble on the road.

"Or this one, madam?" Beltane was saying, to a round-faced woman with a basket of cakes on her arm. "This we call cell-work, or inclosed work, very beautiful, isn't it? I learned the art in Byzantium, and believe me, even in Byzantium itself you'd never see finer. . . . And this very same design, I've seen it done in gold, worn by the finest ladies in the land. This one? Why, it's copper madam—and priced accordingly, but it's every bit as good—the same work in it, as you can well see. . . . Look at those colours. Hold it up to the light, Ninian. How bright and clear they are, and see how the bands of copper shine, holding the colours apart . . . Yes, copper wire, very delicate; you have to lay it in pattern, and then you run the colours in, and the wire acts as a wall, you might say, to contain the pattern. Oh, no, madam, not jewels, not at that price! It's glass, but I'll warrant you've never seen jewels with colours finer. I make the glass myself, and very skilled work it is, too, in my little 'etna' there—that's what I call my smelting stove—but you've not time this morning, I can see that, madam. Show her the little hen, Ninian, or maybe you prefer the horse . . . that's it, Ninian. . . . Now, madam, are the colours not beautiful? I doubt if anywhere in the length and breadth of the land you would find work to equal this, and all for a copper penny. Why, there's as much copper, nearly, in the brooch as there is in the penny you'll give me for it. . . ."

Ulfin appeared then, leading the mules. It had been arranged that he and I would make the short journey to Vindolanda, and return on the morrow, while Beltane and the boy pursued their trade in the town. I paid for the breakfast, then, rising, went across to take leave of them.

"You're going now?" Beltane spoke without taking his eyes off the woman, who was turning a brooch over in her hand. "Then a good journey to you, Master Emrys, and we hope to see you back tomorrow night. . . . No, no, madam, we have no need of your cakes, delicious though they look. A copper penny is the price today. Ah, I thank you. You will not regret it. Ninian, pin the brooch on for the lady. . . . Like a queen, madam, I do assure you. Indeed, Queen Ygraine herself, that's the highest in the land, might envy you. Ninian"—this as the woman moved away, his voice changing to the habitual nagging tone he used to the boy—"don't stand there with your mouth watering! Take the penny now and get yourself a pair of new shoes. When we go north I cannot have you hobbling and lagging with flapping soles as you did all the way—"

"No!" I did not even realize that I had spoken, till I saw them staring. Even then I did not know what impelled me to add: "Let the boy have his cakes, Beltane. The sandals will suffice, and see, he is hungry, and the sun is shining."

The goldsmith's short-sighted eyes were puckered as he stared up at me against the light. At length, a little to my surprise, he nodded, with a gruff "All right, get along," to the boy. Ninian gave me a shining look, then ran off into the crowd after the market-woman. I thought Beltane was going to question me, but he did not. He began to set the goods straight again, saying merely: "You're right, I have no doubt. Boys are always starving, and he's a good lad and faithful. He can go barefoot if he has to, but at least let him have his belly full. It isn't often we get sweet stuff, and the cakes smelled like a feast, so they did."

As we rode west along the riverside Ulfin asked, with sharp concern in his voice.

"What is it, my lord? Is something ailing you?"

I shook my head, and he said no more, but he must have known I was lying, because I myself could feel the tears cold on my cheeks in the summer wind.

Master Blaise received us in a snug little house of sand-coloured stone, built round a small courtyard with apple trees trained up the walls, and roses hiding the squared modern pillars.

The house had once, long ago, belonged to a miller; a stream ran past, its steep fall controlled by shallow watersteps, its walled banks set with little ferns and flowers. Some hundred paces below the house, the stream vanished under a hanging canopy of beech and hazel. Above this woodland, on the steep slope behind the house, full in the sun, was the walled garden that held the old man's treasured plants.

He knew me straight away, though it was many years since we had met. He lived alone, but for his two gardeners and a woman who, with her daughter, cared for the house and cooked for him. She was bidden to get beds ready, and bustled off to do some scolding over the kitchen braziers. Ulfin went to see our mules stabled, and Blaise and I were free to talk.

Light lingers late in the north, so after supper we went out to the terrace over the stream. The warmth of the day breathed still from the stones, and the evening air smelled of cypress and rosemary. Here and there in the tree-hung shadows the pale shape of a statue glimmered. A thrush sang somewhere, a richer echo of the nightingale. At my elbow the old man (*magister artii,* as he now likedto style himself) was talking of the past, in a pure Roman Latin with no trace of accent. It was an evening borrowed from Italy: I might have been a young man again, on my youthful travels.

I said as much, and he beamed with pleasure.

"I like to think so. One tries to hold to the civilized values of one's prime. You knew I studied there as a young man, before I was privileged to enter your father's service? *Those* years, ah, yes, those were the great years, but as one grows older, perhaps one tends to look back too much, too much."

I said something civil about this being of advantage to an historian, and asked if he would honour me with a reading from his work. I had noticed the lighted lamp standing on a stone table by the cypresses, and the rolls lying handily beside it.

"Would you really care to hear it?" He moved that way readily. "Some parts of it, I am sure, would interest you enormously. And it is a part that you can help me to add to, I believe. As it chances, I have it here with me, this roll, yes, this is the one. . . . Shall we sit? The stone is dry, and the evening tolerably mild. I think we shall come to no harm out here by the roses. . . ."

The section he chose to read was his account of the events after Ambrosius returned to Greater Britain; he had been close to my father for most of that time, while I had been involved elsewhere. After he had finished reading he put his questions, and I was able to supply details of the final battle with Hengist at Kaerconan and the subsequent siege of York, and the work of settlement and rebuilding that came after. I filled in for him, too, the campaign that Uther had waged against Gilloman in Ireland. I had gone with Uther while Ambrosius stayed in Winchester; Blaise had been with him there, and it was to Blaise that I had owed the account of my father's death while I was overseas.

He told me about it again. "I can still see it, that great bedchamber at Winchester, with the doctors, and the nobles standing there, and your father lying against the pillows, near to death, but sensible, and talking to you as if you were there in the room. I was beside him, ready to write down anything that was needed, and more than once I glanced down to the foot of the King's bed, half thinking to see you there. And all the while you were voyaging back from the Irish wars, bringing the great stone to lay on his grave."

He fell to nodding then, as old men do, as if he would go back for ever to the stories of times gone by. I brought him back to the present. "And how far have you gone with your account of the times?"

"Oh, I try to set down all that passes. But now that I am out of the center of affairs, and have to depend on the talk from the town, or on anyone who calls to see me, it is hard to know how much I miss. I have correspondents, but sometimes they are lax, yes, the young men are not what they were. . . . It's a great chance that brings you here, Merlin, a great day for me. You will stay? As long as you wish, dear boy; you'll have seen that we live simply, but it's a good life, and there is still so much to talk about, so much. . . . And you must see my vines. Yes, a fine white grape, that ripens to a marvellous sweetness if the year is a good one. Figs do well here, and peaches, and I have even had some success with a pomegranate tree from Italy."

"I can't stay this time, I'm afraid." I spoke with genuine regret. "I have to go north in the morning. But if I may, I'll come back before long—and with plenty to tell you, too, I promise you! There are great things afoot now, and you will be doing men a service if you will put them down. Meantime, if I can, would you like me to send letters from time to time? I hope to be back at Arthur's side before winter, and it will keep you in touch."

His delight was patent. We talked for a little longer, then, as the night-flying insects began to crowd to the lamp, we carried it indoors, and parted for the night.

My bedchamber window looked out over the terrace where we had been sitting. For a long time before I lay down to sleep I leaned my elbows on the sill, looking out and breathing the night scents that came in wave after wave on the breeze. The thrush had stopped singing, and now the soft *hush* of falling water filled the night. A new moon lay on its back, and stars were out. Here, away from lights and sounds of town or village, the night was deep, the black sky stretching, fathomless, away among the spheres, to some unimaginable world where gods walked, and suns and moons showered down like petals falling. Some power there is that draws men's eyes and hearts up and outward, beyond the heavy clay that fastens them to earth. Music can take them, and the moon's light, and, I suppose, love, though I had not known it then, except in worship.

The tears were there again, and I let them fall. I knew now what cloud it was that had lain over my horizon ever since that chance meeting on the moorland road. How, I did not know, but the boy Ninian—so young and quiet, and with a grace in look and motion that gave the lie to the ugly slaveburn on his arm—he had had about him the mark of a coming death. This, once seeing, any man might have wept for, but I was weeping, too, for myself; for Merlin the enchanter, who saw, and could do nothing; who walked his own lonely heights where it seemed that none would ever come near to him. In the boy's still face and listening eyes, that night on the moor when the birds had called, I had caught a glimpse of what might have been. For the first time, since those days long ago when I had sat at Galapas' feet to learn the arts of magic, I had seen someone who might have learned worthily from me. Not as others had wanted to learn, for power or excitement, or for the prosecution of some enmity or private greed; but because he had seen, darkly with a child's eyes, how the gods move with the winds and speak with the sea and sleep in the gentle herbs; and how God himself is the sum of all that is on the face of the lovely earth. Magic is the door through which mortal man may sometimes step, to find the gates in the hollow hills, and let himself through into the halls of that other world. I could, but for that shining edge of doom, have opened those gates for him, and, when I needed it no longer, have left him the key.

And now he was dead. I had known it, I think, after I had spoken in the market-place. My sharp, unthinking protest had been made for no reason that I knew; the knowledge came later. And always, when I spoke like that, men did unquestioningly as I bade them. So at least the boy had had his cakes, and the day's sunshine.

I turned away from the thin, brightening moon, and lay down.

"At least he had the cakes, and the day's sunshine." Beltane the goldsmith told us about it as we shared supper at the town's tavern the next evening. He was unusually silent, for him, and seemed stunned, clinging to our company as, in spite of his sharp tongue, he must have clung to the boy's.

"But—drowned." Ulfin said it on a disbelieving note, but I caught a glance from him that told me he had begun to put events together and understand them. "How did it happen?"

"That evening, at supper-time, he brought me back here and packed the things away. It had been a good day, and the take was heavy; we were sure of eating well. He had worked hard, and so when he saw some boys off down to bathe in the river, he asked if he might join them. He was a great one for washing himself . . . and it had been a hot day, and people's feet kick up a lot of dust, and dung besides, in the marketplaces. I let him go. The next thing was the boys came back, running, with the story. He must have trodden into a hole, and slipped out of his depth. It's a bad river, they tell me. . . . How was I to know that? How could I know? When we came over yesterday the ford seemed so shallow, and so safe. . . ."

"The body?" asked Ulfin, after a pause when he could see that I was not going to speak.

"Gone. Gone downstream, the boys said, like a log on the flood. He came up half a league down-river, but none of them could come near him, and then he vanished. It's a bad death, a puppy's death. He should be found, and buried like a man."

Ulfin said something kind, and after a while the little man's lamentations ran out, and the supper came, and he made shift to eat and drink, and was the better for it.

Next morning the sun shone again, and we went north, the three of us together, and four days later reached the country of the Votadini, which is called in the British tongue Manau Guotodin.

11

Some ten days later, with due stops for trading, we reached Lot's city of Dunpeldyr. It was late afternoon of a cloudy day, and it was raining. We were lucky enough to find suitable lodgings in a tavern near the south gate.

The town was little more than a close huddle of houses and shops near the foot of a great crag on which the castle was built. In times past the crag had contained the whole stronghold, but now the houses crowd, haphazard, between cliffs and river, and on the slopes of the crag itself, right up to the castle wall. The river (another Tyne) curves round the roots of the cliff, then runs in a wide meander across a mile or so of flat land to its sandy estuary. Along its banks the houses cluster, and boats are pulled up on the shingle. There are two bridges, a heavy wooden one set on stone piers, that holds the road to the main castle gate above; and another narrow span of planking which leads to a steep path serving the side gate of the castle. There had been no road-building here; the place had grown without plan, and certainly without beauty or amenity. The town is a mean one, of mud-brick houses with turfed roofs, and steep alleys which in stormy weather become torrents of foul water. The river, so fair only a short distance away, is here full of weed and debris. Between the crag and the river to the east is the market-place, where on the morrow Beltane would set out his wares.

One thing I knew I must do without delay. If, ironically enough, Beltane were to be my eyes inside the castle, neither Ulfin nor I must be seen to go about with him; so, dependent as he was on a servant, someone must be found to replace the drowned boy. Beltane had made no move to do this himself on our journey north, and now was only too grateful when I offered to do it for him.

A short way out of the town gates I had noticed a quarry; not much of a place, but still working. Next morning, carefully anonymous in a shabby cloak of rusty brown, I went there and sought out the quarry-master, a big, genial-looking ruffian who was strolling around among the half-derelict workings, and the equally derelict workmen, like a lord taking the summer air in his country demesne.

He looked me up and down with a fine air of disdain. "Able-bodied servants come expensive, my good sir." I could see him assessing me as he spoke, and coming up with a poor enough answer. "Nor have I one to spare. One gets all the riffraff in a place like this . . . prisoners, criminals, the lot. No one who'd ever be a decent house slave, or be trusted on a farm, or with any kind of skilled job. And muscle comes expensive. You'd best wait for the fair. All sorts come then, hiring themselves and their families, or selling themselves or their brats for food—though, come to that, you'd have to wait for winter and sharp weather to get the cheap market."

"I don't wish to wait. I can pay. I am travelling, and I need a man or a boy. He need have no skills, except to keep himself clean, and be faithful to his master, and have enough strength to travel even in winter, when the roads are foul."

As I spoke his manner grew more civil, and the assessment moved up a notch or two. "Travel? So, what is your business?"

I saw no reason to tell him that the servant was not for myself. "I am a doctor."

My answer had the effect it has nine times out of ten. He started eagerly to tell me of all his various ailments, of which, since he was more than forty years old, he had a full supply.

"Well," I said, when he had finished, "I can help you, I think, but it had better be mutual. If you have a likely hand you can let me have as a servant—and he should be cheap enough, since it's just the riffraff you get here—then perhaps we can do a deal? One more thing. As you will understand, in my trade there are secrets to be kept. I want no blabbermouth; he must be sparing of speech."

At that the rogue stared, then slapped his thigh and laughed, as if at the greatest joke in the world. He turned his head and bellowed a name. "Casso! Come here! Quickly, you oaf! Here's luck for you, lad, and a new master, and a fine new life adventuring!"

A lanky youth detached himself from a gang which was labouring on stone-breaking under an overhang that looked to me to be ready to collapse. He straightened slowly, and stared, before dropping his pick-helve and starting toward us.

"I'll spare you this one, Master Doctor," said the quarry-master genially. "He's everything you ask for." And he went off into fits of mirth once more.

The youth came up and stood, arms hanging, eyes on the ground. At a guess, he was about eighteen or nineteen. He looked strong enough—he would have to be, to survive that life for more than six months—but stupid to the point of idiocy.

"Casso?" I said. He looked up, and I saw that he was merely exhausted. In a life without hope or pleasure there was little point in spending energy on thought.

His master was laughing again. "It's no use talking to him. Anything you want to know you'll have to ask me, or look for yourself." He seized the lad's wrist and held up the arm. "See? Strong as a mule, and sound in wind and limb. And discreet enough, even for you. Discreet as hell, is our Casso. He's dumb."

The youth noticed the handling no more than would a mule, but at the last sentence he met my eyes again, briefly. I had been wrong. There was thought there, and with it hope; I saw the hope die.

"But not deaf with it, I gather?" I said. "What caused it, do you know?"

"You might say his own silly tongue." He started his great laugh again, caught my look, and cleared his throat instead. "You'll make no cure there, Master Doctor, his tongue's out. I never got the rights of it, but he used to be in service down in Bremenium, and the way I heard it, he opened his mouth too wide once too often. Not one to have patience with insolence, isn't the lord Aguisel. . . . Ah, well, but he's learned his lesson. I got him with a job lot of labour after the town bridges were repaired. He's given me no trouble. And for all I know it was house service he was in before, so you'll be getting a bargain with a fine, young—*Hey there!*"

While we had been talking his eye had gone, from time to time, to the gang at work on the stone. Now he started over that way, with some shouted abuse at the "idle scum" who had seized the chance to work more slowly.

I looked thoughtfully at Casso. I had caught the look in his face, and the quick, involuntary shake of the head at the quarry-master's mention of "insolence." "You were in Aguisel's household?" I asked him.

A nod.

"I see." I thought I did, indeed. Aguisel was a man of evil reputation, a jackal to Lot's wolf, who laired in the hilltop remains of Bremenium fortress to the south. Things happened there which a decent man could only guess at. I had heard rumours of his trick of using dumb or blinded slaves.

"Am I right in thinking that you saw what you could not be allowed to report on?"

Another nod. This time his eyes remained fixed on me. It must have been long enough since anyone had tried even this sort of limited communication.

"I thought as much. I have heard stories, myself, of my lord Aguisel. Can you read or write, Casso?"

A shake of the head.

"Be thankful," I said dryly. "If you could, then by this time you would be dead."

The quarry-master had got his gang working again to his satisfaction. He was on his way back to us. I thought quickly.

The youth's dumbness might be no disadvantage to Beltane, who was more than able to do his own talking; but I had been working on the assumption that the new slave must act as his master's eyes while we were in Dunpeldyr. Now I saw that there was no need of this: whatever transpired in Lot's stronghold, Beltane was quite able to report on it himself. His sight was not strong, but his hearing was, and he could tell us what was said; what the place looked like would hardly matter. When we left Dunpeldyr, if the goldsmith needed a different servant, no doubt we could find one. But now time pressed, and here I could certainly purchase discretion, even if enforced, and, I thought, the loyalty that went with gratitude.

"Well?" asked the quarry-master.

I said: "Anyone who has survived service in Bremenium is certainly strong enough for anything I might require. Very well. I'll take him."

"Splendid, splendid!" The fellow waxed loud in his praise of my judgment and Casso's various excellences, so much so that I began to wonder if the slaves were in fact his own to dispose of, or if he was seeing a way to fill his own purse, and would perhaps report the youth's death to his employers. When he began to haggle about price, I sent Casso to collect whatever possessions he had, with instructions to wait for me on the road. I have never seen why, because a man is your captive, or a purchase, he should be stripped of an elementary self-respect. Even a horse or a hound works the better for retaining a pride in itself.

After he had gone I turned back to the quarry-master. "Now we agreed, if you remember, that I would pay some part of the price in medicines. You will find me at the tavern by the south gate. If you come tonight, or send someone to ask for Master Emrys, I will have the medicines ready for you, and leave them to be picked up. And now, about the rest of the price . . ."

In the end we were agreed, and, followed by my new purchase, I made my way back to the tavern.

Casso's face fell when he heard that he was not to serve me, but to go with Beltane; but by the time the evening was through, with the warmth and good food and the lively company that crowded into the tavern, he looked like a plant that, dying in darkness, has been plunged suddenly into sunlit water. Beltane was outspokenly grateful to me, and embarked almost straight away on a long and happy exposition of his craft for Casso's sake. The latter could hardly have found a place in which his mutilation would have mattered less. I suspected that, as the evening wore through, Beltane began to find it a positive advantage to have a dumb servant. Ninian had hardly spoken at all, but neither had he listened. Casso drank it all in, fingering the pieces with his callused hands, his brain waking from the numbness of hopeless exhaustion, and expanding into pleasure as one watched.

The tavern was too small—and we were ostensibly too poor—to have a private chamber, but at the end of the hall, away from the fire, there was a deep alcove with a table and twin settles where we could be private enough. No one took much notice of us, and we stayed in our corner all evening, listening to the gossip that came into the tavern. Facts there were none, but there were plenty of rumours, the most important being that Arthur had fought and won two more engagements and that the Saxons had accepted terms. The High King was to be in Linnuis for some time longer, but Lot, it was said, could be expected home any day now.

In fact he did not come for four more days.

I spent the days withindoors, writing to Ygraine and Arthur, and the evenings in familiarizing myself with the town and its environment. The town was small, and did not attract many strangers, so, since I wanted to avoid attention, I went out at dusk, when folk would mostly be at supper. For the same reason I did not advertise my trade; anyone who approached our party had his full attention claimed by Beltane, and did not think to look further. They took me, I imagine, for a poor scribe of some sort. Ulfin haunted the town gates, picking up what news he could, and waiting for tidings of Lot's approach. Beltane, innocent and unsuspicious, plied his trade. He set up his stove in the square near the tavern, and began to teach Casso the elements of the repairer's art. Inevitably, this drew interest, and then custom, and soon the goldsmith was doing a roaring trade.

This, on the third day, brought just the result we all hoped for. The girl Lind, passing through the market square one day and seeing Beltane, approached and made herself known. Beltane sent her back to her mistress with a message, and a new buckle for herself, and soon got his reward. Next day he was sent for to the castle, and went off triumphantly, with a laden Casso in his wake.

Even had he not been dumb, Casso could have reported nothing. When the two were passed in through the postern gate, Casso was detained to wait in the porter's kennel, while an upper servant conducted the goldsmith to the queen's chambers.

He came back to the tavern at dusk, bubbling with his news. For all his talk of great people, this was the first king's house he had been in, and Morgause the first queen who would wear his jewels. The admiration he had conceived for her in York had soared now to the point of worship; at close quarters, even on him, her rose and gold beauty acted like a drug. He poured his story out over supper, obviously never thinking for a moment that I would not be absorbed in any item of gossip he might retail. Casso and I (Ulfin was still out) were given a word-by-word account of all that was said, of her graces, her praise of his work, her generosity in buying three pieces and accepting a fourth; even of the scent she wore. He did his best, too, with a description of her beauty, and of the splendours of the room where she received him, but here we were dealing with impressions only: the picture he conveyed was a perfumed haze of light and colour; the cool brightness from a window running along the sheen of an amber robe, and lighting the wonderful rose-gold hair; the rustle of silk and the glow and crackle of logs lit against the grey day. And music, too; a girl's voice whispering a lullaby.

"So the child was there?"

"Indeed. Asleep in a high cradle near the fire. I could see it, oh, clearly, outlined against the flames; and the girl rocking it and singing. The cradle was canopied with silk and gauze, with a little bell that chimed as she rocked it, and glinted in the firelight. A royal cradle. Such a pretty sight! I could have wished my old eyes different, for that alone."

"And did you see the child itself?"

It appeared that he had not. The baby had woken once, and cried a little, and the nurse had hushed him without lifting him from the blankets. The queen had been trying a necklet at the time, and without looking round had taken the mirror from the girl's hand, and bidden her sing to the baby.

"A pretty voice," said Beltane, "but such a sad little song. And indeed, I would hardly have recognized the maiden herself, if she had not come to speak to me yesterday. So thin and creeping, like a mouse, and her voice gone thin, too, like something pining. Lind, her name is, did I tell you? A strange name for a maiden, surely? Does it not mean a snake?"

"I believe so. Did you hear the child's name?"

"They called him Mordred."

Beltane showed a tendency here to go back to his description of the cradle, and of the pretty picture the girl had made, rocking it and singing, but I brought him back to the point.

"Was anything said about King Lot's coming home?"

Beltane, that single-minded artist, did not even see the implications of the question. They were expecting him, he told me cheerfully, at any time. The queen had seemed as excited as a young girl. Indeed, she could talk of nothing else. Would her lord like the necklet? Did the earrings make her eyes look brighter? Why, added Beltane, he owed half of the sale to the king's coming.

"She did not seem afraid at all?"

"Afraid?" He looked blank. "No. Why should she? She was happy and excited. 'Just wait,' she was saying to the ladies, just like any young mother with her lord away at the wars, 'just wait till my lord sees the fine son I bore him, and as like his father as one wolf to another.' And she laughed and laughed. It was a jest, you understand, Master Emrys. They call Lot the Wolf in these parts, and take pride in him, which is only natural among savage folks like these of the north. Only a jest. Why should she be afraid?"

"I was thinking of the rumours you spoke of once before. You told me of things you heard in York, and then, you said, there were looks and whispers here among the common folk in the market-place."

"Oh, those, yes . . . well, but that was only talk. I know what you're getting at, Master Emrys, the wicked stories that have been going about. You know that always happens when a birth comes before its time, and there's bound to be more talk in a king's house, because, you might say, more hangs on it. . . ."

"So it was before its time?"

"Yes, so they say. It took them all by surprise. It was born before even the king's own doctors could get here, that were sent north from the army to tend to the queen. It was the women delivered her, but safely, by God's mercy. You remember we were told it was a sickly child? And indeed, I could tell as much from the way he cried. But now he thrives and puts on weight. The maid Lind told me so, when I spoke to her on the way back to the gate. 'And is it true he's the image of King Lot?' I said to her. She gives me a look, as much as to say, That will silence the gossip, but all she says aloud is, 'Yes, as like as can be.' "

He leaned across the table, nodding with cheerful emphasis. "So you see it was all lies, Master Emrys. And indeed, one only has to talk to her. That pretty creature deceive her lord? Why, she was like a bride again at the thought of him coming home. And she would laugh that pretty laugh, like the silver bell on the cradle. Oh, yes, you can be sure the stories were all lies. Put around in York, they would be, by those that had cause to be jealous. . . . You know who I mean, eh? And the child the image of him. They were all saying the same. 'King Lot will see himself in a mirror, just as sure as you see yourself, madam. Look at him, the image, the little lamb. . . .' You know how women talk, Master Emrys. 'The very image of his royal father.' "

So he talked on, while Casso, busying himself with polishing some cheap buckles, listened and smiled, and I, only a little less silent, let the talk go by me while I thought my own thoughts.

Like his father? Dark hair, dark eyes, the description could fit both Lot and Arthur. Was there some faintest chance that fate was on Arthur's side? That she had conceived by Lot, and then seduced Arthur in an attempt to shackle him to her?

Reluctantly, I put the hope aside. When, at Luguvallium, I had felt doom impending, it had been in a time of power. And it did not need even that to tell me to mistrust Morgause. I had come north to watch her, and now the new fragment of information I just heard from Beltane might well have told me what to watch for.

Ulfin came in then, shaking a fine rain from his cloak. He looked across, saw us, and gave a barely perceptible sign to me. I got to my feet, and, with a word to Beltane, went over to him.

He spoke softly. "There's news. The queen's messenger rode in just now. I saw him. The horse was hard ridden, almost foundered. I told you I was on terms with one of the gatehouse guards? He says King Lot's on his way home. He's travelling fast. They're expecting him tonight or tomorrow."

"Thank you," I said. "Now, you've been out all day. Get yourself into dry clothes, and get something to eat. I've just heard something from Beltane that persuades me that a watch on the postern gate might be profitable. I'll tell you about it later. When you've eaten, come down and join me. I'll find somewhere dry to wait, where we won't be seen." We rejoined the others, and I asked: "Beltane, can you spare Casso to me for half an hour?"

"Of course, of course. But I shall need him later on. I was bidden back there tomorrow, with this buckle mended for the chamberlain, and I need Casso's help for that."

"I shan't keep him. Casso?"

The slave was already on his feet. Ulfin said, with a shade of apprehension: "So you know what to do now?"

"I am guessing," I said. "I have no power in this, as I told you." I spoke softly, and above the tavern's roar Beltane could not hear me, but Casso did, and looked quickly from me to Ulfin and back again. I smiled at him. "Don't let it concern you. Ulfin and I have affairs here which will not touch you or your master. Come with me now."

"I could come myself," said Ulfin quickly.

"No. Do as I told you, and eat first. It could be a long watch. Casso . . ."

We went through the maze of dirty streets. The rain, steady now, made muddy puddles, and splashed the dung into stinking pools. Where lights showed at all in the houses, they were feeble, smoking glints of flame, curtained from the wet night by hides or sacking. Nothing interfered with our night-sight, and presently we could pick our way cleanly across the gleaming runnels. After a while the tree-banked slope of the castle rock loomed above us. A lantern hung high in the blackness, marking the postern gate.

Casso, who had been following me, touched my arm and pointed where a narrow alley, little more than a funnel for rain-water, led steeply downward. It was not a way I had been before. At the bottom I could hear, loud above the steady hissing of the rain, the noise of the river.

"A short cut to the footbridge?" I asked.

He nodded vigorously.

We picked our way down over the filthy cobbles. The roar of the river grew louder. I could see the white water of the lasher, and against it the great wheel of a mill. Beyond this, outlined by the reflected glimmer of the foam, was the footbridge.

No one was about. The mill was not running; the miller probably lived above it, but he had locked his doors and no light showed. A narrow path, deep in mud, led past the shuttered mill and along the soaked grasses of the riverside toward the bridge.

I wondered, half irritably, why Casso had chosen this way. He must have grasped some need for secrecy, though the main street was surely, in this weather and at this time, deserted. But then voices and the swinging light of a lantern brought me up short in the shelter of the miller's doorway.

Three men were coming down the street. They were hurrying, talking together in undertones. I saw a bottle passed from hand to hand. Castle servants, no doubt, on their way back from the tavern. They stopped at the end of the bridge and looked back. Now something furtive could be seen in their movements. One of them said something, and there was a laugh, quickly stifled. They moved on, but not before I had seen them, clearly enough, in the lantern's glow: they were armed, and they were sober.

Casso was close beside me, pressed back in the dark doorway. The men had not glanced our way. They went quickly across the bridge, their footsteps sounding hollow on the wet planks.

Something else the passing light had showed me. Just beyond the mill, at the corner of the alley, another doorway stood open. From the pile of timber stocks and sawn felloes outside in the weedy strip of yard, I took it to be a wheelwright's shop. It was deserted for the night, but inside the main shed the remains of a fire still glowed. From that sheltering darkness I should be able to hear and see all who approached the bridge.

Casso ran ahead of me into the warm cave of the shop, and lifted a couple of faggots. Taking them to the fire, he made the motion of throwing them on the ashes.

"Only one," I said softly. "Good man. Now, if you will go back and get Ulfin, and bring him here to me, you can get yourself dried and warm, and then forget all about us."

A nod, then, smiling, a pantomime to show me that my secret, whatever it was, would be safe with him. God knew what he thought I was doing: an assignation, perhaps, or spy's work. Even at that, he knew about as much as I knew myself.

"Casso. Would you like to learn to read and write?"

Stillness. The smile vanished. In the growing flicker of the fire I saw him rigid, all eyes, unbelieving, like the lost traveller who has the clue, against all hope, thrust into his hand. He nodded once, jerkily.

"I shall see that you are taught. Go now, and thanks. Good night."

He went, running, as if the stinking alley were as light as day. Halfway up it I saw him jump and spring, like a young animal suddenly let out of its pen on a fine morning. I went quietly back into the shop, picking my way past the wheel-pit and the heavy sledge left leaning by the pile of spokes. Near the fireplace was the stool where the boy sat who kept the bellows going. I sat down to wait, spreading my wet cloak to the warmth of the fire.

Outside, drowning the soft sounds of the rain, the lasher roared. A loose paddle of the great wheel, hammered by the water, clacked and thudded. A pair of starving dogs raced by, wrangling over something unspeakable from a midden. The wheelwright's shop smelled of fresh wood, and sap drying, and the knots of burning elm. The faint tick of the fire was clearly audible in the warm darkness against the water noises outside. Time went by.

Once before I had sat like this, by a fire, alone, with my mind on a birth-chamber, and a child's fate revealed to me by the god. That had been a night of stars, with a wind blowing over the clean sea, and the great king-star shining. I had been young then, sure of myself, and of the god who drove me. Now I was sure of nothing, save that I had as much hope of diverting whatever evil Morgause was planning as a dry bough had of damming the force of the lasher.

But what power there was in knowledge, I would have. Human guesswork had brought me here, and we should see if I had read the witch aright. And though my god had deserted me, I still had more power than is granted to common men: I had a king at my call.

And now here was Ulfin, to share this vigil with me as he had shared it in Tintagel. I heard nothing, only saw when his body blocked the dim sky in the doorway.

"Here," I said, and he came in, groping his way over to the glow.

"Nothing yet, my lord?"

"Nothing."

"What are you expecting?"

"I'm not quite sure, but I think someone will come this way tonight, from the queen."

I felt him turn to peer at me in the darkness. "Because Lot is due home?"

"Yes. Is there any more news of that?"

"Only what I told you before. They expect him to press hard for home. He could be here very soon."

"I think so, too. In any case, Morgause will have to make sure."

"Sure of what, my lord?"

"Sure of the High King's son."

A pause. "You mean you think they will smuggle him out, in case Lot believes the rumours and kills the child? But in that case—"

"Yes? In that case?"

"Nothing, my lord. I wondered, that's all. . . . You think they will bring him this way?"

"No. I think they have already brought him."

"They have? Did you see which way?"

"Not since I have been here. I meant that I am certain that the baby in the castle is not Arthur's child. They have exchanged it."

A long breath beside me in the darkness. "For fear of Lot?"

"Of course. Think about it, Ulfin. Whatever Morgause may tell Lot, he must have heard what everyone is saying, ever since it became known that she was with child. She has tried to persuade him that the child is his, but premature; and he may believe her. But do you think he will take the risk that she is lying, and that some other man's son, let alone Arthur's, lies there in that cradle, and will grow up heir to Lothian? Whatever he believes, there's a possibility that he may kill the boy. And Morgause knows it."

"You think he has heard the rumours that it may be the High King's?"

"He could hardly help it. Arthur made no secret of his visit to Morgause that night, and nor did she. She wanted it so. Afterwards, when I forced her to change her plans, she might persuade or terrify her women into secrecy, but the guards saw him, and by morning every man in Luguvallium would know of it. So what can Lot do? He would not tolerate a bastard of any man's; but Arthur's could be dangerous."

He was silent for a while. "It puts me in mind of Tintagel. Not the night we took King Uther in, but the other time, when Queen Ygraine gave Arthur to you, to hide him out of King Uther's way."

"Yes."

"My lord, are you planning to take this child as well, to save him from Lot?"

His voice, softly pitched as it was, sounded thin with some kind of strain. I hardly attended; far out somewhere in the night, beyond the noise of the weir, I had heard a beat of hoofs; not a sound so much as a vibration under our feet as the earth carried it. Then the faint pulse was gone, and the water's roar came back.

"What did you say?"

"I wondered, my lord, how sure you were about the child up at the castle."

"Sure of what the facts say, no more. Look at them. She lied about the date of birth, so that it could be put about that the birth was premature. Very well; that could be a face-saver, no more; it's done all the time. But look how it was done. She contrived that no doctor was present, and then alleged that the birth was unexpected, and so quick that no witnesses could be called into the chamber, as is the custom with a royal birthing. Only her two women, who are her creatures."

"Well, why, my lord? What more was there to gain?"

"Only this, a child to show Lot that he could kill if he would, while Arthur's son and hers goes scatheless."

A gasp of silence. "You mean—?"

"It fits, doesn't it? She could already have arranged an exchange with some other woman due to bear at the same time, some poor woman, who would take the money and hold her tongue, and be glad of the chance to suckle the royal baby. We can only guess what Morgause told her; the woman can have no inkling that her own child might be at risk. So the changeling lies there in the castle, while Arthur's son, Morgause's tool of power, is hidden nearby. At my guess, not too far away. They will want news of him from time to time."

"And if what you say is true, then when Lot gets here—"

"Some move will be made. If he does harm the changeling, Morgause will have to see that the mother hears nothing of it. She may even have to find another home for Mordred."

"But—"

"Ulfin, there is nothing we can do to save the changeling. Only Morgause could save it, if she would. It's not even certain that it will be in danger; Lot is not quite a savage, after all. But you and I would only run on death ourselves, and the child with us."

"I know. But what about all the talk up there in the castle? Beltane would tell you about it. He was talking while I got my supper. I mean, the baby being so like King Lot, the living image, they were all saying. Could this of yours just be a guess, sir? And the child be Lot's own, after all? The date could even have been right. They said it was a sickly child, and small."

"It could be. I told you I was guessing. But we do know that Queen Morgause has no truth in her—and that she is Arthur's enemy. Her actions, and Lot's, bear watching. Arthur himself will have to know, beyond doubt, what the truth is."

"Of course. I see that. One thing we could do is find out who bore a male child at about the same time as the queen. I could ask around the place tomorrow. I've made a useful wine-friend or two already."

"In a town this size it could be one of a score. And we have no time. Listen!"

Up through the ground, clear now, the beat of hoofs. A troop, riding hard. Then the sound of them, close and coming closer, clear above the river noises, and soon the town noises as people crowded out to see. Men shouting; the crash of wood on stonework as the gates were flung open; the jingle of bits and the clash of armour; the snorting of hard-ridden horses. More shouting, and an echo from the castle rock high above us, then the sound of a trumpet.

The main bridge thundered. The heavy gates creaked and slammed. The sounds dwindled toward the inner courtyard, and were lost in the other, nearer noises.

I stood up and walked to the doorway of the wheelwright's shop, and looked up to where, beyond the mill roof, the castle towered against the clouded night. The rain had stopped. Lights were moving. Windows flared and darkened as the king's servants lighted him through the castle. To the west side were two windows bright with soft light. The moving lights went there, and stayed.

"Lot comes home," I said.

12

Somewhere a bell clanged from the castle. Midnight. Leaning in the doorway of the wheelwright's shop, I stretched shoulders aching with the damp of the night. Behind me, Ulfin fed another faggot to the fire, carefully, so that no spurt of flame should attract the attention of anyone who might be waking. The town, sunk back into its night-time stupor, was silent, but for the barking of curs and now and again the scritch of an owl among the trees on the steep crag-side.

I moved silently out from the door's shelter into the street near the end of the bridge. I looked up at the black bulk of the crag. The high windows of the castle still showed light, and light from the troopers' torches, red and smoking, moved behind the walls that masked the courtyard below.

Ulfin, at my elbow, drew breath for a question.

It was never asked. Someone, running chin on shoulder across the foot-bridge, ran headlong into me, gasped, gave a broken cry, and twisted to dodge past.

Equally startled, I was slow to react, but Ulfin jumped, grasped an arm, and clapped a hand tightly to stifle the next cry. The newcomer twisted and fought his grip, but was held with ease.

"A girl," said Ulfin, surprised.

"Into the shop," I said quickly, and led the way.

Once there, I threw another piece of elm on the fire. The flames leaped. Ulfin brought his captive, still writhing and kicking, into the light. The hood had fallen from her face and head, and I recognized her, with satisfaction."

"Lind."

She stiffened in Ulfin's grip. I saw the gleam of frightened eyes staring at me above the stifling hand. Then they widened, and she went quite still, as a partridge does before a stoat. She knew me, too.

"Yes," I said. "I am Merlin. I was waiting for you, Lind. Now, if Ulfin looses you, you will make no sound."

Her head moved, assenting. He took his hand from her mouth, but kept his grip on her arm.

"Let her go," I said.

He obeyed me, moving back to get between her and the doorway, but he need not have troubled. As soon as he released her she ran toward me, and flung herself to her knees in the litter of shavings. She clung to my robe. Her body shook with her terrified weeping.

"Oh, my lord, my lord! Help me!"

"I am not here to harm you, or the child." To calm her, I spoke coldly. "The High King sent me here to get news of his son. You know I cannot come to the queen herself, so I waited here for you. What has happened up at the castle?"

But she would not speak. I think she could not. She clung, and shook, and cried.

I spoke more gently. "Whatever has happened, Lind, I cannot help you if I do not know. Come near the fire, and compose yourself, and tell me."

But when I tried to draw my robe from her clutches she clung the harder. Her sobs were violent. "Don't keep me here, lord, let me go! Or else help me! You have the power—you are Arthur's man—you are not afraid of my lady—"

"I will help you if you will talk to me. I want news of King Arthur's son. Was that King Lot who arrived just now?"

"Yes. Oh, yes! He came home an hour ago. He is mad, mad, I tell you! And she did not even try to stop him. She laughed, and let him do it."

"Let him do what?"

"Kill the baby."

"He killed the child Morgause has at the castle?"

She was too distraught to see anything strange about the form of the question. "Yes, yes!" She gulped. "And all the while it was his own son, his very own son. I was there at the birth, and I swear it by my own hearth-gods. It was—"

"*What's that?*" This, sharply, from Ulfin, on watch in the doorway.

"Lind!" I stooped, pulled her to her feet, and held her steady. "This is no time for riddles. Go on. Tell me all that happened."

She pressed the back of one wrist to her mouth, and in a moment or two managed to speak with some sort of composure. "When he came, he was angry. We have been expecting it, but nothing like this. He had heard what people were saying, that the High King had lain with her. You knew that, lord, you knew it was true. . . . So King Lot stormed and raved at her, calling her whore, adulteress. . . . We were all there, her women, but he cared nothing for that. And she—if she had talked sweetly to him, lied, even . . ." She swallowed. "It would have calmed him. He would have believed her. He never could resist her. That's what we all thought she would do, but she did not. She laughed in his face, and said, "But do you not see how like you he is? Do you really think a boy like Arthur could get such a son?' He said, 'So it's true? You lay with him?' She said, 'Why not? You would not wed me. You took that little honey-miss, Morgan, instead of me. I was not yours, not then.' It made him angrier." She shivered. "If you had seen him then, even you would have been afraid."

"No doubt. Was she?"

"No. She never moved, just sat there, with the green gown and jewels, and smiled. You would have thought she was trying to make him angry."

"As she was," I said. "Go on, Lind, quickly."

She had control of herself now. I loosed her, and she stood, still trembling, but with her arms crossed on her breast, the way women stand when grieving. "He tore the hangings off the cradle. The baby started to cry. He said, 'Like me? The Pendragon brat is dark, and I am dark. No more than that.' Then he turned on us—the women—and sent us away. We ran. He looked like a mad wolf. The others ran away, but I hid behind the curtains in the outer chamber. I thought—I thought—"

"You thought?"

She shook her head. Tears splashed, glinting, in the firelight. "That was when he did it. The baby stopped crying. There was a crash, as if the cradle fell over. The queen said, as calm as milk: 'You should have believed me. It was your own, by some slut you tumbled in the town. I told you there was a likeness.' And she laughed. He didn't speak for a bit. I could hear his breathing. Then he said, 'Dark hair, eyes turning dark. The brat *his* slut threw would be the same. Where is he, then, this bastard?' She said, 'He was a sickly child. He died.' The king said, 'You're lying still.' Then she said, very slowly: 'Yes, I am lying. I told the midwife to take him away, and find me a son I dared to show you. Perhaps I did wrong. I did it to save my name, and your honour. I hated the child. How could I want to bear any man's child but yours? I had hoped it was your son, not his, but it was his. It is true that he was sickly. Let us hope that he is dead, too, by this time.' The king said, 'Let us do more than that. Let us make sure.' "

It was Ulfin this time who said quickly: "Yes? Go on."

The girl drew a shuddering breath. "She waited a moment, then she said—in a light, slighting sort of way, the way you dare a man to do something dangerous—'And how could you do that, King of Lothian, except by killing every child born in this town since May Day? I've told you I don't know where they took him.' He didn't even stop to think. He was breathing hard, like someone running. He said: 'Then that is just what I shall do. Yes, boys and girls alike. How else shall I know the truth of this accursed child-bed?' I would have run then, but I could not. The queen started to say something about the people, but he put her aside and came to the door and shouted for his captains. They came running. He shouted it at them, the same. Just those orders, every young baby in the town . . . I don't remember what was said. I thought I would faint, and fall, and they would see me. But I did hear the queen call out something in a weeping voice, something about orders from the High King, and how King Arthur would not brook the talk there had been since Luguvallium. Then the soldiers went. And the queen was not weeping at all, my lord, but laughing again, and she had her arms around King Lot. From the way she talked to him then, you would have thought he had done some noble deed. He began to laugh, too. He said: 'Yes, let them say it of Arthur, not of me. It will blacken his name more surely than anything I could ever do.' They went into her bedchamber then, and shut the door. I heard her call me, but I left her, and ran. She is evil, evil! I always hated her, but she is a witch, and she put me in fear."

"Nobody will hold you to blame for what your mistress did," I told her. "And now you can redeem it. Take me to where the High King's son is hidden."

She shrank and stared at that, with a wild look over her shoulder, as if she would run again.

"Come, Lind. If you feared Morgause, how much more should you fear me? You ran this way to protect him, did you not? You cannot do so alone. You cannot even protect yourself. But if you help me now, I shall protect you. You will need it. Listen."

Above us, the main gates of the castle opened with a crash. Through the thick boughs could be seen the movement of torches, bobbing down toward the main bridge. With the torches came the beat and clatter of hoofs and the shouting of orders.

Ulfin said sharply: "They're out. It's too late."

"No!" cried the girl. "Macha's cottage is the other way. They will come there last! I will show you, lord. This way."

Without another word she made for the door, with myself and Ulfin hard behind her.

Up the way we had come, across an open space, down another steep lane that twisted back toward the river, then along a river path deep in nettles where nothing moved but the rats a-scurry from the middens. It was very dark here, and we could not hurry, though the night breathed horror on the nape like a coursing hound. Behind us, away on the far side of the town, the sounds began. The barking of dogs first, the shouting of soldiers, the tramp of hoofs. Then doors slamming, women screaming, men shouting; and now and again the sharp clash of weapons. I have been in sacked cities, but this was different.

"Here!" gasped Lind, and turned into another twisting lane that led away from the river. From beyond the houses the dreadful sounds still made the night foul. We ran along the slippery mud of the lane, then up a flight of broken steps and out again into a narrow street. Here, all was quiet still, though I saw the glimmer of a light where some scared householder had waked to wonder at the sounds. We ran out from the end of the street into the grass of a field where a donkey was tethered, past an orchard of tended trees and the gaping door of a smithy, and reached a decent cottage that stood away from the rest behind a quickthorn hedge, with a strip of garden in front, and a dovecote, and a kennel beside the door.

The cottage door was wide open and swinging. The dog, at the end of his chain, raved and leaped like a mad thing. The doves were out of the cote and winnowing the dim air. There was no light in the cottage, no sound at all.

Lind ran through the garden and stopped in the black doorway, peering in. "Macha? Macha?"

A lantern stood on a ledge beside the door. No time to search for flint and tinder. I put the girl gently aside. "Take her outside," I said to Ulfin, and, as he obeyed me, picked up the lantern and swung it high. The flame tore up hissing from the wick, vivid and alive. I heard Lind gasp, then the sound caught in her throat. The brilliant light showed every corner of the cottage: the bed against the wall, the heavy table and bench; the crocks for food and oil; the stool, with the distaff flung down beside it and the wool unspinning; the clean hearth and the stone floor scrubbed white, except where the woman's body lay sprawled in the blood that had poured from her slit throat. The cradle by the bed was empty.

Lind and Ulfin waited at the edge of the orchard. The girl was silent now, shocked even out of her weeping; in the lantern's light her face showed blanched and sick. Ulfin had an arm round her, supporting her. He was very pale. The dog whined once, then sat back on his haunches and lifted his nose in a long, keening howl. It was echoed from the clashing, screaming darkness three streets away. And then again, nearer.

I shut the cottage door behind me. "I'm sorry, Lind. There's nothing to be done here. We should go. You know the tavern at the south gate? Will you lead us there? Avoid the middle of the town where the noise is. Try not to be afraid; I said I would protect you, and I will. For the time being you had better stay with us. Come now."

She did not move. "They've taken him! The baby, they got the baby. And they killed Macha!" She turned blind-eyed to me. "Why did they kill Macha? The king would never have ordered that. She was his leman!"

I looked at her thoughtfully. "Why, indeed?" Then, briskly, taking her by the shoulder and giving her a gentle shake: "Come now, child, we must not stay here. The men won't come this way again, but while you are in the streets you could be in danger. Take us to the south gate."

"*She* must have told them the way!" cried Lind. I might not even have spoken. "They came here first! I was too late! If you hadn't stopped me at the bridge—"

"Then you would be dead, too," said Ulfin crisply. He sounded quite normal, as if the night's horrors touched him not at all. "What could you have done, you and Macha? They'd have found you, and cut you down before you'd run to the end of the orchard yonder. Now, you'd best do as my lord says. That is, unless you want to go back to the queen and tell her what's happened here? You can depend on it, she's guessed where you went. They'll be looking for you soon."

It was brutal, but it worked. At the mention of Morgause she came to herself. She threw a last look of horror at the cottage, then pulled her hood about her face, and started back through the orchard trees.

I paused by the grieving dog and stooped to lay a hand on him. The dreadful howling stopped. He sat shivering. I drew my dagger and cut through the rope collar that bound him. He did not move, and I left him there.

Some score of children were taken that night. Someone—wise-woman or midwife—must have told the troopers where to look. By the time we got back to the tavern, by a roundabout route through the deserted outskirts of the town, the horror was over, the troopers gone. No one accosted us, or even seemed to notice us. The streets were full and clamorous. People ran aimlessly about, or peered in terror from dark doorways. Crowds gathered here and there, centered on some wailing woman, and stunned or angry man. These were poor folk, with no way of withstanding their king's will. His royal anger had swept through the town, and left them nothing to do but grieve.

And curse. I heard Lot's name: they had after all been his troopers. But with Lot's name came Arthur's. The lie was already at work, and with time, one could guess, would supersede the truth. Arthur was High King, and the mainspring of good and evil.

One thing they had been spared: there had been no holocaust of blood. Macha's was the only death. The soldiers had lifted the babies from their beds, and ridden off with them into the darkness. Except for a broken head or two, where a father had resisted them, they had done no violence.

So Beltane told me, gasping it out. He met us in the tavern doorway, fully clothed, and trembling with agitation. He seemed not even to notice Lind's presence. He seized me by the arm and poured out his story of the night's happenings. The clearest thing to emerge from it was that the troopers had not long ridden by with the infants.

"Alive still, and crying—you may imagine, Master Emrys!" He wrung his hands, lamenting. "Terrible, terrible, these are savage times indeed. All the talk of Arthur's order, who is to believe such a tale? But hush, say nothing! The sooner we are on the road, the better. This is no place for honest traders. I would have gone before this, Master Emrys, but I stayed for you. I thought you might have been called on to help, some of the men were hurt, they say. They will drown the children, did you know? Dear gods, and to think that only today . . . Ah, Casso, good lad! I took the liberty of saddling your beasts, Master Emrys. I made sure you would agree with me. We should go now. I have paid the landlord, all's done, you may settle with me on the road. . . . And you'll see I bought mules for ourselves. I have meant to for so long, and today with the good fortune at the castle . . . What a mercy, what a mercy! But that pretty lady, who could have thought—but no more of that here! Walls have ears, and these are dreadful times. Who is this?" He was peering short-sightedly at Lind, who clung to Ulfin's arm, half fainting. "Why, surely—is it not the young damsel—?"

"Later," I said quickly. "No questions now. She is coming with us. Meantime, Master Beltane, thank you. You are a good friend. Yes, we should go without delay. Casso, shift the baggage, will you, please? The girl will ride on the pack-mule. Ulfin, you say you have a friend in the guardhouse. Ride ahead, and talk us through. Find which way the troopers went. Bribe the guards if you have to."

As it happened, there was no need. The gates were just being closed when we got there, but the guards made no difficulty about letting us through. Indeed, from the muttered talk that could be overheard, they were as shocked as the townspeople at what had happened, and found it quite understandable that peaceful traders should pack up hurriedly and leave the town in the middle of the night.

A short way down the road, out of earshot of the guardhouse, I drew rein.

"Master Beltane, I have business to see to. No, not back in the town, so have no fear for me. I'll join you later. Do you ride on to the tavern we stayed at on our way north, the one with the bush of broom outside. Remember? Wait for us there. Lind, you will be safe with these men. Don't be afraid, but you will do well to keep silent till I return. Do you understand?" She nodded dumbly. "At The Bush of Broom, then, Master Beltane?"

"Of course, of course. I cannot say I understand, but perhaps in the morning—"

"In the morning, I hope, all will be made clear. For now, good night."

They clattered off. I brought my mule's head up hard. "Ulfin?"

"They took the east road, my lord."

So by the east road we went.

Indifferently mounted as we were, we would not normally have expected to catch up with hard-riding troops. But our mounts were rested, while Lot's men must needs, I thought, still be using the poor beasts that had borne them from the battlefields in the south.

So when, after half an hour's riding, we caught no glimpse, nor heard any sound of them, I drew rein, and turned in the saddle.

"Ulfin. A word with you."

He nudged his mule alongside. In that windy darkness I could not see his face, but something came from him that I could sense. He was afraid.

He had not been afraid before, even at Macha's cottage. And here there could only be one source of fear: myself.

I said to him: "Why did you lie to me?"

"My lord—"

"The troopers did not come this way, did they?"

I heard him swallow. "No, my lord."

"To the sea. I think—it was thought they were going to put the children into a boat, and set it adrift. The king had said he would put them into God's hands, so that the innocent ones—"

"Pah!" I said. "Lot speak of God's hands? He feared what the people might do if they saw the babies' throats cut, that is all. No doubt he'll have to put about that Arthur ordered the slaughter, but that he himself mitigated the sentence, and gave the babes their chance. The shore. Where?"

"I don't know."

"Is that true?"

"Indeed, indeed it is. There are several ways. No one knew for sure. This is the truth, my lord."

"Yes. If anyone had known, some of the menfolk might have tried to follow. So we go back and take the first road to the shore. We can ride along the beach to look for them. Come."

But as I swung my mule's head round, his hand came down on the rein. It was something he would hardly have dared to do, except in desperation. "My lord—forgive me. What are you going to do? After all this . . . are you still trying to find the child?"

"What do you think? Arthur's son?"

"But Arthur himself wants him dead!"

So that was it. I should have guessed long since. My mule jibbed as the reins jerked in my hands. "So you were listening at Caerleon. You heard what he said to me that night."

"Yes." This time I could hardly hear him. "To refuse to murder a child, lord, that is one thing. But when the murder is done for you—"

"There is no need to struggle to prevent it? Perhaps not. But since you were eavesdropping that night, you may also have heard me tell the King that I take orders from an authority beyond his own. And so far my gods have told or shown me nothing. Do you imagine they want us to emulate Lot, and his bitch of a queen? And you have heard the calumny they have thrown upon Arthur. For his honour's sake, even just for his peace of mind, he has to know the truth. I am here for him, to watch and to report. Whatever is to be done, I shall do it. Now take your hand off my rein."

He obeyed. I kicked the mule to a gallop. We pounded back along the road.

This was the way we had originally come to Dunpeldyr by daylight. I tried to remember what we have seen then of the coastline. It is a coast of high cliffs, with wide sandy bays between them. One great headland jutted out about a mile from the town, and even at low tide it seemed unlikely that a man could ride round it. But just beyond the headland was a track leading toward the sea. From there—and the tide, I reckoned, was well out now—we could ride the whole way back along the shore to the mouth of the Tyne.

Faintly, but perceptibly, the night was slackening toward dawn. It was possible to see our way.

Now a cairn of stones loomed on our right. On a flat slab at its base a bundle of feathers stirred in the wind, and the mules showed the whites of their eyes; I supposed they could smell the blood. And here was the track, leading off across rough grassland toward the sea. We swung into it. Presently the track sloped downhill, and there before us was the shore, and the grey murmur of the sea.

The vast headland loomed on our right; to the left the sand stretched level and grey. We turned that way, and struck once more to a gallop.

The tide was out, the rippled sand packed hard. To our right the sea threw a kind of grey light up to the cloudy sky. Some way to the north, set back in the midst of that luminous grey, was the mass of the great rock where the lighthouse stands. The light was red and steady. Soon, I thought, as our mules pounded along, we should be able to distinguish the looming shape of Dunpeldyr's crag to landward, and the level reaches of the bay where the river meets the sea.

Ahead of us a low headland jutted out, its seaward end black and broken, with the water whitening at its edge. We rounded it, the mules splashing fetlock-deep through the creaming surf. Now we could see Dunpeldyr, a mile or two away inland, still alive with lights. Ahead of us lay the last stretch of sand. Shadowy trees marked the river's course, and the ashen glimmer where its waters spread out to meet the sea. And along the river's edge, where the sea-road ran, bobbed the torches of horsemen heading back at a steady canter for the town. The work was done.

My mule came willingly to a halt. Ulfin's stopped, blowing, half a length to the rear. Under their hoofs the ebbtide dragged at the grating sand.

After a while I spoke. "You have your wish, it seems."

"My lord, forgive me. All I could think of—"

"What do I forgive? Am I to bear you a grudge for serving your master rather than me?"

"I should have trusted you to know what you were doing."

"When I have not known myself? For all I know, you have been wiser than I. At least, since the thing is done, and it seems Arthur will bear some part of the blame for it, we can be forgiven for hoping that Morgause's child is dead with the rest."

"How could any of them escape? Look, my lord."

I swung round to look where he pointed.

Away out to sea, beyond a low reef of rocks at the edge of the bay, a sail showed, a pale crescent, glimmering faintly grey in the sea-light. Then it cleared the reef, and the boat moved out to sea. The wind, steadily off-shore, filled the sail, taking the boat out with the speed of a gliding gull. Herod's mercy for the innocents lay there, in the movement of wind and sea, as the drifting boat dipped and skimmed, carrying its hapless cargo fast away from shore.

The sail melted into the grey and vanished. The sea sighed and murmured under the wind. The little waves lapped on the rock and dragged the sand and broken shells seaward past the mules' feet. On the ridge beside us the bent-grass whistled in the wind. Then, above these sounds, I heard it, very faintly, carried to us over the water in a lull of the wind; a thin, keening wail, as unhuman as the song of the grey seals at their meeting-haunts. It dwindled as we listened; then suddenly came again, piercingly loud, straight over us, as if some soul, already leaving the doomed boat, had flown homing for the shore. Ulfin shied as if from a ghost, and made the sign against evil; but it was only a gull sweeping over us, high in the wind.

Ulfin did not speak again, and I sat my mule in silence. Something was there in the dark; something that weighed me down with grief. Not the children's fate only; certainly not the presumed death of Arthur's child. But the dim sight of that sail moving away over the grey water, and the sorrowful sounds that came out of the dark, found an echo somewhere in the very core of my soul.

I sat there without moving, while the wind dwindled to silence, and the water lapped on the rock, and on the sea the wailing died away.

BOOK II

CAMELOT

1

Much as I would have liked to do so, I did not leave Dunpeldyr straight away. Arthur was still in Linnuis, and would want my report, not only on the massacre itself but on what happened afterwards. Ulfin, I think, expected to be dismissed, but, reckoning that to lodge in Dunpeldyr itself would hardly be safe, I stayed on at The Bush of Broom, and so kept Ulfin with me to act as messenger and connecting-file. Beltane, who had been understandably shaken by the night's events, went south straight away with Casso. I kept my promise to the latter: it had been a promise made on impulse, but I have found that such impulses commonly have a source which should not be denied. So I talked with the goldsmith, and easily persuaded him of the advantages of a servant who could read and write; I made it clear, besides, that I was letting Casso go to him for less than his cost to me on condition that my wish was met. I found I had not needed to insist; Beltane, that kindly man, promised with pleasure to teach Casso himself, and then they both took leave of me and went south, aiming once more for York. With them went Lind, who, it seemed, had met a man in York who might protect her; he was a small merchant, a respectable fellow who had spoken of marriage, but whom, for fear of the queen, she had rejected. I took leave of them, and settled down to see what the next few days would bring.

Some two or three days after the terrible night of Lot's return, the wreckage of the boat began to come ashore, and with it the bodies. It was apparent that the boat had driven on rock somewhere and had been broken up by the tide. The poor women who went down to the beach fell to a kind of dreadful squabbling as to which baby was which. The shore was haunted by these wretched women. They wept a great deal and said very little; it was apparent that they were accustomed, like beasts, to take what their lords handed out to them, whether alms or blows. It was also apparent to me, sitting in the alehouse shadows and listening, that in spite of the tale about Arthur's responsibility for the massacre, most folk laid the blame squarely where it belonged, with Morgause, and with Lot, befooled and angry about it. And because men are men everywhere, they were inclined not to blame their king overmuch for his hasty reaction to that anger. Any man, they were soon saying, would have done the same. Come home to find your wife delivered of another man's boy, and small blame to you if you lost your temper. And as for the wholesale slaughter, well, a king was a king, and had a throne to consider as well as his bed. And speaking of kings, had he not made kingly reparation? For this, wisely, Lot had done; and however much the women might still weep and mourn, the men on the whole accepted Lot's deed, along with the golden recompense that followed it, as the natural action of a wronged and angry king.

And Arthur? I put the question one evening, casually, into one such conversation. If the rumours that were being put about were true, of the High King's involvement in the killing, was not Arthur himself similarly justified? If the child Mordred was indeed his bastard by his half-sister, and a hostage to fortune with King Lot (who had not always been his keenest friend), surely it could be said that policy could justify the deed? What more likely way could Arthur find of keeping the great King of Lothian his friend than to ensure the death of the cuckoo in the nest, and take the responsibility for its killing?

At this there were murmurs and head-shakings, which resolved at length into a sort of qualified assent. So I threw in another thought. Everyone knew that in matters like this of policy—and high and secret policy, with a great country like Lothian concerned—everyone knew it was not the young Arthur who made the civil decisions; it was his chief adviser, Merlin. Depend upon it, this was the decision of a ruthless and tortuous mind, not of a brave young soldier who spent his every waking moment in the field against Britain's enemies, and who had little time for bedroom politics—except, naturally, those that every man could find time for. . . .

So, like a seed of grass, the idea was sown, and as quickly as the grass it spread and grew; so that by the time the news came of Arthur's next victorious engagement the facts of the massacre had been accepted, and the guilt for it, whether of Merlin, Arthur, or Lot, almost condoned. It was plain that the High King—may God preserve him against the enemy—had had little to do with it except see its necessity. Besides, the babies, most of them, would have died in infancy of one thing or another, and that without any gifts of gold such as Lot had handed to the bereaved fathers. Moreover, most of the women were soon bearing again, and had perforce to forget their tears.

The queen, also. King Lot was now seen to have behaved in a truly kingly fashion. He had swept home in anger, removed the bastard (whether by Arthur's orders or his own), then got a true heir in the dead boy's place, and ridden off again, his loyalty to the High King undiminished. Some of the bereaved fathers, being offered places in the troop, rode with him, confirmed in their own loyalty. Morgause herself, far from appearing cowed by her lord's violence, or apprehensive of the people's anger, looked (on the one or two occasions when I saw her riding out) sleek and pleased with herself. Whatever the people may have believed about her part in the massacre, she was safe from their ill-will now that she was said to be carrying the kingdom's true heir.

If she grieved for her lost son, she gave no sign of it. It showed, the people said, that she had in truth been seduced by Arthur, and could never have wanted the bastard she had been made to bear. But to me, watching and waiting in drab anonymity, it began to mean something quite different. I did not believe that the child Mordred had been in that boatload of slaughtered innocents at all. I remembered the three armed men, sober and purposeful, who had gone back into the castle by the postern entrance just before Lot's return—and after the coming of Morgause's messenger from the south. The woman Macha, too, lying dead in her cottage beside the empty cradle with her throat cut. And Lind, running out into the dark without Morgause's knowledge or sanction, to warn Macha and take the child Mordred to safety.

Piecing it together, I thought I knew what had happened. Macha had been chosen to foster Mordred because she had borne Lot a bastard boy; it might even have pleased Morgause to watch the baby killed; she had laughed, Lind had told us. So, with Mordred safe, and the changeling ready for the slaughter, Morgause had waited for Lot's return. As soon as she had news of it, her men-at-arms had been sent with orders to dispatch Mordred to yet another safe foster-home, and to kill Macha, who, if her own baby were to suffer, might be tempted to betray the queen. And now Lot was pacified, the town was quiet, and somewhere, I was sure, the child who was Morgause's weapon of power grew in safety.

After Lot had ridden to rejoin Arthur, I sent Ulfin south again, but myself stayed on in Lothian, watching and waiting. With Lot out of the way, I moved back into Dunpeldyr, and tried, in every way I could, to find some clue to where Mordred could now be hidden. What I would have done if I had found him, I do not know, but the god did not lay that burden on me. So I waited for fully four months in that squalid little town, and though I walked on the shore by starlight and sunlight and spoke to my god in every tongue and with every way I knew, I saw nothing, either by daylight or in dream, to guide me to Arthur's son.

In time I came to believe that I might have been wrong; that even Morgause could not be so evil, and that Mordred had perished with the other innocents in that midnight sea.

So at length, as autumn slid into the first chills of winter, and news came that the fighting in Linnuis was done, and Lot would soon be on his way home once more, I thankfully left Dunpeldyr. Arthur would be at Caerleon for Christmas, and would look for me there. I paused only once on my journey, to spend a few nights with Blaise in Northumbria and give him the news, then I travelled south, to be there when the King came home.

He came back in the second week of December, with frost on the ground, and the children out gathering the holly and ivy for decking the Christmas feast. He barely waited to bathe and change from the ride before he sent for me. He received me in the room where we had talked before we parted. This time the door to the bedroom was shut, and he was alone.

He had changed a good deal in the months since Pentecost. Taller, yes, by half a head—it is an age when youths shoot up like barley-stalks—and with breadth to go with it, and the hard lean brownness got from the soldier's life he was leading. But this was not the real change. That was in authority. His manner showed now that he knew what he was doing and where he was going.

But for that, the interview might have been an echo of the one I had had with the younger Arthur, on the night of Mordred's begetting.

"They say that I ordered this abominable thing!" He had hardly troubled to greet me. He strode about the room, the same strong, light lion's prowl of a walk, but the strides were a hand-span longer. The room was a cage restraining him. "When you know yourself how, in this very room, I said no, leave it to the god. And now this!"

"It's what you wanted, isn't it?"

"All those deaths? Don't be a fool, would I have done it like that? Or would you?"

The question needed no reply, and got none. I said merely: "Lot was never remarkable for his wisdom and restraint, and besides, he was in a rage. You might say the action was suggested to him, or at least encouraged, from without."

He threw me a quick, smouldering look. "By Morgause? So I understand."

"I gather Ulfin has told you all the story? Did he also tell you of his own services in the matter?"

"That he tried to mislead you, and let fate overtake the children? Yes, he told me that." A brief pause. "It was wrong, and I said so, but it's hard to be angry at devotion. He thought—he knew that I would have been easy at the baby's death. But those other children . . . Within a month of the vows I made to protect the people, and my name a hissing in the streets. . . ."

"I think you can comfort yourself. I doubt if many men believe that you had anything to do with it."

"No matter." He almost snapped it over his shoulder. "Some will, and that is enough. As for Lot, he had an excuse of a kind; an excuse, that is, that common men can understand. But I? Can I publish it abroad that Merlin the prophet told me the child might be a danger to me, so I had it murdered, and others along with it for fear it should escape the net? What sort of king does this make of me? Lot's sort?"

"I can only repeat that I doubt if you are held to blame. Morgause's women were there within hearing, remember, and the guards knew where their orders came from. Lot's escort, too—they would know he was riding home bent on revenge, and I cannot imagine that Lot remained silent as to his intentions. I don't know what Ulfin has told you, but when I left Dunpeldyr most people were quoting Lot's orders as responsible for the massacre, and those who thought you ordered it think you did so on my advice."

"So?" he said. He really was very angry. "I am the kind of king who cannot even decide for myself? If there is to be blame allotted for this between us, then I should take it, and not you. You know that well enough. You remember as well as I do exactly what was said."

There was no reply to that, either, and I made none. He prowled up the room and back again before he went on:

"Whoever gave the order, you can say if you like that I feel guilt in this. You would be right. But by all the gods in heaven and hell, I would not have acted like that! This is the kind of thing that lives with you, and after you! I shall not be remembered as the king who beat the Saxons out of Britain, but as the man who played Herod in Dunpeldyr and murdered the children!" He stopped. "What is there in that to smile at?"

"I doubt if you need trouble yourself about the name you will leave behind you."

"So you say."

"So I said." The change in tense, or something about my tone, arrested him. I met his look, and held it. "Yes, I, Merlin, said so. I said so when I had power, and it is true. You are right to be distressed at this abomination, and you are right, too, to take some of the blame to yourself. But if this thing goes down in story as your act, you will still be absolved of blame. You can believe me. What else is to come will absolve you of anything."

The anger had died, and he was thinking. He spoke slowly. "Do you mean that some danger will come of the child's birth and death? Something so terrible that men will see the murder as justified?"

"I did not mean that, no—"

"You made another prophecy, remember. You hinted to me—no, you told me—that Morgause's child might be a danger to me. Well, now the child is dead. Could this have been the danger? This smear on my name?" He paused, struck. "Or perhaps some day one of the men whose sons were murdered will wait for me with a knife in the dark? Is that the kind of thing you had in mind?"

"I told you, I had nothing specific in mind. I did not say that the child 'might' be a danger to you, Arthur. I said he would. And, if my word is to be trusted, directly so, and not by a knife in another man's hand."

He was as still now as he had been restless before. He scowled at me, intent. "You mean that the massacre failed of its purpose? That the child—Mordred, did you say?—is still alive?"

"I have come to think so."

He drew a quick breath. "Then he was saved, somehow, from that wreck?"

"It's possible. Either he was saved by chance, and is living somewhere, unknowing and unknown, as you did through your childhood—in which case you may encounter him some day, as Laius did Oedipus, and fall to him in all ignorance."

"I'll risk that. Everyone falls to someone, some time. Or?"

"Or he was never in the boat at all."

He gave a slow nod. "Morgause, yes. It would fit. What do you know?"

I told him the little I knew, and the conclusions I had drawn. "She must have known," I finished, "that Lot's reactions would be violent. We know she wanted to keep the child, and why. She would hardly have put her own child at risk on Lot's return. It's clear enough that she engineered the whole thing. Lind gave us more details later on. We know that she goaded Lot into the furious anger that dictated the massacre; we know, too, that she started the rumour that you were to blame. So what has she done? She has put Lot's fears to rest, and made her own position secure. And I believe, from watching her, and from what I know of her, that at the same time she has contrived—"

"To keep her hostage of fortune." The flush had died from his skin. He looked cold, his eyes like slates with cold rain on them. This was an Arthur that other men had seen, but never I. How many Saxons had seen those eyes just before they died? He said bitterly: "I have been well paid already for that night of lust. I wish you had let me kill her then. That is one lady who had better never come near me again, unless she comes on her knees, and in sack-cloth." His tone made a vow of it. Then it changed. "When did you get back from the north?"

"Yesterday."

"*Yesterday?* I thought . . . I understood that this abomination took place months ago."

"Yes. I stayed to watch events. Then after I began to make my guesses, I waited to see if Morgause might make some move to show me where the child was hidden. If Lind had been able to go back to her, and had dared to help me . . . but that was impossible. So I stayed until the news came that you had left Linnuis, and that Lot would soon be on his way home again. I knew that once he came home I could do nothing, so I came away."

"I see. All that way, and now I keep you on your feet and rail at you as if you were a guard caught sleeping on duty. Will you forgive me?"

"There's nothing to forgive. I have rested. But I should be glad to sit now. Thank you."

This as he pulled a chair for me, and then sat himself in the big chair beyond the massive table. "You've said nothing in your reports about this idea that Mordred was still alive. And Ulfin never mentioned it as a possibility."

"I don't think it crossed his mind. It was mainly after he had gone, and I had time to think and watch, myself, that I thought back and reached my own conclusion. There's still no proof, of course, that I am right. And nothing but the memory of an old foreboding to tell me whether or not it matters. But I can tell you one thing: from the idle contentment that the King's prophet feels in his bones these days, any threat from Mordred, direct or otherwise, will not show itself for a long time to come."

He gave me a look where no shadow of anger remained. A smile sparked deep in his eyes. "So, I have time."

"You have time. This was bad, and you were right to be angry; but it is already barely remembered, and soon will be forgotten in the blaze of your victories. Concerning them, I hear talk of nothing else. So put this aside now, and think about the next. Time spent looking back in anger is time wasted."

The tension broke up at last in the familiar smile. "I know. A maker, never a breaker. How often have you told me? Well, I'm only mortal. I break first, to make room. . . . All right, I'll forget it. There is plenty to think about and plan for, without wasting time on what is done. In fact"—the smile deepened—"I heard that King Lot is planning a move northward to his kingdom there. Perhaps, in spite of laying the blame on me, he feels uncomfortable in Dunpeldyr. . . .? The Orkneys are fertile islands, they tell me, and fine in the summer months, but tend to be cut off from the main all winter?"

"Unless the sea freezes."

"And that," he said, with most unkingly satisfaction, "will surely be beyond even Morgause's powers. So distance will help us to forget Lot and his works. . . ."

His hand moved among the papers and tablets on the table. I was thinking that I should have looked farther afield for Mordred: if Lot had told his queen his plans for taking the court northward, she might have made some arrangement for sending the child there. But Arthur was speaking again.

"Do you know anything about dreams?"

I was startled. "Dreams? Well, I have had them."

A glint of amusement. "Yes, that was a foolish question, wasn't it? I meant, can you tell me what they mean, other men's dreams?"

"I doubt it. When my own mean something, they are clear beyond doubt. Why, has your sleep been troubled?"

"For many nights now." He hesitated, shifting the things on the table. "It seems a trivial thing to trouble over, but the dream is so vivid, and it's always the same. . . ."

"Tell me."

"I am alone, and out hunting. No hounds, just myself and my horse, hard on the track of a stag. This part varies a bit, but I always know that the chase has been going on for many hours. Then, just as we seem to be catching up with the stag, it leaps into a brake of trees and vanishes. At the same moment my horse falls dead beneath me. I am thrown to the turf. Sometimes I wake there, but when I go back to sleep again, I am still lying on the turf, by the bank of a stream, with the dead horse beside me. Then suddenly I hear hounds coming, a whole pack of them, and I sit up and look about me. Now, I have had the dream so many times that even while dreaming, I know what to expect, and I am afraid. . . . It is not a pack of hounds that comes, but one beast—a strange beast, which, though I have seen it so many times, I can't describe. It comes crashing through the bracken and underbrush, and the noise it makes is like thirty couple of hounds questing. It takes no heed of me or my horse, but stops at the stream and drinks, and then goes on and is lost in the forest."

"Is that the end?" I asked, as he paused.

"No. The end varies, too, but always, after the questing beast, comes a knight, alone and on foot, who tells me that he also has killed a horse under him in the quest. Each time—each night it happens—I try to ask him what the beast is, and what is the quest, but just as he is about to tell me, my groom comes up with a fresh horse for me, and the knight, seizing it without courtesy, mounts and prepares to ride away. And I find myself laying hands on his rein to stop him, and begging him to let me undertake the guest, 'for,' I say, 'I am the High King, and it is for me to undertake any quest of danger.' But he strikes my hand aside, saying, 'Later. Later, when you need to, you may find me here, and I shall answer for what I have done.' And he rides away, leaving me alone in the forest. Then I wake, still with this sense of fear. Merlin, what does it mean?"

I shook my head. "That I can't tell you. I might be glib with you, and say that this was a lesson in humility: that even the High King does not need to take all responsibility—"

"You mean stand back and let you take the blame for the massacre? No, that's too clever by half, Merlin!"

"I said I was being glib, didn't I? I have no idea what your dream meant. Probably nothing more than a mixture of worry and indigestion. But one thing I can tell you, and it's the same one that I keep repeating: what dangers lie in front of you, you will surmount, and reach glory; and whatever has happened, whatever you have done, or will do, you will die a worshipful death. I shall fade and vanish like music when the harp is dead, and men will call my end shameful. But you will live on, in men's imagination and hearts. Meanwhile, you have years, and time enough. So tell me what happened in Linnuis."

We talked for a long time. Eventually he came back to the immediate future.

"Until the ways open with spring, we can get on with the work here at Caerleon. You'll stay here for that. But in the spring I want you to start work on my new headquarters." I looked a query, and he nodded. "Yes, we spoke of this before. What was right in Vortigern's time, or even in Ambrosius', will not serve in a year or so from this. The picture is changing, over to the east. Come to the map and let me show you. . . . That man of yours now, Gereint, there's a find. I've sent for him. He's the kind of man I need by me. The information he sent to Linnuis was beyond price. He told you about Eosa and Cerdic? We're gathering what information we can, but I'm sure he is right. The latest news is that Eosa is back in Germany, and he's promising the sun, moon, and stars, as well as a settled Saxon kingdom, to any who will join him. . . ."

For a while we discussed Gereint's information, and Arthur told me what had newly come from those sources. Then he went on: "He's right about the Gap, too, of course. We started work up there as soon as I got your reports. I sent Torre up. . . . I believe the next push will come from the north. I'm expecting word from Caw and from Urbgen. But in the long run it will be here, in the southwest, that we have to make the stand for good and all. With Rutupiae as their base, and the Shore behind them, call it 'kingdom' or not, the big threat must come this way, here and here. . . ." His finger was moving on the relief map of clay. "We came back this way from Linnuis. I got an idea of the lie of the land. But no more now, Merlin. They're making new maps for me, and we can sit over them later. Do you know the country thereabouts?"

"No. I have travelled that road, but my mind was on other things."

"There's little haste yet. If we can start in April, or May, and you work your usual miracle, that should be soon enough. Think about it for me, and then go and look when the time comes. Will you do that?"

"Willingly. I have already looked . . . no, I meant in my mind. I've remembered something. There's a hill that commands this whole tract of country here. . . . As far as I remember, it's flat-topped, and big enough to house an army, or a city, or whatever you want of it. And high enough. You can see Ynys Witrin from it—the Isle of Glass—and all the signal chain, and again clear for many miles both to south and west."

"Show me," he said sharply.

"Somewhere here." I placed a finger. "I can't be exact, and I don't think the map is, either. But I think this must be the stream it lies on."

"Its name?"

"I don't know its name. It's a hill with the stream curling round it, and the stream is called, I think, the Camel. The hill was a fortress before the Romans ever came to Britain, so even the early Britons must have seen it as a strategic point. They held it against the Romans."

"Who took it?"

"Eventually. Then they fortified it in their turn and held it."

"Ah. Then there is a road."

"Surely. This one, perhaps, that runs past the Lake from the Glass Isle."

So I showed him on the map, and he looked, and talked, and went on the prowl again, and then the servants brought supper and lights and he straightened, pushing the hair back out of his eyes, and came up out of his planning as a diver comes up out of water.

"Well, it will have to wait till Christmas is past. But go as soon as you can, Merlin, and tell me what you think. You shall have what help you need, you know that. And now sup with me, and I'll tell you about the fight at the Blackwater. I've told it already so many times that it's grown till I hardly recognize it myself. But once more, to you, is not unseemly."

"Obligatory. And I promise you that I shall believe every word."

He laughed. "I always knew I could rely on you."

2

It was on a sweet, still day of spring when I turned aside from the road and saw the hill called Camelot.

That was its name later; now it was known as Caer Camel, after the small stream that wound through the level lands surrounding it, and curved around near its base. It was, as I had told Arthur, a flat-topped hill, not high, but high enough over the surrounding flatlands to give a clear view on every hand, and steep-sided enough to allow formidable defenses. It was easy to see why the Celts, and after them the Romans, had chosen it as a stronghold. From its highest point the view in almost every direction is tremendous. To the east a few rolling hills block the vision, but to south and west the eye can travel for miles, and northward also, as far as the coast. On the northwest side the sea comes within eight miles or so, the tides spreading and filtering through the marshy flatlands that feed the great Lake where stands the Isle of Glaes. This island, or group of islands, lies on its glassy water like a recumbent goddess; indeed it has from time immemorial been dedicated to the Goddess herself, and her shrine stands close beside the king's palace. Above it the great beacon top of the Tor is plainly visible, and, many miles beyond that, right on the coast of the Severn Channel, may be seen the next beacon point of Brent Knoll.

The hills of the Glass Isle, with the low and water-logged levels surrounding them, are known as the Summer Country. The king was a man called Melwas, young, and a staunch supporter of Arthur; he gave me lodging during my first surveys of Caer Camel, and seemed pleased that the High King should plan to form his main stronghold at the edge of his territory. He was deeply interested in the maps I showed him, and promised help of every kind, from the loan of local workmen to a pledge of defense, should that be needed, while the work was in progress.

King Melwas had offered to show me the place himself, but for my first survey I preferred to be alone, so managed to put him off with civilities of some kind. He and his young men rode with me for the first part of the way, then turned aside into a track that was little more than a causeway through the marshlands, and went cheerfully off to their day's sport. That is a great country for hunting; it teems with wildfowl of every kind. I saw a lucky omen in the fact that almost as soon as they left me, King Melwas flew his falcon at a flock of immigrant birds coming in from the southeast, and within seconds the hawk had killed cleanly and come straight back to the master's fist. Then, with shouting and laughter, the band of young men rode off among the willows, and I went on my way alone.

I had been right in supposing that a road would lead to the once-Roman fortress of Caer Camel. The road leaves Ynys Witrin by a causeway which skirts the base of the Tor, spans a narrow arm of the Lake, and reaches a strip of dry, hard land stretching toward the east. There it joins the old Fosse Way, then after a while turns south again for the village at the foot of Caer Camel. This had originally been a Celtic settlement, then the *vicus* to the Roman fortress, its occupants scraping some sort of living from the soil, and retiring uphill within walls in times of danger. Since the fortress had decayed, their lives had been hard indeed. As well as the ever-present danger to the south and east, they even had, in bad years, to beat off the people of the Summer Country, when the wetlands around Ynys Witrin ceased to provide anything but fish and marsh birds, and the young men craved excitement beyond the confines of their own territory. There was little to be seen as I rode between the tumbledown huts with their rotting thatch; here and there eyes watched me from a dark doorway, or a woman's voice called shrilly to her child. My horse splashed through the mud and dung, forded the Camel knee-deep, then at last I turned him uphill through the trees, and took the steep curve of the chariot-way at a plunging canter.

Even though I knew what to expect, I was amazed at the size of the summit. I came up through the ruins of the southwest gateway into a great field, tilted to southward, but sloping sharply ahead of me toward a ridge with a high point west of center. I walked my horse slowly toward this. The field, or rather plateau, was scarred and pitted with the remains of buildings, and surrounded on all sides by deep ditching, and the relics of revetments and fortified walls. Whins and brambles matted the broken walls, and mole-hills had heaved up the cracked pavingstones. Stone lay everywhere, good Roman stone, squared in some local quarry. Beyond the ruined outworks the sides of the hill went down steeply, and on them trees, once lopped to ground level, had put out saplings and thickets of suckers. Between these the scarps were quilted with a winter network of bramble and thorn. A beaten pathway through sprouting fern and nettle led to a gap in the north wall. Following this, I could see where, half down the northern hillside, a spring lay deep among the trees. This must be the Lady's Well, the good spring dedicated to the Goddess. The other spring, the main water supply for the fortress, lay halfway up the steep road to the northeast gateway, at the hill's opposite corner from the chariot road I had taken. It seemed that cattle were still watered there: as I watched, I saw a herd, slow-moving, come up through the steep gap, and spread out to graze in the sunshine, with a faint, off-note chiming of bells. Their herd followed them, a slight figure whom at first I took for a boy, then saw, from the way he moved, using his staff to lean upon, that it was an old man.

I turned my horse's head that way, and walked him carefully through the tumble of stonework. A magpie got up and flew, scolding. The old man looked up. He stopped short, startled, and, I thought, apprehensive. I raised a hand to him in a sign of greeting. Something about the solitary and unarmed horseman must have reassured him, for after a moment he moved to a low wall that lay full in the sun, and sat down to wait for me.

I dismounted, letting my horse graze.

"Greetings, father."

"And to you." It was not much more than a mumble, in the strong blurring accent of the district. He peered at me suspiciously, through eyes clouded with cataract. "You're a stranger to these parts."

"I come from the west."

This was no reassurance. It seemed that the folk hereabouts had had too long a history of war. "Why'd you leave the road then? What do you want up here?"

"I came on the King's behalf, to look at the fortress walls."

"Again?"

As I stared at him in surprise, he drove his stick into the turf, as if making a claim, and spoke with a kind of quavering anger. "This was our land before the king came, and it's ours again in spite of him. Why don't 'ee let us keep it so?"

"I don't think—" I began, then stopped, on a sudden thought. "You speak of a king. Which king?"

"I don't know his name."

"Melwas? Or Arthur?"

Maybe. I tell you I don't know. What do you want here?"

"I am the King's man. I come from him—"

"Aye. To raise the fortress walls again, then take away our cattle and kill our children and rape our women."

"No. To build a stronghold here to protect your cattle and children and women."

"It did not protect them before."

There was silence. The old man's hand shook on his stick. The sun was hot on the grass. My horse grazed delicately round a thistle head growing low and circular, like a splayed wheel. An early butterfly alighted on a purple head of clover. A lark rose, singing.

"Old man," I said gently, "there has been no fortress here in your lifetime, or in your father's. What walls stood here and looked south and north and westward over the waters? What king came to storm them?"

He looked at me for a few moments, his head shaking with the tremor of age. "It's a story, only a story, master. My granda told it to me, how the folk lived here with cattle and goats and sweet grazing, and wove the cloth and tilled the high field, until the king came and drove them down through yon road into the valley bottom, and there was a grave for them all that day, as wide as a river and as deep as the hollow hill, where they laid the king himself to rest, and his time coming soon after."

"Which hill was that? Ynys Witrin?"

"What? How should they carry him there? It's a foreign country there. They call it the Summer Country, for all it's a sheet of lake water all the year round save through the dry time of midsummer. No, they made a way into the cave and laid him there, and with him the ones who were drowned with him." A sudden, high cackle. "Drowned in the Lake, and the folk watched and made no move to save him. It was the Goddess took him, and his fine captains along with him. Who could have stopped her? They say it was three days before she gave him back, and then he came naked, without either crown or sword." The cackling laugh again, as he nodded. "Your King had best make his peace with her, tell him that."

"He will. When did this happen?"

"A hundred years ago. Two hundred. How would I know?"

Another silence, while I assessed it. What I was hearing, I knew, was a folk memory that had come down tongue to tongue in a winter's tale by some peasant's hearth. But it confirmed what I had been told. The place must have been fortified time out of mind. "The king" could have been any one of the Celtic rulers, driven eventually from the hilltop by the Romans, or the Roman general himself who had stayed here to invest the captured strongpoint.

I said suddenly: "Where is the way into the hill?"

"What way?"

"The door to the king's tomb, where they made the way for his grave."

"How do I know? It's there, that's all I know. And sometimes, on a night, they ride out again. I have seen them. They come wi' the summer moon, and go back into the hill at dawning. And whiles, on a stormy night, when dawn surprises them, one comes late, and finds the gate shut. So he is doomed for the next moon to wander the hilltop alone till . . ." His voice faltered. He ducked his head fearfully, peering. "A king's man, you said you were?"

I laughed. "Don't be afraid of me, father. I'm not one of them. I'm a king's man, yes, but I have come for a living king, who will build the fortress up again, and take you and your cattle, and your children, and their children, into his hand, and keep you safely against the Saxon enemy from the south. And you will still get sweet grazing for your herd. I promise you this."

He said nothing to that, but sat for a while, nid-nodding in the sun. I could see that he was simple. "Why should I be afraid? There has always been a king here, and always will be. A king is no new thing."

"This one will be."

His attention was leaving me. He chirrupped to the cows: "Come up, Blackberry, come up, Dewdrop. A king, and tend the cattle for me? Do you take me for a fool? But the Goddess looks after her own. He'd best tend to the Goddess." And he subsided, mumbling his stick, and muttering.

I gave him a silver coin, as one gives a singer the guerdon for his tale, then led my horse off toward the ridge that marked the summit of the plateau.

3

Some days later the first party of surveyors arrived, to begin their measuring and pacing, while their leader was closeted with me in the temporary headquarters that had been made for us on the site.

Tremorinus, the master engineer who had taught me so much of his trade when I was a boy in Brittany, had died some time ago. Arthur's chief engineer now was a man called Derwen, whom I had first met years back, over the rebuilding of Caerleon in Ambrosius' time. He was a red-bearded, high-coloured man, but without the temper that often goes with that colouring; indeed, he was silent to the point of surliness, and could prove sullen as a mule when pressed. But I knew him to be competent and experienced, and he had the trick of getting men to work fast and willingly for him. Moreover, he had taken pains to be master himself of all trades, and was never above rolling up his sleeves and doing a heavy job himself if time demanded. Nor did he appear to mind taking direction from me. He seemed to hold my skills in the most flattering respect; this was not, I knew, because of any especial brilliance I had shown at Caerleon or Segontium—they were built to pattern on the Roman model, on lines laid down through time, and familiar to every builder—but Derwen had been an apprentice in Ireland when I had moved the massive king-stone of Killare, and subsequently at Amesbury, at the rebuilding of the Giants' Dance. So we got along tolerably well together, and understood each what the other was good for.

Arthur's forecast of trouble in the north had come true, and he had gone up in early March. But during the winter months he and I, with Derwen, had spent many hours together over the plans for the new stronghold. Driven by my persistence, and Arthur's enthusiasm, Derwen had finally been brought to accept what he obviously thought of as my wild ideas about the rebuilding of Caer Camel. Strength and speed—I wanted the place ready for Arthur by the time the campaign in the north should near its close, and I also wanted it to last. Its size and force had to fit his state.

The size was there: the hill's summit was vast, some eight acres in area. But the strength . . . I had had lists made of what material was already there, and, as best I could among the ruins, I had studied how the place had been built before, the Roman stonework on top of layer after layer of earlier Celtic wall and ditching. As I worked I kept in mind some of the fortifications I had seen on my travels abroad, strongpoints thrown up in wilder places than this, and on terrain as difficult. To rebuild on the Roman model would have been a formidable, if not impossible, task; even if Derwen's masons had had the knack of the Roman type of stonework, the sheer size of Caer Camel would have forbidden it. But the masons were all expert at their own dry-stone kind of building, and there was plenty of dressed stone to hand, and a quarry nearby. We had the oak-woods and the carpenters, and the sawyers' yards between Caer Camel and the Lake had been packed all winter with maturing timber. So I had made my final plans.

That they were carried out magnificently everyone can see. The steep, ditched sides of the place they now call Camelot stand crowned with massive walls of stone and timber. Sentries patrol the battlements, and stand guard over the great gates. To the northerly gate a wagon-road climbs between its guarded banks, while to the gate at the southwest corner—the one they call King's Gate—a chariot-way curves up, true-cambered to the fastest wheels, and wide enough for a galloping troop of horse.

Within those walls now, as well kept in this time of peace as in the troubled days I built them for, a city has arisen, gay with gilding and the fluttering of banners, and fresh with gardens and orchard trees. On the paved terraces walk women in rich dresses, and children play in the gardens. The streets are crowded with folk, and full of talk and laughter, the chaffering of the market-place, the quick hoofs of Arthur's fleet and glossy horses, the shouts of the young men, and the clamour of the church bells. It has grown rich with peaceful commerce, and splendid with the arts of peace. Camelot is a marvellous sight, and one which is familiar now to travellers from the four corners of the world.

But then, on that raw hilltop, and among the mess of abandoned buildings, it was no more than an idea, and an idea sprung out of the hard necessities of war. We would start, of course, with the outer walls, and here I planned to use the broken stuff that lay about; tiles from the old hypocausts, flagstones, bedding from the floors, even from the old road-work that had been laid in the Roman fortress. With these we would throw up a revetment of hard rubble which would retain the outer wall, and at the same time support a broad fighting platform laid along the inner side of the battlement. The wall itself would, on the outer side, rise straight out of the steep hillside, like a crown on a king's head. The hillside we stripped of its trees, and seamed with ditches, so that it became, in effect, a steep of breakneck minor crags, to be topped with a great wall faced with stone. For this we would use the dressed tufa found on site, along with materials quarried afresh by Melwas' masons and our own. Above this again I planned to set a massively smooth wall of wood, tied into the stonework and the rubble of the revetment by a strong timber frame. At the gateways, where the approach-roads ran uphill sunk between rocky banks, I designed a kind of tunnel which would pierce the fortified wall, and allow the fighting platform to run unbroken across, above the gates. These gated tunnels, high and wide enough to let horse-drawn traffic through, or riders three abreast, would be hung with huge gates which could fold back against the oak-lined walls. To do this we would have to sink the roadways still farther.

This, and much else besides, I had explained to Derwen. He had been skeptical at first, and only his respect for me had kept him, I could tell, from flat and mulish disagreement—especially about the gates, for which he could see no precedent; and most engineers and architects work, reasonably enough, from well-proved precedent, especially in matters of war and defense. At first he could see no reason to abandon the well-tried model of twin turrets and guard-rooms. But in time, sitting hour by hour over my plans, and conning the lists I had had drawn up of the materials already available on the site, he came to a qualified acceptance of my amalgam of stone and woodworking, and thence to a sort of guarded enthusiasm over all. He was enough of a professional to find excitement in new ideas, especially since any blame for failure would be mine and not his.

Not that blame was likely. Arthur, taking part in the planning sessions, was enthusiastic, but—as he pointed out when deferred to over some technical point—he knew his own business, and he would trust us to know ours. We all knew what the place's function would be; it was up to us to build it accordingly. Once we had built it (he concluded with the brevity of total and unconscious arrogance) he would know how to keep it.

Now, on site at last, and with good weather come early and looking settled, Derwen started work with keenness and dispatch, and before the old herdsman had called the cows home for the first evening's milking, the pegs were driven in, trenches had been started, and the first wagon-load of supplies was groaning uphill behind its straining oxen.

Caer Camel was rising again. The King was coming back.

He came on a bright day of June. He rode up from the village on his grey mare Amrei, accompanied by Bedwyr and his foster-brother Cei and perhaps a dozen others of his cavalry captains. These were now commonly known as the *equites* or knights; Arthur himself called them his "Companions." They rode without armour, like a hunting-party. Arthur swung from his mare's back, threw the reins to Bedwyr, and while the others dismounted and let their horses graze, he trod up the slope of blowing grass alone.

He saw me, and lifted a hand, but did not hurry. He paused by the outer revetment, and spoke to the men working there, then walked out onto the planking that bridged a trench, while the labourers straightened from their tasks to answer his questions. I saw one of them point something out to him; he looked that way, and then all about him, before he left them to mount the central ridge where the foundations for his headquarters had been dug. From there he could command the whole area, and make some sense, perhaps, out of the maze of trenching and foundations, half hidden as it was beneath the web of ropes and scaffolding.

He turned slowly on his heel, until he had taken in the full circle. Then he came swiftly over to where I stood, drawings in hand.

"Yes," was all he said, but with a glowing satisfaction. And then: "When?"

"There will be something here for you by winter."

He sent his eyes round again, a look of pride and vision that could have been my own. I knew that he was seeing, as I could see, the finished walls, the proud towers, the stone and timber and iron that would enclose this space of golden summer air, and make it his first creation. It was the look, too, of a warrior who sees a strong weapon being offered to his hand. His eyes, full of this high and fierce satisfaction, came back to me.

"I told you to use a miracle, and I think you have. That is how I see it. Perhaps you are too much of a professional to feel that way, when you see what was only a drawing on clay, or even a thought in your mind, being built into something real that will last for ever?"

"I believe all makers feel this way. I, certainly."

"How fast it has moved! Did you build it with music, like the Giants' Dance?"

"I used the same miracle here. You can see it. The men."

A quick glance at me, then his gaze went across the mess of churned ground and toiling labourers to where, as orderly as in an old, walled city, the workshops of the carpenters and smiths and masons rang with hammering and voices. His eyes took a faraway and yet inward look. He spoke softly. "I'll remember that. God knows every commander should. I use the same miracle myself." Then, back to me: "And by next winter?"

"By next winter you should have it complete inside, as well as safe to fight from. The place is everything we had hoped for. Later, when the wars are done, there will be space and time to build for other things, comfort and grace and splendour, worthy of you and your victories. We'll make you a veritable eagle's eyrie, hung on a lovely hill. A stronghold to hunt from in war, and a home to breed in in times of peace."

He had half turned from me, to make a sign to the watching Bedwyr. The young men mounted, and Bedwyr approached us, leading Arthur's mare. Arthur swung back to me, brows up.

"So you know? I might have known I could keep no secrets from you."

"Secrets? I know nothing. What secret were you trying to keep?"

"None. What would be the use? I would have told you straight away, but this came first . . . though she wouldn't like to hear me say so." I must have gaped at him like a fool. His eyes danced. "Yes, I'm sorry, Merlin. But I really was about to tell you. I am to marry. Come, don't be angry. That is something in which you could hardly guide me to my own satisfaction."

"I am not angry. What right have I? This is one thing you must decide for yourself. It seems you have, and I'm glad. Is it concluded?"

"No, how could it be? I was waiting to talk to you first. So far it's only been a matter of letters between Queen Ygraine and myself. The suggestion came from her, and I suppose there'll be a lot of talking to do first. But I warn you"—a glint—"my mind is made up." Bedwyr slipped from his saddle beside us, and Arthur took the mare's reins from him. I looked a query, and he nodded. "Yes, Bedwyr knows."

"Then will you tell me who she is?"

"Her father was March, who fought under Duke Cador and was killed in a skirmish on the Irish Shore. Her mother died at her birth, and since her father's death she has been under Queen Ygraine's protection. You must have seen her, but you would not notice her, I expect. She was in waiting at Amesbury, and then again at the crowning."

"I remember her. Did I hear her name? I forget."

"Guenever."

A plover winged overhead, tumbling in the sun. Its shadow floated over the grass between us. Something plucked at the chords of memory; something from that other life of power and terror and bright vision. But it eluded me. The mood of tranquil achievement was unruffled as the Lake.

"What is it, Merlin?"

His voice was anxious, like a boy's who fears censure. I looked up. Bedwyr, beside him, was watching me with the same worried look.

"Nothing at all. She's a lovely girl, and bears a lovely name. Be sure the gods will bless the marriage when the time comes."

The young faces relaxed. Bedwyr said something quick and teasing, then followed it with some excited comment about the building work, and the two of them plunged into a discussion in which marriage plans had no part. I caught sight of Derwen over near the gateway, so we walked that way to talk with him. Then Arthur and Bedwyr took their leave, and mounted, and the other young men turned their fretting horses to ride downhill after their King toward the road.

They did not get far. As the little cavalcade entered the sunken gateway they came head on against Blackberry and Dewdrop and their sisters, making their slow way uphill. The old herdsman, tenacious as goosegrass, still clung to his grazing rights on Caer Camel, and brought the herd daily up toward the part of the field as yet unspoiled by the workings.

I saw the grey mare pause, veer, and start to curvet. The cattle, stolidly chewing, shouldered by, udders swinging. From somewhere among them, as suddenly as a puff a smoke from the ground, the old man appeared, leaning on his staff. The mare reared, hoofs flailing. Arthur pulled her aside, and she turned back hard against the shoulder of Bedwyr's black colt, which promptly lashed out, missing Dewdrop by inches. Bedwyr was laughing, but Cei shouted out angrily:

"Make way, you old fool! Can't you see it's the King? And get your damned cattle out of the way. They've no business here now!"

"As good business as yourself, young master, if not better," said the old man tartly. "Getting the good of the land, they are, which you and your likes can do naught but spoil! So it's you should take your horses off and get your hunting done in the Summer Country, and let honest folks be!"

Cei was never one to know when he should curb his anger, or even save his breath. He pushed his horse past Arthur's mare, and thrust his red face down toward the old man. "Are you deaf, old fool, or just stupid? Hunting? We are the King's fighting captains, and this is the King!"

Arthur, half laughing, began: "Oh, leave it, Cei," then had to control the mare sharply once more as the old goblin bobbed up again at his bridle-hand. The dim eyes peered upward.

"King? Nay, but you can't fool me, masters. 'Tis only a bit of a lad. The king's a man grown. Besides, 'tis not yet his time. He'll come at midsummer, wi' the full moon. Seen him, I have, with all his fighting men." A gesture with his staff that set the horses' heads tossing again. "These, fighting captains? Boys, that's all they be! Kings' fighting men have armour, and spears as long as ash trees, and plumes on them like the manes on their horses. Seen them, I have, alone here on a summer's night. Oh, aye, I know the king."

Cei opened his mouth again, but Arthur put up a hand. He spoke as if he and the old man were alone in the field. "A king who came here in the summer? What are you telling us, father? What men were they?"

Something in his manner, perhaps, got through to the other. He looked uncertain. Then he caught sight of me, and pointed. "Told him, I did. Yes. King's man, he said he was, and spoke me soft. A King was coming, he said, who would tend my cows for me, and give me the grazing for them. . . ." He looked about him, as if taking in for the first time the splendid horses and gay trappings, and the assured, laughing looks of the young men. His voice faltered, and he slid off into his mumbling. Arthur looked at me.

"Do you know what he's talking about?"

"A legend of the past, and a troop of ghosts that he says come riding out of their grave in the hill on a summer's midnight. It's my guess that he's telling an old tale of the Celtic rulers here, or the Romans, or maybe both. Nothing to trouble you."

"Not trouble us?" said someone, sounding uneasy; I think it was Lamorak, a brave and high-strung gentleman who watched the stars for signs, and whose horse's trappings rang with charms. "Ghosts, and not trouble us?"

"And he has seen them himself, on this very spot?" said someone else. Then others, murmuring: "Spears and horsehair plumes? Why, they sound like Saxons." And Lamorak again, fingering a piece of coral on his breast: "Ghosts of dead men, killed here and buried under the very hill where you plan to build a stronghold and a safe city? Arthur, did you know?"

There are few men more superstitious than soldiers. They are, after all, the men who live closest to death. All laughter had vanished, quenched, and a shiver went across the bright day, as surely as if a cloud had passed between us and the sun.

Arthur was frowning. He was a soldier, too, but he was also a king and, like the King his father before him, dealt in facts. He said with noticeable briskness: "And what of it? Show me any strong fortress as good as this which has not been defended by brave men, and founded on their blood! Are we children, to fear the ghosts of men who have died here before us, to keep this land? If they linger here at all, they will be on our side, gentlemen!" Then, to the herdsman: "Well? Tell us your story, father. Who was this king?"

The old man hesitated, confused. Then he asked, suddenly: "Did you ever hear of Merlin, the enchanter?"

"Merlin?" This was Bedwyr. "Why, do you not know—?"

He caught my eye, and stopped. No one else spoke. Arthur, without a glance in my direction, asked into the silence: "What of Merlin?"

The filmed eyes went round as if they could see every man clearly, every listening face. Even the horses stood quiet. The herdsman seemed to take courage from the attentive silence. He became suddenly lucid. "There was a king once who set out to build a stronghold. And like the kings of old, who were strong men and merciless, he looked for a hero, to kill and bury beneath the foundations, and hold them firm. So he caught and took Merlin, who was the greatest man in all Britain, and would have killed him; but Merlin called up his dragons, and flew away through the heavens, safely, and called a new king into Britain, who burned the other one to ashes in his tower, and his queen with him. Had you heard that tale, master?"

"Yes."

"And is it true that you are a king, and these your captains?"

"Yes."

"Then ask Merlin. They say he still lives. Ask him what king should fear to have a hero's grave beneath his threshold. Don't you know what he did? He put the great Dragon King himself under the Hanging Stones, that he did, and called it the safe castle of all Britain. Or so they say."

"They say the truth," said Arthur. He looked about him, to see where relief had already overlaid uneasiness. He turned back to the herdsman. "And the strong king who lies with his men within the hill?"

But here he got no further. When pressed, the old man became vague, and then unintelligible. A word could be caught here and there: helmets, plumes, round shields, and small horses, and yet again long spears "like ash trees," and cloaks blowing in the wind "when no wind blows."

I said coolly, to interrupt these new ghostly visions: "You should ask Merlin about that, too, my lord King. I believe I know what he would say."

Arthur smiled. "What, then?"

I turned to the old man. "You told me that the Goddess slew this king and his men, and that they were buried here. You told me, too, that the new young King would have to make his peace with the Goddess, or she would reject him.

Now see what she has done. He knew nothing of this story, but he has come here with her guidance, to build his stronghold on the very spot where the Goddess herself slew and buried a troop of strong fighters and their leader, to be the king-stone of his threshold. And she gave him the sword and the crown. So tell your people this, and tell them that the new King comes, with the Goddess's sanction, to build a fortress of his own, and to protect you and your children, and let your cattle graze in peace."

I heard Lamorak draw in his breath. "By the Goddess herself, you have it, Merlin!"

"Merlin?" You would have thought the old man was hearing the name for the first time. "Aye, that's what he would say . . . and I've heard tell how he took the sword himself from the depths of the water and gave it to the King. . . ." For a few minutes then, as the others crowded close, talking again among themselves, relieved and smiling, he went back to his mumbling. But then, my final, incautious sentence having got through, he came suddenly, and with the utmost clarity of speech, back to the matter of his cows, and the iniquity of kings who interfered with their grazing. Arthur, with one swift, charged glance at me, listened gravely, while the young men held in their laughter, and the last wisp of trouble vanished in mirth. In the end, with gentle courtesy, the King promised to let him keep the grazing for as long as the sweet grass grew on Caer Camel, and when it did no longer, to find a pasture for him elsewhere.

"On my word as High King," he finished.

It was not clear whether, even now, the old herdsman believed him. "Well, call yourself king or not," he said, "for a lad you show some sort of sense. You listen to them that knows, not like some"—this with a malevolent glance in Cei's direction—"that's all noise and wind. Fighting men, indeed! Anyone who knows aught about fighting and the like knows there's no man can fight with an empty belly. You give my cows the grass, and we'll fill your bellies for you."

"I have said you shall have it."

"And when yon builder"—this was myself—"has got Caer Camel spoiled, what land will you give me then?"

Arthur had perhaps not meant to be taken so quickly at his word, but he hesitated only for a moment. "I saw good green stretches down by the river yonder, beyond the village. If I can—"

"That's no manner of good for beasts. Goats, maybe, and geese, but not cattle. That's sour grass, that is, and full of buttercups. That's poison to grazing."

"Indeed? I didn't know that. Where would be good land, then?"

"Over to the badgers' hill. That's yonder." He pointed. "Buttercups!" He cackled. "King or not, young master, however much folks know, there's always someone as knows more."

Arthur said gravely: "That is something else I shall remember. Very well. If I can come by the badgers' hill, it shall be yours."

Then he reined back to let the old man by, and with a salute to me, rode away downhill, with his knights behind him.

Derwen was waiting for me by the foundations of the southwest tower. I walked that way. A plover—the same, perhaps—tilted and side-slipped, calling, in the breezy air. Memory came back, halting me . . .

. . . The Green Chapel above Galava. The same two young faces, Arthur's and Bedwyr's, watching me as I told them stories of battles and far-off places. And across the room, thrown by the lamplight, the shadow of a bird floating—the white owl that lived in the roof—*guenhwyvar,* the white shadow, at whose name I had felt a creeping of the flesh, a moment of troubled prevision which now I could scarcely recall, except for the fear that the name Guenever was somehow a doom for him.

I had felt no such warning today. I did not expect it. I knew just what was left of the power I had once had to warn and to protect. Today I was no more than the old herdsman had called me, a builder.

"No more?" I recalled the pride and awe in the King's eyes as he surveyed the groundwork of the "miracle" I was working for him now. I looked down at the plans in my hand, and felt the familiar, purely human excitement of the maker stir in me. The shadow fled and vanished into sunshine, and I hurried to meet Derwen. At least I still possessed skill enough to build my boy a safe stronghold.

4

Three months later Arthur married Guenever at Caerleon. He had had no chance to see the bride again; indeed, I believe he had had no more speech with her than what slight formalities had passed between them at the crowning. He himself had to go north again early in July, so could spare no time to travel into Cornwall to escort her to Guent. In any case, since he was High King, it was proper that his bride should be brought to him. So he spared Bedwyr for one precious month to ride down to Tintagel and bring the bride to Caerleon.

All through that summer there was sporadic fighting in the north, mostly a business (in that forested hill country) of ambush and running skirmish, but late in July Arthur forced a battle by a crossing on the River Bassas. This he won so decisively as to create a welcome lull that prolonged itself into a truce through harvest-time, and allowed him at length to travel to Caerleon with a quiet mind. For all that, his was a garrison wedding; he could afford to sacrifice no sort of readiness, so the bridal was fitted in, so to speak, among his other preoccupations. The bride seemed to expect it, taking everything as happily as if it had been some great festive occasion in London, and there was as much gaiety and gorgeousness about the ceremony as I have ever seen on such occasions, even though men kept their spears stacked outside the hall of feasting, and their swords laid ready to lift, and the King himself spent every available moment in counsel with his officers, or out in the exercise grounds, or—late into the night sometimes—poring over his maps, with his spies' reports on the table beside him.

I left Caer Camel in the first week of September, and rode across country to Caerleon. The work on the fortress was going well, and could be left to Derwen to carry out. I went with a light heart. All I had been able to find out about the girl was in her favour; she was young, healthy, and of good stock, and it was time Arthur was married and thinking of getting himself sons. I thought about her no further than that.

I was in Caerleon in time to see the wedding party arrive. They did not use the ferry-crossing, but came riding up the road from Glevum, their horses gay with gilded leather and coloured tassels, and the women's litters bright with fresh paint. The younger of the ladies wore mantles of every colour, and had flowers plaited into their horses' manes.

The bride herself disdained a litter; she rode a pretty cream-coloured horse, a gift from Arthur's stables. Bedwyr, in a new cloak of russet, kept close by her bridle-hand, and on his other side rode the Princess Morgan, Arthur's sister. Her mount was as fiery as Guenever's was gentle, but she controlled it without effort. She appeared to be in excellent spirits, as excited, one gathered, over her own approaching marriage as over the other, more important wedding. Nor did she seem to grudge Guenever her central role in the festivities, or the deference she received for her new state. Morgan herself had state and to spare: she had come, in Ygraine's absence, to represent the Queen, and, with the Duke of Cornwall, to place Guenever's hand in that of the High King.

Arthur, being still ignorant of the seriousness of Ygraine's illness, had expected her to come. Bedwyr had a quiet word with him on arrival, and I saw a shadow touch the King's face, then he banished it to greet Guenever. His greeting was public and formal, but with a smile behind it that she answered with a demure dimple. The ladies rustle and cooed and eyed him, and the men looked on indulgently, the older ones approving her youth and freshness, their thoughts already turning toward an heir to the kingdom. The young men watched with the same approval, coloured with simple envy.

Guenever was fifteen now. She was a shade taller than when I had last seen her, and more womanly, but she was still a little creature, with fresh skin and merry eyes, patently delighted with the fortune that had brought her out of Cornwall as bride of the land's darling, Arthur the young King.

She gave the Queen's excuses prettily, with no hint that Ygraine suffered from anything other than a passing ailment, and the King accepted them smoothly, then gave her his arm, and himself escorted her, with Morgan, to the house prepared for them and their ladies. This was the best of the town houses outside the fortress walls, where they could rest and make ready for the marriage.

He came back to his rooms soon after, and while he was still some way down the corridor I could hear him talking busily to Bedwyr. Nor was the talk of weddings and women. He came into the room already shedding his finery, and Ulfin, who knew his ways, was there ready to catch the splendid cloak as it was flung off, and to lift the heavy sword-belt and lay it aside.

Arthur greeted me gaily.

"Well? What do you think? Has she not grown lovely?"

"She is very fair. She will be a match for you."

"And she isn't shy or mim-mouthed, thank God. I've no time for that."

I saw Bedwyr smiling. We both knew he meant it literally. He had no time to trouble with wooing a delicate bride; he wanted marriage and bedding, and then, with the elder nobles satisfied at last, and his own mind free, he could get back to the unfinished business in the north.

So much he was saying now, as he led the way into the anteroom where the map table stood.

"But we'll talk of that in a moment, when the rest of the Council comes. I've sent for them. There was fresh news last night, by courier. Incidentally, Merlin, I told you, didn't I, that I was sending for your young man Gereint, from Olicana? He got here last night—have you seen him yet? No? Well, he'll be coming with the rest. I'm grateful to you; he's a find, and has proved his value already three times over. He brought news from Elmet. . . . But leave that now. Before they come, I want to ask you about Queen Ygraine. Bedwyr tells me there was no question of her coming north for the wedding. Did you know she was ill?"

"I knew at Amesbury that she was ailing, but she would not talk about it, then or later, and she never consulted me. Why, Bedwyr, what's the news of her now?"

"I'm no judge," said Bedwyr, "but she looked gravely ill to me. Even since the crowning I could see a change in her, thin as a ghost, and spending most of her time in bed. She sent a letter to Arthur, and she would have written to you, she said, but it was beyond her strength. I was to give you her greetings, and to thank you for your letters, and your thought of her. She watches for them."

Arthur looked at me. "Did you suspect anything like this when you saw her? Is this a mortal sickness?"

"I would guess so. When I saw her at Amesbury, the seeds of the sickness were already sown. And when I spoke to her again at the crowning, I think she knew herself to be failing. But to guess at how long . . . even had I been her own physician, I doubt if I could have judged of that."

He might have been expected to ask why I had kept my suspicions from him, but the reasons were obvious enough so he wasted no breath on them. He merely nodded, looking troubled. "I cannot . . . You know that I must go north again as soon as this business is done." He spoke as if the wedding were a council, or a battle. "I cannot go down into Cornwall. Ought I to send you?"

"It would be useless. Besides, her own physician is as good a man as you could wish for. I knew him when he was a young student in Pergamum."

"Well," he said, accepting it, and then again, "Well . . ."

But he moved restlessly, fidgeting with the pins that were stuck here and there in the clay map. "The trouble is, one always feels there is something one should be doing. I like to load the dice, not sit waiting for someone else to throw them. Oh, yes, I knew what you will say—that the essence of wisdom is to know when to be doing, and when it is useless even to try. But I sometimes think I shall never be old enough to be wise."

"Perhaps the best thing you can do, both for Queen Ygraine and for yourself, is to get this marriage consummated, and see your sister Morgan crowned Queen of Rheged," I said, and Bedwyr nodded.

"I agree. From the way she spoke about it, I got the impression that she lives only to see both marriage-bonds safely tied."

"That is what she says in her letter to me," said the King. He turned his head. Faintly, from the corridor, came the sound of challenge and answer. "Well, Merlin, I could ill have spared you for a journey into Cornwall. I want to send you north again. Can Derwen be left in charge at Caer Camel?"

"If you wish it, of course. He will do very well, though I should like to be back myself in good time for the spring weather."

"There's no reason why you shouldn't be."

"Is it Morgan's wedding? Or—perhaps I should have been more cautious? Is it Morgause again? . . . I warn you, if it's a trip to Orkney, I shall refuse."

He laughed. He certainly neither looked nor spoke as if Morgause or her bastard had been on his mind. "I wouldn't put you at such risk, either from Morgause or the northern seas. No, it is Morgan. I want you to take her to Rheged."

"That will be a pleasure." It would, indeed. The years I had spent in Rheged, in the Wild Forest which is part of the great tract of land they call the Caledonian Forest, had been the crest of my life; they had been the years when I had guided and taught Arthur as a boy. "I trust I'll be able to see Ector?"

"Why not, once you've seen Morgan safely wedded? I must admit it will ease my mind, as well as the Queen's, to see her settled there in Rheged. It's possible that by spring-time there will be war in the north again."

Put like that, it sounded strange, but in the context of those times it made sense. Those were years of winter weddings; men left home in spring to fight, and it was as well to leave a secure hearth behind them. For a man like Urbgen of

Rheged, no longer young, lord of great domains, and a keen fighting man, it would be foolish to put off the proposed marriage any longer. I said: "Of course I will take her there. How soon?"

"As soon as things are done here, and before winter sets in."

"Will you be there?"

"If I can. We'll speak of this again. I'll give you messages, and of course you will carry my gifts to Urbgen." He signed to Ulfin, who went to the door. The others came in then—his knights and the men of the Council and certain of the petty kings who had come to Caerleon for the wedding. Cador was there, and Gwilim, and others from Powys and Dyfed and Dumnonia, but no one from Elmet, or the north. This was understandable. It was a relief not to see Lot. Among the younger men I saw Gereint. He greeted me with a smiling gesture, but there was no time for talk. The King spoke, and we sat over our counsels until sunset, when food was brought in, and after that the company took their leave, and I with them.

As I made my way back to my own quarters, Bedwyr fell in beside me, and with him Gereint. The two young men seemed to know one another tolerably well. Gereint greeted me warmly. "It was a good day for me," he said, smiling, "when that travelling doctor came to Olicana."

"And, I believe, for Arthur," I replied. "How is the work going in the Gap?"

He told me about it. There was, it seemed, no immediate danger from the east. Arthur had made a clean sweep in Linnuis, and meantime the King of Elmet held watch and ward for him. The road through the Gap had been rebuilt, right through from Olicana to Tribuit, and both the western forts had been brought to readiness. From talking about this he came to Caer Camel, and here Bedwyr joined him in plying me with questions. Presently we came to where our ways parted.

"I leave you here," said Gereint. He glanced back the way we had come, toward the King's apartments. "Behold," he said, "the half was not told me." He spoke as if quoting from something, but it was something I had not heard. "These are great days for us all."

"And will be greater."

Then we said good night, and Bedwyr and I walked on together. The boy with the torch was a few paces ahead. At first we talked, with lowered voices, about Ygraine. He was able to tell me more than he had said in front of Arthur. Her physician, not wishing to commit anything to writing, had entrusted Bedwyr with information for me, but nothing about it was new. The Queen was dying, waiting only—this was from Bedwyr himself—until the two young women, crowned and in due splendour, had taken their places, and thereafter it would be a strange thing (Melchior had said) if she lasted till Christmas. She had sent me a message of goodwill, and a token to be given to Arthur after her death. This latter was a brooch, finely made of gold and blue enamel, with an image of the mother-goddess of the Christians, and the name, MARIA, inscribed around the edge. She had already given jewels both to her daughter Morgan and to Guenever; these had come in the guise of wedding gifts, though Morgan already knew the truth. Guenever, it seemed, did not. The girl had been as dear, and lately almost dearer, to Ygraine than her own daughter, and the Queen had carefully instructed Bedwyr that nothing must spoil the marriage celebrations.

Not that the Queen, said Bedwyr (who obviously held Ygraine in the greatest respect), had any illusions about Arthur's grief for her; she had sacrificed his love for that of Uther and the kingdom's future, and she herself was resigned to death, secure in her faith; but she was aware how much the girl had come to love her.

"And Guenever herself?" I asked at length. "You must have come to know her well on the journey. And you know Arthur, none better. How will they suit? What is she like?"

"Delightful. She's full of life—in her own way as full as he is—and she is clever. She plied me with questions about the wars, and they were not idle ones. She understands what he is doing, and has followed every move he has made. She was head over ears in love with him from the first moment she saw him in Amesbury . . . in fact, it's my belief that she was in love with him even before that, like every other girl in Britain. But she has humour and sense with it; she's no greensick girl with a dream of a crown and a bedding; she knows where her duty will lie. I know that Queen Ygraine planned this and hoped for it. She has been schooling the girl all this while."

"There could hardly be a better preceptress."

"I agree. But Guenever has gentleness, and she is full of laughter, too. I am glad," he finished, simply.

We spoke of Morgan then, and the other marriage.

"Let us hope it suits as well," I said. "It's certainly what Arthur wants. And Morgan? She seems willing, even happy about it."

"Oh, yes," he said, and then, with a smiling shrug, "you'd think it was a love-match, and that all the business with Lot had never been. You always say, Merlin, that you know nothing of women, and can't even guess at what moves them. Well, no more can I, and I'm not a born hermit, like you. I've known plenty, and now I've spent a month or so in daily attendance on them—and I still don't begin to understand them. They crave for marriage, which for them is a kind of slavery—and dangerous at that. You could understand it with those who have nothing of their own; but here's Morgan: she has wealth and position, and the freedom they give her, and she has the protection of the High King. Yet she would have gone to Lot, whose reputation you know, and now goes, eagerly, to Urbgen of Rheged, who is more than three times her age, and whom she has hardly seen. Why?"

"I suspect because of Morgause."

He shot me a look. "That's possible. I spoke to Guenever about it. She says that since news came of Morgause's latest lying-in, and her letters about the state she keeps—"

"In Orkney?"

"She says so. It does seem true that she rules the kingdom. Who else? Lot has been with Arthur. . . . Well, Guenever told me that lately Morgan's temper had been growing sharp, and she had begun to speak of Morgause with hatred. Also, she had begun to practise what the Queen called her 'dark arts' again. Guenever seems afraid of them." He hesitated. "They speak of it as magic, Merlin, but it is nothing like your power. It is something smoky, in a closed room."

"If Morgause taught her, then it must be dark indeed. Well, so the sooner Morgan is a queen in Rheged, with a family of her own, the better. And what of yourself, Bedwyr? Have you had thoughts of marriage?"

"None, yet," he said cheerfully. "I have no time."

On which we laughed, and went our ways.

So the next day, with a fine sun blazing, and all the pomp and music and revelry that a joyous crowd could conjure up, Arthur married Guenever. And after the feasting, when torches had burned low, and men and women had eaten and laughed and drunk deep, the bride was led away; and later, escorted by his companion knights, the bridegroom went to her.

That night I dreamed a dream. It was brief and cloudy, a glimmer only of something that might be true vision. There were curtains drawn and blowing, and a place full of cold shadows, and a woman lying in bed. I could not see her clearly, or tell who she was. I thought at first that it was Ygraine, then, with a shift of the blowing light, it might have been Guenever. And she lay as if she were dead, or as if she were sleeping soundly after a night of love.

5

So once again I headed northward, keeping this time to the west road all the way to Luguvallium. It was truly a wedding journey. The good weather held all through that month, the lovely September month of gold that is best for travellers, since Hermes, the god of going, claims it for his own.

His hand was over us through all that journey. The road, Arthur's main way up the west, was repaired and sound, and even on the moors the land was dry, so that we did not need to time our journey to seek for stopping-places to suit the women. If, at sunset, no town or village was near, we made camp where we halted, and ate by some stream with trees for shelter, while plovers called in the dusk, and the herons flapped overhead back from their fishing-grounds. For me, it would have been an idyllic journey, but for two things. The first was the memory of my last journey northward. Like all sensible men, I had put regret out of my mind, or thought I had; but when one night someone petitioned me to sing, and my servant brought the harp to me, it seemed suddenly as if I only had to look up from the strings to see them coming into the firelight, Beltane the goldsmith, smiling, with Ninian behind him. And after that the boy was there nightly, in memory or in dreams, and with him the most poignant of all sorrows, the regret for what might have been, and was gone for ever. It was more than simple grief for a disciple lost who might have done my work for me after I was gone. There was with it a wounding self-contempt for the helpless way I had let him go. Surely I should have known, in that moment of stinging, involuntary protest at Cor Bridge, why the protest was made? The truth was that the loss of the boy went far deeper than the failure to win an heir and a disciple: his loss was the very symbol of my own. Because I was no longer Merlin, Ninian had died.

The second wasp in the honey of that journey was Morgan herself.

I had never known her well. She had been born at Tintagel, and had grown up there through the years when I had lived in hiding in Rheged, watching over Arthur's boyhood. Since then I had only seen her twice, at her brother's crowning and at his marriage, and had barely spoken with her on either occasion.

She resembled her brother in that she was tall for her age and dark-haired, with the dark eyes that came, I think, from the Spanish blood brought by the Emperor Maximus into the family of the Ambrosii; but in feature she resembled Ygraine, where Arthur favoured Uther. Her skin was pale, and she was as quiet as Arthur was ebullient. For all this I could sense in her something of the same kind of force, a power controlled, fire banked under her cool ash. There was something, too, of the subtlety that Morgause, her half-sister, showed in such abundance, and Arthur not at all. But this is mostly a woman's quality; they all have it in some degree or another; it is too often their only weapon and their only shield.

Morgan refused to use the litter provided for her, and rode beside me for some part of each day. I suppose that when she was with the women, or among the younger men, the talk must have turned on the coming wedding, and the times to come; but when she was by me she spoke mostly of the past. Again and again she led me to talk of those of my deeds which had passed into legend, the story of the dragons at Dinas Emrys, the raising of the king-stone at Killare, the lifting of the sword of Macsen from the stone. I answered her questions willingly enough, keeping to the facts of the stories, and (remembering what I had learned of Morgan from her mother and Bedwyr) trying to convey to her something of what "magic" meant. As these girls see it, it is an affair of philters, and whispers in darkened rooms, spells to bind a man's heart, or bring the vision of a lover on Midsummer Eve. Their main concern, understandably, is the aphrodisian lore—how to bring, or to prevent, pregnancy, charms for safety in childbirth, predictions about the sex of a child. These matters, to do her justice, Morgan never broached with me; it was to be expected that she was versed in them already. Nor did she seem interested, as the young Morgause had been, in medicine and the healing arts. Her questions turned all on the greater power, and mainly as it had touched Arthur. All that had passed from Uther's first wooing of her mother, and Arthur's conception, to the raising of the great sword of Macsen, she was avid to know. I answered her civilly, and fully enough; she was, I reckoned, entitled to the facts, and (since she was going to be Queen of Rheged, and would almost certainly outlive her husband, and live to guide the future king of that powerful province) I tried to show her what Arthur's aims were for the settled times after the war, and to imbue her with the same ambitions.

It was hard to tell what sort of success I had. After a time I noticed that her talk turned more and more frequently to the hows and wherefores of the power I had owned. I put her questions aside, but she persisted, at length even suggesting, with an assurance as cool as Arthur's own, that I should show some demonstration of it, for all the world as if I were an old wife mixing spells and simples over the fire, or a soothsayer crystal-gazing on market day. At this last impertinence my answer was, I imagine, too cold for her to stomach. Soon afterwards she drew rein and let her palfrey lag back, and thereafter rode the rest of the way with the young people.

Like her sister, Morgan was rarely content with the company of women. Her most constant companion was one Accolon, a splendidly dressed, florid young man with a loud laugh and a high colour. She never let herself be alone with him more than was decent, though he made no secret of his feelings; he followed her everywhere with his eyes, and, whenever he could, touched her hand, or brought his horse sidling so close to her that his thigh brushed hers, and their horses' manes tangled together. She never seemed to notice, and never once, that I could see, gave him other than the same cool looks and answers that she gave to everyone. I had, of course, a duty to bring her unharmed and virgin (if virgin she still was) to Urbgen's bed, but I could have no present fears for her honour. A lover would have been hard put to it to come to her on that journey, even if she had beckoned him. Most nights when we camped, Morgan was attended by all her ladies to her pavilion, which was shared by her two elderly waiting women, as well as her younger companions. She gave no hint that she wished it otherwise. She acted and spoke like any royal bride on her way to a welcome bride-bed, and if Accolon's handsome face and eager courtship moved her she made no sign.

We halted for the last time just short of the limits that are governed by Caer-luel, as the British call Luguvallium. Here we rested the horses, while the servants busied themselves over the burnishing of the harness and the washing of the painted litters, and—among the women—some furbishing of clothes and hair and complexions. Then the cavalcade reformed, and we went on to meet the welcoming party, which met us well beyond the city limits.

It was headed by King Urbgen himself, on a splendid horse which had been a gift from Arthur, a bay stallion decked with crimson and cloth of gold. Beside it a servant led a white mare, bridled with silver and tasselled with blue, for the princess. Urbgen was as splendid as his steed, a vigorous man, broad-chested and strong-armed, and as active as any warrior half his age. He had been a sandy-coloured man, and now his hair and beard, as is the way with sand-fair men, had gone quite white, thick and fine. His face had been weathered by the summers of warfare and the winters of riding his cold marches. I knew him for a strong man, a stout ally, and a clever ruler.

He greeted me as civilly as if I had been the High King himself, and then I presented Morgan. She had dressed herself in primrose and white, and plaited the long dark hair with gold. She gave him a hand, a deep curtsy, and a cool cheek to kiss, then mounted the white mare and rode on beside him, meeting the stares of his retinue, and his own assessing looks, with unruffled composure. I saw Accolon drop back with a hot, sulky look, as Urbgen's party closed round the three of us, and we rode on at a gentle pace to the meeting of the three rivers where Luguvallium lay among the reddening trees of autumn.

The journey had been a good one, but its end was bad indeed, fulfilling the worst of my fears. Morgause came to the wedding.

Three days before the ceremony a messenger came galloping with the news that a ship had been sighted in the estuary, with the black sail and the badge of the Orcadians. King Urbgen rode to meet it at the harbour. I sent my own servant for news, and he was back with it, hot-foot, before the Orkney party could well have disembarked. King Lot was not there, he told me, but Queen Morgause had come, and in some state. I sent him south to Arthur with a warning; it would not be hard for him to find some excuse not to be present. Mercifully, I myself had no need to look far for a similar excuse: I had already arranged, at Urbgen's own request some days before, to ride out and inspect the signal stations along the estuary shore. With some dispatch, and perhaps a slight lack of dignity, I was gone from the city before Morgause's party arrived, nor did I return until the very eve of the wedding. Later I heard that Morgan, too, had avoided meeting her sister, but then it had hardly been expected of a bride so deep in preparations for a royal wedding.

So I was there to see the sisters meet, at the very gate of the church where, with the Christian rites, Morgan was to be married. Each of them, queen and princess, was splendidly dressed and magnificently attended. They met, spoke, and embraced, with smiles as pretty as pictures, and as fixedly painted on their mouths. Morgan, I thought, won the encounter, since she was dressed for her wedding, and shone as the bright center-piece to the feast-day. Her gown was magnificent, with its strain of purple sewn with silver. She wore a crown on her dark hair, and among the magnificent jewels that Urbgen had given her, I recognized some that Uther had given Ygraine in the early days of their passion. Her slim body was erect under the weight of her rich robes, her face pale and composed and very beautiful. To me she recalled the young Ygraine, full of power and grace. I hoped, with fervour, that the reports of the sisters' dislike of one another were true, and that Morgause would not manage to ingratiate herself, now that her sister stood on the threshold of position and power. But I was uneasy; I could see no other reason for the witch to have come to see her sister's triumph and be outshone by her both in consequence and beauty.

Nothing could take from Morgause the rose-gold beauty which, with her maturity, was, if anything, richer than ever. But it was whispered that she was once again with child, and she had brought with her, besides, another child, a boy. This was an infant, still his nurse's arms. Lot's son; not the one for whom, half in hope, half in apprehension, I was looking.

Morgause had seen me looking. She smiled that little smile of hers as she made her reverence, then swept on into the church with her train. I, as Arthur's vicar in this, waited to present the bride. Obedient to my message, the High King was busying himself elsewhere.

Any hopes I had had of being able to avoid Morgause further were dashed at the wedding feast. She and I, as the two princes nearest to the bride, were placed side by side at the high table. The hall was the same one where Uther had held the victory feast that led to his death. In a room of this same castle she had lain with Arthur to conceive the child Mordred, and the next morning, in a bitter clash of wills, I had destroyed her hopes, and driven her away from Arthur's side. That, as far as she knew, had been our last encounter. She was still in ignorance—or so I hoped—of my journey to Dunpeldyr, and my vigil there.

I saw her watching me sideways, under the long white lids. I wondered suddenly, with misgiving, if she could be aware of my lack of defense against her now. Last time we had met she had tried her witch's tricks on me, and I had felt their potency, closing on the mind like a limed web. But she could no more have harmed me then than a she-spider could have hoped to trap a falcon. I had turned her spells back on herself, bearing her fury down by the sheer authority of power. That, now, had left me. It was possible that she could gauge my weakness. I could not tell. I had never underrated Morgause, and would not now.

I spoke with smooth civility. "You have a fine son, Morgause. What is he called?"

"Gawain."

"He has a strong look of his father."

Her lids drooped. "Both my sons," she said gently, "have a strong look of their father."

"Both?"

"Come, Merlin, where is your art? Did you believe the dreadful news when you heard it? You must have known it was not true."

"I knew it was not true that Arthur had ordered the killing, in spite of the calumny you laid on him."

"I?" The lovely eyes were wide and innocent.

"Yes, you. The massacre may have been Lot's doing, the hot fool, and it was certainly Lot's men who threw the babies into the boat and sent them out with the tide. But who provoked him to it? It was your plan from the first, was it not, even to the murder of that poor child in the cradle? And it was not Lot who killed Macha, and lifted the other child out of the blood and carried him into hiding." I echoed her own half-mocking tone. "Come, Morgause, where is your art? You should know better than to play the innocent with me."

At the mention of Macha's name I saw fear, like a green spark, leap in her eyes, but she gave no other sign. She sat still and straight, one hand curved round the stem of her goblet, turning it gently, so that the gold burned in the hot torchlight. I could see the pulse beating fast in the hollow of her throat.

It was a sour satisfaction, at best. I had been right. Mordred was alive, hidden, I guessed, somewhere in the cluster of islands called the Orkneys, where Morgause's writ ran, and where I, without the Sight, had no power to find him. Or, I reminded myself, the mandate to kill him if found.

"You saw?" Her voice was low.

"Of course I saw. When could you hide things from me? You must know that everything is quite clear to me, and also—let me remind you—to the High King."

She sat still, and apparently composed, except for that rapid beat under the creamy flesh. I wondered if I had managed to convince her that I was still someone to be feared. It had not occurred to her that Lind might have come to me; and why should she ever remember Beltane? The necklet he had made for her jumped and sparkled on her throat. She swallowed, and said, in a thin voice that hardly carried through the hubbub of the hall: "Then you will know that, even though I saved him from Lot, I don't know where he is. Perhaps you will tell me?"

"Do you expect me to believe that?"

"You must believe it, because it is true. I don't know where he is." She turned her head, looking full at me. "Do you?"

I made no reply. I merely smiled, picked up my goblet, and drank from it. But, without looking at her, I sensed in her a sudden relaxation, and wondered, with a chill creeping of the skin, if I had made a mistake.

"Even if I knew," she said, "how could I have him by me, and he as like to *his* father as one drop of wine to another?" She drank, set the goblet down, then sat back in her chair, folding her hands over her gown so that the thickening of her belly showed. She smiled at me, malice and hatred with no trace of fear. "Prophesy about this, then, Merlin the enchanter, if you won't about the other. Will this be another son to take the place of the one I lost?"

"I have no doubt of it," I said shortly, and she laughed aloud.

"I'm glad to hear it. I have no use for girls." Her eyes went to the bride, sitting composed and straight beside Urbgen. He had drunk a good deal, and the red stood in his cheeks, but he kept his dignity, even though his eyes caressed his bride, and he leaned close to her chair. Morgause watched, then said with contempt: "So my little sister got her king in the end. A kingdom, yes, and a fine city and wide lands. But an old man, rising fifty, with sons already . . ." Her hand smoothed the front of her gown. "Lot may be a hot fool, as you termed him, but he is a man."

It was bait, but I did not rise to it. I said: "Where is he, that he could not come to the wedding?"

To my surprise she answered quite normally, apparently abandoning the malicious game of chess. Lot, it seemed, had gone east again into Northumbria with Urien, his sister's husband, and was busying himself there overseeing the extension to the Black Dyke. I have written of this before. It runs inland from the northern sea, and provides some sort of defense against incursions along the northeastern seaboard. Morgause spoke of it with knowledge, and in spite of myself I was interested, and in the talk that followed the atmosphere lightened;

and then someone asked me a question about Arthur's wedding and the new young Queen, and Morgause laughed and said, quite naturally:

"What's the use of asking Merlin? He may know everything in the world, but ask him to describe a bridal, and I'll wager he doesn't even know the colour of the girl's hair or her gown!"

Then talk around us became general, with a lot of laughter, and speeches were made, and pledges given, and I must have drunk far more than I was accustomed to, because I well remembered how the torchlight beat and swelled, bright and dark alternately, while talk and laughter surged and broke in gusts, and with it the woman's scent, a thick sweetness like honeysuckle, catching and trapping the sense as a limed twig holds a bee. The fumes of wine rose through it. A gold jug tilted, and my goblet brimmed again. Someone said, smiling, "Drink, my lord." There was a taste of apricots in my mouth, sweet and sharp; the skin had a texture like the fur of a bee, or a wasp dying in sunlight on a garden wall . . . And all the while eyes watching me, in excitement and wary hope, then in contempt and in triumph. . . . Then servants were beside me, helping me from my chair, and I saw that the bride had gone already, and King Urbgen, impatience barely held on a tight rein, was watching the door for the sign that it was time to follow her to bed.

The chair beside me was empty. Round my own the servants crowded smiling, to help me back to my rooms.

6

Next morning I had a headache as bad as anything that the aftermath of magic used to inflict on me. I kept to my rooms all day. On the day following I took leave of Urbgen and his queen. We had sat through a series of formal discussions before Morgause's arrival, and now I could leave the city—how thankfully, it may be guessed—and make my way southwest through the Wild Forest, at the heart of which stood Count Ector's castle of Galava. I took no leave of Morgause.

It was good to be out again, and this time with two companions only. Morgan's escort had been formed mainly of her own people from Cornwall, who had remained with her in Luguvallium. The two men who rode with me were deputed into my service by Urbgen; they would go with me as far as Galava, then return. It was vain for me to protest that I would rather go alone, and would be safe; King Urbgen merely repeated, smiling, that not even my magic would avail against wolves, or autumn fogs, or the sudden onslaught of early snow, which in that mountainous country can trap the traveller very quickly among the steep valley-passes, and bring him to his death. His words were a reminder to me that, armed as I was now with only the reputation of past power, and not the thing itself, I was as subject to outrage from thieves and desperate men as any solitary traveller in that wild country; so I accepted the escort with thanks, and in so doing I suppose I saved my life.

We rode out over the bridge, and along the pleasant green valley where the river winds, bordered with alder and willow. Though my headache had gone, and I felt well enough, a certain lassitude still hung about me, and I breathed the sweet, familiar air, full of pine scents and bracken scents, with gratitude.

One small incident I remember. As we left the city gates, and crossed the river bridge, I heard a shrill cry, which at first I took to be a bird's, one of the gulls that wheeled about the refuse on the river's banks. Then a movement caught my eye, and I glanced down to see a woman, carrying a child, walking on the shingle near the water's edge below the bridge. The child was crying, and she hushed it. She saw me, and stood quite still, staring upward. I recognized Morgause's nurse. Then my horse clattered off the bridge, and the willows hid woman and child from view.

I thought nothing of the incident, and in a short while had forgotten it. We rode on, through villages and farms rich in grazing cattle. The willows were golden, and the hazel groves a-scamper with squirrels. Late swallows gathered along the rooftops, and as we approached that nest of mountains and lakes that marks the southern limits of the great forest, the lower hills flamed in the sun with ripe bracken, rusty-gold between the rocks. Elsewhere the forest, scattered oaks and pines, was gold and dark. Soon we came to the edge of the Wild Forest itself, where the trees crowd so thickly in the valleys that they shut out the sun. Before long we crossed the track that led up to the Green Chapel. I would have liked to revisit the place, but this would have added hours to the journey, and besides, the visit could be made more easily from Galava. So we held on our way, staying with the road as far as Petrianae.

Today this hardly deserves the name of town, though in Roman times it was a prosperous market center. There is still a market, where a few cattle and sheep and goods exchange hands, but Petrianae itself is a poor cluster of daub-and-wattle huts, its only shrine a mere shell of stonework holding a ruinous altar to Mars, in his person of the local god Cocidius. I saw no offering there, except, on the mossed step, a leathern sling, such as shepherds use, and a pile of sling-stones. I wondered what escape, from wolf or wild man, the shepherd was giving thanks for.

Beyond Petrianae, we left the road and took to the hill tracks, which my escort knew well. We travelled at ease, enjoying the warmth of the late autumn sun. As we climbed higher the warmth still lingered, and the air was soft, but with a tingle to it that meant the first frosts were not far away.

We stopped to rest our horses in one high, lonely corrie where a small tarn lay cupped in stony turf, and here we came across a shepherd, one of those hardly hillmen who lodge all summer out on the fell tops with the little blue-fleeced sheep of Rheged. Wars and battles may move and clash below them, but they look up, rather than down, for danger, and at the first onslaught of winter take to the caves, faring thinly on black bread and raisins, and meal cakes made on a turf fire. They drive their flocks for safety into pens built between the rocky outcrops on the hillsides. Sometimes they do not hear another man's voice from lamb-time to clipping, and then on to autumn's end.

This lad was so little used to talking that he found speech hard, and what he did say came in an accent so thick that even the troopers, who were local men, could make nothing of it, and I, who have the gift of tongues, was hard put to it to understand him. He had, it seemed, had speech with the Old Ones, and was ready enough to pass on his news. It was negative, and none the worse for that. Arthur had stayed in Caerleon for almost a month after his wedding, then had ridden with his knights up through the Pennine Gap, heading apparently for Olicana and the Plain of York, where he would meet with the King of Elmet. This was hardly news to me, but at least it was confirmation that there had been no new war-move during the late autumn's peace. The shepherd had saved his best titbit till last. The High King (he called him "young Emrys," with such a mixture of pride and familiarity that I guessed that Arthur's path must have crossed his in times past) had left his queen with child. At this the troopers were openly skeptical; maybe he had, was their verdict, but how, in a scant month, could anyone know for sure? I, when appealed to, was more credulous. As I have said, the Old Ones have ways of knowing that cannot be understood, but deserve to be respected. If the lad had heard this through them. . . .?

He had. That was all he knew. Young Emrys had gone into Elmet, and the lass he'd wedded was with child. The word he used was "yeaning," at which the troopers were disposed to be merry, but I thanked him and gave him a coin, and he turned back to his sheep well satisfied, with only a lingering look at me, half recognizing, I suppose, the hermit of the Green Chapel.

That night we were still well away from the roads, or any hope of a lodging, so when the dusk came down early and dim with mist, we made our camp under tall pines at the forest's edge, and the men cooked supper. I had been drinking water on the journey, as I like to do in mountain country where it is pure and good, but in celebration of the shepherd's news I broke open a new flask of the wine I had been supplied with from Urbgen's cellars. I planned to share this with my companions, but they refused, preferring their own thin ration-wine, which tasted of the skins they carried it in. So I ate and drank alone, and lay down to sleep.

I cannot write of what happened next. The Old Ones know the story, and it is possible that somewhere else some other man has set it down, but I remember it only dimly, as if I were watching a vision in a dark and smoking glass.

But it was no vision; they stay with me more vividly, even, than memory. This was a kind of madness that took me, brought on, as I now know, by some drug in the wine I had taken. Twice before, when Morgause and I had come face to face, she had tried her witch's tricks on me, but her novice's magic had glanced off me like a child's pebble off a rock. But this last time . . . I was to recall how, at the wedding feast, the light thickened and beat around me, while the smell of honeysuckle loaded memory with treachery, and the taste of apricots brought back murder. And how I, who am frugal with food and wine, was carried drunken to bed. I remembered, too, the voice saying, "Drink, my lord," and the green, watching eyes. She must have tried her wiles again, and found that now her magic was strong enough to trap me in its sticky threads. It may be that the seeds of the madness were sown then, at the wedding feast, and left to develop later, when I was far enough away for there to be no blame cast on her. Her servant had been there at the river bridge to see me safely out of the city. Later, the witch had implemented the drug with some other poison, slipped into one of the flasks I carried. There she had been lucky. If I had not heard the news of Guenever's pregnancy, I might never have broached the poisoned flask. As it was, we were well away from Luguvallium when I drank the poison. If the men with me had shared it, so much the worse for them. Morgause would have swept a hundred such aside, to harm Merlin her enemy. There was no need to look further for her motive in coming to her sister's marriage.

Whatever the poison, my frugal ways cheated her of my death. What happened after I had drunk and lain down I can only piece together from what I have since been told, and from the whirling fragments of memory.

It seems that the troopers, alarmed in the night by my groans, hurried to my bed-place, where they were horrified to find me obviously sick and in great pain, twisting on the ground, and moaning, apparently too far gone to be sensible. They did what they could, which was not much, but their rough help saved me as nothing could have done had I been alone. They made me vomit, then brought their own blankets to augment mine, and wrapped me up warmly and made up the fire. Then one of them stayed beside me while the other set off down the valley to find help or lodging. He was to send help back to us, and a guide, then ride on himself down to Galava with the news.

When he had gone the other fellow did what the could, and after an hour or two I sank into a sort of sleep. He hardly liked the look of it, but when at last he dared leave me, and took a step or two away among the trees to relieve himself, I neither moved nor made a sound, so he decided to take the chance to fetch water from the brook. This was a scant twenty paces off, downhill over silent mosses. Once there, he bethought himself of the fire, which had burned low again, so he crossed the brook and went a bit farther—thirty paces, no more, he swore it—to gather more wood. There was plenty lying about, and he was gone only a few minutes. When he got back to the camping-place I had vanished, and, scour the place as he might, he could find no trace of me. It was no blame to him that after an hour or so spent wandering and calling through the echoing darkness of the great forest, he took horse and galloped after his fellow. Merlin the enchanter had too many strange vanishings to his name to leave the simple trooper in any doubt as to what had happened.

The enchanter had disappeared, and all they could do was make their report, and wait for his return.

It was a long dream. I remember nothing about the beginning of it, but I suppose that, buoyed up by some kind of delirious strength, I crept from my bed-place and wandered off across the deep mosses of the forest, then lay, perhaps, where I fell, deep in some ditch or thicket where the trooper could not find me. I must have recovered in time to take shelter from the weather, and of course I must have found food, and possibly even made fire, during the weeks of storm that followed, but of this I remember nothing. All I can recall now is a series of pictures, a kind of bright and silent dream through which I moved like a spirit, weightless and bodiless, borne up by the air as a heavy body is borne up by water. The pictures, though vivid, are diminished into an emotionless distance, as if I were looking on at a world that hardly concerns me. So, I sometimes imagine, must the bodiless dead watch over the world they have left.

So I drifted, deep in the autumn forest, unheeded as a wraith of the forest mist. Straining back now in memory, I see it still. Deep aisles of beech, thick with mast, where the wild boar rooted, and the badger dug for food, and the stags clashed and wrestled, roaring, with never a glance at me. Wolves, too; the way through those high woods is known as the Wolf Road, but though I would have been easy meat they had had a good summer, and let me be. Then, with the first real chill of winter, came the hoar glitter of icy mornings, with the reeds standing stiff and black out of curded ice, and the forest deserted, badger in lair and deer down in the valley-bottom, and the wild geese gone and the skies empty.

Then the snow. A brief vision this, of the silent, whirling air, warm after the frost; of the forest receding into mist, into dimness, breaking into whirling flakes of white and grey, and then a blinding, silent cold. . . .

A cave, with cave-smells, and turf burning, and the taste of cordial, and voices, gruffly uncouth in the harsh tongue of the Old Ones, speaking just out of hearing. The reek of badly cured wolfskins, the hot itch of verminous wrappings, and, once, a nightmare of bound limbs and a weight holding me down . . .

There is a long gap of darkness here, but afterwards sunlight, new green, the first bird-song, and a vision, sharp as a child's first sight of the spring, of a bank of celandines, glossy as licked gold. And life stirring again in the forest; the thin foxes padding out, the earth heaving in the badger-setts, stags trotting by, unarmed and gentle, and the wild boar again, out foraging. And an absurd, dim dream of finding a pigling still with the stripes and long silky hair of babyhood, that hobbled about on a broken leg, deserted by its kind.

Then suddenly, one grey dawn, the sound of horses galloping, filling the forest, and the clash of swords and the whirl of bright axes, the yelling and the screams of wounded beasts and men, and, like a flashing, intermittent dream of violence, a day-long storm of fighting that ended with a groaning quiet and the smell of blood and crushed bracken.

Silence then, and the scent of apple trees, and the nightmare sense of grief that comes when a man wakes again to feel a loss he has forgotten in sleep.

7

"Merlin!" said Arthur in my ear. *"Merlin!"*

I opened my eyes. I was lying in bed in a room which seemed to be built high up. The bright sunlight of early morning poured in, falling on dressed stone walls, with a curve in them that told of a tower. At the level of the sill I caught a glimpse of treetops moving against cloud. The air eddied, and was cool, but within the room a brazier burned, and I was snug in blankets, and good linen fragrant with cedarwood. Some sort of herb had been thrown into the charcoal of the brazier; the thin smoke smelled clean and resinous. There were no hangings on the walls, but thick slate-grey sheepskins lay on the floor, and there was a plain cross of olive-wood hanging on the wall facing the bed. A Christian household, and, by the appointments, a wealthy one. Beside the bed, on a stand of gilded wood, stood a jug and goblet of Samian ware, and a bowl of beaten silver. There was a cross-legged stool nearby, where a servant must have been sitting to watch me; now he was standing, backed up against the wall, with his eyes not on me, but on the King.

Arthur let out a long breath, and some of the colour came back into his face. He looked as I had never seen him look before. His eyes were shadowed with fatigue, and the flesh had fallen in below his cheekbones. The last of his youth had vanished; here was a hard-living man, sustained by a will that daily pushed himself and his followers to their very limits and beyond.

He was kneeling beside the bed. As I moved my eyes to look at him, his hand fell across my wrist in a quick grip. I could feel the calluses on his palm.

"Merlin? Do you know me? Can you speak?"

I tried to form a word, but could not. My lips were cracked and dry. My mind felt clear enough, but my body would not obey me. The King's arm came round me, lifting me, and at a sign from him the servant came forward and filled the goblet. Arthur took it from him and held it to my mouth. The stuff was a cordial, sweet and strong. He took a napkin from the man, wiped my lips with it, and lowered me back against the pillows.

I smiled at him. It must have shown as little more than a faint movement of muscles. I tried his name, "Emrys." I could hear no sound. I fancy that it came as a breath, no more.

His hand came down again over mine. "Don't try to speak. I was wrong to make you. You are alive, that's all that matters. Rest now."

My eye, wandering, fell on something beyond him: my harp, set on a chair beside the wall. I said, still without a thread of sound: "You found my harp," and relief and joy went through me, as if, in some way, all must now be well.

He followed my glance. "Yes, we found it. It's unharmed. Rest now, my dear. All is well. All is well, indeed. . . ."

I tried his name again, and failing, slid back into darkness. Faintly, like movements from the Otherworld of dream, I remember swift commands, softly spoken, the servants hurrying, slippered footsteps and the rustle of women's garments, cool hands, soft voices. Then the comfort of oblivion.

When I awoke again, it was to full consciousness, as if from a long, refreshing sleep. My brain was clear, my body very weak, but my own. I was conscious, gratefully, of hunger. I moved my head experimentally, then my hands. They felt stiff and heavy, but they belonged to me. Wherever I had been wandering, I had come back to my body. I had quitted the world of dream.

I could see, from the change in the light, that it was evening. A servant—a different one—waited near the door. But one thing was the same: Arthur was still there. He had pulled the stool forward, and was sitting by the bed. He turned his head and saw me watching him, and his face changed. He made a quick movement forward, and his hand came down on mine again, a gentle touch like a doctor's, feeling for the pulse in the wrist.

"By God," he said, "you frightened us! What happened? No, no, forget that. Later you'll tell us all you can remember . . . Now it's enough to know that you are safe, and living. You look better. How do you feel?"

"I have been dreaming." My voice was not my own; it seemed to come from somewhere else, away in the air, almost outside my control. It was as feeble as the pigling's pipe when I mended its broken leg. "I have been ill, I think."

"Ill?" He gave a crack of laughter that held nothing of mirth. "You have been stark crazy, my dear king's prophet. I thought you were gone clean out of your wits, and that we should never have you back with us again."

"It must have been a fever of a kind. I hardly remember . . ." I knitted my brows, thinking back. "Yes. I was travelling to Galava with two of Urbgen's men. We made camp up near the Wolf Road, and . . . Where am I now?"

"Galava itself. This is Ector's castle. You're home."

It had been Arthur's home, rather than mine; for reasons of secrecy I had never lived in the castle myself, but had spent the hidden years in the forest, up at the Green Chapel. But as I turned my head and caught the familiar scents of pine forest and lake water, and the smell of the rich tilled soil of Drusilla's garden below the tower, reassurance came, like the sight of a known light through the fog.

"The battle I saw," I said. "Was that real, or did I imagine it?"

"Oh, that was real enough. But don't try to talk about it yet. Take it from me, all is well. Now, you should rest again. How do you feel?"

"Hungry."

This, of course, started up a new bustling. Servants brought broth, and bread, and more cordials, and the Countess Drusilla herself helped me to eat, and then once more disposed me for welcome and dreamless sleep.

Morning again, and the bright, clean light to which I had first woken. I felt weak still, but in command of myself. It seemed that the King had given orders that he was to be fetched as soon as I woke, but this I would not allow until I had been bathed and shaved and had eaten.

When he came at length he looked quite different. The strained look about his eyes had lessened, and there was colour in his face under the brown of weather. Something of his own especial quality had come back, too; the young strength that men could drink from, as at a spring, and be strengthened themselves.

I had to reassure him about my own recovery, before he would let me talk, but he eventually settled down to give me news. "The last I heard," I told him, "was that you had gone into Elmet. . . . But that's past history now, it seems. I gather that the truce was broken? What was the battle I saw? It must have been up these parts, in the Caledonian Forest? Who was involved?"

He eyed me, I thought strangely, but answered readily enough. "Urbgen called me in. The enemy broke across country into Strathclyde, and Caw didn't manage to hold them. They would have forced their way down through the forest to the road. I came up with them, and broke them up and drove them back. The remnants fled south. I should have followed straight away, but then we found you, and I had to stay. . . . How could I leave again, till I knew you were home, and cared for?"

"So I really did see the fighting? I wondered if it was part of the dream."

"You must have seen it all. We fought through the forest, along the river there. You know what it's like, good open ground with thin woodland, birch and alder, just the place for a surprise with fast cavalry. We had the hill at our backs, and took them as they reached the ford. The river was full; easy for horsemen, but for foot-soldiers a trap. . . . Afterwards, when we came back from the first pursuit, people came running to tell me that you were there. You'd been found wandering among the dead and wounded and giving directions to the doctors. . . . Nobody recognized you at first, but then the whispers started that Merlin's ghost was there." A wry little smile. "I gather that the ghost's advice was good, as often as not. But of course the whispers set up a scare, and some fools started throwing stones to drive you away. It was one of the orderlies, a man called Paulus, who recognized you, and put a stop to the ghost stories. He followed you back to where you were living, and then sent to me."

"Paulus. Yes, of course. A good man. I've worked with him often. And where was I living?"

"In a ruined turret, with an ancient orchard round it. You don't remember that?"

"No. But something is coming back. A turret, yes, ruinous, all ivy and owls. And apple trees?"

"Yes. It was little more than a pile of stones, with bracken for bedding, and piles of apples rotting, and a store of nuts, and rags hung to dry on the apple boughs." He paused to clear something from his throat. "They thought at first you were one of those wild hermits, and indeed, when I first saw you myself . . ." His smile twisted. "You looked the part better than you ever looked it at the Green Chapel."

"I can imagine that." And so I could. My beard, before they had shaved me, had grown long and grey, and my hands, lying weakly on the bright blankets, looked thin and old, bones held together with a net of knotted veins.

"So we brought you here. I had to go south again soon after. We caught them up at Caer Guinnion, and fought a bloody engagement there. All went well, but then a messenger came down from Galava with more news of you. When we found you and brought you here, you were strong enough on your feet, but crazy; you didn't know anyone, and you talked about things that made no kind of sense; but once here, and in the women's care, you relapsed into sleep and silence. Well, the messenger came after the battle to tell me that you had never woken. You seemed to fall into a high fever, still talking in the same wild way, then finally lay so long unconscious that they took you for dead, and sent the courier to tell me. I came as soon as I could."

I narrowed my eyes at him. The light from the window was strong. He saw this, and signed to the slave, who pulled a curtain across. "Let me get this clear. After you had found me in the forest and brought me to Galava, you went south. And there was another battle? Arthur, how long have I been here?"

"It is three weeks since we found you. But it is fully seven months since you wandered off into the forest and lost yourself. You were gone all winter. Is it any wonder that we thought you were dead?"

"Seven months?" Often, as a doctor, I have had to give this kind of news to patients who have been long feverish, or lying in coma, and I always see the same sort of incredulous, groping shock. I felt it now myself. To know that half a year had dropped out of time, and such a half year. . . . What, in those months, might not have happened to a country as torn and as embattled as mine? And to her King? Other things, forgotten till now in the mists of illness, began to come back to me.

Looking at him, I saw again, with fear, the hollowed cheekbones and the smudge of sleepless nights beneath his eyes: Arthur, who ate like a young wolf and slept like a child; who was the creature of gaiety and strength. There had been no defeat in the field; his glory there had not suffered even the smear of a shadow. Nor could his anxiety for me have brought him to this pass. There remained his home.

"Emrys, what has happened?"

Once more, in that place, the childhood name came naturally. I saw his face twist as if the memory were a pain. He bent his head and stared down at the blankets.

"My mother, the Queen. She died."

Memory stirred. The woman lying in the great bed hung with rich stuffs? I had known, then. "I am sorry," I said.

"I heard just before we fought the battle at Caer Guinnion. Lucan brought the news, with the token you had left with him. You remember it, a brooch with the Christian symbol? Her death came as no surprise. We had expected it. But I believe that grief helped to hasten her death."

"Grief? Why, has there been—?" I stopped dead. It had come back clearly now, the night in the forest, and the flask of wine I had opened to share with the troopers. And why. The vision stirred again, the moonlit chamber and the blowing curtains and the dead woman. Something closed my throat. I said, hardly: "Guenever?"

He nodded, not looking up.

I asked, knowing the answer: "And the child?"

He looked up quickly. "You knew? Yes, of course you would. . . . It never came to term. They said she was with child, but shortly before Christmas she began to bleed, and then, at the New Year, died in great pain. If you had been there—" He stopped, swallowed, and was silent.

"I am sorry," I said again.

He went on, in a voice so hard that it sounded angry: "We thought you were dead, too. Then, after the battle, there you were, filthy and old and crazy, but the field surgeons said you might recover. That, at least, I had saved from the shambles of the winter. . . . Then I had to leave you to go to Caer Guinnion. I won it, yes, but lost some good men. Then on the heels of the action Ector's courier came to tell me you were dead. When I got here at dawn yesterday I expected to find your body already burned or buried."

He stopped, put his forehead hard down on a clenched fist, and stayed so. The servant, rigid by the window, caught my eye, and went, softly. In a moment or two Arthur raised his head and spoke in his normal voice.

"Forgive me. All the time I was riding north, I kept remembering what you said about dying a shameful death. It was hard to bear."

"But here I am, clean and whole, with my wits clear, and ready to become clearer when you tell me all that has happened in the last seven months. Now, of your kindness, pour me some of that wine, and go back, if you will, to your journey into Elmet."

He obeyed me, and in a while talk became easier. He spoke of his journey through the Gap to Olicana, and what he had found there, and of his meeting with the King of Elmet. Then of his return to Caerleon, and of the Queen's miscarriage and death. This time, when I questioned him, he was able to answer me, and in the end I could give him the chilly comfort of knowing that my presence at court beside the young Queen could have been no help. Her doctors were skilled with drugs, and had saved her the worst of the pain; I could have done no more. The child was ill-conceived; nothing could have saved it, or its mother.

When he had heard what I had to tell him, he accepted this, and himself turned the subject. He was eager to hear what had happened to me, and impatient of the fact that I could remember little after the marriage feast at Luguvallium.

"Can you not remember anything of how you came to the turret where we found you?"

"A little. It comes clear bit by bit. I must have wandered about in the forest and kept myself alive somehow until winter. Then it seems to me as if some rude folk of the hill forest must have taken me in and cared for me. Without that, I doubt if I could have survived the snow. I thought they might be some of Mab's people, the Old Ones of the mountain country, but if so, they would surely have sent word to you."

"They did. Word came, but only after you had vanished again. As is usual, the Old Ones were snowed up in their high caves all winter, and you with them. They went hunting when the snow melted, and came back to their caves to find you gone. It was from them that I first heard that you had run mad. They had had to tie you, they said, but afterwards, at such times, you would be calm and very weak, and so it was at the time when they left you. When they got home, you had gone."

"I remember being bound. Yes. So after that I must have made my way downhill, and ended up in the ruin near the ford—I suppose, in my crazed way, still making for Galava. It was spring; I remember a little of that. Then the battle must have overtaken me, and you found me there in the forest. I recall nothing of that."

He told me again how I had been found, thin and filthy and talking no kind of sense, hiding in the ruined turret, with a kind of squirrel's hoard of acorns and beechnuts, and dried windfall apples put by, and a pigling with a splinted leg for company.

"So that part of it was real!" I said, smiling. "I can remember finding the creature, and healing the leg, but not much else. If I was as sharp set as you say, it was good of me not to eat Master Piglet. What happened to it?"

"It's here in Ector's sties." The first glimmer of humour touched his mouth. "And marked, I think, for a long and dishonourable life. There's not one of the boys would dare lay a hand on the enchanter's personal pig, which looks like growing up into a good fighting boar, so it will end up as king of the sty, which is only proper. Merlin, you've told me all you can remember of what happened after making camp up there on the Wolf Road; what do you remember before that? What made you ill? Urbgen's men said it came on suddenly. They thought it was poison, and so did I. I wondered if the witch had had you followed, after the wedding feast, and one of her creatures had dragged you from your bed that night while the trooper's back was turned. But if that had happened, surely they would have killed you? There was no suspicion of foul play from those two men; they were Urbgen's own, hand-picked."

"None at all. They were good fellows, and I owe them my life."

"They told me that you drank wine that night, from your own flask. They did not share it. They say, too, that you were drunk at the marriage feast. You? I have never seen you the worse for wine. And you sat beside Morgause. Have you any reason to believe that she drugged your wine?"

I opened my mouth to answer him, and to this day I swear that the word on my lips was "Yes." This, as far as I knew it, was the truth. But some god must have forestalled me. Instead of the Yes that my mind had framed, my lips said, "No."

I must have spoken strangely, because I saw him staring, arrested with narrowed eyes. It was a discomforting look, and I found myself elaborating. "How can I tell? But I don't think so. I have told you that I have no power now, but the witch would not know that. She is still afraid of me. She has tried before, not once but twice, to snare me with her women's spells. Both times she failed, and I think she would not have dared try again."

He was silent for a while. Then he said, shortly: "When my Queen died, there was talk of poison. I wondered."

At this I could protest truthfully. "There always is, but I beg you will not regard it! From what you have told me, I am certain there was no such thing. Besides, how?" I added, as convincingly as I could: "Believe me, Arthur. If she were guilty, can you see any reason why I should want to protect Morgause from you?"

He still looked doubtful, but did not pursue it further. "Well," was all he said, "she'll find her wings clipped now for a while. She is back in Orkney, and Lot is dead."

I took this in silently. It was another shock. In these few months, how much had changed. "How?" I asked him. "And when?"

"In the forest battle, I can't say that I mourn him, except that he had that rat Aguisel under his fist, and I believe that I shall have trouble there soon."

I said slowly: "I have remembered something else. During the fighting in the forest I heard them calling to one another that the king was dead. It struck me with helpless grief. For me, there is only one king . . . But they must have been speaking of Lot. Well, yes, at least Lot was a known evil. Now, I suppose, Urien will have it all his own way in the northeast, and Aguisel with him. . . . But there's time enough for that. Meanwhile, what of Morgause? She was carrying a child at Luguvallium, and should have been delivered by now. A boy?"

"Two. Twin sons, born at Dunpeldyr. She joined Lot there after Morgan's wedding. Witch or no witch," he said, with a trace of bitterness, "she is a good breeder of sons. By the time Lot joined us here in Rheged, he was bragging that he had left yet another in her before he quitted Dunpeldyr." He looked down at his hands. "You must have had speech with her at the wedding. Did you find anything out about the other boy?"

There was no need to ask which boy he meant. It seemed that he could not bring himself to say "my son."

"Only that he is alive."

His eyes came up quickly to mine. There was a flash in them, suppressed instantly. But I was sure that it was one of joy. So short a time ago, and he had looked for the child only to kill it.

I said, schooling my voice to hide the pity I felt: "She tells me that she does not know where he is to be found. She may be lying, I'm not sure of that. It must be true that she kept him hidden away from Lot. But she may bring him into the open now. What has she to fear, now that Lot has gone? Except, perhaps, from you?"

He was looking at his hands again. "She need not fear me now on that score," he said woodenly.

That is all I can remember of that interview. I heard someone saying, but the words seemed to go round the curved tower walls like a whispered echo, or like words in my head alone: "She is the falsest lady at this time alive, but she must live to rear her four sons by the King of Orkney, for they will be your faithful servants, and the bravest of your Companions."

I must have shut my eyes then, against the wave of exhaustion that broke over me, for when I opened them again it was dark, and Arthur had gone, and the servant knelt beside the bed, offering me a bowl of soup.

8

I am a strong man, and heal fast. I was on my feet again soon after this, and, some two or three weeks later, thought myself fit enough to ride south in Arthur's wake. He had gone the next morning, riding down to Caerleon. Since then a courier had brought news that longships had been sighted in the Severn estuary, so it looked as if the King would soon have another battle on his hands.

I would have liked to stay a while longer at Galava, perhaps to pass the summer in that familiar country, and to revisit my old haunts in the forest. But after the courier's visit, though Ector and Drusilla tried to keep me, I thought it high time to be gone. The battle now imminent would be fought from Caerleon: indeed, it was possible (the dispatch had said) that the invaders were attempting in force to destroy the war-leader's main stronghold and supply center. I had no doubt that Arthur would hold Caerleon, but it was time I got back to Caer Camel to see how Derwen had been doing in my absence.

It was high summer when I saw the place again, and Derwen's team had done wonders. There it stood on its steep, flat-topped hill, the vision made real. The outer works were complete, the great double wall, of dressed stone topped with timber, running along the rim of the slope to crown the whole crest of the hill. Piercing it at their two opposing corners, the vast gateways were finished, and impressive. Great double doors of oak, studded with iron, stood open, pulled back to wall the tunnels that led in through the thick rampart. Above them went the sentry-way behind its battlements.

Moreover, there were sentries there. Since winter, Derwen told me, the King had had the place invested, so that the work of finishing could proceed inside defended walls. And finished it soon would be. Arthur had sent word that, come July or August, he wanted to be there with the knights-companions and all his cavalry.

Derwen was all for pressing on with the headquarters buildings, and with the King's own rooms, but I knew Arthur's mind better than that. I had given instructions that the men's barracks, and the horse-lines, the kitchens and service quarters must be completed first, and this had been done. A good start had been made, too, on the central buildings: the King, certainly, must lodge under skins and temporary timber, as if he were still in the field, but his great hall was built and roofed, and carpenters were at work on the long tables and benches within.

There had been no lack of local help. The folk who lived nearby, thankful to see a strong place going up near their settlements, had come whenever they could to fetch and carry, or to lend their skills to our own workmen. With them came many who were willing, but too old or too young to labour. Derwen would have sent them away, but I set them to clearing the nettle-grown trenches of a site not far from headquarters where formerly there must have been a shrine. I did not know, and nor did they, to what god it had been consecrated; but I know soldiers, and all fighting men need some center-point, with a light and an offering, to tempt their god down among them for a moment of communion, when strength can be received in return for hope and faith.

Similarly, the spring on the northern embankment, which was enclosed within the outer works of the fortification, I set the women to clearing. This they did eagerly, for it was known that, time out of mind, the spring had been dedicated to the Goddess herself. For many years now it had been neglected, and sunk in a tangle of thorny growth that prevented them from making their offerings and sending up the sort of prayers that women send. Now the woodmen had hacked the thickets down, so I let the women make their own shrine. They sang as they worked; they had been afraid, I think, that their sacred place would be shut away in an enclave of men. I told them not so: when once the Saxon power was broken, it was the High King's plan that men and women should come and go in peace, and Caer Camel would be a fair city set on a hill, rather than a camp of fighting men.

Finally, on the lowest part of the field, near the northeast gate, we cleared a place for the people and their cattle, where they could take refuge, and live, if need be, till danger was past.

Then Arthur came. In the night the Tor flamed suddenly, and beyond the flame could be seen the point of light that was the beacon hill behind. In the early morning sunlight he came riding along the Lake's edge, at the head of his knights. White was still his colour; he rode his white war-horse; his banner was white, and his shield also, too proud for a device such as the others wore. He shone out of the misty landscape like a swan on the pearled reaches of the Lake. Then the cavalcade was lost to sight beyond the trees that crowded the base of the hill, and presently the beat of hoofs came steadily on, and up the new curling road to the King's Gate.

The double gates stood open to receive him. Inside them, lining the newly paved road, waited all those who had built the place for him. So for the first time Arthur, duke of battles, High King among the other kings of Britain, entered the stronghold which was to be his own fair city of Camelot.

Of course he was pleased with it, and that night a feast was held, to which everyone—man, woman or child—who had lent a hand to the work was bidden. He and his knights, with Derwen and myself and a few others, sat in the hall, at the long table so newly sanded that the dust still hung in the air and made haloes round the torches. It was a joyous occasion, without form or solemnity, like a feast on a victory field. He made some kind of speech of welcome—of which I now remember no single word—pitching his voice so that the people pressing outside the doors could hear him; then, once we in the hall had started eating, he left his place at the table's head, and, with a mutton bone in one hand and a goblet in the other, went the rounds of the place, sitting with this group or that, dipping into a pot with the masons or letting the carpenters ply him from the mead-barrel, all the time looking, questioning, praising, with all his old, shining way. In a short while, their awe of him melting, they pelted their questions like snowballs. What had happened at Caerleon? In Linnuis? In Rheged? When would he settle here? Was it likely that the Saxons could press this far and get across the downs? What was Eosa's strength? Were the stories—of this, that, and the other thing—true? All of which he answered patiently: what men knew they must face, they would face; it was the fear of surprise and the arrow in the dark that unmanned the hardiest.

It was all in the style of the old Arthur, the young King I knew. His looks matched it, too. The fatigue and despair had gone; grief had been laid aside; this was once again the King who held all men's eyes, and whose strength they felt they could draw on for ever, and never weaken him. By morning there would be no one there who would not willingly die in his service. That he knew this, and was fully aware of the effect he made, did not detract one whit from his greatness.

As usually happened, we had a word together before sleep. He was housed simply, but better than in a field tent. A roof of leather had been stretched across the beams of his half-finished sleeping chamber, and rugs laid. His own camp bed had been against a wall, with the table and reading lamp he worked with, and a pair of chairs and the clothes chest and the stand with the silver bowl and water-jug.

We had not spoken privately since Galava. He asked after my health, and spoke of the work I had done at Caer Camel, and then of what still remained to do. What had happened in the Caerleon fighting I had heard already, in the talk at table. I said something about the change in him. He looked at me for a moment or two, then, apparently, came to a decision.

"There's something I wanted to say to you, Merlin. I don't know if I have any right, but I shall say it all the same. When you last saw me, at Galava, sick as you were, you must have seen something of what I was feeling. In fact, how could you help it? As usual, I laid all my troubles on you, regardless of whether you were fit to bear them or not."

"I don't remember that. We talked, yes. I asked you what had happened, and you told me."

"I did indeed. Now I am asking you to bear with me again. This time, I hope, I am laying nothing on you, but . . ." A brief pause, to gather his thoughts. He seemed oddly hesitant. I wondered what was coming. He went on: "You once said to me that life divided itself into light and dark, just as time does into day and night. It's true. One misfortune seems to breed another, and so it was with me. That was a time of darkness—the first I had suffered. When I came to you I was half-broken with weariness, and with the weight of losses coming one on the other, as if the world had turned sour, and my luck was dead. The loss of my mother, by itself, could be no great grief to me; you know my heart about that, and to tell you the truth. I would grieve more over Drusilla's death, or Ector's. But the death of my Queen, little Guenever . . . It could have been a good marriage, Merlin. We could, I believe, have come to love. What made that grief so bitter was the loss of the child, and the waste of her young life in pain, and with it, besides, the fear that she had been murdered, and by my enemies. Added to that—and I can admit this to you—was the weary prospect of having to start all over again to look for a suitable match, and going once more through all the ritual of mating, when so much else lies waiting for me to do."

I said quickly: "You surely do not still believe that she was murdered?"

"No. you have set my mind at rest there, as you have about your own sickness. I had the same fear about you, that your death had been my fault." He paused, and then said flatly: "And that was the worst. It came as the final loss, overtopping all the others." A gesture, half-shamefaced, half-resigned. "You have told me, not once but many times, that when I looked for you in need, you would be there. And always, until then, it was true. Then suddenly, at the dark time, you were gone. And with so much still to do. Caer Camel just begun, and more fighting expected, and after that, the settlements and the law-giving, and the making of civil order . . . But you were gone—murdered, I thought, through my fault, like my little Queen. I could not think past it. I did not kill the children at Dunpeldyr, but by God, I could have killed the Queen of Orkney, had she crossed my path during those months!"

"I understand this. I think I knew it. Go on."

"You have heard, now, about my victories in the field during this time. To other men it must have seemed as if my fortunes were rising to their peak. But to me, mainly because of your loss, I felt life at its blackest depth. Not only for grief at the loss of what lies between us, the long friendship—guardianship—I would say love—but for a reason I don't have to remind you of again. You know I have been used to turn to you for everything, except in matters of warfare."

I waited, but he did not go on. I said: "Well, that is my function. No one man, even a High King, can do it all. You are young still, Arthur. Even my father Ambrosius, with all his years behind him, took advice at every turn. There is no weakness in this. Forgive me, but it is a sign of youth to think so."

"I know. I don't think it. This is not what I am trying to say. I want to tell you of something that happened while you were sick. After the battle in Rheged, I took hostages. The Saxons fled into a thick wood on a hill—above the turret where we found you just after. We surrounded the hill, and then drove in on all sides, killing, until the few who were left surrendered. I believe they might have yielded sooner, but I gave them no chance. I wanted to kill. At the last, those few who were left threw down their arms and came out. We took them. One of them was Colgrim's former second-in-command, Cynewulf. I would have killed him then and there, but he had yielded his arms. I loosed him on the promise to take his ships and go; and I took hostages."

"Yes? It was a wise try. We know it did not work." I said it without expression. I guessed what was coming. I had heard the tale already, from others.

"Merlin, when I heard that, instead of going back to Germany, Cynewulf had turned in again to our coasts, and was burning villages, I had the hostages killed."

"It was not your choice. Cynewulf knew. It was what he would have done."

"He is a barbarian, and an outlander. I am not. Granted Cynewulf knew. He may have thought I would not carry out the threat. Some of them were no more than boys. The youngest was thirteen, younger than I was when I first fought. They were brought to me, and I ordered it."

"Rightly. Now forget it."

"How? They were brave. But I had threatened it and so I did it. You spoke of the change in me. You were right. I am not the man I was before this past winter-time. This was the first thing I have done in war that I knew to be evil."

I thought of Ambrosius at Doward; of myself at Tintagel. I said: "We have all done things that we would like to forget. It may be that war itself is evil."

"How could it be?" He spoke impatiently. "But I'm not telling you about it now because I want either your advice or your comfort." I waited, at a loss. He went on, picking his words: "It was the worst thing I have had to do. I did it, and I will abide by it. What I have to say now is this: if you had been there, I would have turned to you, as always, and asked for your counsel. And though you have said that you no longer have the power of prophecy, I would still have hoped—been sure—that you could see what the future held, and would guide me in the path I ought to take."

"But this time your prophet was dead, so you chose your own path?"

"Just so."

"I understand. You offer me this as comfort, that both act and decision can be safely left to you, even though I am here again? Knowing, as we both do, that your 'prophet' is still dead?"

"No." He spoke quickly, strongly. "You have mistaken me. I am offering you comfort, yes, but of a different kind. Do you think I don't know that it has been a dark time with you, too, ever since the raising of the sword? Forgive me if I am meddling in matters I don't understand, but looking back at what has passed, I think . . . Merlin, what I am trying to tell you is this, that I believe your god is with you still."

There was silence. Through it came the flutter of the flame in the bronze lamp, and, infinitely far away, the noises of the camp outside. We looked at one another, he still in early manhood, myself aged and (as I knew) sorely weakened by my recent sickness. And subtly, between us, the balance was changing; had, perhaps, already changed. He, to offer me strength and comfort. *Your god is with you still.* How could he think so? He had only to recall my lack of anything but the most trivial tricks of magic, my want of defense against Morgause, my inability to find out anything about Mordred. But he had spoken, not with the passionate conviction of youth, but with the calm certainty of a judge.

I thought back, for the first time pushing aside the apathy that, since my sickness, had succeeded the earlier mood of tranquil acceptance. I began to see which way his thoughts had gone. One could say they were the thoughts of a general who can lift a victory out of a planned retreat. Or a leader of men who is able, with a word, to give or withhold confidence.

Your god is with you, he had said. With me, perhaps, in the poisoned cup, and the suffering months that had withdrawn me from Arthur's side, and forced him into solitary power? With me (though this he did not know) in the still whisper that had led me to deny the poisoning, and so save from his vengeance Morgause, the mother of those four sons . . . ? With me in the losing of Mordred, whose survival had brought that glow of joy to Arthur's eye? As he would be with me, even, when at length I went to the living burial I feared, and left Arthur alone on middle-earth, with Mordred his fate still at large?

Like the first breath of living wind to the sailor becalmed and starving, I felt hope stir. It was, then, not enough to accept, to wait on the god's return in all his light and strength. In the dark ebbtide, as much as in the flow, could be felt the full power of the sea.

I bowed my head, like a man accepting a king's gift. There was no need to speak. We read one another's minds. He said, with an abrupt change of tone: "How long before this place is complete?"

"In full fighting order, another month. It is virtually ready now."

"So I judged. I can transfer now from Caerleon, foot, horse, and baggage?"

"Whenever you please."

"And then? What have you planned for yourself, until you are needed again to build for peace?"

"I've made no plans. Go home, perhaps."

"No. Stay here."

It sounded like an order. I raised my brows.

"Merlin, I mean it. I want you here. We need not split the High King's power in two before the time comes when we must. Do you understand me?"

"Yes."

"Then stay. Make a place for yourself here, and stay away from your marvellous Welsh cave for a while longer."

"For a while longer," I promised him, smiling. "But not here, Arthur. I need silence and solitude, things hard to come by within reach of such a city as this will become, once you are here as High King. May I look for a place, and build a house? By the time you are ready to hang your sword up on the wall over your chair of state, my marvellous cave will be here, nearby, and the hermit installed, ready to join your counsels. If, by that time, you remember to need him."

He laughed at that, and seemed content, and we went to our beds.

9

Next day Arthur and his Companions rode back to Ynys Witrin, and I went with them. We were going by invitation of King Melwas and his mother, the queen, to attend a ceremony of thanks for the King's recent victories.

Now, although there was a Christian church on Ynys Witrin, and a monastic settlement on the hill near the holy well, the ruling deity of that ancient island was still the Goddess herself, the Mother whose shrine has been there time out of mind, and who is served still by her priestesses, the *ancillae.* It is a cult similar to, but I believe older than, the keeping of the Vestal fire of old Rome. King Melwas, along with most of his people, was a follower of the older gods; and—which was more important—his mother, a formidable old woman, worshipped the Goddess, and had been generous to her priestesses. The present Lady of the shrine (the high priestess, as representing the Goddess, took this title) was related to her.

Though Arthur himself had been brought up in a Christian household, I was not surprised when he accepted Melwas' invitation. But there were those who were. As we assembled near the King's Gate, ready for the ride, I caught one or two looks thrown at him by his Companions, with, here and there, a hint of uneasiness.

Arthur caught my eye—we were waiting while Bedwyr had some word with the guard at the gate—and grinned. He spoke softly. "Do I have to explain to *you?*"

"By no means. You have bethought yourself that Melwas is to be your near neighbour, and has helped you considerably in the building here. You also see the wisdom of pleasing the old queen. And naturally you are remembering Dewdrop and Blackberry, and what you were told about placating the Goddess."

"Dewdrop and—? Oh, the old man's cows! Yes, of course! I might have known you would get straight to it! As a matter of fact I had a message from the Lady herself. The folk of the island want to give thanks for the year's victories, and call a blessing on Caer Camel. I'm living in fear in case someone tells them that I wore Ygraine's token through the fighting at Caer Guinnion!"

He was speaking of the brooch with the name MARIA engraved around the rim. This is the name of the Christians' goddess. I said: "I doubt if it need trouble you. That shrine is as old as the earth it stands on, and whichever Lady you speak to there, the same one will hear you. There is only one, from the beginning. Or so I think. . . . But what will the bishops say?"

"I am High King," said Arthur, and left it at that. Bedwyr joined us then, and we rode out through the gateway.

It was a gentle, grey day, with the promise of summer rain somewhere in the clouds. We were soon clear of the woodland, and into the marsh country. To either side of the road the water stretched, grey and ruffled, as the lynx-paws of the breeze crossed and recrossed it. Poplars whitened in the wayward gusts, and the willows dipped, trailing, in the shallows. Islets and willow-groves and tracts of marshland lay seemingly afloat on the silver surface, their images blurred with the breeze. The paved road, mantled with moss and fern as most roads soon are in that low-lying land, led through this wilderness of reeds and water toward the ridge of higher ground that lay like an arm half-encircling one end of the Island. Hoofs rang suddenly on stone, and the road topped a gentle rise. Ahead now was the Lake itself, lying like a sea moating the Island, its waters unbroken save for the narrow causeway that led the road across, and here and there the boats of fishermen, or the barges of the marsh-dwellers.

From this shining sheet of water rose the hill called the Tor, shaped like a giant cone, as symmetrical as if hand-built by men. It was flanked by a gentler, rounded hill, and beyond that by another, a long, low ridge, like a limb drawn up in the water. Here lay the wharfs; one could see masts like reeds beyond a dip in the green. Beyond the Island's triple hill, stretching into the distance, was a great shining level of water, sown with sedge and bulrush and the clusters of reed thatch among the willows where the marsh people lived. It was all one long, shifting, moving glimmer, as far as the sea. One could see why the Island was called Ynys Witrin, the Isle of Glass. Sometimes, now, men call it Avalon.

There were orchards everywhere on Ynys Witrin. The trees crowded so thickly along the harbour ridge and up the lower slopes of the Tor that only the plumes of wood-smoke, rising among the boughs, showed where the village lay. (King's capital though it was, it could earn no grander title.) A short way up the hill, above the trees, could be seen the cluster of huts, like hives, where the Christian hermits lived, and the holy women. Melwas left them alone; they even had their own church, built near the Goddess's shrine. The church was a humble affair made of wattle and mud, and roofed with thatch. It looked as if the first bad storm would blow it clean out of the ground.

Far different was the shrine of the Goddess. It was said that with the centuries the land itself had slowly grown up around it, and possessed it, so that now it lay beneath the level of men's footing, like a crypt. I had never seen it. Men were not normally received within its precincts, but today the Lady herself, with the veiled and white-clad women and girls behind her, all bearing flowers, waited to welcome the High King. The old woman beside her, with the rich mantle, and the royal circlet on her grey hair, must be Melwas' mother, the queen. Here she took precedence of her son. Melwas himself stood off to one side, among his captains and young men. He was a thickset, handsome fellow, with a curled cap of brown hair, and a glossy beard. He had never married: rumour had it that no woman had ever passed the test of his mother's judgment.

The Lady greeted Arthur, and two of the youngest maidens came forward and hung his neck with flowers. There was singing, all women's voices, high and sweet. The grey sky parted and let through a glint of sunlight. It was seen as an omen; people smiled and looked at one another, and the singing grew more joyous. The Lady turned, and with her women led the way down the long flight of shallow steps into the shrine. The old queen followed, and after her Arthur, with the rest of us. Lastly Melwas came, with his followers. The common folk stayed outside. All through the ceremony we could hear the muttering and shifting, as they waited to catch another look at the legendary Arthur of the nine battles.

The shrine was not large; our company filled it to capacity. It was dimly lit, with no more than half a dozen scented lamps, grouped to either side of the archway that led to the inner sanctuary. In the smoky light the white robes of the women shone ghostly. Veils hid their faces and covered their hair and floated, cloudy, to the ground. Of them all, only the Lady herself could be seen clearly: she stood full in the lamplight, stoled with silver, and wearing a diadem that caught what light there was. She was a queenly figure; one could well believe that she came of royal stock.

Veiled, too, was the inner sanctuary; no one save the initiated—not even the old queen herself—would ever see beyond that curtain. The ceremony that we saw (though it would not be seemly to write of it here) would not be the customary one sacred to the Goddess. It was certainly lengthy; we endured two hours of it, standing crowded together; but I suspect that the Lady wanted to make the most of the occasion, and who was to blame her if thoughts of future patronage were in her mind? But it came to an end at last. The Lady accepted Arthur's gift, presented it with the appropriate prayer, and we emerged in due order into the daylight, to receive the shouts of the people.

It was a small incident, which might have left no mark in my memory, but for what came later. As it is, I can still recall the soft, lively feel of the day, the first drops of rain that blew in our faces as we left the shrine, and the thrush's song from the thorn tree standing deep in summer grass spiked with pale orchis and thick with the gold of the small flower they call the Lady's Slipper. The way to Melwas' palace lay through precincts of summer lawn, where among the apple trees grew flowers that could not have come there in nature, all with their uses, as well I knew, in medicine or magic. The *ancillae* practised healing, and had planted the virtuous herbs. (I saw no other kind. The Goddess is not the same whose bloody knife was thrown, once, from the Green Chapel.) At least, I thought, if I have to live hereabouts, the country is a better garden for my plants than the open hillside at home.

With that, we came to the palace, and were welcomed by Melwas into his hall of feasting.

The feast was much like any other, except (as was natural in that place) for the excellence and variety of the fish dishes. The old queen occupied the central position at the high table, with Arthur to one side of her and Melwas to the other. None of the women from the shrine, not even the Lady herself, was present. What women there were, I noticed with some amusement, were far from being beauties, and were none of them young. Rumour had perhaps been right about the queen. I recalled a glance and a smile passing between Melwas and a girl in the crowd: well, the old woman could not watch him all the time. His other appetites were well enough; the food was plentiful and well cooked, though nothing fanciful, and there was a singer with a pleasant voice. The wine, which was good, came (we were told) from a vineyard forty miles off, on the chalk. It had recently been destroyed by one of the sharp incursions of the Saxons, who had begun to come closer this summer.

Once this was said, it was inevitable which way the talk would go. Between dissection of the past and discussion of the future, time passed quickly, with Arthur and Melwas in accord, which augured well.

We left before midnight. A moon coming toward the full gave a clear light. She hung low and close behind the beacon at the summit of the Tor, marking with sharp shadows the walls of Melwas' stronghold, a fort rebuilt on the site of some ancient hilltop fastness. It was a place for retreat in times of trouble: his palace, where we had been entertained, stood below, on the level near the water.

We were none too soon. A mist was rising from the Lake. Pale wreaths of it eddied across the grass, below the trees, smoking to our horses' knees. Soon the causeway would be hidden. Melwas, escorting us with his torch-bearers, guided us across the pale fog that was the Lake, and up into clear air, onto the ringing stone of the ridge. Then he made his farewells, and set off for home.

I drew rein, looking back. From here, of the three hills that made the island, only the Tor was visible, rising from a lake of cloud. From the shrouding mist near its foot could be seen the red torchlit glow of the palace, not yet quenched for the night. The moon had sailed clear of the Tor into a dark sky. Near the beacon tower, on the rising spiral of the road to the high fortress, a light flickered and moved.

My flesh crept, like a dog's at the sight of a specter. A wisp of mist lay there, high, and across it a shadow strode, like a giant's. The Tor was a known gate to the Otherworld; for a flash I wondered if, with the Sight come back to me, I was watching one of the guardians of the place, one of the fiery spirits who keep the gate. Then my sight cleared, and I saw that it was a man with a torch, running up the steep of the Tor to light the beacon fire.

As I set spurs to my horse I heard Arthur's voice, lifted in quick command. A rider detached himself from the cavalcade and leaped forward at a stretched gallop. The others, silent all at once, followed him, fast but collected, while behind us the flames went up into the night, calling Arthur of the nine battles to yet another fight.

10

The investing of Caer Camel saw the start of the new campaign. Four more years it took: siege and skirmish, flying attack and ambush—except during the midwinter months he was never at rest. And twice more, towards the end of that time, he triumphed over the enemy in a major engagement.

The first of these battles was joined in response to a call from Elmet. Eosa himself had landed from Germany, at the head of fresh Saxon war-bands, to be joined by the East Saxons already established north of the Thames. Cerdic added a third point to the spear with a force brought by longboat from Rutupiae. It was the worst threat since Luguvallium. The invaders came swarming in force up the Vale, and were threatening what Arthur had long foreseen, to break through the barrier of the mountains by the Gap. Surprised and (no doubt) disconcerted by the readiness of the fort at Olicana, they were checked and held there, while the message was sent flashing south for Arthur. The East Saxon force, which was considerable, was concentrated on Olicana; the King of Elmet held them there, but the others streamed westward through the Gap. Arthur, heading fast up the west road, reached the Tribuit fort before them and, re-forming there in strength, caught them at Nappa Ford. He vanquished them there, in a bloody struggle, then threw his fast cavalry up through the Gap to Olicana, and, side by side with the King of Elmet, drove the enemy back into the Vale. From there a movement beyond countering, right back, east and south, until the old frontiers contained them, and the Saxon "king," looking round on his bleeding and depleted forces, admitted defeat.

A defeat, as it turned out, all but final. Such was Arthur's name now that its very mention had come to mean victory, and "the coming of Arthur" a synonym for salvation. The next time he was called for—it was the clearing-up operation of the long campaign—no sooner had the dreaded cavalry with the white horse at its head and the Dragon glinting over the helmets showed in the mountain pass of Agned than the enemy fell into the disarray of near panic, so that the action was a pursuit rather than a battle, a clearing of territory after the main action. Through all this fighting, Gereint (who knew every foot of the territory) was with the cavalry, with a command worthy of him. So Arthur rewarded service.

Eosa himself had received a wound in the fighting at Nappa. He never took the field again. It was the young Cerdic, the Aetheling, who led the Saxons at Agned, and did his best to hold them against the terror of Arthur's onslaught. It was said that afterwards, as he withdrew—in creditable order—to the waiting longboats, he made a vow that when he next set foot on British territory, he would stay, and not even Arthur should prevent him.

For that, as I could have told him, he would have to wait till Arthur was no longer there.

It was never my intention here to give details of the years of battle. This is a chronicle of a different kind. Besides, everyone knows now about his campaign to free Britain and cleanse her shore of the Terror. It was all written down in that house up in Vindolanda, by Blaise, and the solemn, quiet clerk who came from time to time to help him. Here I will only repeat that never once during the years it took him to fight the Saxons to a standstill was I able to bring prophecy or magic to his aid. The story of those years is one of human bravery, of endurance and of dedication. It took twelve major engagements, and some seven years' hard work, before the young King could count the country safe at last for husbandry and the arts of peace.

It is not true, as the poets and singers would have it, that Arthur drove all the Saxons from the shores of Britain. He had come to recognize, as Ambrosius did, that it was impossible to clear lands that stretched for miles of difficult country, and which had, moreover, the easy retreat of the seas behind. Since the time of Vortigern, who first invited the Saxons into Britain as his allies, the southeast shore of our country had been settled Saxon territory, with its own rulers and its own laws. There was some justification for Eosa's assumption of the title of king. Even had it been possible for Arthur to clear the Saxon Shore, he would have had to drive out settlers of perhaps the third generation, who had been born and bred within these shores, and make them take ship back to their grandfathers' country, where they might meet as harsh a welcome as here. Men fight desperately for their homes when the alternative is to be homeless. And, while it was one thing to win the great pitched battles, he knew that to drive men into the hills and forests and waste places, whence they could never be dislodged, or even pinned down and fought, was to invite a long war which could have no victory. He had before him the example of the Old Ones: they had been dispossessed by the Romans and had fled into the waste places of the hills; four hundred years later they were still there, in their remote mountain fastnesses, and the Romans themselves had gone. So, accepting the fact that there must be still Saxon kingdoms lodged within the shores of Britain, Arthur set himself to see that their boundaries were secure, and that for very fear their kings would hold to them.

So he passed his twentieth year. He came back to Camelot at the end of October, and plunged straight away into council. I was there, appealed to sometimes, but in the main watching and listening only: the counsel I gave him I gave in private, behind closed doors. In the public sight the decisions were his. Indeed, they were his as often as mine, and as time went on I was content to let his judgment have its way. He was impulsive sometimes, and in many matters still lacked experience or precedent; but he never let his judgment be ridden by impulse, and he maintained, in spite of the arrogance that success might be expected to bring with it, the habit of letting men talk their fill, so that when finally the King's decision was announced, each man thought that he had had a say in it.

One of the things that was brought up at length was the question of a new marriage. I could see he had not expected this; but he kept silent, and after a while grew easier, and listened to the older men. They were the ones who knew names and pedigrees and land-claims by heart. It came to me also, watching, that they were the ones who, when Arthur was first proclaimed, would have nothing to do with the claim. Now not even his own companion knights could show more loyal. He had won the elders, as he had won all else. You would have thought each one of them had discovered him unknown in the Wild Forest, and handed him the sword of the Kingdom.

You would also have thought that each man was discussing the marriage of a favourite son. There was much beard-stroking and head-wagging, and names were suggested and discussed, and even wrangled over, but none met with general acclaim, until one day a man from Gwynedd, who had fought right through the wars with Arthur, and was a kinsman of Maelgon himself, got to his feet and made a speech about his home country.

Now when you get a black Welshman on his feet and ready to talk, it is like inviting a bard; the thing is done in order, in cadence, and at very great length; but such was this man's way, and such the beauty of his speaking voice, that after the first few minutes men settled back comfortably to listen, as they might have listened at a feast.

His subject seemed to be his country, the loveliness of its valleys and hills, the blue lakes, the creaming seas, the deer and eagles and the small singing-birds, the bravery of the men and the beauty of the women. Then we heard of the poets and singers, the orchards and flowery meadows, the riches of sheep and cattle and the veined minerals in the rock. From this there followed the brave history of the land, battles and victories, courage in defeat, the tragedy of young death and the fecund beauty of young love.

He was getting near his point. I saw Arthur stir in his great chair.

And, said the speaker, the country's wealth and beauty and bravery were all there invested in the family of its kings, a family which (I had ceased to listen closely; I was watching Arthur through the light of a badly flaring lamp, and my head ached)—a family which seemed to have a genealogy as ancient and twice as long as Noah's. . . .

There was, of course, a princess. Young, lovely, sprung from a line of ancient Welsh kings joined with a noble Roman clan. Arthur himself came from no higher stock. . . . And now one saw why the long-drawn panegyric, and the eye slightly askance at the young King.

Her name, it seemed, was Guinevere.

I saw them again, the two of them. Bedwyr, dark and eager, with eyes of love fixed on the other boy; Arthur-Emrys, at twelve years old the leader, full of energy and the high fire of living. And the white shadow of the owl drifting overhead between them; the *guenhwyvar* of a passion and a grief, of high endeavour and a quest that would take Bedwyr into a world of spirit and leave Arthur lonely, waiting there at the center of glory to become himself a legend and himself a grail . . .

I came back to the hall. The pain in my head was fierce. The fitful, dazzling light struck like a spear against my eyes. I could feel the sweat trickling down beneath my robe. My hands slipped on the carved arms of the chair. I fought to steady my breathing, and the hammer-beat of my heart.

No one had noticed me. Time had passed. The formality of the Council had broken up. Arthur was the center now of a group, talking and laughing; about the table the older men sat still, relaxed and easy, chatting among themselves. Servants had come in, and wine was being poured. The talk was all around me, like water rising. In it could be heard the notes of triumph and release. It was done; there would be a new queen, and a new succession. The wars were over, and Britain, alone of Rome's old subject lands, was safe behind her royal ramparts for the next span of sunlit time.

Arthur turned his head and met my eyes. I neither moved nor spoke, but the laughter died out of his face, and he got to his feet. He came over as quickly as a spear starting for the mark, waving his companions back out of earshot.

"Merlin, what is it? This wedding? You cannot surely think that it—"

I shook my head. The pain went through it like a saw. I think I cried out. At the King's move there had been a hush; now there was complete silence in the hall. Silence, and eyes, and the unsteady dazzle of the flames.

He leaned forward, as if to take my hand. "What is it? Are you ill? Merlin, can you speak?"

His voice swelled, echoed, was whirled away. It did not concern me. Nothing concerned me but the necessity of speech. The lamp-flames were burning somewhere in my breast, their hot oil spilling in bubbles through my blood. Breath came thick and piercing, like smoke in the lungs. When I found words at last they surprised me. I had seen nothing beyond the chamber long ago in the Perilous Chapel, and the vision which might or might not have meant anything. What I heard myself saying, in a harsh and ringing voice that brought Arthur up like a blow, and startled every man to his feet, had a very different burden.

"It is not over yet. King! Get you to horse, and ride! They have broken the peace, and soon they will be at Badon! Men and women are dying in their blood, and children cry, before they are spitted like chickens. There is no king near to protect them. Get you there now, duke of the kings! This is for you alone, when the people themselves cry out for you! Go with your Companions, and put a finish to this thing! For by the Light, Arthur of Britain, this is the last time, and the last victory! Go now!"

The words went ringing into total silence. Those who had never before heard me speak with power were pale: all made the sign. My breathing was loud in the hush, like that of an old man fighting to stave off death.

Then from the crowd of younger men came sounds of disbelief, even scoffing. It was not to be wondered at. They had heard stories of my past deeds, but so many of these were patently poets' work, and all, having gone already into song, had taken the high colour of legend. Last time I had spoken so had been at Luguvallium, before the raising of the sword, and some of them had been children then. These knew me only as engineer and man of medicine, the quiet counsellor whom the King favoured.

The muttering was all around me, wind in the trees.

"There has been no signal; what is he talking about? As if the High King could go off on his bare word, for a scare like this! Arthur has done enough, and so have we; the peace is settled, anyone can see that! Badon? Where is it? Well, but no Saxon would attack there, not now. . . . Yes, but if they did, there is no force there to hold them, he was right about that. . . . No, it's nonsense, the old man has lost his senses again. Remember, up there in the forest, what he was like? Crazy, and that's the truth . . . and now moon-mad again, with the same malady?"

Arthur had not taken his eyes off me. The whispers blew to and fro. Someone called for a doctor, and there was coming and going in the hall. He ignored it. He and I were alone together. His hand came out and took me by the wrist. I felt, through the whirling pain, his young strength forcing me gently back into my chair. I had not even known I was standing. His other hand went out, and someone put a goblet into it. He held the wine to my lips.

I turned my head aside. "No. Leave me. Go now. Trust me."

"By all the gods there are," he said, from the back of his throat, "I trust you." He swung on his heel, and spoke. "You, and you, and you, give the orders. We ride now. See to it."

Then back to me, but speaking so that all could hear: "Victory, you said?"

"Victory. Can you doubt it?"

For a moment, through the stresses of pain, I saw his look; the look of the boy who had braved the white flame at my word, and lifted the enchanted sword. "I doubt nothing," said Arthur.

Then he laughed, leaned forward and kissed me on the cheek, and, with his Companions following, went swiftly out of the hall.

The pain lifted. I could breathe and see. I got up and walked after them, out into the air. Those left in the hall drew back and let me through. No one spoke to me, or dared to question. I mounted the rampart and looked outward. The sentry on duty there moved away, not like a soldier, but sidling. The whites of his eyes showed. Word had gone round fast. I hunched my cloak against the wind and stayed where I was.

They had gone, so small a troop to throw against the might of the final Saxon bid for Britain. The gallop dwindled into the night and was gone. Somewhere in that darkness to the north the Tor was standing up into the black sky. No light, nothing. Beyond it, no light. Nor south, nor east; no light anywhere, or warning fires. Only my word.

A sound somewhere in the blowing darkness. For a moment I took it for an echo of that distant gallop; then, hearing in it, faintly, the cry and clash of armies, I thought that vision had returned to me. But my head was clear, and the night, with all its sounds and shadows, was mortal night.

Then the sounds wheeled closer, and went streaming over-head, high in the black air. It was the wild geese, the pack of heaven's hounds, the Wild Hunt that courses the skies with Llud, King of the Otherworld, in time of war and storm. They had risen from the Lake waters, and now came over-head, flighting the dark. Straight from the silent Tor they came, to wheel over Caer Camel, then back across the slumbering Island, the noise of their voices and the galloping wings lost at length down the reaches of the night toward Badon.

With the dawn, beacon lights blazed across the land. But whoever led the Saxon hordes to Badon must hardly have set foot on its bloody soil when, out of the dark, more swiftly even than birds could have flown or fire signalled, the High King Arthur and his own picked knights fell on them and destroyed them, smashing the barbarian power utterly, for his day, and for the rest of his generation.

So the god came back to me, Merlin his servant. Next day I left Caer Camel, and rode out to look for a place where I could build myself a house.

BOOK III

APPLEGARTH

1

To the east of Caer Camel the land is rolling and wooded, ridges and hills of gentle green, with here and there, among the bushes and ferns of the summits, traces of old dwelling-places or fortifications of past time.

One such place I had noticed before, and now, casting about among the hills and valleys, I looked at it once more, and found it good. It was a solitary spot, in a fold between two hills, where a spring welled from the turf and sent a tiny brook tumbling down to meet a valley stream. A long time ago men had lived there. When the sun fell aright you could see the soft outline of ancient walls beneath the turf. That settlement had vanished long since, but since then some other settler, in harder times, had built himself a tower, the main part of which still stood. It had been built, moreover, with Roman stone taken from Caer Camel. The squared shapes of the chiselled stone showed still clean-edged beneath the encroaching saplings and those stinging ghosts that cluster wherever man has been, the nettles. Even these weeds were not unwelcome; they are sovereign for many ailments, and I intended, as soon as the house was done, to plant a garden, which is the chief of the arts of peace.

And peace we had at last. The news of the victory at Badon reached me even before I had paced out the dimensions of my new home. From the account Arthur sent me of the battle it seemed certain that this must be the final victory of the campaign, and now the King was imposing terms, being set on the decisive fixing of his kingdom's boundaries. There was no reason to suppose, his message ran, that there would be any further attack or even resistance for some time to come. I, not having seen the battlefield, but knowing what I knew, prepared to build for a time of peace, where I might live in the solitude I loved and needed, at due remove from the busy center where Arthur would be.

Meanwhile it would be wise to get hold of all the masons and craftsmen I should require before Arthur's own great schemes for his city began to burgeon. They came, shook their heads over my plans, then set cheerfully to work to build what I wanted.

This was a small house, a cottage, if you will, set in the hollow of the hillside, and facing south and west, away from Caer Camel, toward the distant swell of the downs. The place was sheltered from north and east, and, by a curve of the hill below, from the few passers-by on the valley road. I had the tower rebuilt on its old pattern, and the new house constructed against this, single-storeyed, with behind it a square courtyard or garth in the Roman style. The tower formed a corner of this between my own dwelling and the kitchen quarters. At the side opposite the house were workshops and sheds for storage. On the north side of the garth was a high wall coped with tiles, against which I hoped to set some of the more delicate plants. I had long thought of doing what now the masons shook their heads over: the wall was built double, and the hypocaust led warm air into it. Not only in winter would the vines and peaches be safe, but the whole garth would, I thought, benefit from the warmth, as well as from the sunlight it would catch and hold. This was the first time I had seen such an idea put into practice, but later it was done at Camelot, and at Arthur's other palace at Caerleon. A miniature aqueduct led water from the spring into a well at the garth's center.

The men, finding it a pleasant change from the years of military building, worked quickly. We had an open winter that year. I rode to Bryn Myrddin to oversee the moving of my books and certain of the medical stores, then spent Christmas at Camelot with Arthur. The carpenters went into my house early in the New Year, and the work was done and the men free in time to start the permanent building at Camelot in the spring.

I still had no servant of my own, and now had to set myself to find one—not an easy task, for few men can settle happily in the kind of solitude I crave, and my ways have never been those of the ordinary master. The hours I keep are strange ones; I require little food or sleep, and have great need of silence. I could have bought a slave who would have had to put up with whatever I wanted, but I have never liked bought service. But this time, as always before, I was lucky. One of the local masons had an uncle who was a gardener; he had given him, he said, an account of the building of the heated wall, and the uncle had shaken his head and muttered something about new-fangled foreign nonsense, but had since evinced the liveliest curiosity about every stage of the building. His name was Varro. He would be glad to come, said the mason, and his daughter, who could cook and clean, would come with him.

So it was settled. Varro started the clearing and digging straight away, and the girl Mora began to scrub and air, and then, in one of those lucid and lovely spells of early weather, with primroses already showing under the budding hawthorns, and lambs couched warm beside the ewes in the hollows of flowering whin, I stabled my horse and unpacked my big harp, and was home.

Soon after, Arthur came to see me. I was in the garth, sitting in the sunshine on a bench between the pillars of the miniature colonnade. I was busy sorting seeds collected last summer and packed away in twists of parchment. Beyond the walls I heard the stamp and jingle of the King's escort, but he came in alone. Varro went past with a stare and a salute, carrying his spade. I got to my feet as Arthur raised a hand in greeting.

"It's very small," were his first words, as he looked about him.

"Enough. It's only for me."

"Only!" He laughed, then pivoted on his heel. "Mmm . . . if you like dog-kennels, and it seems you do, then I must say it's very pleasant. So that's the famous wall, is it? The masons were telling me about it. What are you planting there?"

I told him, and then took him on a tour of my little garth. Arthur, who knew as much about gardens as I about warfare, but who was always interested in making, looked and touched and questioned; he spent a lot of time at the heated wall, and on the construction of the small aqueduct that fed the well.

"Vervain, Camomile, Comfrey, Marigold . . ." He turned over the labelled packets of seed lying on the bench. "I remember Drusilla used to grow marigolds. She gave me some concoction of them when I had the toothache." He looked round him again. "Do you know, there is already something of the same peace here that one had at Galava. If only for my sake, you were right in refusing to live in Camelot. I'll feel I have a refuge here, when things are pressing on me."

"I hope you will. Well, that's all here. I'll have my flowers here, and an orchard outside. There were a few old trees here already, and they seem to be doing well. Would you like to come in now and see the house?"

"A pleasure," he said, in a tone so suddenly formal that I glanced at him, to see that his attention was not on me at all, but on Mora, who had come out of a doorway and was shaking a cloth in the breeze. Her gown was blown close against her body, and her hair, which was pretty, flew in a bright tangle round her face. She stopped to push it back, saw Arthur, blushed and giggled, then ran indoors again. I saw a bright eye peep through a crack, then she caught me watching, and withdrew. The door shut. It was apparent that the girl had no idea who the young man was who had eyed her so boldly.

He was grinning at me. "I am to be married in a month, so you can stop watching me like that. I shall be the most model of married men."

"I am sure of it. Was I watching you? It's no concern of mine, but I should warn you that the gardener is her father."

"And a tough fellow he looks. All right, I'll keep my blood cool until May. God knows it's landed me in trouble before, and will again."

" 'A model married man?' "

"I was talking about my past. You warned me that it would reach into my future." He said it lightly; the past, I guessed, was well behind him now. I doubted if thoughts of Morgause still troubled his sleep. He followed me into the house and, while I found wine and poured it, went on another of his prowling tours of discovery.

There were only two rooms. The living-chamber took two-thirds of the length of the house, and its full width, with windows both ways, on garth and hill. The doorway opened on the colonnade that edged the garth. Today for the first time the door stood open to the mild air, and sunlight fell warmly across the terra-cotta tiles of the floor. At the end of the room was the place for the fire, with a wide chimney to take the smoke outside. In Britain we need fires as well as heated floors. The hearthstone was of slate, and the walls, of well-finished stone, were hung with rich rugs I had brought back with me from my travels in the East. Table and stools were oak, from the same tree, but the great chair was of elm wood, as also the chest under the window, which held my books. A door at the end of the room led to my bedchamber, which was simply furnished with bed and clothes chest. With some memory, perhaps, of childhood, I had planted a pear tree outside the window.

All this I showed him, then took him to the tower. The door to this led off the colonnade in the corner of the garth. On the ground floor was the workroom or stillroom, where the herbs were dried, and medicines made up. There was no furniture but a big table, and stools and cupboards, and the small brick stove with its oven and charcoal burner. A stone stair against one wall led to the upper room. This was the chamber I meant to use as my private study. Here there was nothing as yet but a work-table and chair, a couple of stools and a cupboard with tablets and the mathematical instruments I had brought from Antioch. A brazier stood in one corner. I had had a window made looking out to the south, and this was covered with neither horn nor curtain. I do not readily feel the cold.

Arthur moved round the tiny room, stooping, peering, opening boxes and cupboards, leaning on his fists to gaze out of the window, filling the small space with his immense vitality, so that even the stout, Roman-built walls seemed barely to contain him.

In the main chamber, once more, he took a goblet from me and raised it. "To your new home. What will you call it?"

"Applegarth."

"I like that. It's right. To Applegarth then, and your long life here!"

"Thank you. And to my first guest."

"Am I? I'm glad. May there be many more, and may they all come in peace." He drank and set the goblet down, looking about him again. "Already it is full of peace. Yes, I begin to see why you chose it . . . but are you sure it is all you want? You know, and I know, that the whole of my kingdom is yours by right, and I do assure you I'd let you have half of it for the asking."

"I'll let you keep it for the present. It's been too much trouble for me to envy you overmuch. Have you time to sit for a while? Will you eat? The very idea will frighten Mora into an epilepsy, because you can be sure she has been out to ask her father who the young stranger is, but I'm certain she can find something—"

"Thank you, no, I've eaten. Have you just the two servants? Who cooks for you?"

"The girl."

"Well?"

"Eh? Oh, well enough."

"Which means you haven't even noticed. For God's sake!" said Arthur. "Let me send you a cook. I don't like to think of you eating nothing but peasant messes."

"Please, no. The two of them round me by day are all I want, and even they go to their own home at night. I do very well, I assure you."

"All right. But I wish you would let me do something, give you something."

"When I find something I want, be sure I'll ask you for it. Now tell me how the building is going. I'm afraid I've been too occupied with my dog-kennel to pay much attention. Will it be ready for your wedding?"

He shook his head. "By summer, perhaps, it might be fit to bring a queen to. But for the wedding I'll go back to Caerleon. It will be in May. Will you be there?"

"Unless it's your wish that I should be there, I would prefer to stay here. I begin to feel I've had too much travelling in the past few years."

"As you wish. No, no more wine, thank you. One thing I wanted to ask you. You remember, when first the idea of my marriage was mooted—the first marriage—you seemed to have some doubts about it. I understood that you had had some sort of presentiment of disaster. If so, you were right. Tell me, please—this time, have you any such doubts?"

They tell me that when I guard my face, no man can read what is in my mind. I met his eyes level. "None. Need you ask me? Have you any doubts yourself?"

"None." The flash of a smile. "At least, not yet. How could I, when I am told that she is perfection itself? They all say she is lovely as a May morning, and they tell me this, that and the other thing. But then, they always do. It will suffice if she has a sweet breath and a compliant temper . . . Oh, and a pretty voice. I find that I care about voices. All this granted, it couldn't be a better match. As a Welshman, Merlin, you ought to agree."

"Oh, I do. I agree with everything Gwyl said, there in the hall. When do you go to Wales to bring her to Caerleon?"

"I can't go myself; I have to ride north in a week's time. I'm sending Bedwyr again, and Gereint with him, and—to do her honour, since I can't go myself—King Melwas of the Summer Country."

I nodded, and the conversation turned then on the reasons for his journey north. He was going, I knew, mainly to look at the defensive work in the northeast. Tydwal, Lot's kinsman, held Dunpeldyr now, ostensibly on behalf of Morgause and Lot's eldest son, Gawain, though it was doubtful if the queen's family would ever leave Orkney.

"Which suits me very well," said the King indifferently. "But it creates certain difficulties in the northeast."

He went on to explain. The problem lay with Aguisel, who held the strong castle of Bremenium, in a nest of the Northumbrian hills, where Dere Street runs up into High Cheviot. While Lot had ruled to the north, Aguisel had been content to run with him, "as his jackal," said Arthur contemptuously, "along with Tydwal and Urien. But now that Tydwal sits in Lot's chair, Aguisel begins to be ambitious. I've heard a rumour—I have no proof of it—that when last the Angles sent their ships up the Alaunus River, Aguisel met them there, not in war, but to speak with their leader. And Urien follows him still, brother jackals, playing at being lions. They may think they are too far away from me, but I intend to pay them a visit and disillusion them. My excuse is to look at the work that has been done on the Black Dyke. From all I hear, I should like a pretext to remove Aguisel for good and all, but I must do it without rousing Tydwal and Urien to defend him. The last thing I can afford, until I am sure of the West Saxons, is a break-up of the allied kings in the north. If I have to remove Tydwal, it may mean bringing Morgause back to Dunpeldyr. A small thing, compared with the rest, but the day she sits in a mainland castle again cannot be a good day for me."

"Then let us hope the day will never come."

"As you say. I'll do my best to contrive it so." He looked round him again as he turned to go. "It's a pleasant place. I'm afraid I shan't have time to see you again before I ride, Merlin. I go before the week is out."

"Then all the gods go with you, my dear. May they be beside you, too, at your wedding. And some day, come and see me again."

He went. The room seemed to tremble and grow larger again, and the air to settle back into tranquillity.

2

And tranquillity was the sum of the months that followed. I went over to Camelot soon after Arthur's departure for the north, to see how the building work was going; then, satisfied, left Derwen to complete it, and retired to my new-made fastness with almost the same feeling of home-coming as I felt at Bryn Myrddin. The rest of that spring I spent about my own affairs, planting my garden, writing to Blaise, and, as the country-side burgeoned, collecting the herbs I needed for a renewal of my stores.

I did not see Arthur again before the wedding. A courier brought me news, which was brief but favourable. Arthur had found proof of Aguisel's villainy and had attacked him in Bremenium. The details I did not know, but the King had taken the place and put Aguisel to death; and this without rousing either Tydwal or Urien, or any of their kinsmen against him. In fact, Tydwal had fought beside Arthur in the final storming of the walls. How the King had achieved this, the report did not say, but with the death of Aguisel the world would be cleaner, and, since he died without sons, a man of Arthur's choosing could now hold the castle that commanded the Cheviot pass. Arthur chose Brewyn, a man he could be certain of, then went south to Caerleon well content.

The Lady Guinevere duly arrived in Caerleon, royally escorted by princes—Melwas and Bedwyr and a company of Arthur's knights. Cei had not gone with the party; as Arthur's seneschal his duty lay in the palace at Caerleon, where the wedding was celebrated with great splendour at Pentecost. I heard later that the bride's father had suggested May Day, and that Arthur, after the briefest hesitation, had said, "No," so flatly that eyebrows were raised. But this was the only shadow. All else seemed set fair. The pair were married late in the month on a glorious day of sunshine, and Arthur took a bride to bed for the second time, with, now, days and nights to spare. They came to Camelot in early summer, and I had my first sight of the second Guinevere.

Queen Guinevere of Northgalis was more than "well enough and with a sweet breath"; she was a beauty. To describe her, one would have to rob the bards of all their old conventions; hair like golden corn, eyes like summer sky, a flower-fair skin and a lissom body—but add to all this the dazzle of personality, a sort of outgoing gaiety, and a way of communicating joy, and you will have some idea of her fascination. For fascinating she was: on the night she was brought to Camelot I watched her through the feasting, and saw other eyes than the King's fixed on her throughout the evening. It was obvious that she would be Queen not only of Arthur, but of all the Companions. Except perhaps Bedwyr. His were the only eyes that did not seek hers constantly; he seemed quieter even than usual, lost in his own thoughts, and as for Guinevere, she barely glanced his way. I wondered if something had happened on the journey from Northgalis that stung his memory. But Melwas, who sat near her, hung on her every word, and watched her with the same eyes of worship as the younger men.

That was a beautiful summer, I remember. The sun shone blazing, but from time to time the sweet rains came and the soft wind, so that the fields bore crops such as few men could remember, and the cattle and sheep grew sleek, and the land ripened toward a great harvest. Everywhere, though the bells rang on Sundays in the Christian churches, and crosses were to be seen nowadays where once cairns of stone or statues had stood by the wayside, the country folk went about their tasks blessing the young King for giving them, not only the peace in which to grow their crops, but the wealth of the crops themselves. For them, both wealth and glory stemmed from their young ruler, as, during the last year of the sick Uther's life, the land had lain under the black blight. And the common folk waited confidently—as at Camelot the nobles waited—for the announcement that an heir was begotten. But the summer wore through, and autumn came, and, though the land yielded its great harvest, the Queen, riding out daily with her ladies, was as lissom and slender as ever, and no announcement was made.

And here in Camelot, the memory of the girl who had conceived the heir and died of him troubled no one. All was new and shining and building and making. The palace was completed, and now the carvers and gilders were at work, and women wove and stitched, and wares of pottery and silver and gold came into the new city daily, so that the roads seemed full of coming and going. It was the time of youth and laughter, and building after conquest; the grim years were forgotten. As for the "white shadow" of my foreboding, I began to wonder if it had indeed been the death of the other pretty Guenever that had cast that shadow across the light, and seemed to linger still in corners like a ghost. But I never saw her, and Arthur, if he once remembered her, said nothing.

So four winters passed, and Camelot's towers shone with new gilding, and the borders were quiet, the harvests good, and the people grew accustomed to peace and safety. Arthur was five and twenty, and rather more silent than of old; he seemed to be away from home more, and each time for longer. Cador's duchess bore him a son, and Arthur rode down into Cornwall to stand sponsor, but Queen Guinevere did not go with him. For a few weeks there was whispered hope that she had a good reason for refusing the journey; but the King and his party went and returned, and then left again, by sea, for Gwynedd, and still the Queen at Camelot rode out and laughed and danced and held court, as slim as a maiden, and, it seemed, as free of care.

Then one raining day of early spring, just as dusk fell, a horseman came thudding to my gate with a message. The King was still away, and was not looked for yet for perhaps another week. And the Queen had vanished.

The messenger was Cei the seneschal, Arthur's foster-brother, the son of Ector of Galava, a big man, some three years older than the King, florid and broad-shouldered. He was a good fighter and a brave man, though not, like Bedwyr, a natural leader. Cei had neither nerves nor imagination, and, while this makes for bravery in war, it does not make for good leadership. Bedwyr, the poet and dreamer, who suffered ten times over for one grief, was the finer man.

But Cei was staunch, and now, since he was responsible for the ordering of the King's household, had come himself to see me, attended only by one servant. This, though he bore one arm in a rough sling, and looked tired and worried out of his slow mind. He told me the story, sitting in my room with the firelight flickering on the ceiling rafters. He accepted a cup of mulled wine, and talked quickly, while, at my insistence, he removed the sling and let me examine his injured arm.

"Bedwyr sent me to tell you. I was hurt, so he sent me back. No, I didn't see a doctor. Damn it, there hasn't been time! Anything could've happened, wait till I tell you. . . . She's been gone since daybreak. You remember how fair it was this morning? She went out with her ladies, with only the grooms and a couple of men for escort. That was usual—you know it was."

"Yes." It was true. Sometimes one or more of the knights accompanied the Queen, but frequently they were occupied on affairs more important than squiring her on her daily rides. She had troopers and grooms, and nowadays there was no danger, so near Camelot, from the kind of wild outlaw who had frequented lonely places when I was a boy. So Guinevere had risen early on what promised to be a fine morning, mounted her grey mare, and set out with two of her ladies, and four men, of whom two were soldiers. They had ridden out across a belt of dry moorland bordered to the south by thick forest. To their right hand lay the marshlands, where the rivers wound seaward through their deep, reedy channels, and to the east the land showed rolling and forested toward the high lift of the downs. The party had found game in plenty; the little greyhounds had run wild after it, and, said Cei, the grooms had their hands full riding after them to bring them back. Meantime, the Queen had flown her merlin after a hare, and had followed this herself, straight into the forest.

Cei grunted as my probing fingers found the injured muscle. "Well, but I told you that it was nothing much. Only a sprain, isn't it? A pulled muscle? Will it take long? Oh, well, it's not my sword arm. . . . Well, she galloped the grey mare in, and the women stayed back. Her maid's no rider, and the other, the lady Melissa, is not young. The grooms were coming back with the greyhounds on the saddle, and were still some way off. Nobody was worrying. She's a great horsewoman—you know she even rode Arthur's white stallion and managed it?—and besides, she's done it before, just to tease them. So they took it easy, while the two troopers rode after her."

The rest was easy to supply. It was true that this had happened before, with no chance of ill, so the troopers spurred after the Queen at no more than a hand-gallop. They could hear her mare thudding through the thick forest ahead of them, and the swish and crackling of the bushes and dead stuff underfoot. The forest thickened; the two soldiers slowed to a canter, ducking the boughs which still swung from the Queen's passing, and guiding their horses through the tangle of fallen wood and water-logged holes that made the forest floor such dangerous terrain. Half cursing, half laughing, and wholly occupied, it was some minutes before they realized that they could no longer hear the Queen's mare. The tangled underbrush showed no trace of a horse's passing. They pulled up to listen. Nothing but the distant scolding of a jay. They shouted, and got no answer. Annoyed rather than alarmed, they separated, riding one in the direction of the jay's scolding, the other still deeper into the forest.

"I'll spare you the rest," said Cei. "You know how it is. After a bit they forgathered, and by then, of course, they were alarmed. They shouted some more, and the grooms heard them, and went in and joined the search. Then after a while they heard the mare again. She was going hard, they said, and they heard her whinnying. They struck their spurs in and went after her."

"Yes?" I settled the injured arm into the freshly tied sling, and he thanked me.

"That's better. I'm grateful. Well, they found the mare three miles off, lame, and trailing a broken rein, but no sign of the Queen. They sent the women back with one of the grooms, and they went on searching. Bedwyr and I took troops out, and for the rest of the day we've been quartering the forest as best we could, but nothing." He lifted his good hand. "You know what that country's like. Where it isn't a tangle of tree and scrub that would stop a fire-breathing dragon, it's marsh where a horse or a man would sink over his head. And even in the forest there are ditches as deep as a man, and too wide to leap. That's where I came to grief. Dead fir boughs spread over a hole, for all the world like a wolf-trap. I'm lucky to have got away with just this. My horse got a spike in the belly, poor beast. It's doubtful if he'll be good for much again."

"The mare," I said. "Had she fallen? Was she mired?"

"To the eyeballs, but that means nothing. She must have galloped through marsh and mire for an hour. The saddle-cloth was torn, though. I think she must have fallen; I can't see the Queen falling off her else—unless she was swept off by a bough. Believe me, we must have searched every brake and ditch in the forest. She'll be lying unconscious somewhere . . . if not worse. God, if she had to do such a thing, why couldn't she do it when the King was at home?"

"Of course you have sent to him?"

"Bedwyr sent a rider before we left Camelot. There are more men out there now. It's getting too dark to find her, but if she's been lying unconscious, and comes round, maybe they'll hear her calling. What else can we do? Bedwyr's got men down there with dragnets. Some of those pools are deep, and there are currents in that river to the west . . ." He left it there. His rather stupid blue eyes stared at me, as if begging me to do a miracle. "After I took my toss he sent me back to you. Merlin, will you come with me now, and show us where to look for the Queen?"

I looked down at my hands, then at the fire, dying now to small flames that licked round a greying log. I had not put my powers to the test since Badon. And how long before that since I had dared to call on the least of them? Nor flames, nor dream, nor even the glimmer of Sight in the crystal or the water-drops: I would not importune God for the smallest breath of the great wind. If he came to me, he came. It was for him to choose the time, and for me to go with it.

"Or even just tell me, now?" Cei's voice cracked, imploring.

Time was, I thought, when I would only have had to look at the fire, like this, to lift a hand, like this . . .

The small flames hissed, and leaped a foot high, wrapping the grey log with blazing scarves of light, and throwing out a heat that seared the skin. Sparks jumped, stung, with the old welcome, quickening pain. The light, the fire, the whole living world flowed upward, bright and dark, flame and smoke and trembling vision, carrying me with it.

A sound from Cei flicked my attention back to him. He was on his feet, backed away from the blaze. Through the ruddy light pouring over him I saw that he had gone pale. There was sweat on his face. He said hoarsely: "Merlin—"

He was already fading, drowned in flame and darkness. I heard myself say: "Go. Get my horse ready. And wait for me."

I did not hear him go. I was already far from the firelit room, borne on the cool and blazing river that dropped me, light as a leaf loosened by the wind, in the darkness at the gates of the Otherworld.

The caves went on and on for ever, their roofs lost in darkness, their walls lit with some strange subaqueous glow that outlined every ridge and boss of rock. From arches of stone hung stalactites, like moss from ancient trees, and pillars of rock rose from the stone floor to meet them. Water fell somewhere, echoing, and the swimming light rippled, reflecting it.

Then, distant and small, a light showed; the shape of a pillared doorway, formal and handsome. Beyond it something—someone—moved. In the moment when I wanted to go forward and see I was there without effort, a leaf on the wind, a ghost in a stormy night.

The door was the gateway to a great hall lighted as if for a feast. Whatever I had seen moving was no longer there; merely the great spaces of blazing light, the coloured pavement of a king's hall, the pillars gilded, the torches held in dragon-stands of gold. Golden seats I saw, ranged round the gleaming walls, and silver tables. On one of these lay a chessboard, of silver, dark and light, with pieces of silver gilt standing, as if half through an interrupted game. In the center of the vast floor stood a great chair of ivory. In front of this was a golden chessboard, and on it a dozen or so gold chessmen, and one half-finished, lying with a rod of gold and a file where someone had been working to carve them.

I knew then that this was no true vision, but a dream of the legendary hall of Llud-Nuatha, King of the Otherworld. To this palace had they all come, the heroes of song and story. Here the sword had lain, and here the grail and the lance might one day be dreamed of and lifted. Here Macsen had seen his princess, the girl whom in the world above he had married, and on whom he had beggotten the line of rulers whose latest scion was Arthur . . .

Like a dream at morning, it had gone. But the great caves were still there, and in them, now, a throne with a dark king seated, and by him a queen, half-visible in shadows. Somewhere a thrush was singing, and I saw her turn her head, and heard her sigh.

Then through it all I knew that I, Merlin, this time of all the times, did not want to see the truth. Knowing it already, perhaps, beneath the level of conscious thought, I had built for myself the palace of Llud, the hall of Dis and his prisoned Persephone. Behind them both lay the truth, and, as I was the god's servant and Arthur's, I had to find it. I looked again.

The sound of water, and a thrush singing. A dim room, but not lofty, or furnished with silver and gold; a curtained room, well lighted, where a man and a woman sat at a little inlaid table and played at chess. She seemed to be winning. I saw him frown, and the tense set of his shoulders as he hunched over the board, considering his move. She was laughing. He lifted his hand, hesitating, but withdrew it again and sat awhile, quite still. She said something, and he glanced aside, then turned to adjust the wick of one of the lamps near him. As he looked away from the board, her hand stole out and she moved a piece, neat as a thief in the market-place. When he looked back she was sitting, demure, hands in lap. He looked, stared, then laughed aloud and moved. His knight scooped her queen from the board. She looked surprised, and threw up her hands, pretty as a picture, then began to set the chessmen afresh. But he, suddenly all impatience, sprang to his feet and, reaching across the board, took her hands in his own and pulled her toward him. Between them the board fell over, and the chessmen spilled to the floor. I saw the white queen roll near his foot, with the red king over her. The white king lay apart, tumbled face downward. He looked down, laughed again, and said something in her ear. His arms closed round her. Her robe scattered the chessmen, and his foot came down on the white king. The ivory smashed, splintering.

With it the vision splintered, broke in shadow that wisped, greying, back into lamplight, and the last glimmer from the dying fire.

I got stiffly to my feet. Horses were stamping outside, and somewhere in the garth a thrush was singing. I took my cloak from its hook and wrapped it round me. I went out. Cei was fidgeting by the horses, biting his nails. He hurried to meet me.

"You know?"

"A little. She is alive, and unhurt."

"Ah! Christ be thanked for this! Where, then?"

"I don't know yet, but I shall. A moment, Cei. Did you find the merlin?"

"What?" blankly.

"The Queen's falcon. The merlin she flew and followed into the forest."

"Not a sign. Why? Would it have helped?"

"I hardly know. Just a question. Now take me to Bedwyr."

3

Mercifully, Cei asked no more questions, being fully occupied with his horse as we slithered and bounded, alternately, over the difficult ground. Though, in spite of the rain, there was still sufficient light to see the way, it was not easy to pick a quick and safe route across the tract of water-logged land that was the shortest way between Applegarth and the forest where the Queen had vanished.

For the last part of the way we were guided by distant torchlight, and men's voices, magnified and distorted by water and wind. We found Bedwyr up to the thighs in water three or four paces out from the bank of a deep, still runnel edged with gnarled alders and the stumps of ancient oaks, some cut long ago for timber, and others blasted with time and storm, and growing again in the welter of smashed branches.

Near one of these the men were gathered. Torches had been tied to the dead boughs, and two other men with torches were out beside Bedwyr in the stream, lighting the work of dragging. On the bank, a short way along from the oak stump, lay a pile of sodden debris running with water, which glinted in the torchlight. Each time, one could guess, the nets would come up heavily weighted from the bottom, and each time all the men present would strain forward under the torchlight to see, with dread, if the net held the drowned body of the Queen.

One such load had just been tipped out as Cei and I approached, our horses slithering to a thankful stop on the very brink of the water. Bedwyr had not seen us. I heard his voice, rough with fatigue, as he showed the net-men where next to sink the drags. But the men on the bank called out, and he turned, then, seizing a torch from the man beside him, came splashing toward us.

"Cei?" He was too far gone with worry and exhaustion to see me there. "Did you see him? What did he say? Wait, I'll be with you in a moment." He turned to shout over his shoulder: "Carry on, there!"

"No need," I said. "Stop the work, Bedwyr. The Queen is safe."

He was just below the bank. His face, upturned in the torchlight, was swept with such a light of relief and joy that one could have sworn the torches burned suddenly brighter. "Merlin? Thank the gods for that! You found her, then?"

Someone had led our horses back. All around us now the men crowded, with eager questions. Someone put a hand down to Bedwyr, who came leaping up the bank, and stood there with the muddy water running off him.

"He had a vision." This was Cei, bluntly. The men went quiet at that, staring, and the questions died to an awed and uneasy muttering. But Bedwyr asked simply:

"Where is she?"

"I can't tell you that yet, I'm afraid." I looked around me. To the left the muddy channel wound deeper into the darkness of the forest, but westward, to the right, a space of evening light could be seen through the trees where it opened out into a marshy lake. "Why were you dragging here? I understood the troopers didn't know where she fell."

"It's true they neither heard nor saw it, and she must have fallen some time before they got on the track of her mare again. But it looks very much as if the accident happened here. The ground's got trampled over now, so you can't see anything much, but there were signs of a fall, the horse shying, probably, and then bursting away through these branches. Bring the torch nearer, will you? There, Merlin, see? The marks on the boughs and a shred of cloth that must have come from her cloak. . . . There was blood, too, smeared on one of the snags. But if you say she's safe . . ." He put up a weary hand to push the hair from his eyes. It left a streak of mud right down his cheek. He took no notice.

"The blood must have been the mare's," said someone from behind me. "She was scratched about the legs."

"Yes, that would be it," said Bedwyr. "When we picked her up she was lame, and with a broken rein. Then when we found the marks here on the bank and among the branches, I thought I saw—I was afraid I knew what had happened. I thought the mare had shied and fallen, and thrown the Queen into the water. It's deep here, right under the bank. I reckoned she might have held on to the rein and tried to get the mare to pull her out, but the rein broke, and then the mare bolted. Or else the rein got caught on one of the snags, and it was only some time later that the mare could break loose and bolt. But now . . . What did happen?"

"That I can't tell you. What matters now is to find her, and quickly. And for that, we must have King Melwas' help. Is he here, or any of his people?"

"None of his men-at-arms, no. But we fell in with three or four of the marsh-dwellers, good fellows, who showed us some of the ways through the forest." He raised his voice, turning. "The Mere men, are they here still?"

It seemed that they were. They came forward, reluctant and over-awed, pushed by their companions. Two men, smallish and broad-shouldered, bearded and unkempt, and with them a stripling boy—the son, I guessed, of the younger man. I spoke to the elder.

"You come from Mere, in the Summer Country?"

He nodded, his fingers twisting nervously in front of him at a fold of his sodden tunic.

"It was good of you to help the High King's men. You shall not be the losers by it, I promise you. Now, you know who I am?"

Another nod, more twisting of the hands. The boy swallowed audibly.

"Then don't be afraid, but answer my questions if you can. Do you know where King Melwas is now?"

"Not rightly, my lord, no." The man spoke slowly, almost like one using a foreign language. These marsh people are silent folk, and, when about their own business, use a dialect peculiar to themselves. "But you'll not find him at his palace on the Island, that I do know. Seen him away hunting, we did, two days gone. 'Tis a thing he does, now and again, just him and one of the lords, or maybe two."

"Hunting? In these forests?"

"Nay, master, he went fowling. Just himself, and one to row the boat."

"And you saw him go? Which way?"

"Southwest again." The man pointed. "Down there where the causeway runs into the marsh. The land's dry in places thereabouts, and there be wild geese grazing in plenty. There's a lodge he has, a main beyond, but he won't be there now. It's empty since this winter past, and no servants in it. Besides, the news came up the water this dawning that the young King was on his way home from Caer-y-n'a Von with a score of sail, so he would be putting in at the Island, maybe with the next tide. And our King Melwas surely must be there to greet him?"

This was news to me, and, I could see, to Bedwyr. It is a constant mystery how these remote dwellers in the marshes get their news so quickly.

Bedwyr looked at me. "There was no beacon lighted on the Tor when news came about the Queen. Did you see it, Merlin?"

"No. Nor any other. The sails can't have been sighted yet. We should go now, Bedwyr. We'll ride for the Tor."

"You mean to speak with Melwas, even before we seek the Queen?"

"I think so. If you would give the orders? And see these men recompensed for their help?"

In the bustle that followed, I touched Bedwyr's arm and took him aside. "I can't talk now, Bedwyr. This is a high matter, and dangerous. You and I must go alone to seek the Queen. Can you manage this without being questioned?"

He frowned, searching my face, but said immediately: "Of course. But Cei? Will he accept that?"

"He's injured. Besides, if Arthur is due, Cei should be back in Camelot."

"That's true. And the rest can ride for the Island, to wait for the tide. It'll be dark enough soon for us to slip away from them." The day's strain hacked abruptly through his voice. "Are you going to tell me what this is all about?"

"I'll explain as we ride. But I want no one else to hear, not even Cei."

A few minutes later we were on our way. I rode between Cei and Bedwyr, with the men clattering behind us. They were talking lightheartedly among themselves, wholly reassured, it seemed, by my word that all was well. I myself, though still knowing only what the dream allowed me, felt curiously light and easy, riding at the urgent pace Bedwyr set through the treacherous ground, without thought or care, not even feeling saddle or bridle-rein. It was not a new feeling, but it was many years since it had come to me; the god's will streaming past, and myself going with it, a spark blown between the lasting stars. I did not know what lay ahead of us in that watery dusk, but only that the Queen and her adventure were but a small part of the night's destiny, shadows already blown aside by this great forward surge of power.

My memory of that ride is all confusion now. Cei's party left us, and shortly afterwards we found boats, and Bedwyr embarked half the party by the short route across the Lake. The rest he divided, some by the shore road, others by the causeway that led directly to the wharf. The rain had stopped now, and mist lay everywhere with the night coming; above it the sky was filling with stars, as a net with flashing silver fish. More torches were lit, and the flat ferries crammed with men and horses were poled slowly through misty water that streamed with reflected light like smoke. As the roops on shore broke and re-formed, their horses shoulder-deep in the rolling mist, we saw the glimmer of a distant torch mounting the Tor. Arthur's sails had been sighted.

It was easy then for Bedwyr and myself to slip away. Our horses plunged down from the hard road, cantered heavily through a league of wet meadowland, and gained the fast going of the road that led southwest.

Soon the lights and sounds of the Island sank behind us and away. Mist curled from the water on either hand. The stars showed the way, but faintly, like lamps along a road for ghosts. Our horses settled into their stride, and soon the way widened, and we could ride knee to knee.

"This lodge to the southwest." His voice was breathless. "Is that where we go?"

"I hope so. Do you know it?"

"I can find it. Is that why you needed Melwas' help? Surely, when he knows of the Queen's accident, he'll let our troops search his land from end to end. And if he's not at the lodge now—"

"Let us hope he is not."

"Is that a riddle?" For the first time since I had known him, his voice was barely civil. "You said you'd explain. You said you knew where she was, and now you're looking for Melwas. Well, then—?"

"Bedwyr, haven't you understood? I think Guinevere is at the lodge. Melwas took her."

The silence that followed was more stormy than any oath. When he spoke I could hardly hear him. "I don't have to ask you if you're sure. You always are. And if you did have a vision, I can only accept it. But tell me how, and why?"

"The why is obvious. The how I don't yet know. I suspect he has been planning this for some time. Her habits of riding out are known, and she often goes to the forest that edges the marsh. If she encountered him there, when she was riding ahead of her people, what more natural than that she should stop her mare and speak to him? That might account for the silence, while the troopers tried to find her at first."

"Yes . . . And if he gripped the rein and tried to seize her, and she spurred her mare on . . . That would account for the broken rein and the marks we found by the banks. By all the gods, Merlin! It's rape you're talking about. . . . ! And you said he must have been planning this for some time?"

"I can only guess at it," I said. "It seems likely that he must have made a few false casts before the chance came; the Queen unattended, and the boat ready nearby."

I did not pursue my own thoughts further. I was remembering that lamplit room, so carefully prepared for her; the chess game; the Queen's demure composure, and her smiling look. I was thinking, too, of the long hours of daylight and dusk that had passed since she had vanished.

So, obviously, was Bedwyr. "He must be mad! A petty king like Melwas to risk Arthur's anger? Is he out of his mind?"

"You could say so," I said dryly. "It has happened before, where women are concerned."

Another silence, broken at length by a gesture, dimly seen, and a change in his horse's stride. "Slow here. We leave the roadway soon."

I obeyed him. Our horses slowed to a trot, a walk, as we peered around us in the mist. Then we saw it, a track leading, apparently, straight off into the marsh.

"This is it?"

"Yes. It's a bad track. We may have to swim the horses." I caught a glance back at me. "Will you be all right?"

Memory plucked at me. Bedwyr and Arthur, in the Wild Forest, riding, necks for sale, as boys will, but always with a care for myself, the poor horseman plodding at heel.

"I can manage."

"Then down here." His horse plunged down the narrow twist of mud among the reeds, then took the water like a boat launching; mine went after it, and we were forging, wet to the thigh, through the smooth water. It was a strange sort of progress, because the mist hid the water; hid even our horses' heads. I wondered how Bedwyr could see the way, then glimpsed, myself, far out across the gleam of water and banks of mist, and the black shapes of trees and bushes, the tiny glimmer of light that meant a dwelling. I watched it inching nearer, my mind racing this way and that with the possibilities of what must be done. Arthur, Bedwyr, Melwas, Guinevere . . . and all the time, like the deep humming that a harp builds up below an intricate web of music, was that other pressure of power which was driving me toward—what?

The horses heaved out of the water and stood, blowing and dripping, on a ridge of dry land. This stretched for some fifty paces ahead of us, and beyond it, some twenty paces farther, was the house, across another channel of water. There was no bridge.

"And no boat either." I heard him swear under his breath. "This is where we swim."

"Bedwyr, I'll have to let you do this last bit alone. But you—"

"Yes, by God!" His sword whispered loose in its scabbard.

I shot a hand out and gripped his horse's bridle above the bit. "—But you will do exactly as I tell you."

A silence. Then his voice, gentle and stubborn: "I shall kill him, of course."

"You will do no such thing. You will save the High King's name and hers. This is Arthur's business, not yours. Let him deal with it."

Another silence, a long one. "Very well. I will be ruled by you."

"Good." I turned my horse queitly into the cover of a clump of alder. His, perforce, followed, with me still gripping the bit. "Now wait. Look yonder."

I pointed to the northeast, the way we had come. Far away in the night across the flat marshlands a cluster of lights showed, high up, like stars. Melwas' stronghold, alight with welcome. Unless the king himself was there, home from hunting, it could only mean one thing: Arthur had come back.

Then, the sound so magnified by the water that it made us start, came the click and creak of a door opening nearby, and the soft ripple of a boat moving through the water. The sounds came from behind the house, where something invisible to us took to the water and moved away into the mist. A man's voice spoke once, softly.

Bedwyr moved sharply, and his horse flung up its head against my restraining hand. His voice was strained. "Melwas. He's seen the lights. Damn it, Merlin, he's taking her—"

"No. Wait. Listen."

Light still showed from the house. A woman's voice called something. The cry had in it some kind of entreaty, but whether of fear, or longing, or sorrow at being left alone, it was impossible to tell. The boat's sound dwindled. The house door shut.

I still held Bedwyr's bridle. "Now, go across and bring the Queen, and we will take her home."

4

Almost before I had finished speaking he was off his horse, had dropped his heavy cloak across the saddle, and was in the water, swimming like an otter for the grassy slope before the door. He reached it, and began to draw himself up from the water. I saw him check, heard a grunt of pain, a stifled gasp, an oath.

"What is it?"

He made no reply. He got a knee to the bank, then pulled himself slowly, with the aid of a hanging willow, to his feet. He paused only to shake the wet from his shoulders, then trod up the slippery slope to the house door. He went slowly, as if with difficulty. I thought he was limping. As he went, his sword came rasping from the sheath.

He hammered on the door with the hilt. The sound echoed, as if from an empty house. There was no movement; no reply. (So much, I thought sourly, for the lady who waits for rescue.)

Bedwyr hammered again. "Melwas! Open to Bedwyr of Benoic! Open in the King's name!"

There was a long pause. It could be felt that someone within the house was waiting with held breath and beating heart. Then the door opened.

It was opened, not with a slam of defiance or bravery, but slowly, a crack only, which showed the small light of a taper, and the shadow of someone peering out. A slight figure, lissom and straight, with loose hair flowing, and a long gown of fine stuff with a creamy sheen.

Bedwyr said, and it came strangled: "Madam? Lady! Are you safe?"

"Prince Bedwyr." Her voice was breathless, but low, and apparently composed. "I thank God for you. When I heard you coming I was afraid. . . . But then, when I knew it was you . . . How did you come here? How did you find me?"

"Merlin guided me."

I heard the swift intake of her breath clear from where I stood holding the horses. The taper lit the pale shape of her face as she turned her head sharply, and saw me beyond the water. *"Merlin?"* Then her voice was once more soft and steady. "Then I thank God again for his art. I thought no one would ever come this way."

That, I thought, I can well believe. I said aloud: "Can you make ready, madam? We have come to take you back to the King."

She did not answer me, but turned to go in, then paused, and said something to Bedwyr, too low for me to catch. He answered, and she pushed the door wide, and gestured him in after her. He went, leaving the door standing open. Inside the room I saw the pulsing ebb and flow of light that meant a fire. The room was softly lit by a lamp, and I caught glimpses through doorway and window of a room more richly furnished than any long-neglected hunting lodge could have shown, with gilded stools and scarlet cushions, and, through another half-open doorway, the corner of a bed or couch, with a coverlet thrown across a tumble of bed-line. Melwas had prepared the nest well for her, then. My vision of firelight and supper table and the friendly game of chess had been accurate enough. The words that would tell Arthur moved and raced and re-formed in my brain. The mist smoked up round the house like white ghosts, white shadows . . .

Bedwyr emerged from the house. His sword was back in its sheath, and in one hand he carried a lamp; the other held a pole such as marsh-men use to push their flat-bottomed craft through the reeds. He approached the water's edge, moving cautiously. "Merlin?"

"Yes? Do you want me to swim the horses over?"

"No!" sharply. "There are knives set below the water. I had forgotten that old trick, and drove a knee straight into them."

"I thought you were limping. Are you badly hurt?"

"No. Flesh wounds only. My lady has dressed them for me."

"All the more reason why you can't swim back, then. How do you propose to get her over here? There must be some place where I can land the horses safely. Ask her."

"I have. She doesn't know. And there's no boat."

"So?" I said. "Has Melwas any gear that will float?"

"That's what I was thinking. There's sure to be something we can use; and the costlier the better." A shadow of amusement lightened the grim voice. But neither of us cared to comment on the situation across twenty feet of echoing water with Guinevere herself within earshot.

"She's dressing herself," he said shortly, as if in answer to my thought. He set the lamp down at the water's edge. We waited.

"Prince Bedwyr?"

The door opened again. She was in riding dress, and had braided her hair. Her cloak was over her arm.

Bedwyr limped up the bank. He held the cloak for her, and she drew it close and pulled the hood to cover the bright hair. He said something, then vanished indoors to reappear in a short while, carrying a table.

I suppose the next few minutes, if anyone had been in the mood to appreciate it, would have been rich in comedy, but as it was, Queen Guinevere on one side of the water, and myself on the other, stood in silence and watched Bedwyr improvising his absurd raft, then, as an afterthought, pitching a couple of cushions into it, and inviting the Queen to board it.

This she did, and they came across, an undignified progress, with the Queen crouched low, holding on to one carved and gilded table leg, while the Prince of Benoic poled the contraption erratically across the channel.

The thing came to the bank, and I caught a leg and held it. Bedwyr scrambled ashore, and turned to help the Queen. She came gracefully enough, with a little gasp of thanks, and stood shaking out her stained and crumpled cloak. Like her riding dress, it had been soaked and roughly dried. I saw that it was torn. Something pale shook from the folds and fell to the muddy turf. I stooped to pick it up. It was a chessman of white ivory. The king, broken.

She had not noticed. Bedwyr pushed the table back into the water, and took his horse's bridle from me. I handed him his cloak and said formally to the Queen, so formally that my voice sounded stiff and cold: "I am glad to see you well and safe, lady. We have had a bad day, fearing for you."

"I am sorry." Her voice was low, her face hidden from me under the hood. "I took a heavy toss when my mare fell in the forest I—I don't remember much after that, until I woke here, in this house . . ."

"And King Melwas with you?"

"Yes. Yes. He found me lying, and carried me here. I was fainting, I suppose. I don't remember. His servant tended me."

"He would have done better, perhaps, to have stayed by you till your own people came. They were searching the forest for you."

A movement of the hand that held the hood close about her face. I thought it was trembling. "Yes, I suppose so. But this place was near, just across the water, and he was afraid for me, he said, and indeed, the boat seemed best. I could not have ridden."

Bedwyr was in the saddle. I took the Queen's arm, to help her up in front of him. With surprise—nothing in that small composed voice had led me to suspect it—I felt her whole body shaking. I abandoned the questioning, and said merely: "We'll take this ride easily, then. The King is back, did you know?"

I felt the shudder run through her, like an ague. She said nothing. Her body was light and slender, like a girl's, as I put her up in front of Bedwyr's saddle.

We went gently on the way back. As we neared the Island, it could be seen that the wharf was ablaze with lights, and milling with horsemen.

We were still some distance off when we saw, lit by their moving torches, a group of horsemen detach themselves from the crowd, and come at the gallop along the causeway. A man on a black horse was in the lead, pointing the way. Then they saw us. There were shouts. Soon they came up with us. In the lead now was Arthur, his white stallion black with mud to the withers. Beside him on the black horse, loud with relief and concern for the Queen, rode Melwas, King of the Summer Country.

I rode home alone. There was nothing to be gained, and too much to be lost, by confronting Arthur and Melwas now. So far, by Melwas' quick thinking in leaving the marsh house by the back way, and being present to greet Arthur as his ships put in to the wharf, the affair was saved from scandal, and Arthur would not be forced, whatever his private feelings when he found or guessed at the truth, into a hasty public quarrel with an ally. It was best left for the present. Melwas would take them all into his firelit palace and give them food and wine, and perhaps lodge them for the night, and by morning Guinevere would have told her story—some story—to her husband. I could not begin to guess what the story would be. There were elements in it which she would be hard put to it to explain away; the room so carefully ready for her; the loose robe she had worn; the tumbled bed; her lies to Bedwyr and myself about Melwas. And more than all, the broken chessman and its evidence of a true dream. But all this would have to wait until, at the very least, we were off Melwas' land, and no longer surrounded by his men-at-arms. As for Bedwyr, he had said nothing, and in the future, whatever his thoughts, his love for Arthur would keep his mouth shut.

And I? Arthur was High King, and I was his chief adviser. I owed him a truth. But I would not stay tonight, to face his questions, and perhaps evade them, or parry them with lies. Later, I thought wearily, as my tired horse plodded along the shore of the Lake, I would see more clearly what do do.

I went home the long way round, without troubling the ferryman. Even if he was willing to ply so late, I did not feel equal to his gossip, or that of the troops who might be making their way back. I wanted silence, and the night, and the soft veils of the mist.

The horse, scenting home and supper, pricked his ears and stepped out. Soon we had left the sounds and lights of the Island behind us, the Tor itself no more than a black shape of night, with stars behind its shoulder. Trees loomed, hung with mist, and below them lake water lapped on the flattened shingle. The smell of water and reeds and stirred mud, the steady plod of hoofs, the ripple of the Lake, and through it all, faint and infinitely distant, but tingling like salt on the tongue, the breath of the sea-tide, turning to its ebb here at its languid limit. A bird called hoarsely, splashing somewhere, invisible. The horse shook his damp neck, and plodded on.

Silence and still air, and the calm of solitude. They drew a veil, as palpable as the mist, between the stresses of the day and the night's tranquillity. The god's hand had withdrawn. No vision printed itself on the dark. About tomorrow, and my part in it, I would not think. I had been led to prevent trespass by a prophetic dream; but what "high matters" the sudden renewal of the god's power in me portended I could not tell, and was too weary to guess at. I chirrupped to the horse, and he quickened his pace. The moon's edge, above a shaw of elms, showed the night black and silver. In a short half-mile we would leave the Lake shore, and make for home along the gravel of the road.

The horse stopped, so suddenly that I was jerked forward on his neck. If he had not been so far spent, he would have shied, and perhaps thrown me. As it was he balked, both forefeet thrust stiffly in front of him, jarring me to the bone.

Here the way ran along the crest of a bank that skirted the Lake. There was a sheer drop, half the height of a man, down to the water's surface. The mist lay thickly, but some movement of air—perhaps from the tide itself—stirred it faintly, so that it swirled and rose in peaks like cream in a tub, or flowed, itself like water, thickened and slow.

Then I heard a faint splashing, and saw what my horse had seen. A boat, being poled along a little way out from shore, and in it someone standing, balancing as delicately as a bird balances on a rocking twig. Only a glimpse I had, dim and shadowlike, of someone young-seeming and slight, in a cloak-like garment that hung to the thwarts and over the boat's edge to trail in the water. The boy stooped, and straightened again, wringing the stuff out. The mist coiled and broke round the movement, and its pallid drift reflected, briefly, the starlight. I saw his face. I felt shock thud under my heart like an arrow to its target.

"Ninian!"

He started, turned, stopped the boat expertly. The dark eyes looked enormous in the pale face.

"Yes? Who's that?"

"Merlin. Prince Merlin. Do you not remember me?" I caught at myself. Shock had made me stupid. I had forgotten that when I fell in with the goldsmith and his assistant on the road to Dunpeldyr I had been in disguise. I said quickly: "You knew me as Emrys; that is my name. Myrddin Emrys from Dyfed. There were reasons why I couldn't travel under my own name. Do you remember now?"

The boat rocked. The mist thickened and hid it, and I knew a moment's blind panic. He had gone again. Then I saw him, still there, head on one side. He thought and then spoke, taking time about it, as always.

"Merlin? The enchanter? That is who you are?"

"Yes. I am sorry if I startled you. It was a shock seeing you like this. I thought you were drowned, that time at the Cor Bridge when you went swimming in the river with the other boys. What happened?"

I thought he hesitated. "I am a good swimmer, my lord."

There was some secret here. It did not matter. Nothing mattered. I had found him. This was what the night had been moving toward. This, not the Queen's trespass, was the "high matter" toward which the power had driven me. Here was the future. The stars flashed and sparkled as once they had flashed and sparkled on the hilt of the great sword.

I leaned forward over the horse's neck, speaking urgently. "Ninian, listen. If you don't want to answer questions, I'll ask none. All right, so you ran away from slavery; that doesn't matter to me. I can protect you, so don't be afraid. I want you to come to me. As soon as I saw you first, I knew what you were; you're like me, and, by the Sight that God has given me, I think you will be capable of the same. You guessed it, too, didn't you? Will you come to me, and let me teach you? It won't be easy; you're young yet; but I was younger still when I went to my master, and you can learn it all, I know. Trust me. Will you come and serve me, and learn as much of my art as I can give you?"

This time there was no hesitation at all. It was as if the question had been asked and answered long ago. As perhaps it had. About some things there is this inevitability; they were in the stars from the last day of the Flood.

"Yes," he said, "I'll come. Give me a little time, though. There are things to—to arrange."

I straightened. My rib-cage hurt from the long breaths I drew. "You know where I live?"

"Everyone knows."

"Then come when you can. You will be welcome." I added, softly, as much to myself as to him: "By God himself, you will be welcome."

There was no reply. When I looked again, there was nothing but the white mist with the starlight on it, bitter-white, and from below, the lap of the lake water on the shore.

Even so, it took me till I got to my own house to realize the very simple truth.

When I had seen the boy Ninian, and yearned to him as to the one human being I had known who could go with me wherever I had gone, it had been years ago. How many? Nine, ten? And he had been perhaps sixteen. Between a youth of sixteen and a man in his middle twenties there is a world of change and growing: the boy I had just recognized with such a shock of joy, the face I had remembered a score of times with grief—this could not be the same boy, even had he escaped the river all those years ago, and lived.

As I lay that night in bed, wakeful, watching the stars through the black boughs of the pear tree, as I had done when a child, I went through the scene again. The mist, the ghostly mist; the upward starlight; the voice coming as an echo from the hidden water; the face so well remembered, dreamed over these ten years; these, combining suddenly to waken a forgotten and futile hope, had deceived me.

I knew then, with tears, that the boy Ninian was truly dead, and that this encounter in the ghostly dark had only mocked my weariness with a confused and cruel dream.

5

He did not come, of course. My next visitor was a courier from Arthur, bidding me to Camelot.

Four days had passed. I had half expected to be summoned before this, but, when no word came, assumed that Arthur had not yet decided what move to make, or that he was bent on hushing the affair up, and would not force a public discussion even in council.

Normally a courier passed between us three or four times a week, and any messenger whose commission took him past my house had long since formed the habit of calling at Applegarth to see if I had a letter ready, or to answer my questions. So I had kept myself informed.

I heard that, unbelievably, Guinevere was still on Ynys Witrin, where some of her ladies had joined her as guests of the old queen. Bedwyr, too, was still lodged in Melwas' palace; the knives had been rusty, and a couple of the wounds they made had become inflamed; added to this, he had taken a chill from wet and exposure, and was ill now with fever. Some of his own men were there with him, guests in Melwas' hall. Queen Guinevere herself, so said my informant, visited him daily, and had insisted on helping his nurses.

Another fragment of information I gathered for myself. The Queen's merlin had been found dead, hanging from its jesses in a high tree, near the place where Bedwyr had dragged the channel.

On the fifth day the summons came, a letter bidding me to confer with the High King about the new council hall, which had been finished while he was in Gwynedd, I saddled up and left immediately for Camelot.

Arthur was waiting for me on the western terrace of the palace. This was a wide paved walk, with formal garden beds wherein some of the Queen's roses bloomed, and pansies and the pretty summer flowers. Now, in the chilly spring afternoon, the only colour came from the daffodils, and the pale dwindling heads of the fair-maids.

Arthur stood by the terrace wall, looking out toward the distant, shining line that was the edge of the open sea. He did not turn to greet me, but waited until I was beside him. Then he glanced to make sure that the servant who had brought me to him had gone, and said abruptly:

"You will have guessed that it's nothing to do with the council hall. That was for the secretaries. I want to talk with you privately."

"Melwas?"

"Of course." He swung round with his back to the parapet, half leaning against it. He regarded me frowningly. "You were with Bedwyr when he found the Queen, and when he brought her back to Ynys Witrin. I saw you there, but when I turned to find you, you had gone. I am told, moreover, that it was you who told Bedwyr where to find her. If you knew anything about this affair that I do not, then why did you not wait and speak with me then?"

"There was nothing I could have told you then that would not have stirred up trouble that you could well do without. What was needed was time. Time for the Queen to rest; for you to talk with her; time to allay men's fears, not inflame them. Which you seem to have done. I am told that Bedwyr and the Queen are still on Ynys Witrin."

"Yes. Bedwyr is ill. He took straight to bed with a chill, and by morning was in a fever."

"So I heard. I blame myself. I should have stayed to dress those cuts. Have you talked with him?"

"No. He was not fit."

"And the Queen?"

"Is well."

"But not yet ready to make the journey home?"

"No," he said shortly. He turned away again, looking toward the distant gleam of the sea.

"I take it that Melwas must have offered some sort of explanation?" I said at length.

I expected the question to strike some kind of spark, but he merely looked tired, grey in a grey afternoon.

"Oh, yes. I talked with Melwas. He told me what had happened. He was fowling in the marshes, himself with one servant, a man called Berin. They had taken their boat into the edge of the forest, up the river that you saw. He heard the commotion in the forest, and then saw the Queen's mare plunge and slide in the mud of the bank. The Queen was thrown clear into the water. Her own people were nowhere to be seen. The two men rowed to her and pulled her out. She was unconscious as if she had struck her head in the fall. While they were doing this they heard her people go by at some distance, without coming near the river." A pause. "No doubt at this point Melwas should have sent his man after them, but he was on foot and they were mounted, and besides, the Queen was drenched and fainting, and very cold, and could hardly have been carried home, except by boat. So Melwas had the servant row to his lodge, and make a fire. He had food there, and wine. He had expected to go there himself to pass the night, so the place was ready."

"That was fortunate."

I kept the dryness from my voice, but he gave me a flick of a glance, sharp as a dagger. "Indeed. After a while she began to recover. He sent the servant with the boat to Ynys Witrin to bring help, and women to tend her, with either horses and a litter, or else a barge that could carry her in comfort. But before he had gone far the man returned to say that my sails were in sight, and that it looked as if I would land with the tide. Melwas judged it best to set off at once himself for the wharf to meet me, as his duty was, and to give me the news of her safety."

"Leaving her behind," I said neutrally.

"Leaving her behind. The only craft he had was the light skin boat that he used for his fowling trips. It was not fit for her—certainly not in the state she was in. You must have seen that for yourself. When Bedwyr brought her to me, she could do nothing but weep and shiver. I had to let the women take her straight away and put her to bed."

He pushed himself away from the parapet, and, turning aside, took half a dozen rapid steps away and back again. He broke off a sprig of rosemary, and pulled it to and fro in his hands. I could smell its peppery, pungent scent from where I stood. I said nothing. After a while he stopped pacing and stood, feet apart, watching me, but still pulling the rosemary in and out between his fingers.

"So that is the story."

"I see." I regarded him thoughtfully. "And so you spent the night as Melwas' guest, and Bedwyr is still there, and the Queen is lodged there as well . . . until when?"

"I shall send for her tomorrow."

"And today you sent for me. Why? It seems that the affair is settled, and your decisions have been made."

"You must know very well why I sent for you." His voice had a sudden rough edge to it that belied his previous calm. "What do you know that 'would have stirred up trouble' if you had spoken to me that night? If you have something to say to me, Merlin, say it."

"Very well. But tell me first, have you spoken with the Queen at all?"

A lift of the brows. "What do you think? A man who has been away from his wife for the best part of a month? And a wife who was in need of comfort."

"But if she was ill, being nursed by the women—"

"She was not ill. She was tired, and distressed, and she was very frightened."

I thought of Guinevere's composed, quiet voice, the careful poise, the shaking body.

"Not of my coming." He spoke sharply, answering what I had not said. "She feared Melwas, and she fears you. Are you surprised? Most people do. But she does not fear me. Why should she? I love her. But she was afraid that some evil tongue might poison me with lies. . . . So until I went to her, and listened to her story, she could not rest."

"She was afraid of Melwas? Why? Was her story not the same as his?"

This time he did answer the implication. He sent the mangled spring of rosemary spinning out over the terrace wall. "Merlin." It came quietly, but with a kind of hard-held finality. "Merlin, you do not have to tell me that Melwas lied to me, and that this was a rape. If Guinevere had been so badly hurt when she fell that she lay fainting for most of the day, then she could hardly have ridden home with you, or been as whole and sound as she was when I lay with her that night. She had sustained no hurt at all. Nothing but fear."

"She told you that his story was a lie?"

"Yes."

If Guinevere had told him a different tale, I thought I knew what she had not made clear. I said slowly: "When she spoke with Bedwyr and myself, her story was the same as Melwas'. Now you say that *the Queen herself* told you it was rape?"

"Yes." His brows twitched together. "You don't believe either story, do you? Is that what you are trying to tell me? You think—by God, Merlin, just what do you think?"

"I don't yet know the Queen's story. Tell me what she said."

He was so angry that I thought he would leave me then and there. But after a turn or two along the terrace he came back to where I waited. He had almost the air of a man approaching single combat.

"Very well. You are my counsellor, after all, and it seems I shall be in need of counsel." He drew in his breath. The story came in brief, expressionless sentences. "This is what she says. She did not take a fall at all. She saw her falcon stoop, and catch its jesses in a tree. She stopped her mare, and dismounted. Then she saw Melwas, in his boat by the bank. She called to him for help. He came up the bank to her, but did nothing about the merlin. He started to talk to her of love; how he had loved her since the time they had travelled up from Wales together. He would not listen when she tried to stop him, and when she made to mount again he took hold of her, and in the struggle the mare broke free and bolted. The Queen tried to call out for her people, but he put a hand over her mouth, and threw her down into the boat. The servant thrust if off from the bank, and rowed them away. The man was afraid, she says, and made some sort of protest, but he did as Melwas bade him. He took her to the lodge. It was all ready, as if he expected her . . . or some other woman. You saw it. Was it not so?"

I thought of the fire, the bed, the rich hangings, the robe Guinevere had worn. "I saw a little. Yes. it was prepared."

"He had had her in his mind so long. . . . He had only been waiting his chance. He had followed her before—it was well known that she had a habit of outriding her people." There was a film of sweat on his face. He put the heel of his hand up to his brow and wiped it away.

"Did he lie with her, Arthur?"

"No. He held her there all day, pleading with her, she says, begging for her love. . . . He began with sweet speeches and promises, but when they got him nowhere, he grew crazed, she says, and violent, and began to see his own danger. After he had sent his man away, she thinks he might have forced her, but the servant came quickly back to tell his master that my sails had been sighted, and Melwas left her in panic, and hurried to me to tell his lies. He threatened her that if she spoke the truth to me, he, Melwas, would say he had lain with her, so that I would kill her as well as him. She was to tell the same story as he would tell. Which you say she did, to you."

"Yes."

"And you knew it was not true?"

"Yes."

"I see." He was still watching me with that fierce but wary look. I was beginning to realize, but without much surprise, that even I could not keep secrets from him now. "And you thought she might have lied to me. That was the 'trouble' you foresaw?"

"Partly, yes."

"You thought she would lie to me? To me?" He repeated it as if it were unthinkable.

"If she were afraid, who could blame her for lying? Yes, I know you say she is not afraid of you. But she is only a woman, after all, and she might well be afraid of your anger. Any woman would lie to save herself. It would have been your right to kill her, and him, too."

"It is still my right to do that, whether there was a rape or not."

"Well, then—? Could she have known that you would even listen to her, that you would be King and statesman before you allowed yourself to be the vengeful husband? Even I stand amazed, and I thought I knew you."

A flicker of grim amusement. "With Bedwyr and the Queen on the Island as hostages, you might say my hands were tied. . . . I shall kill him, of course.

You know that, don't you? But in my own time, and on some other cause, when all this is forgotten, and the Queen's honour cannot suffer from it." He swung away, and put his two hands on the parapet, looking out again across the darkening stretch of land toward the sea. Somewhere a beam broke through the clouds, and a shaft of dusky light poured down, lighting a distant stretch of water to a piercing gleam.

He spoke slowly, into the distance. "I've been thinking over the story I shall put about. I shall take a tale midway between Melwas' lie and what the Queen told me. She was there all day with him, after all, from dawn till dusking. . . . I shall let it be given out that she fell from her horse, as Melwas said, and was carried unconscious to the hunting lodge, and there lay, shaken and fainting for most of the day. Bedwyr and you must bear this out. If it were known that she was not hurt at all, there are those who would blame her for not trying to escape. This, though the servant had the boat under his eye all day, and even if she could have swum, there were the knives. . . . She could, of course, have threatened them with my vengeance, but she saw that as the road only to her own end. He could have kept her there, and had his pleasure and then killed her. You know that her people had already accepted the fact of her death. Except you. That was what saved her."

I said nothing. He turned.

"Yes. Except you. You told them she was alive, and you took Bedwyr to her. Now, tell me how you knew. Was it a 'seeing'?"

I bent my head. "When Cei came for me, I called on the old powers, and they responded. I saw her in the flame, and Melwas, too."

A moment of suddenly sharpening concentration. It was not often that the High King searched me for truth as he was wont to search lesser men. I could feel something of the quality that had made him what he was. He had gone very still. "Yes. Now we come to it, don't we? Tell me exactly what you saw."

"I saw a man and a woman in a rich room, and beyond the door a bedchamber, with a bed that had been lain in. They were laughing together, and playing chess. She was clad in a loose robe, as if for night, and her hair was unbraided. When he took her in his arms the chessboard spilled, and the man trod on the pieces." I held out a hand to him, with the broken chessman. "When the Queen came out to us, this was caught in the fold of her cloak."

He took it, and bent his head over it, as if studying it. Then he sent it spinning after the sprig of rosemary. "So. It was a true dream. She said there was a table, and chessmen of ivory and ebony wood." To my surprise, he was smiling. "Is this all?"

"All? It is more than I would ever have told you, had I not owed it to you as your counsellor."

He nodded, still smiling. All the anger seemed to have gone. He looked out again over the dimming plain with its gleams of brightness and the shaft of wheeling light. "Merlin, a little while ago you said, 'She is only a woman.' You have told me many times that you know nothing of women. Does it never occur to you that they lead lives of dependence so complete as to breed uncertainty and fear? That their lives are like those of slaves, or of animals that are used by creatures stronger than themselves, and sometimes cruel? Why, even royal ladies are bought and sold, and are bred to lead their lives far from their homes and their people, as the property of men unknown to them."

I waited, to see his drift. It was a thought I had had before, when I had seen women suffer from the whims of men; even those women who, like Morgause, were stronger and cleverer than most men. They were made, it seemed, for men's use, and suffered by it. The lucky ones found men they could rule, or who loved them. Like the Queen.

"This happened to Guinevere," he went on. "You yourself said just now that I must still be a stranger to her in some respects. She is not afraid of me, no, but sometimes I think that she is afraid of life itself, and of living. And most certainly she was afraid of Melwas. Don't you see? Your dream was true. She smiled, and spoke him fair, and hid her fear. What would you have had her do? Appeal to the servant? Threaten the two of them with my vengeance? She knew that was the road only to her own end. When he showed her the bedchamber, to let her change her wet clothing (he takes women to that house sometimes, it seems, out of sight of the old queen his mother, and clothes are kept there, with things such as ladies like), she thanked him merely, then locked the door on him. Later, when he came to bid her to meat, she pretended faintness, but after a while he grew suspicious, then importunate, and she was afraid he would break the door, so she ate with him, and spoke him fair. And so, through the long day, till dusk. She let him think that, with nightfall, he would have his pleasure, while all the time she hoped for rescue still."

"And then it came."

"Against all hope, and thanks to you, it came. Well, that is her story, and I believe it." That quick turn of the head again. "Do you?"

I did not answer straight away. He waited, showing neither anger nor impatience—nor any shadow of doubt.

When at length I spoke, it was with certainty. "Yes. She told the truth. Reason, instinct, 'Sight' or blind faith, you can be sure of it. I am sorry I doubted her. You were right to remind me that I don't understand women. I should have known she was afraid, and knowing that, I might have guessed that what poor weapons she had against Melwas, she would use. . . . And for the rest—her silence until she could speak with you, her care for your honour and the safety of your kingdom—she has my admiration. And so, King, have you."

I saw him notice the form of address. Through his relief came a glint of laughter. "Why? Because I did not fly out in a high royal rage, and demand heads? If the Queen, in fear, could play-act for a day, surely I could do it for a few short hours, with her honour and my own at stake? But not for longer. By Hades, not for longer!" The force with which he brought his clenched fist down on the parapet showed just what he had held in check. He added, with an abrupt change of tone: "Merlin, you must be aware that the people do not—do not love the Queen."

"I have heard whispers, yes. But this is not for anything she is, or has done. It is only because they look daily for an heir, and she has been Queen for four years, without bearing. It's natural that there should be disappointed hopes, and some whispering."

"There will be no heir. She is barren. I am sure of it now, and so is she."

"I feared it. I am sorry."

"If I had not planted other seed here and there," he said with a wry smile, "I might share some of the blame with her; but there was the child I begot on my first Queen, not to speak of Morgause's bastard by me. So the fault—if it is that—is known to be the Queen's, and because she is Queen, her grief at it cannot be kept private. And there will always be those who start whispers, in the hope that I will put her away. Which," he added with a kind of snap, "I shall not."

"It wouldn't occur to me to advise it," I said mildly. "What does occur to me is to wonder if this is the shadow that I saw once lie across your marriage bed. . . . But enough of that. What we must do now is bring her back into the people's love."

"You make it sound easy. If you know how—"

"I think I do. You swore just now by Hades, and it broke a dream I had. Will you let me go to Ynys Witrin, and bring her back to you myself?"

He started to ask why, then half laughed and shrugged. "Why not? Maybe to you it is as easy as it sounds. . . . Go, then. I'll send word for them to prepare a royal escort. I'll receive her here. At least it saves me having to see Melwas again. Will you, with all your wise counsels, try to stop me from killing him?"

"As effectively as a mother hen calling the young swan out of the water. You will do as you think fit." I looked out across the water-logged plain, toward the Tor and the low-lying shape of its neighbour island, where the harbour lay. I added, thoughtfully: "It's a pity that he sees fit to charge harbour dues—and exorbitant ones at that—to the war-leader who protects him."

His eyes widened speculatively. A smile tugged at his mouth. He said slowly: "Yes, isn't it? And then there's the matter of the toll on the road along the ridge. If my captains should by any chance refuse to pay, then no doubt Melwas will bring the complaint here himself, and who knows, it may even be the first that comes to the new council chamber? Now, since that is what I told the scribe you were coming for, shall we go and see it? And tomorrow, at the third hour, I'll send the royal escort, to bring her home."

6

With Bedwyr still on Ynys Witrin, the royal escort was led by Nentres, one of the western rulers who had fought under Uther, and who now brought his allegiance and that of his sons to Arthur. He was a grizzled veteran, spare of body, and as supple in the saddle as a youth. He left the escort fidgeting under its Dragon banners on the road below my house, and came riding himself up the curving track by the stream, followed by a groom leading a chestnut horse trapped with silver. Horse and trappings alike were burnished to a glitter as bright as Nentres' shield, and jewels winked on the breastband. The saddle-cloth was of murrey, worked with silver thread.

"The King sent this for you," he said, with a grin. "He reckons your own would look like a dealer's throw-out among the rest. Don't look at him like that, he's much quieter than he appears."

The groom gave me a hand to mount. The chestnut tossed his head and mouthed the bit, but his stride was smooth and easy. After my stolid old black gelding he was like a sailing-boat after a poled barge.

The morning was cold, in the wake of the north wind that had frozen the fields since mid-March. At dawn that day I had climbed to the hilltop beyond Applegarth, and had felt against my skin that indefinable difference that heralds a change of wind. The hilltop thorns were no more than breaking into bud, but down in the valley one could see the green haze on the distant woods, and the sheltered banks nearby were thick with primroses and wild garlic. Rooks cawed and tumbled about the ivied trees. Spring was here, waiting, but held back by the cold winds, as the blackthorn flowers were locked in the bud. But still the sky was overcast and heavy, almost as if threatening snow, and I was glad of my cloak with all its regal splendours of fur and scarlet.

All was ready for us at Melwas' hall. The king himself was dressed in rich dark blue, and was, I noticed, fully armed. His handsome face wore a smile, easy and welcoming, but his eyes had a wary look, and there were altogether too many men-at-arms crowded into the hall, besides the full company outside, brought down at readiness from his hilltop fortress, to throng into the orchard-fields that served the palace for garden. Banners and bright trappings gave the welcome a festive air, but it was to be seen that every man wore both sword and dagger.

He had, of course, expected Arthur. When he saw me his look at first lightened with relief, then I saw the wariness deepen, and tight lines draw themselves around his mouth. He greeted me fairly, but very formally, like a man making the first move of a gambit at chess. I replied, with the long, studied speech of Arthur's deputy, then turned to the old queen, his mother, who stood beside him at the end of the long hall. She showed no such caution as her son's. She greeted me with easy authority, and made a sign toward a door on the right of the hall. There was a stir as the crowd parted, and Queen Guinevere came in among her ladies.

She, too, had expected Arthur. She hesitated, looking for him in the glitter of the packed hall. Her gaze passed me, unseeing. I wondered what god had moved her to wear green, spring green, with flowers embroidered on the breast of her gown. Her mantle was green, too, with a collar of white marten, which framed her face and gave her a fragile look. She was very pale, but bore herself with rigid composure.

I remembered how, that night, I had found her shaking in my grasp; and on the thought, as if I had been dipped in cold water, I saw that Arthur had been right about her. She might be a queen in bearing and in courage, but under it all there was a timid girl, and one looking, all the time, for love. The gaiety, the ready laughter and high spirits of youth, had masked an exile's eager search for friendship among the strangers of a court vastly different from the homely hearth-stone of her father's kingdom. I would never, wrapped in Arthur as I had been for twenty years, even have troubled to think about her, except as his people thought: a vessel for his seed, a partner for his pleasure, a glowing pillar of beauty to shine, silver beside his gold, on the hilltop of his glory. Now I saw her as if I had never seen her before. I saw a girl, tender of flesh and simple enough of spirit, who had had the fortune to marry the greatest man of the age. To be Arthur's Queen was no mean burden, with all that it entailed of loneliness, and a life of banishment in an alien country, with, as often as not, no husband near to come between her and the flatterers, the power-hungry schemers, those envious of her rank or beauty, or—perhaps most dangerous of all—the young men ready to worship her. Then there would be those (and you could trust them to be many) who would tell her, over and over again, about the "other Guinevere," the pretty Queen who had conceived from the King's first bedding of her, and for whom he had grieved so bitterly. It would lose nothing in the telling. But all this would have been nothing, would have passed and been forgotten in the King's love, and her new, exciting power, if only she had been able to conceive a child. That Arthur had not used the Melwas affair to have her put aside, to take a fertile woman to his bed, was proof indeed of his love; but I doubted if she had yet had time to see it so. He had been right when he told me that she was afraid of life, afraid of the people round her, afraid of Melwas; and—I could see it now—more than any of them she was afraid of me.

She had seen me. The blue eyes widened, and her hands moved up to clasp the fur at her throat. Her step checked momentarily, then, once more held in that pale composure, she took her place beside the queen, on the side away from Melwas. Neither she nor the king had glanced at one another.

There was a resounding silence. Someone's robe rustled, and it sounded like a tree in the wind.

I walked forward. As if Guinevere had been the only person there, I bowed low, then straightened.

"Greetings, madam. It's good to see you recovered. I have come, with others of your friends and servants, to escort you home. The High King is waiting to receive you in your palace of Camelot."

The colour washed into her face. She only came up as high as my throat. I have seen eyes like hers on a young deer pulled down and waiting for the spear. She murmured something, and fell dumb. To cover it, and give her time, I turned to Melwas and his mother, and went smoothly into a courtly, over-elaborate speech, thanking them for their care of Queen Guinevere. It had become patent, while I was speaking, that Melwas' mother still had no idea that anything might be wrong. While her son watched me with a bold look glossing over that mixture of wariness and bravado, the old queen answered me with equally courtly thanks, messages for Arthur, compliments for Guinevere, and, finally, a pressing offer of hospitality. At that the young Queen looked up, briefly, then her eyelids hid her eyes again. As I declined, I saw her hands relax. I guessed that there had been no chance, since that parting in the marshes, for Melwas to speak with her and try to find out what she had told Arthur. I think, indeed, that he was going to insist on our staying, but something in my eyes stopped him, and then his mother, accepting the decision, came with obvious eagerness to the question that interested her.

"We looked for you that night, Prince Merlin. I understand that you were led by your vision to find the Queen, before even my son got back to the Island with the news. Will you not tell us, my lord, what this vision was?"

Melwas had jerked to attention. His bold look defied me to elaborate. I smiled, and my gaze bore his down. Without my prompting, the old woman had asked the very question that I wanted. I raised my voice.

"Willingly, lady. It is true that I had a vision, but whether it came from the gods of air and silence who have spoken to me in the past, or from the Mother Goddess to whose worship the shrine beyond those apple trees is sacred, I cannot tell. But I had a vision that led me straight through the marsh-land like a fledged arrow to its mark. It was a double vision, a bright dream through which the dreamer passes to a darker dream below; a reflection seen in deep water where the surface colour lies like glass over the dark world beneath. The visions were confused, but their meaning was clear. I would have followed them more quickly, but I think the gods willed it otherwise."

Guinevere's head came up at that, and her eyes widened. Again, in Melwas', that spark of doubt. It was the old queen who asked: "How otherwise? They did not want the Queen found? What riddle is this, Prince Merlin?"

"I shall tell you. But first I will tell you about the dream that came to me. I saw a king's hall paved with marble, and pillared with silver and gold, where no servants waited, but where the lamps and tapers burned with scented smoke, bright as day. . . ." I had let my voice take on the rhythm of the bard who sings in hall; its resonance filled the room and carried the words right out through the colonnade to the silent crowds outside. Fingers moved to make the sign against strong magic; even Guinevere's. The old queen listened with evident satisfaction and pleasure; it was to be remembered that she was the chief patroness of the Goddess's sacred shrine. As for Melwas, as I spoke I watched him move from suspicion and apprehension into bewilderment, and, finally, awe.

To everyone there, already, the dream had taken on a familiar pattern, the archetype of every man's journey into the world from which few travellers return.

". . . And on the precious table a set of gold chessmen, and nearby a great chair with arms curled like lions' heads, waiting for the King, and a stool of silver with doves' claws, waiting for the Lady. So I knew it for Llud's hall, where the sacred vessel is kept, and where once the great sword hung that now hangs on Arthur's wall in Camelot. And from over-head, in the sky beyond the hollow hill, I heard them galloping, the Wild Hunt, where the knights of the Otherworld course down their prey, and carry them deep, deep, into the jewelled halls of no return. But just as I began to wonder if the god was telling me the Queen was dead, the vision changed. . . ."

To my right was a window, high in the wall. Outside was a prospect of sky, cloudy above the tops of the orchard trees. The budding apple boughs showed lighter, in their young sorrel-and-green, than the slaty sky. The poplars stood pale like spears. But there had been that breath of change in the morning; I felt it still; I kept my eye on that indigo cloud, and spoke again, more slowly.

". . . And I was in an older hall, a deeper cavern. I was in the Underworld itself, and the dark King was there, who is older even than Llud, and by him sat the pale young Queen who was reft from the bright fields of Enna and carried out of the warm world to be the Queen of Hell; Persephone, daughter of Demeter, the Mother of all that grows on the face of the earth. . . ."

The cloud was moving slowly, slowly. Beyond the budding boughs I could see the edge of its shadow drawing its veil aside. From somewhere a breeze came wandering to shiver the tall poplars that edged the orchard.

Most of the people there would not know the story, so I told it, to the obvious satisfaction of the old queen, who must, like all devotees of the Mother's cult, be feeling the cold threat of change even here in this, its ancient stronghold. Once, when Melwas, doubting my drift, would have spoken, she silenced him with a gesture, and (herself perhaps with more instinctive understanding) put out a hand and drew the Queen closer to her side. I looked neither at the dark Melwas nor at Guinevere, pale and wondering, but watched the high window out of the side of my eye, and told the old tale of Persephone's abduction by Hades, and the long, weary search for her that Demeter, the Mother Goddess, undertook, while the earth, robbed of its spring growth, languished in cold and darkness.

Beyond the window the poplars, brushed with the early light, bloomed suddenly golden.

"And when the vision died I knew what I had been told. Your Queen, your young and lovely Queen, was alive and safe, succoured by the Goddess and waiting only to be carried home. And with her coming, spring will come at last, and the cold rains will cease, and we shall have a land growing rich once again to harvest, in the peace brought by the High King's sword, and the joy brought by the Queen's love for him. This was the dream I had, and which I, Merlin, prince and prophet, interpret to you." I spoke straight past Melwas to the old queen. "So I beg you now, madam, to let me take the Queen home, with honour and with joy."

And at that moment, the blessed sun came bursting out and laid a shaft of light clear across the floor to the Queen's feet, so that she stood, all gold and white and green, in a pool of sunshine.

We rode home through a brilliant day smelling of primroses. The clouds had packed away, and the Lake showed blue and glittering under its golden willows. An early swallow hawked for flies, close over the bright water. And the Spring Queen, refusing the litter we had brought for her, rode beside me.

She spoke only once, and then briefly.

"I lied to you that night. You knew?"

"Yes."

"You do see, then? You really do? You see all?"

"I see a great deal. If I set out to look, and if God wills it, I see."

The colour came into her face, and her look lightened, as if something had set her free. Before, I had believed her innocent; now I knew it. "So you, too, have told my lord the truth. When he did not come for me himself, I was afraid."

"You have no need to be, now or ever. I think you need never doubt that he loves you. And I can tell you, too, Guinevere my cousin, that even if you never bear an heir for Britain, he will not put you aside. Your name will stand alongside his, as long as he is remembered."

"I will try," she said, so softly that I could hardly hear it. Then the towers of Camelot came in sight, and she was silent, bracing herself against what was to come.

So the seeds of legend were sown. During the golden weeks of spring that followed, I was more than once to hear men talking under their breaths of the "rape" of the Queen, and how she had been taken down almost to the dark halls of Llud, but brought back by Bedwyr, chiefest of Arthur's knights. So the sting of the truth was drawn; no shame attached to Arthur, none even to the Queen; and to Bedwyr was credited the first of his many glories, the story growing, and its hero gaining in stature, as his hurts healed and at last were well.

As for Melwas, in the way these things have, if the "Dark King" of the Underworld became linked in men's minds with the dark-avised King whose stronghold was the Tor, it was still without blame to Guinevere. What Melwas thought nobody knew. He must have realized that Guinevere had told Arthur the truth. He may have grown tired of being cast as the villain of the story, and of waiting (as everyone was waiting) for the High King to move against him. He may even have cherished hopes, still, that he might in some dim future come to possess the Queen.

Whatever the case, it was he who made the next move, and by doing so gave Arthur his way. One morning he rode to Camelot, and, perforce leaving his armed escort outside the council hall, took his seat in the Chair of Complaining.

The council hall had been built on the style of a smaller hall that Arthur had seen on one of the visits paid to the Queen's father in Wales. That had been merely a larger version of the daub-and-wattle round house of the Celts; this in Camelot was a big circular building, impressively built to last, with ribs of dressed stone, and between them walls of narrow Roman brick from the long-abandoned kilns nearby. There were vast double doors of oak, carved with the Dragon, and finely gilded. Inside, the place was open, with a fine floor of tiles laid out from the center, like a spider's web. And like the outer ring of a web, the walls were not curved, but sectioned off with flat panelling. These panels were covered with matting of a fine golden straw to keep out the draughts, but in time would be ablaze with needlework; Guinevere already had her maids set to it. Against each of these sections stood a tall chair, with its own footstool, and the King's was no higher than the next man's. This place was to be, he said, a hall for free discussion between the High King and his peers, and a place where any of the King's leaders could bring their problems. The only thing that marked Arthur's chair was the white shield that hung above it; in time, perhaps, the Dragon would shimmer there in gold and scarlet. Some of the other panels already showed the blazons of the Companions. The seat opposite the King's was blank. This was the one taken by anyone with a grievance to be settled by the court. Arthur had called it the Chair of Complaining. But in later years I heard it called the Perilous Chair, and I think the name was coined after that day.

I was not present when Melwas tabled his complaint. Though I had at that time a place in the Round Hall (as it came to be called), I seldom took it. If his peers were equal there to the King, then the King must be seen to match them in knowledge, and to give his judgments without leaning on the advice of a mentor. Any discussions Arthur and I had were held in private.

We had talked over the Melwas affair for many hours before it came to the council table. To begin with, Arthur seemed sure that I would try to stop him from fighting Melwas, but here was a case where the cold view and the hot coincided. To Arthur it would be satisfying and to me expedient that Melwas should suffer publicly for his actions. The lapse of time, and Arthur's silence, with the legend I had invoked, ensured that Guinevere's honour would not be in question; the people had taken her once more into their love, and wherever she went flowers strewed the way with blessings thrown like petals. She was their Queen—their darling's darling—who had almost been taken from them by death, and had been saved by Merlin's magic. So the story went among the common folk. But among the more worldly there were those who looked for the King to move against Melwas, and who would have been quick to despise him had he failed. He owed it to himself, as man and as King. The discipline he had imposed on himself over the Queen's rape had been severe. Now, when he found that I agreed with him, he turned, with a fierce joy, to planning.

He could, of course, have summoned King Melwas to the council hall on a trumped-up excuse, but this he would not do. "If we harass him until he makes a complaint himself, it comes to much the same thing in the sight of God," he said dryly. "but in terms of my conscience—or my pride, if you like—I will not use a false charge in the Round Hall. It must be known as a place where no man need fear to come before me, unless he himself is false."

So harass him we did. Situated as the Island was, between the High King's stronghold and the sea, it was easy enough to find causes. Somehow or another there came to be constant arguments about harbour dues, rights of free way, levies and taxes arbitrarily imposed and hotly contested. Any of the petty kings would have grown restive under the constant stream of minor vexations, but Melwas was even quicker to protest than most. According to Bedwyr (to whom I owed an account of the council meeting), it was apparent from the start that Melwas guessed he had been deliberately brought before the King to answer the older, more dangerous charge. He seemed eager to do so, but naturally enough allowed no hint of this to come into words: that must have meant his certain death for treason by the vote of the whole Council. So the grievances over dues and taxes, the arguments over the right levies for the protection offered by Camelot, took their long-drawn and tedious course, while the two men watched one another as swordsmen do, and at last came to the heart of the matter.

It was Melwas who suggested single combat. How he was brought toward this was not quite clear; my guess was that he took very little steering. Young, keen-tempered, a good swordsman, knowing himself to be in grave danger, he must have leaped at the chance of a quick decisive solution that gave him a half-hope of success. He may have counted on more. His challenge came at last, hotly: "A meeting to settle these matters here and now, and man to man, if we are ever to agree as neighbours again! You are the law, King; then prove it with your sword!"

Uproar followed, arguments flying to and fro across the hall. The older of those present found it unthinkable that the King should risk himself, but all had by this time some inkling that there was more at stake than harbour dues, and the younger knights were quite frankly eager to see a fight. More than one of them (Bedwyr was the most insistent) offered himself as combatant in Arthur's place, until finally the King, judging his moment, got decisively to his feet. In the sudden silence he strode to the round table at the hall's center, lifted the tablets where Melwas' grievances were listed, and sent them smashing to the floor.

"Now bring me my sword," he said.

It was midday when they faced one another on the level field in the northeast quarter of Caer Camel. The sky was cloudless, but a steady cool breeze tempered the warmth of the day. The light was high and even. The edge of the field was deep in people, the very ramparts furred with folk. At the top of one of Camelot's gilded towers I saw the cluster of azure and green and scarlet where the women had gathered to watch. The Queen, among them, was in white, Arthur's colour. I wondered how she was feeling, and could guess at the still composure with which she would hide her fear. Then the trumpet sounded, and silence fell.

The two combatants were armed with spears and shields, and each man had sword and dagger at his belt. Arthur was not using Caliburn, the royal sword. His armour—a light helmet and leather corselet—showed neither jewel nor device. Melwas' dress was more princely, and he was a shade the taller. He looked fierce and eager, and I saw him cast a look toward the palace tower where the Queen stood. Arthur had not glanced that way. He looked cool and infinitely experienced, listening apparently with grave attention to the herald's formal announcement.

There was a sycamore tree to one side of the field. Bedwyr, beside me in its shade, gave me a long look, and then drew a breath of relief.

"So. You're not worried. Thank God for that!"

"It had to come to this in the end. It's best. But if there had been danger for him, I would have stopped it."

"All the same, it's folly. Oh, I know that he wanted to, but he should never risk himself so. He should have let me do it."

"And what sort of showing would you make, do you suppose? You're still lame. You could have been cut down, if not worse, and then the legend would have had to start again. There are still simple folk who think that right is with the strongest sword."

"As it is today, or you'd not be standing idly by. I know. But I wish . . ." He fell silent.

"I know what you wish. I think you will have your wish, not once but many times, before your life's end."

He glanced sharply at me, started to say something more, but then the pennon fell, and the fight had begun.

For a long time the men circled one another, spears poised for the throw, shields ready. The light advantaged neither. It was Melwas who attacked first. He feinted once, then, with great speed and strength behind the throw, hurled the spear. Arthur's shield flashed up to deflect it. The blade slid screaming past the boss, and the spear buried itself harmlessly in the grass. Melwas, snatching for his sword-hilt, sprang back. But Arthur, in the same moment as he turned the spear aside, flung his own. By doing so he cancelled the advantage that Melwas' first throw had given him; but he did not draw his own sword; he reached for the other's spent spear, upright by him in the turf, pulled it up, and hefted it, just as Melwas, abandoning his sword-hilt, sent the King's spear also whizzing harmlessly from his shield, and turned, swift as a fox, to pick it up in the same way and face spear with spear once more.

But Arthur's weapon, harder flung, and more desperately parried, flew spinning to one side, to bounce level along the turf and skid away from Melwas' hand. There was no hope of snatching it up before Arthur could throw. Melwas, shield at the ready, feinted this way and that, hoping to draw the other's spear and so regain the advantage. He reached the fallen weapon; he stooped for it where it lay, the shaft half-propped to his hand by a clump of thistles. Arthur's arm moved, and the blade of his spear flashed in the light, drawing Melwas' eye. Melwas ducked, throwing his shield up into the line of the cast, at the same time swerving down to grab the fallen weapon. But the King's move had been a false one; in the unguarded moment when Melwas stooped sideways for the other spear, the King's, thrown straight and low, took him in the outstretched arm. Arthur's sword whipped into his hand as he followed the spear.

Melwas staggered. As a great shout hit the walls and echoed round the field he recovered, grabbed the spear, and hurled it straight at the King.

Had he been any less fast, Arthur must have closed with him before he could use the spear. As it was, Melwas' weapon struck true when the King was halfway across the space between them. Arthur caught it on his shield, but at that short range the force was too great to turn. The long shaft whipped in a half-circle, checking the King's rush. With the sword still held in his right hand, he tried to tear the spear-point from the leather, but it had gone in close by one of the metal stays, and jammed there, caught by its barbs. He flung the shield aside, spear and all, and ran in on Melwas, with nothing to guard his naked side but the dagger at his left hand.

The rush gave Melwas no time to recover himself and grab a spear for a third cast. With the blood streaming down his arm, he dragged out his sword, and met the King's attack, body to body, with a slithering clash of metal. The exchange had left them still evenly matched, Melwas' wound, and the loss of strength in his sword arm, against the King's unguarded side. Melwas was a good swordsman, fast and very strong, and for the first few minutes of the hand-to-hand struggle he aimed every stroke and slash at the King's left. But each one met iron. And step by step the King was pressing him; step by step Melwas was forced to give in front of the attack. The blood ran down, weakening him steadily. Arthur, as far as could be seen, was unhurt. He pressed forward, the ringing blows coming fast and hard, the whining whip and parry of the long dagger chiming between. Behind Melwas lay the fallen spear. Melwas knew it, but dared not glance to see where it lay. The dread of fouling it, and falling, made him slower. He was sweating freely, and beginning to breathe like a hard-ridden horse.

One of those moments came when, breast to breast, weapon to weapon, the men stood locked, totally still. Round the field the crowd was silent now, holding its breath.

The King spoke, softly and coldly. No one could hear what he said. Melwas did not reply. There was a moment's pause, then a swift movement, a sudden pressure, a grunt from Melwas, and some kind of growled answer. Then Arthur disengaged smoothly, and, with another low-spoken sentence, attacked afresh.

Melwas' right hand was a blur of glossy blood. His sword moved more slowly, as if too heavy for him. His breathing laboured, loud as a stag's in rut. With a great, grunting effort he brought his shield smashing down, like an axe, at the King. Arthur dodged, but slipped. The shield's edge took him on the right shoulder, and must have numbed the arm. His sword flew wide. There was a gasp and a great cry from the watching people. Melwas gave a shout, and swung his sword up for the kill.

But Arthur, now armed only with a dagger, did not spring back out of range. Before anyone could draw breath he had jumped forward, straight past the shield, and his long dagger bit into Melwas' throat.

And stayed still, followed only by a trickle of blood. No thrust followed. He spoke again, low and fierce. Melwas froze where he stood. The sword dropped from his lifted hand. The shield fell to the grass.

The dagger withdrew. The King stepped back. Slowly, in the sight of all that throng, the King's men and his own, and of the Queen watching from her tower, Melwas, King of the Summer Country, knelt on the bloody grass in front of Arthur, and made his surrender.

Now there was no sound at all.

With a movement so slow as to be almost ceremonial, the King lifted his dagger, and cast it, point down, to quiver in the turf. Then he spoke again, more quietly even than before. This time Melwas, with bent head, answered him. They spoke for some time. Finally the King, still with that ceremony of gesture, reached a hand, and lifted Melwas to his feet. Then he beckoned the defeated man's escort to him, and, as his own people came crowding, turned away among them and walked back toward the palace.

In later years I heard several stories about this fight. Some said that it was Bedwyr who fought, not Arthur, but that is patently foolish. Others asserted that there was no fight, or Melwas would surely have been slain. Arthur and Melwas, they said, were brought by some mediator in the Council to agree on terms.

That is not true. It happened exactly as I have told it. Later I learned from the King what had passed between the two men on the field of combat: Melwas, expecting death, was brought to admit the truth of the Queen's accusation, and his own guilt. It is true that it would not have served for Arthur to kill him, but Arthur—and this on no advice from me—acted with both wisdom and restraint. It is a fact that after that day Melwas was loyal to him, and Ynys Witrin was reckoned a jewel in the tally of Arthur's sovereignty.

It is a matter of public record that the King's ships paid no more harbour dues.

7

So the year went by, and the lovely month came, September, my birth-month, the wind's month, the month of the raven, and of Myrddin himself, that wayfarer between heaven and earth. The apple trees were heavy with fruit, and the herbs were gathered and drying; they hung in sheaves and bunches from the rafters in the outhouses at Applegarth, and the still-room was full of ranked jars and boxes waiting to be filled. The whole house, garden, tower and living quarters, smelled sweetly of herbs and fruit, and of the honey that welled from the hives; even, at the end of the orchard, from the hollow oak where the wild bees lived. Applegarth, it seemed, reflected within its small boundaries the golden plenty of the kingdom's summer. The Queen's summer, men called it, as harvest followed hay-time, and still the land glowed with the Goddess-given plenty. A golden age, they said. For me, too, a golden age. But now, as never before, I had time to be lonely. And in the evenings, when the wind was in the southwest, I could feel it in my bones, and was grateful for the fire. Those weeks of nakedness and hunger, and exposure to the mountain weather in the Caledonian Forest, had left me a legacy that even a strong body could not shake off, and were pricking me forward into old age.

Another legacy that time had left me; whether as a lingering after-effect of Morgause's poison, or from some other cause, I had, from time to time, brief attacks of something that I might have called the falling sickness, save that this is not a malady that comes in later years if it has not been felt before. The symptoms, besides, were not like those in cases that I had seen or treated. The fit had come three times in all, and only when I was alone, so none knew of it but myself. What happened was this: resting quietly, I had drifted off, it seemed into sleep, only to wake, cold and stiff and weak with hunger—though not inclined to eat—many hours later. The first time it was a matter of twelve hours or so only, but I guessed from the giddiness, and the light, exhausted feeling, that it had not been normal sleep. On the second occasion the lapse of time was two nights and a day, and I was lucky that the malady had struck me when I was safely in my bed.

I told no one. When the third attack was imminent I recognized the signs; a light, half-hungry sensation, a slight giddiness, a wish to rest and be silent. So I sent Mora home, locked the doors, and took myself to my bedchamber. Afterwards I felt as I sometimes had after a time of prophecy, borne up like a creature ready for flight, with senses rinsed and clean as if new-made, colours and sounds coming as fresh and brilliant as they must to a child. Of course I took to my books for enlightenment, but finding no help there, I put the matter aside, accepting it, as I had learned to accept the pains of prophecy, and their withdrawal, as a touch of the god's hand. Perhaps now the hand was drawing me closer.

There was no fear in the thought. I had done what he had required of me, and when the time came, would be ready to go.

But he did not, I reckoned, require me to sacrifice my pride. Let men remember the royal prophet and enchanter who retired from men's sight and his King's service in his own time; not a dotard who had waited overlong for his dismissal.

So I stayed solitary, busying myself with the garden and my medicine, writing and sending long letters to Blaise in Northumbria, and being cared for well enough by the girl Mora, whose cooking was from time to time enriched by some gift from Arthur's table. Gifts went back from me, too; a basket of some especially good apples from one of the young trees; cordials and medicines; perfumes, even, that I concocted for the Queen's pleasure; herbs for the King's kitchen. Simple stuff, after the fiery gifts of prophecy and victory, but somehow redolent of peace and the age of gold. Gifts of love and contentment; now we had time for both. A golden time indeed, untroubled by foreboding; but with the prickling sense I recognized of some change to come; something undreaded, but ineluctable as the fall of the leaves and the coming of winter.

What it was, I would not allow myself to think. I was like a man alone in an empty room, contented enough, but listening for sounds beyond the shut door, and waiting with half a hope for someone to come, though knowing in his heart of hearts that he would not.

But he did.

He came on a golden evening, in about the middle of the month. There was a full moon, which had stolen, like a ghost, into the sky long before sunset. It hung behind the apple boughs like a great misty lantern, its light slowly waxing, as the sky around it darkened, to apricot and gold. I was in the stillroom, crumbling a pile of dried hyssop. The jars stood clean and ready. The room smelled of hyssop and of the racks of apples and plums laid on the shelves to ripen. A few late wasps droned, and a butterfly, snared by the room's warmth, flattened rich wings against the stone of the window-frame. I heard the light step behind me, and turned.

Magician they call me, and it is true. But I neither expected his coming nor heard him until I saw him standing there in the dusk, lit by the deepening gold of the moon. He might have been a ghost, so did I stand and stare, transfixed. The meeting in the mist on the Island's shore had come back to me frequently, but never as something real; with every effort of recall it became more and more of a dream, something imagined, a hope only.

Now the real boy was here, flushed and breathing, smiling, but not quite at ease, as if unsure of his welcome. He held a bundle which, I supposed, must contain his goods. He was dressed in grey, with a cloak the colour of beech-buds. He had no ornaments, and no weapons.

He began: "I don't suppose you remember me, but—"

"Why should I not? You are the boy who is not Ninian."

"Oh, but I am. I mean, it is one of my names. Truly."

"I see. So when I called you—"

"Yes. When you spoke first, I thought you must know me; but then—when you said who you were—I knew you were mistaken, and—well, I was afraid. I'm sorry. I should have told you straight away, instead of running away like that. I'm sorry."

"But when I told you that I wanted to teach you my art, and asked you to come to me, you agreed to do so. Why?"

His hands, white on the bundle, clenched and twisted in the fold of the cloth. He hung still on the threshold, as if poised to run. "That was . . . When you said that he—this other boy—had been the—the kind of person who could learn from you . . . You had felt it all along, you said, and he had known it, too. Well—" he swallowed, "—I believe that I am, too. I have felt, all my life, that there were doors in the back of the mind that would open on light, if one could only find the key." He faltered, but his eyes did not waver from mine.

"Yes?" I gave him no help.

"Then when you spoke to me like that, suddenly, out of the mist, it was like a dream come true. Merlin himself, speaking to me by name, and offering me the very key . . . Even when I realized that you had mistaken me for someone else, who was dead, I had a wild thought that perhaps I could come to you and take his place. . . . Then of course I saw how stupid that was, to think I could deceive you, of all people. So I did not dare to come."

"But now you have dared."

"I had to." He spoke simply, stating a fact. "I have thought of nothing else since that night. I was afraid, because . . . I was afraid, but there are things that you have to do, they won't let you alone, it's as if you were being driven. More then driven, hounded. Do you understand?"

"Very well." It was hard to keep my voice steady and grave. There must have been some note in it of what my heart felt, because, faint and sweet from the upper room, I heard the answer of my harp.

He had heard nothing. He was still braced, braving me, forcing himself into the role of suppliant. "Now you know the truth. I'm not the boy you knew. You know nothing about me. Whatever I feel, here in myself"—a hand moved as if to touch his breast, but clenched itself again on the bundle—"you may not think I'm worth teaching. I don't expect you to take me in, or spend any time on me. But if you would—if you would only let me stay here, sleep in the stableplace, anything, help you with—well, with work like that"—a glance at the pile of hyssop—"until perhaps in time you would come to know . . ." His voice wavered again, and this time died. He licked dry lips and stood mute, watching me.

It was my gaze that faltered, not his. I turned aside to hide the joy that I could feel mantling my cheeks. I plunged my hands wrist-deep in the fragrant herbs, and rubbed the dry fragments between the fingertips. The scent of hyssop, clean and pungent, rose and steadied me.

I spoke slowly, to the herb jars. "When I called to you by the Lake, I took you for a boy with whom I travelled north many years ago, and who had a spirit that spoke to mine. He died, and ever since that day I have grieved for his death. When I saw you, I thought I had been mistaken, and that he still lived; but when I had time to think about it, I knew that now he would be a boy no longer, but a grown man. It was, you might say, a stupid error. I do not commonly make such errors, but at the time I told myself it was an error bred of weariness and grief, and of the hope that was still alive in me, that he, or such another spirit, would one day come to me again."

I paused. He said nothing. The moon had moved beyond the window-frame, and the door where the boy stood was almost in darkness. I turned back to him.

"I should have known it was no error. It was the hand of the god that crossed your path with mine, and now has driven you to me, in spite of your fear. You are not the boy I knew, but if you had not been just such another, you can be sure I would not have seen you, or spoken to you. That night was full of strong magic. I should have remembered that, and trusted it."

He said eagerly: "I felt it, too. You could feel the stars like frost on the skin. I'd gone out to catch fish . . . but I let them be. It was no night for death, even for a fish." Dimly, I saw that he smiled, but when he drew breath, it came unsteadily. "You mean I may stay? I will do?"

"You will do." I lifted my fingers from the hyssop, and let it trickle back onto the cloth, dusting my fingertips together. "Which of us, after this, will dare to ignore the god who drives us? Don't be afraid of me. You are very welcome. No doubt I'll warn you, when I have time to be cautious, of the heavy task you're undertaking, and all the thorns that lie in the way, but just at this moment I dare say nothing that will frighten you away from me again. Come in, and let me see you."

As he obeyed me, I lifted the unlit lamp from the shelf. The wick caught flame from the air, and flared high.

In full light I knew that I could never have mistaken him for the goldsmith's boy, but he was very like. He was taller by a thumb's breadth, and his face was not quite so thin in outline. His skin was finer, and his hands, as fine-boned and clever-looking as the other boy's, had never done slave's work. His hair was the same, a thick dark mane, roughly cut just short of his shoulders. His mouth was like, so like that I could have been deceived again; it had the gentle, dreaming lines that—I suspected—masked a firmness, even obstinacy, of purpose. The boy Ninian had shown a quiet disregard of anything that he did not want to notice; his master's discourses had gone unheeded over his head while he took refuge in his own thoughts. Here was the same soft stubbornness, and in these eyes, too, the same half-absent, dreaming look that could shut the world out as effectively as dropped eyelids. They were grey, the iris rimmed with black, and had the clarity of lake water. I was to find that like lake water they could reflect colour, and look green or blue or black-stormy as the mood came. Now they were watching me with what looked like a mixture of fascination and fear.

"The lamp?" I said. "You've not seen the fire called before? Well, that's one of the first things you'll learn; it was the first my own master taught me. Or is it the jars? You're looking at them as if you thought I was bottling poison. I was packing the garden herbs for winter's use."

"Hyssop," he said. I thought there was a glint of mischief, which in a girl I might have called demure. " 'To be burned with brimstone for inflammations of the throat; or boiled with honey to help pleurisy of the lungs.' "

I laughed. "Galen? Well, it seems we have a flying start. So you can read? Do you know—? No, it must wait till morning. For the present, have you had supper?"

"Yes, thank you."

"You said that Ninian was 'one of your names.' What do you like to be called?"

"Ninian will do . . . that is, unless you would rather not use it. What happened to him, the boy you knew? I think you said he was drowned?"

"Yes. We were at Corstopitum, and he went swimming with some other boys in the river beside the bridge where the Cor flows into the Tyne. They came running back to say he had been swept away."

"I'm sorry."

I smiled at him. "You will have to work very hard to make good his loss. Come, then, we must find you a place to sleep."

That was how I acquired my assistant, and the god his servant. He had had his hand over both of us all that time. It seems to me now that the first Ninian was but a forerunner—a shadow cast before—of the real one who came to me later, from the Lake. From the start it was apparent that instinct had deceived neither of us; Ninian of the Lake, though knowing little of the arts I professed, proved a natural adept. He learned quickly, soaking up both knowledge and art as a cloth soaks up clear water. He could read and write fluently, and though he had not, as I in my youth had had, the gift of languages, he spoke a pure Latin as well as the vernacular, and had picked up enough Greek to be able to read a label or be accurate about a recipe. He had once, he told me, had access to a translation of Galen, but knew nothing of Hippocrates beyond hearsay. I set him to reading in the Latin version I had, and found myself, in some measure, sent back to school by the score of questions he asked, of which I had taken the answers so long for granted that I had forgotten how they were reached. Music he knew nothing of, and would not learn; this was the first time I came face to face with that gentle, immovable stubbornness of his. He would listen, his face full of dreaming light, when I played or sang; but sing himself, or even try to sing, he would not; and after a few attempts to teach him his notes on the big harp, I gave it up. I would have liked it if he had a voice; I would not have wanted to sit by while another man made music with my harp, but now with age my own voice was not as good as it had once been, and I would have liked to hear a young voice singing the poems I made. But no. He smiled, shook his head, tuned the harp for me (that much he could and would do), and listened.

But in everything else he was eager and quick to learn. Recollecting as best I could the way old Galapas, my master, had inducted me into the skills of magic, I took him, step by step, into the strange and misty halls of art. The Sight he had already in some degree; but where I had surpassed my master from the start, Ninian would do well if in time he could equal me, and he was still a stranger to the flights of prophecy. If he went half as far as I, I would be content. Like all old men, I could not believe that that young brain and gentle body could withstand the stresses that I myself had withstood many times. I helped him, as Galapas had done me, with certain subtle yet safe drugs, and soon he could see in the fire or the lamp, and wake from the vision afterwards no more than weary, and, at times, disturbed by what he had seen. As yet he could not put truth together with vision. I did not help him to; and indeed, in those peaceful months of his apprenticeship there was little happening of enough moment to set prophecy stirring in the fire. Once or twice he spoke to me, in a kind of confusion, about the Queen, and Melwas and Bedwyr and the King, but I put the visions aside as obscure, and pursued them no further.

He steadfastly refused to tell me about himself or whence he came. He had lived most of his life, he said, on or near the Island, and allowed me to gather that his parents had been poor dwellers in one of the outlying Lake villages. Ninian of the Lake, he called himself, and said it was enough; so as such I accepted him. His past, after all, was nothing; whatever he was going to be, I would make. I did not press him; I had had enough, as a bastard and a child with no known father, of the shame of such questioning; so I respected the boy's silences, and asked no more than he would tell me.

All the practical side of healing, the study of anatomy, and the use of drugs, he was interested in, and good at. He could also, as I never could, draw with real skill. He began, that first winter, for sheer delight in the work, to compile a local herbal of his own, though most of the seeking and identifying of the plants, which is more than half the doctor's art, would have to wait till spring. But there was no hurry for it. He had, he told me, for ever.

So the winter passed in deep happiness, each day too short for all it could be filled with. To be with Ninian was to have everything; my own youth again, eager and quick to learn, with life unfolding full of bright promise; and at the same time the pleasures of quiet thought and of solitude. He seemed to sense when I needed to be alone, and either withdrew physically from my presence to his own room, or fell silent, and apparently into some deep abstraction, which left my thoughts free of him. He would not share the house with me, preferring, he said, to have rooms of his own where he need not disturb me, so I had Mora get ready the upper rooms that would have housed the servants, had any lived with me. The rooms were above the workshop and storeroom, facing west, and, though small and low under the rafters, were pleasant and airy. I did wonder at first if Mora and he had come to some sort of understanding; they spent a lot of time talking together in the kitchen, or down by the stream where the girl did some of the washing; I would hear them laughing, and could see that they were easy together; but there was no sign of intimacy, and in time I realized that Ninian, from things he let fall in talk, knew as little about love as I myself. Which, from the way the power grew in him, palpably week by week, I took to be only natural. The gods do not give two gifts at once, and they are jealous.

Spring came early the next year, with mild sunny days in March, and the wild geese going overhead daily, toward their nesting sites in the north. I caught some kind of chill, and kept to the house, but then one fine day went outside to sit in the little garth, where the doves were already busy about their love-making. The heated wall made the place as pleasant as a fireside; there were rosy cups of quince against the stone, and winter irises full out at the wall's base. In the gardens beyond the stable buildings I could hear the thud of Varro's spade, and thought idly of the planting I had planned. Nothing was in my mind beyond vague, pleasant plans of a domestic sort, and the sight of the pink sheen on the breast feathers of the doves, and the sleepy sound of their cooing. . . .

Later, looking back, I wondered if for a brief hour my malady had blanketed me from consciousness of the present. It would have pleased me to think so. But it seems probable that the malady that overtook me was age, and the weakness left by the chill, and the lulling drug of contentment.

Quick footsteps on a stone stair startled me awake. I looked up. Ninian came hurrying down from his room, but with uncertain steps, as if it were he, not I, who was half-drugged, or even ill. He kept a hand on the stone wall, as if without its guidance he would have stumbled. Still unsteadily, he crossed the colonnade, and came out into the sunshine. He paused there, with a hand to one of the pillars for support. His face was pale, his eyes enormous, the black pupils swimmingly overspreading the iris. His lips looked dry, but there was damp on his forehead, and two sharp lines of pain gouged down between his brows.

"What is it?" I began in alarm to get to my feet, but he put out a hand to calm me, then came forward. He sank down on the flags at my feet in the sun.

"I've had a dream," he said, and even his voice was unlike itself. "No, I wasn't asleep. I was reading by the window. There was a spider's web there, still full of drops from last night's rain. I was watching it as it shook in the sunlight. . . ."

I understood then. I put a hand down to his shoulder and held it steadily. "Sit quiet for a moment. You will not forget the dream. Wait there. You can tell me later."

But as I got to my feet he shot a hand out and grabbed at my robe. "You don't understand! It was a warning! I am sure of that! There's some sort of danger—"

"I understand quite well. But until the headache goes, you will remember nothing clearly. Now wait. I'll be back soon."

I went into the stillroom. As I busied myself mixing the cordial I had only one thought in my mind. He, sitting reading and thinking, had had vision brought to him in a dewdrop's spark of light; I, waiting idly and with passive mind in full sunlight, had seen nothing. I found that my hand shook a little as I poured the cordial for him; it would take love, I thought, to stand peacefully aside and watch the god lift his wing from over me, and take another into its shadow. No matter that the power had brought pain and men's fear and sometimes hatred; no one who has known power like that has any wish to abdicate it to another. Not to anyone.

I carried the goblet out into the sunlight. Ninian, still curled on the flagstones, had his head down, a fist pressed tightly against his brow. He looked very slight and young. He raised his head at my step, and the grey eyes, swimming with tears of pain, looked at me blindly. I sat down, took his hand in mine, and guided the goblet to his mouth. "Drink this. It will make you feel better presently. No, don't try to talk yet."

He drank, then his head went down again, this time against my knee. I laid a hand on his hair. For some time we sat like that, while the doves, disturbed by his coming, flew down again onto the coping of the wall, and once more took up their gentle courtship. Beyond the stables the monotonous sound of Varro's spade went on and on.

Presently Ninian stirred.

I lifted my hand. "Better?"

He nodded and raised his head. The lines of pain had gone. "Yes. Yes, it's quite gone. It was more than a headache; it was like a sharp pain right through the brain. I've never felt anything like that before. Am I ill?"

"No. You are merely a seer, an eye and a voice for a most tyrannous god. You have had a waking dream, what men call a vision. Now tell me about it, and we shall see if it is a true one."

He drew his knees up, clasping them with both hands. He spoke, looking past me at the wall with the black branches and red cups of the quince. His eyes were still dark, dilated with vision, and his voice was low and even, as if reciting something learned by rote.

"I saw a stretch of grey sea, whipped with storm winds, breaking white over rocks like wolves' fangs. There was a beach of pebbles, grey, too, and streaming with rain. The waves came in over the beach, and with them came broken spars and casks and torn sails— pieces of wreckage. And people; drowned bodies of men and women. One of the men's bodies rolled near me, and I saw he had not been drowned; there was a deep wound in his neck, but the blood had all been washed away by the sea. He looked like an animal that has been bled. There were dead children, too, three of them. One was naked, and had been speared. Then I saw, out beyond the breakers, another ship, a whole ship, with sails furled in the wind, and with oars out, holding her steady. She waited there, and I saw that she was low in the water as if heavily laden. She had a high, curved prow, with a pair of antlers fastened to it; I couldn't see if they were real, or carved in wood. I could see her name, though; it was *King Stag*. The men in the ship were watching the bodies tumbling on shore, and they were laughing. They were a long way off across the sea, but I could hear what they said, quite clearly. . . . Can you believe that?"

"Yes. Go on."

"They were saying, 'You were guided, by God! Who could have told that the old scow was so richly found? Luck like yours, and a fair division of the spoils, and we'll all make our fortunes!' They were speaking to the captain."

"Did you hear his name?"

"I think so. They called him Heuil."

"Was that all?"

"No. There was a sort of darkness, like a mist. Then the *King Stag* had gone, but near me on the shore there were horsemen, and some of them had dismounted and were looking at the bodies. One man lifted a piece of broken planking with something on it that might have been the name of the wrecked ship, and carried it across to where another was sitting on his horse. He was a dark man, carrying no device that I could see, but he was obviously their leader. He looked angry. He said something, and the others got to their horses again, and they all galloped up off the beach, through the dunes and the long grasses. I was left there, and then even the dead bodies were gone, and the wind was blowing into my eyes and making them water. . . . That was all. I was looking at the spider's web, and the drops had melted in the sunlight. A fly was caught there, shaking the web. I suppose that was what woke me. Merlin—"

He stopped abruptly, and cocked his head to listen. Now I could catch, from the road below, the sounds of a troop of horsemen, and a distant command to halt. A single rider detached himself, and approached at a rapid canter.

"A messenger from Camelot?" I said. "Who knows, perhaps this is your vision coming home."

The horse stopped. There was the jingle of the bridle being thrown to Varro. Arthur came in through the archway.

"Merlin, I'm glad to see you about. They told me you had been ill, and I came to see for myself." He paused, looking at Ninian. He knew, of course, that the boy was with me, but they had not met before. Ninian had refused to go with me to Camelot, and whenever the King had visited me, had made some excuse and retired to his rooms. I did not press him, knowing the awe that the people of the Lake villages felt for the High King.

I was on my feet, just beginning, "This is Ninian," when the boy himself interrupted me. He came to his feet in one swift movement, as fast as a snake uncurling, and cried out:

"That's the man! That's the one! It was a true dream then, it was true!"

Arthur's brows shot up, not, I knew, at the lack of ceremony, but at the words. He looked from Ninian back to me. "A true dream?" He said it softly. He knew the phrase of old.

I heard Ninian gasp as, through the dregs of the vision, he came back to the present. He stood there blinking, like someone thrust suddenly into bright light. "It's the King. So it was the King."

Arthur said, sharply now: "So what was the King?"

Ninian, flushing, began to stammer. "Nothing. That is, I was just talking to Merlin. I didn't know you at first. I—"

"Never mind. You know me now. What is this about a true dream?"

Ninian looked appealingly at me. Telling me his dream was one thing; making his first prophecy to the King's face was quite another. I said across him, to the King: "It seems that an old friend of yours is indulging in piracy, or some villainy uncommonly like it, somewhere in his home waters. Murder and robbery, and peaceful traders looted and then wrecked, and no one left alive to tell the story."

He frowned. "An old friend of mine? Who, then?"

"Heuil."

"Heuil?" His face darkened. Then he stood for a few moments in thought. "Yes, it fits. It fits. I had news a while back from Ector, and he said Caw was failing, and that wild brood of his looking around them like idle dogs for something to tear. Then three days ago I heard from Urbgen, my sister's lord in Rheged, of a village on the coast attacked and looted, and the folk killed or scattered. He was inclined to blame the Irish, but I doubted that; the weather's been too rough for anything but local raiding. Heuil, is it? You don't surprise me. Shall I go?"

"It seems you had better. My guess is that Caw is dead, or dying. I can't believe that Heuil would dare, otherwise, to do anything to provoke Rheged."

"Your guess?"

"That is all."

He nodded. "It seems likely. In any case, it will answer very well. I had been almost ready to invent some pretext for a foray to the northward. With Caw's grip slackening, and that black dog Heuil collecting a following that could contest his brother's claim to the rulership of Strathclyde, I would like to be there to see things for myself. Piracy, eh? You did not see where?"

I glanced at Ninian. He shook his head. "No," I said, "but you'll find him. You will be there, on the shore, while the wreckage and the bodies still lie there. The raiders' ship is *King Stag*. That's all we know. You should be able to fasten the guilt where it belongs."

"I'll do that, never fear." He was grim. "I'll send north to Urbgen and Ector tonight to expect me, and I'll ride myself in the morning. I'm grateful. I've been looking for an excuse to cut my lord Heuil out of the pack, and now you give me this. It may be just the chance I need to get another agreement ratified between Strathclyde and Rheged, and throw my weight in behind the new king. I don't know how long I shall be away. And you, Merlin? All is really well with you?"

"All is very well."

He smiled. He had not missed the glance that had gone between Ninian and myself. "It seems you have someone to share your visions with, at last. Well,

Ninian, I am glad to have met you." He smiled at the boy, and said something kind. Ninian, staring, made some sort of answer. I had been wrong, I saw, about him; he was not awed by the presence of the King, and there was a quality in the way he looked at Arthur, something I could not quite put a name to; none of the worship that I was used to seeing in men's eyes, but a steady appraisal. Arthur saw it, looked amused, then dismissed the boy and turned back to me, asking for messages for Morgan and Ector. Then he said his goodbyes and went.

Ninian looked thoughtfully after him. "Yes, it was a true dream. The dark leader on the white horse, with the white shield shining, and no blazon on it but the light of the sky. It was Arthur beyond doubt. Who exactly is Heuil, and why does the King want an excuse to cut him down?"

"He's one of the sons of Caw of Strathclyde, who has been king on Dumbarton Rock since before I can remember. He's very old, and has sired nineteen sons on various women. There may be daughters, too, but those wild northern men make little of their girls. The youngest of the brood, Gildas, has recently been sent to my old friend Blaise, whom you know of, to learn to read and write. He, at least, will be a man of peace. But Heuil is the wildest of a wild breed. He and Arthur have always disliked one another. They fell out and fought, once, over a girl, when Arthur was a boy in the north country. Since then, with Caw's health failing, the King has seen Heuil as a danger to the balance of peace in the north. He would do anything, I think, to harm Arthur, even ally himself with the Saxons. Or so Arthur believes. But now that Heuil has taken to rapine and murder, he can be hunted down and destroyed, and the greater danger will be averted."

"And the King takes an army north, just like that, on your word?" There was awe in his face now, but not the awe of kings or their counsels. He was, for the first time, feeling the power in himself.

I smiled. "No, on yours. If I seemed to take the credit for the seeing I am sorry. But the matter was urgent, and he might not have believed you as readily."

"Of course not. But you saw it, too?"

"I saw nothing."

He looked startled. "But you believed me straight away."

"Of course. Because I did not share it, it doesn't mean it was not a true dream."

He looked worried, then rather scared. "But, Merlin, do you mean that you knew nothing about this before I told you my dream? I mean, about Heuil's turning pirate . . . I should say, his intention to turn pirate? That you sent the King off to the north on my word alone?"

"That is what I mean, yes."

A silence, while worry, apprehension, excitement, and then joy showed in his face as clearly as the reflection of light and cloud blowing across the waters of his native lake. He was still taking in the implications of power. But when he spoke he surprised me. Like Arthur, he saw straight past those implications to others, that were my concern, not his. And his next words were an exact echo of Arthur's. "Merlin, do you mind?"

I answered him as simply. "Perhaps. A little, now. But soon, not at all. It's a harsh gift, and perhaps it is time that the god handed it on to you, and left me in peace to sit in the sun and watch the doves on the wall."

I smiled as I spoke, but there was no answering glimmer in his face. He did a strange thing then. He reached for my hand, lifted it to his cheek, then dropped it and went back upstairs to his room without another word or look. I was left standing there in the sun, remembering another, much younger boy, riding downhill from the cave of Galapas, with the visions swirling in his head, and tears on his face, and all the lonely pain and danger hanging in the clouds ahead of him. Then I went indoors to my own room, and read beside the fire till Mora brought the midday meal.

8

Arthur rode out next day for the north, and thereafter we got no more news. Ninian went about the place with a half-dazed look, compounded, I think, of wonder at himself and the "true vision," and at me for not seeming distressed at the way it had passed me by. For myself, I admit I was divided; looking back on that day, I knew that I had been lingering in the edges of the poisoned dream that was my sickness; but even after Arthur's visit and acceptance of Ninian's prophecy, nothing had come to me out of the dark, either of proof or denial. For all that I seemed to feel, in the rich quiet of the days, a tranquil approval. It was like watching a shadow that slowly, as the distant clouds move, withdraws from one field or forest, and passes on to shroud the next. I had been shown, gently enough, where happiness now lay; so I took it, preparing the boy Ninian to be as I had been, and myself for some future half seen and guessed at many times, but now seen more clearly and no longer dreaded, but moved toward, as a beast moves toward its winter sleep.

Ninian, more even than before, seemed to withdraw into himself. On one or two occasions, lying wakeful in the night, I heard him cross the garth soft-footed, and then run, like a young thing released, down the valley to the road. Twice, even, I sought to follow him in vision, but he must have taken care to cloud himself from me, for I saw no farther than the roadway, then the slight figure running, running, into the mist that lay between Applegarth and the Island. It did not trouble me that he had secrets, any more than it troubled me to hear him and the girl Mora talking—sometimes at great length—in the stillroom or the kitchen. I had never counted myself lively company, and with age tended to be even more withdrawn. It only pleased me that the young people should find common interests, and keep each other contented in my service.

For service it was. I worked the boy harder than any slave. This is the way of love, I find; one longs so fervently for the beloved to achieve the best ends that he is spared nothing. And that I loved Ninian there could no longer be any doubt; the boy was myself, and through him I would go on living. As long as the King should need the vision and the power of a King's prophet, he would find it, as ready to his hand as the royal sword.

One evening we built the fire up high against the chill wind of April, and sat beside it, watching the flames. Ninian settled straight down in his usual place, on the rug before the hearth, chin on fist, the grey eyes narrowed against the flames. Gradually, on the fine pale skin, the gleam of sweat showed, a film which caught the firelight and limned his face with a pure line, damping the edges of his hair, and fringing the black lashes with rainbows. I, as lately more and more often, found myself watching him, rather than reaching after my own power. It was a mixture of deep contentment, and a cruelly disturbing love that I made no attempt either to check or to understand. I had learned the lessons of the past; I went with the time, believing that I was master enough of myself and my thoughts to do the boy no harm.

There was a change in his face. Something moved there, reflection of grief or distress or pain, like something seen faintly in a glass. Sweat was running into his eyes, but he neither blinked nor moved.

It was time I went with him. I stopped watching him, and turned my eyes to the fire.

I saw Arthur straight away. He was sitting his big white horse at the edge of the sea. It was a pebbled strand, and I recognized the crag-fast castle above: Rheged's sea-tower, which commands the Ituna estuary. It was dusk, and the stormy sky piled indigo clouds behind a grey sea lighter than its own horizon. Foam-filled waves dashed down on the stones and raced hissing up the shore, to die in creamy froth and drag back through hissing pebbles. The white stallion stood fast, with the foam swirling round his fetlocks; his splashed and gleaming flanks, and Arthur's grey cloak blown with the horse's mane, looked part of the scene, as if the King had ridden out of the sea.

A man, a peasant by the look of him, was by Arthur's bridle, talking earnestly, and pointing seaward. The King followed the gesture, then sat straight in the saddle, his hand to his eyes. I saw what he was looking at: a light, far out toward the horizon, tossing with the tossing sea. The King asked a question, and the man pointed again, this time inland. The King nodded, something passed from hand to hand, then he turned his stallion's head and lifted an arm. The white horse went up the sea path at a gallop, and through the thickening mists of the vision I could see the troopers pressing after him. Just before the vision faded I saw, at the head of the cliff, lights pricking out in the tower.

I came back to the firelit room to find that Ninian was there before me. He was kneeling, or rather crouching, on the rug, with his head in his hands.

"Ninian?"

No movement but a slight shake of the head. I gave him a moment or two, then reached for the cordial I kept to hand.

"Come. Drink this."

He sipped, and his eyes thanked me, but still he did not speak.

I watched him for a few minutes in silence, then said: "So it seems that the King has reached the shores of the Ituna, and has found out about the pirates. He rests in Rheged's seatower, and with morning, I have no doubt, he will be hard on Heuil's tracks. So what is it? Arthur is safe, your vision was true, and he is doing what he set out to do."

Still nothing, but that look of white distress. I said quickly: "Come, Ninian, don't take it to heart so. For Arthur this is a small matter. The only hard thing about it is that he must punish Heuil without offending his brothers; and even that won't be too difficult. It's a long time since Heuil—metaphorically speaking—spat on his father's hearthstone and went out to do his mischiefs in his own way. So even if old Caw is still alive, I doubt if he'll repine; and as for the elder sons, I've no doubt Heuil's death would come as a relief." I added, more sharply: "If it was tragedy you saw, or disaster, it's all the more important to speak of it. Caw's death we expected; whose, then? Morgan, the King's sister? Or Count Ector?"

"No." His voice sounded strange, like an instrument meant for music that is blown through by a gritty wind. "I did not see the King at all."

"You mean you saw nothing? Look, Ninian, this happens. You remember that it happened the other day, even to me. You must not let it distress you. I've told you before, you must wait for the god. He chooses the time, not you."

He shook his head. "It isn't that. I did see. But not the High King. Something else."

"Then tell me."

He gave me a desperate look. "I can't."

"Look, my dear, as you do not choose what you are shown, so neither do you choose what you will tell. There may come a time when you use your judgment in the halls of kings, but with me you tell me all that you see."

"I cannot!"

I waited a moment. "Now. You saw in the flames?"

"Yes."

"Did what you saw contradict what came before, or what I think I have just seen?"

"No."

"Then if you are keeping silent out of fear of me, or fear that I may be angry for some reason—"

"I have never been afraid of you."

"Then," I said patiently, "there can surely be no reason to keep silent, and every reason to tell me what you think you saw. It may not be the tragedy you so obviously think it is. You may be interpreting it wrongly. Has that not occurred to you?"

A flash of hope, soon shut out. He took a shaky breath, and I thought he would speak, then he bit his lip and remained silent. I wondered if he had foreseen my death.

I leaned forward and took his face in my hands and forced it up toward me. His eyes came reluctantly up to meet mine. "Ninian. Do you think I cannot go where you have just gone? Will you put me to that trouble and stress, or will you obey me now? What was it that you saw in the flame?"

His tongue came out to wet dry lips, and then he spoke, in a whisper, as if he was afraid of the sound. "Did you know that Bedwyr is not with the High King? That he stayed behind in Camelot?"

"No, but I could have guessed it. It was obvious that the King must leave one of his chief captains to keep his stronghold and guard the Queen."

"Yes." He licked his lips again. "That's what I saw. Bedwyr in Camelot—with the Queen. They were—I think they are—"

He stopped. I took my hands away, and his eyes fell, how thankfully, away from mine.

There was only one way to interpret his distress. "Lovers?"

"I think so. Yes. I know they are." Then, in a rush now: "Merlin, how could she do this thing? After all that has happened—after all he has done for her! The Melwas affair—everyone knows what happened there! And Bedwyr, how could he so betray the King? The Queen—a woman to look aside from such a man, such a King . . . If only I could believe that this was no true dream! But I know it's true!" He stared at me, with eyes still dilated with the dream. "And, Merlin, in God's name, what must we do?"

I said slowly: "That I cannot tell you yet. But put it from you if you can. This is one burden that you must not be asked to share with me."

"Will you tell him?"

"I am his servant. What do you think?"

He bit his lip again, staring into the fire, but this time, I knew, seeing nothing. His face was white and wretched. I remember feeling vaguely surprised that he should, apparently, blame Guinevere more for her weakness than Bedwyr for his treachery. He said at length: "How could you tell him such a thing?"

"I don't know that yet. Time will show me."

He lifted his head. "You're not surprised." It sounded like an accusation.

"No. I think I knew, that night when he swam across to Melwas' lodge in the Lake. And afterwards, when she nursed him. . . . And I remember how, when she first came to Caerleon for her wedding, Bedwyr was the only one of the knights who would not look at her, nor she at him. I think they had already felt it, on the journey from Northgalis, before ever she saw the King." I added: "And you might say that I was told clearly enough many years ago, when they were still boys together, and no woman had yet come, as women will, to disturb their lives."

He got abruptly to his feet. "I'll go to bed," he said, and left me.

Alone, I went back into the flames. I saw them almost straight away. They were standing on the western terrace, where I had talked with Arthur. Now the palace was in darkness, but for the dispersed sparkle of the stars, and one shaft of lamplight that lay slanting over the tiles between the tubs of budding rose-trees.

They were standing silent and stock-still. Their hands were locked in each other's, and they were staring at one another with a kind of wildness. She looked afraid, and tears stood on her cheeks; his face was haunted, as if the white shadow sapped his spirit. Whatever kind of love had them in its claws, it was a cruel one, and, I knew, neither of them as yet had dared to let it kill their faithfulness.

I watched, and pitied, then turned from the smoking logs and left them to their privacy.

9

Eight weeks later the King came home. He had caught up with Heuil, beaten him in fair fight, burned his ships, and levied a fine which would keep him singing small for some time to come.

Once again he had crushed back his instincts in favour of policy. He had been met on his journey north with the tidings that Caw of Strathclyde had died, quietly in his bed. Quietly, that is, for Caw; he had spent the day hunting and half the night feasting, then, when the inevitable penalties struck his ninety-year-old body in the small hours of the dawning, had died, surrounded by such of his sons and their mothers as could get to the death-bed in time. He had also named his heir, the second son Gwarthegydd (the eldest had been badly maimed in fighting some years back). The messenger who brought Arthur the news also carried assurances of Gwarthegydd's friendship. So Arthur, till he had met and spoken with Gwarthegydd, and seen how he stood with his brother Heuil, would not put the friendship at risk.

He need not have been so careful. It was said that when Gwarthegydd heard the news of Heuil's defeat he let out a guffaw almost as hearty as his father's great bellow, and drank down a full horn of mead to Arthur's health. So the King rode north with Urbgen and Ector into Dumbarton and sat down with Gwarthegydd for nine days, and watched him crowned at the end of it. Then, well satisfied, he rode south again. He went by the east road to Elmet, found the Vale and the Saxon lands quiet, then crossed the country by the Pennine Gap to Caerleon. There he stayed for a month, and in the first days of June came home to Camelot.

It was time. Again and again in the fire I had seen the lovers, tossed between desire and faith, Bedwyr fine-drawn and silent, the Queen with great eyes and nervous hands. They were never again alone: always with them her ladies sat and sewed, or his men rode in attendance. But they would sit or ride a little way apart from the rest, and talk and talk, as if in speech, and now and again a light and desperate touch, there was comfort to be had.

And they watched day and night for Arthur's coming: Bedwyr, because he could not quit his post of torment without the King's leave; Guinevere with the forebodings of a lonely young woman who is half in awe of her husband, but has to depend on him for protection and comfort and what companionship he has time to give.

He was home in Camelot for ten days or so before he came to see me. It was a soft bright morning in June. I had risen soon after dawn, as was my habit, and went walking across the rolling hilltops above the house. I went alone; there was usually no sign or Ninian until Mora called him to breakfast. I had walked for an hour, thinking, and pausing from time to time to gather the plants I was looking for, when, beyond a fold of the downs, I heard hoof-beats, coming easily.

Don't ask me how I knew it was Arthur; one hoof-beat is very like another, and there was no foresight in the air that day; but love has stronger wings than vision, and I merely turned and waited for him, in the lee of one of the groves of thorn that here and there break the pale sweep of the high downlands. The thorn trees crowned the edge of a little valley where ran a track as old as the land itself. Up this, presently, I saw him coming, sitting at ease on a pretty bay mare, and with his young hound, Cabal's successor, at heel.

He lifted a hand to me, turned the mare up the slope, then slid from the saddle, and greeted me with a smile.

"Well, so you were right. As if I had to tell you that! And now I suppose I don't even have to tell you what happened? Have you ever thought, Merlin, what a dull thing it is to have a prophet who knows everything before it has happened? Not only can I never lie to you, but I can hardly even come to you afterwards and boast about it."

"I'm sorry. But I assure you, this time, your prophet waited for your dispatches just as eagerly as anyone else. Thank you for sending the letters. . . . How did you find me? Have you been to Applegarth?"

"I was on the way there, but a fellow with an ox-cart—one of the sawyers—said he had seen you come this way. Are you going farther? I'll walk with you if I may."

"Of course. I was just going to turn for home. . . . Your letters were very welcome, but I still want to hear everything at first hand. It's strange to think that old Caw has gone at last. He's been sitting on that crag of his at Dumbarton for as long as I can remember. Do you think Gwarthegydd can hold his own now?"

"Against the Irish and the Saxons, yes, I wouldn't doubt him there. How he makes out with the seventeen other claimants to the kingdom is another matter." He grinned. "Sixteen, I suppose, since I clipped Heuil's wings for him."

"Make it fifteen. You can hardly count young Gildas, since he went to serve Blaise as his clerk."

"That's true. A clever boy, that, and was always Heuil's shadow. I fancy that when Blaise dies he'll be headed for a monastery. Perhaps it's as well. Like his brother, he has never loved me."

"Then it's to be hoped he can be trusted with his master's papers. You should get some of your own scribes to set your records down."

He cocked a brow at me. "What's this? A prophet's warning?"

"Nothing of the kind. A passing thought, merely. So Gwarthegydd is your man? There was a time when he threw Caw off and wooed the Irish kings."

"He was younger then, and Caw's hand was heavy. That's over. I think he will be well enough. What really matters at this stage is that he agrees with Urbgen. . . ."

He talked on, telling me all the burden of the weeks away, while we walked slowly back across the downs, with the mare following, and the great hound coursing, nose down, in widening circles round our path.

In essence, I thought, listening, nothing had changed. Not yet. Less and less did he need to come to me for counsel, but, as always since his boyhood, he needed the chance to talk over—to himself as much as to me—the course of events, and the problems of the newly built concourse of kingdoms as they arose. Usually, at the end of an hour or two, after a conversation to which I might have contributed much, or sometimes nothing at all, I could both hear and see that the knots were in a fair way to being unravelled. Then he would rise suddenly, stretch, give me farewell, and go; an abrupt disappearance with anyone else, but between us there was no need for more. I was the strong tree on which the eagle alighted in passing, for rest or thought. But now the oak showed a withered bouth or two. How long would it take the sapling to be up to his weight?

He had come to the end of his narrative. Then, as if my thoughts had communicated themselves to him, he gave me a long look, with trouble in it. "Now, about you. How have you been during these last weeks? You look tired. Have you been ill again?"

"No. My health need not trouble you."

"I've thought more than once about my last visit to you. You said that it was this—" he hesitated over it, "—your assistant who 'saw' Heuil and his rabble at their work."

"Ninian. Yes, it was."

"And you yourself saw nothing?"

"Yes," I said. "Nothing."

"So you told me. I still find that strange. Don't you?"

"I suppose so. But if you remember, I wasn't well that day. I suppose I had not fully recovered from that chill I caught."

"He's been with you—how long?"

"He came in September. That makes it, what? Nine months?"

"And you have taught him all you know?"

I smiled. "Hardly. But I have taught him a good deal. You need never lack a prophet, Arthur."

He did not smile in response. He was looking deeply troubled. He walked on across the flinty turf, with the mare's nose at his shoulder, and the hound running ahead. It was quartering the acres of furze with their loads of scented yellow blossom. Wherever it went it dislodged the tiny blue butterflies in clouds, and scattered the glossy scarlet of the ladybirds. There had been a plague of them that spring, and the furze bushes held them in their hundreds, like berries on the thorn.

Arthur was silent for a space, frowning at his thoughts. Then he came, apparently, to a sudden decision. "Do you trust him?"

"Ninian? Of course. Why not?"

"What do you know about him?"

"As much as I need to," I said, perhaps a little stiffly. "I told you how he came to me. I was certain then, and I am still certain, that it was the god who drew us together. And I could not have an apter pupil. Everything I have to teach him he is more than eager to learn. I don't have to drive him; I have to hold him back." I glanced at him. "Why? I would have thought you had seen the proof of his aptitude. His vision was true."

"Oh, I don't doubt his aptitude." He spoke dryly. I caught the faintest of emphasis on the last word.

"What then? What are you trying to say?" Even I was not prepared for the degree of cold surprise in my voice.

He said quickly: "I'm sorry, Merlin. But I have to say this. I doubt his intentions toward you."

Though he had signalled the blow, it still struck with paralyzing force. I felt the blood leave my heart. I stopped and faced him. Around us the scent of the gorse rose, sweet and strong. With it, unconsciously, I recognized thyme and sorrel and the crushed fescue as the bay mare put her head down and tore at a mouthful of grass.

I am not lightly made angry, least of all with Arthur. It was only a moment or two before I could say, levelly: "Whatever you have to say, you had certainly better say now. Ninian is more than my assistant, he bids fair to be my second self. If I have ever been a staff to your hand, Arthur, he will be such another when I am dead. Whether or not you like the boy—and why should you not, you hardly know him?—you may have to accept him so. I shall not live for ever, and he has the power. He has power already, and it will grow."

"I know. That is what troubles me." He looked away from me again. I could not judge if it was because he could not face me. "Don't you see, Merlin? He has the power. It was he who had the vision. And you did not. You say you were tired, you had been ill. But when did your god ever take that into account? This was no trivial 'seeing'; it was not something that normally you would have missed. Because of it I was already there, on the borders of Rheged, when Caw died, and was able to support Gwarthegydd and prevent God knows how much trouble among those warring princes. So why did no vision come to you?"

"Must I keep repeating it? I—"

"Yes, you were ill. Why?"

Silence. A breeze came across the miles of downland, smelling of honey. Under it, through the immense stillness of the day, the grasses rustled. The mare cropped eagerly; the hound had come back to its master's feet and sat there, tongue lolling. Arthur stirred, and began to speak again, but I forestalled him.

"What are you saying? . . . No, don't answer. I know quite well what you are saying. That I have taken in this unknown boy, become infatuated, opened to him all the secret lore of drugs, and something of magic, and now he schemes to take my place and usurp my power. That he cannot be acquitted of using my own drugs against me. Is that it?"

Something of a smile touched his lips, though without lightening his grim look. "You never did deal in ambiguities, did you?"

"I never hid the truth, least of all from you."

"But then, my dear, you do not always see all the truth."

For some reason the very gentleness of the reply touched me with foreboding. I looked at him, frowning. "I am willing to accept that. So now, since I hardly imagine that all this springs from some vague suspicion, I must assume that you know something about Ninian that I don't. If that's so, why not tell me, and let me be the judge of its importance?"

"Very well. But—" Some change in his expression made me turn and follow his gaze. He was looking past me, away beyond the shoulder of the down, where a little valley held a stream fringed with birch and willow. Beyond this rose the green hill that sheltered Applegarth. Among the willows I caught a glint of blue, and then saw Ninian, who must have been up early after all, stooping over something at the edge of the stream. He straightened, and I saw that his hands were full of greenstuff. Watercress grew there, and wild mint among the king-cups. He stood for a moment, as if sorting the plants in his hands, then jumped the stream and ran away up the far slope, with his blue cloak flying out behind him like a sail.

"Well?" I said.

"I was going to say, let's go down there. We have to talk, and there must be more comfortable ways of doing it than standing face to face on top of the world. You unnerve me still, you know, Merlin, even when I know I'm right."

"That wasn't my intention. By all means let us go down."

He tugged the mare's head up from the grass, and led the way downhill to where the little wood crowded along the stream's edge. The trees were mostly birches, with here and there a twisted trunk of alder, overgrown with bramble and honeysuckle. One birch tree lay newly fallen, clean with silver bark. The King loosed a buckle from the mare's bit, tied one end of the rein to a sapling, then left her to graze, and came back to sit beside me on the birch trunk.

He came straight to the point. "Has Ninian ever told you anything about his parentage? His home?"

"No. I never pressed him. I suspected base origins, or at any rate bastardy—he hasn't the peasant look or way of speech. But both you and I know how little those questions can be welcomed."

"I have not had your scruples. I have wondered about him since that day when I met him with you at Applegarth. Since I came home I have asked about him."

"And found out what?"

"Enough to know that he has been deceiving you from the beginning." Then, striking a fist to his knee, with a sudden violence of exasperation: "Merlin, Merlin, are you so blind? I would swear that no man could be so deceived, except that I know you. . . . Even now, a few minutes ago, watching him down here by the stream, you saw nothing?"

"What should I see? I imagine he had been collecting alder bark. He knew we needed more, and you can see where that tree has been stripped. And he was carrying watercress."

"You see? Your eyes are good enough for that, but not to see what any other man in the world would have seen—if not straight away, then within days of meeting him! I suspected it in those first few minutes there in your courtyard, while you told me the 'true dream,' and then when I made inquiries I found that it was true. We both watched the same person running uphill just now. You saw a boy carrying watercress, but what I saw was a girl."

I cannot recall at what point during his speech I knew what he was going to tell me; before he got halfway it came like a truth already known; the heat before the lightning strikes, the silence after the lightning that is filled with the coming thunder. What the wise enchanter with his god-sent visions had not perceived, the young man, versed in the ways of women, had seen straight away. It was true. I could only marvel, dumbly, that I had been so easy to deceive. Ninian. The dim-seen figure in the mist, so like the lost boy that I had greeted her and put the words "boy" and "Ninian" into her head before she could even speak. Told her I was Merlin; offered her the gift of my power and magic, gifts that another girl—the witch Morgause—had tried in vain to prise from me, but which I had hastened eagerly to lay at this stranger's feet.

Small wonder that she had taken time to think, to arrange her affairs, to cut her hair and change her dress and gather her courage, before coming to me at Applegarth. That she had refused to share the house, preferring the rooms off the colonnade with their separate stair; that she had taken no interest in Mora, but that the two of them were so easy together. Mora had guessed, then? I swept the thought aside as others crowded. The speed with which she had learned from me; the power, with all its suffering, already accepted with dread, with resignation, and finally with willing joy. The grave, gentle look, the gestures of a worship carefully offered, and as carefully constrained. The way she had gone from me when I spoke so lightly of women disturbing men's lives. Her swift condemnation of Guinevere, rather than of Bedwyr, for giving way to a hurtful love. Then, with quickening memory, the feel of her dark hair under my hand, the sweet bones of her face, and the grey eyes watching in the firelight, and the disturbing love that had so troubled me, and now need trouble me no more. It came to me, like the sunlight breaking through the birch trees on the forgotten bluebells of the copse where, long ago, a girl had offered me love, then mocked me for impotence, that this time no jealous god need come between us. At last I was free to give, along with all the rest of the power and effort and glory, the manhood that until now had been the god's alone. The abdication I had feared, and feared to grudge, would not be a loss, but rather a new joy gained.

I came back to the sunshine and a different birch-wood and the faded bluebells of June, to see Arthur staring.

"You don't even look surprised. Did you guess?"

"No. But I should have done; if not by any of the signs that were obvious to you, then by the way I felt . . . and feel now." I smiled at his look. "Oh, yes. An old fool, if you like. But now I know for certain that my gods are merciful."

"Because you think you love this girl?"

"Because I love her."

"I thought you were a wise man," he said.

"And because I am a wise man, I know too well that love cannot be gainsaid. It's too late, Arthur. Whatever comes of it, it is too late. It has happened. No, listen. It has all come clear now, like sunlight on water. All the prophecies I have made, things in the future that I have foreseen with dread . . . I see them approaching me now, and the dread has gone. I have said often enough that prophecy is a two-edged sword; the gods are delphic; their threats, like their promises of fortune, turn in men's hands." I lifted my head and looked up through the gently moving leaves. "I told you that I had seen my own end. There was a dream I had once, a vision in the flame. I saw the cave in the Welsh hillside, and the girl my mother, whose name was Niniane, and the young prince my father, lying together. Then through and over the vision I saw myself, grey-haired, and a young girl with a cloud of dark hair, and closed eyes, and I thought that she, too, was Niniane. And so she was. So she is. Do you see? If she has any part in my end, then it will be merciful."

He got to his feet so abruptly that the hound, curled there, jumped aside, ridge-backed and looking round for danger. Arthur took three steps away from me, and three back to stand in front of me. He drove one fist into the other palm with such violence that the mare, a dozen paces away, started and then stood, ears erect, trembling. "How do you expect me to sit here and listen to you talking of your death? You told me once that you would end in a tomb, alive, you thought it would be in Bryn Myrddin. Now, I suppose, you will ask me to let you go back there so that this—this witch can leave you there entombed!"

"Not quite. You have not understood—"

"I understand as well as you do, and I think that I remember more! Have you forgotten Morgause's curse? That women's magic would snare you at the end? And what was promised you once by the Queen Ygraine, my mother? You told me what she said. That if Gorlois of Cornwall died, then she would spend the rest of her life praying to any gods there are that you would die betrayed by a woman."

"Well?" I said. "And have I not been snared? And have I not been betrayed? And this is all it is."

"Are you so sure? Forgive me for reminding you yet again that you don't know women. Remember Morgause. She tried to persuade you to teach her your magic, and when you would not, she took power another way . . . the way we know about. Now this girl has succeeded where Morgause failed. Tell me one thing: if she had come to you as herself, as a woman, would you have taken her in and taught her your skills?"

"I can't tell you that. Probably not. But the point is, surely, that she did not? The deception was not hers in the first instance; it was forced on her by my error, and that error in its turn was forced on me by the chance that led me first to meet and love the boy Ninian who was drowned. If you cannot see the god at work there, I am sorry."

"Yes, yes—" impatiently, "—but you have just reminded me that this is a delphic god. What you see now as a joy may be the very death you have dreaded."

"No," I said. "You must take it the other way. That a fate long dreaded can prove, in the end, merciful, like this 'betrayal.' My long nightmare of entombment in the dark, alive, may prove to be such another. But whatever it is, I cannot avoid it. What will come, will come. The god chooses the time and the form. After all these years, if I did not trust in him, I would be the fool you think me."

"So you'll go back to this girl, keep her by you, and go on teaching her your art?"

"Just that. I could hardly stop now. I have sown the seeds of power in her, and as surely as if it were a tree growing, or a child I had begotten, I cannot stop it. And the other seed has been sown, for good or ill. I love her dearly, and were she ten times an enchantress, I can only thank my god for it, and take her to me more nearly than before."

"I cannot bear to see you hurt."

"She will not hurt me."

"If she does," he said evenly, "witch or no witch, lover or no lover, I shall deal with her as she deserves. Well, it seems there is no more to be said. We had better go back. That basket looks heavy. Let me take it for you."

"No, a moment. There is one more thing."

"Yes?"

He was standing straight in front of me where I still sat on the birch log. Against the delicate boughs of the birches and the shifting of the leaves in the soft breeze he looked tall and powerful, the jewels at shoulder and belt and sword-hilt glittering as if with their own life. He looked, not young, but full of the richness of life, a man in the flower of his strength; a leader among kings. His face was contained. There was nothing to tell me what he would say, what he might do, after I had spoken.

I said slowly: "Since we have been talking of last things, there is one other thing I have to tell you. Another vision, which it is my duty to bring to you. It's something that I have seen, not once but several times. Bedwyr your friend, and Guinevere your Queen, love one another."

I had been looking away from him as I spoke, not wanting to see how the wounding stroke went home. I suppose I had expected anger, an outburst of violence, at the very least surprise and furious disbelief. Instead there was silence, a silence so drawn out that at length I looked up, to see in his face nothing of anger or even surprise, but a kind of sternly held calmness that tempered only compassion and regret.

I said, not believing it: "You knew?"

"Yes," he said, quite simply, "I know." There was a pause, while I looked for words and found none. He smiled. There was something in the smile that did not speak of youth or power at all, but of a wisdom perhaps greater, because more purely human, than is ascribed to me. "I do not have vision, Merlin, but I see what is before my eyes. And do you not think that others, who guess and whisper, have not been at pains to tell me? It sometimes seems to me that the only ones who have given no hint by word or look have been Bedwyr and the Queen themselves."

"How long have you known this?"

"Since the Melwas affair."

And I had never guessed. His kindness to the Queen, her relief and growing happiness, had told me nothing. "Then why did you leave Bedwyr with her when you went north?"

"To let them have something, however little." The sun was in his eyes, making him frown. He spoke slowly. "You have just been telling me that love cannot be ruled or stopped. If you are prepared to accept love, knowing that it may well bring you to your death, then how much more should I accept this, knowing that it cannot destroy friendship or faith?"

"You believe that?"

"Why not? Everything else you have ever told me has been true. Think back now over your prophecies about my marriage, the 'white shadow' that you saw when Bedwyr and I were boys, the *guenhwyvar* that touched us both. You said then that it would not blur or destroy the faith we had in one another."

"I remember."

"Very well. When I married my first Guenever you warned me that the marriage might be unwholesome for me. That little girl 'unwholesome'?" He laughed, without mirth. "Well, now we know the truth of the prophecy. Now we have seen the shadow. And now we see it falling across Bedwyr's life and mine. But if it is not to destroy our faith in one another, what would you have me do? I must give Bedwyr the trust and freedom to which he is entitled. Am I a cottager, with nothing in my life but a woman and a bed I am to be jealous of, like a cock on his dunghill? I am a king, and my life is a king's; she is a queen, and childless, so her life must be less than a woman's. Is she to wait year by year in an empty bed? To walk, to ride, to take her meals with an empty place beside her? She is young, and she has a girl's needs, of companionship and of love. By your god or any god, Merlin, if, during the years of days that my work takes me from court, she is ever to take a man to her bed, should I not be thankful it is Bedwyr? And what would you have me do, or say? Anything I say to Bedwyr would eat at the root of the very trust we have, and it would avail nothing against what has already happened. Love, you tell me, cannot be gainsaid. So I keep silent, and so will you, and by that token will faith and friendship stay unbroken. And we can count her barrenness a mercy." The smile again. "So the god works for us both in twisted ways, does he not?"

I got to my feet. The birches moved and the sun poured down. The stream glittered against my eyes, so that they watered.

I said quietly: "You see? This the final mercy. You no longer need either my strength or my counsel. Whatever you may need after this of warning or prophecy, you can still find at Applegarth. As for me, let your servant go in peace, back to my own home and my own hills, and whatever waits for me there." I picked the basket up and handed it to him. "But in the meantime, will you come back with me to Applegarth, and see her?"

10

When we reached Applegarth it seemed deserted. It was still very early. Varro had not yet come to start work, and I had seen Mora from a distance, making her way toward the village market with her basket on her arm.

The mare knew the way to the stables, and trotted off, with a clap on the flank. We went into the house. The girl was there, sitting on her accustomed stool in the window embrasure, reading. Not far from her, on the stone sill, perched a redbreast, picking up the crumbs she had scattered.

She must have heard the horse, and assumed either that I had ridden that morning, instead of walking, or that a messenger had come very early from Camelot. She had obviously not expected the King himself. When I went into the room she looked up, with a smile and a "Good morning," and then, seeing Arthur's shadow fall across the doorway behind me, got to her feet and let the book roll together between her hands. "I'll leave you to talk, shall I?" she said, and turned, in no haste, to go.

I started to warn her. "Ninian—" I began, but then Arthur came quickly past me into the room, and stopped just inside the door, his eyes on her face.

Be sure that I was staring, too.

Now that I knew, I wondered how I had not always known. For eighteen, it was hardly a man's face; an immature eighteen might have had that smooth cheek and sweet mouth, and her body under the shapeless clothing was as slim as a boy's, but the hands were not a young man's hands, nor were the slender feet. I can only think that my own memory of the boy Ninian had kept me, blindly, to the image of him as he had been at sixteen: my desire to have him had been strong enough to let me re-create him, first in the dimly seen ghost of the Lake, then in this girl, so near to me, so closely watched, and yet not seen, through all the past long months. And then, perhaps (I thought), she had been able to use a little of my own magic against me, to keep me blind—and so to keep herself beside me, until her purposes were served.

She stood straight as a wand, facing us. I suppose it needed no magic for her to tell that we knew. The grey eyes met mine for the fraction of a moment, when she faced the King.

What happened then is difficult to describe. There was the quiet, everyday room, filled with the scents and sounds of the summer morning; sweet briar and early roses and the gilly-flowers she had planted outside the window; last night's burned logs (the nights could still have a chill in them, and she had insisted on making a fire for me to sit by); the sweet sub-song of the redbreast as he flew up into the apple boughs outside. A summer room, where, to anyone of normal perceptions, nothing passed at all. Just three people, in a pause of silence.

But to me the air tingled suddenly over the skin, like water when lightning strikes. I felt the flesh creep on my bones, and the small hairs on my arms fur up;

my nape stirred like the ruff of a dog in a thunder-storm. I do not think I moved. Neither the King nor the girl seemed to notice anything. She watched him gravely, unalarmed, I might have thought unmoved and barely interested, if I had not been getting these fearsome currents washing over and through my flesh as the tide washes over a rock lying on the shore. Her grey eyes held his; his dark ones bored into her. I could feel the force as the two of them met. The air trembled.

Then he nodded, and put up a hand to loosen the cloak from his shoulder. I saw her mouth move with the shadow of a smile. The message had passed. For my sake, he would accept her. And for my sake, she would stand the trial. The room steadied, and I said: "Let me," and took his cloak from him to lay it down.

The girl said: "Shall I bring you some breakfast? Mora left it ready, but you were late, so she went to market. She says the best things are taken if she is not there early."

She went. The platters were laid ready on the table, and we took our places. She brought bread, and the crock of honey, and a pitcher of milk along with one of mead. She set the latter down at the King's hand, then without a word took her usual place across from me. She had not looked at me again. When I poured a cup of milk for her she thanked me, but without lifting her eyes. Then she spread honey on her bread, and began to eat.

"Your name," said the King. "Is it Niniane?"

"Yes," she said. "but I was always called Nimuë."

"Your parentage?"

"My father was called Dyonas."

"Yes. King of the River Islands?"

"The same. He is dead now."

"I know that. He fought beside me at Viroconium. Why did you leave your home?"

"I was sent to the Lady's service, in the Isle of Glass. It was my father's wish." The glimmer of a smile. "My mother was a Christian, and when she lay dying she made him promise he would send me to the Island; I know she intended me for the service of the church there. I was only six years old, but he promised her. He himself had never held with what he called the new God; he was an initiate of Mithras—his own father took him there in the time of Ambrosius. So when the time came for him to keep his promise to my mother, he did indeed take me to the Island, but to the service of the Good Goddess, in the shrine below the Tor."

"I see."

So did I. As one of the *ancillae* of the shrine she would have been there on the occasion of Arthur's thanksgiving after Caer Guinnion and Caerleon. Perhaps she had glimpsed me there, beside the King. She must have known that, for her, there was small chance of coming any nearer to the prince-enchanter, and learning any of the greater arts. Then on that misty night I had put the key into her hand. It had taken courage to grasp it, but God knew she had plenty of that.

The King was still questioning her. "And you wanted to study magic. Why?"

"Sir, I cannot say why. Why does a singer first want to learn music? Or a bird want to try the air? When I first went to the Island, I found some traces of it, and learned all they had to teach, but still I was hungry. Then one day I saw . . ." She hesitated for the first time. "I saw Merlin in the shrine. You will remember the day. Later, I heard he had come to live here at Applegarth. I thought, If only I were a man I could go to him. He is wise, he would know that magic is in my blood, and he would teach me."

"Ah, yes. The day we gave thanks for our victories. But if you were there, how is it that you failed to recognize me, the first time you saw me here?"

She went scarlet. For the first time her gaze dropped from his. "I did not see you, sir. I told you, I was watching Merlin."

There was a flat pause of silence, as when a hand is laid across the harp-strings, killing the sound. I saw Arthur's mouth open and shut, then the flash of a vivid laughter in his face. She, looking steadfastly at the table, saw nothing of it. He shot me a look brimful of amusement, then drained his cup and sat back in the chair. His voice never altered, but the challenge had gone; he had lowered his sword.

"But you knew that Merlin was not likely to accept you as a pupil, even if the Lady could be persuaded to let you leave her cloisters."

"Yes. I knew that. I had no hope. But after that I settled even less easily into the life there among the other women. They seemed, oh, so contented to be penned there with the small magics and the prayers and spells, and looking backward always toward the times of legend. . . . It's hard to explain. If there is something within oneself, something burning to be free, one knows of it." A look straight at him, equal to equal. "You must have known it. I was still unborn, hammering at the egg, to get out into the air. But the only way I could have escaped from the Island would have been if some man had offered for me, and for that I would not have gone, nor would my father have made me."

He gave a brief nod, of acceptance and, I thought, of understanding. "So?"

"It wasn't easy, even, to find time to be alone. I would watch and wait my chance, and slip out sometimes, only to be alone with my own thoughts, and with the water and sky. . . . Then, on the night when Queen Guinevere was missing, and the Island was in uproar, I—I'm afraid all I thought of was my chance to get out without being missed. . . . There was a boat I sometimes borrowed. I went out. I knew no one would see me in the mist. Then Merlin came along the Lake road, and spoke to me." She paused. "I think you must know the rest."

"Yes. So when chance—the god, you would say, if you are Merlin's pupil—made Merlin mistake you for the boy Ninian, and ask you to come and learn from him, you made the second chance for yourself."

She bent her head. "When he spoke first, I was confused. It was like a dream. Afterwards I realized what had happened, that he had mistaken me for some boy he had known."

"How did you get free of the shrine in the end? What did you tell the Lady?"

"That I had been called for higher service. I did not explain. I let her think I was going back to my father's house. I think she imagined that I had to go back to the River Isles, perhaps to be married to my cousin, who rules there now. She did not ask. She put no rub in my way."

No, I thought to myself; that imperious lady would be glad to rid herself of an adept who must have bidden fair to out-shine her. Among those white-robed girls this young enchantress must have shone out like a diamond in white flax.

Behind me, the redbreast flew back to his perch on the window-sill, and tried a stave of song. I doubt if either Nimuë or Arthur heard it. His questions had changed direction: "Do you need fire for the vision, or can you see, like Merlin, in the small drops of dew?"

"It was in dewdrops that I saw the vision of Heuil."

"And that was a true one. So. It seems you already have something of the greater power. Well, there is no fire, but will you look for me again, and tell me now if there is any other warning in the stars?"

"I can see nothing to order."

I bit my lip. It was my own voice as a young man, confident, perhaps a little pompous. He recognized it, too. He said gravely: "I am sorry. I should have known."

He got to his feet then, and reached for the cloak that I had laid across a chair. There was a perceptible flaw in her composure, as she hurried to help him with it. He was saying goodbye to me, but I hardly heard him. My own composure bade fair to be in ruins. I, who was never at a loss, had not had time to think what I must say.

The King was in the doorway. The sun caught him and sent his shadow streaming back between us. The great emeralds on Caliburn's hilt flashed in the light.

"King Arthur!" said Nimuë sharply.

He turned. If he found her tone peremptory he gave no sign of it.

She said: "If your sister, the lady Morgan, comes to Camelot, lock up your sword and watch for treachery."

He looked startled, then said harshly: "What do you mean by that?"

She hesitated, looking in her turn surprised by what she had said. Then she lifted her palms out, in a gesture like a shrug. "My lord, I don't know. Only that. I am sorry."

"Well . . ." said Arthur. He looked across at me, lifted his brows, then shrugged in his turn, and went out.

Silence, so long that the robin hopped right into the room and onto the table where the breakfast lay, barely touched.

"Nimuë," I said.

She looked at me then, and I saw that although she had stood in no awe of the King, she was afraid to meet my eyes. I smiled at her, and saw to my amazement the grey eyes fill with tears.

I put out both my hands. Hers met them. In the end there was no need of words. We did not hear the King's horse go down the hill, or, much later, Mora come back from market to find the breakfast still uneaten.

BOOK IV

BRYN MYRDDIN

1

So, toward the end of my life, I found a new beginning. A beginning it was in love, for both of us. I had no skill, and she, vowed from childhood to be one of the Lake maidens, had hardly thought of love. But what we had was enough and more than enough. She, for all she was many years younger than I, seemed happy and satisfied; and I, calling myself in private dotard, old fool, wisdom dragged at mockery's chariot wheels, knew that I was none of these: between myself and Nimuë was a bond stronger than any between the best-matched pair in the flower of their age and strength. We were the same person. We were part of each other as are night and daylight, dark and dawn, sun and shadow. When we lay together we lay at the edge of life where opposites fuse and make new entities, not of the flesh, but of the spirit, the issue as much of the ceaseless traffic of mind with mind, as of the body's pleasure.

We did not marry. Looking back now, I doubt if either of us even thought of cementing the relationship in this way; it was not clear what rites we could have used, what faster bond we could have hoped for. With the passing of the days and nights of that sweet summer, we found ourselves closer and yet more close, as if cast in a common mould: we would wake in the morning and know we had shared the same dream; meet at evening and each know what the other had learned and done that day. And all the time, as I believed, each of us harboured our own private and growing joy: I to watch her trying the wings of power like a strong young bird feeling for the first time the mastery of the air; she to receive this waxing strength, and to know, with love but without pity, that at the same time the power was leaving me.

So the month of June flew by, and then high summer was with us. The cuckoo vanished from the brakes, the meadowsweet was out with its heavy honey smell, the bees droned all day in the blue borage and the lavender. Nimuë called to Varro to set a saddle on the chestnut—Arthur had made her a present of him—then she kissed me and rode off toward the Lake. It was, of course, known now that the former servant of the Goddess was with Merlin at Applegarth. There must have been speculation and gossip, some of it no doubt malicious—and (I was sure) all of it amazed at the impulse that had taken a young and lovely girl into the ageing enchanter's bed. But the High King had stated publicly, and had moreover made it clear by gifts and visits, that our relationship had his approval; so even the Lady of the shrine had not attempted to close her doors against Nimuë, she had, rather, made her welcome, in the hope (Nimuë suggested with amusement) that the shrine might fall heir to some of Merlin's secrets. Nimuë herself did not often leave Applegarth, either for the Island or the court at Camelot. But she was hardly to be blamed if she was a trifle flown with the power and excitement of these first months, and as a young bride enjoys showing off her new status among her maiden colleagues, so, I guessed, Nimuë was eager to revisit her friends among the Goddess's *ancillae.* She had not yet been to the court of Camelot without me; I guessed what she did not say, that even with the King's support she was doubtful of her reception there. But on three occasions she had been back to the Island, and this time, she told me, she would see about the promise of some plants from the garden near the holy well. She would be back at dusk. I saw her off, then checked over my bag of medicines, put on a straw hat against the sun, and set out across the hill to visit the house of a woman who was recovering from a bout of fever. I went blithely. The day was fine but fresh, and lark-song poured down from a clear sky like rillets of bright water. I reached the hilltop and followed the track between gorse bushes ablaze with flowers. A flock of goldfinches fluttered and dipped through a patch of tall, seeding thistles, making the sweet, plaintive call that the Saxons call "chirm," or "charm." The breeze smelled of thyme.

That is all I remember. Next—it seemed all in a moment—the world was dark, and the stars were out, with that clear sparkle that one can feel pricking down into the eyes and brain. I was lying on my back, flat on the turf, staring up at them. The gorse bushes were all round me, humped and dark, and gradually, as if sense were coming back from a limitless distance, I felt the stab of their prickles biting into hands and arms. Starlight sparked from the dew. Everywhere there was a great silence, like a held breath. Then above me, high in the black sky, another point of light began to grow. The darkness lit. Into this single, waxing point of light the smaller stars, like metal dust to a lodestone, like a swarm into the hive, fled, till in all the sky there was no other light. My eyes dazzled. I could not move, but lay there, it seemed alone on the curve of the world, watching the star. Then, intolerably bright, it started from its place, and swiftly, like a brand flung across the sky, it arched from the zenith to the earth's edge, trailing behind it a great train of light shaped like a dragon.

I heard someone call out: "The Dragon! The Dragon! See where the Dragon falls!" and knew the voice was my own.

Then lights, and hands, and Nimuë's face, white in the lantern light, with Varro behind her, and a youth I vaguely recognized as the shepherd who watched his flock on the down. Then voices. "Is he dead?" "No. Come, quickly, cover him. He's cold." "He's dead, mistress." "No! Never! I'll never believe it! Do as I say!" Then, with anguish: "Merlin, Merlin!" And a man's voice, fearfully: "Who will tell the King?"

After that a gap of time, and my own bed, and the taste of hot wine and herbs infused in it, and another long gap, this time of sleep.

Now we come to the part of my chronicle that is the most difficult to tell. Whether or not (as the popular belief went) the falling comet with the dragon's tail betokened the true end of Merlin's greater powers, I know that, looking back at the days and nights—more, the weeks and months—that followed, I cannot tell for certain whether what I remember was reality, or a dream. It was the year of my journeying with Nimuë. Looking back now, I see it, scene after scene, like reflections sliding past a boat, blurred and repeated, and broken, as the oars stir the water's glass. Or like the moments just before sleep, when scene after scene swims up into the mind's eye, the true memories like dreams, and the dreams as real as memory.

I still only have to close my eyes to see Applegarth, serene in the sun, with the silver lichen thick on the old trees, where the green fruit, slowly swelling, shone like lamps, and in the sheltered garth lavender and sage and sweet briar breathed their scent into the air as thickly as smoke. And on the hill behind the tower the thorn trees, those strange thorns that flower in winter and have small flowers with stamens like nails. And the doorway where the girl Nimuë first stood shyly, with the light behind her, like the gentle ghost of the drowned boy who might have been a greater enchanter than she. And the ghost itself; the "boy Ninian" who still haunts my memories of the garth, alongside the slender girl who sat at my feet in the sun.

For perhaps a week after my falling fit on the hilltop, I spent most of my time sitting on the carved seat in the garth. Not from weakness, but because Nimuë insisted, and I needed time to think.

Then one evening, in the warm dusk, I called her to me. She nestled down in her old place, on a cushion at my feet. Her head was against my knee, and my hand stroked the thick hair. This was growing now, and had reached her shoulder-blades. I wondered daily at my old blindness that had not seen the curves of her body, and the sweet lines of throat and brow and wrist.

"You've been busy this week."

"Yes," she said. "Housewife's jobs. Cutting the herbs and bunching them to dry."

"Are they done?"

"Just about. Why?"

"I've been idle all this time while you have been working, but I have been thinking."

"About?"

"Among other things, Bryn Myrddin. You have never been there. So before the summer ends, I think we must leave Applegarth, you and I—"

"Leave Applegarth?" She started away from me, looking up in dismay. "Do you mean live at Bryn Myrddin again . . . both of us live there?"

I laughed. "No. Somehow I don't see that happening. Do you?"

She subsided against my knee, her head bent. She was silent for a while, then she said, muffled: "I don't know. I've never glimpsed even a dream of it. But you have told me that you will die there. Is that what you mean?"

I put out a hand again and touched her hair. "I know I have said that that will happen, but I've had no warning of it yet. I feel very well, better than for many months. But look at it like this: when my life does end, yours must begin. And for that to happen you must do one day as I did, and enter the crystal cave of vision. You know this. We've spoken of it before."

"Yes, I know." She did not sound reassured.

"Well," I told her cheerfully, "we shall go to Bryn Myrddin, but at the end of our journey. Before we get there we shall have travelled widely, and seen many places and many things. I want you to visit the places where I have passed my life, and see the things I have seen. I have told you as much as I can; now you must see as much as I am able to show you. Do you understand?"

"I think so. You are giving me the sum of your life, on which to build my own."

"Exactly that. For you, the stones on which to build the life you want; for me, the crown and harvest."

"And when I have it all?" she asked, subdued.

"Then we shall see." Amused, I caressed her hair again. "Don't look like that, child, take it lightly. It's a wedding journey, not a funeral procession. Our travels may have a purpose, but we'll take them for pleasure, be sure of that. I've had this in mind some time; it wasn't just suggested by this last sick turn of mine. We've been happy here in Applegarth, and no doubt we shall be happy here again, but you are too young to fold your wings here year after year. So we'll go travelling. I have a suspicion that my real object is just to show you the places I've known and loved, for no more serious reason than that I have known and loved them."

She sat up, looking easier. Her eyes began to sparkle. She was young. "A kind of pilgrimage?"

"You could call it that."

"Tintagel, you mean, and Rheged, and the place where you found the sword, and the lake where you laid it to wait for the King?"

"More than that. God help us both, we must sail to Brittany. My story and the High King's has been bound up—as yours will be, too—in that great sword of his. I have to show you where the god himself first came to me, with the first sign of the sword. Which is why we should go soon. The seas are calm, but in another month or so the gales will start."

She shuddered. "Then by all means let us go now." Then, suddenly, all uncomplicated pleasure, a young woman setting out on an exciting journey, with no other thought in her head: "And you'll have to take me to Camelot. I really haven't got anything fit to wear. . . ."

So next day I spoke to Arthur's courier, and not very long after that Arthur himself came to tell me that escort and ship were ready, and that we could go.

We set sail from the Island at the end of July, and Arthur and the Queen rode down to the harbour to see us on our way. Bedwyr was with us, his face a mixture of relief and misery: he had been sent to escort us across the sea, and he was like a man released from the torment of a drug which he knows will kill him, but for which, night and day, he craves. He was charged with dispatches from Arthur to his cousin King Hoel of Brittany, and would escort us as far as Hoel's court at Kerrec.

When we came to the quay the ship was still loading, but soon all was ready, and Arthur bade us farewell, with an admonition to Nimuë to "take care of him" which brought forcibly back to me memories of the voyage I had made with Arthur himself a squalling baby in his wet-nurse's arms, and King Hoel's escort scowling at the noise, and trying to give me due greeting through it all. Then he kissed Bedwyr, with nothing apparent in his look save warm affection, and Bedwyr muttered something, holding him, before turning to take his leave of the Queen. Smiling by the King's side, she had command of herself; her light touch of Bedwyr's hand, and the serene "Godspeed" she wished him showed barely more warmth than that given to Nimuë, and rather less than to me. (Since the Melwas affair, she had shown a pretty gratitude and liking, such as a girl might have for her elderly father.) I said my goodbyes, cast a wary eye at the smooth summer sea, and went on board. Nimuë, already pale, came with me. It needed no prophetic vision to foretell that we would see nothing of one another until the ship docked in the Small Sea.

It is no part of this tale to follow our travels league by league. Indeed, as I have explained, I cannot do so. We went to Brittany, that I know, and were welcomed there by King Hoel, and spent the autumn and winter in Kerrec, and I showed Nimuë the roads through the Perilous Forest, and the humble inn where Ralf, my page, guarded the child Arthur through the dangerous hidden years. But here already the memories are confused; as I write I can see them all, crossing each other like ghosts that crowd, century by century, into an old dwelling house. Each is as clear as the others. Arthur as a baby, asleep in the manger straw. My father watching me in the lamplight, asking, "What will come to Britain?" The druids at their murderous work in Memet. Myself, a frightened boy, hiding in the cattle-shed. Ralf riding post-haste through the trees with messages from Hoel to send to me. Nimuë beside me in the budding woods of April, lying on green turf in a forest glade. The same glade, with the white doe fleeing like magic, to draw danger away from Arthur. And across this, confusedly, other memories or other dreams: a white stag with ruby eyes; the deer fleeing through the dusk under the oaks at Nodens' shrine; magic on magic. But through all, like a torch relit for another quest, the stars, the smiling god, the sword.

We stayed away till summer, this much I know for certain. I can even record the day of our arrival back in Britain. Cador, Duke of Cornwall, died that year, and we disembarked in a country deep in mourning for a great soldier and a good duke. What I cannot recall is which of us—Nimuë or myself—knew that it was time to be gone, or which harbour to sail for. We landed in a little bay a league or so from Tintagel, on Dumnonia's northern coast, two days after Cador's death, to find Arthur there already, with all his train. Having seen our sail, he came down to the wharf to meet us, and before ever we landed we saw the covered shields, the lowered pennons, and the unadorned white of mourning, and knew what had brought us home.

Scenes like these swim up, brightly lit with hardly a shadow. But then comes the candlelit chapel where Cador's body lay in state, with monks chanting; and the scene dislimns, and once again I am standing at the foot of his father's bier, waiting for the ghost of the man I had betrayed. Even Nimuë, when once I spoke to her of this, could be no help to me. For so long now we had shared thought and dream alike that she herself could not (she told me) separate the sight of Tintagel in the summer, with the gentle wind lifting the sea against the rocks, from my stormy tales of time past. Tintagel mourning for Duke Cador recently dead seems less real to either us than the storm-beaten stronghold where Uther, lying with Gorlois' wife Ygraine, begot Arthur for Britain.

And so it was with the rest of the time. After Tinagel we went north. Memory, or dream here in the long darkness, shows me the soft hills of Rheged, the hanging clouds of forest, the lakes ringing with fish, and, reflected in the glass of its own lake, Caer Bannog, where I hid the great sword for Arthur to find. Then the Green Chapel, where later, on that legendary night, Arthur lifted it at last into his hand.

So, as I had done in earnest years ago, we lightly followed the sword, but something—some instinct I could no longer be sure was prophetic, or even wise—bade me keep silence about the other quest which, sometimes, I had glimpsed in the shadows. It would not be for me; it would come after me; and the time was not yet. So I said nothing of Segontium, or the place where still, deep in the ground, lay buried the other treasures that had come back with the sword to the West.

At last we came to Galava. It was a happy end to a pleasant journey. We were welcomed by Count Ector, an Ector grown stout with age and good living since the peace, who presented Nimuë to the lady Drusilla (with a wink at me) as "Prince Merlin's wife, lass, at long last." And beside him was my faithful Ralf, flushed with pleasure, proud as a peacock of his pretty wife and four sturdy children, and avid for news of Arthur and the south.

Nimuë and I lay together in the tower room where I had once been carried to recover from Morgause's poison. It was some time after midnight, as we lay watching the moon touch the hilltops beyond the window, that she stirred, turning her cheek into the hollow of my shoulder, and said softly:

"And what, after this? Bryn Myrddin and the crystal cave?"

"I think so."

"If your own hills are as beautiful as these, perhaps I shan't mind, after all, deserting Applegarth . . ." I heard a smile in her voice . . . "at least in summer."

"I promised you that it wouldn't come to that. Tell me this: for the last stage of your wedding journey, would you rather travel down the western roads, or take ship from Glannaventa, and go by sea to Maridunum? I'm told the seas are calm."

There was a short pause. Then she said: "But why ask me to choose? I thought—"

"You thought?"

Another pause. "I thought you had something still to show me."

It seemed that her instinct was as true as my own. I said: "What, then, my dear?"

"You have told me all the story of the sword, and you have shown me now all that happened to it, this wonderful Caliburn that is the symbol of the King's power, and by which he holds his kingdom. You have showed me the places of vision which led you to find it; where you hid it until Arthur should be ready to raise it, and where at last he did raise it. But you have never told me where you yourself found it. I had thought that this would be the last thing you would show me, before you took me home."

I did not reply. She raised herself in the bed, and lay on an elbow, looking down at me. The moonlight slid over her, making her a thing of silver and shadow, lighting the lovely lines of temple and cheekbone, throat and breast.

I smiled, tracing the line of her shoulder with a gentle finger. "How can I think and answer you when you look like that?"

"Easily." She answered the smile, not moving. "Why have you never told me? It's because there's something else there, isn't it, that belongs to the future?"

So: instinct or vision, she knew. I said slowly: "You spoke of a 'last thing.' Yes, there is still one mystery, the only one; and yes, it is for the future. I haven't seen it clearly myself, but once, before he was King, I made a prophecy for Arthur. It was between the finding and the raising of the sword, when the future was still hedged around with fire and vision. I remember what I said . . ."

"Yes?"

I quoted it: "I see a settled and shining land, with corn growing rich in the valleys, and farmers working their fields in peace as they did in the time of the Romans. I see a sword growing idle and discontented, and the days of peace stretching into bickering and division, and the need of a quest for the idle swords and the unfed spirits. Perhaps it was for this that the god took the grail and the spear back from me and hid them in the ground, so that one day you might set out to find the rest of Macsen's treasure. No, not you, but Bedwyr . . . it is his spirit, not yours, which will hunger and thirst, and slake itself in the wrong fountains.' "

A long silence. I could not see her eyes; they were full of moonlight. Then she whispered: "The grail and the spear? Macsen's treasure, hidden again in the ground, to be the objects of a quest as great as that of the sword? Where? Tell me where?"

She looked eager; not awed, but eager, like a runner in sight of the goal. When she does see the chalice and the spear, I thought, she will bend her head before their magic. But she is only a child, and still sees the things of power as weapons in her own hand. I did not say to her: "It is the same quest, because what use to anyone is the sword of power without the fulfilment of the spirit? All the kings are now one King. It is time the gods became one God, and there in the grail is the oneness for which men will seek, and die, and dying, live."

I did not say it, but lay for a while in silence, while she watched me, unmoving. I could feel the power coming from her, my own power, stronger now in her than in my own hands. For myself, I felt nothing but weariness, and a kind of grief.

"Tell me, my darling," she said, whispering, intent.

So I told her. I smiled at her, and said, gently: "I will do better than tell you. I shall take you there, and what there is to see, I shall show you. What is left of Macsen's treasure lies below the ground in the ruined temple of Mithras at Segontium, that is called Caer-y-n'a Von, below Y Wyddfa. And now that is all that I can give you, my dear, except my love."

I remember that she said: "And that would have been enough, even without the rest," as she stooped to put her mouth on mine.

After she slept I lay watching the moon, full and bright, becalmed, it seemed for hours, full in the center of the window-frame. And I remembered how, long ago, as a child, I had believed that such a sight would bring me my heart's desire. What that had been in those days—power, prophecy, service, love—I could barely remember. Now all that was past, and my heart's desire lay here, sleeping in my arms. And the night, so full of light, was empty of the future, empty of vision; but still, like breathing ghosts from the past, came the voices.

Morgause's voice, the witch's voice spitting her curse at me: "Are you so sure you are proof against women's magic, Prince Merlin? It will snare you in the end."

And across it, Arthur's voice, vigorous, angry, full of love: "I cannot bear to see you hurt." And then: "Witch or no witch, lover or no lover, I shall deal with her as she deserves."

I held her young body close against my own, and kissed her sleeping eyelids, very gently. I said to the ghosts, to the voices, to the empty moonlight: "It was time. Let me go in peace." Then, commending myself and my spirit to God who all these years had held me in his hand, I composed myself for sleep.

This was the last thing that I know to be truth, and not a dream in darkness.

2

When I was a small child at Maridunum I had slept with my nurse in a room in the servant's wing of my grandfather's palace. It was a ground-floor chamber, and outside the window grew a pear tree, where at evening a thrush would sing, and then afterwards the stars would come pricking out into the sky behind the branches, looking for all the world as if they were lights entangled in the tree. I used to lie watching them in the quiet of the night, and straining my ears to hear the music which, I had been told, the stars make as they move along the sky.

Now at last, it seemed, I heard it. I was lying, warmly shrouded, on—I thought—a litter, which must, from the swaying motion, be being borne along under a night sky. A great darkness wrapped me in, and far above me arched a night sky teeming and wheeling with stars, which rang like small bells as they moved. I was part of the ground that moved and echoed to my pulses, and a part of the enormous darkness that I could see above me. I was not even sure if my eyes were open. My last vision, I thought, feebly, and my heart's desire. My heart's desire was always this, to hear, before I died, the music of the stars. . . .

Then I knew where I was. There must be people near me; I could hear voices talking softly, but seemingly at a great distance, like voices when one is sick with fever. Servants were carrying the litter; their arms brushed me with warmth; the beat in the ground was the soft tread of their sandals. This was no vision lighted by the singing spheres; I was only a sick old man, earth-bound, being carried home by stages, in the helpless silence of my malady. The music of the stars was no more than the bells on the harness of the mules.

How long it took I cannot tell. At length the litter levelled at the head of a long climb, and an archway of warm firelight met me, and more people, and voices everywhere, and someone weeping, and I knew that somehow, out of another falling-fit of the malady, I had been brought home to Bryn Myrddin.

More confusion after that. Sometimes I thought that Nimuë and I were still on our travels; I was showing her the streets of Byzantium, or walking with her on the heights above Berytus. She brought me the drugs she had made, and held them to my mouth. It was her own mouth that was on mine, tasting of strawberries, and her lips murmured sweet incantations above me, and the cave filled with smoke from handfuls of the precious frankincense. There were candles everywhere: in their mellow wavering light my merlin perched on the ledge by the cave's entrance, waiting for the god's breath on his feathers. Galapas sat by the brazier, drawing my first maps for me in the dust, and beside them, now, knelt the boy Ninian, poring over them with his grave and gentle eyes. Then he looked up, and I saw that it was Arthur, vivid and impatient, and ten years old . . . and then Ralf, young and sullen . . . and then at last the boy Merlin, going at his master's bidding up into the crystal cave. And so came the visions; I saw them again, the dreams that had first stormed into my child's brain here in this very cave. And this time Nimuë held my hand, and saw them with me, star for star, and held the cordial afterwards to my lips, while Galapas and the child Merlin, and Ralf and Arthur and the boy Ninian, faded and vanished like the ghosts they were. Only the memories remained, and they, now, were locked in her brain as they had been in mine, and would be hers for ever.

Through it all, though I had no sense of it, time was passing, and the days wore through, and still I lay in that strange limbo of helpless body and vividly working mind, while gradually, as a bee sips the honey from a flower. Nimuë the enchantress took from me, drop by drop, the distillation of all my days.

Then one early dawn, with the sound of birds singing outside, and the warm summer breeze bringing the scent of flowers and summer hay into the cave, I woke from a long sleep, and found that the malady had left me. Dream time was over; I was alive, and fully awake.

I was also alone, in darkness, save where a long quill of sunlight drilled through a gap left where they had pulled the tumble of rocks down across the cave mouth, and had gone away, leaving me in my tomb.

I had no way of knowing how long I had lain in the waking death. We had been at Rheged in July, and it was still apparently high summer. Three weeks, or at most a month . . . ? If it had been longer, I would surely be weaker. As it was, until the last profound sleep, which must have been taken for death, I had been cared for and fed with my own cordials and medicines, so that, though stiff, and very weak, I had every chance of life. There was no hope of my being able to move any of the stones that sealed my tomb, but there was a good chance that I might be able to attract the attention of someone passing this way. The place had been a shrine, time out of mind, and the folk came regularly up the valley with offerings for the god who watched the sacred spring beside the cave. It was possible, now, that they would hold the place even more holy, knowing that Merlin, who had held the High King in his hand, but who had been their own enchanter, giving his time and skill to tend their hurts and those of their animals, was buried here. They had brought gifts daily, of food and wine, while he was alive; surely they would come with their offerings, to appease the dead?

So, stifling my fear, I raised myself and tried, through the swirling weakness of my new waking state, to judge what I must do.

They had laid me, not in the crystal cave, which was a small hollow high in the wall of the main cavern, but in the main cavern itself, on my own bed. This had been draped in some stuff that felt rich and stiff, and gave back, to the same probe of light, the glimmer of embroidery and precious gems. I fingered the pall that covered me; it was of some thick material, soft and warm, and beautifully women. My fingers traced the pattern worked on it: the Dragon. And now I could see, at the four corners of the bed, the tall, heavily wrought candlesticks that gave off the gleam of gold. I had been left, apparently, with pomp and with royal honours. Had the King been here, then? I wished I could remember him. And Nimuë? I supposed I had my own prophecies to thank that this was all the burial they had accorded me, and that they had not given me to the earth, or to the fire. The thought was a shiver over the skin, but it prompted me to action. I looked at the candles. Three of them had burned down almost to lumps of shapeless wax, and then died. The other, blown out perhaps by some chance draught, was still a foot or so tall. I put a finger to the nearest, where the wax had run down; it was still soft. Twelve hours, I calculated, or at most fifteen, since they had been lighted, and I had been left here. The place was still warm. If I was to keep alive, it must be kept that way. I leaned back against the stiff pillow, drew the pall with its golden dragon up over my body, fixed my eyes on the dead candle, and thought: We shall see. The simplest of magics, the first I ever learned here in this very place; let us see if this, too, has been taken from me. The effort sent me, exhausted, back into sleep.

I woke to see the sunlight, dim now and rosy, lighting a far corner of the cave, but the cave itself was full of light. The candle burned steadily, with a warm golden flame. It glimmered on two gold coins lying on the pall; I remembered, vaguely, the weight of them tumbling from my eyes as I woke and moved. It also showed me something more to the purpose: the ritual cakes and wine that had been left beside the bier as offerings to the dead. I spoke aloud to God who kept me, then, sitting on the bier, with the grave-clothes round me, ate and drank what had been left.

The cakes were dry, but tasted of honey, and the wine was strong, running into me like new life. The candlelight, dealing its own faint warmth, dispelled the last wisps of fear. "Emrys," I found myself whispering, "Emrys, child of the light, beloved of kings . . . you were told that you would be buried quick in darkness, your power gone; and look, here it has come to pass, and it is not fearful after all; you are buried, and quick, but you have light and air and—unless they have rifled the place—food and drink and warmth and medicines. . . ."

I lifted the candle from its heavy sconce and carried it into the inner caves which were the storerooms. Everything was just as I had left it. Stilicho had been a more than faithful steward. I thought of the wine and honey-cakes left beside the "bier," and wondered if, besides, the caverns had been scoured and garnished, then carefully furnished for the dead. Whatever the reason for leaving things as they were, there, row on row, box on box, were the precious stores, and in their places the flasks and jars of drugs and cordials, all that I had not taken with me to Applegarth. There was a real squirrel's hoard of food, dried fruit and nuts, honeycombs gently seeping into their jars, a barrel of olives in oil. No bread, of course, but in a crock I found, bone-hard, some thick oatcake made long ago by the shepherd's wife and given to me; it was still good, being dry as board, so I broke it up and put some of it to sop in wine. The meal garner was half full, and with oil from the olive-barrel I could make meal cakes of a sort. Water, of course, I had; soon after I had come to take up residence in the cave I had had my servant lead a pipe of water from the spring outside to fill a tank; this, kept covered, ensured clean water even through frost and storm. The overflow, channelled to run down to a fissured corner of a remote inner chamber, served as a privy. There were candles aplenty in store, and tinder with the flints on the ledge where I had always kept them. There was a sizable pile of charcoal, but I hesitated, for fear of smoke or fumes, to light the brazier. Besides, I might need the warmth in the time ahead. If my reckoning of time was right, in a short month the summer would be over, and autumn setting in with its chill winds and its killing damp.

So at first, while the warm airs of summer still breathed through the cave, I used light only when I needed to see to prepare my food, and for comfort sometimes, when the hours dragged in darkness. I had no books, all having been taken to Applegarth. But writing materials were to hand, and as the days went by and I gained strength and began to fret in the idleness of captivity, I formed the idea of trying to set down in some kind of order the story of my boyhood and the times I had lived through and helped to mould. Music, too, would have been something to be made in darkness, but the standing harp had gone with my books to Applegarth, and my own small harp had not been brought with the other riches, to furnish the house of the dead.

Be sure that I had given thought to escaping from my grave. But those who had laid me there and given me, in honour, the sacred hill itself, with all that lay within it, had used the hill itself to seal me in; half the mountain-side, seemingly, had been levered down to fall across the cave's entrance. Try as I would I could not shove or scrape a way through. No doubt someone with the right tools might have done it in time, but I had none. We kept spades and axes always in the stable below the cliff.

There was another possibility, which I considered time and again. As well as the caves that I used, there were other, smaller chambers which opened off one another, branching deep into the hill. One of these inner caves was little more than a chimney, a rounded shaft running up through the rock levels, to reach the air in a little corrie of the hill above. Here a low cliff, many years back, had, under the pressure from tree-roots and storms, split open to let light, and sometimes small rocks and rain-water, down into the hollow below. Through this fissure now the cave-dwelling bats made their daily flights. In time the pile of fallen stones in the cave had built up into a kind of buttress, reaching perhaps a third of the way up toward the "lantern," as I might term the hole above. When, hopefully, I looked to see if this rough stair had been extended, I was disappointed: above it, still, lay a sheer pitch three times the height of a man, and above that the same again, sloping at first steeply, and then more gently, to reach the gap of daylight. It was just possible that a fit and agile man could have climbed out unaided, though in places the rock was damp and slimy, and in others manifestly unsafe. But for an ageing man, recently in his sick-bed, it was impossible. The sole comfort of the discovery lay in the fact that here, literally, was a "chimney"; in the cold days to come I could light the brazier there with safety, and savour warmth and hot food and drink.

I did think, naturally, about making a fire of some kind, in the hope that the smoke might attract the attention of the curious, but there were two things against this. First, the country people who lived within sight of the hill were used to seeing bats go up daily from the hillside, looking for all the world like plumes of smoke; the second was that I had little to spare of fuel. All I could do was conserve the precious stores I had, and wait for someone to make a way up the valley to visit the holy well.

But nobody came. Twenty days, thirty, forty, were notched on my tally stick. I recognized with reluctance that where the simple folk had come to pray to the spirit of the well, and offer gifts to the living man who healed them, they were afraid of the enchanter lately dead, and of the new haunting of the hollow hill. Since the valley led nowhere but to the cave and the spring, no travellers used it. Nothing came into the high valley, except the birds (which I heard) and, I supposed, the deer, and once a wolf or a fox that I heard snuffling in the night at the tumble of stones that blocked the cave's entrance.

So the tallied days dragged by, and I stayed alive, and—what was harder—kept fear at bay in every way I knew. I wrote, and wrestled with plans for escape, and did what domestic tasks the days demanded; and I am not ashamed to remember that I drugged the nights—and sometimes the desperate days—with wine, or with opiates that stupefied the senses and dulled time. Despair I would not feel; through all that long life in death I held to one thing, as to a ladder let down from the light above me: throughout my life I had obeyed my god, had received power from him, and rendered it back again; now I had seen it pass to the young lover who had usurped me; but though my life was apparently done, my body had been kept—I could not tell how or why—from either earth or fire. I was alive, and had regained both strength and will, and, prison or no, this was the hollow hill of the god himself. I could not believe that there was not some purpose still to be fulfilled.

I think it was with this in mind that I nerved myself at length to climb into the crystal cave.

All this while, with my strength at low ebb and the power (I knew) gone from me, I had not been able to face the place of vision. But one evening when, with my store of candles running low, I had sat too long in darkness, I brought myself at last to climb the ledge at the back of the main cavern, and, bent double, to creep into the crystal-lined globe.

I went, I believe, for nothing more than the comfortable memories of past power, and of love. I took no light with me, and looked for no vision. I simply lay, as I had done when a boy, belly down on the rough crystals of the floor, letting the heavy silence enclose me, and filling it with my thoughts.

What they were I cannot now remember: I suppose I was praying. I do not think I spoke aloud. But in a while I became conscious—as, in a black night, a man realizes, rather than sees, the coming dawn—of something that answered to my breathing. Not a sound, only the faintest echo of a breath, as if a ghost was waking, taking life from mine.

My heart began to thud; my breathing sharpened. Within the darkness the other rhythm quickened. The air of the cave hummed. Round the crystal walls ran, echoing, a whisper that I knew.

I felt the easy tears of weakness start into my eyes. I said aloud: "So, after all, they brought you back to your own place?" And, from the darkness, my harp answered me.

I groped forward toward the sound. My fingers met the live, silken feel of wood. The carved fore-pillar nestled into my hand as I had seen the hilt of the great sword slide into the King's grip. I backed out of the cave, silenced the harp's faint plaining against my breast, and picked my way carefully down again into my prison.

This was the song I made. I called it "Merlin's Song from the Grave."

Where have they gone, the bright ones?
I remember the sunlight
And a great wind blowing;
A god who answered me,
Leaning out from the high stars;
A star that shone for me,
A voice that spoke to me,
A hawk that guided me,
A shield that sheltered me;
And a clear way to the gate
Where they wait for me,
Where surely they wait for me?

The day wanes,
The wind dies.
They are gone, the bright ones.
Only I remain.

What use to call to me
Who have neither shield nor star?
What use to kneel to me
Who am only the shadow
Of his shadow,
Only the shadow
Of a star that fell
Long ago.

No song comes brand-fire-new and finished from the first playing, so that now I cannot recall just on which occasion, as I was singing it, I became conscious of an unusual sound that had been, as it were, tapping at the door of my brain for several staves. I let the chords die, laid a hand along the strings, and listened.

The beating of my heart sounded loud in the still, dead air of the cave. Below it went another throbbing, a distant beat coming seemingly from the heart of the hill. I can hardly be blamed, shut as I had been for too long from the ordinary traffic of the world, if the first thoughts that came crowding were winged with instinct born of ancient beliefs—Llud of the Otherworld, the horses of the Wild Hunt, all the shadows dwelling in the hollow hills. . . . Death for me at long last, on this still evening at the end of summer? Then, in less time than it takes for two short breaths, I had arrived at the truth—and it was already too late.

It was the traveller I had waited for, and at length despaired of; he had ridden up above the cave, and halted by the cliff where the lantern opened on the air, and had heard the music. There was a pause, broken only by the sharp strike of nervous hoofs on stone as the horse fretted, held and sidling. Then a man's voice, calling out:

"Is there anyone there?"

I had already laid the harp aside and, with what speed I could, was scrambling through the half-dark toward the cave below him. As I went I tried to call out, but it was a moment or so before my thudding heart and dry throat would let me answer. Then I cried out:

"It is I, Merlin! Don't be afraid, I'm no ghost. I'm alive, and trapped here. Break a way out for me, in the King's name!"

My voice was drowned by the sudden confusion of noise from above. I could guess what had happened. The horse, sensing, as beasts do, some strangeness—a man below ground, the unnatural sounds coming apparently from the fissure in the cliff, even my anxiety—gave a long, pealing whinny and plunged, scattering stones and small gravel and setting other echoes rattling. I shouted again, but either the rider did not hear or he took the horse's fear for an instinct truer than his own; there was another sharp clatter of hoofs and cascading stones, then the beating gallop retreated, faster than it had come. I could not blame the rider, whoever he was; even if he did not know whose tomb lay beneath him, he must have known the hill was sacred, and to hear music from the ground, at dusk, on the crest of such a hill . . .

I went back to pick up the harp. It was undamaged. I put it aside, and with it the hope of rescue, then set myself grimly to prepare what could, for want of a worse word, be called my supper.

3

It was perhaps two nights after this, or maybe three, when something woke me in the night. I opened my eyes on total darkness, wondering what had disturbed me. Then I heard the sound. Stealthy scrapings, rattlings of stone, the patter of earth falling. They came from the lantern, high in the inner cave. Some beast, I thought, badger or fox or even wolf, scratching its way toward the smell of food. I drew the covers round me, and turned over and shut my eyes again.

But the sounds went on, stealthy, persistent, and now impatient, a fierce scrabbling among the stones that spoke of more than animal purpose. I sat up again, taut with sudden hope. Perhaps the horseman had come back? Or he had told his story, and some other, braver soul had come to investigate? I took breath to shout, then paused. I did not want to scare this one away like the first. I would wait for him to speak to me.

He did not; he was intent merely on scraping his way in through the opening in the cliff. More stuff fell, and I heard the chink of a crowbar, and then, unmistakably, a smothered curse. A man's voice, rough-spoken. There was a pause, as if he was listening, then once again the sounds began, and this time he was using some sort of heavy tool, a mattock or a spade, to dig his way in.

Not for worlds would I have shouted now. No one bent simply on investigating a strange story would do so in such stealthy secrecy; the obvious thing to do would be what the horseman had done, to call out first, or to wait quietly and listen, before attempting to force a way into the lantern. What was more, no innocent man would have come, for choice, alone and at night.

A few moments' reflection brought me the probable truth. This was a grave-robber; some outlaw, perhaps, who had heard rumours of a royal grave in Merlin's Hill, and who had doubtless had a look at the cave mouth, decided it was too thoroughly blocked, and had settled on the shaft as being the easier and less conspicuous way of entry. Or perhaps a local man who had watched the rich procession pass, and who had known for years of the cliff and its precarious entry to the hill. Or even a soldier—one of those who, after the ceremonies, had helped to block the cave mouth, and who had been haunted since by recollections of the riches there entombed.

Whoever he was, he must be a man of few nerves. He would be fully prepared to find a corpse laid here; to brave the stench and sight of a body some weeks dead; even to lay hands on it and rob it of its jewels before he tumbled it from the gem-encrusted pall and gold-fringed pillow. And if he should find, instead of a corpse, a living man? An old man, weakened by these long days underground; a man, moreover, whom the world believed to be dead? The answer was simple. He would kill me, and still rob my tomb. And I, stripped of my power, had no defenses.

I rose silently from the bed, and made my way through to the shaft. The digging sounds went on, steadily now, and through the widened opening at the top of the shaft I could see light. He had some sort of lantern there, which dealt him light enough. It would also prevent him from noticing the faint glimmer of a rushlight from below. I went back to the main chamber, kindled a light carefully behind a screen, then set about the only preparations I could make.

If I lay in wait for him with a knife (I had no dagger, but there were knives for preparing food) or with some heavy implement, it was by no means certain that I would be quick enough, or powerful enough, to stun him; and such an attack would make my own end certain. I had to find another way. I considered it coldly. The only weapon I had was one that in times past I had found to be more powerful than either dagger or cudgel. The man's own fear.

I took the blankets off the bed and folded them out of sight. I spread the jewelled pall over, smoothed it, and set the velvet pillow in place. The gold candlesticks still stood where they had been put, at the four corners of the bed. Beside the bed I set the gold goblet that had held the wine, and the silver platter studded with garnets. I took the gold coins, the ferry-man's fee, from where I had laid them, wrapped myself in the king's mantle that they had left for me, blew out the light, and lay down on the pall.

A rending sound from the shaft, a scatter of rubble onto the cavern floor, and with it a rush of fresh night air, told me that he was through. I shut my eyes, placed the gold coins on the lids, smoothed the long folds of my mantle, then crossed my arms on my breast, controlled my breathing as best I could, and waited.

It was perhaps the hardest thing I have ever done. Often before I had faced danger, but never without knowing one way or the other what the risks were. Always before, in times of stress or terror—the fight with Brithael, the ambush in the Wild Forest—I had known there was pain to face, but in the end victory and safety and a cause won; now I knew nothing. This stealthy murder in the dark, for a few jewels, might indeed be the ignominious end which the gods, with their sidelong smiles, had showed me in the stars as my "burial quick in the tomb." It was as they willed. But, I thought (not coolly at all), if I have ever served you, God my god, let me smell the sweet air once more before I die.

There was a soft thud as he landed in the shaft. He must have a rope with him, tied to one of the trees that grew from the cliff. I had been right; he was alone. Faintly, under the weight of the gold on my eyelids, I could see the warming of the dark that meant he had brought his lantern with him. Now he was feeling his way, carefully, across the uneven floor toward the chamber where I lay. I could smell his sweat, and the reek of the cheap lantern; which meant, I thought with satisfaction, that he would not catch the lingering odours of food and wine, or the smell of the recently doused rushlight. And his breathing gave him away; with even greater satisfaction I knew that, bravado or no, he was afraid.

He saw me, and stopped in his tracks. I heard his breath go in as harshly as a death-rattle. He had nerved himself, one would guess, to face a decaying corpse, but here was a body like that of a living or newly dead man. For seconds he stood, hesitating, breathing hard, then, remembering perhaps what he had heard of the embalmers' art, he cursed again softly under his breath, and tiptoed forward. The light shook and swung in his hand.

With the smell and sound of his fear my own calmness grew. I breathed smoothly and shallowly, trusting to the wavering of his lantern and its smoking light not to let him see that the corpse moved. For an age, it seemed, he stood there, but at last, with another sharp rattle of breath and an abrupt movement like a horse under the spur, he forced himself forward to my side. A hand, unsteady and damp with cold sweat, plucked the gold coins off my eyelids.

I opened my eyes.

In that one brief flash, before movement or blink or breath, I took it all in: the dark Celtic face lit by the horn lantern, the coarse clothing of some peasant levy, the pitted skin slithering with sweat, the greedy slack mouth and the stupid eyes, the knife in his belt, razor-sharp.

I said, calmly: "Welcome to the hall of the dead, soldier."

And from its dark corner, at the sound of my voice, the harp whispered something, on a sweet, fading note.

The gold coins fell, ringing, and rolled away into darkness. The lantern followed, to be smashed into smoking oil on the floor. He let out a yell of fear such as I have not often heard in my long life, and once again, from the darkness, came the mockery of the harp. Yelling again, he took to his heels and ran, stumbling blindly out of the cave and making for the shaft. He must have made a first vain attempt to climb his rope; he cried out again as he fell heavily back to the rock-strewn floor. Then fear lent him strength; I heard the sobbing breaths of effort receding upward as he swarmed to the top. His footsteps ran and slipped down the hillside. Then the sounds died, and I was alone again, and safe.

Safe, in my grave. He had taken the rope. In fear, perhaps, that the enchanter's ghost could swarm after him and follow, he had dragged it up after him. The gap he had made showed a ragged window of sky, where a star shone, remote and pure and indifferent. Cool air blew in, and the cold, unmistakable smell of dawn coming. I heard a thrush from the cliff-top.

God had answered me. I had smelled the sweet air again, and heard the sweet bird. And life was as far from me as before.

I went back into the inner chamber and, as if nothing had happened, began my preparations for another day.

And another. And a third. On the third day, having eaten and rested and written and calmed my mind as far as I could, I once more examined the chimney shaft. The wretched grave-robber had left me a shred of new hope: the pile of fallen stones was higher by almost three feet, and though he had pulled his rope up after him, he had left me another, which I found lying, loosely coiled, at the base of the shaft. But the hopes that this raised were soon proved false; the rope was of poor quality, a cord no more than four or five cubits in length. I could only assume that he had intended to tie his spoils together—he could never have hoped to carry even one of the candlesticks out with him on his climb—fasten them to the main rope's end, and draw them after him. I calculated that even to bear away the four candlesticks, the thief would have had to make four journeys up and down the shaft. The cord would never, even had it been long enough to throw and loop over some rocky projection, have been strong enough to bear my weight. Nor could I—scanning yet again the damp and crumbling side of the chimney—see any such safe projection or foothold. It was possible that a young man or an agile boy might have managed the climb, but although I had been a strong man all my life, with a strong man's endurance, I had never been an athlete, and now, with age and illness and privation, the climb was quite beyond me.

One other thing the thief had done: where, before, I would have had to reach the high lantern and then set to work to dig and scrabble a way through—

an impossible task without tools and ladder—now the way lay open. All I had to do was get to it. And I had a length of good cord. It would come hard, I thought, if I could not contrive some kind of scaffolding which would take me as far as the sloping section of the chimney, and from there, perhaps, I might be able to rig some kind of makeshift ladder. Much of the cave's furnishing had gone, but there was still the bed, a stool or two, and a table, the casks, and a stout bench forgotten in a corner. If I could find some way to break them up, fasten the pieces together with cord, or with torn strips of blanket, wedge them with sherds from the storage jars . . .

All the rest of that day, and the next following, working directly under the light thrown down from above, I toiled at my makeshift scaffold, bearing a wry thought for Tremorinus, my father's chief engineer, who had first taught me my craft. He would have laughed to see the great Merlin, the engineer-artificer who had outpaced his master, and had lifted the Hanging Stones of the Giants' Dance, cobbling together a structure of which the sorriest apprentice would have been ashamed. All I needed to do, he would have said, was to take my harp like Orpheus, and play to the fragments of the broken furniture, and watch it build itself like the walls of Troy. This had been his theory, stoutly held in public, about the way I had managed the lifting of the great trilithons of the Dance.

By nightfall of the second day I had rigged a sort of rough scaffolding roofed with the stout plank of the bench, which might serve as a base for a ladder. It was nine feet high, and fixed firmly enough with a pile of stones holding it in place. I had only, I reckoned, another twenty-five feet to build.

I worked until dusk, then lighted the lantern and made my wretched meal. Then, as a man turns to the comfort of a lover, I lifted the harp into my arms and, without thoughts of Orpheus or Troy, played until my eyelids drooped, and a false chord warned me that it was time to sleep. Tomorrow would be another day.

Who could have guessed what kind of day? Tired from my labours, I slept deeply, and woke later than usual to the light of a bright thread of sunshine, and the sound of someone calling my name.

For a moment I lay still, thinking myself still caught in the mists of a dream that had mocked me so often before, but then I came fully awake to the discomfort of the cavern floor (I had broken my bed up for use) and the voice again. It came from the lantern, a man's voice, overpitched with nerves, but with something familiar about the queerly accented Latin.

"My lord? My lord Merlin? Are you there, my lord?"

"Here! Coming!"

In spite of aching joints, I was on my feet as swiftly as any boy, and ran to the foot of the shaft.

Sunshine was pouring down from above. I picked my way, stumbling, to the foot of the rude structure that almost filled the base of the shaft. I craned upward.

Framed in the gap of brilliant sky was a man's head and shoulders. At first I could distinguish little against the brightness. Me, he must be able to see clearly, unkempt, bearded, no doubt pale as the ghost he must have feared to see. I heard his shivering gasp of breath, and the head drew back.

I cried out: "Stay for me, for God's sake! I'm no ghost! Stay! Help me out of here! Stilicho, stay!"

Almost without thinking, I had identified his accent, and him with it. My old servant the Sicilian, Stilicho, who had married Mai the miller's daughter, and kept the mill on the Tywy at the valley's foot. I knew his kind, credulous, superstitious, easily afraid of what they did not understand. I leaned against the upright of the scaffolding, gripped it with shaking hands, and fought for a composure that would reassure him. His head came cautiously back. I saw the black eyes staring, the sallow pallor of his face, the open mouth. With a self-control that shook me with another wave of weakness I spoke in his own language, slowly and with apparent calm:

"Don't be afraid, Stilicho. I was not dead when they left me here in error, and all these weeks I have been trapped here in the hill. I am not a ghost, boy; it truly is Merlin, alive, and very much in need of your help."

He leaned nearer. "Then the King—all those others who were here—?" He stopped, swallowing painfully.

"Do you think that a ghost could have built this scaffolding?" I asked him. "I hadn't despaired of escaping. I've lived here in hope, all through these weeks, but by the God of all gods, Stilicho, if you leave me now without helping me from here, I swear I shall be dead before the day is out." I stopped, ashamed.

He cleared his throat. He sounded shaken, as well he might, but scared no longer. "Then it really is you, lord? They said you were dead and buried, and we have been mourning you . . . but we should have known that your magic would keep you from death."

I shook my head. I forced myself to go on talking, knowing that with every word he was coming nearer to accepting my survival as true, and nerving himself to approach the tomb and its living ghost. "Not magic," I said, "it was the malady that deceived you all. I am no longer an enchanter, Stilicho, but I have God to thank that I am still a strong man. Otherwise these weeks below the earth would surely have killed me. Now, my dear, can you get me out? Later we can talk, and decide what's to be done, but now, for God's sake, help me out of here and into the air. . . ."

It was a grim business, and it took a long time, not least because, when he would have left me to go for help, I begged him, in terms of which I am now ashamed, not to leave me. He did not argue, but set himself to knotting the long, stout rope which he had found still attached to an ash sapling in the rock above the lantern. He finished it with a loop for my foot, then lowered it carefully. It reached the platform, with some length to spare. Then he let himself down into the shaft, and in a short space of time was beside me at the foot of the scaffolding. I think he would have gone on his knees, as his habit had been, to kiss my hands, but I gripped him so tightly that instead he held me, supporting me with his young strength, and then helped me back into the main cavern.

He found the one remaining stool for me, then lit the lantern and brought me wine, and after a while I was able to say, with a smile: "So now you know that I am a solid body, and no ghost? It was brave of you to come at all, and braver still to stay. What on earth brought you to this place? You're the last person who I'd have thought would go visiting a tomb."

"I wouldn't have come at all," he said frankly, "but that something I heard made me wonder if you were not dead after all, but living here alone. I knew you were a great magician, and thought that perhaps your magic would not let you die like other men."

"Something you heard? What was that?"

"You know the man I have to help me at the mill, Bran, he's called? Well, he was in town yesterday, and brought home some tale of a fellow who'd drunk himself silly in one of the taverns, and the story was going about that he had been up to Bryn Myrddin, and that the enchanter had come out of the tomb and spoken to him. People were standing him drinks and asking for more, and of course the tale as he told it was plainly lies, but there was enough to make me wonder . . ." He hesitated. "What did happen, lord? I knew someone had been here, because of the rope on the tree."

"It happened twice," I told him. "The first time it was a horseman riding over the hill . . . you can see how long ago, I marked it on the tally yonder. He must have heard me playing; the sound would carry up through the hole in the cliff. The second time was four—five?—days, since, when some ruffian came to rob the tomb, and opened the cliff as you saw it, and let himself down with the rope." I told him what had happened. "He must have been too scared to stop and untie his rope. It's a mercy you heard his story, and came up before he got his courage back, and came back for it—and perhaps dared the tomb again."

He gave me a sidelong, shamefaced look. "I'll not pretend to you, lord. It's not right you praising me for courage. I came up yesterday evening. I didn't want to come alone, but I was ashamed to bring Bran, and Mai wouldn't go within a mile of the place. . . . Well, I saw the mouth of the cave was just as it had been, and then I heard the harp. I—I turned and ran home. I'm sorry."

I said, gently: "But you came back."

"Yes. I couldn't sleep all night. You remember when you left me once to guard the cave, and you showed me your harp, and how it played sometimes by itself, just with the air moving? And how you gave me courage, and showed me the crystal cave and told me I would be safe there? Well, I thought of all that, and I thought of the times you were good to me, how you took me out of slavery and gave me freedom and the life I have now. And I thought: Even if it is my lord's ghost, or the harp playing by magic, alone in the hollow hill, he would never harm me. . . . So I came again, but this time I came by daylight. I thought: If it is a ghost, then in sunlight it will be sleeping."

"And so I was." The thought touched me, like a cold dagger's point, that if I had drugged myself last night, as I had so often done, I might have heard nothing.

He was going on: "I walked over the hill this time, and I saw the new broken stone showing white in the corrie where the little air-shaft comes out. I went to look. I saw the rope then, tied to the ash tree, and the big gap in the cliff, and when I looked down the shaft, I saw the—" he hesitated, "—the thing you built there."

I had not thought to feel amusement ever again. "That is a builder's scaffold, Stilicho."

"Yes, of course. Well, I thought, no ghost made that. So I shouted. That's all."

"Stilicho," I said, "if ever I did anything for you, be sure you have paid me a thousand times over. In fact, you have saved me twice over. Not only today; if you hadn't left the place the way I found it, I should have died weeks back, from starvation and cold. I shall not forget it."

"We've got to get you out of here now. But how?" He looked around him at the stripped cave and the broken furnishings. "Now we've spoken, and you're feeling stronger, lord, shall I not go and bring men and tools, and open the doorway for you? It would be the best way, truly it would."

"I know that, but I think not. I've had time now to consider. Until I know how things stand in the kingdoms, I can't suddenly 'come to life.' That is how the common people will see it, if Prince Merlin comes back from the tomb. No part of the story must be told until the King known. So, until we can get a private message to him—"

"He's gone to Brittany, they say."

"So?" I thought for a moment. "Who is Regent?"

"The Queen, with Bedwyr."

A pause, while I looked down at my hands. Stilicho was sitting cross-legged on the floor. In the lantern's light he looked still much like the boy I had known. The dark Byzantine eyes watched me.

I wetted my lips. "The Lady Nimuë? Do you know who I mean? She—"

"Oh, yes, all the world knows her. She has magic, as you used to—as you have, lord. She is always near the King. She lives near Camelot."

"Yes," I said. "Well, I am sorry, my dear, but I cannot have it known before the King comes back from Brittany. Somehow, between us, we shall have to get me out of the shaft. I have no doubt that if you will bring the tools up out of the stable, we'll manage something."

And so we did. He was back in something under half an hour with nails and tools and the small stock of timber that had been left in the stable. It was a bad half hour for me: I had no doubts that he would return, but the reaction was so intense that, left alone again, I sat there on the stool, sweating and shaking like a fool. But by the time the stuff was pitched down the shaft, with himself following it, I had myself in hand, and we set to work and, with me sitting idly on the stool watching and directing, he put together a ladder of a sort and fixed it to the platform I had made. This reached the sloping section of the chimney. Here, as an adjunct to the knotted rope, he cut pieces of wood which with the help of cracks and protuberances of rock he wedged at intervals against the side of the chimney to act, if not as steps, then as resting-places where one could set a knee.

When all was done he tested it, and while he did so I wrapped the harp in the remaining blanket, and with it my manuscripts and a few of the drugs that I might need to restore my strength fully. He climbed out with them. Finally I took a knife and cut the best of the jewels off the pall, and dropped them, together with the gold coins, into a leather bag which had held herbs. I slipped the thong of the bag over my wrist, and was waiting at the scaffold's foot when at last Stilicho reappeared at the top, laid hold of the rope, and called for me to begin my climb.

4

I stayed a month with Stilicho at the mill. Mai, who had held me formerly in trembling awe, once she saw that this was no terrifying wizard, but a man sick and in need of care, looked after me devotedly. I saw no one besides these two. I kept to the upper chamber they gave me—it was their own, the best, they would hear of nothing else. The hired man slept out in the granary sheds, and knew only that some ageing relative of the miller's was staying there. The children were told the same, and accepted me without question, as children will.

At first I kept to my bed. The reaction from the recent weeks was a severe one; I found daylight trying, and the noises of every day hard to bear—the men's voices in the yard as the grain barges came in to the wharf, hoofs on the roadway, the shouts of the children playing. At first the very act of talking to Mai or Stilicho came hard, but they showed all the gentleness and understanding of simple folk, so things gradually became easier, and I began to feel myself again. Soon I left my bed, and began to spend time with my writing, and, calling the elder of the children to me, began to teach them their letters. In time I even came to welcome Stilicho's ebullience, and questioned him eagerly about what had happened since I had been shut away.

Of Nimuë he knew little beyond what he had already told me. I gathered that her reputation for magic, in the weeks since my going, had grown so quickly that the mantle of the King's enchanter had fallen naturally upon her shoulders. She spent some of her time at Applegarth, but since the Lady's death had gone back to the Island shrine, to be accepted without question as the new Lady of the place. One rumour seemed to indicate that the status of the Lady would change with her. She did not remain on the Island, a maiden among maidens: she paid frequent visits to the court at Camelot, and there was talk of a probable marriage. Stilicho could not tell me who the man was said to be, "But of course," he said, "he will be a king."

With this I had to be content. There was little other news. Most of the men who came up-river to the mill were simple workmen, or barge masters, whose knowledge was only local, and who cared for little beyond getting a good price for the goods they carried. All I could gather was that the times were still prosperous; the kingdom was at peace; the Saxons kept to their treaties. And the High King, in consequence, had felt free to go abroad.

Why, Stilicho did not know. And this did not, for the moment, matter to me, except that it must mean my own continued secrecy. I thought the matter over again, after my return to health, and the conclusions I came to were the same. No purpose could be served by my public return to affairs. Even the "miracle" of a return from the grave would do no more for the kingdom and its High King than my "death" and the transfer of power had done. I had no power or vision to bring him; it would be wrong to indulge in a return which would tend to discredit Nimuë as my successor, without bringing anything fresh or even valid to Arthur's service. I had made my farewells, and my legend, such as it was, had already begun to gather way. So much I could understand from the tales that, according to Stilicho, had already added themselves to the grave-robber's tale of the enchanter's ghost.

As for Nimuë, the same arguments applied. With what wisdom I could command in the matter, I saw that the love we had had together was already a thing of the past. I could not go back, expecting to claim again the place I had had with her, and to tie jesses to the feet of a falcon already in flight. Something else held me back, something I would not recognize in daylight, but which mocked me in dreams with old prophecies buzzing around like stinging flies. What did I know of women, even now? When I remembered the steady draining of my power, the last, desperate weakness, the trancelike state in which I had lain before the final desertion in darkness, I asked myself what that love had been but the bond that held me to her, and bade me give her all I owned. And even when I recalled her sweetness, her generous worship, her words of love, I knew (and it took no vision to do so) that she would not lay her power down now, even to have me back again.

It was hard to make Stilicho understand my reluctance to reappear, but he did accept my desire to wait for Arthur's return before making plans. From his references to Nimuë he was obviously not yet aware that she had been more to me than a pupil who had taken up the master's charge.

At length, feeling myself again, and not wanting to impose any longer on Stilicho's little household, I prepared to set off for Northumbria, and set Stilicho to make arrangements for me. I decided to go north by sea. A sea voyage is something I never willingly undertake, but by road it would be a long, hard journey, with no guarantee of continued fine weather, and besides, I could hardly have gone alone; Stilicho would have insisted upon accompanying me, even though at this time of year he could ill be spared from the mill. Indeed, he tried to insist on going with me by ship, but in the end let himself be overruled; this not only by expedience, but because I think he believed me still to be the "great enchanter" whom he had served in the past with such awe and pride. In the end I had my way, and one morning early I went quietly downstream on one of the barges, and embarked at Maridunum on a north-bound coastal ship.

I had sent no message to Blaise in Northumbria, because there was no courier I could trust with the news of "Merlin's return from the dead." I would think of some way to prepare him when I came near the place. It was even possible that he had not yet heard news of my death; he lived so retired from the world—held to the times only by my dispatches—it was conceivable that he had only just unrolled my last letter from Applegarth.

This, as it turned out, was the fact; but I did not find out yet for a while. I did not get to Northumbria, but travelled no farther north than Segontium.

The ship put in there on a fine, still morning. The little town sunned itself at the edge of the shining strait, its clustered houses dwarfed by the great walls of the Roman-built fortress that had been the headquarters of the Emperor Maximus. Across the strait the fields of Mona's Isle showed golden in the sun. Behind the town, a little way beyond the fortress walls, stood the remains of the tower that was known as Macsen's Tower. Nearby was the site of the ruined temple of Mithras, where years ago I had found the King's sword of Britain, and where, deep under the rubble of the floor and the ruined altar of the god, I had left the rest of Macsen's treasure, the lance and the grail. This was the place I had promised to show Nimuë on our way home from Galava. Beyond the tower the great Snow Hill, Y Wyddfa, reared against the sky. The first white of winter was on its crest, and its cloud-haunted sides, even on that golden day, showed purple-black with scree and dead heather.

We nosed in to the wharf. There were goods to unload, and this would take time, so I went thankfully ashore, and, after a word at the harbour-master's office, made for the wharfside inn. There I could have a meal, and watch the unloading and loading of my ship.

I was hungry, and likely to get hungrier. My idea of any voyage, however calm, is to get below and stay below, without food or drink, until it is over. The harbour-master had told me that the ship would not sail before the evening tide, so there was ample time to rest and make ready for the next dreaded stage of the journey. It did cross my mind to wish I might have time to make my way up once again to the temple of Mithras, but I put the thought aside. Even if I were to revisit the place, I would not disturb the treasure. It was not for me. Besides, the privations of the journey had tired me, and I needed food. I made for the inn.

This was built round three sides of a court, the fourth being open to the wharf, for the convenience, I suppose, of carrying goods straight from the ships into the inn's storerooms, which served as warehouses for the town. There were benches and stout wooden tables under the overhanging eaves of the open courtyard, but fine though the weather was, it was not warm enough to persuade me to eat out of doors. I found my way into the main room, where a log fire burned, and ordered food and wine. (I had paid my passage with—appropriately—one of the gold coins which had been the "ferryman's fee"; this had left me change besides, and caused the ship's master to accord me a respect which my apparent style hardly called for.) Now the servant hastened to serve me with a good meal, of mutton and fresh bread, with a flask of rough red wine such as seamen like, then left me in peace to enjoy the warmth of the fire and watch through the open door the scene at the quay-side.

The day wore through. I was more tired than I had realized. I dozed, then woke, and dozed again. Over at the wharf the work went on, with creak of windlass and rattle of chain and straining of ropes as the cranes swung the bales and sacks inboard. Overhead the gulls wheeled and cried. Now and again an ox-cart creaked by on clumsy wheels.

There was little coming and going in the inn itself. Once a woman crossed the courtyard with a basket of washing on her head, and a boy hurried through with a batch of bread. There was another party staying, it seemed, in chambers to the right of the court. A fellow in slave's dress hurried in from the town, carrying a flat basket covered with a linen cloth. He vanished through a doorway, and a short while later some children came running out, boys, well dressed but noisy, and with some kind of outlandish accent I could not place. Two of them—twins by their look—settled down on the sunlit flagstones for a game of knucklebones, while the other two, though ill-matched for size, started some kind of mock fight with stocks for swords, and old box lids for shields. Presently a decent-looking woman, whom I took to be their nurse, came out of the same doorway and sat down on a bench in the sun to watch them. From the way the boys, now and then, ran to gaze toward the wharf, I guessed that their party was perhaps waiting to join my ship, or continue its voyage on another vessel that was tied up a few lengths away along the quay.

From where I was sitting I could see the master of my ship, and at his elbow some sort of tallyman with stilus and wax. The latter had written nothing for some time, and on board the activity seemed to have ceased. It would soon be time to get back to my uneasy bed below decks, and wait miserably until the light breezes carried us northward on the next stage of the journey.

I got to my feet. As I did so I saw the master raise his head, with a movement like that of a dog sniffing the air. Then he swung round to look upward at the inn roof. Straight above my head I heard the long creak of the weathervane swinging round, then whining to and fro in small uneasy arcs as the suddenly rising breeze of evening caught it. To and fro it went, then settled into silence in front of a steady wind. The wind went across the harbour like a grey shadow over the water, and in its wake the moored ships swayed, and ropes sang and rattled against the masts like drumsticks. Beside me the fire flickered and then roared up the open chimney. The master, with a gesture of impatient anger, strode for the ship's gangway, calling out orders. Mingled with my own annoyance was relief; the seas would roughen quickly in this wind, but I would not be on them. With the fickle violence of autumn, the wind had veered. The ship could not sail. The fresh wind was blowing straight from the north.

I walked across to speak to the master, who, watching the sailors stow and rope the cargo against the new weather, glumly confirmed that there was no question of sailing until the wind blew our way again. I sent a boy to bring up my gear, and went back to bespeak a room at the inn. That there would be one vacant I knew, for the ill wind had apparently blown good for the other lodgers in the place. I could see sailors making ready on the other ship, and back at the inn there was a rush and bustle of preparation. The children had vanished from the courtyard, and presently reappeared, cloaked and warmly shod, the smallest boy holding his nurse's hand, the others frolicking around her, lively and noisy and obviously excited at the prospect of the voyage. They waited, skipping with impatience, while the slave I had seen, with another to help him, came out loaded with baggage, followed by a man in the livery of a chamber-groom, sharp-voiced and authoritative. They must be people of consequence, in spite of their strange speech. About the tallest of the boys, I thought, there was something vaguely familiar. I stood in the shadow of the inn's main doorway, watching them. The innkeeper had bustled up now, to be paid by the chamber-groom, and then a woman, his wife, perhaps, came running with a package. I heard the word "laundry," then the two of them backed away from the doorway with bow and curtsy, as the principal guest at length emerged from the chamber.

It was a woman, cloaked from head to foot in green. She was slightly built, but bore herself proudly. I caught the gleam of gold at her wrist, and there were jewels at her throat. Her cloak was lined and edged with red fox fur, deep and rich, and the hood, too. This was thrown back on her shoulders, but I could not see her face; she was turned away, speaking to someone behind her in the room.

Another woman came out carefully, carrying a box. This was wrapped in linen, and seemed heavy. She was plainly dressed, like a waiting woman. If the box contained her mistress's jewels, these were persons of consequence indeed.

Then the lady turned, and I knew her. It was Morgause, Queen of Lothian and Orkney. There could be no mistake. The lovely hair had lost its rose-gold glimmer, and had darkened to rose-brown, and her body had thickened with child-bearing, but the voice was the same, and the long slant of the eyes, and the pretty, folded mouth. So the four sturdy boys, ruddy and clamorous with the outlandish accent of the north, were her children by Lot of Lothian, Arthur's enemy.

I had no eyes for them now. I was watching the doorway. I wondered if, at last, I was going to see her eldest son, her child by Arthur himself.

He came swiftly out of the doorway. He was taller than his mother, a slim youth who, though I had never seen him before, I would have known anywhere. *Dark hair, dark eyes, and the body of a dancer.* Someone had once said that of me, and he was like me, was Arthur's son Mordred. He paused beside Morgause, saying something to her. His voice was light and pleasant, an echo of his mother's. I caught the words "ship" and "reckoning," and saw her nod. She laid her pretty hand on his, and the party started to move off. Mordred glanced at the sky, and spoke again, with what looked like a hint of anxiety. They went by within feet of where I was standing.

I drew back. The movement must have caught her attention, for she glanced up, and for the merest fraction of a moment her eyes met mine. There was no recognition in them. But as she turned to hurry for the ship I saw her shiver, and draw the furred cloak about her as if she felt the wind suddenly cold.

The train of servants followed, and Lot's children: Gawain, Agravaine, Gaheris, Gareth. They trod over the gangplank of the waiting ship.

They were going south, all of them. What Morgause purposed there I could not guess at, but it could be nothing but evil. And I was powerless to stop them, or even to send a message ahead of them, for who would believe a message from the dead?

Then the innkeeper and his wife were beside me, wanting to know my pleasure.

I did not, after all, ask to sleep in the rooms that the Queen of Orkney and her train had just vacated.

The wind still blew from the north next day, cold, strong, and steady. There was no question of my own ship's continuing north. I thought again of sending some message of warning to Camelot, but Morgause's ship would easily outpace a horseman, and to whom, in any case, could I send? To Nimuë? To Bedwyr or the Queen? I could do nothing until the High King was back in Britain. And by the same token, while Arthur was still abroad, Morgause could do him no evil. I thought about it as I made my way out of the town, and set off along the track that led below the fortress walls toward Macsen's Tower. It would be an ill wind indeed if I could get no good of it at all. Yesterday's rest had refreshed me, and I had the day in hand. So I would use it.

When I had last been in Segontium, that great military city built and fortified by Maximus whom the Welsh call Macsen, it had been all but a ruin. Since then, Cador of Cornwall had repaired and re-fortified it against attackers from Ireland. That had been many years ago, but more recently Arthur had seen to it that Maelgon, his commander in the west, kept it in repair. I was interested to see what had been done, and how; and this, as much as anything else, took me along the valley track. Soon I was well above the town. It was a day of sunshine and chilly wind, and the city lay bright and washed with colour below me in the arm of the dark-blue sea. Beside the track the fortress walls rose stout and well kept, and within them I could hear the clash and bustle of an alert and well-maintained garrison. As if I had still been Arthur's engineer, proposing to report to him, I marked all that I saw. Then I came to the south side of the fortress, where ruin and the four winds had been allowed their way, and paused to look up the valley slope toward Macsen's Tower.

There was the track, once trodden by the faithful legionnaires, but probably now used only by sheep or goats and their herds. It led up the steep hillside to the swell of stony turf that hid the ancient, underground shrine of Mithras. For more than a hundred years the place had been ruinous, but when I had been there before, the steps that led down to the entrance had still been passable, and the temple itself, though patently unsafe, still recognizable. I started slowly up the track, wondering why, after all, I had come to see it again.

I need not have wondered. It was not there. There was no sign either of the mound that had hidden the roof or of the steps that had led downward. I did not need to look far to find the cause. At the head of the slope where the temple had lain, the restorers of Segontium, levering away the great stones of the fortress wall for their rebuilding, and quarrying here and there for smaller metal, had set half the hillside rolling in a long slope of scree. In this had seeded and grown half a hundred small trees—thorn and ash and blackberry—so that even the track of the fallen scree was hard to trace. And everywhere, like the weft of a loom, the narrow sheep-trods, white with summer dust, criss-crossed the hillside.

I seemed to hear again, faintly, the receding voice of the god.

"Throw down my altar. It is time to throw it down."

Altar, shrine and all, had vanished into the locked depths of the hill.

There is something not quite believable about any change of this kind. I stood there for some time, casting about for the bearings I knew. There was no question of the accuracy of my memory; a line straight from Macsen's Tower on the hill above to the southwest corner of the old fortress, and another, from the Commandant's house to the distant peak of Y Wyddfa, would intersect one another right over the site of the shrine. Now, they intersected one another right in the middle of the scree. I could see where, almost at that very point, the bushes were sparse, and the boulders showed gaps between, as of a space below.

"Lost something?" asked a voice.

I looked round. A boy was sitting perched above me, on a fallen block of stone. He was very young, perhaps ten years old, and very dirty. He was tousled and half-naked, and was chewing a hunk of barley bread. A hazel stick lay near him, and his sheep grazed placidly a little way up the hill.

"A treasure, it seems," I said.

"What kind of treasure? Gold?"

"It might be. Why?"

He swallowed the last bit of bread. "What's it worth to you?"

"Oh, half my kingdom. Were you going to help me find it?"

"I've found gold here before."

"You have?"

"Aye. And once a silver penny. And once a belt buckle. Bronze, that was."

"It seems your pasture is richer than it looks," I said, smiling. This had once been a busy road between fortress and temple. The place must be full of such trove. I looked at the boy. His eyes were clear and lively in the dirty face. "Well," I added, "I don't actually want to dig for gold, but if you can help me with some information, there's a copper penny in this for you. Tell me, have you lived here all your life?"

"Aye."

"Kept sheep in this valley?"

"Aye. Used to come with my brother. Then he got sold to a trader and went on a ship. I keep the sheep now. They're not mine. Master's a big man over to the hill."

"Do you remember—" I asked it without hope; some of the saplings were surely ten years grown. "Do you remember when this landslide came? When they were rebuilding the fort, perhaps?"

A shake of the tousled head. "It's always been like this."

"No. It wasn't always like this. When I was here before, many years ago, there was a good track along the hillside here, and deep in the side of the hill, just over yonder, was an underground building. It had once been a temple. In old times the soldiers used to worship Mithras there. Have you never heard tell of it?"

Another shake.

"From your father, perhaps?"

He grinned. "Tell me who that is, I'll tell you what he said."

"Your master, then?"

"No. But if it's under there"—a jerk of the head toward the scree—"I know where. There's water under. Where the water is, that'll be the place, surely?"

"There was no water when I—" I stopped. A prickling ran over my flesh, like a cold draught. "Water under where?"

"Under the stones. There. Way under. Twice a man's height, by the feel of it."

I took in the small dirty figure, the bright grey eyes, the hazel stick at his feet. "You can find water under the ground? With the hazel?"

"It's easiest wi' that. But I get the feeling sometimes, just the same, on my own."

"And metal? Is that the way you found gold here before?"

"Once. It was a nice bit of a statue or something. A dog, sort of. The master took it off me. If I found some more now I wouldn't tell him. But mostly it's copper, copper coins. Up there in the old buildings."

"I see." I was thinking that when I found the shrine it had already been a deserted ruin for a century or more. But when it was built, no doubt it would have been beside a spring. "If you will show me where the water lies below the stones, there will be silver in it for you."

He did not move. I thought he looked wary. "That's where it is, this treasure you're looking for?"

"I hope so." I smiled at him. "But it's nothing that you could find for yourself, child. It would take men with crowbars to shift those stones, and even if you led them to the place, you would get nothing of what they found. If you show me now, I promise that you will be paid."

He sat still for a moment or two, scuffling his bare feet in the dirt. Then, groping inside the skin kilt that was his only garment, he produced, flat on a dirty palm, a silver coin. "I was paid, master. There's others knew about the treasure. How was I to know it was yours? I showed them where to dig, and they lifted the stones and took the box away."

Silence. Here in the lee of the hill the wind had no way. The bright world seemed to spin far away, then steady, and come back. I sat down on a boulder.

"Master?" The boy slipped from his perch and padded downhill. He stopped near me, peering, but still poised warily, as if for flight. "Master? If I did wrong—"

"You did no wrong. How could you know? No, stay, please, and tell me about it. I shan't hurt you. How could I? Who were they, and how long ago did they take the box away?"

He gave me another doubtful look, then appeared to take me at my word. He spoke eagerly. "Only two days since. It was two men, I don't know them, slaves they were, and they came with the lady."

"The lady?"

At something in my face he stepped back half a pace, then stood his ground. "Aye. Came two days ago, she did. She must have had magic, I think. Went straight to it, like a bitch to the porridge-pot. Pointed almost to the very place, and said, 'Try there.' The two fellows started shifting the rocks. I was sitting up there. When they'd been at it for a bit, they were moving the wrong way, so I went down. Told her what I told you, that I could find things. 'Well,' she says, 'there's metal hid somewhere hereabout. I've lost the map,' she says, 'but I know it's here. The owner sent me. If you can show us where to dig, there's a silver coin in it for you.' So I found it. Metal! It took the hazel clean from my hand, like a big dog snatching a bone. A powerful kind of gold there must have been there?"

"Indeed," I said. "You saw them find it?"

"Aye. I waited for my pay, see?"

"Of course. What was it like?"

"A box, so by so." Gestures sketched the size. "It looked heavy. They never opened it. She made them lay it down, then she laid her hands right across it, like this. I told you she had magic. She looked right up there, right into Y Wyddfa, as if she was talking to the spirit. You know, the one that lives there. It made a sword once, they say. The King has it now. Merlin got it for him from the King of the hills."

"Yes," I said. "Then?"

"They took it away."

"Did you see where they went?"

"Well, yes. Down toward the town." He shuffled his toes in the dirt, regarding me with clouded eyes. "She did say the owner sent her. Was that a lie? She was very sweet-spoken, and the slaves had badges with a crown on. I thought she was a queen."

"So she was," I said. I straightened my back. "Don't look like that, child, you have done nothing wrong. In fact, you have done more than most men would have done in your place: you told me the truth. You could have earned another silver coin if you had kept your mouth shut, showed me the place, and gone on your way. So I shall pay you, as I promised. Here."

"But this is silver, master, And for nothing."

"Not for nothing. You gave me news that must be worth half the kingdom, or even more. A king's ransom, don't they call it?" I got to my feet. "Don't try to understand me. Stay here in peace, and watch your sheep and find your fortune, and the gods be with you."

"And with you too, master," said he, staring.

"It may be," I said, "that they still are. All they have to do now is to send another ship in the wake of the first one, and take me south."

I left him looking wonderingly after me, with the silver coin clutched tightly in the dirty hand.

A south-bound ship docked next day at noon, and sailed again with the evening tide. I was on board, and stayed prostrate and suffering until she came, five days later, safely into the Severn Channel.

5

The winds stayed strong, but variable. By the time we reached the Channel, the weather had settled to fair, so we did not put in at Maridunum, but held straight on up the estuary.

Enquiries had told me that the *Orc,* Morgause's ship, had been bound for Ynys Witrin, putting in at least twice on the way. It was possible, since by good luck mine was a fast ship, that Morgause and her party might not be too far ahead of me. I suppose I might have bribed the master of my ship to put in at the Island also, but nothing could have saved me there from recognition, with the consequent uproar that I had striven to avoid. Had I known when I saw Morgause that she had the things of power with her from the Mithraeum, and had still (since the boy's judgment seemed good) some magic in her hands, I would have felt bound, whatever the risks, to sail with her in the *Orc,* though I might never have survived the voyage.

I had no means of knowing when Arthur was expected home, and if I had to stay in hiding until he came, Morgause would probably be able to reach him before I did. What I was hoping for, as I travelled south so closely in her wake, was that I could somehow reach Nimuë. I had faced what might be the result of that. A return from the dead is rarely a success. It was very possible that she might herself want to stop me from reaching Arthur again, and reclaiming my place in his affection and his service. But she had my power. The grail was for the future, and the future was hers. Warn her I must, that another witch was on the way. The rape of Macsen's treasure had sounded some note of danger which I could not ignore.

To my relief my ship passed the mouth of the estuary that led to the Island's harbour, and held on up into the narrowing Severn Channel. We put in at length at a small wharf at the mouth of the Frome River, from which there is a good road leading straight to Aquae Sulis in the Summer Country. I had paid my passage this time with one of the jewels from my grave-clothes, and with the change from this I bought myself a good horse, filled the saddlebags with food and a change of clothing, and set off at once along the road toward the city.

Except in those places where I was very well known, I thought there was small chance now of my being recognized. I had grown thinner since my entombment, my hair was now quite grey, and I had not shaved my beard. For all that, I planned to skirt towns and villages if I could, and lie at country taverns. I could not lie out; the weather was turning colder every day, and, not much to my surprise, I found the ride exhausting. By the evening of the first day I was very ready to rest, and put up thankfully at a small, decent-looking tavern still four or five miles short of Aquae Sulis.

Before I even asked for food, I sought news, and was told that Arthur was home, and at Camelot. When I spoke of Nimuë they answered readily, but more vaguely. "Merlin's lady," they called her, "the King's enchantress," and elaborated with one or two fanciful tales, but they were not sure of her movements. One man said she was in Camelot with the King, but another was sure she had left the place a month back; there had been, he said, some trouble in Rheged; some tale about Queen Morgan, and the King's great sword.

So Nimuë, it seemed, was out of touch; and Arthur was home. Even if Morgause did land on the Island, she might not hasten straight to confront the King. If I made all haste, I might reach him before she did. I hurried with my meal, then paid my shot, had them saddle up once more, and took again to the road. Though I was tired, I had come a scant ten miles, and my good horse was still fresh. If I did not press him, I knew that he could go all night.

There was a moon, and the road was in repair, so we made good time, reaching Aquae Sulis well before midnight. The gates were locked, so I skirted the walls. I was stopped twice, once by a gate guard calling to know my business, and once by a troop of soldiers wearing Melwas' badge. Each time I showed my brooch with its Dragon jewel, and said curtly, "King's business," and each time the brooch, or my assurance, told, and they let me by. A mile or so after that the road forked, and I turned south by southeast.

The sun came up, small and red in an icy sky. Ahead, the road led straight across the bleak hill land, where the limestone shows white as bone, and the trees are all racked north-eastward away from the gales. My horse dropped to a walk, then to a plod. Myself, I was riding in a dream, gone in exhaustion beyond either stiffness or soreness. Out of mercy to both weary animals, I drew rein by the next water-trough we passed, tossed hay down from the net that hung at the saddle bow, and myself sat down on the trough's edge and took out my breakfast of raisins and black bread and mead.

The light broadened, flashing on the frosty grass. It was very cold. I broke the cat-ice on the trough, and laved my face and hands. It refreshed me, but made me shiver. If the horse and I were to stay alive we must soon move on. Presently I bitted up again, and led him to where I might mount from the edge of the trough. The horse threw up his head and pricked his ears, and then I heard it, too; hoofs approaching from the direction of the city, and at a fast gallop. Someone who had left the city as soon as the gates had opened, and was coming in a hurry, on a fresh horse.

He came in sight: a young man riding hard, on a big blue roan. When he was a hundred paces off, I recognized the insignia of the royal courier, and, clambering stiffly down from the trough's edge, moved into the road and held up a hand.

He would not have stopped for me, but here the road was edged on the one side by a low ridge of rock, and the other by a steep drop, with the trough blocking the narrow verge. And I had turned my horse so that he stood across the way.

The rider drew rein, holding the restless roan, and saying impatiently: "What is it? If you're fain for company, my good man, I can't provide it. Can't you see who I am?"

"A King's messenger. Yes. Where are you bound?"

"Camelot." He was young, with russet hair and a high colour, and (as his kind have) a kind of prideful arrogance in his calling. But he spoke civilly enough. "The King's there, and I must be there myself tomorrow. What is it, old man, is your horse gone lame? Your best plan is—"

"No. I shall manage. Thank you. I would not have stopped you for a triviality, but this is important. I want you to take a message for me, please. It is to go to the King."

He stared, then laughed, his breath like a cloud on the icy air. "For the King, he says! Good sir, forgive me, but a King's messenger has better things to than take tales from every passer-by. If it's a petition, then I suggest you trot back to Caerleon yourself. The King's to be there for Christmas, and you might get there in time, if you hurry." His heels moved as if he would set spurs to his horse, and ride on. "So by your leave, stand aside and let me by."

I did not move. I said quietly: "You would do well to listen, I think."

He swung back, angry now, and shook his whip free. I thought he would ride over me. Then he met my eyes. He bit back what he had been going to say. The roan, anticipating the whip, bounded forward, and was curbed sharply. It subsided, fretting, its breath puffing white like a dragon's. The man cleared his throat, looked me up and down doubtfully, then fixed his eyes on my face again. I saw his doubt growing. He made a concession and a face-saver at the same time.

"Well—sir—I can listen. And be sure I'll take any message that seems up to my weight. But we're not supposed to act as common carriers, and I have a schedule to keep."

"I know. I would not trouble you, except that it is urgent that I reach the King, and as you have pointed out, you will get there rather more quickly than I. The message is this: that you met an old man on the road who gave you a token, and told you that he is on his way to Camelot to see the King. But he can only make his way slowly, so if the King wishes to see him he must come to him by the way. Tell him which road I am taking, and say that I paid you with the ferryman's guerdon. Repeat it, please."

These men are practised at remembering word for word. Often the messages they take are from men who cannot write. He began to obey me, without thought: "I met an old man on the road who gave me a token, and told me that he is on his way to Camelot to see the King. But he can only make his way slowly, so if the King wishes to see him, he must— Hey, now, what sort of a message is that? Are you out of your mind? The way you put it, it sounds as if you're sending for the King, just like that."

I smiled. "I suppose it does. Perhaps I might phrase it better, if it will make a more comfortable message to deliver? In any case, I suggest you deliver it in private."

"I'll say it had better be in private! Look, I don't know who you are, sir—and it's my guess you're somebody, in spite of, well, not looking it—but by the god of going, it had better be a powerful token, and a good guerdon, too, if I'm to take a summons to King Arthur, however privately."

"Oh, it is." I had wrapped my Dragon brooch in linen, and fastened it into a small package. I handed him this, and with it the second of the gold coins that had sealed my eyelids in the tomb. He stared at the gold coin, then at me, then turned the package over in his hand, eyeing it. He said doubtfully: "What's in it?"

"Only the token I spoke of. And let me repeat, this is important, and it's urgent that you should give it to the King in private. If Bedwyr is there with him, no matter, but no other person. Do you understand?"

"Ye-es, but . . ." With a movement of knees and wrist he wheeled the roan horse half away from me, and with another movement too fast for me to prevent, he broke open the package. My brooch, with the royal Dragon glinting on the gold ground, fell into his hand. "This? This is the royal cypher."

"Yes."

He said, abruptly: "Who are you?"

"I am the King's cousin. So have no fear of delivering the message."

"The King has no cousin, other than Hoel of Brittany. And Hoel doesn't rate the Dragon. Only the . . ." His voice trailed away. I saw the blood begin to drain from his face.

"The King will know who I am," I said. "Don't think I blame you for doubting me, or for opening the package. The King is well served. I shall tell him so."

"You're Merlin." It came out in a whisper. He had to lick his lips and try twice before he could make a sound.

"Yes. Now you see why you must see the King alone. It will be a shock to him, too. Don't be afraid of me."

"But . . . Merlin died and was buried." He was perfectly white now. The reins ran slack through his fingers, and the roan, deciding to take advantage of the respite, lowered its head and began to graze.

I said quickly: "Don't drop the brooch. Look, man, I'm no ghost. It is not every grave that is the gate of death."

I had meant that as a reassurance, but he went, if possible, more ashen than before. "My lord, we thought . . . Everybody knew . . ."

"It was thought that I had died, yes." I spoke briskly, keeping it matter-of-fact. "But all that happened was that I fell into a sickness like death, and I recovered. That is all. Now I am well, and will re-enter the King's service . . . but secretly. No one must know until the King himself has had the news, and spoken with me. I would have told no one but one of the King's own couriers. Do you understand?"

This had the effect, as I had hoped, of bringing back his self-assurance. The red came back into his cheeks, and he straightened his back. "Yes, my lord. The King will be—very happy, my lord. When you died—that is, when you—well, when it happened, he shut himself up alone for three days, and would speak to no one, not even to Prince Bedwyr. Or so they say."

His voice came back to normal while he was speaking, warming, I could see, with pleasurable excitement at the thought of the good news he would have to carry to the King. Gold was the least of it. As he came to an end of telling me how Merlin had been missed and mourned "the length and breadth of the kingdom, I promise you, sir," he pulled the roan's head up from the frosty grass, and set it dancing. The colour was back bright in his face, and he looked excited and eager. "Then I'll be on my way."

"When do you expect to reach Camelot?"

"Tomorrow noon, with good fortune, and a good change of horses. More probably, tomorrow at lamp-lighting. You couldn't give my horse a pair of wings while you're about it, could you?"

I laughed. "I should have to recover a little further before I could manage that. One moment more, before you go . . . There's another message that should go straight to the King. Perhaps you bear it already? Did you get any news in Aquae Sulis of the Queen of Orkney? I heard that she was travelling south by ship to Ynys Witrin, no doubt on her way to court."

"Yes, it's true. She's arrived. Landed, I mean, and on her way now to Camelot. There were those who said she wouldn't obey the summons—"

"Summons? Do you mean that the High King *sent* for her?"

"Yes, sir. That's common knowledge, so I'm not talking out of turn. As a matter of fact I won a small wager on it. They were saying she wouldn't come, even with the safe-conduct for the boys. I said she would. With Tydwal sitting tight in Lot's other castle, and Arthur's sworn man, where could she look for refuge if the High King chose to smoke her out?"

"Where, indeed?" I said it absently, almost blankly. This I had not foreseen, and could not understand. "Forgive me for detaining you, but I have been a long time without news. Can you tell me why the High King should summon her—and apparently under threat?"

He opened his lips, shut them again, then, obviously deciding that telling the King's cousin and erstwhile chief adviser was no breach of his code, nodded. "I understand it's a matter of the boys, sir. One in particular, the eldest of the five. The queen was to bring them all to Camelot."

The eldest of the five. So Nimuë had found Mordred for him . . . where I had failed. Nimuë, who had gone north on "some business for the King."

I thanked the man, and stood back, moving my horse out of his way. "Now, on your way, Bellerophon, as best you can, and 'ware dragons."

"I've got all the dragons I need, thanks." He gathered the reins, and raised a hand in salute. "But that's not my name."

"What is it, then?"

"Perseus," he said, and looked puzzled when I laughed. Then he laughed with me, flourished his whip, and sent the roan past me at a gallop.

6

The need for hurry was past. It was likely that Morgause would reach Arthur before the courier, but about that I could do nothing. Though it still disturbed me to know that she had with her the things of power, the sharpest of my worries was gone: Arthur was forearmed; she was there by his orders, and her hostages with her. It was also probable that I myself would be able to see and talk with him before he had dealt with Morgause and Mordred. I had no doubt at all that Arthur, the moment he saw my token and heard the message, would be on the road to find me. Meeting the courier had been a stroke of excellent fortune; even in my prime I could not have ridden as these men ride.

Nor was it urgent, now, that I should get in touch with Nimuë. Of this, in an obscure way, I was glad. There are some tests that one shrinks from making, and some truths that one would rather not hear. I think that if I could have concealed my existence from her I would have done so. I wanted to remember her words of love and grief at my passing, not see in fresh daylight her facc of dismay when she saw me living.

For the rest of that day I went slowly, and, well before sunset on a still, cold afternoon, came to a wayside inn, and stopped there. There were no other travellers staying, for which I was glad. I saw my horse stabled and fed, then ate the good supper provided by the innkeeper's wife, and went early to bed, and a dreamless sleep.

All the next day I stayed indoors, glad of the rest. One or two folk passed that way: a drover with his flock, a farmer with his wife on their way home from market, a courier going northwest. But again, at nightfall, I was the only guest, and had the fire to myself. After supper, when the host and his wife withdrew to their own place, I was left alone in the small, raftered room, with my pallet of straw drawn near the fire, and a stack of logs nearby to keep the place warm.

That night I made no attempt to seek sleep. Once the inn was sunk in silence, I pulled a chair near to the hearth and fed fresh wood to the flames. The goodwife had left a pot of water simmering at the edge of the fire, so I mixed hot water with the remains of the supper's wine, and drank it, while around me the small sounds of the night took over: the settling of the logs in the fire, the rustle of the flames, the scuttle of rats in the thatch, the sound, far away, of an owl hunting in the icy night. Then I set the wine aside and closed my eyes. How long I sat there I have no idea, or what form the prayers took that brought the sweat to my skin and set the night noises whirling and receding into a limitless and stinging silence. Then at last, the light of the flames against my eyeballs, and through the light the darkness, and through the darkness, light . . .

It was a long time since I had seen the great hall at Camelot. Now it was lit against the dark of an autumn evening. An extravagance of waxlight glittered on the gay dresses of the women, and the jewels and weapons of the men. Supper was just over. Guinevere sat in her place at the center of the high table, lovely in her gold-backed chair. Bedwyr was on her left. They looked happier, I thought, high of heart and smiling. On the Queen's right, the King's great chair was empty.

But just as the chill had touched me, of not seeing him who was all I desired to see, I saw him. He was walking down the hall, pausing here and there to speak to a man as he passed. He was calm, and smiling, and once or twice set them laughing. A page led him; some message, then, had been sent up to the high table, and the King was answering it himself. He reached the great door, and, with a word to the sentries, dismissed the boy and stepped outside. Two soldiers—guards from the gatehouse—waited for him there, with, between them, a man I had seen before: Morgause's chamber-groom.

The latter started forward as soon as the King appeared, then stopped, apparently disconcerted. It was obvious that he had not expected to see Arthur himself. Then, mastering his surprise, he went down on a knee. He started to speak, in that strange northern accent, but Arthur cut across it.

"Where are they?"

"Why, at the gate, my lord. Your lady sister sent me to beg an audience of you tonight, there in the hall."

"My orders were that she should come tomorrow to the Round Hall. Did she not receive the message?"

"Indeed, my lord. But she has travelled far, and is weary, and in some anxiety of mind about your summons. She and her children cannot rest until she knows your will. She has brought them—all—with her tonight, and begs you of your grace that you and the Queen will receive them—"

"I will receive them, yes, but not in he hall. At the gate. Go back and tell her to wait there."

"But, my lord—" Against the King's silence, the man's protests died. He got to his feet with a kind of dignity, bowed to Arthur, then withdrew into the darkness with the two guards. More slowly, Arthur followed them.

The night was dry and still, and frost furred the small clipped trees that lined the terraces. The King's robe brushed them as he passed. He was walking slowly, head down, frowning as he had not let himself frown in the hall full of men and women. No one was about except the guards. A sergeant saluted him and asked a question. He shook his head. So with neither escort nor company he walked alone through the palace gardens, past the chapel wall, and down the steps by the silent fountain. Then through another gate with its saluting sentries, and onto the roadway which led down through the fortress to the southwest gate.

And, sitting by the blaze in the faraway tavern, with the vision driving its nails of pain through my eyes, I cried out to him with a warning as plain as I could make it:

Arthur. Arthur. This is the fate you begot on that night at Luguvallium. This is the woman who took your seed to make your enemy. Destroy them. Destroy them now. They are your fate. She has in her hand the things of power, and I am afraid. Destroy them now. They are in your hand.

He had stopped in the middle of the way. He raised his head as if he could hear something in the night sky. A lantern hanging from a pole threw light on his face. I scarcely knew it. It was somber, hard, cold, the face of a judge, or an executioner. He stood for a few minutes, quite still, then moved as suddenly as a horse under the spur, and strode down toward the main gate of the fortress.

They were there, the whole party. They had changed and robed themselves, and their horses were fresh and richly caparisoned. Torchlight showed the glint of gold tassels and green and scarlet harness. Morgause wore white, a robe trimmed with silver and small pearls, and a long scarlet cloak lined with white fur. The four younger boys were to the rear, with a pair of servants, but Mordred was beside his mother, on a handsome black horse, its bridle ringing with silver. He was looking around him curiously. He does not know, I thought; she has not told him. The black brows, tipped like wings, were smooth; the mouth, a still mouth, folded like Morgause's, kept its secrets. The eyes were Arthur's, and my own.

Morgause sat her mare, still and upright, waiting. Her hood was thrown back, and the light caught her face. It was expressionless and rather pale; but the eyes glittered green under the long lids, and I saw the kitten's teeth savaging her underlip. I knew that, under the cool exterior, she was disconcerted, even afraid. She had ignored Arthur's messenger, and deliberately brought her little train to Camelot at this late hour, when all would be assembled in the great hall. She must have reckoned on bring her royal brood to the steps of the high throne, and perhaps even presenting Arthur's son in public, so forcing the King's hand before his Queen and all the assembled nobles and their ladies. These, she could be sure, would have stood the allies of a lonely queen with a brood of innocents. But she had been stopped at the gate, and now, against all precedent, the King had come out alone to see her, with no witness but his soldiers.

He came down now under the torchlight. He stopped a few paces away, full in the light, and said to the guards: "Let them come."

Mordred slid from his horse's back, and handed his mother down. The servants took the horses and withdrew to the gatehouse. Then Morgause, with a boy to either side of her, and the three younger ones behind, went forward to meet the King.

It was the first time they had met since the night in Luguvallium when she sent her maid to lead him to her bed. Then he had been a stripling, a prince after his first battle, gay and young and full of fire; the woman had been twenty years old, subtle and experienced, with her double web of sex and magic to entrance the boy. Now, in spite of the years of child-bearing, there was still something left of whatever had drawn men's eyes and sent them mad for her. But she was not now facing a green and eager boy; this was a man in the flower of his strength, with the judgment that makes a king, and the power to enforce it, and with it all something formidable, dangerous, like a fire banked down that needs only a breath of air to set it blazing.

Morgause went down to the frosty ground in front of him, not in the deep curtsy that one might have expected from a suppliant who had need of his forgiveness and grace; but kneeling. Her right hand went out and forced the young Mordred, likewise, to his knees. Gawain, on her other side, stood, with the other children, looking wonderingly from his mother to the King. She left them so; they were Lot's, self-confessed, big-boned and high-coloured, with the fair skin and hair bequeathed by their mother. Whatever Lot had done in the past, Arthur would visit none of it on his children. But the other, the changeling with the thin face and the dark eyes that had come down through the royal house from Macsen himself . . . she forced him to his knees, where he stayed, but with his head up, and those dark eyes darting round him, looking, it seemed, all ways at once.

Morgause was speaking, in the light, pretty voice that had not changed. I could not catch what she said. Arthur stood like stone. I doubt if he heard a word. He had hardly glanced at her; his eyes were all for his son. Her voice took an edge of urgency. I caught the word "brother," and then "son." Arthur listened, still-faced, but I could feel the words flying like darts between them. Then he took a step forward, and put out a hand. She laid hers in it, and he raised her. I saw among the boys, and in the men who waited at the gate, a subtle relaxation. Her servants' hands did not drop from their hilts—they had studiously not been near them—but the effect was the same. The two older boys, Gawain and Mordred, exchanged a look as their mother rose, and I saw Mordred smile. They waited now for the King to give her the kiss of peace and friendship.

He did not give it. He raised her, and said something, then, turning, led her a little way aside. I saw Mordred's head go round like a hunting dog's. Then the King spoke to the boys:

"Be welcome here. Now go back to the gatehouse, and wait."

They went, Mordred with a backward look at his mother. For a moment I saw terror in her face, then the mask of calm came down again. Some message must have passed, for now the chamber-groom came forward, in a hurry, from the gatehouse, bearing in his hands the box that they had brought from Segontium. The things of power . . . unbelievably, she had brought them for the King. Unbelievably, she hoped to buy her way to his favour with the treasure of Macsen. . . .

The man knelt at the King's feet. He opened the box. The light shone down on the treasure that lay within. I saw it all, as clearly as if it lay at my feet. Silver, all silver; cups and bracelets, and a necklet made of silver plaques, designed with those fluid and interlocking lines with which the northern silversmiths invoke their magic. There was no sign of Macsen's emblems of power, no grail studded with emeralds, no lance-head, no dish crusted with sapphire and amethyst. Arthur gave it barely a glance. As the chamber-groom scuttled back into the shelter of the gatehouse, the King turned again to Morgause, leaving the gift lying on the frosty ground. And as he had ignored the gift, so he ignored all that, until now, she had been saying. I heard his voice quite clearly.

"I sent for you, Morgause, for reasons which may not be clear to you. You were wise to obey me. One of my reasons concerns your children; you must have guessed this; but you need not fear for them. I promised you that none of them should be harmed, and I shall keep my promise. But for yourself, no such promise was made. You do well to kneel and sue for mercy. And what mercy can you expect? You killed Merlin. It was you who fed him the poison that in the end brought him to his death."

She had not expected this. I saw her gasp. The white hands fluttered, as if she would have put them to her throat. But she held them still. "Who has told you this lie?"

"It is no lie. When he lay dying, he himself accused you."

"He was always my enemy!" she cried.

"And who is to say he was wrong? You know what you have done. Do you deny it?"

"Of course I deny it! He hated me, always! And you know why. He wanted no one to have power over you but himself. We sinned, yes, you and I, but we sinned in innocence—"

"If you are wise, you will not speak of that." His voice was dry and icy. "You know, as well as I do, what sins were committed, and why. If you hope for any mercy now, or ever, you will not speak of it."

She bowed her head. Her fingers twisted together. Her pose was humble. When she spoke, she spoke quietly. "You are right, my lord. I should not have spoken so. I will not encumber you with memories. I have obeyed you, and brought your son to you, and I leave your heart and conscience to deal rightly with him. You will not deny that *he* is innocent."

He said nothing. She tried again, with the hint of her old sideways, glinting look.

"For myself, I admit that I stand accused of folly. I come to you, Arthur, as a sister, who—"

"I have two sisters," he said stonily. "The other one has just now tried to betray me. Do not speak to me of sisters."

Her head went up. The thin disguise of suppliant was shed. She faced him, a queen to his king. "Then what can I say, except that I come to you as the mother of your son?"

"You have come to me as the murderer of the man who was more to me than my own father. And as nothing else. You are no more to me, and no less. This is why I sent for you, and what I shall judge you for."

"He would have killed me. He would have had you kill your own son."

"That is not true," said the King. "He prevented me from killing you both. Yes, I see that shakes you. When I heard of the child's birth, my first thought was to send someone up to kill him. But, if you remember, Lot was before me. . . . And Merlin, of all men, would have saved the child, because he is mine." For the first time passion showed through a crack in his composure. "But he is not here now, Morgause. He will not protect you again. Why do you think I refused to receive you in the open hall tonight, in the presence of the Queen and the knights? That is what you hoped for, is it not? You, with your pretty face and voice, your four fine boys by Lot, and this youth here with those dark eyes, and the look of his royal kindred . . ."

"He has done you no harm!" she cried.

"No, he has done me no harm. Now listen to me. Your four sons by Lot I will take from you, and have them trained here at Camelot. I will not have them left in your care, to be brought up as traitors, to hate their King. As for Mordred, he has done me no wrong, though I have wronged him sorely, and so have you. I will not add sin to sin. I have been warned of him, but a man must do right, even to his own hurt. And who can read the gods accurately? You will leave him with me also."

"And have you murder him as soon as I am gone?"

"And if I do, what choice have you but to let me?"

"You've changed, brother," she said, spitefully.

For the first time, something like a smile touched his mouth. "You might say so. For what comfort it is to you now, I shall not kill him. But you, Morgause, because you slew Merlin, who was the best man in all this realm—"

He was interrupted. From the gatehouse came a clatter of hoofs, the quick challenge from the sentries, a breathless word, then the creak and crash of the gates opening. A horse, tagged with foam, clattered through, and came to a halt beside the King and stood. Its head went down to its knees. Its limbs trembled. The courier slid down from the saddle, grabbed at the girth to keep his own limbs from folding under him, then went carefully on one knee, and saluted the King.

It was hardly a comfortable interruption. Arthur faced about, his brows drawn, and anger in his face. "Well?" he asked. His voice was even. He knew that no courier would have got through to him at such a moment, and in such a state, unless his business drove him. "Wait, I remember you, don't I? Perseus, is it not? What news can you possibly bring from Glevum that makes it worth your while to kill a good horse, and break in on my private councils?"

"My lord—" The man cleared his throat, with a glance at Morgause. "My lord, it is urgent news, most urgent, that I must deliver privately. Forgive me." This half to Morgause, who was standing like a statue, hands to her throat. Some wisp of forgotten magic, trailing, may have warned her what the news might be.

The King regarded him in silence for a moment, then nodded. He called out an order, and two of the guards came forward, halting one on either side of Morgause. Then he turned, with a sign to the courier, and walked back up the roadway with the man following him.

At the foot of the palace steps he paused and turned.

"Your message?"

Perseus held out the package I had given him. "I met an old man on the road who gave me this token, and told me that he is on his way to Camelot to see the King. But he can only make his way slowly, so if the King wishes to see him, he must come to him. He is travelling by the road that runs over the hills between Aquae Sulis and Camelot. He told me—"

"He gave you this?" The brooch lay in the King's hand. The Dragon winked and glittered. Arthur looked up from it, his face colourless.

"Yes, my lord." The clipped recital hurried. "I was to tell you that he paid me for my service with the ferryman's guerdon." He held out his hand with the gold coin in the palm.

The King took it like a man in a dream, glanced at it, and handed it back. In his other hand he was turning the brooch this way and that, so that the Dragon flashed in the torchlight. "You know what this is?"

"Indeed, my lord. It's the Dragon. When I saw it first I asked what his right to it was, but then I knew him. My lord, yes . . ." The King, his face quite bloodless now, was staring. The man licked his lips, and somehow got the rest of the message out. "When he stopped me, yesterday, he was near the thirteenth milestone. He—he didn't look too good, my lord. If you do ride to meet him, it's my guess he won't have got much beyond the next inn. It stands back from the road, on the south side, and the sign's a bush of holly."

"A bush of holly." Arthur repeated it with no expression at all, like a man talking in his sleep. Then, suddenly, the trance that held him shattered. Colour flooded his face. He threw the brooch up in the air, flashing and turning, and caught it again. He laughed aloud. "I might have known! I might have known. . . . This is real, at any rate!"

"He told me," said Perseus, "he told me he was no ghost. And that it wasn't every tomb that was the gate of death."

"Even his ghost," said Arthur. "Even his ghost . . ." He whirled and shouted. Men came running. Orders were flung at them. "My grey stallion. My cloak and sword. I give you four minutes." He put out a hand to the courier.

"You will stay here in Camelot till my return. You have done more than well, Perseus. I'll remember it. Now go and rest. . . . Ah, Ulfin. Tell Bedwyr to bring twenty of the knights and follow me. This man will direct them. Give him food, and tend his horse and keep him till I come again."

"And the lady?" asked someone.

"Who?" It was plain that the King had forgotten all about Morgause. He said indifferently: "Hold her until I have time for her, and let her speak to no one. No one, do you understand me?"

The stallion was brought, with two grooms clinging to the bit. Someone came running with cloak and sword. The gates crashed open. Arthur was in the saddle. The grey stallion screamed and climbed the torchlit air, then leaped forward under the spur, and was out of the gate with the speed of a thrown spear. It went down the steep, winding causeway as if it had been a level plain in daylight. It was the way the boy Arthur had once ridden through the Wild Forest, and to the same assignation. . . .

Morgause, her virgin white spattered with thrown turf and sods, stood stiffly between her guards, as men-at-arms clattered past her. The boys were in their midst, and Mordred among them. They vanished toward the palace without a backward look.

For the first time since I had known her, I saw her, no more than a frightened woman, making the sign against strong enchantment.

7

Next morning the innkeeper and his wife, to their alarm and distress, found me lying on the cooling hearth, apparently in a faint. They got me into bed, wrapped winter-stones to warm me, piled blankets around me, and got the fire going once more. When, in time, I wakened, the good folk looked after me with the anxious care they might have accorded their own father. I was not much the worse. Moments of vision have always to be paid for; first with the pain of the vision itself, then afterwards in the long trance of exhausted sleep.

Reckoning out the distances, I let myself rest quietly for the remainder of that day, then next morning, putting my hosts' protests aside, had them saddle my horse. They were reassured when I told them I would not ride far, but only a mile or so down the road, where a friend could be expected to meet me. I further allayed their fears by asking them to prepare a dinner "for myself and my friend."

"For," I said, "he loves good food, and the goodwife's cooking is as tasty as any, I'll swear, at the King's court of Camelot."

At that the innkeeper's wife laughed and bridled, and began to talk of capons, so I left money to pay for the food, and went my way.

After the spell of hard frost, the weather had slackened. The sun was up, and dealing some warmth. The air was mild enough, but still everywhere was the hint of winter's coming; in the bare trees of the heights, the fieldfares busy in the berried holly, redwings flocking on the bushes, nuts ripe in the hazel coppices. The bracken was fading gold, and there were still flowers out on the gorse.

My horse, after his long rest, was fresh and eager, and we covered the first stretch of road at a fast canter. We met no one. Soon the road left the high crest of the limestone hills, and slanted downward along a valley-side. All along the lower reaches of the valley the slopes were crowded with trees in the flaming colours of autumn; beech, oak and chestnut, birch in its yellow gold, with everywhere the dark spires of the pine trees and the glossy green of holly. Through the trees I caught the glint of moving water. Down by the river, the innkeeper had told me, the way forked. The road itself held straight across the river, which here was paved in a shallow ford, and just beyond the water another way led off to the right, through the forest. This was a little-used track, and a rough one, which cut off a corner to rejoin the gravelled road some miles farther toward the east.

This was the place I was making for. It was a full mile since I had seen any sort of dwelling; the ford was as private for our meeting as a midnight bedchamber. I dared not go farther to meet him. Whenever Arthur had to ride, he made all speed, and cut all corners. Not knowing the forest track, I could not count on his using it, so might miss him if I took one way or the other.

It was a good place to wait. Down in the hollow the sun shone warmly, and the air was mild but fresh. It smelled of pines. Two jays wrestled and scolded in a shaw of hollies, then flew low across the road with a flash of sky-blue in their wings. Distantly, in the woods to the southeast, I heard the long rasping noise that meant a woodpecker at work. The river whispered across the road, running gently, no more than a foot deep across the Roman setts of the ford.

I unsaddled my horse and slacked his bit, then unbuckled an end of the rein, tied it to a hazel stem, and left him to graze. There was a fallen pine a few paces from the river's edge, full in the sun. I set the saddle down by the tree trunk, then sat down beside it to wait.

My timing had been good. I had waited there barely an hour when I caught the sound of hoofs on the gravel road. So he had kept to the high road, not cutting the corner through the forest. He was not hurrying, but riding easily, no doubt resting his horse. Nor was he alone. Bedwyr, hard on his heels, had perhaps been allowed to come up with him.

I walked out into the road and stood waiting for him.

Three horsemen came trotting through the forest, and down the gentle slope leading to the far side of the ford. They were all strangers; moreover, they were a kind of man who nowadays was rare enough. In times past, the roads, especially those in the wilder lands to the north and west, were rife with danger for the lonely traveller, but Ambrosius, and Arthur after him, had swept the main posting-roads clear of outlaws and masterless men. But not quite, it seemed. These three had been soldiers; they still wore the leather armour of their calling, and two of them sported battered metal caps. The youngest of them, sprucer than the others, had stuck a sprig of scarlet berries behind one ear. All three were unshaven, and armed with knives and short-swords. The oldest of them, with streaks of grey in a heavy brown beard, had an ugly-looking cudgel strapped to his saddle. Their horses were sturdy mountain cobs, cream, brown and black, their hides thick with dirt and damp, but well fed, and powerful. It did not need any prophet's instinct to know that here were three dangerous men.

They halted their horses at the river's brink and looked me over. I stood my ground and returned the look. I had the knife at my belt, but my sword was with the saddlebags. And flight, with my horse stripped and tethered, was out of the question. If truth be told, I was still no more than faintly apprehensive; there had been a time when no one, however wild and desperate, would have dared lay a finger on Merlin; and I suppose that the confidence of power was still with me.

They looked at one another, and a message passed. It was danger, then. The leader, he with the greying beard and the black horse, walked the beast forward a pace, so that the water swirled past its fetlocks. Then he turned, grinning, to his fellows.

"Why, look you, here's a brave fellow, disputing the ford with us. Or are you the Hermes, come to wish us Godspeed? I must say, you're not what one expects of the Herm." This with a guffaw in which his fellows joined.

I moved aside from the center of the road. "I'm afraid I can't claim any of his talents, gentlemen. Nor do I mean to dispute the way with you. When I heard you coming I took you for the outriders of the troop that is due this way very soon. Did you see any sign of troopers on the road?"

Another glance. The youngest—he of the cream cob and the woodbine spray—set his horse at the water and came splashing out beside me. "There was no one on the road," he said. "Troopers? What troopers would you be expecting? The High King himself, maybe?" He winked at his companions.

"The High King," I said equably, "will be riding this way soon, by all accounts, and he likes the law of the roads looked to. So go your ways in peace, gentlemen, and let me go mine."

They were all through the ford now, ranged round me. They looked relaxed and pleasant enough, good-tempered even. Brown Beard said: "Oh, we'll let you go, won't we, Red? Free as air to go you'll be, good sir, free as air, and travelling light."

"Light as a feather," said Red, with a laugh. He was the one with the brown horse. He shifted the belt round from his thick thighs, so that the haft of his knife lay nearer to his hand. The youngest of the three was already moving toward the fallen pine where the saddlebags lay.

I began to speak, but the leader kicked his horse in closer, dropped the reins on its withers, then suddenly reached down, catching hold of me by the neck of my robe. He gathered the stuff in a choking grip, and half lifted me toward him. He was immensely strong.

"So, who were you waiting for, eh? A troop, was it? Was that the truth, or were you lying to scare us off?"

The second man, Red, thrust his horse near on the other side. There was no faintest chance of escaping them. The third one had dismounted, and, without troubling to undo them, had a long knife out and was slitting the leather of the saddlebags. He had not even glanced over his shoulder to see what his fellows did.

Red had his knife in his hand. "Of course he was lying," he said roughly. "There were no troops on the road. Nor any sign of them. And they wouldn't be coming by the forest track, Erec, you can be sure of that."

Erec reached back with his free hand and slipped the knobbed cudgel from its moorings. "Well, so it was a lie," he said. "You can do better than that, old man. Tell us who you are and where you're bound for. This troop you're talking about, where are they coming from?"

"If you let me go," I said with difficulty, for he was half choking me, "I will tell you. And tell your fellow to leave my things alone."

"Why, here's high crowing from an old rooster!" But he relaxed his hold, and let me stand again. "Give us the truth, then, and maybe do youself a bit of good. Which way did you come, and where's this troop you were talking about? Who are you, and where are you bound?"

I began to straighten my clothes. My hands were shaking, but I managed to make my voice steady enough. I said: "You will do well to loose me, and save yourselves. I am Merlinus Ambrosius, called Merlin, the King's cousin, and I am bound for Camelot. A message has gone before me, and a troop of knights is riding this way to meet me. They should be close behind you. If you go west now, quickly—"

A great guffaw of laughter cut me off. Erec rocked in his saddle. "Hear that, Red? Balin, did you get it? This is Merlin, Merlin himself, and he's bound for the court at Camelot!"

"Well, he might be, at that," said Red, shaking with mirth. "Looks a proper skeleton, don't he? Straight from the tomb, he is, and that's for sure."

"And straight back to it." Suddenly savage, Erec seized me again and shook me violently.

A shout from Balin gave him pause. "Hey! Look here!"

Both men turned. "What have you got?"

"Enough gold to get us a month's food and good beds, and something to go in them, forby," called Balin cheerfully. He threw the saddlebag down to the ground, and held up his hand. Two of the jewels glinted.

Erec drew in his breath. "Well, whoever you are, our luck's in, it seems! Look in the other one, Balin. Come on, Red, let's see what he's got on him."

"If you harm me," I said, "be sure that the King—"

I stopped, as if a hand had been laid across my mouth. I had been standing there, perforce, hemmed between the two horses, staring up at the bearded face bent down over me, with the high bright sky behind him. Now, across that sky, with the sun striking bronze from its black gloss, went a raven. Flying low, silent for once, tilting and sidling on the air, went the bird of Hermes the messenger, the bird of death.

It told me what I had to do. Till now, instinctively, I had been playing for time, as any man will play, to ward off death. But if I succeeded, if I made the murderers pause and hold their hands, then Arthur, riding alone, and on a weary horse, with nothing in his heart but the thought of meeting me, would come on them there, three to one, in this lonely place. In a fight I could not help him. But I could still serve him. I owed God a death, and I could give Arthur another life. I must send these brutes on their way, and quickly. If he came across my murdered body here, he would go after them, no doubt of that; but he would know what he was doing, and he would have help.

So I said nothing. Balin started on the other saddlebag. Erec seized me again, dragging me close. Red came behind me, tearing at the belt that held my wallet, with the rest of my gold stitched into its lining. Above me the knotted bludgeon swung high.

If I reached for my own weapon, they might kill me sooner. My hand went back for the knife in my belt. From behind, Red's hard hand caught and held my wrist, and the knife spun to the ground. The bones of my hand ground together. He thrust his sweating face over my shoulder. He was grinning. "Merlin, eh? A great enchanter like you could show us a thing or two, I'm sure. Go on then, save yourself, why don't you? Cast a spell and strike us dead."

The horses broke apart. Something flashed and drove like light across the sky. The cudgel flew wide and fell. Erec's hand loosed me, so suddenly that I staggered, and fell forward against his horse. Bending above me still, the brown-bearded face wore a look of surprise. The eyes stared, fixed. The head, severed cleanly by that terrible, slashing blow, bounced on the horse's neck in a splatter of blood, then thudded to the ground. The body slumped slowly, almost gracefully, onto the cob's withers. A gush of blood, bright and steaming, flooded over the beast's shoulder and splashed down over me where I reeled, clinging to the breast-band. The horse screamed once, in terror, then reared and slashed out at the air, tore itself free, and bolted. The headless body bobbed and swayed for a bound or two before it pitched from the saddle to the road, still spouting blood.

I was thrown hard down on the grass. The cool dampness struck up through my hands, steadying me. My heart thumped; the treacherous blackness threatened, then withdrew. The ground was thudding and shaking to the beat of hoofs. I looked up.

He was fighting the two of them. He had come alone, on his big grey horse. He had outstripped Bedwyr and the knights, but neither he nor the stallion showed any trace of weariness. It was a wonder to me that the three murderers had not broken and fled at the very sight of him. He was lightly armed only—no shield, but a leather tunic stitched with metal phalerae, and a thick cloak twisted round his left arm. His head was bare. He had dropped the reins on the stallion's neck, and controlled him with knee and voice. The great horse reared and wheeled and struck like another battle-arm. And all around horse and King, like a shield of impenetrable light, whirled the flashing blade of the great sword that was mine and his: Caliburn, the King's sword of Britain.

Balin flung himself on his horse, and spurred, yelling, to his fellow's aid. A ribbon of leather flying from Arthur's tunic showed where one of them had slashed him from behind—while he was killing Brown Beard, probably—but now, try as they might, they could not pass that deadly ring of shining metal, or close in past the stallion's lashing hoofs.

"Out of the way," said the King, curtly, to me. The horses plunged and circled. I started to drag myself to my feet. It seemed to take a long time. My hands were slimy with blood, and my body shook. I found that I could not stand, but crawled instead to the fallen pine, and sat there. The air shook and clashed with battle, and I sat there, helpless, shaking, old, while my boy fought for his life and mine, and I could not summon even the mortal strength of a man to help him.

Something glinted near my foot. My knife, lying where Red had struck it from my hand. I reached for it. I still could not stand, but threw it as hard as I could at Red's back. It was a feeble throw, and missed him. But the flash of its passing made the brown horse flinch and swerve, and sent its rider's blow wide. With the slither and whine of metal, Caliburn caught the blade and flung it wider, then Arthur drove the great stallion in and killed Red with a blow through the heart.

There was a moment when the sword jammed and could not be withdrawn, and the body, falling, made a dead weight on the King's sword arm. But the grey stallion knew about that, too. Balin, trying to wheel the cream cob to take the King in the rear, met teeth and armed hoofs. An upward slash laid the cream's shoulder open. It swerved, screaming, and turned against rein and spur to flee. But Balin—brave ruffian that he was—wrenched its head back by main force, just as the King dragged his sword clear of Red's body and wheeled back, right-handed, into fighting range.

I believe that in that last moment Balin recognized the King. But he was given no time to speak, much less beg for mercy. There was one more vicious, brief flurry, and Balin took Caliburn's point in his throat, and fell to the trampled and bloody grass. He writhed once, gasped, and drowned on a gush of blood. The cob, instead of running, now that it was no longer constrained, simply stood with head hanging and shaking legs, while the blood ran down its shoulder. The other horses had gone.

Arthur leaped down, wiped his sword on Balin's body, shook the folds of his cloak from his left arm, and came across to me, leading the grey. He touched my bloodstained shoulder.

"This blood. Is any of it yours?"

"No. And you?"

"Not a scratch," he said cheerfully. He was breathing only a little faster than usual. "Though it wasn't quite a massacre. They were trained men, or so it seemed to me, when there was time to notice. . . . Sit quietly for a moment; I'll get you some water."

He dropped the stallion's reins into my hand, reached to the pommel for the silver-mounted horn he carried there, then trod lightly toward the river. I heard his foot strike something. The quick stride stopped short, and he exclaimed. I turned my head. He was staring down at the wreck of one of my saddlebags, where, in the scatter of spilled food and slashed leather, lay a strip of torn velvet, heavily stitched with gold. One of the jewels that Balin had torn from it lay winking beside it in the grass.

Arthur swung around. He had gone quite white.

"By the Light! It's you!"

"Who else? I thought you knew."

"Merlin!" Now he really was trying for breath. He came back to stand over me. "I thought—I hardly had time to look—just those murdering rascals butchering an old man—unarmed, I thought, and poor, by the look of the horse and trappings . . ." He went on both knees beside me. "Ah, Merlin, Merlin . . ."

And the High King of all Britain laid his head down on my knee, and was silent.

After a while he stirred and lifted his head.

"I got your token, and the message from the courier. But I don't think I really quite believed him. When he first spoke and showed me the Dragon it seemed right . . . I suppose I'd never thought you could really die, like mortal men . . . but on the way here, riding alone, with nothing to do but think—well, it ceased to be real. I don't know what I pictured; myself ending up again, perhaps, in front of that blocked cave mouth, where we buried you alive." I felt a shiver go through him. "Merlin, what has happened? When we left you for dead, sealed in the cave, it was the malady, of course, giving the appearance of death; I realize that now. But afterwards? When you woke, alone and weighed down with your own grave-clothes? God knows, that would be enough to bring another death! What did you do? How survive, locked alone in the hill? How escape? And when? You must have known how sorely I was bereft. Where have you been all this while?"

"Not so great a while. When I escaped, you were abroad. They told me you had gone to Brittany. So I said nothing, and lodged with Stilicho, my old servant, who keeps the mill near Maridunum, and waited for your return. I'll tell you everything soon—if you will get me that drink of water."

"Fool that I am, I was forgetting!" He jumped up and ran to the river. He filled the horn and brought it, then went down on one knee to hold it for me.

I shook my head and took it from him. "Thank you, but I'm quite steady now. It's nothing. I was not hurt. I am ashamed to have been of so little help."

"You gave me all I needed."

"Which was not much," I said, half laughing. "I could almost feel sorry for those wretches, thinking they had an easy kill, and bringing Arthur himself down on them like a thunderbolt. I did warn them, but who could blame them for not believing me?"

"You mean to tell me they knew who you were? And still used you like that?"

"I told you, they didn't believe me. Why should they? Merlin was dead. And the only power I have now is in your name—and they didn't believe that, either. 'An old man, unarmed and poor.' " I quoted him, smiling. "Why, you didn't know me yourself. Am I so much changed?"

He considered me. "It's the beard, and, yes, you are quite grey now. But if I had once looked at your eyes . . ." He took the horn from me and got to his feet. "Oh, yes, it is you. In all that ever mattered, you are unchanged. Old? Yes, we must all grow old. Age is nothing but the sum of life. And you are alive, and back with me here. By the great God of heaven, I have you back with me. What should I fear now?"

He drained the horn, replaced it, and looked around him. "I suppose I had better tidy up this mess. Are you really all right now? Could you tend my horse for me? I think he could be watered now."

I led the stallion down to the water, and with it the cream cob, which was grazing quietly, and made no attempt to escape me. When they had drunk I tethered them, then got some salve from my pack and doctored the cut on the cob's shoulder. It rolled an eye back at me, and the skin of its shoulder flickered, but it showed no sign of pain. The cut bled still, but sluggishly, and the beast was not walking lame. I loosed the girths of both horses, and left them grazing while I retrieved the scattered contents of my saddlebag.

Arthur's way of clearing up the "mess"—three men violently dead—was to haul the bodies by their heels to a decent hiding-place at the forest's edge. The severed head he picked up by the beard and slung it after. He was whistling while he did it, a gay little tune I recognized as one of the soldiers' marching songs, which was frank, not to say over-explicit, about the sexual prowess of their leader. Then he looked around him.

"The next rain will clear some of this blood away. And even if I had a spade or mattock, I'm damned if I'd spend the time and trouble in digging that carrion in. Let the ravens have them. Meanwhile, we might as well impound their horses; I see they've stopped to graze away up the road there. I'll have to wash the blood off first, or I'll never get near them. You'd better abandon that cloak of yours, it'll never be the same again. Here, you can wear mine. No, I insist. It's an order. Here."

He dropped it over the pine log, then went down to the river and washed. While he remounted and went cantering up the road after the other horses, I stripped off my cloak, which was already stiffening with blood, and washed myself, then shook out Arthur's cloak of royal purple, and put it on. My own I rolled up and pitched after the dead men into the undergrowth.

Arthur came back at a trot, leading the thieves' horses.

"Now, where is this inn with the bush of holly?"

8

The innkeeper's boy was out in the road, watching for me. I suppose he had been posted there to give the goodwife warning of when the "meal fit for the King's court" would be wanted. When he saw us coming, two men and five horses, he stood staring awhile, then went with a skip and a jump back into the inn. When we were still seventy paces short of the place, the innkeeper himself came out to see.

He recognized Arthur almost straight away. What drew his eye first was the quality of the King's horse. Then came a long, summing look at the rider, and the man was on his knee out on the road.

"Get up, man," said the King cheerfully. "I've been hearing good things of the house you keep here, and I'm looking forward to trying your hospitality. There's been a little skirmish down by the ford—nothing deadly, just enough to get up a bit of an appetite. But that will have to wait a little. Look after my friend here first, will you, and if your goodwife can clean his clothes, and someone can tend to the horses, we'll cheerfully wait for the meal." Then, as the man began to stammer something about the poverty of his house, and the lack of accommodation: "As to that, man, I'm a soldier, and there've been times when any shelter from the weather could be counted a luxury. From what I've heard of your tavern, it's a haven indeed. And now, may we come in? Wine we cannot wait for, nor fire. . . ."

We had both in a very short time. The innkeeper, once he had recovered himself, came to terms quickly with the royal invasion, and very sensibly set all aside except the immediate service that was needed. The boy came running to take the horses, and the innkeeper himself piled logs on the fire and brought wine, then helped me out of my soiled and blood-splashed robes, and brought hot water, and fresh clothes from my baggage roll. Then, at Arthur's bidding, he locked the inn door against casual passers-by, and got himself off to the kitchen, there, one imagined, to instill a panic frenzy into his excellent wife.

When I had changed, and Arthur had washed, and spread his cloak to the blaze, he poured wine for me, and took his place at the other side of the hearth. Though he had travelled fast and far, and with a fight at the end of it, he looked as fresh as if he had newly risen from his bed. His eyes were bright as a boy's, and colour sprang red in his cheeks. Between the joy of seeing me again and the stimulus of the danger past, he seemed a youth again. When at length the goodwife and her husband came in with the food, making some ado about setting the board and carving the capons, he received them with gay affability, so easily that, by the time we had done, and they had withdrawn, the woman had so far forgotten his rank as to scream with laughter at one of his jests, and cap it herself. Then her husband pulled at her gown, and she ran out, but laughing still.

At last we were alone. The short afternoon drew in. Soon it would be lamp-lighting. We went back to our places one on either side of the blaze. I think we both felt tired, and sleepy, but neither of us could have rested until we had exchanged such news as could not be spoken of in front of our hosts. The King had, he told me, ridden the whole way with only a few hours' respite for sleep, and to rest his horse.

"For," he said, "if the courier's message, and the token he brought, told a true tale, then you were safe, and would wait for me. Bedwyr and the others came up with me, but they, too, stopped to rest. I told them to stay back and give me a few hours' grace."

"That could have cost you dear."

"With that carrion?" He spoke contemptuously. "If they hadn't caught you unarmed and unawares, you could have dealt with them yourself."

And time was, I thought, when without even a dagger in my hand I could have dealt with them. If Arthur was thinking the same, he gave no sign of it. I said: "It's true that they were hardly worth your sword. And talking of that, what have I been hearing about the theft of Caliburn? Some tale about your sister Morgan?"

He shook his head. "That's over, so let it wait. What's more to the point now is that I should know what has been happening to you. Tell me. Tell me everything. Don't leave anything out."

So I told my story. The day drew in, and beyond the small, deep-set windows the sky darkened to indigo, then to slate. The room was quiet, but for the crack and flutter of the flames. A cat crept from some corner and curled on the hearth, purring. It was a strange setting for the tale I had to tell, of death and costly burial, of fear and loneliness and desperate survival, of murder foiled and rescue finally accomplished. He listened as so many times before, intent, lost in the tale, frowning over some parts of it, but relaxed into the warmth and contentment of the evening. This was another of the times that comes vividly back to me in memory whenever I think of him; the quiet room, the King listening, the firelight moving red on his cheek and lighting the thick fall of dark hair, and the dark watching eyes, intent on the story I was telling him. But with a difference now: this was a man listening with a purpose; summing up what he was told, and judging, ready to act.

At the end he stirred. "That fellow, the grave-robber—we must find him. It shouldn't be hard, if he's cadging drinks from that story all over Maridunum . . . I wonder who it was who heard you the first time? And the miller, Stilicho; I've no doubt you'll want me to leave that to you?"

"Yes. But if you could ride over that way some time, perhaps when you're next in Caerleon? Mai will die of terror and ecstasy, but Stilicho will take it as no more than his due, who served the great enchanter . . . and then boast about it for the rest of his days."

"Of course," he said. "I was thinking, while I was on the road; we'll go straight on from here to Caerleon now. I imagine you're not yet ready to go back to court—"

"Not now, or ever. Or to Applegarth. I have left that for good." I did not add "to Nimuë"; her name had not been mentioned by either of us. So carefully had we avoided it that it seemed to ring through every sentence that was spoken. I went on: "I've no doubt you'll fight me to the death over this, but I want to go back to Bryn Myrddin. I'll be more than glad to stay with you in Caerleon until it can be made ready again."

Of course he objected, and we argued for a while, but in the end he let me have my way, on the (very reasonable) condition that I did not live there alone, but was cared for by servants. "And if you must have your precious solitude, then you shall have it. I shall build a place for the servants, out of your sight and below the cliff; but they must be there."

" 'And that is an order?' " I quoted, smiling.

"Certainly. . . . There'll be time enough to see about it; I'll spend Christmas at Caerleon, and you with me. I take it you won't insist on going back there till the winter is past?"

"No."

"Good. Now, there's something in your story that doesn't agree with the facts . . . that business you described in Segontium." He glanced up, smiling. "So that was where you found Caliburn? In the soldiers' shrine of the Light? Well, it tallies. I remember that you told me, years ago, just before we left the forest, that there were other treasures there still. You spoke of a grail. I still remember what you said. But the gift Morgause brought to me was no treasure of Macsen's. It was silver goods—cups and brooches and torques, the sort of thing they fashion in the far north. Very handsome, but not as you described the treasure to me."

"No. I did catch a glimpse of it, there in the vision. It was not Macsen's treasure. But the shepherd boy was certain that it was taken, and I believe him."

"You don't know?"

"No. How could I, without power?"

"But you had this vision. You watched Morgause and the boys accost me at Camelot. You saw the silver treasure she gave me. You knew the courier had come, and that I was on my way to you."

I shook my head. "That was not power, not as you and I have known it. That is Sight only, and that, I think, I shall have until I die. Every village sibyl has it, in some degree or another. Power is more than that: it is doing and speaking with knowledge; it is bidding without thought, and knowing that one will be obeyed. That has gone. I don't repine now." I hesitated. "Nor, I hope, do you? I have heard tales of Nimuë, how she is the new Lady of the Lake, the mistress of the Island's shrine. I am told that men call her the King's enchantress, and that she has done you service?"

"Indeed, yes." He looked away from me, leaning forward to adjust a log on the burning pile. "It was she who dealt with the theft of Caliburn."

I waited, but he left it there. I said at length: "I understood she was still in the north. She is well?"

"Very well." The log was burning to his satisfaction. He set his chin on a fist, and stared at the fire. "So. If Morgause had the treasure with her when she embarked, it will be somewhere on the Island. My people saw to it that she did not go ashore between Segontium and her landing there. She lodged with Melwas, so it should not be beyond me to have it traced. Morgause is being held under guard until I get back. If she refuses to speak, the children will hardly be proof against questioning. The younger ones are too innocent to see any harm in telling the truth. Children see everything; they will know where she left the treasure."

"I understand that you're going to keep them?"

"You saw that? Yes. You would also see that your courier came just in time to save Morgause."

I thought of my own effort to reach him with my dreaming will, when I thought she would use the stolen grail against him. "You were going to kill her?"

"Certainly, for killing you."

"Without proof?"

"I don't need proof to have a witch put to death."

I raised a brow at him, and quoted what had been said at the opening of the Round Hall: " 'No man nor woman shall be harmed unjustly, or punished without trial or manifest proof of their trespass.' "

He smiled. "Well, all right. I did have proof. I had your own word that she tried to kill you."

"So you said. I thought you said it to frighten her. I told you nothing."

"I know. And why not? Why did you keep it secret from me that it was her poison that sent you to your death in the Wild Forest, and then left you with the sickness that was almost your death again?"

"You've answered that yourself. You would have killed her, after the Wild Forest. But she was the mother of that young son, and heavy with another, and I knew that one day they would come to you, and become in time, your faithful servants. So I did not tell you. Who did?"

"Nimuë."

"I see. And she knew—how? By divination?"

"No. From you. Something you said in your delirium."

Everything, she had taken from me; every last secret. I said merely: "Ah, yes. . . . And do I take it that she also found Mordred for you? Or did Morgause bring him into the open, once Lot and I were dead?"

"No. He was still hidden. I understand that he was lodged somewhere in the Orkney Islands. Nimuë had nothing to do with that. It was by the purest chance that I heard of him. I got a letter. A goldsmith from York, who had done work for Morgause before, travelled that way with some jewels he hoped to sell her. These fellows, as you know, get into every corner of the kingdom, and see everything."

"Not Beltane."

His head came up, surprised. "You know him?"

"Yes. He's as good as blind. He has to travel with a servant—"

"Casso," said the King. Then, as I stared: "I told you I got a letter."

"From *Casso?*"

"Yes. It seems he was in Dunpeldyr when—ah, I see, that was when you met them? Then you will know they were there on the night of the massacre. Casso, it appears, saw and heard a good deal of what went on; people talk in front of a slave, and he must have understood more than he was meant to. His master could never be brought to believe that Morgause had anything to do with events so dreadful, so went up to Orkney to try his luck again. Casso, being less credulous, watched and listened, and managed at length to locate the child who went missing on the night of the massacre. He sent a message straight to me. As it happened, I had just heard from Nimuë that it was Morgause who caused your death. I sent for her, and saw to it that she brought Mordred with her. Why are you looking so dumbfounded?"

"On two counts. What should make a slave—Casso was a quarryman's labourer when I first found him—write 'straight to' the High King?"

"I forgot I had not told you: he served me once before. Do you remember when I went north into Lothian to attack Aguisel? And how hard it was to find some way of destroying that dirty jackal without bringing Tydwal and Urien down on my head, swearing vengeance? Some word of this must have got around, because I got a message from this same slave, evidence—with facts that could be proved—of something he had seen when he was in Aguisel's service. Aguisel had misused a page, one of Tydwal's young sons, and then murdered him. Casso told us where to find the body. We found it; and others besides. The child had been killed just as Casso had told us."

"And afterwards," I said dryly, "Aguisel cut out the tongues of the slaves who had witnessed it."

"You mean the man is dumb? Well, that might account for the free way men seem to talk in front of him. Aguisel paid dearly for failing to make sure he could not read or write."

"Neither he could. When I knew in Dunpeldyr he was both dumb and helpless. It was I who, for a service he had done me—or rather, for no reason that I remember, except perhaps the prompting of the god—arranged to have him taught."

Arthur, smiling, raised his cup to me. "Did I call it 'pure chance'? I should have remembered who I was talking to. I rewarded Casso after the Aguisel affair, of course, and told him where to send any other information. I believe he has been useful once or twice. Then, over this last thing, he sent straight to me."

We spoke of it for a while longer, then I came back to present matters. "What will you do with Morgause now?"

"I shall have to settle that, with your help, when I get back. Meanwhile I shall send orders that she is to be kept under guard, at the nunnery at Amesbury. The boys will stay with me, and I'll have them brought down to Caerleon for Christmas. Lot's sons will be no problem; they're young enough to find life at court exciting, and old enough now to do without Morgause. As for Mordred, he shall have his chance. I will do the same for him."

I said nothing. In the pause, the cat purred, suddenly loud, and then stopped short on a sighing breath, and slept.

"Well," said Arthur, "what would you have me do? He is in my protection now, so—even if I could ever have harmed him—I cannot kill him. I haven't had time to think this thing through, and there'll be time enough later to discuss it with you. But it has always seemed to me that once the boy had survived Lot's murderous purge, I would sooner have him near me, and under my eye, than hidden somewhere in the kingdom, with the threat that that might entail. Say you agree with me."

"I do. Yes."

"So, if I keep him by me, and grant him the birthright that he must have thought he would never see—"

"I doubt if that has crossed his mind," I said. "I don't think she has told him who he is."

"So? Then I shall tell him myself. Better still. He'll know that I needn't have accepted him. Merlin, it might be well. You and I both remember what it was like to live our youth out as unfathered bastards, and then to be told we were of Ambrosius' blood. And who am I to take on me yet again the wish for my son's death? Once was too much. God knows I paid for it." He looked away again into the flames. There was a bitter line to his mouth. After a while he lifted a shoulder. "You asked about Caliburn. It seems that my sister Morgan took herself a lover; he was one of my knights, a man called Accolon, a good fighter and a fine man—but one who could never say no to a woman. When King

Urbgen was here with Morgan, she cast her eyes on Accolon, and soon had him at her girdle, like a greyhound fawning. Before she came south she had got some northern smith to make a copy of Caliburn, and while she was here in Camelot she managed to get Accolon to exchange this for the sword itself. She must have reckoned, in a time of peace, on getting herself free of the court and back to the north before the loss was discovered. I don't know what favours she granted Accolon, but certainly when she went north again with King Urbgen, Accolon took leave and went with them."

"But why did she do this?"

His quick, surprised look made me realize how rarely I had had to ask such a question. "Oh, the usual reason: ambition. She had some idea of putting her husband on the high throne of Britain with herself as his queen. As for Accolon, I'm not sure what she promised him, but whatever it was, it cost him his life. It should have cost hers, too, but there was no proof, and she is Urbgen's wife. Her being my sister should not have helped her, but he knew nothing of the plot, and I cannot afford to have him as my enemy."

"How did she hope to get away with it?"

"You had gone," he said simply. "She must have had word from Morgause that you were ailing, and she was making ready for her time of greatness. She reckoned that any man who held the sword could command a following, and if the King of Rheged were to raise it . . . Before that, of course, I was to have been killed. Accolon tried. He picked a quarrel and fought me. It was the substitute sword, of course; the metal was brittle as glass. As soon as I tested it for use, I knew there was something wrong, but it was too late. At the first clash it broke off short below the hilt."

"And?"

"Bedwyr and the rest were shouting 'treachery,' but they hardly needed to. I could see from Accolon's face that treachery was there. For all that his sword was still whole, and mine was broken, I think he was afraid. I drove the hilt into his face, and killed him with my dagger. I don't think he made any resistance. Perhaps he was a true man, after all. I like to think so."

"And the true sword? How did you know where it was?"

"Nimuë," he said. "It was she who told me what had happened. Do you remember that day, at Applegarth, when she told me to beware Morgan and the sword?"

"Yes. I thought she must mean Morgause."

"So did I. But she was right. All the time Morgan was at court, Nimuë hardly left her side. I wondered why, because it was obvious there was no love lost between them." He gave a rueful little laugh. "I'm afraid I took it as a women's quarrel . . . she's not overly fond of Guinevere, either . . . but she was right about Morgan. The witch corrupted her when she was no more than a girl. How Nimuë got the sword back I don't know. She sent it down from Rheged with an armed escort. I haven't seen her since she went north."

I started to ask something more, but he suddenly raised his head, listening.

"And here comes Bedwyr, if I'm not mistaken. We've had little enough time together, Merlin, but there will be other times. As God is good, there will be other times." He got to his feet, put his hands down, and raised me. "Now we have talked enough. You look exhausted. Will you go to your rest now, and leave me to face Bedwyr and the others, and give them the news? I warn you, it won't be a quiet party. They're likely to clean our good host out of anything drinkable he has in his cellars, and take the night to drink it. . . ."

But I stayed with him to receive the knights, and afterwards to drink with them. Nobody, all through the long, noisy celebration, mentioned Nimuë to me, and I did not ask again.

9

We spent another full day resting at The Bush of Holly. A party went back to the ford to bury the dead men, and from there on to Camelot with messages from the King. Another party was sent to Caerleon to give warning of the King's approach. Then, while I rested, the young men went hunting. Their day's sport provided an excellent dinner, and their servants and pages, who came up with us that day, helped the innkeeper and his wife cook and serve it. Where everyone slept that night, I have no idea; I suspect that the horses were turned out, and that the stable was even fuller than the inn. On the following day, to our hosts' evident regret, the royal party moved off for Caerleon.

Even after the building of Camelot, Caerleon had kept its status as Arthur's western stronghold. We rode in on a bright, windy day, with the Dragon standards snapping and rippling from the roofs, and the streets leading up to the fortress gates crowded with people. At my own insistence, I rode cloaked and hooded, and to the rear of the party, rather than beside the King. Arthur had finally been brought to accept my decision not to take my place near him again; one cannot go back on an abdication, and mine had been complete. He still had not mentioned Nimuë's part in that, though he must have been wondering (along with others, who also avoided mentioning her name to me) just how much of my power she had managed to assume. Of all people, she should have "seen" that I was above ground again, and with the King; should have known, in fact, that I had been put still living into my tomb. . . .

But no one asked questions, and I was not prepared to supply what I believed to be the answers.

In Caerleon they had allotted royal chambers to me, next to Arthur's own. Two young pages, eyeing me with the liveliest curiosity, conducted me to the rooms through corridors crowded with bustling servants. Many of them knew me, and all had obviously heard some version of the strange story; some merely hurried past, making the sign against strong enchantment, but others came forward with greetings and offers of service. At last we reached my rooms, sumptuous apartments where a chamberlain awaited me, and showed me a splendid array of clothing sent by the King for me to choose from, with jewels from the royal coffers. A little to his disappointment I set aside the cloth of gold and silver, the peacock and the scarlet and the azure, and chose a warm robe of dark-red wool, with a girdle of gilded leather, and sandals of the same. Then, saying: "I will send light, my lord, and water for your washing," he withdrew. A little to my surprise he signed to the two boys to leave the chamber with him, and left me there unattended.

It was already past the time of lamp-lighting. I went over to the window, where the sky was deepening slowly from red to purple, and sat down to wait for the pages to come back.

I did not look round when the door opened. The flickering light of a cresset stole into the chamber, sending the evening sky receding, darkening beyond its weak young stars. The page moved softly round the room, touching lamp after lamp with flame, until the chamber glowed.

I felt tired after the ride, and heavy with reaction. It was time I roused myself, and let myself be made ready for the feasting tonight. The boy had gone out to set the cresset back in its iron bracket on the corridor wall. The chamber door was ajar.

I got to my feet. "Thank you," I began. "Now, if of your goodness—"

I stopped. It was no page. It was Nimuë who came swiftly in, then stood backed against the door, watching me. She was clad in a long gown of grey, stitched with silver, and there was silver in her hair, which was loose, and flowing down over her shoulders. Her face was white, and her eyes wide and dark, and while I stood gazing, they suddenly brimmed over with tears.

Then she was across the room and had me fast in her arms, and was laughing and crying and kissing me, with words tumbling out that made no sense at all except the one, that I was alive, and that all the time she had been grieving for me as dead.

"Magic," she kept saying, in a wondering, half-scared voice, "it's magic, stronger than any I could ever know. And you told me you had given it all to me. I should have known. I should have known. Ah, Merlin, Merlin . . ."

Whatever had passed, whatever had kept her from me, or blinded her to the truth, none of it mattered. I found myself holding her close, with her head pressed against my breast, and my cheek on her hair, while she repeated over and over, like a child: "It's you. It's really you. You've come back. It is magic. You must still be the greatest enchanter in all the world."

"It was only the malady, Nimuë. It deceived you all. It was not magic. I gave all that to you."

She lifted her head. Her face was tragic. "Yes, and how you gave it! I only pray that you cannot remember! You had told me to learn all that you had to tell me. You had said that I must build on every detail of your life; that after your death I must be Merlin. . . . And you were leaving me, slipping from me in sleep . . . I had to do it, hadn't I? Force the last of your power from you, even though with it I took the last of your strength? I did it by every means I knew—cajoled, stormed, threatened, gave you cordials and brought you back to answer me again and again—when what I should have done, had you been any other man, was to let you sleep, and go in peace. And because you were Merlin, and no other man, you roused yourself in pain and answered me, and gave me all you had. So minute by minute I weakened you, when it seems to me now that I might have saved you." She slid her hands up to my breast, and lifted swimming grey eyes. "Will you tell me something truthfully? Swear by the god?"

"What is it?"

"Do you remember it, when I hung about you and tormented you to your death, like a spider sucking the life from a honey-bee?"

I put my hands up to cover hers. I looked straight into the beautiful eyes, and lied. "My darling girl, I remember nothing of that time but words of love, and God taking me peacefully into his hand. I will swear it if you like."

Relief swept into her face. But still she shook her head, refusing to be comforted. "But then, even all the power and knowledge you gave me could not show me that we had buried you living, and send me back to get you out. Merlin,

I should have known, I should have known! I dreamed again and again, but the dreams were full of confusion. I went back once to Bryn Myrddin, did you know? I went to the cave, but the door was blocked still, and I called and called, but there was no sound—"

"Hush, hush." She was shivering. I pulled her closer, and bent my head and kissed her hair. "It's over. I am here. When you came back for me, I must have been drugged asleep. Nimuë, what happened was the will of the god. If he had wanted to save me from the tomb, he would have spoken to you. Now, he has brought me back in his own time, and for that, he saved me from being put quick into the ground, or given to the flames. You must accept it all, and thank him, as I do."

She shivered again. "That was what the High King wanted. He would give you, he said, a pyre as high as an emperor's, so that your death would be a beacon to the living the length and breadth of the land. He was wild with grief, Merlin. I could hardly make him listen to me. But I told him I had had a dream, and that you yourself had said that you wished to be laid in your own hollow hill, and left in peace to become part of the land you loved." She put a hand up to brush tears from her face. "And it was true. I did have such a dream, one of many. But even so, I failed you. Who did what I should have done, and helped you to escape? What happened?"

"Come over here, to the fire, and I'll tell you. Your hands are cold. Come, we have a little time, I think, before we need go into the hall."

"The King will stay for us," she said. "He knows I am here. He sent me to you."

"Did he?" But I put that aside for the present. In a corner of the room a brazier burned red in front of a low couch covered with rugs and skins. We sat side by side in the warm glow, and, to her eager questions, I told my story yet again.

By the time I had finished her distress was gone, and a little colour had crept back into her cheeks. She sat close in my arm, with one of my hands held tightly in both her own. Magician or mortal man, there was no shadow of doubt in my mind that the joy she showed was as real as the glow of the brazier that warmed us both. Time had run back. But not quite: mortal man or magician, I could sense secrets still.

Meantime she listened and exclaimed, and held my hand tightly, and presently, when I had done, she took up the story.

"I told you about the dream I had. It made me uneasy; I began to wonder, even, if you had been truly dead when we left you in the cave. But there had seemed no doubt; you had lain so long without movement, and seemingly without breath, and then all the doctors declared you dead. So in the end we left you there. Then, when the dreams drove me back to the cave, all seemed normal. Then other dreams, other visions, came, which crowded that one out and confused it. . . ."

She had moved away from me while she was speaking, though she still held my hand between her own. She lay back against the cushions at the end of the couch, looking away from me, into the heart of the glowing charcoal.

"Morgan," I suggested, "and the theft of the sword?"

She gave me a quick glance. "I suppose the King told you about that? Yes. You heard how the sword was stolen. I had to leave Camelot, and follow Morgan, and take back the sword. Even there, the god was with me. While I was in

Rheged a knight came there from the south; he was travelling to visit the queen, and at night, in Urbgen's hall, he told a strange tale. He was Bagdemagus—Morgan's kinsman, and Arthur's. You remember him?"

"Yes. His son was sick a while back, and I treated him. He lived, but was left with an inflammation of the eyes."

She nodded. "You gave him some salve, and told him to use the same if the eyes troubled him again. You said it was blended with some herb you had at Bryn Myrddin."

"Yes. It was wild clary, that I brought back from Italy. I had a supply at Bryn Myrddin. But how did he think he was going to get it?"

"He thought you meant that it grew there. He may have thought you had planted a garden, as we did at Applegarth. Of course he knew that you were buried there in the hill. He didn't admit to us that he was afraid, but I think he must have been. Well, he told us his story, how he had ridden across the hilltop, and heard music coming seemingly up out of the earth. But then his horse bolted in terror, and he didn't dare go back. He said he hadn't told anyone his story, because he was ashamed of his flight, and afraid of being laughed at; but then, he said, just before he came north, he had heard some tale in Maridunum about a fellow who had seen and spoken with your ghost. . . . Well, you know who that was, your grave-robber. Taken both together, and along with my persistent dreams, the story spoke aloud to me. You were alive, and in the cave. I would have left Luguvallium that night, but something else happened that forced me to stay."

She glanced across at me, as if waiting for me to nod, knowing what was to come. But I said merely: "Yes?"

There was the same brief flash of surprise that Arthur had shown, then she bit her lip, and explained.

"Morgause arrived, with the boys. All five. I was hardly a welcome guest, as you may guess, but Urbgen was civility itself, and Morgan was afraid of what she had done, and almost clung to me. I believe she thought that as long as I was there Urbgen's anger wouldn't be vented on her. And of course, I suppose, she hoped that I might intercede with Arthur. But Morgause . . ." She lifted her shoulders as if with cold.

"Did you see her?"

"Briefly. I could not stay there with her. I took my leave, and let them think I was going south, but I did not leave Luguvallium. I sent my page, secretly, to speak with Bagdemagus, and he came to see me at my lodgings. He's a good man, and he owed you his son's life. I did not tell him that I believed you were still living. I told him merely that Morgause had been your enemy, and your bane, and that Morgan had showed herself a witch also, and the enemy of the King. I begged him to spy, if he could, on their counsels, and report to me. You can be sure that I had already tried to reach Morgause's mind myself, and had failed. All I could hope for was that the sisters might talk together, and something could be learned from that about the drug that had been used on you. If my dream was right, and you still lived, the knowledge might help me save you yet. If not, I would have more evidence to give the King, and procure Morgause's death." She lifted her hand to my cheek. Her eyes were somber. "I sat there in my lodgings, waiting for him to come back, and knowing all the time that you might be dying, alone in the tomb. I tried to reach you, or even just to see, but whenever I tried to see you, and the hill, and the tomb, light would break across the vision and dash it aside, and there, moving down the light, floated a grail, clouded like a moon hidden in storm or mist. Then it would vanish, and pain and loss would break through the dream till I woke distracted, and crying, through the longing and sorrow, to dream again."

"So you were warned of that? My poor child, left to guard such a treasure . . . Did Bagdemagus warn you that Morgause had heard of it, and meant to steal it?"

"What?" She looked at me blankly. "What do you mean? What had Morgause to do with the grail? It would have soiled the god himself if she had even looked at it. How was she to know where to find it?"

"I don't know. But she took it. I was told so, by someone who watched her do it."

"Then you were told a lie," said Nimuë roundly. "I took it myself."

"It was you who took Macsen's treasure?"

"Indeed it was." She sat up, glowing. In her eyes two little braziers, reflected, shone and glittered. The candid grey eyes looked, with the red points of light, like cat's eyes, or witch's. "You told me yourself where it lay buried; do you remember that? Or were you already gone into your own mists, my dear?"

"I remember."

She said soberly: "You told me that power was a hard master. It was the hardest thing I have ever done, to go to Segontium, instead of travelling south again to Bryn Myrddin. But in the end I knew I had been bidden to do it, so I went. I took two of my servants, men I could trust, and found the place. It had changed. The shrine had gone, under a landslip, but I took the bearings you had given me, and we dug there. It might have taken a long time, but we had help."

"A dirty little shepherd boy, who could hold a hazel stick over the earth, and tell you where the treasure was hidden."

Her eyes danced. "So, why do I trouble to tell you my story? Yes. He came and showed us, and we dug down, and took the box away. I went up into the fortress then, and spoke with the Commandant, and slept there that night, with a guard on my room. And during the night as I lay in my bed, with that box beneath it, the visions came teeming. I knew that you were alive, and free, and that you would soon be with the King. So in the morning I asked for an escort to take the treasure south, and set off for Caerleon."

"And so missed me by two days," I said.

"Missed you? Where?"

"Did you think I 'saw' the shepherd boy in the fire? No, I was there." I told her then, briefly, about my stay in Segontium, and my visit to the vanished shrine. "So when the boy told me about you and your two servants, like a fool I assumed it was Morgause. He didn't describe the woman, except that she—" I paused, and looked across at her with raised brows. "He said she was a queen, and the servants had royal badges. That was why I assumed—"

I stopped. Her hand, holding mine, had clenched suddenly. The laughter in her eyes died; she looked at me fixedly, with a strange mixture of appeal and dread. It did not need the Sight to guess the part of the story that she had not told me, or why Arthur and the rest had avoided speaking of her to me. She had not usurped my power, or had a hand in trying to destroy me: all she had done, once the old enchanter had gone, was to take a young man to her bed.

I seemed to have been expecting this moment for a very long time. I smiled, and asked her, gently: "Who is he, this king of yours?"

The red rushed into her cheeks. I saw the tears sting her eyes again. "I should have told you straight away. They said they hadn't told you. Merlin, I didn't dare."

"Don't look like that, my dear. What we had, we had, and one cannot drink the same draught of elixir twice. If I had still been half a magician, I should have known long ago. Who is he?"

"Pelleas."

I knew him, a young prince, handsome and kind, with a sort of gaiety about him that would help to offset the haunted somberness that sometimes hung around her. I spoke of him, commending him, and in a while she grew calmer, and began, with growing ease, to tell me about her marriage. I listened, and watched, and had time, now, to mark the changes in her; changes, I thought, due to the power that she had had so drastically to assume. My gentle Ninian had gone, with me into the mists. There was an edge to this Nimuë that had not been there before; something quietly formidable, a kind of honed brightness, like a weapon's edge. And in her voice, at times, sounded a subtle echo of the deeper tones that the god uses when, with authority and power, he descends to mortal speech. These attributes had once been mine. But I, accepting them, had taken no lover. I found myself hoping, for Pelleas' sake, that he was a strong-minded young man.

"Yes," said Nimuë, "he is."

I started out of my thoughts. She was watching me, her head on one side, her eyes alight once more with laughter.

I laughed with her, then put out my arms. She came into them, and lifted her mouth. I kissed her, once with passion, and once with love, and then I let her go.

10

Christmas at Caerleon. Pictures come crowding back to me, sun and snow and torchlight, full of youth and laughter, of bravery and fulfilment and time won back from oblivion. I have only to shut my eyes; no, not even that; I need only glance into the fire and they are here with me, all of them.

Nimuë, bringing Pelleas, who treated me with deference, and her with love, but who was a king and a man. "She belongs to the King," he said, "and then to me. And I—well, it's the same, isn't it? I am his before ever I can be hers. Which of us, in the sight of God and King, is ever his own man?"

Bedwyr, coming on me one evening down beside the river, which slipped along, swollen and slate-grey, between its winter banks. A fleet of swans were proving the mud at the water's edge among the reeds. Snow had begun to fall, small and light, floating like swansdown through the still air. "They told me you had come this way," said Bedwyr. "I came to take you back. The King stays for you. Will you come now? It's cold, and will get colder." Then, as we walked back together: "There's news of Morgause," he said. "She has been sent north into Lothian, to the nunnery at Caer Eidyn. Tydwal will see to it that she's kept fast there. And there's talk of Queen Morgan's being sent to join her. They say that King Urbgen finds it hard to forgive her attempt to embroil him in treachery, and he's afraid that if he keeps her by him the taint will cling, to him and to his sons. Besides, Accolon was her lover. So the talk goes that Urbgen will put her away. He has sent to Arthur for permission. He'll get it, too. I think Arthur will feel more comfortable with both his loving sisters safely shut up, and a good long way away. It was Nimuë's suggestion." He laughed, looking at me sideways. "Forgive me, Merlin, but now that the King's enemies are women, perhaps it is better that he has a woman to deal with them. And if you ask me, you'll be well out of it. . . ."

Guinevere, sitting at her loom one bright morning, with sun on the snow outside, and a caged bird singing on the sill beside her. Her hands lay idle among the coloured threads, and the lovely head turned to watch, down beside the moat, the boys at play. "They might be my own sons," she said. But I saw that her eyes did not follow the bright heads of Lot's children, but only the dark boy Mordred, who stood a little way apart from the others, watching them, not as an outcast might watch his more favoured brothers, but as a prince might watch his subjects.

Mordred himself. I never spoke with him. Mostly the boys were on the children's side of the palace, or in the care of the master-at-arms or those set to train them. But one afternoon, on a dark day drawing to dusk, I came on him, standing beside the arch of a garden gateway, as if waiting for someone. I paused, wondering how to greet him, and how he might receive his mother's enemy, when I saw his head turn, and he started forward. Arthur and Guinevere came together through the dead roses of the garden, and out through the archway. It was too far away for me to hear what was said, but I saw the Queen smile and reach out a hand, and the King spoke, with a kind look. Mordred answered him; then, in obedience to a gesture from Arthur, went with them as they moved off, walking between them.

And, finally, Arthur, one evening in the King's private chamber, when Nimuë brought the box to show him the treasure from Segontium.

The box lay on top of the big marble table that had been my father's. It was of metal, and heavy, its lid scored and dented with the weight of the stuff that had fallen on it when the shrine crumbled to ruin. The King laid hands to it. For a few moments it resisted him, then suddenly, light as a leaf, it lifted.

Inside were the things just as I remembered them. Rotten canvas wrappings, and, gleaming through them, the head of a lance. He drew it out, trying the edge with a thumb, a gesture as natural as breathing.

"For ornament, I think," he said, rubbing the jewels of the binding with his hand, and laying it aside. Then came a flattish dish, gold, with the rim crusted with gems. And finally, out of a tumble of greyed linen fallen to dust, the bowl.

It was the type of bowl they call sometimes a cauldron, or a grail of the Greek fashion, wide and deep. It was of gold, and from the way he handled it, very heavy. There was chasing of some sort round the outside of the bowl, and on the foot. The two handles were shaped like birds' wings. On a band round it, out of the way of the drinker's lips, were emeralds and sapphires. He turned and held it out to me with both hands.

"Take it and see. It is the most precious thing I have ever seen."

I shook my head. "It is not for me to touch."

"Nor for me," said Nimuë.

He looked at it for a moment longer, then he put it back in the box with the lance-head and the dish, gently wrapping the things away in the linen, which was worn thin, like a veil. "And you won't even tell me where to keep such splendour, or what I am to do with it?"

Nimuë looked across at me, and was silent. When I spoke, it was only a gentle echo of what I had said before, long ago. "It is not for you, either, Arthur. You do not need it. You yourself will be the grail for your people, and they will drink from you and be satisfied. You will never fail them, nor ever leave them quite. You do not need the grail. Leave it for those who come after."

"Then since it is neither mine nor yours," said Arthur, "Nimuë must take it, and with her enchantments hide it so that no one can find it except that he is fitted."

"No one shall," she said, and shut the lid on the treasure.

After that, another year dawned cold, and drew slowly into spring. I went home at April's end, with the wind turning warm, and the young lambs crying on the hill, and catkins shivering yellow in the copses.

The cave was swept and warm again, a place for living, and there was food there, with fresh bread and a crock of milk and a jar of honey. Outside, by the spring, were offerings left by the folk I knew; and all my belongings, with my books and medicines, my instruments and the great standing harp, had been brought from Applegarth.

My return to life had been easier than I had anticipated. It seems that to the simple folk, as indeed to the people in distant parts of Britain, the tale of my return from death was accepted, not as plain truth, but as a legend. The Merlin they had known and feared was dead; a Merlin lived on in the "holy cave," working his minor magics, but only a ghost, as it were, of the enchanter they had known. It may be they thought that I, like so many pretenders of the past, was some small magician merely claiming Merlin's reputation and his place. In the court, and in the cities and the great places of the earth, people looked now to Nimuë for power and help. To me the local folk came to have their sores or their aches healed; to me Ban the shepherd brought the sickly lambs, and the children from the village their pet puppies.

So the year wore on, but so lightly that it seemed only like the evening of a quiet day. The days were golden, tranquil and sweet. There was no call of power, no great high clean wind, no pain in the heart or pricking of the flesh. The great doings of the kingdom seemed no longer to trouble me. I did not hunger or ask after news, for when it came, it was brought by the King himself. Just as the boy Arthur, racing up to see me in the shrine of the Wild Forest, had poured out all the doings of every day at my feet, so did the High King of Britain bring me all his acts, his problems and his troubles, and spread them out there on the cave floor in the firelight, and talk to me. What I did for him I do not know; but always, after he had gone, I found myself sitting, drained and silent, in the stillness of complete content.

The god, who was God, had indeed dismissed his servant, and was letting him go in peace.

One day I drew the small harp to me, and set myself to make a new verse for a song sung many years ago.

Rest here, enchanter, while the fire dies.
In a breath, in an eyelid's fall,
You will see them, the dreams;
The sword and the young king,
The white horse and the running water,
The lit lamp and the boy smiling.

Dreams, dreams, enchanter! Gone
With the harp's echo when the strings
Fall mute; with the flame's shadow when the fire
Dies. Be still, and listen.

Far on the black air
Blows the great wind, rises
The running tide, flows the clear river.
Listen, enchanter, hear
Through the black air and the singing air
The music . . .

I had to leave the song there because a string broke. He had promised to bring me new ones, next time he came.

He came again yesterday. Something had called him down to Caerleon, he said, so he had ridden up, just for an hour. When I asked him what the business was in Caerleon, he put the question aside, till I wondered—then dismissed it as absurd—if the journey had been made merely to see me. He brought gifts with him—he never came empty-handed—wine, a basket of cooked meats from his own kitchen, the promised harp-strings and a blanket of soft new wool, woven, he told me, by the Queen's own women. He carried them in himself, like a servant, and put them away for me. He seemed in spirits. He told me of some young man who had recently come to court, a noble fighter, and a cousin of March of Cornwall. Then he spoke of a meeting he was planning with the Saxon "king," Eosa's successor, Cerdic. We talked till the dark drew in, and his escort came jingling up the valley track for him.

The he rose, lightly, and, as always now when he left me, stooped to kiss me. Usually he made me stay there, by the fire, while he went out into the night, but this time I got up and followed him to the cave entrance, and waited there to watch him go. The light was behind me, and my shadow stretched, thin and long, like the tall shadow of old, across the little lawn and almost to the grove of thorn trees where the escort waited below the cliff.

It was almost night, but over beyond Maridunum in the west, a lingering bar of light hinted at the dying sun. It threw a glint on the river skirting the palace wall where I was born, and touched a jewel spark on the distant sea. Near at hand the trees were bare with winter, and the ground crisp with the first frost. Arthur trod away from me across the grass, leaving ghost-prints in the frost. He reached the place where the track led down to the grove, and half turned. I saw him raise a hand.

"Wait for me." It was the same farewell always. "Wait for me. I shall come back."

And, as ever, I made the same reply:

"What else have I to do but wait for you? I shall be here, when you come again."

The sound of the horses dwindled, faded, was gone. The winter's silence came back to the valley. The dark drew down.

A breath of the night slid, like a sigh, through the frost-hung trees. In its wake, faintly, like no sound but the ghost of a sound, came a faint, sweet ringing from the air. I lifted my head, remembering, once more, the child who had listened nightly for the music of the spheres, but had never heard it. Now here it was, all around me, a sweet, disembodied music, as if the hill itself was a harp to the high air.

Dark fell. Behind me the fire dimmed, and my shadow vanished. Still I stood listening, with the calmness over me of a great contentment. The sky, heavy with night, drew nearer the earth. The glimmer on the far sea moved, light and following shadow, like the slow arc of a sword sliding back to its sheath, or a barge dwindling under sail across the distant water.

It was quite dark. Quite still. A chill brushed my skin, like the cold touch of crystal.

I left the night, with its remote and singing stars, and came in, to the glow of the fire, and the chair where he had been sitting, and the unstrung harp.

THE LEGEND

When King Uther Pendragon lay close to death, Merlin approached him in the sight of all the lords and made him acknowledge his son Arthur as the new king. Which he did, and afterwards died, and was buried by the side of his brother Aurelius Ambrosius within the Giants' Dance.

Then Merlin had a great sword fashioned, and fixed by his magic art into a great stone shaped like an altar. There were gold letters on the sword which said: "Whoso pulleth out this sword of this stone, is rightwise king born of all England." When at length it was seen by all men that only Arthur could pull the sword from the stone, the people cried out: "We will have Arthur unto our king, we will put him no more in delay, for we all see that it is God's will that he should be our king, and who that holdeth against it, we will slay him." So Arthur was accepted by the people, high and low, and raised to be king. When he was crowned, he made Sir Kay the seneschal of England, and Sir Ulfius was made his chamberlain.

After this were many years of wars, and battles, but then came Merlin on a great black horse, and said to Arthur, "Thou hast never done, hast thou not done enough? It is time to say Ho! And therefore withdraw you unto your lodging and rest you as soon as ye may, and reward your good knights with gold and with silver, for they have well deserved it." "It is well said," quoth Arthur, "and as thou hast devised, so it shall be done." Then Merlin took his leave of Arthur, and travelled to see his master Blaise, that dwelt in Northumberland. So Blaise wrote the battles word by word, as Merlin told him.

Then one day King Arthur said to Merlin, "My barons will let me have no rest, but needs I must take a wife." "It is well done," said Merlin, "that ye take a wife. Now is there any that ye love more than another?" "Yea," said King Arthur, "I love Guinevere, the king's daughter, Leodegrance of the land of Cameliard, the which holdeth in his house the Table Round that ye told he had of my father Uther." Then Merlin advised the King that Guinevere was not wholesome for him to take to wife, and warned him that Lancelot should love her, and she him again. In spite of this the King determined to wed Guinevere, and sent Sir Lancelot, the chief of his knights and his trusted friend, to bring her from her home.

On this journey Merlin's prophecy came to pass, and Lancelot and Guinevere loved one another. But they were helpless to realize their love, and in time Guinevere was married to the King. Her father, King Leodegrance, sent the Round Table to Arthur as a wedding gift.

Meanwhile Arthur's half-sister Morgause had borne her bastard son by the King. His name was Mordred. Merlin had prophesied that great danger should come to Arthur and his kingdom through this child, so when the King heard of the birth he sent for all the children born upon May-day, and they were put into a ship and set adrift. Some were four weeks old, some less. By chance the ship drove against a rock where stood a castle. The ship was destroyed, and all in it died except Mordred, who was found by a good man, and reared until he was fourteen years of age, when he was brought to the King.

Soon after the wedding of Arthur and Guinevere the King had to leave the court, and in his absence King Meleagant (Melwas) carried the Queen off into his kingdom from which, as men said, no traveller ever returned. The only way into her moated prison was by two very perilous paths. One of these was called "the water bridge" because the bridge lay under water, invisible and very narrow. The other bridge was much more perilous, and had never been crossed by a man, made as it was of a sharp sword. No one dared go after her but Lancelot, and he made his way through unknown country, until he came near Meleagant's lodge that had been built for the Queen. Then he crossed the sword bridge, and sustained grievous wounds therefrom, but he rescued the Queen, and later, in the presence of King Arthur and the court, he fought and killed Meleagant.

Then it befell that Merlin fell in a dotage on one of the damosels of the Lake, whose name was Nimuë, and Merlin would let her have no rest, but always he would be with her. He warned King Arthur that he should not be long above earth, but for all his craft he would be put alive into the earth, and he warned him also to keep his sword and the scabbard safely, for it would be stolen from him by a woman that he most trusted. "Ah," said the King, "since ye know of your adventure, why do you not put it away by your magic arts, and prevent it?" "That cannot be," said Merlin. "It is ordained that ye shall die a worshipful death, and I a shameful death." Then he left the King. Shortly after this Nimuë, the damosel of the Lake, departed, and Merlin went with her wherever she went. They went over the sea to the land of Benwick, in Brittany, where King Ban was king, and Elaine his wife had with her the young child called Galahad. Merlin prophesied that one day Galahad should be the most man of worship in the world. Then after this Nimuë and Merlin left Benwick, and came into Cornwall. And the lady was afraid of him because he was a devil's son, and she did not know how to make away with him. Then it happened that Merlin showed her a cave in a rock which could be sealed with a great stone. So by her subtle working she made Merlin go under that stone to show her the magic that dwelt there, but she cast a spell on him so that he could not ever come out again. And she went away and left him there in the cave.

And anon a knight, a cousin of the King's called Bagdemagus, rode out from the court, to find a branch of an holy herb for healing. It happened that he rode by the rock where the Lady of the Lake had put Merlin under the stone, and there he heard him lamenting. Sir Bagdemagus would have helped him, but when he went to the stone to lift it, it was so heavy than an hundred men could not have moved it. When Merlin knew he was there, he told him to save his labour, for all was in vain. So Bagdemagus went, and left him there.

Meantime it had happened as Merlin had foretold, and Arthur's sister Morgan le Fay had stolen the sword Excalibur and its sheath. She gave these to Sir Accolon with which to fight the King himself. And when the King was armed for the fight there came a maiden from Morgan le Fay, and brought to Arthur a sword like Excalibur, with its scabbard, and he thanked her. But she was false, for the sword and the scabbard were counterfeits, and brittle. So there was a battle between King Arthur and Accolon. The Lady of the Lake came to this battle, for she knew that Morgan le Fay wished ill to the King, and she wanted to save him. King Arthur's sword broke in his hand, and only after a grievous fight did he get his own sword Excalibur back from Sir Accolon and defeat him. Then Accolon confessed the treason of Morgan le Fay, King Urien's wife, and the King granted mercy to him.

And after this the Lady of the Lake became the friend and guardian of King Arthur, in the stead of Merlin the enchanter.

AUTHOR'S NOTE

According to legend, of which the main source is Malory's *Morte d'Arthur,* Merlin stayed above ground only a short while after Arthur was crowned. The period of battles and tournaments that follows the coronation can surely be taken to represent the actual battles fought by the historic Arthur. All that we know of the real war-leader, Arthur the Soldier *(dux bellorum),* is that he fought twelve major battles before he could count Britain safe from the Saxon enemy, and that eventually he died, and Mordred with him, at the battle of Camlann. The much-quoted account of the twelve battles occurs in the *Historia Brittonum* written by the Welsh monk Nennius in the ninth century.

> Then Arthur fought against them in those days, with the kings of the Britons, but he himself was the leader of battles. The first battle was at the mouth of the river which is called Glein. The second, third, fourth and fifth, on another river, which is called Dubglas, and is in the region of Linnuis. The sixth battle was on the river which is called Bassas. The seventh was a battle in the wood of Celidon, that is Cat Coit Celidon. The eighth was the battle at Castellum Guinnion, in which Arthur carried the image of Saint Mary, ever Virgin, on his shoulders, and the pagans were put to flight on that day and there was a great slaughter of them through the power of our Lord Jesus Christ and through the power of Saint Mary the Virgin, his mother. The ninth battle was fought at the City of the Legions. The tenth battle he fought on the river, which is called Tribuit. The eleventh occurred on the mountain, which is called Agned. The twelfth was the battle on Mount Badon, in which there fell together in one day 960 men in one onset of Arthur, and no one laid them low save himself alone. And in all the battles he remained victor.

Only two of these battles can be located with any kind of certainty: that in the Caledonian Forest—the Old Caledonian Forest that stretched down from Strathclyde into the modern Lake District—and the one at the City of Legions, which could be either Chester or Caerleon. I have contented myself with using Nennius' own place-names, and identifying only one other, the battle of the River Tribuit. It has been suggested that this is an early name of the River Ribble. There is a place where the old Roman road crosses the Ribble and heads toward the Aire Gap (the "Pennine Gap"). This is called Nappa or Nappay Ford, and local tradition remembers a battle there. The nearby camp that I have called "Tribuit" was at Long Preston; the other two in the Gap were of course Elslack and Ilkley. I also made use of a tradition that Arthur fought at High Rochester (Bremenium) in the Cheviots. Apart from these two "battle sites" I have inserted none in the map.

Blaise. According to Malory, Blaise "wrote down Arthur's battles word for word," a chronicle which, if it ever existed, has vanished utterly. I took the liberty of building in a destructive agent in the person of Gildas, the young son of Caw of Strathclyde and brother of Heuil. These are historic personages. We are told that Arthur and Heuil hated one another. Gildas the monk, writing in about A.D. 540, refers to the victory of "Mount Badon," but without mentioning Arthur by name. This has been interpreted as a sign, at the least, of disapproval of a leader who had shown himself no friend to the Church.

Merlin's illness. The episode in the Wild Forest is taken from the story of Merlin's madness as told in the *Vita Merlini,* a twelfth-century Latin poem commonly ascribed to Geoffrey of Monmouth. This is in part a retelling of the older Celtic "Lailoken" tale of the madman who roamed the Caledonian Forest. Merlin-Lailoken was present at the battle of Arfderydd (the modern Arthuret, near Carlisle), where his friend, the king, was killed. Driven mad by grief, he fled into the forest, where he eked out a wretched existence.

There are two poems in *The Black Book of Carmarthen* that are attributed to him. In one he describes the apple tree that shelters and feeds him in the forest; in the other he addresses the piglet which is his sole companion.

Guenever and Guinevere. Tradition asserts that Arthur had two wives of the same name, or even three—though this was probably only a conveniently poetic round number. The rape of Guinevere by Melwas (or Meleagant) occurs in the mediaeval romance *Lancelot* of Chrétien de Troyes. In Chrétien's story Lancelot has to cross a sword bridge leading to the hollow hill of faery—a version of the ancient rape fantasy that we find in the tales of Dis and Persephone, or Orpheus and Eurydice.

Guinevere, according to the mediaeval legends, suffered abduction from time to time as a matter of course, and equally as a matter of course was rescued by Lancelot. A modern reader can see how the stories rose around "the much-abducted queen." Mediaeval singers found in "King Arthur and his Court" a rich source of story-telling, and in time a long series of tales came to be hung around the central figures, much as the television series-writers hang their scripts today. Gradually, in the legends, Arthur himself fades into the background, and various new "heroes" take the center of the stage: Lancelot, Tristram, Gawain, Gereint. Lancelot, being purely fictional (and an invention some centuries later than the "Arthurian fact"), is made to fill the role of the Queen's lover so essential to the mediaeval romancers and their convention of courtly love.

But it is tempting to believe that the first of the "rape stories," the Queen's abduction by Melwas, was founded on fact. Certainly Melwas existed, and remains have been found of the right period that indicate strongholds on and near Glastonbury Tor. In my tale Bedwyr, whose name is linked with Arthur's long before "Lancelot" ever appears, takes the Lancelot role. In the character of Guinevere, as here drawn, I believe I was influenced by Chaucer's treatment of the "false" Criseyde.

Nimuë (Niniane, Vivien). Nor is there any necessity to attribute the same sort of "falseness" to Merlin's lover, Nimuë. The "betrayal" theme of this legend springs from the need to explain the death or disappearance of an all-powerful enchanter. My version of Merlin's end is based on a tradition which obtains still in parts of the "Summer Country." It was sent me many years ago by a Wiltshire correspondent. This version of the tale is that Merlin, with age drawing on, desired to hand on his magic powers to someone who could be Arthur's adviser after his death. For this he chose his pupil Nimuë, who showed herself adept. This tale not only allows the great enchanter his dignity, and a measure of common sense, but also explains Nimuë's subsequent influence over Arthur. The King would hardly otherwise have kept her near him, or accepted her help against his enemies.

Ninian. The "boy Ninian" episode was suggested by another incident found in the *Vita Merlini.* Here Merlin sees a youth buying shoes, and pieces of leather to repair them with to make them last longer. Merlin knows that the youth will have no need of the new shoes, as he will be drowned the same day.

Cerdic Elesing. The Anglo-Saxon Chronicle records that Cerdic and Cynric his son landed at Cerdices-ora with five ships. Cerdic was Elesing (the son of Elesa, or Eosa). The date given is A.D. 494.

Whatever doubt there may be about the dates of Cerdic's battles, or the locations of his first conquests (Cerdices-ora is thought to be Netley, near Southampton), all the chroniclers seem to agree that he was the founder of the first West Saxon monarchy from which Alfred was to claim descent. For Cerdic, and for the changing of the burial customs that Gereint suggests on page 679, see Hodgkin's *History of the Anglo-Saxons,* Vol. I, Section IV.

Llud-Nuatha, or Nodens. The shrine of Nodens is still to be seen, at Lydney in Gloucestershire.

Merlin's song on pages 682–683, "He who is companionless," is based on the Anglo-Saxon poem *The Wanderer.*

Finally, for the many gaps in my knowledge of this enormous subject I can only beg forgiveness, and paraphrase what H. M. and N. K. Chadwick wrote in the preface to their *Growth of English Literature:* "If I had read more widely I should never have completed this book." More: if I had even known how much there was to read, I would never have dared to start to write at all. By the same token I cannot list all the authorities I have followed. But I can hope, in all humility, that my Merlin trilogy may be, for some new enthusiast, a beginning.

M.S.

Edinburgh, 1975–1979

A NOTE ABOUT THE AUTHOR

MARY STEWART, one of the most popular novelists writing today, was born in Sunderland, County Durham, England. After boarding-school, she received a B.A. with first class honours in English Language and Literature from Durham University and went on for her M.A. Later she returned to her own University as a Lecturer in English. She married in 1945. Her husband is Sir Frederick Stewart, who is Chairman of the Geology Department at Edinburgh University, and a Fellow of the Royal Society.

Lady Stewart's career as a novelist began in 1954 with the publication of *Madam, Will You Talk?* Since then she has published fifteen successful novels, including *The Last Enchantment,* the third book of this magical trilogy about the legendary enchanter Merlin and young Arthur. Her books for young readers, *The Little Broomstick* (1971) and *Ludo and the Star Horse* (1974), quickly met with the same success as her other novels. In 1968, she was elected Fellow of the Royal Society of the Arts. In 1971, the Scottish Chapter of the International PEN Association awarded her the Frederick Niven prize for *The Crystal Cave.* In 1974, the Scottish Arts Council Award went to *Ludo and the Star Horse.*